After Long Silence

The Presences mean something different to each of Jubal's colonists. In some, these towering crystals inspire awe, in others fear. A small band must break through the long silence between humanity and the Presences to strike a new alliance – and bring about the end of a tyrannical dynasty.

Shadow's End

A mysterious force, which emanates from the region of space known as Ularia, may threatened the human race with extinction – entire populations have vanished from the occupied worlds of the remote Hermes Sector; all except the human population of the planet Dinadh . . .

Six Moon Dance

Many years ago, humans settled the world of Newholme and ruthlessly bent the planet to their will. But now the ground itself shakes with ever-increasing violence, and the official arbiter of the Council of Worlds has come to investigate rumours of a terrible secret that lies buried deep within Newholme's past . . .

Also By Sheri S. Tepper

Land of The True Game

King's Blood Four (1983)
Necromancer Nine (1983)
Wizard's Eleven (1984)

Marianne

Marianne, the Magus and the
    Manticore (1985)
Marianne, the Madame and the
    Momentary Gods (1988)
Marianne, the Matchbox and the
    Malachite Mouse (1989)

Mavin Manyshaped

The Song of Mavin Manyshaped
    (1985)
The Flight of Mavin Manyshaped
    (1985)
The Search of Mavin Manyshaped
    (1985)

Jinian

Jinian Footseer (1985)
Dervish Daughter (1986)
Jinian Star-Eye (1986)

Ettison

Blood Heritage (1986)
The Bones (1987)

Awakeners

Northshore (1987)
Southshore (1987)

Other Novels

The Revenants (1984)
After Long Silence (1987)
The Gate to Women's Country (1988)
The Enigma Score (1989)
Grass (1989)
Beauty (1991)
Sideshow (1992)
A Plague of Angels (1993)
Shadow's End (1994)
Gibbon's Decline and Fall (1996)
The Family Tree (1997)
Six Moon Dance (1998)
Raising the Stones (1990)
Singer from the Sea (1999)
The Fresco (2000)
The Visitor (2002)
The Companions (2003)
The Margarets (2007)

Sheri S. Tepper
SF GATEWAY OMNIBUS

AFTER LONG SILENCE
SHADOW'S END
SIX MOON DANCE

GOLLANCZ
LONDON

First published in Great Britain in 2013 by Gollancz
An imprint of the Orion Publishing Group
Orion House, 5 Upper St Martin's Lane,
London WC2H 9EA

An Hachette UK Company

A CIP catalogue record for this book
is available from the British Library

ISBN 978 0 575 11600 9

1 3 5 7 9 10 8 6 4 2

Typeset by Input Data Services Ltd, Bridgwater, Somerset

Printed and bound by CPI Group (UK) Ltd, Croydon, CR0 4YY

The Orion Publishing Group's policy is to use papers
that are natural, renewable and recyclable products and
made from wood grown in sustainable forests. The logging
and manufacturing processes are expected to conform to
the environmental regulations of the country of origin.

www.orionbooks.co.uk
www.gollancz.co.uk

CONTENTS

ENTER THE SF GATEWAY . . .

Towards the end of 2011, in conjunction with the celebration of fifty years of coherent, continuous science fiction and fantasy publishing, Gollancz launched the SF Gateway.

Over a decade after launching the landmark SF Masterworks series, we realised that the realities of commercial publishing are such that even the Masterworks could only ever scratch the surface of an author's career. Vast troves of classic SF & Fantasy were almost certainly destined never again to see print. Until very recently, this meant that anyone interested in reading any of those books would have been confined to scouring second-hand bookshops. The advent of digital publishing changed that paradigm for ever.

Embracing the future even as we honour the past, Gollancz launched the SF Gateway with a view to utilising the technology that now exists to make available, for the first time, the entire backlists of an incredibly wide range of classic and modern SF and fantasy authors. Our plan, at its simplest, was – and still is! – to use this technology to build on the success of the SF and Fantasy Masterworks series and to go even further.

The SF Gateway was designed to be the new home of classic Science Fiction & Fantasy – the most comprehensive electronic library of classic SFF titles ever assembled. The programme has been extremely well received and we've been very happy with the results. So happy, in fact, that we've decided to complete the circle and return a selection of our titles to print, in these omnibus editions.

We hope you enjoy this selection. And we hope that you'll want to explore more of the classic SF and fantasy we have available. These are wonderful books you're holding in your hand, but you'll find much, much more . . . through the SF Gateway.

www.sfgateway.com

INTRODUCTION
from The Encyclopedia of Science Fiction

Sheri S. Tepper (Born 1929) is a US writer whose first genre publications were poems under her then married name Sheri S. Eberhart, the earliest being 'Lullaby, 1990' in *Galaxy*, in 1963. She then fell silent as an author, beginning to write again only once she was in her 50s, producing SF and fantasy as Tepper.

Her first-written novel, a long, complex work of SF, eventually appeared as *The Revenants* (1984). Her first-published novel was *King's Blood Four* (1983), the first of the long and very interesting True Game series, which continued with *Necromancer Nine* (1983) and *Wizard's Eleven* (1984). This initial trilogy was prequelled by another trio: *The Song of Mavin Manyshaped* (1985), *The Flight of Mavin Manyshaped* (1985) and *The Search of Mavin Manyshaped* (1985). A third sequence comprises *Jinian Footseer* (1985), *Dervish Daughter* (1986) and *Jinian Star-Eye* (1986). In terms of internal chronology, the middle trilogy precedes the first; the third runs partly parallel with the first and continues beyond.

Readers knew almost at once that something very unusual was happening in these books, but most serious critics ignore paperback fantasy trilogies, and it took some years before Tepper was spoken of much at all. In the True Game books some of the human colonists on a planet also inhabited by Aliens have, long before the story opens, developed a wide range of PSI POWERS which have shaped a baroquely intricate society: the second trilogy's Mavin Manyshaped, for example, comes from a clan of SHAPESHIFTERS. The world itself, it emerges in the Jinian trilogy, has a Gaia-like planetary consciousness. The best term for these books would be Science Fantasy. They show an astonishing assuredness of narrative voice; for Tepper is that unusual kind of writer, the apparently *born* story-teller. Further evidence of her narrative fluency (and her seemingly endless inventiveness) came with the Marianne fantasy trilogy: *Marianne, the Magus and the Manticore* (1985), *Marianne, the Madame and the Momentary Gods* (1988) and *Marianne, the Matchbox and the Malachite Mouse* (1989).

Tepper's first novel of SF proper was initially split by the publisher into two volumes, *The Awakeners: Northshore* (1987) and *The Awakeners: Volume 2: Southshore* (1987), but was soon sensibly released as *The Awakeners* (1987). As a work of speculative sociobiology and ecology it is ebullient, but the plotting of this tale of a theocratic riverside civilization where it is forbidden to travel eastwards is sometimes a little awkward. The same year saw the shorter and more confident *After Long Silence* (1987), a melodrama set on a planet whose crystalline native lifeforms are very dangerous, and can be lulled only by music.

From this point Tepper concentrated on SF. Her first truly ambitious SF work was *The Gate to Women's Country* (1988), which surprised some readers for the ferocity with which it imagined a POST-HOLOCAUST world where social separation by GENDER is almost complete, but where the supposedly meek women outmanoeuvre the really dreadful men on almost all grounds. All Tepper's subsequent work is fierce; indeed, with hindsight, the same controlled anger is visible in the apparently affable science-fantasy books of her early career that can more easily be found later, even in a moderately uplifting tale like *A Plague of Angels* (1993), which allows its protagonists to survive the long ordeal of coming to a balanced understanding of a world complexly crafted out of SF and fantasy conventions.

The next year saw the beginning of her major SF work to date, the loosely and thematically connected Marjorie Westriding trilogy: *Grass* (1989), *Raising the Stones* (1990) and *Sideshow* (1992). To describe the trilogy by naming its villains somewhat distorts the ease and glow of these books' telling, and labours their melodramatic elements (which are only sometimes insistent): the villains are Nature-ruiners, fundamentalist religionists and – it is a category which comprehends the previous two – Mankind (whom Tepper sees as almost doomed by their own sociobiological nature); only the final volume – after the planet Elsewhere, five millennia hence, is freed from a tyrannous attempt to maintain by force a fetishized dream of human diversity – offers some relief. Tepper interrupted this trilogy with *Beauty* (1991), part MAGIC REALISM, part fairy tale, part SF, in which Sleeping Beauty is taken by TIME TRAVEL – because she has witnessed some visitors from the future – to a savagely DYSTOPIAN twenty-second century and meets (in various guises, including that of Prince Charming) the Beast; this is a book about despoliation as a consequence of CLIMATE CHANGE and other DISASTERS, including, again, the incapacity of male humans to change their behaviour: in the end, the planet has no chance. In the first volumes of the Marjorie Westriding sequence and in *Beauty* the effective END OF THE WORLD, for all these reasons, can be placed about a century hence; *Shadow's End* (1994) returns directly to this scenario, with environmental destruction again primarily caused by a dire marriage of fundamentalist religion and maleness: in this case at the hands of religionists whom she calls Firsters, after their insistence that only humans, of all creatures in the galaxy, have any right to live.

Later novels sharing these concerns – sometimes with an excessive intensity – include *Gibbon's Decline and Fall* (1994) and *The Fresco* (2000) and *The Waters Rising* (2010), where that intensity has become simplisitic. More tolerantly, *Six Moon Dance* (1998) allows Old Earth to survive (by the skin of its teeth) in the background, focusing instead on a colony planet whose native indigenes do all the physical labour for humans but are 'perceived' as invisible. The story, however, becomes far more complex than its beginning chapters suggest, and its subtleties of social analysis – along with some highly intricate GODGAME manoeuvres by a sentient distributed network evolved beyond real comparison with computers – make it perhaps Tepper's finest late work. Also very notable is *The Margarets* (2007), whose title describes the seven distinct AVATARS or DOPPELGANGERS, occupying differing contexts on different planets, into which the tale's protagonist Margaret becomes divided, as though her various strands of childish lifestyle fantasy had been actualized by a tangling of similar PARALLEL WORLDS; meanwhile humanity has a bad case of arrested development (especially in matters of ecology) caused by unpleasant aliens, but may with difficulty be saved.

Tepper requires the engine of story to provide impulsion for the other things she can do, which tends to tilt her work towards melodrama and excess, and thus to obscure a little her remarkable sophistication. In the space of only a few years she became one of SF's premier world-builders; the diversity of invented societies in *Sideshow* – this diversity being the actual point of the book – is breathtaking, as is the vivid ecological mystery of *Grass*, the bizarre discovery of a *bona fide* 'god' in *Raising the Stones*, and the planetary dance that climaxes *Six Moon Dance*. She was one of the most significant new – and new FEMINIST – voices to enter 1980s SF, and a figure whose daunting singlemindedness about the disasters threatening this planet have significantly affected the world of SF.

Tepper has grown increasingly angry with our treatment of the planet and of ourselves, sometimes with a clarity that can become almost cartoonish, so it is a great pleasure to be reminded, in the three novels here brought together, that she is a consummate world-builder, and that the lessons she teaches are, in the end, humane. *After Long Silence* is set on a planet partially colonized by humans, but whose native inhabitants take us in their stride. In the end only music – music played from the heart's depths – can sing across the gaps of unknowing; and families are reunited, and the wicked are punished. *Shadow's End* does expose us to nightmare, a human-based space empire that has been 'homo-normed' according to the 'Firster' philosophy that humans (effectively human males) have sole rights to the universe, which they transform into a solitude. But the universe, as amply illustrated in this long tale, is too big for that to happen, too deep, too old, too wise. Though some of the same hard arguments shape the tale, the intricacies of

Six Moon Dance again trump any sense that we are being told too much. On a colony planet, where sex roles are amusingly reversed, strange aliens are discovered, seismic disturbances march in time to the thrust of testosterone, a wise crone saves all. It is a mix of stories only possible in a mature genre, for Tepper has mixed a dozen stories together here. Like her best work, it is a bucking bronco of a book, a sign that SF writers can continue to make it new. Her best work rides us into the sunrise.

For a more detailed version of the above, see Sheri S. Tepper's author entry in *The Encyclopedia of Science Fiction*: http://sf-encyclopedia.com/entry/tepper_sheri_s

Some terms above are capitalised when they would not normally be so rendered; this indicates that the terms represent discrete entries in *The Encyclopedia of Science Fiction*.

AFTER LONG SILENCE

1

When Tasmin reached for the gold leaf, he found the box empty. The glue was already neatly painted onto the ornamented initial letter of the Enigma score, and it would dry into uselessness within minutes. He spent a fleeting moment wanting to curse but satisfied himself by bellowing, 'Jamieson!' in a tone that was an unequivocal imprecation.

'Master Ferrence?' The boyish face thrust around the door was wide-eyed in its most 'Who, me?' expression, and the dark blond hair fell artfully over a forehead only slightly wrinkled as though to indicate 'I'm working very hard, now what does he want?'

Undeceived by all this, Tasmin waved the empty box and snarled, 'One minute, Jamieson. Or less.'

The acolyte evidently read Tasmin's expression correctly for he moved away in a nicely assessed pretense of panic mixed with alacrity. The gold leaf was kept in a storeroom up one flight, and the boy could conceivably make it within the time limit if he went at a dead run.

He returned panting and, for once, silent. In gratitude, Tasmin postponed the lecture he had been rehearsing. 'Get on with what you were doing.'

'It wasn't important, Master.'

'If what you were doing wasn't important, then you should have checked my supplies. Only pressure of urgent work could have excused your not doing so.'

'I guess it was important, after all,' Jamieson responded; a quirk at the corner of his mouth the only betrayal of the fact that he had been well and truly caught. He let the door shut quietly behind him and Tasmin smiled ruefully. The boy was not called Reb Jamieson for nothing. He rebelled at everything, including the discipline of an acolyte, almost as a matter of conviction. If he weren't almost consistently right about things; if he didn't have a voice like an angel ...

Tasmin cut off the thought as he placed the felt pad over the gold leaf and rubbed it, setting the gilding onto the glue, then brushed the excess gold into the salvage pot. It was a conceit of his never to do the initial letter on a master copy until the rest of the score and libretto was complete. Now he could touch up the one or two red accents that needed brightening, get himself out of his robes and into civilian clothes, and make a photostat of the score for his own study at home – not at all in accordance with the rules, but generally winked at so long as the score didn't leave his possession. The finished master manuscript would go into a ceremonial filing binder and be delivered to Jaconi. They would talk a few minutes about the Master Librarian's perennial hobby horse, his language theory, and then Tasmin would borrow a quiet-car from the citadel garage and drive through the small settlement of Deepsoil Five, on his way home to Celcy.

Who would, as usual, greet his homecoming with sulks for some little time.

'This whole celibacy thing is just superstition,' she pouted, as he had predicted. 'Something left over from old religious ideas from Erickson's time. We've all outgrown that. There's no reason you shouldn't be able to come home at night even if you are copying a score.'

The phrases were borrowed; the argument wasn't new; neither was his rejoinder. 'That may be true. Maybe all the ritual is superstition and nonsense, Celcy love. Maybe it's only tradition, and fairly meaningless at that, but I took an oath to observe every bit of it, and it's honorable to keep oaths.'

'Your stupid oath is more important than I am.'

Tasmin remembered a line from a pre-dispersion poet about not being able to love half as much if one didn't love honor more, but he didn't quote it. Celcy hated being quoted at. 'No, love, not more important than you. I made some oaths about you, too, and I'm just as determined to keep those. Things about loving and cherishing and so forth.' He tilted her head back, coaxing a smile, unhappily aware of the implications of what he had just said but trusting her preoccupation with her own feelings to keep her from noticing. Sometimes, as now, he did feel he stayed with her more because of commitment than desire, but whenever the thought came to him he reminded himself of the other Celcy, the Celcy who, when things were secure and right, seemed magically to take this Celcy's place. She didn't always act like this. Certain things just seemed to bring it out.

'I sure don't feel loved,' she said sulkily. He sighed, half in relief. She might not take less than a day to forgive him for having been away for the seventeen days it had taken to orchestrate and copy the new Enigma score – or, more accurately, the putative Enigma score since it hadn't been tested on the Enigma yet, and might never be – but she would come around eventually. Nothing he could do would hurry the process. If he ignored her, it would take even longer, so he set himself to be pleasant, reminding himself of her condition, trying to think of small things that might please her.

'What's going on at the center? Something you'd like to see? Any good holos?'

'Nothing good. I went to a new one that Jeanne Gentrack told me about, but it was awful.' She shivered. 'All about the people on the Jut, starving and trying to get out through the Jammers after their Tripsingers were assassinated by that crazy fanatic.'

'You know you hate things like that, Celcy. Why did you go?'

'Oh, it was something to do.' She had gone alone, of course. Celcy had no women friends and was too conventional to go with a man even though Tasmin wouldn't have objected. 'I'd heard it was about Tripsingers, and I thought you might like it if I went.' She was flirting with him now, cutely petulant, lower lip protruding, wanting to be babied and cosseted, making him be daddy. He would try to kiss her; she would evade him. They would play this game for sometime. Tonight she would be 'too tired' as a punishment for his neglect, and then about noon tomorrow she might show evidence of that joyously sparkling girl he had fallen in love with, the Celcy he had married.

He put on a sympathetic smile. 'It's great that you'd like to know more about my work, love, but maybe seeing a tragic movie about the Jut famine isn't the best way to go about it.' Of course, she wasn't interested in his work, though Tasmin hadn't realized it until a year or two after they were married. Five years ago, when Celcy was eighteen, her friends had been the children of laborers and clerks, and she had thought it was a coup to marry a Tripsinger. She had listened to him then, eyes shining, as he told her about this triumph or that defeat. Now all their friends were citadel people, and Tasmin was merely one of the crowd, nothing special, nothing to brag about, just a man engaged in uninteresting activities that forced him to leave her alone a lot. He could even sympathize with her resentment. Some of his work bored him, too.

'It's not just that she's bored, Tas,' his mother had said, fumbling for his hand through the perpetual mists that her blindness made of her world. 'Her parents died on a trip. Her uncle took her in, but he had children of his own, and they wouldn't be normal if they hadn't resented her. Then, on their way to Deepsoil Five, there was a disaster, one wagon completely lost, several people badly maimed. Poor little Celcy was only eight or nine and hardly slept for weeks after they got here. She's frightened to death of being abandoned and of the Presences.'

He had been dumbfounded. 'I never knew that! How did you?'

She had frowned, blind eyes searching for memory. 'I think Celcy's uncle told me most of it, Tas. At your wedding.'

'I wonder why she never mentioned it to me?' he had mused aloud.

'Because she doesn't want to admit it or remember it,' his mother had answered in that slightly sharpened voice reserved for occasions when Tasmin, or his father before him, had been unusually dense. Tasmin remembered his father, Miles Ferrence, as a grim, pious man who said little and expected much, given to unexpected fits of fury toward the world and his family, interspersed with equally unexpected pits of deep depression. Miles had gone into peril and died at the foot of the Black Tower the year after ... well, the year after Tasmin's older brother had ... Never mind. Tasmin had been surprised at how difficult it was to mourn his father, and then had been troubled by his own surprise.

Celcy was still talking about the holodrama, her voice becoming agitated and querulous. 'I couldn't see why they didn't build boats and just float down the shore. Why did they have to get out through the Jammers.'

He closed his eyes, shutting out other thoughts and recollections, visualizing the map of the Jut. The far northwest of Jubal, an area called New Pacifica. A peninsula of deepsoil protruding into a shallow bay. At the continental end of this Jut were two great crystal promontories, the Jammers – not merely promontories but Presences. Between them led a steep, narrow pass that connected the Jut to the land mass of New Pacifica and the rest of Jubal, while out in the bay, like the protruding teeth of a mighty carnivore, clustered the smaller – though still very large – offspring of the Jammers, the Jammlings.

'Jammlings,' he said. 'Scattered all through the water. I don't think there's a space a hundred yards wide between them anywhere. The Juttites would have needed a Tripsinger to get through there just as they did to get between the Jammers.'

'Oh. Well, none of the characters said that in the holo. They just kept getting more and more starved until they got desperate.' Her face was very pale and there were tiny drops of moisture on her forehead. 'Then they tried rushing past the Jam ... the Jam ... the Presences, and somebody tried to sing them through and couldn't and everybody got squashed and ripped apart and ... well, you know. It was bloody and awful.' Her voice was a choked gargle.

Well, of course it was, an inner voice said. As you should have known, silly girl. He pulled her to him and quelled the voice sternly, annoyed with himself. Her hysteria was real. She had been genuinely upset by the drama. Sympathy was, called for rather than his increasingly habitual impatience. 'Hey, forget it. All past history and long gone. Now that you're pregnant, you need more cheerful influences.' With a flourish, he produced his surprise. 'Here, something I picked up.'

'Oh Tasmin!' She slipped the ribbon to one side and tore at the paper, pulling the stuffed toy from its wrappings and hugging the gray-green plush of the wide-eyed little animal. 'It's so cunning. Look at that. A viggy baby. I love it. Thank you.' She stroked the feathery antennae, planting a kiss on the green velour nose.

He suppressed the happy comments he had been about to make. The toy had been intended for the baby, a symbol of expectation. He should have said something to that effect before she opened it. Or perhaps not. She was more pleased with it than a baby would be.

He tried with another gift. 'Except for a preceptor trip next month, I've told the Master General I won't be available for any extended duty until after the baby comes. How about that?'

'I wish it was already next month,' she went on with her own thoughts, only half hearing him.

'Why? What's next month?'

'Lim Terree is coming to do a concert. Less than three weeks from now. I really want to hear that ...'

Lim Terree.

He heard the name, then chose not to hear it. Not to have heard it.

Instead, he found himself examining Celcy's smooth lineless face, staring at her full lips, her wide bright eyes, totally unchanged by their five years of marriage. She was so tiny, he chanted to himself in his private ritual, so tiny, like a doll. Her skin was as smooth as satin. When they made love, he could cup each of her buttocks in one of his hands, a silken mound. When they made love his world came apart in wonderful fire. She was his own sweet girl.

Lim Terree.

She was pregnant now. An accident. The doctor had told them she couldn't possibly get pregnant unless she took the hormones he gave her, but she wouldn't take the drug. Could not, she said. It made her sick. Impossible that she could be pregnant, and yet she was. 'Sometimes we're wrong,' the doctor had said. 'Sometimes these things happen.' A miracle.

Tasmin was amazed at his own joy, astonished at his salesmanship in convincing her it would be fun to have a child of their own. Too soon for a test yet, but he hoped for a son. Celcy wouldn't mind his caring for a boy, but she would probably hate sharing him with a little girl. 'Fear sharing him,' he told himself, remembering his mother's words. 'Not hate, fear.'

He coughed, almost choking. He couldn't just go on staring at his wife and ignoring what she had said. He had to respond. 'When did you hear he was coming?'

'There are big posters down at the Center. "Lim Terree. Jubal's entertainment idol. Straight from his triumphant tour of the Deepsoil Coast." I got his most recent cube and it's wonderful. I don't know why you couldn't do concert versions, Tasmin. Your voice is every bit as good as his. He started as a Tripsinger, too, you know.'

7

He let the implications of this pass. It wasn't the first time she had implied that his profession was not very important, something that anyone could do if they were foolish enough to want to. *Mere* Tripsinger was in her tone if not in her words, betraying an ignorance shared by a significant part of the lay population on Jubal. She was wrong about Lim, though. He hadn't been a Tripsinger, mere or otherwise.

Lim Terree.

'I know him,' he said, his voice sounding tight and unnatural. 'He's my brother.'

'Oh, don't make jokes,' she said, the petulant expression back on her face. For a moment she had forgotten her recent neglect. 'That's a weird thing to say, Tasmin.'

'I said he is my brother. He is. My older brother. His real name is Lim Ferrence. He left Deepsoil Five about fifteen years ago.'

'That's just when I got here! He was a Tripsinger *here*?'

Not really, he wanted to say. 'You were only a school child when he left. And yes, he did some trips out of here.'

'Did he really do the Enigma? Everyone says he did the Enigma.' She was suddenly eager, glowing.

It was hard to keep the resentment out of his voice. 'Celcy, I don't know who "everyone" is. Of course Lim didn't sing the Enigma. No one has ever got by the Enigma alive.'

She cocked her head, considering this. 'Oh, people don't always tell the truth about things. Tripsingers are jealous of each other. Maybe he went with just a small group and got through, but it was never recorded or anything.'

He made a chopping, thrusting-away gesture that she hated, not realizing he had done it until he saw her face. 'Lim Terree did not do the Enigma trip. So far as I remember he led two caravans east through the Minor Mysteries, one out to Half Moon and back, and one through the Creeping Desert to Splash One on the Deepsoil Coast and that was it. He didn't come back from that one.'

'Four trips?' She gave him a skeptical look, making a mocking mouth. 'Four trips? Come on, Tasmin. Sibling rivalry, I'll bet. You're jealous of him!' Then she hastily tried to undo some of the anger he realized he had let show in his face. 'Not that I can blame you. He's so good looking. I'll bet the girls mobbed him.'

Not really, he wanted to say again. They – most of them, at least the ones his own age – knew him for what he was, a man who … better not think about that. He wasn't even sure that it was true anymore. Dad had screamed and hammered his fist, calling Lim filthy, depraved. Was that it? Depraved? Something like that, but that was after Lim had gone. Tasmin had only been sixteen, seventeen when Lim left. Lim had been five years older. Memory didn't always cleave to the truth, particularly after someone had gone. Perhaps none of what he thought he remembered had really happened.

'I don't remember,' he equivocated. 'I was just a kid, just getting out of basic school. But if you want to go to his concert, love, I'll bet he has some tickets he'd make available – for his family.' Which seemed to do the trick for she stopped sulking and talked with him, and when night came, she said she was too tired but didn't insist upon it after he kissed her.

Still, their love making was anything but satisfying. She seemed to be thinking about something else, as though there were something she wanted to tell him or talk to him about but couldn't. It was the way she behaved when she'd spent money they didn't have, or was about to, or when she flirted herself into a corner she needed his help to get out of. He knew why she did those things, testing him, making him prove that he loved her. If he asked what was bothering her before she was ready to tell him, it would only lead to accusations that he didn't trust her. One of these days, they'd have to take time to work it out. One of these days he would get professional help for her instead of endlessly playing daddy for her in the vain hope she'd grow up. He had made himself this promise before. Somehow there never seemed to be time to keep it – time, or the energy to get through the inevitable resentment. Looking at her sleeping face, he knew that Celcy would regard it as a betrayal.

Sighing, unable to sleep, he took his let-down, half hostile feelings onto the roof. It was his place for exorcising demons.

Virtually every house in Deepsoil Five had a deck or small tower from which people could watch approaching caravans or spy on the Presences through telescopes. He had given Celcy a fine scope three years ago for her birthday, but she had never used it. She didn't like looking at the Presences, something he should have realized before he picked out the gift. Back then he was still thinking that what interested him would interest her.

'A very masculine failing.' His mother had laughed softly at his rueful confession. 'Your father was the same way.' And then, almost wistfully, she added, 'Give her something to make her feel treasured. Give her jewelry next time, Tas.'

He had given her jewelry since, but he'd kept the scope. Now he swung it toward the south. A scant twenty miles away the monstrous hulk of the Enigma quivered darkly against the Old Moon, a great, split pillar guarding the wall between the interior and the southern coast. Was the new score really a password past the Presence? Or would it be just one more failed attempt, ending in blood and death? The Enigma offered no comment, simply went on quivering, visibly occulting the stars at its edge in a constant shimmer of motion.

He turned to the west in a wide arc, ticking off the Presences along the horizon. Enigma, Sky Hammer, Amber Axe, Deadly Dozen, Cloud Gatherer, Black Tower, the Far Watchlings, then the western escarpment of crowded and mostly unnamed Presences. A little south of west were the Twin Watchers. The Watcher score was one of the first Passwords he had ever learned – a fairly simple piece of singing, with phonemes that were easy to get one's tongue around. 'Arndaff duh-roomavah,' he chanted softly, 'sindir dassalam awoh,' wondering as he occasionally did if there was really any meaning in the sounds. Official doctrine taught there was not, that the sounds, when properly sung and backed up with appropriate orchestration, merely damped the vibration in the crystalline Presences, thus allowing caravans to get through without being crushed. Or dismembered. Or blown away by scattering shards of crystal.

Although ever since Erickson there had been people who believed implicitly in the language theory. Even now there were a few outspoken holdouts like Chad Jaconi, the Master Librarian, who believed that the sounds of the librettos were really words, and said so. Jaconi had spent the last forty years making a dictionary of tripsong phonemes, buying new translators from out-system, trying to establish that the Password scores were, indeed, a language. Every time old Jaconi thought he'd proved something, however, someone came along with a new libretto that contradicted it. There were still Explorer-singers out there with recorders and synthesizers and computers, crouched just outside the range of various Presences, trying endless combinations to see what seemed to work, coming up with new stuff even after all these years. Tasmin had actually heard the original cube made a hundred years ago by Ben Erickson, the first Explorer to get past the Far Watchlings to inland Deepsoil, an amazing and utterly mysterious, if not mystical, achievement. How could anyone possibly have arrived at the particular combination of phonemes and orchestral effect by trial and error! It seemed impossible.

'It had to be clairvoyance,' Tasmin mused, not for the first time. 'A crystal ball and a fine voice.'

Erickson had sung his way past the Presences for almost fifty years before becoming one more singer to fall to the Enigma. During those years he had made an immortal name for himself and founded both the Order of Tripsingers and the Order of Explorers. Not bad accomplishments for one man. Tasmin would have been content to do one-quarter as well.

'Tassy?' A sad little whisper from the stairway. 'I woke up and you weren't there.'

'Just getting a little air, love.' He went to her at the top of the stairs and gathered her into his arms. She nestled there, reaching up to stroke his face, whispering secret words into his ears, making his heart thunder and his arms tighten around her as though he would never let her go. As he picked her up to carry her downstairs, she turned to look out at the line of Presences, jagged against the stars.

'You were looking at those things. I hate them, Tasmin I do.'

It was the first time she had ever said she hated the Presences, and his sudden burst of compassionate understanding amazed him. They made love again, tenderly, and afterward he cuddled her until she went back to sleep, still murmuring about the concert.

'He really is your brother? He'll really give us tickets?'

'I'm sure he will.'

In the morning, Tasmin wondered whether Lim might indeed make some seats available as Tasmin had promised. To be on the safe side, he bought a pair, finding himself both astonished and angry at a price so high as to be almost indecent.

The streets of Splash One were swarming with lunch-seekers and construction workers, military types, and bands of belligerent Crystallites, to say nothing of the chains of bewildered pilgrims, each intent on his or her own needs, and none of them making way for anyone else. Gretl Mechas fought her way grimly through the crowds, wondering what in the name of good sense had made her decide to come down to Splash One and make the payment on her loan in person. She could have sent a credit chit down from the priory in Northwest City by messenger, by comfax, by passenger bus – why had she decided to do it herself?

'Fear,' a remembered voice intoned in answer. 'Debt is a terrible thing, Gretl. Never get into debt.' It was her father's voice, preserved in memory for Gretl's lifetime.

'Easy for you to say,' she snarled. Easy for anyone to say. Hard to accomplish, however, when your only sister sent an emergency message from Heron's World telling you that she'd lost an arm in an accident and couldn't pay for her own regeneration. In advance, of course. No one did regeneration anymore unless they were paid in advance. And equally, of course, if you needed regeneration, no one would lend you any money either, except on extortionate terms that sometimes led to involuntary servitude. The stupid little twit hadn't thought she'd need regeneration insurance. Naturally not, when she had Gretl to call on.

'Shit,' she said feelingly, finding her way through the bruising crowds to the door of the BDL building, ignoring the looks that followed her. People had been looking at Gretl since she was five, men particularly. Perhaps it was her skin, like dark, tawny ivory. Perhaps it was her hair, a mahogany wealth that seemed to have a life of its own. Perhaps it was figure, or face, or merely some expression of lively unquenchable interest in those wide, dark eyes. But men always looked. Gretl didn't look back, however. Her heart *was* with a certain man back on Heron's World, where she'd be, too, as soon as this contract was over.

'What was that name again,' the credit office clerk asked, mystified. 'Here, let me see your code book.'

Gretl handed it over. One got used to this on Jubal. It cost so much to bring in manufactured materials that everything on Jubal was used past the point of no return. Nothing ever worked quite right ...

'It's been paid,' the clerk said with a look of knowing complicity.

'Paid?' she blurted in astonishment, only half hearing the clerk. 'What do you mean, paid?'

'Your loan has been paid in full,' the clerk said, glancing suspiciously from under her eyelashes. 'You didn't know?'

'I sure as hell didn't. Who paid it?'

The clerk fumbled with the keys, frowning, then shaking her head.

'Well?'

'Justin,' the clerk whispered.

'Who?'

'Oh, come on, lady.' The whisper was angry.

'I asked who that was. For God's sake, girl, tell me. I've only been on this planet for a few months, and I haven't any idea ...'

The clerk nodded, a tiny nod, upward and to the right. Gretl looked up. Nothing there but the glass-enclosed offices of the Brou Distribution Ltd., or BDL, hierarchy. In one of them, a curtain quivered. 'Him,' whispered the clerk, suddenly quite pale. 'Harward Justin.'

'The Planetary Manager?' Gretl fell silent, full of a sick uneasiness. She had met him. When she was here to arrange the loan, and only for a moment in passing. He had stopped at the desk where she was waiting, introduced himself, asked her to have lunch with him. She had refused.

A man with no neck, she recalled. Greasy rolls of fat from his jaw to his shoulders. Eyes that looked like half frozen slush peering at her between puffy lids. A drooping, sensual mouth. Wet, she remembered. He had licked his lips continually.

Abruptly she asked, 'Do you have an envelope?'

The clerk gave her a curious glance as she passed one over. Gretl inserted the payment she had been about to make, scribbled a few words on the outside, then handed it to the clerk.

'I am not interested in other people paying my debts,' she said. 'I'll repay my loan on the terms I specified. See that Mr. Justin gets this.'

She turned and strode away, the inner queasiness giving way to amazement and then anger. Wait until Don Furz heard about this! Unbelievable! The gall of the man!

She had almost reached the door when the hand fell on her shoulder.

He was a tall man, an expressionless man, an uninterested man. He did not look at her as other men usually looked at her. It was almost as though he did not see her as a person at all. He said very little, but he did not release her as he said it.

'My name is Spider Geroan. I work for Harward Justin, and he'd like to see you. Now.'

2

During Tasmin's orchestral effects class, it turned out that the air pump had been rigged to make farting noises, always good for a laugh. Practice for the neophytes shuddered to a halt while Tasmin dismantled the instrument.

'That particular sound is used, so far as I'm aware, only in the run through the Blind Gut,' he remarked to the class. 'The only instructive thing about this incident is that there are sounds that work better when produced instrumentally rather than by synthesizer, which is why we have drums, bells, pumps, and other paraphernalia ...'

'You're running perilously close to expulsion, Jamieson,' he growled when the class was over. 'That equipment is your responsibility.'

'Some of the pre-trippers are kind of uptight,' the boy remarked, not at all disturbed at the threat. 'I thought a laugh might help.'

There was something in that, enough that Tasmin wasn't inclined to press the matter. As was often true, Jamieson had broken the rules to good effect. This close to robing and first trip, many of the neophytes did get nervous and found it hard to concentrate. 'Sabotaging equipment just isn't a good idea,' Tasmin admonished in a fairly mild tone. 'Some idiot kid fooled around with a Jammer drum once, seeing if he could sound like some 'Soilcoast singer, and it got put into a trip wagon just as it was. Do you need me to tell you what happened?'

'No, sir.' Slightly flushed, but so far as Tasmin was able to discern, unrepentant, Jamieson agreed. 'I remember.'

'Well, double check that air pump. Be damn sure it does what it's supposed to do before you leave it.'

Jamieson moved to change the subject. 'Are we taking any of the first trippers out, Master?'

'On first New Moon, yes. There are only three I'm a neutral preceptor for, three I haven't had in my own classes – let's see, James, Refnic, and that Clarin girl with the astonishing voice ...'

'Renna. Renna Clarin.' Jamieson cocked his head, considering.

'Right. Anything I should know?'

'James will fade, definitely if there's a clinch, and probably anyhow. He spends half his life wetting his pants and the other half drying himself off and asking if anybody noticed. Refnic's reliable. The tougher things are, the

14

more he settles. I don't know that much about Renna Clarin except she looks funny bald. She transferred in.'

Tasmin ignored the impudence, as Jamieson had known he would. 'Evidently female neophytes don't have their heads shaved at Northwest, and it came as a shock to her when she got shaved down here. She had excellent personal references. Her records from Deepsoil Seven choir school were good.'

Jamieson shrugged eloquently, a balletic gesture starting at his shoulders and ending at his fingertips, which twitched a little, showing their contempt for good records. Excellent choir school recommendations might mean little except that a candidate had an acceptable voice or got along well with the Choir Master. Jamieson himself had had terrible choir school grades and had set a new school record for demerits, a fact that Jamieson knew Tasmin was well aware of. Again he changed the subject. 'What's the route?'

'Oh, I think we'll do my usual first trip loop. Past the Watchers on the easy side, down through the False Eagers, along Riddance Ridge to the Startles. Then down the deepsoil pass to Harmony, stay overnight there, give them a good scary look at the Tower while you and I sing them past, then back through the Far Watchlings.'

'If it was me,' Jamieson said, greatly daring, 'I'd use James on the Startles. He likes that score and he can't do much wrong there.'

'Rig him to pass, that it? Then what happens the first time some caravan depends on him?'

'Oh, I just thought a little more experience maybe …' Jamieson's voice trailed off, embarrassed. He obviously hadn't thought at all. Now he flushed and ducked his head in a hinted apology, a courtesy he accorded Tasmin but very few others.

'Think about it,' Tasmin recommended, testing the final adjustment of the air pump. He sat back then, musing. 'Jamieson.'

'Sir?'

'You're of an age to pay attention to the 'Soilcoast singers. What do you know about Lim Terree?'

'Oh, hey, apogee. Way up in the ranking. Best-seller cubes, last three out. The girls are brou-dizzy over him.'

'What's his music like?'

Jamieson gave this some thought. 'Kind of hard to describe. There's a lot of Tripsinger stuff in it, but he takes way off from that. Of course, all the 'Soilcoast singers bill their stuff as being real Passwords, but you couldn't get anywhere with it. I don't think you could, anyhow.'

'What do you mean?' Tasmin was really curious. He had so deeply resented Lim's misuses of Password material that he had not kept up with the 'Soilcoast singer cult, although he knew it was extensive and bled money at every pore. 'What do you mean, you couldn't get anywhere with it?'

Jamieson pursed his lips, gestured toward a chair, and Tasmin nodded permission to sit. 'You know the score for the Watchers? Minor key intro, two horns, and a tuned drum. Diddle, diddle, diddle in the strings in that rhythmic pattern, then the solo voice comes in with the PJ, ah the Petition and Justification, right? Kind of a simple melody line there, pretty straightforward, not like those key and tempo shifts in the Jammer sequences? Well, Lim Terree does a kind of takeoff on that. He uses the melody of the P, ah the Petition and Justification, but he kind of – oh, embroiders it. Trills and little quavers and runs and grace notes. Where you sing "Arndaff duh-roomavah," it comes out "Arn-daffa-daffa-daffa-duh-uh-uh-uh-duhroo-duhrooma-vah-ah-ah."' It was a marvelous, tumbling cataract of sound.

Jamieson had a good voice. Tasmin tried briefly and without success to convince himself he was listening to an obscenity. The phrase had been hypnotic.

'And it goes on like that?'

'The phrase "sindir dassalam awoh" takes about three minutes with all the cadenzas and rhythmic repetitions and stuff. If you tried that out on the Watchers … well, I just don't think it would get you very far. They'd blow and you'd be gone.'

'I see what you mean. What's the attraction then?'

'Well, it's great music. Really. Lots of noise and what they do on stage is pretty erotic. He wears something that looks sort of like a Tripsinger robe, only fancier, open down the front practically to his downspout.' Jamieson leapt up, gestured as though unzipping himself from a spraddled stance, at once potent and aggressive, making Tasmin see what he was talking about. 'The orchestral stuff is wild, too. Loads of percussion and heavy power assists.' He collapsed into the chair again, legs over the arm.

'Which couldn't be used on a real trip.'

'Not unless you had a trip wagon the size of a coastal broubarge to hold the power source.'

'So, how's he going to do a concert here? He'd never get that power by the Presences. And even if the Presences would let it past, which they won't, the widest trail on Riddance Ridge barely passes a standard brou wagon.'

'Most of it'll probably be holo. He'll be live against his own recorded setup with maybe one or two live backup musicians along.'

'Why would he bother? If things are so great in the Deepsoil Coast, why come inland?'

The acolyte shrugged, a minimal shoulder twitch. 'I can't figure it. Too much exposure, maybe? I read the fanstats sometimes. There's a lot of competition among what they call the Big Six. Terree's oh, about number three, down from one or two a year ago. This new kid Chantry is a favorite with the Governor's crowd, and he's gone up like a balloon. Maybe Terree figures he'll be more of a novelty after he comes back from an inland trip.'

'Tripsinger Lim Terree,' Tasmin quoted from an imaginary poster. 'Back from a six-month tour of duty leading desperate caravans in the interior ...'

Jamieson grinned. 'Something like that, yeah. Why all the interest, Master Ferrence?'

'Oh,' Tasmin fell silent. 'I knew him once, years ago. He came from around here.'

'No joke! Really? Well, I guess it'll be old friends at the bar then.'

'Not really. I didn't know him that well.'

'I wonder why he didn't let me know he was coming?' Tasmin's mother stared toward him in wonder, though for years Thalia Ferrence had seen nothing but blurred outlines through those wide eyes. 'It seems odd he wouldn't let me know.' Her voice was aching and lost, with an agonizing resurgence of familiar pain, made strange only by renewed intensity.

He probably didn't know you were still alive, Tasmin thought, not saying it. 'Lim was probably too embarrassed, Mother. Or, maybe he didn't know Dad was gone and thought he might not be welcome.'

'His father would have forgiven him. Miles knew it was nothing that serious.' She shook her head, smiling. She seemed determined to reform Miles Ferrence in memory, determined to create a loving and forgiving father where Tasmin could remember only hostility and harsh judgment.

Not only her eyes that can't see, Tasmin reflected. Her heart can't see either. Maybe that's part of being a wife and mother, having a blind heart. If she's blind to Lim's faults, well, she's blind to mine as well. He tried to feel generous about her warmth to Lim but couldn't. Something about it sickened him. Sibling rivalry? That would be Celcy's easy answer to everything. No, it was the senseless expenditure of emotion on someone unworthy of it that offended him.

Or jealousy. It could be that. He could be jealous of Lim. It would be nice to have only oneself to worry about instead of juggling three or four sets of responsibilities. Celcy. Work. His mother, whose blindness could be helped at one of the 'Soilcoast medical centers if he could only get her there and pay the bills. Since Miles Ferrence had died, BDL provided no more medical care for her.

Not that she ever reproached him. 'Your wife has to come first, Tas. Just come see me when you can. I love it when you do.'

Now she leaned forward to take his hand and stroke it. 'Are you going out on a trip soon?'

'First New Moon, Mom. First trip for some recently robed singers. Be gone two days is all. I don't like to leave Celcy alone very long, not in her condition.'

'She's not still pregnant, is she?'

'Why – ' He had started to say 'of course, she is' and found the words sticking in his throat. 'Why did you think she wasn't?'

'Oh, I don't know.' That perceptive stare again, as though the mind saw what the eyes could not. 'It just seemed sort of unlikely. Tell her she's welcome to stay with me while you're away.'

He patted his mother's hand, knowing that she knew he would tell Celcy and Celcy wouldn't care. Sibling rivalry wasn't the only kind of rivalry she knew about.

On the first of New Moon he led a small caravan out of the ceremonial gate of the citadel, itchily anticipating the transition from reality to marvel. Deepsoil Five was reality. Celcy, who had been entirely marvelous at one time, was mostly reality these days. Work was entirely reality. Though the citadel tried to evoke a sense of exhalation and mystery, its ornamented ritualism had become increasingly matter-of-fact over the years. Chad Jaconi called the constant ceremonies 'painfully baroque' compared to the sense of the marvelous that had permeated Tripsinging when he was young. Maybe it was something you could feel only when you were young. Tasmin didn't feel it at all when he was in the citadel.

The marvel, the mystery – and almost always the exaltation – came when he left deepsoil. He anticipated the moment with a kind of hunger, never knowing exactly when it would happen, always sure it would.

He led the group through the sparsely populated area to the west of the citadel, past heavily planted fields of euphoric brou, Jubal's only export crop. Behind them lay the citadel, the food crop fields, the dwellings, the nondenominational chapel, the service and entertainment center. Behind them lay Deepsoil Five: very ordinary, very real, very day-to-day . . .

And all around them lay dream country.

They stopped at the edge of a brou field to put soft shoes on the mules while Tasmin picked pods for each of them, a privilege that Brou Distribution Ltd granted only to 'licensed Tripsingers going into peril.' The pomposity of the phrase never failed to amuse Tasmin. Any kid who was fast on his feet could pick brou under the noses of the field guards, and often did. In the last analysis, however, no matter how pompous the organization was, they all worked for BDL; BDL who maintained the citadels and paid for the caravans and the Tripsingers to get them through, and for the Explorers to find the way, and for the farmers to grow the food they all ate, and all the infrastructure that kept the whole thing moving. Tripsingers, Explorers, mule breeders, service center employees, hundreds of thousands of them, all working, in the end, for BDL.

'May we achieve passage and safe return,' Tasmin intoned, cleaving to the ritual, distributing the pods.

'Amen.' A stuttered chorus from the first-timers amid a crisp shattering of dry pods. They chewed and became decidedly cheerful. Tasmin smiled, a little cynically. The brou-dizzy would have worn off by the time they came near a Presence.

Soon the planted fields gave way to uncultivated plains, sloping gently upward toward the massif that formed a sheer-sided wall between the deep-soil pocket of Five and all the shallow soiled areas beyond. The stubby, imported trees gave way to taller growths, mythically slender and feathery, less like trees than like the plumes of some enormous bird. They smelled faintly spicy and resinous, the smell of Jubal itself. Among the grasses, smaller shrubs arrayed themselves like peacock's tails, great fans of multicolored, downy leaves, turning slowly to face the sun. Out in the prairie, singly or in groups, stood small Watchlets no taller than a man. They glowed like stained glass, squeaking and muttering as the wagon passed. Tasmin noted one or two that were growing closer to the road than was safe. He had not brought demolition equipment along on this trip, and in any case he preferred to pass the word and leave it to the experts. He made quick notes, sighting on the horizon.

The balloon-tired wagon was quiet. The mules wore flexible cushioned shoes. There were no rattling chains or squeaking leathers. More than one party had met doom because of noisy equipment – or so it was assumed. They rode silently, Jamieson on the seat of the wagon, Tasmin and the students on their soft-shod animals. Part of the sense of mystery came from this apprehensive quiet. Part came from the odors that always seemed to heighten Tasmin's perception of the world around him. Part came from the intrinsic unlikelihood of what they would attempt to do.

That unlikelihood became evident when they wound their way to the top of the mighty north-south rampart and looked down at what waited there. At Tasmin's gesture, they gathered closely together, the mules crowded side to side.

'What you see before you, people,' Tasmin whispered, 'is the so-called easy side of the Watchers.' He didn't belabor the point. They needed only a good look at what loomed on either side of their path.

Before them the road dropped abruptly downward to curve to the left around the South Watcher. A few dozen South Watchlings stood at the edge of the road, tapering monoliths of translucent green and blue with fracture lines splitting the interiors into a maze of refracted light, the smallest among them five times Tasmin's height. Behind the Watchlings began the base of the South Watcher itself, a looming tower of emerald and sapphire, spilling foliage from myriad ledges, crowned with flights of gyre-birds that rose in a whirling, smoke-like cloud around the crest, five hundred feet above.

On the north side of the road a crowd of smaller North Watchlings shone in hues of amethyst and smoke, and the great bulk of the North Watcher hung above them, a cliff formed of moonstone and ashy quartz, though chemists and geologists argued that the structure of the Watcher was not precisely either of these. In his mind, Tasmin said 'emerald' and 'moonstone' and 'sapphire.' Let the chemists argue what they really were; to him whether they were Presences hundreds of feet tall, or 'lings a tenth that size, or 'lets, smaller than a man, they were all sheer beauty.

Between the Watchers, scattered among the Watchlings, was the wreckage of many wagons and a boneyard of human and animal skeletons, long since picked clean. Behind the Watchers to both north and south extended the endless line of named and unnamed Presences that made up the western rampart of Deepsoil Five, cutting it off from the rest of the continent except through this and several similar passes for which proven Passwords existed.

Jamieson feigned boredom by sprawling on the trip wagon seat, although he himself had only been out twice before. Refnic, James, and Clarin perched on their mules like new hats at spring festival, so recently accoutered by the citadel Tripmaster as to seem almost artificial, like decorated manikins. 'Put your hoods back,' Tasmin advised them quietly. 'Push up your sleeves and fasten them with the bands. That's what the bands are for, and it gets your hands out in the open where you need them. I know the sleeves are stiff, but they'll soften up in time.' Tasmin's own robes were silky from repeated washings and mendings. The embroidered cuffs fell in gentle folds from the bands, and the hood had long ago lost its stiff lining. 'Put the reins in the saddle hook to free your hands. That's it.'

With heads and arms protruding from the Tripsingers' robes, the students looked more human and more vulnerable, their skulls looking almost fragile through the short hair that had been allowed to grow in anticipation of their robing but was still only an inch or so long. They could not take their eyes from the Watchers, a normal reaction. Even experienced caravaners sometimes sat for an hour or more simply looking at a Presence as though unable to believe what they saw. Most passengers traveled inside screened wagons, often dosed with tranquilizers to avoid hysteria and the resultant fatal noise. These students were looking on the Presences at close range for the first time. Their heads moved slowly, scanning the monstrous crystals, from those before them to all the others dwindling toward the horizon. South, at the limit of vision, a mob of pillars dwarfed by distance marked the site of the Far Watchlings with the monstrous Black Tower hulked behind them, the route by which they would return. They knew that there, as here, the soil barely covered the crystals. Everything around them vibrated to the eager whining, buzzing, squeaking cacophony that had been becoming louder since they moved toward the ridge.

The Watchers knew they were there.

'Presumably you've decided how you want to assign this?' Tasmin usually let his first trippers decide who sang what, so long as everyone took equal responsibility. 'All right, move it along. Perform or retreat, one or the other. The Presences are getting irritated.' Tasmin controlled his impatience. They could have moved a little faster, but at least they weren't paralyzed. He had escorted more than one group that went into a total funk at the first sight of a Presence, and at least one during which a neophyte, paralyzed with fear, had flung himself at a Presence.

'Clarin will sing it, sir, if you don't mind. James and I will do the orchestral effects.' Refnic was a little pale but composed. Clarin seemed almost hypnotized, her dark brows drawn together in a concentrated frown, deep hollows in her cheeks as she sucked them in, moistening her tongue.

'Get on with it then.'

The mules hitched to the trip wagon were trained to pull at a steady pace, no matter what was going on. Refnic climbed into the wagon and settled at the console while James crouched over the drums. Clarin urged her animal forward, reins clipped to the saddle hook, arms out.

'Tanta tara.' The first horn sounds from the wagon, synthesized but not recorded. Somehow the Presences always knew the difference. Recorded Passwords caused almost instant retaliation. The drum entered, a slow beat, emphatic yet respectful. Duma duma duma. Then the strings:

'Arndaff duh-roomavah,' Clarin sang in her astonishingly deep voice, bright and true as a bell. 'Arndaff, duh-roomavah.' With the first notes, her face had relaxed and was now given over to the music in blind concentration.

The squeaking buzz beneath their feet dwindled gradually to silence. The mules moved forward, slowly, easily on their quiet shoes, the muffled sound of their feet almost inaudible.

Flawlessly, the string sounds built to a crescendo. The drum again, horns, now a bell, softly, and Clarin's voice again. 'Sindir, sindir, sindir dassalam awoh.'

The mules kept up their steady pace, Clarin riding with Tasmin close behind, then the wagon on its soft-tired wheels, and the two riderless animals following. The synthesizer made only those sounds it was required to make. Muffled wheels and hooves were acceptable to the Presences, though any engine sound, no matter how quiet, was not. No mechanical land or aircraft of any kind could move about on Jubal except over deepsoil where the crystalline Presences were cushioned by fifty meters or more of soft earth from the noise going on above them. Since such pockets of soil were usually separated from other similar areas by mighty cliffs of ranked Presences, there was no effective mechanical transportation on the planet except along coastal areas and over the seas.

'Dassalom awoh,' Clarin sang as they moved around the curve to the left. 'Bondars delumin sindarlo.' Few women could manage the vocals for the Passwords needed around Deepsoil Five, though Tasmin had heard there were a lot of female Tripsingers in the Northwest. He gave her a smile of encouragement and gestured her to continue, even though they were in safe territory. If there had been a caravan with them, the Tripsingers and trip wagon would have pulled aside at this point and gone on with the Petition and Justification variations until every vehicle had passed. Tasmin felt she might as well get the practice.

Clarin began the first variation. If anything at all had been learned about the Presences, it was that they became bored rather easily. The same phrases repeated more than a few times were likely to bring a violent reaction.

At the end of the second variation, Tasmin signaled for the concluding statement, the Expression of Gratitude. Clarin sang it. Then there was silence. They pulled away from the Watchers, no one speaking.

A thunderous crack split the silence behind them, a shattering crash echoed from the far cliffs in retreating volleys of echoes. Tasmin swung around in his saddle, horrified, thinking perhaps the wagon had not come clear, but it was a good ten meters beyond the place where the smoking fragments of crystal lay scattered. Behind them, one of the Watchlings had violently shed its top in their general direction.

'Joke,' muttered Jamieson. 'Ha, ha.'

Clarin was white-faced and shivering. 'Why?' she begged, eyes frightened. 'Why? I didn't miss a note!'

'Shhh.' Tasmin, overwhelmed with wonder, could not speak for a moment. He took her arm to feel her shaking under his hand, every muscle rigid. He drew her against him, pulled the others close with his eyes and beckoning hands, whispered to her, and in doing so spoke to them all. 'Clarin, I've never heard the Watcher score sung better. It wasn't you. What you have to remember is that the Presences – they, well, they're unpredictable. They do strange things.' He stroked the back of the girl's head, like a baby's with the short hair.

'Joke,' murmured Jamieson again. 'It was laughing at us.'

'Jamieson, we can do without that anthropomorphic motif!' Tasmin grated, keeping his voice level and quiet with difficulty. He didn't want to talk, didn't want to have to talk, wanted only to feel the adrenaline pulsing through him at the shuddering marvel of the Presences. With an effort, he

focused on the frightened first trippers. 'These are crystals, very complicated crystals. Certain sound combinations cause them to damp their own
signals and stop their own electrical activity. It's complex, it's badly understood, but it isn't supernatural.'

'I wasn't thinking supernatural,' Jamieson objected, the everlasting rebel.
'Laughter isn't supernatural!'

'It is if a crystal mountain does it,' Tasmin said with finality, aware of the
dichotomy between what he said and what he felt. What he said was doctrine, yes, but was it truth? He didn't know and he doubted if any of those
promulgating the position knew for sure. Still, one didn't keep a well-paid
position in the academic hierarchy by allowing unacceptable notions to be
bandied about in front of first-timers, or by speculating openly about them
oneself, particularly when the BDL manual laid out the official position in
plain language. It was in BDL's interest that the Presences be considered
merely ... mineral. What was in BDL's interest was in Tasmin's interest.
He contented himself with a fierce look in Jamieson's direction that was
countered with one of bland incomprehension. The trouble was that he and
Jamieson understood one another far too well.

He gave Clarin a shake and a pat, then watched with approval as she sat up
on the mule and wiped her face. She was very pale but composed. Her hair
made a dark shadow on her skull, and the skin over her high, beautifully
modeled cheekbones was softly flushed. She had made a quick recovery.

'Ooh, that makes me seethe,' she grated. 'I'd like to ...'

'To demolish a few Presences, right? I know the feeling. Look at them,
though, Clarin! Look down there!'

He pointed down the long slope in front of them where the False Eagers
stood. She followed his gaze. Light scintillated from the Eagers in ringed
rainbows, coruscating and glittering, a rhapsodic symphony of color, the
flocks of gyre-birds twisting around them, a swirling garment of changeable
smoke.

'Would you want to destroy that?' he asked.

'No,' she said at last. 'I really wouldn't.'

'To say nothing of PEC orders to the contrary,' Jamieson remarked dryly.
'The Planetary Exploitation Council strictures do prohibit demolition of
anything except deepsoil encroachment.'

'Little ones,' she sighed. "Lets or 'lings. Nothing like that.'

'Nothing like that,' Tasmin agreed. 'Now, I'd like you to pay some attention to the aspect of the Watchers from this direction.' He dropped into
his dry, lecture-time voice, trying to turn their attention to something
besides the possibility of totally arbitrary annihilation. 'The score is different coming from the west, of course, and it's an uphill climb, which means
a longer reach, musically. It's called the "trouble side," though the westside

score is actually simpler, both vocally and in orchestral effects. I'd suggest we get a move on. We have the False Eagers, the Startles, and Riddance Ridge to pass yet today before we go down the deepsoil pass to Harmony.'

The first-timers took turns on the winding road beside the Eagers, a repetitive canon on one simple theme. James started well enough, but he got worse as the trip progressed. Refnic sang them through the Startles with practiced ease. As Jamieson had predicted, James froze in mid PJ on Riddance Ridge during an a capella series of phrases without any orchestral effects to cover the quiet. There was a moment of hideous silence. The ground began to tremble beneath them, but just as Tasmin opened his mouth to pick up the vocal Jamieson began singing, missing hardly a syllable, his voice soaring effortlessly. The ground beneath them quieted. When they had come across, Tasmin stopped them and passed his field glasses around, pointing out the wreckage of wagons that lay in a weathered tumble at the foot of the ridge.

It was hard to make a point in a whisper, but Tasmin could not let it wait. 'James, that's the result of too little knowledge, too many assumptions, bad preparations, or Tripsingers who freeze. There's nothing wrong with being a good backup man. The orchestral effects are just as important as the vocals. If you can't depend on yourself for the vocals, for Erickson's sake, don't risk your life and those of other people.' James was white with shame and frustration. He had been badly frightened by the explosion at the foot of the Watchers, but so had they all. Jamieson's face was bland. He was too bright even to hint at I-told-you-so.

After the trip, Harmony was blessedly dull, a small deepsoil pocket, entirely agricultural. Still, the food and beds were good, and Tasmin took half an hour to pay a condolence call on his mother's sister Betuny, a woman not close enough to ever have been called 'aunt.' Her husband had died only recently, and Tasmin brought a letter from his mother. After this duty call, he returned to the Trip House to find Renna Clarin on the porch waiting for him. She had wrapped a bright scarf around her head and wore a matching robe, vividly striped. For the first time he noticed how lovely she was, a thought that caught him with its oddness. He was not accustomed to thinking of the neophytes as lovely.

'I wanted to thank you, sir.'

'For what, Clarin? You did a good job out there.'

'For ... for not jumping all over me when I got scared.'

She was standing slightly above him on the porch, a tall girl with a calm and perceptive manner. Without the Tripsinger's robe she looked thinner, more graceful, and he remembered the feel her body against his when he had hugged her. One always hugged students at times of peril, but he realized with a flush that she was the first female student he had ever precepted. 'So you were scared?' he asked softly. 'Really scared?'

'Really scared.' She laughed a little, embarrassed at the admission.

'So was I. I often am. After a while you … you look forward to it. When you're really scared, the whole world seems to … brighten.'

She considered this, doubtfully. 'That's hard to imagine.'

'Trust me. It happens. Either it happens, or you get into some other line of work.'

She flushed, thanked him again, and went down the hall to her room. In his own room, Tasmin lay awake, conscious of the towering escarpments all around the town, gathered Presences so quiet that one could hear choruses of viggies singing off in the hills. Echoes of that surge of emotion hitting him that morning were with him still, a welling apprehension, half pleasurable, half terrifying. It had seldom come so strongly. It had seldom lasted so long. He lay there, his body tasting it, listening to the viggies singing until almost midnight.

He had his first-trippers up and traveling as soon as there was enough light. They stared at the Black Tower long enough to be impressed with the sheer impossibility of the thing while Tasmin, Jamieson close behind him, read silently from the prayers for the dead. The remains of Miles Ferrence lay somewhere in that welter of crystal trash at the bottom of the tower. After Miles Ferrence had died, Tasmin had gone back to the original explorer's notes and done a new Black Tower score, dedicated to the memory of his father. He had really done it to please his mother, and so far no one using it had died. Today he got them through by singing it himself, with Jamieson doing backup.

After the Black Tower, the Far Watchlings seemed minor league stuff, good practice, but with nothing very interesting about them. James asked to be excused. The sense of awe and mystery that Tasmin had been reveling in departed as they came through the last of the Watchlings and saw Deepsoil Five awaiting them at the bottom of the long slope. Back to reality again. Tasmin heaved a deep breath. He would be home in time for supper.

'How did your boysies do?' Celcy said, patting his face and reaching up to be kissed. 'Were they in frightfully good voice?'

'All but one, yes.' He didn't really want to talk about James. Or, for some reason, Clarin.

'Oh, poor poopsie, did he get popped off?'

'Celcy, that's not funny. And it's in damn poor taste.' He snapped at her, regretting it instantly.

Her good spirits were undampened, however. 'I'm sorry, Tasmin. Really. I just wasn't thinking. Of course, he didn't get popped off with you there.

That's what you're there for, isn't it? To keep the boysies safe and sound.'

'Among other things.'

'I missed you. I missed you a lot.' She opened his robe and came inside it, against him, pummeling his ribs with her fists. 'Did you hear me, did you?'

'I heard you.' He laughed, suddenly joyous. 'I heard you, Celcy.'

'So. Do something about it.'

His weariness left him. The aftertrip letdown was postponed. She was as giddy and playful as a happy child, eager to please him, and the evening passed in a tangle of lovemaking and feasting.

'I have been cooking dinner all day,' she announced at one point, pouring him a third glass of wine. 'All day long, without surcease!'

He rubbed his stomach ruefully. If he hadn't married Celcy for quite other reasons, he might have married her for her cooking. 'You're very good to me.'

'That's because,' she said, running her hands under his shirt. 'Because.'

There was an interlude.

And then, sleepily, 'Tassy, sweetie, *he* called.'

'Who?' He could not for the moment imagine whom she might be talking about, and then it came to him with a blow of almost physical force. 'Lim? He's here?' He had to be on Deepsoil Five or he couldn't have called.

'He's up at the power station. They're camping there for a day or two to get some equipment fixed, he said. Then they'll come on into town. He talked to me for the longest time, and he's the sweetest man! Tassie, you never told me how wonderful he really is. He wanted to know all about you and me and how we met and everything.'

There was a cold, hard lump, at the base of Tasmin's throat. He tried to swallow it away, but it wouldn't go.

'What else did he want?'

'To give us tickets to the show, of course. To have dinner with us after.'

'Did he ask about Mother?' It was the wrong thing to have asked. Her mood changed abruptly.

'Yes. He asked if she and your father were still living at the same place, and I told him your father died, but she was still there. It's funny he wouldn't know that, Tassy, about your father. I imagine he'll call her, too.'

Tasmin doubted it very much. When Lim had left Deepsoil Five, he had gone without a word. It wasn't until almost four years later that they had found out he was alive and well on the Deepsoil Coast, doing nightclub concerts of trip songs, moving young women to passionate abandon, making money with both hands. After Tasmin's father died, his mother could have used some of that money, but Lim had never offered, not even after Tasmin wrote ...

Funny. In the letter, he had told Lim that Mother was in need, but he had not said his father was dead. He had supposed Lim knew. And yet, how would he have known?

'What else did you tell him?'

'Oh, just that we wanted tickets. I said lots and lots, so we could bring all our friends ...'

Your friends, he thought. Your boyfriends and their wives. Celcy had lots of boyfriends, most of them married. Just friends, nothing to get jealous or upset over. Just boyfriends. No girlfriends, though. All women were rivals, no matter how young or old. Poor Celcy. Dear Celcy.

'You said dinner?'

'After the show, he said. He wants to talk to you.'

Jaconi caught him at lunch, very full of his newest theory. 'I'm convinced I've found a repetitive sequence, Tas! A similarity that crops up in over ten percent of all successful Petitions and Justifications.'

'Don't be pedantic, Jacky. Call them PJs like everyone else does.'

The older man flushed, ran his fingers through his gray beard as though he were combing mice out of it. 'Habit. Trying to stay dignified in front of the students. Hell, you were my student.'

'I remember. And you were a good teacher, too. You should have stayed with it instead of taking the library job.'

'Well, it gives me time to – you know. I know you call it my hobbyhorse, Tas, but it isn't just that. Really. Some days I think I'm that close.' He held up a pinched thumb and finger, almost meeting. 'That close. I know we're actually talking to the things! It almost seems I can understand what the words are ...'

'Until someone comes along with a new PJ?'

'No, that's been the trouble up until now. I've been assuming all the ... PJs should have a common element, right? But what if Erickson was right? What if it is really language.' Jaconi's voice dropped to a conspiratorial whisper, and he looked around to be sure no one was listening. 'I mean, we don't always say the same things under similar circumstances. Suppose I step on your toe. I could say, "Gee, I'm sorry," or "Excuse me," or "That was clumsy of me," or "Oh, shit," or any one of a dozen other things, all equally appropriate.'

'That's true.' Tasmin was interested, despite himself.

'Always before, I was looking for identical elements. All those translators I bought, I was always looking for words or phrases or effects that were the same and had the same effect. But if we don't always say the same thing to convey the same emotion, then maybe the Presences don't either and what I should be looking for is clusters. Right?'

'It sounds logical.'

'Well, so that's what I'm looking for now. I may even have found some. There are similar elements in about ten percent of all PJs.'

'What do you mean, similar?'

'Tone progressions of vowel sounds, mostly. With similar orchestrals. Horns and drums. There's percussion in ninety-five percent of the clusters and horns in over eighty percent, and the other twenty have organ effects that are rather like horn sounds.'

Jaconi's description had set of a chain of recollection in Tasmin's mind, and he reached for it, rubbing his forehead. 'Jacky, I brought you the new Enigma score a week or so ago.'

'You poor guy. I looked it over after you left it and it was a bitch.'

'Well, yeah, it was complex, but not that bad, really. The Explorer's notes were excellent; I've never seen better. It did have a long sequence at the first of the PJs, though, lots of vowel progressions in thirds and fifths and per-cussion and horns.'

'Who came up with it?'

'Some explorer who normally works way up in the north-west. Don Furz? Does it ring a bell?'

'Furz's Rogue Tower Variations. Furz's Creeping Desert Suite. Furz's Canon for Fanglings.' He pronounced it 'Farzh.'

'Oh, *Farzh.* I should have realized.'

'When's it scheduled for trial?'

'It isn't. The Master General wanted it on file, that's all.'

'No volunteers?'

'That's a bad joke, Jacky. We've been trying the Enigma for about a hundred years and what's the score by now? Enigma, about eighty. Tripsingers, zero. We won't have a volunteer unless we have someone set on suicide.'

Celcy had spent the week prior to the concert creating a new dress. Deepsoil Five was hardly a hotbed of fashion, and she often made her own clothing, copying things she saw in holos from the Coast where the influences of the star ships coming and going from Splash One and Two kept the style chang-ing. Her current effort was brilliant orange, shockingly eye-catching with her black hair and brown skin, particularly inasmuch as it left bits of that skin bare in unlikely places.

'You're beautiful,' Tasmin told her, knowing it was not entirely for him that she'd created the outfit. She took his admiration for her physical self for granted.

'I am, aren't I?' She twirled before the mirror, trying various bits of jewelry, settling at last on the firestone earrings he had given her for their fifth anniversary after saving for two years to do so. He still felt a little guilty every time he saw her wear them. The money would have helped a lot on what he was saving for his mother's medical treatment, but Celcy had really wanted them, and when she got things she wanted, she was as ecstatic as a birthday child. He loved her like that, loved the way she looked in the gems. They, too, glittered with hot orange flares.

He stood behind her, assessing them as a couple, he tall, narrow faced and tow-haired, like a pale candle, she tiny and glowing like a dark torch. Even in the crowded concert hall after the lights went down, she seemed to burn with an internal light.

He had told himself he would detest the music, and he tried to hate it, particularly inasmuch as he recognized the Password bits, the words and phrases that had cost lives to get at, here displayed purely for effect, used to evoke thrills. Here, in a Tripsinger citadel town, Lim had sense enough not to bill anything as a tripsong, not to dress as a Tripsinger, and to stay away from the very familiar stuff that anyone might be expected to know. Except for those very sensible precautions, he used what he liked, interspersing real Password stuff with lyrics in plain language. Even though Tasmin knew too much of the material, he still felt a pulse and thrill building within him, a heightening of awareness, an internal excitement that had little or nothing to do with the plagiarized material. The music was simply good. He hated to admit it, but it was.

Beside him, Celcy flushed and glittered as though she had been drinking or making love. When the concert was over, her eyes were wide and drugged looking. 'Let's hurry,' she said. 'I want to meet him.'

Lim had made reservations at the nicest of the local restaurants. None of them could be called luxurious by Deepsoil Coast standards, but the attention they received from other diners made Celcy preen and glow. Lim greeted them as though he had never been away, as though he had seen them yesterday, as though he knew them well, a kind of easy bonhomie that grated on Tasmin even as he admired it. Lim had always made it look so easy. Everything he did, badly or well, he had done easily and with flair. Tasmin found a possible explanation in widely dilated eyes, a hectic flush. Lim was obviously on something, obviously keyed up. Perhaps one had to be to do the kind of concert they had just heard. Tasmin looked down at his own hands as they ordered, surprised to find them trembling. He clenched them, forced his body into a semblance of relaxation, and concentrated on being sociable. Celcy would not soon forgive him if he were stiff and unpleasant.

'Place hasn't changed,' Lim was saying. 'Same old center. I thought they'd have built a new auditorium by now.'

Tasmin made obvious small talk. 'Well, it's the same old problem, Lim. Caravans have a tough enough time bringing essential supplies. It would be hard to get the BDL Administration interested in rebuilding a perfectly adequate structure, even though I'll admit it does lack a certain ambience.'

'You can say that again, brother. The acoustics in that place are dreadful. I'd forgotten.'

'I just can't believe you're from Deepsoil Five,' Celcy bubbled. 'You don't look all that much like Tasmin, either. Are you really full brothers? Same parents for both of you?'

There was a fleeting expression of pain behind Lim's eyes, gone in the instant. 'Ah, well,' Lim laughed. 'I got all the looks and Tasmin got all the good sense.' His admiring and rather too searching glance made this a compliment to her, which she was quick to appreciate.

'Oh, no.' Celcy sparkled at him. 'It takes good sense to be as successful as you've been, Lim.'

'And you must think Tasmin's pretty good looking, or you wouldn't have married him.'

They were posing for one another, advance and retreat, like a dance. Celcy was always like this with new men. Not exactly flirtatious, Tasmin sometimes told himself, at least not meaning it that way. She always told him when men made advances, not denying she liked it a little, but not too much, sometimes claiming to resent it even after Tasmin had seen her egging some poor soul on. Well, Lim wouldn't be around that long, and it would give her something to remember, something to talk about endlessly. 'He really liked me, didn't he, Tas. He thought I looked beautiful ...'

'Speaking of success,' Tasmin said mildly, raising a glass to attract Lim's attention. 'Now that you're very much a success, could you offer some help for Mother, Lim? She's not destitute, but I'd like to send her to the coast. The doctors say her vision can be greatly improved there, but it costs more than I can provide alone. And now with Celcy pregnant ...'

She glared at him, and he caught his breath.

'Sorry, love. Lim is family, after all.'

'I just don't want our private business discussed in public, Tas. If you don't mind.'

'Sorry.' Her anger was unreasonable but explainable. As ambivalent as she felt about having a baby, of course, she would be equally ambivalent about being pregnant or having Lim know she was. Tasmin decided to ignore it. 'About Mother, Lim? You are going to see her while you're here, aren't you?'

Lim was evasive, his eyes darting away and then back. 'I'd really like to, Tas. Maybe tomorrow. And I'd like to help, too. Perhaps by the end of the season I'll be able to do something. Everyone thinks this kind of work mints gold, but it's highly competitive and most of what I make goes into equipment. If you'll help me out with a little request I have, though, things should break loose for me and I'll be able to put a good-size chunk away for her.' He was intent again, leaning forward, one hand extended in an attitude Tasmin recognized all too well. The extended wrist was wrapped in a platinum chronocomp set with seven firestones. Not the yellow orange ones, which were all Tasmin had been able to afford for Celcy, but purple blue gems, which totaled in value about five times Tasmin's annual salary.

Tasmin felt the familiar wave of fury pour over him. Let it go, he told himself. For God's sake, let it go.

'What request?' Celcy, all sparkle-eyed, nudging Tasmin with one little elbow, eager. 'What request, Lim? What can we do for you?'

'I understand there's a new Don Furz Enigma score.'

'That's right,' Tasmin said, warily.

'And I understand you have access to it.'

'I made the master copy. So?'

His face was concentrated, his eyes tight on Tasmin's own. 'I need an edge, Tas. Something dramatic. Something to make the Coast fans sit up and scream for more. Everyone knows the Enigma is a killer, and everyone knows Don Furz has come up with some surprising Passwords. I want to build my new show around the Enigma score.'

Tasmin could not answer for a long moment, was simply unable to frame a reply.

'Oh, that's exciting! Isn't that exciting, Tas? A new Lim Terree show built about something from Deepsoil Five. I love it!' Celcy sipped at her wine, happier than Tasmin had seen her in weeks.

And he didn't want to spoil that mood for her. For a very long time he said nothing, trying to find a way around it, unable to do so. 'I'm afraid it's out of the question,' Tasmin said at last, surprised to find his voice pleasantly calm, though his hands were gripped tightly together to control their quivering. 'You were at the citadel for a time, Lim. You know that untested manuscripts are not released. It's forbidden to circulate them.'

'Oh, hell, man, I won't use it as is. It would bore the coasties to shreds. I just need it ... need enough of it for authenticity.'

'If it isn't going to be really authentic, you don't need it at all. Make up something.'

'I can't do that and use Furz's name. The legal reps are firm about that. I've got to have something in there he came up with.' Lim looked down. Tasmin, in surprise, saw a tremor in his arms, his hands. Nerves? 'That's just the lead in, though. There's something else.' Lim gulped wine and cast that sideways look again, as though he were afraid someone was listening.

'I've met someone, Tas. Someone who's put me on to something that could get us into the history books right up there next to Erickson. No joke, Tas. You and Cels can be part of something absolutely world shattering. Something to set Jubal on its ear ...'

'Oh, don't be stiff about it, Tas.' Celcy was pleading now, making a playful face at him. 'He's family and it's all really exciting! Let him have it.'

'Celcy.' He shook his head helplessly, praying she would understand. 'I'm a Tripsinger. I'm licensed under a code of ethics. Even if we ignored the risk to my job, our livelihood, I swore to uphold those ethics. They won't permit me to do what Lim wants, I'm sorry.'

'Hell, I was a Tripsinger, too, brother,' Lim said in a harsh, demanding tone. 'Don't you owe me a little professional courtesy? Not even to make a bundle for old Mom, huh?' Said with that easy smile, with a little sneer, a well-remembered sneer.

The dam broke.

'What you spent for that unit you've got on your wrist would get Mom's eyes fixed and set her up for life,' Tasmin said flatly. 'Don't feed me that shit about putting it all into equipment because I know it's a lie. You were never a Tripsinger. You broke every rule, every oath you took. You set up that ass Ran Connel to help you fake your way through the first trip, then after you were licensed you led four trips, and your backup had to bail you out on all of them. You got through school by stealing. You stole tests. You stole answers. You stole other people's homework including mine. Whenever anyone had anything you wanted, you took it. And when you couldn't make it here, you stole money from Dad's friends and then ran for the Coast. The reason I have to support Mom as well as my own family is that Dad spent almost everything he had paying off the money you took. You never figured the rules applied to you, big brother, and you always got by on a charming smile and that damned marvelous voice!'

Celcy was staring at him, her face white with shock. Lim was pale, mouth pinched.

Tasmin threw down his napkin. 'I'm sorry. I'm not hungry. Celcy, would you mind if we left now?'

She gulped, turning a stricken face on Lim, 'Yes, I would mind. I'm starved. I'm going to have dinner with Lim because he invited us, and if you're too rude to let childish bygones be bygones ...' Her voice changed, becoming angry. 'I'm certainly not going to go along with you. Go on home. Go to your mother's. Maybe she'll sympathize with you, but I certainly don't.'

He couldn't remember leaving the restaurant. He couldn't remember anything that happened until he found himself in a cubicle at the citadel dormitory, sitting on the edge of the bed, shivering as though he would never stop. It had all boiled up, out of nothing, out of everything. All the suppressed, buried stuff of fifteen years, twenty years ...

Over twenty years. When he was seven and Lim was twelve, Dad had given Tasmin a viggy for his birthday. They were rare in captivity, and Tasmin had been speechless with joy. That night, Lim had taken it out of the cage and out into the road where it had been killed, said Lim, by a passing quiet-car. When Tasmin was eight, he had won a school medal for music. Lim had borrowed it and lost it. When he was sixteen, Tasmin had been desperately, hopelessly in love with Chani Vincent. Lim, six years older than she, had seduced her, got her pregnant, then left on the trip to the Deepsoil Coast from which he had never returned. The Vincents moved to Harmony, and from there God knows where, and Dad had been advised by several of his friends that Lim had stolen money – quite a lot of it. With Dad it had been a matter of honor.

Honor. Twenty years.

'Oh, Lord, why didn't I just say I'd think about it, then tell him I couldn't get access to the damn thing.' He didn't realize he had said it aloud until a voice murmured from the door.

'Master?' It was Jamieson, an expression on his face that Tasmin could not quite read. Surprise, certainly. And concern? 'Can I help you, sir?'

'No,' he barked. 'Yes. Ask the dispensary if they'd part with some kind of sleeping pill, would you. I'm having a – a family problem.'

When he woke before dawn, it was with a fuzzy head, a cottony mouth, and a feeling of inadequacy that he had thought he had left behind him long ago. He had ruined Celcy's big evening. She wouldn't soon let him forget it, either. It was probably going to be one of those emotional crises that required months to heal, and with her pregnant, the whole thing had been unforgivable. The longer he stayed away, the worse it would be.

'You childish bastard,' he chided himself in the mirror. 'Clod!' The white-haired, straight-nosed face stared back at him, its wide, narrow mouth an expressionless slit. It might be more to the point to be angry at Celcy, he thought broodingly, but what good would it do? Being angry with Celcy had few satisfactions to it. 'Idiot,' he accused himself. 'You can sing your way past practically any Presence in this world, but you can't get through one touchy social situation!' His eyes were so black they looked bruised.

He borrowed a quiet-car from the citadel lot and drove home slowly, not relishing the thought of arrival. When he got there, he found the door locked. Few people in Deepsoil Five locked their doors, but Celcy always did. He had to find the spare key buried under one of the imported shrubs, running a thorn into his finger in the process.

She wasn't at home. He looked in their bedroom, in the study, in the kitchen. It was only when he went to the bathroom to bandage the thorn-stuck finger that he saw the note, taped to the mirror.

'Tasmin, you were just so rude I can't believe it to your very own brother, I gave him the score he wanted, because I knew you'd be ashamed of yourself when you had some sleep and he really needs it. He really does, Tas. It was wrong what you said about his not being a Tripsinger, because what he found out will make us famous and we're going to the Enigma so he can be sure. You'll be proud of us. It would be better with you, Lim says, but we'll have to do it just ourselves.

'You were mean to spoil our party, after I decided to go ahead and have the baby just because you want it even though I don't, and I'm really mad at you.'

So, that's what she hadn't been telling him. That's what she had been hiding from him. A desire to end the pregnancy, not go through with it. The letters of the note were slanted erratically, as though blown by varying winds. 'Drunk,' he thought in a wave of frozen anger and pity. 'She and Lim stayed at the restaurant, commiserating, and they got drunk.' There were drops of water gleaming on the basin. They couldn't have left long ago.

He went to his desk to shuffle through the documents he had brought home for study. The Enigma score was missing.

Surely Lim wouldn't. Surely. No amount of liquor or brou would make him do any such thing. He wasn't suicidal. He couldn't have forgotten his own abysmal record as a Tripsinger; he wouldn't try the Enigma. He was too pleased with himself. Surely. Surely.

Tasmin ran from the house. It was possible to drive to within about three miles of the Enigma, but deepsoil ended suddenly at that point. From there on, travelers went at their peril. With cold efficiency he checked the gauges. The batteries would carry him that far and back. There were standard field glasses in the storage compartment.

He was through the foodcrop fields in a matter of minutes and into the endless rows of carefully tended brou. Ten miles, fifteen. BDL land. Miles of it. BDL, who controlled everything, who would not like this unauthorized approach to the Enigma.

Who would have his hide if he wrecked their car, he reminded himself, focusing sharply on a five-foot Enigmalet that had appeared from nowhere, almost at the side of the road, miles out of its range. Sometimes the damned things seemed to grow up overnight! As 'lets they were easy to dispose of, and someone should have disposed of this one. When they got to 'ling size, it was a very different and difficult thing.

He could see the Enigma peaks clearly. The great Presence was bifurcated almost to its base, rearing above the plain like a bloody two-tined fork. Five miles more. At the end of it he found his own car parked against the barricade. He could feel the ground tremble as he set his feet on it, and he hastily removed his shoes and took the glasses from the compartment. How high would Lim have dared go? How high would Celcy go with him, and how high would he dare go after them?

The world shivered under his feet, twitching like the hide of a mule under a biting fly. It wanted him off. It wanted him away. Moreover, it wanted those others off as well. He bit his lip and kept on. It was three miles to the summit from where one could actually see the faces of the Enigma itself, shattered plane of glowing scarlet, fading into a wall that extended east and west as far as had ever been traveled, a mighty faceted twin mountain that stood in an endless forest of Enigmalings, looming over the plains along the empty southern coast.

He climbed and stopped, scarcely breathing, climbed again. To his left, a pillar of bloody crystal squeaked to itself, whined, then shivered into fragments. He cried out as one chunk buried itself in a bank a foot from his head. One of the smaller fragments must have hit him. He wiped blood from his eyes. Other pillars took up the whine. He controlled his trembling and went on. Surely Celcy wouldn't go on. As frightened of the Presences as she was? She wouldn't go on. Unless she had no choice. Lim had always taken what he wanted. Perhaps now he was simply taking Celcy, because he wanted her.

He reached the top of a high, east-west ridge from which he could peer through a gap in the next rise. A narrow face of scarlet crystal shone to the left of the gap and another to the right, the twin peaks of the Enigma. From somewhere ahead, he heard a voice ...

Lim. Singing. He had a portable synthesizer with him, a very good one. All around Tasmin, the shivering ceased and quiet fell. Desperately, he climbed on, scrambling up the slope, finding the faint path almost by instinct. Something traveled here to keep his trail clear. Not people, but something.

The voice was rising, more and more surely. Silence from the ground. Absolute quiet. Tasmin tried to control his breathing; every panting breath seemed a threat.

Then he was at the top.

The path wound down to a small clearing between the two faces of the Enigma. Celcy sat on a stone in the middle of it, pale but composed, her hands clasped tightly in front of her as though to keep them from shaking, her face knitted in concentration. Lim stood at one edge, his hands darting over the synthesizer propped before him, his head up, singing. On the music rack of the synthesizer, the Enigma score fluttered in alight wind.

Tasmin put his head in his hands. He didn't dare interrupt. He didn't dare go on down the path. He didn't dare to call or wave. He could only poise himself here, waiting. Silently, he sang with Lim. The Petition and

Justification. God, the man was talented. It should take at least three people to get those effects, and he was doing it alone, sight reading. Even if he had spent several hours reviewing the score before coming out here, it was still an almost miraculous performance. He had to be taking something that quickened his reaction time and heightened his perceptions. There was no way a man could do what he was doing otherwise ...

'Go on down,' he urged them silently. 'For God's sake, go on down. Get down to the flatland. Get out of range.'

Celcy's eyes were huge, fastened upon Lim as though she were in a concert hall. Through the glasses he could see the eggshell oval of her face, as still as though enchanted or hypnotized. She did not look like herself, particularly around the eyes. Perhaps Lim had given her some of the drug he'd been taking? Go on down the trail, Celcy. While he's singing, go on down. Or come back up to me.

But Lim wouldn't have told her to go on. He wouldn't have thought how he was to go on singing and carrying the synthesizer and reading the music all at once. Perhaps she could carry the music for him. Lim began the First Variation.

'Move,' he begged them, biting his lower lip until the blood ran onto his chin. 'Oh, for God's sake, Lim, move one way or the other.' Lim's back was to him; Celcy's hands were unclenched now, lying loosely in her lap. Her face was relaxing. She was breathing deeply. He could see the soft rise and fall of her breast.

Second Variation. Lim's voice soared. And the Enigma responded! Unable to help himself, Tasmin's eyes left the tiny human figures and soared with that voice, up the sides of the Enigma, his glance leaping from prominence to prominence, shivering with the glory that was there. He had not seen a Presence react in this way before. Light shattered at him from fractures within the crystal, seeming to run within the mighty monolith like rivers of fire, quivering. Leaping.

A tiny sound brought his eyes down. Celcy had gasped, peering up at the tower above them, gasped and risen. Tasmin barely heard the sound of that brief inhalation, but Lim reacted to it immediately. He turned, too quickly for a normal reaction, his eyes leaving the music. Tasmin saw Lim's face as he beamed at Celcy, his eyes like lanterns. Oh, yes, he was on something, something that disturbed his sense of reality, too. Reacting to Celcy's action, Lim abandoned the Furz score and began to improvise.

Tasmin screamed, 'Don't. *Lim!*'

The world came apart in shattering fragments, broke itself to pieces and shook itself, rattling its parts like dice in a cup. Tasmin clung to the heaving soil and stopped knowing. The sound was enormous, too huge to hear, too monstrous to believe or comprehend. The motion of the crystals beneath him and around him was too complex for understanding. He simply clung, like a tick, waiting for the endless time to pass.

When he came to himself again, the world was quiet. Below him, the small clearing was gone. Nothing of it remained. Blindly, uncaring for his own safety, he stumbled down to the place he thought it had been. Nothing. A tumble of fragments, gently glowing in the noon sun. Silence. Far off the sound of viggies singing. At his feet a glowing fragment, an earring, gold and amber.

'To remember her by,' he howled silently. 'Joke.'

He wanted to scream aloud but did not. The world remained quiet. There was blood in his eyes again; he saw the world through a scarlet haze. Under his feet was only a tiny tremor, as though whatever lived there wished him to know it was still alive.

'I'm going,' he moaned. 'I'm going.' So a flea might depart a giant dog. So vermin might be encouraged to leave a mighty palace. 'I'm going.'

As he turned, he stumbled over something and picked it up without thinking. Lim's synthesizer. Miraculously unbroken. Tasmin clutched it under one arm as he staggered over the ridge and down the endless slopes to the place he had left the car. Not a single pillar whined or shattered. 'Joke,' he repeated to himself. 'Joke.'

Then he was in the car, bent over to protect the core of himself from further pain, gasping for air that would not, did not come.

3

He heard his mother's voice as though through water, a bubbling liquidity that gradually became the sound of his own blood in his ears.

'That acolyte of yours? Jamieson? He was worried about, you, so he called me, and we went to your house and found the note she left you, Tas.' His mother's hand was dry and frail, yet somehow comforting in this chill, efficient hospital where doctors moved among acolytes of their own. 'He got a search party out after you right away. They found you in the car, out near the Enigma. You'd been knocked in the head, pretty badly. You've got some pins and things in your skull.' She had always talked to him this way, telling him the worst in a calm, unfrightened voice. 'You'll be all right, the doctors say.'

'Celcy?' he'd asked, already knowing the answer.

'Son, the search party didn't go up on the Enigma. You wouldn't expect that, would you? They'll get close shots from the next satellite pass, that's the best they can do.' She was crying, her blind eyes oozing silent tears.

'They won't find anything.'

'I don't suppose they will. She did go there with Lim, didn't she?'

He nodded, awash in the wave of pain that tiny motion brought.

'I can't understand it. It isn't anything I would have thought either of them would do! Celcy? The way she felt about the Presences? And Lim! He wasn't brave, you know, Tas. He always ran away rather than fight. You know, when he was a little fellow, he was so sweet. Gentle natured, and handsome! Everyone thought he was the nicest boy. You adored him. The two of you were inseparable. It was when he got to be about twelve, about the time he entered choir school, he just turned rotten somehow. I've never known why. Something happened to him, or maybe it was just in him, waiting to happen.'

'You were right about Celcy's not wanting to have a baby,' he murmured, newly sickened as he remembered. It wasn't only Celcy who had died. 'I thought she'd become excited about it, but she really didn't want it.'

'Oh, well, love, I knew that,' she said sympathetically. 'You knew it, too. A girl like that doesn't really want babies. She was only a little baby herself. All pretty and full of herself; full of terrible fears and horrors, too. Afraid you'd leave her as her parents did. Hanging on to you. Not willing to share you with anything or anybody. Not willing to share you with a child. She needed you all for herself. When I read her note, I wondered if she would have been able to go through with it after all. I'm sorry, Tas, but it's true.'

It rang true. Everything she said was true, which simply made Celcy's scribbled confession more valiant. 'She was going to have the baby because I wanted it. She did things for me that no one ... no one ever knew about.' He breathed, letting the pain wash over and away. 'When she wasn't afraid – she wasn't at all like the Celcy you always saw. I wanted her not to have to be so ... so clinging. But I loved her. I got impatient sometimes, but so much of it was my fault. I never took the time with her I should have, the time to make her change. I just loved her!'

It came out as a strangled plea for understanding, and his mother answered it in the only way she could to let him know she knew exactly what he meant, her voice filled with such an access of pain that his own agony was silenced before it.

'I know, Tasmin. I loved Lim, too.'

Under the circumstances, the Master General was inclined to waive discipline.

'I don't want any more unauthorized removal of manuscripts, Tasmin. I know it's often done, but the rule against it stands. The fault wasn't prox-imately yours, but the responsibility was. You have been punished by the tragedy already. Anything further would be gratuitously cruel.'

Tasmin was silent for an appropriate time. He was not yet at the point where he could feel anything. He was sure a time would come that would demon-strate the truth of what the Master General had said about responsibility.

'Master.'

'Yes, Tasmin.'

'I was actually on the Enigma when it blew.'

'So I've been told. You have the devil's own luck, Tasmin.'

'Yes, sir. The fact is, sir, my bro ... Lim Terree was singing the Furz score. He had a portable synthesizer, I'd swear it was an Explorer model, and he was good, sir. He really was good. I haven't heard any better ...'

'If you're trying to justify ...'

'No, sir, you misunderstand. The score was *effective*. It wasn't until he forgot himself and started improvising that the Enigma blew.'

'Effective!'

'Yes, sir. There wasn't a quiver. He got through the first variation and well into the second before he deviated from the score. If they'd been able to go on down the far side, they'd have been well away.' He choked, remembering Celcy's face as she had looked joyously at the singer. 'Well away, sir. Well away.'

There was a long silence. 'I'm fascinated, Tasmin. And quite frankly, I'm surprised and puzzled. I remember Lim when he was here. I wouldn't have said this was in character at all. Your wife was a very attractive girl. Could she have – oh, egged him on, so to speak?'

Tasmin shook his head, 'No, sir. She was terrified of the Presences. She wouldn't even look at them through a 'scope.'

'How do you explain it?'

'I can't, sir. I really can't.'

'But the score was effective, a real Password.'

'Yes, sir. I think so, sir.'

'Well. Thank you for bringing this to my attention, Tasmin. I'm sincerely sorry for your loss.'

'Thank you, sir.'

And then home again. Sick leave. Dizziness and nausea and a constant gray feeling. Jamieson dropping in each evening to fill him in on what was going on. A Jamieson oddly tentative and uncharacteristically kind.

'James dropped out of Tripsinging. He's going to specialize in orchestrals.'

'Good.'

'Refnic's moving to the Jut. They've still got a shortage of Tripsingers there, even after – what is it now, six years? I guess most singers are still afraid of the Crystallite fanatics. Anyhow, Refnic's going.'

'Good for him.'

'Clarin's staying in Deepsoil Five. When I finish my acolyte's year, I thought you might like to have her. She'd like to work with you. You know, Master Ferrence, there's a lot to her.'

It was as though Jamieson was offering him something he could not quite see. Tasmin tried to respond but couldn't. Jamieson left it at that.

The synthesizer lay on the table in his study where the medical team had dropped it off. There were prints of the satellite pictures, too. The Master General had known he would want to see them even though they showed nothing at all except tumbled crystal.

The synthesizer was the best one Tasmin had ever seen, if not an Explorer model, something close. It had some kind of transposition circuits in it that

Tasmin wasn't familiar with. He fooled with it for over an hour before he was able to get it into play, and then what emerged was a mishmash that must have accumulated over weeks or months. Lim's voice. Rehearsals. Lim's voice again, cursing at a technician. 'Damn you, I've told you twenty times I want....' Then again, 'Get it right this time or get off the job ...'

Fragments of music. Real Tripsinging, as pure as air. Lim's improvisations. The Enigma score. Celcy's voice. '... Tasmin will be so proud! Everyone will know who we are, won't they? You, and Tasmin, and even me.'

Then back to the recording session, Lim's voice again. 'You'd think after all this time they could say something meaningful ... that was petulant of you ... pisses me off when they don't know who I am ...'

And finally great swaths of music, a full concert of it, uninterrupted hours of Lim's music, indomitable and triumphant.

When it was over, Tasmin sat in the silence of the house for most of the night, staring at nothing.

'It wasn't you, Tassy. It wasn't your fault.' Tasmin's mother wept, agonized by his guilt.

'In a way it was. If the Enigma score hadn't been at the house, she couldn't have given it to him. If he hadn't had it, he couldn't have gone there.' He reached for her hand, taking it in his, wishing she could see him.

'Tassy, it was he who asked for it, and she who gave it. All you did was ... ' His mother stared in his direction, intimidated by his silence.

'All I did was break a rule. Me. The one who was always telling her how important the oaths were. The one who always talked about honor.

'What you did was make a mistake. Not a dishonorable one. You only wanted the score to study. It was just a mistake, not a matter of honor ...'

'Mother, it feels like a matter of honor to me. I can't explain it. I know I'm not guilty of having any evil intent. I know I'm not guilty of anything perverse or dreadful, but I can't just let it rest. If I'd obeyed the rules, there wouldn't have been a mistake. Celcy would be alive. And Lim.'

'All right,' she spat at him, her decade's old resignation giving way at last to something alive and angry. 'So you did something wrong. God forbid you should ever do anything wrong. Everyone else, but not you. You're so much above mistakes. So damn good. And now you're going to punish me because you made a mistake.' She began to weep, tears running down her face in runnels from those wide, blind eyes. 'You're all I have left!'

'The money I got for the house will take care of you,' he said at last, unable to meet her pain with anything but this chilly comfort. 'I bought a BDL annuity, and I've written to Betuny in Harmony. She sent word by the last

caravan through. She's coming from Harmony. One of the laymen from the
Citadel will look after you until she gets here.'

'We never really got along.'

'You will now. She's your sister, and she's very grateful to have a place
since her husband died.'

'She thinks I'm crazy.' It was half a laugh.

'Let her think what she likes. And I won't be gone forever.'

'I wish I understood why you have to go at all.'

He wanted to tell her, but it would only have confused her as much as it
confused him, so he said none of the things he had been thinking for days.
Instead he murmured, 'I have to know why, Mother. I can't go back to my
own life until I know why. Right now all I can think of is questions with no
answers. Please – if you won't give me your blessing, at least tell me it's all
right.' He did not want to weep. He had already wept enough.

'It's all right,' she said, drying her eyes on her sleeve. 'It's all right, Tasmin.
If you feel you have to, I guess you have to. I just wish you'd forgive yourself
and let it go. We can all blame ourselves because people die. I blamed myself
over your father. And over Lim.'

'I know you did. This is just something I have to do.'

'All right.' She twisted the handkerchief in her hands, wringing it, reach-
ing up to run it under her eyes. 'Just be sure you take warm clothes with you.
And plenty of food ...' She laughed at herself. 'I sounded so ... motherlike.
We never outgrow it. We just go on fretting.'

'I will, Mother. I'll take everything I need.'

He went out to the quiet-car and sat in it, too weary to move for the
moment, thinking aloud all the things he had wanted to say but had not.

'I've always been your good boy, Mother. Yours and Dad's. I never asked
questions. I always did what I was told. If I broke any rules, they were always
little rules, for what I thought were good reasons. I loved someone, even
though I knew she loved me in a different way. I wanted a child, and she
wanted to be my child. Still, I really loved her, and sometimes – oh, sometimes all that love came back to me a hundredfold. And I thought if I went
on being good, life would be like that always. Something bright and singing,
something terrible and wonderful would come to me. Like my viggy Dad
gave me when I was seven. Like the medal I won. Like Celcy the way she was
sometimes. Something joyful.

'And instead there's this thing caught in my throat that won't go down.
Two people dead, and I don't know why. One I loved, one I hated, or maybe
loved, I don't know which. Maybe the other way around. All the things I
thought I wanted ... I don't know about them anymore ... I thought Celcy
was everything to me, and yet I didn't ever take the time to get things
growing between us. I thought I loved her, yet right there at the end. I was

thinking about the Enigma! Why? Why was I thinking about the music instead of about her?

'What did Lim know or think that was so important to him? What was he trying to prove? What made her go with him? *Why did she die!*'

'Celcy,' he cried aloud, as though she would answer him, forgive him. 'Why, Celcy?'

The Enigma listened, then it didn't. Jamieson called what the Watchling did during our last trip a joke. He was it was laughing at us. Maybe it was. Lim said he knew something, something to knock Jubal on its ear...

He started the car. There was a mount waiting for him at the citadel. The things he was taking with him were already there, packed by the Tripmaster's own hands into two mule panniers and slung on Tasmin's saddle. All the supplies a Tripsinger needed to travel alone, a rare thing in itself and one for which the Master General had been evasive about granting permission.

On the seat beside him was another bag that Tasmin had packed for himself. His favorite holo of Celcy was there, and the note she had written him, and the earring that was all the Enigma had left him of her.

The toy viggy baby was there, too. He didn't know why he was taking it, except that it couldn't go with the house and he couldn't bear to throw it away.

He laid his hand on the bag. Through the heavy fabric, Lim's recording synthesizer made a hard, edgy lump. One puzzle was inside that lump, preserved. His brother's music. Unexpected and glorious, not what he had thought it would be, not a music the Lim he thought he knew could ever have created.

The other puzzle was inside himself, in a place he couldn't reach, something he had to touch, could not rest until he touched...

Why had she gone there? Despite her terror? What possible reason could there be?

Whose fault was it? Why had she and the baby died at all?

4

The Ron River stretched its placid length along a gentle deepsoil valley sloping down to Deepsoil Five from the north. In the valley, deepsoil was no
more than a mile wide at any point, less than that in most places. There were
isolated farmsteads along the Ron, small crofts tenanted by eremitic types,
many of them engaged in crop research for BDL. Most were doing research
on brou, but some were engaged in improving the ubiquitous and invaluable
settler's brush, a native plant that had been repeatedly tinkered with by the
bioengineers, a plant on which both mule and human depended during long
journeys and which, it was said, the viggies and other local fauna ate as well.

Tasmin was greeted variously as he went, sometimes with friendliness
and other times with surliness. He returned each greeting with a raised
hand and distant smile. He did not want to stop and talk. There was nothing
to talk about. Certainly not about the weather or the scenery. The weather
was what it always was on this part of Jubal, sunny, virtually rainless.

As for the scenery, there was little enough of it. Wind sang in the power
lines stretching from the reservoir down to Deepsoil Five; the distant hydroelectric plant squatted at the top of the visible slope like a dropped brick;
the fields were neatly furrowed; each dwelling was impeccably maintained.
Like a set of blocks, Tasmin thought. All lines crossed at right angles. Even
the Ron had had its major meanders straightened, its banks sanitized. Few
crystals. No singing. No peacock tailed trees turning toward the sun. No
trees of any kind.

A demolition crew was working at one point on the road, lowering a
heavy mesh cone over an intruding 'ling. A noise box directed a loud burst
of low frequency sound at the shrouded crystal, and the pillar exploded into
a thousand fragments within the mesh cone. Tasmin spent a few idle minutes watching the crew gather up the knife-edged pieces and truck them
a few thousand yards to a vacant spot of prairie, well away from the road.
In time, every shard would seed another 'let and a new forest of crystals
would grow. From the color of the one destroyed, Tasmin thought it might
be a Watchling, probably from the North Watcher. That particular ashy
shade was rare elsewhere. How it had come here was anyone's guess. A piece
picked up on a wheel or popped into a wagon, perhaps. A shiny gem thrust
into a pocket and then carelessly thrown away. Then the dews of night

had dissolved minute quantities of mineral in the soil, and the crystal had grown, but how it had reached 'ling size without demolition was someone's culpable oversight. The thing had been twelve feet tall!

By evening, he had passed the hydroelectric plant and the dam, circled the shining lake, and reached the top of the long ridge that backed the reservoir. Here the flora was more typical of Jubal, the fan-shaped trees relaxing into their night-time fountain shapes as the sun dropped. His lungs filled with the faintly spicy aroma he loved.

He had almost decided to place his camp in a small clearing among a grove of the plumy Jubal trees when he heard a voice behind him.

'Master Ferrence? Camp is set up over here, sir.'

'Jamieson? What the dissonant hell are you doing here?' He turned to see the boy standing beside an arched tent, which was so well hidden among the trees that he had missed it on his walk through the grove.

'Acolyte's oath, Master.'

'Don't be ridiculous! Acolyte's oath only applies in the citadel.'

'Not according to Master General, Master Ferrence. He says I owe you most of a year yet, and where you go, I go. So says Master General with some vehemence.' The boy was downcast over something, not his usual ebullient self.

'How did you know which way I was going?'

'You and the Tripmaster discussed it. He told Master General and Master General told me. I left a few hours before you planned to.'

'I don't suppose it would do any good to ask you to go back and say you couldn't find me.'

'Master General would just send me looking. He said so already.' The boy turned away, gesturing toward the pile of wood laid by and the cookpot hung ready. 'We've got some fresh meat.'

Tasmin followed him in a mood of some bewilderment. It had certainly not been his intention to travel in company, and had he chosen company, he would not have chosen Jamieson. Would he? 'Master General didn't say anything to me.'

'He didn't want to argue with you. He told us to make ourselves useful and not intrude on your privacy.'

'Us?'

'Me and Clarin, sir.'

'Clarin!'

'Yes, sir?' The girl came out of the tent, touched her breast in a gesture of respect, and stood silently waiting.

'You don't have acolyte's oath as a reason,' he snarled, deeply dismayed. Clarin!

'Master General said I might have oath, sir. If your journey takes you past Jamieson's year, sir, then you would be starting on mine.'

'I didn't even say I'd take you as acolyte!'

'Well, but you didn't say you wouldn't, sir, so Master General ...'

Tasmin shook his head and said nothing more. He was too weary and too shocked to deal with the subject. The pins in his skull had set up a tuneless throbbing at the first sight of Jamieson, and he wondered viciously if the Master General would have been so generous with acolytes if he knew the effect they had on Tasmin's injured head. He had been peaceful, settling into the wonder of Jubal, letting it carry him. Now ... Damn!

He sat down beside the laid fire and watched while Jamieson and Clarin moved around the camp, making it comfortable. His acolyte seemed subdued, and Tasmin could appreciate why. An almost solitary trip into the wilds of Jubal would hardly appeal to Jamieson's gregarious nature. Though it wasn't mere social contact Jamieson craved. The boy would rather chase girls than eat, but he'd rather sing than chase girls, and he liked an audience when he did it. The thought of Jamieson's discomfort and unhappiness damped his own annoyance with a modicum of sympathy. Obviously, this hadn't been the boy's idea.

Clarin led Tasmin's mule off toward the patch of settler's brush just beyond the trees. The mule would eat it now; they might be eating it later – the roots and stalks would sustain life for human travelers, though no method of preparation did much to improve the taste. Clarin returned, leaving the mule munching contentedly.

'Why in God's name ...' he muttered.

Clarin threw a questioning glance in Jamieson's direction. The boy avoided meeting her glance. 'I believe the Master General didn't think you should be alone, sir.' She was respectful but firm.

'What did he think I was going to do? Throw myself at the foot of a Presence, like some hysterical neophyte or crazy Crystallite, and yodel for the end?'

Jamieson still refused to look at her. Something going on there, but Tasmin was too weary to dig it out.

'I don't know, sir. I think he just thought you needed company.'

Tasmin snorted. He didn't want company. He wanted to sink himself in Jubal. Breathe it. Taste it. Lie wallowing in it, like a bantigon in a mudhole. Wanted to be alone.

Which wasn't healthy. Even in his current frame of mind, he knew that. Well, did he need company? Certainly it would be easier traveling with three. There were routes that were passable to a single singer, particularly a good singer – and Tasmin was good, his peers and his own sense of value both told him that. However, two or three singers could do better, move faster.

46

'Did the Tripmaster enlighten either of you as to where I was going to end up on this trip?' he asked resignedly.

'No, sir.' Jamieson was heating something over the fire, still subdued.

'The Deepsoil Coast.' Where Lim Terree had lived. Where he had talked to people, left clues to himself. Lim's territory.

'What!' Jamieson turned, almost upsetting the pot, not seeing Clarin glaring at him as she set it upright once more and took his place tending it. 'No joke? Apogee! I've always wanted to go there!' His face was suddenly alive with anticipation.

'We're a long way from there. Weeks.'

'Yes, sir. I know.'

'What route?' asked Clarin, stirring the pot without looking at it, the light reflecting on her hair. It had grown into tiny ringlets, Tasmin noted, and she looked more feminine than he had remembered. In her quiet way, she seemed to be as excited as Jamieson.

'The only way I could get the Master General to agree to my going at all was to offer to do some mapping on the way. We've got some old scores he wants me to verify. Little stuff, mostly. Challenger Canyon. The Wicked Witch of the West. The Mad Gap.'

Jamieson put on his weighing look. 'Mapping is Explorer business. Besides, nobody travels that way.'

'Which is why he can't get an Explorer to do it. They have more important things to do. For some reason, Master General wants the scores verified. Nobody's been that way for ten or twenty years. Nobody's used the Mad Gap password for about fifty. I had quite a hunt to find a copy of the score, as a matter of fact. We have no idea whether the Passwords will still work.' It sounded weak, even to Tasmin, and yet Master General had been adamant about it. Something going on there? Tasmin would have bet his dinner that the hierarchy of the Order was up to something.

Jamieson was unaccountably subdued again. 'It sounds like it will take forever,' he said with self-conscious drama.

'Not forever. A few weeks, which is what I said to start with. Good practice for you two.'

'I suppose.' The boy growled something to himself, and Clarin muttered a reply.

'You don't sound overjoyed.'

Jamieson grunted, 'Right at the moment – I'm sorry. I shouldn't mention personal things.'

'Mention away.' Tasmin stretched out on his bedroll, feeling through his pack for the flask of broundy he usually carried.

'Right at the moment I'm mainly concerned that Wendra Gentrack will still be single when I get back to Deepsoil Five. She was madder than anybody I've ever seen when I told her ... told her I had to go.'

'Ah,' Tasmin murmured. Wendra Gentrack was a very social young lady. Daughter of Celcy's friend Jeannie and of Hom Gentrack, one of BDL's Agricultural Section Managers. 'You have an understanding?'

'I have had what I regarded as an understanding, yes. She seems to have whatever seems to be most fun for her on any given day.'

'I told Jamieson he was brou-dizzy,' the girl said from her place beside the fire. 'Wendra is virtually brain dead.'

Jamieson poked the fire viciously, pulled the kettle off and set out three bowls. 'Are you ready to eat now?' he asked Clarin in a poisonous tone. 'Would that activity possibly occupy your mouth with something besides giving me advice I didn't ask for?'

Oh, marvelous, Tasmin thought. All I need. A juvenile feud. Without thinking, he said, 'There are relationships that strike others as being inappropriate, Clarin, which are, in fact, very rewarding to those involved.'

She flushed, and he realized with sudden shock what he had just said. He felt his face flame, but kept his eyes locked on hers. 'We're evidently going to be traveling together. There is only one way I can see that this will work. From this moment you both have equal acolyte status. I expect citadel courtesy between the two of you as well as toward me. Right?'

They nodded. He thought Clarin had an expression of relief, although perhaps it was more one of quiet amusement. Amusement? At what?

Doggedly, he went on. 'And, Jamieson, I do understand how you feel about leaving 'Five just now. Believe me, I do. I would send you back if there were any way to do it.' And I will keep trying to think of a way, he told himself grimly.

'Now, what have you fixed for our supper?'

They sprawled near the fire with their bowls, a savory dish of fresh vegetables and grain served with scraps of broiled meat. A little wind came down the slope behind them, bringing the scent of Jubal and the sound of viggies singing. 'I had a viggy once,' mused Tasmin. 'For a few hours.'

'No joke? I didn't know anyone could catch them.'

'No, they can be caught. They just die in captivity, is all. But this was a young one that was found with broken legs along the caravan route. Somebody splinted the legs and kept the viggy and it lived. Later they sold him to my father.'

'Did it sing?' Clarin asked, her voice hushed.

'Not while I had it. It might have. It ... got away.'

There was a long silence, interrupted only by the sound of chewing, the clatter of spoon on bowl.

'Master?'

'Clarin.'

48

'You know I transferred in from Northwest.'

'Yes. I never knew why.'

'Oh.' She seemed to be searching for a reply that would be appropriately impersonal. 'My voice was too low for a lot of the scores up there. Nine out of ten of them are soprano scores, and I'm no soprano. The Masters thought I'd have a better chance of being steadily employed down around Five or even Northeast, over toward Eleven. It wasn't until I got to Five that I ever heard much about the Crystallites. And then you mentioned Crystallites a little while ago. Are they really set on killing off all Tripsingers, or is that just a horror story?'

'Well, there was that one notorious assassination on the Jut about six years ago,' Tasmin replied. 'I'm sure you've heard of that, even though you'd have been very young at the time. It was no campfire tale. All twelve Tripsingers at the local chapter house were killed by a band of Crystallite fanatics. The Jut has no food source of its own. The Jut Tripsingers made regular trips to bring in supplies by caravan, but there had been bad weather and food was already short. They were killed just as they were about to leave on a provisions run. There were about one hundred people there, and when they tried to get out between the Jammers, they all died but two. We have their accounts of what happened, and some accounts found on the Jut, written by people who died ...'

'And the Crystallites?'

'They got away, clean away. As far as I know, no one has ever found out how. They had to have had help, that's certain. Help from outside, somewhere. Anyhow, that was really the first occasion when anyone heard much about Crystallites.'

'I don't understand them!'

'They seem to have picked up Erickson's beliefs and carried them to a ridiculous extreme,' Tasmin said. 'Erickson believed the Presences are sentient, and by that he meant conscious, capable of understanding. He believed when we do a PJ we actually use meaningful words, even though we don't know what the meaning is. He started the Tripsingers as a quasi-religious order – the Worshipful Order of Tripsingers – and we've still got a lot of the old religious vocabulary and trappings left.

'The Crystallites picked up the belief in the sentience of, Presences and built on it. In their religious scheme, the Presences are not merely sentient but godlike. The Crystallites believe either that Tripsinging is diabolical or that all Tripsingers are heretics, I'm not sure which. Quite frankly, their theology doesn't seem to be very consistent or well thought out. Sometimes I think two or three people just invented it without bothering to do a first draft. At any rate, they seem to consider it blasphemous for people to speak to the Presences at all. Not up close, at any rate. If we do so, we're tempting the gods who may, if they grow sufficiently, agitated, destroy everything.' Tasmin smiled at her. Stated thus baldly, it sounded silly. At the foot of the Black Tower, staring up, it often seemed quite reasonable.

'What do the Crystallites want us to do?'

Jamieson answered in a sarcastic, singsong voice. 'They want us to stay on the coast, build cathedrals, burn incense, sing prayers all day, and bring in pilgrims from the known universe. Pilgrims who slap down consumer chits with both hands just to look at a Presence through a scope and even more to get within a few miles of one. That's about it.'

'Stated with Jamieson's usual contempt for complexity,' Tasmin chided, 'but essentially true. They have quite a commercial empire built around pilgrimage. And, sad to say, the emergence of the Crystallites seems to have been what caused BDL to revise its own position on the Presences.'

Clarin thought about this. 'Oh, of course! If people really thought the Presences were sentient, and if the Planetary Exploitation Council thought so, too, then BDL probably couldn't have exploitation rights to Jubal anymore. BDL might be deported, and it wouldn't like that one little bit. But ... if BDL defines the Presences as non-sentient ...'

'Not *if*,' said Jamieson. '*Since*. BDL's been defining the Presences as non-sentient for fifty years. Even though we all know they are ...'

'Jamieson!'

The boy threw up his hands, saying in an argumentative tone, 'Well, we do, Master Ferrence. I don't know a single 'Singer who believes they're non-sentient. No matter what he may say on the outside, inside he knows.'

'He or she,' said Clarin in a patient tone. 'There are women singers, too, you know.' It was obviously not the first time she had reminded Jamieson of this.

Tasmin sighed. Did he really want to spend effort cleaving to the BDL line on this trip? Did he want this continuing tug of war with Jamieson? Jamieson, who was, Tasmin reminded himself, one of the most talented singers it had ever been Tasmin's duty to try and whip into some kind of acceptable shape. Reb Jamieson? The everlasting mutineer? Who sang as he sang at least partly because he believed the Presences heard and understood what he sang? And Clarin. Clarin the what? He looked at her, but her face was turned down and he saw only the unlined curve of her forehead and the busy working of her hands on her bootlaces.

He chose peace. 'All right, Jamieson, say what you like on this trip. Say it to me. Say it to Clarin; she seems to have good sense. Say that the BDL has been trying to redefine the Presences as non-sentient for the last fifty years so BDL won't be threatened with expulsion. Say that most of us, Tripsingers and Explorers, don't really believe that. Say it here by the campfire. But don't, for God's sake, say it out loud in the citadel when we get back, or in any other

citadel we may stop at. I won't flame in on you if you'll be halfway discreet.'
He astonished himself with an enormous yawn.

The boy nodded, his face bright red in the fire glow. 'Even though we all
know they're sentient, it's different from being sure. I mean if anybody could
prove it, the Planetary Exploitation Council might make BDL pack up and
get out, so BDL won't let that happen.'

'BDL means you and me, too,' sighed Tasmin. 'If we're being honest, none
of us wants it to happen. So, be halfway discreet.'

'It's a kind of hypocrisy, isn't it?' Clarin asked softly.

Jamieson shook his head at her warningly.

'It's interesting,' mused Clarin. 'I hadn't paid much attention to all of this
Crystallite business. We were very isolated up Northwest, and it's closer there
to the 'Soilcoast than it is to the interior. There are a number of Crystallite
temples on the 'Coast, though. I do know that.'

'Lots of temples,' Tasmin agreed drowsily. 'And lots of pilgrims coming in.
Business versus business. Brou Distribution Limited against the Crystallites.'

'Us in the middle,' said Jamieson, nodding.

'Sleep,' Tasmin suggested again, rising and moving toward the tent.
Inside the cloverleaf tent the packs were distributed, each in a separate little
wing, privacy curtains half lowered. Tasmin's bedroll was stretched out for
him, the cover turned down. Clarin's touch. Clarin? A complex person,
he thought. It took a good deal of courage to come halfway across Jubal,
come as a stranger to a new citadel in an area where women were not as
well accepted as Tripsingers as they were in the Northeast. Well. He would
undoubtedly get to know Clarin rather well.

Sighing, he lowered himself onto his bedroll and dropped the curtain,
thinking about the whole BDL-Crystallite fracas. 'Us in the middle,' he
said, intoning Jamieson's sentiment as though it were some kind of bedtime
prayer rather than the invocation of a troublesome truth.

5

The Explorers Chapter House at the Priory in Splash One made up in class for what it lacked in homey comforts. Or so Donatella Furz had always thought. Built in the first enthusiastic flush of planetary exploitation – back in the time before BDL realized how limited access to Jubal was actually going to be – it was a symphony of rare woods inlaid with Jubal coral, squat pillars of vitrified earth, and enormous beveled glass windows looking out onto the sea and the city. Donatella's room had three such, a protruding roomlet facing in three directions, furnished with an elegantly laid table and two comfortable chairs. Eating breakfast in this extravagant bay window was an experience in both seeing and being seen. Half of Splash One seemed to be aware that it had a more or less famous personage among its more ordinary citizens, and a good number of them seemed to know where she was staying. Five or six young gawkers were gathered on the opposite sidewalk when she wakened that morning. They had gathered in front of a dilapidated struc- ture, which seemed to be half saloon and half something else, both halves in danger of imminent collapse. 'Looky, looky, Don Furz, the Explorer knight,' their gestures said, though they didn't shout at her, which she appreciated. When she sat down to breakfast, the same ones or substitute ones were still there, pointing and nudging one another.

Among whom, she warned herself silently, might be one with a laser pistol or an old-fashioned garotte or just a plain steel knife. The last one had had such a knife. Donatella still had it in her Explorer's case, wrapped in a bloody shirt, and she had a half-healed slash in her left arm to remind her of the cost of naive enthusiasm.

She finished her brou-pod tea, set the cup down with a little click of final- ity, and wiped her lips. Rise, she instructed herself. Rise to the occasion. Smile at the people. Wave. Go back in the room where they can't see you. Do not, repeat, do not shut the curtains. Only someone with something to hide would shut the curtains.

Why in heaven's name had she decided to stay at the Chapter House? She hadn't remembered it being this public, this exposed. And why in heaven's name had they built the stupid Priory right in the middle of town? She asked the services man this question when he came for her dishes.

'I think the town grew up around it, Ma'am. Some of the nearby buildings have gone up during the past year. Sixty or seventy years ago, as I understand it, the Priory was quite secluded.' He busied himself with the table and with a quick inspection of the room. As he left, he paused by the door to say, 'I am, by the way, instructed to ask if you have any special wishes during your visit? Special food or drink, entertainment?'

She knew the man's job description included entertainment of several very specific sorts, but despite his obvious charm and intelligence, he didn't appeal to her except as a source of information. If she needed to avail herself of a service employee sexually, she'd stick to Zimmy.

'How about a concert?' she asked, apparently with her usual dangerously naive enthusiasm channeled this time. Used for advantage. 'Chantry or Pit Paragon – one of those.' She gave him an eager, expectant look.

'It's not considered ...' He frowned, his darkly handsome face expressing disapproval neatly mixed with a proper degree of subservience, torso ever so slightly bent toward her, respect and good advice, impeccably offered. Oh, he was slick, this one.

'Oh, hell, man, I know what it's considered. Slumming, right? Undignified? Why would an Explorer knight want to listen to some revisionary rip-off of the sacred calling?'

He grinned, and she suddenly liked him better.

'Tell you what, what's your name?'

'Blanchet, Ma'am.'

'All right, Blanchet, we won't scandalize the natives by appearing in public as ourselves. You shop for me today. Buy me a wig. Let's see. Something red, I think.' She turned to catch a glimpse of herself in the mirror, smoothing the wide, short bell of golden hair with one hand. Dark blue eyes. Straight nose, a little too long she had always felt. All that climbing about had kept her figure slim, what there was of it. She could get away with a red wig. 'Are they still wearing masks at public events down here? Well, buy me a small one that'll hide my eyes and nose. And a dress. I need a bright blue dress.'

The man was openly laughing now. 'Size, Ma'am?'

'One of those wraparound things with the straps that go all which a ways. They only come one size, you know what I mean? Stretch to fit? In some cases, stretch to rip?'

He nodded. 'Is that all, Ma'am?'

'Concert tickets. Any one of the top six will do fine, and you might keep your mouth shut about it, if you're allowed to do that. No point in distressing your Prior or mine ... or the Explorer King.'

'I can be discreet.'

'You'll find me most generous if you are.'

He bowed himself out with the breakfast dishes, almost certainly going to report directly to someone from the Exploration Department. Probably the local Prior, who would want to know what the visiting knight was up to. So, let him report: The Explorer knight had a taste for night life; the Explorer knight wanted a new dress; the Explorer knight didn't want to be recognized. Everything on the list slightly against the conventions and everything perfectly harmless. The conventions would have had her making a ceremonial procession of herself, dressed in tall boots and worn Explorer leathers, avoiding questionable entertainment and signing autographs with a slightly distant smile. Theoretically, they should suspect her more if she were more compliant. Surely someone on the edge of treason wouldn't be dressing up for a 'Soilcoast singer concert.

She gritted her teeth in concentration. Since someone had tried to kill her, she had to assume that everything she did was watched, every word she said was overheard. Making contact was up to her trusted friend. All she had to do was get herself out in public where it could be done without being noticed. The Chapter House would be watched for the agreed-upon signal – a red wig and a blue dress. Pray God her trusted friend had managed everything according to plan.

And pray God the arrangement had been made with Lim Terree.

When evening came, she decided she rather liked the effect of the red wig, an almost devil-may-care gaiety, in no sense diminished by the impish half mask with the feathery eyebrows. And the blue dress, which clung satisfactorily, was a success also, drawing attention away from her face. Blanchet would accompany her, of course. Explorer knights, male or female, always had at least one escort when in the larger 'Soilcoast cities, if for no other reason than to keep the celebrity seekers in order. If she and Blanchet were lucky, they would be taken for just another couple out on the town; tourists from Serendipity or even from out-system, perhaps; or minor BDL officials in from a deepsoil pocket, a dirt town. They would have dinner, see the sights, attend the concert, and return to the Chapter House. Where she either would or would not invite Blanchet to share her bed for the night. He was an attractive enough man. But he wasn't Link. He wasn't even Zimmy.

She poured herself a drink and sat down on the couch that fronted the extravagant windows, far enough back in the room that she could not be seen. There were at least ten gawkers outside her window now, all staring upward as though hypnotized. In a few minutes she would go and lean out of the window, wave to them, call out 'Hi, how are you? Great night, isn't it?' Watching for any move in her direction, any weapon. Anything that might betray another assassin.

Though there might not be another one. Not yet. Whoever had sent the first assassin could not know that the would-be killer was dead. For all the sender knew, the assassin might be alive and well and ready to try again. She could say that phrase to herself calmly, 'try again,' say it almost without fear. It was only when she took the thought further, 'try again to kill Don Furz,' that her stomach clenched into a knot and bile burned in her throat. 'Try again to kill Don Furz because Don Furz knows something she is not supposed to know.'

Not that she'd been trying to find out any such thing! She had been sitting in the large underground library of the Chapter House, three floors below where she was sitting right now, poring through some old papers for references to the Mad Gap. Her Prior thought there might be some early Explorer comments that would suggest a useful method of approach. The Gap was currently impassable. BDL wanted it passable. Thus, Donatella Furz, who thought she remembered reading something about it years ago, was immured in dusty papers and unintelligible correspondence, bored to tears, yawning over the ancient stacks, and longing for dinner. She was skimming the letters between a virtually unremembered third decade Explorer and his Prior when she came upon a page in a completely different handwriting. The half-stretched yawn died on her face and she stared at it in disbelief. She did not need to see the signature to know whose it was. Erickson! She had seen faxes of that handwriting a thousand times. She had seen the handwriting itself a hundred times in the Erickson Library at Northwest City, a library that was supposed to contain every extant scrap of original Erickson material.

But here it was, a letter in the master's own hand! It had obviously been misfiled and had lain unread for the last seventy years. Misfiled by whom? Reading the entire letter made it very clear. Misfiled by Erickson himself.

It was a letter to the future, couched in such subtle and evasive terms that only an Explorer – and one of a particular turn of mind at that – would find it intelligible. It hinted at possibilities that Donatella Furz found stunning in their implications. 'I have further outlined this matter,' the letter concluded. 'Reference my papers on the Shivering Desert, filed with the Chapter House in the Priory of Northwest.'

Northwest was her home House. When she had fruitlessly completed the Mad Gap research, too excited to concentrate on it any longer, she returned to Northwest City and found the papers Erickson had referred to. They took some finding because they weren't included in the Erickson material at all. They were buried in the middle of an endless compilation of permutations used in the Shivering Desert, an area that had been totally passworded for eighty years and was, therefore, uninteresting.

'Buried in boredom,' she told herself. 'He picked two places no one would look for decades, and he buried them there.' The pertinent notes were on two pages of perma-paper. Donatella folded them and hid them in the lining of her jacket, then spent hours poring over them in the privacy of her room.

She had taken the papers with a sense of saving them, though protocol would have required her to report them to the Prior at once. Later she examined her motives, finding much there that disturbed her, but coming at last to the conclusion that she thought the papers were safer with her than they would have been with the Department of Exploration.

Even then she had had sense enough to leave other, harmless papers out in her room to explain her study, in case anyone was watching, or wondering.

Erickson had not expected his eventual reader to believe him without proof. At the conclusion he said in effect, 'If you want to test this theory, do thus and thus at some unpassworded Presence. If you do it right, you'll see what I mean.'

Don had chosen to try it on the Enigma. Everyone and his favorite mule had tried the Enigma, and permission to approach it was almost impossible to obtain. It had taken six months before she had the opportunity to get to the Enigma from the southern coast. She did what Erickson suggested – and more!

When she returned, it was with the recording cubes and notes for the Enigma Score, and she was dizzy with what she knew, bubbling with it. Erickson had only known half of it. If he had had a synthesizer like the current ones ... She had hugged the knowledge to herself, glorying in it. Only Donatella Furz knew the whole truth, the truth about Jubal. No one else knew. No one!

Only some time later did she realize that in seventy years there might have been others who knew or suspected, but if they had, they had been ruthlessly suppressed – only after someone had tried to kill her.

On her return, she had arranged for the Enigma notes to be sent to a Tripsinger citadel for transcribing and orchestration – 'Send it to that man in Deepsoil Five,' she had suggested. 'Tasmin Ferrence. The one who did that great score on the Black Tower.' Then she had reported a possible breakthrough to the Prior of her Chapter House and had done it with due modesty in language full of 'perhaps' and 'this suggests.' She had made all the proper moves in the proper order; none of them should have aroused suspicion. If only she could have kept it at that! But no matter what motions she went through, what modest little remarks she made when congratulated, she could not hide her elation. Inside herself, she was bubbling with what she knew, what she thought, what she wanted to prove, what she had proved. She had not been so foolish as to blurt it out to anyone – it was obviously information that some people would want to suppress – but neither had she been sensible enough to keep her obvious euphoria hidden.

Who might have observed that euphoria?

Explorers Martin and Ralth, while they were out at dinner one night. 'Touch me, boys, because the day will come when you'll tell people, "I knew her before she was famous."'

'What are you up to now, Don?' asked Martin, sounding bored. 'Another new variation for the Creeping Desert? Don't we have enough Creeping Desert variations already?'

'Bigger than that,' she had replied with a laugh. 'Much bigger.'

'You've got a Gemmed Rampart score that really works,' suggested Ralth. 'Or a foolproof way to get through the Crazies.'

'Why not?' She had giggled.

'Which?'

'Why not both? Why not everything?'

They had laughed incredulously. They had ordered more wine. There had been laughter and arguments among the three Explorers and congratulations on the Enigma score.

Well, what else had she said that night? Nothing. Nothing at all. One bragging phrase. 'Why not everything?' Had there been enough in that conversation to give someone the idea that Donatella Furz knew something they would rather she didn't know? Not really. It could all be put down to her euphoria. Even an untested score for a Presence as famous as the Enigma lent a certain cachet to her name. She hadn't really said anything at all!

Who else had she talked to? Zimmy. A services employee. A Northwest Chapter House man. Not unlike this Chapter House man, Blanchet, except that Zimmy belonged to Don. He was only hers, he kept saying, and had been only hers for some years now, eager to please her, intelligent in meeting her needs for comfort and affection. Zimmy. She thought of him with both fondness and pleasure. What had she said to Zimmy? Nothing much. 'Oh, Zimmy, if you knew what I know.' Something like that. He hadn't even paid much attention.

And who else? The woman in Northwest City who usually cut her hair.

Don's head had been bent forward while the woman depilated the back of her neck, quite high, so that the bottom of the wide bell of her hair would come just to the bottom of her ears. 'How can you do it?' the woman had chattered. 'All alone, out among the Presences. I would pee my pants, truly, lady knight, I would.'

'It isn't as dangerous as people have thought it was.'

'No, it is more. I know it must be. To hear the Great Ones speak, to attempt to pacify them. Oh, a terror, lady knight, truly, a terror '

The woman's use of the words 'Great Ones' should have stopped Donatella in her tracks. Those were the words used by Crystallites to refer to the Presences, but Don simply hadn't noticed. 'It won't be long before we'll all be able to walk among the Presences much more safely. Not long at all.' Don had raised her head, seeing herself and the woman in the mirror.

'Oh, you think some great discovery? Some marvel?' The woman peered at her in the mirror, her black eyes gleaming with something acquisitive and desperate.

And at that point Don had realized what she was saying and had drawn up sharply. 'No, no discovery, no marvel, Sophron. Simply the slow accumulation of knowledge ...'

Who else had she talked to?

Chase Random Hall, the Explorer King. Could anything she had said to him in the dining room of the Chapter House, during the informal time of day when everyone was on a first-name basis, could anything there have been interpreted as something threatening?

'Randy, you ever think the day may come we'll all be out of work?'

'Mind your manners, silly girl. Don't be obscene.'

'No, I mean wouldn't it be terrific if we found The Password?' 'The Password' was the apotheosis on Jubal and had been for a hundred years. It was like 'The Millennium' or 'The Second Coming,' a terrible end said to be devoutly desired by some, the single score that would open every pass and permit free travel everywhere.

'I think it's a disgusting thought, one I would appreciate not having raised again in my hearing.' Randy had been effete in his youth and was effete still, but there was no arguing with his successes. Now he smoothed his elegantly trimmed moustaches and smiled at her in his best monster-eating-up-a-little-girl smile: glittering eyes in a brown, brown face with his terribly white teeth, teeth that made one weak even while they made one shiver, anticipating voracious kisses. They were inevitable, those teeth, like death. 'Do you like living dangerously, stupid child?'

'Is it that dangerous to speculate about The Password?' She had said it lightly. Surely she had said it lightly!

'A little idle speculation here in the Chapter House, over drinks, perhaps not. Anything more than that, decidedly. As a moment's thought – if you are capable of such – should have informed you. Think, silly girl. If you had The Password, there are at least twenty people I could name who would kill you to keep it quiet.'

She knew her face had changed then. Changed with horror, in memory. People who would kill! She remembered her friend Gretl Mechas. Or rather, Gretl's body as it had been when Donatella identified it. Remembering this, she turned away. She had had enough of this conversation.

But then he had asked, 'Would you like to go to bed with me, Donatella?'

'I am the King Explorer's to command,' she had said, stiffly, taking refuge in a ritual answer. This was a new gambit.

'Not at all eager, are you?'

'I ... I have other affections, Randy.'

'Don't we all know it. Your affections are the talk of the House and most unworthy of you. Speaking of danger then, stupid child, what's the news about the Mad Cap?' And they had talked shop as she detailed her attempts to find a Password through the Gap before moving on to other things. Why had he mentioned going to bed together? Everyone knew Randy preferred men, though he would possess a woman if he thought it useful. Had he thought she might be useful? But not quite useful enough? Had he slipped when he spoke of people killing other people? Was he interested in her reaction? Or was it merely a very effective way to change the subject?

It had been an odd, a very odd conversation. With her well-schooled memory for exact words and phrases, exact tones and progressions of tones, she could play it over in her head, again and again, but it made no more sense now than it had then.

Her ruminations were interrupted by tapping at the door. Blanchet came in, dressed to the toenails in a one-piece glitter-suit with a plumed hat and multiple chains of Jubal coral around his neck. She made an appreciative sound. 'Don't you look marvelous.'

'My poor best will be hardly good enough, Ma'am.' He gave her an admiring look. 'The outfit becomes you.'

'So long as I don't become the outfit.' She laughed. 'Having got into it, there may be some difficulty getting out. The outfit and I may be inextricable. You'd better not call me "Don" this evening. That might give our truancy away. Call me Tella. My brother always called me that.'

'Very well, Tella. My name is Fyne Iron Blanchet, and my close friends call me Fibe. Or Fibey.'

'Fyne Iron?'

'Family names both. I don't think my mother ever thought what it would sound like.'

'Well, it sounds very ... metallurgical.'

'So I've always felt.' He offered her his arm and they went down the lift to ground level where a city car awaited them. The gawkers were still staring up at her window. None of them seemed to notice her. 'Shall I drive?'

'Please. You know Splash One far better than I. It keeps growing! Every time I've been here before I've gotten myself hopelessly lost.'

He suited himself to her mood, not talking merely to make conversation but concentrating on his driving. Splash One had grown explosively in recent months, so much so that concentration was a necessity. She stared out at a city raw and gawky in its burgeoning adolescence.

Half the streets were torn up, more were barricaded, though no one paid any attention to the barricades. Stiff, square-cornered new buildings of reinforced brick thrust up beside curvilinear older ones of rammed earth, the hard burnt brown making harsh edges against soft gray. The older buildings were covered with signs offering bargains in entertainment, in used equipment, in new and used clothing, new and used furniture, apartments, rooms. Most of the staff at the military base just outside of the city had dependants housed here in Splash One, and domiciliary space was at a premium.

The newer buildings were labeled with small directories at the entrances; government offices, BDL division offices, purchasing agents, suppliers' representatives, research labs. Every sidewalk was jammed with people; every window had one or two persons leaning out of it, waving, talking to those in the street. Some of those in the streets were engaged in trade of an unmistakable kind, and Don stared.

'Prostitutes?' she asked, breaking her preoccupied silence. There had never been prostitutes on Jubal. At least, none that were visible.

Blanchet nodded. 'Recent imports. They say that somebody high up got paid off.' He didn't need to specify which somebody. The word among BDL employees was that the Governor had both hands out for himself, which was unnerving. PEC appointed governors were supposed to be unimpeachable, and it made one wonder how high the rot had spread.

At the end of a short side street a building loomed, gleaming like gold and culminating in a high, ornately curved dome. Crowds of people passed in and out through the monstrous doors.

'What in Jubal is that?' she asked, turning to peer over her shoulder.

'Crystallite Temple.'

'It's *huge!*'

'It's huge and there are about four more like it up and down the 'Soilcoast. You don't have one in Northwest City yet?'

'No. And I don't look forward to having one. Where do they get the money?'

'Pilgrims. Contributions. If you haven't seen some of the evangelical cubes the Crystallite hierarchy sends out, you've missed something. Very slick, Tella. The money pours in as though it were piped. The people at the top aren't like the ones you see running around on the streets. The assassins, fanatics, and insurgents are a scruffy lot, but those in charge of the temples are something else again. Very smooth. You ought to see them.' His mouth compressed into a grim line.

'Well, let's. We're not in any hurry, are we?'

He gave her a surprised look, but obediently brought the car to a halt and walked with her back toward the Temple yard. The paved area was scattered with small groups of pilgrims, each wearing a knot of orange ribbon to identify his status, each group led by a soberly robed guide. Blanchet inconspicuously attached himself and Donatella to the rear of one straggling group as they followed the orange ribboned ones into the enormous structure.

Donatella only with difficulty kept herself from exclaiming. Around them were towering pillars, vaulted ceilings high above, dazzling fountains of light and smoke. 'Where do they get all this!' she demanded in a whisper. 'How could they get this kind of equipment when we're still short of medical supplies and simple things like computers or lift machinery?'

Blanchet kissed his palm in a derisory gesture and she subsided. Obviously someone had been paid off. And why did it surprise her? She turned as Blanchet nudged her, pointing unobtrusively at three figures that had just come onto an elevated platform at the top of a broad flight of stairs. Two men, one woman. The men could have been brothers, both with extravagant manes of white hair, both tall and well built, robed in glittering, vertically striped garments and wearing high domed crowns. The combination made them appear to be about twelve feet tall. The woman, on the other hand, glittered in quite another way. Her breasts were exposed under sparkling necklaces of gems, and her draped skirt seemed to be woven of gold thread, the extensive train slithering behind her like the body of a heavy snake. She, too, was crowned and plumed.

'Chantiforth Bins and Myrony Clospocket,' Blanchet whispered. 'Half brothers, I understand, with a long, slippery history. Now Supreme Pontiff and High Priest. And the High Priestess, Aphrodite Sells. The three of them are the real power behind all the Crystallites on Jubal.'

'Are they the power behind the assassinations, too? And the terrorism?'

'They claim not. Though they say they "understand" the frustration that leads their followers to commit such acts.'

On the high platform the glittering woman called out a short phrase, which brought the congregation to immediate silence. She had a voice like a knife, as cutting as a shard of crystal.

Don watched for a short time as the three sparkling figures began a ritual that was obviously familiar to most of those in the audience who were cheerfully bellowing the responses. 'I've seen enough,' she murmured. 'Let's get out of here.'

They returned to the car, unspeaking, and continued the interrupted trip, passing the farmer's market, a bustling enclave of trucks, mule wagons, booths stacked high with produce, milling vendors, customers, and sightseers, all in one swirling, noisy throng. Across from the market were the fish stalls, a long line of booths fronting the enclosed ponds of the local fish farms, smelling richly of the sea. Beyond the ponds stood the tilting masts of the merchant fleet. Don remarked at the number of ships. 'There are more private boats than BDL has!'

Blanchet nodded solemnly. 'BDL isn't the sole power in Splash One and Two anymore. At least that's the inside word. More than half the traffic last year was noncommercial. Military, a lot of it. Plus all the pilgrims the Crystallites bring in. And they've added some staff to the Governor's office.'

Don started to say, 'That's silly, he doesn't do anything,' then thought better of it. Her friend Link had been attached to the Governor's office. She contented herself by asking, 'Why?'

'Because of the Jut Massacre.'

'That was six years ago!'

'Well, you know how long it takes the Planetary Exploitation Council to move.'

'I wasn't aware that the PEC moved at all. I thought they merely existed, like the Core Stars.' It was safe to say that, she thought. Lots of people said things like that.

'The story is that the Jut Massacre moved them. Somebody up there had a son or grandson among the slain, and it made them take the Crystallites seriously. You know they're reopening the question of native sentience.'

It was safer for her to say nothing at all. 'Look at that building,' she marveled. 'It's all of six stories tall. It's a fortress!' The huge gray structure looked like a monolith, almost windowless, surrounded by high, crenelated walls.

'You've seen it before, but probably not from this angle. It used to have an open square in front of it, right at the eastern edge of town. It's the BDL Headquarters. Behind it is the Tripsingers' citadel, and the Governor's official residence is adjacent, there.' He indicated a palatial, terraced edifice set among gardens. 'The reason they've added to the Governor's staff is to take care of this upcoming PEC inquiry. And they've beefed up the military in case of further threats from the Crystallite rank and file, though what earthly use we have for this many troopers is anybody's guess. In the process they've made Jubal the garrison planet for the entire system. Everyone assumes someone bribed someone, because the base on Serendipity has been closed and transferred here. And the military have brought their spouses and kids and intimate friends. All of whom need housing and services and food. The town is a mess.'

'It certainly is,' she agreed.

'Splash Two isn't any better, from what I hear. Nor are any of the smaller cities. Population of the 'Soilcoast cities is supposed to be in excess of two million. Since we haven't the resources to build up, we're spreading out. I'm told at this rate of growth, deepsoil space will run out in a few years. The farmers are already screaming at the cost of land, and we need all the farmlands to feed the people. The whole thing doesn't make sense.'

'Amazing,' she murmured, shaking her head. 'Simply amazing. I think of Northwest City as fairly urban until I come down here. We're really cushioned from all this growth up there, and I can't say I'm not glad. What's that ruckus down there?'

'Hmm. There's a Crystallite street demonstration going on. Well, you've seen the temple. Might as well see the other side of it. Hear the singing?'

She heard the tuneless wailing, not something that either an Explorer or Tripsinger would have considered singing. 'What are they up to?'

'I'll drive slowly enough that you can see, but put your mask in your lap and don't stare at them. These are the shock troops, and they aren't averse to civil disorder. They throw things at people who look like they might be enjoying themselves. As far as they're concerned, anyone enjoying himself on Jubal is bound to be a heretic!' The car moved smoothly down the avenue, and Don watched the mob from the corners of her eyes.

Half a dozen cadaverous figures clad only in loin cloths and sandals were haranguing a scanty and fluid crowd of sightseers. Don caught the words, 'blasphemous impertinence' and 'the day of punishment is coming,' and 'we cannot be moved!' As the car came even with the crowd, one of the chanting figures lit a torch, held it high for a moment, then threw it down. Behind the crowd, flames leapt up in a blue hot cone.

People screamed and fled, and Don stared in disbelief at the cross-legged figure burning on the sidewalk, its wide white eyes shining in ultimate agony through the flames. 'My God,' she said, retching. 'My God. They're burning a person!'

'An immolation?' Blanchet asked, mouth drawn into a rictus of distaste and horror. He speeded the car to move them away. 'Sorry. It's been a moon or more since they did one of those here in the city. Are the soldiers on top of it?'

She looked back. Uniformed figures were moving purposefully through the crowd, one with a fire extinguisher.

'Soldiers are there. Why do they burn themselves?'

'To show the authorities they aren't afraid of death, or pain, or torture, or imprisonment. To show they can't be controlled by police methods. We've got a small scale holy war on our hands. It's just that no one in government seems to realize it yet. People are taking bets on whether the Governor has been paid not to act. And these public immolations are bad enough. The secret, ritual killings are worse ...'

'Ritual killings?' she faltered, afraid of what he was going to say to her.

'Killings by torture. Women carved up ...'

'Blanchet, don't. Please don't. One of them was a friend of mind. Gretl Mechas. She was cut to ribbons. They said it took hours for her to die. I had to identify her body and I couldn't identify anything except her clothes. Oh, Lord, no one in Northwest called it a ritual killing.'

'Maybe it wasn't. Sorry, Tella. Your friend wasn't the only one. There have been others. Always women or young boys.'

The horrible sight of the immolation, the hideous memory of her friend, as well as Blanchet's comments on the current political scene had ruined Don's desire for dinner or entertainment. Oh, Gretl! Lovely, warm, friendly

Gretl. Why! And she couldn't take time to grieve over Gretl tonight. She had to remind herself that there were other, urgent reasons for her to be abroad in the city.

'Where are we going for dinner?' she asked, keeping her voice flatly matter of fact and not caring what the answer might be.

'The Magic Viggy,' he told her, shaking his head. 'I'd planned it as an appropriate place to take someone with red hair and a very blue dress. I'm afraid it will seem rather trivial, now.'

It did seem trivial. They ate imported food at extortionate prices. They drank, albeit abstemiously. Blanchet would have been quite happy to fill her glass more often, but Don let it sit three-quarters full during most of dinner. She didn't need to be more depressed, which the wine would eventually do. They chatted. Though Blanchet was a well-informed and interesting companion she had trouble later recalling what they had discussed. Magicians and clowns moved about, playing tricks, distributing favors. A neighboring table was occupied by a noisy crowd of elderly sightseers. There was a lot of clutter. When they were ready to leave, Don missed her bag and found it on the floor, half buried under a bouquet of flowers that a magician had pulled from her hair.

'Like a circus,' she said. 'Like a carnival.'

'The most popular place in town,' he agreed. 'Now, I have tickets to Chantry.'

'Not Lim Terree?' she asked, cocking her head. 'I really liked him last time I was here.'

'Oh, hadn't you heard?' he asked. 'It was on the news here a few days ago. Lim Terree is dead.'

She made an appropriate expression of dismay without letting the shock show on her face. She felt herself go pale and cold, but the flickering lights in the restaurant hid that. By the time they reached the street, she was in command of herself once more, able to sit through Chantry's concert and pretend to enjoy it. When it was over, she asked to return to the Chapter House, and once there, claimed weariness and was left alone, though Blanchet expressed regret for that decision as she smiled herself away from him. How desirable to be alone! Except, she reminded herself, for whatever listening and watching devices were undoubtedly placed here and there in her rooms.

She rummaged in her bag, as though for her handkerchief, her fingers encountering something that crackled crisply. She palmed it in the handkerchief, wiped her nose, then thrust the note under her pillow as she turned down the bed. Nightly ritual, she told herself. The whole bedtime score with all variations. Shower. Teeth brushed. Hair brushed. Nightgown. Emergency kit on the bedside table. No Explorer would ever go to sleep without the emergency kit within reach. Then, pick up the new exploration digest, delivered to her door in her absence, and read the professional news for a while. A new theory of variation. Which wasn't new. Yawn. Let the eyes fall closed. Rouse a little. Put out the lights.

She let a little time go by, then silently brought the emergency kit under the covers and turned on its narrow beamed light. The note she had put in her purse before leaving, informing her friend that someone had tried to kill her, was gone. In its place were two others. The letters were minuscule, hard to read.

'Terree informed and supplied as per our plans. He is obtaining Enigma score in Five. Took him some time to set up tour. Should return at end of Old Moon.'

This was dated weeks previously and was on a tiny sheet of paper, no larger than one-quarter the palm of her hand. Folded inside it was another sheet, even smaller, dated a few days prior.

'Word received two days ago, Lim Terree dead on Enigma. Trying to find out what happened. Make contact.'

Both were signed with a twisted line that returned upon itself to make three links of a chain. She put out the light, replaced the kit on the bedside table, then methodically tore the two notes into tiny pieces and ate them.

In the office of the Prior, Fyne Blanchet finished his report with a yawning comment. 'I don't know what all the fuss is about. She's all right. I talked about the things you wanted me to, but she didn't say anything much. There's no evidence of her knowing anything I don't. She didn't gripe about corruption or say she was going to murder the governor or anything, just a few snide remarks, the same as anyone.'

'She didn't ask you to stay.'

'A lot of them don't. Hell, she's got it on with that guy at the Northwest Chapter. Five years? What's his name, Zimble? So, she's monogamous. Lots of women are. Besides, she was really upset over that burning. She saw the whole thing. She didn't eat much, and she was pale all through the concert.'

The Prior grunted, thought. After a time, he said, 'She has some people she usually sees here in Splash One.'

'So?'

'So, she would normally want to visit them.'

'And?'

'If she doesn't visit them or any one of them, it might mean something.'

Blanchet yawned. He felt the Prior was clutching at straws. Donatella Furz was nothing to worry about. And what was the Prior so worried about?

Blanchet, who kept his curiosity strictly in check when it was profitable to do so, told himself he really didn't know. Or care.

'Fibey,' she said the next morning over her breakfast fish, 'I've got three old friends here in town. I'd like to see them while I'm here. Could you arrange that for me?'

'Certainly, Ma'am. Any particular order? Lunch dates? Dinner dates?'

'No. Nothing in particular. Whatever's convenient for them. There's an old family friend, actually sort of a cousin of my mother's. Name's Cyndal Prince, and last time I was here she lived over in that development south of town, along the bay. Then there's Link Emert. He's still with BDL, but he's recently been attached to the Governor's office. Liaison of some kind. And then there's my niece, Fabian Furz.'

'Your brother's daughter?'

'One and only. Bart died about five years ago, one of those wasting diseases no one in the interior knows anything about, and by the time he got to the "Soilcoast, it was too late to do anything. You'd think by now they'd have improved the medical system in the Deepsoil towns, wouldn't you?'

'I think it's a materiel question, Ma'am.'

'Oh, I know, I know. No way to ship the big diagnostic machines in. No way to take in the life support systems. Shit. They take in anything else that suits them, in itty bitty pieces, if necessary, with a whole troop of mechanics to put it together again. Oh, well, no reason to fuss about it now. Bart's long gone, and my bitching won't bring him back. Anyhow, if you could get hold of those people and set up dates for me, this afternoon or tomorrow morning, I'd appreciate it. I'll call you just before noon, if that's convenient.'

'You have other plans for this morning?'

'I, Blanchet, am going to have my annual medical checkup. That's why I'm here. Orders from up top.'

There was no shortage of diagnostic machines at the Splash One medical center. No shortage of technicians either, Don thought, as she was prodded, poked, bled, and otherwise sampled for the tenth time in as many minutes. 'This is the last one,' the anonymous white-coated person said with at least a semblance of sympathy. 'You can get dressed now.'

The physician, who appeared harried and abstracted, leafed through the chart twice before looking up at Don with a furrowed brow. 'You didn't have that wound on your arm last time. No record of it in your history. Well, there wouldn't be. It's obviously fresh.'

'Yes, it's a recent injury.'

'When? How?'

'Oh, about ten days ago. A fall. A 'ling blew its top when I was on a narrow trail, and I fell against a sharp edge. I reported it to the Prior when I got back to the Chapter House. It should be in the record update.'

'Oh, I see it. Yes. Well, just checking. Healing clean, is it?'

'Seems to be healing well, yes.'

'Do you want the scar removed?'

'Perhaps later. It still takes two or three weeks of regeneration treatment to take scars off, doesn't it?'

'With the small machines, which is all we have available, yes. About that.'

'Well, I don't have time right now. I've got several explorations to do for BDL before Old Moon's out. I've got some leave coming up next Dead Moon, though. Maybe I'll do it then.'

'Suit yourself. If you want it done in Northwest City, don't go to the BDL medical center there. Word to the wise, right? Go to this woman. You'll have to pay for it, but you'll be better satisfied.' The physician handed over a note with a name on it.

Don made an appreciative noise, both for the information and because she had been afraid there would be close questioning about the injury. Not that it wasn't very much like a dozen crystal cuts she'd had over the years. It could have been a crystal cut.

But it wasn't.

Shortly after she had returned to Northwest from the Enigma, she had calmed down and begun to realize how dangerous her position might be. This realization was followed by a period of indecision during which she had found an excuse to make a quick trip to Splash One, ostensibly only to attend a government house reception. During the reception, she had managed to get lost on the way to the women's convenience long enough to hold a lengthy whispered conversation in a dark and supposedly vacant office, guaranteed by her friend to be free of ears or eyes.

'I don't suppose it would do any good to suggest you just forget the whole thing?' her friend had murmured.

'I've explained why that won't work,' she had said. 'This information has to get out. It has to be made public.' They both knew it. Don's friend had worked for an intelligence agency at one time and was well aware that this was the kind of information that had to be publicized. As public information, it was a danger to no one. As a secret, it was a death trap. And the consequences to the planet if the information was kept quiet were too terrible for either of them to contemplate.

'BDL isn't going to like it.'

'That's why I can't do it,' Don had whispered. 'They pretty well control me. I know damned well any Priory reports where I go, what I do. Not just me. All Explorers. No. It's got to be someone else who does it. Someone BDL doesn't control.'

Together they had crafted a hasty plan, every step of which made the danger more and more clear. When they parted, it was as co-conspirators. Wheels were in motion, very secret wheels. Donatella returned to Northwest with a sense of mixed relief and apprehension, taking refuge in routine duties, everyday activities. Behind her in Splash One, her friend would move things along.

There had been one loose end. She had had to fill out a 'lost or stolen equipment' report to cover the synthesizer that she had taken to Splash One and returned without. But after that, nothing had happened. For weeks, nothing at all.

Until ten days ago when she had been sent out on a routine two-day trip to explore a pocket of deepsoil behind an offshoot ridge of the Redfang Range. It had seemed an odd assignment, even at the time. The offshoot, Little Redfang, was only half a day's travel from Northwest. The Passwords to a good part of the range were Donatella's own work, and most of them had been part of the repertory for almost a decade. All that was wanted this time was some minor variation that would get wagons through the Fanglings in a slightly different direction from that taken formerly – a route that Don could see no sensible justification for – and virtually any apprentice Explorer could have done the job.

Still, an assignment approved by one's Prior was an assignment not to be argued with. She remembered being preoccupied with her personal problem, worrying at it relentlessly as she rode. The plan was dependent on so many variables, so many little things she couldn't control. She was having second thoughts, trying to decide if she should make another trip to Splash One or whether it was too late at this point to do anything but ride it out. Indecision was not an ordinary thing with Donatella; it irritated her. Explorers couldn't be indecisive. Those that were didn't last long. The morning's trip made the matter no clearer, moreover, and by noon she reached the peril-point and had to force herself to set the subject aside. She told herself she would think about it again that night, over her campfire.

It took most of the afternoon working with synthesizer and computer, trying permutations of a few phrases that seemed likely, to come up with a new score on the music box that quieted things down very nicely. It was a fairly simple variation of a score she knew well, one she felt competent to use in singing herself through the range – just as a test, and certainly not something that was required of an Explorer – and it was early evening when she started.

The way she chose was a narrow ledge along a towering face and above a sheer drop into a gorge of living crystal. The gorge gleamed with amber and hot orange lights through its generally winey mass. All the Redfang Range was bloody, as evil looking in its way as the Enigma, though a whole lot simpler to get through. Her narrow ledge wouldn't do as a trip-trail, but it would serve to get her into the deepsoil pocket, after which she would find some way out that wagons could travel. As she sang her way along the ledge, she told herself that hell must look much like the gorge below her. The lower the sun dropped, the more it looked as though it were on fire.

She didn't hurry during the transit. Afterward she realized it was entirely likely that someone had followed her from the peril-point. Certainly that someone knew something about Tripsinging, for the attack came at pre-cisely that moment when she moved out of peril. A black clad, black masked form, barely visible in the dusk, came from slightly to one side and behind her.

If it hadn't been that she turned just at that moment in response to some tiny sound; if it hadn't been that the sun glinted on the knife blade as she turned, she would not have seen her attacker at all.

As it was, she dropped without thought, rolled, pulled up her legs to pro-tect her belly and her arm to protect her throat, felt a moment's searing pain along the arm, kicked up and out with both legs, and saw the figure soar over her into the air above the gorge. She had reacted without thought, reacted as she had been taught, as she had practiced a thousand times in the self-defense courses that, since the Jut Massacre, all Explorers had had to take over and over again.

The weapon clattered onto the ledge, but the attacker fell endlessly, with-out a sound.

For a short time after that, Don was so busy applying emergency care to her gashed arm that she had no time to wonder about the attacker. When the bleeding was stanched, she huddled over a tiny fire, terrified that the assassin might not have been alone. Then, when no further assault came, she began to wonder why she had been attacked at all.

At first light she had attempted to climb to the place the body lay, so far below as to be virtually invisible. If she could find out who, she might find out the reason.

After an hour or two, she gave up. Someone might get into the gorge with a parachute or a balloon. They would not get out again.

Since then it had remained a mystery. Someone had tried to kill her. She didn't know who, and she wasn't sure why. Not a torture killing like Gretl's; nothing weird about it; just a straightforward attempt at murder!

A Crystallite assassin? That's why Explorers studied self-defense, after all, because of the threat posed by fanatics. It could have been. In which case, the intended victim might not have been Don Furz particularly, but simply any Explorer. However, Crystallite assassins were said to scream religious slogans during attacks. Certainly they had done so during the Jut Massacre and in several other assassinations since. This person, male or female, had been silent.

Was it someone who knew what Don had found out? One of those twenty the Explorer King had mentioned? Then how had he or she found out? What did they know?

Was it someone from BDL?

What would her trusted friend think about it? She had been unable to pass the word along until yesterday.

Now she realized the doctor was looking at her oddly, obviously wondering at her long preoccupation. 'I was just trying to figure out some way to have the scar removed now,' she said to explain her abstraction. 'But it can't be done. There just isn't time. Other than the scar, how am I?'

'You're thirty-three years old, in perfect health, in beautiful shape, with no evidence of any disease whatsoever. You've got the muscles of a stevedore and the reaction time of a prime jetball ace. What else can I tell you? Here's a copy of the report. The duplicate will be placed in your record.' He cocked his head and looked at her quizzically.

Don grinned. No matter how often she told herself it was foolish, she always approached the annual medical exam with the suspicion it would find her in some lingering illness. Each time, the report relieved her anxiety, and she took the copy now with a sense of reprieve.

She called Fyne Blanchet from a booth in the lobby of the medical building.

'I made a lunch date for you with your elderly relative,' he said. 'She's a little hard of hearing, so I hope she got it straight.'

'When and where, Blanchet?'

'Thirteen hundred at the Fish House on Bayside Street. She told me, among many other things, that she doesn't eat red meat.'

'Who can afford red meat? I can't.' Pasture land was strictly limited on Jubal, and red meat was the epitome of luxury. Fowl was more usual. Fish, more common yet.

'I'm waiting for a call back from your niece, and Link Emert would love to have cocktails with you after work. He says seventeen hundred at the 'Ling Lounge, just down the block from his office.'

'Fine. I'll check back with you after lunch.'

Lunch at the Fish House was as predictable as any meal with Cyndal. Close inspection of the menu to determine whether there was anything on it she could not eat. Each such item read aloud. Querulous inquiry into the morals of anyone who would eat said item. Further finicky attention given to ordering copiously from among items that she could eat. And, finally, greedy consumption of said items, right down to the polish on the plate, while discoursing upon the flavor of every mouthful.

If anyone had an ear trained on Cyndal, Don hoped they enjoyed the experience.

'Very nice, Donatella. Very generous of you. What do you hear from your dear mother?'

'Just the usual, Cousin Cyndal. She's still greatly involved with the local gardening group there in Deepsoil Twelve. She asked to be remembered to you.'

'Such a lovely woman, your mother.'

Donatella, who had quite another view of her parent, smiled and said nothing. When she left the restaurant, the waiter came running after her with her bag, which she, as usual, had forgotten.

'Blanchet? Did you get hold of Fabian?'

'Dinner tonight or breakfast tomorrow, whichever you prefer.'

'Oh, make it dinner tonight. Then I'll have the morning to sleep in and luxuriate before starting back to Northwest. Tell her – tell her to pick a place and I'll meet her there at twenty hundred. I'm going to do some shopping before I meet Link Emert. Thanks, Blanchet.'

When she arrived at the 'Ling Lounge, she found Link already ensconced behind a table, his mobile chair hidden by it. Link usually arrived early in order to make his disability less apparent.

'Donatella!' He half rose, pushing up with his arms to give the appearance of someone with legs that worked, then seated himself again to reach out for her hand. She did not lean down to kiss him. He had been very explicit about the pain that caused him, so she didn't do it. Also, her hair was flattened and drawn back severely and she was wearing a not very becoming suit that made her legs and torso shapeless.

'I don't want to want you anymore,' he had said to her once, the words hissing out between clenched teeth. 'Don't you understand, Don! It hurts to want you. It hurts to want anything!'

So, she looked as unwantable as possible, within the bounds of what might be acceptable in a place with the effrontery to call itself the 'Ling Lounge. Predictably, it was decorated with phoney 'lings, plastic crystals that reached from floor to ceiling. Variations on Tripsinger themes pounded from speakers. 'Interesting place,' she said, gesturing with disdain. 'How long has this been here?'

'Oh, less than a year. It's an appalling tourist trap, plain and simple, but the drinks are good.'

'Tourists! Lord. That's a word I'd read about but never thought to hear in Jubal, Link. Tourists!'

'More of them all the time, Don. There's even some guy down in Bay City who advertises interior trips for tourists, with Tripsingers and the whole score.'

'He's out of his mind!'

'No. He takes them out by the Deadheads, sings them through with some mish mash, then gives them a look at the Crazies, "accidentally" blows up a Crazeling or two, and brings the tourists back all agog. They think they've been in peril.'

'And he makes it with both hands.'

'So I hear. What are you drinking, Donatella, my love? It's been almost a year since I've seen you, you know that?' He said 'my love' casually, as though it didn't matter, but her heart turned over at the words, as it always had. He was thinner. His eyes were sunken. That once glowing face looked pallid. Even his lips were colorless. She shook herself and smiled, pretending not to see.

They ordered drinks. They talked. Little things. Inconsequentialities. Recent explorations. Link's work as Explorer liaison to the Governor's office. The recent announcement that the CHASE Commission was coming to Jubal.

'What the hell is the CHASE Commission?' she asked.

'The Planetary Exploitation Council has set up a new commission to decide once and for all whether there is sentient native life on Jubal.'

'Oh, I did know about it. I just didn't remember the name. The services man talked about it last night. And somebody mentioned it at that reception I came down for, last time I was here in town.' Donatella's real reason for coming to Splash One had occupied her mind to such an extent that she had been barely able to focus on social rituals. 'As I recall on that occasion I forgot who the Governor's wife was and introduced her to someone as Gereny Vox.'

'Donatella!' He sounded genuinely shocked. By no stretch of resemblance could the well-known mule breeder be compared in either face or figure to Honeypeach Thonks. Gereny was a completely genuine, if rough-edged, person of considerable charm. Lady Honeypeach was a self-created and ominous device.

'It was just a slip of the tongue. I knew right away I'd got it wrong, and I apologized all over the place. She was very sweet about it, in a poisonous way.' Don laughed unconvincingly. It had been a horrible gaffe, one she'd heard about later from the Explorer King and one that, in its way, had perhaps helped to obscure what else she might have been doing in Splash One. 'Well, how are they going to go about deciding the sentience question?'

72

'They're going to hold hearings in a few weeks, just as they did fifty years ago, what else?'

'Remind me what CHASE stands for.'

'The Commission on Humans and Alien Sentience: Exploitation.'

'Are they going to try to prove human sentience first?' She choked with laughter. 'I've had some question about that recently. I have a few nominees for no sentience at all, starting with the Governor.'

'Hush, child. You make treasonous utterance. The Governor's stepson is chairman of the commission. Ymries Fedder. He named the commission, I understand.'

'Oh, yes. Honeypeach's son.' It seemed appropriate to say nothing more, and she contented herself with quirking one eyebrow at Link. He quirked back and she sighed. As always, they understood each other precisely. As always, she ached to hold him. As always, she mourned for him, longed for him. And as always, she kept a cheerful face and let none of it show. He had been in that chair for five years, ever since the trip on which an unexplored Presence blew with Link directly in the way. He should have died, would have died except for Don. Afterward he had accused her of sentencing him to life imprisonment, and she had offered to help him out of it. No Explorer could do less, no lover more. The offer still stood. He had not taken her up on it yet. Thank God.

And as always when she saw him, her mind went frantic, trying to think of a way for a rather minor employee of the Department of Exploration to lay hands on something like a hundred thousand chits. Which is roughly what it would cost to get Link to Serendipity and pay for regeneration of his legs. Half that amount would import a set of bio-prostheses, which would at least let him walk!

No sense thinking about it. She'd thought about it before. Ten years' salary. Damn BDL and their priorities! Brou first, everything else second. And the Explorer Kings, who should be fighting for medical care as part of the contract, seemed content to piddle around with the amenities package. She kept her face calm, crying inside.

Two hours went by and she looked at the comp on her wrist. 'Got to run, Link. In one hour I've got a date with my niece, remember her? Fabian? With the Planetary Welfare Office.'

'I saw Fabian just last week. She came into the Governor's office for something or other ... what was it? Oh, I remember. She's working on a settlement plan for the fringe people who get left behind when various military personnel are transferred out-system.'

'Fringe people?'

'Ah ... what shall we say. Unofficial dependants. Uncontracted spouses. The troopers bring them in. Then when they ship out, they decide for one reason or another to go unencumbered.'

'Unofficial divorce.'

'In a manner of speaking. Kids, too, of course.'

'Bastards,' she said, with feeling. 'Link. Thanks for the drinks.' She took his hand in her own, casually, squeezed it, only for a moment, smiled and rose.

'Donatella!' He called her back. 'You forgot your bag.'

She returned to the Chapter House to shower and change her clothes, entering by the back door and slipping up the stairs when no one was watching, not furtively, simply as though in a hurry. She had no particular wish to explain her unattractive garb to anyone, least of all Blanchet. By the time he arrived with the drink she ordered, she was showered and dressed for dinner, albeit less spectacularly than on the previous night.

'Did you have good visits with your friends?'

'Cousin Cyndal is not really a friend,' she confessed with every semblance of candor. 'Cousin Cyndal is a pain in the downspout. However, if I don't see her when I'm here, my mother doesn't let me forget it. Seeing Link Emert is also a pain, of a different kind. I keep remembering him the way he was before the accident.'

'Ah.' Blanchet was sympathetic. 'Well, you'll enjoy the evening more, perhaps.'

'Oh, Lord,' she replied, 'I hope so. It's always good to see Fabian. She's fun.'

And Fabian was. She told stories of the 'fringe people' that made Don alternately laugh and cry; made outrageous conversation with the waiters who delivered their crisp cooked vegetables, wonderfully flavored with strips of broiled fish and fowl; and ended the evening in reminiscences and general conversation. As they left the restaurant, Don said, 'Damn, I forgot my bag again,' and Fabian laughed. 'You always have, every time I've ever been with you, so I picked it up for you. Here.'

And back to her room again, duty done. Same procedure with the purse as last night. It was the first chance she had had.

The note was in the bag. Under the bedcovers she read the tiny letters.

'Note received. Terree's brother, Tasmin Ferrence, said to be on way to 'Soilcoast. Has music box. I will contact. Careful.'

And the curvy line that made the signature. Chain, or CHAIN, if one wanted to be accurate. The investigative and enforcement arm of the PEC, that was CHAIN. Donatella spent a futile moment wishing that CHAIN was indeed present on Jubal, in force, rather than merely represented by one fairly powerless former employee.

Back to the note. Careful. What did that mean? Careful. Of course she was careful.

Still, the single word appended to the note made her uneasy. Instead of falling immediately asleep as she usually did – as all Explorers did if they wished to be properly concentrated on each day's task – she squirmed rest-lessly in the noisy dark, staring at the lights from the saloon-cum-amuse-ment park across the street. Refracted through the beveled glass of her windows, the lights made red-purple lines across her bed. There were the sounds of a crowd outside, little muffled by the closed windows. The bustle of people moving along the avenue, shouts of revelry and of annoyance, replies, laughing or threatening or haranguing. Like those fanatics. She remembered the burning Crystallite, eyeballs crisping through a curtain of fire, and set the thought aside with a shudder. Think of something else. Think of Link. Link with his face so carefully controlled. No accusations. Not for years. And yet she would be lying to herself if she thought he had adapted. Of course he hadn't. He was still the same Link, trapped, trapped forever, and she as trapped without him.

If only. If only she had a hundred thousand chits. If only she could get a hundred thousand chits. He deserved it. BDL owed it to him.

She could not rest. She was not even sleepy. If she had been even drowsy, she might not have heard the sound, so tiny a noise, a click where a click didn't belong.

At the window in the bathroom. Opening on an airshaft, as she recalled. Three stories up.

She did not wait for the click to be repeated. Explorers did not wait. Those who waited, died. Instead, she rolled out of the bed, heaping the covers into a vaguely body-shaped roll behind her and stood behind the open bathroom door. She had no weapon. A mental inventory of the room yielded nothing of use. The bathroom now, yes. There were useful things there. Spray flasks of various things: dry-wash, antiperspirant, depilatory. She visualized where she had left them, the dry-wash or the edge of the bath, set aside, not useful here in Splash One where there was plenty of water. The antiperspirant was in the cabinet. The depilatory was on the back of the convenience, where she had sat to do her legs and the back of her neck. An almost full bottle.

The click was repeated, this time with a solidly chunking sound as though something had given way. The latch on the bathroom window, no doubt. She began to breathe quietly, deeply. Whoever was breaking in would listen for that. Deeply. Regularly. Breathe.

The figure came through the bathroom door so silently that she almost missed it. Only the movement across the bars of light betrayed it. On feet as silent, she slipped around the door and into the bathroom, feeling for the flask, the barest touch, not wanting to make a sound. She picked it up carefully, her face turned toward the room, trying to see in the intermittent flares of livid light.

The figure was at the bed. It leaned forward, reaching. No knife this time. Something else. A growl, almost like an animal as it realized she wasn't there. It turned toward the switch, and suddenly the room was flooded with light. The hooded figure spun around, saw her, lunged toward her, and she sprayed the depilatory full in its eyes, falling sideways as she did so.

It made no sound except a gagging spit. It kept coming, blindly, reaching for the place she had moved toward. Bigger than she. Stronger, too, most likely. It was like a deadly game of feely-find. The creature couldn't see, but it could hear her. She went across the bed in a wild scramble, then out the door into the hall, leaving it open. The stairwell was directly ahead of her. She breathed, 'No, no, don't,' just loudly enough to be heard, then stepped sideways and knelt by the wall. As the maddened figure rushed toward her voice, she stuck out her foot, and the careening shape plunged over it, head-first down the stairs. Don darted back into her room and shut the door.

The crashing sound brought colleagues and visitors out into the hall. Don joined them, sleepily tying the belt of her robe. 'What was that noise? Did you hear it? What happened?' Voices from below were raised in incredulous excitement.

A man. Must have fallen down the stairs. No, a man's body. He's dead.

What was he doing in the Chapter House? Did anyone know him?

Why was he dressed that way?

A thief? Who would rob a Chapter House? Explorers didn't carry valuables.

The excited interchange bubbled on while Don half hung across the bannister, staring at the black lump on the floor below. Someone had removed the mask, and a blankly anonymous face stared up at her with dead and ruined eyes. Someone who had known where she was. Someone who had known she was alone. How fortuitous for someone that the intruder had broken his neck. Now no one could ask him who had sent him.

6

Three mule riders approaching Splash One early one morning from the direction of the Mad Gap would have been enough to attract the attention of the locals. Three mule riders followed by a small swarm of Crystallites, all of whom were hooting, cursing and throwing mud, was enough not only to attract attention but to bring the nearest military detachment into overwhelming action. The Crystallites were promptly face down in the mud they had been using as ammunition, their hands and feet locked behind them, and tranquilizer guns were being applied unstintingly to various exposed portions of their anatomies.

'Sorry about that,' the Captain in command of the group said to Tasmin, offering him a clean towel from the riot wagon. 'They're getting worse all the time. If the Governor doesn't act soon, our commanding officer, Colonel Lang, probably will. Hope it won't be too late.'

'How late would it have to be to be too late?' asked Clarin in a bitter voice, trying to get the mud out of her curly hair with scant success. That last mud ball had a rock in it. A red lump the size of a hen's egg was rising on her forehead, and she looked as disheveled as she did angry. 'Our Master, here, preferred we not use our whips on them.'

'I saw your troop coming,' Tasmin said to the officer in a mild voice. 'I thought we could outrun them until you arrived.'

Jamieson was regarding the prone figures vindictively, running his quirt through his hands. Tripsinger mules were so well trained it would be unthinkable to use quirts on them; the device was merely costume. Despite this, Jamieson's intent could be read in his face.

'They'd love it if you took the whip to 'em,' the Captain said, gesturing his permission. 'Do, if it'll make you feel better. They consider that quite a mark of holiness, being beaten on. That's why we use the trank-guns. They hate that. Keep 'em tranked up for ten days or so, force feed 'em, then turn 'em loose fatter than they were. They just hate it.' He spat reflectively, as Jamieson unobtrusively put the quirt out of sight. The officer held out his hand. 'Name's Jines Verbold.'

Tasmin took the proffered hand. 'It's good to meet you, Captain Verbold. I'm Tripsinger Tasmin Ferrence. These are my two acolytes, Reb Jamieson and Renna Clarin.'

The Captain nodded to each of them. 'Did I misread something, Master Ferrence, or did you three just come down the hills from the Mad Gap?'

'We did. Is there something wrong with that?'

'I didn't know anybody could get through the Gap.'

Tasmin expressed amazement. 'I used an old, old Password, Captain. I suppose it could have been lost, though that's hard to believe. It's been in my library since my father's time, maybe even his father's. I think it's an original Erickson. It never occurred to me it wasn't generally known.'

'Well, that'll be news to please some people I know of. They've had people trying the Gap, trottin' up there and then trottin' down again, for about the last year.'

'It's those crazy key shifts in the PJ,' said Clarin thoughtfully as she rummaged in one pocket. Something moved beneath her fingers, and she scratched it affectionately. 'And those high trumpet sounds. They aren't anything you'd think of, normally.'

'And how Erickson thought of them, God knows,' laughed Tasmin. He felt a rush of sudden elation. Despite the mud-flinging fanatics, the incident was an omen, a favorable omen. Things were going to go right in Splash One. He was going to find out everything he needed to know. The weight of mystery would be lifted. There would be no more questions. He turned to the acolytes, wondering if they felt as euphoric as he did to be at the end of the journey.

Jamieson evidently felt something. The boy's face shone with interest as he looked down onto the city. During their travels, he seemed to have become less preoccupied with the girl he had left behind and increasingly interested in where they were going and what they were doing. Or perhaps it was the girl who was with them, although Tasmin had not seen him make any obvious move in her direction. Still ... propinquity. An excellent remedy for absent friends, propinquity – although it would be hard to know whether Jamieson had been encouraged or not, Clarin being so self-contained. She was an inveterate pettifier – Tasmin would have bet she had a crystal mouse in her pocket right now, one she'd caught stealing food from the camp. She was friendly and always thoughtful, but cool. Tasmin had come to appreciate her during this trip. He approved of her restrained manner, her calm and undemanding demeanor, though he did so without ever considering what that approval implied.

'I said,' the officer repeated, breaking in on Tasmin's thoughts, 'I said, where are you staying?'

'The citadel,' he replied, almost without thinking. Where else would a Tripsinger stay but there, among his own kind? 'If they have room for us.'

'Do you know your way there?'

'Not really. I've been in Splash One before, but it was years ago, when I did a lot of trips to the Coast.' This city looked nothing like the smallish town he remembered. This city swarmed, bubbled, erupted with ebbs and flows of citizenry, trembled with noise. 'Thank God for one hundred meters of deepsoil,' he murmured only half-aloud, intercepting Clarin's empathetic glance.

'It's amazing, isn't it?' she agreed. 'I saw it two years ago on my way down from Northwest to Deepsoil Five. I think it's doubled in size since then.'

'Well, it's enough changed that I'm going to send a man with you as a guide,' the Captain told them. 'There are Crystallites in the city, too, and they consider anyone in Tripsinger robes as targets of opportunity. I'm in charge of a stockade of troublemakers, a whole disciplinary barracks full, and I swear they're less trouble than these damn fanatics. I suggest you leave the mules in the citadel stables after this and wear civilian clothes in town. It's not foolproof protection, since they may recognize your faces, but it'll help.'

'What are we allowed to do,' Jamieson asked, 'to protect ourselves?'

'Anything you bloody well can,' Verbold replied. 'Up to and including killin' a few of 'em. Like I said, once the Governor gets off his rounded end, we'll have a clearance order on 'em and that'll put an end to it.'

'Clearance order?' Clarin asked.

'For the maintenance of public safety, yes, Ma'am. The relocation camp's already built, down the Coast about ten miles. Power shielded and pretty much escape proof. Put 'em in there and let 'em have at each other if they have to have at somebody. Everyone knows it has to be done. What's keeping his excellency is beyond us – all of us. Somethin' devious no doubt.' He pulled a face, begging their complicity. It had not been a politically astute thing to say.

'Any rumors about the delay?' Jamieson demanded.

'Oh, there's always rumors,' the Captain said, turning away brusquely. He had said too much. Besides, they knew what the rumors were: The Governor was being given a share of the pilgrimage money; he was being paid off by the fanatics.

Tasmin shook his head at Jamieson, and he subsided. Tasmin did not want to discuss planetary politics or the Planetary Exploitation Council here on the public way, surrounded by soldiers who might repeat anything that was said, in or out of context, accurately or not. What the Captain chose to say was the Captain's own business, but Tasmin had a lifelong habit of caution. He leaned from the saddle to take the officer's hand once more. 'Thank you, Captain. I'll tell the Master General of the citadel how helpful you've been.' The Master General of the Splash One Citadel was also the Grand Master of the Tripsinger Order, Thyle Vowe. Favorable mention to Vowe was not an inconsiderable favor, and the Captain grinned as he stepped back and saluted them on their way.

They reached the citadel without further incident, were welcomed, then lauded when it became known that Tasmin had come down from the Mad Gap with a long lost Password. There was good-natured teasing of the citadel librarian, some not so good-natured responses from that official, followed by room assignments for the travelers, provision for cleaning the clothes they had with them, and obtaining more anonymous garments to be worn in town. Grand Master Thyle Vowe, it seemed, was at the Northwest Citadel and would not return for some days. Tasmin wrote a note, including some laudatory words about Captain Verbold – including his probable political sympathies – and left it for him. It was late afternoon before all the details were taken care of and Tasmin could get away.

The two acolytes were lounging in the courtyard, obviously waiting for him, Clarin, predictably, with a gray-furred crystal mouse – so called because its normal habitat was among the crystal presences – running back and forth on her shoulder.

'Private business,' Tasmin said, trying to be more annoyed than he actually was. Now that the time had come, he was having a fit of nerves, and the false hostility in his voice grated even upon his own ears.

'No, sir,' said Clarin, apparently unmoved as she pocketed the mouse. 'You've told us all about it, and we need to go with you. We can help you find Lim Terree's manager or agent or whatever he is.' She was saying no more than the truth. In the long evenings over the campfire, they had learned more about one another than any of them would have shared in the stratified society of the citadel. They were almost family – with the responsibility that entailed.

Tasmin, suddenly aware of that responsibility, found that it made him irritable. 'I can do that alone.' Could he? Did he want to?

'You might be set upon, Master. We've inquired. It's best for Tripsingers to go in company, so the Master General of this citadel has ordered.' Jamieson was factual, a little brusque, avoiding Tasmin's eyes. With sudden insight, Tasmin realized the boy was not speaking out of mere duty and would be wounded if he were rebuffed.

He took refuge in brusqueness of his own. 'I hope you two haven't been chirping.'

'Master Ferrence!' The boy was hurt at being accused of being loose mouthed.

Jamieson's pain shamed Tasmin for his lack of courtesy, and he gritted his teeth. 'Did you get a car?'

'Yes, sir. That greenish one over there.'

'Looks well used, doesn't it?' The vehicle appeared to have been used to haul hay, or perhaps farm animals; it sagged; the bubble top was scratched into gray opacity.

'Well, there were only two to choose from, and the other one was pink.' Jamieson gave him a sidelong glance, assaying a smile of complicity, still with that expression of strain.

Tasmin flushed. Did he have the right to reject friendship when it was offered? Was he so determined upon his hurt he would hurt others to maintain the appearance of grief? He reached out to lay his hand on Jamieson's shoulder, including Clarin in his glance. 'If you're so damned set on being helpful . . .' Tasmin had already made a few calls from his room, locating one of the backup men Lim had had with him in Deepsoil Five and obtaining from him the name of Lim's agent. 'We're looking for a man named Larry Porsent, and we're supposed to find him in the Bedlowe Building, Eleventh Street and Jubilation Boulevard.' Under his hand, Jamieson relaxed.

The streets were scarred with new and half-healed trenches; the building they sought was under construction with the first two floors occupied even while all the turmoil of fabrication went on above. They dodged hod carriers and bricklayers and representatives of half a dozen other construction specialties as they climbed the stairs to the second floor.

'When do you suppose they'll start putting lifts in these buildings?' Jamieson complained. 'I've done nothing in this city yet but climb stairs. They've got Clarin and me in dormitories five flights up.'

'They'll put in lifts when lift mechanisms are defined as essential,' Tasmin said indifferently. He had been given a pleasant suite on the second floor of the citadel, overlooking a walled garden. 'Or when there gets to be enough demand to fabricate them locally. Right now, it takes tenth place behind a lot of other needed supplies like medical equipment and farm machinery and computers. There's the office.'

The name was painted in lopsided letters on a raw, new door. Inside they found the tenant crouched on the floor, trying to assemble a desk. He was a short, plump man with a polished pink face that gleamed with sweat and annoyance as he tried to fit a part into a slot that obviously would not hold it. 'Larry Porsent,' he introduced himself, clambering to his feet with some difficulty. 'What can I do for you?'

'I'm Tasmin Ferrence.'

'Yes.' There was no indication the man recognized the name.

'I'm Lim Terree's brother.'

The man scowled. 'I'll be damned. Really? I didn't know he had a brother. Didn't know he had any kin at all. Except his wife, of course, and the kid.'

'Wife!'

'Well, sure. You mean you didn't know? Well, of course you didn't know or you wouldn't be surprised, right. I'm kind of slow on the launch today.

81

Not my day. Not my season, if you want the truth. Perigee time. Lim's death just about finished me off.'

'He was a major client?'

'He was damn near my only client. He wanted all my time, and I gave it to him. Would've worked out fine, too, if he hadn't gone crazy. I mean, since you're his brother and kin and all – these your kids? Nice lookin' kids. Why in the name of good sense would a man take every credit he's saved up in ten years and spend everything he's got settin' up a tour of the dirt towns! You can't make that pay. Everybody knows you can't make it pay. I told him. I told his wife, Vivian, and she told him.' He ran both hands through his thinning hair, then thrust them out as though to beg understanding. 'Why would a man do that?'

'You mean, the tour to Deepsoil Five wasn't a financial success?'

'Hell, man, no tour to the dirt towns is a financial success! They're always a dead loss. Only time we do 'em, ever, is if BDL banks 'em for us. I mean, any of us, any agent, any performer. BDL pays it out every now and then, just for the goodwill, but there's no audience there. How much can you make, stacked up against what it costs to get there?'

Jamieson asked, 'You're telling us that Lim Terree used his own money to pay for the trip?'

'Everything he had. Down to the house and his kid's savings fund. And since you're his brother, I can show you a few bills that didn't get paid if you're interested in clearing his good name.'

Tasmin shook his head, dizzied by this spate of unexpected information. 'Lim had a very expensive comp on his wrist when I saw him last.'

'He did, indeed. And I wish I had it now. That was a gift, that was. Guess who from? Honeypeach herself. The Governor's lady.' He spat the word. 'Poor old Lim couldn't sell it or he was dead. He couldn't lose it or he was dead. All he could do was wear it and try to stay out of her bed. People that upset Honeypeach end up buried. She's a crystal-rat, that one. Teeth like a Jammling, and she wanted to eat him.'

'Terree's wife,' Clarin said, sympathetically aware of Tasmin's confusion. 'Where would we find her?'

'You'll find her at home, such as it is, over the fish market, down at the south end. Or you'll find her in the market, guttin' and scalin'. She and the kid have to eat, and Lim sure left her without the wherewithal. She left a registered job with the Exploration records office to have Lim's kid, and they sure won't take her back …'

'I may have some other questions,' Tasmin said, shaking his head. 'Right now I'm too confused by all this to know. We can find you here daytimes?'

'If I can make it through the next few days, you can. I've got a few comers lined up. One of 'em's bound to break orbit. None of 'em are Lim Terree, though, I'll tell you that. He was a genius. A damned genius. He could do more with a music box than any other three people. If you find out what made him crazy, I wish you'd let me know.' He dropped to his knees and began working on the assembly once more, oblivious to their departure.

In the car there was a careful silence. Tasmin was trying to fit what he had just learned into the structure he had postulated, and it did not fit. A penniless Lim Terree. A man who had told the truth when he said he hadn't the funds to help Tasmin with their mother's needs. Why?

'Do you know where the fish market is, Reb?'

The boy flushed with pleasure. Tasmin seldom addressed him by his sobriquet. 'Clarin and I studied the city map for a while. I think I can find it.'

He did find it, after several false turns, although finding a place to put the car was another thing. The market was long and narrow, extending across the length of the fish farms and the fleet moorings. The wares on display included both native and farmed out-system fish, finned and shelled and naked skinned. Though Jubal had a paucity of land life – a few small animals like viggies, a few birdlike and insect-like creatures – its shallow oceans burgeoned species, and the rainbow harvest made up most of the protein needs of the human inhabitants. They struggled through the crowd toward the south end of the market, asking as they went for Vivian Terree.

Tasmin knew her as soon as he saw her. She was so like old pictures of his mother that she could have been related by blood. That same triangular face, the same deeply curved and oddly shaped mouth in which the lower lip appeared to be only half as long as the upper one, giving her a curiously exotic appearance. That same long, silvery hair – though Vivian wore it braided and pinned to keep it out of her way. Lim must have been attracted by that unbelievable resemblance.

'Vivian?' Tasmin asked.

She pushed a wisp of hair from her forehead with one wrist, keeping the bloody fingers extended. Her other hand held a curved knife. 'Yes?'

'I'd like to talk with you, if you have a minute.'

'I don't have a minute. I don't have any time at all. They don't like us having conversations while we're supposed to be working.' Her face and voice were so full of worry and pain there was no room for curiosity.

'I can wait until after work. My name's Tasmin Ferrence. I'm Lim's brother.'

She stared at him, her eyes gradually filling with tears. The knife hand trembled, as though it wanted to make some other and more forceful gesture. 'Damn you,' she said in a grating whisper. 'Damn you to hell.'

In his shock, Tasmin could not move. Clarin stepped between them as though she had rehearsed the movement. 'Don't say that, Vivian. I don't know why you would say that. Tasmin was only a boy when his brother left home, and he doesn't know any reason for you to say anything like that. See. Look at his face. He doesn't know. Whatever it is, he doesn't know.'

The woman was crying, her shoulders heaving. Tasmin straightened, looked around to meet the eyes of an officious and beefy personage stalking in his direction. He moved to meet this threat. 'Are you the supervisor here?'

The man began to bluster. Tasmin drew himself up. 'I am Tripsinger Tasmin Ferrence. I am on official business for the citadel. I need to talk to this woman, Vivian Terree, and I intend to do so. You can either cooperate or I can report your lack of cooperation to the citadel. The choice is entirely up to you.'

The bluster changed to a whine, the whine to a slobber. Tasmin left him in mid-cringe. 'Clarin, find out where we can talk.'

Vivian led them out of the market and around to the rear where a flight of rickety stairs took them to the second floor. The tiny apartment was as splintery and dilapidated as the stairs, with narrow windows that did nothing to ventilate the scantily furnished two rooms or ameliorate the overwhelming stench of fish.

The baby was playing quietly in a crib. A boy child, about two or a little older. He turned to look at them curiously as they entered, holding up his arms to his mother. 'D'ink.'

'Lim's son?'

'Lim's. Of course.' She filled a cup and held it to the baby's lips. 'Little Miles.'

The name came as a shock. Named after their father? Lim's and Tasmin's father?

'Lim didn't live here?' Tasmin fumbled.

'We didn't live here. We had a house, a nice house, on the rocks over the bay. There was a little beach for Miles to play on. Lim borrowed against it.'

Miles? 'You lost it?'

'I guess I never really had it.' She turned on him, glaring. 'We would have had it if he hadn't done that crazy thing. He borrowed against the house. Against everything we had. A hundred-day note. Due and payable at the Old Moon. He was dead by then.' She leaned over the child, weeping.

Tasmin looked at Clarin, pleadingly.

'Let me take the baby out on the stairs,' she said to Vivian. 'You and Tasmin need to talk.' She went out with Jamieson, and he could hear them playing a rhyme game on the landing while the sea birds shrieked overhead.

'Vivian. I don't ... I don't know why Lim did that. His agent told me about it. I don't understand it.'

'He had to get to you.'

'To me? I hadn't even seen him in fifteen years! I wrote to him and he didn't even answer!'

'You wrote to ask him for money. Why should he send money to you!'

Tasmin bit back the obvious answer, controlled himself.

'Vivian, I don't know why. Mother was in need; I thought Lim was making it with both hands.'

'Let your damned father take care of her!'

'He died. Years ago. Not long after Lim left.' After Lim had left, Miles Ferrence had almost seemed to court disaster.

She was shaking. 'Dead?' She got up, moved into the next room. Tasmin could hear water running. In a moment she returned. Her hands and face were wet. She had washed off the fish blood. 'Dead?' she asked again.

'Why does it matter?'

'I suppose it doesn't, now. Everything he went through. Trying to prove himself to that rotten old man!'

'You didn't even know him!'

'I know about him.' She began to weep again. 'He was ... he was terrible. Oh, God, he hurt Lim so.'

'Well, Lim hurt him.'

'Later. Later Lim hurt him. Later Lim tried to. To get even a little. Because it didn't seem to matter. Poor Lim.'

'I don't understand.'

'How old are you?' she asked suddenly, eyes flashing.

'Thirty-two.'

She counted, shaking her head. 'Lim was thirty-seven, almost thirty-eight. He was only twelve when it happened. So, you were only seven. Maybe you didn't know. I guess you didn't.' She bent forward, weeping again.

'Vivian, please. Talk to me. I don't know what happened. I don't know what you're saying. Yes, my father was a very unpleasant person sometimes. Yes, I think he was harder on Lim than he was on me because Lim was older.'

'Hard! I could forgive it if he'd just been hard.'

'I don't know what you're talking about. I'd like to understand, but I don't. I just don't.'

'You really don't know?'

'I really don't know.'

She got up, wiping her eyes, and wandered around the room, picking things up, putting them down again. She went to the door and looked out at the child, sitting on Jamieson's lap being patty-caked by Clarin. The mouse was on her shoulder once more, and the baby couldn't decide what to look at, Clarin's hands or the little animal.

'When Lim was twelve,' Vivian said, 'he went to choir school.'

Tasmin nodded. All Tripsingers and would-be Tripsingers went to choir school.

'There was this man, the assistant choir master. Lim told me his name was Jobson. Martin Jobson.'

'The name doesn't mean anything to me, Vivian.'

'He was probably long gone by the time you ... Well, he was one of those men – what do you call it?' She paused, her face very pale. 'A man who screws little boys?'

Tasmin ran his tongue around a suddenly dry mouth. 'You mean a pedophile?'

'He did it to Lim.'

'Oh, Lord. How awful ...'

'He could have gotten over that I think. He really could. He said he could have gotten over that, and I believe him. But Lim went home and told his father, your father.'

Tasmin shut his eyes, visualizing that confrontation. She did not need to go on. He knew what she would say.

'Your father told him it must have been his fault, Lim's. Your father said he must have asked for it. Invited it. Seduced the man, somehow. Your father told him he was ruined. Debauched. That's the word Lim always said, debauched. He told Lim he was filthy. Perverted. That he couldn't love him anymore.'

'No,' Tasmin murmured, knowing it was true. 'Oh, no.'

'Your father had this viggy he was going to give Lim, and he gave it to you instead. Because you were a good boy. Pure, he said.'

'My viggy ...'

'Lim let it loose. If he couldn't have it, he wouldn't let you have it either. He went crazy, he said. He heard the viggy singing to him, words he could understand, like a dream. He had delusions. After that ... after that it didn't matter what he did. He was already ruined. That's what he thought ...'

'So when he ran away ...'

'He was just getting even. A little.'

'Ah.' It was a grunt. As though he had been kicked in the stomach. He got up and went to the door, moved outside it onto the narrow porch, and bent over the railing. The blue-purple of the bay stretched away to the headlands on either side, and beyond the bay, the ocean. At the limit of his vision he could see the towering buoys of the Splash site. Star ships came down there. Ships whose thunder was cushioned from the planet by an enormous depth of ocean. Things came and went, but the foundations of the world remained unshaken.

Unlike men whose foundations trembled when new things came upon them. Unlike brothers, when they learned the loved and despised was not despised at all and had not been loved enough.

'God,' he said. It was a prayer.

'Master?' Jamieson stood beside him, his hand out, his face intent with concern.

'I'm all right.' He moved back into the shabby room. 'Vivian. I'll help. I'll help you all I can. You and the baby.'

'How?'

'I don't know. Not just yet. But I will help. Would you go to Deepsoil Five? My mother would make you very welcome there ... no! Don't look like that. She didn't know. I swear to you, she did not know. My father ... he was a cruel man in many ways, Vivian, but neither she nor I knew anything about what you've told me. Lim never told us.' He put his arms around her.

'He still loved his father,' she said, weeping. 'And he was ashamed.'

Clarin came in with containers of hot tea, obtained from a vendor down in the bustle. Jamieson went out and returned with crisply fried chunks of fish, the chortling baby high on his shoulders, exclaiming, 'Fiss, 'ot fiss.' Both the acolytes inspected Tasmin as though for signs of illness or damage, and he made an attempt at a smile to reassure them. They were not reassured.

They sat without speaking for a time. Eventually, Vivian said something about the baby, her face softening as she said it.

Tasmin asked, 'Do you know what Lim was doing, Vivian? Why he did it?'

'He had to get to you,' she replied. 'That's all I really know. He needed something by Don Furz, and you had it. And he told me if he could get that, we'd be wealthy. His family would be proud of him, and we'd be wealthy.'

'Nothing else? Only that?'

'That's all. It was a secret, he said. A terrible secret.'

She knew nothing more. They left her there, promising to return. Tasmin gave her what money he had with him, enough to last a few days. 'Don't go back to the market,' he told her. 'You don't need to do that.'

On the way to the car he fished in his pocket, bringing Celcy's earclip out at last. He stood by the car, staring at it for a long moment. All he had left of her. All.

'Jamieson.'

'Sir?'

'You're a clever fellow, Reb. Somewhere in all this mess there will be someone who buys gems. I paid four hundred for a pair of these. Firestones are more valuable here than they are in the interior. You ought to be able to get at least a hundred for this one clip, just on the value of the stones. That's enough to buy passage for a woman and a child, isn't it?'

It was Clarin who replied. 'Yes, Sir. More than enough.' There was an ache in her voice, but Tasmin did not notice it. She was fighting herself not to put her arms around him, but he did not notice that either. His face was so tired and bleak, she would have done anything at all to comfort him. The best she could do was do nothing.

'Can you do that, too?' Tasmin asked. 'Get passage. Earliest possible trip with someone reliable. On the Southern Route, I think. It's longer, but there hasn't been a fatality on that route for quite a while.'

'Yes, Sir.' Jamieson and Clarin shared what Tasmin had come to identify as 'a look.'

'I'm all right. You heard the whole thing from the stairs, I know. It's ... well, it's a shock to find someone you've—'

'Hated?' Clarin tilted her head to one side, examining him through compassionate eyes.

'I guess. It's a shock to find someone you've hated didn't deserve it. It turns the blame inward.'

'No more your fault than his,' said Clarin, blinking rapidly. 'Excuse me, Sir, but your father must have been a bastard.'

'He was.' Tasmin sighed. 'In many ways he was, Clarin, he was.'

'And then what?' asked Jamieson. 'Shall we go back on the same trip?'

'Go back?' he shook his head, for a moment wondering what the boy was talking about. 'To Deepsoil Five? Of course not, Jamieson. The mystery is still there, isn't it? I still don't know what Lim was doing. I still don't know why Celcy died!'

'Where next, Sir?'

'To Don Furz. That's the only clue we have left.'

Donatella Furz returned to the Chapter House at Northwest late in the afternoon of the agreed-upon day, having come up the coast in a small BDL transport ship and inland from there in a provisions truck. Zimmy would be expecting her, undoubtedly with something special set up by way of dinner and amusement. She needed him, needed to talk to him. Events of the past three days had been as confusing as they were frightening. She kept thinking of Gretl, even though what was happening to her was nothing like what had happened to Gretl except in its atmosphere of obdurate menace. At the moment of peril she had had no time to be frightened. Only afterward, considering it, thinking how close to death she had come both times, did the cold sweat come on her and her stomach knot.

Now she had to confide in someone. Someone close. Who else could it be but Zimmy? She found herself rehearsing the conversation she would have with him, his exclamations of concern. He already knew about Gretl – everyone at the Priory knew about Gretl – he'd understand her fear. Even thinking of telling him made her feel better, as though the very fact she could share her troubles and dangers somehow lessened them. If she could trust anyone, she could trust him. Even though she hadn't told him anything yet, she would now. She had to be able to talk to someone!

Zimmy, however, was not waiting for her.

She didn't want to make an undignified spectacle of herself over the man – he was a services employee, after all, and the Explorer King had said enough on that score already – so she showered and changed and went down to the common room for a drink and the odd bit of chitchat. Chase Random Hall was in his usual place, a high backed chair with the unmistakeable air of a throne. She nodded in his direction and received a nod in return.

'All well, Don?' he called, bringing every eye in the room to rest on her.

Damn the man. 'All well, Randy,' she returned with a brilliant smile. 'The doctor says I'll live.' She circulated, exchanging the gossip of Splash One for the gossip of Northwest. The evening meal was announced, and still no Zimmy. Now she began to worry, just a little. Had he forgotten the date of her return? He would be full of apologies and consternation if that was the case, busy taking little digs at himself. Or had something happened to him? She turned away from the thought. It was enough that people were trying to kill her; surely there was no reason for anyone to try to kill Zimmy. Of course, there were always accidents.

'I don't see Zimble around,' she said to her dinner mate.

'Zimmy? Oh, he went out. Let's see, I saw him go out the little gate about midafternoon. Shopping, he said, and then an amateur show with friends.'

'Ah.' She kept her voice carefully casual. 'After what I saw in Splash One, I grow concerned about any absent face.' The conversation switched to Gretl Mechas, and she quickly changed the subject. They talked of Crystallites, suspected and proven, and she remained puzzled. He must have forgotten. Though Zimmy usually didn't forget. Not anything. He was the kind of man who remembered every word of conversations held years before; the kind of man who sent greetings on obscure anniversaries; the kind of man who kept gift shops in business. He had a little notebook full of people's birthdays. This minor talent, or vice, would have made him merely a sycophantic niggler were it not for his humor and charm. No, she could not imagine Zimmy forgetting.

She was in the lounge at a corner table, half hidden by her table mates, when he returned. She saw him in the hallway, checking the message board. Ralth was halfway through a complicated story that she chose not to interrupt, so she did not call out or make any gesture, but merely noticed Zimmy from under her lowered lids. Zimmy turned, his mobile face twisted into a laughing response to someone's remark.

And saw her.

Don let her lids drop closed, frightened at what she had surprised in his face. Shock. Shock and astonishment. He had not expected to see her here. He had not expected to see her anywhere. She gasped and put a hand to her throat, not looking up. Something hard pressed up. She gulped.

'Don? What's the matter?' Ralth was looking at her with concern.

'I swallowed the wrong way. Got so intrigued by your story, I forgot to breathe.' She laughed and looked up. There he was. Zimmy. Now he was beaming at her. Waving. If she hadn't seen him for that split second, she would have believed in his apparent pleasure at the sight of her. She waved back, as though she hadn't a care in the world.

Inside, a part of her screamed.

If he had not expected to see her at all, then he had expected her not to be here. Not to be anywhere. To be dead.

Zimmy. So. Well and yes, Donatella. He is a Chapter Horse man. A hired man. Here for your comfort. Did you think love would change all that? Did you think he loved you just because he said so? A hired man is a hired man, that is, a man who works for money, loves for money.

Who had paid him?

Ralth's story concluded to general and amused disbelief. She excused herself and went to greet Zimmy, hiding her inner turmoil, pretending. 'Zimmy! Lord, it's good to be back. Splash One is a madhouse.' Her throat was tight, but her voice sounded normal.

'You look all pale around the eyes, lovely. Why don't you go up and get into something more comfortable and I'll give you a nice back rub.' He gave her a sly, sideways glance, code for something erotic. No, oh, no.

'Come on up,' she said. 'Just for a few minutes, though. I'm dead to the world. Couldn't sleep down there in Splash One. Too noisy.' She was going on past him, walking up the stairs, still talking. 'Zimmy, do you know what I saw?' She described the Crystallite immolation, shuddering dramatically. Once in the room, she sat on a chair and took her shoes off, motioning him to the other chair.

'Don't you want a nice back rub? You'd sleep better.'

'Zimmy, old friend, I will tell you the exact truth. There was a man at the Splash One Chapter House you wouldn't believe.' She described Blanchet, focusing on certain attributes of his that were only conjectural, hinted at surfeit of all things sexual, and concluded, 'So I really just want to fall into bed. Alone.'

His chin was actually quivering. Tears were hanging in the corners of his eyes. God, the man should be awarded a prize for drama. Donatella made herself lean forward, made herself pat him on the knee. 'Oh, Zimmy. Come on now. It didn't mean anything. It wasn't like us. But I am tired. Run on, now. Don't let Randy see you being all upset or he'll give you a public lecture.'

She yawned, opened the door for him despite his pretty protestations, and locked it when he was out of earshot.

God. He was good. She had almost believed him. If it hadn't been for that one, split second ...

She would bet anything she owned that if he was not directly responsible for the attempts on her life, he was deeply involved.

Who did he work for? In this house, he worked for the manager of services. The manager of services worked for the Prior. The Prior worked for the head of the BDL Department of Exploration – what was that man's name, a new man. Bard Jimbit. Bard Jimbit worked for Harward Justin, Planetary Manager. All of them worked for BDL.

Or perhaps he worked for the Explorer King, unofficially, for Randy's position was one of honor, not actual authority. He had risen to that position, one of three or four current Explorers in various parts of Jubal to do so, through election by his peers. The Kings were elected to represent the Explorers in dealings with BDL, to conduct contract negotiations and resolve disputes. Kings were supposed to be nonpolitical, though everyone knew that a very political favor-trading process led to election. It was part of the whole ritual nonsense the order had been saddled with by Erickson. Theoretically, Don owed fealty to the King, fealty being anything from giving up her seat at dinner to going to bed with him if he demanded it. Chase Random Hall was too clever to cause ill feeling by demanding anything. He got what he wanted without demanding. Did he also want her dead?

Who did want her dead? How had Lim Terree actually died? In an accident" Or had he fallen to some black-hooded figure coming out of the night? She got up and checked the lock on the door, then wandered around the room, casually examining the walls and ceiling. Listening devices? Were there listening devices in the walls? Were there eyes? Had someone watched her in this room as she pored over Erickson's notes? Were those notes safe where she had hidden them in the closet, in the lining of her boots? It was an odd, unsettling feeling to search for spies here in Northwest. She had expected there to be eyes and ears in Splash One; she had not really thought there would be any here.

And why not?

Because this was home.

Who, here at home, had paid Zimmy?

Who, here at home, wanted her dead?

It was almost dawn before she fell asleep.

In the luxurious Executive Suite of the BDL building in Splash One, Chase Random Hall was the dinner guest of Harward Justin, Planetary Manager for BDL. They were not known to be friends, but Justin sometimes commented that he found the Explorer King a witty and amusing companion, whose views on the needs and desires of the Explorers were valuable to management.

At least, such was the overt reason Justin gave for their occasional get-togethers. The covert basis for their real relationship was one of mutual self-interest. Just now they were discussing the upcoming contract negotiations for the Explorers Guild.

'We'll start meeting next week on the new contract,' Randy said, sniffing at his broundy glass. 'I suppose you want me to go through the motions.'

'I've heard the usual nonsense that the Explorers will demand increased medical care,' Justin said in his heavy, humorless voice. Justin was a bulky, powerful-looking man of sinister calm. He never allowed himself to do anything that threatened that appearance in public, although his private pleasures were less restrained. His pleasures were indulged in by himself, but his angers were attended to by others, usually by his agent, Spider Geroan. 'Very expensive medical care.'

The Explorer King sought consultation from the bottom of his glass. 'They're getting serious about it, Justin.'

'Who is?'

'A good many of them. Our little friend Don Furz, for one. Her lover's still in that chair, you know. Five years now.'

'She's only one person.'

'There are others.'

'Not many. Reprogram them onto the amenities issue again. It's a hell of a lot cheaper to pay for a few additional services employees than it is to ship people to Serendipity and pay for regeneration. Tell them about the progress we've already made. There's minor regeneration already available here on Jubal.'

'We have machines only for things like eyes, fingers, wiping off scars. Doesn't mean much if you're missing a leg or an arm.'

Justin scowled. 'The Explorer contract is not going to make a damned bit of difference, Hall! Go through the motions.' The threat in his voice was patent. 'Tout them onto amenities and don't worry about it.'

'So it won't make any difference,' the King said. 'Which means ...'

'Which means you should ask very few questions, Hall, and engage in no speculation at all.'

Justin's voice was oily with malice, but the King chose not to hear it. 'The Governor is leaving it perilously late.'

'Moving against the Crystallites, you mean?' Justin made a cynical smirk.

The Governor was doing what Justin had told him to do. 'He may want a major incident.'

'He'll get it. It's inevitable.'

'He may feel that he must have something irrefutable, unarguable. A notorious assassination, perhaps. Something to justify the forceful use of troops.' Justin tilted the glass and drank the last drop of broundy, then touched the button that would summon one of the mute and deaf waiters who served the Executive Suite.

'Presumably the CHASE group can't start hearings until the Crystallites have been moved into the relocation camp?'

'They'll be moved in time, just before CHASE is ready to meet. The Governor's stepson, Ymries Fedder, will be chairman.' Justin was not quite happy about this, but there had been some necessary favor trading in the ivory halls of PEC. Governor Wuyllum Thonks had friends there, though Justin could not imagine why.

The King mused, 'I presume the findings are already determined. The commission will find there is no reason to believe any sentience exists in the Presences ...'

'After which event,' Justin said with a chilly and ruthless smile, 'I think we would find we have more economical access to the interior than we've had heretofore.'

There was an appreciative silence. 'The Tripsingers are going to be very upset,' said the King. 'To say nothing of the Explorers.'

'Do you really care?' Justin asked carelessly.

'Each time I check the balance in my account on Serendipity, I care less.' He made circles on the table with his glass. Hall felt broundy was an overrated drink. The effect was pleasant, but the taste left much to be desired. He preferred fruit-based liquors, imported ones. 'The account comes to a very nice sum. For which I should continue to give my best efforts. And that brings me back to Donatella Furz.'

'You've brought her up before. What are you suggesting, Randy? That she has uncovered some cache of secrets? That she has discovered The Password? That she has arrived, at some fundamental truth that has eluded the rest of us?' Justin shook his head and leaned back in his chair, accepting a full glass from a blank-faced servitor.

'Oh, unload it, Justin. You understand well enough what I'm worried about. If she has learned something basic to do with language, with sentience, we're slashed off. You, me, all of BDL.'

Harward lifted a nostril. Foolish man to think his little worries had not been anticipated by those both more intelligent and more powerful than he. Foolish little man. Still, he made his voice sympathetic as he said, 'Has she said anything to indicate that is true?'

The King thought for a time, then shook his head reluctantly. 'No. I have a man very close to her, and he says she's got something, but she's been chary. He has no proof of what it is, not yet.'

'Well then?' Harward allowed himself a tiny sneer.

'She was wounded a few trips ago. A bad slash on her arm.'

'Not an unheard-of occurrence for an Explorer. Broken crystals are like knives, I understand.'

'I'd wager it was a knife. Somebody tried to get rid of her.'

'Ah. And this makes you suspicious?'

'Wouldn't it you?'

'It would make me ask you, Randy, why you take such an interest?'

Randy snarled. 'The Enigma has been tried and tried again. She didn't just go out there and solve it all by herself with her little music box.'

'Erickson did.'

'Not the Enigma?'

'I mean that Erickson solved various passwords all by himself with his little music box. Why are you so determined that Furz did not?'

'I know her. I know how her mind works. She isn't capable of that. She's bright, but she's not Erickson.'

Which was pure jealousy talking, Justin thought. Chase Random Hall was one of the most politically astute Explorers on Jubal, but he was not one of the most talented. 'Well, as far as that goes, the score may not work. I understand it isn't even scheduled for testing. It may be a complete boggle.'

The King shook his head, a hungry snarl at the corner of his mouth, elegantly shaped brows curving upward in an expression of disagreement. 'It's no boggle. The Prior over at our Chapter House had a communique from the Master General of the citadel in Deepsoil Five. The thing works.'

'So?'

'Just now would be a bad time for Donatella to come up with something linguistic, wouldn't it?'

'Avery bad time. If it got out. On the other hand, Hall, it would also be a bad time for anything awkward to happen to her It's important that the CHASE report not be subject to question later on. Don Furz is very high on the list of witnesses to be called. A questionable accident might arouse a good deal of suspicion, and we don't want that.'

'I just thought ...'

'Don't. Don't think, Randy.' Justin wanted no underling working at cross purposes. He would make his own final arrangement regarding Donatella Furz. One that would forward his plans. The Explorer knight was very well known. Her assassination would indeed be notorious. He regarded Hall with a sneer. 'You dislike her, don't you?'

'Donatella?' Randy laughed, a brittle cackle with no mirth in it. 'How can you say such a thing? She's a charming woman. Very lovely. Bright. Dedicated.'

'You dislike her, don't you?' the Planetary Manager said again, still amused.

'My dear Justin,' Hall sneered. 'However did you guess?'

Harward Justin showed his teeth, an expression that the Explorer King knew far too well. When he spoke again, it was with ominous softness. 'Don't let your dislike override your good sense, Hall. I've explained that I don't want anything awkward happening to her just now. Spider Geroan still works for me. You wouldn't want to forget that.'

The Explorer King smiled. It took every ounce of self-control he had to create that smile. He had met Spider Geroan only once, had seen Spider Geroan's handiwork only once. He never, never wanted to see either again.

7

His excellency Governor Wuyllum Thonks was at ease with his wife and child in the little retiring room of Government House, having dined well and drunk better yet.

'Wully,' Lady Honeypeach Thonks addressed him, tapping the table with her jeweled nail protectors while perusing a printed list, 'do I have to invite that awful Vox woman to the soiree? She smells like horses.'

'It wouldn't be politic to leave her out,' said a quiet voice from across the room where Maybelle Thonks looked up from her book to continue the admonition. 'Not if you're inviting all the rest of the BDL higher echelon.'

'The rest of them don't smell. And it's really none of your business, Mayzy. You usually don't even show up.'

'I wish you wouldn't call me Mayzy, Peachy. I really hate it.' Maybelle frowned and returned to the printed page. Twitting Honeypeach, her so-called stepmother, was a dangerous occupation, and Maybelle kept resolving not to do it. Still, she did it. It was like a scab she had to pick at. Damn the woman!

Her stepmother raised one foot and did not answer. The foot was being groomed by a kneeling servitor, and its condition seemed to be of paramount interest. 'I don't like that color polish, girl. Try the pinky one.' She bent forward to stroke the outer edge of a big toe. 'Still a tiny bit of callus there. Rub it a bit more.' She returned to the list. 'I've invited Colonel Roffles Lang for you, Mayzy.'

'He's at least fifty. Why not one of the younger officers, if it's for me?' Actually, Maybelle had already made arrangements for an escort, although it would be extremely dangerous to say so.

'I have to invite him anyhow.'

And you want the younger ones for yourself, Maybelle thought, returning to her book. Some people said that Maybelle's father, the Governor, was an expert in masterly inaction, which was code for being well paid to do nothing. Certainly in the case of his wife his inaction was legendary. Maybelle wondered if it were masterly. Perhaps he enjoyed watching Honeypeach lying in wait for her quarry? Or did he enjoy it when she finally caught them? Was he there, watching, at the kill? Maybelle shuddered and tried to bury herself in *The History of the Jubal System*, Chapter Two, 'Serendipity and Jubal, the Sister Planets.'

'Would you like me to invite some of the Explorer knights, Wully?'

'That pretty one from Northwest,' he grunted. 'You know.'

'Donatella Furz?' Honeypeach smiled sweetly, again examining her foot and giving approval of the color varnish being applied to her nails. 'Anybody but, love. She killed my sweet Limmie, that one did.'

'Oh, honestly.' Maybelle put down the book and rose to the bait. 'She did not. Lim Terree died on the Enigma, singing a new score that Don came up with, that's all. He wasn't a Tripsinger, for God's sake. He should never have tried it. He was drugged up and he got himself killed. Don had nothing to do with it. I know her, and she's great.'

'Where did you get all that?' her father asked, something threatening in his unexpected attention, as though some mighty and slumbrous reptile had come angrily awake. 'All that about Terree? That was private information from the Grand Master's office to mine. I didn't release that information.'

'Well, your whole staff was talking about it,' Maybelle replied, refusing to be cowed. 'They were naturally interested. All of them know that Lim Terree was one of Honey's proteges.'

Which is, she concluded to herself, a euphemism to end all euphemisms. Though, come to think of it, Terree had seemed to keep his distance. Unlike some others. Chantry, for example. Chantry was going to be eaten alive. There would be nothing left of him but his teeth. Men that strolled into Honeypeach's lair came out as carrion.

The Lady Honeypeach noted the word *protege* and made a mental tally in her get-even book. Maybelle had quite a number of such tallies after her name. But then, so did others. Donatella Furz among them. 'I won't ask Furz,' she told Wuyllum. 'I don't like her. She killed my Limmie and she was rude to me at the PEC reception. But I will ask those new people. The ones who had the Mad Gap password.'

'If you mean the Tripsinger and acolytes from Deepsoil Five, you're too late,' murmured Maybelle. 'They're leaving for Northwest today.'

Honeypeach made a face. From the Governor's palace, she often used the scope to look right into the courtyard of the citadel. The blond Tripsinger had looked a lot like her poor Limmie. All that mass of silvery hair, that narrow, esthetic looking face, and those long, straight legs. Very edible. Very, very edible.

8

Tasmin and the acolytes decided to transport their mules to Northwest. Riding the animals was not sensible. It would take six to ten days for the journey, during which Don Furz could be sent almost anywhere. A truck towing a mule trailer could make it in one or two, depending on the ferry schedule.

'We can borrow mules at Northwest Citadel,' Tasmin reminded them for the third time. 'We don't have to take our own.'

'I like Jessica,' said Clarin. 'I like her a lot, and I'd just as soon not leave her here if you don't mind.'

He didn't argue. The trust between Tripsinger and mount had to be absolute. Gentle, unflappable, sensible – Tripsinger mules were all of these, as well as being sterile, which PEC rules demanded. The mares and jacks were kept at widely separated sites on the 'Soilcoast and breeding was by artificial insemination. Similar precautions were used in breeding foreign fish and fowl. Until there was a final declaration on the question of sentience, no imported creatures were allowed to breed freely on planets under PEC control.

Except people of course. The assumption had been that if it was necessary to evacuate the planet, every human would be deported. Most livestock, fowls, and fish would be slaughtered before the humans left. The mules would not be – it was generally accepted that the Tripsingers simply wouldn't stand for that – but in one generation they would be dead. The imported trees and shrubs were sterile. The vegetable crops would be killed except for settler's brush, which was a native species with only slight improvements. If the new commission they had been hearing about was to declare there was native sentience on Jubal and rule for disinvolvement, Jubal could be left as it had been before humans came.

Except that BDL wouldn't let that happen.

'Take Jessica,' Tasmin said. 'Take your own mule, Clarin. I confess to a fondness for Blondine, as well.'

'Not mine,' growled Jamieson, fondling his animal's ears. 'This old long-ear hasn't got a drop of sense.' The mule turned and gave him a severe and searching look, which the boy repaid with a palm full of chopped fruit. 'I'll see what I can round up in the way of transportation.'

'Clarin and I will get the equipment packed,' Tasmin said. They had already made arrangements for Vivian to travel to Deepsoil Five in a wagon train leaving almost at once. Tasmin had sent a message ahead to his mother, though he knew it might not reach her before Vivian did. Messages were sent by heliographic relay between widely separated parts of the planet, but the signal posts were only sporadically manned. Satellite relay worked if the transmitter was directly above the target receiver, but except on the coast or over water, both transmitters and receivers often burned out mysteriously. The Presences simply did not tolerate electromagnetic activity within a considerable distance, as a number of pilots had learned to their fatal dismay in the early years.

Clarin assisted Tasmin in repacking their equipment, checking each item as they went. 'You didn't leave this box like this, did you?' she asked, pointing to Lim's synthesizer, standing open on the table.

'Servants,' he mouthed softly. 'They poke into everything. The story is that BDL pays for all kinds of information. Probably nine out of ten servants in the citadel are selling bits and pieces to BDL informers for drinking money.'

She flushed. 'Someone told me that before. I'd forgotten. It seems so silly. We all work for the same people.'

'Not really,' he said, still softly. 'If you ask me whom I work for, I'll tell you I work for the Master General of my citadel, and ultimately for the Grand Master of the Order. Explorers work for their priories. I know BDL pays for all of it ultimately, but I don't think of myself as working for BDL. Maybe that's self-serving. There's a lot about BDL I just can't stomach.'

She seemed thoughtful, and he waited for the question he knew was coming, wondering what it would be this time. She had displayed a sustained though delicately phrased curiosity about Tasmin's life, but they had pretty well covered his history by now.

'Why do they call him Reb?' she asked.

'Who?' He was surprised into blankness.

'Jamieson. Why do they call him Reb?'

'Because he is one. He was a rebel in choir school. He's been a rebel in the citadel. He's been in trouble more than he's been out of it.' Tasmin smiled at a few private memories.

She sat on the bed and fumbled in her pocket, taking out her green-gray crystal mouse, which sniffed at her fingers with a long, expressive nose as it inflated its song-sack to give a muffled chirp. 'You know Jamieson wasn't sent after you by the Master General.'

'He wasn't?'

'He demanded to come. Because he thought you needed him.'

Tasmin was dumbfounded. 'What was all that about the girl he left behind?'

'So much smoke. We rehearsed it. So you wouldn't think it was his idea. He thought you'd send us back if it was his idea.'

Tasmin dropped to a chair, astonished. 'How did you get dragged in?'

'That was the Master General. He said if Jamieson was right, if you needed someone, you needed someone besides Jamieson because a steady diet of Jamieson was too much for anyone.' Her mouth quirked as she petted the mouse, curled now in one palm, cleaning itself.

Tasmin stared at her. That kid. That boy. That ... his eyes filled.

Seeing this she turned, going back to the former subject. 'Why did they let him stay in the Order if he was so much trouble?'

'Because more often than not he's been right. And because he's a fine musician, of course.' And because he loves Jubal, Tasmin thought. Maybe as much as I do.

'Is he right about ... about the Presences?' This was obviously the question she had really wanted to ask in the first place.

'What do you think?'

'It isn't what I think. I *feel* he's right. I guess inside somewhere, I *know* he's right. But if he's right, that makes everything else ...'

'Hypocritical?' he suggested. 'You used that word before, I think.' He sat down, looking at her closely. Her eyes were tight on his. The matter was important to her. He decided to give it his full attention.

'Well, I suppose it is hypocritical. I guess we – we Tripsingers – we go along with what BDL demands because it makes it possible for us to go on doing what we love to do. On the surface, in public, we pretend the Presences aren't sentient because that statement allows us to move around on Jubal. Underneath, we believe they are sentient, and that belief is what makes moving around on Jubal worthwhile! We assent to hypocrisy, because it doesn't seem to make that much difference. I guess it's because we don't see anything consequential happening just because we give lip service to non-sentience It doesn't change anything. We still go through the motions Erickson laid down for us, the quasi-religious, very respectful stuff he ordained, so while we say they're not sentient, we act as though they are sentient. We have to. Otherwise we might lose Jubal, and Jubal's in our blood.'

She sat down opposite him, her face eager. 'I've felt that, you know. What is it like, for you?'

He lowered himself onto the bed, dangling a sock from one hand, thinking. What was it like for him?

'It's like going into paradise,' he said. 'We say going into peril, but I've always thought paradise must be very perilous. Anything beautiful, anything that takes hold of your heart and shakes it – that's perilous.

'The peril takes hold of you even before you leave, sometimes. You see the ceremonial gate opening. Everything inside you gets very still. You start to ride, the fields flowing by, slowly changing to Jubal lands. You smell the Jubal trees, and as you go up the trail, they turn, almost as though they're following you. The ground begins to shiver, only a little, then more. Something is speaking in the ground, something enormous ...'

'I know,' she whispered. 'You go on and the words being spoken in the ground get bigger and bigger until they fill your head. Until you see the Presence before you, glittering. Light comes out of it like daggers, like swords. They pierce you, and you begin to sing. ... It's like bleeding music instead of blood.'

He nodded. She knew. Oh, yes. She knew.

'And if you do it right, quiet comes,' he concluded for her. 'Something listens.'

There was an aching understanding between them, a sympathy that was almost agony. He flushed and dropped his eyes, awash with an emotion he would not allow himself to feel. When she had spoken, he had felt her in his arms, as she had been there on the trail below the Watchers, trembling in his arms. He gritted his teeth, pushing the feeling away. It made him feel disloyal to the memory of Celcy each time he had one of these fleeting feelings.

After a time she pocketed the mouse and said, 'Logically, if something listens, something should reply.'

He shook his head, smiling ruefully. 'That's what Chad Jaconi says. He's spent forty years trying to make sense out of Password scores. I don't know how many so-called universal translator setups he's bought from out-system.'

'Did he ever get anything?'

'Nothing sensible.'

'What about the other side of the conversation? The Presence side?'

'Gibberish. For decades, people have recorded the sounds the Presences make. They've tried every known translator device. All they get is some kind of noise, Chad says. White noise or brown noise or something. Squeaks, howls, snores, gurgles. Nothing useful. Nothing with meaning.'

'What about the viggies? They sing. Maybe they're sentient.'

'A lot of people tried to establish that. There were a number of viggies captured in the early years, well treated so far as anyone could tell, and they almost all died – overnight sometimes. A very rare few were said to have lived in captivity. The one I had, the one Lim let loose, was supposed to say a few words, "pretty viggy" and "viggy wants a cooky," but there's no record of any of the things the PEC looks for in determining sentience. No tool-making. No proof of language. No burial of the dead. And, of course, there's simply no way to go among them and study them as our naturalists would like to do. They're nocturnal, elusive, die when captured, and they don't talk. So much for viggy sentience ...'

There was a tap at the door and Jamieson thrust his head in. 'I've found an empty brou truck that's leaving for Northwest in half an hour.'

'Right,' Tasmin agreed, rising. 'Let this stuff go, Clarin, I'll finish packing here. You two get your own gear.'

There was a brief delay while the truck was fitted with a proper hitch to pull the trailer Tasmin had borrowed from the mule farm. Since there was only space in the truck turret for two passengers, Jamieson chose to ride with the mules. They set out early in the afternoon.

First came the city outskirts, mud houses, mud stores, untidy gardens, these separated from similar stretches by great swatches of hard surfaced road, with more of it building. 'Military construction,' bellowed the driver over the noise of their travel. 'Somebody decided they needed better roads to move the military around. That's why bricks are so short. They've got all the solar furnaces out here surfacin' road.'

They passed several of the furnaces, huge mirrors hung on complicated frameworks that both tracked the sun and focused the resultant beam. Behind the furnaces, road surface smoked hotly, fading from red to black.

Once past the construction, though the road was narrow and bumpy, they made better time. They were traveling through fields of grain and narrower strips lined with root crops. Occasionally they could see pens of fowl or small meat animals, chigs or bantigons, omnivores native to Serendipity. Tasmin's mouth watered. He had an insatiable hunger for grilled bantigon. Fried bantigon. Bantigon pie. On this meat-poor planet, Tasmin was an unregenerate carnivore. Clarin, watching him salivate, gave him a sympathetic look. She, too, enjoyed fresh meat.

They reached a wide, shallow river and were ferried across. They passed a small town on their right, then more fields and farms, and another small town on their left. They were bending away from the sea, toward the uplands. Ahead of them were the only deepsoil hills yet discovered on Jubal, great sandy dunes pushed up by the sea winds and over-grown with settler's brush and feathery trees. They wound among the hills, startling tiny native animals who fled across the road, once surprising a group of viggies who fled whooping as the truck came near, turning their heads backward to peer behind them with enormous pupilless eyes, ears wagging and feathery antennae pointing at the truck. At the top of the hill, the largest viggy inflated his song-sack and boomed reproachfully at them before the group fled out of sight.

'I had no idea they came this near cultivated lands,' Tasmin said as he stared at the retreating gray-green forms. In all his trips he had actually seen viggies only five or six times, though he had heard them almost nightly all his life.

'See 'em all the time along the coast,' said the driver. 'Six, eight at a time. Had engine trouble along here once. Had to stop and spend the night on the road. Heard 'em singing real close by. Must've gone on all night. Lots of other critters around here, too. Ones you don't see very often.'

When they came out of the hills, the sun was behind them, falling slowly into the sea. 'We'll spend the night in Barrville,' the driver advised. 'There's a BDL agri-station there. Imagine they'll put you up.'

Sandy Chivvle, the local manager, did indeed put them up, glad of the company and eager to show someone what was being done with the ubiquitous brou. She insisted that seeds from this batch be tested against seeds from that batch, and by the time supper was put before them, none of them cared if they ate or not. The night passed in a cheerful haze.

Laden with reports to be delivered to Jem Middleton, head of the BDL Agricultural Division, they left early in the morning, somewhat headachey and lower in spirits. The driver dosed them with hot tea from a thermos flask, and they rumbled along endless fields of brou, the pale green-gray of newly planted fields alternating with the dark gray-green of mature crops, passing lines of loaded trucks headed the other way. They came into Northwest City a little after noon.

They unloaded the mules and then inquired at the neighboring BDL center for Jem Middleton. They found him in the bowels of the building in a remote room in which there was a welter game in progress. At least there were cards and stacks of consumer chits on the table, though the open document cases on the side table argued that something else might have been going on. To Tasmin's surprise, perhaps to his dismay, one of those present was the Grand Master of the Tripsinger Order, Thyle Vowe.

'Tasmin Ferrence! As I live and sing, if it isn't the wonder of Deepsoil Five! And your acolytes, too. Well, this is a surprise. I heard you were coming to Splash One, but I didn't think we'd see you up here. Heard about that Mad Gap thing. Makes me feel like an absolute fool. Should have checked the old files on it someplace besides Splash One, but I never thought of it. Let's see, you'd be Jamieson, wouldn't you? Heard a lot about you.' And the white-haired Master knuckled Jamieson sharply on the upper arm, grinning at him expansively. 'And you'd be Clarin, the little gal with the astonishin' bass voice, right? Heard about you, too. Word is that Tasmin Ferrence always gets the mean ones – bright but mean.'

Clarin submitted to the Grand Master's fatherly caress with what Tasmin regarded as commendable patience. It was almost as though she knew him, or knew of him.

'Tasmin, come meet some people! You know Gereny Vox, don't you?

Best mule breeder we've ever had and I've lived through six of 'em. The plain faced, gray-haired woman reached a hand across the table, nodding as Tasmin took it and murmured greetings. The Grand Master went on. 'This here's Jem Middleton. Jem's the head of the Agri Division for BDL, heck of a nice guy, good welter player, too. You want to watch him if you ever get into a game, boy. And this other fella is Rheme Gentry. Rheme's new on the Governor's staff from off-world and still sufferin' from Jubal shock. Good lookin' fella, isn't he? Lord, if I'd had teeth and hair like that, I'd of cut me a swath through the ladies. Not Rheme. Very serious fella, Rheme.'

The lean and darkly handsome man he referred to shook his head in dismay at this introduction, acknowledging Tasmin's greetings with a rueful nod.

'Now, want to sit in on the game? What about somethin' to eat? What can I get you to drink?'

Tasmin could not keep himself from grinning. The Grand Master had that effect on people. 'Thank you, no, Sir. I'm only here to deliver some papers to Jem Middleton from his manager out at Barrville.'

'Damn that girl,' Middleton growled, drawing great furry brows together in a solid line across his massive and furrowed forehead. 'Always gettin' her damn reports in on time. Now I'll have to get to work.'

'But since you're here in Northwest, Sir,' Tasmin said to the Grand Master, 'perhaps you could arrange an introduction for me. To an Explorer knight named Don Furz.'

There was a silence in the room, only a brief one, not one of those appalling silences that sometimes occurred during social gatherings following some gaffe, but enough of a pause that Tasmin wondered whether he had put a foot wrong. His prearranged excuse could do no harm. 'I wanted to express my admiration for the workmanlike way the Enigma notes were prepared. I had the honor of doing the master copy of the score ...'

The silence broke. Thyle Vowe was all affability once more. 'Ever met Don Furz?'

'No, sir. I haven't had that pleasure.'

'Well, why don't we find out where you can maybe find Don Furz. Gereny, would you mind?'

The roughly clad, gray-haired woman gave him a quizzical look and went to the wallcom. After a few muttered phrases, she returned, a puzzled, half angry expression on her face.

'Don's been sent on a short trip up to the Redfang Range and is expected to return tonight. Something about an alternate route?' She exchanged a quick look with both Vowe and Middleton.

Thyle Vowe seemed very thoughtful at this, turning to rummage among the papers on the nearby table. 'Tell you what, Tasmin. The Redfang's only a few hours from here. Why don't you and your young friends ride up that way and meet Don? I'll give you a map so you won't go astray.' He rummaged a moment more, than handed Tasmin a small chart, pointing at it with a plump, impeccably manicured finger. 'Take the road back of the citadel, ride straight east for about half a mile, then take this turning north. Stay on that road, and it'll deliver you right at the foot of the Redfang canyon by the time it gets dark, if you don't run into Don on the road. Better get a quick start.' He was moving them toward the door.

Jem Middleton interrupted. 'Just a minute, Ferrence. I wouldn't want you to run into any trouble up that way you couldn't handle. Rarest thing on Jubal, next to red meat, is crystal bears, but darned if I didn't get word there's been a crystal bear sighted up toward Redfang. You'd better take a stun rifle along, just in case.' And he was on his feet, pulling a rifle out of a tall cupboard and thrusting it into Tasmin's hands. 'You can return it whenever you get back.' Then they were in the corridor once more with the door shut firmly behind them.

'What does he think he's playing at?' Jamieson demanded, outraged. 'Crystal bears! Nobody's seen a crystal bear for fifty years.'

'Shhhh,' Clarin demanded. 'Something's going on here, Reb. Keep your mouth shut and your eyes open. Do you trust the Grand Master, Master Ferrence?'

Tasmin gave her a grateful look of concurrence. Something was indeed going on here. 'Trusting the Grand Master would be my inclination,' Tasmin replied, a little tentatively. The four people in the room behind them might have been playing welter, but those open, paper-stuffed cases argued they had been doing something else. As did the fact that some of the face-down hands had had four cards while others had had six. As for the rifle, Tasmin had only fired a stun rifle during the annual proficiency shoots. Rifles were not even routinely supplied to caravans any longer, though they had been standard issue some twenty years ago. The story about crystal bears was nonsense. No one had seen a crystal bear for decades. There was some question as to whether anyone had ever seen a crystal bear or whether they were entirely mythical, and everyone in that room knew it. Unless – one were to substitute *Crystallite* for crystal bear. In which case had been telling him something without telling him anything ...

'Yes,' he said in a grim decision. 'I trust him.'

'Well, then let's trust him. Let's do what he suggested.' Clarin looked at the rifle with dismay. 'We don't want to walk around carrying that.'

'Put it under your robe, Clarin. Yours is stiffer than mine. You can wait at the gate while Jamieson and I bring the mules.' Tasmin shook his head at himself as he hurried away across the compound, turning back to see Clarin lounging casually against one wall, the rifle tucked behind her.

The mules were eager to travel after their half day in the trailer. When they had ridden far enough from the city that the rifle would not occasion comment, Tasmin fastened it to the rings of his saddle, trying twice before he got it right. Lord, no one except the military used rifles anymore.

'Crystal bears,' mumbled Jamieson, still seething. 'Who does he think you are, Master? Everts of the Dawn Patrol?' This was a favorite holodrama of Jubal's children. 'When was the last time anyone saw a crystal bear?'

'There's some doubt anyone ever did, actually,' said Tasmin dryly. 'Fairy tale stuff. Early explorers claimed to find a lot of things back in crystal country. Crystal bears were just one of the menagerie. Some of the earliest explorers said viggies could talk and mice could sing.'

'Well, they can,' Clarin objected, patting her pocket. A muffled chirp followed the pat. 'At least sort of. Why would Jem Middleton have had a rifle right there in his office?' Clarin asked.

'Exactly,' Tasmin replied. 'Why?'

They rode through ascending lands, scattered fields of human crops giving way to Jubal country, the ramparts of the Redfang rising before them as the sun sank behind their left shoulders and the road grew narrower and dimmer. After the last of the farms they passed no one.

'No Don Furz,' said Jamieson, giving voice to the obvious.

'Do you get the idea that maybe the Grand Master and the others were afraid of that?' Clarin asked.

'The road tops a ridge just ahead,' Tasmin answered, his voice carefully unemotional. 'We'll probably get a look down into Redfang canyon from there.'

From the ridge top, the road dropped into a basin surrounded on three sides by mixed stony outcroppings and the 'lings and 'lets of the Redfang, then curved to the right around a flat-topped pillar of stone.

There was someone on the pillar!

A gray clad figure scurried back and forth, toppling stones down the precipitous sides. Even from this distance they could hear the grunts of effort, the shattering rattle of stone on stone.

At the foot of the pillar, half a dozen shadowy figures were attempting to scale the rocky walls. The intent of the attackers was clear, and there was desperation in the movement atop the rock. As they watched, one of the plummeting stones tore a climber loose and carried him onto the shattered stones at the loot of the almost vertical face. Other climbers redoubled their efforts to reach the embattled one.

Without a moment's hesitation, Jamieson yodeled 'brother, brother, brother,' the recognition called gathering strength from the echoes that cascaded in its wake, shattering the silence of the canyon, demanding that any Explorers or Tripsingers within hearing identify themselves. An answering cry came from the pillar top, telling them which side they were on.

Tasmin slid off his mule, dragging the rifle from its scabbard and throwing himself down behind a convenient looking rock. His best rifle scores had always been from the prone position, and he settled into the earth with a wriggle, flicking on the power switch and putting his eyes to the goggle scope all in one motion, tracking the lighted dot across the face of the butte. When it slid across one of the climbing figures he squeezed once, twice, then began tracking once more. One pull would drop a man. Two would keep him dropped for a while. He tracked and pulled again.

Jamieson and Clarin were clattering down the trail toward the pillar at a reckless gallop, the unshod hooves of the mules creating a cataract of echoes, a continuous thunder. The 'brother, brother, brother,' yodel, leaping the octaves to stir a threatening vibration from the surrounding 'lings, added to the cumulative rumble of avalanching sound that gave the effect of a mounted troop. At the base of the pillar the attackers broke and ran.

Tasmin tracked a fleeing shape, pulled, tracked another, and pulled again before the remaining attackers were lost behind a forest of crystal pillars. Crystallites? They were very quiet for Crystallites. By the time Jamieson and Clarin reached the pillar, all the attackers had disappeared. Tasmin stood up, brushing gravel from his chest and belly, and restored the rifle to its scabbard, noting with angry but somehow detached astonishment that the intensity dial was set to 'kill.' He hadn't set it there. He hadn't touched it. Regulation setting was 'stun.' Always.

At the foot of the slope, three people moved among the fallen. Clarin, Jamieson, and the shadow figure from the top of the bluff who had come down to join the acolytes. Tasmin mounted and rode to join them. As Tasmin drew nearer, he saw it was a woman who was turning one of the fallen bodies face down with a gesture of anger or dismay. She came toward him, golden hair fluttering in the light breeze, dark blue eyes fixed angrily on his own.

'I wish to hell you hadn't felt you had to kill them all!' she announced.

Then, with surprise, 'You're Tasmin Ferrence, aren't you? Your acolyte said "Ferrence," but I didn't make the connection.' And then, surprisingly. 'I hope to hell you've got my music box.'

Tasmin was gaping at her when Jamieson said 'Master,' in the tone of an adult interrupting the play of children. He was peering over their heads in the direction the fleeing attackers had gone. 'I hate to bring it up, but the noise back in those 'lings indicates they haven't gone away. There were at least ten of them, Sir, and with due respect, you only dropped four.'

'You think they're coming back?'

'I don't think all that hollering presages imminent departure.'

'The Explorer expresses her thanks, Tripsinger,' the woman said. 'My mule's over behind that rock, and the best place for us is back in the range, quickly.' She ran toward the mule, and they followed her, hearing the noise building behind them as they went. 'Those bastards caught up with me right after I came out of the range,' she shouted over the noise. 'There were only four of them at first, but then they seemed to drop out of the rocks like gyrebirds off a 'ling. I only had time to get up on that pillar. Two minutes later, they'd have had me. Or, if you'd been two minutes later, they'd have had me anyhow!'

Only when they were halfway to the range did Tasmin notice the typical Explorer outfitting of both beast and rider and realize who she was. 'You're Don Furz?' he exclaimed.

She gave him a quick look. 'Who did you think?'

'I didn't know Don Furz was a woman.'

'It won't be anything long if we don't get back into the range. Your mules aren't soft-shod. We'll stop just inside.' She kicked her animal into a run, and they trailed after her, entering the range between two bloody towers that hummed and whispered ominously. 'Pay no attention to them,' Don shouted. 'They won't blow if we hurry!' She galloped on, making a quick turn to the right, then to the left, pulling up in a shower of gravel.

'Get your mules shod, quick,' she said, pulling the cover from her Explorer's box and unfolding the panels around her waist and across her thighs. 'We're going down that canyon to the left. The Password is new. I just came up with it this afternoon.'

'Then they can't follow us,' Jamieson said with satisfaction as he stretched soft shoes over mule hooves.

'They may try,' Clarin contradicted. 'They weren't making any noise before, but they're certainly making it now.' A cacophony of shouts, chants, and religious slogans echoed in the canyon behind them.

'There weren't any witnesses before,' Don said. 'Now there's the possibility we may get away and talk about this. They want us to believe they're Crystallites.'

'You don't think they really are?'

'Those bodies weren't dressed like Crystallites, and they weren't half starved like the Crystallites I've seen,' Don commented impatiently. 'Finished? Good, come along behind and I'll get us through.'

She rode toward a branching canyon, stroking the music box as she went. Her voice was good, not up to Tripsingers' standards, of course, but then it didn't need to be. Explorers rarely sang their way past the Presences, and in any case it didn't take a great deal to get a single person and mule through most places. Tasmin noted with amusement that Clarin was taking notes on her own machine as she rode. He watched her expression, fascinated. The music was there, on her face. Her eyes moved, opened, shut, swung one way and then another as though she saw the notes. Her mouth pursed, opened, widened, pursed once more as it tasted the music. Her hand snapped up and to one side, then back again, all unconsciously. It was like watching someone struggling – perhaps struggling to give birth? Or to conquer something, possess something. Or to be possessed by something! That was probably closer, and Tasmin wondered what his own face looked like when he sang.

Well, if Don Furz didn't sing them out, Clarin could. And Jamieson could, of course, without notes, having heard it only once, though his face showed none of what went on inside.

The score was effective enough, a little thin in places. There were several small tremors, nothing serious. Tasmin saw Clarin rescoring on her box, making lightning decisions as to what effects were needed to flesh out the notes and make them hold for Tripsinging purposes. She was faster at orchestration than Jamieson was. Not that they would ever need such a score. This canyon looked very much like a dead-end to nowhere.

Above them loomed the bloody pillars of the range, almost black in the dusk, with the jagged tooth of Redfang itself behind them. These were not Fanglings they went among. They were far too large for that, and Tasmin wondered briefly if they had been individually named and whether the same basic Password worked for them all.

The sounds of pursuit faded behind them. They came out of peril, down from the crystal pass to find a pocket of deepsoil, a hundred square yards of Jubal trees and shrubs gathered around a tiny spring, which filled a rock cup with reflected starlight.

They dismounted wearily, making no effort to set up camp. 'How safe are we here?' Tasmin asked.

Don wiped her forehead with an already dirty sleeve. 'Well, if they can get a singer or two to help them, they might come in after us after a few hours' work. More likely, they'll use the standard route and come in east of us, then work this way. If they have access to a set of satellite charts of this area, it won't take them long to figure it out.' She stared back the way they had come, her back and shoulders rigid.

'We shouldn't stay here then.'

'Just long enough to rest the animals and get some food for ourselves.' She was still standing, still rigidly staring.

Tasmin put his hand on her arm. She turned slowly, glaring at him with angry, despairing eyes.

'This is the third time they've tried,' she said. 'The third time. They almost killed me twice before.' She shook his hand away. 'That is my synthesizer you've got. Lim gave it to you, didn't he? You're his brother. I didn't know that ...' Her voice was ragged, jerky with half suppressed emotion.

'Hush,' Tasmin said firmly. 'Get hold of yourself, Explorer. Clarin's already brewing tea. I suggest we sit down quietly, have a cup together while you explain what all this is about.'

She shook her head, an unconscious gesture of negation.

'We did save your life,' drawled Jamieson, looking up from his position by the fire where he was blowing strips of dried settler's brush into reluctant flame, his face speckled with soot. 'I know you don't trust anyone. Probably don't know who's coming at you next, but we are the good guys, really.'

Don laughed, a slightly hysterical laugh. 'I keep escaping by the narrowest margins. As though I had a slightly incompetent guardian angel. Why in heaven's name did you show up when you did?'

'I believe someone thought you might be in trouble,' Tasmin told her, digging in his pocket for the message the Grand Master had sent and explaining briefly how they had happened to seek her out near Redfang. 'They gave us the rifle just before we left.'

'On a very transparent pretext,' Jamieson commented.

'And it was set on kill,' Tasmin concluded. 'It was irresponsible of me not to have checked it before firing, but ...'

'But we were in a bit of a hurry,' Jamieson concluded, irrepressibly.

'Jamieson!' Clarin said patiently. 'Slash it off.'

'You don't really act like assassins.' Donatella sighed as she opened the message. 'But then, Zimmy didn't either.' She sank to the ground near the fire. 'I don't know what this means.'

'What does it say?'

She spread the small sheet of paper on a rock by the fire and read its contents aloud.

'*The Grand Master is aware.* What does that mean?'

'He's certainly being careful, isn't he?' said Tasmin. 'I think he's telling us he knows something, but he's not putting anything on paper that would prove anything against him. Let's get back to you, Explorer Furz. You've been attacked, but you've escaped. You're still alive. On the other hand, my brother is dead. My wife is dead ...'

'Your wife! What did she have to do with—'

'Leave that aside for the moment. Evidently the reason they're dead has something to do with you. That's why I'm here. The acolytes are here because one of them is presumptuous and the other got dragged in by the ears.' Jamieson flushed, and Tasmin went on. 'I suggest that now's a very good time to find out where we all stand.'

'I don't know where to start,' she said hopelessly.

'At the beginning,' suggested Clarin. 'Where did it all start?'

'In the library of the Priory at Splash One,' Don said quietly. 'When I found a letter Erickson had written ...'

Half an hour later, she fell silent, the others still staring at her. There were

110

things missing from her story. She knew it and they knew it. Still, they had the general outline.

'Let me see if I understand this,' Clarin said. 'You found documents of Erickson's that indicated a method of proving that the Presences are sentient.'

Don nodded.

'You took some steps, as yet unspecified, to verify this information. As a consequence of this verification, you came up with the notes for the Enigma score.'

Don nodded again, slowly.

'And at that point, you decided you had to tell someone what you knew.'

'No,' Don sighed. 'At that point I just bubbled around like boiling sugar for a time, while everyone patted me on the head. Then I got some sense and I decided to keep my mouth shut.'

'You didn't say that!' Jamieson complained, while Tasmin gave him a sidelong look.

'It was a fleeting decision,' she explained. 'Figure it out for yourself, acolyte. If I come up with proof of sentience, somebody will have to do something about it. The Planetary Exploitation Council has to take some action, don't they? I think everyone assumes that once sentience is established, on any planet, not just Jubal, humans have to get out.'

'Not everywhere. Not always,' Tasmin said.

'No, not everywhere, not always, but those are the rare exceptions. So, why should I want to tip the Tripwagon? I earn my living here, just the way you do. My friends are here. My livelihood is here. Besides – it's Jubal! It's home! I don't want to leave here. So after I came down out of the clouds, the first thing I decided to do was keep my stupid mouth shut. Of course, that was after I went giggling around for several days like a damned fool. Anybody who looked at me probably knew I'd found something.' She sighed again, rubbing grubby hands up the sides of her face, leaving long smears of soil.

Clarin passed cups of steaming tea and commented, 'Presumably you decided differently after a while.'

'After I'd had a chance to think, yes. We all know the CHASE Commission is due to meet here very soon. And everyone knows it's rigged. Lord, the chairman of the commission is the Governor's own stepson, and everyone knows that BDL owns the Governor. So, it's pretty sure the results of the commission hearings are prearranged. And we all know what BDL wants those to be. Non-sentient. So then I got to thinking about what will happen after the CHASE Commission reports.'

'And,' Jamieson said impatiently.

'And what will happen is that BDL won't go on paying Explorers and Tripsingers when they don't have to.'

Jamieson gave her a puzzled look. 'I don't understand.'

Tasmin nodded. What she said reinforced some suspicions of his own. 'If the CHASE Commission reports non-sentience, the PEC strictures will be removed. They're the usual strictures imposed by the PEC on any planet where indigenous sentience is a question.'

'Non-destruction of habitat,' quoted Clarin. 'Something like that.'

'Exactly like that,' Tasmin nodded.

Jamieson still looked puzzled.

'If the strictures are removed,' Clarin explained to him, 'then BDL can destroy whatever they like.'

Jamieson's mouth fell open. 'They wouldn't! The Presences are absolutely unique!'

'It's never stopped humans before,' Tasmin said, thinking of the histories he had read in the citadel. Rivers turned into sewers. Mountains leveled into rubble. All for the profit of the great agglomerates. 'Not where profit is concerned. Think how profits could be increased if BDL didn't have to use Explorers or Tripsingers or wagon trains. Think how much brou could be moved if they could fly the cargo in and out.'

'It stinks,' said Clarin with feeling.

'It stinks,' agreed Donatella. 'But it's obvious once you start thinking about it. So, quite selfishly I'd decided to keep my mouth shut, but then I realized it wouldn't make any difference. Most likely I was going to be out of work and off-planet no matter what happened, and so was everyone else I knew. At that point, I decided to do what I should have decided in the first place. For Jubal's sake, not mine.'

'To get the word out,' Clarin continued. 'However, you suspected that if you simply spoke out, you would probably be silenced.'

'I think it was a reasonable assumption,' Don said, gesturing back the way they had come. 'You saw them.'

Clarin leaned back on one arm and continued her recapitulation. 'At this point the story gets a little confusing for me. You contacted a friend, whom you do not identify to us …'

'For that friend's own protection,' Don assented, half angrily. 'You say you're the good guys, but how the hell do I know.'

'All right. I'll pay chits for that. So, you contact this friend, and you and the friend work up this plan. You decide to get one of the Top Six 'Soilcoast Singers to get the word out for you. You're going to feed this singer certain information, which will then be used as the basis for a show.'

'Part of the information was in the Enigma score, and I was the only one who had it at that point. We tried to figure out a way the singer could get the score without tracing it back to me. Then my friend told me Lim Terree could get the score from his brother in Deepsoil Five, Tripsinger Tasmin Ferrence, because I'd already sent it to you for scoring . . .' Her voice trailed away. 'I hadn't known you were his brother. Getting it from you seemed less culpable. I didn't think anyone would be surprised if he got it from someone in his own family. It wouldn't seem like . . .'

'Like a conspiracy,' Tasmin finished for her. 'It wouldn't make BDL suspicious.'

She nodded gratefully. 'I thought not. Our plan was that by the time anyone at BDL smartened to what was going on, everyone on Jubal would be talking about the show. Oh, people would doubt that what was in the show was real information, but it would still be widespread by then. Too widespread to stop. And the talk alone would make the PEC pay attention, whether they believed it or not. Then, too, there'd be holo cubes made and distributed. It wouldn't be controllable. Too many people would know.'

Clarin asked, 'It wasn't part of your plan that Lim Terree would go up on the Enigma?'

'Lord, no! He wasn't a Tripsinger. It wasn't even a proven score yet. He was just supposed to get the score from his brother in a way that would seem natural and unthreatening and then bring it back to Splash One.'

'And it wasn't your intention that he should pauperize himself getting to Deepsoil Five? He did, you know. His wife and child are destitute.' Clarin sipped at the last of her tea, watching Don's face.

'I didn't know.' Don leaned forward, burying her head in her hands. 'Nothing went right, did it? I had no idea he'd done that. My friend arranged the whole thing. I should never have . . .'

'Never mind, Don,' Tasmin said gently. 'It wasn't your fault. Not any more than it was mine or my father's or Lim's own. He was trying desperately to prove himself. He put everything he had into this – more than he had. Your friend's only mistake was to count too heavily on someone whose own demons were riding him. There's more than enough guilt to go around, but you don't deserve much of it.'

'Meantime,' Clarin said, going on with her precis, 'two attempts were made on your life. One here in the Redfang Range, one sometime later in the Chapter House at Splash One. But you say you do not know who is attempting to kill you.'

'It's true. I don't. I've been over and over everything I said to anyone from the beginning. As I said, I did bubble around a little bit, right at the first, but I never actually said anything. Maybe someone could suspect that I know something I shouldn't, but no one can know, not for sure.'

'For some people, suspicion is enough,' Tasmin commented. 'More than enough. Crystallites, for example. Though I should think they would welcome proof of sentience.' He waited for a comment from Don but heard none. 'Surely you must suspect someone.'

'Someone with BDL, obviously,' she said uncomfortably. 'We all know how unscrupulous they are. He is.'

'He being?'

'Justin. The more profit out of Jubal, the more goes in his own pockets. At least, so I've heard.'

'In his pockets, and the Governor's. Some say it even goes to the PEC.'

'I don't like to believe that,' Don said wearily. 'The point is, what am I going to do now?' She stood up and walked around the little fire, swinging her arms, rotating her head, working the kinks out. 'I don't know where to go, what to do. All I can think of is to use the com network to send information to everyone I can think of and hope it gets generally disseminated before they catch up to me.'

'I doubt they're going to let us out of here long enough for you to do that,' Clarin remarked. 'We're bottled up.'

'Oh, we can get out,' Don said. 'I know this Range well. Even if they come in after us, there are all kinds of little side canyons and slots you can't even see from the satellite charts. But if we get out, what?'

'I'm still trying to figure out what's going to happen,' Jamieson said in a puzzled voice. 'There are some pieces that don't seem to fit.'

'What do you mean?'

'Well, we met an officer when we were coming into Splash One, and he told us all the Crystallites would be rounded up pretty soon for the sake of public order. They make a lot of noise, he Crystallites, but there aren't all that many of them. Then when we were coming up to Northwest, the driver talked about the military and the roads. They've closed the base on Serendipity and moved the sector garrison here. The Deepsoil Coast is already overcrowded. Jubal can hardly feed its population now, while Serendipity has surpluses all over the place. It doesn't make any economic sense at all. And what I'm wondering is, what are they going to use all those troopers for!'

'It's almost as though they expected general disorder, isn't it?' asked Tasmin in a deceptively mild voice. He had been staring out over the ranges while suspicions gradually solidified within him.

'What kind of general disorder? Who are those troopers going to be used against?'

'Well, considering that BDL will probably start destroying Presences shortly after the CHASE Commission delivers its report, I would judge the troops are to be used against us,' Tasmin said.

'Us!'

'Tripsingers. Explorers. All the dependants and ancillary services. All those who earn their living from us, the storekeepers, farmers, and mule breeders. Thousands of us, Reb. If we see the destruction of a few Presences, most of us will forget lip service to BDL. We might get violent.'

'Damn it, we *would* get violent,' the boy asserted.

'I think BDL knows that. If I were Harward Justin, I'd be planning to destroy a lot of Presences within minutes of the CHASE report. Before there could be any general uprising. Then I'd use the troops to keep order.'

'So what do we do?' Don asked again. 'Sit here and die? Try to get out? To do what?'

'Figure something out,' said Clarin definitely. 'We'll figure something out, Don. But it would help a great deal if you would start by trusting us more than you have.'

Donatella shook her head as though she did not understand.

'Oh, come on, Don. You've talked around and around it, for hours. You've told us you found this proof. You've told us you checked the proof. You've told us you have real, factual information. You've told us everything – except what the process was and what the information is. I don't see how we can help you if we don't know.'

The Explorer knight rose, stalked away from the fire and stood at some distance from it, her back to them, as rigid as when they had first arrived at the quiet pocket. The fire threw flickering lights along her back, glimmering in her pale hair. 'If anyone finds out, they'll kill me,' she said.

'They're trying to kill you anyhow. We didn't bring the threat with us. It's already here. I don't think they'll try any harder if they know what the real information is.'

Don returned to the fire, rather wild-eyed, like some feral, dirty-faced creature bent over a primordial altar, her face haggard in the leaping light. 'You won't believe it,' she said at last. 'I didn't.'

'Try us,' suggested Jamieson.

'I talked to the Enigma,' she said. 'And it talked back.'

Dead, disbelieving silence.

'You're joking!' Jamieson said, choking.

'I told you you wouldn't believe me.'

'Talked? In words?'

'In words. Real words. And the Enigma talked back. In words.'

Silence again. Silence that stretched into moments, each staring at the other, uncertain, unable to believe ...

At last Tasmin's voice. 'That was a *translator* in the box!'

'A new one,' she answered softly. 'Very powerful. My friend got it for me. I took the label off.'

'I thought it was a transposition program.'

'No reason you should have known it was a translator. But the translation is there, in the box. An actual conversation between a person and a Presence.

A conversation that makes a kind of sense, too, which is remarkable considering that it's a first of its kind. That's what we were giving Lim Terree. That's why he went to such lengths to get the score from you, Ferrence. He knew what we had.'

'God!' Shocked silence once more.

'So, you see,' she said, 'we have to do something. And all I can think of is what I said before. Spread the word as widely as possible, assuming we could even get access to the com-net, and then hide out until the fallout is over.'

'That wouldn't work,' said Jamieson.

'I don't understand.'

'It doesn't matter that you know the Presences are sentient. You have no witness. The information you've got could have been faked. So long as the CHASE Commission is rigged to give a report of non-sentience, BDL can depend on the military to enforce that ruling, no matter what the truth is. The troopers don't care. Even if you told people and some of them believed you, it wouldn't do any good. BDL would stifle them.'

'Maybe not,' said Clarin.

Jamieson gave her a challenging look.

'No, really Reb. You haven't taken it all in yet. Listen to what the woman said! She talked to the Enigma. It talked back. If we can actually understand the words of the Presences, there are some very great voices here on Jubal that simply can't be stifled!'

9

Bird-cloud, Silver-seam, Sun-bright, Star of the Mountain, Blue Glory Child of the Twelfth Generation, listening in the quiet of the evening ...

To: Bondri Gesel the Wide-eared, Messenger of the Presences.

Bondri singing, along with his troupe in four part harmony, to the outer Silver-seam, the skin, as it were, of the great Presence: 'Peace, calm of wind, flow of water, gentleness of tree-frond turning, joy of sunlight, contentment of moonlight and star.'

Which did not serve. Silver-seam, Bird-cloud, Star of the Mountain, and so forth returned the song in a series of aching anharmonics: 'Discontinuity. Distant: shore thundering. Close, whispering of change. Proliferation of Loudsingers. Disturbance of one's edges and bits. Fingers itch. Noises in air and earth. Discomfort in the roots. Confusion. Query to Bondri: establish causation?

Bondri the Wide-eared, who had traveled fifty days with his troupe to carry a message to the inner Silver-seam, now paused, his song-sack in limp folds, shaken to the center of his being.

Prime Priest Favel, bent and trembling on his poor old legs, whispered, 'Has this ever happened before?'

Bondri flapped his ears in negation, signaling quiet to the troupe. 'No Great One has ever asked such questions before. No Great One has really seemed aware of us before, aged one. What shall I sing?'

'Equivocate,' suggested the Prime Priest. 'Say nothing much at some length. Tell Silver-seam you will seek reasons.'

Bondri sang in canon form, which allowed the troupe to follow his lead. After going on at some length, Bondri concluded: 'Causation currently unknown. Who knows what passes among the Loudsingers? Who can smell the sunlight? Who can taste the wind? Thy messengers will ascertain.'

He had uttered no word of the inner message he had come so far to deliver, even though it was a brief one: 'Red Bird to the top of Silver Mountain.' Most of the inner messages the viggies carried were no more lengthy than this particular one, which had come from the Great Blue Tooth, Horizon Loomer, Mighty Hand, the Presence humankind called the East Jammer. Prime Priest Favel, who had learned human speech in captivity among the Loudsingers in his youth, was fond of naming the Great Ones with human titles, using human words that he said were thought-provoking in their very imprecision. There had seemed to be no point in attempting to deliver the message that East Jammer had sent. Inner Silver-seam would not even have heard it so long as its skin was quivering like this or while this strange questioning was happening – though the latter seemed stilled, at least for the moment.

'Should I try to quiet it for the message?' Bondri hummed to the priest.

He received a gesture in reply, why not.

Bondri swelled his throat into a great, ruby balloon and sang again to the skin, sang of calm, signaling the troupe to begin an antiphon on the theme of evening, one composed by Bondri's own ancestor in a season of incessant and troubling storm. It was one of the most efficacious of the surface songs. The troupe composed itself for best projection and howled harmoniously, throats swelled into sonorous rotundity, putting all their energy into it at length and to little effect. The very air quivered with annoyance. Bird-cloud, Silver-seam, Sun-bright, Star of the Mountain, and all – known among humankind as the North Watcher – was not tranquil and would not become so.

'Cacophony, dissonance, melodic lines falling apart,' whispered a part leader to Bondri. 'Great Bird-cloud is annoyed with his messengers.' High Priest Favel stood to one side, bent and waiting, making no comment, though Bondri threw him a nervous glance.

There was no help for it. Bondri stood forward and chirped a staccato phrase. 'Tumble down threatens hereabout, dangerous for viggy-folk, go and stay away, away a time, quick, quick.' He turned to the old priest. 'Your perceptiveness must come quickly.'

This was the sense of Bondri's message, though these were not the words. The words had other meanings – leader to troupe, experienced singer to novices in the presence of a Prime Priest of the people – and there were implications of the time of day and the season, modifications of language required by the site in which the words were spoken. When one of the Companions of the Gods quoted another, there was no need for the hearer to ask when or to whom the words were spoken or in what weather or circumstance. The words themselves said it all. The word *taroo* – *go* – *was* sung in the early morning. It became *tarou* at midmorning and tarouu at noon. It was *itaroo* sung in sunlight and *etaroo* sung in light mist. *Atarouualayum* conveyed the going of a mated pair, sans giligee, at midmorning in driving rain, somewhat north of the Shadowed Cliffs ... in spring.

So now, Bondri's words conveyed a chill autumn evening in the vicinity of the North Watcher during which a familial troupe of viggies – males females, giligees, and young, all, except the very newest trade daughters, sharing the same thought patterns – had approached the Great One to deliver a message but could not get past the skin to deliver it and were putting themselves in peril if they didn't move. Bondri felt compelled to reissue the warning to which Prime Priest Favel had not yet harkened.

'Your (autumn chilled but most valued) perceptiveness? The (mighty but not quite trustworthy) Presence in whose (arbitrary and sometimes simply vengeful) decisions we trust grows (dangerously and maliciously) agitated. Best (imperative) we depart.'

The priest flicked his elbows in agreement, and Bondri made the wing sign in turn to the pouchmate pathfinders of the troupe, who slithered off at once down an almost invisible track along the side of the North Watcher. This was a proven track on which movement was possible without alerting the Great One. The crystalline structure beneath it had no fractures, no vacancies, no dislocations, no planar defects or interstitials – none of those deviations from uniform crystal-line structure that in the Presences served the function served by neurons and neuro-transmitters in fleshly creatures. Not that the viggies, or as they called themselves, 'etaromimi,' knew that. They did know that the track was solid, stolid, and without sensation. In a few hundred yards it would debouch upon a pocket of safe soil where a small grove of trees provided a place to rest. The Prime Priest was very old and needed surcease.

'Is far enough?' hummed one of the troupe. 'Silver-seam can make great destruction, very far.'

Bondri was by no means sure it was far enough, but it was as far as the Prime Priest was likely to get, given the state of his legs. They had been broken in his youth and had never healed properly. While they were broken, he had been captured by the Loudsingers and held captive long enough to learn their language. Much later one of the young Loudsingers, blessed be his familial patterns of thought forever, had kindly released Favel to his people. That Loudsinger's name was Lim Ferrence, and his was one of the names of honor whose patterns were recalled by Bondri's troupe during times of recollection.

Behind them on the slope, several of the Great One's fingers blew their tips with a crash and volley of tinkling glass.

''Lings,' murmured Favel, giving the fingers their human name. ''Lings.'

None of the debris came near the viggies, and Bondri sighed in relief. The Great Ones were not always sensible about assigning fault. If a viggy did something to displease them, their skins or fingers might kill quite another viggy in retaliation. It was almost as though the skins did not know the difference between one individual and another. Or did not know there was a difference. They were the same with the Loudsingers. Sometimes the Great Ones would incubate annoyance for a very long time, exercising vengeance long after the original culprit had gone away or died. At least, this is the way it seemed to Bondri, even though the Prime Priest told him otherwise.

'It is the difference between their insides and outsides,' panted the Prime Priest, making Bondri realize he had been vocalizing. 'The surfaces of their minds are shallow and quick to irritate. They slap at us as we twitch at a woundfly, unthinking. In the Depths, where the great thoughts move at the roots of the mountains, they are slow to reason and, I believe, largely unconscious of us. I have often thought there is little connection between the two parts of them.'

'Except for the way Silver-seam behaved tonight,' caroled Bondri. 'Strangely.'

'Strangely indeed! It seemed well aware of us, did it not? As though some midmind had come awake.'

It had indeed seemed quite aware of them, a very uncomfortable thought. 'Blessed be (all Presences, large and small, their fingers and skin-parts) they,' said Bondri, antennae erect and curved inward over his head, warding away any ill fortune that the priest's remark might otherwise attract.

'Oh, by all means,' sighed Favel. 'Yes.'

'May I assist your aged and infirm and overly chilled perceptiveness?'

'If you would be so (gracious in this season) kind, youngster. I get creakier with every moon.'

'We would be honored to carry you.'

'That much is not necessary. A shoulder to lean on would be welcome.'

The troupe sped down the track, moving as quickly as possible consonant with the requisite care. Dislodging bits of crystal trash often made the Great Ones very angry, particularly if it was done noisily. Pieces had to be picked up gently and set aside, and that took time, but long practice made the troupe both quick and silent.

By the time dark fell, they had reached the grove of trees.

'Where are we?' the Prime Priest asked, settling himself into a soft pocket of earth and fluffing his fur to retain body heat. 'I do not recognize this route.'

'Back side of Silver-seam,' Bondri reported. 'Just east of the Tineea Singers, Those-Who-Welcome-Without-Meaning-It, named by the Loudsingers, the False Eagers. An easy transit, your perceptiveness.'

'Perhaps by tomorrow, an easy transit. At the moment, an impossible one. I cannot move farther. Have we food?'

'Wet food and dry. Comfort yourself while we prepare.'

Preparation took little time. There were edible stalks to peel, grain heads to thresh, a few seed pods to open with a sharpened bone. It was not viggy bone. The bones of the viggies were fragile and light, and in any case the ritual of disposal made viggy bone inaccessible for any useful purpose. On the other hand, the hard strong bones of the Loudsingers and their animals were often found at the roots of the Great Ones and were much sought after. Viggies had been anatomizing human and mule corpses for generations, and there was little they did not know about human anatomy. The giligees, particularly, were interested in this knowledge. Sometimes among the wreckage of Loudsingers, animals, and wagons, there were bits of metal, also. Sharp or toothed edges made from this material were even more treasured. Bondri carried several bits of metal in his vestigial pouch just below his song-sack, gifts from his people, mostly salvaged at the foot of Highmost Darkness, Lord of the Gyre-Birds, Smoke Master, the one the humans called Black Tower.

The Prime Priest munched on peeled stalks of settler's brush and made polite conversation, as befit a time of food sharing. 'One could almost forgive the humans (outlanders, weird strangers who say unmentionable and disgusting things with words that are not true, thereby incurring the taboo) for coming to Our-Land-of-the-Gods,' he sang. 'They have brought good food.'

'Some of it,' admitted Bondri, whose troupe had only recently acquired the habit of raiding human fields and gardens. 'The little seeds at the top of the long stems are good, even though they are only ripe one time of the year. And the various thick roots and sweet leaves are good, and those juicy bulbs that grow on their trees. The big seeds aren't good. Brou they call them.'

'I don't think they use the big seeds for food.'

'I've heard that sung,' Bondri conceded. 'I've heard they mash the big seeds at a place near the sea, mash them, and put them in containers, and send them away in boats. Our-fisher-kin-who-ran-from-the-sea-bringing-fish say the mashed seeds go off-world.'

'That is true,' the Prime Priest acknowledged in a minor key. 'During my captivity, I saw it with my own eyes. The Loudsingers eat brou to make them cheerful.'

'They do not made us cheerful. The big seeds are very dangerous.'

'Arum,' the Prime Priest nodded, his throat sack swelling and collapsing in sadness. 'I lost all of one pouch to them. The pouch boss went down into the Loudsinger fields. She was at that age where they taste everything, and her pouchmates followed her. One taste and fff. Hopeless. Nothing could be done.' He sat silently, mourning. When a mated pair and the giligee could produce a pouchful only every six or seven years the loss of an entire set of pouchmates was difficult to bear. Next time the chosen giligee would go well back into the country to incubate, well away from deep-soil. And the giligee would stay there until his daughters were of reasonable age, beyond that curious, mouthing stage when everything went between the back teeth. It was difficult to live away from deepsoil, but one or more of the older children could go with the giligee, as helper. There was always etaromimi-bush, called by the Loudsingers settler's brush, if there was nothing else.

'Your perceptiveness?'

'Yes, Bondri.'

'You haven't told me where you wish to go.'

'The gods are distressed. You see it for yourself, Bondri, First Singer, Troupe Leader. Just as the North Watcher – Silver-seam and so forth – just as it quivers and blows its fingers, so do other of the Great Ones. Highmost Darkness, Lord of the Gyre-Birds, Smoke Master, the one the humans call Black Tower has been particularly disturbed. And now this questioning? This complaint of tumult! Who can it be who makes this tumult? Who are the sensible creatures? There are only three possibilities. The gods themselves. Or the Loudsingers. Or us. Only we three are sensible creatures to make causes of things. Can there be any other answer?'

Bondri admitted there could be no other.

The Priest chewed thoughtfully, rubbing at his legs with his bony fingers. 'I go toward a place of meeting. Prime Priests will be there from south and north. We will talk of this. It is very disturbing. One does not know what truth is.'

Bondri shuffled his feet back and forth in the dust. 'Is it possible, perceptiveness, that it is the gods themselves?'

The Prime Priest waved his ears in negation. 'Nothing is certain. It could be that this confusion emanates from the Mad One. Song has come that the Mad One spoke to a Loudsinger.'

There was a sharply indrawn breath from the viggies, who had been eavesdropping politely, trilling an occasional phrase antiphonally to indicate attention. A Presence had broken the ban! Spoken to a Loudsinger! Done what every viggy was forbidden to do!

'How? If the Loudsinger had not the words of calm for the skin and the words of greeting for the inner one?'

'There is rumor,' Favel sang, 'that the Loudsinger, a female Loudsinger, had the words.'

'How did she come by them?' The entire troupe held its breath, waiting for the answer to this.

The old viggy sighed. 'Do not ask what you already know must be true. If she had them, she had them from us. Are we not etaromimi, Goers Between the Gods? Have the trees suddenly taken up singing?'

The old priest had used the humorous mode, which called for appreciative laughter, though with the intonation requiring slight shame, and this evoked an embarrassed cadenza from the troupe. Now he waved his ears at them, a cautionary gesture. 'We had best giggle (melodically) now. Later may be only occasions for (disharmonic) sorrow.'

'There was that time,' Bondri intoned, the words conveying a time some fifty years before, in the spring of the year, when one troupe had been surprised by a (foreign, weird, off-world) creature. 'He had a (noise creator, song stealer, abomination) machine.'

'Do any now live who remember that time?' crooned the troupe in unison and with deep reverence.

'None,' hymned the priest, closing the litany of recollection. 'Only the holy words remember.' The words were quite enough, of course. Though individual viggies died, words were immortal. Words and melodies and the lovely mathematics of harmony, these were the eternal things, the things of the gods. So long as they were remembered accurately – and the Prime Priests had the job of remembering them all – everything could be reconstructed as it had happened at the time. The surprise. The fleeing. The creeping back to see what the strange creature was doing. The horror as they heard the stolen song, captive in the machine, the attempt to rescue the song – to no avail. Several had died in the effort, but the song was still captive. Captive, no doubt, until this very day. And now, perhaps that same (grieved for, sorrowed over) song had been used against its will to speak to the Mad One, the Presence Without Innerness, the Killer Without Cause, called by the Loudsingers, the Enigma.

'Poor (predestined to sorrow, condemned, doomed) creatures,' caroled a young giligee, solo voice. 'If the Mad One has done this thing, the next time it will kill. The Mad One always talks once, then kills the next time. The Loudsinger(s) will undoubtedly die.' The giligee voice soared, and Bondri closed his eyes in appreciation of that voice, even as he shivered at the words.

'True,' quavered the old priest, taking a comforting bite of fruit. 'If any Loudsingers go trying to sing to the Enigma again, undoubtedly the Enigma will kill them all.'

10

In his hovel on the outskirts of Splash One, Brother-minor Jeshel, whip-hand of the Society of Crystallites, Worshippers of the Holy Ones, Gods Incarnate on Jubal, finished beating his handmaid and looked around for someone else who might need admonishment. Brother Jeshel was almost certain the Gods Incarnate had spoken to him in a dream. He seemed to remember something of the kind happening, and had his handmaid not interrupted him, he would have remembered it clearly enough to tell The Three and maybe be allowed to testify to a vision in temple.

Sister Sophron lay on the floor, half naked and weeping.

'Get up,' he snarled. 'And don't wake me up like that again.'

'A messenger came,' she sobbed. 'From her. I didn't know what else to do.'

'The messenger could wait. Cover yourself. You're disgusting like that.'

Since Sister Sophron had not removed her gown, the accusation was unjust. Nonetheless, she pulled the rent fabric to cover her back and shoulders and tried to tie it in front, noting in passing that several of the ties were pulled off. Brother-minor Jeshel had wakened in a rage.

'What does he want?'

'The messenger?'

'Who else are we talking about, slut! Of course, the messenger.'

'He says he's from her, the wife.'

'Ah. Tell him I'll talk to him in a bit. Get yourself dressed. You'll need to get yourself into town, to your job.'

Shuffling and holding the gown together at her waist, Sister Sophron left the room. She did not meet the messenger's eyes when she repeated Jeshel's remarks, nor did she look back to see how they were received. At the moment she could think only of getting to the privy before she threw up. It wasn't right of Jeshel to beat her when she was like this. She had thought it would be better on Jubal, but it was no better, not at all. Brother-minor Jeshel was no different from comrade-insurgent Jeshel. He used slightly different words, that was all. Back on Serendipity Jeshel had said 'Revolt' and 'The Cause' and 'The-rotten-management, with all its boot-lickers.' Now he said 'Presences' and 'Evangelism' and 'The-rotten-BDL with all its flunkeys' – Tripsingers and Explorers included – but it still came down to yelling and burnings and killing people from behind. It still came down to Sophron earning their living while Jeshel conspired. It still came down to blood and bombs and being beaten on when you were pregnant. Vomiting copiously, Sister Sophron cursed Brother-minor Jeshel and wished for the moment she had never told him what that Explorer knight had said when Sophron had been cutting her hair.

Behind her in the filthy hall, Rheme Gentry made a face to himself and went on humming quietly. He was very weary, having returned from Northwest only very late last evening, but he would not sit down. There was nothing clean enough to sit on. Eventually Jeshel would show up, dirty and uncombed, probably bug infested as well, though that would be difficult on this planet. There were no human parasites. Perhaps Jeshel had evaded quarantine in order to have some shipped in. Rheme had not yet met Brother-minor Jeshel, but he had heard about him: a lower level functionary in the Crystallite hierarchy, but one reputedly responsible for a good deal of general terrorism and disruption. After sending Tasmin Ferrence to find, and one hoped to assist, Don Furz, the four conspirators, Vowe and Vox, Middleton, and Gentry, had discussed various Crystallites as a possible source of information, and Brother Jeshel had been their unanimous choice. Rheme, it was decided, should put on a modest disguise and a false name to interrogate the man. Rheme amused himself by thinking what his uncle would say to all this. The director of CHAIN wouldn't be delighted at the risk, that much was sure.

He set that uncomfortable thought aside and considered various names for the group that was getting itself together here on Jubal. They might name it the Quarternine Conspiracy, Or perhaps the Card Game Connivance. The most accurate title could be Four Against the Tide. Although according to Thyle Vowe it would be vastly more than four when the Tripsingers learned what was going on – those who didn't already suspect.

Besides, it was wrong to think of it as a conspiracy. A counterconspiracy, rather. A counterintelligence group. This allowed for some additional names. The Jubal Operation. He rather liked that one.

'What'a you want?' The voice was unaccommodating. Gentry turned to see the Crystallite standing behind him, as lank haired, stubble faced, and smelly as had been described.

'My name is Basty Pardo,' Gentry advised him. 'The Governor's lady is interested in how her little project is coming along.' His name had been Basty Pardo once, and he was certain that the Governor's lady was interested in a good many things. Rheme avoided lies whenever possible.

Brother Jeshel grunted. Gentry was a type he hated instinctively. He was clean and fit looking, with good teeth. Such men couldn't be up to any good, so far as Brother Jeshel was concerned, but he couldn't insult the man. Not now. Not yet. He chose divagation.

'I'm interested in how my own little project is coming along! Some troopers took some of my people the other day. Out toward the Great Ones we was watchin' over. Heretics came right by the Great Ones, and when we chastised 'em, the troopers came. She told us she'd keep the troopers off us.'

Rheme put on his voice of cold command. 'If you're talking about your attack on the Tripsinger and his acolytes who came through the Mad Gap, it was stupid of your people to interfere. The Governor can keep the troops off your neck so long as you don't assault people, Jeshel, but once you start throwing things, the troopers will move. Nobody can stop them.'

Jeshel glared at him in astonishment. The pretty boy could talk hard at any rate. 'The Governor can command 'em.'

'Not when it's a case of public order. They have standing orders for situations like that. The Governor can keep the troopers from rounding you up – at least for a while – but he can't give you immunity. You know that.' It all had a fine authoritative sound, and Rheme wondered briefly if he was saying anything at all true or relevant to the situation. In most situations, sounding authoritative was good enough.

Jeshel grunted. The assault on the Tripsinger had been a calculated risk. He hadn't really expected to get away with it, but his people were getting restless, eager for some real confrontation. There had to be an incident soon, something major, or some of them would start to backslide.

'The Governor's lady wants to know what's going on,' Rheme repeated impatiently, hoping the man would respond. It would be dangerous to stay too long or to talk much more than he already had. A wrong word and the filthy fanatic would catch on to the fact that Rheme knew next to nothing and was fishing for information.

'I don't know. It was only yesterday. I sent some people, but they haven't come back yet.'

Nor had Donatella Furz come back yet, at least she had not by the time Rheme left Northwest City. Nor had the starkly handsome Tripsinger and his acolytes, come to that. 'Did you send some of your followers?' This seemed a safe question.

'Nuh. Not real members. Some people I know.'

'You think ... ah ... this time they'll succeed?'

'I sent enough of 'em. Four of 'em. If she got sent out yesterday, like was promised, my people should'a caught up with her about dark.'

'Heavens.' Rheme took out his handkerchief and fastidiously wiped his hands and brow, deciding to risk it. 'That should be enough to deal with one Explorer, shouldn't it? But then, we have to remember, you didn't succeed either time before.'

'What'a you mean, either time?' Jeshel scowled at the smaller man, a suspicious snarl crossing his lips. 'Wasn't any other time. This is the only one.'

'Is it only once? Well, it may be. The Governor's lady uses other people as well. Well, I'll give her your message. Meantime, tell your people to stay out of trouble, Jeshel. Burn themselves up all they like, but don't throw rocks? Hmmm?'

Outside in the street, Rheme unlocked his car in the face of twenty scowling Crystallites who had materialized from various hovels and alley openings, carefully not looking at any of them. They were the kind of beasts that were threatened by a direct look. When he drove off, it was to the clatter and splat of missiles hitting the car, but he felt cheered that it was nothing worse than that.

Though his own temporary office was at Government House, he drove directly to BDL Headquarters and parked in the back, not in the courtyard. That courtyard, like that of the citadel next door, was under fairly consistent surveillance by Honeypeach herself who liked to know who was going and coming from Splash One. Inside the building, he slipped down a flight of back stairs and into an untenanted cross hallway. At the end of it was an unmarked door, and he knocked softly, in an insistent pattern.

'Gentry?' someone whispered.

'Me,' he agreed, slipping through the door as it opened a crack. 'Good heavens, do we have to go through all this whisper and skulk?'

Gereny Vox lifted one eyebrow. 'There's no eyes or ears in this room, Rheme. It's maybe the only room in the whole BDL building you can say that about. Reason there's no eyes is that this is the mule breeding files down here. Who the hell cares about the mule farm files, right? I've got a reason to be here. You don't. Better say it quick and get gone.'

He sighed, wiping his forehead once again. 'Get word to Thyle that you were right. Honeypeach traded favors with Brother Jeshel to get Don Furz killed. He sent four men, but it's the only time he has sent anyone.' He wiped his forehead and ran his finger inside his high, tight collar. 'Gereny, it's hotter than the Core Stars down here.'

'Keeps the files from gettin' musty. You got anything else?'

'No. How did you find out about Honeypeach anyhow?'

She spat, ritually, without moisture. 'Two dumb stall cleaners at the stables here in Splash One, yakkin' about stuff while they should be shovelin' shit. Didn't see me in the stall fixin' Tinkerbell's leg. Both of 'em sort of Crystallites. Not the hard core kind, but the hangers-on. Well. One of 'em has a brother, and he says his brother's been sent with some other guys off to Northwest. To do in some Explorer knight, so he said. They were all paid a good bit to go. Said the knight would be sent out on a mission and they could kill her when she was on her way back, because the Governor's wife wanted her dead.' She spat again. 'I told Thyle and he called you and Jem for a meetin'. You were late, but you heard the rest of it. We guessed it was Don Furz, she bein' the only one much in the public eye up there, but we didn't know 'til I called the Priory it was all goin' to happen so soon.'

'I may be able to find out a little more, as I'm not known around here yet, and nobody but the four of us knows I work for the PEC. Are you getting anywhere?'

'We're puttin' two and two together.'

'According to Jem there seem to have been two attempts on the Explorer's life in the past, plus the one yesterday,' Gentry mused. 'What made Jem suspicious that somebody tried to kill Furz before?'

'Jem's got a birdy over in BDL Exploration Division.'

'Birdy?'

'A little spy. Somebody low down in the ranks, somebody no one pays any attention to. Probably some data clerk or communications expediter. Jem didn't say who, and we didn't ask. Well, the birdy says the orders sending Furz out to Redfang the first time weren't to standard. Somebody's approval missin', something not right. And Jem found out today the orders sending her out there this last time weren't any more legitimate than the first ones. Both sets were boggled.'

'Boggled?'

'Faked! Some wallmouse creepin' out at night to boggle orders. Who do you suppose? The Explorer King? I'd put my chits there. Easy enough to tell, Gentry. You've got the connections. Find out whether Chase Random Hall has accounts on Serendipity. If he's got money there, it's nine times sure he's your wallmouse, sendin' his own Explorer off to get killed.' Her face writhed briefly at the thought of this betrayal.

Rheme Gentry made a quick note. 'Don't count on my being able to find out anything, Gereny. Mail to Serendipity's being censored or just lost, even the diplomatic stuff from Government House. BDL controls the ships, and except for a few odds and ends, messages aren't getting through.'

'Now how do you know that?'

'I had acknowledgment signals worked out, things to be planted in the system news, outside the BDL net, and they aren't showing up. Jubal's getting zipped up tight, Gereny. I'll see what I can find out about Hall, but I wouldn't fasten on him too quickly. It could be someone else. Hall's a little conspicuous. I'd bet on someone less noticeable.'

'Poor Donatella,' Gereny mused. 'Nice gal. Met her three or four times, always pleasant. No snoot to her, like some of those Explorers. Hope she's all right.'

'Well, we'll hope Tasmin Ferrence got there in time to help her out. Jeshel said he sent four ruffians, but if they were the quality I saw hanging around in the Crystallite quarter, the stun rifle should have increased the odds in our favor. Those two attempts before bother me, though. Brother Jeshel claims no part in those ...

'Even if it is the Explorer King, I'll bet he's not acting on his own. I'd like to know who's giving the orders.'

Price Zimble sat at the feet of the Explorer King, gently stroking the King's knees and calves. Chase Random Hall, while relishing the sensation, affected not to notice this intimacy.

'Then what did you do?' the King asked. 'After Donatella got back from Splash One?'

'I hung around,' said Zimmy. 'I've been hanging around for days.'

'She hasn't asked for you since?'

'Not once.'

'You've been through her room?'

'Over and over again. There's nothing there, Chase. A few odds and ends of papers and things she's working on, and her own things. That's all.'

'No messages?'

'None that aren't ordinary. You know. Ralth asking her to have dinner, or Martin inviting her for a drink, or something like that. A thank you note from her old cousin down in Splash One.'

'It could be code.'

'Code! For heaven's sake, Randy. It said, "Dearest Donatella, thank you so much for the nice lunch. Do give my best to your mother. Love, Cousin Cyndal." If you can make code out of that ...'

The King made an irritated moue, his mouth twisting unattractively. 'Nothing more about the man down in Splash One, the one that died in the Chapter House?'

'Nothing. No one knows who he is or who sent him. Unless you do.'

'Don't be silly, Zimmy. Justin sent him. Who else?' His voice was not as sure as the words.

'What do you want me to do now?'

'In the unlikely event she comes back from this Redfang trip ...'

'Unlikely event?' Zimmy opened his eyes very wide in ingenuous surprise.

'Somebody saw to it she got sent, idiot, and it wasn't me. I saw the orders! They were boggled. Why did the powers that be send her off into the Redfang anyhow? There's nothing there that really needed doing.'

'Powers that be?' Zimmy was all innocence.

The Explorer King sounded irritated. Parts of the puzzle didn't fit. He the King, had been told not to do anything to Don Furz. But someone was doing something to Don Furz. Who? And why? He didn't look closely at Zimmy. If he had, he might have surprised a glimmer of amusement in Zimmy's eyes.

'Don't ask questions, Zimmy. The less you know the better off you are. And if she does come back, be there and don't look surprised.'

'Well, of course, Randy,' said Zimmy with a hurt expression. 'I have better sense than that.'

✳

Maybelle Thonks listened to her stepmother singing and cringed inside. Honeypeach only sang when in the ascendency, and Maybelle hated to guess whose bloody and recumbent bodies her father's wife must be currently and unmelodically stomping over.

'Problem?' asked Rheme Gentry. He had just come out of the Governor's office with a stack of papers, which he placed on his desk. 'Anything the Governor's aide can do to help?'

'Honeypeach is singing.'

'Ah?'

'It probably means she's just killed somebody.'

'May Bee.' It was said softly, but unmistakably as a warning.

'Well, it does.'

He whispered. 'It may, but we are not going to say so. Not inside Government House. Not anywhere where we might be overheard. Are we?' He took her hand and led her out onto the wide terrace, which extended along two sides of the house, well away from concealing shrubbery or roof overhangs.

When they were clear of the building, she said, 'Rheme, how do you stand it?'

'Well, I confess I was somewhat dismayed when I arrived to take the job as your father's aide and learned exactly what his wife thought that entailed.'

'How did you keep out of her clutches?'

'I told her I had picked up a virulent and sexually transmitted infection on Rentree Four, that it was currently in remission but still quite communicable, and that the symptoms of the disease in women included complete atrophy of the breasts and other genitalia.'

'Rheme! Did you really? You did. My God, I never would have ... how marvelous.'

'I further told her that she needn't worry about her stepdaughter because I found women of your type unattractive. I told her I disliked light brown hair and hazel eyes because they reminded me of my evil aunty, the scourge of my youth.'

'You beast.'

130

'As a result, she has not worried, and you and I are allowed to be much together. Of course, she may be watching you eagerly for signs of atrophy. One doesn't know.'

'You didn't answer my first question. How do you stand it? You know what daddy's up to.'

'I do, indeed. He is up to making a very large fortune for himself before the bottom falls out here on Jubal. He is taking money from the Crystallites with one hand and from BDL with the other. When BDL does whatever it is planning to do, which I haven't totally figured out yet, there will be big trouble, following which there will probably be an inquiry. In advance of the inquiry your father will resign to enjoy his retirement on Serendipity or Eutopia or New Havah-eh or some such place.'

'It's dishonorable.'

'Not a word that your father has used much, Maybelle. One thing I confess that I don't understand is why you are as you are while he is what he is.'

'Because I had Mother around for over twenty years. And he's had Honeypeach. She corrupts people. Not that daddy needed much corrupting. He's had her since she was fifteen. Can you believe that? Her son, Ymries Fedder, is really my father's son, too. It's why Mother left him, when she finally found out about it.'

'And you are here only because your mother died.'

'I'm here because I had nowhere else to go. Mother's family disowned her when she married the honorable Wuyllum. The honorable Wuyllum was sending support for me, but he quit when Mother died. She and I were living on Serendipity, but as an off-worlder I couldn't even get a work permit there.'

'You could work here.'

'Doing what?'

'Your father could put in a word with BDL. There should be some kind of registered job available.'

'He won't. I've begged him. He doesn't want me to have any resources at all except what he provides. He's a terrible man, Rheme. He possesses people. Mother had told me some things, but I didn't have any idea what he's really like until I got here. He doesn't do anything much with people, but he likes to own them. Every now and then he'll twitch the chain, just to be sure it's still attached.' She turned away, biting her lip to keep the tears back.

'You could marry me.'

'Yes, I could. The idea is a very attractive one, too. But it would be the end of your job here, believe me. We'd have to leave.'

'That wouldn't be the end of the universe, May Bee.'

'Not if we got away. We might not, Rheme. I know you think I'm

131

overstating things, but things happen to people who don't do what Daddy or Honeypeach want them to do. Sometimes they have accidents and die. Sometimes they just disappear.'

'Ah,' he said again, not arguing with her. After his interview with Brother Jeshel, he no longer doubted her – not that he ever had.

'I get so ... so angry. I love this place – not Government House, but Jubal. I met an explorer, Donatella Furz, at one of the receptions. I told her I'd never seen the countryside, and she took me out into the crystal country. It's beautiful, very strange and mystical. It's obvious what's going to happen to it. It's going to be destroyed. By my father. By BDL. I keep thinking there must be something I could do.'

'Thou and I,' he mused, looking back into Government House through the door they had left open behind them. Honeypeach Thonks was standing in that doorway, staring at her stepdaughter with the look that a hungry gyre-bird might fasten on some bit of tasty carrion. Rheme bowed in her direction, a bit more deeply than custom required. When he got his head up again, she was gone. 'Yes,' he mused softly, so that only Maybelle could hear. 'We're going to have to do something.'

On the roof of the Crystallite Temple in Splash One, just to one side of the high mud brick, plastic gilded dome, there was a comfortable apartment reached by a twisting stair hidden in one of the massive pillars that supported the vaulted ceiling. It was accessible only to a few servants and the three residents: Chantiforth H. Bins, Myrony Clospocket, and Aphrodite Sells, these three being both the heart and soul of the Crystallite religion on Jubal. It was the place they spent most of their time between services, except for infrequent and well-disguised forays into the less savory night life of Splash One.

'Jeshel's stirrin' up the fuckin' rabble again,' remarked Myrony, his bald pate gleaming in the light of the late afternoon sun as he put down the corn-control and moved toward the glass doors that opened on a spacious roof terrace. 'Our man over in BDL reports he assaulted some fuckin' Tripsinger a few days ago. I wish you'd sit on him, Bins. You're the High Pontiff, and that's the only one he listens to. He's goin' to provoke Thonks to do somethin' foolish before we're ready.'

The multitudes would have been surprised to see their High Priest at home, Myrony's shiny pate unwigged, his sonorous voice fallen into the vulgar accents of his youth. Myrony had been born and reared in a scumpocket on Zenith, an entertainment world known more for its depravity than for its devotion to theology. That he had risen so far into godliness from this beggarly beginning spoke volumes for his tenacity and ruthlessness, if not for his conscience.

'Old Sweet Wuyllum won't do anything until we're ready,' murmured Aphrodite through perfect teeth and lips, which pursed into a kiss as she peered into the mirror and preened over the glitter of the new firestone necklace. She had been Myrony's associate on a dozen worlds, and she knew him better than anyone still living. 'Thonks knows whose hand stuffs his pocket.'

'Not necessarily so, Affy,' Chantiforth Bins corrected her in comfortably avuncular tones. Though his association with the other two was more recent than theirs with one another, he had long ago adopted a familiar and confidential tone with them both. 'The Governor could be forced to move. Myrony's right. We need to sit on Jeshel unless Wuyllum tells us he needs an incident. And then we need to do a quick sunder and be off planet by the time it happens.'

'Harward Justin's not going to let anything happen to us,' the woman remarked, stretching luxuriously while stroking the gemstones. The necklace was a gift from Justin, and Aphrodite had her own reasons for believing the BDL boss would take care of them. Her ego was so strong that she had never considered any other outcome of their relationship. Though she didn't realize it, her complaisance was a personality trait that Justin much appreciated, since he felt it made her totally predictable. He would have been reinforced in this opinion by her remarks. 'Justin likes the good job we've done for him,' she said, smiling at her own reflection and giving the gem one Last pat. She did not enjoy remembering the earning of the gift, but having it made up for that. 'It's the first time we've ever hired out to start a religion, you know that It's been what you might call interesting.'

'Given the free hand we had, it wasn't bad,' Chantiforth admitted.

'It wasn't workin' worth shit until Justin brought In those shiploads of trash from Serendipity,' Myrony remarked. 'Didn't have two converts to rub together until then. You have to hand it to Justin. He knew the kind of people would go for it. Jeshel and his bunch are just right.'

'Jeshel and his bunch are going to scream contra-tenor when they get interned with all the rest,' Chantiforth objected. 'Justin may be sorry he's got them on his hands then.'

'Let Jeshel scream. Let him say anything he hikes. He has no idea who we really are, and less than no idea where we're going to be. The army'll take care of Jeshel.' Chantiforth Bins rose and crossed to the high windows that looked out over the city. 'I'm going to miss this place.'

'Not me,' Aphrodite said. 'The food's lousy, the noise never lets up, and the only music they have is that damn Tripsinger howling. Me for the Spice Coast on 'Dipity.'

'I think we all agree it was worth it though.' Bins turned from the window with a smile, rubbing his fingers together suggestively. 'Biggest one we've done together. Didn't all those pilgrims bleed money?'

Aphrodite puckered her forehead. 'Pity there won't be any more pilgrims when BDL crashes everything. And you're right, Chants. We need to do a sunder well ahead of the shutdown. No telling what some PEC flunky might end up doing. There might be some kind of a last-minute shift that could leave us where we're not supposed to be. Whenever that CHASE Commission gets here, we need to start moving. Couple of months? Or maybe sooner, from what I hear. And we need to watch our money, too. Even though it's on Serendipity, something could go wrong. There's about six million now. Split three ways, Chants-love, that's two million for each of us. Which is not too utterly threadbare for three years' part-time work.'

'More than three fuckin' years total,' growled Myrony. 'Chanty and me had to set up the Jut Massacre, remember? That was a little iffy. I didn't like bein' that close to those fuckin' Presences. And there was some rumor-mongerin' even before that.'

Aphrodite shrugged. 'It didn't exactly take your full time, My. You and Chanty managed to get in on that Heron's World slash-up in between. You guys made me real mad on that one, you know! I'm some kind of shredded settler's brush, you couldn't cut me in on that?' She stood up and drifted lazily to the window, looking out over the low parapet to the snarling hubbub of the city.

'You weren't around,' Myrony snarled, giving her a nasty look. 'You were busy. Seems to me there was something I heard about some diplomatic papers that disappeared.'

'Never mind,' she said, turning to wave her hands at him, shushing him. 'I don't want to be reminded.'

Below them in the vaulted sanctuary, a bell rang repeatedly, the measured dong, dong, dong seeming to tighten the very atmosphere around them.

'Evening services,' said Chantiforth, rising and moving toward the rack where his robe and crown were hung. 'Damn I'm getting tired of this. It was kind of fun at first, but I've had it to my back teeth.'

'All you have to do is look impressive,' Myrony objected. 'It's my nigh' for the sermon.'

'Mine for dispensing revelations,' Aphrodite remarked. 'I think I'll wear that new mantle with the blue feathers. What'll the message from the Presences be tonight?'

'Work for the fuckin' hour cometh,' Myrony suggested with an unpriestly sneer as he reached for the full white wig that stood on a stand by the door.

'Repent for the day is at hand,' sniggered Chantiforth.

'What'd'you think they really say?' she asked, stretching. 'The Presences? Y'ever thought about that?'

The two men, tall, white haired, benevolent looking as saints, gave her equally empty stares, as though wondering if she had gone mad.

'No,' she sighed. 'I guess you guys never thought about that.'

Don Furz looked down on the Redfang valley from a high pass, her head barely lifted above the line of crystal prominences, swiveling slowly as she examined the lowlands with a pair of excellent glasses. She stopped several times and stared intently, adjusting the glasses for focus, then moved on. When she had scanned the entire valley, she wriggled back down the pass to join Tasmin and his acolytes, who were lying beside the trail playing with Clarin's crystal mouse.

'They're there,' she said crisply. 'At least two bunches of them.'

'The same ones as last night?' Tasmin asked, handing the mouse to Clarin and getting to his feet.

'They look the same. Who knows? One group is right down at the bottom of the trail, as though they were waiting for us. The other one is moving along down the center of the valley, as though they don't even know the other one is here.'

'Did you see robes? Tripsinger robes?'

'In the group moving down the valley, yes. Two of them. But no robes at the bottom of the trail.'

'Which way is the 'Singer group headed?'

'There's a passworded trail east of them. It'll take them in behind the Redfang range, about five miles south and east of us.'

Tasmin frowned. 'We can wait until the 'Singer group goes on into the range, then we can cross their trail behind them and out of sight of the ones below us.'

'There's a route I know.' She nodded. 'If we can get behind the 'Singer group, I can get us into a fast north-south corridor.'

Tasmin nodded approval. 'Then once we're far enough south to avoid immediate trouble, we can split up. Some of us need to get to Thyle Vowe. I wish his message had been just slightly less enigmatic, that he'd told us just what it is he's aware of, but we have to operate on the assumption he knows or at least suspects what's going on Whether he does or not, we need help and there's nowhere else to get it.'

'I never intended to involve others,' Donatella complained. 'It makes me feel hideously responsible.'

'You didn't involve us, not purposely. The acolytes and I have talked this over, Explorer.' He rose and stretched, the full sleeves of his robe dropping back to his shoulders as he reached for the sky. Then he turned to her, shaking his robes down around him. 'We ... or I should say, I started this journey to solve a couple of personal mysteries – things I needed to know about Lim, about my wife. I still want answers to those, but right now there are more urgent things.' He turned away. It seemed a desecration to stop his search for the cause of Celcy's death, and yet he could do nothing else.

'First things first,' Clarin said encouragingly, filling the silence and giving him time to recover. She had pocketed the mouse and was now assembling her gear.

'Right,' Tasmin agreed, attempting a rather weary smile. 'We've talked it over, and we want to help you do precisely what you were trying to do. On the face of it, telling all Jubal that the Presences are sentient is the most important thing we could do just now.'

Clarin nodded, running her fingers through her short, curly mop. 'We agree about that. However, Tasmin and Jamieson and I – we all feel the need to be prudent. Once the CHASE Commission meets and reports, there will be no time for other efforts. The case has to be airtight. We have to be able to prove everything we allege. And so far, as Jamieson mentioned, we have only your word for everything. There could be another explanation for the attack on you, and that's the only thing we've seen with our own eyes.' She shouldered her pack and went off to load it on the waiting mule.

'But I told you ...' Donatella interrupted.

Jamieson said firmly, 'You've told us about your arrangement with Lim Terree but there could be other explanations for that as well.' He went up the trail to load his own mule.

'I've played you the Enigma cube!' she protested to Tasmin.

'You have no witnesses to making that cube, and it could have been faked,' Tasmin replied in a sympathetic tone. 'And quite frankly, it is ... well, enigmatic.' Seeing her expression he added hastily, 'We don't disbelieve you! You're right, they are words, and they are sequential words. They just don't seem to be substantially responsive to what you were saying. Or thought you were saying.'

'I was scared to death,' she admitted. 'I hurried more than I should have. There were these constant tremors. And the Enigma's words sounded ... well, they sounded a little hostile.'

Tasmin nodded. 'We thought so, too, which is actually one of the best arguments there could be that the thing *isn't* faked. Presumably, a fake would have made better sense and have been more ingratiating. For the record, we believe you. Others won't, not necessarily. There has to be proof. It has to be as obvious to the people we will give it to as it is to you.' He walked over to the mules where Clarin and Jamieson waited, listening attentively. 'We have to have more than your word. There need to be witnesses.'

Donatella Furz looked from one expectant face to the other, uncertain and angry. 'How do you expect me to …'

'Oh, very simple.' said Jamieson with a radiant smile. 'We're going to talk to the Enigma, too.'

11

Harward Justin made his home in a luxurious apartment on the top floor of the BDL building. At one time he had considered living elsewhere, but he had rejected the idea. It was convenient to be able to call upon BDL service employees when one needed a cook or housekeeper or cleaning crew. With BDL people, he need not concern himself with maintenance, discipline, or remuneration, though he occasionally intervened in such matters. Justin was a believer in the stick, rather than the carrot, and the personnel department's idiot insistence upon paying people more than they were worth often stuck in his craw.

Still, using BDL services people worked well enough for his day-to-day needs. Since they did not live in, he was not required to feed them. When they were gone, he had a great deal of privacy. And it was in privacy that he indulged the needs that required other and very special servants.

A neighboring windowless space had been walled off and cut up into two corridors of apartments and cubicles. This warren was connected to his own rooms with a locked and guarded door. Justin's personal servants lived there – the ones provided for him by Spider Geroan.

Most people feared and hated Spider Geroan. Justin found him both interesting and admirable. He detected in Geroan's manner a kind of kinship. Even Geroan's face, which Justin had always felt resembled the face of a recent corpse, devoid of all life though not yet noticeably decayed, pleased Justin. He saw in that face a reflection of himself as he willed himself to be, remote and implacable. He found in Geroan a depth of silent understanding he had never received from any other human being. Justin suspected that others – 'them,' the world at large – would consider his amusements childish, on a level with cutting up live animals or terrorizing smaller children, the things boys did and then grew out of. However, Geroan did not seem to think him immature in his pleasures. Geroan knew all about the servants' quarters. Geroan had recruited most of the inhabitants. Geroan knew exactly why Justin wanted them. Or one of them, from time to time.

Tonight, Justin was considering a particular one as he waited at the connecting door while the guard unlocked it. Inside this door to the left, another door led to the apartments of the professional servants: the doctor, the masseuse, the four social courtesans who acted as hostesses when Justin entertained, each with private and well-equipped quarters. To the right were the cells, tiny cubicles provided only with basic sanitation equipment. At one time he had thought to fill this corridor, but he hadn't done so. Many of the doors stood open, revealing empty rooms. He went to a closed door, third on his left, and thrust it open. It was numbered with a '6,' and it opened only from the outside.

The occupant was huddled against the wall.

'Stand up,' he ordered her.

She did not seem to have heard him. Cursing, he pulled her to her feet and she swayed against the wall, almost falling. She was dressed in filthy veils which left her breasts and crotch uncovered. At one time she would have tried to cover herself. She did not, any longer. She did not need to, any longer. The once voluptuous body, the once shapely legs were now mere bony caricatures. What had been a wealth of mahogany hair was now a greasy mop, hanging in lank strings.

'Beddy-bye,' he said to her, his code word, the word he had made her fear.

There was no response. No movement in the dull eyes. No twitch on the face.

Cursing again, he struck her and she fell against the wall to lie there without moving.

'They're not going to come after you, you know!' he shouted. 'They all think you're dead. They've thought so for months. The same night I brought you here, we got a body that Geroan had worked over and put it with your clothes out behind the Priory. Everyone thinks it was you!'

There was not a flicker of response.

Harward stormed out of the room, letting the door lock itself behind him.

He let himself into the other corridor. The doctor's apartment was second on his right. This time Harward made a perfunctory gesture of knocking before he entered. Professional servants worked better if one allowed them a pretense of privacy.

The man inside rose from the chair he had occupied, a finger marking his place in the book he held. He was neatly dressed in Justin's livery, a gray-faced man of about thirty-five. His hands trembled. 'Yes, Mr. Justin,' he murmured.

'Room number six,' Justin demanded. 'What's the matter with her?' Part of the doctor's duties was to provide medical attention to those in both corridors.

'Gretl?'

'Number six,' hissed Justin.

'She's dying,' the doctor said, his voice quavering. The quaver irritated Justin. If she was dying, it was her own fault. He had intended her to be one of his courtesans, but she'd failed to please him.

'Why? What's the matter with her?'

The doctor's voice became calm and quite emotionless. Only the trembling hands betrayed him. 'She's half starved. She's been repeatedly raped and abused, and she wishes to die.'

'Stop her.'

'I'm afraid there is nothing I can do. I can force feed her if you like, or put her on euphoric drugs if you wish. She might go on living then, at least for a while. She'll never look like anything much, of course.'

Justin curled his lip in irritation. Of course he didn't want the woman on euphorics. The woman's happiness was not what he had in mind.

'Get rid of her,' he said.

'I can't ... I can't do ...'

'You can. Or I'll have someone call on your wife, Doctor Michael. Maybe you'd like to have her in room six?'

The doctor was silent.

Justin turned to go.

'Mr. Justin ...'

'What!'

'I've been here for a year ...'

'So?'

'You told me after I'd been here for one year, you'd consider letting me see the children ...' Now the face betrayed the man. A certain liquid glaze of the eyes. A quiver at the corner of the mouth.

Justin's lip curled once more, this time with a deep and abiding satisfaction.

'Yes,' he assented very softly and lovingly. 'I certainly will do that, Doctor. I certainly will consider it.'

The man's face broke. 'Are they ... are they all right?'

'Why wouldn't they be?'

'Please, Sir—'

'Doctor!' The voice was a whip crack.

The man bowed his head, wordlessly.

'Your being a good boy,' said Justin, licking his lips, 'is what keeps your family the way it is.'

There was no response. Justin left him there, shaking very slightly, his finger still in the open pages of the book.

Justin talked to himself, quietly and convincingly. He was well rid of the woman. She'd been a disappointment, so forget her. What he'd really wanted to do was prove a point, and he'd done that. Nobody said no to Harward Justin and got away with it. As for the doctor, he would give the man a little hope. Not much, just a little. Make him think his family's life was connected to what he did, how he acted. Make him believe that. Maybe show him a holo of his wife and kids. It would have to be faked, of course. Since one didn't want wives running around asking inconvenient questions, the doctor's wife had been dead since the day Geroan had picked the doctor up. As for the children ...

His ruminations were interrupted by the murmur of a well-known voice coming via annunciator from the reception hall, four stories below. Justin started and swore. Think of the devil. The voice on the annunciator was that of Spider Geroan. He was on his way up.

'Well, Spider.' Justin greeted him with a twisted smile and an affable squint of his slushy toad's eyes. 'Nice of you to come and let me know the job's done.'

'Unfortunately, no.'

There was a silence, more uncomfortable than ominous. Spider Geroan had no fear of Justin's displeasure. A physical anomaly made him immune to pain, and he could not remember ever having felt affection or feared death. He was proof against threats. His only pleasures were both arcane and agonizing for others; his only reason for living was a narrow but persistent curiosity. His motionless face betrayed no interest in what he had just said, but then it never betrayed any interest in anything. It was one of the things Justin liked about Geroan.

So now, Justin asked in the sympathetic tone one might use in inquiring after the health of a dear and valued friend, 'I'm sorry to hear that, Spider. What happened?'

'You wanted Don Furz's killing to look like a Crystallite attack?'

'I did. I do, yes. She's very well-known, something of a cult personality. Her killing will be the final outrage that will move the Governor to lock up the Crystallites.'

The assassin nodded. 'I sent a small group of well-trained men armed with knives. Your little man in the Priory boggled a set of orders, just as you directed, and got the Explorer sent up into the Redfang. My men were ready to take her as soon as she got far enough out that she couldn't retreat back among the Presences. While we waited for the appropriate moment, someone else went for her. Four of them. My men joined in, but a bunch of armed Tripsingers came along and drove them off.'

'Tripsingers! Armed? How many?'

'My men said six. I doubt that. There were probably three. From the descriptions, one of them was likely Tasmin Ferrence, from Deepsoil Five. He was in Northwest City just hours before, and he mentioned to a truck driver that he wanted to meet Furz. There were two acolytes with him, probably his own. They were carrying at least one rifle. I don't know how or why they were armed, not yet, but I'll find out.'

Justin sucked on his teeth impatiently. 'So, what happened?'

'Several of my men were killed; the rest were driven off. Furz and the Tripsingers retreated into the Redfang Range.'

'She got away *again!*'

'*They* got away.' There was a slight emphasis on the *they*. Geroan had been paid to get the woman, but now he wanted them all. 'Only temporarily.'

'You sent someone after them?'

'Of course. You've paid to get rid of her, and you'll get what you paid for, Justin. It's ridiculous that it should be requiring so much effort. I've already sent some of my people into the Redfang after them, along with a couple of hired Tripsingers.'

'If you get to Furz, you'll have to kill Ferrence, too, and the Tripsingers won't stand for your killing their colleagues.'

'They won't be asked for their approval.' His voice was almost weary, as though the subject bored him. No muscle of his face quivered, and Justin found this stoniness admirable. Still, he persisted. Just sometimes dreamed of evoking surprise on that face, just once.

'They may attack your people.'

'If they do, they'll be disposed of.'

'Then your men won't be able to get out!'

Geroan turned his back. So, the men wouldn't be able to get out. They were expendable.

Justin subsided. 'Who were the men who beat you to it?'

'One of them lived for a short while. I asked him.'

'And?'

'He said he got his money from the Crystallites, but it came originally, so he understood, from Honeypeach Thonks.'

'Thonks's whorelady? Why would Honeypeach want to kill Donatella Furz?'

Geroan had wondered the same and had been sufficiently curious to institute a few inquiries. 'I'm told the Governor's lady was enamored of one of the Top Six 'Soilcoast singers.'

'Rumored, hell, man. Honeypeach was and is enamored of all six of them and any twelve other men, women, or mules, anytime, anywhere. You mean Lim Terree? The one who died? You're right about part of it at any rate. He did die while using a Furz score. Still, isn't it farfetched to think that was the reason?'

'Perhaps. Her motivation could be mere pique. During a big reception here in Splash One some months ago, Donatella Furz introduced Honeypeach as Gereny Vox.'

Even Justin could appreciate the humor in this. He barked, 'So? A slip of the tongue? You have people who would report a slip of the tongue?' He shook his head, wonderingly. Spider Geroan was the best in the business, and his success was known to be based on detailed and accurate intelligence, but could he really place credence in such tiny things?

'Perhaps her own self-esteem is as important to her as your secrets are to you, Justin.'

Justin snorted. It was hard enough for him to imagine how an ex-erotic dancer and part-time prostitute on Heron's World could get pregnant by an ambitious bureaucrat, bear him a son, and end up displacing the Governor's well-bred wife to become the first lady of a not inconsiderable planet. That the same woman would be particularly jealous of her reputation surpassed belief. 'I don't think it's a question of self-esteem, Geroan. It's a matter of vanity, plain and simple. Honeypeach believes everyone on Jubal knows her and either admires or envies her or both. If they don't, they should. She doesn't give a damn about her past. It's her present and future she cares about, and having people look at her is important to her. That's why the 'Soilcoast singers are almost her private property – vanity. It's why she makes the honorable Wuyllum keep his pretty daughter tied down – though I'm trying to talk her out of that.' Justin licked his lips. 'The woman wants no competition. Sometimes she has to be encouraged to allow a little.'

'Well, we'll soon eliminate whatever competition Furz may offer. If my men don't catch up to her within the next two days, I'll go after her myself. I cannot remember an occasion on which someone escaped my efforts three times. It cannot be allowed. My sense of what is fitting will not permit it to happen again.' The words were like drops of water falling onto stone, emotionless, without particular force, and yet the will behind the voice would eat away just as the drops of water would, forever if necessary. If Geroan ever brooded, which Justin doubted, he was perhaps doing it now. 'Just as a sop to my curiosity, Justin, how did you find out the woman is a danger to you?'

'You have your sources, Geroan. I have mine.' The assassin waited, unmoving, and his implacable silence made Justin uncomfortable. 'Oh, very well. Someone got a translator program for her from off-world. The procurement clerk saw the item on a bill of lading and reported it to me. I have a short list of items that are always reported to me whenever they show up, and translators are at the top of the list. Then Donatella reported her synthesizer missing in Splash One, and the Prior there reported that fact, through channels. "Lost" equipment is something else I interest myself in, for obvious reasons. Those two facts drew my attention to Donatella Furz. Then the services man at her home Priory told the Explorer King she was excited and elated about something. And she dropped a few remarks to him that indicated more than a passing interest in the ultimate Password. Besides which, she came up with an Enigma score, and the damn thing works. Given that combination, what would you think, Geroan?'

The assassin merely stared, saying nothing for a moment. Geroan was almost incapable of surprise, but Harward Justin had just surprised him. Geroan had underestimated him. Justin's information net had to be almost the equal of Spider's own. The only clue that Spider had and Justin had not mentioned was the rather equivocal information that the hairdresser, Sophron, had come up with.

After Geroan had gone, Harward spent a few minutes in futile cursing. Donatella Furz led a charmed life. He had no idea how she had escaped the first two times. Both assassins had been provided by Geroan himself, but it would do no good to rail at Geroan. And though Justin would feel much more secure if she were dead, perhaps it was sufficient that she had been driven back into the ranges, out of communication with anyone on the 'Soilcoast. It was unlikely she could stir up any trouble before Ymries and the CHASE Commission would arrive. Once the hearings started, how could she do any damage?

Some other excuse would be found to round up the Crystallites. Chanty Bins could get his pet terrorist to plant a bomb or something, then the rabble Crystallites would be rounded up and put out of the way. Of course, Chanty Bins and his cronies would need a few days' notice to get off-planet before the general roundup. They'd done a good job of setting up the whole Crystallite operation, and he might be able to use them again somewhere else ...

Unless – unless he decided he didn't want them to leave at all, which might be safer for Justin in the long run. The three of them must have accumulated a considerable credit account on Serendipity by now – four millions or more, Justin estimated from what he knew of the take at the temples. The account wouldn't be hard to tap if he set his mind to it, particularly if Bins and his colleagues weren't getting in his way while he did it. Four millions or more was a nice bit of lagniappe.

He considered this for some time, along with thoughts about the armed Tripsingers, without quite making up his mind what he intended to do about either. His disappointment in his special servants was quite forgotten.

Word went out from Spider Geroan's place, atop one of the older buildings in Splash One, that the spider was tugging on his web. The strings of that web, highly placed and low, twitched themselves nervously wondering if anything they had caught would be of interest to the spider. Though sometimes it was better to have nothing interesting at all than to have only part of something that Spider Geroan badly wanted.

One of Geroan's webs shivered almost immediately.

'It's Price Zimble, Spider, Sir. Word is you want reports. I have nothing new of use, honored one.'

'Surely you've talked to the Explorer knight since her return, services man.'

'Only briefly, honored Geroan. She hasn't sent for me since she got back.'

A long pause for thought. 'You couldn't possibly have said or done anything before she left that would have given her a clue we'd been talking about her, could you, Zimmy?'

'Never, honored Geroan. Of course not. It wasn't me that tipped her, if anything tipped her. It was something that happened in Splash One.'

'Funny thing,' murmured the Spider.

'What's that, honored Geroan?'

'Some of my people went up to Redfang, Zimmy. Looking for the Explorer knight up there. Found her, too, just like you arranged for our friend Justin. Of course, you hadn't arranged anything for Justin until you'd checked with me first, had you? Because the Spider's webs only work for the Spider, don't they? They don't play the outside against the middle do they, Zimmy? Right?'

'Right, Spider, Sir. I didn't do a thing until you gave me the start, Sir. Then I did the orders Justin wanted. They were perfect, just perfect. Looked official, they did, Sir.' Zimmy sounded more nervous than usual while talking to Geroan.

'Funny thing.'

Silence.

'My people found some other people up there, too. Some other people looking for the Explorer knight. Some other people who knew right where to look.'

'She ... she must've told someone she was going. She ...'

'Oh, I don't think the Explorer told them,' said the Spider. 'Funny thing. Isn't it.'

Geroan disconnected without saying goodbye. Donatella Furz had evaded his assassin in Splash One. Had that attempt failed, perhaps, because Zimmy had said something to alert her? And had Zimmy sold information to Honeypeach Thonks? Information that was supposed to belong exclusively to Geroan? Perhaps Zimmy had outlived his usefulness.

But then again ... Zimmy was a very good web into the Northwest Priory. A very good web to Chase Random Hall. Not a bad bit of web, everything considered. Perhaps he merely needed a bit of discipline. Spider Geroan found a bit of discipline often did wonders. He considered this for a time, deciding what kind and amount of discipline might be most effective, until his next web called to report.

This was a gemstone broker who worked in the vicinity of the fish market, who wanted to report a young man who had sold a firestone earclip.

'Orange stones, nothing very special, but nice. Gave the kid a hundred twenty for the clip. I've got some gems almost like it. Close enough to make up another clip. I'll get five hundred for the two, easy.'

'Kid?' queried Geroan patiently. 'What kid.'

'Tripsinger kid. A what-you-call-'em, acolyte. One of the young ones that doesn't do trips by himself yet, you know.' He went on to describe Jamieson in some detail.

'From where?'

'Didn't say. He did say he wanted the money for passage to Deepsoil Five though. For a woman and a baby. Just chattin', you know the way they do, when they're tryin' to sell somethin'.'

'What woman? What baby?'

The broker stuttered, 'I c-c-could try to find out, honored Geroan. Could try. Don't know much where to start, though.'

'The acolyte came to you, why?'

The broker muttered again. 'I d-d-dunno.'

'Because he saw your place, stone-skull. That means he was nearby, in the area.'

'M-m-maybe just havin' some lunch. Lots of people come down to the market for the fish. You know.'

'Maybe for fish. But maybe looking for someone. Maybe found someone. Start by asking if there was a Tripsinger around your place looking for a woman and a baby.'

Another of Geroan's webs was a cleaning woman in the citadel at Splash One. She came in person, desperately full of bits and pieces, hoping something would satisfy the Spider.

'The Tripsinger from Deepsoil Five had two sets of robes with him, and so did each of the two acolytes, Spider, Sir. Underwear, tunics, socks, boots, and spare boots. Worn, too. Like they'd been living on the country for some time. Skinny mules. Like they get when they set settler's brush for a long while. The machines of the acolytes had Deepsoil Five labels. His machine did, too, but that's a funny thing, he had two of them.'

'Two of what?'

'Two machines. Music machines, like they carry to make the Tripsongs. He had two. One like the ones the kids had – like all the regular Tripsinger boxes, with the citadel label on it and the warning against unauthorized use, you know – and a different one. I looked it over, but it didn't have any label on it.'

'Describe it,' asked Geroan, his interest piqued. This fit in nicely with Justin's suspicions.

'It was greenish instead of gray. It had two handles on the sides instead of one on top. The keys and dials and things opened up on a fold-down panel, three folds. The regular ones just have two and they fold up, not down. And the speakers fold out on top, not on the sides, like the regular ones do.'

'Nothing else? No words, trademarks, maker's tags?'

She shook her head.

'And they went where?'

'Northwest City. The acolyte, the boy, he found a truck that was going there. I was cleaning the hall and heard him say so.'

Geroan nodded his thanks, and the woman left, relieved. She expected no payment and rejoiced merely to be let alone for a time by Spider Geroan.

After that, Geroan simply sat, hands folded on his belly, thumbs moving in endless circles around one another as he thought and plotted and thought more.

It was late afternoon when the follow-up call came from the gem broker.

'The Tripsinger was lookin' for a woman named Vivian Terree. She had a kid, a baby. You want 'em?'

'Find out where they are. Find out if they're planning to leave Splash One. Let me know.'

There were other calls, back and forth, as the spider tugged on other webs and the information flowed in, culminating in a final call to Harward Justin.

'The Explorer synthesizer that Donatella Furz reported missing seems to have ended up in Tasmin Ferrence's possession.'

'A Tripsinger?'

'He had an Explorer model, green, two handled, with a threefold panel. At least he had it when he turned up in Splash One. I don't know where it is now.'

Harward made note of this, along with the fact that the Tripsinger had been looking for a specific woman and child. Then he sat, putting all the information together.

Donatella Furz had had an Explorer box with a special translator insert. That box was now in the possession of a Tripsinger from Deepsoil Five. Lim Terree had died near Deepsoil Five. Tasmin had come hunting for Terree's wife and baby. Tasmin had shown up, armed, in time to help Donatella Furz escape a very well laid trap.

Connections. Nine times out of ten, it was safest to assume complicity whenever there were connections.

The time was growing close, very close. He could conceive of only one source of threat to his plans. Not the Explorers. They were under control. The Tripsingers, however, could be trouble. So far, there was only this one man– Tasmin Ferrence. Just one. If there were more ...

Anything Justin did would have to be done at once. He had trusted to underlings too many times already. And so had Spider Geroan.

Besides, there was all that money on Serendipity.

He summoned a trusted secretary. 'Get hold of Chantiforth Bins and make an appointment for him to see me early tomorrow morning. Then call Spider Geroan and ask him to be here at the same time.'

His last call of the night was to the satellite surveillance teams. By morning, he would know almost precisely where Don Furz and her new friends were to be found.

12

In Deepsoil Five, Thalia Ferrence had adapted reasonably well to the presence of her sister, Betuny, who had arrived from Harmony with scant possessions. Since her arrival, however, Thalia had acquired the habit of strolling off several times during the day and almost always at dusk to the low wall that separated the shrubby garden of her house from a narrow roadway and the brou fields beyond. When she had been much alone, she had ached for company. Now that her sister had come to keep her company, she ached to be alone. Betuny was all right. She cooked well enough, Old recipes from their childhood that Thalia relished as much for the nostalgia they evoked as for their slightly disappointing flavor. Betuny maintained the house well, too, being scrupulous about keeping each thing in an accustomed location so that Thalia would not stumble or fall over unexpected barriers.

But Betuny chattered, commenting endlessly on everything, and Thalia found herself wearying of her sister's voice, wanting nothing, neither food nor a neat house nor company, so much as silence. Betuny had a theory about Lim's death. Betuny thought she understood Celcy's character. Betuny considered it wicked of Tasmin to have gone off like that. Betuny philosophized about the Presences. Betuny knew a way to raise the money to have Thalia's eyes fixed – every day a new commentary or a new plan, each more fly-brained than the last, each day the same voice, going on and on and on.

So, Thalia had announced her need of a few moment's meditation from time to time, flavoring the announcement with a spice of religious fervor, and Betuny had manners enough to accept that, albeit reluctantly, though she could not really respect it. She had, however, gone so far as to drag out an old chair and put it in the corner of the wall where Thalia could find it easily. Thalia could sit there for an hour at a time, musing, her head on her folded arms atop the low barricade, listening to the soft sounds of doors opening and closing, women calling children in to supper or to bed, the shushing pass of quiet-cars, and more often than not a chorus of viggies sounding much closer than she remembered hearing them when she could see.

There were few loud or aggressive sounds, and the voice that accosted her from across the wall one evening came as a shock even though she had heard the slow gravelly crunch of feet approaching down the road.

'Are you Thalia Ferrence?'

She nodded, uncertain. It was a cold hard voice, not one she recognized, and she was very good at recognizing voices.

'Tasmin Ferrence's mother?'

She nodded again, paralyzed with fear. Had something happened to Tasmin? She started to ask, but the voice went on relentlessly.

'Are you blind?'

She bridled. 'That's not a nice thing ...'

'Never mind. I see you are, lucky for you. You have a daughter-in-law? A grandchild?'

'No,' she said. 'My daughter-in-law is dead. And the baby she was carrying.'

'Not Tasmin's wife. The other one. The one who changed his name. Lim's wife.'

She could hardly speak in her eagerness, her joy, her disbelief. 'Lim had a wife? A child?'

'You didn't know?'

'No. I didn't know. Where are they?'

There was a snort, more of annoyance than amusement. 'That's what I was going to ask you.' Then the crunch of retreating feet.

'Wait,' she cried. 'Wait! Who are you? How do you know?'

No answer. Nothing but the usual soft sounds, the far-off chorusing of viggies. She rose to feel her way along the path and into the house. She was, after all, the widow of a Tripsinger and the mother of another. There were certain courtesies that the citadel ought to be able to provide. After considering carefully what she would ask – no, demand! – she coded the com and asked to speak to the Master General of the Citadel.

She found it strange that although he did not know about Lim's wife or child, he had many questions to ask about the man who had told her of them.

The troupe of Bondri Gesel had come far from the slopes of the North Watcher – Silver-seam and all relevant honorifics – when the senior giligee approached Bondri while keening the preliminary phrases of a dirge. Words were hardly necessary under the circumstances. The old Prime Priest was barely able to stagger along, and even when they carried him, they had to jiggle him to keep his breath from catching in his throat.

'Bondri, Troupe-leader, Messenger of the Gods, one among us has a brain-bird crying for release.' So sang the giligee.

Bondri sagged. 'Prime Priest Favel,' he hummed, subvocalizing. The giligee wagged her ears in assent. Well, there was nothing for it but to halt for a time. The Prime Priest deserved that, at least. Every viggy needed a quiet time to set the mind at rest and prepare the brain-bird. 'We make our rest here,' Bondri sang, leader to troupe admitting of no contradiction. The giligee was already circulating among the others, letting those know who had not the wits to see it for themselves.

'I am glad of a rest,' the Prime Priest warbled, breathily. 'Glad, Bondri Gesel.'

'So are we all,' Bondri replied gently. 'See, the young ones have made you a comfortable couch.' He helped the old viggy toward the low bench of fronds, which the young ones had spread on a shelf of soil overlooking the valley beyond. From this vantage point one could look back on the Tineea Singers, the Ones Who Welcome Without Meaning It, arrayed against the sky, almost equidistant from one another and too close for easy passage among them. The Singers had gained their name in immemorial times; no viggy worth his grated brush bark would try to sing a way among them, though young ones sometimes dared each other to try. The song that worked for one did not work for the next, and they were too close to separate the sounds. The Loudsingers had a way to get through, but the only safe viggy way was around.

'The Ones Who,' mused Prime Priest Favel. 'I have not been this way in a generation. I had forgotten how beautiful they are.'

Bondri looked at them, startled into perception of them as newly seen. Indeed, when not considered as a barrier, they were very beautiful. Pillars of diamond lit with rainbow light, their varying heights and masses grouped in such a way that the heart caught in the throat when one saw them at dawn or at dusk. 'They are beautiful,' Bondri agreed. 'But perverse. They do not respond honestly to us.'

'Like a young female,' Favel sighed. 'Singing tease.'

Bondri was surprised at this. 'Tease?'

'Yes. She is too young for mating yet, she has nothing to give, really, but she rings tease. The Loudsingers have a word for it. Flirt. She sings flirt.'

'Tineea,' Bondri sang softly. 'The songs of maidenhood.'

'The Ones Who are like that. They flirt, tease, sing tineea to entice us. But they have nothing yet to give us. Perhaps one day, they will.'

'That is true,' whispered Bondri. Newly awakened to loveliness, he stood beside the old priest for a long time more, wondering if The Ones Who could perceive their own beauty.

'Enjoy the aspect, old one,' he said as he returned to the others of the troupe.

'Is he at peace?' inquired the giligee as she busily grated brush bark, using a crystal-mouse jawbone as a grater, onto several criss-crossed and immature tree fronds. When heaped with grated bark, the fronds would be folded, then twisted to press out the refreshing bark juice, a drink for all in the troupe to share. Both the mouse jaw and the tree fronds were in keeping with viggy law concerning tools. Tools were expected to be natural, invisible, undetectable, as were the etaromimi themselves.

'Prime Priest Favel admires The Ones Who,' Bondri warbled, watching as the first juices trickled into an ancestor bowl.

'Take him drink,' the giligee said. 'It is your giligee's bowl, Bondri. A good omen.'

Bondri picked up the bowl and looked at it. It was a good bowl, clean and gracefully shaped. It was a good omen, bringing to his mind many memories of his giligee. He shared a few of these with the nearby troupe members before mounting the hill once more.

'Whose bowl is this?' Favel asked courteously, allowing Bondri to identify the bowl and sing several more little stories concerning his giligee. The time she climbed the tall frond tree and couldn't get down – that had been before Bondri was even depouched the first time. The way she used to cock one ear, making everyone laugh. Bondri was smiling when he left the old priest, and Favel, left behind to sip his bark sap, was contented as well. It was good to share memories of the troupe.

Memory was such a strange thing. A viggy would experience a thing and remember it. Another viggy would experience the same happening and remember it as well. And yet the two memories would not be the same. On a night of shadow and wind, one viggy might sing that he had seen the spirit of his own giligee, beckoning from beside a Jubal tree. Another viggy might sing he had seen only the wind, moving a veil of dried fronds. What had they seen, a ghost or the fronds? Where was the truth in memory? Somewhere between the spirit and the wind, Favel thought.

When the troupe traveled down a tortuous slope, one would remember pain, another joy. After a mating, one would remember giving, another would remember loss. No one view would tell the truth of what occurred, for truth always lay at the center of many possibilities.

'Many views yield the truth,' Favel chanted to himself, very softly. This was the first commandment of the Prime Song. Only when a happening had been sung by the troupe, sung in all its various forms and perceptions, could the truth be arrived at. Then dichotomy could be harmonized, opposition softened, varying views brought into alignment with one another so that all aspects of truth were sung. Not Favel's view alone, but the view of dozens, the view of all members of the troupe, if one had a troupe.

Oh, one must. One must have a troupe. Favel blessed the hour he had been adopted into Bondri's troupe. As a male, he should have lived out his life in the troupe to which he was depouched, but the continuity of his life had been broken when the second commandment of the Prime Song was broken.

The second commandment was almost a corollary of the first. 'Many views yield truth,' said the first part of the Prime Song. 'Therefore, be not alone,' said the second.

Favel had been alone. He had been alone for a very long time, which meant there were gaping, untruthful holes in his memory of his life. When he sang these parts of his life, there were no other views to correct and balance his own – no joyous counterpoints to relieve his pain, no voices of hope or curiosity to relieve his own terrified horror. Favel had been a broken one – broken and abandoned.

It had happened long ago – how long ago? Fifteen years? Twenty? A lifetime. Favel had been a young male then, almost of mateable age, had long since given up trailing his giligee in favor of being with the adventurers, as the young ones thought of themselves. It had been in Bondri's pouch troupe, the troupe of Nonfri Fermil, Nonfri the Gap-toothed with the beautiful voice, and it was Nonfri's trade daughter Trissa that Favel had set his song upon.

She had not been in the troupe long, only long enough to get over her first pain of separation, only long enough to learn a few of the troupe's memories so that she did not sit utterly silent during evening song. To Favel, she was Trissa of the frilled ears, for the edges of her wide ears were ruffled like new leaf fronds, the soft amber color of dawn, only slightly lighter than her songsack. Her eyes were wide and lustrous, but so were those of all the people. Her voice, though – ah, that Favel could remember, but he had to sing it to himself all alone, for none in Bondri's troupe had ever known her. 'Softly resonant,' he sang quietly to himself, 'plangent in the quiet hours, rising like that of the song mouse to trill upon the sky.' Ah, Trissa. She had sung tineea and turned his soul.

A small group of youngsters had gone one evening to gather brush. Some of the elders of the troupe had a taste for bark sap, and the young ones were searching for a juicy growth. Favel was older than the gatherers and too shy of his awakened senses to invite his own group to go with him, so he broke the second commandment of the Prime Song and went alone. Alone to lie in the brush and watch Trissa, hear Trissa. Alone to imagine himself and Trissa mated.

Her group started back, laden with juicy brush. Favel, hidden at the foot of a 'ling, waited for them to pass. One of them, a silly young male, threw a bit of crystal at the 'ling, the very 'ling that Favel lay beneath, hidden in the grasses. The 'ling had been excitable. It had broken.

When he woke, there was blood on his head and his legs were broken beneath the shattered 'ling. When he pulled himself to the place the troupe had been, the troupe had departed. Days passed, and nights, and he found himself beside a Loudsinger trail. Days passed again, and nights, and a Loudsinger caravan came by.

After that was pain as the Loudsinger tried to set his legs, then less pain, and finally only the songbreaking agony of loneliness as he waited to die.

'Why did you not die, Favel?' Bondri had asked him later.

'I was too sick to die,' he had replied. 'My brain-bird could not settle on it.' And it was true. Despite the ban, despite the taboos, Favel had not died. Perhaps curiosity had kept him alive.

Favel learned Loudsinger talk. It gave him something to do, and it was not particularly difficult. One word served many purposes. No word was particularly precise. The Loudsingers made no attempt to find truth, each merely asserting his or her own vision of history. 'I remember it this way,' one would say in a disagreeable tone. 'You're wrong, this is the way it went,' making Favel writhe at the rude arrogance of such statements.

The man was named Mark Anderton, and he kept Favel in a cage made of stuff Favel could not bite through. Favel considered the question of taboo and finally allowed himself to chitter words and phrases at him in order to get food.

'Listen to my little frog-monkey,' Anderton would say. 'Like a ruckin' p'rot, in't it.'

'What's a p'rot?' someone always asked.

'Urthian bird. Talks just like people,' he would say, with a guffaw. 'I got me a Jubal p'rot.'

'See the pretty viggy,' they would chant, stuffing bits of meat through the bars at Favel. 'See the pretty viggy.'

'Pretty viggy,' Favel would say, without expression, grabbing for the meat, while the Loudsingers broke themselves in half laughing. He was breaking the taboo by not dying, but he was not breaking the taboo when he used words. They did not know he understood what he said.

'Ugliest thing on six worlds,' one said. 'Pretty viggy my pet ass.'

Favel had never considered whether he was pretty or not. It wasn't something generally considered important. Trees were beautiful, of course. Presences, most of them, were beautiful. Voices were beautiful, some more and some less. But viggies?

It was a new thought, one that perplexed him. Had he thought Trissa was beautiful? After much thought he admitted to himself that he had. Yes, the sight of her had gladdened his song. She had been beautiful.

In time Mark Anderton had tired of having a viggy and had sold Favel to another man, who had sold him in turn to Miles Ferrence as a gift for his oldest son.

There were two sons – and how weirdly strange it had seemed to Favel to have sons – and a woman and a man in Miles Ferrence's troupe, and by that time Favel had figured out how it was the Loudsingers got by without giligees. There was something strange about the Ferrence troupe, something wrong. Some days there was such ugliness in the voices that Favel buried his head under his arms, trying not to hear. Favel's cage was hidden on a high shelf for a time. Then he was given to the youngest boy, but the oldest boy took the cage into the night and set him free.

'I am Lim Ferrence,' he had told Favel. 'I am not debauched. I am Lim Ferrence, and I can sing as well as anybody, better than anybody, and I am not debauched, and if I can't have you, nobody can have you, so you go back where you came from ...'

As soon as he was far enough from the cage to make recapture unlikely, Favel had stood forth and sung his thanks to Lim Ferrence, seeing the blank oval of the boy's face staring into the darkness, incredulous at this torrent of song. 'I owe you a debt,' Favel had sung. 'I owe you a debt unto the tenth generation ...' He had sung it in Loudsinger language, breaking the taboo. A debt of honor took precedence over any taboo, but afterward he had wondered if the young Loudsinger had even understood.

The debt should have been paid long ago. Why hadn't that debt been paid?

Favel mused, hearing the soft sounds of the giligee who was grating the bark, the young ones who were pressing the sap, the gatherer females who were sorting through their pouches of seeds and roots. The sound of a troupe. How long had he wandered before he found a troupe once more, a troupe that would take him in?

Long, memory told him. 'Long, lonely,' he sang, his voice rising over the troupe-song below him, so that the others muted their voices and sang with him, letting him know they knew the truth of what he sang. Long, lonely, and wandering. He had not paid the debt then because he could not. He had not the means.

Until he met the troupe of Bondri Nettl, which took him in and learned his memories as though he had been a young trade daughter. Because he had a retentive memory and knew the language of the Loudsingers, he became a priest, then a Prime Priest. Now there were several troupes who knew bits of the Loudsinger language and viggies of many troupes who knew the memories of Favel, who knew the long loneliness of Loudsinger captivity – though they would never know the truth of it for Favel did not know that truth himself. Sometimes Favel wished he could sing to Lim Ferrence and Miles and the younger son, Tasmin, and the strange woman, Thalia. Perhaps they would have seen enough of what really happened to make a truthful telling.

Bondri Nettl was gone now. Bondri Gesel was his heir. And though he had searched for the troupe of Nonfri Fermil, their paths had not crossed in all the years. There had never been another like Trissa, with the frilled ear edges and song that stopped his heart.

There was a flutter in his mind as he thought of this. A little flutter, as though something were trapped there. He understood, all at once, without any preliminary suspicions, why it was the troupe had stopped and why it was he had been given this comfortable couch on which to rest.

Below, where the members of the troupe nibbled and drank, the giligee heard a silence where the Prime Priest had lain. She looked up to meet his eyes.

'Tell Bondri Gesel the Prime Priest believes it is time to depart,' Favel said, trying with all his mind to remember everything, absolutely everything he had ever done.

Bondri heard. In this sparsely grown location, it would not be a fully ceremonial departure, but neither would it lack care. Bondri was not one to scamp the niceties, nor would he allow slackness in his troupe.

Within moments some of the young ones were leaping off to gather fronds for the Couch of Departure, and even before they came leaping back, waving the fronds above them, the old priest had sighed, sagged, and bent his head into the posture of submission. When the fronds had been laid out, he staggered toward them, disdaining the assistance members of the troupe tried to give him.

'I hope that giligee of yours is halfway skillful,' he hummed to Bondri as he laid himself down. 'Making no bloody mess of it.'

'Very skillful, old one. It did my own giligee not long ago. It was very clean. You, yourself drank from her cup.'

'Well, I'll be glad of that. I've seen some botched ones in my time.'

'No fear, Prime Priest. The giligee of Bondri Gesel will do you honor.'

'May I find both honor and sustenance in your troupe, Bondri Gesel.'

'I am gratified, old one.'

The giligee was hovering at the edge of things, a bit nervously, but it came forward quickly enough when Bondri gestured, and the troupe began the Last Chants as though rehearsed. Well, in a way they were. They had done them several times not long since.

Bondri knelt for the Final Directives.

'Remember the Loudsinger language I've taught the troupe, Bondri. My spirit tells me you will have need of it. I lay this upon you.'

'I will remember, your perceptiveness. I will remember the language as I will remember your name, rehearsing both in the dawn hours.'

'I owe a debt,' the priest continued in a whisper. 'A debt to the person or troupe of the Loudsinger, Lim Ferrence, who released me from bondage. I lay that debt upon you, Bondri Gesel.'

'The debt is assured and guaranteed,' the troupe sang, voices soaring and throat sacks booming. 'Taking precedence over all other things. Assured unto the tenth generation.'

'None of that tenth generation stuff,' the Prime Priest went on, a trifle agitated. 'I have already let it go too long. I want it paid out soon, Bondri. It will be on my conscience otherwise. It might prevent my development.'

'I will fulfill immediately,' Bondri sang, the rest of the troupe following his lead. So sung, it was more than an oath. It became a sacred undertaking, overriding all taboos. And 'immediately' meant before they did anything else at all.

Favel went on with one or two other little bequests, nothing difficult, subsiding at last into shut-eyed silence. Bondri took Favel's head between his hands and gestured with his ears. The giligee came forward to kneel with its teeth to the back of the Prime Priest's neck. Bondri inflated his throat sack to its fullest. At one signal, the troupe burst into full voice, drowning out the weak cries the old priest made as he departed. When the giligee had the brain-bird lying licked clean and naked on the fronds, the troupe witnessed its transfer into the giligee's pouch, then all assisted in cleaning Favel's delicate skull. It made an ancestor cup of remarkable delicacy and graceful shape. The eye holes were handles of delightful elegance. Bondri drank from it first singing of certain memories he shared with Favel, then each of the troupe did likewise. As they sang the memories, the priest's apprentices made fire – a very laborious process used only for a departure – and all took part in the ceremonial burning of Favel's remains. There wasn't enough fuel where they were to guarantee that no bones remained, but the wound flies and gyre-birds could be depended upon to do the rest. When everything was done well as it could be done, carefully not looking behind them in order that there be no improper memories, the troupe began to run away south.

They had an immediate debt to pay, and the site of fulfillment would begin at the place the Loudsingers called Deepsoil Five.

Aphrodite Sells, astride a mule named Lilyflower, cursed the mule, the trail, the company, and the direction in which they were going.

'Shut it,' urged Myrony Clospocket. 'Another fuckin' squeak out of you, Affy, and I swear I'll slit your throat.' He fingered the knife at his waist, sounding very much as she remembered him from years before, like something elemental with mindless violence breeding just beneath his skin.

'You don't like it any better than I do,' she complained. 'We should have done a quick sunder, My.'

'We should have done it a week ago, a month ago, before Justin got after us. I've decided he's up to something nasty. We'll be fuckin' lucky if we get off Jubal at all.'

'Justin just said he needed us to take care of this one thing. He said we were the only ones he could trust, us and the Spider.' She sounded doubtful, even to herself. When Justin had given them their orders, he had not been his usual flattering self. 'It has to be important, My. He never would've risked a flier to get us in there otherwise.'

'Risk, hell! He blew up half a dozen fuckin' Presences and then sent the flier in over where they'd been. You can pray to God nobody finds, out what he did before the CHASE Commission makes its fuckin' report.'

'If Justin did it, he did it so's he wouldn't get caught. And it must be important.'

'That's what he said, and I paid chits for it at the time. That's Justin. He can make shit sound like syrup. He can hold a fuckin' mule-fruit out in front of you and swear it's roast bantigon until your mouth waters. Oh, yeah, I paid chits for the idea then. That was before I'd been out in this fuckin' country on this fuckin' mule for five days.'

'It can't be that new to you. You said you were on the Jut for the massacre.'

'Shut it, I told you. You want those fuckin' Tripsingers to hear you talking about the Jut?'

'They're ahead of us by half a mile, My. You are in a state.'

'Spider Geroan isn't ahead of us. He's behind us, and I swear to God that man's got ears can hear a viggy fart a mile away.' Myrony Clospocket shifted on the mule, substituting one aching set of muscles for another. 'Besides, when Chanty and me was on the Jut, it was only for two days, and we got picked up by a quiet-boat and sung through the Jammers real fast when the killing was over. It was Colonel Lang that got it done. Same colonel who's back in Splash One right now while we're out here killin' ourselves.'

'I should've gone with Chanty,' she mumbled, wiping sweat from under her ears and across her forehead. 'At least the way he's going down there in the south is a standard route.'

'You didn't want to go with Chanty,' he snarled, mimicking viciously. 'Oh, no, little Affy didn't want to get mixed up with kidnapping babies and killing women'

'I don't like killing,' she said with some dignity. 'I never have. You and Chantiforth Bins know that very well, Myrony. I never did a job with you where there was any killing, and I haven't done any on this one. Besides, I think it shits to go grabbing babies. Why's this woman and her kid important anyhow?'

'Justin thinks she may be important to that Tripsinger from Deepsoil Five, that's all. Important enough, maybe he'll trade for her.'

'Most unlikely,' she drawled, putting on her pulpit voice. 'Most unlikely for any man to put himself in peril to save some woman, particularly some woman isn't even his wife or anything.' She wiped sweat again and glared at the handkerchief, grimed with the sticky dust of the trail. 'Besides, I thought you and Geroan were going to take care of the Tripsinger and the Explorer. When and if we catch up to them, that is.'

'If is right. According to Justin, they had them located. Located, hell. By the time we got dropped off, they were god knows how far ahead of us. All we were supposed to do was buzz in, splash 'em from a distance with these new rifles and get ourselves back to Splash One, ready for the sunder. Oh, yeah, Justin had it all plotted.'

'You didn't say splash them to me, My. You said take care of ...'

'What the fuckin' hell did you think we meant, Affy? Invite 'em to a tea party? Convert 'em into bein' good little Crystallites?'

She was silent for a time, finally asking with at least an appearance of meekness, 'Well, when we catch up to them and you dispose of the Tripsinger, then nobody needs the woman and kid, do they!'

'Insurance,' he growled, almost beneath his breath, hearing the crunch of hooves narrowing the distance between themselves and Spider Geroan. 'The woman and the kid are just insurance, Affy, and mind your fuckin' tongue.'

Inside one of the massive walls of the BDL building, a lean and dusty figure lifted a soil-filled bucket high above her head and felt the weight leave her hands as it was hauled away.

'That's enough for now,' came a whisper from above. 'Come on up, Gretl.' There was the sound of water running. The dirt dug out of the mud brick wall was being disposed of, washed into the sewers of Splash One.

Gretl Mechas started to object, then sagged against the wall of the vertical shaft, unable to muster the strength to move. She could not have continued, even if he had been willing. The makeshift mallet and chisel fell from her hands.

'Gretl?'

'Coming,' she said at last, setting her foot on the first of the laboriously inserted pegs that formed a spiral ladder in the chimney-like shaft. When she came to the top, Michael, the doctor, reached for her hand and pulled her out, like a cork out of a bottle. They stood in what had been Gretl's cell when she had been alive. Now that she was dead – for the second time – it was presumably empty, at least temporarily. Michael placed a mud-covered bit of planking conveniently near the opening, then moved the cot back almost to cover it.

'How much farther do we have to go down?' she sighed.

He ran the length of hauling rope between his hands, measuring off the yards. 'Another twenty feet, maybe. That should bring us into the cellars.' He dropped the bucket and coils of rope into the shaft. 'I can get us down another foot or so tonight, after I'm sure he's asleep.'

'You're sure he's got a tunnel?' She asked the question for the twentieth time and he gave her the answer he had given each time before.

'According to the guards I overheard, yes. It was put in when the building was constructed. It runs out to the east, through the farmland. There's a door out there. According to the men, it's so well hidden from the outside, it isn't even locked.'

'We should be able to move faster now that I'm dead,' she said tonelessly, wiping the dust from her eyes. 'I won't have to listen for that damned door every minute, wondering if he's coming down the hall.'

The doctor nodded, fetching a damp cloth from the attached convenience so she could wash the dust from her face. 'There's no one else alive in this corridor, Gretl. Unless he brings someone new in here, I think you're safe. And from what the ladies say, he's preoccupied with other things right now.'

'Ladies,' she snorted weakly.

'They hate him just as much as you do. They just had a lower breaking point, that's all.' He stroked her hair. 'You did your part very well. You looked as though you were dying.'

'You were right. He didn't want me any more when he couldn't get any response. It was hard not to show anything, Michael. Oh, God, but I do hate him.'

'I know.'

'I've meant to ask, how did you make him believe I was dead?'

'The same way he made everyone out there believe Gretl Mechas was dead before. There's no shortage of bodies. There are two or three rooms down the corridor that have bodies in them. I just bagged one of those and gave it to the guards. They weren't likely to look. They saw what they expected to see, just as your friends did when they saw your clothes on that other poor soul, whoever it was.' Michael's voice shook with despair. 'The place is full of death. Justin breathes death. My wife and the kids are dead. I know it. God, I hoped for so long, but I saw it in his eyes this last time.'

'Why did he pick you?'

'The historic press published a story on me. I'd developed some new treatments for diseases of aging using biological products I'd found here on Jubal. Nothing very significant, but the historic news blew it up into something. He asked me to work for him full time as his personal physician. I thought that was ridiculous and said so ...'

'Justin told me once that no one can say no to him.'

160

'He said the same thing to me. "Nobody gets away with saying no to Harward Justin," and "What's mine stays mine."'

'What's his stays dead,' she whispered. 'Did he think you could keep him alive forever or something?'

'Who knows what he thought. I can't extend his life, no matter what. So far I've been lucky. He hasn't been sick. And, of course, when the escape shaft is done ...' His head came up, listening. 'I hear something. Better get through onto my side in case he pays me a visit.' He crawled head first into the opening, bent his body into a 'U' shape and! came up through a similar opening on the other side of the wall, behind a couch in his own apartment. Behind him, Gretl hovered, listening to furniture-moving sounds. In al moment she heard him whispering, 'False alarm. Do you have enough food? I have more for you here if you need it.'

'Not hungry,' she mumbled.

'Have to be,' he told her. 'Both of us have to be. For strength: Strength to be dead, Gretl. Strength to get us out of here.'

'All right,' she said, reaching through the thick wall to take the wrapped package. Then she placed the plank over the hole and moved the bare cot to cover it. When the doctor had come to 'do away with her,' he had wedged the latch on her door so it wouldn't close. Later, while she was below in the shaft they had been digging for months, he had given the guards her 'body.' The guards weren't watchful, and they certainly weren't intelligent.

She slipped to the far end of the corridor and into an empty room, carefully wedging the latch, saliva filling her mouth at the smell of the package in her hands. She would have a bath. And a meal. And then sleep. And then it would be night, and she would start digging again.

Thalia Ferrence sat in her chair by the wall, dreaming of a grandchild. The Grand Master had called to tell her that he had learned about the woman, that she and the child were on their way to her. The child and Lim's wife, Vivian. Thalia hadn't told Betuny yet. Betuny would be upset, afraid that Thalia wouldn't need her anymore. Perhaps Thalia wouldn't really need Betuny anymore, but she'd deal with that later just now, it was too pleasant to anticipate, to dream, to imagine all the wonderful things implied in a daughter coming, and a baby. And to think about old times, too. She had done that a lot lately.

She had allowed herself a celebratory glass of broundy, something she seldom did, and now sat in her chair at the end of the garden, her arms folded on the low wall, the setting sun shining full on her face so that she felt the soft warmth of it as she half dreamed about old times long past, wishing she could see the brou fields and the towering Presences once more. She could see them in a sense, but they loomed so large in her remembered vision that she wondered if she had not created them. She wanted to check reality against her memory and had spent a long hour floating dreamily over this, as though the truth were something she needed to arrive at – a key to some future imagining that could not be achieved otherwise. She could no longer be sure what was true, what had actually happened. What had been the truth about Lim, about Miles? Was Tasmin actually what she thought he was? Had Celcy been? Was this woman who was coming going to be a part of her life? Was this world the world she remembered, or was it only a dream she had invented? How would she know?

The voice, when it came, though it asked a similar question, was not like that other voice that had accosted her. This voice was so soft and insinuating it could have been part of her brooding dream.

'Are you the mother of Lim Ferrence?'

The broundy was flowing in her veins. 'Lim Terree he called himself,' she said, almost chanting and with a half smile curving her lips. 'But I was his mother, yes.' The voice that had spoken to her was a strange voice, almost like a child's voice, but with an odd accent. It could be a dream voice. Certainly it did not seem to be a real one.

There was a moment's silence, as though she had said something confusing.

'Was?' the voice asked at last. 'Implies former time? Not now?'

'He is dead,' she said. 'Dead. He died on the Enigma.'

A tiny consternation of sounds. She was reminded of birds talking, that chirrupy, squeaky noise, but in a moment the child's voice spoke again, almost like singing.

'What kin did he leave behind?'

'I thought it was just me, you know. I thought I was his only real kin, the only one who still cared, and remembered, and grieved. Oh, there is Tasmin, of course. His brother, but Tasmin couldn't be expected to care. Yes, I thought it was only me, but it seems he had a wife, and a child. They're coming here. Soon. Someone came to inquire about them, and then when I asked the citadel, they found out for me ...' Her dream gave way to a sharp pang of anxiety. 'I hope, nothing's happened to them.'

Again that dream pause. Something brushed her face, like a feather, something soft, cool, and infinitely gentle. Then the voice. 'Why should something happen to them?'

'I don't know. It's that man who came. His voice. He didn't tell me his name. He said it was lucky I was blind. He wanted to know where Lim's wife was, and his baby. I told them I didn't know Lim had a wife and a baby. The man wasn't polite. He didn't even say goodbye.'

That small consternation of sound once more. 'Did you think it was a threat to your son's wife?'

'It seemed odd they would want to know where she was. It seemed odd anyone would want to know. What is she to anyone? The Master General said she was only a woman, no position, no family. Working in the fish market, he said. And the baby, only a baby.' Thalia brooded over the wonder of a woman and a baby who were only that. Not Tripsingers. Not people with busy-ness or resentments to take them away, but only people. A woman. A child.

Then the voice once more, soft as gauze, so soft she could scarcely tell from what direction it came, unaware it came from all about her, from two dozen throats, soft as a whisper. 'How was she to come to you, Mother of Lim Ferrence?'

'By the southern route. Southwest of the Enigma. To the Black Tower.' Her eyes filled with tears. She had been worrying over that route. Miles had died at the Black Tower.

Her weeping hid the tiny sound of those that departed. In the grayed light of dusk none had seen them come, and none saw them go.

West of Deepsoil Five, the troupe of Bondri Gesel found a trail through the Far Watchlings, called by the viggies Those Joyously Emergent. Although narrow, it was an insensitive trail, one that required little song and on which great haste might be made.

'We were right about the Enigma,' several members of the troupe were singing. 'The Mad One has killed again. Lim Ferrence, honored be his name, cannot be repaid, for the Enigma has killed him. Oh, how foolish to attempt song with the Enigma.'

Bondri hissed in irritation, and their song faded away. He didn't wish to think of the Enigma just now. If Favel were still here to sing it over with, perhaps they could have arrived at some conclusion, but this was truly a matter for the priests. He sang so, briefly, to a tinkling chorus of assent.

'How are we sure that the Loudsinger and her child are in danger?' caroled one of the young viggies, an attractive female whom Bondri had had his eyes on for some time as a proper trade daughter for the troupe of Chowdri, to the south.

'The mother of Lim Ferrence was not sure,' Bondri admitted. 'She but suspected danger. Still, she has no eyes, and ...'

'Contradiction,' sang the senior giligee. 'She has eyes, oh Bondri Gesel, Wide-eared one. Her eyes are not in repair, it is true, but they could be fixed. This pouched one could fix them.'

163

Bondri made a small noise, indicating both consternation at being inter-rupted and a degree of doubt. He knew of no incident in which a giligee had worked on a Loudsinger.

'Truly, oh Bondri Gesel. This one has taken their bodies apart many times. The mother of Lim Ferrence, honored be his name, has only a small malfunction. It could be made proper.'

The giligee had touched Lim Ferrence's mother with its antennae. If the giligee said such a thing could be done, then it could be done. 'Remember what you have said,' intoned Bondri, wondering just how far a viggy could go in breaking the taboo. 'If we do not find the child, it may be we will pay our debt in this way.'

'I interrupted the Troupe Leader,' chirped the giligee. 'Please return to your song.'

'The woman cannot see,' Bondri warbled, this time in the conditional mode. 'Our ancestors say of those without eyes that the spirit must see what the flesh cannot, is this not so?'

'Verily, these are true words,' sang the troupe.

'So, her ears told her the man made a threat, though perhaps his words did not convey his true intention.'

'Blasphemy,' sighed the troupe. 'Obscenity.' To the viggy, words that did not convey reality were worse than no words at all. Once this tendency of the Loudsingers to singe falsehood had been determined, the taboo had been invoked. How could viggies sing; with those who did not care about truth?

'Pity them,' intoned Bondri. 'For they are lost in darkness of unmean-ing.' He paused, an obligatory beat, then continued, 'So the mother of Lim Ferrence feels her son's mate and their descendent child are in danger. She does not even know she feels it, yet her inward parts know. If such danger truly threatens and can be forefended, Prime Priest Favel's debt is paid even though Lim Ferrence has been killed.'

There was appreciative murmuring, followed by a burst of purely recre-ational rejoicing. After a time, they halted for grooming and food. Bondri took advantage of the halt to peek into the pouch of the giligee who had honorably corrected him. The pink thing that squirmed there in its nest of pouch-tendrils looked very lively. The brain-bird of Prime Priest Favel was developing well.

'We're being followed,' said Jamieson, getting down from his mule with an exclamation of pain and annoyance as he grabbed for one ankle. 'Damn! I keep hitting that place.'

'Shhh,' said Clarin. 'I told you last night to let me put a bandage on it.'

'It didn't need one.'

'It does if you keep hitting it every time you get on and off your mule, Reb. For heaven's sake!'

'Oh, all right. Put some kind of a pad on it if it will make you feel better.'

'Me? It's you who keeps hitting it.'

'All right,' said Tasmin, wearily as he rolled up his bedding and inflatable mattress. 'The two of you slash it off, will you. You say we're being followed?'

'I rode back and found the highest point I could, Master Ferrence, then looked along the backtrail as you suggested. They were there, all right. Six riders. The only reason I could see them is they're coming down that long traverse along the cliff, the one we were on yesterday morning. About half-way down, the trail splits, you remember? Right there, one of them got down and snooped along the ground, obviously hooking for trail signs. Then they came the way we did.'

'Have you any idea who?'

'Two Explorers, Master. Way out in front, as though they don't want to associate with the ones behind.'

'And the ones behind?'

'Riding in couples. A man and maybe a woman, then farther back, I think two men.'

'I don't suppose you could see who they are?'

'I could see the Explorers' leathers. The woman seemed to be wearing something glittery in her hair, beads maybe. Maybe it isn't a woman at all, but that's the impression I got.'

'Well, it was only a matter of time before someone came after us.' Tasmin cursed silently, wondering who. Wondering why. Wondering how they had found this trail. The group that had pursued them originally had been easy to evade, and they had hoped there would be no further pursuit. Now, this.

The long north-south corridor between two escarpments of Presences that Donatella Furz had found for them had made the traveling simple and very quick, since they had not needed to sing their way through. Now they would need to travel even more quickly.

Don came out of the grove of trees where their small tents were pitched, her face flushed with annoyance or anger or some mixture of both. 'Did I hear you say someone is tracking us?'

Tasmin nodded. She grimaced, then turned to take a folded chart from the pack on the ground, spreading it on a convenient rock and kneeling over it. 'Damn! I didn't think anyone would find us in here.'

'They probably found our trail all the way back in the Redfang and tracked us in here, Don. There are two Explorers with the group.'

She shook her head. 'Well, I found this corridor. I suppose it would be arrogant of me to think no one else had the wits to find it.'

'Did you tell anyone about this passage?'

'I probably did. I would have noted it on the file charts in my room, too. I think I told Ralth. Hell, for all we know, Ralth may be one of the Explorers with them.'

'Whoever they are, they probably don't know they're hunting you, Don. Whoever sent them will have fed them a tale.'

She perused the chart, chewing her lips. 'You still want to split up?'

Clarin made a face of denial, but Tasmin said, 'Yes.' He said it very firmly. He had become too aware of Clarin. She seemed always to be at his side, ready with whatever he needed next. Or he was always at hers. It was hard to know which. He found himself turning to her, depending on her. If she had her way, she would not leave them, but he was going to insist on it. Clarin and Jamieson both. It was the only thing that made sense. He bit down the feelings this raised in him. It could be a final parting, and they all knew it. It was bearable only if he did not admit it to himself. 'I want Jamieson and Clarin to do their best to get to Splash One.'

Don pointed at the chart. 'The best way back to the Soilcoast from here is to take the Shouting Valley cutoff, about half a day ahead of us.'

'Why do you want me to go to Splash One?' Clarin asked Tasmin in a subdued, faintly rebellious voice.

'You've got to get to Vowe,' Tasmin answered. 'I want you to tell him everything we know, everything we suspect, everything we've even thought of in passing. We need whatever protection he can give us. He's got to be ready for whatever we do, and if you don't get to him, we have no other way to let him know.'

'Also, I want you to take him a recording of the Enigma stuff,' Donatella said. 'I made a copy cube last night. I'll keep my box, the one with the translator in it. You take my new one.'

'We've got synthesizers,' Clarin objected.

'I know you do, but Explorer boxes are different. They're programmed to try variations. You sit off about a mile away from a Presence and start with something that almost works or worked somewhere else. Then you try variations until you get one that doesn't rock the needle, see. We don't publicize it, but that's how you do it, mostly.'

'I thought Presences always reacted adversely to recordings,' Jamieson remarked suspiciously.

'They do, if it's close up. But at that distance, it only seems to tickle them. Like a subconscious response, one they're not even aware of. When you've got a variation that doesn't rock the needle, then you play it over until you know it well enough to sing yourself through or at least to get up close and try it first person.' She patted the box, almost as though it had been a mule. 'If often works, for the easy ones. Not for the Enigma, of course.'

'You never told us what Erickson's clue was to getting the Enigma score, did you?' Clarin asked.

Donatella shook her head. 'And I'm not going to. Not yet. Better for you if yon don't know. If it looks like you're going to be captured, destroy the cube. That way you won't know anything that can help anyone.'

'We'll know where you and Tasmin are going.'

'Yes,' said Tasmin. 'And if you're taken, tell them anything they want to know. Tell them where we're going. Well watch out for ourselves. You don't know anything except that Don Furz thinks she talked to a Presence and is going to the Enigma to find out for sure. Tell them that.'

'You'll get through all right,' Don said. 'I've got proven Passwords for almost everything west of here stored in the box, and the charts are clearly labeled. You'll have to duck around the Giant's Toenails. Can't get by there without a Tripwagon full of effects, but if you detour to the south, there's a back way.'

'Where are you two going when you leave the Enigma?' Clarin asked.

'From there, depending upon what we get, either to Deepsoil Five or back to the Deepsoil Coast,' Tasmin replied.

Silence. Her face was calm, but he could see her hurting, rebellious eyes. Oh, Clarin. Clarin.

'Clarin.' More than anything he wanted to comfort that pain. Foolish. She was almost young enough to be his daughter.

'Yes.'

'Listen. At least one of us has to go with Don as a witness. I'm the logical person because I'm enough older than you and Reb to have a reputation that guarantees me a certain amount of credibility. Also, getting back to Splash One for the hearings is going to require help. I can get that from the citadel in Deepsoil Five, and I carry more weight there than either you or Reb.'

'I could go with you and Don.'

'Then Jamieson would be alone. And if whoever is following us chooses to split up and send some of them after him, or if there's someone trying to intercept us from the west, then Jamieson's dances would be decreased.'

'You're right,' she said. 'Sorry.'

'And when we get to Vowe?' asked Jamieson, equally subdued.

'Just tell him. Put it in his hands. He'll know what he can do with it. If he can do anything with it. Pray God he'll believe you.'

'Oh, he'll believe me,' said Clarin. 'He'll believe every word I tell him.'

'You *did* know him before,' Tasmin said. 'I thought so. When we met him there in Northwest.'

'He's ... he's an old family friend,' she said. 'He didn't let on because it makes it ... difficult.'

'Enough of this,' Don said. 'Let's take a few minutes to familiarize you two with this box. Then let's be on our way. According to what Jamieson says, they're only one day behind.'

'Do you have any idea who they are, Donatella?'

She shook her head. 'Forget the Explorers. They could be anyone. From Northwest or anywhere. As you say, they could even be my friends. The others? I have no idea. The only woman I've offended is Honeypeach Thonks, but I can't imagine her on a mule, hunting me down in the backcountry.' She beckoned the two acolytes to her and began a quick, detailed exposition.

Jamieson and Clarin were both quick to pick up the intricacies of the Explorer box. It was different from the Tripsinger synthesizers only in detail, and they demonstrated considerable proficiency at the end of an hour, enough, at least, that Don nodded her head in approval. 'Good enough. We'd better move out quickly.'

Tasmin had already packed the mule saddles, and they took a few moments to hide the remnants of their fire before leaving. Not that it would do any good. If the tracker behind them could find evidence of their passage on the barren trail down the cliff, he would find evidence here as well.

They rode on southward, the hooves of the unshod mules making a musical clopping that was hypnotic. If they had traveled on some other business, if they had traveled without pursuit, Tasmin felt he could have gloried in this strange corridor that Don Furz had found amidst the towering Presences. They were on every side, seeming to look down into the valley where the group walked, violet and ochre, ruby and sapphire, emerald and ashen – a thousand gathered giants, occasionally quaking the air with their muttered colloquies.

'What are they saying?' he asked Don.

'Nothing, so far as I know.'

'Doesn't your new translator pick up words?'

'It *did*, at the Enigma, and in answer to what I sang! But this muttering doesn't translate to anything. All the translator does is snore and snarl and moan.'

You have tried the new translator on it then? Once? More than once?'

'I've tried the translator for hours at a time during every trip since the Enigma. Nothing.'

'Then these along here aren't sentient?' Somehow that didn't seem an appropriate premise.

'I wouldn't draw that conclusion,' remarked Clarin. 'Perhaps they simply aren't talking.'

'Or won't,' said Jamieson. 'I still need proof.'

'You were so sure they were sentient,' Clarin objected.

'That doesn't mean they'll talk to us,' he replied. 'If you were one of them, would you?'

They all stared up at the Presences. Cliffs of coruscating rose. Towers of glittering amber. Mighty ramparts of shimmering sapphire, lambent with refracted light. Walls of gray, shattered with silver. Barricades of scintillating flame.

'Ahhh.' The sound came from Clarin, the sound of someone wounded, or a sound of lovemaking, a climactic ecstasy of sound, half muffled. The expression on her face was the one she got sometimes when she was singing.

Tasmin's hands shivered on the reins, wanting to reach for her. 'We can't linger,' he said in his driest voice. 'Come, we can't stop.' Donatella was looking at him strangely, and he avoided her eyes. His whole being felt stretched, pulled into gossamer, encompassing the world.

An act of self-hypnosis, his tutorial mind advised him. A so-called religious experience. Simply be quiet and it will depart.

As it did, slowly, over the following long hours in the saddle.

They came to the fork in the trail. Donatella checked the charts the others were carrying, checked their machine once more, then sat beside Tasmin as Jamieson and Clarin rode away, small figures growing smaller, dwindling down the west-pointing canyon, not looking back, going away to the cities of the Deepsoil Coast and possibly ... what?

'It's unlikely anyone is looking for them, as individuals,' Donatella said, trying to be comforting, trying to convince herself. 'They're safer without us, Tasmin. Come, let's do what we can to wipe out their tracks.'

'I pray so,' he said, aching with a loss he had not thought to feel so soon again. It was like the loss of Celcy, and yet unlike. This time it was as though something of himself had gone. 'I pray so.'

Rheme Gentry, while ostensibly much occupied with the Governor's private business, was actually engaged in two equally demanding activities. On the one hand, he was feeding every item of available information to Thyle Vowe, for his assistance in trying to outwit 'that bastard at BDL.' On the other hand, he was trying desperately to figure out a way to get a vital message to Serendipity and save Maybelle Thonk's life, or at the very least, her health and sanity, in the process.

Things were drawing to a climax on Jubal. The Honorable Wuyllum was increasingly preoccupied with getting certain items of private – and public – property shipped away to Serendipity, and this required a good deal of falsification of papers inasmuch as BDL had shut down all off-planet shipments except for the necessary flow of brou. Getting anything but brou into space took some doing, though Rheme was getting to be an expert at it. Justin hadn't quite shut off courtesies to the Governor's office. Not yet. Why, the young singer, Chantry, had been shipped out the week before at Honeypeach's insistence, babbling, half conscious, and likely to remain that way. Regeneration didn't work all that well on the nervous system.

'My poor Chantry just collapsed,' Honeypeach said at frequent intervals, 'from overwork, poor baby.'

From drugs, Rheme thought. Drugs and stimulants – which any man needed if he were to get involved with Honeypeach – and too many demands on a nervous system that was, after all, merely biological and normal, not made of transistors and metal parts. Honeypeach simply wasn't interested in normal people or normal biology or normal sex. Honeypeach liked whips and drugs and various electronic devices. Honeypeach liked sex in threes and fours and dozens. Honeypeach liked to watch while others suffered and gyrated, often people Honeypeach said she liked a lot coupled with people she didn't like at all. Rheme knew the signs. Honeypeach had a certain look in her eye when she was choosing who was next, and Maybelle was in line for forced participation. That alone would have told him that the Governor and the Governor's lady were counting the days until departure. Honeypeach would not have focused on Maybelle unless it no longer made any difference what she did or was seen to do.

The honorable Wuyllum had shown no signs of being either aware of this or upset by it. His daughter by his first wife was evidently not seen as a possession of particular value. Rheme Gentry was trying to change that.

'Has the Governor considered what he might be interested in doing after retirement?' he asked in his blandest voice.

'Why should I have thought of any such thing?' Wuyllum growled suspiciously.

'An opportunity on Serendipity has come to my attention,' Rheme answered in his most syrupy voice. 'One which the Governor might be interested in. A very wealthy family agglomeration, which is looking for an alliance of mutual profit, and which has a marriageable son …'

'Son?' Wuyllum was being very slow on the load, and Rheme cursed to himself while his face went on being disinterested. 'About Maybelle's age,' he said. 'May one speak frankly?'

Wuyllum stared at him for a moment or two before grunting permission. Rheme felt sweat start along the back of his neck and under his arms.

'It cannot escape one's attention that your daughter and her stepmother are not sympathetic,' he said, still in that disinterested tone that he had rehearsed over and over again at the end of the garden, beyond the ears. 'It's perfectly understandable, too, your wife being so very young and lovely. At your daughter's current age and level of social experience, however, the is quite marriageable. One could recommend her to many very wealthy families seeking alliances of various kinds, many of which would be to the Governor's advantage. Also, such a marriage would remove a present source of annoyance to the Governor's lady.'

Wuyllum grunted again, a faint light of understanding leaking outward from his face. 'I might consider that,' he said at last.

'If the Governor considers such a possibility in his own best interest, the young lady could be sent on to Serendipity in order that she become fully acquainted with the social set there. It is my understanding she left Serendipity while still too young to take part fully in social affairs.'

'She was twenty-two,' the Governor snorted. 'No more sex smell to her than to a mule.'

Rheme affected not to have heard. 'Since the families of which we are speaking are interested in reproduction, they prefer women who are ... somewhat naive and unspoiled. One might say "conservatively reared." The Governor's daughter gives that impression ... now.'

A light dawned. 'Need to keep her that way, do we? That's what you're sayin', isn't it? Got to keep her away from Honeypeach's party fun, heh?' The Governor's face twisted into a nasty sneer. 'And I suppose you'd want to go along to 'Dipity. Kind of a chaperon, heh?'

'I'd prefer not, Sir, if you don't mind.' Rheme allowed a brief expression of distaste to cross his face, wondering if he were overdoing it. Wuyllum was no fool. Obviously not. He was as thick-skinned and slow to move as some cold-blooded primordial reptile, but where his own self-interest was concerned, he had an absolute genius for understanding the implications of everything around him. 'We're very busy here and I really would prefer not.' Let Wuyllum think that Rheme had tired of the girl's attentions. Let him think whatever he damned well liked, but let Rheme get Maybelle off Jubal and away from Honeypeach Thonks. 'I can find the name of some appropriate woman on Serendipity ...'

The Governor grunted again, suspicion allayed, then turned his attention to other items of business.

That evening voices were raised in the private quarters of his excellency. Rheme, who was huddled with Maybelle in the far corner of the garden repeating the message that he intended Maybelle to carry with her to Serendipity, heard the voices and rejoiced.

'What've you been getting up to with Maybelle, heh?' the Governor asked his wife, his voice coming clearly through the drawn curtains.

'I don't even like Mayzy,' his wife confided. 'She spent too much time with that vanilla milk woman to be interesting.'

'If you're talkin' about my first wife, woman, you'd better have the sense to know who she was. She was the daughter of the Lifetime Ambassador to Gerens, and she came from one of the wealthiest families on Heron's World.'

'And they slashed her off with nothing when she married you, Wuyllum, don't forget that.'

'Doesn't matter. Maybelle was reared by her mama. She's prime stuff, according to people who know.'

'Prime what? Prime settler's brush gruel? She's nothing, Wully. Milky, like her mama. Nothing at all. I don't even know why Justin wants to meet her again.'

'Now you listen to me, Honeypeach. I'm telling you once, and only once. I'm sendin' Maybelle back to Serendipity now. Settin' her up back there with a little place of her own, heh? Hire some snooty woman to be chaperone, get her into society. And between now and the time she leaves, and after we get there, I don't want her touched, you understand? Heh?'

There was an uncomfortable silence, broken by a whimper of pain. Honeypeach was accustomed to inflicting pain, but she was not accustomed to feeling it. 'Who'd want to touch her? And what would you do if I did?'

'I'd ask Harward Justin for the loan of Spider Geroan, woman. You've got your uses. I don't mind your foolin' around to suit yourself, long as you don't meddle with me. Meddle with me, and you'll find yourself havin' a date with Spider Geroan and comin' home outside your own skin lookin' in. You understand me?' The voice was expressionless, without anger, but the whimpering reply told the listeners that Honeypeach had heard it.

In the garden, Maybelle shivered in Rheme's arms. 'God, what did you tell him?'

'How marriageable you are, girl. What a nice, fertile mama you'll make for some herediphilic family on Serendipity.' Rheme was actually deeply disturbed by the overheard conversation. He had not liked the lady's mentioning Justin, and he had not liked the Governor's mentioning Spider Geroan. It had implications for his own life and safety that he found ominous. 'Now pay attention, May Bee, and remember what I'm telling you. Once you're on Serendipity, you're to go directly to those people I've told you about. You're to tell them you're from Basty *Pardo*. Give them the message, just as I gave it to you. They'll see the message gets sent on, and they'll keep you safe.'

'I can't bear to leave you,' she sobbed. 'God, Rheme, there may be a war here.'

'Oh, there will be a war here,' he said grimly. 'And I'll get through it a lot easier if I know you're all right.'

'This vital message of yours, who's it for?'

He was silent, wondering whether he should tell her anything at all except what she needed to know. Meeting her rebellious expression, he knew she needed to know enough to give her a sense of participation. Maybelle was very young, in her attitudes and personality. When he had spoken of her as being untouched, he had said no more than the truth. Still, she had a vivid perception of right and wrong, and it would be wrong of him to use her without her knowing why.

'The work of the Planetary Exploitation Council's been corrupted for years,' he said at last. 'There was a lot of money credit involved, credit that came from the exploiter agglomerates. The corruption didn't involve many of the PEC members, actually, but the others were too complacent to see what was going on. However, the massacre at the Jut started some tongues wagging because one of the people killed was the son of one of the Council members. She got together some of the newer, younger members and began to agitate for an investigation. You know the PEC has an enforcement body, CHAIN, called that for no good reason. If the letters stand for anything, no one knows what. Speaking from personal knowledge, CHAIN is quite incorruptible. It's headed up by an old fox named Pardo ...'

'Any relationship to Basty Pardo?' she asked.

'An uncle, actually. Well, the General – he's retired, but everyone still calls him the General – advised some of the PEC members, and the Council managed to muster a majority of vote support for investigation. CHAIN began by hiring some investigators, a few like me, love. Enough to find out what's really going on.'

'So you really are a PEC agent! I thought you were joking. Then it isn't hopeless.' Her face lit up, that glowingly childlike look he had grown to love. Sternly, he kept his hands away from her. No sense making it harder than it was.

'It isn't hopeless providing this message can get off-planet and reach the right people, May Bee. But Justin has the planet sealed off. I didn't expect that. Shortsighted of me, but I just didn't expert it. All communications are monitored. No one and no thing is being allowed to leave without a priority voucher, and no priority vouchers are being issued except for the few hued by Justin himself or those we've wangled through the Governor's office. You're the Governor's daughter, and you're known to be hopelessly naive and gauche and remote from anything important. You don't even take part in most social events. Everyone thinks you're a little odd and I've been hinting for weeks that you're perhaps a trifle stupid. You're simply the least suspect person we know.'

He touched her cheek, smiling, not letting her know how truly desperate he felt the need was. Everything that was happening on Jubal told Rheme that only force would work, and yet so far as he knew, no one in CHAIN had taken that into account. The Governor would go off-planet in his own good time, and the PEC authorities could pick him up on Serendipity or wherever he landed. But Justin wouldn't leave, and Justin wouldn't resign, and Justin wouldn't obey an order from the PEC.

No, Justin would dig in. Justin would start a war on Jubal rather than be taken into custody. Justin would have to be dug out, or blasted out, or Jubal would have to be put under siege.

And by the time the siege was over, it could be too late for a few million people. And for Jubal as well.

13

It was midafternoon. Left to themselves, Tasmin and Donatella had ridden farther south and laid a few false side trails, which they hoped would be confusing to the followers.

'The valley gets narrower from here on,' Don said. 'We won't be able to escape them, Tasmin, except by keeping ahead of them. What are you doing with those mule shoes?'

Tasmin looked up from the shoes he was fiddling with. 'I traded these off Clarin's and Jamieson's animals,' he said. 'The pattern on each set is a little different. If we put them on two feet of each of our mules, maybe they'll think there are still four of us.'

'Do you think they'll pay chits for that?' Donatella asked him, one eyebrow raised in doubt, as he slipped two of the marked shoes over the mule's hooves, like slippers. 'Do you think they'll really believe there are still four mules?'

'They might. Unless they're smarter than some people are, yes.' He tried for a rueful laugh. 'I just invented the trick, Explorer. It made me feel I was doing something. I deceive myself probably. It's either do something or fret. Fretting makes my stomach ache. Maybe they won't realize how inventive we are.'

She acknowledged this with a slight, barely ironic smile. 'It could work. I don't recall anyone talking much about doing tracking on Jubal. What is there to track? On Heron's World, of course, they do. Lots of hunting on Heron's World.'

'You've been to Heron's World?'

'Of course not, Tripsinger. I was born here. My mother got a bonus for me, as a matter of fact. I was her third.'

'It saves shipping when you can manufacture locally,' he responded.

'Many thanks, Tripsinger.'

'No strain intended, Don. I was just wondering how you knew so much about Heron's World.'

'Library stuff. Adventure stories.'

'Adventure stories?' he laughed. 'After being an Explorer on Jubal?'

'You know it's not always that exciting,' she said. 'Sometimes it's anything but.'

175

'As when?' he asked.

She had stories, her own stories, others' stories, tales of defeat and pain. They were not the stories Explorers told one another, and she didn't know why she told Tasmin except that they were stories needing telling and she might not have another chance. During the trip, she had learned all about him and Celcy. Now she wanted to talk about her and Link.

'Some things you bury,' she said. 'I believe in burying many things. Not denying they happened, you understand, but just getting rid of them. Putting them away somewhere where you don't stumble over them every day. But with Link ... there's no way I can bury that. I used to delight in the Presences. Since one of them almost killed Link ... since then I don't like them as much.'

He considered this, wondering why it didn't apply to him. Celcy had died on the Enigma, and yet he, Tasmin, stilt felt as he always had about the Presences. Perhaps women were different. His mother had always told him that they were. 'And you've been alone since then?' he asked her.

'Not exactly alone. I have good friends. And there was a talented services man in Northwest City. I took advantage of his good nature from time to time. Zimmy. Of course, Zimmy was spying on me, as I should have known he would. I saw his face the last time I returned to Northwest. You'd have to know Zimmy for it to make sense, but he didn't expect me to be back.'

When she explained how she knew, Tasmin commented, 'Not a lot to go on. Just the expression on a man's face.'

'I said you'd have to know Zimmy. Believe me, he expected never to see me again.'

Tasmin's eyes narrowed and his mouth stretched in a silent grimace. 'Who's the one who gave the orders, Don? Who hired him?' The man who hired Zimmy had hired the assassin. The man who hired the assassin was the man who had driven Don Furz underground, causing her to conspire with Lim. And that man was ultimately responsible for Lim's and Celcy's death.

'The top of BDL, most likely. Harward Justin is an evil man. I know that about him for sure.'

'I've never met Harward Justin.' But that's where the ultimate responsibility probably lay. Tasmin nodded to himself over this. If there was fault, that's where it lay.

She shivered. 'I met him once. Luckily, I'd just comeback from a trip and I looked like a wet viggy.'

'Why luckily?'

'I've been told I'm attractive. And I've been told that Justin has an appetite for attractive women. And he doesn't let them tell him no.'

For a moment he thought she was going to say something more about this, but she fell into an abstracted and painful silence that it would have seemed impertinent to interrupt.

By late afternoon, they had begun to climb once more, and well before dark they had reached a crest of hills lined with tiny amber 'lets, no higher than their knees. Far to the east stood the golden Presence from which these small crystals had come.

'An old streambed,' Donatella explained. 'It washed the seed crystals down here in almost a straight line. I believe that's how a lot of the straight ramparts formed originally. A million years ago, there was nothing there but a river. Now there's a mountain range.'

'We're moving onto high country,' he agreed. 'I want to get a view behind us if I can.'

He dismounted and lay among the crowded 'lets, peering through his glasses back along their trail. At last he spotted them, moving figures well inside the limit of vision. 'They're there. Still coming, and they're past the side trail where Clarin and Jamieson turned off.'

'How many?'

'All six. None of them have gone after the youngsters. I don't know whether to be glad or sorry.'

'They're closer than when Jamieson saw them, aren't they? Only two or three hours behind.'

'My guess would be yes.'

'If we only had a moon, we could keep going late tonight, walk and lead the mules.'

'They may keep coming anyhow,' he said, staring through the glasses back the way they had come. There was something implacable about the lead rider, something relentless in the angle of his body. He exclaimed, 'Damn!'

She peered through her own glasses. Now for the first time, they saw, trailing the group, a mule hostler with a string of unburdened animals.

'They have fresh mounts,' Don whispered. 'No wonder they're moving so fast. If they catch us before we reach the south end of the valley ...'

'We can't outrun them,' Tasmin said. 'We'll have to think of something else.'

He thought as they rode, stopping twice to pick over bunches of green settler's brush, which he whittled at on the way.

'What in hell are you doing?' Donatella asked.

'Being inventive again, Donatella. I'll let you know if it works,' he told her, trying to sound more confident than he felt. Half an hour later he had four flat disks of settler's brush, thick spirals of narrow branches, made to fit tightly inside mule shoes.

He showed them to her. 'We're going to tie these onto our feet, just as soon as we find someplace we can hide the mules. Then we're going to go on, leaving a false mule trail, until we can find a place to hide ourselves – a small place that they won't think of searching, because they'll be looking for people and mules, not people alone.'

'Hide the mules where?'

'I don't know where. I'm praying we can find a place.'

They did find a place, across a little stream and up a draw, a dense grove of Jubal trees in a tiny box canyon on the opposite side of the narrow valley from the trail. They rode their animals down to the stream, leaving a clear trail, and taking time to water the animals well. Then they led the animals over rock up the curving draw and tied them deep among the trees. On their return, they wiped out all prints, then donned the false mule shoes and walked back to the trail from the stream, leaving clear but infrequent imprints.

'We'll come back for them when the pursuit passes us by,' Tasmin asserted, allowing no doubt to creep into his voice.

Donatella stopped on the trail to wipe her forehead and settle the straps of her pack. They had left most of their gear on the mules, taking only what was needed for survival. 'What if we didn't get the tracks into that grove completely wiped out? What if they don't believe the tracks? What if they go down into that draw?'

'Then they'll have two more mules and most of our equipment. But they still won't have us. Now we have to leave as much trail as we can before dark.'

Walking on the false mule shoes was neither easy nor quick. Twice in the following hour they spied on their pursuers, who were drawing frighteningly close. The second time, Donatella saw them clearly and she put the glasses down with an expression of horrified surprise that she didn't offer to explain. Tasmin let her alone. Attempting a mulelike pace while keeping his balance on the false mule feet required total concentration.

They had not gone far enough to satisfy him when it began to grow dark. 'We can't go much farther, Donatella. The soil is getting shallower along here. If we just keep going, we may find ourselves on a barren slope when they catch up with us. I wish I knew for sure what they intended. It might make a difference ...'

Her abstracted silence broke with a rush of words. 'I know what they intend. Killing. Torture. One of them is a man I know about, Tasmin. I saw him through my glasses, saw him clearly. I've seen that face before. I know who he is.' Her voice faded to silence, as though the name could not be uttered.

'Tell me,' he ordered.

'His name is Geroan,' she answered. 'He works for BDL, for Harward Justin. He's an assassin. A hired killer.'

'How do you know?'

'A friend of mine met him. She told me about Spider Geroan.' Donatella had turned white herself, from something more than mere recollection of what a friend might have said. Tasmin waited for her to go on, but she bit her lip and was silent.

'We have the rifle,' he offered.

'We daren't use it. The moment we use it, they'll be sure we're here. And we only have one rifle. They probably have six or seven.'

'True,' he nodded. 'You're right. They can't know we're here. Not yet. Not for sure.'

'It's been a long time since I came this way, but I don't think there's anything ahead of us to help. It gets more and more barren the farther up this valley we go, and narrower. There's no way out on either side. Just precipices with no passes through them. The only ways out are back, the way we came, where the pursuers are right now, or at the southern end . . .'

Where they were seemed barren enough, a slope of hard igneous rock that looked as though it had not changed since it had been spewed out molten except to be sparsely netted with soil-filled cracks. There were only a few stunted Jubal trees, their meager fans trembling in the chill wind. Occasionally there were veins of softer, lighter stone running parallel with the trail: pale, sedimentary strata, the bottom of some ancient sea, layered between stripes of the harder stone by cycle after cycle of vulcanism and alluvium, one replacing the other.

As they moved on, these veins tilted into a wall on their right, at first low, then towering, a striped and undulating outcropping where the softer strata had been eaten away to leave shadowed pockets between the wind-smoothed shelves of harder rock.

As his eyes and mind searched for a hiding place, Tasmin chewed over what Donatella had said about the man following them. There had been fear in her voice, abject fear, more fear than would have been occasioned by no more than she had told him. It was not merely that the man was an assassin. Tasmin started to ask her, then caught himself. She was already afraid. Talking about it might only make it worse.

He turned his mind to the stone, concentrating on it, searching for something his traveler's sense told him must be there, somewhere . . .

'Stop,' he cried The trail curved to the right around the slope where wind had chewed deeply between the layers, making horizontal crevices that held darkness in their depths. One of these pockets, slightly above their heads, was almost entirely hidden behind fragments fallen from the shelf above. 'There,' he pointed. At one side of the shelf a hole gaped, thicker than their bodies, accessible from the trail by a tumbled stairway of fallen rock.

He was halfway up the stones before she reacted enough to follow him. He was inside the cleft, exploring its sloping depth, before she reached the shelf. 'Come in,' he whispered, wary of the echoes his voice might rouse. 'It slopes back, away from the trail. Some of the rocks have rolled back here. Help me push some of them up to narrow the hole we came through!' He thrust one of the stones toward her, and she rolled sideways to push it still farther. Within moments they had cleared themselves a hidden crawlspace with ledges of stone above and below and walls of broken rock around them. The wind came through the crevices with many shrill complaints and the late light of evening fell slantingly in frail, reedlike beams, lighting Don's pale face and wide, apprehensive eyes.

'It'll be fairly dark by the time they get here,' he said, one hand squeezing her shoulder. 'I'm going out and lay additional mule tracks, around the corner and down a bit farther. They may use lights to see the trail, but in the dusk this wall will look solid, as though this crack were full of stone.'

He slipped out and onto the trail, seeking out tiny patches of soil that would take clear imprints of the false hooves. When he had gone half a mile farther, he came to a split in the trail, which he traveled until it petered out onto rock, and more rock stretching endlessly away to the south. Then he pocketed the mule shoes, climbed the wall and scrambled back the way he had come, careful to leave no visible trace, grateful for the wind that might be presumed to have blown their tracks away.

She was waiting for him with stones ready to plug the hole behind him. Their two mattresses were already inflated on the roughly rippled stone. 'Thank God for an inflatable mattress,' she murmured. 'We'll have to be quiet. It'll be easier with something soft under us.' Her voice broke into a gasping sob.

He pulled her toward him, almost roughly. 'You've been strange ever since you saw them,' he said. 'Ever since you saw that man. There's more to it than you've told me.' He stretched out on his own mattress and drew her down beside him, watching her face. One eye was lit from the side by a last vagrant beam of sunset light, that eye tear-filled and spilling. 'Tell me.'

She gasped. Her teeth were gritted. He saw the muscle at the corner of her jaw, clenched tight.

'Will you tell me,' he asked. 'Don't you think I should know?'

'I had a friend,' she said. 'A good friend. Her name was Mechas, Gretl Mechas. She came from Heron's World, on contract to the Department of Exploration. Not an Explorer. She was in procurement and accounting. They housed her in the Priory in Northwest because there was extra space there. We got to know one another very well ...'

Tasmin waited, waited longer, then said, 'Go on.'

'She got word her sister was in need of something back on Heron's World. Gretl never told me what it was. She seemed a little annoyed about it, in fact, like the kid had gotten herself into Home kind of trouble. Anyhow, Gretl needed money to send home. She went down to Splash One, to the BDL credit authority. She could have done it all by com, but Gretl was like that. She liked to do things personally.'

'Yes.'

'When she got back she told me she'd met Harward Justin. He'd stopped by the loan desk while she was there, and he'd been pretty persistent in asking her to have lunch with him. She told me she'd refused him though he hadn't made it easy. You'd have to have seen Gretl in order to visualize this properly, Tasmin. She was stunning. Men did pester her, but she didn't take it seriously because she was in love with someone back on Heron's. She laughed about it when she told me. She said Justin looked like a Jubal toad-fish, fat and greasy and with terrible little eyes ...

'Anyhow, when she went to make her first payment, they told her Justin had paid off the loan. She owed him, personally. She left her payment in an envelope for him, but as she was leaving, that man – that Spider Geroan – accosted her and told her Justin wanted to see her.'

'Yes.'

'She was very strong-willed, Gretl. Indomitable. Spider Geroan took her to Justin's office, there in the BDL building. Justin told her how he wanted her to pay the debt, and she told him she would pay her debt on the terms she had incurred when she took it, nothing else.

'When she got back she was angry. I'd never seen her so angry before. And she told me what Justin said. Justin told her he'd paid her debt, now she owed him. He told her people had to pay him what they owed him, or else. He said if she wouldn't have him, then Geroan could have her. And he laughed when he said it.

'She told me about it, shaking her head over it, furious, not able to believe the man. She reported it to the Priory office and to the Explorer King, both personally and in writing. Technically, it was a violation of the union contract. The contract doesn't allow sexual harassment ...

'Two days later they found her in the alley out behind the Priory, there in Northwest. Her flesh cut in little pieces, all over, like noodles. Head, face, everywhere. Her clothing and personal things were dumped on top of the body. Except for her clothing, we couldn't have identified her. I tried to believe it was someone else, but the clothes were hers. No one could have recognized her. Whoever did it had rubbed something into the cuts to keep her from bleeding to death right away. And then dumped her there. Like a message.'

'And you think it was Geroan?'

'I know it was. I went to the protector that investigated her death and I screamed at him to find who was responsible. I told him about Harward Justin trying to use her, about his threatening her. The protector got me out of there, took me for a walk, and he whispered to me that if I didn't want the same thing to happen to me, I'd keep my mouth shut. He was scared, Tasmin. Really scared. He said they knew who did it, who'd been doing it for years, but they couldn't touch him because he had people to swear he was in Splash One when it happened. He even showed me pictures of the man. His name was Spider Geroan, they said, and he worked for Harward Justin. Then I remembered what Gretl had told me. She wouldn't give Justin what he wanted, so he told Spider he could have her ...'

'She'd been raped I suppose,' Tasmin said, sickness boiling in his stomach.

'No,' she choked. 'Nothing so normal as that. Geroan isn't interested in sex. He isn't even interested in dominance, which is what most rape is anyhow. No, the protector said Geroan has something wrong with his nervous system. He can't feel pain, so it fascinates him. Watching people in pain is the only pleasure he has ...'

Donatella shuddered into gulping sobs, and he took her in his arms, pulling his blanket over them both. There was a sound, and they tensed, listening. It came again. Far down the trail, the way they had come, a voice shouting. Had they found the mules? He shivered. Why else would they call out?

Following that so and, he felt only fear, her fear, shared, her trembling and his, their bodies cold under the hasty covering, their senses strained for the first breath of sound that would presage the arrival of the adversary, the enemy, perhaps Geroan, who would use them for an arcane and terrible pleasure, perhaps someone else merely seeking their deaths and not particular about how these deaths were to be brought about.

He was caught in the story she had told about Spider Geroan. What did such a man think or feel, or remember? Did he humiliate and degrade his victims so he could come to despise them, making murder seem a deserved end rather than a despicable corruption? Did he feel anything about them? Did he remember at all? Was his pleasure physical? Was it transitory? Was there some quiet orgasm of the mind that substituted for pleasure of the senses? Since he could not feel pain, could he feel anything? How did one communicate with someone who could not feel at all?

It would be, he thought, like being killed slowly by a machine. Pleading would mean nothing. The device would be programmed to inflict pain, and it would not care what the victim said or did.

Tasmin clenched his teeth tight to keep from shaking. He had always feared pain. The prospect of pain filled him with horror. He imagined blood, wounds, deep intrusions into organs and bone. Bile filled his throat and he gulped, then blanked it out. His way of dealing with the horror was not to think of it. He had seen students, mad with fear of the Presences, run directly toward them, and he wondered what it would take to break his own mind and make him behave in such a way. He had learned to blank out such thoughts, and he did so now, erasing them, thinking only of darkness and quiet.

Donatella was remembering the body of her friend and was wondering whether she had the courage to take her own life before she fell into Geroan's hands. Her knife was under the mattress, where she could reach it. She was not sure reaching it would be enough. She clung to Tasmin, thinking of begging him to help her, not let her be taken by that man. The terror built into a spasm of shaking, and then ebbed away, leaving her limp.

Her face was buried in his shoulder, against his naked skin where his shirt had come unfastened under his Tripsinger's cloak. Her cheek was on his chest, her breath moving softly into the cleft of his arm, where the hairs quivered, as in a tiny wind.

The tickling breath came into the blankness Tasmin had evoked, came as a recollection, a summer hillside, grass beneath him, Jubal trees along the ridge, himself lying with his arms around Celcy and the warm, moist breeze of summer cooling the pits of his shoulders. Celcy's head was on his chest, her lips on his skin. Now, as then, he felt the hairs moving in a dance of their own and responded to the diminutive titillation as he had then, by turning a little, moving her body more solidly onto his own, moving his arm more closely around her. One of her legs fell between his, a sudden, unexpectedly erotic pressure, and he raised his own leg in surprise, bringing it into intimate contact with her.

She gasped, becoming very still, and he felt the quick heat between them. They breathed together, her lips opening on his skin, her hand moving between them to pull her shirt away. Then the skin of her breasts was naked against his own, her nipples brushing his chest as she thrust herself up from him to tug at the belt around her waist.

He felt a ripple across his belly as the silken belt that had held her full trousers tight around her slender form pulled free. He saw the sash through half closed eyes, a ribbon of scarlet. Then there was nothing between his leg and the furry mound of her groin except the fabric of his trousers.

Blood beat in his ears. He shut his eyes, not wanting to think or see, wishing he could shut his ears as well and let the surging feeling wash over him in silent darkness, with only the sunlit meadow filling all the space around him. She made no sound, merely raised away from him a little so he could free himself from his clothing, only as much as necessary, soundlessly. There was no time for anything more than that, no time for anything between them except this urgency, no time for avowals or questions or even words. They existed separately, in a place remote from time or occurrence.

Their bodies slid together in a continuous, gulping thrust, then lay joined, scarcely stirring, needing scarcely to shift, the tiniest motion amplified between them as though by some drug or device into a cataclysm of feeling. She pushed only a little, the smallest thrust of her body toward him and away, and they were gasping, uncontrolled, grasped inexorably by a continuous quiver that swept them up and over a towering wave of sensation to leave them floundering in the trough, blood hammering in their ears.

'Aaah,' she moaned in an almost soundless whisper. 'Aaaah.'

'Shhh.' He whispered in return. 'Celcy ...' The fear was gone. His body was disassembled. There was a violent pain behind his ears from the spasms that had seized his neck and jaw in a giant's vise, but even this seemed remote and unimportant.

Then there was the sound of a voice, the rattle of gravel, and the vision of meadowlands shattered as his eyes snapped open. Coming toward them was the crunch of hooves, a voice cursing monotonously.

Their bodies lay flaccid, boneless, like two beings mashed into one creature, that creature scarcely aware. Through a chink in the piled stones, Tasmin could see through slitted eyes a dim segment of the path extending back the way they had come. A line of mules. Two Explorers, one of them on foot examining the trail with a lantern, then the man Donatella had said was Spider Geroan with a another rider behind him, dark and silent as a shadow. Then the string of riderless mules. They went past in a shuffle of feet, a roll and rattle of gravel. After a long gap a bald man and a tired, smudge-faced woman approached.

The final hooves came closer, passing the ledge with a scratch and click of stone against stone, then went on to the south. The voice they had heard before cursed again, at repetitive length. The woman answered, briefly and whiningly, the two finally complaining their way into silence behind the rocky rampart.

The pain in Tasmin's head departed, leaving a vacancy behind. Her body clenched on him like a squeezing hand, and he moved once more, this time slowly, languorously, lifting her with his body, holding her there with his hands while he dropped away, then pulling her down once more, over and over again, impaling her, holding her tight to him as he rolled over upon her and thrust himself into her. The wave came again, slowly, building and cresting, carrying them with it into the dark depths of a strange ocean.

The first time it had been Celcy. This time it was no one at all. He sought a name and could not find one as nonsense words flicked by, babbling rhymes, childlike sounds. Perhaps the name he wanted was an exotic word in some foreign tongue, a question without an answer.

'Mmmm,' she sighed.

He did not know who it was. Who either of them were.

They slept as their fleeting hunger had dropped them, disarrayed, close coupled, slowly moving apart as the night wore on until dawn found them still side by side, but separate. When Tasmin awoke, it was to a strange dichotomy, a bodily peace surpassing anything he had known for months coupled with an anxiety for which he could not, for the moment, find an object.

When he saw who lay beside him, both body and mind were answered. She opened her eyes to see his own fixed on her, accusingly.

'We aren't dead,' she said in response to this unspoken indictment. 'I expected to be dead by this morning.'

His instant reaction had been a twitch of revulsion, a feeling very much akin to guilt. The feeling passed as he said Donatella's name to himself, leaving only a faint residue of grief behind. 'You're disappointed,' he murmured, feeling hysterical laughter welling within him. 'Ah, Donatella, you do sound a little put out.'

She flushed. 'It's not that. It's just that I ...'

He felt a surge of sympathy. 'You wouldn't have ... I know. Neither would I. We thought we were going to die. Or maybe our bodies thought so. Well – it happened. Forget it.'

There was a silence. She seemed to be considering this. 'Yes. I think you're right. It didn't matter what I did. I would never need to explain it, not to myself, not to anyone, because there wouldn't be any tomorrow ...'

He was stung into an irrational objection. 'It may be petulant of me, but did it really take that to make you want to make love to me?' He tried to smile to take the sting out of his words, but the wound to his vanity was there. Amazing! He was wounded because a woman he hardly knew felt she needed to explain away her actions regarding him.

'You know better,' she said sharply. 'You, of all people! It didn't take that to make me want to make love to you. It wasn't really making love, Tasmin, and it wasn't really you. I haven't made love, not for years. Not to anyone. Not since ...'

'Not since?'

'Not since Link.' She sat up, pulling the blanket around her while she fumbled with her disordered clothes, crouching for a moment to shake herself into some semblance of order, tugging at her tunic searching for her sash. 'We weren't casual lovers, Link and I. We were fellow Explorers. Colleagues. Friends. For him, there isn't any more. For me there isn't either. Not really.'

'I thought you told me about that man, what's his name? The services man?'

'Zimmy? Zimmy was just ... like getting my hair done. When things got too tight. Too rough. He was talented in that way, Zimmy. With him it wasn't love, it was skill. Technique. It wasn't making love.'

'And last night wasn't either.'

'In a way it was.'

'Only a way?' His irrationally hurt pride was giving way to curiosity.

She gave him a long, level look. 'In a way it was because I forgot you aren't Link. You're not Link, Tasmin. You're a lovely man and I think a dear friend, but you're not Link.'

'And you're not Celcy,' he said, wanting to get through her self-absorption, perhaps to wound her, only a little.

'Celcy's dead,' she said flatly. 'You need to forget. Part of you knows that, Tasmin. How long will you go on being married to Celcy? You called me by her name, you know. How long are you going to go on allowing yourself to love only if you pretend it's Celcy doing it? There are other people, you know. Clarin, for instance. She's in love with you.'

'Don't be ridiculous,' he said, thrusting his way through the stones that had hidden them. 'She's a child.'

'Child my left elbow. What is she? Eighteen, nineteen?' They slid down onto the trail, adjusting shoes and straps. 'What are you? My age, about? Thirtyish?'

'Thirty-two.'

'She's no child,' Donatella muttered.

He rejected all this. He had no intention of forgetting Celcy! 'Don't you need to forget Link and go on living, too?'

'No!' The cry came out uncontrollably, her hands went up in a pushing gesture, demanding that he take the words back. 'He's alive. If I could get him to Serendipity, if I could afford the fees, he could have regeneration. Everything that made Link himself is still there. It's only his body that won't let him out. It isn't the same as if he were dead!'

He felt a wave of empathy. 'Money? That's it, isn't it. That's what love comes down to sometimes. A fortune to space him to Serendipity, and you'll never have it. A fortune to get my blind mother to Splash One and pay for the treatment, and I don't have that. So, your Link stays in a support chair and my mother can't see.'

He didn't want to talk about this anymore. 'Have you stopped to think that if we're successful at proving the Presences sentient, we'll probably be shipped to Serendipity – for transshipment elsewhere, if nothing else. All of us. Every human person on Jubal. Which will include your friend Link, won't it? And my mother.'

She looked dazed. 'It … it never occurred to me.'

'We'd still have the treatment to pay for, but at least we'll he where it can be obtained.' He laughed, a little harshly but with some satisfaction as he saw her look of concern for him turn to one of confusion and dismay, and then to irritation.

'Oh, God, Tasmin, what are we talking about this for?'

'Exactly,' he murmured to himself, thankful that she was getting off the subject. Clarin! Of all idiotic ...

'I can't handle all this,' she went on. 'We may not even be alive tomorrow. We've got to get to the Enigma and Deepsoil Five. It'll take half a day to pick up the mules and get back where we are, and now they're ahead of us.' She shrugged her arms through the straps of the pack and started down the rocky shelf.

'Yes, but they don't know that yet,' he said, trailing her a half step behind. 'Which gives us the tiniest bit of an edge, Donatella. I think the time has come for us to break out of this valley and head straight for the Enigma.'

'We have to backtrack for the mules anyhow, and there are some routes east. Rough transit, though. No Passwords for a good part of this country east of us. Let me thing about it.' She rubbed her head. 'When we get to the mules, I'll take a look at the charts.'

He agreed, shrugging the straps into a more comfortable position. The trail sloped downward to the place they had left the mules. And the mules would be rested. If they went to the east ... 'Pray God Jamieson and Clarin get to Thyle Vowe ...'

'You're placing a lot of hope in a couple of children,' she said sarcastically.

'Clarin's no child,' he said absently, only then realizing what he had said.

At that moment, Clarin and Jamieson were re-entering the north-south valley in a mood of defeat. Clarin was frankly crying, tears of weariness and frustration, and Jamieson's face showed a similar, although more controlled emotion.

'We'll never catch up to them,' she said hopelessly. 'And now the trackers are between them and us.'

'We know where they're going,' Jamieson replied. 'So, we'll meet them there. Or we'll get ourselves to Deepsoil Five and ask the Master General to help us someway. I don't know, Clarin. I wish you'd stop crying.'

'I'm tired! We haven't slept since we left Tasmin and Don, and there's no point in trying to pretend I'm rested and cheerful. I'm scared, too. God, Jamieson, with what we found out, aren't you? I'll cry for a while and get it out of my system. A good cry is almost as good as a night's sleep.'

'It's very hard for me to control myself when you do that. I find myself wanting to hug you.'

'Up a gyre-bird's snout,' she remarked rudely, wiping her face with grubby hands. 'Since when?'

'Oh, I don't know,' he mused. 'You're huggable.'

'Not by you, Jamieson.'

He turned away so she would not see his face. 'Got your mind set on him, don't you?'

'I don't know what you're talking about.'

'Up a bantigon's end flap you don't. You're wasting your time, Clarin. He was brou-dizzy over his little wife when she was alive, and he still is.'

Clarin sighed and wiped her face on her sleeve. 'All right, Reb. Just between us, yes. I'm tracked on the man. He's a little stiff, a little humorless. Some days I think he's got a Tripsinger score where his sex urge ought to be. But when he talks, it's like he's reading my mind.'

'You're what he ought to have had, Clarin. But he didn't. He had a little girl who never had the least idea what was going on in his head. You never met her, but I did.'

'What was she like?'

'Like? She was ... she was a lot like Wendra Gentrack. Edible. And sweet. Like some baby animal, soft, and giggly. Kind of fearful. Not interested in much. A good cook. Beautiful looking. She only had one way to act toward men, flirtatious. She didn't mean anything by it. She fluffed up even for me, and I'm nobody.'

'I wouldn't say that,' she objected softly.

He shook his head in mock protest, going on. 'What I mean is, you got this very strong urge to take care of her, even when she didn't need it. She'd give this little breathless laugh or sigh, like a child, and you'd feel your chest swelling with protective fervor.' He laughed. 'Not like you, Clarin. Not independent.'

'No, I haven't noticed myself arousing any of that protective fervor.'

'She couldn't relate to women at all – always had her claws out. And that was fear, I figured out. She had any woman between the ages of eight and eighty slotted as a possible competitor. Poor Master Ferrence could only sneak over to see his mother when she wasn't looking. I'd always figured it was lucky we didn't have any women Tripsingers at Deepsoil Five, or she'd have made his life miserable.'

'She's dead,' Clarin said. 'That sounds hard, but it's the simple truth, Reb. She's dead. She's not going to come back from the bottom of the Enigma. She's gone. Eventually, he'll realize that. If there is any eventuality. I keep forgetting there may not be ...'

'You're planning on being around if he does?'

'If any of us are still alive, you bet your sex life I do.' She managed a rueful smile, then stiffened. Her eyes had caught a tiny motion, far down the valley.

'Give me the glasses,' she said, with an imperative gesture. 'Quick!'

She stared, searching the clearing where the movement had caught her eye.

'It's them,' she said, disbelieving. 'Tasmin and Don.'

'Alone?'

'All alone. On foot. Coming back this way. They must have hidden the mules. Or lost the mules. Or the way's blocked down them; as it was for us.' She urged her tired animal into a trot. 'Come along, acolyte. We're not as alone as I thought we were.'

Jamieson's report to Tasmin of their effort to find an open route to the west made it clear they had no other choice than to return. 'We were cut off,' Jamieson snarled. 'We tried three routes west, and every one of them had an encampment of troops arrayed across it. Guards, sentries, whatever. With life detectors of some kind, too. They damn near caught us!'

'Every trooper with weapons bristling all over him,' Clarin said. 'We've thought all along that Justin had the troopers in his pocket. Now we know for sure. Half the garrison is camped between us and the 'Soilcoast. They had Explorers with them. Jamieson spied out one group last night.'

'They were talking about guarding the routes out of the Presences,' Jamieson said. 'Except for regular brou caravans, anyone coming from the west is supposed to be stopped. The troopers were arguing with the Explorers whether it would be acceptable to engage in a little robbery and rape in the process. The Explorers were really tense about the whole thing – sitting back-to-back kind of tense. Somebody in that setup is going to get killed!'

'How did the Explorers get mixed up in this?'

'I got the impression they didn't really know what was going on, Master Ferrence. They'd been hired to bring the troopers in because no Tripsingers were available.'

'Not available!' Tasmin's exclamation was sheer reflex. Tripsingers were always available!

Clarin sighed. She looked exhausted, damp ringlets of hair scalloping her cheeks and forehead. 'Thyle Vowe has obviously sent the word to the citadels that Tripsingers are not to lead Troopers anywhere. The word may not have reached the interior yet, but there's been plenty of time for Vowe to tie up the Coast.'

'It would explain what happened,' Tasmin agreed thoughtfully.

Clarin's voice shook as she said, 'Listen, Tasmin. We haven't told you the worst thing yet. The troopers were doing a lot of talking about the equipment they had with them.'

'Demolition equipment,' explained Jamieson. 'White noise projectors and chemical explosives with various kinds of propulsion devices. I snooped around a little while Clarin yodeled down a canyon to draw them off. She sounded exactly like about twenty Tripsingers on a practice trip through the Crazies. The troopers thought there were at least a dozen of her, all female, so the putative rapists went zipping off in pursuit.'

'Clarin!' cried Tasmin. 'What happened?'

'They ran into some 'lings and about half of them got killed,' she said with a calmness that was belied by her shaking hands and bloodless lips. 'I was lying above them on a parapet I'd got through to by using Don's machine.'

'It gave me plenty of time,' Jamieson said, irrepressibly. 'I got a good look at the equipment they're carrying. I also got away with a copy of their map.' He drew it from one of the deep pockets of his robe and unfolded it, spreading it on the ground before them. It was a satellite map of the area stretching from Deepsoil Five on the east to the Deepsoil Coast on the west and from the southern coast to the Jut.

'Justin isn't going to waste any time,' Clarin said, pointing to the markings on the map. The Watchers, the Startles, the Creeping Desert, the Mad Gap, the list went on and on, all marked for destruction, with a line of march leading from demolition site to demolition site as the road was cleared before them. They wouldn't need any Tripsingers. There wouldn't be anything to get in their way!

Tasmin shivered. He felt suddenly cold, as though it was his own body someone had scheduled for destruction. As soon as the Commission findings were announced, Justin would begin!

Don interrupted his musing, angrily. 'I recognized the voice of that woman on the trail last night. Her name is Sells. She's some high mucky muck among the Crystallites. I heard her speak once in the Crystallite Temple in Splash One. What was she doing with Geroan?'

He replied, 'Well, you know that Geroan works for Justin. I think you can assume that the Crystallites also work for Justin. Probably they always have.'

'The Crystallites!'

'I imagine Harward Justin had the commission arranged for even before the Jut massacre,' he said. 'The massacre was simply the opening shot in the BDL war, the dramatic "incident" he needed to reopen the sentience question.'

'He's a monster! All those people ...'

'Do you think Justin cares? After what you told me about him?'

'Is he the one at the top?'

'He's at the top on Jubal, that's certain.' And at the top of my particular list, he thought. 'Which doesn't help us at the moment.' He nodded at Jamieson and Clarin. 'You two did a good job. Don't look so downcast.'

'I don't know what to do next,' Clarin sighed, then sighed again, patting a pocket, complaining tearfully like a child. 'And I lost my mouse.'

She looked up at Tasmin, wishing in that instant she could make him respond as Celcy had evidently done. She could use a little comforting, a little protection.

He started to extend his hand toward her, then stopped himself, accusing himself, accusing Donatella. He couldn't hug Clarin now, not after what Don had said. The whole thing was ridiculous. He had no place in his life for Clarin, not now, not when a world hung in the balance.

Clarin turned away, confused by the expression on his face, a rejection that she had done nothing to provoke. She blinked back tears and walked away from them, barely noticing the ironic twist of Donatella's lips. Jamieson came after her, standing beside her as she stared back down the valley, the way they had come.

'You need some sleep, lady.'

She did not see the yearning on his face. She responded only to his words. 'Amen, Reb. Sleep. And two or three other little things I can think of.'

From behind them, Tasmin's voice came in its usual matter-of-fact intonation, as though there was no whirlpool of feelings boiling among them, as though there had been no crisis, no imminent threat, no assassins after them, no map of disaster, no anything that mattered at all. 'Get a little rest, Clarin, Jamieson. There won't be any for the next few days. Don and I have picked a route out of this valley. With what you've told us, we can't waste any time. We'll have to head straight for the Enigma.'

14

The office of the Grand Master in the tower of the citadel at Splash One was a disaster area – or so Thyle Vowe thought, looking it over.

'Can't we throw some of this stuff away,' he asked plaintively from among the litter of cube copy, handwritten notes, and files of untidy correspondence.

Gereny Vox looked up from the box she was packing. 'If you're not interested in having documents to base a case on later, sure. We could just burn the place down and get rid of it all.'

'It's all in the computers anyhow,' he said doubtfully, not really believing it.

'You sure? You sure Justin doesn't have a mouse here in the citadel somewhere, wiping away anythin' that Justin wouldn't want to come out later on? Listen, Thyle! If I can find Crystallites workin' in my own stables, you can find a mouse or two chirpin' away here in the citadel. Believe me. Anyhow, I'm almost through.'

'Where did you and Jem decide to put the stuff?'

'We found an empty brou warehouse near the docks in Tallawag. It's far enough north of Splash One not to get interfered with, and it's close enough we can hide out there a while if we need to.'

'An empty warehouse? That'd be scarce as red meat! How'd you find one of those.'

'Well, somebody favorable to our side of things boggled a few records is what happened. So far as BDL's facility files're concerned, the place is packed with obsolete equipment. So far as the equipment inventory files're concerned, it's full of dried brou. So far as the brou shipment schedule files're concerned, it was emptied last flight out. The auditors might catch up to it in a year or two, but by then it shouldn't matter. Right now it's got my mule breedin' files and Jem's agridiv files, and anythin' else he or Rheme Gentry thinks is important enough to hold onto – includin' at least six copies of all the evidence Rheme's come up with in the Governor's office – along with all the stun rifles we could steal from the armory and all the charge cubes we could steal from troop supply. There's some mighty corruptible folks out there, Thyle. Makes you real sad, seein' what the world's come to.'

'You're sly, Gereny,' he said admiringly. 'That's what you are. You and Jem are a pair. And you takin' pay from BDL, too.'

'Pair of old mules is what we are,' she said comfortably. 'Just because BDL fills our feed trough doesn't mean we won't kick 'em if they need it. We may not be able to prove sentience, which is what I bet Don's up to, but we'll sure as hell prove corruption. You heard anything about Don yet?'

'Just enough to worry me quite a bit.'

'That girl of yours get any information back to you?'

'Not a word. No, I sent a couple of 'Singers up Redfang way the day after we sent Tasmin Ferrence. My 'Singers found bodies, more of 'em than there should have been, but none of 'em people we were worried about. They found tracks, too, headed back into the range. Four sets. I figure that means Don Furz is in good company.'

'Includin' Renna.'

'I do worry some about her,' he confessed.

'Well, why'd you send your own daughter off on a fool trip like that?'

'Because she was with Tasmin and his other acolyte, and because accordin' to you there were only three or four Crystallites to worry about – instead of about a dozen assassins, which is what there turned out to be accordin' to the tracks – and because Renna and I agreed nobody was to know she's my daughter because she says it makes her life difficult. I gave her my word. She started callin' herself Clarin and moved away from Northwest where people knew about it. Clarin was her mama's name. My Princess. Did you see what those pagans did to her hair, down there in Five? She had the prettiest hair ...'

'You don't want citadels cuttin' neophytes' hair, all you have to do is tell 'em so. You think somethin's happened to her?'

'No,' he grumped. 'No, I don't. Tasmin's clever. And that Jamieson is cleverer than two Tasmins. He could sing his way by the Black Tower in the dark with a high wind blowing. And Renna's no fool-child, herself. No, I think they got driven back into the range and are bottled up in there. They'll get to a citadel eventually. Hope they've got sense enough to stay there until all this is over.'

He went into a silent communion with his worries, fumbling papers from one pile to another until Gereny asked, 'You knew the discipline stockade was found empty, and all the hard cases have disappeared along with most of the regular troops and a whole batch of weaponry?'

'Captain Jines Verbold told me, yes. Came to me at home, kind of snuck around so's nobody'd see him, said it happened without his knowledge or help, and I believe him. Verbold says his men are the only ones left around, barely enough of 'em to round up the Crystallites – which he had orders to do. Colonel Lang is showin' his true colors, Gereny.'

'Well, what are you doin' about it?'

'I've got every citadel on alert. I've cut off Tripsingers, so he can't use them to get anyplace. Trouble is, Gereny, there wasn't any pressure to get Tripsingers. Which means ...'

'Which means Justin figures he won't need 'em, right?'

'Doesn't need and doesn't want. That's the way I see it, yes. So, I've sent Tripsingers here and Tripsingers there, the ones with the best rifle scores, and I've sent some noise projectors and what not. Way I got it figured, this is pretty rough country and those troops haven't seen action in a long, long time. One good rifleman ought to be able to pin down a lot of troops, don't you think? Blow up some 'lings on top of 'em. Delay 'em some','

'Delay 'em maybe. I don't think you'll stop 'em.'

'No, Gereny, I don't either. We'll need some help to do that.'

'Did your Captain tell you the troops had some Explorers with 'em?'

The Grand Master scowled at her. 'Chase Random Hall has had both hands out for a long time. He probably called in a few loyalty chits, told a few more lies. Some fool young Explorers think loyalty's more important than good sense.' Thyle ran both hands through his white hair and sighed. 'Hall's been their union rep for years, sold 'em out on almost every issue, and they still vote for him and pay him his fealty. Makes you wonder what some people use for brains.'

'Rheme's trying to get a message out asking for a gunship, is he?'

'Why the hell else are we gettin' ready to evacuate the citadel, Gereny? Say the PEC figures it has enough evidence of corruption it gets itchy and calls for Justin's resignation and the Governor's. Up until just recent, Rheme was gettin' a lot of information out, and I figure the PEC might figure it had about enough evidence by now. Say Justin or Wuyllum or both orders out the whole army to defend 'em and refuse to budge. Be dumb of either of 'em, but they might do it anyhow.'

'Not the Governor. Rheme says he's gettin' ready to run. Any time now.'

'Well, Justin then. Say Justin digs himself in and won't move. It'd be like him. So, then, say the PEC decides to slash off BDL headquarters as a sort of object lesson. That happens I don't want to be sittin' here in the citadel, right on their doorstep, examinin' my belly button as my last view of anythin' mortal.'

'"Tisn't a bad belly button,' Gereny remarked in a discriminating tone.

'Lots've flesh I'd rather be lookin' at,' he replied, pinching a portion of Gereny's.

'You old bantigon,' she remarked fondly. 'Well, if you want to spend any of your declinin' years chasing women, you'd better go through this pile of stuff and tell me what we need to keep.' She put another file in a carton and thumped it to settle the contents. 'And you'd better start thinkin' up real good excuses to move everybody out without Honeypeach Thonks gettin' suspicious. She watches this place like she was a gyre-bird and we'd been dead for three days.'

'I know she does,' he said uncomfortably. The close surveillance Honeypeach exercised over the citadel in Splash One had been one of his major concerns. 'I figured she'd be gone by the time we needed to move. Thought I might leave movin' 'til the last minute, Gereny, love. Assumin' there's goin' to be a last minute.'

Vivian Ferrence lay on a mattress inflated over a layer of crates in the bottom of a brou wagon, baby Miles bouncing on her stomach. Their journey had gone on for many days, and the anxieties of Splash One were beginning to give way to less painful feelings, though in an erratic and undependable fashion. She no longer had to worry whether Miles would have enough to eat on a given day. The food provided by the trip cook was monotonous but adequate. Flat bread. Beans or cheese or bean cheese. Dried fish or meat. A small ration of fresh fruits and vegetables. Once every four or five days, a bit of roasted fresh meat when one of the bantigons from the crate in the back of the cook wagon was slaughtered. There was milk for Miles, as well, artificial and reconstituted, but full of appropriate minerals nonetheless.

And there were cookies. The trip cook, Brunny, had an affinity for children, and cookies seemed mysteriously to materialize whenever Miles toddled around the cook wagon after lunch or during the evening halts.

During the night there were the peaceful stars and sleep that was better than she had had at any time recently. During the day, there was Tripsinging and the glory of the Presences. She had not been afraid. Even considering how Lim had died, she had not been afraid. Her acceptance was almost fatalistic, she realized. If she died on this journey, she would at least have had this period of peace and sufficient food and a warm bed. And memories. Lots of memories.

Night before last, just at sunset, they had seen a red sparkle on the eastern horizon, twin spires of iridescent scarlet. 'That's the Enigma,' the Tripmaster had announced. 'Be nice if there was a trail that way. It'd cut off about fifty miles. As it is, we turn north up ahead a ways, go on up through Harmony anti past the Black Tower. You can see the very tip of Old Blacky, sticking up there over that purple peak. Then Deepsoil Five, same day.'

Deepsoil Five. The feelings of peace fled, and Vivian became anxious once more. Why? She had accepted what Tasmin had told her. He hadn't known, his mother hadn't known. Much though she believed they should have known, she could not condemn them for something that had been between Lim and his father. Or, she could condemn them but chose not to. Chose, rather, to let baby Miles have a family – if only her mind could stop there, but it never did. It always went on, 'let Miles have a family even though they betrayed his daddy and ended up killing him.'

No matter how often she told herself that she did not condemn them, she ended up by doing exactly that. Betrayal, she moaned. Killing. Violent accusations against absent people she didn't even know. Each time she arrived at this point in her circular agony, she cried bitterly, then told herself all over again that they hadn't really done it. Tasmin had been seven years old when it happened; he had been only sixteen or seventeen when Lim left. Could she really hold a seven-year-old boy responsible? And Thalia, Tasmin's mother – she had been going blind even then. Perhaps that had been all the trauma she could handle. Her husband couldn't have been any help to her. Perhaps she had been unable to see anything at all.

So, alternately accusing and exonerating, Vivian had spent the recent hours gradually working herself out of the emotional maelstrom and into something approaching calm. Now, with the end of the journey in sight, that calm was disrupted and all the feelings of pain and anger were stirred once more.

'I have to stop this,' she whispered half-aloud. 'I have to stop it.'

''Top it,' said Miles. ''Top it, Mama.'

'I will,' she promised, laughing at him through teary eyes. 'I will. Are you going to go get some cookies from Mr. Brun?'

'Cookies,' Miles verified with a nod of his head. 'Yes. Cookies wit' nuts.'

'Where do you suppose Mr. Brun gets nuts?' she asked in pretend amazement.

'Viggy nuts,' crowed Miles, giggling. It was a story Brunny told him, about the viggies bringing nuts to trade for candy. Actually, there were no nuts on Jubal, and the sweet, hard nuggets in Brunny's cookies were merely sugary chunks of baked proto-meal, but Miles loved the viggy story.

'That's right.' She laughed with him, sitting up as the wagon slowed and stopped. 'Supper time, almost.' She was hungry tonight. She had noticed herself being a lot hungrier over the past week or so That was good. She had lost a lot of weight in the fish market, lost a lot buying food only for Miles because there wasn't enough money for food for them both. Lim wouldn't have known her, she had become so haggard. She didn't want Lim's mother to see her that way.

'But it doesn't make any difference,' she murmured to herself. Lim's mother was blind. She couldn't see. It didn't matter.

'All down. Mules to water,' cried the Tripmaster.

'Mools a wattah,' echoed Miles. 'Awl down.'

'All right, love. We'll get down.' She fumbled for her shoes and Miles's, finding them between two crates, and she was busy fastening straps when the Tripmaster arrived at the rear of the wagon.

'Everything all right, Mrs. Ferrence?'

'Everything's fine, Tripmaster.'

'Brunny says to bring the baby on over for his evening treat.' He regarded her curiously from pale, almost colorless eyes. He had known Lim Ferrence, he had told her, long ago, in school in Deepsoil Five. Without waiting for curious questions, she had told him what had happened to Lim when Lim was only a child. It was a kind of catharsis, telling it. The Tripmaster had said nothing more, nothing since, not about Lim, but he had been uniformly solicitous of her and the baby. 'Only a couple day, more, and we'll arrive. You lookin' forward to gettin' there?'

'I am, yes,' she half lied. 'I've never met Lim's mother.'

'She's blind, you know.'

'Yes, I know. Tasmin told me.'

'Pity. I remember her, too, before she was blind, that is. One of the prettiest women I'd ever seen. Lim always bragged on her. You look like her, you know. Like she did then.'

She was shocked. 'I didn't know!'

'Oh, yes. Same shape face. Same eyes and mouth. Same hair. You could be her daughter.' He stumped off, leaving her behind with her mouth open.

'Cookies,' demanded Miles.

She got down from the wagon and walked toward the cook wagon, Miles's sturdy legs bringing him steadily along at her heels. When he had received his cookies, she stood with him while he ate them, staring up at the long, dun-colored slopes around them. Open country. Groves of Jubal trees, turned to face the setting sun, plumes fanned wide. Far off, at the top of the western slope, she saw something moving, a speck on the horizon, miles and miles away against low clouds lit by sunset glow. 'Riders,' she pointed.

The cook followed her pointing finger, frowning. 'I don't see nothin'.'

'They were there,' she insisted. 'Riders.'

'Better tell Tripmaster,' Brun advised. 'There's not supposed to be anyone out here right now but us.'

The Tripmaster grunted when she told him, looking a little worried. 'Trouble?' she asked, apprehensively. 'Something wrong?'

'Oh, no. No. I should think not. It's just that there's been a good deal of ... oh, call it unrest. Over this CHASE Commission thing, most of it. People taking sides, and the Crystallites gettin' worse and worse.'

She shuddered. 'Sometimes I have bad dreams about Crystallites.'

'Don't we all. Well, I don't like people movin' around unless I know who they are.'

The man moved away and she and the boy returned to their wagon. She could sleep either in the wagon where they had traveled or under it or in a tent, if she preferred. There was little rainfall on this part of Jubal. What moisture there was came from the coast in vast, cottony fogs that rolled in at evening and burned away with the first light of morning, leaving the Jubal trees sodden with accumulated dew. When light came, every frond lifted, funneling the precious moisture down the trough-shaped veins and into hollow reservoirs below ground. More than one traveler had saved his life by drinking the bitter liquid when no other moisture was available, though no one would drink it by choice. If there was fog, it would be better to sleep in a tent, but there was no sign of fog tonight.

'Tent up?' asked Miles.

'I don't think so,' she told him. 'I think we'll take our mattresses over in that big grove of Jubal trees, little boy. Jubal trees smell so nice.' There would be a little privacy there, as well. She felt the need of a good, all-over wash, and her hair needed braiding.

'Smell nice,' he agreed. 'Jubal trees smell so nice.'

She gathered up their scattered belongings. They had so little that it would fit into one shoulder sack. Their few extra clothes and her books were in a crate at the bottom of the wagon. The sack and the mattress were not even a heavy load as she dragged them to the grove, some distance east of the wagons.

Miles helped her by dragging his own half-sized mattress after her, plopping it down beside hers within the grove. When it was dark, the trees would change from fan shape to a fountain shape, more efficient for fog catching, Vivian assumed, just as the fan shapes were more efficient for gathering sunlight. The result would make a shadowy grove that looked quite unlike the daytime one.

'Smell it, Mama,' Miles said now, bouncing on his bed and waiting for the trees to shift.

The sun was a ball, then a half drop, then merely a thin arc upon the horizon. Then nothing, and the trees let go with a rustling sigh, a long shushing. The fronds fell outward from the middle, and what had been two-dimensional shapes became plumy clouds gathering darkness beneath them.

'Supper,' she told Miles. 'Let's get supper quick, then we can come back here and watch the stars come out.'

There were viggies singing as they finished their meal and helped Brunny put away the disarranged implements and supplies.

'Where you stretched out for the night?' the Tripmaster asked. 'Over in that Jubal grove? Looks like a nice place if there's no fog. Not much danger tonight.' He looked up at the clear sky, hands busy with his trip log. 'Sleep well.'

By the time they returned to the mattresses under the Jubal trees, the first stars were trembling in the high eastern sky.

'You need to go behind a bush?' she asked.

'I went,' Miles said. 'All by myself.'

'Fine. Then you're going to sleep all night, without waking up, aren't you?'

'All night,' he agreed, snuggling onto the mattress. 'Tell Miles a story.'

She told a story until his eyes closed and his breathing became slow and quiet. Then she told a story to herself, as she gave herself a slow, cool sponge bath, as she brushed and rebraided her hair, as the stars came out to make a glittering diagonal band across the heavens, a story about tomorrow, about the future. She snuggled into her mattress, head pillowed on an arm, to drift in and out of sleep.

The sudden light and shout from the direction of the wagons was an intrusion.

'Tripmaster!' A bellow. A well-schooled bellow, in a modulated voice. She had heard that voice before. Miles stirred in his sleep, and she put out a hand, ready to muffle him if he woke. Why? Because the Tripmaster had said he didn't like people moving around when he didn't know what they were doing. Because he had said something about Crystallites, and that voice had something to do with Crystallites!

A sleepy mumbling. Brunny's voice, then the Tripmaster himself, drawling sleepily.

'Well, well, ain't it that big mucky-muck Crystallite Chantiforth Bins? High Pontiff or some such, an't it? What in the name of all that's holy are you doing out here in Presence country? I thought you Crystallites believed in keeping your distance.'

'Well, we do,' said the voice. 'Except when one of our own is in trouble, Tripmaster. Which I have reason to believe is the case.'

'Is that the truth? Now who would that be?'

'Member of our congregation. Had a baby under un-sanctified conditions, fell on hard times, sold herself into bondage to the blasted BDLers. I've come to buy her bond and take her home.'

There was silence. Vivian lay in baffled silence. The story made no sense. There was no woman on this trip who had sold herself into service.

'Don't think I know the party you're speakin' of,' said the Tripmaster. 'No passengers this trip.'

'Oh, come now, Tripmaster. I know BDL pays your salary, but I'm prepared to be more generous than you can imagine. The woman's name is Vivian. Vivian Ferrence? And she has a little boy.'

Vivian was screaming silently into her hand, fighting to keep herself silent and unmoving in the grove. The Tripmaster had said no passengers. Why had he said that?

'Well, you're weeks too late, Bins. We had that lady with us for a time with her child, but she left us at the Deepsoil Twelve cutoff. There was a caravan there goin' by the northern route, one with women and children on it, and she chose to go with them. Kind of lonesome lady, lost her husband recently. Wanted some other women around, and I can't say's I blame her ...

'By the way, that fella with you has that stun rifle pointed kind of in this direction. He plannin' to shoot some of us, or what?' The Tripmaster had been talking very loudly, loudly enough so that no one in the camp could have missed a word.

Hearty laughter. 'He's just mistrustful, Tripmaster. He wouldn't put it past you to lie to us.'

'Well, easy enough to prove,' the Tripmaster bellowed. 'There's me and my backup 'Singer. There's six drivers here, includin' the cook, and there's six wagons. You can look in all six of 'em.'

Vivian kept silent, thinking frantically. Had she left anything behind. Any toy? Any little shoe? Any blanket or bit of clothing?

'He covered himself,' she explained silently. 'The Tripmaster said we were with the caravan for a while. If you left anything, it was from then. Be still, Vivian. Be very still.'

So she was still, though she could not even identify the threat. She had had nothing to do with the Crystallites. She had heard Chantiforth Bins in the temple. Everyone went to the temple. It was a major attraction. What was he doing here? Why was he looking for her, for the baby? Why was she shaking in fear he would find her?

'Be still,' she ordered herself. 'Trust the Tripmaster. Be very still.'

Chantiforth Bins was speaking again, over the sound of rummaging, over the muttering between him and his man ... men? More than one. Two, maybe three. 'I don't find her, that's for sure, Tripmaster. Well, since she left you so long ago, you won't mind our going along with you into Deepsoil Five, will your We can wait for her there.'

'Suit yourself, Bins. But suit yourself with those rifles in their scabbards. We'll have enough trouble gettin' by the Black Tower without your making us nervous.'

There were multiple clicks and snaps as the rifles were put away. The men were staying. Staying. And when morning came, when light came, the Jubal trees would make fans of themselves, facing east. And Miles might jabber, she couldn't stop him. Then they would find her.

The Tripmaster was leaving the vicinity of the wagons.

Bins's voice called, 'Where are you going, Tripmaster?'

'I'm goin' to do what I need to do, Bins. You want to come along?'

Bins motioned to one of the men with him, who sauntered after the Tripmaster into a small grove well to the north of the one Vivian occupied. The Tripmaster had carried a latrine spade. After a time, they returned to the wagons. There was desultory talk. The firelight dimmed. Silence came.

Perhaps someone was on watch, perhaps not. She could not tell. Several of the drivers went to the grove also. The last time a driver went, no one went with him.

Before she had married Lim, Vivian had worked for the Exploration Division, a lowly job to be sure, though a registered one, requiring concentration and accuracy as she fed the reports of the Tripsingers and Explorers into the master library of BDL. Some of her co-workers did not even read what they transmitted, their fingers doing the job all by themselves. Vivian, however, had read a lot of it and and lived every word. She had inside her head the experiences of half the Tripsingers and Explorers on Jubal. She knew what mistakes they had made, what errors of judgment. She knew when they had been clever, too.

Now she asked herself what one of the clever ones would have done, sitting with her head bowed on her clenched hands as she thought. After a time her face cleared and she released the valve on her mattress and allowed the air to bleed away, so slowly it seemed to take forever, not making a hiss. Then Miles's mattress, slowly, so slowly. He slept on. Miles was a good sleeper. She picked him up, cradling him in her arms, his limp mattress under him, then crept through the grove to the side away from the wagons. She needed a declivity, even the smallest trough would do, and she needed distance, to the east.

Behind her someone coughed, and she stopped, agonized. Silence fell again and she went on, up the long rise of ground to the east. She went slowly, keeping her feet from crunching, yard after slow yard.

When she looked back, the fire among the wagons was only a dim star. Beside her were two Jubal trees, the outliers of a considerable grove, and behind them the ground fell away in a gentle bowl At the bottom of the bowl, she laid Miles down and slowly, very slowly, reinflated his mattress.

She tucked the blanket loosely around him, then went back the way she had come, measuring the distance with frequent turns to look over her shoulder. When she returned, she carried her shoulder bag and dragged her own mattress behind her to wipe out the footprints she knew she had made.

When she settled into the hollow beside the baby, he murmured in his sleep. Exhausted, she lay beside him with her open eyes fixed on the eastern horizon.

Light came at last, waking her suddenly. Despite her apprehension, she had dozed off. She could not see the camp from where they were. Leaving Miles still deeply asleep, she crawled up the slope, poking her head up behind the lower fronds of a Jubal tree. The wagons were there, much farther away than she would have believed. People were moving around. Chantiforth Bins was stalking here and there, poking into things, searching every nearby grove. Within moments of sunrise, he was in the grove she had been sleeping in, marching through it and out the side nearest her to peer up the slope.

'Any sign?' he called to someone.

'Viggies've been in here,' someone answered. 'Footprints all over everything. Nothin' else.'

Viggies! She gasped with relief. Her own tracks had been hidden then. Brunny was moving around the cook wagon, his loose coat wagging around him. After a time, clutching his coat, he went off to the same grove the Tripmaster had used the night before, also carrying a latrine shovel. No one offered to go with him.

Miles moved. Vivian crouched beside him, ready to silence him if necessary. It might not be necessary. Sometimes Miles slept well into the morning ...

As he did this time. The wagons were some distance away before he woke.

When she could no longer see the wagons, Vivian assumed the wagons could no longer see her and went down to the campground, hoping that someone would have found some way to leave food and water. The place was as clean as any campsite the Tripmaster had ever left.

'No cooky?' asked Miles hungrily. 'Where's Brunny?'

Her eyes filled with tears. What had the Tripmaster hoped to do? Had he hoped to take the interlopers into Deepsoil Five and then return for her? Or send someone from Harmony? What would it be, minimum? Three days? Five? Surely he must have ...

She put Miles down with an exclamation and ran toward the grove where both the Tripmaster and Brunny had gone. She found it almost at once, a little mound. Tentatively, she dug into it with a dried frond.

Shit.

She wrinkled her nose, disgusted. Well, of course. She shoved the half dried feces aside and kept on digging.

Deep in the hole she found a water bottle, a small carton of rations, and a little plastic sack. In the sack was a note for her and something for Miles.

'We'll be back for you,' Brunny had written. 'Stay put.'

'Cookies,' said Miles with satisfaction.

Staying put for the morning was no problem. The afternoon became less pleasant, with a strong, grit-bearing wind from the south. Vivian left Miles huddled beneath a sheltering Jubal tree while she searched the surrounding area for cover. To the northwest were ramparts of Presences, pale yellow and gray-blue with forests of 'lings gathered at their bases, dwindling southward almost to the trail. Directly north was the pass to Harmony, a long, 'ling-littered slope, almost barren of growth. Nearby, groves of Jubal trees and meadows of knee-high grass lined the trail on both sides. Farther east, another escarpment was first amber, then orange, then vivid red, peaking at its point of ultimate scarlet into the sheer facades of the Enigma. So much she either knew, had seen herself, or had learned from her over-the-shoulder observations of the charts.

To the south, the groves of the trees dwindled to nothing, and the sedimentary rock of a coastal desert took over, only an occasional pillar-like Presence breaking the flat monotony, the ruled-line of the horizon.

The rock was broken by potholes. Within minutes of beginning her search, Vivian found half a dozen of them, none of them much larger than her head. A bit deeper into the rock desert, the holes became larger, and about a quarter of a mile from the trail, in the middle of a patch of fine sand, she found a hole with nicely stepped sides, a sandy bottom, and an overhang on the south edge – a perfect shelter from the strong south wind.

It was warm in the hole, also. The stone walls gathered the rays of the sun and held the warmth. They would give it up slowly, even in the chill of the night. All day they sat in the sand at the bottom of the hole, Vivian manufacturing trucks for Miles out of ration cartons and bits of string, Miles building roads in the sand, both of them retreating under the ledge when the wind blew chill. It was a better hiding place than the grove of trees had been, and from the lip of the hole she could see anyone or anything approaching while it was still miles away. She did not consider that anyone might approach in the dark or in the fog. She had not even seen one of the notorious fogs of the southern coast.

When it came, it was not much to see. The first hint of it was the clamminess of the blankets that wakened her, blankets suddenly soggy and cold in the darkness. She had gathered dried tree fronds for fire, if it became necessary to have fire, and she lit a small pile of them with the firestarter from the rations kit. They smoldered with a dense, eye-burning smoke that would not rise above the lip of the hole, and she threw sand over the charred branches, cursing at them. Better to be cold than half asphyxiated, she thought, not realizing quite how cold it would get. Once that realization struck home, she pulled Miles onto her larger mattress and half deflated the smaller one to make a tent over them, thriftily setting the water jug beneath one folded corner and listening to the plop, plop, plop as condensation from the fog ran into it. A Tripsinger had done that once. She had read about it in his report. She sat cross-legged, with Miles in her lap, making a tent pole of her body and head, both blankets wrapped around them. After an endless time, she even dozed.

It was the voices that wakened her. Soft voices in the dark, calling her.

But not by name. At first the strangeness of that did not strike her. Only when she had come fully awake did the voices seem odd and mysterious.

Until then they had been a component of dream.

'We search for the wife of Lim Ferrence,' the voices said. Sang. Chanted.

'Lim Terree,' another voice contradicted with a soft soprano warble. 'The mother said he called himself Lim Terree.'

'So she did,' the voices sang. 'We search for the wife of Lim Terree.'

She did not answer, could not have answered. These were ghost voices from a world of spirits and haunts, a childhood world of reasonless fear.

'Perhaps she is afraid,' said the second voice. It sounded like a woman's voice, or a child's. Not a man's voice. Vivian's heart hammered. She had to say something. Perhaps they had cone to help her. Help Miles.

'What do you want?' she called, her voice a thin shriek on the edge of terror.

'Do not be afraid, please,' the voices sang. 'The mother of Lim Terree thought you were in danger. We have come to help you.'

'Some men came,' she cried. 'Looking for me. For my little boy.'

'Ah,' the voices sang. 'Can you move? Can you walk? Are you strong and well?'

'Yes. Yes. I'm all right.'

The voices murmured in some other language. A few voices first, then several, then many. A chorus. Whatever it was they were singing, they did it several times over until it satisfied them. In some obscure way, it satisfied Vivian, too. When they were through with the song, it was completed. Even she could hear that.

'We have sung this predicament,' the voices told her. 'You cannot walk in the dark. You have not the means, as we have. You would hurt yourself and the little one. So, when it is light, you must come to the red mountains. We will come behind and wipe away the tracks you will leave.'

'The red mountain? The Enigma!'

'Yes. So you call it.'

'It's where Lim died,' she cried. 'I don't want to go there!'

'Not quite there,' they murmured. 'Only near there. It is safe there. No Loudsingers . . . no humans come there.'

'I wanted to go to Deepsoil Five,' she cried. 'Lim's mother is there.'

'We think the men who looked for you are also there. It is not safe there. Later we will take you there.'

The fog became silent once more. After a time, she thought she had dreamed it. When light came at last, she knew it had not been a dream. In the fine sand all around the edge of the hole were the strange four-toed prints of viggy feet. She had never heard that they could speak. In the light of day, she could not believe they had spoken.

Her disbelief immobilized her and would have kept her from moving, except for the light that came darting from the trail toward Harmony.

Morning had come; the fog had slowly burned away; she had seen the tracks and marveled at them, uncertain whether to be curious or terrified. No one had ever alleged viggies to be harmful. The few specimens who had been caught in the early years of exploitation had all died, most of them very quickly. No rumor of violence attached to them at all. They were virtually unseen, a constant presence to the ear, an unconsidered irrelevancy otherwise.

But no one had ever said they could talk. It was this that made her suspicious. Suppose they were not really viggies at all.

'But they were here,' she told herself. 'Right here, not four feet from me. If they'd wanted to, they could have snatched me up or killed me or whatever they wanted.'

Still, she was undecided. Then, as she was having a slow look around from the lip of the hole, she saw the glint of light up the trail toward Harmony. Flash. Then again, flash. She watched for a long time until it came again, three, four times. Light reflecting off lenses. Up that trail, at the limit of vision, someone was watching this place.

Had they been watching yesterday?

She slid down into the hole and began to pack their few belongings. A little way east of them was a narrow ridge, paralleling the trail, running eastward along it. If she could get behind that, no one could see her from the trail.

She watched first, waiting until the flashes came, then came again, then did not come. Then she was out of the hole and trotting toward the east with Miles staggering along behind. When they came to a grove of Jubal trees, she picked up Miles and darted into the grove to lie behind a tree and watch the Harmony trail.

After a time, flash, and flash again. This time she carried Miles as she trotted quickly away to the next grove. She had begun to get the feel of it. Someone was taking a look every quarter hour.

It took four more dashes between groves to attain the ridge. Then they were behind it.

'More game,' suggested Miles, who had become fond of diving behind trees.

'Not right now, my big boy,' she told him. 'Right now, we're just going for a long walk. Can you do that?'

He nodded, mouth pursed in a bargaining expression. 'Cooky?'

'When we stop for lunch, I'll give you a cooky. How's that?'

'Fine.'

Long before they stopped for lunch he was worn out and asleep on her shoulder. Long before they arrived at the red mountains, while they were still miles from them, she was equally worn. Evening found them curled in a circle of settler's brush, eating cold rations and drinking less water than they wanted, then falling into exhausted slumber.

'Come,' the voice said, almost in her ear. 'You cannot sleep now. Men are seeking you. Come.'

This time she saw them, in the thinnest glimmer of New Moon light, occulted by the shadow of Serendipity to a mere scythe of silver. They were furred and large-eyed, with wide, mobile ears. Their necks were corrugated with hanging flaps of bright hide, shadowed red and amber and orange, and their heads were decked with long, feathery antennae that looked like nothing so much as the fronds of Jubal trees. They were all around her, singing, singing in her own language, and she was not afraid of them.

'Where are the men?' she whispered. 'How far back?'

'They saw you come this way,' the viggies sang. 'Even though we wiped the lands clean of your feet, still they search.'

'What are we to do?'

'We will take you where they cannot go, woman of Lim Terree, honored be his name.'

They guided her. She carried Miles, and two of the viggies ran along at her sides, their hands on her thighs, pushing or tugging ever so slightly to keep her on the right path. Bondri had introduced himself, as they went he named off the others of the troupe. Sometimes they slowed, sometimes to allow others of the troupe to clear a way ahead, sometimes to allow those who had been clearing the way behind to change jobs with others. Always they sang, sometimes in their own language, sometimes in hers. So she learned the story of Favel, the broken one, and of his release by the Loudsinger child. She wanted to laugh, then to cry. Lim hadn't done it out of generosity. He hadn't done it out of sympathy for the poor viggy, either. He'd done it out of spite and wounded feelings and jealousy and pain. She tried to tell Bondri this, and he listened with one ear cocked backward to hear her.

'Good,' he said at last. 'This is what Favel wanted. Another view to make his song more true.'

It made no sense to her. Only that they were saving her, and Miles. That made sense.

They went eastward to the end of the ridge, then northward, into the crystal range. Now the viggies were singing in their own tongue exclusively, quieting the earth that trembled beneath them, opening ways that would be closed to those who followed. Some of the troupe climbed to the tops of peaks and yodeled into the night, while all those below opened their ears wide, listening.

'What are they doing?' she asked Bondri.

'The troupe of Chowdri goes around near here. They keep watch on the Mad One, the one you call the Enigma. I have a daughter to trade with

Chowdri, and we will sing of Favel's death so the word may go east and south.' He did this all in one breath, a kind of recitatif, and she shook her head in amazement. Lim had been an accomplished musician, perhaps a genius. But Bondri could do things with his voice Lim could never have attempted. Of course, Lim hadn't had a song-sack on his neck to hold several extra lungfuls of air, either.

At dawn they stopped. The Engima towered above them, a little to the east, like two bloody swords stabbed upward into the sky. Several weary viggies ran up from the south, singing as they came.

'The men have gone back they way they came, still looking. They did not find any sign of the woman or the child. They say they will go to Deepsoil Five, that the woman must eventually come to Deepsoil Five.'

Well, she had left some of her few belongings on the wagon, in a carton. Undoubtedly whoever was after her and Miles had found them.

'They cannot come in here,' Bondri said. 'Your people have no words to let them into this place.'

'But I cannot stay with your people forever, Bondri Wide Ears! Someday I must go to my own people.'

'Someday is someday. We will sing that later. Just now we eat.'

Miles woke up. He looked at the viggies with total wonder, then politely offered Bondri his last cooky. Bondri took it gravely and ate half, returning half. In return, Bondri gave him a cup of bark sap, which Miles shared with his mother. When she had drained the cup, she looked at it carefully, paling as she did so.

'What ... what is this?'

'An ancestor cup,' Bondri replied. 'This one belonged to Favel, who honored your husband's name. Favel who laid his debt upon us that good should be returned for good.'

Gently, she laid the skull cup down. Nothing in the Tripsingers' reports had prepared her for this, but native good manners did what preparation could not. 'I am honored,' she whispered, listening carefully while Bondri sang several songs of Favel's life. She joined the troupe in eating settler's brush, though she gave Miles his breakfast from rations he was more accustomed to.

And when they had finished, she joined the troupe in singing the song of her own rescue. That she had little or no voice did not seem to disturb the viggies. Miles more than made up for her.

'He has a good voice, your son,' they sang to her. 'When he is big, he will be a troupe leader.'

'If he lives to get big,' she whispered. A giligee patted her shoulder and crooned in her ear.

At midmorning, word was received from Chowdri's troupe, and they began to work their way east, ever closer to the Enigma.

'Isn't this dangerous?' she asked Bondri. 'Aren't we going into peril?'

'Not into peril,' he sang. 'Not to the Mad One's roost. Only to the edge of the skin where the songs keep it quiet.'

'Skin?' she asked, not sure she had understood.

'The outer part," Bondri explained, searching his more limited Loudsinger vocabulary. 'The hide, the fur, the ...' he found a word he liked, 'the integument.'

'Of the Presence."

'Yes. The part that only twitches and slaps, like your skin, Lim's mate, when a wound fly crawls on it. The skin of the Mad One is not mad. Only the brain of it is mad, and we will not come close to that.'

By evening they had come closer to the Enigma than Vivian wanted to, and yet the troupe of Bondri Gesel showed no discomfort. Six of the viggies were delegated to sing quiet songs to the skin, and these six were replaced from time to time by six others, one at a time slipping into and out of the chorus so that it never ceased. The music was soothing, soporific. Vivian found herself yawning, and Miles curled up under a Jubal tree and fell deeply asleep, even without his supper.

'You should stay awake,' Bondri suggested. 'Chowdri is on his way here. He has a good tongue. We sing well together.'

The troupe of Chowdri joined them after dusk but before the night was much advanced. There were choral challenges and answers, contrapuntal exercises, long, slow passages sung by the two troupe leaders, and finally a brisk processional during which the singers tapped on their song-sacks to make a drumming sound. Chowdri had brought food. Chowdri *was* less amazed to see Vivian than Bondri thought he should be, and this occasioned some talk.

'We have one, too.' sang Chowdri importantly. 'A very little one. Not depouched yet.'

'A Loudsinger child!' Bondri was incredulous. 'A true Loudsinger child?'

'My senior giligee found it in a body,' Chowdri sang. 'A female who was killed by the Mad One. My giligee went at once to find bones on the Enigma, before the gyre-birds came, and she found this little one, inside the woman, the way they grow. No bigger than a finger. We have sung that the taboo does not apply to such little ones.'

'What did he say?' Vivian asked.

Bondri translated.

'I don't understand,' she said. 'What does he mean?'

Bondri beckoned to his own giligee, who came forward and allowed Bondri to open its pouch and point within. 'There,' he sang. 'In the pouch. This is the brain-bird of Favel. Here, also, grow the little ones from mating.

Our females carry them inside for only a little time, not like you Loudsingers. Favel told me all about it.'

'Brain-bird?' she faltered.

'Excuse me, Chowdri,' sang Bondri. 'My guest has a difficulty that I must correct before we sing further together.'

'Males and females mate,' he sang to her. 'You understand this?'

Vivian fought down a hysterical giggle and told him yes, that she understood, that Loudsingers did a similar thing.

'After a few days, the female seeks out the giligee and sheds the little one, like a little worm. The giligee takes the little thing into its pouch. The tendrils of the pouch close it in and give it nourishment. It lives and grows there. When it is big, it is depouched. It is a female.'

'Always?' she wondered.

'Always,' he said firmly. 'We know it is not so with you, but with us it is always female. The female lives and is traded as a daughter to some other troupe and mates and does female things. Then the time comes her brain-bird cries for release. The giligee bites out the brain-bird and puts it in the pouch again. It grows again. This time it is male.'

'Always,' she nodded to herself in amazement.

'Always. In every female there is a male waiting to grow. It grows up and mates and does male things. And when its own brain-bird cries for release, the giligee takes it once more. And this time, the last time, it grows to be a giligee.'

'And when its brain-bird cries for release again?'

'There is no brain-bird in a giligee. They get very old and finally die. Then we make an ancestor cup as we do for all, and put them beside a Presence and sing their songs.'

'So Chowdri's giligee has a human baby in it? You know whose baby that is, don't you? That's Tasmin's baby. Lim's brother. Tasmin Ferrence. The woman must have been his wife. Celcy. And Lim was there. Lim was on the Enigma. Maybe he didn't die!'

Bondri turned away in some haste and began a burst of song, which his troupe joined, then Chowdri's troupe, the two groups singing away at one another as though to compile an encyclopedia of song. When the melody dwindled at last and Bondri returned to Vivian, he looked very sad and old, his song-sack hanging limp.

'He is truly dead. I am sorry, Lim's mate, but he is truly dead. The giligee took some of his bone to make a bark scraper. Do you want his ancestor cup? I know it is not the Loudsinger way, but the giligee can get it if you want it.'

She shook her head, weeping. There for a moment, she had been full of irrational hope. Well. Miles was alive, and she was alive, and it seemed that Tasmin's baby was alive also.

'How long will the giligee keep it?' she whispered.

'Until it is done,' Bondri sang, shrugging. 'It is not nearly finished yet.'

'Will … will the giligee give it to us – to Tasmin's family – when it is finished?'

Bondri seemed to be considering this. 'I believe it will. I will take debt with Chowdri's troupe to assure it. In that way, the debt of Favel will be repaid to the family of Lim Terree. We have saved his wife and his child and his brother's child. That is a good repayment.'

'Repayment in full,' the troupe sang. 'Repayment at once, as Favel required. Proud the troupe of Bondri Gesel to have repaid a debt of honor.'

15

Maybelle Thonks squatted on her luggage in the small tender and stared across half a mile of slupping ocean to the spider-girdered tower in which the charred hulk of the *Broumaster* hung, readying for lift. The little boat in which she sat was packed with cartons and bags, all of which had been searched by BDL security men before they had been loaded. Maybelle had been searched as well.

'For your protection, Ma'am,' the female guard had sneered. 'Sometimes people plant things on other people.'

'How in hell do you think anyone could have planted anything *there*?' Maybelle had hissed in her ear, shocked. 'For the love of good sense, woman!'

'Just routine,' the guard had said, suddenly aware who she was violating.

'You've been through my luggage, through my clothes, through my cosmetics. You've been all over my body like a bad sunburn. What the hell do you think I'm carrying, a bomb?'

'Just routine,' she mumbled again, handing Maybelle an intimate bit of her clothing.

Fuming, Maybelle reassembled herself and turned to check her belongings, which were now in a state of total disarray. She did a quick inventory of the jewelry case. One pair of rather valuable earclips missing. The security guard had used only one hand for parts of the search. The other one had undoubtedly been busy filching jewelry. Maybelle toyed with the idea of accusing the woman. What would it gain her? Delay. Which she didn't want. Which might even have been the motive for the theft.

Pretend not to notice it, she had told herself. *You're probably being watched right now, so lock up the cases and pretend not to notice*. Which she had done, just in time for the porter to take the cases down to the tender.

Now she was bounding around on Jubal's purple ocean, almost at the launch site and herself seemingly the only passenger for Serendipity. Well, that's what Rheme had said. No one was getting off of Jubal these days. No body and no thing.

Except for brou. And the things the Honorable Wuyllum had stolen. And the things Honeypeach had stolen. And a few cartons near her feet that were tagged as belonging to Aphrodite Sells.

'The rats are deserting the sinking ship,' she quoted, without having any clear idea what rats were. Something little and scaly, with unpleasant teeth, that came onto ships simply in order to leave them, ships like the ones on Serendipity, shallow and gently curved, with long, triangular sails.

'We'll miss you, Mayzy,' Honeypeach had said. 'You have no idea how much.' There had been a threat in that, which Maybelle had pretended not to hear.

'Settle yourself in,' her father had directed. 'Pick the best part of the capital city and rent yourself some kind of expensive-looking place. Rheme's arranged for some woman to help you; he'll give you her name.' That was all the Honorable Wuyllum had to say on the matter, but then he was much preoccupied with stripping Jubal of as much wealth as possible in the few days or weeks that remained.

'That's funny,' said the boatman. 'The loading ramp's not down.'

'What does that *mean*?' she asked, a queasy feeling rising from her stomach to the bottom of her throat and resting there as though it had no intention of moving.

'It means we can't get onto the ship,' he muttered. 'Dumb shits.' He hit a button on the control panel and a horn blatted over the sound of wave and wind.

Maybelle put her hands over her ears. The horn went on blaring for some time. When it was cut off, she heard an answering howl from the tower.

'Return to port. Ship is lifting in the hour and will accept no passengers or additional cargo, by order of the launch commander.'

'Tell him who's on board,' Maybelle directed between dry lips.

'He knows,' the boatman mumbled in a surly voice. 'You think he don't know!' Still, he put the amplifier to his lips and told the tower who he was carrying.

'Return to port,' the tower blared. 'Ship is lifting in the hour ...'

Maybelle fell back onto the seat. There had been that vicious tone in Honeypeach's voice when she had said goodbye. Something eager, lascivious, and sniggering. If anyone could have arranged this disappointment, Honeypeach could. All she would have to do was call Justin ...

'We have to go back,' the boatman said. 'We'll get fried if we stay out here when she lifts.'

Maybelle had nothing to say. What was there to say? What would she do when she reached shore? Run? Run where? She huddled on the seat, oblivious to the blare of the tower or the liquid slosh of the waves, lost in apprehension. When they came within sight of the dock, she saw the ebony and gold of the guards from Government House. Someone had sent them to meet her. Someone had known she wouldn't be leaving.

The sound of a hailing voice brought her head around. A small fishing boat lay just off their port bow. The plump figure at the helm was shouting at them. The tender boatsman slackened speed, let the boat come almost to a stop.

'Miss Maybelle Thonks?' the helmsman cried. Plump. With gray hair. She thought she had seen him somewhere before, though she could not see much of his face behind the goggles and high-wound scarf.

'Yes,' she nodded, petrified with fright.

'Mr. Gentry asked us to pick you up, Miss. If you wouldn't mind.' He smiled at her in a grandfatherly manner.

She cast a quick look again at the dock. Household guards still there, and among them someone else. Someone in an extravagant hat and drifting multicolored veils. Honeypeach. Oh, yes.

'I'll go with this man, boatman,' she said in her rarely used imperative voice, covering fear with a pretense of arrogance. 'Hold the boats together while I toss my luggage in.'

She transferred herself from tender to fishing boat, hearing angry shouts from the dock over the slupping waves. It wasn't until she was in the other boat, together with all her belongings, that she realized anyone could have used Rheme's name. By then it was too late to do anything about it. The wake of the BDL boat was disappearing in the direction of the dock, and the boat she was in was speeding north along the shore.

16

Tasmin, Donatella, Clarin, and Jamieson left the north-south valley by striking southeast through a gap that the charts identified as the Ogre's Stair. There was no Password and they had an anxious time getting past the Presence. Donatella thought she had a Password that could be adapted, but the Ogre was not amenable. They were about to give up in anger and frustration when Clarin stopped them.

'Let me,' she said opening her music box and kneeing her mule to the forefront. 'Tasmin, help me.'

She touched the keys and began singing. It took Tasmin only a moment to realize what she had done. Once or twice Don's previous efforts had seemed to quiet the Stair. Clarin had taken those brief phrases and wound them together, amplifying and extending the melody, attaching a harmonic line from quite another score, and then orchestrating the whole thing as she went. Tasmin picked up the harmonic line and began to sing it, their two voices rising together.

He had never sung with her before.

It was as sensual as touching her. More. It was like making love. He knew this, understood it, and set it aside, refusing to think of it, even as his voice went on and on. The music had its own logic, just as lovemaking did. Its own logic and its own imperatives. It wasn't necessary to think or explain. The thing was of itself, a perfection.

The mules began to move forward on their own. Don and Jamieson followed, their mouths open. Jamieson was stunned at what he was hearing. He had sung with Clarin, but it had not been like this.

Clarin's voice had almost a baritone-contralto range, as softly mellow in the lower ranges as an organ pipe, as pure in the higher ones as a wooden flute. Tasmin's range was smaller, lower, the quality of his voice richer, more velvety. The two blended as though they were one.

When they reached the end of the initial melody, Clarin raised the key and began a variation.

Tasmin followed her, effortlessly.

Beneath them the Ogre's Stair was motionless.

They reached the top on a soaring, endless chord that drifted away into the sky, becoming nothing. The Stair was behind them. As they left it, it sang to them, three tones of enormous interrogation.

Tasmin and Clarin rode on, not noticing, not hearing, oblivious to the world around them.

Don did not have her translator working.

'Good Lord,' she breathed, looking toward Jamieson, astonished to find him pale and shivering, tears in his eyes.

'Jamieson,' she murmured. Clarin and Tasmin were riding on, not looking at one another, silent. 'Jamieson?'

'Just once,' he mumbled to her. 'Just once. If I could ...'

She nodded, understanding. There was nothing she could say. Poor Jamieson. Too much propinquity. She squeezed his shoulder sympathetically. He loved the girl, and she loved Tasmin, and Tasmin loved – what? Celcy? Jubal?

By the time they reached the bottom of the slope, Clarin was herself once more. She had dug a package of sweet stores out of her pocket and now offered them around.

'The people tracking us know we're headed south. And since the only thing you did to stir up suspicion was to come up with the Enigma score, they may realize we're headed that way.'

Don agreed. 'When they get out of that valley we left, they'll hit a major east-west shipping route, with virtually no problems on the way.'

'We'll simply have to get there first,' Tasmin said, lifting a mule foot and staring at it as though fascinated. He was still lost in the music, still finding it hard to connect with reality. 'We've lost a little time dealing with the Ogre, but as I read the charts, I think we can make a fairly short traverse of the Blinders, just east of us, and come into one of the main east-west routes ourselves.'

'The one that comes through Deepsoil Two, Six, Eight, and Nine?' Jamieson asked in a fairly normal voice. 'That's an easy run. I know every Password on that route.'

'Good for you, Reb. And Nine is just through the Mystic Range from Harmony.' He thumped the mule and tightened the cinch, then took a candy from Clarin and sat down beside her. 'We need to move fast. Justin's got the interior shut off, and he wouldn't have done that unless he expected the CHASE Commission to arrive momentarily. As soon as he gets their verdict, he'll send word to the troops, and anything we have to say will come much too late.'

Jamieson nodded. 'What do you think we have, at best? A few days? A few weeks? That, at most, if we're going to show them anything while they're here. We've got to collect our evidence and then get back to the Deepsoil Coast at a dead run.'

With the situation thus delineated, unaccountably they all felt better. The situation was fully as bad as they had thought it was and they were all agreed on it, which relieved each of them of having to worry it out individually. Don even managed a quirky smile at the sight of Clarin trying to replace her lost crystal mouse by baiting a new and elusive beast with candy. It evaded capture, and they mounted once more, setting out at a good pace toward the Blinders.

After that, they did not seem to pause, not for days. Sleep came and went in brief periods of exhausted slumber, forgotten all too soon, along with snatched meals and hasty relief stops. Jamieson fought them through the Blinders, finding an amazing strength from somewhere, this time leaving them with mouths open. They left the last of the crystal towers in the evening when the refracted light from the setting sun made it almost impossible to see anything in any direction and found themselves on the open trail to Deepsoil Two with only easy Passwords between themselves and the dirt town. In Two, Tasmin requisitioned four additional mules from the citadel, letting their own animals trail along unburdened for most of the following day as they caught up with and joined a caravan headed east and stayed with it all the way into Deepsoil Six. The caravan rested for eight hours, but Tasmin and company slept only five, rising in the dark to continue on the way, timing their departure to let them come to the first intervening Presences at dawn.

Clarin caught a crystal mouse in the 'lings above Deepsoil Eight.

She had it half tamed by the time they reached Nine, feeding it crumbs and singing repetitive melodies to it, to which the others dreamed as they rode.

Jamieson sang them through the Startles, above Harmony to the west, and they planned to sleep that night in the caravansery. There was no citadel in Harmony, but the caravansery manager put himself out to be as useful as possible, fetching food and towels and assorted oddments to a running commentary.

'Nice to have a group of 'Singers here again,' he said, his chins and bellies wobbling in emphasis. 'Had a bunch earlier you wuttn't believe.'

'Tripsinger trouble?' Tasmin asked, disbelievingly. 'I haven't heard that we've got any troublemakers, currently.'

'Naah, the Tripmaster was all right, him and his assistant. Wagon men was all right, too. The cook even helped me fix a meal for the lot of 'em. No, it was those others with 'em.'

'Passengers?'

The fat man shook his head, first chins then bellies swaying like waves generated from a common source somewhere around the ears. 'Don't think so, no. Four men with mules o' their own, come along after the caravan lookin' for some woman and baby. Tripmaster sait the woman left 'em back outsite o' Twelve. Crazy, if she went that way. Lots longer that way. Have to go through Thirteen and Fourteen on yer way up to Six, then come the way you come from there. Take almost twice't as long.'

'You didn't happen to hear who it was they were looking for, did you?' asked Tasmin, dry-mouthed.

'Woman's name was Terree. Same's that Soilcoast singer got himself kilt on the Enigma …'

'These men didn't happen to say who they were, did they?' Donatella asked.

'Oh, no neet to tell me the name o' the one of 'em. Bins, he was. Chantiforth Bins. My wife buys ever cube those tamnt Crystals put out. True believer, she is, just so long as she won't have to get up off her lollyfalooz to do nothin' about it. Ever time I come in the room, it's that cube rantin' and ravin' like some bantigon with a buttache. I've seen him till I'm sick of him. Heart him, too, and he toesn't make any more sense up clost than on the cube. I knew he was lyin' the minute he startit talkin'.'

'But he didn't find the woman.'

'Nah. She was long gone. Way I think, that Tripmaster he hit her somewheres.'

'Hit her!'

'Right. Like hit her in the trees or hit her in a hole in the ground so's those fella's cuttn't hurt her none. Her'n the baby.'

'The answer to all our problems,' said Jamieson, sotto voce, leaning heavily on Clarin. 'Hit 'em in a hole in the grount.'

'I'll hit you in a hole in the grount if you're not careful,' murmured Clarin, smiling at him.

'Where's the Tripmaster now?' Tasmin asked, trying to glare at them and succeeding only in looking weary.

'Gone on t'Five. 'Forn he went, he ast me to get 'long there and help her out. Whispert it, kind of. The Tripmaster that was.'

'When was this?' Tasmin said, dangerously patient.

'Was yesterday since. Trouble was, I can't go til these ones go away.'

'Did the Tripmaster say where they came up to the wagon train? Bins and his bunch?'

'Oh, yes. Come up on it down at the turn off where one roat comes up here t'Harmony and one goes east to nothin' much. I think that's right. Course, you might ask 'em. They're all of 'em asleep in there.' And he pointed to one of the dormitory rooms, halfway down the long hall. 'They lookt for her but din't fint her. Sait they're goin' on t'Teepsoil Five, first thin' tomorrow.'

'Armed?' asked Jamieson.

The caravansery manager shook his head. 'Don't think so. No arms I saw.'

'I guess we don't sleep?' Donatella asked, only half a question.

'I guess you're right,' said Tasmin. 'Do you have any Bormil tea?' he asked the caravansery manager. 'Or Tsamp? something that will keep us awake for a while?'

'Now, what kint o' caravansery wuttn't have Tsamp,' the manager nodded. 'Sure I got Tsamp. You want it powdert or cookt in somethin'?'

They settled on Tsamp in broth, drinking enough of it that their nerves were screamingly alert when they left Harmony, headed south.

When the sun came up, they found themselves at the fork of the trail, a long ridge leading away to the east, groves of trees speckling the shallow soil between the westward trail and the Presences, and not a sign of Vivian or the baby. They called and searched for an hour, then spent some time hailing with the machines, and then, in a mood of fatalistic exhaustion, turned east and rode for the Enigma.

Tasmin had seen it before, from the north side, from between the twin needles, between the two insolent daggers of bloody ice. He had looked down onto the little flat that lay between those daggers like a stained handkerchief between two gory swords, and he had seen that handkerchief fold away around Celcy, around Lim, wrapping away those arrogant enough to test the Enigma.

Now he saw the same place from below.

A polished ramp of crystal wound upward toward that same little flat. All the shards and shattered fragments had been cleared away. It gleamed like cut glass, like ruby or dark garnet with paler edges, as though its blood had coagulated in some places and had run with water in others, dark clots and pale tints intermingled where something bled into the sea of that great crystal, bled forever and was forever washed away. .

Within the bloody traceries glinted the web of fracture, the delicate tracery of dislocation, of tilted planes and vacant edges, shivering with dawn light.

'Where did you go before, Don?' Tasmin asked. 'When you talked to it?'

'Up there,' Donatella answered. 'It was a dim, gray day, with fog in the air. Not like today. I ... I don't recall being afraid then.'

'Are you now?'

'Lord, yes, aren't you? That thing is glaring at us.'

'I expected to be afraid. But then I've only been here once, and my experience was a different one from yours.'

'What do we do?' Clarin asked. 'Now you can tell us, Donatella. What was your clue? What did Erickson give you that took you up there?'

Donatella turned and adjusted her music box, finding a particular setting and playing it so softly they barely heard it, a haunting melody, rising and falling in quiet repetition, as though water ran upon stone, eating it away. 'An-dar-ououm, an-dar-ououm.' It was the Enigma score, and yet it was neither synthesizer nor human voice.

'Viggies?' asked Jamieson. 'Is that viggies?'

'I'll cut in the translator,' she said. 'Now listen.'

The same melody, translated. 'Let the edges sleep. Let one half sleep,' sang the translator, 'let it sleep in peace, let it rest, let it rest, let water run deep, let the edges grow, let the way come clear, soft, soft, let the fingers sleep, let one half sleep.'

She cut off the machine. 'There's more. Not a lot more words, but a lot more music, and very repetitive. That's what Erickson suggested – that I record a group of viggies near a Presence without a Password. Well, I got lucky. I hid. I heard them singing off in the night, and I recorded that first thing.

'However, the translator could only give me a few words. I doubt if any translator, up until now, could have done even that. It told me it needed more, lots more. So, I hid in a hole in that cliff up there for over a week, recording viggy songs and chatter and describing what they were doing until the translator had enough that it could start to give it to me clearly. We got words for water and fingers and sleep right away, but it took some time to get the rest. The viggy language is more complex than you can imagine. Once I had the translation, I learned their words, then came here and sang the thing. That's what I used. I sang that to the Enigma, all of it, for about an hour. I don't have much voice, but it didn't take much. You heard it. Simple.'

'And you were recording whatever sounds the Presence made?'

'Of course. At first, only noise. Whatever different kinds of noise there are. Like back in the valley, like most places, just a garble, a kind of whistling, chuckling, squeaking, snoring noise. But as I sang, it quieted down. I'd already figured out what questions I wanted to ask. *Do you have a name for yourself you would like me to use*? I thought that would get us off on the right foot. So, as soon as everything was quiet, I sang that. Loudly.'

'And the answer was, as I recall from when you played it for us, *Messengers know to whom they come*. Right?' asked Jamieson.

'Right. Not exactly responsive, but it did make sense. So, I thought I'd give it some information at that point. I sang, *I am not one of the usual messengers*.'

Clarin said, 'And the reply to that was *None of them are*.'

'That's right. Up until that point, everything had been very peaceful. Then I started to go on to my next question. The minute I started, it shook. Just a little, and only on one side, but I thought – well, I thought, hell, I had enough. I'm no linguist, no philologist, no specialist in alien communication. Suppose I slashed it off, all unwitting. So I went back to the first song, the peaceful water one, and I sang that while I backed off.'

'So your intention is to repeat that sequence?' Clarin asked again, staring upward. 'With us as witnesses.'

'Why didn't we try it on some other Presence, something closer to where we were?' Jamieson wanted to know, also staring upward. There was something ominous about the bloody glare coming from the Enigma, something threatening about the darting, dancing light.

'I tried the viggy music on some other things, and it didn't work. Evidently it's specific to this Presence. And I haven't had time to record any other viggy songs and try anywhere else.'

'Would you say the viggies are sentient?' Clarin asked.

'I didn't think so before,' Don cried. 'I thought of that, of course, because the translator was taking their babble and making words out of it. Nobody has ever seriously alleged that they were. They're so elusive. It would have been hard to prove. But, yes. Once the translator began to make words out of their songs, I believed they were. Not that they've offered to talk to me to prove it.'

'Which isn't the point right now anyhow,' said Tasmin. 'Anybody want to stay down here?' He looked Jamieson full in the eye. 'You should, you know, Reb. Stay here with Clarin and the translator. You'll be able to hear, but you should be out of danger. Then if something happens to Don and me, you two can still carry the word.'

'Master Ferrence?'

'Yes, Reb.'

'With all due respect, Sir. Of the two of us, I'm quicker. I agree that some of us should stay down here. You, Sir. And Clarin.' His eyes were clear as he said it. He didn't look toward Clarin, though Donatella knew he wanted to.

'He's right,' Donatella agreed. 'You're good, Tasmin. But he's better.'

'Ah, the confidence of youth,' Tasmin said, smiling weakly. They were right, of course. He should be able to accept it without its hurting, but damn it, it did hurt. Jamieson had never been afraid to try things, even forbidden things, even foolish things. And it told. He had learned, learned along the edges where Tasmin had always forbidden himself to go.

'Luck, Reb,' he said at last, biting his lip. 'Go ahead.'

'Loudsingers,' gasped one of the troupe of Chowdri, galloping wildly into the camp, antennae waving. 'Loudsingers on the Mad One.'

'Who dares?' cried Chowdri. 'What Loudsinger dares? Has not the Mad One killed enough of them?'

'Same one as last time,' the messenger chanted, breathlessly. 'The female one. And one called Tasmin and one called Reb and one called Clarin.'

'Tasmin!' called Bondri, thrusting through the surrounding troupe members, Vivian close behind him. 'Tasmin Ferrence?'

'They are holding a song captive in a box,' the messenger cried. 'I heard it. The female one has it.'

The troupes rose with one accord. 'I cannot let Tasmin Ferrence come to harm,' Bondri chanted. 'He is part of the debt.'

'Neither can the song be left captive,' Chowdri asserted, showing his fangs.

'Let me talk to him,' Vivian cried. 'I'll make him understand, Bondri. There's no need for violence.'

'Hurry then,' he sang. 'Go quick. I will bring the baby.'

'Down there,' said Chantiforth Bins, pointing to a ridge along the side of the Enigma. 'See them, Myrony? Spider? Just to the left of that tall splinter.'

Chantiforth Bins had gone on to Deepsoil Five from Harmony, and in Deepsoil Five he had found Myrony and Spider Geroan – along with Aphrodite Sells and two unhappy Explorers. The Explorers had left for the Deepsoil Coast. Affy was still in Deepsoil Five with Spider's man. Chanty, Myrony, and Spider had decided to come to the Enigma and give it one more try before returning to the Coast themselves. After all, where else could their various quarries be heading?

Now they stood almost where Tasmin had when he saw Lim and Celcy die, looking down on the area between the Enigma towers from the north. Beneath them the ground quivered in a ceaseless tremor.

'I see 'em,' Myrony admitted nervously. 'Now what?'

'Slash 'em off and get back to Splash One,' Chantiforth said, lifting his rifle.

'No,' said Spider Geroan.

'Whattaya mean, no,' Myrony objected. 'That's what we came for, Geroan. Get rid of the Tripsinger and the Explorer, and there both of 'em are, down by the splinter.'

'That's the wrong one,' said Spider Geroan. 'He's only an acolyte. Where's the right one? Ferrence?'

'Ah,' Myrony remarked. 'Yer right, ya know. There's the fuckin' Tripsinger. I see his robe. Down there at the bottom, with the girl. He's out o' range.'

'So, slash off these two, then go down and get those two, what's the fuss.' Chantiforth was in a hurry. Things were happening back on the Deepsoil

Coast. Things that might threaten the profit from this whole job if he didn't get there soon to protect his rights. He lifted the rifle again.

'No,' said Spider again. 'You hit these two up here, those down there two are going to see it. They'll run off, back into the range most likely, where we can't follow.' Spider narrowed his eyes in concentration.

'I told you we should' a brought those Explorers.'

'What good would that have done?' As ever, Spider's voice was quite expressionless. 'They said there was no way they could get us by the Enigma, and everyone in Deepsoil Five agreed with them. You can't use a noodle to beat bantigons, Bins. It's all going to work out anyhow.'

'Damned if I see how. The fuckin' man is out o' range.'

'She's the one that came up with the Enigma score,' Chantiforth observed. 'She's going to sing it right now, isn't she? What else would she be here for? Well. That gives us some time.'

Spider nodded. 'While they're occupied, we'll sneak down behind these lings. You and Myrony hide there, as near the Explorer and the acolyte as you can get. I'll go on down and get into range for Ferrence before you slash off these two.'

'What about the girl with Ferrence?'

'I'll keep her,' Spider said, affecting not to notice the expression of revulsion that crossed Bins's face. It had been a very long trip, and he had not had any amusement for a long time, had not had that particular excitement that came with watching the one thing he had never experienced. He examined Clarin through his glasses. Good. He liked that type, that age. They were strong and agile, capable of many contortions and pleas before they died.

'You'll yodel when you're ready?' Myrony asked. 'I don't likc bein' around those fuckin' Presences for very long.' They started toward the gap in the Crystal through which Tasmin had stared down. 'Wait!'

'What's the matter with you?' Chantiforth demanded.

'We take out these two first, then go on down where Spider is, and he's done the Tripsinger, then this Presence starts to shake and jiggle, how do we get back over the top here to get back to town? Affy's there, waitin' for us.'

'He's right, you know,' Bins said to Geroan. 'Our mules are back there in Deepsoil Five. And all our supplies. I'm not eager to live off the country all the way back to the Coast. Even if we don't go to the Coast, it's a long hike around by way of Harmony.'

Spider ruminated. 'All right. I'll make a small change in plan. Do it just the way we'd said. You go on down a little way and cover these two in case there's trouble. I'll go all the way down and take out the Tripsinger and the girl first. These two up here won't be paying any attention; they'll be busy with their boxes. I'll come back up, meet you, then we'll all come back up here to the top before we slash off the Explorer and the acolyte. Kind of spoils it for me, but that's the way we'll do it.' Though it did not show on his face, Spider was disappointed. He did not tolerate disappointment well, and only by substituting a mental image of Aphrodite Sells for Clarin in his plans for the next day or so was he able to feel quite comfortable.

The others had no objection. They stood quietly, checking their weapons, waiting for the tremors to cease.

✳

'There,' sang Bondri. 'That one is Tasmin Ferrence. Prime Priest Favel said he had hair that color.'

'Yes,' agreed Vivian. 'That's Tasmin all right. Keep the baby here, Bondri, will you?' And she slipped out of the grove of settler's brush and made her way toward Tasmin and Clarin.

Behind her, the viggy messenger who had brought the earlier word returned again 'More Loudsingers,' he sang softly to the assembled troups. 'On the Mad One's back. High against the sky.'

✳

'Ready?' asked Donatella, her fingers poised over the box.

'Ready,' nodded Jamieson, grinning. He stared around him at the little flat place between the towering scarlet peaks. He wanted to remember it, just as it was. His mind felt like there were flames leaping over it, laughing flames. He remembered every score he had ever sung, every one he had ever seen! 'Ready,' exultantly.

Their hands came down together and the music began.

✳

'The men at the top of the Mad One have weapons,' sang the messenger. 'They are pointing them at the people of Tasmin Ferrence.'

✳

'Tasmin,' cried Vivian. 'Tasmin, you've got to get your people down from up there. Please!'

✳

'Move now,' Spider Geroan directed. The quivering of the ground had lessened enough that they could move securely upon it. 'Move fast, and keep out of sight.'

'Let the troupes of Bondri and Chowdri surround the men with weapons,' urged Bondri. 'A debt of honor is about to come unstuck.'

'It is not our debt,' demurred Chowdri.

'It is the debt of Prime Priest Favel,' Bondri trilled. 'Prime Priests are of all troupes.'

The troupes sang this for a few moments in several variations. No one could deny that it was true. Though some sang that a debt incurred before a viggy became Prime Priest might not be binding on all troupes, this was a minority voice, which became only a haunting anharmonic in the finished song.

'Go then,' urged Chowdri, somewhat grudgingly. 'Go to the Mad One, the Presence Without Innerness, the Killer Without Cause, called by the Loudsingers, the Enigma. Fulfill the debt.'

'Vivian! How did you get here?'

'The viggies brought me, Tasmin. Listen, there's no time for questions. The viggies say that the Enigma will kill anyone who tries to sing it quiet. The Enigma is crazy.'

'Donatella did it before.'

'Not really. It wasn't awake, and she got on and then off before it woke up, is all. It's wide awake today. Tasmin, get her off of there.'

While Tasmin was still staring at Vivian, trying to make sense of what she was saying, Clarin did not wait. Some deep apprehension within herself was verified by Vivian's first words, and she darted up the slope at a dead run while Tasmin watched helplessly from below, unable even to follow for Vivian was now clinging to his arm. 'Tasmin, do you have a recording of a viggy song? Tasmin! Do you?'

He tried to focus on her question. 'Yes. Donatella played it just a little while ago.'

'You've got to give it back to them, Tasmin.'

'Give it back!'

'Wipe it out. Something. They'll try to take it from you, Tasmin, and some of them could be killed. They saved me. They saved Miles. *They've got Celcy's baby, Tasmin*! Oh, don't ask how, why. Don't ask questions, just tell me you will.'

The music was builiding slowly into a rhythmic pattern, Jamieson's voice softly soaring, leaping, like the wind. Beneath the sound, the Enigma quieted, shivering almost into silence. Still, there was a quiver.

'It took me almost an hour last time,' Donatella whispered.

Jamieson nodded, never losing the line of melody. His eyes swung between the two towers of the Enigma. As they moved between the two, he saw Clarin coming up the trail. 'She's in a tearing hurry,' he told himself, still singing. There was someone with Tasmin on the flatland, pointing and gesturing ...

'It's still shakin' a little,' whispered Myrony.

'Well, wait until it quits,' Chantiforth replied. They were working their way down toward the pillars that bordered the clearing where Jamieson was singing. Spider had started before them and was halfway down to the scree slopes on which Tasmin stood.

'Somebody coming up,' hissed Chanty. 'Lie flat and be still'

They peered between tumbled bits of crystal, watching Clarin as she came toward them up the mountain, panting and pulling herself along at speed. Just a little below them she stopped, positioning herself against a pillar, gasping for breath.

'What in hell,' thought Jamieson, not for a moment interrupting the song. Clarin was gesturing, imperatively. He began a repetition, a phrase that was sung again and again, in ascending keys, only to hear her voice moving with him.

'An-dar-ououm,' he sang.

'Bro-oo-ther,' she sang in thirds below, clear as a bell.

The danger call! The recognition call! His eyes darted around him, he turned. Nothing!

'An-dar-ououm,' he sang, his voice rising.

'Bro-oo-ther,' in thirds.

Jamieson beckoned to Donatella and began to move down, away, away from the bloody ground between the spires, down toward Clarin, never stopping the song.

'An-dar-ououm,' he sang again, voice soaring.

'An-dar-ououm,' came half a hundred voices from all around him.

Viggies! In the shadow of crystal he could see their eyes glowing behind the ruby orbs of inflated song-sacks. 'An-dar-ououm, an-dar-ououm. '

Then he and Donatella were beside Clarin, the three of them moving downward, swiftly, letting the viggies take the song.

'What's the matter?' Donatella demanded. 'Why did you cry "brother"?'

'Save your breath. Don. Just get down and out of the way of this thing. According to the viggies, it's going to blow.'

'Blow! It's quiet as a tomb, and getting quieter all the time.' Donatella stopped, turned as though to go back up the mountain. 'Is that *viggies* singing?'

'Trying to give us time to get out of the way. Us and themselves. Move, will you.' Clarin grabbed Donatella's arm and forcibly turned her. 'Move, down. If we're wrong you can always come back ...'

Then they were down off the ramp and running toward Tasmin and Vivian and Miles and a dozen young viggies who were all staring at the Enigma and at one another with open mouths, immobilized by strangeness.

A quiver.

A small quiver, as though a rug had been pulled beneath their feet. The song was running away, trickling off the mountain on a wave of viggy feet, fleeing. The rug moved once more, this time a good tug. Donatella staggered. The viggies threw themselves down, gesturing, calling in Loudsinger language, 'Down, down, hold on, tumble down coming.'

And then it came, thunder, the mountain heaving, the spires shimmering, seeming actually to bend and sway as all around them the smaller pillars shattered and roared.

Fragments spun across the sky, glittering shards of bloody light, edged like knives.

Chunks rained from the top of 'lings, bounding, shattering, ricocheting in hissing trajectories.

Against the sky the twin tines of the Enigma shouted, a howling cataract of threat and danger.

The Translator, set at the top of its volume, roared.

'You'd think after all this time they could get it right.' Donatella's voice become the voice of a giant.

Then *'That was petulant of* you.' Donatella's monstrous voice again.

Then *'It pisses me off when they don't know who I am ...'* Donatella's voice. As it had been Lim's voice, that other time.

On the height, two figures staggered to their feet, one of them carrying a rifle. A spinning shard took off his head, the shard no redder than the blood that spouted high in a momentary jet. The other figure fell and was swallowed up in a dancing fountain of razor-edged boulders.

Where Tasmin and the others clung, the earth heaved and hit them in the face, falling away beneath them again, shaking, again, again, again.

Then silence.

Vivian, Miles, Donatella, Tasmin, Clarin, Jamieson.

The viggies had gone.

Vivian, Miles, Donatella, Tasmin, Clarin ...

'Where's Jamieson?' grated Tasmin. 'Where is he?'

'He was right behind me,' Clarin sobbed. 'Right behind me.' She levered herself to her feet, staggering. 'Back there.'

Back there was only piled crystal.

From behind a tumble of sanguinary glass, glittering with malice, a dusty thing rose to its feet, teeth exposed in a grimace of hate. It put a weapon to its shoulder and snarled at them through the blood on its face. 'Stand where you are.'

'I have to find Jamieson,' said Tasmin stupidly. 'I've got to find him.'

'I said stand where you are! Or I'll shoot the lot of you.'

'Spider Geroan,' Donatella whispered. 'Oh, God. Spider Geroan.'

'Get over here,' Spider said, gesturing with the weapon at Clarin. 'Get over here, or I'll kill the rest of them right now, starting with him!'

As though hypnotized, Clarin moved toward him.

'Clarin! No!' Tasmin's voice.

She twitched.

'Keep moving, girl, or I'll take him out. I swear I will.'

She moved on. When she was within reach of him, he grabbed her, turning her to face them, one of his arms around her throat, the other fumbling to place a knife at the side of her face.

'Now,' said Spider Geroan. 'Who did that?'

'Who ... who did what?' Donatella asked.

'Who set off that thing!'

'No one,' she said. 'It just blew.'

The knife at Clarin's face made a tiny motion and she cried out, a thin, black trickle oozing down her cheek.

'None of that!' he grated. 'Somebody did it.'

Tasmin struggled to make his voice calm. The man before him was mad. Perhaps had always been mad. 'Clarin went up to tell Jamieson and Don that the Enigma doesn't act rationally,' he said. 'Vivian brought us that message. We didn't know it before ...'

'So you got scared and ran, and that did it,' Geroan asserted, moving the knife again. Clarin cried out again, a high, toneless shriek.

'It was already doing it,' Don said. 'Couldn't you feel it? The shaking never really stopped!'

Spider breathed heavily for a moment. First, he wanted to get even with whichever one of them had done it to him. Then he wanted to do this girl. Then ... then he'd figure out what next. In the meantime, he moved the knife again, almost reflexively, hearing the answering cry of pain with something approaching pleasure.

Tasmin's stomach clenched and he bit down on his tongue to keep from screaming.

'Distract him,' murmured Don. 'Think of something.'

'I have to find Jamieson,' Tasmin called frantically. 'Or none of us can get out of here.'

Spider looked up, the knife stopped moving. 'What do you mean?'

'Let me find him,' Tasmin shrieked. 'He's like my son.'

In the shadows of the rocks, Bondri Gesel. 'Like his son? What does that mean? Let me alone.' This to a giligee who was stanching the blood from a cut on his shoulder. 'Let me alone and find this Jamieson. He is one of Tasmin Ferrence's troupe, and the debt is not yet paid.'

'He could be your son and it wouldn't matter,' Spider snarled lifting the hand with the knife to wipe his own eyes. He felt no pain from the cuts on his face and neck, but the blood was a nuisance and made him irritable. 'He could be your brother or your mother and it wouldn't matter. You've been a bother, Tripsinger. You and the Explorer there. I've come to stop the bother.'

He choked Clarin against his chest with his knife hand and picked up the rifle once more. There were too many of them to play with. He would save only one. The girl. Clarin. Though he didn't feel like it, really. Maybe he would, later.

In the shadows of the rocks, Bondri Gesel. 'That Loudsinger is going to kill them,' he roared at the top of his song-sack. 'The debt is coming unstuck again; get rid of that Loudsinger with the weapon.'

Something seized Spider's knife hand and tore it away from Clarin's face. Clarin rolled away, and as Spider leaped toward her, he tripped over something and fell down. It was a furry thing, and it didn't get out of his way. Another furry thing was hanging on the end of the rifle and he couldn't raise it. Something grabbed him by his legs and sank needle teeth into his thighs. There was no pain, but the thing hung on him, handicapping his movement. Another thing grabbed for the rifle, two more, tearing it away from him. The things clinging to his legs tripped him again. Dozens more of them sat on him. One stared deep into his eyes, brushing his forehead with long, feathery things growing out of its head. He struggled, but there were too many of them.

'This one is defective,' said the senior giligee. 'Bondri Gesel, this Loudsinger is defective. He has no pain feelings at all. Perhaps that is why he acts as he does.'

Bondri regarded the Loudsinger with disfavor. The Prime Song urged good returned for good, and when possible, good returned as an example for others, even when bad had been intended. However, the song also directed that those who kill without good reason must be disposed of in order that others may live in tranquility. Then there was the question of the taboo. There was no good reason to break the taboo for this man. Now he looked down into Spider Geroan's expressionless eyes and attempted to apply the Song.

'Can you fix him?' he sang. 'Can you fix him so he can feel?'

'Simple,' caroled the giligee.

'Well, then, fix him,' he said, with a sense of satisfaction that he did not even attempt to understand. 'And when you have finished, tell the troupe they can eat him.'

By the time the first astonished screams came from Spider Geroan, Tasmin and the others had found Jamieson and carried him far enough away from the Enigma to avoid any further 'tumble down.' When they had gone far enough that they could hear no further noise from that direction, they slumped on the flat, motionless earth without moving, watching in dull amazement as a giligee everted her pouch over Clarin's wounded face and began to mend it.

Jamieson lay nearby, a circle of giligees around him. He was, according to Bondri, somewhat broken, but the giligees thought he could be fixed.

One of those giligees, at Vivian's suggestion, had shown Tasmin what was in her pouch. 'It isn't finished yet,' she had apologized. 'But it's developing nicely. The female Loudsinger says it is your young?' What was there was very small, but very pink and lively.

'I can't believe it,' Tasmin said over and over. 'I can't believe it.'

Bondri could not figure out why he could not believe it. He had seen it. So had everyone else. And they had sung it to him two or three times. Bondri was getting impatient. He had not raised the question of the captive song, but he nudged Vivian from time to time, until at last she cleared her throat.

'Tasmin. Bondri asks that you free the song you have captive.'

'It's the only proof I've got,' Donatella objected.

'No one's going to believe just that,' Clarin said. 'We've got nothing, Don. The Enigma blew. It didn't talk to you.'

'It did before,' she cried.

Bondri inflated his sack. These people did not sing in an orderly fashion. They did not get things straightened out and properly harmonized; they jumped from one thing to another, over and over. 'Please,' he boomed.

'One thing at a time. First, the captive song. Then what other things are of concern.'

'The record of the viggy music is no good to us,' said Tasmin. 'Come on, Don. They've saved our lives.'

'All right,' she cried. 'I don't care. I was probably deluded anyhow.'

Tasmin opened the machine. 'Would you like us to erase it?'

'Erase? I would like you to set it free!'

Vivian reached across Tasmin's hands to press the controls. 'Let it play out, Tas. Then burn the cube. That's what they do with their dead. The cube will be dead then, and the song will be free.'

'So.' Bondri nodded his approval. 'We will join the song.'

As it played from the synthesizer, the viggies sang with it. Am-dar-ououm. A song of quiet. When it was done, Tasmin placed the cube in the fire where it expired in a flash of sparks.

'So.' Bondri sighed.

'Why did the Enigma blow?' Tasmin asked Bondri, singing it.

'Because it is the Mad One, which has two minds. You heard it. On your machine.'

'On the machine?'

'On your machine. Which speaks in Loudsinger language with the voice of that one.' He pointed to Donatella.

Tasmin clutched his head. 'It uses your voice, Don?'

'It uses whoever's voice is using it. When Lim had it, it used his.'

'Then that bellowing from the translator, it wasn't you?'

'It was the Mad One,' sang Bondri. 'It was angry that you did not address it by name. You, female Loudsinger,' he pointed to Don, 'had asked it before what its name is, but you did not remember ...'

'I don't understand,' she whispered.

Chowdri was annoyed. These people didn't understand anything! 'Bondri and I will sing it to you,' he chanted. 'Now listen!'

'You came to the Enigma before. Months ago. You used a stolen song to quiet the skin of the Enigma, is that not so? That is so. Then you asked it a question. You asked it what name it had for itself.'

Donatella nodded. Tasmin brought himself out of his self-absorption and listened. Even Clarin half sat up, making the giligee beside her snort in disapproval.

'The Enigma replied,' sang Chowdri. 'We heard it do so. It sang, "Messengers know to whom they come."'

'Was that a reply?' chanted Tasmin.

'It was the name the Enigma called itself. *Messengers know to whom they come.* Perhaps the Enigma thinks it is a messenger to all the Presences, and so it says this mad thing.

'Then the female told it something. "I am not one of the usual messengers," and the Enigma replied, "None of them are." There are no usual messengers to the Enigma. Messengers do not come to the Enigma. Thinking of this made the Enigma angry, and you, you female Loudsinger, wisely you went away very quickly. Is this not a true song?'

'It is a true song,' sang Donatella in a tone of resignation. 'That's what happened.

'This time,' sang Bondri, 'you came again and quieted the skin. It is a sunny day, much light flows into the Enigma making it hot. The Enigma is awake and irritable. It expected you to address it by name. It had told you its name. You did not address it by name. You merely went on with skin quieting, even though the Enigma was awake. It became irritated …'

'You mean that's what happened with Lim? He did the same thing?' Tasmin's jaw dropped. 'It wasn't because he stopped following the score?'

'When the Presence wakes, you must call it by name,' sang Chowdri and Bondri together, the troupe behind them in full chorus. 'Every child knows that!'

Silence, while they thought about it. It was Clarin who asked the question at last. 'Then all we had to do was call it what it told us its name was? *Messengers know to whom they come*?'

'Perhaps,' sang Chowdri, solo voice. 'Except that the Mad One is mad.'

'What does that mean?'

'It changes what it calls itself. Sometimes every hour, every day. Sometimes not so often. And sometimes it will not tell anyone what its name is.'

'So,' said Don. 'It got angry, and it blew.'

'It snapped its fingers at you,' sang Chowdri. 'And we had only finished cleaning up from last time.'

'It shouted,' Tasmin said. 'It shouted out that after all this time, we ought to be able to get it right.'

'One half of it sang that,' agreed Bondri.

'Then it was the other half that said, "That was petulant of you."'

'True. The other half is less irritable. It remonstrates with the first half. But it was the first half of the Enigma that said, "I become annoyed when these creatures do not know who I am." The Enigma said these same things to Lim Terree. The Mad One sometimes says the same things over and over. We believe the Mad One is mad because it has two halves that are partly separate and partly the same.'

'It was there all the time,' Tasmin said. 'I heard those words, but I thought it was Lim who said them.'

'You could have asked us,' said Bondri irrationally. 'The other Great Ones are not mad, most of them. Some are silly, but most of them are not mad.

Except that they are very irritated just now, and it must be because of the things the Loudsingers are doing!'

'But you've never spoken to us before,' Clarin sang. 'Why?'

'Because you do not sing the truth,' Bondri chanted, the troupe joining him to make this manifest. 'To sing to those who do not sing the truth, this is taboo.'

'But you broke this taboo!'

'Because of the debt we owed for Prime Priest Favel, for your brother who released him from captivity in the long ago. A debt of honor takes precedence over taboo.' He stood up, gathering his troupe around him. 'Now we go, and the taboo is once again as it should be. I have paid the debt of Prime Priest Favel. Vivian and the child are saved. You, Tasmin Ferrence, are saved. Your almost child is also saved, or will be when it is finished. I have returned good for good.'

Don cried out, a pleading sound of negation. Tasmin thought bleakly of what was in store for Jubal, his mind frantically searching for some way to stop the departure of the viggies.

'There is still a debt,' he gasped. 'A debt owed by Bondri Gesel.'

Bondri drew himself up, fangs exposed. 'What debt!'

'When my brother released Prime Priest Favel from captivity, a debt was incurred. Is this not so?'

'It is so.'

'And is a song not as important as a Prime Priest?'

Bondri cocked his head. It was not a question he had considered before. A giligee trilled a response, a female took up the refrain, then two males in countermelody. They sang it for some time. Finally Bondri responded. 'A song is almost as important as a Prime Priest.'

'Did I not free a song from captivity, Bondri Gesel? Do you not owe me a debt?'

This time the singing went on for the better part of an hour. Tasmin went to the place Jamieson lay, running his hands along the boy's face and body. 'Will he live?' he whispered to the intent giligees.

'Oh, yes,' one of them trilled in return. 'He will live. I think we have him mostly fixed. Tomorrow, maybe, he will walk.' She sat with her pouch everted, and Tasmin withdrew his gaze from that mass of thin tendrils that had penetrated Jamieson's body and were busy deep inside, doing incredible things.

He went to sit beside Clarin. The wounds on her face were closed. She lay huddled in a blanket, shivering from time to time. He put his hand under the blanket, on her neck. She jerked away from him.

'Shhh,' he said. 'It's all right, Clarin. All right.'

She began to cry. He gathered her up in his arms.

'Shhh.' His heart turned over at the sound of her weeping.

'No one ever hurt me before. Not purposely.'

'He was a machine, Clarin. Pretend it was a machine. Not anyone worth hating. He's dead.'

'They ate him!' she turned her head away, retching.

'It's a meat-poor planet, Clarin. According to Vivian, they eat very little meat. They eat fresh fish whenever they get to the seashore, or whenever their fisher kin run inland with a catch, and they dry fish to carry with them. They don't eat carrion or carrion eaters, which eliminates a lot of the other wildlife.'

'It just ... just takes getting used to. What are we going to do now?'

'As soon as the viggies quit singing, I'll let you know.'

When they finished singing, it was to announce that freeing the song had indeed brought a debt with it. Neither of the troupe leaders was happy about this. Tasmin wondered how much of the decision had been brought about by viggy curiosity concerning the Loudsingers. Perhaps the troupes had not wanted to return immediately to the taboo.

He said nothing of this. Instead, he drew Clarin up beside him, held her until she quit shaking, and then said, 'Bondri Gesel, Troupe leader, great singer. I beg a boon from you. I beg that you listen while I try to sing truth to you. Me, and this person with me here.' He gestured at Clarin. 'Jamieson sings more truth than I do, but he cannot sing just now. Will you listen while I try?'

Bondri, annoyed, conferred with the troupe. The troupe was a good deal more compliant than he was.

'What are we singing?' whispered Clarin, a trace of color coming back into her cheeks.

'We're singing the destruction of Jubal,' Tasmin said. 'If we don't get some help here, everything we feared is still going to come to pass.'

In later years the troupes of viggies who moved from the pillars of the Jammers to the towers of the east, resang on festival occasions the First Truth Singing of the Loudsingers. Not that it was a very polished performance, but it rang with a passionate veracity that the viggies much admired. Of course, there were only two who really sang, plus one who gave them some musical support, so the ultimate truth of the song might have been in doubt, were it not for verification by later happenings. Nonetheless, the viggies remembered that night.

Tasmin stood up and sang the story of the PEC, of human exploitation of many planets. He sang of the Prime Song of humans, and of the disobedience that many showed that Song. Beside him, Clarin – the viggies assumed she was his mate, they sang so alike and so well together – sang of greed and pride, things that the viggies understood to some extent. She sang of lying, which they did not understand but were willing to take on faith. Then together they sang of what they had learned, of the lies told about the Presences, of the great destruction that was sure to come.

At this point, the viggies joined the song, query and reply, antiphonally, circling, circling again, as it grew more and more true. 'If,' they sang, 'then what?' and Tasmin replied. 'Then if,' they sang, 'what then?' and Clarin told them.

They sang of the good guys, Jamieson who lay wounded with the gili-gees working on him, Thyle Vowe, Grand Master of the Tripsingers, who worshipped the truth – Clarin sang this, much to Tasmin's surprise – of Tripsingers and Explorers, and those people of peace who tilled the soil and loved Jubal. These people would not be allowed to stay, they would go in any case, but they would not want Jubal destroyed behind them.

And lastly, they sang the names of villains. Spider Geroan, who had been healed of his affliction and then eaten. The Crystallites, who were liars. The troopers who blocked the way east. And finally, Hayward Justin, Planetary Manager, who would destroy the Presences, very soon unless something was done.

And finished singing.

There was a long silence, unbroken. None of the members ventured song. At last it was the senior giligee, the one who carried Prime Priest Favel's brain-bird, who called in a high, clear soprano that soared above them like a gyre-bird.

'Come, Troupe leader. We must go to the Highmost Darkness, Lord of the Gyre-Birds, Smoke Master, the one the humans call Black Tower, and ask it what to do.'

17

They came to the Black Tower on the following day. Jamieson was unable to ride. Tasmin had held the boy before him on the saddle, cradling him like a baby while he slept.

The troupes of Bondri and Chowdri had come by their own paths, swifter trails than the one followed by the humans. When Donatella and Clarin arrived, some distance ahead of Tasmin, Jamieson, and the spare mules, they found the troupes already singing.

The humans made camp. None of them had eaten recently, and food, while uninteresting, was a necessity. The smell of heating rations woke even Jamieson.

'I thought I was dead,' he said wonderingly. 'It came down on top of me.'

'You probably would have been,' Tasmin whispered, lifting the boy's head to the cup. 'Except for the giligees.'

'Except for the what?'

A long explanation followed, which had not really ended when Bondri Gesel came into their campsite, shaking his head.

'We sang to the Black Tower,' he chanted in a weary monotone. 'It did not want to listen. It is full of annoyance and irritation. It is worse than when we were at the one you call the Watcher. It is not the skin that speaks, nor the deep parts. It is some middle part that is new to us, a part full of questions and anger. Something has happened to make it very angry, Tasmin Ferrence. Presences have been bothered!'

'Bothered?' asked Tasmin, uncertain what the viggy meant.

'To the north. Loudsingers came. They made noises and shattered the fingers of many Presences, passing through the air in the confusion. The Presences were slow to wake, but now they are wakening. On all the world, they are wakening.'

'The people following us,' said Don. 'I wondered how they got onto us so fast. They came in by air!'

Bondri went on. 'We have sung to the Highmost Darkness. We have told it everything we know. Then we sang everything you sang to us. It wants to sing to you.'

'Me?' Tasmin asked.

'You. And the Explorer and the young female and this one. All of you.'

Jamieson heaved himself into a sitting position. 'I'm not sure I'm up to singing.' He was staring at the viggy in complete absorption, turning to Tasmin. 'Who did you say this was?'

Tasmin introduced them. 'Bondri, this is Jamieson, my friend. Bondri Gesel, leader of the viggies.'

The young human and the viggy nodded their heads precisely at the same moment and to the same angle. Evidently ceremony knew no species. Tasmin fought down a snort of bleak amusement.

'Bring him anyhow,' said the viggy. 'The Black Tower wants to look at him.'

'Look?' faltered Jamieson. 'They can see?'

'Not with eyes,' admitted Bondri. 'But they see, yes. When they want to.'

'And you've told them all about what's happening, with BDL and all?'

'We are not sure Highmost Darkness, Smoke Master, Lord of the Gyre-Birds understands, because we do not understand. That is why it wants to see you.' And Bondri turned away, stamping his feet a little as he went, head high and throat sack half distended.

'He's miffed,' said Jamieson in awe.

'He is that,' agreed Tasmin as he got to his feet and joined the others in a straggling procession toward the Black Tower, the music box with the translator program at the ready.

'How is it,' the Tower asked, after laborious introductions had taken place, 'that you have not proclaimed (sung, announced) our sentience before – if you have known it (contained a concept for) as you say you have known it.'

Bondri translated this into Loudsinger language. They checked it against the translator. Viggy and machine were more or less in agreement. Bondri was waiting somewhat impatiently for a human response.

Tasmin looked helplessly toward Clarin. They were assembled so near the monstrous monolith that it actually seemed to bend above them. The sounds that came from it came from here, there, everywhere. They had no sense of location. It was not like looking into a human – or a viggy – face. There was no way in which the question could be simply answered. There was no time for equivocation, for polite, diplomatic evasions. These words were the first between two totally different types of sentient creatures. Though they did not have the language of the viggies, which could speak only truth, Tasmin felt desperately that he should try.

Clarin nodded to him, eyes fastened on his. 'Tell it,' she said. 'Tell it the truth. Find the words, somehow, and tell it the truth.'

'What do you want me to sing?' whispered Bondri. 'It is a very important question the god has asked.'

'I don't want you to sing,' Tasmin cried. 'I want to tell it myself. Me. And Clarin and Jamieson. I want to tell it exactly what we mean to say!'

'Do the Loudsingers have the words?'

'No, Bondri. You know we don't have the words. We have to have a while to get the words.'

'Then I will tell the Highmost Darkness that the Loudsinger is preparing an answer.'

The troupe sang a short phrase, three times repeated, and a cascade of sound belled from the Tower.

'It understands the difficulty this question poses,' said Bondri. 'The Great One found intriguing alternatives in encoding it linguistically and can extrapolate there would be alternative possibilities in answer. It allows you time.'

Shaking their heads over this, trying to believe they were living a reality rather than a dream, they gathered around Donatella's synthesizer. Tasmin bent above the keyboard, making quick notations as the translator gave him each key concept. Clarin was beside him. Jamieson heaved himself up, tottering, and Vivian ran to hold him up.

'Lie down, young man. You're not fit to be up.'

Jamieson grinned. 'You think I'm going to let that old man do all the singing, Vivian?' He staggered a little. 'I'll get stronger if I move around.'

He went to peer over Tasmin's shoulder. Tasmin looked up, shook his head disapprovingly, then turned back to the machine. After a time, Jamieson leaned closer, to help.

Occasionally the translator beeped, clucked, and refused to offer anything at all. When this happened, Tasmin turned to Bondri and asked, 'How would you say ...' or 'Is this how you say ...?' Bondri offered him word or correction, and Tasmin returned to his work.

What concepts would the Black Tower have? No organic ones, surely. One could not talk of hearts, of blood, of pain. Did they feel pain? Did they have honor? Did they understand truth? There were honorifics aplenty, so they had some concept of glory and power, but what did even these mean to them? They did understand beauty, so much was clear. There was not a phrase sung by the viggies that was not beautiful, and that could not be accidental. There was not a word or phrase in a successful Password that was not beautiful either, and that should have told them something. Though perhaps it told them only that viggy and human had similar esthetics.

It emerged that the Presence had no concept of its own crystallinity. Its mind existed within the great crystal as the mind of humans existed within its cells. Was the human mind aware of its cellular nature, of its neurons and receptors? Only from the outside did that kind of awareness come. And what were the minds of the Presences after all but vast arrays of dislocations, molecular vacancies, self-reproducing line, and planar defects generating energy along infinitesimal fault lines, molecular neurons rather than biological ones, atoms of chromium instead of dopamine, with vacancies in the infinite grid serving as receptor cells?

And yet they were aware. They knew inside from outside. They spoke from their own universe to a universe outside themselves. It would suffice – as a starting point.

Slowly, lines of musical notation grew beneath Tasmin's hands. More slowly yet, the words were chosen.

'I can't do that,' sighed Jamieson, indicating a soaring line of vocalization. He was able to stand without help, able to move with only minor discomfort. Or so he told himself, refusing to admit how much of his competence at the moment was mere adrenaline. But he couldn't sing that …

'I can,' said Clarin. Her voice was factual, without expression, and yet her eyes were alive with concentration.

'Yes, better let Clarin do that. You take the other part. This will be yours, Clarin,' Tasmin muttered, slashing the notation pen across the staff, notes blooming in its wake. 'Here's another one for you, Clarin. The main theme is mine. I'm leaving the embellishments to you two.'

Jamieson grunted, making notes on his own machine, subvocalizing certain phrases to set them in mind.

Tasmin scowled, erased, notated once more. 'This cadence, here. Take it slow; don't hurry it. Extend this syllable out, out, that's the base. Build on that, don't lose it. Come up on the vibrato softly, then let it grow, make it tremble …'

'Wait a minute,' Clarin muttered, reaching for the pen and pointing at the screen. 'Here, and here, do it this way.' The glowing notes and words shivered and changed. Tasmin considered. Yes, it was better. Was it enough? Only the attempt would tell.

'I don't get this bit,' Jamieson said. 'Shouldn't it fall into the minor, TA-daroo, like that? You've got it on the next syllable …'

'No, it works. You initiate the harmonic line and Clarin comes in here, and me, here.'

'What are they doing?' Bondri whispered to Donatella.

'I'm not sure,' the Explorer answered. 'I've never seen anyone do it before.'

'How can they make a song without singing it?'

'It's just something they do,' she replied.

An hour wore away, and most of another. Words and phrases were changed in meaning by others that came before or after, by subtle modifications in emphasis or key. They sang very softly to Bondri, phrase by phrase, and he nodded, wondering at the strangeness of this. What would the Great Ones make of this concept of difference? Of dominance of one group by another group? To the Great Ones, all viggies were alike, the same. The Great Ones seemed to know nothing of individuality. What would they think? What would they do?

Bondri turned to the senior giligee for comfort.

'All will be as all will be,' it sang, quoting the fifth commandment of the Prime Song. 'Be at peace, Bondri Wide Ears.'

'That's easy for you to sing,' Bondri mumble-hummed, quoting Jamieson. This human language had some interesting things in it. Sarcasm, for instance. And irony. Bondri was very taken with both.

'All right,' Tasmin cried at last. 'Pay attention, class. We're almost sight reading this one, so hold your concentration. Get it right the first time, because we may not have a second chance. Donatella, help us with these effects – on this line right here ...'

'You expect me to sight read this!' she exclaimed incredulously.

'You can do it,' announced Clarin through tight lips.

'It'll take all four boxes,' Jamieson said. 'Tasmin leads.'

'Pronounce that word again,' Tasmin was asking Bondri. 'Dooo-vah-loo-im.' He made another notation of accent on the keyboard. 'Did you feed it to the other boxes, Jamieson?'

'All in but that last change. All right.'

They stood apart, breathing deeply, the boxes supported on their retract-able stands. Tasmin keyed the first sounds he had scored, a low, brooding bass, pulsing beneath the words he was singing, the words he was thinking. It would not be enough to sing nonsense syllables. They had sung nonsense words for generations. This time he had to know what he meant.

The bass built into a mighty chord of pure sound, non-instrumental in feeling, then faded away almost to silence as Tasmin began to sing.

'Here in this beautiful land,' he sang, 'we lived on lies.' This was a phrase Bondri had helped them with: a condition that is not real, a word that is warped.

'Lies,' sang Clarin and Jamieson, weaving the sound of *lies* into a disso-nance, which throbbed for one moment and then resolved into an expectant harmonic.

'Powerful ones let us move in these lands only if we lied.' Tasmin had wanted the word *freedom*. Neither Bondri nor the translator could come up with anything. Did the Great Ones have any concept of freedom? How would they?

'If we told the truth, they would force us [the word meant shatter or demolish] away from these lands of glory. Our voices would be silenced, our praise songs fallen into quiet.

'The lies they put into our mouths were these ...'

Donatella bent frantically over her box making a wild clamor of bells. Beneath Jamieson's fingers, trumpet sounds soared into incredible cascades of sound. Drums beat in an agitated thunder under Clarin's hands.

Three voices rose as one, separating into distinct upward spiraling tendrils of song. 'They forced us to say there were no Presences [great beings, mighty non-mobile creatures]. They told us to say the Great Ones were no more than empty stones.'

Silence. A tentative fluting. 'Why? Why did they do this?' Jamieson's voice rose in a lilting cusp of sound, questioning, seeking, wheeling like a seeking gyre-bird, tumbling in the air, a question that moved so quickly it could not be caught or denied. 'Why?'

From the troupe of Bondri Gesel, an antiphon, unrehearsed, spontaneous as a fall of water. 'Why? What creature could do this thing?'

A return to the ominous base, the annunciatory drum.

'The laws of man [this small, mobile creature not made as the Great Ones are made, other than the messengers of the gods] are clear,' Tasmin sang. 'Where sentient creatures already are [beings like the Great Ones in thinking, making concepts] humans may not go except as those same creatures will allow.'

A hushed phrase, sung in unison, echoed by the troupe of Bondri Gesel. 'We singers respect [obey, honor] the law.'

'But the powerful ones do not respect the law,' Clarin trumpeted.

Silence. A cymbal, tapped. A woodblock sound, like the inexorable drop of water.

'We, we the singing creatures, the speaking creatures, we respect the law and yet we lied ...'

Three voices rising in one great harmonic chord. 'Because our concepts would be broken if we left the Great Ones. We did it out of fear, out of hope, out of love.'

Voices trailing into silence. Liquescent flute sounds dripping away. A last faint call of a grieving trumpet, as though from a distant rampart, being abandoned. A last tap of slack headed, fading drum. Quiet.

What a definition of hypocrisy, Clarin thought, almost hysterically. A symphony on human mendacity.

From the Black Tower, not a quiver.

The four of them stared up at the enormous height, their faces strained with the concentration of the song, gradually relaxing, becoming slack. Jamieson staggered and collapsed on the ground, smiling apologetically at Donatella before he passed out. The giligees gathered around him again, chirping angrily.

Tasmin wondered weakly if they'd gotten any of the words right. The word for love, for instance. Bondri had, said it that way, but Bondri had had an odd expression on his wide face when he said it. Tasmin started to ask Bondri whether the word had ever even been used with the Presences.

And was knocked to his knees by the song coming from the Black Tower.

He could not understand a word of it. The translator chirped and gurgled, words fled across the screen only to be replaced with others. Words accumulated, multiple meanings were tried and discarded. Missing sense was filled in on the basis of speculation, words in parentheses bubbled and disappeared. Others came in their places.

'Interesting! (occupying of intelligence). More interesting (even than) the exercise (amusement, occupation) we have (been engaged in). Small mobile creatures (having such) concepts has not (been considered). Our messengers have not (troubled us, announced to us) concepts. Northern entities (parts?) find this (intriguing), Southern parts (entities?) even now begin (debate upon) concepts implied. Deep buried sections (parts? entities?') where the (great water lies) also include themselves. Wonderful! Quite wonderful! *Imperative: Explain love. Explain hope. Explain fear.'*

Just in case they missed it, the Black Tower sang it twice more, in variations. The translator compared versions two and three with version one and settled upon a single message.

Bondri had huddled down beside Clarin, the two of them arguing over an explanation of love that would make sense to a crystalline being. An unlikely duo to be doing such a thing, Tasmin thought at first. Then, remembering certain things both Bondri and Clarin had done in the past, he thought perhaps they were the best ones to do so. Bondri was going on about loving sets of offspring, loving a good giligee, loving the troupe.

Clarin didn't talk with the viggy long. Using the translator, she began singing about hope and fear, with the troupe of Bondri Gesel as backup. 'Those of us with short lives,' she vocalized, in a line of extended melody, 'much regret ending, becoming nothingness. This regret is fear. Those of us with fragile bodies that can be broken, much regret that breaking. This regret is also fear. We fear ending and breaking. We fear the ending of those we think of as parts of ourselves. Others are those who are not broken with us or ended with us. Thinking of others as part of self is called love.

'So, in our minds we create patterns in which there is no fear. These patterns are called hope ...'

Donatella was stretched out on the ground, simply listening, her face remote and musing. When she saw Tasmin looking at her, she remarked, 'She makes it all sound so simple, Tasmin. They'll probably understand her, too. I told you they talked, Tasmin. I told you. God, I wish Link could be here ...'

Later, falling over themselves from exhaustion, they tried to sleep, but Bondri Gesel kept waking them.

'The Great One wishes you to explain pain once more, Loudsinger.' 'The Great One asks that you tell again of the difference between bad and good.'

'In answer to a previous question, you used certain Loudsinger words the Great One does not understand. The Great One wants to know more about "standard business practices."' 'The Great One wants to know if you have something the same as hoosil. I told the Great One that was anger, but it wants *you* to tell it. It sang your particular label. This means the Great One now knows we are each a separate creature, Tasmin Ferrence. It never thought that before. None of them ever thought that before.'

Tasmin accepted this through a haze of fatigue. 'I noticed the translator had some trouble deciding between parts and entities. As though the Presence isn't quite sure about boundaries between things.'

'The viggies noticed this, too, Tasmin Ferrence.'

'You sound amazed, Bondri Gesel.'

'I am ... what is that word Jamieson gave me? I am dumbfounded, Tasmin Ferrence. I am based in silence.' Bondri bounded away, obviously elated, only to return later, waking them all to get yet another answer and to answer a question or two himself.

'What was that business about the northern and southern parts, Bondri? I didn't understand that,' asked Jamieson.

'The one you call the Black Tower touches the ones you call the Watchers, deep beneath the soil. Far to the west it touches the ones you call Mad Gap. It touches the False Eagers and Cloud Gatherer and all the Presences of the Redfang Range. Beneath the lands, Tasmin Ferrence, all the Presences touch one another. Or perhaps not quite all. Perhaps they are all part of one thing. A thing that is everywhere, beneath the Deepsoil, far down, even beneath the seas. We think this is so. Or perhaps they only talk with one another. This is why, we viggies think, the Great One is not sure about edges of things. The Black Tower is not sure where it ends and other things begin. It is not madness, like the Enigma, but it is strangeness ...'

Morning.

Donatella, still triumphant, to Jamieson. 'I told you they talked.'

'You didn't tell me they talked all the time.' Jamieson was unable to get up, and no one would let him try. Still, he seemed to be alert, with a clear understanding of what was going on. He asked Tasmin, 'What do we do now? Have we got enough proof for the commission?'

'We haven't talked to it yet about what Justin is planning to do ...'

'Has already done,' snapped Don. 'At least partly.'

This took the entire morning. Some things were understood almost immediately. The Black Tower understood destruction. It did not understand 'maximizing profits,' however, which Tasmin had taken some time to translate though he used the Urthish word for it, too. When the Tower finally understood cost benefits, it had a fit of hoosil, which required them to leave the vicinity for over an hour. At the end of the hour, the concept had been spread through the vast network and they were told that all the Presences both understood it and were equally annoyed by it as it pertained to them. What came out always equaled what went in, so far as the Presences were concerned. Taking more out than went in was immoral, unmathematical, and illogical. Things did not balance properly if more went in than out, or vice versa.

'Of course, they're completely right,' Donatella said. 'Do we want to talk about closed and open systems? Maybe that can wait.'

'It'll have to wait,' Tasmin told her. 'We'll all getting to the point that our voices are giving out.'

'Now what?' intoned Bondri Gesel, sounding weary but indomitable. The troupe had spent the morning telling each other what was happening, just to get it on record, and they had not been able to arrive at a finished song. Some of the words did not seem to be entirely accurate or true. The senior giligee was having a fit over that. Giligees were conservative anyhow, and this one was carrying the brain-bird of Prime Priest Favel, which made it even more conscious of doing things right.

'I hate to say this, Bondri, but do you suppose we could teach the Black Tower to speak some Urthish? The human language? We have some words that are very cumbersome to translate.'

'It should be very easy for them to learn the whole language,' Bondri sang. 'The Great One has already asked us to begin.' Bondri sounded offended by this.

'Your own language is far superior,' Tasmin offered placatingly. 'Truly.'

'Oh, we know it is. More accurate. More specific.'

'Exactly.'

'Your language, on the other hand, has a lot of words we don't have at all. It has more room in it.'

'That's true.'

'That's what the Great One says. The Great One says it is a good language for puzzles, because it can mean many things.'

'The Great Ones like puzzles, do they?'

'For millions of years they have done puzzles, Tasmin Ferrence. They have divided themselves into parts. What you would call teams. They have used us to carry puzzle moves from one part to another, so the other team would not know what move they are making. They made us for this, or so our Prime Song says. Now you are their new puzzle, Tasmin Ferrence. You and all the Loudsingers. We viggies think it will be interesting to watch them figure you out.'

'I want them to speak Urthish for only one reason, Bondri Gesel.'

'We know,' said the troupe leader. 'When they speak to your powerful ones, there must be no misunderstanding what they say.'

Now Tasmin was dumbfounded. 'They intend to speak to our "powerful ones"?'

'They do, Tasmin Ferrence. As soon as you give them all the words in your language and tell them where these powerful ones are to be found.'

'All the words?'

'Are they not in the machine somewhere? The female, Clarin, said they were in the machine.'

'The dictionary! In the translator, yes.'

'Can this be played to the Great Ones?'

'I suppose it can.' The Presences themselves had thought of this? Well, it would certainly save the human voices. 'I understood that recorded things were unacceptable to them.'

'Irritating to the skins, yes, Tasmin Ferrence. But they can tolerate it if they are awake.'

Tasmin exchanged a wondering glance with Clarin, who said, 'Before they speak to the powerful ones, Bondri Gesel, ask the Tower if they will speak, very quietly, to persons from the citadels of the Tripsingers?'

'They will do this, even though they say your language is ugly, Clarin. It has some very bad sounds in it.'

'Would they understand an apology?'

'They already know. They say you are a young race that has not had time to smooth yourself. You are still very bumpy.' Bondri made a smile-like face, fangs showing at the edges of his mouth, a trifle malicious, Tasmin thought, before continuing. 'Your language is bumpy, and it is obvious some of your individual persons are also bumps that need to be smoothed away. Or eaten, perhaps.' Bondri licked his lips, enjoying Clarin's near success at hiding a shudder. 'Undoubtedly you have other bumps as well. However, they find even that interesting. There is no end to the interest that the Great Ones have stored up.'

Jamieson could not travel. The giligees would not let him travel. Tasmin knelt beside him, his hand on the boy's shoulder, watching the rise and fall of his chest, the flutter of eyelids, moving with the dream he was in.

The pressure of Tasmin's hand brought him from sleep. 'Master Ferrence,' Jamieson said, wakening all at once.

'Reb.'

'I'm sorry to plop out on you this way.'

'I shouldn't have let you sing to the Tower.'

'You and who else would've tried to stop me?'

'There was a Tripsinger here a while ago from Deepsoil Five, Reb. They heard the Tower roaring and sent someone to find out what was going on. I've asked him to send some people out to be with you, and with the Tower. The giligees will stay with you at least until then ...'

'Have a good trip, Master Ferrence. Make it fast.'

'We will. I'm sorry you can't be there for the end of it, however it ends.'

'It'll end here, too, one way or the other.' Jamieson grinned at him, then heaved a deep breath, as though it hurt him to do so. 'Master Ferrence.'

'Yes, Reb.'

'Remember, once I told you there was a lot to Clarin, Sir. I told you she wanted to work with you.'

'Well – she got her chance.'

'More than that, Sir. Tasmin.' That heaving breath again. 'She loves you. I got it out of her. I wish you'd kind of remember that. As a favor to me.'

Tasmin could not think of anything to say. He clasped Jamieson's shoulder in his hand once more and left him there.

A caravan moved from Deepsoil Five westward, laden with brou. It came to the Watchers. The Tripsinger put back his hood and rolled up his sleeves. In the Tripwagon, the backup man leaned forward to touch the synthesizer.

Trumpet sounds. A tap of drums.

'Arndaff-du-roomavah,' the Tripsinger sang.

'Brother, brother, brother,' replied the South Watcher. 'Return to the citadel and tell the Master General this Presence is his brother and wishes to speak with him.'

The wagons halted.

The Tripsinger fell silent, amazed and dizzy, totally unbelieving.

Not a 'ling quivered. The ground was silent.

'Are you deaf?' the North Watcher rumbled. 'Do what your brother says.'

Outside the Jut, a wagon train moved eastward along the 'Soilcoast road. It came to the Jammers. The Tripsingers readied themselves, a trifle nervously as every Tripsinger had done since the massacre. The ground was quiet, suspiciously quiet. They did not know what to make of that, and regarded each other with unease. The first notes sounded from the Tripwagon, only to be drowned by quite another music.

'Brother, brother, brother,' sang the Jammers in close harmony. 'Return to your citadel and tell your Master General to check his armory and be ready for trouble. Also, tell him to keep quiet about it until he hears from us.'

At the Redfang Range, a lonely Tripsinger sat high within the fire-like glimmer of the ranked pillars, awash in orange light. Night was coming, and he had caught no sight of anyone the Grand Master was interested in. Rumors were the Grand Master's own daughter was in here somewhere, but if that were true, she wasn't showing herself. Sighing, he put his glasses in his pack and started down the trail.

As he went into peril, he picked over the controls of his box, singing the Password in a passable voice, a bit wearily. He had been sitting high on the pass all day, and it had been a funny day. Spooky. Absolutely quiet. No movement in the Presences at all. He yawned, garbling the first words, his mouth gaped wide. It stuck that way. Someone else was singing ...

'Brother, brother, brother,' the Presence beside him vocalized softly in flutelike tones. 'Tripsinger, go tell the Master General of your citadel to get word to the Grand Master of the Worshipful Order that I, Redfang, want to speak with him.'

And then, almost as an afterthought.

'Are you recording this, youngster? Your Master General may want proof.'

The CHASE Commission was assembled in Splash One, conducting its scheduled meetings with considerable pomp. Among the audience were a number of VIPs, a few from Jubal, though most – including representatives from both the current and historic press as well as advisers and so-called neutral observers from the PEC – were from off-planet. Those from Jubal included the Honorable Wuyllum Thonks, not yet departed for he had not the means to depart, and his less than honorable lady, present for the same reason, although she did not understand why Wuyllum was at all worried. The only thing that had upset Honeypeach in a long, long time was Maybelle's disappearance. Justin wanted her and Justin was getting nasty about it. Honeypeach licked the corners of her mouth and visualized what she would do when she found the girl. Maybelle had to come out of hiding sometime.

Grand Master Thyle Vowe was also in attendance, though several of his friends and colleagues were not. Gereny, for example, and Jem. And that sweetheart of Rheme's, the Governor's daughter, the one that Vowe had personally pulled off that boat before Honeypeach Thonks could lay hands on her. Luckily Rheme had alerted them to provide a backup escape, just in case she didn't get away. These three and some others had established quite a redoubt in the half-empty warehouse in the fishing village of Tallawag. That it was an unlikely place for them to hide could have been testified to by several minions of Honeypeach's who had been searching for Maybelle ever since Vowe had abducted her. So far, they hadn't even come close.

Watching Honeypeach steam had given Vowe enough satisfaction to carry him over the deadly boredom of the hearings. He was of the opinion that the hearings were designed to be deadly, planned to be uninteresting in the extreme. Witness after witness testified to attempts to make sense out of Presence noises, some of them philologists who spoke pure jargon with no recognizable meaning. No one mentioned viggies. No one even thought of viggies. Vowe wondered at this. He had always had suspicions about viggies.

Harward Justin squatted at one side of the hearing room, low-bottomed as a toad, his slushy eyes swiveling from side to side of the room, his thin mouth stretching in a gratified grimace whenever a witness made a particularly telling point. For all the boredom, the place was crowded and concentration was intense.

Thus when someone jostled the Grand Master, he did not immediately respond. It took the elbow in his ribs twice more before he looked down to see a note held in the hand of an anonymous donor who was looking everywhere but at the Grand Master.

'Emergency. Northwest Citadel, soonest.' The name appended was Jasum Porlees, Master General of the Northwest Citadel. He and Thyle Vowe had been, boys in choir school together.

The Grand Master let a little time elapse, then squirmed through the crowd to the door. Outside on the steps, the same anonymous man was standing, staring out over the city and talking almost without moving his mouth. 'There's an air car waiting for you at the garage, Grand Master. Your friend says hurry.'

It was only when Thyle Vowe was halfway to the garage that he realized the man who had been talking to him was Rheme Gentry.

'Your daughter's all right,' said the Master General of the Northwest, soon after Thyle Vowe's arrival. He poured a cup of tea for the Grand Master and waited for the inevitable question.

'Where is she, Jasum?'

'Somewhere near the Black Tower. Or maybe most of the way here, by now. Probably coming pretty fast, since they won't have to sing their way by anything.'

'Won't have to what? What in hell are you talking about?'

'You're not going to believe who told me, Thyle. Best way to tell you is to show you. Are you up for a short mule ride into the Redfang Range?'

The commission had heard witnesses for ten days and part of an eleventh. Finally it recessed for a day or two before reconvening to consider its findings. Some of the members took advantage of this interruption to see something of Jubal while there was still, in one member's words, something to see. The destruction that would occur following their pronouncement was fully understood by certain members of the commission, although not by Honeypeach's stepson, the chairman, Ymries Fedder. He had been brou-sotted in his apartment since arrival, and the commission had been chaired by its vice chairman, a junketeering bureaucrat from Heron's World.

Harward Justin retired to the BDL building to take care of a few details. Wuyllum Thonks was waiting for him there.

'What the hell are you doing here, Thonks?'

'That's what I'd like to know. What am I doing here? Honeypeach and I were supposed to be off this place a week or more ago.'

'After the findings are announced, Governor, you can be on the first ship out. Along with the commission members. I had to seal things up to prevent any last-minute problems.'

'And when will the first ship out be leaving?'

'Three or four days. Maybe five if they want to make it look good. Some of them are sightseeing right now. They may take an extra day or two.'

'You don't anticipate any trouble?'

'I always anticipate trouble, Thonks. That's why it never bothers me.' Justin smiled, a slithering of lips across irregular teeth, making Wuyllum think of snakes writhing over stones. 'Trouble is just another thing to plan for, Governor.'

Wuyllum shivered for no discernable reason. 'I'll tell Honeypeach.'

'Speaking of your charming wife.' Justin smiled again, a particularly reptilian smile. 'Honeypeach promised to introduce me to your lovely daughter, but seemingly she's disappeared. Did you ever find her?'

'Not yet.' Wuyllum waved the question away, refusing to consider the implications of what Justin had just said. 'Maybelle had planned to return to Serendipity. It's her home, you know. When she was disappointed about the journey, she probably went to stay with friends. No doubt she'll turn up. Well. We'll be expecting space, Justin. On the first ship out. You'll let us know.'

'Remind your charming wife about the introduction, Thonks. I certainly want to meet your daughter before you leave. The Governor's residence is right next door. Call me when you find her.'

The Governor left, ashen-faced. He did not care terribly what might happen to Maybelle. He was, however, suddenly very worried that he might not be able to find her. Justin, for some inscrutable reason of his own, had just placed a price on Wuyllum's departure.

As soon as Justin was alone, he commed Colonel Lang, commander of the troops on Jubal. The men and the equipment were ready. As soon as the commission announced its findings, they could start blasting their way into every dirt town east of the coast.

'Colonel Lang?'

'Manager Justin.'

'It comes to mind, Colonel, that there may be some demonstrations when the commission announces its findings.'

'Is that so, Sir? Everything seems very peaceful.'

Justin sneered. The man was being slow on the load. 'Well, the findings haven't been announced yet, have they?'

'That's why I'm wondering why there should be disorder, Sir. If we don't know what the findings are, then we can't know what the response will be, can we?'

The officer's voice had been very dry, almost insolent, and Justin cursed himself. Damn the man's nerve! He was right, though. Any preemptive action, particularly while the commission members and observers were still on the planet, might be interpreted as exactly what it was.

'So long as you're ready for any eventuality, Colonel.'

'Oh, indeed, Sir. Always ready for any eventuality.'

Colonel Lang punched the com out. Every company of troopers moving toward the east had trailed behind it a string of relay points. Orders could be sent down those relay stations within hours. Once the commission's findings were known, orders to begin destruction would be received by the troopers without delay and Colonel Lang intended to join in the fun. However, just to avoid any problem later on, the Colonel did not intend to send those orders until the commission's findings were formally announced.

At another military office in Splash One, Captain Jines Verbold put down the snoop-ear that had been tuned to the Colonel's call.

'Harward Justin,' he explained unnecessarily to his visitor.

'I thought so,' said Rheme Gentry. 'He's getting nervous, now that everything's coming to a climax.'

'When's all this climaxin' goin' to take place?'

'After the commission reconvenes to consider its findings, but before those findings are announced. While the observers are still here needless to say. Probably tomorrow.'

'It would've been nice to have a little more notice,' the Captain said mildly. 'Not complainin', you understand. Just commentin'.'

'Sorry, Captain. We've only known about it ourselves for the past day or two. We've acquired some unexpected allies. It was … well, to say the least, it was a surprise.'

'You wouldn't care to tell me …'

'Can't. Sworn to secrecy. You'll know when it happens.'

'You want to tell me where?'

'You know where the commission members are housed, Captain?'

'Justin fixed up an old BDL residential building out at the east edge of town.'

'Right. I'd keep an eye on that if I were you.'

'How can I help?'

'Captain, it would be useful if there were a few troops on Jubal that Justin couldn't get at for a while. Just in case some very important orders arrive, you know? Orders that replace the current chain of command? Since you were given the assignment of keeping order here in the city, you're elected. Of course, your opinions have been noted, too, along the way.'

'My big mouth,' murmured the Captain.

'Let's say you let it be known where your sympathies lay. Well, as I said, it'd be a very good thing if there was a good-size body of men elsewhere. Elsewhere, but not too far away. Say, oh, an hour's move, if possible. Needless to say, they should be ready for action on receipt of orders.'

'Who – ah, who might they expect to get orders from?'

'Someone very high up, Captain. Someone outranking the Colonel by a good bit.'

'Sayin' they're my men, I'd be in the clear then?'

'Oh, yes, Captain. You'll be in the clear. Better than in the clear. Your cooperation with legitimate authority will be noted.'

'If I can stay out of Colonel Lang's way until then.'

'Yes. There is that.'

'I'm not sure enough of the men would back me in outright mutiny.'

'I understand the problem.'

Verbold frowned, drumming his fingers on his desk as he considered the situation. 'You know, Justin has his own security forces. BDL people. They're spread all over, watchin' everyone, runnin' back to the BDL building carryin' tales. I suppose you know that Justin doesn't trust just anybody. That bunch is hard and mean, and I wouldn't want to tangle with 'em.'

'Hm. Damn. I'd forgotten that. Is there anything you could do to be sure they are where they won't give you any trouble? Say, at BDL headquarters.'

'Ah.' Captain Jines Verbold thought quietly for a time, stroking his chin. 'If his security forces are in the building, then you've got all the maggots in one hole, don't you? Well, I might call Justin and tell him to be sure his own men are guarding BDL because ...'

'Because you've had rumors of ah ... an assassination attempt among ... ah, covert Crystallites,' suggested Rheme. 'People who didn't get rounded up when the others did. People he didn't identify, because he didn't buy them in the first place. Real converts. Real religious fanatics.'

'Oh, yes. Covert Crystallites. Why, I've been hearing about this assassination business from covert Crystallites for some time. Yes. I must let Justin know. He'll pull his men in, and then I think I'll take mine out on maneuvers tonight. Out, but not too far out.'

'Do that,' agreed Rheme, dryly. 'Just be sure I've got a way to reach you.'

During the night, a fog came up. When morning arrived, there were cottony mists hiding the environs of Splash One. At the building on the outskirts of the city, which had been remodeled for their use, members of the CHASE Commission and various observers from the PEC got out of bed, looked through their windows, and sighed. Many of them had not slept particularly well. There had been strange tremors in the night, shiverings and rollings. Not enough to panic anyone, but enough to rouse some and cause bad dreams in others.

On a usual morning breakfast would be served on the terrace. On a foggy morning like this, the somber dining room would probably be substituted, to no one's satisfaction. In preparation for this event, and others that would follow, members washed themselves and cleaned their teeth, scratched themselves and engaged in other, more individual, wake-up practices. Some of the commission members considered what findings they would give. Others didn't bother. In their cases, the findings had already been paid for and needed no consideration.

Among the ancillary personnel, and one of those last to arrive on Jubal, was a tall, moustached gentleman of unmistakably military bearing, who openly carried PEC observer identification. There was another, rather different set of papers in a hidden compartment in his traveling case. This morning, as part of his preparation for the day, this observer removed the papers from hiding and transferred them to a breast pocket, where they would be readily available. They bore, on the lower left-hand corner, the linked ellipses that were the sign of CHAIN.

Outside of town on a low hill, Tasmin got off his mule and helped Clarin down as well. Donatella had not yet arrived, but they expected her shortly.

'Foggy,' said Clarin.

'He said it would be.'

'Why do you call him he?' she asked. 'I mean, why do you call it he?'

'I don't know. It had a deep voice. Mostly. I guess that's why.'

'I guess that's why I did, too. Then I got mad at myself for doing it.'

'Do you think the new one is ready?'

'He ... it ... the Black Tower said it would be.'

'What's its name?'

'Nobody said. I guess we'll ask it.'

'Where's Bondri?' Tasmin asked.

'Could be anywhere. Most likely is anywhere. He'll come when we call him. He says.'

'I kept thinking the viggies were going to reinstitute the taboo.'

'Not after their Great Ones told them not to. According to Bondri, our whole tribe has become a debt of honor, Tasmin.'

'Tribe?'

'Tripsingers. Explorers. Us. We're the good guys.'

'The bad guys have all the guns, though.' He was staring at the city before him, a thoughtful look on his face.

'What are you thinking about?'

'Donatella's lover. Link. She told the giligees about him. They may be able to fix him.'

'I wonder if the debt would extend that far.'

'No. They sang about that for quite a while and decided it was a private matter. They have a word for private reproductive or affectional matters, but I've forgotten what it is. Anyhow, she'd have to pay for it.'

'With what?'

'Meat. Bantigons, I guess. They say they like bantigon. Hell, so do I.'

'Look. The fog is burning off,' she said.

They watched as the slow veils lifted. Donatella rode up beside them and joined the quiet scrutiny.

'There it is,' whispered Clarin.

'Where?'

'Over there. A kind of greenish shadow between us and the residence where the CHASE people are.'

'God! It's so big I didn't even see it.'

'With the top of it hidden that way, it looks like a huge new building, sort of.'

As the fog rose, the new Presence came clearly into view. Green as new grass in the dim light, growing more glowingly emerald as the mist burned away. Two hundred feet high, perhaps. A narrow tower of living crystal in which the light danced and played.

'They didn't grow it that fast!'

'No, it's been there, deep down. They pushed it up from underneath, according to Bondri.' Donatella yawned, shaking her head.

'Without an earthquake?'

'According to Bondri, just a few shivers.'

'Where did you see Bondri?'

'He's back there,' Donatella gestured. 'He says he'll come out later on. Right now he and the troupe want to watch and sing, so they can remember it right!'

When it became obvious the fog was burning away, the manager of the hostelry told the dining room supervisor to serve breakfast on the terrace as usual. The supervisor set up the tables and the buffet, never lifting her eyes from the level of utensils and plates. The commission members and observers, when they arrived, sought hot drinks and companionship. Fog still lay mistily above them, a low ceiling of shifting veils that hid any distant view. It was several minutes before the gentleman of military bearing, who was somewhat older and less gregarious than the rest, said in a tone of astonishment, 'Was that there yesterday?'

The others looked out and then up, seeing a bulky structure nearby, its top hidden in the fog. They continued to stare as the mists shifted away, perceiving the crystal tower for the first time. It wasn't a building, as some of them had assumed when they had subconsciously noticed the bulk. It wasn't a building, and it hadn't been there the day before.

Some of the members, those who had been paid to bring in certain, predetermined findings, began to entertain horrible suspicions.

These suspicions were verified a moment later.

'Good morning, members of the CHASE Commission and observers from the Planetary Exploitation Council,' caroled the looming green tower in impeccably articulated harmonic fifths. 'For your convenience, you may address me as Emerald Eminence. I am here to testify before you as to the sentience of the Presences on Jubal.'

Everyone, including the observers from the PEC, later agreed that by the time the viggies appeared on the terrace, in full chorus with an Urthian libretto, their obvious sentience was an anticlimax.

Within moments of the first appearance of the new Presence, Justin was aware of it. The residence provided for the CHASE Commission had been well equipped with eyes and ears. Justin was not one to leave anything to chance.

Now he stared at the small holostage on his desk in furious disbelief. The image of the Emerald Eminence appeared tiny and irrelevant and he heard the words coming from it with angry incredulity. Nothing had prepared him for this. No one had even suggested that this could happen. It was a trick! Had to be. It had to be explained to the commission members as a trick. Somehow it had to be explained away ...

But he couldn't wait on that! He picked up the com and punched for Colonel Lang.

'Send the orders to destroy,' he snarled.

'The commission report isn't in,' the Colonel objected, testily. The Colonel had eyes and ears of his own.

'You can send the orders to your troops and apologize later, telling them you thought the commission had reported, or you can refuse, in which case I have some papers to be transmitted to your superior officers within the hour. I think these papers would solve the Jut Massacre mystery to everyone's satisfaction. No one has ever known how the assassins got off the jut ... until now.'

Colonel Lang's voice cracked with rage. 'You'd implicate yourself, Justin!'

'You think I care? I'm going to hold this planet, Lang. I'm going to take it over. I'm going to get rid of all the roadblocks and take it for myself. There won't be any sentience to question when I'm through with it, and I've got some friends in very high places. Now what are you going to do?'

There was only a moment's reluctant silence. 'I'll send word to the troops.'

'Fine. Do that.'

There was a disturbance somewhere in the building. Justin went to the door of his office and listened to the uproar from the reception area below. Raised voices, one screeching, the other bellowing. Honeypeach Thonks and Wuyllum. So, they had also seen the Presence speaking to the commission and had come for asylum. Justin showed his teeth. Let them. It might come to the point that any pair of hands that could recharge a rifle would be an asset.

Justin summoned his chief of security and barked half a dozen hasty orders. Thanks to Verbold's timely warning about the assassination attempt, all the men were present. There were enough forces and weapons inside the walls to hold the BDL building against anything the planet had available to bring against him. And in addition to that, the building had a few nasty surprises built in, surprises that Justin had arranged for, even though he had never really thought he'd have to use them.

By the time he finished – first with the Presences and then with Jubal – any power that might have opposed him would be gone!

Partway up the vertical shaft that burrowed down six floors through the BDL building walls, Gretl Mechas leaned her head against the wall and listened. The bottom of the shaft was now within inches of the goal. The last few buckets full of shattered mud brick had been hauled up and poured away. Now she could hear great disturbance inside the building, much shouting, feet hammering to and fro. Taking a deep breath, she began to ascend the peg ladder to the servant's quarters, almost a hundred feet above where Michael waited. It was time.

18

Since Jamieson and Clarin had first encountered them blocking the way west, the troopers had methodically worked their way farther into the ranges. Although led initially by Explorers, most groups had long since lost their guides. As the intent of the troops had become clear, the Explorers had vanished. This did not greatly disturb the officers, who had been well briefed by Colonel Lang, although it occasioned a mild spookiness among the ranks, inclining them to start at the least sound and move hastily away from anything that resembled a Presence.

'You don't understand,' a young lieutenant remonstrated with his men. 'When we get the orders, we're going to blow them up. They won't be able to do anything to us if they're blown up!'

From time to time a shadowy, dusk-hidden figure might approach a nervous group to ask some such question as, 'How much of them do you suppose is showing? Most of the Presence is underground. If we blow up the top, what's the bottom part going to do?'

The shadowy figure would then drift away, leaving the enlisted men to pass this question on to their fellows. They didn't know who had asked them – just 'somebody.' The officer, aware that hysteria had gone a bit further than consonant with discipline, tried to find the somebody with no success, and the Tripsinger who had started the rumor moved back into the ranges to think up something else, equally troublesome.

This kind of harassment, which was widespread, made the Tripsingers who did it feel slightly better, but did almost nothing to mitigate the danger to the Presences. The troops kept on moving eastward, and when the orders from Colonel Lang began to reach them, there were bodies of well-equipped men dallying along within a few hours' march of almost twenty major Presences.

The orders told them they needed delay no longer.

Sergeant (sometime) Halky Bend had been detailed to lead a small group of men at a fast pace, guided by an unwilling Explorer knight, by a circuitous route to the Watchers. The route was no good for wagons or mules, but men on foot could make it. Bend had been released from the disciplinary barracks in order to lead the group because he was known to move quickly, he was thought to be indomitable, and he had been in the stockade only for breaking most of the bones in a woman's face, not for any serious breach of military discipline.

When the orders came, Halky, his men, and the Explorer – who had been marching for some days at the end of a short and uncomfortable rope – were still miles from the Watchers.

'Get a move on,' Halky instructed the Explorer, both verbally and physically. 'Accordin' to this map, we've got five miles to go yet!'

His instructions were interrupted by the return of a man who came back over an eastern ridge at a run, hollering, 'Sar'n, Sar'n,' as though he'd spotted a diamond mine. When they arrived at the top of the ridge, it was easy to see why. The False Eagers lay below them, ranked towers of glittering gems. Halky's lips parted in a lascivious smile. He licked them with a suddenly dry tongue, then spread the map to see whether anyone had identified this opportunity for him.

The glittering spires of the Eagers were regarded as one of the visual wonders of the known universe; they were not listed on the map as a target; they threatened no shipping route; no one had thought to guard them. To Halky Bend, however, they were an irresistible lure.

Halky had left Heron's World just one step ahead of the planetary police. He had stolen nothing much, killed nobody important, and engaged in no large-scale fraud or blackmail. Halky's crimes were often not motivated by profit at all. He simply liked to break things. His earliest years had been made joyous by destruction. His first orgasm had been accompanied by the incomparable clatter of huge windows falling before a fusillade of stones. He and several adolescent cronies had twice managed to shatter millennia-old stained-glass windows in a historic church and get clean away, though later and more ambitious exploits, which brought together certain incendiary devices and several large public buildings, brought the police closing on his heels. Well aware of this, he had joined the military and shipped out.

Now as he stared at the marvelous scintillation of the Eagers, he heard in his mind the tinkle and crash of broken crystal, the satisfying impact one felt when hitting something that would not bend or give way and could not hit back. With a feeling not so much akin as identical to sexual lust, he announced target practice. The troop set up their simple mortars and fired a few rounds to get the range. Thousand-year crystals shattered and fell. Diamond towers shivered into glittering shards. A cry as of agonized reproach came from the ground, and hearing this the troopers whooped and cheered, bringing the mortars to bear upon the few Tineea Singers that were still intact. Within the hour, the Eagers were no more.

While everyone was having fun, the Explorer escaped.

Within the next hour, every Presence on Jubal knew the Eagers were gone. They told every Tripsinger and every viggy within range of their voices. As soon as the Explorer found friends, every Presence, every Tripsinger, and every viggy also knew the name of Halky Bend.

A large company under the command of Colonel Roffles Lang himself, was brought by coastal flier to the southern coast and then inland as far as was safe to do so. The company needed to march only a little farther north to reach the Enigma and begin an assault on it. Tripsingers from Deepsoil Five fought in defense of the shrieking Presence alongside a dozen Explorer knights, but they could not get close enough to the well-armed troops to cause them any real damage. The Enigma shuddered, screamed in two voices, and fell at last into a mountain of scarlet glass, a bloody wound on Jubal's skin. The Tripsinger defenders retreated northward to the citadel at Deepsoil Five, which they felt they would have to defend before long. Colonel Lang regarded the results of the action with satisfaction and sat down to look at the map. There were other targets listed on their route of march: Sky Hammer, the Amber Axe, the Deadly Dozen, Cloud Gatherer, and then, finally and most importantly, the Black Tower. The Presences were so close together that Lang felt they could probably all be destroyed within a day. In fact, he could leave the closer and lesser targets to a junior officer and quick-march with a select group to take care of the Black Tower himself.

Stopping in the Redfang Range on their way to the Jammers, a gun crew took sight on the Redfang and saturated the area with explosive charges. When they were finished, only rubble remained – rubble and the far-off sound of viggies grieving.

Outside Splash One, the CHASE Commission members, all of whom had seen and heard both the Emerald Eminence and the viggies, stubbornly insisted on arguing their findings for what remained of the day.

'A trick,' asserted one dewlapped man with darting and suspicious eyes who had been paid well for his participation on the commission and had already spent the money. He was convinced the credit would have to be returned if he did not do what he had been paid to do, and he did not have it to give back. 'It was a trick,' he said firmly, eyes flicking from left to right to left again.

'What about the viggies?' someone demanded for the tenth time.

The viggies were inarguable. The viggies were sitting there, occasionally bouncing in their comfortable chairs, looking interested and asking questions. Enough of the commission members clung to their commitments, however, that it was not until very late that night that the exact wording of the findings was agreed upon. Since it was so late, the commission retired without announcing what those findings were.

In the bowels of the BDL building, Harward Justin blew the dust from a cracked notebook he had dug from the back of a long-closed drawer and flipped the pages to find the checklist he had written there years ago. Reading from it, item by item, he crossed the room to a locked control board, which he tugged at in futile impatience for a moment before fumbling in his pocket for keys. He had not been in this room for almost ten years. He had not really thought the time would ever come when he would need it.

Staggering footsteps on the stairs brought him away from the control board, teeth bared, furious at the interruption. Wuyllum Thonks was stalking down the stairs as though he were at home in the gardens of Government House, Honeypeach behind him, both wearing expressions of angry disdain.

'Justin,' complained Honeypeach. 'We've just been watching troopers marching in from somewhere. They've surrounded us. I don't think it's Colonel Lang's men. I haven't seen him. But they do have guns and things. And I can't reach Ymries at all, I've tried and tried ...'

Wuyllum added his own comments. 'It'd be smart to go on out and give ourselves up, Justin. Put a good face on it, show them we're innocent. They'll never convict us of anything anyhow. Not you or us, not with the friends we have and the money we can put into our defense. If we stay in here, they may assault the building! We could all get killed.'

'Shut up,' snarled Justin. 'You and your whorelady get out of here, Wuyllum. I've given you guest rooms. Go stay there.'

Ignoring the insult to his lady, Wuyllum went on. 'At least tell your security people to let us out. If you don't want to give up, all right ...'

'Justin!' cried Honeypeach, 'why, how could you say such a horrible thing ...'

Justin turned, arm out, catching her across the face with the full force of his weight, crumpling her against the wall. 'I said to get that slut out of here,' he instructed Thonks. 'I've still got a chance if I can bring enough of those damned crystals down in a hurry, and I'm not going to waste time fooling with you or your trull. If you want to go on living, get away from me.' He turned away from them, not bothering to see whether Wuyllum dragged the bloodied Honeypeach away.

The installation before him controlled a battery of chemical rockets, rockets without electronic components, rockets carrying nothing that could be altered or burned out by the mysterious interventions of Jubal. The Watchers, the Mad Gap, the Enigma, the Black Tower, and half a hundred other Presences had been pretargeted by these missiles. Though Verbold's troops had probably demolished some or even many of these Presences, the fact that troops now surrounded the BDL building argued that the destruction orders had already been countermanded. Justin could not depend on the troops to clear the transportation routes on Jubal ...

But if the troops couldn't, the rockets could. Let the rockets fly and the routes to the dirt towns would be open. There wouldn't be any Presences left on this part of Jubal! Even if he had to lie low for a while, he could come back to pick up the pieces. With all that money on Serendipity – his own and what his phoney Crystallites had squirreled away – there was plenty to start again. Even if he had to leave Jubal for a while ...

With the redundancies he'd programmed in to prevent accidents, it would take an hour's work to set up the firing sequences. Once they were set, however, Justin could leave them to their work. He had a bolt hole, an escape tunnel dug ostensibly as a sewer line when the BDL headquarters was built. At the far end of it was a cavernous garage, and in that garage was a quiet-car. Eastward, about two hours' drive, there was a refuge he had prepared years before He could hide there until he could get off-planet to collect the money that would let him come back and start again. He had planned for trouble. Justin always planned for trouble. Just as he planned for Jubal!

His plans for Jubal were not going to be forestalled by a few talking crystals and a mutinous commission. His lips drawn back into an animal snarl, Justin set to work.

'Stalemate,' said Rheme Gentry to Tasmin. 'Justin's holed up in the BDL building. I'm afraid of what he has in there. Logically, we should take the place out now, but we don't have the weapons here to knock it down – all the heavy weaponry on the planet is with Lang's men. We won't even have enough men to mount an assault until Lang's troops return, assuming they do. All we can do is keep Justin and his men penned up in there until the General can get some help from off-planet.'

'The General?'

'My uncle. Zorton Pardo. He's the commander of CHAIN, and if you don't know what that is, neither does anyone else. It's the very quiet, almost invisible enforcement arm of the PEC. I sort of work for him. He showed up here as one of the PEC observers. He's taken command of the troops on Jubal. But my message never got off-planet, and with a typical lack of foresight, he didn't bring a gunship with him.'

'Has he stopped the destruction!'

'Orders have gone out. It may take a while for them to arrive. You know that, Tripsinger.' Rheme's face was blotched and gray with fatigue. 'And if Justin does what I think he means to, it won't make any difference.'

Tasmin put his face into his hands. The Enigma was gone. Redfang was gone. The Eagers were gone. All the Presences had trumpeted the destruction of the Eagers. Tasmin remembered the Eagers. He remembered traveling through them with Clarin, when he was first aware of Clarin. He remembered going home from them to Celcy, when Celcy was still alive. The memories swirled and twined to become joined in his mind, twisted together like a striped candy, infinitely sweet, nauseatingly sad, a pain that clenched the guts like a cancer, eating him – women and Jubal, love and love – the one destroyed, the other destroyed. His woman, women, this place. Everything he loved. This man, he said to himself with hating fury, this man is destroying, has destroyed everything. Harward Justin!

'What d'you think he's got in there?' Tasmin gasped.

'We know what he has. I've picked up some of the original construction workers, and they're happy to tell us everything they ever knew. He's got over a hundred pretargeted chemical rockets without any fancy electronics at all. No seeker components. No hunters. They're aimed just as you'd aim a projectile rifle. By aiming the launch tubes.'

'He's going to set them off,' Tasmin said definitely.

'He may, yes.'

'Not may. Will. That's exactly what he'll do. He's like an animal when you corner it. He'll go down fighting with everything he has.' Tasmin's mind spun, jittered. He knew his perception of Justin was true. 'Justin's theory would be he could always pick up the pieces. Break Jubal into enough pieces, no one else will care about it, then he'll salvage what's left. Or he'd think that if he committed enough destruction, he could get away in the confusion. Either way, Rheme, he's going to set them off.'

'How do we stop him?' Rheme asked helplessly.

Tasmin concentrated, his nose wrinkling almost like an animal's. 'Evacuate the area around the BDL building,' he demanded. 'Move. Right now. Get the troopers away from there.'

'What do you ...' Rheme stopped as he saw he was talking to Tasmin's fleeing back. He was headed away at a run, toward the Eminence. Cursing briefly, Rheme turned to do what Tasmin had suggested.

Tasmin found Don and Clarin beside the Eminence, together with Bondri Gesel. He hailed them breathlessly.

Two verbal acknowledgments, one quaver of song, and a deep musical tone that was somehow interrogative.

He blurted out what Rheme had told him, what he himself suspected, repeating and stuttering, trying to make both Bondri and the Eminence understand projectiles, what they were, where they were, what they might do. 'There!' he pointed. 'Behind the BDL building wall.'

'More destruction?' queried the Eminence, the mighty voice trembling, shivering. With fear? Apprehension? Fury? It was the Eminence that had told them the Eagers were gone, the Enigma, Redfang, the Amber Axe – the list had seemed endless.

'It can be stopped if you can move the rockets. Or break down the installations where they are. Or break the controls that go to them …'

Silence. Then a voice almost gentle, speaking words Tasmin did not understand.

'The Great One wishes to know if there are any individuals – persons – near that place,' Bondri asked.

From where they stood, they could look down into the city. Rheme had taken Tasmin seriously. The area around the BDL building and Government House had been evacuated of civilians when the troopers surrounded it. Now even they were retreating, moving away quickly, herding a few stubborn civilians before them.

'Tell the Great One no one is there except those evil ones who have caused the destruction,' Tasmin told Bondri.

'The Great One used our language because he needed to know what is true,' apologized Bondri.

'Tell the Great One that I understand.'

There was further conversation in the viggy tongue, then Bondri gestured toward the long eastern slope above the city. 'The Presences will try to stop further destruction. You could watch from up there,' he suggested. 'That place should be safe.'

Tasmin moved in the direction the viggy had indicated. He felt hollow, burned out inside, as though his perceptions formed a thin shell around vacancy. Clarin and Don were behind him, leading their mules and his. The animals had been grazing at the foot of the Eminence, no more concerned by its size or the noise it made than by any other on Jubal. Bondri and some of his troupe went off to one side. It was nearing dawn. Only one full day since the Eminence had heaved itself up out of the cracking deepsoil. One day since the Eagers had gone. Tasmin cursed. From behind him, Clarin reached out, then dropped her hand. There was nothing anyone could say to him now. Since he had heard about the Eagers, he had been shut down, almost as he had been when Celcy died. It was as though everything that had happened had been focused on one point somewhere inside him. Only that one point had validity for him now.

They came to a rocky ledge about half a mile from the edge of the city. A narrow belt of farms lay west of them, then a short street lined with low storage buildings, another street of small stores, and finally the wall that marked the eastern boundary of the three great structures: Government House, the empty citadel, and the BDL building. Around this wall, Captain Verbold's troops had been established in a solid line, well protected behind hastily built barricades. Now the barricades were abandoned. The troops were on building tops and at street corners some distance away. There were none on the near side at all.

Tasmin glared at the wall as though it were his enemy. Behind the wall was Harward Justin. If something happened to that wall, if that wall came down, Harward Justin would run. He would run. Tasmin licked his lips, amazed at the flavor of that thought, the flavor of seeing Justin run, skittering like a crystal mouse, dodging, evading, eventually being caught. Oh, the catching. Tasmin's muscles tensed, as though he prepared to leap. Adrenaline poured into his veins, and he tasted it, tasted the thought of doing something himself instead of sitting idly by while everyone and everything else acted.

Oh, yes, Justin would run. And if he did, it would have to be in this direction.

Tasmin stared around himself, searching the ground between where they were standing and the city, peering here and there, his head twisting, eyes glittering.

'What makes you so sure he'll come this way?' asked Clarin.

He turned in amazement. Don had moved away, toward the viggies, but Clarin was sitting calmly on her mule, dark hair tumbled around a clean-washed and expressionless face. 'You are watching for Justin, aren't you?' she asked.

'How did you know?'

'Because our minds are alike, Tasmin. Because he's the one,' she said. 'The one you can blame it all on.'

'Do you object?' he grated, unreasonably angry.

She shook her head, kept her face calm, eluded his wrath. 'What makes you believe he'd come this way?'

'The city's all torn up,' he snarled, not realizing he had thought it all out. 'If he has a tunnel, it couldn't go in the direction of the city. They keep digging foundations and substreets and drainage trenches. He couldn't have had a tunnel going into the city and kept it hidden. It would have to come this way.'

She smiled, a tiny, barely curved lipline. 'Amazing, Tasmin. My father told me you were clever.'

'Your father?'

'Thyle Vowe is my father. Never mind. So you really think Justin will come.'

'If he can move, he'll come.'

'You could be hurt. Killed.' She said it calmly, as though it didn't matter. He didn't hear her.

Colonel Lang's detail arrived at the Black Tower early in the morning, tired but still functioning. A few of the men had been killed, fallen to Tripsinger sniper fire or shattered into bloody fragments by a too close approach to troublesome 'lings, but the dead were no more than Lang had been willing to sacrifice. He had been more concerned about losing his weaponry, but it had arrived virtually intact. Now he directed his men to within a quarter mile of the Tower and there set up his mortars.

Jamieson, fairly well recovered from his injuries on the Enigma, lay on a ledge to one side of the Tower. For the last few days, Jamieson had been living his own resurrection, as though in heaven and granted the privilege of talking with God. He and the Presence had spent long hours in colloquy, hours that were as ecstatic as any Jamieson could remember. Now he lay on the ledge with Tripsingers from Deepsoil Five scattered around him, determined to defend the Presence against whatever came. The men were equipped with weapons that the armorer of the citadel – who had been working on them frantically for days – had assured them would have more than twice the range of the usual stun rifles. Below the Black Tower, Highmost Darkness, and so forth, the two giligees who had stayed behind with Jamieson were preparing to leave. They had not been diligent about their preparations, and Jamieson called to them that the attack was imminent.

'Get out of there,' he demanded. 'Tumble down.'

'Stayed to be sure you were fixed,' sang the giligees softly. They had become very fond of Jamieson. He had a voice better than most viggies and was very good to sing with. Listening to Jamieson and the Black Tower had been edifying. They had much to sing to the troupe when they were reunited.

'I know,' he caroled. 'I am grateful. But you must move now. Those troopers down there are setting up mortars.'

The giligees had not seen mortars nor sung them. They had no idea what Jamieson was talking about and were already surfeited with new Urthish words and phrases. Politely but without haste, they started up the narrow trail to the place Jamieson waited.

On the prairie below, Colonel Lang estimated the range of the Tower and ordered his gunner to fire a round. It landed slightly below the giligees, knocking them off their feet, half burying them in shards.

With a cry Jamieson leapt to his feet and ran down the trail, frantically digging out the unharmed giligees and tossing them above him onto a ledge that led back into the ranges. 'Hurry,' he screamed at them. 'Run.'

'Threat!' sang the Black Tower in an enormous voice. 'Destruction.'

Jamieson gulped a lungful of air and sang, 'Do not fear. We will protect ...'

At the side of the Tower a Tripsinger tried his new rifle on the gunner, drilling a neat hole through him.

Colonel Lang cursed, corrected the aim, and dropped another shell into the mortar.

Jamieson was reassuring the Black Tower, singing all his love and determination, his voice more glorious in this epiphany than it had ever been. He saw the shell coming out of the corner of his eye. He was still singing when it hit.

Near the BDL building, Tasmin felt a tremor beneath his feet. Clarin hastily got out of the saddle and sat, pulling the mules down beside her. Obediently, they collapsed with their tong necks stretched along the ground. 'Get down, Tasmin.'

'What's happening?'

'Whatever the Eminence intends to happen.'

The tremor grew into a rocking, a shattering, a tumbling of soil. Before them, the long row of earthen brick storehouses collapsed into a heap of mud rubble.

'Not quite,' Clarin breathed. 'Not quite enough.'

It began again, first a ripple, then a wave, the second reinforcing the first, harmonic vibrations that amplified with each return. The wall around Government House began to twist and topple. Still not enough.

Then more! Vast undulations rolling them first one way, then the other. Trees dancing a wild pavane on the prairie beside them, tipping and bowing. Buildings in the city shaking and trembling. The world so awash with mighty sound that they were deafened by it, making each individual destruction seem to occur in eerie silence. The golden dome of the temple coming apart, dropping in ragged chunks that seemed to take forever to fall.

Tasmin wondered if it had been full of pilgrims. Worshippers of the Great Ones. The Great Ones who were bringing the city down on top of their heads.

And again the mighty shaking, the harmonics of one huge oscillation reinforcing another.

The tower at the corner of the BDL building crumpled in upon itself like wet paper. One corner of the main building sagged and fell. The grounds within the wall shifted and jigged, stones leaping over the ground like waterdrops on a griddle.

Tasmin put his glasses to his eyes, bracing his elbows on the ground as the lenses swung wildly. There was motion in the courtyard of the BDL building, someone at the gate that separated it from Government House. The Honorable Wuyllum, quite alone. No Someone staggering along behind him, clutching at him. Honeypeach?

Clarin muttered an imprecation. She, too, was watching Honeypeach Thonks who was covered with blood from a wound on her head. The Honorable Wuyllum turned and kicked at her, then fled as she pursued him through the gate, across the expansive terraces, and into Government House.

It came down upon them. All at once. As though the bottom layer of it had been pulled away. Within the walls, nothing stood, no wall, no fragment of corner, no towering chimney, and then the walls themselves fell.

And finally the BDL building went, tumbling in upon itself in the shivering tide of motion as though it had been built of sand.

'The citadel ...' he breathed.

'Empty,' she said. 'My father told me it was empty.'

They both saw the dark opening in the earth at the same time. The soil was still shivering when Clarin's arm went out, her finger pointing toward it even as Tasmin stood up and mounted his mule. The opening expanded. A camouflaged doorway, well east of the fallen area. And out of it came a large man in a small quiet-car, driving speedily away toward the east, toward them, where they waited.

'Clarin ...'

'Yes.'

'Get away. He'll be armed.'

'I want to ...'

'If anything happened to you, I couldn't bear it. It would kill me. There's been enough. Please, Clarin.'

She said nothing more. He sensed her motion rather than saw it. He would not take his eyes off the man before him.

It was dawn. The morning light shone straight into Harward Justin's eyes, blinding him. He was within yards of Tasmin before he saw the silhouetted

266

figure of mule and man, the blocky outline of a rifle at the man's side. He had been shaken out of his usual concentration by the earthquake. Without thinking, he wrenched the steering lever to turn back the way he had come, not stopping to realize that the rifle was in its scabbard, that he could have outrun the mule.

Tasmin leaned forward and kicked the mule into a run. He could not hope to catch the man – could not hope to. Did hope to. Wanted to get his hands around that bulbous neck. Fracture that thick, oil-rich skull like a nut, squeeze it.

The car sped back. Justin fumbled on the seat beside him, but the hand weapon he had laid ready had fallen onto the floor when the car made its sudden turn. The car teetered, almost overturning, and he gave up trying to reach the weapon in favor of reaching the secret tunnel from which he had emerged. Directly before him on the scarcely visible track lay the entrance to the hidden cavern, the door still open. There was a large open area behind that door. Once inside that area, he could turn the car. Once inside, he could get at his weapon. The car plunged into darkness. Not far behind, Tasmin pursued it ...

Something hit him from one side. Someone. Launched at him from one side, knocking him off the mule. Someone shouting at him.

'Tasmin, Tasmin, for God's sake it's going to blow don't go in there after him it's going to blow ...'

The earth came apart as it had come apart once before on the Enigma, except that this was not the Enigma, this was Deepsoil, solid as rock, eternal as stone, now broken and riven, with fire belching into the sky as a hundred huge rockets tried to launch themselves and blew apart under countless tons of shattered stone. Rocks fell around them in a clattering hail. Someone screamed in pain. What was left of the rulers' enclave of Splash One shivered into microscopic dust rising on a white-hot wind. The cloud boiled, towered, heaved itself into the sky, blocking the sun. A dusk-like shadow fell.

Tasmin lay on his back, staring at it.

Someone beside him was moaning.

Clarin. Cradling her arm and crying from pain and shock.

'I think it's broken,' she wept. 'A rock fell on it ...'

He got up, slowly, feeling himself to see if his own parts were present. From the hill behind him came a trill, then a harmonic hymn. Bondri Gesel and the troupe, who had felt it coming, had sung a warning and would now record it all in song.

When Tasmin turned back to Clarin, the giligee was already there, working on her arm.

'You are making a habit of hurting yourself,' it sang to Clarin, even as it looked up at Tasmin with angrily speculative eyes.

Tasmin shook his head. Somewhere under all that rubble was a man he had wanted to kill. Still wanted to kill. The emptiness in himself was not filled. Nothing could have lived through that. Justin must be dead, and yet he, Tasmin, was not at all satisfied.

The troops who had just arrived at the Great Blue Tooth, Horizon Loomer, Mighty Hand, the Presence humankind called the East Jammer, had not received any order that countermanded the original one. They set up and got off several very well aimed shells, which knocked a few large chunks off the Jammer. Gyre-birds rose in a whirling, agitated cloud. The ground shook. The men cheered. The Jammer cheered in return, its enormous voice increasing in volume and rising in pitch. The troops found themselves groveling on the ground, hands over ears, screaming at the noise, which did not end until they stopped moving altogether.

Rage had led the Jammer to this unplanned retaliation. Quiet malice led it to communicate the success of the tactic to all other Presences.

At the foot of the Black Tower, one of the giligees whom Jamieson had saved ran frantically among the Tripsingers and Explorers whose sniper fire had successfully kept the troopers at bay.

'Highmost Darkness wants you to move away,' it squeaked in their ears, so excited by the action that it could no longer maintain calm song. 'Black Tower wants you to move. Fast, away, away.'

'They'll destroy it,' grated one of the Tripsingers, wiping blood from his forehead where a flying crystal chip had cut him. They had managed to hold the gunners at bay. They had managed to kill a good many of them. The Colonel who had set off the shell that had killed Jamieson had left some time ago, marching hastily away toward the south with a handful of men, but he had left enough men behind to pound the Tower to rubble once they got close enough.

'No. Black Tower won't let them. It knows how, now, but you must go away. Quickly. Eastward, back into the ranges. Go, and cover your ears.'

The defenders fled, covering their ears as they had been directed. The sound began almost immediately, a painful intensity of sound, and they increased their speed to get away from it as soon as possible. As they got farther away, the sound increased and went on increasing, always only bearable, and they did not stop running.

The troopers, who had not been given permission to run, were soon unfitted for further attack. Some of the weapons detonated by themselves, quite harmlessly so far as the Tower was concerned, though the recumbent and unconscious men would not have agreed.

Thereafter, there was no more destruction.

The CHASE Commission, delayed by explosions in the city, which rocked the building they were in and blanketed the participants with dust, convened belatedly at noon for the sole purpose of announcing their findings.

Sentience: of two types.
Human persons, including their livestock and crops
are to be allowed to remain on Jubal
only at the invitation of the sentient species.

The commission members relaxed. It was done. Facing a corner, the iron-jawed man silently chewed his lips, relieved that he need no longer stand almost alone. If certain people wanted their money back, they'd have to whistle for it. He didn't have it anymore. One and then another of the members began moving toward the doors. Now if they could only get off the planet.

To the east of and far below the piled rubble of the BDL building, Harward Justin awoke to an almost darkness, a cavernous, echoing emptiness in which shadows moved and gathered. After an unfocused time of half consciousness, he began to concentrate on the light. He could see several flickers from where he lay, dancing light that gleamed from along the floor and walls. Fires. Small fires. Nothing dangerous. Nothing threatening. He tried to get up and found himself pinned by one arm. The car had overturned, throwing him clear except for the right arm. He struggled to drag himself free and almost fainted from the pain that surged through his shoulder and chest. Something there was injured, broken ...

He was in the garage, he told himself. He had come back into the garage, and then the rockets had gone off. The garage was still intact. Of course, he had built it and the tunnel to take anything except a direct hit from something major – something nuclear, perhaps. He stared at the flickering light. Perhaps they were electrical fires. By squirming a little he could see a narrow and broken line of light in one direction – the large doors through which he had driven the car, now fallen almost closed and partly buried. In the opposite direction there was only a dark hole, a black ellipse. That was the tunnel back into the wreckage. He stared into it, not really aware for a time that what he heard coming from its depths was voices. Voices. The only people who had been in the headquarters except himself were the security people. Those on the lower levels must have escaped.

'Hi!' he called. 'I'm down here.'

There was silence, then a whispering. Then silence once more.

'I'm caught under this car,' he shouted again. 'Get off your asses and get over here.'

Now he heard the voices again, the shuffle of feet. The car blocked his vision. He couldn't see who it was. Only the feet coming. Bare feet. Why would security men have bare feet? Then another set, shoes this time. He relaxed. Not only those two, however. There were others ...

'Mr. Justin,' said a voice from beside the car. 'Harward Justin?' A woman's voice?

He turned, fighting the pain, turning his eyes upward in their sockets to see who it was. A woman. A haggard, burning eyed woman.

'Number six,' he said in disbelief. 'Number six.'

'Gretl,' the woman corrected him gently, her eyes quite mad. 'Gretl Mechas. With some of your other friends ...'

It was late in the evening before Rheme Gentry came to the General's room to greet his uncle.

'Has the destruction been stopped?' the General asked.

Rheme Gentry nodded wearily. 'We understand it has. Little thanks to us. The Presences found a way to defend themselves.'

'Are they holding that against us?'

'No. Not according to Tasmin Ferrence and his group. Tasmin and friends have turned out to be our main spokesmen. Them and the viggies.' Rheme shook his head, surprised to find tears coursing down his cheeks. 'The damned troops destroyed the Eagers,' he cried. 'And Redfang!'

'You're crying,' said his uncle, shocked.

'Oh, General ... You just haven't been here long enough.'

'No. It's obvious I haven't.'

'In fact, I'm not sure I know what brought you here at all.'

'There were two things that brought me, Rheme. One was not hearing from you. Considering your unremitting and frequently irrelevant verbosity, I found that somewhat ominous. The other reason was that I did hear from someone else. I got a letter a few weeks ago, evidently just before Justin shut down communications entirely. It was from a former employee of mine, a remarkable woman who used to be the head of our cryptanalysis division. Cyndal Prince. Cyndal retired and came here to Jubal where her only living relatives were. A sister, I believe, and a niece and nephew. Any letter I get from Cyndal, I send over to Crypto as a matter of course. She had some interesting things to say, as usual, beautifully encoded, information she couldn't have gotten through Justin's censorship by normal channels. Taking the two things together, I felt my presence might be useful.' He regarded the wet-faced man before him with sympathy. 'Now, if you can set emotion aside for the moment, I'd like your opinion on what we need to do next.'

Rheme wiped his face. 'You reconvened the committee as a committee of inquiry?'

'Yes. They found as seemed appropriate. We have indictments against Justin, against the Governor, his wife, against a whole throng of lesser villains. Most of whom, I'm afraid, have escaped justice by dying rather sooner than we'd intended.'

'Lang's still alive. Some of the troops, including Lang and the bunch that destroyed the False Eagers, have refused to come in as ordered.'

'How do you know that?'

'Viggies. Tripsingers. They hear things, then they tell a Presence, and the next thing you know, the Emerald Eminence knows all about it.'

'So?'

'So, we have to take some of the loyal troops and go after them. We can't let them roam around like brigands.'

'You don't think the viggies and the Presences will take care of them?'

'I'm sure they would, eventually. It will look a lot better to PEC and be more honorable if we do it ourselves, however.'

'Where is Colonel Roffles Lang now?'

'He's somewhere south of where the Enigma used to be with a couple hundred troopers. He's proclaimed himself commander of all humans on Jubal.'

'Oh, has he,' the General mused with an audible sniff. 'Well! I agree that it will look better if we discipline our own. And since we may have to leave Jubal very soon, it should be done at once. I've promoted Captain Verbold to Colonel, Commander of the Garrison, effective immediately. Sort through the troops you have and the ones that are coming back. Work with him and get the matter in hand.'

The matter had been put in hand by the following morning, and Colonel Verbold was much in evidence as troops began to assemble outside the city.

Donatella Furz, who had been alerted by both Clarin and Rheme, circled through the gathering men; her long legs ticking off the distance as she searched for one particular participant. She found him at last, red-eyed, obviously somewhat brou-sotted, sitting in the shade of his own mule as he cleaned his rifle.

'Tasmin,' she said calmly. 'I've been looking for you.'

He grunted at her.

'What do you think you are doing?'

'Going with the troopers,' he mumbled. 'Get everything cleaned up.'

'Wasn't Justin's death enough for you?'

He glared at her. 'I don't know what you're talking about.'

She sat down beside him. 'I'm talking about vengeance, Tasmin. Clarin said you really wanted to kill Justin. I can understand that. He did rather slip through your fingers ...'

'Bastard,' he growled.

'But that doesn't make this more sensible.' She gestured around them at the assembling ranks.

'Colonel Verbold said I could go.' He sounded like an unreasonable five-year-old.

'No, what he said was that he couldn't stop you tagging along. However, he did mention his displeasure to Rheme, who mentioned it to Clarin, and both of them told me.'

'I've got to ...' He fumbled for words, unable to find them.

'You've got to get it out of your system,' she said for him.

'Celcy,' he blurted. 'She died.'

'Yes, she died. And Urn's dead. And the Eagers are gone, and the Enigma, and Redfang, and a couple of dozen others. I can't say I blame you for wanting to kill Justin and trying your best, even though you damn near got yourself killed in the process. Still, Justin had a lot less to do with Celcy's death than he did with Gretl's, for instance, but I'm not out here with a stun rifle set on high-fry, trying to do a mop-up job that troopers are trained for and we're not.'

'Gretl wasn't your wife. Celcy was mine.'

She stared at the pig-headed man before her with a combination of pity and irritation. Part of this was her fault. If she hadn't lectured him, hadn't gotten his back up over Celcy, if she hadn't made him aware of and, therefore, guilty over his attraction to Clarin, maybe matters would simply have taken their proper course and he would have let himself forget. Damn!

'Tasmin, do you value our friendship enough to go into that tavern over there and have a glass with me? Broundy, maybe? Hot tea?'

'You won't change my mind.'

'After we talk, you do what you like, Tasmin. I won't try and stop you. I promise.'

Unwillingly, he shouldered his weapon and followed Donatella through the scattered groups of men. When they were seated at the back of the almost-empty place with steaming drinks before them, she regarded him thoughtfully, trying to find a key to that locked, barricaded door he was using for a face.

He was sotted, exhausted, agitated, and pale. Jamieson and Clarin had both mentioned that he had lost weight since Celcy's death, and Don thought he had lost even more since she had first met him. He didn't look well. Obsessed, perhaps. Maybe just stubborn. Maybe merely guilty.

'Why did you pick her, Tasmin? Out of all the women in Deepsoil Five. Why did you pick Celcy?'

Of the many questions she might have asked, he had not expected this one. The stubborn rejection he had ready would not serve. 'Well ... I didn't pick her, not really. I met her. She was working at the commissary. She was admiring some little trinket, and I bought it for her. I made some remark about buying a pretty thing for a pretty girl ...' He tried to focus on Don, having some difficulty in doing it, but his voice was clear.

'And then?'

'Well, one thing led to another. You know.'

'Tell me.'

'Next time I went in there, I asked her to have lunch. She told me about her family, how she lived. It sounded ... bleak.'

'You felt sorry for her?'

'In a way. She was trapped in that life. It was extremely limited.'

'And, of course, she was sexy.'

He flushed. 'That's my own affair, don't you think?'

'I think we've shared enough of ourselves that we can talk about it, Tasmin. Take it as agreed. She was sexy. She made you feel – powerful. Protective.'

'I suppose.'

'Did you ever really look at her, Tasmin? Did you really evaluate how much of her you liked? Did you make a conscious choice, based on how well you got along? Did you ever compare her with other women?'

He made an impatient gesture, which she immediately and correctly interpreted.

'There weren't any other women. You were completely tied up in yourself and your work, and you weren't looking for someone who could live happily with you. She was pretty and sexy and she was doing a menial job, which you regarded with aristocratic distaste. She was there. She needed someone, and you responded.'

'I suppose,' he said, flushing. 'You make it sound superficial, but all that conscious choice business is pretty cold-blooded, isn't it?'

'Is it? I don't know, Tasmin. I've never been married. All I know is, given your nature, you probably take a lot of care in the fitting of your Tripsinger robes. You were probably very selective about picking a mule from the stables. I knew you take infinite care in checking out your synthesizer, because I've seen you do it. After all, those things are important and essential to you. But according to you, you didn't give that much care to seeking a wife. You simply found her, like a bit of crystal in your path. You let her get accustomed to you, let her learn to depend on you without ever making any conscious decision to do so. Then, having done that, you couldn't in good conscience let her down.'

He glared at her. Nothing she had said was really incorrect, and yet she infuriated him.

'You are admirable in many respects, Tasmin. And honorable. But you are sometimes so damn stubborn it takes my breath away.'

'You've no right to say that,' he blurted. 'I left Deepsoil Five to find out why she died. I've traveled God knows how many miles trying to find out why she died. One thing led to another thing, and they all led to Harward Justin – him and his minions. You say Justin isn't that responsible? Then you tell me why she died.'

'She could have died, Tasmin, because she knew you were disappointed in her and she wanted to do something you would wholly approve of.'

'You're saying I killed her ...'

'I'm saying that when any of us get into relationships where one person totally depends on another, we kill something. Ourselves, perhaps. Or them.'

'We got along!'

'Of course you did! Good Lord, Tasmin, between you and Jamieson, I've heard all about your life together. You were in love with Jubal, and she was scared to death of it. You were fascinated by the Presences, and she was in sheer terror of them. You were always forgiving her for it. Always making excuses for her. Always patronizing her. She may have died because she wanted to live up to your expectations, Tas. Oh, maybe she was brou-sotted at the time, I hope so, so that she didn't know what was coming – maybe in her fogged up mind she decided to do one marvelous thing that you would have to admire.'

He gaped at her, unable to find words.

'It's true. You were at least as responsible as anyone else. But all you want to do is blast someone to make yourself feel better. First it was Lim, but he was dead. Then it was me, but you decided it wasn't my fault. Then it was Harward Justin, but he got Idled without your help, much. Now who is it going to be? Some mutinous trooper who doesn't know a Presence from a piece of rock salt?'

Donatella was crying, partly for herself. 'Quit looking for someone to blame, Tasmin, and get on with your life ...' She understood his feelings very well. She had been through it herself, with Link. She got up and left him there, staring at the steam rising from the cup in front of him.

When the troops marched out, Tasmin did not go with them. He was outside the city, at the foot of the Emerald Eminence, singing with Bondri Gesel.

'Donatella said it,' he sang, 'but it isn't true ...'

They sat in quiet sunlight while machines thundered in the city, clearing away rubble, finding bodies, occasionally finding one that lived. Tasmin couldn't identify what was going on inside himself, a kind of freshness coming, as though someone had opened a window inside him so that a chill, pure wind blew into him. It hurt. It was very cold and it hurt.

'It wasn't the whole truth, what Donatella said.' He gasped again. 'You know about us, Bondri. With us – each of us sees the truth our own way, from our own totally egocentric point of view, and then we insist on that. It's like kids, fighting. You did. I didn't. You did, too. You viggies don't have those kinds of arguments. When you sing it, it comes out.' He felt hurt that she seemed to do this, and she was wounded at his lack of consideration, but neither intended such an outcome."

'Yes, you perceive us properly,' sang Bondri Gesel. 'We would sing that, more or less.'

'I guess that one the words of memory are set into our minds in a specific way, that's how we remember. We can't remember the thing happening, we just remember the words we told ourselves about it. I told my mother once that I didn't want a blind woman for my mother, and she remembered that for years. Every time she remembered it, she cried. She said blind is what she was, and if I said what I did, it meant I didn't want her. I don't think that's what I meant, and yet it's true. She was right. There was no way to separate what she was from her blindness. I had to accept her blindness if I was going to accept her. There's no way to separate people into pieces of themselves and only accept the pieces we want. If the viggies had been singing to her, what they said wouldn't have hurt her, for they would have said it all – not just part of it ...

'I'm beginning to think I talk to myself only in skin quieters, Bondri. What I say isn't necessarily what I mean. It isn't even the truth. It just gets me by ...'

'Ah,' sighed Bondri Gesel. 'It's important to you? You really want to sing your Celcy, Tasmin Ferrence. Sing your Celcy as we would sing one of ours?'

Tasmin put his head in his hands, wetting his palms with tears. 'Yes. I would like to sing the truth of her, Bondri. Because how do I know what happened to her until I know what she really was? I can't believe she went there because of me ...'

Bondri shook his head, an astonishingly human gesture. 'Don Furz should not have tried to sing her to you alone, Tasmin Ferrence, because she did not know her. Even you should not sing her alone, Tasmin Ferrence. Who else was there, Tasmin Ferrence? She had no children. From what you say, your males saw only her quality of tineea. You have a word, *flirtation*. It is the same. It is a little dance the females do when they are too young to mate. The *tineea*. It says, admire me. Flatter me. Sing pretty things to me. Expect nothing from me, for I have nothing yet to give. It is this quality of tineea I hear in your song of her.'

'There was more to her than that!'

'Yes. There is always more.'

'She was going to bear my child.'

'Is this difficult or dangerous among humans?'

'Not particularly, no. But she didn't want to do it. She was doing it only for me.'

'Ah. Well, then, we might sing the song of a child who reluctantly began to grow up for love of her mate. It is already a better song than tineea alone.'

'She went to the Enigma, even though she was terrified of the Presences.'

'You speak often of terror when you speak of her. Was she often frightened?'

'She was always frightened. Her parents died when she was little. She was abandoned. Her uncle raised her, but he had children of his own. I was the first person she ever had that she belonged to – that belonged to her. She was afraid she would lose me, terrified, of that – of everything.'

'Ah. Well. This is a different matter. Now we will sing of her valiance, of her courage, to be so afraid and yet to try to conquer it.'

'She gave Lim what he needed when I refused it.'

'We will sing of generosity.'

'She loved me. If Don's right, she died because she loved me.'

'We will sing of devotion.'

Courage. Generosity. Devotion. They were not words he would ever have picked for Celcy, and yet he could not say they were not true. 'I kept saying to myself that I would find the time to be with her more, time with her enough to reassure her that she wouldn't lose me, enough so that she could start to grow up. She might have become a person quite different from the one people saw.'

'We will sing of possibilities, Tasmin Ferrence. We will sing of what she might have become, given time.'

Tasmin sighed, a breath that filled him completely, that left him completely suddenly aware of truth. 'Sing what she might have become. That's it. That's the part that hurts so. That I didn't give her time to become it before she died.'

'So we will sing.'

Tasmin cried, then laughed, weakly, wiping the tears away. 'Is it true, what you sing, Bondri? Are your songs true?'

'Truth is what we sing, Tasmin Ferrence.' On Tasmin's arm the viggy fingers lay, four of them, three and a thumb, petting him. 'You did not know her well enough, Tasmin Ferrence. And then she died. All things die. You did not know her as you should have, as you would have done. You cannot sing her now. You blame yourself. So, that becomes your song. You can sing that you blame yourself for not taking time. Bondri's troupe will listen and help you sing. "He blames himself," we will sing, "but it is not his fault. He did what he could do." It is not fault. It is a debt you owe. You cannot pay it to her, but her child lives. You can learn to sing that child. And to that child, if you will sing devotion and courage and generosity long enough, that, too, will be true. If you will sing what she might have become, then the child will grow, knowing these things about his mother. And what starts now as a song full of time that never was, becomes, in time, the truth.'

Tasmin thought about it, slowly nodding his head. So. So. So. What starts as an enigma score, becomes the truth.

'Think about it, Tasmin Ferrence.'

'I'll think about it, Bondri. When Jamieson gets back, I'll talk to him about it. He knew Celcy. And he knows me so well ...'

The viggy gasped as though hurt. It was a very human sound, full of a deep and abiding pain.

'Tasmin, my friend. This morning I was told of something very sad and grievous that now I must sing to you ...'

Thyle Vowe asked Tasmin to speak for the Tripsingers in negotiations with the Presences. Donatella was invited by her colleagues to represent the Explorers. After thinking about it only briefly, Don declined.

'Let Tasmin represent us,' she said to her colleagues. 'I can't do anything for you that he won't do. And I have something else I have to take care of.'

As soon as services were reestablished, she withdrew a good part of her savings from the BDL credit authority and spent the lot on bantigons, which she offered to the five giligees in Bondri's troupe. She had two friends she wanted them to work on. Link, of course. And Gretl Mechas, who had shown up out of the settling dust, like a wraith, half naked and quite mad.

After her initial shock and surprise at seeing Gretl, Don had asked few questions. Months ago she had identified a tortured body as being that of Gretl Mechas, doing so because it was found with Gretl's clothes, not because she had actually recognized any part of it. Now, even as she realized it had been some other poor creature's body, put there so that no one would look for Gretl, she also realized that Gretl might have preferred that that anonymous body had been hers, that she had been, in fact, dead, gone, out of it. On the surface, Don accepted this, even while she plotted with the giligees. 'You want me to let your family know, don't you?' she suggested, carefully staying away from the subject of Gretl's lover. 'Back on Heron's World?'

Gretl started to say no, then nodded yes. 'Yes. Tell Mother I'm alive. Not ready to come home yet. Maybe not for quite a while. Never maybe. Maybe sometime. Yes. But alive.' Alive, her mind said, wishing her soul could be convinced of that. She consented to go to the viggies because Don suggested it and because she was not able to decide to do anything else. After what she and the others had done to Harward Justin, she did not know if she would ever be fit to do anything normal and human again. And yet, at the end it had been Gretl who had convinced the others to let him die.

Link had been slow to agree to Don's offer. At length, however, he had consented to go into the ranges with Don and Gretl and spend a time there with the giligees.

When ten long days had passed, the giligees had not yet done for Gretl what they hoped, eventually, to do. Gretl stayed with them. Link, despite his doubts, had been a simpler matter. He returned to Splash One with Don, weak and staggering, but walking. Each day he became stronger. Don watched his strength return, wondering why she did not feel the euphoria she had expected; then knowing why, never mentioning it to him. Now that Link could explore again, it seemed likely there would be nothing to explore. The dream had come true; the reason for the dream had departed. The irony of this escaped neither of them. They spent a great deal of time in each other's company, gently making love and purposely saying very little, as though their emotions were a forest of 'lings they needed to thread their way through, very carefully.

After several days of this, Donatella did make time to have lunch with her Cousin Cyndal.

'I was so sorry to hear about Lim's wife and baby,' Cousin Cyndal said, with an air of competence and without looking at the menu. 'When Lim and I arranged the whole thing, he never said a word to me about the financial side of things. I feel responsible.'

'You weren't responsible. Trace it back, Cyndy, and the responsibility for the whole thing falls apart into chance and everyone's individual devils. Except for Harward Justin, no one was at fault. I could have picked any other Presence to try Erickson's suggestion on, but because it was big, and tough, and had stumped all the experts, and I had more ego than was good for me, I picked the Enigma. If I'd done it with any of the others – the Black Tower, the Watchers, even the Jammers – it would have been all right. I could blame myself, too.'

'That's fruitless.'

'I know. It's only marginally better than blaming someone else.'

'How's Link?'

'Getting used to being himself again.'

'Are you going to stay together?'

'We haven't decided. Since neither of us knows what kind of life we're going to lead, or even where we're going to lead it, it's a little premature to make that decision.'

'My, you're being logical.'

'I've been lecturing on the subject.' Donatella remembered her diatribe to Tasmin and changed the subject. 'Did anyone ever suspect you, Cyndal?'

'Your elderly cousin, Cyndal? That fussy old woman? Of course not. No one here on Jubal knows what I did for a living before I came here. Just because I'm old doesn't mean I'm feeble, but they don't know that.'

Donatella flushed.

'Now,' said Cousin Cyndal, 'let's see if there's anything on this menu I can eat.'

'So 'lings are part of the skin of the Presences, are they?' Thyle Vowe grumped to his daughter.

''Lings and 'lets and the surface of the large crystals as well,' Clarin told him.

'And all we were doing all these years was singing lullabies, were we?' He growled in disgust.

'I'm sorry, Daddy, but that's about what we were doing. Very complicated lullabies, of course. The reason we could never translate the noises the Presences made was because they were just noises. Snores and squeaks and scratches. Just like you or me in the middle of a nap, coughing, sneezing, scratching an itch. In the hundred years we've been here, we never got the Presences awake enough to talk.'

'Shit,' erupted the Grand Master. 'It makes a man wonder about the purpose of life.'

'Yes,' agreed Clarin, thinking about Jamieson and how much he had wanted to talk to the Presences, how much he had been looking forward to it. 'Yes. It makes one wonder.'

A time came when everything had been said several times, when negotiations were completed, when ships had departed and other ships had arrived, when the worst of the grieving was over, when the dead had been buried – at least those whose bodies had been found, which did not include Harward Justin – when the matter that had begun with the Enigma score could be considered to be almost over. When that penultimate time came, Tasmin went looking for Clarin.

He found her in the library of the citadel in Splash One. She was reading through accounts of old journeys, many of them first journeys, full of the mystery and wonder that had been Jubal. Her hair had grown long enough that it fell over her forehead, shadowing her eyes. He could not read her expression.

'I was trying to remember how it was, before we knew what it was all about,' she said. 'You and Jamieson and I talked about how we felt. The marvel. The anticipation.'

'It's still there,' he said.

'Not for us,' she said, laying the book down and looking up at him with that long, level look he thought of as so typical of her.

'Why do you say that?'

'Oh, Tasmin, you know what the findings were as well as I do.'

'You haven't spoken with your father, then. I sent word to him this morning.'

'No, I haven't talked with him.'

'If you had, he would have told you that we're not leaving. At least he and I are not leaving. Most of the Tripsingers won't be leaving.'

'You mean they really ... the Presences really want us to stay?'

'They find us interesting, Clarin. They find our perception of them particularly interesting. They see us pretty much the way I'm beginning to see the viggies. The viggies – or at least the giligees – can go right into our bodies and tell us all about them. Things we didn't know. We can do the same for the Presences. They had no concept at all of what they were until we came along and told them.'

'That's right. You've been negotiating.'

'The Presences see no reason for us to go, so long as we're sensible about Jubal. They don't intend to keep their midbrains awake much of the time – evidently their philosophical life, down deep, occupies most of their interest – and they say we'll still be needed to keep them from rolling over on us in their sleep. The ones that were destroyed are growing again, very quickly. Their roots are still there. They tell us there will be another Redfang in a few decades. Another set of Eagers.'

'But what would we do? To earn a living?'

'There's still a market for brou. BDL won't be available to handle it off-planet, of course, but some agglomerate will take us on. The provisional setup we have now will give way to our own planetary government. The viggies want us to stay because we provide good food. We'll need Explorers. Less than a quarter of Jubal is even mapped.' He took a deep breath, eyes shining. 'Clarin, all that country out there! Presences we don't know! Things we've never seen! All that wonderful ...' He caught sight of her unresponsive face and sighed. 'The Presences even asked our advice about the viggies.'

'The viggies?'

'There's the question of their eating some humans. Seemingly a back country troupe of viggies caught and ate a trooper named Halky Bend. I don't know why, except that the Presence said it was justified. Things like that worry the Presences a little. They're aware we don't eat people, or viggies. They know something about taboos. They have some of their own ...' His voice trailed away into silence. She wasn't reacting. 'So,' he concluded weakly, 'there's lots for us to do here.'

'I'm not sure I want to be studied,' she said, apropos of nothing.

'Studied?'

'Of course. The scientists will be all over Jubal. Just think! The first non-organic intelligences!'

'They may come, but they won't be able to sing their way past a waste receptacle,' he said. 'They'll need us, Clarin.'

'Oh, I know that. But I don't want to be their subject.'

'You?'

'Us. Oh, yes. They'll study us along with the Presences, us and the viggies. They'll write learned papers on "The Interactions of Human and Nonorganic Intelligences."'

'So?'

'It's just ...' Her objections sounded specious, even to her. She flushed and examined her hands intently.

He put a package in her lap. 'Here's something I found.'

She looked at him quizzically, opened it. The soft gray-green plush stared up at her. 'A viggy baby,' she said softly. 'For your baby, Tasmin.'

It was a moment before he could respond. 'Yes, for the baby. I've been wondering what to name him.'

'I think there's only one possible name. Call him Lim Jamieson.'

'Lim.' He turned away to the window, tears in his eyes. 'Jamieson.'

'You owe an indebtedness. There's only one way to pay it. Honor their names. Care for their troupes. That's what Bondri would say.'

'What about Celcy?' he asked her, looking her carefully in the face. 'What do I owe her?'

'You've already paid your indebtedness to Celcy,' she said. 'You never hurt her, at least not purposely. Everyone I've talked to says she was as happy and contented being married to you as it was possible for her to be. And now she's gone.'

'Don says she died because she wanted to do one, totally admirable thing.'

'That's possible,' she said calmly. 'There are other possibilities, Tasmin. An infinite number of them. With some things it doesn't matter what is true.'

'I thought it did, to me.'

'Only because you were feeling guilty about it. You wanted something to exonerate you. Or maybe something to canonize her. Then when you found the truth about Lim, you felt even worse. None of that was your doing, Tasmin.'

He laughed, very softly.

'I said something funny?'

'No. You sing one song, and Don sings another, and Bondri sings a third, and I sing another one yet. I suppose we could get my mother in on this. And Jeannie Gentrack, and the other friends we had in Deepsoil Five. At the time, Celcy's death seemed so silly, so futile, so meaningless. It made me so angry. More angry than sad, as I look back on it. I've wanted and wanted to know why she died, and I don't know any more than when we left.'

'And do you know something even stranger, Tasmin? If you could bring Celcy back and ask her, she couldn't tell you.'

'That's true,' he said with sudden enlightenment. 'She probably couldn't.'

'It doesn't matter. Nothing would change on the basis of your understanding about what happened then. What does matter is that you're going to get a baby soon, her baby. And you're going to go on living here on Jubal. And your mother is. And Vivian and Urn's child.'

'And you,' he said.

'I haven't decided yet.'

'Clarim Did you tell Jamieson once that you loved me?'

Her eyes filled. 'Yes. I did. He shouldn't have told you.'

'It was the last thing he said to me, Clarin. He asked me to keep it in mind, for his sake.'

She wept.

'All these conversations I've been having with people, Clarin – they haven't taught me anything that I didn't already know. Only two people on this journey taught me something I didn't know. You and Jamieson. I didn't know anyone could feel as I did about Jubal, care the way I did about Jubal. I set myself apart from people really, separate, in a class all by myself.' He laughed ruefully. 'Don asked me why I picked Celcy, why I didn't try to find someone more suitable. There was a simple reason. It never occurred to me that anyone could be what I needed. I was elite, Clarin. Solitary in my mystical splendor. I thought I was all alone. Jamieson had to force himself on me to teach me I had no monopoly on wonder. Jamieson ... and you.'

The tears spilled. 'I miss him,' she whispered.

'So do I. You're right. If I owe Lim, I owe Jamieson, too. He told me where my heart was.'

'Are you trying to say you love me?'

'I'm trying to say I love you both. Loved him. Love you. Not the way I thought I loved Celcy. Something quite different from that ...'

'I don't want to be your child.'

'No. I didn't think you did. I don't want that, either.'

'Will you get confused, about who I am, Tasmin?'

He thought about this. It was so easy to get confused about who people were. Each person was so many persons. One could only try. He lifted her from the chair, holding her tightly against him. She felt as she had that time at the foot of the Watcher, trembling. She smelled the same. He remembered their voices rising together as they ascended the Ogre's Stair. Two voices, like one. Like himself. If he knew himself, he knew her. If he knew himself ...

'If I get confused,' he promised, 'I'll ask Bondri to help me sing you, Clarin.'

SHADOW'S END

BEHOLD NOW BEHEMOTH
which I made with thee. ...
He is the chief of the ways of God.
The Book of Job

1

Dawn on Dinadh.

Deep in the canyonlands shadow lies thickly layered as fruit-tree leaves in autumn. High on the walls the sun paints stripes of copper and gold, ruby and amber, the stones glowing as though from a forge, hammered here and there into mighty arches above our caves. Inside the caves, the hives spread fragrant smoke, speak a tumult of little drums, breathe the sound of bone flutes. Above all, well schooled, the voice of the songfather soars like a crying bird:

'The Daylight Woman, see how she advances, she of the flowing garments, she of the golden skin and shining eye. ...'

I do not speak with Daylight Woman. I revere her, as do all Dinadhi, but it is Weaving Woman I plead with, am pleading with. Origin of all patterns, I pray, let my shuttle carry brightness!

Each morning before first light, songfather comes to the lip of our cave, where it pushes out, pouting above the darkness below. There he stands, hearing the far faint sounds of daysongs from the east, raising his voice when first light touches the rimrock above, using his song to coax the light down the great wall. Today I stand unnoticed in the shadow beside the hive, listening as the song flows north and east and west into a dozen canyons, past a hundred hives, stirring reverberations and resonances, joining a great warp and woof of sound that follows Daylight Woman's eternal march westward. Dawnsong, so the songfather tells us, endlessly circles our world like the belt that runs from the treadle to the wheel, and thus Dinadh is never without welcome to the Lady of Light.

One time we had another lady. One time we had another father, too, but they were relinquished long ago, when the terrible choice was made. Though the songfathers assure us we were made for that choice, we people, we women, sometimes I grieve over it. Sometimes in the night, darkness speaks to me, and the stars call my name. Saluez, they cry, Saluez, look at us, look at all the mysteries in the night. ...

But still we have appropriate and sufficient deities. We have Weaving Woman and Brother and Sister Rain, and many others. And Lady Day. In darkness, one could step into error. In cloud or fog – rare enough anywhere on Dinadh – one could stray from the right path. Led by Daylight Woman, we walk only the chosen trail, the wise way, and each morning and evening the songfathers celebrate her shining path.

'The lighted path, the chosen way,' intones Hallach, in the words I had anticipated. I hear those words coming back from farther north, where the canyon rim is lower and comes later into the light. Though it sounds like an echo, it is being sung by the songfather of Damanbi. From where I stand I can hear light welcomed not only from Damanbi but also from beyond it, from Dzibano'as and Hamam'n. When the wind blows from the east, we hear the song from Chacosri, around the corner in Black-soil canyon.

I am not the only listener. Inside the hive everyone is gathered behind the doorskins listening, waiting the time of release. Children jitter impatiently. Some men and women paint their faces to ready themselves for the day. Old people with many tasks confronting them stand stolidly, wishing the welcome finished.

And I, Saluez? I wish it could go on forever. I wish the moment could stand frozen in time and not move at all.

'See her rise,' sings Hallach. 'See her dance in garments of fire. See dark withdraw, exposing the world to her grace.'

It is planting season, a time to consider fecundity; so songfather sings now to Brother Big Rain, begging for storm upon the heights, and to Sister Deep Rain, begging for long slow drizzle that will wet the canyons and fill the springs. He mentions the top spring and pool, the lower spring and pool, the waterfall that spreads its moist lace over the rock, the wetness of the bottomland where the summer crops will grow. He sings to Weaving Woman of the pattern of foods eaten at different seasons.

No doubt songfather is eager for summer food, as we all are. We are all sick of winter-fungus, life-bread, grown in the hives during cold time, using the warmth of our bodies, the waste of our bodies to feed itself. It has no taste. It keeps us alive, but it gives no pleasure. During winter, all the pleasurable food must be saved for others, for there are worse things than mere tastelessness.

But soon the time of winter-fungus will be past. First-water has already been carried to the fruit trees, to wake them from winter. Now songfather sings of damp soil, the feel of it, the perfume of unfolding blossoms, continuing this litany until light falls on his face. He opens his soft, fleece outer robe and his patterned cotton inner robe, exposing bare flesh to the light, closing his eyes as he feels the warmth move from chest to belly to thigh. When it reaches his knees, he looks downward through slitted lids, not to miss the moment the sun touches his feet. The final words of the song must be timed properly.

'... even as she has commanded, step into her day! Go forth!'

The song ends as all morning songs end, when light lies on the feet of the singer. Hah-Hallach, songfather of Cochim-Mahn, turns and steps forward onto daylight, seeing the way clearly. The musicians on the roof of the song-study house have been waiting for this. The bone flute shrieks, the panpipes make their breathy sound, the gongs tremble, the little drums, with a final flourish, tum-te-tum into silence. Only then the poisoned doorskins are set aside by careful hands, and people pour from the hive, the sound of day voices bubbling up like water in the spring. Now are talking voices, voices for the light, stilled since dark came. They speak of planting maish and melons. They ask who left a water bowl outside all night. They rise in annoyance at children, and children's voices respond after the manner of children.

And I? I wait until songfather sees me standing there, where I have been since before light, my head bent down, trying not to tremble, for it would not be fitting for songfather to see me tremble.

'Songfather,' I murmur.

'Girl,' says Hah-Hallach, who until yesterday called me Saluez, sweet Sally-girl, who until yesterday was Grandpa, who until yesterday would have put arms about me, holding me.

Am I different today from yesterday? I am still Saluez, granddaughter of his heart, so songfather has said to me, manytime, many-time. Am I changed? Am I not still myself, the self I grew to be? Until yesterday, I knew who Saluez was. Until yesterday, when Masanees told me it was certain:

'You are with child,' she said, gripping my shoulders to help me control my shaking.

I cried then. I was too proud to scream, but I cried, and Masanees wiped my face and cuddled me close as only women will cuddle me close now, only women who know. I had not wanted to be this way. I was not ready for this. Some say there are herbs one can take, but such things are only whispered. The songfathers do not allow it; they say we were made for fecundity, such is the purpose of the pattern, so the Gracious One has spoken. They tell us how all nature is made the same, every tree with its fruit, every blossom with its bee. So every girl must take a lover, once she is able.

I said no, no, no. My friend Shalumn said no, no, no. We were enough for one another, she and I. But this young man said yes, yes, yes. And that young man said yes, yes, yes. And Chahdzi father looked at me beneath his eyebrows, so. So, I picked the one who was least annoying, and it was done. I had a lover. If all went well, soon I would have a husband. When the seed sprouts, Dinadhis say, then the gardeners join their hands and dance. Their hands, and other parts as well. I take no great pleasure in that thought. First loving is, as the old women say, fairly forgettable. Nor is there any pleasure in the thought of what comes between.

So, now I am with child and am no longer favorite anything to Hallach, songfather. Now I become part of the promise, part of the covenant, part of the choice. For this time between the planting and the dancing, only that. Nothing more.

'A day has been appointed for you,' says songfather, not looking at me.

I feel myself shake all over, like a tree in wind, like a newborn little wool-beast experiencing the coldness of air for the first time. Is it fear I feel, or is it anger at their pushing me so? 'Soon you will be old enough. Soon you will have a lover. Soon you will have a husband. It is the way of Dinadh.' I learned these words when I was first able to talk. Now it is all I can do to stand until the shudder passes, leaving me chilled beneath the sun.

'You are prepared?' It is the ritual question.

'Songfather,' I say, 'I am prepared.' The words are the correct words. I have been trained since babyhood to say those words, but no amount of training has made them sound sincere, not even to me! What is it I am supposed to be prepared for? No one will say. They whisper. They hint. But no one ever says!

'You were made for this,' he says solemnly. 'As the Gracious One has told us, you were made for the giving of this gift. Who will go with you?'

I say, 'Masanees, sister-mother.' Masanees has done this thing before, several times, successfully! She is of my mother's generation, though my mother is gone.

Hah-Hallach knows all this. 'She will watch over you,' he says, approvingly.

'Yes, songfather.' I suppose she will.

'Attend to the day. Soon you will go and our songs will go with you.' He strides past me, toward the song-study house.

So. The Gracious One has been mentioned in passing. I have fulfilled my destiny and said my words. The songfather has said his words. Sweet-Sally and Grandpa have said no words at all. The thing is resolved upon, whatever the thing is, and all Dinadhi know their parts in the pattern. They are they, and I am Saluez, who turns and goes back into the hive, for there is much preparation to be made.

Still I cannot keep my head from going back, far back to let my eyes look high, there, among the rimrock, among all those piles of stones where stands the House Without a Name. It has stood there since the Dinadhi came to this place. One stands above every hive. This was the choice we were offered by the Gracious One. This is the choice we made, so songfather says. We people of Dinadh.

But deep inside me I say no! No! This is not the choice I made. I had no part in it. You songfathers made this choice for me, and I have no part in it at all!

Songfather spoke to me at Cochim-Mahn on Dinadh. In another place another man spoke to another woman. That place was the city of Alliance Prime on the world now called Alliance Central. The world had once been called earth, when Alliance Central was only a department, a bureaucracy, that grew and grew until all the earth was covered by Alliance Central and no one called it earth anymore. So I have been taught, as all Dinadhi children are taught, for Dinadh is a member of the Alliance.

The powerful man was the Procurator himself, and the woman was Lutha Tallstaff. She was part of a happening thing and I was part of the same happening thing, a branching of the pattern, as we say, though she and I knew nothing of one another at the time. While we live, say the weavers, we are only the shuttles, going to and fro, unable to see the pattern we are making, unaware of other shuttles in the weft. After years we can look back to see the design we have made, the pattern Weaving Woman intended all along. A time comes when one sees that pattern clear, and then one says, remember this, remember that; see how this happened, see how that happened. Remember what the songfather said, what the Procurator said.

What he first said was, 'You knew Leelson Famber.'

It was a statement of fact, though he paused, as one does when expecting an answer.

Lutha Tallstaff contented herself with a slight cock of her head, meaning all right, so? She was annoyed. She felt much put upon. She was tired of the demands made upon her. Anyone who would send invigilators to drag her from her bath and supper – not literally *drag*, of course, though it felt like it – to this unscheduled and mysterious meeting at Prime needed no help from her! Besides, she'd last seen Leelson four years ago.

'You knew Famber well.' This time he was pushing.

Skinny old puritan, Lutha thought. Of course she had known Leelson well.

'We were lovers once,' she replied, without emphasis, letting him stew on that as she stared out the tall windows over the roofs of Alliance Prime upon Alliance Central.

A single ramified city-structure, pierced by transport routes, decked with plazas, fountains, and spires, flourished with flags, burrowed through by bureaucrats, all under the protective translucence of the Prime-dome, higher and more effulgent than those covering the urbs. The planet had been completely homo-normed for centuries. Nothing breathed upon it but man and the vagrant wind, and even the wind was tamed beneath the dome, a citywide respiration inhaled at the zenith and exhaled along the circumference walls into the surrounding urbs with their sun-shielded, pallid hordes. Lutha, so she would tell me, had a large apartment near the walls: two whole rooms, and a food dispenser and sleeping cubicles and an office wall. The apartment had a window scene, as well, one that could create a forest or a meadow or a wide, sun-drenched savanna, complete with creatures. Lutha sometimes wondered what it would be like to actually live among other creatures. Came a time she and I laughed ruefully about that, a time when we knew all too well what it was like!

On that day, however, she was not thinking of creatures as she remained fixed by the Procurator's expectant eyes. He was waiting for more answer than she had given him thus far.

She sighed, already tired of this. 'Why is my relationship with Leelson Famber any concern of yours?'

'I . . . that is, we need someone who . . . was connected to him.'

Only now the tocsin. 'You knew Leelson Famber,' he'd said. 'You *knew* him.'

'Why!' she demanded with a surge of totally unexpected panic. 'What's happened to him?'

'He's disappeared.'

She almost laughed, feeling both relief and a kind of pleasure at thinking Leelson might be injured, or ill, or maybe even dead. So she told me.

'But you were lovers!' I cried in that later time. 'You said you were made for each other!'

So we believe, we women of Dinadh, who sit at the loom to make an inner robe for our lovers or our children or our husbands or ourselves, beginning a stripe of color, so, and another color, so, with the intent that they shall come together to make a wonderful pattern at the center, one pattern begetting another. So people, too, can be intended to come together in wonder and joy.

So I pleaded with her, dismayed. 'Didn't you love him? Didn't he love you?'

'You don't understand,' she cried. 'We'd been lovers, yes! But against all good sense! Against all reason. It was like being tied to some huge stampeding animal, dragged along, unable to stop!' She panted, calming herself, and I held her, knowing very well the feeling she spoke of. I, too, had felt dragged along.

'Besides,' she said, 'I was sick of hearing about Leelson! Him and his endless chain of triumphs! All those dramatic disappearances, those climactic reappearances, bearing wonders, bearing marvels. The Roc's egg. The Holy Grail.'

'Truly?' I asked. Even I had heard of the Holy Grail, a mystical artifact of the Kristin faith, a religion mostly supplanted by Firstism, though it is practiced by some remote peoples still. 'Practiced,' we say of all religions but that of the Gracious One. 'Because they haven't got it right yet.' It is the kind of joke our songfathers tell.

But Lutha shook her head at me, crying angrily, saying well, no, not the Holy Grail. But Leelson had found the Sword of Salibar, and the Gem of Adalpi. And there was that business about his fetching home the Lost King of Kamir. Well, we knew what came of that!

Perhaps the Procurator understood her ambivalence, for he lurched toward her, grimacing. 'Sorry!' He chewed his lip, searching for words, his twisted body conveying more strain than the mere physical. 'I perceive the fact of his disappearance does not convey apprehension.'

'His disappearance alone does not make me apprehensive,' Lutha drawled, emulating his stuffy manner. Though it annoyed the Fastigats, who claimed intuition as a province solely theirs, even laymen could play at inferences. 'I gather from *your* obvious distress, however, that his disappearance does not stand alone.'

Seeming not to notice her sarcasm, he gestured toward the wide chairs he had ignored since she entered the room. 'Sit down, please, do. Forgive my rudeness. I haven't had time for niceties lately. Let me order refreshment.'

'If it pleases you.' She was starved, but damned if she'd let him know it.

'I hope it will please us both. Today … today could use some leavening of pleasure, even if it is only a little fragrance, a little savor.'

She seated herself as he murmured rapidly into his collar-link before scrambling into the chair across from her, a spindly lopsided figure, his awkwardness made more evident by the skintight uniform. When in the public gaze, draped in ceremonial robes or tabards or togas or what-have-you, even elderly bureaucrats could look imposing enough, but without the draperies, in official skinnies with their little potbellies or saggy butts fully limned, many of them were a little ridiculous. Even the Fastigats. So she said of him.

He, peering nearsightedly at her, saw wings of white hair at either side of her face, stark against otherwise char-black tresses, a bed-of-coals glow warming the brown matte skin at lip and cheek: forge lights, comforting or burning. He saw her square, possibly stubborn jaw. He looked into her eyes, a dark warm gray, almost taupe, showing more anger and pain than he had expected. No doubt the Procurator saw it all. If he cared about such things, no doubt he thought what I thought: how lovely! Though perhaps he had less reason than I to value loveliness.

So he looked at her but did not speak again until the almost invisible shadows had fetched fragrant teas and numerous small plates of oddments, something to suit every taste. Lutha averted her eyes from the food items that were still moving or all-too-recently dead and concentrated on the tray of small hot tarts set conveniently at her elbow. The aroma and taste were irresistible.

'You have some problem concerning Leelson Famber?' she prompted, brushing crumbs from her lips with one of the folded finan skins provided as napkins, soft and silky to the touch. On its own world, the finan is rare, almost extinct. Using its skins for napkins would be a conceit had the animal not been made for that purpose, as the Firsters aver. They are the hierarchs of homo-norm, of whom there are many, even upon Alliance Central. Besides, the finans' genetic pattern had been saved in the computers at Prime. So Lutha told me.

Instead of answering, the Procurator asked, 'Are you familiar with what is now called the "Ularian crisis"?'

Familiar, Lutha thought. Now there was a word. The crisis had been when? Almost a century ago. And on the frontier, to boot. Why in the world would a linguist like herself – a document expert, yes, but withal a mere functionary – be expected to be 'familiar' with such distant and ancient history?

She put her mind in neutral and stared at the table, noticing the foods she found most attractive were now closer to her and the disgusting dishes had been removed. How did the shadows know? Was her face that easy to read? Or were the shadows taught to interpret the almost imperceptible twitches and jerks most people made without realizing it. Were they empaths, like Fastigats? Perhaps they actually were Fastigats, turned invisible as penance for some unseemly behavior. Fastigats were great ones for seemliness.

What had the old man been talking of? Of course. 'Ularian crisis,' she said. 'Around twenty-four hundred of the common era, a standard century ago, give or take a little. Alliance frontier worlds in the Hermes Sector were overrun by a race or force or something called Ularians.' She paused, forehead wrinkled. 'Why was it named that?'

'The first human populations that vanished were in a line, a vector, that led toward the Ular Region,' he replied.

She absorbed the fact. 'So, this something wiped all human life off a dozen worlds or systems or—'

The Procurator gestured impatiently at this imprecision.

She gave him a half smile, mocking his irritation. 'Well, a dozen somethings, Procurator – you asked what I knew and I'm telling you.' She resumed her interrupted account, 'Sometime later the Ularians went away. Thereafter, briefly, occurred the Great Debate, during which the Firster godmongers said Ularians didn't exist because the universe was made for man, and the Infinitarians said Ularians could exist because everything is possible. Both sides wrote volumes explaining Ularians or explaining them away – on little or no evidence, as I recall – and the whole subject became so abstruse that only scholars care one way or the other.'

The Procurator shook his head in wonder. 'You speak so casually, so disrespectfully of it.'

She considered the matter ancient history. 'I shouldn't be casual?'

He grimaced. 'At the time humans – at least those who knew what was going on – feared for the survival of the race.'

'Was it taken that seriously?' she asked, astonished.

'It was by Alliance Prime, by those who knew what was happening! All that saved us from widespread panic was that the vanished settlements were small and few. Publicly, the disappearances were blamed on environmental causes, even though people vanished from every world in Hermes Sector – that is, every one but Dinadh.'

She shrugged, indicating disinterest in Dinadh. She who was to learn so much about Dinadh knew and cared nothing for it then.

The Procurator went on. 'My predecessors here at Prime could learn nothing about the Ularians. The only evidence of the existence of an inimical force was that men had disappeared! Prime had no idea why they – or *it* – attacked in the first place.'

He leaned forward, touching her lightly on the knee. 'Did Leelson ever speak to you of *Bernesohn Famber*?'

She was suddenly intrigued. 'Oh, yes. Leelson's great-grandpop. One of the greatest of all Fastigats, to hear Leelson tell it. A genius, a biochemist.'

'Do you remember the name Tospia?'

Lutha smiled. 'Bernesohn's longtime lover. A Fastiga woman, of course.' She frowned. 'A diva in solo opera. Leelson played some of her sensurrounds for me. Very nice, though I think the senso-techs were owed as much credit as Tospia herself. To my taste, one person's performance sensed six times, however differentiated and augmented, does not have the interactive passion of six separate actors. I've yet to experience one that has true eroticism.'

The Procurator peered at her over the rim of his cup. 'But Leelson never mentioned Bernesohn and the Ularians?'

She gave the question to her subconscious, which came up empty. 'I recall no connection.'

He settled himself with a half-muffled groan. 'I beg your patience:

'A century ago, there were twelve human populations on planets in Hermes Sector. Eleven of these were only settlements, six of them homonormed, the other five at the survey stage. The twelfth world, Dinadh, had a planetary population. Dinadh is a small world, an unimportant world, except that it is near us in a spaciotemporal sense, though not in an astrophysical one. Everything into and out of Hermes Sector, including information, routes through Dinadh and did, even then.

'So, it was customary for freighters to land there, whether going or coming, and one did so a century ago, bringing the news that two of the settlements in Hermes Sector had vanished. Prime sent six patrol ships carrying investigative teams; two ships returned with news of further vanishments; the other four did not return. We sent more men to find the lost men – frequently a mistake, as in this case. None of them returned. Dinadh's government, such as it is, refused to consider even partial evacuation, which would have been the best we could do. Evacuating a populated planet is impossible. There aren't enough ships to keep up with the birthrate.' He sighed.

'And?' she prompted.

'Dinadh is the only occupied planet of its system, the only one suitable for occupation. The Alliance did the only thing it could think of, englobing the system with unmanned sentinel buoys. We might as well have done nothing, for all the good it did. No one came out of the sector toward Dinadh. Every probe we sent into the sector from Dinadh simply disappeared.

'Ten standard years went by; then twenty, then thirty. Planets applying for colony rights were sent elsewhere. Then, thirty-three standard years after the crisis, the sentinel buoys picked up a freighter crossing the line *from* Hermes Sector into Dinadhi space! The holds were stuffed with homo-norm equipment. The crew claimed they had found it abandoned and therefore salvageable, after falling into Hermes Sector accidentally, through a rogue emergence. Later we checked for stellar collapse and found an enormous one about the right time—'

'Stellar collapse?'

'The usual cause of rogue emergences is stellar collapse. The dimensional field twitches, so to speak. Things get sucked in here and spat out there. Well, the crew was brought here, and more questions were asked. It turned out they'd picked up equipment from four worlds in the sector and had noticed nothing at all inimical. We sent volunteer expeditions to investigate. All of them returned shrugging their shoulders and shaking their heads. Nothing. No sign of what had happened to the human population thirty-odd years before, and no signs of aliens at all. We assumed the Ularians, whatever they or it had been, had departed.'

'So there were no survivors?' mused Lutha.

He shook his head. 'Oh, we looked, believe me! We had no information about Ularians, no description of them, no actual proof that they existed, which gratified the Firster godmongers, you may be sure, for they'd claimed from the beginning there were no such things as Ularians. Since government is always delicately poised vis-à-vis godmongers, we were extremely interested in what survivors might tell us, but we never found a thing in Hermes Sector. Oh, there were some children who turned up on Perdur Alas around twenty years ago, but they were probably emergence castaways also.'

'Unlikely they'd have been there for eighty years. They'd have had to be third or fourth generation.'

'Quite right. All this is mere diversion, however.'

'You started by asking me about Bernesohn Famber,' she said impatiently.

'The *relevant* fact is that Bernesohn Famber was on one of the ships that went into Hermes Sector right after the vanishments.'

'One of the lost ships.'

'No! One that came back. Bernesohn was erratic and secretive. A genius, no doubt, but odd. Sometimes he didn't appear outside his quarters for days and days. His colleagues didn't expect to see him regularly, so they didn't realize he was gone! When the ship got back here, they didn't have any idea where or when he'd gone. We couldn't find him.'

The Procurator leaned back in his chair. 'Imagine our discomfiture sometime later when we learned he was living on Dinadh.'

'How did you find that out?' Lutha asked.

'Well, a year or so after Bernesohn disappeared, Tospia, his longtime companion, gave womb-birth to twins. In Fastiga.'

Lutha knew where Fastiga was. It might be called a suburb of Prime. Leelson's mother lived there.

The Procurator went on. 'Tospia's twins were entered in the Famber lineage roster, but nobody at Prime made the connection.'

She said impatiently, 'You intend to make the point, I presume, that the twins were conceived after Bernesohn's disappearance?'

The Procurator assented. 'Years later a sensation sniffer for one of the newslinks did a so-called biography of Tospia – unauthorized, need I say – in which he alleged that Bernesohn Famber could not have fathered the twins. Tospia threw a memorable and widely publicized tantrum and sued the sniffer for misprision of media freedom, asserting that Bernesohn had been living on Dinadh and that she had visited him there.'

The Procurator set down his cup and went on:

'Enormous consternation, as you might imagine! Alliance officers were sent to Dinadh immediately to debrief Bernesohn about the Ularians.'

'And?'

He shrugged, mouth downturned. 'And the Dinadh planetary authorities turned them all away, saying that Bernesohn had bought a hundred-year privacy lease, that even though he was no longer at his leasehold, his lease was still in effect and no one could be admitted but family members, thank you very much. His "family members" were notably uncooperative, and since our only reason for questioning Bernesohn was the Ularian threat, which was seemingly over, we couldn't demonstrate compelling need. In the absence of compelling need, we had no authority to invade a member planet, and that's what it would have taken.'

He nodded to himself, then resumed in a thoughtful voice: 'Of course, we drew what inferences we could. We assumed Bernesohn had gone there because he expected to find something on Dinadh, but if he'd come up with anything useful, he hadn't told Prime about it.'

'You said he was no longer at his leasehold?'

He sighed, turning his cup in his hands. 'All Dinadh said about the matter was that they "had welcomed him as an outlander ghost."'

'Which means?'

'We presume it means he died. And there the matter has rested until now. ...' His voice trailed off disconsolately.

'But?'

'But, now they're back.'

Lutha stared at him, disbelieving. 'The Ularians?'

He nodded, swallowed, shredded the finan-skin napkin between his fingers. 'Almost a hundred standard years! Why not fifty years ago? It was then Prime decided it was safe to open up Hermes to colonization once more. There are three populated worlds and several colonies in there; there are homo-norm teams on half a dozen other worlds, and survey teams everywhere worthy of survey.'

'And?'

'And two of the colonies are gone. Like last time.'

Lutha turned away from his distress, giving herself time to think, holding her cup over the table and feeling it grow heavier as it was filled with tea by an almost invisible shadow.

'What has all this to do with Leelson?' she asked.

'Now we're desperate to know whatever Bernesohn Famber knew. As long as Bernesohn's privacy lease has any time to run, however, the only people Dinadh will allow to poke about among Bernesohn's belongings are family members. Family is a very big thing on Dinadh. Since Leelson is descended from Bernesohn, Leelson is Bernesohn's "family," so far as the Dinadhi are concerned.'

Now Lutha understood what they were asking of her. 'You need Leelson, but Leelson has disappeared.' She tapped her fingers, thinking. 'Did you think I might know where Leelson is? Or did you have some idea the Dinadhi would accept me as Leelson's "family"?'

'I don't think you know where Leelson is, no. I know the Dinadhi will accept you as family. You are Leelson's wife as they define wife.'

When Lutha told me this, I laughed. It was true, in a way. She was Leelson's wife as we on Dinadh define wife. Some of the time.

'Because we were lovers?' she asked him.

'Because you bore his child,' the Procurator said.

She felt the blood leave her face, felt it drain away to disclose a familiar

300

sorrow, an endless ache. 'My son is a private matter.'

He sighed. 'Believe me, Lutha Tallstaff, under other circumstances I would not challenge your privacy. The Ularians give us no choice. Do you remember Mallia Stentas? From Keleborn?'

Lutha answered distractedly, 'We were at upper school together. She became a manager for some agricultural consortium. ...'

'You may mourn her now – she and her lifemates and all their many children – gone from Tapil's World. And the people on Up-dyke-Chel. They are not merely dead, but dust in the wind, vanished and gone, no stone to mark the place they were. Whatever the Ularians may be, when they come upon a world, they leave behind no monuments. ...'

He stood, walked across the room to the wall retriever, and flicked it into life. 'Tapil's World,' he murmured. 'Beamed by our recorders.'

An empty town materialized before them. Everywhere evidence of interruption. A doll lying abandoned by a fence. A child's wagon, half-full of harvested vegetables, standing at the side of a fenced garden. A sun hat caught in a thorny shrub. A fuzzy native animal – either useful for something or a neutered pet, as it would not have escaped homo-norming otherwise – hopping slowly along a hedge, crying plaintively. Kitchens with food half-prepared, rooms with tables still littered, desks still piled. The probe came down over one desk, focusing on a holo that stood there. Herself. Mallia and herself, young scholars, arms around one another, grinning into eternity.

'Damn you,' Lutha said without heat.

'I want you to feel it,' he admitted. 'It could be your house. It could be you, and your son. It could be all humanity.'

During our time together, Lutha described his voice, full of a sonorous beauty, like the tolling of a funeral bell. He was working Fastigat stuff on her, wringing her emotions like a wet towel, making her all drippy. Leelson had done that from time to time, worked Fastigat stuff on her, though he had done it for their mutual pleasure.

'Nothing like a romantic moon,' she told me. 'A little wine, and a silver-tongued Fastigat to make the worlds move.'

'It does not take wine or a Fastigat to move the world,' I told her, thinking of my own love.

'I am relieved to hear it,' she said then, laughing as she wept. We had then a good deal of reason to weep.

But even then, during her meeting with the Procurator, she thought all that Fastigat stuff unnecessary. The memory of Mallia alone wrung her quite enough.

So, she took a deep breath and said to this old, conniving man: 'You want me to go to Dinadh, is that it?'

The Procurator nodded. 'We want someone to go, and the only people they will allow are Leelson, his mother, or you. Leelson's mother has refused to go. Leelson himself, we can't find. That leaves you. You're already proficient in basic Nantaskan. Dinadh speaks a dialect of Nantaskan. And I'll send a Fastigat with you.'

'Please. No,' she cried.

He reached toward her, pleadingly. 'Lutha. Please. We'll pick someone who isn't ... intrusive. Someone tactful.'

She snorted.

'Some Fastigats can be,' he said in an offended tone.

'The Dinadhi will allow me a companion?' She sneered. 'Someone nonfamily?'

'If he goes as your assistant or servant, yes. You'll need some such to help with your son. You'll have to take the boy.'

She laughed again, this time incredulously. 'You're joking, of course.' He knew how ridiculous the idea was. Even the invigilators who had summoned her to this meeting had been aware of the problem Leely presented. They'd brought a whole crèche team with them to take care of Leely while she was away.

He shook his head at her, leaning forward to pat her knee, an avuncular gesture. 'Believe me, Lutha, I wouldn't ask it if it weren't necessary. The Dinadhi won't accept you without the boy.'

'You expect me to drag a child across half a dozen sectors to ...' This child, she said to herself. This particular child, with his particular problems.

'Spatiotemporally, it's not half a dozen sectors,' he told her. 'I wish it were, quite frankly. We'd be safer!'

She made herself relax, slowly picked up the cup once more, finding it fresh, steaming hot.

'Will you go?' he asked.

'Do I have a choice?' she grated. 'If I don't go, you'll—'

'Nothing,' he assured her. 'Really nothing. We have the power to compel you, but compelling you would be useless. We need your willing, intelligent cooperation. It's up to you whether you give it or not.'

As though that old devil conscience would have let her say no! 'You know me,' she said angrily. 'You knew I wouldn't say no. Didn't you?'

As he did. As Fastigats did. Lutha told me all about Fastigats. Fastigats get to know people very quickly, very well, very completely, as had this bald, quirky old empath across from her who hadn't come right out and told her he was one of them. Who hadn't needed to, any more than Leelson had, when they had been together.

✳

'You're going to be fine,' Leelson had said often during her later stages of pregnancy, soothing her in moments of dismay.

'I know,' she'd snapped. 'Women have been having babies for hundreds of thousands of years.'

'Well, yes. But I don't regard that as particularly comforting, do you?' He made a face at her, making her laugh. 'Stars have been blowing up into novas for billions of years, but that doesn't make their near vicinity desirable.'

'If you intend a similarity, I am offended,' she said. 'Though I may have assumed the proportions of a nova, I have no intention of bursting. I merely scream when I stand up, because it hurts to stand up! This may sound like an explosion, but actually—'

'We are not Firsters. You could have – ' he interrupted gently.

'Don't tell me. Of course I could have.' Could have chosen not to be pregnant. Could have chosen to delay the development of the fertilized egg. Could have had the baby developed in a biotech uterus, given crèche birth. She hadn't chosen that. Why not? She didn't know why not! Why had he gotten her pregnant in the first place? Fastigats could control that if they wanted to! Obviously, he hadn't wanted to!

'Well then?' Leelson being reasonable.

'I keep thinking it must be boring for you.' Great Gauphin, it was boring enough for her.

'A new experience is seldom boring. Womb-birth is becoming quite rare, and rare happenings appeal to the collector's taste. All Fastigats are collectors.'

She didn't say what she was thinking, that the whole thing had been an accident. That she'd had second thoughts about it, but then Leelson's mother had said – Leelson had said ...

The less thought about all that the better. Still, she was peevish when Leelson seemed more fascinated by the pregnancy than he was by her. She said this, laughing at herself.

'It's not true,' he assured her. 'I am passionately fond of you, Lutha Tallstaff. You are like a dinner full of interesting textures and flavors, like a landscape full of hidden wonders. I am not ignoring you in all this.'

True. When one had a Fastigat for a lover, one could not complain of being ignored. One's every whim was understood; one's every mood was noted. For the most part, one's every desire was satisfied, or thwarted, only to make the satisfaction greater when it occurred. If a Fastigat lover was not forthcoming, it was not through lack of understanding. Sometimes Lutha felt (so she told me) she was understood far too well. Sometimes she longed for argument, for passionate battle, for a sense of her own self back again. Pride kept her from showing it, that and the fear that Leelson would accommodate her. Only a fool would take on an opponent who could block every thrust before it was made.

It was easier during those early months after Leely was born, for then Leelson switched at least part of his searching intelligence from her to the child, leaving Lutha to her udderish moods and mutters while he hovered over the infantender, forehead creased, feeling his way into that little mind.

'Like a maze,' he'd said, almost dazedly. 'All misty walls and dazzling spaces. Hunger or discomfort comes in like jagged blobs of black, and the minute he eliminates or burps or takes the nipple, he's back to dazzling spaces again.'

'No faces?' she'd asked, disappointed. Babies were supposed to recognize faces. Like baby birds, back when there had been birds, recognizing the special markings of their own species. Eyes, nose, mouth: that configuration was supposed to be instinctively recognized by humans. Lutha had read about it.

'Well, I can't feel faces,' he'd replied. 'No doubt they're there.'

Later he postulated that Leely recognized something else or more than faces. Some quality unique to each person, perhaps. Some totality.

'He's not one of us, I'm afraid. Not a Fastigat.' Leelson had shaken his head ruefully over the four-month-old child. It was then Lutha admitted to herself what she had refused to consider before: Leelson was disappointed at not having a Fastigat son. Virtually all Fastigat sons were empaths, at least. If she'd had a daughter, it wouldn't have mattered!

'Hardly fair,' she'd muttered, wanting to weep. 'Sexist!'

He'd smiled charmingly, the way he did. Fastigats were almost always charming. 'Not my fault, Lutha. I didn't design it. It's sex-linked, that's all.'

'You'd think biologists—'

He hadn't let her finish. 'Well, of course our women say attempting to make female Fastigats is meaningless, because any normal woman is a sensitivity match for a male empath, any day.'

He'd made her laugh, hiding his own disappointment. Perhaps even then he'd known – or at least suspected – this disappointment wasn't to be the only one.

Time came soon enough, of course, when suspicion was fulfilled and Leelson went away. Unforgivably away. Without announcement or preamble. One morning she had wakened to find him gone. He'd left a note, of course, if one could call five words a note. Not much after their years together.

'You must feel abandoned. Betrayed!' This from Lutha's older sister, Yma, sector-famed, thespian absolute.

The accuracy of this made Lutha blaze hotly as she denied it. 'I do not! Leelson's and my relationship lasted a long time. Neither of us is from a contractual culture, so why would I feel betrayed!' She said it as though she meant it. In fact, she did feel betrayed and abandoned, not that she could possibly admit it to Yma. How could he? She couldn't have left Leelson! How could he have left her?

Yma went on. 'Perhaps not a contract, but still …'

'But still nothing, Yma. I had a child because I wanted a child.' That was partly true. She kept her lip from trembling with considerable effort. After the initial shock, she had wanted a child.

'Well, of course you did, darling, but it was a genetic risk. With him.'

'Fastigat men father normal children on non-Fastigat women all the time!'

Yma couldn't leave it at that. 'Well, there are no aberrations in your family line.'

'You don't know that!' Lutha cried.

'Oh, yes I do and so do you. Even though we've never met them, we know all about Papa's side of the family. They're all totally ordinary, ordinary, ordinary!' To Yma, nothing could be worse.

Lutha did indeed know a great deal about Papa's family, and his many siblings and half siblings out on the frontier. Frontier worlds began with a colony ship, a few hundred crew members, and a hundred thousand human embryos. Thirteen or fourteen years later the original embryos were boys and girls who began procreating on their own, using the crèche equipment on the ship. A few decades, the colony might number in the millions! Twenty children per woman was not uncommon, virtually all of them crèche-born. In a homo-normed world, there were few impediments. No dangerous diseases, little danger from weather, no danger from plants or animals – in fact few plants and no animals at all.

'Mama Jibia does go on and on about the kinfolk,' Lutha admitted.

'She's never said anything indicating they're anything but boring. And Mama's family, we know all about, both sides, four generations back. Her mother is Lucca Fineapple, and we've met her. Remember?'

'The religious grandma,' said Lutha with vague discomfort at the memory. 'Who visited us on her way through the sector.'

'Exactly. You do remember! We thought her very strange! Well, women who depilate and tattoo their entire bodies *are* strange. But that's simply attitudinal; biologically she's quite all right. And Mama Jibia is always telling stories about Lucca's mother – Nitha Bonetree, remember, the one who first ran away to the frontier?'

'Which is where Lucca was born, and Mama too. I guess I remember some of that. Mama Jibia always said we'd inherited our talents from Nitha's line.'

'It isn't the detail that matters in any case! The only thing that matters is there's no problem in your family on either side back four generations. And

Leelson should *not* have left you to provide the entire care for the boy, as though it were somehow your fault!'

Lutha felt herself turning red, felt the tears surging, heard the anger in her words. 'I had always intended to be responsible for my child. It was *my* choice.'

Was it? Was it indeed? Then why couldn't she remember making it! She asked me this and I laughed. I couldn't remember either. It had just happened. One couldn't really question it. Lutha said even Yma knew she'd gone too far. Wisely she let the matter drop.

Lutha never mentioned to Yma the credit drafts regularly deposited to her account from Fastiga. Fastigats did not father by chance. As a society, they fathered no unknown or unacknowledged children, and all children fathered by Fastigats received support from Fastiga. It was a matter of honor, one of the primary differences, so said Fastigats, between Fastigats and lesser men.

Fastigats didn't even sign certificates of intent. Their honor was so untarnished they were exempt from the requirement imposed on all other citizens of Central, to have five responsible, self-supporting coparents on record by the fourth month of pregnancy.

Lutha and Yma and Mama Jibia and two male cousins had signed for Leely. No one cared who had children, or how many, but one of the basic rights of Alliance citizens was not to be responsible for other people's. The penalties for dereliction of responsibility were severe, and the credit drafts from Fastiga were infuriatingly beyond the call of duty. Even more infuriating were the Fastigat uncles and male cousins who visited at intervals, observed Leely's growth and development, then went away again. Meantime, Leely grew bigger and stronger and older and Lutha became more tired and desperate.

'You ought to consider the alternatives,' Yma said, every time they met. 'Really, Lutha. You ought to. ...'

The Fastigat uncles and cousins also urged her to consider alternatives. Santeresa's World, they'd suggested, where the whole planet made its living caring for the sick, the injured, the disabled. It was expensive, but Fastiga would pay for it. Lutha had refused. Her child was not an alternative. End of statement. End of consideration, no matter how her life narrowed around her day by day and even her necessary professional duties gave way to Leely's needs. She could not decide to let him go any more than she had decided to have him. Though she had. She must have!

For years now she had kept a fragile calm, slathering sentimental oil on every emotional linkage, making her life move like some old cog-and-belt-driven machine, creaking and wobbling from one day to the next. And now, here, all at once, this skinny old fart, this Fastigat servant of the Alliance, this bureaucrat, had thrust an additional duty among her gears, grinding her to a screaming halt!

She abandoned simile and summoned anger, making herself rage at being forced to do the Alliance's will. Was this a penalty, for having known Leelson? Another one?

The anger wouldn't hold. It was too hard to hide from herself the anticipation she felt at the promise of somewhere to go, the relief at the idea of someone to help her. The promise of succor and change.

So Lutha planned a journey, even as I, Saluez, planned a journey, though hers was far longer than mine. In a sense, at least, hers was longer, though mine wrought greater changes. For me a night soon came when Shalumn and I wept on each other's shoulders, I out of fright, she out of fear of losing me. The following morning I bent beneath the brow-strap of my carrying basket and went up the rocky trail with Masanees. High on a shelf above Cochim-Mahn, I panted, waiting for her to catch up with me. Masanees is not as agile as she once was. She has not yet received Weaving Woman's reward, that comfortable time of life when she need no longer fear conceiving, but she is no longer young. I am young. I am twelve in Dinadh years, twenty standard years. Too young for this, perhaps. But no. Women younger than I, much younger than I have made this trip. If a woman is old enough to conceive, she is old enough for this. So the songfathers say. 'Soil which accepts seed is ready for the plow!'

'Whsssh,' Masanees breathed as she came up to the stone where I waited. 'Time for a breather. That path gets steeper every year.'

'Have you come up before this year?' I asked, knowing the answer already.

Masanees nodded. 'With Dziloch. And last year with Kh'nas.'

'Imsli a t'sisri,' I murmured. *Weave no sorrow.*

'None,' Masanees replied cheerfully. 'They're both fine. We did it right.'

I tried to smile and could not. I was not reassured. Each year some did not return from the House Without a Name. Each year some went behind the veil, down into shadow. Each time the women no doubt thought they had done it right. Who would go there otherwise?

There was no point in saying it. Saying it only increased terror. I had been told one should, instead, sing quietly to oneself. A weaving song, dark and light, pattern on pattern. Turning away up the hill, I chanted quietly to myself in time with my plodding feet.

The House Without a Name stands on a promontory above Cochim-Mahn. One can see a corner of it from the shelf where the songfather stands, only a corner. One would not want to see it all. One would not want to look at it as part of one's view of the world. It is easier to ignore it, to pretend it isn't really there. One can then speak of the choice in measured tones, knowing one need not fear the consequences. As songfathers do.

'*That which we relinquished, death and darkness in the pattern.*

'*That which we took in its place, the House Without a Name ...*'

That's how the answer to the riddle goes, the one no one ever asks out loud, the riddle my grandmother whispered to me in the nighttime, as her grandmother had whispered it to her. 'What is it men relish and women regret?' Grandma asked, preparing me. Letting me know without really letting me know. Frightening me, but not terrifying me.

It's the way we do things now. We hint. We almost tell, but not quite. We let young people learn only a little. If they never know it thoroughly or factually, well, that makes the choice easier. If they do stupid things because they don't know enough, that's expected.

As a result, ignoring the house becomes habit and I was able to ignore my approach to it until we arrived at the stone-paved area outside the door. Then I had to admit where I was.

'Shhh,' whispered Masanees, putting her arms around me. 'It's all right. We've all been through it, child. It's all right.'

Still I shivered, unable to control it. 'I'm scared,' I whispered, shaming myself.

Evidently I wasn't the only one to have said something like that, for Masanees went on holding me.

'Of course you're scared. Of course you are. The unknown is always scary. Sooner we get to it, sooner it'll be over. Come now. Be a good, brave girl.'

She pushed the door open. The house had a pitched roof, but there were wide openings under the eaves where birds had flown in and out and little nut-eaters had scrambled down to make their mess among the other droppings.

'First we had to make all clean,' said Masanees. The brooms were lashed to her pack, and I followed her example as we gave the place a good sweeping and brushing, including the tops of two low stone tables that stood side by side. One table had a stone basin in its center. We wiped it clean and filled it with water we'd carried up from below. Then we emptied the packs at either side of the basin, and I exclaimed at the sight of such bounty! Meal cakes, beautifully colored and baked in fancy shapes. Strips of meat dried into spirals around long sticks of candied melon. Squash seeds roasted and salted. Dried fruits. More candied fruits. Masanees showed me how to lay it all out in patterns, varying the colors, making it bright and attractive. There is always a store of such foods kept in the hive, she said, even when we have nothing to eat but winter-fungus. Even when *we* hunger, these ritual foods are kept sacred so *they* will not hunger.

When everything was done on the one table, she cast me a look from the corners of her eyes, and I knew whatever was going to happen to me, Saluez, would happen now. She spread a folded blanket upon the other table and helped me lie facedown upon it. She gave me a ring of basketwork and told me to put my face firmly down in it. She shackled my wrists and ankles to the rings in the stone.

'Ready?' asked Masanees.

I jerked at the shackles. I could feel my eyes, wide. I knew the whites were showing, knew I was beginning to panic.

'Shh, shh. It's all right. Here. Drink this.' She raised my head and held the cup to my lips.

'I'll be all right,' I cried mindlessly, not drinking.

'You'll be all right,' Masanees agreed, tipping the cup. 'Come on, Saluez. It's easier so.'

I made myself drink. My arms and legs jerked against the bonds. Gradually they stopped moving and lay quiet. I could hear. I could feel. I could breathe through the basketwork, but I did so quietly. The basket ring encircled my face, and beneath my eyes was only the stone of the table.

I heard the heavy door close as Masanees left. I knew what was outside, nearby, hanging from the branch of an ancient tree: a wooden mallet beside a gong. I heard her feet pause, heard her voice saying words I knew, heard the metal struck by the mallet, a slow series of blows that reverberated among the canyons, a long plangent sound, not sweet but seductive. One, two, three. Then a long pause. Then one, two, three again. The series went on. Triplet, then pause. Triplet, then pause. Then a responsive sound. Was it what she expected? It seemed very loud to me.

My limbs wanted to jerk, to pull free. They could not move. The sounds outside increased. ...

I heard her feet hurry off. Somewhere nearby, hidden in the trees, she would conceal herself to wait, and watch, until she could return to let me go. ...

I do not like remembering that time. Sometimes the whole thing comes back on me, all at once, before I have had a chance to shut it out. I cry out, then. I stand shivering. People pretend not to see me, turning their eyes away until I have shaken the memory off and closed the door upon it. I do not like remembering that time, so I shall remember something else instead.

I shall remember when I was a child in Cochim-Mahn.

Dinadhi girl-children have much to learn. Clay between the hands and the whirl of the wheel. Wool and cotton between the fingers and the twist of the spindle. The weight of brush and broom, the long hours at the loom. The feel of the grindstone under one's palms, the bend of the back when dropping seeds into the holes made by the planting stick. The setting of the solar cooker to gather all the sun's heat. The forward thrust of the head against the tump line, bringing down wood for the winter. A woman must be always busy if her family is to be clad and shod and fed and kept warm, so a girl-child is taught to be constantly busy as well.

Once each left-thumb day – it is how we count days: little-finger day, lesser twin, longer twin, point-finger day, thumb day; right hand first, then left, making a double hand; five double hands to the month; twelve months to the year, plus the eight or nine extra days Daylight Woman gives us at harvest time. As I say, once every left-thumb day, my mother went to the sanctuary cells of Bernesohn Famber, taking me with her as her mother had taken her. Famber was not there, of course. He had become an outlander ghost a long time before, in the time of my great-grandmother. Still, he had paid for a hundred-year lease, paid for cells allocated to him and secured against intrusion or extradition for one hundred standard years. The price for such a lease includes food and cleaning. The food mostly came from off-planet, but the cleaning was done by us.

Each tenth day we took brooms and brushes and soft old rags and went into his cell, which is around the back of the main hive, on the cave-floor level, in a kind of protrusion built out from the body of the hive. We don't like outlanders stumbling about among us in the hive, so our leasehold has its own entrance. In case an outlander needs help at night, there is a corridor that comes into a storeroom of the hive, but it is seldom used except by those who serve the outlanders.

The Cochim-Mahn leasehold is three cells built around a toilet place. We don't use the manure of outlanders in our fungus cellars. There is some feeling it might kill the fungus. Instead we buy these closet things from the Alliance for our leaseholders to use, and when they get used up, we trade for new ones. So Bernesohn Famber's place was a little corridor with five doors in it, one to the hive storeroom, one to the toilet, and three more to the three cells. The cell nearest the front, nearest the lip of the cave, had a door to the outside as well. All of the rooms had lie-down shelves around the sides. One back room was where Famber had slept, one he had used for storage, and the one with the door to the outside had his worktable and a comfortable chair and many strange devices and machines. These, Mama told me, were recorders and computers and analyzers, to help Bernesohn Famber with his work.

'What was his work?' I always asked, each and every time.

'Finding out about Dinadh,' she always said, winking at me. Grown-ups wink like that when they hint something about the choice. Or the House. Or the other world we had, before we came here. Things we are not supposed to talk about.

'Did he find out?' I asked.

'Nobody knows,' she said, marching back through the cells to the back one, where she started with the broom and I followed with the brush, sweeping down the smooth mud walls, brushing off the sleeping shelves, making a little pile of dust and grit that got bigger the farther we pushed it from cell to cell, until at last we could push it right out the door onto the floor of the cave. Then I took the broom and pushed it across the cave floor, farther and farther forward, until it came to the edge and fell over, all that dust and grit and sheddings of the hive falling down like snow on the canyon bottom.

Sometimes, while Mama was sweeping, I'd sit and look at the machines, longing to push just one button, just to see what would happen. It was forbidden, of course. Such things were not Dinadhi things. We had to live without things like that. We had *chosen* to live without them. We had *chosen* to give them up in return for what we were promised instead.

After we cleaned Bernesohn Famber's leasehold, sometimes we went down to the storerooms to pick something for supper. In summers, there are all kinds of things, fresh or dried melon, fresh or dried meat, different kinds of vegetables and fruit, pickled or fresh or dried. There is almost always grain, head grain or ear grain, eaten whole or cracked or ground for making bread. We have seeds for roasting, and honey too. We brought bees with us, from the other world.

In late winter and early spring, though, there's mostly fungus from the cellars, pale and gray and tasting like wood. The only good thing about fungus is that it's easy to fix. It can be eaten fresh or dried, raw or cooked. We usually put some salt and herbs on it to make it taste like something. Most all of our cookery is done in the mornings, when the sun is on the cave. We use solar reflectors for cooking. The whole front edge of the cave is lined with them, plus all the level spots to either side, and any time of the morning you can see women scrambling across the cliff wall to get at their own ovens and stewpots.

After food is cooked, it's kept warm in padded boxes until eating time. None of our food is very hot, except in wintertime. Then we have fires in the hive, and we over them. It would take too many trees to have fires in summer. That was part of the promise and the choice as well. We have to protect the trees and certain plants because the beautiful people need them.

Even though girls had much to learn, sometimes Mama would tire of teaching me and say, 'Go on, go play,' and then I'd have to try to find somebody else whose mama had said, 'Go play,' to them too.

Shalumn and I played together mostly. We played babies and we played wedding and we played planting and harvest, smoothing little patches in the dust and grooving them like ditches, and putting tiny rocks down for the vegetables. We had dolls, of course, made out of reed bundles, covered with cloth, with faces painted on. We didn't play with the boys, not once we were old enough to know who was a boy and who was a girl. Boys played sheepherder and songfather and watermaster, and they had games where somebody always won and somebody always lost. Shalumn and I played bed games together, and once Mama caught us at it and whipped us both on our bottoms. I still have a little line there, on one side, where the whip cut. After that we were careful.

I remember those as pleasant times, but I can't make them sound like much. Nothing much happens with children on Dinadh. We don't have adventures. If we tried to have an adventure, we'd probably die right away. Maybe better ... better I think of some other story. Not my life or Lutha Tallstaff's life, but someone else's. Another person entirely, the third one of us. The one Lutha and I met together. Snark the shadow.

At the end of each workday the Procurator dismissed his shadows, allowing them to descend the coiled ramps that led from occupied areas to Shadowland beneath. There each shadow entered the lock as he was programmed to do.

'Strip off your shadow suit,' said the lock.

The shadow stripped off the stiff suit with all its sensors and connectors, hanging it in an alcove in one side of the booth.

'Place your hands in the receptacles.'

The shadow placed.

'Bend your head forward to make contact with the plate.'

The shadow bent.

Light, sounds, movement. Snark stood back from the plate, shaking her head, as she always did, bellowing with rage, as she always did.

'Leave the cubicle,' said the voice, opening the door behind her, opposite the one she'd come in by.

'Goddamn bastards,' screamed Snarkey, hammering at the cubicle wall. 'Shitting motherfuckers.'

The floor grew hot. She leapt and screamed, resolved to obey no order they gave her. As always, the floor grew too hot for her, and she leapt through the door just in time to avoid being seared.

'It's the mad howler,' said slobber-lipped Willit from a distant corner of the locker room. 'Snarkey-shad herself, makin' noises like a human.'

'Shut the fuck up,' growled Snark.

Willit laughed. Others also laughed. Snark panted, staring about herself, deciding who to kill.

'Slow learner,' commented Kane the Brain, shaking his head sadly.

Snarkey launched herself at Kane, screaming rage, only to find herself on the floor, whimpering, her thumb in her mouth.

'An exceptionally slow learner,' repeated the former speaker, kicking Snark not ungently in the ribs. 'Poor old Snark.'

'Good baby-girl shadow.' Willit sneered as he passed on his way to the door. 'Play nice.'

Snark sobbed as the room emptied.

'Have you quite finished?' asked the mechanical voice from a ceiling grille.

'Umph,' she moaned.

'I'll ask one more time. Have you quite finished?'

'Yessir.' The word dragged reluctantly from her throat, burning as it came.

'Then get up and get dressed. The locker room will be steam-cleaned in five minutes. Besides, you are no doubt hungry.'

She was hungry. Procurator had hosted a banquet today, and shadows had served the food, seeing it, smelling it, seeing other people eat it. Shadows didn't eat. Shadows didn't get hungry or sleepy or need the toilet. Sometimes they got in the way of things and were killed, but if so, they did it quietly. Ordinary people didn't stare at shadows, it wasn't civilized, any more than wondering about them was. Shadows were a peculiar possession of bureaucrats in office in Alliance Prime, and that's all anyone really needed to know unless one was a shadow oneself.

The metallic voice preached at her. 'If you'll make it a habit to eat just before you go on shift and immediately after, you'll feel less hunger and you'll be less uncontrolled. If you are less uncontrolled, you won't find yourself rolling around on the floor making infant noises and attracting the scorn and derision of your fellows.'

'Damn motherfuckers ain' my fellows.'

'What did you say?'

'I said I feel little collegiality for those sharing my conditions of servitude.'

In the sanctuary, when Snark was a little kid, the grown-ups had talked High Alliance. She could talk like that anytime. If she hadn't been able to remember back that far, she could mimic her fellow-shad, Kane the Brain. Kane talked like an official butthead.

The voice said, 'You aren't required to feel collegiality. You are only required to behave as though you do.'

Snark panted, letting the rage seep away. Each time she came off shift, it was the same. Everything that had happened to her, every glance that had slid across her without seeing her, every gesture she was supposed to notice, every need she was expected to anticipate, all of them boiled inside her all day, rising higher and higher, until the cubicle took the controls off and she exploded.

Which was wasting time, she told herself. Wasting her own time. She only had one third of her time to herself, as herself. One third she was a shadow, under full control. One third she was asleep, also under control. The rest of the time, here in Shadowland, she could feel however she wanted to feel, do whatever she wanted to do. She could eat, talk, have sex – if she could find somebody willing. She could read, attend classes, engage in hobbies. If she wanted to kill somebody, have sex with somebody unavailable, the simulation booth would accommodate her. The booth would help her do anything! Anything except kill people so they stayed dead.

If they didn't stay dead, what was the point! So she'd asked herself before. What was the point of living like this?

'You are at liberty to end it,' Kane had told her. 'The fourth human right is the right to die.'

'Th'fucks that mean?' she'd screamed the first time she'd heard Kane on this subject.

Kane had explained it all. Kane had even escorted Snark to a disposal booth and explained the controls. 'Simple, for the simpleminded,' Kane had said. 'Enter, close door, press button. Wait five minutes to see if you change your mind. When the bell rings, press button again. Zip. All that's left are a few ashes. No pain, no blood, no guts, no untidiness whatsoever.'

So said Kane, but the last thing Snark wanted was a neat disposal booth and a handful of ashes. Where was the joy in no pain, no blood? Who got anything out of that? That was no way to kill anybody, not even yourself! God, if you were going to kill yourself, at least make it a real mess! Make 'em clean up after you!

'Why you all the time wanting to kill folks?' Susso, one of her sometime sex partners, wanted to know.

'Get in my nose,' she'd snarled. 'Push against me!'

'Everybody gets in your nose,' Susso said. 'All the time. The only way you could be happy is if you killed everybody in the world and had it all to yourself.'

It wasn't true. There'd been some good kids at the sanctuary when they'd first brought Snark there. Snark hadn't wanted to kill them. She'd liked them. She'd been what? Nine or ten maybe? Old enough to tell them things. And to tell the supervisor as well.

'Where are you from, little girl?'

'From the frontier.'

'Don't tell lies, little girl. Children don't come from the frontier.'

'It's not a lie! I did so!'

'Don't contradict me, little girl. Don't be a nasty, contradictory little liar.'

Her name hadn't been Snark then. It had been something else. And she hadn't wanted to kill people then. That came later, after they'd named her Snark the liar, Snark the thief. Not Snark the murderer, though. She'd never actually killed anybody, though she'd wanted to. Just her luck they'd caught her before she'd done it.

The judgment machines were clear about that: 'You are sentenced to life-time shadowhood because of your emotional need to breach the first and second rights of man.'

'They got no right,' Snark had snarled to Susso. 'They got no right.'

'Why don' they?' he'd asked. 'As much as you.'

'They're machines,' she'd told him. 'On'y machines. I'm a person, a human. The universe was made for me!'

Susso had shaken his head. 'You been listenin' to some Firster godmonger on the newslink, girl. Some belly-sweller. Some prick-waver. Forget Firsters. They don't talk for this world. Not for Alliance Central, they don't. Too many Fastigats on Alliance Central. Fastigats don't listen to Firsters. This world is different. This world has shadows, and most of the time shadows aren't human. One third the time, shadows got the right to live like they want except they try an' hurt somebody. The rest o' the time, shadows got no rights. That's the way this world is!'

Snark knew that. When the invigilators had dragged her before the huge, unbearably shiny robo-judge, they'd read her the words printed across its front: EQUAL JUSTICE; THE SAME REMEDY FOR THE SAME CRIME, EVERY TIME.

'On Alliance Central, human rights are those rights our people grant one another and enforce for one another,' the machine said in its solemn, mechanical voice. 'There are four human rights universally recognized. The first of these is the right of all individuals to do what they choose with an absolute minimum of interference. Man is not required to meet any stand-ard of behavior so long as he is not adversely sensed by any other human. The second right is that of choosing one's dependants. Persons may not be taxed or otherwise forced to support dependants they have not chosen, though they are absolutely required to care for those they have signed for. The third right is to be protected from those who would infringe upon the first two rights through interference or unlawful dependency. Thievery, of which you have been convicted, is a crime of interference and dependency. You have put others to inconvenience and you have supported yourself at others' expense. You may be brought into alignment with social norms if you so choose. Do you so choose?'

Of course she hadn't so chosen. And she never would! Which she'd said, not quite that politely.

Imperturbably, the machine had gone on: 'If one chooses not to be aligned, the fourth human right is to die. Do you choose to die?'

She hadn't chosen that either.

'On Alliance Central, persons choosing neither to be aligned nor to die have only one alternative remaining – to become shadows.'

Or, as Kane the Brain said later, 'Spend two thirds of your time asleep or serving the bureaucracy so they'll let you think you're doing what you want one third of your time!'

Which is what Snark had ended up doing. No fix for her. No having her mind changed so she wouldn't want to steal anymore. No having her chemistry changed so she wouldn't want to maim or kill. No, better be herself one third of the time than never be herself at all.

'So go to the simul and kill somebody,' Susso had yelled at her when she'd tried to damage Susso and found herself curled up on the floor, thumb in mouth. 'Go to the simul and slap people around, kill people, that's what you want. Do it! But you can't do it out here!'

It sounded great, but nobody stayed dead in a simul! How could you get any satisfaction killing somebody who didn't stay dead? You wake up the next day, the same person is still walking around, looking through you. No matter you'd disposed of him in the simul, you'd still be smelling him. And even when Snark was in the simul, something inside her just knew the people in there weren't real, even though they looked just like the ones, sounded just like the ones Snark hated!

Sounded like Kane, talking like he did. Or looked just like that bastard Willit, egging her on that way, making her end up with her thumb in her mouth. Sounded like that bastard Procurator, him with his fancy tea parties. If Snark wanted, she could bring up the Procurator in the simul booth, or that black-haired woman he'd had with him the other day, Lutha Tallstaff. There she'd sat, hair perfect, face perfect, dressed in clothes you could kill for, holding out a cup to be filled, never noticing who it was that filled it! Never noticing who brought the food, who served it! Not a nod. Not a smile. Pretending Snark really was invisible!

Bitch! What she'd like to do to that bitch! She could tie her up and make her watch while Snark carved the old bastard into slices. Then, when it got to be her turn, let her feel what it was like not to exist! Let high-and-mighty Lutha Tallstaff learn what it felt like to be chopped up into bloody pieces, made into nothing!

Whimpering in eagerness, ignoring her hunger, Snark ran from the locker room in the direction of the simul booth.

The day I went to the House Without a Name, Chahdzi, my father, spent the morning cleaning the upper pool. In the afternoon it was his responsibility to carry food down into the canyon, so all day he kept an eye on the shadow at the bottom of the canyon, judging the progress of the day. If he was to return before dusk, he would need to stop work on the upper pool when the shadow touched the bottom of the eastern wall, or perhaps, for safety's sake, a little time before.

When the shadow was where he thought it should be, he went up the short ladders to the cave floor, took a sack of Kachis-kibble from the storehouse, put it over his shoulders, fastened it onto the carrier belts that crossed his chest, swung himself around the ends of the ladder, and began the descent to the canyon floor. Tonight he needed to speak to songfather about the old outlander ghost who was causing so much inconvenience. When he had done that, perhaps he could also discuss certain conflicts in his own life that needed patterning. Had these conflicts been decreed by Weaving Woman? If so, could they be sung and acknowledged? Could his annoyance be exorcised in song? Or must it remain silent, part of the corruption inevitably incurred when the terrible choice had been made?

I, Saluez, know this, because I know how he thought. My father often spoke to me of his troubles, of his confusions. He did not get on well with Zinisi, his wife (who was not my mother). Always he resolved to speak to *his* father, to songfather about it. Always he delayed. Sometimes he spoke of his ambition to become a songfather himself, a das-dzit, a patterner, a seer-of-both-sides. I asked him once why, if seeing both sides was important, only men could be songfathers? Did not women have a side? He said he would ask songfather, but he never did.

There were two ladders leading down to the first spring, two ladders more to the first pool, where he'd been scraping algae that morning. Six more ladders led to the second spring and pool, the big one that was still under construction, and then two to the bottom, where the orchards and gardens and grain fields were. From there it was an easy walk down the canyon to the feeding stones where the beautiful people would come to feed at dusk. *Lovely on wings, the Kachis*, he hummed beneath his breath. *Lovely on wings, both powerful and wise.*

'See them come on their wings of light,' he sang softly. 'See them emerge from the shadows of the trees. Beautiful on wings ...' Though sometimes he wondered if he really wanted ... No. That had been decided long ago.

He muttered these same phrases to me, sometimes. Whispering as though he didn't intend me to hear. Or, perhaps, intended that I should hear without being certain he intended it. A hint, rather than a word. Which is the same way certain other information was transmitted. No one had really said it.

When he came to the level of the spring, he slowed his climb, taking extra care. There the water falls into the first pool from such a height that it is often blown onto the ladder rungs and into the carved climbing holes, making the footing treacherous. Wetness spread beside him, dripping from the higher to the lower rocks, in some places running in tiny moss-edged diagonals across the almost vertical surfaces of the stones. This was rain that had fallen far from here, high up, soaking into the flesh of the mesa to emerge at last like blood from a wound.

Arriving at the first pool, he stopped to ease the straps over his shoulders as he listened to the spring dripping musically into the shallow puddle at the lip. From the shallow it runs back into the cavern where he'd been working. There the water glints, sending wavering glimmers of reflected light up the smooth vertical shaft that emerges before the hive. This is the household pool from which the people of Cochim-Mahn take water for cooking and hivekeeping. Several large round pots hung before him, tipped on their sides in their rope cradles, ready to be lowered into the water. As he rested, a pot dropped downward, filled, leveled, and then jerked upward, dripping and sloshing as it went. He could hear women singing, *Yeeah-mai, Eeah-mai*, as they turned the spool to wind the rope. Our water, our blood; our water, our blood.

Beneath the sound of their voices chortled the sound of the second spring, the larger one, so powerful at this time of year that it actually spurts from the side of the mountain, arching out between two chunks of green stone to fall chuckling into the big pool the people of Cochim-Mahn have been building for a long, long time. Generations of our people have carved out the mountain behind the water-lip, caulking the cracks to make a place for the water to rest away from the sucking wind and the thirsty sun. Huge stone pillars have been left to hold the mountain up, and among these monstrous trunks the water lies smooth as a mirror, stretching far back into the darkness, deep in some places as four or five tall men.

Between first pool and second, the ladders are shorter and quite dry. My father made quick work of them. The main water gate stands beside the second pool, where well-caulked wooden pipes lead downward to the tanks below. There, also, is the stone house of the seasonally elected water-master, one who will assure fair distribution of crop water. This early in the year the house was empty, no water was being used except the bucketsful that had been carried to the fruit trees. From far back in the darkness, my father could hear the tap of hammers. There, behind a cofferdam, several of our kinsmen were cutting more stone away, making the storage pond even larger.

The last ladders are the longest, down to the canyon floor where a trickle of meltwater, all that had escaped the traps of the hives upstream, ran between green banks dotted with flowers. From here it is an easy trot to the feeding stones.

The stones are huge and flat. Later in the season, when true warmth comes, the people of the nearer towns spend a day here, scrubbing away the grease and winter-filth and scenting the place with fragrant smoke and fresh herbs. My father ignored the smell as he set the open end of the sack at the lip of the dished stone, then turned to spill its contents behind him. He left without looking back. It is not polite to look at other persons' food or at persons who are eating; so it is not polite to observe the Kachis either. Looking at another person's food implies that one has not had enough.

Looking at another person's food is like begging. Only babies and dogs look at people eating.

He set out at a trot for the ladders. Behind him he heard nothing. He slowed. Stopped. Turned. Nothing. Usually there was a call from a tree-clustered canyon and an answering chirrup from somewhere nearer. Usually he had to hurry to be away from the feeding rocks before dusk.

But tonight, nothing. The Kachis were elsewhere. Unwillingly, my father turned his eyes where the rim of the canyon gleamed high and bright in the last of the light, toward the House Without a Name.

Dusk on Dinadh.

Below in the canyon was only darkness. Beneath the arch of the cave, shadows gathered. In the hive, nighttime quiet stopped the tongues of children, men and women began to whisper. The evening song was done. Chahdzi had returned from the canyon. All the door-skins were down but one. Of all the people of Cochim-Mahn, only Hallach still stood outside upon the lip of stone. Hallach and the two women of his family who had gone to take him food and drink.

'Songfather, this woman brings you evening food,' whined son's daughter, my half sister, Hazini.

'Songfather, this woman brings you water for your mouth,' hummed daughter's daughter, Shalumn. My friend Shalumn.

She remained my friend. Even afterward, she talked to me sometimes. Or, she talked to the wall, knowing I was where I could hear her. So I learned how things were, how things happened, how she read Hallach's face and his movements, seeing what he really felt written upon him.

So, she said, Hallach turned and held out his hands. Shalumn poured the water into them, murmuring rapidly as she did so. 'Blessings upon the pattern of water, water that fecundates, that cleanses, that cools, that blesses, that heals, that becometh a tool in the dedicated hands of the Dinadhi.'

He sipped from his hands, rinsing away the words of song so they would not be contaminated by mere food, then dried his hands upon the folds of his cotton inner robe. He approved of Shalumn's abbreviated litany. If Hazini had poured the water, she would have chattered out the entire water-blessing catalog rather than ending expeditiously with the all-purpose phrase *becometh a tool in the hands.* ... And while Hazini had gone on and on, Hallach songfather would have had to stand hungry, which would not have bothered Hazini, who was bony as a lightning-killed tree and ate only so much as a small picky bird. Hazini did not understand hunger.

Hallach took the bowl Hazini offered, casting his eyes upward. There was light upon the height, still time to eat outside before real darkness came. He sat down, his back politely turned so the girls would not offend custom by catching sight of his food, an important courtesy in times of famine, though one not rigorously observed during the present days. There was no current shortage of food in Cochim-Mahn.

The women had raided the last of their winter stores to provide stew for tonight, stew full of the flavors of smoked meat and dried roots. A bright stripe of flavor among all those dark stripes of fungus! He scooped a mouthful onto a round of hearth-bread and let the softened meat pleasure his tongue.

'Songfather?' Hazini said in a self-important voice. 'This woman has learned the rest of the rain names and would recite them for songfather.'

'Umph,' Hallach said around a mouthful. 'Not tonight, Hazini. It is not a proper time.'

She made a disrespectful sound behind him, almost a rudeness.

He put down his food and turned to look at her. Her lips were compressed into that pinched line Hallach found so annoying. Just like Chahdzi's second wife, Zinisi. Pinch-pinch, whine-whine, never satisfied with anything. Pretty, though. The way she turned her head and looked at men under her lashes, with that half smile, letting that whiny little voice come out like a seeking tendril to wind around their loins. Songfather remembered how Zinisi had wooed poor Chahdzi, the poor widower. 'Chaa-dzi. Can liddle Zinisi have the pretty feathers, Chaa-dzi?' Poor Chahdzi hadn't been able to resist her. Now look at him! With only Saluez to listen to him, only Saluez to . . .

Hallach felt sudden fury. He fixed Hazini with a songfather glare. 'Girl, do not make that tightness with your mouth. You cannot recite sacred names from a mouth like that.' Rage filled him. He dared not stop to question why. 'Also, your voice is too whiny. It must be full and generous if you are to pray to Daylight Woman and Weaving Woman and Great Lightning Wielder.'

Shalumn's mouth puckered as though she might laugh, but as Hallach turned toward her she bowed hastily, hiding her face. Hazini, shocked into movement, turned and ran back toward the great dark slab of the hive.

Hallach, ignoring Shalumn for the moment, turned back to his food. He did not ask himself where this rage had come from. He knew. Saluez. Feelings he was supposed to have put behind him. Affections a songfather might not indulge in. His anger was unworthy of him, but nonetheless, he felt no remorse at chiding Hazini. The Gracious One had decreed this conflict from the time they had come to Dinadh. Age must discipline youth.

Men must teach women the proper way of things. Some must lose that others may gain. Cold against heat, dry against wet, life against death, every quality must strain to contain its opposite, the whole requiring songfathers to sing the pattern into balance.

Though sometimes it was hard to accept ... what happened.

Hallach shifted uncomfortably. It wasn't wise to think about that either. Such thinking smacked of doubt, and of course he didn't doubt. She'd be fine. She was his ... his son's daughter. Of course she'd be fine.

No longer at all hungry, he set the half-emptied bowl aside.

Shalumn saw all this and drew her own conclusions. She moved slightly toward him, her hesitancy reminding him she had not been dismissed. Hallach held one finger upright, stopping her where she stood.

'Saluez,' he said, a mere whisper. It would not have been proper for a songfather to ask about a mere girl, but he had not asked. He had merely said a name.

Shalumn had seen Masanees return. Shalumn had seen her leave again, with two of the sisterhood. Then, in the dusk, they had returned again, a cluster of women who had carried someone, someone alive, perhaps, or dead, perhaps, but who had in either case gone into a side entrance to the hive and down into a shadowy place below, a place Shalumn could not go, where even songfathers could not go.

No one had mentioned this to songfather, and he could not ask. He had not asked, and Shalumn did not move or speak. She did not look up. Her eyes remained down. There were certain things a woman would never say to a man. Not any man.

After a moment Hallach waved the finger at her, letting her take the bowl and go.

It was many days later that I came upon Shalumn in a corridor. She knew me by the borders painted upon my outer robe. Had she not painted them? Had the robe not been her gift to me? Now she turned away, as she must, and began to speak to the corridor wall. She told the wall about songfather, and Hazini, and how songfather had looked and what songfather had said. She knew I was standing in an alcove just behind her. She knew I could hear.

'Songfather looked very sad,' she said. 'Songfather looked very strange. I went away then, stumbling a little. I wept. I miss my friend.' She gulped, and I saw her wipe her face with her hand. 'I miss my love. I will always miss my love.' She walked away then, not glancing at me, but her cheeks were wet.

Shalumn's were the only tears I saw shed for me. Songfather could not show grief. Chahdzi could not show grief. Hazini would not grieve, nor Zinisi, nor any of the people of the hive. Weaving Woman sends the shuttles to and fro, light and dark, youth and age, good and ill, wisdom and stupidity. Belief and doubt, also. Belief and doubt.

Often the pattern is not as we ourselves would weave it.

2

Masanees brought Saluez back to the hive and her story stopped. Time went by, yes, but Saluez did not care much about that. She did not hunger or thirst. The women around her forced her to eat and drink. Her prayers to Weaving Woman had not been answered. Her shuttle had not carried light. Her pattern was dark, only dark, and no one could see its end. There was no story of Saluez.

What was true of me was true also of Snark. During that time, she had no story. She was as she was, and little changed from day to day. We were stopped, our shuttles still, our colors waiting. During this time, the story was Lutha's story, the pattern was Lutha's pattern.

'My name is Trompe Paggas,' the Fastigat said into Lutha's annunciator. 'I've been assigned as your assistant.'

She opened her door to the surging traffic. A hurrying passerby bumped her visitor hard enough to carom him into her, and clutching one another, they almost fell into her rooms. She stumbled to the door and shut it against the noise of the crowded concourse while her disheveled guest brushed himself off. He seemed more annoyed than the minor trampling warranted.

'How do you stand it?' he growled.

'Stand what?' She was puzzled.

'Living in all this mob!'

Her face cleared. It wasn't a mob. It was just the ordinary workaday crowd, but this man was used to Fastiga, where things were managed differently, or to Prime, which was, if anything, too sparsely populated. Trompe Paggas had even put on a coverall so he wouldn't be contaminated by rubbing up against people. Now, before he had even divested himself of this garment, he said, 'You're ambivalent about me.'

She laughed, the sounds fluttering up her throat like startled birds. This was so familiar, so like Leelson, this Fastigat habit of holding her feelings up before her, as though she didn't know how she felt unless he told her! Even his gently concerned tone of voice was the same, even his expression, kindly and questioning.

'Trompe, don't tell me. Please. Let that be a rule between us. Of course I'm ambivalent about you. I'm ambivalent about everything! About the trip.

About taking Leely. About finding out something, or not finding out anything. About the Ularians wiping out humanity!'

'Ambivalent, even about the prospect of destruction?' he asked, shocked.

'Sometimes. Sure. Some days, doesn't it seem like a good idea we should all be wiped out? Some days, don't we make a royal mess of things?' As an official translator, she was aware of that mess, if he wasn't. Words of impassioned rage and raw desperation flowed through her workstation every day. Broken treaties. Misinterpreted promises. Endless renegotiation. Forged certifications. Lies and evasions. She laughed again, seeing his expression.

'No,' he said soberly. 'It does not seem like a good idea. All problems can be solved. It merely takes the will and attention to do so.'

She shrugged, smiling: he was so very Fastigat!

'All right, I won't make problems. I realize you'll know how I feel. I'll tell you right now, you probably won't ever know how Leely feels about anything. Let's accept that. Your job will be to use your abilities to help me cope while we search for anything Bernesohn Famber might have left on Dinadh. You're not here to *tell me* how I feel or help me deal with my emotions or any of that Fastigat stuff. I've had that. I don't need it.'

He shrugged, making a face like a Leelson face. Physically, he was as unlike Leelson as possible, being short and chunky and dark instead of tall, slender, and bright-haired. A man of gold, Leelson. A man of iron, this. In his favor, he had astonishingly alert blue eyes and was also quite young. Younger than Lutha, at any rate.

'Can I see the boy?' he asked.

She pointed. The door between the office room and the sleeping room was open. He went through it with her behind him.

Leely was standing naked before the window scene, which was dialed to *forest*. His clothes lay as he'd dropped them in the corner. He had decorated the wall near the window with a feces finger painting, an extraordinary impression of the blown trees in the forest scene. He turned toward them with a lovely smile and a lilting laugh.

'Dananana,' he purred. 'Dananana.'

'Excuse me,' she murmured to Trompe. 'If you'll give me a moment.'

Trompe nodded expressionlessly.

She was aware of him watching her as she keyed the room-bot, cleaned Leely, and got the clothes back on him. No matter where she put the fasteners, he managed to get his clothes off, little contortionist! And look at the skin of his chest and shoulders, all blotchy from chill. Well, no harm done. The room-bot had the floor and walls cleaned by the time Leely was dressed again.

'That's my sweet boy,' she murmured, hugging him and putting him down once more, handing him the child-sized paint sticks she'd gone to such trouble to find.

'Dananana,' he said, patting her face with one hand as he threw the sticks across the room with the other. 'Dananana.'

'How old is he?' Trompe asked from the doorway. His face showed nothing, but he knew the answer. He was only checking.

She stiffened. 'Almost six.' Leely was just past his fifth birthday.

'Big for his age.' Trompe's voice held no emotion, but she could feel something. Disapproval? Or what? 'He must weigh what?'

'He's heavy for his age. But, as you know, Leelson is tall and muscular, and my family also runs to size, so Leely will probably be a big man.'

Now she knew what he was thinking. *How will she cope then? When he's a big man, what will she do*? His mouth opened, then closed again, the words unspoken. Well, at least he learned fast. And what right did he have to disapprove?

'What kind of treatments have you tried?' he asked.

She fought down her annoyance. Even though he'd been briefed, he wanted her to talk about it so he could feel what she felt, find his way into her psyche. Damn all Fastigats! Would he be more help if he understood?

She gritted her teeth and said in a patient voice, 'I'm sure you were told, but both Leelson and I had a genome check early in my pregnancy. Both of us are within normal limits. Leely's pattern differs from ours only within normal limits. Physically, he's fine.'

'And mentally?'

Had the man no eyes? She kept her voice calm as she answered.

'Well, sometimes he won't leave his clothes on. He won't learn to use the potty, though he does like to eliminate outdoors. He has no speech, obviously. And he doesn't seem to classify. He reacts to each new animal, person, or thing in pretty much the same manner, with curiosity. If one food chip is tasty, he doesn't assume similar-looking ones are. He regards each thing as unique.'

'Really?'

'Give him a red ball, he'll learn that it bounces and squeezes. He may treasure it. If he loses it and I give him another red ball, he has to start from scratch. Though it looks identical to me, somehow he knows it isn't the same thing he had before.'

'Strange.'

She nodded. It was. Strange.

'I understand they've tried splicing him.'

It wasn't a question, but she answered it anyhow. 'The geneticists spotted a few rare variations that they thought might be connected to behavior, and they tried substituting some more common alleles. Among Leely's unique attributes, however, is a super-efficient immune system. Each time extraneous genetic material is introduced, his body kills it. It may take him a day, or a week, but he manages it every time. That means that even if we hit upon whatever variant might help, it would take him a very short time to get rid of it. And, of course, it may not be in the chromosomes. It may be elsewhere in the cells.'

The geneticists had suggested a complete cellular inventory, but she had resisted that. Perhaps she didn't really want to know. If they found something ... Well, how very final that would be!

Trompe said, 'I imagine the doctors are very interested in him! The immune system, I mean.'

'Extremely interested. Particularly inasmuch as he also heals very quickly. At first thought, these traits would seem to be extremely valuable—'

'But only the healing, the immunity.'

'Right. If they could be separated from the rest of his pattern, but no one knows what particular combination of combinations has resulted in that trait.'

'So, whatever's wrong, it can't be fixed.'

She stiffened. 'I object to the word. Leely is all right the way he is! You may as well know that Leelson Famber and I disagreed on that point.'

He narrowed his eyes at her. 'But ... how intelligent is he?'

'I believe he has a different level of intelligence,' she said belligerently. One of her most vehement arguments with Leelson had been on that subject. She tried to be fair. 'Though it's hard to be sure because our idea of intelligence is so dependent upon the use of language. He scores quite high on some nonverbal tests, those that don't depend solely on classification.'

'I don't understand.'

'What I said earlier! He doesn't classify things. He can't look at a pile of blocks and pick out all the blue ones. Mere blueness isn't a category for Leely. Nor mere roundness, mere squareness, mere ... whatever. Each thing is its own thing.'

'With its own name?'

'Who knows? If he could talk, perhaps that would be true. He's past the age when most children either learn a language or create one.' She heard the pain in her voice, knew Trompe heard it too.

'So?' He was looking at her curiously, figuring her out.

Lutha took firm control of her voice. She had to sound objective and calm. She would not start out on this arduous project with a companion who felt she was irrational.

'Since he's so very healthy, I've considered he might be a new and fortunate mutation. Perhaps he will learn language later than most children.'

There was no legitimate reason for her to believe that, but she believed it anyhow, passionately, with her whole heart. Leelson had said that for every positive mutation, there were undoubtedly thousands of useless or lethal ones. Intellectually, she accepted that. So far as Leely was concerned, she could not. He couldn't be … useless.

She pulled her mind away from that thought. She didn't want Trompe Paggas to think she was – what? Deluded. A mother who was blind and fond to the point of stupidity? Speak of something else!

Trompe gave her the opening. 'He didn't like those colors you gave him. Why was that, do you suppose?'

'A mistake on my part,' she admitted ruefully. 'He loves to paint, as you saw, and I thought the colors would be tempting. I was wrong. They don't please him for some reason. They have the wrong texture or smell. He does quite nice renderings in feces, as you've seen. Or in gravy, or mud.'

'Organic media,' mused Trompe. 'Probably with organic smells.'

'Perhaps he identifies by smell, categorizes by smell. I don't know. Maybe he has another sense entirely.'

A superhuman sense, she didn't say, though she thought it. A more-than-human sense. She caught herself and flushed. She'd mentioned these thoughts to a few family members, a few friends, all of whom thought she was pushing the limits of reality. And sometimes – yes, sometimes she knew she would trade eventual superhumanity for a Leely who would learn to use the potty and keep his clothes on!

'No need to get upset, Lutha. I understand.' Trompe was smiling at her, squeezing her shoulder. 'Fine. I was briefed. I was just digging for some kind of overall understanding, but we've obviously said enough.' He seated himself and adopted an expression that said he was getting down to business.

'It's going to be hard for you,' he said.

She nodded, admitting as much.

Trompe tapped his front teeth with a thumbnail. 'The Procurator wishes you to know you may have all the help you need, both in preparing to go and to keep your business alive while you're gone. Meantime, I made some inquiries of my own. I thought Leelson might be, you know, simply avoiding the issue, but he's truly gone. No one I spoke to had any idea where he was.'

'Limia could go,' said Lutha, referring to Leelson's mother.

'Easier than you,' he agreed. 'I wonder why she won't?'

Both sat silently for a time.

'Let's ask her,' he said. 'Let's go ask her!'

'Now?' she cried. 'I can't leave—'

He interrupted her with a finger to her lips. 'I'll call a creche team to take care of Leely, and why not now? If Limia won't go, I think we both should know why. We'll run on over to Fastiga and find out.'

South of Alliance Prime the enclave of Fastiga lay beneath its own separate dome, the towers of the men jutting aggressively above the sprawling domiciles of the women. Nothing separated them but multilevel sculpture gardens and fantastically ritualized behaviors, both well observed.

In the domiciles the languorous hours between the evening meal and the erotic observances of deep night were set aside for the reception of visitors. Fires were lit in the halls of lineage, dusty bottles were opened and decanted into elegant crystal, children were sent to their own quarters to bedevil their adolescent minders, womenfolk put on their most seductive draperies, and everyone gossiped about everyone else. Fastiga women were much interested – some said obsessed – by lineage. All Fastigats claimed common ancestors; they were all one clan; only the precise degree of kinship was subject to analysis, but of such minor quibbles nightlong conversations could be built.

Trompe brought Lutha up from clangorous, crowded traffic levels below ground to the murmuring quiet of a house she had visited once before. And had not intended to visit again, she acknowledged to herself as he fetched her a glass of wine and ushered her to a sheltered corner of the hall of lineage. It was a secluded niche mostly hidden from the other visitors.

'Leelson brought me here once,' she said, aware of a sudden bellicosity, the flaring embers of old anger.

He nodded, as though he already knew. Well, Fastigats did know. They knew entirely too much.

'It may take me a while to get to Limia,' he murmured. 'Custom demands I work my way around the room. Don't move. I'll be back.'

He left her. She settled into the chair, which was both comfortable and private. The wings on either side hid her from anyone who was not directly opposite, and there was more uninhabited room around her than in her whole apartment and three or four others like it. Behind her, she could hear two Fastiga women making conversation, unaware they were overheard.

'There's Olloby Pime, with her Old-earth friend,' said one voice. 'So hairy, Old-earthers. I had an earther lover once. Did I ever tell you, Britta? So relaxing. Such a treasure. Poor thing had no idea what I was feeling, and I can't tell you how refreshing that was.'

Britta paused before responding. 'I perceive your satisfaction, Ostil-ohn, but my own experience would lead me to believe such a liaison would be rather frustrating.'

Britta and Ostil-ohn, said Lutha to herself. Ostil-ohn, who had had a terrestrial but non-Fastigat lover.

Ostil-ohn, who was saying:

'Oh, my dear, no. For example, if I wasn't in the mood for sex, instead of being coaxed and wooed and pestered for simply hours and having to heat up out of sheer inevitability, I could just pretend I was wild with desire to begin with.'

'He didn't know the difference?'

'Not at all! He hadn't the tiniest flicker of perception, so he got on with it, and I sighed and yelped a bit, and shortly it was over, while meantime I'd gone on thinking what I was thinking about before he started!'

'But, Ostil-ohn, this implies ... what if you were in the mood and he wasn't?'

'Ah, well, there are drawbacks to every relationship. It's true one gets in the mood much less often than with Fastigats.'

Britta snorted.

'I wonder where Limia Famber is,' Ostil-ohn murmured next. 'I haven't seen her lately.'

Lutha leaned back, listening intently.

'One assumes she has not been taking part in public life since her son disappeared.'

'I shouldn't think she was surprised! What did she expect? Leelson was destined to disappear. Takes after his father in that regard.'

'Ostil-ohn! You're being cruel. Grebor Two didn't disappear purposely. Any more than *his* father did!'

'Listen, when three generations of Fambers stick around only long enough to father one child, then take off and are never seen again, one may be forgiven for assuming a genetic tendency toward vanishment!'

A pause indicating that Britta was considering this. 'Three generations?'

'Actually four, if you count uncles. Leelson; his father, Grebor Two; his grandfather, Grebor One; and his great-granduncle.'

'Who was his great-granduncle?'

'Paniwar Famber, son of Bernesohn and Tospia. That's five generations, because Paniwar was an only too.'

'Paniwar was *not* an only. Paniwar had a twin sister, Tospiann. Boy and girl—'

'I meant only *son,*' interrupted Ostil-ohn.

'—and Bernesohn had flocks of children with other women!'

A moment's silence. 'That's right. I'd forgotten.'

'Paniwar had more than one child, too, though it was a scandal! He got some little tourister girl pregnant when he was just a boy. She wanted him to marry her, can you imagine! When he told her Fastigats *don't,* she went to some remote place and had the child secretly, making Paniwar guilty of improper fathering! The talk went on for years!'

'My dear, it wasn't a little tourister girl. I remember now. It was someone famous on the frontier! He was only a boy, she was twice his age, and that's what the talk was about!'

Ostil-ohn murmured, 'Whoever. I'll modify my statement. When four generations of Fambers stick around only long enough to father one *acknowledged son* and then take off never to be seen again, one may be forgiven for assuming it's genetic.'

Britta said, 'Limia would argue with you. She doesn't acknowledge the boy Leelson fathered. He had it out of that translator woman he took up with. You know. We met her once. Lutha something. Tall-staff. Basically earthian stock.'

'Did I meet her?'

'But of course you did,' Britta insisted. 'Leelson brought her here. Then Limia went to see her!'

'Oh, yes. To warn her off, don't you suppose? Limia was furious! And what is it about the child? Something not right?'

Lutha's face flushed. Damn them. What right had they to discuss Leely!

Britta went on. 'It isn't Fastigat. It's not even normal earthian. I haven't seen it, though some of the men have. Oh, look, there's someone who'd know. Trompe Paggas. Trompe knows everything!'

Lutha looked up, saw Trompe moving toward her, gave up any attempt at concealment, and rose to her full height. She turned to the matrons she'd been eavesdropping upon with a pleasant smile and a nod.

Both had the grace to flush, though only Ostil-ohn was capable of speech. She murmured politely as Lutha moved to join Trompe, and then the two woman put their heads together once more, to share the full delicious horror of what they'd just done.

Leelson Famber's mother was in no mood to talk with Lutha Tall-staff. When Trompe insisted, she made them wait a discourteous amount of time before inviting them to her private quarters. During that time she dressed herself with some care and prepared herself mentally for what she supposed would be a request on the Tallstaff woman's part for additional help with her idiot child.

It turned out, however, that Lutha Tallstaff had something else in mind.

'I've been asked by the Alliance to go to Dinadh,' Lutha announced. 'With my son.'

Limia sat back, surprised both at the announcement and at the propriety of Lutha's language. 'My son,' she'd said. Many women might have said 'Leelson's son.' Or 'our son.' 'Leelson's and my son.' Or even, courtesy forbid, 'your grandson.'

Limia sat back in her chair, feeling an unintended frown creeping onto her forehead. 'Yes,' she said, smoothing both her face and her voice. 'What has that to do with me?'

'I don't want to go,' said Lutha. 'I've agreed to do so only if no other way can be found.'

'Other way?'

'The Dinadhi will allow entry to you. The Procurator says you've refused to go.'

'Yes.'

'I thought perhaps you didn't understand how important the matter is and how very difficult the trip will be for me.'

'I am an old woman. You are a young one.' Among Fastigats, with their reverence for age, this was all that needed saying. Seemingly, it was not enough for the Tallstaff woman.

Lutha explained, 'In order to be allowed to investigate Bernesohn Famber's life there, I have to be connected with his lineage. This means I have to take my son with me.'

Limia's gorge rose at the word *lineage*, but she kept her voice calm. 'Surely that is not onerous.'

Lutha threw a glance in Trompe's direction.

Smoothly he said, 'Lutha Tallstaff correctly assesses that the visit to Dinadh will be more than merely onerous, mistress. It will be extremely difficult.'

Limia rose and stalked across the floor, her long skirts foaming around her ankles. With her back to the younger woman, she allowed herself a bitter smile. 'Leave us, Trompe.'

'Mistress...'

'Leave us!'

She waited until she heard the sound of the door sliding shut behind him. 'I came to call upon you,' she said, turning to Lutha. 'At your office. Remember?'

'Of course.'

'When I first heard you were pregnant. I believe I told you then something of the family history.'

'I respect the meaning lineage has for you, madam, but as I said at the time, family histories are most interesting to members of the family in question. You'd made it clear you would never consider me as any part of your family.'

'I told you of the saying among Fastigats? Do you remember?'

'I remember it, madam. "Mankind, first among creatures. Fastigats, first among mankind. Fambers, first among Fastigats."'

Lutha thought it unbearably arrogant, then and now. 'I thought it hyperbole, madam. Fastigats are not known as Firsters.'

'Ninety-nine percent of all Firsters are vulgar, but even they may occasionally assert a truth. It is a truth that the universe was made for man, not as Firsters exemplify man but as Fastigats exemplify man. Evolution moves in our direction. It is our pride and our duty. You would have been wise to respect our history and traditions, though you were outside them. I mentioned to you that Leelson's line is composed of only sons.'

A fact that seemed to be generally known, considering what Lutha had overheard downstairs.

'I thought that interesting, but not compelling, madam. At best it is a statistical anomaly.'

'I asked you – no, I begged you not to go on with your pregnancy.'

'As I told you at the time, it was not something I had planned.' She hadn't, and she had no explanation for not having done so. None at all. Against every tenet of her rearing, against every shred of her own resolution, it had simply happened.

Limia went on implacably: 'You chose to ignore what I had to say. I explained that Leelson's child would have a better chance of being valued by his father and by me if born to a Fastiga woman and, if a son, with the Fastigat skills. I spoke from conviction, from concern. As you now admit, you felt my reasoning was not meaningful, not compelling. Why, now, should your conviction be compelling to me? Why, now, should your difficulties or problems be my concern?'

Lutha stared out the window behind the woman, not wanting to look her in the face. Everything she said was true. The only omission from Limia's account was Leelson's reaction when Lutha had told him of his mother's visit. He had been angered, infuriated. Let Limia keep her opinions to herself. If he wanted to father a child on Lutha, that was his business! At that moment Lutha had loved him most, for he had not spoken like a Fastigat but like a lover.

One could not say to Limia Famber, however, that the child had been Leelson's choice. Limia Famber wasn't interested in what her son had wanted. *Had* wanted. Then.

Very well. There was still one final question she needed to ask. Lutha breathed deeply, counting the breaths, holding her voice quiet as she said, 'There is an additional possibility. Leelson himself could make this trip far easier than I, and he would have no reason to refuse. Do you have any idea where he might be?'

Limia laughed harshly. 'Don't be a fool, woman! Do you think I would be so grievously upset if I knew where Leelson was? If I knew he was anywhere, alive? If I knew that, I could assume he has time yet to beget another child. If I knew he was still among the living, I would not despair of his posterity.'

The sneering tone made Lutha tremble, only partly with anger. She could actually fear this woman!

'It is early to despair of his posterity,' she said at last. 'Leely is only five.'

The older woman regarded her almost with pity. 'Leely! Your misbegot provides no posterity, not for our line, not even for yours, if you cared about such things. My kinsmen have seen your *Leely*, at my request. Believe me, it is because of your Leely that I despair!'

Some weeks after I returned from the House Without a Name, a veiled woman stopped me in the corridor, asking that I meet her behind the hive that evening. I knew her voice. From her veil, I knew she was one like me.

I did as she asked, leaving the hidden quarters in the bowels of the hive and encountering her near the back wall of the cave, whence she guided me through a hidden cleft and along a narrow trail that led downward to a turning behind a rock where there was a dark crevice.

'Puo-toh,' came the whisper from the crevice. *Who goes?*

'Pua-a-mai etah,' my guide replied. *Goes a newly wounded one.*

'Enter,' said the whisperer, lifting a foliage curtain from within the crevice. 'Follow.'

My guide held the foliage while I went beneath. It fell into place behind me as I went down a path that twisted among great stones. This was a water path, smoothed by the rains of a thousand years, dimly lit by occasional candles on metal spikes driven into the stone. I wondered if the lights were there for my benefit, for my guide did not seem to need them. She moved as easily in darkness as she did in the infrequent puddles of light.

We came to a blanket door, the two blankets slightly overlapping.

'Remove your veil and come in,' she said.

She raised both hands to the flap of her veil, loosing it and thrusting it aside as she went through the blanket and around the draft wall that stops the outside air from blowing in. Behind it was the cave itself. It was dim inside, lit only by the small fire burning upon the central hearth under a metal hood. It was also warm, which meant it was well plastered, with all its holes and crevices stuffed with stone and covered with a layer of mud. As I looked around I realized the walls had been not only sealed, but smoothed. Walls and benches had been painted with white clay to reflect the light, and there were designs drawn there, ones I had never seen before. The mortar chimney that led the smoke away went beneath the lie-down bench, curved with it, and came up against the far wall, where a little door gave access to the shelf where the start-fire is built, to get the warm air rising. Once air is going up the straight chimney, one shuts the start-fire door, and the heated hearth air is pulled under the bench, warming the place we sit or sleep.

It was a warm cave, carefully planned, carefully built, as carefully as any hive cell I had ever seen. The air was fragrant, scented by spices stewing over the fire. I knew there would be breathing holes somewhere, a few at the bottom of the cave, beside the fire, to suck new air in as the warm air rose. We do the same in the hive.

On the curving bench sat a score of women, all with their hoods pushed back, their veils down. Only once had I seen my face in a mirror since my day at the House Without a Name. Once had been enough. Now I stared as though into fifty mirrors, seeing my face again and again, with variations. Here was a missing eyelid, there a ragged lip, there nostrils chewed at the edges. There were ears missing, cheeks pocked and scarred and riven. Foreheads and scalps and jaws with only skin across the bone.

When I had wakened in the hive, the bandages had already been in place. Veiled women had told me what had happened. No one knew why. It happened sometimes. It was no fault of Masanees or any of the other attendant women. Every detail of the ritual had been reviewed, again and again. Did you do this? Did you do that? Did you lie with your face firmly in the basket ring? Was there plenty of food and drink? Yes and yes, everything had been done as it was supposed to be done, as it had been done over and over for generations of years.

'Welcome,' said an old woman. 'To our sisterhood.'

The others bowed and murmured. Welcome. Welcome.

'Are you still with child?' asked the eldest.

I nodded. So far as I knew, I was. I was no longer about to be married; I was no longer considered marriageable; but I was still with child.

'When your birthing time comes, you will come here,' said the woman.

This was a surprise! I looked around the circle, seeking some reason. Those who could, smiled comfortingly at me.

'We have all had the experience,' one of the women said. 'Most of us are from Cochim-Mahn, but some are from Dzibano'as and Hamam'n and Damanbi. When the moons are full, we delegates come to offer comfort to our new sister, walking in the day from hive to hive, staying overnight with our sisters who then join our travels the following day. Tonight we have with us women even from Chacosri, around the canyon corner. We all know what you are suffering. Many of us have had children. When your time comes, come here.'

'We are a sisterhood,' said another to me, kindly. 'We are a sisterhood of wounds. We must care for ourselves, for the others are afraid of us.'

'Afraid!' I cried. I knew it was so. Walking veiled in the corridors of the hive, I had seen it on their faces, even on Father's face, Grandfather's face. I had seen it on Shalumn's face, though her fear was outweighed by pity. I did not want to believe it. 'Why afraid?'

'Because we do not fit the promise made by the Gracious One,' whispered another. 'Because we seem to cast doubt upon the choice. Because they are afraid we will bring the abandoned gods among them again.'

And then they put their arms around me, and I wept, and they said soft words and let me weep, and the singing began and went around and around the fire, old songs to fit the designs upon the walls, songs so old the ordinary people of the hives had forgotten them, songs of our former father, our former mother, songs of the time when the shadows had welcomed us and we did not go in fear or hope of the Kachis or the ghosts.

It is time to introduce new color into the robe we are weaving. I have woven Lutha and Leelson and Leely, Saluez and Snark. Now I will fill a new shuttle with heavier threads than ours. I will weave the King of Kamir.

I had never met a king before, and when eventually I did, at first I thought he did not look like much. Still, his pattern would be rich and vivid, a storm design set against our simple stripes of joy and pain. While Lutha Tallstaff was traveling toward our meeting, while I sang in the cave of the sister-hood, he, the King of Kamir, thought mighty thoughts and made the fabric tremble!

Jiacare Lostre, the King of Kamir who had been lost (who had tried desperately and unsuccessfully to stay lost), sat cross-legged on the chalcedony throne of Kamir-Shom-Lak considering with measurable satisfaction the demise of Leelson Famber and all his lineage. Famber's siblings and their children and all their children. Famber's parents and their siblings and all their children. Beginning, however, with Leelson himself, with Leelson's wife or mate, if any, and his offspring.

Despite the burdens of kingship, which had piled up during his absence, Jiacare had found time to recruit and dispatch an appropriate assassination team: Mitigan, a professional killer from Asenagi, a Firster who saw no dichotomy between profession and religion; Chur Durwen, another Firster, a talented youngster from Collis who was well on his way to high professional status; plus the brothers Silby and Siram Haughneep, the king's own bodymen, sworn servitors to the royal family. Oh, definitely a four-assassin target, the family Famber, all of whom would learn painfully and lengthily that 'finding' lost kings who did not wish to be found was not the wisest of occupations.

Words penetrated his preoccupation.

'... and so, Your Most Puissant and Glorious Effulgence, it is no longer possible to reserve the forests of Tarnen, though they are Lostre-family possessions, since they are needed by Your Majesty's peasantry in Chalc as pastures for their cattle.'

The Minister of Agriculture lowered his databoard and peered over the top of it at His Royal Highness, who stared rigidly past the minister at the tapestries behind him.

'This is a serious question,' murmured the Minister of Agriculture, as though to himself.

'I'm sure,' said His Effulgence from a tight throat. 'Too serious to be delayed for my benefit. Why didn't you just get on with it?'

'The Scroll of Establishment of Kamir-Shom-Lak requires that all matters concerning the general welfare be presented to the king for his approval or advice.'

'Since my advice is invariably ignored, I don't advise,' said the king.

'The Great Document does not require that Your Effulgence advise. It merely requires that matters be presented in case Your Majesty might choose to do so,' said the minister, with an unsympathetic yawn.

'Take it as written that I do not choose. I neither advise nor approve. Nor will I ever approve of any matter brought before me. Certainly I do not approve of cutting the forests of Tarnen. They are the last forests remaining upon Kamir.'

'As Your Majesty knows, the removal of forests is one of the necessary steps in homo-norming a planet. Kamir has delayed far longer than most planets. Why, on Kamir, we still have animals!'

The king became very pale. 'We have a few, yes. There are fifty species of birds in the forests of Tarnen, including the royal ouzel, whose feathers grace our crown, whose image is graven upon our planetary seal. There are numerous species of insects and animals. There are ferns, orchids—'

'None of which is required by man,' the Minister of Agriculture interrupted. 'We have been over this, Your Majesty. In accordance with Alliance regulations, before we may establish outgrowth colonies, our home planet must be homo-normed at least to Type G. That means—'

'I know what it means! It means no trees, no birds, no animals. Why don't we skip over a step? Why don't we save the forests by eliminating the cattle, which we will do sooner or later when we set up the algae farms required by Class G.'

'We have preserved the patterns of the forest species, Your Effulgence. They are in our files as required by the homo-norming laws.'

'They won't be alive! No flutter of wings, no plop of little green bodies into water, no silver glitter beneath the ripples. There will be only men and the crops to feed men!'

'The stored species can be enlivened whenever there is sufficient space and food for them. Just now, however, there is widespread hunger in the area of Chalc. As Your Majesty is aware, food and medicines are already stringently rationed everywhere on Kamir.'

'Except among the aristocracy.'

'Your ministers cannot be expected to govern if they are hungry or worried over the welfare of their families.'

'Suggest that the peasants of Chalc restrict their fecundity.'

'Humanity comes first. Fecundity is the blessing of the universe, which was made for man.'

'What universe is that?'

The Minister of Agriculture flushed, slightly embarrassed. 'One gets into the habit—'

'I am not one of your Firster constituents, Minister. I am a faithful son of Lord Fathom, ancient and enigmatic, god of the Lostres.' He took his eyes from the tapestries and looked directly into the minister's eyes. 'Listen to me for a moment. You have traveled. You are a sophisticated man. You have been to Central, as I have. What do you think of it?'

'Your Effulgence ...'

'Be honest! What do you think of it?'

'It seems a very efficient place.'

'Did you feel at all crowded?'

'Well, one does feel a bit—'

'Did you go to the Grand Canyon of Old-earth?'

'Yes. I confess, I didn't see what the fuss was about.'

'You rode down in a transparent elevator. Through the glass you saw the strata, each one labeled as to age. At the bottom you experienced a sensur-round of the way it used to be, a few centuries ago. You were told that the canyon now houses over a billion people. Do you want that for the forests of Tarnen?'

'But it's inevitable, Your Effulgence! There will be frontiers for our great-grandchildren, perhaps, but for us, now, there is still space to fill! So long as there is space to fill, we must go on having babies. So Firstism teaches us.'

The king sighed deeply. 'Save the teachings for the fecund masses, Minister. Why don't you give the peasants some land in the Orbive Hills.'

'There is no arable land left in the Orbive. There has been widespread erosion. ...'

The king nodded slowly. 'Oh, yes. Because your father chose to allow fire-wood cutting in the Orbive instead of providing solar stoves. Because his father permitted unlimited herd growth among the Chalcites to woo their votes. Just as his father, your great-grandfather, first Kamirian convert to the Firster cause, defeated the attempt by the Green Party to limit human population upon Kamir. And so sealed our fate forever.'

The minister flushed angrily. 'As Your Majesty says.'

'*My* grandfather told *your* grandfather that the herds would die and the people would die.'

The minister's mouth twisted into a half smile. 'Your Majesty's grand-father is remembered for his sagacity. Now that the herds are dying and the people are dying, however, there is a public outcry which will not be stanched by mere laying of blame on persons long dead. Hungry people do not care what our grandfathers did. So long as one inch of Kamirian soil remains, the people will believe that using it will solve their problems. Only when all the land is gone and destroyed will they permit the next step in homo-norming, and Your Majesty knows it as well as I.'

The king uncrossed his legs and put them flat upon the throne, his hands flat beside them, wondering if by will alone he could sink into that stone, obliterate himself, become nothing. He said, sighing deeply, 'Do as you will. I do not approve. Take that as written, and let me abdicate.'

'The Scroll of Establishment of Kamir-Shom-Lak specifies a hereditary king, Your Majesty, and it has no provision for abdication.'

'I have a younger brother. Several, in fact.'

'So long as Your Effulgence is alive ...' The threat in this was implicit. Kings might die, but they could not run away. Kings had died, as a matter of fact, under more or less mysterious circumstances. He did not mind dying. He did mind what they would no doubt do to him first, to make him say something they could use for a reason. Conspiracy against the welfare of Kamir. Kamir, that he loved as some men love women!

'How many more of you are there today?' asked the king. 'How many more ministers out there in the anteroom, crouched slavering over the few remaining fragments of our planet?'

The minister stiffened. 'Seven, Your Highness.'

'Tell them they may go. I don't approve of anything they're doing.'

Angered, the minister growled: 'The Firster godmongers pray for you daily in your blindness, Majesty. Man is meant to procreate! We were given the universe to fill. What are a few animals, a few trees in the face of our destiny?'

'Tell the rest of them to go home,' the king said desperately. 'Tell them in future they must condense their reports to something less than five minutes. In future, I will listen to nothing longer. I will set a timer.'

'But Your Highness can not possibly comprehend the ramifications of the problems from a condensed—'

'Why should I comprehend?' he cried, pressed past endurance. 'I don't comprehend. I will never comprehend. I see a different world than you ministers see. On ascending to this throne, I took an oath to rule the world of Kamir. That world, though much diminished, still had seas and forests and animals. You are destroying that world. Greater comprehension would only increase my sense of futility.' The Lost King rose from his throne, turned his back upon his minister, and stalked to a nearby window that stood open to let in the fresh breezes of early spring.

He had escaped on a day much like this – it had been late fall, not spring, but on a similar day – slipping out this very window in the darkness before dawn, across the velvet lawns, into the trees. Once Tarnen was gone, this royal park would contain all the trees left on Kamir. He had thought of that as he had walked through them that day toward his cache of clothing and

338

money and documents, hidden away bit by inconspicuous bit over a long, long time of preparation. He had emerged on the far side of the trees dressed as an Elithan, and he had slipped into the crowd that always stood there, staring at the palace, to stand for a time himself, staring at the palace, before he went away.

He had taken ship for Elitha, unremarked, unnoticed, calling himself Osterbog Smyne, a common Elithan name. He had reached Elitha. Oh, with what eagerness had he taken up a new life as a nobody on Elitha. If not for that damnable Leelson Famber, Osterbog Smyne would be on Elitha still, keeping a fruit stall, taking his holidays in the forests, watching birds, maybe even going fishing, far from ministers and reports and briefings and the whole irrelevant, endless fal-de-rol of kingship.

'Your Majesty is so deep in thought, one assumes he is considering marriage and the production of an heir,' said a pontifical voice from behind him. So. The Minister of Agriculture had called for assistance, and here was Lord Zhoun, the Prime Minister, the quintessence of boredom, the paradigm of duty undesired.

Jiacare Lostre murmured, 'I've told you, I've no intention of begetting a child to carry on this charade. The planet is within a year or so of being Class G. Soon you'll be directing the aristocracy to turn in their pets for euthanizing. Soon will come Class-J domed cities, which will grow, and grow, until they make a glittering ceiling over the final convulsions! You know how it will end, how it always ends. The Scroll of Establishment contains no requirement that I be part of the process.'

'Common sense would indicate—'

'Common sense, hah! Focus on one of my no-doubt-eager brothers or nephews. Groom half a dozen of them for this thankless ascendancy.'

'Your Majesty, please ...'

'Prime Minister, please!'

'You used to call me Uncle.'

'You used to call me Jickie, Lord Zhoun, and you used to tell stories of adventure and mystery. You used to like to go riding. Remember horses? You even took me fishing once. When father was alive, you were quite a nice fellow.'

'When your father was alive, he attended to his duty.'

'In a manner of speaking, Uncle. My father, though beset by uncontrollable and inappropriate affection for small girls, was in most respects a very good king. He had no convictions to confuse him. He was impressed by ritual and dedicated to traditions. He complied with them well, but then he had certain talents I do not.'

'Jickie!'

'It's true, Uncle. Father was quite open with me. As I had four older brothers, he felt free to tell me things he would never have told the heirs. First, he had taught himself not to care about anything but sensation. Then he taught himself to sleep while sitting bolt upright, eyes wide open. He could do this either while upon the throne or upon horseback, and he was invariably asleep while you and the others read your interminable accounts of continuing destruction. He told me this, enjoying his cleverness, without realizing the effect it had on me. Of course, he never thought I'd ascend the throne.

'Unfortunately, I lack his simplicity. My existence is entirely symbolic, yet I am expected to behave as though my thoughts and acts had significance. My office could be filled by an android. Indeed, an android would do my job far better. It could be programmed, as my father was. It could smile gently and pay no attention to the destruction going on around it.'

'I thought when Leelson Famber found you—'

'You paid Famber to bring me back!' the king snarled. 'You paid him!'

The Prime Minister shook his head, confused at the vehemence of this reaction. 'Actually, no, Jickie, we didn't. We were worried about you! We paid Fastiga a fee to ascertain what had happened to you. They assigned him to the task, that's all.'

'Ah.' The Lost King turned on his minister with an expression both wild and strange. 'You didn't mention that when I returned. Nor since, come to that.'

'You never asked,' said the Prime Minister, astonished into a loss of aplomb. 'You never asked, Jickie.'

The king turned back to the window, unable to hide his emotions: anxiety, rage, regret, what? All those Fambers, even now being disposed of! Well, few enough of them compared with the population of a planet. And were they not foremost among Firsters? And were not Firsters his enemies, now and forever?

The window beside him reflected his pale face, a ghostly image superimposed over the distant trees. That long Lostre nose. That triangular Lostre mouth. The very face of dynasty hiding the person of . . . whom?

Who had he been, there on beautiful Elitha? Who might he have become? Famber the Fastigat hadn't actually forced him to return. Once found, however, he had thought . . . Or had he thought?

'Why?' asked the Prime Minister in a concerned voice. 'What difference does it make who hired him, or for what?'

After a moment the Lost King shrugged. 'None, really. The free agent is as culpable as the director of that agent. That's Kamir law, isn't it?'

'Yes. With certain reservations. What have you done?'

The king turned, a vague and rather nasty smile on his face. 'Nothing, Prime Minister. Nothing that is not entirely traditional for kings.'

Shortly after that, in the office of the Procurator, Snark the shadow stood immobile against the wall, alert to any need expressed or unexpressed on the part of the Procurator's guests.

There were three of them, ponderous all, two Fastigats and a non-Fastiga woman, counselors to Alliance Prime, heavy with the weight of years and experience, heavy with cynicism and doubt, heavy, at the moment, with anger and despair.

'Two more worlds,' said the oldest of them, a gnarled tree of a man. So Snark thought of him, Twisted-tree. Shadows were not introduced, and the three knew each other well enough to have needed no introductions among themselves. In the absence of other names, Snark labeled the two men Twisted-tree and Thunder-man. The woman's name she knew: Chief Counselor to Prime for Planetary Management Poracious Luv.

Thunder-man rumbled, 'The latest communique came just this morning. Two more worlds wiped clean in Hermes Sector, yes.'

'Survivors?' asked Poracious Luv.

'We're not looking for any. Except as they may show up on the monitors.'

'Weren't there survivors last time?' she asked.

The Procurator murmured, 'No proven survivors. Some children were found.'

'Didn't they say?'

'I don't know. I don't think I ever read the report.' The Procurator waved his hand impatiently. What had happened last time really wasn't germane. 'What's being done?' he demanded.

Thunder-man went on. 'Last time, a century ago, there was only one populated planet in Hermes Sector, Dinadh. There were also a few outposts and colonization teams. This time there are four systems containing a dozen worlds, most of which have been homo-normed to Class D, basic treefarm grass-pasture biome, with all native life eliminated except for a few tough but relatively unimportant species. Yes.'

'And?'

'And Dinadh, the single world of its own system, doesn't want to be involved. They've refused intervention. The other populated systems are cooperating in what we call an evacuation. It's purely symbolic. We can't really evacuate the population; we couldn't even keep up with the birth rate. We're giving first priority to people who have friends here in Prime. In addition to the symbolic gesture, we've actually removed advance teams from several worlds.' Thunder-man referred to his notes. 'From planet Mandalay and the first moon of Cabal in Jerome's system; and from a planet in Goan's system, Perdur Alas.'

'Where the hell will you put evacuees?' asked the Procurator in a whisper. 'Every habitable world is full to the shores!'

'There's a used-up planet a bit nearer in, across the space time border in Janivant Sector, yes. Borthal's World. The original population on Borthal's colonied out a couple of generations back, shortly before it hit crit-popple and ah ... perished.'

'Crit-popple?' Poracious Luv murmured, her lips quirking.

The Procurator cleared his throat. 'Some of the younger administrators have their own jargon, Madam Luv. We used to say things like, "absolute carrying capacity," or "sanity limitation." Lately it's become critical population level, crit-popple.'

Thunder-man went on: 'As I was saying, there's no flora or fauna left on Borthal's, but we've seeded the seas with resistant photocellulars for oxygen production, and we're stockpiling foodstuffs there now. Practically speaking, there won't be that many evacuees. Most of them will be children, and we can only get a few tens of thousands off.'

The three visitors sat in gloomy silence.

Poracious Luv murmured, 'How long is the Alliance going to go on promising a continually expanding frontier?'

'Don't talk dirty,' boomed Twisted-tree. 'You talk like that, somebody'll hear you.'

'Somebody's already heard me,' she snorted. 'The Celosians don't care if I talk population limitation for the Pooacks. The Pooacks don't care if I talk population limitation for the Schrinbergians. So long as I don't mean them, they don't care. Sometimes, late at night, I have these dreams about all the animals. ...'

'Animals?' asked the Procurator. 'What animals?'

'All of them. The ones in pattern storage. In the files. Whales. Elephants. Grampuses. Winged things, some of them. I have these dreams. The souls of all the animals are speaking to me, condemning mankind as the greatest beast of the field. They make a kind of hollow roar, like the sound of the sea.'

'This is no time to be fanciful!' Twisted-tree announced. 'Besides, I find your words offensive. Man is not an animal.'

She made a rude gesture. 'You Firsters have been top-ahead ever since you came up with that "universe made for man" claptrap.'

Twisted-tree snarled, 'Fastigats are not Firsters, madam, any more than kings are commoners. As kings and commoners may share pride of identity while being otherwise unlike, so we and Firsters share certain opinions. Neither they nor we are the first to have those opinions, and the Firsters are saying no more than we have always said. The universe was made for man.'

The Procurator said, 'Firsters are oversimplifying, of course. "Humanity first" leaves certain refinements unaccounted for. Still, their numbers are growing.'

The big woman grumbled, 'They're making their politics sense-able, that's why. Have you seen their sensurrounds?'

The Procurator shook his head, making a little moue of distaste.

She went on: 'They portray exciting journeys to newly homo-normed planets where the senser lives happily ever after with no shortages, lots of room, plenty of food, and a couple of dozen live, healthy children.'

The Procurator laughed knowingly. 'Sensing is believing!'

Poracious Luv gave him an indignant look. 'Once they've sensed the Firster version, they don't want to hear anything about your so-called refinements. They don't want to know the ordinary Firster has about as much chance of going to the frontier as he has of surviving once his world hits – what did you call it? – crit-popple? And, of course, you Fastigats may continue in your ivory-tower opinions because it won't happen here.'

Twisted-tree flushed slightly. Thunder-man looked offended. The Procurator, through long practice, ignored what she had said. Alliance Central wasn't officially a 'world.' It was a government. Freedom-of-procreation laws that applied to Alliance worlds could not apply here. The administration would not remain in power if Alliance Central ever hit crit-popple. There were ways to assure that it did not. Required emigration for larger families. Shadowhood for overactive males. A little something in the water supply. A little something else in the air.

Poracious Luv's hand twitched toward her cup. Snark moved like invisible lightning, taking away the used cup, filling a clean one, putting it where the avid hand could fall upon it. Poracious drew in the hot fragrant brew as though breathing it, half emptying the cup. It was time to change the subject.

'Is there any news from Dinadh?' she asked.

'Lutha Tallstaff is on her way there now,' said the Procurator. 'It will be some time before we hear anything from there. How about the recorders we had hidden all through Hermes Sector? Did they function properly? Did we get anything useful?'

Twisted-tree growled, 'They functioned well, yes. We have excellent records of thousands of colonists going about their business. Then we get deterioration of the audio segment, then brief exclamations, drawn breaths, yes. We see people staring fearfully around themselves. Then we see a gray veil, and the next moment we have good views of a planet without human life.'

'That quickly?'

'More quickly than I can tell it. Subsequently, the recorders stop functioning.'

Twisted-tree said gloomily, 'They stopped functioning on Mandalay and Jerome's System, yes.'

Silence once more except for the almost surreptitious inhalation of tea.

After a time the Procurator offered, 'If they are taking the people first, perhaps some kind of device implanted *in* the people themselves would give us useful information.'

'Political suicide,' hissed Poracious. 'If it were ever found out we'd used workers or colonists . . .'

'What if they were volunteers?' asked the Procurator.

The woman shook her head. 'Even so. There are populated worlds out there, worlds with representation here at Prime. Those representatives are already giving us hell because we didn't start evacuation the minute we knew the Ularians were back. Never mind that it's impossible to evacuate a settled world. We take off a thousand; the same day they have a thousand and ten babies! They don't want to hear we can't do it, even though that's what we've told them right along. Blind faith in somebody stepping in to fix things eliminates a lot of emotional stress, so blind faith is what most people have!

'Now that they're facing the fact nobody can fix things, they're on the screaming prod; and if they found out we'd put recorders into people we knew would be taken, they'd have us for breakfast, broiled.'

'But we need information,' the Procurator murmured.

'Well, we can't use colonists.' Her eyes came to rest on Snark, seeming to see her through her garb, through her shadowhood. Poracious Luv's gaze went past Snark, on to the several other shadows in the room, resting briefly on each. 'Not colonists, Procurator. But . . .'

His eyes followed hers. 'Shadows?' he asked in a hushed voice. 'You mean shadows?'

'Why not?'

'Why not? Because it denies the first right of man! As shadows, they can live part of their lives normally. But on a frontier world . . .'

'How do we know they wouldn't be better off?' Poracious asked in a silky tone. 'We don't know what the Ularians do with them. Maybe they transport them to other, more suitable worlds.'

'Tchah,' he snorted.

'We could always claim we believed so, and who could prove we didn't?' asked Thunder-man. 'Besides, in a time of war, there have to be sacrifices. Whom would you rather sacrifice?'

'The first rule of governance is never to choose who to sacrifice,' snarled the Procurator. 'Or, at least, never to be seen to choose. Death and dismemberment must always be . . . inadvertent. Everybody's fault or nobody's fault!'

'What are you suggesting?' Thunder-man asked the woman, ignoring the Procurator's words. 'Replacing a real preliminary team with one made up of shadows?'

Poracious Luv nodded thoughtfully. 'Exactly. If I heard you correctly, we took preliminary teams off three worlds. One of them was Perdur something?'

He glanced at his notes. 'Perdur Alas,' he confirmed.

Twisted-tree drummed his fingertips on his chair arm, scanning his data-board. 'The team there was only a few hundred strong. How many shadows are there?'

'I'm sure there will be enough,' said Poracious significantly. 'By the time we get them ready to go.'

The Procurator folded his hands in his lap and stared at his guests. Was he capable of this? He murmured, 'You'll recall we use simulation booths to control the shadows, to vent their hostility. The booths are a modified form of sensurround. Shadows are accustomed to the satisfaction they get in the booths. There are no simul booths on Perdur Alas.'

'No, and you can't put any there,' said Poracious. 'The Firsters would have a fit.'

The Procurator shook his head slowly, considering.

'There aren't that many Firsters,' said Twisted-tree.

'There are altogether too many,' whispered the Procurator. It was true. They had an influence that was out of all proportion to their numbers, and those numbers were growing.

Thunder-man said, 'Firsters have enough trouble accepting sensurround. They'd have a fit if they knew about simul booths.'

Poracious nodded. 'You're right. We may get away with sending shadows, but we'd never get away with the other. Someone would talk. Some shipping coordinator or installation tech.'

'Then you're talking about deep conditioning,' the Procurator objected. 'The very conditioning the shadows have rejected!'

'How much can be accomplished with deep conditioning?' asked Poracious. 'Can we make anything much of them?'

The Procurator mused, half aloud. 'Look around you, madam! Half the people on the streets have been conditioned to some degree, though they've done it voluntarily. Most professionals are educated at least partly through deep conditioning. The only difference between them and the shadows is that they've asked for it and the shadows have vehemently rejected it.'

'Forget that for the moment,' she urged. 'Just tell me what can be realistically expected.'

He mused. 'We can't make a master mathematician out of a discalculic, but we can enormously multiply natural aptitudes. It has always been interesting to me that many shadows are very bright. We could assign them jobs in accordance with their aptitudes.'

'Advance teams are mostly bio-generalists anyhow,' muttered Thunder-man.

'But it's got to look natural, and the group must include women,' said Poracious. 'I suppose there are women shadows.'

'There are.' The Procurator sighed.

'You don't like the idea?' she asked.

'It may seem foolish to worry about a few lives, about depriving people of their guaranteed human rights, or about the appearance of impropriety when we're threatened with extinction, but I am sworn to uphold the rights of man,' protested the Procurator, somewhat stiffly. 'I can't just—'

'It seems to me the rights of man include the right to go on living,' growled Twisted-tree. 'If we're wiped out, it won't matter what we do now, yes? To protect ourselves, we need information, and this is one way, maybe the only way, to get it!'

'We could be open about it,' the Procurator said plaintively. 'People would understand. . . .'

'No, they wouldn't.' Twisted-tree grinned without humor. 'They'd jump at any excuse to depose us, because that's what people do. Yes. During a crisis, people pull together; they're afraid rocking the boat will dump them over the side, but still, crises make people fearful, which makes them angry, which makes them hostile. When the crisis is over, the opposition decides to see what was done that might be called illegal. Yes. Then executions happen. Exile happens. If we survive this, it should not be to face such a fate! Therefore, we do whatever offers the slightest hope, but we protect appearances while we do it, yes.'

'He's right,' mused Poracious. 'Later, when survival is assured, the little opposition scholars will start digging. Make sure there are no records of this, Procurator. And damn few recollections!'

The Procurator sighed. It was true. What they said was indisputably true. 'Shadows, then. On Perdur Alas, as soon as we possibly can.'

'Strip off your shadow suit,' said the lock in its metallic, impersonal voice.

Shadow stripped.

'Place your hands in the receptacles.'

Shadow placed.

'Bend your head forward to make contact with the plate.'

Shadow bent.

Light, sounds, movement. Snarkey stood back from the plate, shaking her head as she always did, bellowing with rage as she always did, though this time with more reason.

'Leave the cubicle,' said the voice, opening the door behind her, opposite the one she'd come in by.

'Goddamn bastards,' screamed Snark, leaping from the cubicle, turning to shake her fist at it.

Behind her someone laughed, and she grew abruptly cold as she turned and glared.

'The mad howler back once again,' said Willit. 'Good day, old Snarkey-shad.'

'I nominate you,' growled Snark with a toothy smile.

Willit laughed, uncertainly. Snark went on smiling viciously as the laugh dwindled.

'Whaddayou mean, you nominate me?'

'The name Ularians mean anything to you, shad?' Snark sneered.

'Monsters,' said a voice from a corner. 'From outer space.' The speaker giggled.

'No game?' muttered Willit disbelievingly. 'Monsters?'

'Monsters,' said Snark. 'And they wiped out most of the frontier.'

'That's history,' said Willit doubtfully.

'That's today, buttface. They're back. And the bureaucrats want to find out more about them. So they're gonna put people on a frontier planet, people with chips in 'em, so the skinsuits can tell what happens to the people when the Ularians eat 'em or blow 'em to forever. And guess who, shitheads?'

Silence. Snark glared at them with satisfaction. That had shut the crawlers up. She screwed up her mouth and yowled, 'I nominate all of you.'

'Who the fuck's gonna listen to you naming anybody,' muttered Willit. 'Ma Ugly herself! Who're you, the Procurator all of a sudden?'

Snarkey laughed. 'Who you think they're goin' to take? They need a few hundred men and women. How many of us you think there are down here?'

'I never counted.' Willit, suddenly apprehensive.

Snark didn't answer. Let the bastards stew. Look at 'em. Every one of 'em trying to think up reasons it wouldn't be him or her.

The hell it wouldn't.

In the simul booth, Snark lay snug, the flexible carapace enclosing her, the multiple loops and feedbacks pulsing gently. This time, this one time, she hadn't come in with murder in mind. This time, this one time, she hadn't come in with anything in mind at all except running away, the way she used to run away when she was little. Sometimes she thought her whole life had been running away from things or places or people to other things or places, and it was one of these she dreamed of now, maybe the best place ever, from a long time ago, somewhere far.

There was grass. The grass was important, the smell of it and the feel of it. There were thickly needled evergreen trees and shrubs growing close and tight along a wall. There was an earthen half tunnel burrowing beneath the scratchy branches, a tunnel that could be hidden behind her, and in the heart of the shrubbery lay a nest thickly carpeted with dried needles and soft ferns where a bit of film stuff was wrapped around a dirty old blanket to keep it dry. She could lie wrapped in the blanket with the film stuff outside that, warm and dry no matter if it rained, peering through a tiny hole in the leaves almost like looking through a telescope. Out there the big stone building loomed over the fields and garden plots and barns, and she could watch what went on: the young ones doing their work, the grown ones walking among them, smiling their dangerous smiles. They had their hands hidden in their pockets, holding weapons, just waiting until one of the kids did something wrong, the way Snark always did something wrong.

The journey always started here, in this hidden place, with her looking out. The people out there might even be looking for her, calling her name, but they couldn't find her. Even if they told the kids to find her, they couldn't. Long delirious moments would go by, with Snark relishing her safety, feeling the warmth around her, the contentment. Her eyes would close, finally, shutting out the world, the people, the stone house. Her breathing would slow. Her heart would slow, too, into quiet, purposeful *bump, bump, bump.* Then even that noise would fade and she would be ... elsewhere.

To begin with, she was always on a moor. That's where the journey started. It didn't matter how she got there; the dream didn't bother with that. She was simply there, on an almost flat highland covered with low, scrubby-scratchy bushes between aisles of softer bracken that were interrupted by shallow, moss-surrounded peat-dark ponds. When she thought about the place at all, she thought perhaps it was a place she had been once, a place she had seen, smelled, walked in. Maybe it was the place she'd been born to, where her own people were. She never thought she'd made it up. It was too real for that.

Sometimes she found herself standing there almost naked. Other times she had stout boots and a rain cape with a hood that covered her, and when dressed like this, she could lie well hidden on the moor itself, her body shadowed by the brushy growths or obscured by the bracken. Still, if she did that – and sometimes it seemed someone told her it would be all right if she did – she knew she could be tracked eventually. They could smell her. They could come whistling through the evening air, seeking anything warm-blooded, calling in those tempting voices that always seemed to know her name. No. Even though the moor was safe in comparison to most other places, it wasn't safe enough.

So she never gave in to the relief she felt when she arrived. Relief was only a momentary feeling, not enough by itself. She had to cross the moor, had to dodge along the folds in the ground, following the bracken aisles, keeping her feet out of the ponds, staying as dry as possible as she worked her way toward the horizon, where the world ended against a gray span of featureless sky. Later it might change to blue or even violet, it might glow with sunset or darken to lapis night, but when she arrived, when she crossed the moor, it was always the same: gray and clear, without depth or measure.

At a certain point on her journey she would hear the sea. A murmur only, a soft susurrus against the rattle of the bracken and the squodge of her footsteps. The whisper would grow louder, though never really loud, until she reached the edge where the world fell away in rooty edges above cliffs of gnarl, where the seabirds made screaming dizzy clouds beneath her as they wheeled wildly out, spiraling from their precipice perches over the hammered surface of the sea.

Then panic came, always. Even if she wasn't closely pursued in the dream, even if she had lots of time to walk slowly along the sheer drop, noticing the sparkle of the waters and the whirling gyre of the birds, panic always overcame her. She wouldn't find the right place! It would be better to jump now, jump before they caught up with her. Otherwise they might catch her, and that would be worse. Every time she came here she had to fight down the urge to jump, shut it out, stop thinking about it. She had to turn to her left to walk as close to the edge as possible, eyes hunting for landmarks, putting her feet carefully onto stone and pebbly places, leaving no track to be seen, knowing all the time that her smell remained, floating on the air, hanging there for the hunters to find!

Eventually, long after she'd become convinced she had missed it, she came to the curiously twisted rock looming at the edge of the cliff. It was always there, alongside a shrubby tree with an outflung trunk.

Then she had to be agile and quick. Once, long ago, someone had carried her. Then, she'd locked her arms around someone's neck and that someone had made the jump. Now she was old enough to jump by herself, out from the edge of the cliff, catching the protruding trunk, holding on tightly as it sagged below the level of the rim, and then ... then she had to grasp the rooty growth that extended from the cliff face and pull herself in!

In was through the narrow entry of a cave, a little sandy-floored crevice not much bigger than two or three Snarks, where the floor was softened with dried bracken and flat stones lay piled near the opening. The stones were for stacking in the entrance until only tiny airholes remained. Soft animal skins waited to be pulled around her. Someone ... someone had given her the skins, but she could not remember who. It didn't matter. When she was curled there, wrapped there, she was warm and completely safe. No one, not even the trackers, could find her there.

From her position of warm safety, she sometimes heard them coming, their voices keening over the sound of the waters, louder and louder until they were wailing into the ocean wind from just above the place where she lay. They had smelled her as far as the edge, but they smelled her no more. She had flown away like a sea-bird. She had vanished. Her hole was not visible from above. When the stones were stacked in the opening, it was not visible from the sea below or from the gulf of air. So far as the flying things knew, she was gone.

The spray blew gently into her face. The sound of the seabirds came softly to her ears. At night she could see the stars through the hole in the stone. Sometimes it was enough merely to be there, merely to be safe, and it was tempting to lie there, not eating, not drinking, letting life go away somewhere else, letting herself wither into nothing, quietly, contentedly, safe. Being dead was safer yet, she knew that, but life still pulled at her. Besides, the cave supported life. At the back of the crevice, water leaked down onto a hollowed stone beside a tight chest full of hard bread and dried fruit and strips of smoked meat. She could stay in safety for days and days at a time, without dying. It was a good place.

Later, after she was ... found, picked up by ... whoever it had been; later, after she was somewhere else, after she was at the stone house with the wall; later, when she burrowed into the shrubbery to be safe, to be hidden, it was the moor she dreamed of. Rather than go back to the stone house, sometimes she stayed in the dream for a very long time. It didn't matter how long she stayed. When she came back eventually, they still had to feed her, even if they didn't want to. Any child who was sent to the stone house, they had to take care of. They had to feed her. They weren't allowed to kill her.

That still left a lot of stuff they could do if they felt like it, if you broke the rules, if they caught you. It was always Snark who got caught, even when it wasn't Snark who'd done it. When a matron asked who did it, who bloodied the nose, who ripped the shirt, who broke the chair, somebody always giggled and said, the Snark did it. The Snark hit me. The Snark pushed me. The Snark bit me and bloodied my nose. Always when she had and often when she hadn't.

So she figured she might as well. If they were going to say she did, she might as well. And she might as well do it right, once and for all. Might as well use something sharp or heavy, so afterward they couldn't point fingers, couldn't name names, couldn't go running to the older ones yelling Snark, Snark did it.

In the simul booth, she groaned, heaved, grew red with fury at her persecutors.

Peace, whispered the booth. *It's all right. You don't need to kill anyone. Don't need to hit anyone, hurt anyone, bloody anyone. Peace. No one can find you here. You're safe here. It's better here than where you were before. ...*

Here. Here at the edge of the cliff it was. Everywhere else the two feelings were all mixed up. Scared-hate. Threat anger. Fear-rage. She couldn't separate them. They were one feeling. What she feared she hated, what she hated she would kill. ...

Peace, whispered the booth.

If she could just kill whatever-it-was, whoever-it-was, so it would stay dead forever. Then, then ...

Peace, the booth insisted.

Peace. See the jar your mother put there, in the niche. See the pictures on it. There is Father Endless and Mother Darkness. There are the peacemakers, the peace bringers. Here, with them watching over you, you needn't kill or harass or bother. Here, with them watching over you, you are safe.

Eventually, the booth had its way. Snark quit fighting and slept. There in the simul booth, safe in the carapace, she slept, dreaming she was in the shrubbery at the sanctuary, wrapped in her old blanket, sleeping. And in that dreamed sleep, she dreamed she was in the even safer place at the edge of the moors. Sleep within sleep within sleep, dream within dream, she dreamed of becoming safer and safer still.

3

Lutha, Leely, and Trompe arrived upon Dinadh at our only port, Simidi-ala (the Separated Place), which stands in an area of desolate coastland beside Dinadh's only sea. This is the one place on Dinadh where there are garages for vehicles, where complicated things brought from off-planet may be repaired, where foreign wares may be housed. The stretch of coastline including the neighboring bay is called Tasimi-na-Dinadh, that is, the Edge of Dinadh, and visitors are told that when they came 'across the Edge' and 'through the Separation,' they have left behind them, symbolically at least, those things eschewed by Dinadh.

What things are eschewed by Dinadh? All those things that might draw us nearer other worlds. All those things that might make others look at us more closely, that might cause curiosity or speculation. These we eschew in favor of duty, gravity, privacy, knowing our place. Also beauty and order and reverence for ... our chosen ways.

Lutha and Trompe were informed of this, there at Simidi-ala. Lutha looked over the head of her sleeping child as the latest of several inform-ants departed, fretting over the time already spent in fruitless waiting. It is Dinadh's way to make people wait and spend time and fret a little. Let them decide at first whether they wish to come to Dinadh at all. Let them think long about spending all those years with us. If they cannot stand a little frus-tration in Simidi-ala, they will never stand a winter in a hive!

'Why do people keep coming by and looking at us and then going away again?' Trompe demanded.

'You're the empath,' Lutha breathed. 'You figure it out!'

'They're curious about us,' he said. 'About why we're here. And they're very curious about Leely.' He sighed and rolled his head onto his shoulders, trying to ease aching muscles. He blinked sleepily and sat up straighter. Someone was coming.

The approaching Dinadhi was dressed as we all are, as Lutha and Trompe and Leely themselves were, in robes of fine, creamy cotton, high shoes woven of thin leather strips and soled with the durable, flexible wood of the paran tree, and over all a robe of soft leather – in summer, thin and light; in winter, heavier, with the wool still on – with bright patterns painted down the front and around the cuffs of the sleeves. These patterns are one's own, painted by the wearer, so even veiled women may be identified by their specific patterns. I have learned from Lutha and Snark what women wear on other planets, frilly thises and lacy thats, but we have no stockings, no intimate undergarments. Lutha tells me that all the time she spent on Dinadh she felt she was walking around in her night clothing. I told her we do not wear night clothing. Wool and leather we have. Cotton we have. That is all that we have.

Lutha said they were surprised to find our garments exceptionally comfortable. Even Leely objected to them less than he did to his ordinary wear. They had managed to keep him dressed during most of the trip out.

'Sorry to have kept you waiting,' murmured the official, seating himself beside them and setting his feet squarely together. 'There've been several someones here looking for you, and when you arrived, we thought it wise to have a small conference and share our perceptions of the matter.'

'Looking for me?' asked Trompe, sitting up straighter and opening his eyes wide.

The official shook his balding head and stroked his beard from the point where it was gathered into a carved bone ring below his chin, down the glossy tassel to his waist. All our men who work at the port wear their beards like that so we will know who they are, so we will pray for them, exposed as they are, to the influences of outsiders.

The official said, 'Two were here yesterday, looking for the wife of Leelson Famber, and Leelson Famber's children. They said they came to seek peace and ultimate truth upon Dinadh and wished to meet with Leelson Famber's family while they were here.'

'While they were here seeking truth,' said Trompe heavily.

'Who?' asked Lutha, suddenly wide-awake. 'And what do you mean, children?' She indicated her sleeping son. 'To my knowledge, this is the only child Leelson ever fathered.'

The official smiled again. 'We leasehold officers are accustomed to applicants of many kinds and degrees of fear or fervor, gush or melancholy. The two I speak of are of another stripe. Though Mitigan of Asenagi and Chur Durwen of Collis make proper application for right of residence, neither their desire for sanctuary nor their wish to learn from the songfathers rings true. Instead of a manner either fervid or meditative, both men display an attitude of aplomb, of alert disinterest, of customary unsurprise.'

Trompe slitted his eyes.

The official shrugged. 'We are parochial, but we are not naive. To our eyes, they have the appearance of mercenaries.'

'What did you tell them?' demanded Trompe.

The official smiled. 'Nothing except that the wife of Leelson Famber was not here. That no children of Leelson Famber were on Dinadh. As was true at the time.'

'Did they accept that?'

'No. They wanted to see our records.'

Trompe snorted.

The official smiled. 'As you are no doubt aware, there are no such things on Dinadh. We don't record things. We remember them. We don't have files or archives or libraries, we have rememberers. We don't have maps, we have guides. We don't write books, we tell tales. We don't even have money, as you understand money. The only reason we allow outlanders on the planet at all is to get hard currency credit for off-planet purchases.'

'Did you remember anything for them?' Lutha asked.

'Nothing. But neither did we discourage their remaining upon Dinadh. Hundred-year leases do not grow on trees.'

'I don't suppose you found out what they're really here for. Or where they're from?'

'We watched them, we listened, trying to find out why they were really here, but they spoke a language we have no record of. A secret language, our translators think. An assassin's tongue.'

'So, where are they now?' Trompe demanded.

'Across the port. In one of the other hives. We thought we'd let you get on your way before we send them anywhere else.'

Lutha sighed.

Trompe said, 'How much will you charge to tell them nothing?'

The official shook his head chidingly. 'We don't play games of that sort, Outlander Paggas. That leads to a pattern of darkness, and we try to avoid such. The only reason for our mentioning these people is that we thought you might know of them, know who they are, why they are here. Seemingly, you do not, so they will not be allowed to infringe upon your privacy – or, I should say, the privacy of Bernesohn Famber, whose lease has still two standard years to run.'

'You'll send them away?'

'They have the same privilege as any other applicant. If they wish to buy a lease, they may buy one. The only cells available at the moment are in hives some distance from Cochim-Mahn, where Bernesohn Famber dwelt among us.'

'You're saying we won't encounter them.'

'I'm saying it would be extremely unlikely. Now, your other visitor presents a somewhat different situation.'

'Other visitor?' Lutha raised her brows.

'Thosby Anent. Supposedly he is a broker in craft items, of which Dinadh creates a small array. He pretends to be a broker, and we pretend to believe him. He is actually a spy for the Alliance, and he was here yesterday, asking for you.'

'But we are here for the Alliance,' Lutha erupted, spontaneously and unthinkingly.

The Dinadhi beamed at her. 'Of course you are. How nice of you to admit it. It relieves us of the burden of fiction! Old Anent is harmless, but I may not force him on you. Will you see him?'

Trompe shrugged assent.

'Rest here. I'll send him along, and then the vehicle manager to start you on your way.'

'And your name, sir?' Trompe asked.

'Merely a humble patterner, doing his duty.' He went away, leaving Trompe and Lutha to stare at one another, and then at the elderly man making his way across the floor toward them. He was somewhat gray and dried-out looking, with pale watery eyes of so light a blue they seemed almost white, when they could be seen through the wreath of smoke around his head.

'Thosby Anent,' he murmured, taking the pipe from his mouth and peering over his shoulder even as he cupped his hand beside his lips, a perfect parody of conspiracy. 'Covert agent of Alliance Prime, at your service.'

'What do you mean, covert agent?' asked Lutha. 'Why would the Alliance have a covert agent here?'

'Why, why,' he stuttered, 'to receive information. To forward it to Alliance Prime. They sent me because there's some conspiracy here. Something going on. They needed someone of my experience. I knew you must have been sent to ...' He made an inclusive gesture.

'I see,' said Trompe fretfully, pinching the flesh between his eyes into a ridge as he felt for what was actually going on inside the oldster's mind. He seemed perfectly sincere, feeling a little outraged dignity, a little pomposity. A minor functionary living on dreams of glory. 'How did you know we'd been sent to ...?' He aped the other's inclusive gesture.

'The ship,' the man whispered. 'It was an official ship.'

As it had been, without question. Well. Trompe bowed formally. 'Thank you for your offer. If we learn anything at all, we will bring it directly to you.'

'I thank you sir. I will keep my, ah ... *network* in readiness. Should you, by any chance, happen upon something urgent, the code word is *vigilance.*' He pursed his lips and nodded rapidly to himself several times. '*Vigilance.*'

'I see,' said Lutha, trying to keep from laughing.

Leely chose that moment to stroke her face and mutter his customary polysyllable.

'So this is the young man,' Thosby said, peering at Leely like a squirrel peering at a nut, as though wondering where to begin nibbling. 'They were speaking of him in the corridor. So this is he.'

'He is,' said Lutha. 'And we've come a long way, and we're tired. If you gentlemen will excuse us.' She stood up and took Leely away with her to what was called on Dinadh the female privacy facility.

Trompe bid Thosby Anent farewell, though it took several more conspiratorial exchanges to do so. As Thosby went the vehicle man arrived.

'Are you the last one we have to deal with?' demanded Trompe in a weary voice.

'The last person here at the port, yes,' the man replied. 'I am about to rent you a vehicle at an exorbitant price, and sell you a guidebook, also quite expensive, by which means you may reach the hive where Bernesohn Famber had – or, I should say, has – a lease on a certain number of cells. On Dinadh, leases survive the lessees. Kin may claim them as inheritance and may sell the remaining rights, with our approval, of course. So, Famber's place is still there, undisturbed, his belongings as they were the day he left, in the hive of Cochim-Mahn, where the songfather has been told to expect you.'

'How long a journey to Cochim-Mahn?'

'It will take you several days. There are hostels along the way.'

'It seems a long time. Why can't we fly?'

'Flight is permitted only in certain, well-defined cases of emergency.'

'And why is that?' asked Trompe.

The vehicle man shrugged. 'Have you seen persons sitting at their ease in the afternoon, drinking, perhaps, or talking with one another, when an insect comes suddenly buzzing and darting about their faces? Have you seen how they slap at it, wave it away, how it plagues them? Or in the evening, beside the lamp, when one is reading, and a flapping thing comes to the light?'

Trompe nodded.

'So our mother world feels about unnatural flying things buzzing about her face.'

'But she doesn't object to unnatural things crawling on her?' Trompe exploded.

'On her clothing,' corrected the vehicle man. 'We can all put up with a few tiny things crawling about in our clothing. So long as they do it quietly and do not bite!'

'Which pretty well put us in our place!' Trompe remarked to Lutha when she returned. 'In effect, we're mites in the seams of Dinadh's garments. Harmless ones, of course.'

Lutha went to one of the pore-like openings in the outer wall and stood looking out. 'Several of the female port workers came in to use the facilities

356

while I was there. They were curious. Mostly about Leely.'

'Trying to talk to him?'

'Just watching him. He did a portrait of one of them on the wall.'

'In what medium, dare one ask?' He allowed himself a hint of distaste, hoping she would look at him, speak to him, Trompe, rather than to the air over his shoulder as she seemed always to do.

She ignored his tone. No Fastigat would use such a tone unless he were eager for argument, and she was not interested in argument. 'In some pinky-colored dirt he found in a flowerpot in there. He peed in it to make mud.'

Trompe turned away, frustrated. 'They were impressed?'

'They seemed to be.' She fell silent for a moment. They had been impressed. More than merely impressed. Awed, perhaps. 'There was a great deal of discussion about Weaving Woman. ...'

'A goddess, as I recall,' he said distantly.

'A goddess, yes.'

'One they feel rather guilty about,' he said.

'Guilty?'

'Hmm. I note some who, when they speak of her, brood with a sort of self-reproach.'

'Then you note more than I do. All I know about Weaving Woman indicates she's an indwelling spirit of art and craftsmanship. The women using the facilities spoke of Leely as her child.'

'Which means?'

She shrugged. The women's concentration had been a little frightening, but she chose not to mention that. Instead she gestured vaguely. 'From what I recall of the culture chips I reviewed on the way out, Weaving Woman is pattern, which probably includes portraiture and sculpture, portrayal of any and everything.'

Trompe turned the idea around, seeing if it had any focus for him, then let it go with an impatient grunt. It was time to get moving. They had already wasted too much time.

At the garages below, the manager of vehicles gave them precise instructions. The vehicles were economical, but of low performance. They could not be driven off the roads, which the hives kept clear of overhanging foliage by cutting winter firewood along them. If visitors traveled without a guide, the route would be programmed into the vehicle before departure and could not be deviated from thereafter. The doors of the vehicle would be locked before they departed from Simidi-ala and would not unlock until they reached the first hostel. The same would apply between hostels. One did not get out of the vehicle between destinations.

'What if we have a mechanical breakdown?' Trompe asked.

'Press the alarm button in the vehicle and wait. The time will afford an excellent opportunity for meditation. Eventually someone will come to fetch you.'

'We can't hike to the nearest village?'

'All worlds have their threats. We make rules to protect visitors from the threats present on Dinadh. Outside the vehicle, you might be injured, or even killed. Then your world would bring a complaint against our world. And our world would have to defend the complaint before the high Alliance courts. We would have to hire experts qualified to present cases before that court. We are a poor people. We cannot afford the expenses of litigation.'

Trompe muttered about this exchange to Lutha, concluding, 'So much for exploration! Even though the route is programmed in, the vehicles aren't automatic, oddly enough. Evidently we can stop to rest or admire the view wherever we like, we just can't get out!'

'You rejected the idea of a guide?' she asked curiously.

He made a face. 'The people here want us to hire a guide. They want it so firmly I feel we'll find out more without. During the trip we'll get a feel for the place, enough to be well acclimated when we arrive at Cochim-Mahn.'

'So be it, then.' She smiled, indicating acceptance. She would have preferred to go quickly and get the matter over with, but it didn't really matter. They could go without a guide.

The vehicle, though clumsy looking, was commodious, with both a sanitary compartment and a well-stocked food-service console. The food was off-planet, Lutha noted, prepackaged elsewhere and imported. Every meal they'd been served at the Edge had been off-planet food. Which made one wonder if planetary food was tasty enough for off-worlders. Or if there was enough of it. Of course, at the price they had paid to rent the vehicle, they could have been fed on ambrosia with enough left over to pay a year's expenses on Central!

'Now if Leely will just leave his clothes on,' Trompe remarked.

His slightly sarcastic tone reminded Lutha of Leelson. Though she understood it, it angered her nonetheless. Fastigats could always empathize, always understand, except with Leely. They had no idea how or why he felt as he did. They were offended, as though they had reached out and been rudely rebuffed. She bit back an angry response. If Leelson himself had felt frustration, then Trompe was certainly entitled to a similar feeling.

'Pity you have to be bothered with all this,' she said, thinking it a pity she herself had to be.

He made an impatient gesture. 'Sorry. This is my job after all. You really couldn't have managed alone.'

'No,' she said, mimicking his tone and surprised at the depth of her furious agreement. 'I really could not have managed alone.'

Though their destination was a considerable distance north, they had first to go eastward from the coast, up a series of switchbacks on the face of a more or less vertical cliff until they reached the level highland that we, who live here, call the skylands. At first they were relieved to have reached the level road, but soon they found they made no more progress than previously as they traveled first eastward, then westward, then eastward again between the deep gorges that interdigitated the skylands from either side.

'This is ridiculous,' Trompe muttered, making yet another hundred-sixty-degree turn.

'Dinadh at one time had a great deal more water than it has now,' remarked Lutha. 'These canyons must have been cut by sizable rivers.'

She peered down at the threadlike trickles glittering in the depths among clean-edged patches of green, letting her eyes move upward to the mesa tops, all of them like the one they were traversing, covered with low forest broken by occasional grassy glades.

'Trompe. Stop!'

He stopped obediently. 'What?'

'Animals.' They were approaching an open glade where a group of small, woolly, long-necked animals grazed under the watchful care of herdsmen. 'What are they doing?'

'Eating grass,' said Trompe. 'Haven't you seen an animal before?'

'I never have. Oh, sensurround, of course, but not a real one. What are the herdsmen doing? Twirling those things?'

'Spindles. They're spinning thread from wool, or perhaps from wild cotton. It's in the chips I gave you.'

She nodded as Trompe started the vehicle once more, as they went slowly by. The herdsmen had a stout little wain with shutters at either end and head-high sections of woven-mesh panel racked at its sides. As they passed the group Lutha waved, receiving only the barest of blank-faced nods in return.

'Was Dinadh this arid when the first settlers came?' Trompe asked as he maneuvered the vehicle along a road uncomfortably close to a sheer drop on one side. 'Or did it change after?'

Lutha let her subconscious seek the information. 'It was as it is now. The first Alliance scholars to visit the planet were told the Dinadhi had come from another world and they "remembered" emerging onto this world from their previous one through a hole in the ground. It's not an unusual origin myth. Other cultures have similar ones.'

'They were probably on one of the fabled "lost ships,"' Trompe conjectured. 'There've been enough of those to go around.'

She shrugged. 'There have been "lost ships," but this is the only uniden-
tified colony. I looked it up before we left Central. Except for the population
on Dinadh, the Alliance ethnologists have always been able to identify the
planet of origin, and that's true even when populations have ended up far
from their original destinations.'

'But not here.'

'According to the stuff the Procurator gave me. No one knows for sure
how the Dinadhi got here.'

'No missing ship with a Dinadhi-like society?'

'No record of one.'

'No similar societies from which this could be an unrecorded offshoot?'

'One theory had it they came from a frontier society beyond Hermes
Sector. The world was called Vriat or Breadh; something like that. The
colony on it disappeared.'

'The Ularians?'

'Nobody knows what happened. They just disappeared, that's all.'

'There have been a lot of Nantaskan-speaking worlds that colonied out.
Arriving from any of them makes more sense than this hole-in-the-ground
story.'

She glanced at him sidewise. 'There is a real site for the supposed emergence, Trompe. As a matter of fact, it's in a wide valley not many days' travel
from Cochim-Mahn. Or so the maps say, at any rate.'

'A sacred site, no doubt,' he said flippantly.

'Oh, very sacred! It's the omphalos. Extra-special rites every third year, a
Dinadh year being six hundred and a fraction days. Every third year they
draw an additional day out of the omphalos, the navel of time. That doesn't
quite do it, so every sixtieth year they have to pull two days. Tahs-uppi, the
ceremony's called.'

'Meaning what? You're further along with the language than I am.'

She mused. 'Tahs-uppi. Tasimi means the edge or the border. Well, actually it means "our borders'," plural possessive. Tahs probably means something like end, or limit. There's a word ... uppas, uppasim, uppasimi.' She
fell silent.

'So?'

'I was trying to figure out the ending. It has something to do with selection, I think. Part of the litany of Weaving Woman gives her the name
of K'loch mahn uppasimi. Selector of our patterns. Well, not quite that.
Chooser, intrinsic.'

'I don't quite get that.'

'Well, in our language we wouldn't say the rain chooses to fall. It just naturally falls. Weaving Woman *is* pattern, she doesn't choose it.'

'So the name means what? The end of pattern?'

'The crux, the fulfillment. That would fit. Every hundred standard years, more or less, they reach the fulfillment of the pattern, pull out an extra day or so, and start over.'

'With feasting, I suppose. Processions.'

'More likely fasting and prayer. Actually, I don't know. The chips you gave me merely mention Tahs-uppi and gave the date for the preceding one. When a ceremony is very holy, taboo, it's hard for an outsider to learn the details.' She stared down into the abyss they were skirting. 'The pattern is due to end fairly soon. Maybe we'll get a chance to ask about it.'

'I wonder what would happen,' Trompe mused, turning the vehicle away from the canyon and toward the forest, where the road disappeared around patches of thorny growths, 'if they didn't find one.'

'Find one what?' she asked, startled.

'An extra day. When they went to fish one out of the navel hole.'

She laughed. 'You're an idiot, you know, Trompe. What an idea.' She chuckled, thinking about it, a kind of black joke on the Dinadhi. The high priest, or whoever, dipping into the omphalos with his what? His wand? His day hook? Slowly withdrawing it to the sound of drums and flutes, only to find it empty. No extra day. Gradually, as she thought on it and considered the implications, she stopped finding the idea at all funny.

Toward evening they arrived at the hostel, the first one between Simidi-ala and Cochim-Mahn.

'And not a moment too soon,' Lutha muttered as she parked the vehicle and heard the doorlocks make a solid thunk as they disengaged. 'I'm exhausted.'

Leely was sitting up, looking around himself with some interest.

Lutha got out, sniffed the fragrant air, sighed, stretched, held out her arms to the boy, who came slowly into them, head turning as he tried to see everything at once.

They were at the top end of yet another of the endless canyons, its branches and ramifications receding into the distance: carved buttes, slender pillars and towers, stepped ziggurats of stone, vertical walls pocked with caves, some of them occupied by busy hive communities or by the lonely bulk of abandoned hives, all thrown into brilliantly colored contrasts of fire and shade by the level rays of the setting sun. Sound came softly from the canyons, voices and drums, the high shriek of a bone flute, the hissing rain-sound of rattles.

'Evensong,' Lutha said. 'Farewell to Lady Day. And that, too, is about time.'

'We're more tired than we should be,' said Trompe as he slowly removed their belongings from the vehicle. 'The trip wasn't that arduous.'

She agreed with a weary brush at a lock of hair that dangled at her forehead. 'Indeed, Trompe. We are scarce begun and I am so weary I can hardly see. What is it about this place?'

He considered the question soberly. 'I think it's the fact that we have no sense of distance traveled toward our goal. It's been like a maze. One goes and goes, then comes a turn, and one goes back almost the way one came. It takes hundreds of lateral marks back and forth among these canyons before we make much progress toward the goal. I'm conscious of frustration in myself. I can certainly feel it in you.'

'That's it,' she said, almost relieved to have identified her feelings. 'Trompe, you're right. It's all the same – mark after mark of thorn forest and herds of woolly beasts, then the road emerges onto an utterly astonishing prospect. We look out on marvel, complete with rising song and smoke from the occupied hives and mysterious silence from the abandoned ones—'

'More abandoned ones than I expected,' he interjected.

'—then we turn back, almost the way we came; mark after mark of thorn forest once more, another astonishing prospect, then turn again, like a shuttle in a loom. Back and forth. Back and forth. After a time one's sense of astonishment wanes.'

'But the landscape demands astonishment, nonetheless, so one is left feeling naughty to be so ungrateful.' Trompe grinned wearily at her. 'At least, that's how I felt! One more breathtaking view and I would gag. Especially considering we could have flown the distance in an hour or so.'

She sagged under Leely's weight as the boy gripped her more tightly around the neck, murmuring his usual 'Dananana,' moistly in her ear.

'He's hungry,' she said.

'How do you know?'

'I just know. Or perhaps I assume he is because I am. Let's go in and see what the menu offers.'

What the Dziblom-nahro offered was a flavorful stew of grain and peppers, flat polygons of unleavened bread served with a dish of salted herbs and another of a fruity sweet-sour-hot sauce, plus a small helping of roasted meat, no doubt from the same woolly, deer-like creatures they had seen in flocks along their journey.

'Not bad,' Trompe murmured.

'Should be quite acceptable,' Lutha murmured in return. 'It's the basic menu for human diets on most non-ocean worlds. Grain. Vegetables. Fruit. A little meat. Evidently this is a nondairy cuisine. No milk. No cheese.'

'The flocks we saw on our way here today had tiny udders between the front legs. Milk animals need more nourishment than animals raised for meat, wool, or hides, and Dinadh probably doesn't produce enough grain to feed animals.' He leaned forward and poured another cupful of the beverage that accompanied their meal. 'Water or water flavored with mashed dried fruit as a drink. There's probably no grain or fruit left over for fermented or distilled drinks, either. Definitely a subsistence diet, trembling always on the edge of famine.'

'Which might explain the Dinadhi dependence upon their gods,' she commented softly, casting a look across the empty room at the yawning young woman who had served them while politely averting her eyes. 'They need to feel they have done all the right things to assure their continued well-being.'

'You draw this conclusion from the language?'

'The use and frequency of religious words and phrases helps place the culture.'

'How?'

Lutha made a little moue. 'The precept is that consistent and frequent use of a limited lexicon, oral and gestural, denotes the presence of a rigorous sect, possibly one with a well-defined canon of positive and negative observances—'

'Thou-shalts and shalt-nots?'

'Right. Add to this adversarial language—'

'Adversarial?'

'Adversarial or exclusionary language – words that mean "them," as opposed to "us." I don't mean simple reference to identity. I mean trash words. Like the words the Firsters apply to non-Firsters – animal-lovers, ape-people, tree-worshipers, greenies. ...'

He laughed. 'Those are the mild ones.'

'Well, you get the idea. Fearful people develop their religions as protective devices, ways to manipulate hostile environments, formulas for identifying and defeating their enemies. The more fearful people are, the more enemies they have, the more adversarial language they use. My race is proud; yours is uppity. My people are the elect; yours is damned. My religion is true; yours is false. I worship god; you're possessed by demons.'

'Surely that's very common?'

'Of course it is! Only very secure people are able to think non-adversarially. As a linguist, I have to keep in mind that fearful people are dangerous. When backed into corners, they bite! Before I start translating some document, I need to know what words and phrases might be heard as corner-backers.'

'So you look for trash words and adversarial and exclusionary language. How?'

She nodded thoughtfully. 'If possible, you lay hands on transcriptions of meetings, observances of public holidays, special religious services, any session where the people aren't talking *to* outsiders but are talking about them. You run those records through a content analyzer looking for god words. You also want to know how manlike the god is. Fearful people prefer manlike gods, deified humans, or gods that take human shape or do human things, gods they can imagine being friends with, or asking for a favor.'

'People don't go into battle shouting the name of the Ethical First Principle?'

'Not usually. Also, the god often resembles his followers in behavior and feelings. Angry people have angry gods and vindictive people have vindictive gods, and so forth.'

Lutha indicated the serving woman who leaned against a doorpost, eyes half-closed. 'When our serving woman spoke of the gods, however, she wasn't talking about deified humans. During our supper she mentioned Weaving Woman and Brother Corn and the Fruit Maidens and half a dozen other deities, none of them manlike, none of them adversarial. *But*, finally, when she left us to our dinner, she said, "May the Gracious One hold us all in beauty," and by using the word for "us all," she excluded the mentioned being.'

'Meaning she wants the pattern to benefit her and her family and friends, but doesn't want it to benefit us?'

Lutha frowned. 'No. The only creature specifically excluded was the other creature mentioned, the Gracious One. The language is adversarial by omission!'

He laughed. 'Sorry, Lutha, but I don't get that.'

'Listen. There are a dozen Dinadhi words for "all," or "us all." For example, there's a word that means us all, everything living in the universe. There's another word that means all us Dinadhi, and still another word that means all us humans here in this room. When you use an "us all" word, if you mention anyone in particular in the same phrase, it means that person is excluded. You can say, "Simidi-ala and *us all* Dinadhi are faithful worshipers," and actually mean, "Except for Simidi-ala, we on Dinadh are faithful worshipers." Or you can say, "Martha and *us all* were laughing at the jokes," which actually means, "We were all laughing except Martha, who has no sense of humor."'

'If you use any word that means "us all," but mention someone by name, that person is excluded?'

'Right. If you want to include that person, you don't mention him, her, or it by name or you use the other set of words that just means "all." What our serving woman actually said was, "May the Gracious One allow all other persons to continue in beauty."'

'The implication being ...?'

'By the Great Org Gauphin, Trompe, I don't know! Either that the Gracious One is unbeautiful, or that the Gracious One can't appreciate beauty, or that the Gracious One is not concerned with beauty. How did she feel when she said it?'

'I wasn't paying attention,' he said, slightly shamefaced.

Lutha shook her head. 'Whatever it is, it doesn't concern us!'

'We're not the scapegoat, in other words.'

'Right. And that's remarkable, Trompe. Outsiders are almost always suspect.'

They rose from the table as the servitor bestirred herself to collect their dishes. Lutha gathered Leely into her arms and started for the porch outside the window where they had been sitting.

'Lady . . .' The woman spoke from behind them. 'Are you going out?'

'I had thought it would be pleasant,' Lutha replied in careful dialect. 'Should I not do so?'

'If you go to enjoy the air, do not leave the porch. Stay behind the grille. Such is the proper pattern of dusk behavior.'

Lutha bowed, thanking her, then murmured a translation for Trompe's benefit.

'This time I was paying attention. Her emotion had something to do with safety,' he mused, when they were outside, looking through the grille into the clearing and past it to the thorn forest. 'Or a taboo of some kind. One of those negative commandments you were talking about?'

'I have no idea. Suppose we sit awhile in these comfortable-looking chairs and enjoy the evening. I'm weary, but not sleepy yet.'

'Can I take the boy? He looks very heavy.'

'Leave him. He's all right, aren't you, Leely-baby? Of course he is, all snuggled down on Mommy's shoulder. Sit, Trompe. As the girl says, enjoy the air. One thing we will have to say about Dinadh; it has wonderful air.'

They sat, breathing the resinous fragrance of day-warmed trees, the cool water-scented wind that came up from the canyons. The sky was pure lapis, not yet black, with several large planets pulsing in the last glow at the horizon. Empty planets, Lutha told herself. With a few abandoned mines. And beyond this single system, everything else wiped clean by the Ularians.

'Dana,' whispered Leely, pointing with one chubby hand. 'Danana.'

'What is it?' whispered Trompe.

Lutha shook her head. She couldn't tell what it was. Something emerging from the forest: flowing draperies, melting mists. A wraith? A ghost? A creature oozing from among the trees into the clearing, seeming almost to glow in the dusk. Soon it was joined by others, half a dozen, ten, beings that lifted on their wings, circling.

Ethereally slender, androgynous in form, fairylike in effect. As Lutha's eyes adjusted to the dark, she could see more clearly the delicate arms, the twig-thin fingers, the pearly membrane of the wings. They danced at the edge of the forest, arms beckoning.

'Tempting to get a closer look,' murmured Trompe. 'If we hadn't been warned off.'

The young woman who had warned them stood in the window, watching as they were watching.

'What are they?' Lutha asked.

The girl replied softly. 'Kachis. Sim'midi-as-yah.'

'Them, the beautiful people,' Lutha translated in a whisper as the girl turned abruptly and went back into the building. 'Which doesn't tell us much.'

'Which tells us a good deal,' said Trompe soberly. 'Her voice didn't betray it, but her feelings did. She's ... awestruck. And ... hopeful. And ... afraid.'

'Frightened?' Lutha asked. 'Surely not.'

'I'm a Fastigat, lady. Remember?'

Lutha regarded the slowly circling forms, pale against the shadows of the forest. Their eyes were large, seeming almost to glow, though it was more likely they simply reflected ambient light as did the eyes of many nocturnal creatures. The forms were almost human, the faces those of smiling children, though they all seemed to be male, if the long, semi-erect organs paralleled earthian forms. They called and beckoned, their delicate feet prancing upon the grasses. Ridiculous to be afraid of these, Lutha thought.

'Perhaps she was afraid of something else.'

Trompe shook his head. No, the girl had not been frightened of anything else. Whatever that strange mix of feelings meant, it had been occasioned by these, these beautiful people.

'Well then,' said Lutha, intensely matter-of-fact. 'She is awestruck because they are taboo. That is why she told us to stay upon the porch, behind the rail. To prevent our contravening some local custom.'

Trompe nodded soberly. 'If she prevents our contravening something, it's something more than mere custom.'

Chur Durwen of Collis, who had without the least concern dipped deep into the King of Kamir's coin to pay for a hundred-year sanctuary leasehold on Dinadh, now considered whether he might not have been cheated on the deal. After three days' travel, he seemed no closer to his goal than he had been in Tasimi-na-Dinadh. Now they were stopped at yet another hostel, and Chur Durwen carried his belongings into the place in sullen silence.

'How much longer?' he demanded of the guide when he returned to the vehicle for another load.

The guide shrugged. 'It depends how much sun on the car. It depends how fast we go. It depends whether all the bridges are passable.'

Chur Durwen turned to Mitigan and made an angry face, hiding it from their guide. 'They ought to homo-norm this world!'

'Have you noticed that the herds are almost the only animals on Dinadh? I'd swear this place has already been homo-normed, despite the denials of every Dinadhi I've asked. What hasn't been done will no doubt be done, in time.'

'In time! Everything's in time! Forever time!'

'There, there,' soothed the man from Asenagi as he removed his belongings from the vehicle. 'We'll get there when we get there, colleague.'

The other snorted. 'When we get there, we won't be any closer to where we want to be than we are now!'

'Patience! Eventually, we'll learn where Bernesohn Famber had his leasehold, which could be where Leelson Famber is or was, if the Haughneeps haven't killed him elsewhere already. That place will probably be where Famber's child or children are.'

'We should have picked up some rememberer and shaken the information out of him.'

Mitigan shook his head with an amused smile. 'How would we know which one to pick up, which one had the "files" we're interested in? Ah? They don't all remember everything, obviously.'

'Surely the ones who remember were there in the port, where we arrived. I mean, Famber had to come through there, just as we did.'

'I have no idea. We're not sure Leelson ever came here! Our informant at Alliance Prime said Leelson's family was coming here, but we're not sure when. We're sure Bernesohn Famber came, but that was a hundred years ago. One pleasant thing about this rememberer system of theirs is that it is self-limiting. Old stuff gets weeded out as rememberers die.'

'If Leelson Famber or his son came here, it was recently. He wouldn't be weeded out! If he's here, these people would know where!'

'Right. So we pick one at random and ask him? Without being discovered? Without any suspicion attaching to us? And with one carefully guarded port the only way off Dinadh?'

'Not a good idea,' admitted Chur Durwen.

'Not unless we want our exit slammed in our face. No, if we want to ask a rememberer, we'll have to go to their central place, their capital or holy city, where their so-called index men dwell. Of course, we have no idea where that is. Assuming we can find out, assuming we can get there, then we'll need to abduct one of the index men, hoping he's the right one, one who can lead us to the rememberer we need. He might only lead us to a local subindexer. It might take as many as four or five steps to get us where we want to be.'

Chur Durwen grimaced.

The other said, 'I think it's simpler just to do as we planned. Go where they send us, keep our ears and eyes alert, ask questions. When we've got a clue, we'll leave. These canyons will be easy to get lost in. We know how to live off the country. Nobody's going to find us unless we want them to. Eventually, we'll find who we're after. King Lostre set no time limit. We're being paid for our time as well as for the job, so we're in no hurry. It's always safest to take one's own sweet time.'

Their guide went stumping off toward the hostel, shouting something unintelligible.

'As the zossit flies, we'd have arrived two days ago,' muttered Chur Durwen.

'As the zossit flies on this planet, we wouldn't. It has no zossits. It has no large flying creatures at all, only tiny ones.' Mitigan picked up his pack and settled it on one shoulder.

From inside the hostelry came the clangor of a gong, a disruptive sound, quickly smothered, like a cough at a concert.

'Food,' Mitigan said, turning toward the gray building.

From the forest behind them came a voice, an interrogative note, a questing, almost human cry.

Their driver appeared beside the door.

'Come in,' he called. 'Now.'

'Such a hurry,' Chur Durwen muttered to himself. 'The usual nonsense. Hurry up and wait.'

Mitigan had not moved. He stood staring into the trees. 'I heard something ... wings. Didn't I just say there were no large birds?'

'Now!' insisted the guide peremptorily.

The man from Asenagi turned and trudged after his colleague, hearing behind him the flutter of wings coming purposefully through the trees.

Perdur Alas was a celestial anomaly, a planet on which life had stuck at the level of fish, bird, and shrub without any obvious cause for the lack of further diversification. Currently the planet held a limited variety of sea and land plants, enormous schools of a few varieties of fish, and sizable flocks of even fewer scaled bird forms that seemed to have evolved directly from air-breathing flying fish without intermediate land-dwelling stages. Biologically speaking, Perdur Alas was extremely simple. So far as homo-norming went, simplicity made the job easier, which explained the small size of the preliminary team recently evacuated from the planet.

When the pseudo-team of ex-shadows arrived, they were set down beside a new encampment, raw as a wound, just beginning to scab over with ferny and brushy growths. A thousand or so paces to the west a pallid sea swooshed gently onto a rocky shelf at the base of the cliffs. A little north of west the cliffs sagged onto a scanty crescent of graveled beach, the only beach a day's journey in either direction. Farther north, ranks of east-west ridges cut the sky, the nearest jagged, the more distant sparsely freckled with prototrees. Bracken-like and furze-like growths covered everything not covered by blue or purple mosses, making a moorland that stretched unbroken to the eastern and southern horizons.

When the preliminary work was done, the birds and plants would be gone. The planet would have trees suitable for lumber and grasses suitable for pasture. It would have grains, edible root, leaf, and fruit crops, plus at least one draft and one dairy animal and perhaps – if the colonists were not Firsters – one or two animals from the category 'small-furry-dociles' or pets. There was no need for insects or birds in Class-C homo-norm. All plants were designed to be wind-pollinated, and Perdur Alas was windy enough.

The arriving team knew this without needing to consider the implications, though bio-assay tech Snark surprised herself shortly after landing by thinking that a million things could be added to Perdur Alas before it had the same complexity as most untouched Class-A planets. Her next thought was one of recognition. This planet, in all its simplicity, was entirely familiar to her.

'Quarters this way,' announced team leader Kane, hoisting an equipment case onto his shoulder and stumping off toward the team housing at one side of the encampment.

The pseudo-team, though differing from the original team in physical appearance, was identical as to numbers, sex, and functions. Now most of them straggled after Kane without comment. Each of them had a role to play. Kane's was to keep everyone else working. Snark's was to compare current organisms with those included in Class-C category, using an automatic inventory device, to determine which species should be adapted or eliminated and what others should be introduced to make the world suitable for man. A few members of the team had been conditioned as tank-farm workers, assigned to grow and process food. Others were assigned as housekeeping staff, while others yet would provide maintenance duties and staff communications.

Each of them would occupy the same work space and sleep space as his or her counterpart on the former team. Each of them knew the routine for each day's labors. They knew what the departed team had known about the work already done. In addition, they knew, and had had it proved to them on the way out, that they could not injure one another. As in Shadowland, if one formed any intention toward violence, one found oneself curled into the fetal position, thumb in mouth, just as formerly. They knew who they were. They also remembered what they had been, though that matter did not seem relevant and was often forgotten for quite lengthy periods. Each of them had almost invisible scars behind which implanted devices made records of everything seen, heard, smelled, tasted, felt. The devices did not intrude upon thought. Their thoughts, though rare, were their own.

As the team moved off toward the camp the pilot and engineer of the vessel stood at the foot of the loading ramp watching, not noticing Snark, who had stopped to pick up a replacement filter for the bio-assay machine and now stood just inside the open cargo bay.

'Funny bunch,' the pilot said. 'You ever notice their eyes?'

'How could you help but notice? You listen to their mouths going on, this that, this that, all sounding pretty good, then you look at the eyes and see these wild animals glaring at you.'

'Crazy people? With implants, maybe?'

'I dunno. One thing sure. They're out here on the edge of nowhere and the Ularians are coming.'

'Hush,' said the engineer. 'We were told—'

'We were told not to talk. I'm not talking. Hell, how far is it back to where anybody can hear me!'

'I hear you,' said the other, stiffly. 'And both of us could get asked what we saw, what we heard. From anybody.'

Snark read the look on the engineer's face to mean, 'And if they ask me, I'll tell them you were shooting off your mouth!'

'Yeah, well,' said the pilot in sudden discomfort. 'We'd best get started back. It feels pretty exposed here. Like somebody might be watching us.'

Snark slipped out of the cargo bay as they went up the ramp, then stood below, watching them. She was remembering another ship, like this ship. Herself going up a ramp just like this one.

Before the lock closed, the pilot risked one more look at the humans moving among the graceless buildings below and mumbled a final comment. To shadows, reading lips was nothing at all, and Snark read the words clearly.

'Bait! That's what they are. Bait.'

Lutha and Trompe discovered their vehicle could not actually 'arrive' at the hive of Cochim-Mahn. It could be driven to a point roughly opposite and above our hive, where the road ended at the edge of the cliffs. A flat triangular chunk of metal hung from the roof beam of the vacant guest house, and before doing anything else, Trompe struck it several times. They both waited as the resultant resonance trembled above the depths, seeming to hang interminably before fading into the daysounds of wind and creature.

We heard it, of course, though songfather hadn't waited for it. He knew when they were coming. I hadn't waited for it either. Despite what had happened to me, it was still my duty to clean the quarters of Bernesohn Famber, which I had done, along with airing blankets and sleeping pads for those who were expected.

After a brief wait, Lutha shrugged at the lack of response and carried Leely into the guest house. It had two cramped rooms, a sanitary arrangement added on the back, and a food dispenser wedged into a corner, all very dim behind tightly closed shutters. She stretched and bent, working out the kinks, then lay down on the padded bench, Leely beside her, and fell into a doze. She might have opened the shutters in order to admire the carved and crenellated canyon, the effect of shade and sun as the occasional clouds came sailing over, but both Lutha and Trompe, so she told me later, were sick unto death of canyons.

'I think someone's coming,' Trompe said after a considerable silence. He lay as he had thrown himself down, in a posture of exaggerated exhaustion, and did not remove his forearm from his eyes as he spoke.

'How do you know?' asked Lutha.

'Hmm.' It was a doubtful sound, as though he didn't know himself how he knew. 'I'm picking up put-upon feelings. Someone out there is feeling overworked and irascible. Angry or aggrieved about something, too. Not us. Or, not us specifically.'

'Ah.' She rose and went out back to consult the sanitary system, returning brushed and furbished. 'Still not arrived? When will he get here?'

'Now he's standing among the trees. Politeness, I think. Waiting until we notice him.'

'If you weren't a Fastigat, that might take some time.'

'I think his next step may be some throat clearing or modest coughs, growing louder with time.'

Indeed, as she opened the door, the sound she heard was an apologetic cough that seemed to ask, 'Was I wanted?'

'I am Lutha Tallstaff,' she said across the clearing. 'Mother of Leely Famber, direct-lineage son of Bernesohn Famber. With me is my assistant, Trompe.'

'And your son?' asked my father, Chahdzi, who stood beneath the trees.

The upper part of his face was painted blue, the line running horizontally just below his eyes and across the bridge of his nose. Lutha tried to recall anything she might have read about that. Nothing. A local custom, she thought, which was accurate. Persons undertaking dangerous tasks paint their eyes yellow, asking others to pray for them. Persons who must deal with outsiders paint their faces half-blue, so we will watch and listen carefully, in case they show signs of deviance. And so on.

'Leely is in here, asleep,' she said.

My father stepped from the shade of the trees and came forward. 'I am Chahdzi, son of the songfather of Cochim-Mahn. It is my assigned task to serve you as guide to the leasehold of Bernesohn Famber.' Without invitation, he came across the shallow porch and into the room, where he took a long look at Leely, to make sure he was a real, living person. 'We have to walk and climb a long way,' he said in explanation. 'The boy will be heavy to carry.'

'He can walk,' said Lutha. 'He can run and climb.' Like a little goat. 'Most of the way, at least.'

'Partway. But of such complexity, interesting patterns are made,' he said in the falsely cheerful tone one adopts for reassuring children.

'I suppose it does,' she said doubtfully. Certainly this whole business was complex enough. 'When do we go?'

'Since you were expected today, I left Cochim-Mahn this morning. It took me all of today to get here to meet you, and now it is late. Soon Lady Day departs with all her blessings and the time of whispering comes. When the Lady comes again, we will go.'

'Shortly after dawn tomorrow then,' commented Trompe.

The man shivered, almost undetectably, and nodded. 'I will sleep in here, or perhaps in your vehicle.'

'Because,' said Lutha, moved by an obscure impulse, 'because it is better not to be out in the dark?'

Again that shiver, almost unnoticeable. 'Because of the pattern, matron,' he said in a dignified voice. 'Which alternates dark and light, activity and quiet, whisper and shout, sleep and waking ...'

'Do I offend in asking about the night?' she asked. 'I am curious about ... the things that go about in the dark.'

'Bernesohn Famber was also curious, or so I am told by the rememberers. Outlanders are often curious about Dinadh and the Dinadhi. Why do we paint our faces and sometimes our bodies? Why do we sing all the time? Why do we do this, or that? We tell you all the same things. All is part of the pattern; the light and the dark.' He gestured vaguely. 'If one wishes to learn details, one must consult a songfather who is schooled in such things. I am a simple person, a mere yahsdi' imicha dimicha'a.'

She translated mentally. One-who-is-assigned-to-do-what-needs-doing. A man of all work, perhaps. A handyman. She started to ask him how far they would have to go on the morrow, the words drying in her mouth as she saw his face, suddenly alert, listening.

She cocked her head. There was a sound, distant, but not faint. A song, rising from the canyon.

'Forgive me,' said Chahdzi. 'I will return shortly.'

He left the room and went out into the open, where he threw his arms open to the sky and began a breathy song, evidently addressed to thin air.

'What's he doing?' asked Trompe.

'You're the empath,' she said.

'All I can pick up is a feeling of concern, a desire which he is repressing.'

She listened, translated, nodded. 'He's singing to Weaving Woman, begging her to keep the patterns clear and straight.'

Afar, the song faded into silence, only the echoes remaining for a moment more. Chahdzi stood with bowed head. In a few moments he turned and came back to them.

'How far do we have to go then, tomorrow?' Lutha asked.

He shook his head, as though reminding himself of where he was. 'A day. A long day spent in going quickly. Which is why I look at the boy, to see how fast we can go. Climbing down the walls is not easy.'

'Perhaps we won't get there in one day,' she said casually.

'One must,' he said. Impersonal imperative. One must, that's all.

'Dangerous to be out after dark, is it?' Trompe's head was cocked, picking up all the little signals.

Chahdzi smiled, ducking his head slightly. 'Danger has a place in the pattern, surely. And pain. Slidhza b'dasya a yana chas-as imsli t'sisri.'

Again Lutha translated to herself, fumbling with the word order. *A wise person doesn't use his own shuttle to weave sorrow.* Or perhaps, a wise shuttle won't weave grief.

'I do not understand,' she said.

He shrugged again, a habitual gesture. 'It is foolish to create dark patterns for ourselves, matron. Weaving Woman will include enough darkness, whether we wish or no. Let us hope for a bright pattern tomorrow, if we are her beloved children.' He pointed to the child. 'That one is. Everyone says so.'

'Now, why is that?' Trompe asked, amazed.

'He knows.' Chahdzi smiled. 'Everyone says he knows.'

'Knows what?' asked Lutha, wonderingly. 'Knows what, Chahdzi?'

'Knows,' he said softly. 'What is. Patterns. What comes next.'

Though his words were not unlike other comments the Dinadhi had made about Leely, they were no more explanatory. The boy himself showed no signs of knowing what needed doing, unless sleeping was it.

'Will you eat with us?' asked Lutha.

'I accept your generous offer of food,' he said, looking away from her in obvious discomfort.

His tone made her realize that he would have gone hungry had she not offered, and also that one did not say 'eat with us' on Dinadh. Damn! She hadn't given sufficient thought to some of the stuff she'd found in the culture chips!

'Since I do not know your taste,' she said carefully, 'will you do us the courtesy of choosing for yourself?'

He went happily to the food unit, where he stood for a long time in contemplation of the listed menu, mumbling to himself.

'I like very much the taste of cheese,' he said, pointing at a certain item and using their own word, *cheese*, which evidently did not exist in his own language. 'But I cannot eat of it unless ...'

She came to his assistance, reading labels. 'It's all right. Everything in here is dosed with the necessary enzymes. Trompe and I have commented that you have no dairy beasts on Dinadh.'

'It is said we brought milk creatures from our former world,' he murmured. 'But here, Weaving Woman could not permit them. Here our pattern changed.'

'Human-owned flocks of grazers and browsers have ended a good many patterns,' grunted Trompe. 'Once man killed off the natural predators and let them multiply.'

'So it is said,' agreed Chahdzi, glancing at Lutha from the corner of his eyes as she manipulated the food-service unit. Something light for herself and for Trompe. She would feed Leely when he wakened. As for Chahdzi, who was obviously apprehensive that they might watch while he ate, she would make the matter simple.

She handed him the warmed packet of cheese and cereal-food, saying, 'Perhaps you would enjoy your meal on the porch?'

'Indeed.' He bowed gravely and took it away with him, leaving Trompe and Lutha to eat their own selections in silent company. Chahdzi might be out of sight, but he was not out of earshot, so Lutha did not mention her annoyance at the thought of a long climb on the morrow and Trompe did not remark upon the feelings he picked up from Chahdzi: awe, hope, terror, anger. The same feelings he'd detected in the serving girl at the hostel. The same strange combination.

As they ate, Lutha dug out a handful of culture chips and scanned the indices, muttering to herself.

'Nothing there on the subject?' Trompe asked, sotto voce, elaborately nonspecific concerning which subject.

'Not a ... nothing,' she replied. 'You'd think—'

'The language chips I gave you were prepared by the people at Tasimi-na-Dinadh,' he murmured thoughtfully. 'All properly indexed for use by possible leaseholders and no doubt somewhat edited ...'

'A sales pitch, in other words,' she muttered.

He nodded. 'They were the most recent chips the Procurator had, though he also gave me some old ones made by independent researchers. I didn't pass them on to you because they looked like heavy going. They're really old, and they aren't indexed at all.'

'Please,' she said. 'Are they in your pack?'

'Finish your food,' he said gently. 'I'll get them in a minute.'

After Chahdzi had thanked them again for food and sequestered himself in their vehicle, after Leely had had his supper and fallen asleep once more, Trompe dug out the chips he had promised: old ones, nicked at the corners, their labels faded.

'You say the Procurator gave you these?' she asked doubtfully.

'Well, he gave me the Dinadh file, and they were in it. He did remark that the newer chips were more up-to-date.'

'They're so up, all usefulness has been edited out of them,' she snorted. 'They're completely superficial. All the taboos are avoided, so we can't tell what we should or shouldn't say, may or may not do! For example, we've seen the beautiful people are ubiquitous, but the chips don't even mention them. These are the ones I should have studied.'

'Maybe,' he said soberly. 'But they seemed very ponderous to me.'

Peevishly, she disregarded this as irrelevant. Fastigats weren't researchers. They didn't spend their time making laborious correlations from ancient records; they didn't sift history for nuances. They drew their conclusions from the here and the now, from whatever or whoever was feeling and emoting in the vicinity. Well, nonetheless.

She accessed one of the chips at random and began plowing through it, realizing after some little time that Trompe had been right. It was heavy going. This researcher had come to Dinadh as to virgin territory and had weeded nothing out. He or she had included everything uncut, every branch and twig and tangled root. Who knew what was alive and important, what had died long ago or had compacted into impenetrable peat?

She yawned, tried to focus, forced herself to concentrate, and finally gave up in disgust, no longer annoyed at Trompe. He was right. This was ponderous indeed. She would seek nuances later perhaps, but not tonight. Leely and Trompe had the better idea. One should sleep when one could!

4

The first night on Perdur Alas, Snark bedded down in the dormitory with the other shadows, waking frequently, listening for some unusual sound, but hearing only breathing, snores, restless movements, and sighs. She herself slept little. The chip within her recorded her wakefulness. Someday, somewhere, someone might review these feelings, experience her perceptions. Everything the chip detected was beamed to a tiny satellite hidden beside a moonlet, and from there was relayed to the nearest occupied planet – Dinadh, probably, where the hated Lutha Tallstaff had gone – and from there to somewhere else and somewhere else again, all the way back to Alliance Prime and the damned Procurator. Perhaps even now someone on Dinadh was monitoring what had been done today on Perdur Alas and wondering why this particular shadow was awake.

Snark tried to care and could not. They had no right, she told herself, quite correctly. She knew it and they knew it: they had no right. The words were familiar, but the rage they usually evoked would not come. Those sent to Perdur Alas had been conditioned against rage, against rebellion.

No one had thought to condition any of them against childhood fantasies. On the third night, Snark lay down among the others as before, but when they slept, she rose and went out into the night. All day she had been smelling the moor. The smell had filled her to the exclusion of other perceptions, had preoccupied her with feelings long dreamed and totally familiar. Perhaps these woody and ferny growths had come from the same place as the ones she had smelled as a child. Perhaps this moor had been designed to be like one she had seen long ago, her dream moor, complete with tea-brown pools and rustling bracken. Perhaps that world and this one had shared a common designer or a common heritage.

Even as she said to herself, *perhaps, perhaps*, she knew there was no happenstance involved. Similarity didn't matter. Only this place mattered, its odors that smelled like, its growths that looked like, its moor that felt like the moor she had dreamed. This could be the actual refuge she had found as a child – or dreamed she had found. If one went west across this stretch of rolling ground, one would come to cliffs above the sea. They would be the same cliffs, the same sea. During the workaday world of daylight there had been no opportunity to explore. Now in a dark relieved only by the pearly glimmer of tiny moonlets, shining through the night like so many lopsided paper lanterns, she would find the old cliff, the old sea, the old place she knew so well.

Every step of the way could have been dictated from memory! Surely she had seen a pool of this shape before! Surely she had caught her foot on just such a root and been sent sprawling in just this way, with this particular herb crushed beneath her cheek to surround her with identical pungency. Surely the sound of the sea had come at just this point and no other, the swelling and sighing of the surf as it rolled small stones on the rocky shelf below. Surely all of this was the same, her own childhood place, wherever and whenever it had been, come here again.

She wasn't even surprised. However astonishing similar things might be, identical things were not. One could be astonished at the close resemblance of brothers but not at that of identical twins. So she couldn't be astonished at this moor, for it was not merely like. It *was* the one she had known, and that was all there was to it. The two, though they seemed separate in time and space, were the same place.

So musing, believing herself half dreaming, she came to the edge of the cliff at last, feeling a familiar panic, a fleeting urge to jump. Why? Why the panic? Why ... because there was something following her. Something seeking her. Now? Or then?

She puzzled over this as she turned left along the rimrock. This was the way she had always turned. The cliff was as she remembered, and the soughing of the sea. She wandered slowly along the precipice, around this stone and that twiggy growth, searching, believing she had missed it, as she had always believed –

Only to come upon it suddenly: the outcropping of stone, the branch extending into space, the bare, pale, polished place upon the wood where her hands, someone's hands, had rubbed the bark away to make a smoothness. Without thinking, without decision, she leapt out, hands extended to grasp, the springiness of the wood coming as a shock to the muscles of her arms as she bounced pendant beneath it like a toy jerking upon a string. No hole, she told herself in sudden panic. No hole in the cliff. Nowhere to go from here.

The fear was only momentary. The entry was there, a darker crevice among the striations of the cliff face. And a protruding stone where she needed to put her foot. And a ropy rootlet hanging down ...

She didn't really remember this part. In her dream, she felt the details of the cave rather than smelled or heard or saw them. This cave felt sandier; it had no bracken bed. It felt smaller, too, but then, it would have seemed larger to the child she had been when she had dreamed it first. The trickle of water was there at the back, making a modest puddle on its hollowed stone, seeping away down a mossy crack. She remembered caches of food. There were none in this cave. She remembered warm animal skins, and they, too, were missing. She could bring food. She could bring blankets and armfuls of cut bracken to cushion her rest. From this time forward, she would go to bed with the others, but when they slept, she would sneak away to spend the dark hours here, in this refuge above the sea.

Now she lay down on the sandy floor, her body taking the curved form so often imposed upon it, knees up, thumb in mouth, hip seeking a familiar hollow. The stones beside the entry were piled as she had left them in dream. She reached with one hand to stack them, the larger ones on the bottom, the smaller above.

Moving the stones disclosed a niche. In the niche was a painted jar with a lid. Snark's eyes drifted across it, hardly seeing it. Though she hadn't remembered the jar before, hadn't recalled its presence or patterns, she did so now. The jar had always been there, its egglike shape of white clay covered with dark swerving lines, wings, and faces. She even knew the names of those portrayed. Father Endless and Mother Darkness. Mother had put the jar there. Someone . . . someone named Mother had put the jar there. And inside were the bones of . . .

Whose bones? Why there?

She fell asleep before she could answer the question.

Just before dawn she had a momentary panic when she prepared to leave the cave and realized she didn't know how. She remembered coming here, yes, time after time, escaping here, yes, finding refuge here, cuddling down warmly, nose to the gap in the piled rocks, smelling the sea wind, hearing the birds when they woke before dawn to plunge out in their screaming spirals above the sea. She could remember eating here, jaws moving in slow mastication while the birds screamed and dived. She could remember sucking up the slow seep of water as it accumulated on the hollowed stone. She even remembered squatting on the minuscule ledge, skinny butt jutting over the gulf as she peed down the face of the cliff, her own tiny stream joining the vast ocean below, but she had no memory at all of ever leaving this place.

So, how did she get out? The branch that had dropped her down had sprung back to its position above, out of reach. The cliff overhung the ledge. Above was invisible, unreachable. She sat, fighting panic, thinking it out. She needed something to draw the branch down. Once she had hold of the branch, she could pull herself up. So, she would use her belt, with a stone tied to the end to give it weight.

She tried this, but her belt was too thick, too inflexible. She took off her shirt and tore strips from it, braiding them together for strength, succeeding at last in drawing the branch down, close, where she could reach it. As she bounced and juddered, working her way up to the rim of the stone, she resolved next time to bring a strong line with a weight affixed so she would have the proper tool to get out. She must have had such a tool before. She could not imagine why she had forgotten it until now. Unless perhaps, before, someone else had drawn the branch down for her. Unless, before, she had been only a child.

She returned to the dormitory complex just in time to get into bed before the others woke. Perhaps the watchers on Dinadh knew she had been away, but none of the Shadowland people did. Certainly Snark did not tell them.

The shadows had been given the knowledge they needed to act as their roles required, and for some of them this had been the equivalent of an advanced education in biotechnology. Though the information had been imposed, they could use it, fumblingly at first and with more assurance as time went by. They had not been given a course in morals and ethics. No one had thought to prevent their stealing. What was there to steal on Perdur Alas?

Snark stole food and blankets to start with. Over the next dozen nights she equipped her refuge. She stole food enough for a lengthy stay. She made her bracken bed, a blanketful cut each night on her way to the cliff, a new blanket carried there each night until the entire floor of the cave was cushioned and comfortable. Though she remembered animal skins from the time before, the blankets were as warm and they smelled better. She brought two lengths of line with weights at one end, keeping one in her pocket and one in the niche next to the opening – just in case she lost the one she was carrying.

She did nothing that significantly changed the original dream until she had fulfilled it meticulously. Only then did she add other supplies, things the adult Snark thought might be useful: night glasses for spying, an emergency beacon, a box of vegetable and fruit seeds from the agricultural lab. Suppose, she told herself, suppose I get left here all by myself! Suppose the Ularians get all the others, but I'm hiding and they can't find me. Suppose they don't get me! I'd need the beacon so humans could come rescue me. I'd need to grow food. I'd need to stay alive!

The words, the very tone was familiar. Someone had said the same to her once, long ago. Fleetingly she realized the idea of rescue was ridiculous. Why would they come to rescue a totally dispensable shadow? A shadow who had been put here as bait in the first place? Does the worm on the hook expect to be rescued simply because the fish have eaten all the other worms?

Perhaps, she told herself. Perhaps, if the worm had information about the fish. Perhaps then. Suppose she *saw* the fish, the Ularians. Then there'd be reason to pick her up. The monitor would sense what she sensed, but he couldn't read her mind. The monitor might think she'd found out something important! Whether she did or not, she could say she had. If she said it out loud, the monitor would hear what she said.

So, she would try to see them, if they came, and whether she did or not, she would say loudly that she had found out something. Dangerous, that. How did one find anything out except through one's senses. If she merely deduced, it would have to be from evidence. From things seen and heard. Could one pretend to see? Pretend to hear?

Such questions preoccupied her. Rarely she thought about men. Susso had come with the other shadows. Maybe she ought to tell Susso about her cave. Invite him to come along.

The idea was transient, the motivation unconvincing. Sex was pleasurable, sure, but survival was sweeter still. Susso wouldn't keep his mouth shut. Then the others would get involved. They'd interfere. They'd stop Snark leaving. Stop her coming here. Better not say anything to Susso. Who needed men anyhow?

'Inventory's almost done,' said Kane, when they had been on the planet thirty or forty days. 'Tomorrow we'll start the ag-study.'

'I'm missing supplies in ag-lab,' one of the women said plaintively. 'One whole carton of vegetable seeds is missing.'

'They probably miscounted,' said Kane carelessly. 'They probably did.'

They were the predecessors, the other team, the real team, acknowledged but unconsidered. They had been here. They had gone. Now *we* were here. No one ever said, 'When we're finished and gone.' No one ever said, 'When the job's done.' They had been conditioned against such expectations. The job was interminable. The task was lifelong. And though lifelong might be short indeed, they were conditioned against anxiety.

'You got enough seeds left to do the job?' Kane asked. 'That's all that matters.'

She had enough for the job. No one paid any attention to her earlier comment. They went to their daily tasks with perfect gravity and understanding, though it was all accomplished in dreamlike slow motion. Even eating was slow. Every movement, every task was set for them. Go from 1 to 2; 2 leads to 3; 3 leads to 4. Nothing was done because they wanted to or thought of it themselves. They didn't worry; they didn't fight. They scarcely spoke. Sometimes two of them would couple in the night with spurious urgency, but even such brief convulsions were muted and soon forgotten.

Very occasionally Snark remembered the simul booth back in Shadowland, but she couldn't bring herself to want it much. She sometimes remembered raging, remembered shouting, remembered fighting – or trying to. It was all another dream, not unlike this dream of being on Perdur Alas. Each day took care of itself. And now that Snark had found her own place, which was real and remote from dreaming, each night took care of itself as well.

Deprived of his shadows, the Procurator had not yet grown accustomed to pouring his own tea. Often more liquid slopped onto the table than stayed in the cup, on this occasion giving him reason to swear gustily as an underling entered, one Mikeraw.

'Sorry, sir,' the underling murmured.

'You didn't do it,' grouched the Procurator. 'I did. I am clumsy and incapable! We had grown too dependent upon shadows, Mikeraw. Far too dependent!'

Mikeraw, who was lowly in rank and non-Fastigat, had never been served by shadows. He contented himself with a murmured agreement as he helped the Procurator mop both himself and the tabletop.

This accomplished, Mikeraw bowed, murmuring, 'I thought you should see this, sir. It seems to impinge—'

'What? What is it?' He reached for the proffered document.

'An agent upon Dinadh, sir. Reporting rumor, sir.'

'An Alliance agent?'

Mikeraw flushed slightly. 'As a matter of fact, no, sir. We have an agent there, but he doesn't report much. This is from a Gadravian agent.'

'The Gadravians take a lot on themselves!'

'They insist they are loyal members of the Alliance and are merely providing us with appropriate redundancy in intelligence matters. As in this case.'

'This case? Case of what, man?'

Mikeraw cleared his throat. 'It is rumored the King of Kamir has sent assassins to Dinadh to eradicate the Famber lineage, sir.'

The Procurator sat down with a thump.

'Famber? Leelson Famber? Why in the name of all that's holy and intractable ... ?' The King of Kamir was a joke, of course. Everyone knew of the King of Kamir. He was proverbial. 'Useless as the King of Kamir.' Said of lackadaisical students and lie-about workmen, as well as of tools that didn't function or equipment that fell apart. For the first time the Procurator considered that the king might rather resent this reputation. Might have resented it enough to have wished to put it behind him.

He gaped unattractively while thinking. Suddenly aware of this, he gave his mouth something to do, asking, 'It was Leelson who found him, wasn't it?'

'Yes, sir. When the king disappeared, the government of Kamir retained

Fastiga to investigate, and Fastiga assigned Leelson Famber.'

'Excrement,' muttered the Procurator. 'Oh, excrement.'

'I thought, inasmuch ...'

'Quite right. Quite right. Good man. Well, it puts Lutha Tallstaff in the broth, doesn't it? And any Fastigat with her. On behalf of the boy, of course. The assassins might not bother him, and maybe not her, but they will the boy. Unless Trompe Paggas gets in the way!'

'I've consulted the relevant documents, sir, that is, the laws of Kamir as they might apply in this situation. I came up with the thought that we might approach the king himself to obtain a royal writ.'

'Calling the assassins off, you mean?'

'Yes, sir.'

'And then what?'

'Send the writ to Dinadh ...' His voice trailed off, and he shifted from foot to foot, uncomfortably.

'Assuming one could get such a writ, who would deliver it on Dinadh, and to whom?' asked the Procurator.

The underling shrugged. He didn't know.

The Procurator sighed. 'Fastiga,' he murmured. 'Whoever goes to Kamir can't be from Fastiga.'

'Why not from Fastiga, sir?'

'The bureaucrats would suspect a Fastigat. They do, you know.'

'Perhaps we could send another assassin, sir?'

'You say?'

'Send a corsair to catch a corsair, isn't that the saying?'

'Not in my language, it isn't.'

'In mine, sir.'

'And where are you from?'

'Far Barbary, sir.'

'Well, that explains it. All pirates there, aren't they?'

'Not much anymore, sir. Once were, of course. My own great-grand-father, in fact.'

'And how did you end up here?'

The man stared at his boots, reddening.

The Procurator accurately read his embarrassment.

'Government is merely another kind of piracy, is that it?' The Procurator guffawed, tears welling in his eyes. 'I take no offense. It's true, my boy. Politicians are pirates, of a sort!'

'I wasn't going to say so, sir. Though my father does.'

'And your grandfather, too, no doubt. Well. You could be right. Send a corsair to fetch a corsair, an assassin to fetch an assassin. In which case, who's our assassin?'

'We'll need to ask the King of Kamir, sir. He seems to have an inexhaustible supply.'

It was, as a matter of fact, Councilwoman Poracious Luv who went to Kamir on behalf of the Alliance. She demanded an audience with the king and received it without delay. Jiacare Lostre, King of Kamir, was so enervated by his day-to-day life, he didn't even make her wait. He would have consented to meet with an offal-eater from Hapsobog to break the tedium, and he found little fault with this wallowing bulk, this monstrous bosom heaving at him, even though she insisted on boring him with a brief history of the Ularian crisis, which he cared nothing about.

His kingly prerogative allowed him to tell her so, yawning.

'I don't think Your Majesty understands,' she said, growing quite pink about the jowls as she held out a pleading arm from which the quivering flesh hung in braceleted rolls.

'My Majesty does understand quite well,' he said. 'I just don't give a damn if we're condemned a wee bit sooner than our present course will equally condemn us.'

She chewed her lower lip, wondering why in heaven's name the Procurator had picked her for this mission.

'There are those who feel differently,' she murmured.

'Not I,' he said. 'Not while I'm pinioned here!'

'Are you?' she asked, suddenly interested despite herself. 'By what?'

Her obvious interest caught him by surprise, and he became expansive. 'Tradition, madam. And the force of law. I am coerced in many divers ways, by suasion horrible to contemplate, by threats against the comforts of my kin, of whom, despite my boredom, I am fond. My mother's life is hostage 'gainst my own, and so my sister's – who, in happier times, was very dear to me.'

'You did have happier times, then?'

He snorted. 'I had four brothers older than myself, all four of whom aspired to mount this seat. Efficiently they entered on the task of murdering each other, leaving me to sit upon a throne I much despised.'

'So much so you ran away from it.'

He flushed. 'I planned escape, achieved it! Ah, but then I was dragged back to duty as bad boys are driven to their books by masters' canes. Like them, I swot and grimace and complain. ...'

She gnawed at the inside of her cheek, a habit that gave her the look of some ponderous ruminant.

'Would you be more sympathetic if I could arrange for your ... release?'

The king actually smiled. 'Oh, madam, how my sympathy would wax, like moons grown fat on light. Away from here, my lips, most eloquent, would speak your cause.'

'My cause, as you put it, is simply to stop your assassins, Majesty. My ultimate cause may be something else again, but for the nonce, it's only that. The Famber lineage must not be worried by threats of assassination, not, at least, until we've found what we need concerning Bernesohn Famber.'

The king regarded his fingernails with gravity. 'From all that lengthy tale you bored me with, it seems rather too late to look for him.'

'For Bernesohn, yes. For whatever information he had, possibly not. We pray not.'

'How would you think to get me out of this?' He gestured widely, including his kingdom, the planet, all the clutter and cumber of the monarchy of a dying world.

Poracious Luv shook her head. 'I don't know yet. I'll have to think on it, perhaps seek some advice. We have excellent counselors. Sometimes they can be quite Machiavellian. Assuming we can think of something that will work, you'll give me the writ?'

'Oh, Madam Luv, I'd carry it myself.'

She brightened with sudden inspiration. 'Would you, now? Then, sir, that may be the answer you are seeking! Consider. It is likely the assassins will be turned aside only by you, true? It may be no one can save our desperate inquiry except yourself? It may be, therefore, that the saving of humanity is in your hands? Including the lives of all those upon Kamir? All the mamas and sisters and children of your ministers, for example?'

He stared at her from beneath swollen lids, startled once again from his ennui. 'That would be true if ministers had kin. Reason declares that such men come from eggs abandoned by the deadly cockatrice, that they hatch forth among the desert sands, the word *tradition* peeping from their beaks e'en as they crack their shells. Myth has it that they strike their prey to stone, and that is true. This world will be but stone when they are through.'

She regarded him quizzically. 'Your Majesty exaggerates slightly. When humans use up a world, there are usually some bacteria left, even some hardy plants. In any case, your ministers are not free agents. They are responsible to a larger constituency – to all the people of Kamir who lust for life, who have encumbrances of kindred and friendship. Such people will not willingly accept extinction, no matter how traditional it might be.'

'So much is true. I've heard that even weighty governors are wary of the people they abuse.'

'So! Use your people to gain your freedom! That is, if you're truly resolved not to return to kingship. Our Procurator says the same man who will hail a leader in time of crisis will kill him once the crisis is over.'

'Again, true,' said the king with appreciation. 'For though he'll play at resolution when death hangs upon a hair, once danger's passed, all his anxieties, like vicious fleas, do burrow bloodily. An itchy man is prey to discontent; he'll suage his flea bites with the blood of kings.'

'Surely the common man wouldn't want that!'

'What common men want most is beer and sex, without disturbances.'

'So if it were necessary for *you*, yourself, to leave Kamir in order to save the people from disturbance ...'

'It is unlikely that the counselors would fight to keep me here. When all Kamir is threatened with despair, a king may make a kingly sacrifice!'

'One hopes such sacrifice may be relatively painless,' murmured Big Mama.

'Even pain,' said the king, with no intention of being prophetic, 'even pain is preferable to dying of unrelieved ennui.'

'She has who?' the Procurator asked Poracious Luv's messenger, believing he had misunderstood her.

'Jiacare Lostre, the king himself,' the messenger replied. 'He and Poracious went before his ministers and told them Kamir was in danger. The council pooh-poohed the idea. The king told them that in that case they wouldn't mind if he told the people of Kamir all about the Ularians being just next door in Hermes Sector. Poracious said the Alliance would help him publicize the matter.'

'Somewhat exceeding her authority,' murmured the Procurator.

The messenger muffled an undiplomatic snort. 'As Madam herself said, it got the job done. The ministers knew there'd be widespread panic, possibly insurrection. They've let the king go. He and Madam were to have left for Dinadh the day after I left for Alliance Central.'

'Amazing.'

'Actually, the council of ministers didn't fight as hard as Madam Luv thought they might. She felt they'd really wanted an excuse to get rid of Jiacare. He has a younger brother, Fenubel, who's much easier to get along with. They've already installed him as regent.'

'Interesting,' the Procurator murmured. 'You're rejoining Madam Luv?'

'Yes, sir.'

'Talk to my adjutant outside. Make whatever arrangements are necessary. Things are getting complicated. I think I'd better go with you.'

In the hostel above Cochim-Mahn, Chahdzi woke Trompe very early, before it was quite light.

'It is not good to move before the daysong has been sung,' he told the Fastigat soberly, emphasizing his words with peckish nods, like an anxious hen. 'Still, we must go all in one day, and we must leave now to accomplish that.'

Trompe got Lutha and Leely up, and they made a hurried meal before taking up their packs and moving toward the canyon trail, arriving there just as the sun peeked over the farther canyon wall. They heard the dawn-song as they had heard it before during their journey, a rising smoke of melody, wavering, expanding, until all the world could hear it.

The narrow trail led them on a winding way downward among forest trees, coming out of the trees again and again to make hundred-eighty-degree turns and move into the trees again. At the beginning of the journey, on the outer edge of one curve, they saw far off across the canyon a strange house rising above the rim, barely distinguishable from the natural rock around it. The house was laid with dry stone, without mortar, and had a pitched roof with openings beneath the eaves. It resembled several other such structures Lutha had noted on their way toward Cochim-Mahn. She put glasses to her eyes and watched an elderly woman approaching the building, head down.

'What do you call that building?' Lutha asked, pointing it out.

'A House Without a Name,' said Chahdzi, his tone forbidding further questions.

Lutha, who was looking back at the elderly woman, merely grunted. The woman moved in an unusual way. As though apprehensive. As though fearful. Fearful of what? What was inside?

Trompe, picking up on her perception, followed her gaze back along the road, too late. They had come around a curve and could see the place no longer.

Chahdzi spoke as though continuing some former conversation. 'You see how this trail winds back and forth, into this side canyon and out again, each time a little farther down the great canyon but requiring much time in the walking. If we could go across, it would take only a little time, but there is no way to go across safely.'

Lutha fumed silently. If the Dinadhi were sensible and efficient, they could go across, but the Dinadhi weren't sensible or efficient, so everything was done the long way, the slow way, the laborious way.

The patterned way, she reminded herself, cautioning against impatience. She settled the padded straps on her shoulders. When they stopped next, she would arrange the retriever at the top of her pack, set it on audio only, and listen to one of the grimy old language chips Trompe had given her the night before. No sense wasting the time entirely!

It was noon before they came halfway down the great wall, stopping on a promontory from which they could look directly south, across a spacious canyon bottom where a lake gleamed, and into the mouths of four other canyons. These four plus the canyon in which they stood made the five points of a star, with themselves at the northeastern point. They could look down the southern arm, a little way into the eastern and western arms, but they could see only the far wall and opening of the canyon to their right.

As they took food from their packs to make a hasty lunch, Chahdzi told them the lake was called 'the Gathered Waters,' and was neither deep nor lasting. Present in spring and early summer, it dwindled to almost nothing in fall or early winter when there was not enough water to fill the declivity.

The sun stood at its zenith, lighting the southmost canyon to its bottom but leaving those at either side still shaded. The sun also lighted the great stone cave eaten into the western wall of the canyon across from them, making the hive within it glow like gold.

'There is ba h'din, the hive, of Cochim-Mahn,' Chahdzi said. 'There is the leasehold of Bernesohn Famber. Below, stretching toward the Gathered Waters, is the greenblessing, the farm and fruit lands of our people. And now we have rested long enough. We must walk again.'

Though Lutha saw a glimmer of water along the canyon bottom and in the shallow lake, she saw no green, blessed or otherwise. Her glasses brought it within vision: a soft fur of trees and vegetation nestled in a wilderness of red stone. Narrow ribbons of greenery, at some places only a few paces across. It seemed scarcely enough to feed the people of the looming hive.

Wordlessly, they got the straps of their packs across their shoulders once more. From this point on, the trail was much grown up with small thorny shrubs and tough grasses, and Chahdzi led the way.

'No one uses this trail much, do they?' Lutha asked.

Chahdzi took time to reflect before answering. 'When Bernesohn Famber was there, people came again and again, as he chose, to bring equipment and supplies that were unavailable in Cochim-Mahn. Once his wife came here to him, also. The animals go up in spring and come down in fall. Other people come, now and then.'

Chahdzi seemed to feel this explained the situation fully, for he offered nothing more. Lutha soon found this understandable. The way had steepened; the footing was intermittently treacherous. It was sensible to avoid conversation in order to give all one's attention to where one stepped and what one was holding on to.

During the morning and for the first hour after their noon stop, Leely scampered along behind them or between them, interrupting his journey to stare at a flying bird or the shape of a cloud. In early afternoon, however, he sat down with a sighing 'Dananana,' and refused to move farther.

'Here's where I earn my fee,' said Trompe, picking the child up and placing him on his shoulders.

'I will take him when you are tired,' said Chahdzi. 'We cannot stop for him to rest.'

Light now came from the west, glaring into their eyes as they wound their way down and down.

'Some of the canyons don't get enough light to be habitable, do they?' Lutha asked, suddenly aware of differences among the various chasms.

'They must be wide enough to let the sun in,' agreed Trompe. 'Best of all are the wide east-west canyons with a sloping southern wall. Worst are the narrow north-south ones, with steep walls. In those the evening song would follow hard upon the song of morning. In those Lady Day finds little pleasure and shadow breeds.'

Lady Day would take little comfort from the canyon beyond the Gathered Waters, south of them. Already its western wall threw heavy shadow halfway up the eastern precipices, leaving the depths in darkness. Each day it would be lit for a short time at midday. The rest of the time it would be a dim and forbidding region. Lutha stared into its shadows and shivered, turning her attention elsewhere.

'Trompe and I saw many abandoned hives on our way here. Why so many?'

Chahdzi cleared his throat. 'H'din ha'disha. Empty hives, yes, they become … vacant when the Dinadhi move about. From one place to another.'

'Why?'

He shrugged. 'Perhaps a spring dries up.' His tone shut off further discussion.

Trompe cast a quick glance at Lutha, pursing his lips, shaking his head. Chahdzi was uncomfortable with the question.

She read his expression and let the matter drop, turning her attention to the landscape below her, where the delicate green of new leaves sprouted beside the transient water, a silver shoestring of oasis in this rocky land. They were close enough now that she could identify fruit trees, the branches almost hidden behind a flourish of blossoms.

When they stopped to drink from their flasks, Chahdzi took Leely, who was by now asleep, fastening him to his back with crossed belts that might have been made for the purpose. They went on, more quickly as the day waned and the sun fell, climbing downward until Lutha thought she would drop from the pain in her legs where the muscles rebelled at every step. She told herself another thousand steps and she would rebel, danger or no. She began counting, storing up her pain against the explosion she intended. She had reached eight hundred and something when the trail leveled and they debouched upon the level gravel soil of the canyon bottom.

'Now' – Chahdzi sighed – 'it will be easier.' He was sweating and pale.

'Let me take Leely,' said Trompe.

'Let Leely walk,' said Lutha. 'He's awake. He's just being lazy.'

The boy screamed at being put down, and when the three adults started ruthlessly off without him, he ran after them, raging incoherently. Lutha stopped his mouth with a cookie, which occupied him until they were almost at the stream. The sun had sunk below the rim of the canyon above them, and the great cave with its hive was deep in shadow.

Chahdzi took a small stoppered bottle from his pack and directed them to take a small mouthful each, even Leely. Then, while they sputtered at the acrid taste, he said, 'Take a deep breath and go fast. Only a little more now, but the darkness comes swiftly.'

'I'm ready to drop,' said Lutha.

'You may not,' he said softly. 'Not yet. Only a little more. Quickly.'

They pushed themselves into an exhausted stagger that accelerated into a heart-pumping plunge, fueled by Chahdzi's stimulant, as they splashed through the narrow stream, tending a little southward to a place immediately below the great cave. Now they were in shadow. Now they could see the hive itself, see the few people assembled upon the lip of stone, peering down at them.

'Ladders!' said Lutha, disbelievingly.

'Only a few,' said Chahdzi, gesturing her to climb first. 'Go, rest, go, rest. Keep moving.'

They climbed. They climbed forever. Leely screamed. Lutha cursed under her breath. One ladder led to another, led to another yet. A few were slimy with spray. And then they were on the flat, sagging with exhaustion.

A high tenor voice soared:

'*See our Lady depart. See her dance westward, upon the rock-rimmed mountains, beautiful her feet among the trees. ...*'

A tiddle of bone flutes, a rattle of little drums sounded from the wide-windowed loft of a tower nearby. Seemingly the rush was over. People were moving about purposefully, with no appearance of panic, men and women both, difficult to tell what sex they were in the loose robes, their hair cut alike, their faces painted this way or that. Some wore only the underrobe, the back hem pulled between their legs and up over the belt in front. Others' robes flowed free. A few had put on leather outer robes, these evidently for ceremonial reasons, for the singer and the musicians were among those so clad.

'Now what?' breathed Trompe.

'The leasehold of Bernesohn Famber is at the back,' said Chahdzi, sounding more cheerful than he had at any time during the day. 'Only a few steps.'

He led them along the south side of the great hive, past numerous pore windows and a few skin doors, each made of a drum-tight hide lashed to a frame of poles. Then there were no more windows and doors in the walls, and they entered upon Bernesohn Famber's private space: limited on the north by the featureless wall of the hive, on the south by the curving wall of the cave, on the west by his own living space, a small, single-story wing extruded from the hive: mud-colored, dome-roofed, softly rounded. Unlike the doors of our people, the annex door was made of planks, heavily strapped, hinged, and latched. The door had a lock. The single window was shuttered from inside.

'Is there a key?' Trompe asked, trying the door.

The latch rattled beneath his hand, and I, Saluez, opened the door from within.

They stared at me, Lutha and Trompe and the child.

I stood before them, my face veiled, holding a broom.

'What in hell?' demanded the tall, golden-haired man who came up behind me. 'What in the hell are you doing here?'

'Dananana,' cooed Leely.

'Leelson,' gasped Lutha, surprise warring with fury on her face. 'Leelson! Damn it all to hell, what are *you* doing here!'

We expected these people. We had been told to prepare for their arrival, so I had been inside the leasehold, cleaning it. I had fetched extra sleeping pads, extra blankets. I had brushed down all the walls and benches and had swept all the dust into a pile just inside the outer door. I had my hand upon the latch when it rattled, so I opened it. Lutha stood there, with Trompe and her child. I knew at once who they were, for we had been expecting them and I had seen them on the trail across the canyon earlier in the day. My father, Chahdzi, stood with them, but when he saw me, he turned and went away without speaking.

I stepped out of the way, drawing my pile of dust aside with my broom.

'What the hell *are* you doing here?' demanded Trompe, moving aggressively toward the man, who had been with us for some time.

Lutha scooped up Leely and came inside. Her face was twisted with effort; she was trying to scream or curse, but her voice would not come. She managed only a snarling croak, only a step or two inside the door, before she slumped against the wall, her face going blank. I knew at once they had been given the emergency drink, the one we carry when we are out in the world and need to reach the hive before darkness. The drug does that, when it wears off. It leaves bodies limp and minds shut down. I took her arm and helped her sit down, and behind us the darkness came, as though a blanket had been dropped across the light.

I had a pot of tea already prepared as a restorative. I filled a cup and held it to Lutha's lips. After a moment's hesitation, she drank.

'Let's get the door shut,' said Leelson, suiting his action to the words before opening the inside shutters to let the last of the dusk seep in between the bars.

Across the canyon, on the trail they had descended by, pallid forms were gathering.

'You arrived just in time,' said Leelson from the window.

Trompe shambled over to stand beside him, staring at the sight. I turned my face away.

'My god,' said Trompe. 'How many of them are there?'

More white forms streamed in from the darkness of the southern canyon, a constant milky flow, a torrent of wings and fluttering membranes.

'Well,' Lutha said in a gargled whisper. 'Was this the reason for our hurry? This assemblage?'

Since she spoke in my own language, I took it she was asking me. I bowed, murmuring, 'On this world we do not talk of the things of night. Not in daytime voices. It is not wise.'

'Would they do us harm?' she murmured between sips.

'Darkness is inimical to light by its very nature,' I whispered. 'All the beings of darkness, also. Living man may dream or hope as he will, but he must walk in the light. The wise man chooses his way and does not thereafter put himself outside his own pattern.' This is the kind of thing the song-fathers say, words to make one think one has been told something when, in fact, one has been told nothing at all. These are words to comfort children and strangers.

She barely nodded, the last effects of the drink draining away into exhaustion. 'What you're saying is ...'

She would not accept mere allusion. I bowed my head and spoke sense. 'In the dark hours, a man should be at home beside the fire, speaking softly. See how all the animals and birds of day go to rest and to quiet; see how they lie hidden, how they whisper in their lairs. Are we less wise than they? Have we no hive, no hole, no cavern to hold us? And why would we choose to be elsewhere than in our homes?'

'We might choose for curiosity's sake, perhaps,' said Trompe, in my language, though awkwardly. 'A desire to know.'

'We become what we know,' I said bitterly. 'If a woman wishes to stay alive, she must be careful what she knows.'

'Enough,' breathed Lutha in her weary voice. 'I'm afraid we're all too tired to appreciate the finer points of Dinadhi philosophy. What's your name, by the way?'

I bowed. 'Saluez,' I said. 'Saluez of the Shadow. Your servant, madam.'

'Assigned to me? Us?'

'To clean the Famber leasehold. To fetch what you may need, any of you.'

She dismissed me with a gesture, as though I had not even been there. I did not know then that there were shadows on her world, too, that because I had used the word, her reaction was to treat me as one of them. One took no notice of them. Both my words and my veil confused her, mostly because she was so tired. She dismissed me and turned to the others, and for a time thereafter it was as though I did not exist.

Leelson existed, however. Leelson Famber had been with us on Dinadh for some time. She had things to say to him!

'As for you, Leelson Famber, I think you owe us an explanation! Me, particularly!' She spoke our language as though, once started on it, she lacked energy to change.

'My presence is more explicable than yours,' he said in his own tongue. 'I came as legitimate lineage son of Bernesohn Famber—'

'You came without bothering to tell anyone at Alliance Prime!' Trompe exploded.

'Or your mother!' snarled Lutha. 'Who is very busy just now advancing your Firster cause by despairing of your posterity and blaming it all on me.'

He looked at them, astonished, his expression gradually changing from irritation to understanding.

He sat down, drawing Lutha beside him onto one of the cushioned mud benches along the walls. 'On my way from Kamir back toward Central, I overheard some crewmen talking of the vanishment of a homo-norm team in Hermes Sector. It reminded me of the last time that had happened, the Ularian thing a century ago. I knew great-great-grandpop had been looking into it, and I knew he'd disappeared here on Dinadh. It was, in a sense, on the way, so I decided to make a brief stopover on the chance he might have left some information here. It was a spur-of-the-moment decision, and I thought I'd be back before anyone got in an uproar. ....'

He made a gesture of annoyance. 'And it certainly never occurred to me the Dinadhi would accept Leely as ... as lineage son.'

Across the valley the forms swarmed, swirling outward from the cliff face. They would not be content with the far side of the canyon for long. I moved to the shutters and closed them, returning to my former place. The people in the room did not notice me.

Lutha made an impatient gesture to Trompe, as though saying, 'There! See!'

'I didn't perceive the threat as imminent!' Leelson said emphatically.

'I don't know what you call imminent, but the world you heard about was only the first. Several more Hermes Sector worlds have been wiped clean,' snarled Trompe.

Leelson looked up in astonishment. 'When?'

'Just before Trompe and I were sent here,' Lutha said. 'One of the colonists was an old friend of mine. The Procurator used her death as a goad to move me on this journey. God, Leelson! If I'd only known you were here!'

She fumed, her face set and hard, her anger – which had hottened with Leelson's reference to the boy – warring with her exhaustion. I wondered which god she had invoked. We do not consider it polite to call upon a god as one would a servant. We are careful to use the correct names and polite address.

As for Leely, he had climbed onto the wall bench nearest me and lay there staring at the ceiling, murmuring over and over, 'Dananana, Dananana.' I sat down beside him, drawing no attention to myself. We members of the sisterhood learn to do that.

'Did it never occur to you,' Lutha snarled, 'that Alliance Prime needed to know where you were?'

'If this attack followed the same pattern as a century ago, there'd have been plenty of time to advise Prime.'

'And what pattern was that?' Trompe demanded.

'The first thing that went then was a supply facility on a moon near the far side of the Hermes Sector. It was a standard year before anything else happened, and another year went by before populations were removed from anywhere farther in.'

Trompe snarled, 'Well, the Ularians didn't follow the previous pattern. They've completely destroyed or transported colonies on three of the worlds closest to Dinadh. That's what alerted Prime.' He sighed, running his fingers through his hair. 'I suppose your intentions are understandable, though it would have saved a good deal of trouble if someone had known where you were.'

Leelson nodded glumly, accepting this assessment.

Trompe asked, 'Since you've been here a while, I suppose we should ask if you've found out anything useful.'

Leelson darted his eyes toward me and did not reply.

I rose and bowed, saying politely, 'I will leave you now. Food stores have been augmented in anticipation of your arrival.'

'*You* knew they were coming?' Leelson demanded in outrage. '*You* didn't tell me?'

'If you had asked, you would have been told,' I replied, turning away from him toward Lutha. 'Other supplies should be adequate for your stay.'

I swept my pile of dust before me as I went out of the room and through the little hall to the door that connected with the hive. It, too, was made of wood, with a lock upon it. I swept my way through, shut the door loudly, then opened it a crack. No one noticed. I was able to hear everything they said.

'Damn them,' Leelson was muttering. 'Insular, taciturn, withholding information like that! I could have forestalled your journey. ...'

Trompe said, 'Calm down, Leelson. We're here now and we're on the same mission you are, so there'll be no conflict. Forget I asked any questions. We're too tired to think about it now. I hope there's space for all of us to sleep.'

I heard Lutha murmuring agreement, then scuffings and murmurs as they moved about, exploring the cells. There were plenty of wall benches, plenty of cotton sleeping pads. Bernesohn Famber had used one room for storage, but the other two rooms were large enough for all of them. In the hive, they would have housed a dozen of us, but evidently outlanders needed more privacy than we Dinadhi.

'Leely and I'll take this room,' said Lutha from the back room where Leelson had been sleeping. 'I presume there's other sleeping space for you men.'

'Plenty of sleeping space,' Leelson murmured, moving in and out.

Though the dispenser could deliver hot food, I had cooked food for their evening meal and left it in food boxes on the shelf. Someone found the boxes, for I heard the sounds of their opening, the little homely noise of spoons and bowls. Those who were eating did so slowly and silently. Perhaps they were too tired to have appetite or enjoy flavor.

Through the door, I watched while Lutha took Leely into the room she had chosen and Trompe retreated to the storeroom where he'd made up a bed for himself. By opening my door a little wider, I could see into the room where Leelson was. He had spread his own bed on the bench under the window and had opened the shutters a crack, to let in the evening air. I drew in a deep breath and held it, forbidding myself to go in and close the shutters once more. Not while he was awake. He lay for a long time, eyes open, but at last he wearied, closed the shutters himself, and settled to sleep.

My own sleeping place was near the door, near the outlanders, where, without moving, I could see through the crack. Something was going to happen, because of them or to them, so I had brought my pad and blankets from below. We veiled women have few enough amusements, few enough stories to tell one another. We need to see and hear everything!

The sound of someone moving about woke me in the mid hours of the night. I saw Lutha come out into the little hallway, where she stood looking in on Leelson. Though I could see only his hand, his sleeve, it was enough to tell me he had, as usual, slept only a little before rising to busy himself with Bernesohn's equipment. Often he spent the night so, muttering to himself and making notes. His back was toward Lutha, and she spent a long time staring at him, fury and longing battling on her face. Later she told me her feelings for him were like surf, love and lust pounding at her, only to recede, leaving pools of chilly, clear anger behind.

I grew weary watching her silent battle, and I had shut my eyes when she spoke at last:

'I can't understand why you didn't tell someone!'

The legs of the chair scraped on the floor. It was Bernesohn's chair, the only chair I had ever seen except in Simidi-ala. We do not use chairs in the hives.

He growled, 'You can come in, Lutha.'

She bit her lip as she went into the room to join him. Though I could not see them, I could hear them clearly.

He said, 'What I can't understand is your bringing the child out here.'

She blurted, 'I wasn't given a choice, Leelson!'

'I'm sure the Procurator didn't force you.'

'He gave me to understand my doing what he asked might have something to do with human survival,' she snarled. 'Which would move most of us, even those of us who aren't Fastigats or Firsters.' She came back into the doorway, half in, half out of the room.

He spoke from behind her. 'Your coming, I understand. I said I couldn't understand your bringing the child.'

Her expression was disbelieving. 'Listen to yourself. Damn it, Leely is Famber lineage—'

'No,' said Leelson firmly. 'He is not Famber lineage. Not according to Fastigat custom.'

'Your own people are supporting him!'

'Fastigat responsibility is one thing. Famber lineage is another. Each has its own parameters.'

'You only say that because he's not ...'

'Normal? Of course. Fastigat lineage, under Fastigat law, requires a basic condition of humanity. That's where we separate from the Firsters. They would accept Leely, we won't. Humanity, under Fastigat law, has a specific definition.'

She glared at him. 'You're saying your own son is not human!'

'Lutha—'

'Leelson!'

They fell silent simultaneously. I thought at first they were concerned about being overheard, but perhaps it was only to get control of themselves that they stopped when they did.

'My belief concerning the child is at least as sensible as yours,' he said at last, rather sadly. 'You're trying to hope him into superhuman status, into some new avatar of humanity. We Fastigats, on the other hand, say simply he does not meet our definition.'

'You don't think he's human!' she charged again.

'No.'

'Even though you and I are—'

'Lutha, we've said this—'

'I don't care. ...'

He sighed deeply, wearily. He said:

'Genetic programming sometimes goes awry and produces a non-replica. At the cellular level, such mistakes are eradicated. We remove warts; we cure cancers. At a slightly higher level, we remove extra limbs resulting from incomplete twinning. We do all this without great emotional hurricanes. But when the mistake is at a neurocortical level, when the body looks human, or even rather human, emotions get mixed in—'

She interrupted him with an outthrust arm, rigid and furious.

'Let's not discuss it,' he suggested. 'We won't agree, Lutha. We can't. Let's agree to accept each other's position. If you had to bring him, you had to bring him. I'll accept that you believed it was necessary.'

She moved into the room and out of my sight. I sneaked into the dark hallway and stood where I could watch them. She was facing the closed shutters, her arms crossed, her hands clutching her shoulders, hugging herself, perhaps cautioning herself. He had gone back to the table and was sorting through the record chips Bernesohn Famber had left strewn about. My mother had gathered them up and put them in boxes, but some of them had already been nibbled by corn-rats. Cornrats can survive only because we have made hives safe for ourselves, making havens for them in the process.

'Bernesohn didn't believe in labels,' Leelson murmured. 'I've been going through chips for the last three days, and I've yet to find anything that's identified. He also didn't believe in filing categories. Some of these chips have a dozen different things on them.'

Lutha wasn't willing to give up the former topic. 'The people here in Cochim-Mahn knew you were here, didn't they? Chahdzi knew you were here. Hell, probably the people in the Edge knew you were here!'

'Of course. Chahdzi brought me here, just as he did you, and I came through the Edge, just as you did. I was surprised that the housekeeper did not tell me you were coming.'

'Why didn't they tell us? I could have been partway home by now!'

'Well, it's the same question I asked Saluez, isn't it? You didn't ask them if I was here. I didn't ask them if someone else was coming.' He shook his head at her. 'If they'd volunteered the information, you'd have left without paying for the hover you no doubt rented, and the guides, and the supplies.

Dinadhi don't do anything that discourages custom. They need hard currency too much.'

He inserted a file chip into the retriever and pressed it firmly home.

A woman stood in the center of the room, her voice making a fountain of sound, lovely as falling water in an arid land. Then another woman stood beside her, singing, a voice joined to itself, a duet of pure wonder. The scent of something flowery and spicy filled my nose. I tasted wine. My body ached with wanting. ...

It was only a fragment, over in a moment. Sensurround, they call it. Magic. Oh, to think of that being here all these years! If I had only known!

'Tospia,' breathed Lutha. She took a deep breath, then another. She was trembling. I could see it from where I stood. But then, so was I.

'You played that one for me a long time ago,' she said, her voice yearning.

He did not answer for a moment, but when he did, the words came crisply, without emotion. 'Since there are no labels, I never know whether I'll find an aria, a shopping list, a lubricious monologue, or something significant.'

He removed the song chip from the retriever and began clicking other chips into it, one by one. Voices muttered. Vagrant scents came and went. I tasted herbs, mud, smoke.

'You've found nothing so far?' she asked. She had gained control of herself and her voice was as impersonal as his own.

'One fragmentary memorandum. I marked it. It's here somewhere. I'll run across it in a moment.'

I got out of sight as she wandered back into the bedroom where Leely lay sprawled, running her fingers along the walls, along the small, barred air-vent openings. At the storage cubicles, she began a meticulous search. Top to bottom, left to right, missing none, scamping none.

In the third compartment of the second row, she found a set of holograms and a display stand. I knew what they showed. Herself. Herself and Leelson. Different places. Different times. None of them with Leely.

In the next compartment below, she came upon clothing she evidently recognized, for she held it up, smiling, shaking her head. A rainbow-beaded vest. A belt of iridescent leather. Shirts and trousers and a long, warm coat of rare earthsheep's wool. At least Leelson had said it was earthsheep, though none of them existed on earth – Alliance Central – anymore.

I disappeared into my storeroom when I heard Trompe moving around. He came to Lutha's door, demanding, 'What?'

'Looking for anything Bernesohn may have left, but all this stuff belongs to Leelson,' she replied.

In the next room, Leelson inserted a chip that whined and scratched before speaking clearly and plainly. During the past several days I'd heard it more than once. The voice was scratchy and a little cantankerous. At hearing it, both Lutha and Trompe crossed into the room where Leelson was.

...'fore leaving make record of ... following significant findings ... Ularians ... reason for Dinadh's immunity ... oldest settled world in the sector ... only one, here or elsewhere, where the present inhabitants are mumble-mumble as to origin.

'Is that the memorandum you mentioned?' asked Lutha while the chip made scratchy, whining noises.

'This is the only one I've found that says anything about the Ularians,' said Leelson. 'Unfortunately, there are only a few clear places. Something has chewed on the chip.'

He fiddled with the machine; it repeated the last phrase several times, *to origin, to origin, to origin.*

... narrowed field of inquiry ... taken steps to ... remedy situation ... considering factors that seem ... Dinadhi omphalos and abandoned gods ... tell Tospia ... rejoinder of my lineage ...

The reader went on blurting fragmentary words and phrases interrupted by harsh scratching and stretches of gibberish.

Leelson, Trompe, and Lutha stared at one another.

'I've played that one several times,' said Leelson. 'I've jotted down the clear words and phrases, here. Any ideas?'

'It's enigmatic at best,' said Lutha at last. 'Was he anticipating legal action? Rejoinder is a word I've only run across in legal documents.'

Leelson shrugged. 'The bit about rejoinder to the question of his lineage may refer to the court action Tospia brought against the news sniffer over the paternity of the Famber twins. Did you know about that?'

Lutha said, 'The Procurator mentioned it. Tospia visited Bernesohn here, returned to Central, had twins, and their parentage was questioned.'

'Questions of lineage, as you've discovered for yourself, would have annoyed Bernesohn no end. His voice sounds annoyed. Also, there's a good bit of frustration and weariness, but no real excitement. Possibly because he's tired. As though he'd been digging and digging for something.'

'The answer that wasn't here, perhaps?' Lutha sighed. I knew what she was thinking. To have come all this way for nothing.

'Or because he'd found out what he needed to know,' said Trompe thoughtfully. 'He could have learned what he needed to know and done something about the Ularians. He says he took steps to remedy the situation.'

'The record didn't say he took steps to remedy "the situation,"' contradicted Lutha. 'There's a pause there....'

Trompe paid no attention. 'My god, Leelson. The only *situation* was the Ularian business. If he had a remedy ...'

Lutha sat down, murmuring, 'He speaks of abandoned gods. I've heard nothing of abandoned gods while we've been here on Dinadh.'

Oh, but I had. Whispered by grandmothers to granddaughters, mentioned in old songs sung by sisterhoods.

Lutha went on: 'He also speaks of the omphalos. Had he any maps of Dinadh?'

Leelson nodded. 'Here? A whole file of them. But why maps?'

'Place-names often survive while language changes around them. Sometimes the names of places give us the only evidence of languages that have otherwise disappeared. God names are sometimes applied to places, therefore a place-name might be a clue to what he calls an abandoned god.'

She ran her hands through her hair, pressing her fingertips into her forehead. I could feel her ache in my own forehead as she said:

'The only other thing that comes to mind is that Bernesohn disappeared from here, where we are. We know hover cars can't get down into the canyon. We know the Dinadhi use fliers only for emergencies – kind of emergency unspecified. So, wherever he went, he probably had to go on foot. Since he mentioned the omphalos, is it credible that he went there?'

I heard the rustle as Leelson unfolded the maps. I myself had seen them, had unfolded them, studied them, all the wonderful maps. Printed upon them were all the roads, lines of green; the ocean, a blotch of blue; the endless twisting edges of the canyons, black squiggles; and the names of places in curly lettering. The omphalos was shown there, too, shaded in violet and crimson, important colors, sacred colors. When duty had required me to tend to this place by myself, after Mother departed and before Leelson came, I had many times sat at that table and traced the way, how I would go if I were going to the omphalos. To Tahs-uppi. To the renewal. To say goodbye.

I could feel the map in my hands, soft from handling. I could visualize it, much fingerprinted, bearing many notations in a microscopic hand.

Lutha saw what I had seen.

'Somebody's used this,' she said. 'Bernesohn. He's annotated it.'

'Used it a lot,' said Trompe.

'If Bernesohn Famber went somewhere on foot,' Lutha persisted, 'how did anyone find out he was gone?'

Leelson replied. 'They told me the housekeeper came in here to clean or bring new supplies. She found the last supplies hadn't been used, so the hive was told to keep watch. When no one saw him for a year, they named him an outlander ghost and said he was wandering among the canyons. They invited him to join the people of Cochim-Mahn.'

'What does that mean?' asked Lutha.

'I asked the same question. They told me they invite all the ghosts to join them, and furthermore, that most of them do so. They wouldn't clarify the matter, so don't ask. I don't know and I can't pick up anything clear from their emotions.'

He could have picked up a good deal from mine. I got up from the place I was hiding and went to the door. I wanted to hear what they were saying about the omphalos.

They stood around the table, looking down at the map. Lutha's fingers traced wandering lines of canyons and the tips of mesas, all ramified like the branches and twigs of trees pointing off in all directions. Canyons run down all the sides of the mesas; mesas limit all the edges of the canyons. Except at the sea. And at the omphalos.

'Look at this,' said Leelson softly as he pointed to the southward leading canyon. 'What does that mean? "Simi'dhm'a."'

She raised her head. Later I was to learn what that posture meant, that alertness. Her mind was searching, searching.

'Separated,' she said. 'Separated something. What would the root word be? Dhuma?'

'Could be.'

'The word for songfathers is hahm-dhuma. So this would be what? Separated father?'

He thought about it. 'Ghost?' he suggested. 'A parent who's died?'

She shook her head. 'That doesn't have the right feel to it. I need a lexicon. Either that or I need a lot longer with the old chips. Tomorrow we'll ask Chahdzi. Maybe he'll tell us. '

'I will tell you,' I said from behind them.

They turned as one, surprised, perhaps a little hostile.

'There is a dark canyon, where the sun scarcely touches. It is Simi'dhm'a, which now means lost and lonely, though once it meant abandoned ones. Importances left behind.'

'Left behind where?' whispered Lutha. 'Where, Saluez?'

'On the other world. Before we came here. On the world of Breadh. It was there we left Mother Darkness and Father Endless.'

They looked at me. I could feel the two men probing at me, trying to feel as I felt, feeling as I felt but not knowing why. Lost, they were. Not understanding.

'Why?' Lutha breathed. 'Why did you leave them behind, Saluez?'

'Because of them,' I whispered, gesturing at the shuttered windows.

Leelson moved to the window. I hurried to turn off the lamp, an outlander lamp, one that runs on stored sunlight.

They watched as Leelson shifted the lever that controlled the shutters, opening them only a crack.

'Careful,' I whispered. 'Oh, be careful.'

Fragile fingers slid between the slats. Luminous eyes peered in at us.

Teeth as delicate and sharp as needles bit at the edges of the slats. My flesh knew those teeth. I cried out.

Lutha turned to me, reached for me, catching my veil with the bracelet she wore. My veil dropped. They saw my face. Lutha hesitated for only a moment, then drew me close to her and held me.

Leelson closed the lever.

From the darkness outside came the cries of petulant children, denied a treat. It was the sound I had heard after Masanees had sounded the gong. I had not heard the sound of wings, one or two approaching quietly, as was customary, but these same cries, the noisy approach of many, talking among themselves. And when they came in, they had not gorged themselves on the banquet prepared for them before settling on my back to do what they had come for. No. Instead they had grabbed my hair, pulled at me, raised my head, insisted upon getting at my face.

'They!' said Leelson with certainty. 'They did that to you!'

They had, yes, but I did not reply. Instead I stood with my head on Lutha's shoulder and let myself cry. I had not seen the beautiful people since the House Without a Name. Perhaps I had hoped never to see them again.

On Perdur Alas, Kane the Brain came in from the day's labor in the fields, where they'd been planting various food and fiber crops for the ag-test. He was carrying a bundle on his shoulder, something wrapped in his own jacket, and he put it on the table in the lab, saying to no one in particular, 'We found this thing in a cave out there.'

Snark was filing germination records, but she put the pile down and came over to see what it was. A jar, not unlike the jar in her cave.

'That's Father Endless,' she said, tracing the pattern. 'And Mother Darkness. And these are the horizons of sleep.'

'How do you know that?' Kane demanded, not too urgently. 'You've never seen it before!'

'I've seen them before,' said Snark, remembering all at once that this was true. 'My mother told me about them. On Breadh our people believed in them, but then our people listened to the words of the tempter and put their gods aside. My family was of the T'loch sdi, the old order.' The words came of themselves. Labels. An identity, for herself, for her mother, for certain other children, certain other mothers and fathers. The old order.

'What does that mean?'

She quoted what she had been told:

'We were faithful to our beliefs. Faithful to Father Endless, to Mother Darkness. When we died, we died into their keeping, for that was part of the everlasting pattern. We did not allow the tempter to sway us. Even after many generations on the new world, we remained faithful. And at last we ran away from the new world, fled from the new commandment. We came here. That is, my parents came here.'

'You weren't born here.' Willit sneered. There was no real venom in his voice. The challenge was only habit.

'No. I think I was only a baby, though. I grew up here. Keeping away from the scourges of the tempter, until the ship came and took us survivors away.'

'Survivors!'

She rubbed her head fretfully. 'Me. And the other children. Five of us. All the adults were gone by then.' Gone to Father Endless and Mother Darkness. Gone into the womb between the worlds. To the place where everything dwells in timelessness.

Willit started to say something sneery, but Kane stopped him. 'Snark. Why did they call you survivors?'

'Because they didn't believe we had lived here. They thought we'd survived a shipwreck, taken off in a survival pod, got twisted into a wormhole, and ended up here. They thought we were castaways. I knew we weren't, but they said the five of us couldn't have lived here otherwise.

'It was on the ship they said we were survivors. Then, later, they put me in the home. But the people at the home didn't know ... who I was. They said I was a liar.'

'Right,' barked Willit. 'They knew you, kid.'

'I wasn't lying,' she said.

'There's no world called Breadh,' said Kane. 'Not in this sector. You were probably sent here from one of the other worlds, when the Ularians came. If you were the only ones left, what happened to the others?'

Snark thought about it. Part of it was clear and close. Scourges. They'd had to stay away from the scourges. And from something else, too. She shrugged. She couldn't really remember.

'Survivors from Ularians. I be damned,' said Kane.

'And what are these damned Ularians when they're not hiding under a rock?' asked Willit.

'Nobody really knows.' Kane looked at the jar he'd found. 'Nobody knows who they are. There were no survivors. Not unless Snark was one.'

'You mean she really could have been? A survivor?'

It was all very casual, not very meaningful, and everyone went back to work without agonizing over it. In Snark, however, the discovery of the jar began a chain of recollection. She remembered faces, voices. She remembered things people had said. She remembered words. The returned ones. The faithful.

That child Snark: How long had she been here, before they found her? Had it been only a few days? A few seasons? Had it been years? Whether born here or not, certainly she had grown here. Someone had provided clothing. There had been the animal skins, the fleeces in the cave, the clay jars. Where had the skins come from, with their woolly fleece? There were no animals like that on this world.

No. They'd been wearing the animal skins when they came! But they had brought no tools, no food. Who had told her that? Someone had. How had they grown food? Had they grown food?

How much was reality? How much was dream? That night, curled in her blankets in the cave at the edge of the sea, she asked herself that question again and again, finding no answer. In the niche in the wall, the patterned jar kept its enigmatic silence. There were bones in it, she was sure of that. Whose bones they were, she did not really want to remember.

5

On Dinadh, Leelson and Trompe asked me questions until I could answer no more questions. 'Saluez? Saluez?' they begged, until at last I wept. All the pain I had refused to feel, all the tears I had stored away, everything came flooding out, drowning me.

'Leave her alone,' Lutha said angrily to the two men. 'Later on we'll find out what we need to know. We're too tired now. We will talk when it is light.'

Everything was easier when it was light. Perhaps she knew that better than they. I let her lead me back into the entryway, through the door I had left ajar, to my bed in the storeroom of the hive.

'Do you sleep here?' she asked, her tone saying what her words did not, that it was a poor place for a woman to sleep.

'It is ... private,' I whispered. 'And it is closer to my duties than the other place, below, for women like ...' For women like me.

'Why, Saluez?' she begged, her voice a whisper. 'Why did they do this to you?'

I choked, thrusting her away, trying to put her off, noting the way she had said it. Not 'What happened to you?' but 'Why did they do it?' How could I say why? How could I tell her when I did not know myself? She caught herself up, becoming very quiet before she laid her fingers upon my mutilated mouth. Tender fingers. Gentle hands.

'Never mind,' she said. 'Tomorrow.'

Tomorrow would offer no more explanations than tonight, but I let it be.

She left me. I lay down upon the shelf, pulling the woolen blanket over me, turning my head upon the cotton pillow to find a certain position in which my face was mostly hidden but was not thrust hard against the fabric. I didn't want anyone to see my face if they happened upon me sleeping, but actually covering it brought pain. There is a venom in their teeth, and any touch can set it afire. The pain sometimes lasts for years, so my sisters say. If I find exactly the right position, the pain diminishes almost to nothing; I can fall asleep and, sleeping, forget, and sometimes even wake without remembering, believing for a few blessed moments I am as I used to be. ...

The man who was father to my child is Slozhri T'ri. Turry. In Lutha's language, his name means Worrier. He worried at me from the time we

404

were children together. His mother is ... was a second mother to me. My only mother after my own was gone. Poor Chahdzi father. He has had little fortune with his womenfolk. Saluez, his first daughter, now come into this shame. And my mother, his first wife, long since gone into the night and returned as our departed kindred do. She left human form while giving birth to my little brother. I was only a baby then. So, after a time father took another wife, Zinisi, a s'mahs, which is to say a screech bird, one who has made his life a misery. His second daughter ... Well, if any man can bear being close enough to Hazini to get her pregnant, the beautiful people will likely let her be. Likely her flesh is bitter as her tongue.

Even so, perhaps she is the better daughter. Perhaps she will be the better wife to someone. Someone will be a better wife to Turry, too, and he can worry at her for a time.

He has not asked to see me. Sometimes men do ask, so the sisterhood says, advising against it. Better not to see, not to be seen. Better to have one's child among one's sisters, better to nurse it and wean it and send it up into the hive to be reared by its father's people or by one's own people. Better never to let it call you mother. Better watch it from corners, from behind doorskins, seeing it grow, praying that Weaving Woman will do better for the child than for the mother. Better to take all one's joy in the sisterhood. In the special food and drink, stored by the sisters selfishly, for themselves, for their own pleasure and no one else's. In the special songs and stories one hears only there, the special weavings made only among the sisterhood. In the special herbs gathered and dried only there so the sisters may have peace ...

Small pleasures, stored against the darkness of despair. Taste something savory. Smell a little sweetness. Let a sister rub your shoulders where they ache, or brew a special pot of tea, or even join in making bodily delight as some of the sisters do, as I would do if Shalumn were among us. That is the greatest loss. Love is the greatest loss. We make a life of remnants, of details, and so each hour's shadow is delayed, another day, another day. But, oh, the nighttime is hurtful when you lie down and your body longs for the body of the beloved. When your breasts tingle and your nipples get hard and you taste the beloved's skin on your tongue and between your legs, you are on fire. Even being pregnant does not stop that. Animals have more sense. They do not go on rutting and mating once the female has kindled. They do not stand knee-deep in sweet grass and long for apples. But we, we people do. We go on longing and longing and longing, and all the beautiful people and all their teeth and talons do not change that!

So I lay breathing like a bellows, panting, trying to imagine I was as I used to be and she was beside me, we two moving together in the bed dance.

All ... all for nothing.

I sat up, tears flowing, unstoppable, as though another dam had broken. There was a water pitcher in the corner. I put my head over the basin and poured the cold water through my hair, gasping when it ran around my ears and into my eyes. Beside the basin was the packet the sisterhood had given me. At first I had taken it, thanked them, told myself I would not use it, but more and more I did use it. Now I took one of the leaf rolls and lit it at the candle, drawing the smoke deep into me.

'Say, "Mother Darkness, come to me," the sisters had said.

'Mother Darkness, come to me.'

'Say, "Father Endless, come to me."'

'Father Endless, come to me.'

'Say, "Mother and Father of peace, come to me."'

'Mother and Father of peace, come to me,

Tomorrow will be easier.

And the day that follows easier yet.

And I will grow to age in tranquillity,

In contentment approaching you,

   whom my kindred have forgot.'

After a time my body went away somewhere, flying, as though lifted by a blessed wind. I lay down on the bed and nothing hurt. Oh, when I was a child, I would never have dreamed the pleasure that comes from the mere absence of hurt. Such a sweetness was, for the time, enough. I set the rolled leaf in the covered, spouted bowl beside the bed and turned my nose into the braided skein of smoke. I breathed and breathed, watching the guttering candle dwindle into dark. And I slept.

On Perdur Alas, Snark made her way toward the sea. Her hands were empty, for all the things needful for her survival had long since been stored in the cave. The stealing was over. The scurrying and sneaking were over. Behind her in the camp the other shadows slept, weary at the end of a tiresome day spent weeding the test gardens. The seeds of a sedge-like native plant came floating on every breeze, sprouting in mere hours to form a network of thick stolons in which nothing could grow but themselves. They had to be sprayed, early and often. They had to be cleared by hand from around the food seedlings. Despite this annoyance, the ag-tests were coming along. They knew now what would grow, or at least what would germinate and sprout, though it would still be some time until the harvest. A small victory among workers who did not care enough to count victories. The planet could be homo-normed. It would support human life.

There were other coups that had been counted, and these were Snark's own. Though technical knowledge had been forced upon her, it seemed to fit her mind as mate fits mate, making a comfortable fullness instead of an aching vacancy. It was like being transported from a barren desert into an orderly jungle, where every byway was lined with interesting bits of information, where techniques and processes grew on every tree, like fruit. She had been moved to create a microorganism to fixate nitrogen on plant rootlets. She had grafted genetic instructions for a flavorful grain onto the basic stock of one of the furze-like plants of the moor. There had been excitement in these experiments, in thinking of them and finding within herself the knowledge to accomplish them. She had felt elation, a hen cackle of victory at each successful outcome.

Tonight she was late in her journey, delayed by a stack of report forms. She had been tempted to stay in the dormitory with her fellows, but the retreat to the sea's edge was habit now. Let it go on. Whatever changes the day might bring, let comfortable habit sustain each evening.

'Sustain,' she said to herself, as though quoting. Someone else had said that. 'Sustain each evening with comfortable ...' No. Not comfortable. Essential. Essential habit.

Whichever it was, she went through moonlit darkness toward the sea, past the tea-dark pools and the marshy places, through the rustling bracken, toward the roll of stones upon the sea shelves, the incessant grinding of gravel beside the waves. Which was, tonight, making a curious sound.

She stopped, confused. A curious sound. Not the usual one. This was flattened, muffled sounding. As though some enormously thick bandage had been pressed down upon the world.

She crouched, making herself as small as possible, then crept silently into a nearby tangle of bracken from which she peered out through slitted eyes. Near on her left, she heard a *clack-chitter-chitter-clack* as a small shelled creature made its laborious way across an outcropping of stone. From some distance to her right came the shrill cries of the seabirds in their spiraling gyre above the hammered sea. She was not far from the rim of the cliff. Not far from the cave itself. Perhaps a few hundred yards, all told. Still, better not move. Better merely wait to see what this oddness portended.

Whatever-it-was went on being odd. She turned her head seaward. The bird cries piped without resonance. Even the sound of the waves was wooden and flat, reaching the ear as a single impulse, a slap with no following susurrus. Everything seemed damped. And then, moving to the left, between her and the sea, a wallowing darkness, a silent, heaving immensity.

The thing had no edges! She could not see its shape. Though it swallowed stars, they were not thickly enough strewn to show an outline. At the advancing edge, a star winked out, then another, and at the trailing edge one winked into being, then another. Huge it was. Like a building. Yet moving ... moving soundlessly. Invisibly.

She burrowed her face in her hands and did not look up for a time. When she did so again, the darkness had turned inland, toward the camp. Before her the stars winked out, one by one.

She could run, perhaps, and warn them! She could sneak quickly along under the bushes and get there in time to tell them ... what? That a monstrous shadow was coming?

Her flesh tingled, as though an electrical field had been generated around her. Her hair stood on end. Her breath left her lungs in a sudden rush as the air pressure increased, more, and more, and more, then was suddenly gone, leaving her gasping into her cupped hands, desperately achieving silence.

The shadow was between her and the camp, approaching it from the south. She squirmed silently, turning so that she faced the camp. Everywhere, shadows.

Shadows. Immensities.

One approached from the north. And another yet, from the southeast. Wallowing darknesses, with no distinguishable features, no identifying characteristics ...

Except the taste coating her tongue. Like carrion and cold and something hideously oily-rancid. She held her nose. It was not smell. The taste flowed between her teeth, making her salivate profusely, a copious, mucilaginous spit that trailed sickeningly from the corners of her mouth and refused to be spat away. The taste of moldy mastodon. The flavor of Behemoth. The savor of absolute immensity.

'Are you getting this?' her shadow mind mocked the distant observer, the monitor on Dinadh, the evaluator at Alliance Prime. Despite terror and discomfort, her rebellious ego thumbed its nose at that distant watcher, wherever, whenever it might be. 'God, I hope you're getting this. This is them, fellows. The Ularians. Just taste them!'

She almost screamed, for she felt it then. A vibration in the soil beneath her. Perhaps she heard it too. So deep a sound. Once and again. And again. The sound of earthquake breeding but not breaking. The sound of unimaginable hooves, slowly treading.

A shriek from the direction of the camp, only momentarily human. More surprise than pain. Cut off in midhowl. The darknesses gathered thickly there, around the camp.

And at this evidence of purpose concentrated away from herself, Snark scurried silently on all fours toward the sea, toward her landmark stones and her polished branch, throwing only one terrified glance behind her when she arrived there, seeing nothing toward the camp but the absence of stars, hearing nothing, smelling nothing, but tasting ... oh, that foul grizzly smell, that flavor of old fur, long and matted, of bloody hooves and a hugeness past belief.

She dropped into the cave in one frenzied movement, then thrust her head outside to spit into the ocean far below, scraping her tongue with her fingers, taking out her knife and using the back edge of that to scrape with, only then able to stop retching. The taste was still there, but diminished. Here it was diluted by the sea air, by its salt tang and chill cleanliness.

She crawled under her blankets and was still as any animal petrified by fear, self-hypnotized into quiet. Time passed. The plod of those unimaginable feet came again, then once more. In her reverie, the shapes against the stars assumed form, like a puzzle her unconscious kept probing at. Maybe they weren't really that big. Maybe they had like ... wings. Bats looked a lot bigger than they really were. And birds. Perhaps, in the daylight, one could see that they were quite imaginable, only with wings. If they returned in daylight.

Except that winged things did not plod in that obdurate, inescapable way. Did not stalk across a world as though it were a pasture.

Light flushed the horizon and she squinted her eyes shut against it, refusing to admit the audacity of daylight. It was still night, she told herself. Still safe dark, hiding dark, friendly dark.

Sunlight allowed no such fiction, for she had forgotten to wall herself in. The sequined surface of the sea flashed into her eyes, blinding her. She emerged slowly, cautiously, drew down the branch, and lifted herself to peer above the rimrock across the moor. There was the camp, as she had left it, all the landmarks as she had last seen them. Nothing else. No residue of the disgusting taste. The flatness gone. Sounds once more familiar. Echoes coming from far hillsides and nearby stones. She crawled onto the rim and lay there quietly, waiting. Nothing. Nothing. Whatever it had been, whatever they had been, they had gone. For now.

It took a long time for her to decide to go to the camp, for she knew from the beginning what she would find. A vacancy. Everyone gone. Kane the Brain and slob-lipped Willit and even Susso. No blood. No mess. Not even the feathery ash a disposal booth would have left behind. Nothing at all.

Crumpled blankets on the beds, fallen into body shapes. Here a light left on, where someone had been up, maybe on the way to or from the toilets. And yes, there a pair of slippers, a stride apart, where the feet had been lifted from them all at once, the nightsuit fallen into a heap between them. Living things, human things gone, but their belongings untouched.

Except for the test gardens. There were barren plots. Not all of them. Not all the tests. Just some. This one and that one, apparently at random.

But, of course, it would not be at random. This clean-edged selective destruction could not be by chance. The plots destroyed had been selected; they would have to have something in common!

Snark dug into her pocket for her notebook and dictated into it, listing the plots destroyed, grains type 178 and 54 and 209. Root crops 89 and 102 and 5 and 27. Virtually all the leaf crops, leaving only half a dozen standing. Destroyed because of what? Dangerous? Or merely not nutritious? Or perhaps not smelling nice to whatever the monstrous shadow had been. Or not tasting nice. Or not something nice, some other sense that Snark could not even imagine. Perhaps the destroyed crops made the monstrous shadows itch? Or made their eyes water. Assuming they had eyes. Which one would be wrong to do. The missing crops made their enormous membranous vorticals twinge, that was it.

She found herself thrashing on the ground, laughing hysterically. The sounds she was making frightened her, and she stopped all at once, horrified at herself. She choked the sound with her own hands, terrified at her own panic. She had been conditioned! She shouldn't be able to feel anything of the kind!

Conditioned to be among others, she told herself. Conditioned to be one of a group. Not to be alone. Not like this. She clicked on her notebook once more, setting down her thoughts, her impressions. 'The sound was damped, like big curtains hung in open space might do,' she said. 'Absorbing sound waves.' After a moment's thought, she described what she had unconsciously resolved about their shape. 'Winged,' she said. 'I think they must have wings, or some membrane of some kind that covers a wide area. But ... I got the feeling of shagginess. Of fur ...'

The laboratories were undisturbed. Her grain furze grew glossily green and spiky in its hydroponic tank. The lights above it were still on. The generator hadn't been touched.

If she were to make changes, would the darknesses notice? If she moved something here, now, would they return and realize someone had escaped their raid?

Who could tell? Better change nothing. Better move nothing. Or, better yet, move some tiny inconspicuous thing and see if they noticed.

She had left a bundle of furze-grain seedlings stored in the back of a cold-frame. They were in an unlabeled container. Probably the darknesses had not even seen it. In case they had, she divided some other seedlings and put the container back, now holding something else. She would plant the seedlings near her cave, where in time they might stand between herself and hunger.

There were food stores, too, that she could shift, leaving everything looking much as before. When she returned to the cave, she did so heavily laden. Everything had to be swung into the cave at the end of a rope and then tucked away in crannies before she, herself, had room to stretch out. It was late afternoon before she was finished. Too late, that day, to plant the seedlings. Tomorrow she would get them in. Not in rows or patches, but one by one, among the native plants they much resembled. And tomorrow, if the darknesses did not return, she would take more food, carefully, just as she'd learned as a child. Leaving no trail. Making everything look just as it had before.

From my room in the hive, I heard Lutha and Leelson and Trompe talking. It was early morning. They thought I was still asleep, I suppose, for they were talking about me.

'The emotion was shame,' said Trompe in an argumentative tone.

'Also anger,' Leelson insisted. 'She was ashamed, but also angry.'

'Wouldn't you be?' demanded Lutha. 'My God, gentlemen. Wouldn't you be? The anger part I can certainly understand.'

'So can we,' said Leelson in a tone even I thought to be patronizing. 'It's the shame part we're finding intriguing.'

'What they did to her was a rape,' said Lutha furiously. 'Our persons are in our faces. When we show ourselves to the public, we show our faces. That's what we recognize about one another, those of us who see, at any rate. Our faces portray our personas. Her persona was violated, just as in rape. Rape evokes emotions of shame and anger because of the violation.'

'Why was it done?' Trompe asked.

She replied, 'We won't understand it until we find out a lot more about this society.' She paused, breathing furiously, enraged on my behalf. Even from where I lay on my bed, I could hear her fuming.

'And I *will* find out,' she said firmly.

I thought she might indeed, for she seemed a very determined woman. I would have told her what she wanted to know if I could. But could I say, yes, it was my own fault, for sometimes I have doubts, and my sisters in sorrow tell me they, too, have doubts. But, so my sisters say, we are not alone in this! Our mothers, siblings, cousins, our dearest friends, they have doubts. Most of those who emerge unscathed from the House Without a Name, they, too, have doubts. Doubts are not peculiar to those who have been maimed, so why ... why we? Was our doubt of a particular kind?

More had been maimed lately, so the sisters said. In our great-grand-mothers' time, almost no one was maimed, but now it is more than half! Why? What was happening? The sisterhood argued over this again and again, finding no answer. What does one say? I was guilty of doubting. I did not doubt more than others, or differently from others, but I was selected for punishment. My punishment was particularly horrid because ... because of who did it to me. ...

Lutha was right. There is no rape on Dinadh, but I can imagine it would be as shaming, as cruel as this. In a way, it was like what the two Fastigats were doing to me, questioning me, searching at me, examining me, bending their Fastigat sense upon me. That, too, was rape. They increased my shame and sorrow for no good reason, for they could not learn something I did not know.

It is better to do as the sisters recommend, to say nothing at all, to admit nothing. Let them seek elsewhere, among others for answers. And if they find answers, let them tell me.

A voice from the door.

'Saluez? Are you awake?'

Lutha.

I sat up, pulling my veil into place. 'I was up earlier,' I confessed.

'Leelson and Trompe and I've been talking,' she said. 'We have an offer we wish to make you, in return for your help.'

I had heard nothing of an offer. What offer?

She said, 'It's possible ... your face can be fixed. Restored ...'

'No,' I cried, thrusting away with both hands. 'No. Do not say that!'

She looked shocked, horrified. 'But surely ...'

'I would have to leave Dinadh,' I cried hysterically. 'I would have to go away from my people. They would not let me live here if you healed me.'

'But ... but I thought ...'

'It was my fault,' I cried. I who had decided to say nothing! I, who knew it was not my fault! 'My face is evidence of my sin. Do you think you can erase my sin by healing me? Do you think my people will let me live among them if I am healed!'

She backed away from me in confusion. Leelson came from the study and put his hand on her shoulder. 'What?' he demanded.

She turned and led him into the room, shutting the door firmly behind them. And I sat on the edge of my bed and cried. Oh, if I were healed, Shalumn might be mine again. Oh, if I were healed, I would have to go away. Oh, if I were healed, it would change nothing, it would change everything!

After a time I dried my face, straightened my veil, and went to knock upon the closed door.

'I will help you,' I said when they opened it. 'But you must not talk of ... what you said earlier. Not at all. Not ever!' I could not bear it. It set all my hard-won peace at nothing.

They stared at me, all three of them. The boy was curled on a bench beneath the window, playing with his fingers. They cared, but he did not.

'Why?' asked Leelson. 'Why will you help us?'

'You say there is great danger for everyone, perhaps for Dinadh too. Perhaps the outlander ghost found something to avert this danger, so I will help you search for the outlander ghost or for what it was he knew.'

Leelson ran his hands through his hair. He was a handsome man,

Leelson. Tall, bright-haired, with one of those rugged, rocky outlander faces that always seem strange to us Dinadhi, who are round-faced and smoother looking. The boy looked something like him. More like him than Lutha. But he had a big-eyed strangeness to him, something I thought I should recognize.

'Where could Bernesohn Famber have gone, Saluez?'

It was a foolish question. He knew as well as I. 'You heard his own voice,' I replied. 'He spoke of the southern canyon, of the omphalos. You yourself said he must have walked. That is where he walked.'

Leelson frowned as he seated himself. 'All right, let's take it point by point. Last night you told us certain gods were abandoned on your former world.'

I nodded. Unwisely, I had said it.

'And these gods were abandoned for' – he gestured toward the window – 'the beautiful people.'

'We chose the Kachis instead,' I said. 'Our songfathers chose them.'

'Why?' asked Lutha.

'It is not something we speak of,' I told them. 'I have already said more than is proper. We chose them, that is all. We abandoned certain of our gods, and chose these instead, and came here to this world.'

'Through the omphalos?'

'Through the omphalos.'

They looked at one another in that way they have, like grown-ups amused by the fanciful tales of children.

'She believes it,' said Trompe, staring at me.

Why would I not believe it? It was true.

'If you'll allow a non-Fastigat a comment,' said Lutha in a dry voice. 'As a linguist, I've become aware that there are many kinds of truth – factual truths, scientific truths, spiritual truths, psychological truths. It is no doubt spiritually true that the people of Dinadh emerged from the omphalos. That being so, it doesn't matter whether it's factually true or not.' She smiled at me, saying I might believe as I liked, she would not question it.

'Why do you say that?' Trompe demanded.

She turned to him, gesturing. 'I say it because we can only deal with so many variables at a time! Bernesohn didn't mention emergence stories, he spoke of a place! A geographical location. We need not concern ourselves with what's true or false *about* the place, at least not until we get there.'

I bowed my head. Exactly. What was true or false did not concern them. Only their duty concerned them, as only my duty now concerned me. My duty and my child to come. The future, to which life itself owes a duty. 'To fit into the pattern,' say the songfathers. 'Each life owes a duty to fit in.'

Even men who know many lies occasionally tell the truth.

'We must go there, then,' said Leelson. 'To the place.'

'It is forbidden,' I told them. 'No outlanders are allowed at the omphalos. Only Dinadhi without stain may attend Tahs-uppi, and the ceremony will be very soon.'

They simply stared at me, knowing what I was feeling. How strange to have people know as these men knew. They knew what I had said was not all I meant.

'But you're going to take us there,' said Leelson at last, prompting me.

'I will guide you,' I whispered. 'If you want to go.'

'But I have a map,' he said, holding it up for me to see. 'Do I need a guide?'

'You don't have a way to travel,' Lutha said. 'That's what she means.'

'You would not last an hour after dark,' I said quietly. 'There are ways and ways. You need someone who knows the ways.'

Not that I knew the ways. I'd never been out after dark, but I'd spoken with herders who had. Leelson moved to the desk, Trompe to the bench, Lutha to her child, all thinking, all deciding, as though this wandering motion helped them think. Perhaps it did.

'They'd know we were gone,' said Lutha, pulling Leely into her lap. 'They'd come after us.'

'How would they know?' I asked. 'I am your servitor. I take care of your needs. If I do not report that you are gone, who is to know?'

'They would see we aren't here, see we aren't moving around.'

'They don't look at you anyhow," I said. 'That's what I am assigned to do. I look at you so the others don't have to. We do not look at outlanders, we of Dinadh!'

'They would know *you* aren't here,' said Trompe.

Lutha said softly, 'They don't look at her, either.'

Behind my veil, my mouth twisted. It was true. If Chahdzi or songfather did not see me for a number of days, they would think I was staying out of sight. The sisters below would know they had not seen me there, in our place, but they would not search for me. They knew I served these outlanders. They would wait until my duty was done and I came to them.

'So they wouldn't know we were gone,' said Trompe.

'No,' I said. 'They would not know. Not for some time. Songfather may not know until he himself arrives at the omphalos and finds you there.'

'The ceremony is soon?' Lutha demanded.

'Very soon,' I told them. 'Within days.'

'Can we get there first?'

'Not by much,' I admitted. 'A few days, at most.'

'How do we get there at all?'

'There are wains here in the canyon, wains that make a safe enclosure for people, with woven panels to make a safe pen for the gaufers that pull them.

When the songfathers attend Tahs-uppi, that is how they go. We must take a wain and six gaufers to pull it.'

'Gaufers?' asked Lutha.

'Woolbeasts. The young are gaufs. Gaufers are the neutered ones.'

I could see her tucking these words away against later need.

'How do we get these gaufers down from the heights?' asked Leelson.

'We don't. There are still some here, because all the flocks have not been moved up the trail yet. We must steal them before the flocks are taken up.'

'Food stores?' murmured Trompe.

'There is much food here in the dispenser,' I told them. 'Though it is outlander food, I imagine I can figure out how to cook it over a fire.'

They thought about this for some time. Lutha went on cuddling the child. Trompe stared out across the floor of the cave to the canyon. Leelson fiddled with things on the desk, moving them about, here and there. When Leelson turned to me at last, it was not to ask how, but why.

'If this journey is forbidden,' he said, 'you may be putting yourself at grave risk.'

Behind my veil I smiled. 'What can they do to me that has not already been done? Perhaps they will kill me! They will not do it until after the child is born, and I do not care if they do it then.'

Perhaps it was only what Lutha calls bravado, but I think I was telling the truth.

I am not much practiced at stealing. We Dinadhi do not steal, not much. Oh, children, sometimes, a little dried fruit more than our share. A handful of nuts. A finger dipped surreptitiously into the honey pot. What else? What is there? Only what we make with our own hands.

So, considering how to steal a wain and gaufers was a novel thing for me. It had a certain stomach-churning excitement to it. Leaving the outlanders to mutter and worry behind me, I went out onto the lip of the cave and sat with my legs dangling over the edge. Below me, behind screened openings in the canyon wall, the herds have their winter caves. There before the time of First Grass the females bear their young. When all the gaufs have been born and are steady on their legs, the herds are driven up one of the trails onto the grassy forested lands above. Wains are not taken back and forth. They are too bulky and heavy to drag up and down the trails. So there are wains on the heights for the herders to live in, and there are wains in the canyons for the songfathers to travel to and from the little ceremonies at each other's hives and the big ceremonies like Tahs-uppi.

At the Coming of Cold, the herds come down again, into the caves, where they eat the dried remnants of our gardens, the vines and stalks and even the weeds we have pulled and set aside for them. When they have eaten it all, they eat fungus, as we do, growing as tired of it as we do and becoming eager for the fresh green of the heights. Most of the herds had gone up already, but a few small flocks were left.

Getting six gaufers away from the herders would be possible. Harnessing them would probably be difficult, though I thought I could figure it out. Harnessing them, hitching them, driving them, all that to be figured out and accomplished without being observed. Which meant at night.

'What are you thinking?' asked Lutha, coming to sit beside me.

I told her my thoughts, describing the caves, pointing downward where this one was, and that one, shaking my head at the danger, at the difficulty.

'When we came to Cochim-Mahn,' she said, 'we left the hostel and started down the trail when it was barely light. Chahdzi said it wasn't quite proper to start before the dawnsong, but we did it, nonetheless. Suppose we take the animals very early in the morning, just at dawn.'

'The herders would not hear us then,' I agreed. 'They sleep in the hive, and they do not come out until the daysong.'

'So, if you locate the animals we need, and if Leelson finds a wain, and if we take all our supplies down, a little at a time ... well, then, in a few days ...'

'It must be sooner than that,' I told her. 'There are only a few animals left in the caves.'

'Well, we'll begin at once,' she said. I heard apprehension in her voice. It would have been surprising if she had not felt it. I did.

'At once,' I agreed. 'It will take time to carry our supplies down the ladders.'

She sighed deeply. 'Do you know the way to the omphalos?'

'No. But I have heard the stories of the journey, over and over since I was a child. How the wains go, and what people see on the way, and how the ...' I had been about to mention what the beautiful people did at Tahs-uppi. That was forbidden. Instead I said weakly, 'I've heard how the songfathers draw out the extra days, to balance the seasons.'

'What did they look like, these extra days?' she asked, half smiling.

I shook my head at her. 'No one knows. All those present hide their faces. It would be improper to look.'

'Improper to look at a lot of things around here,' she muttered to herself as she rose and went back into the leasehold, to tell the others. I went down the ladders to see if our plan could be made real or would remain only talk.

The herd caves smell only a little, because the droppings are taken away at once to the caverns where fungus is grown, just as our human waste is taken in the hive. So, when I came to the caves, there were herders moving about with their shovels, cleaning the pens and pretending not to see me. Perhaps they did not see me. I tried to remember if I had seen veiled women before I became one myself, remembering times in childhood when adults had whispered to me that it was not wise to look, not wise or polite to see. So I had not seen. Now I was not seen.

So much the better. I could take my time. I could linger. I could see where the stoutest gaufers were, two in this pen, three in that, one in the third. When they are neutered, their horns curl tightly instead of growing out to the sides. That way we may drive them in pairs, side by side, without their bumping. The neutered ones get heavier, too, and tamer, for they are constantly handled. There were seven or eight good ones in the pens, and they nosed the woven panels at the front of the caves, soft noses wrinkling, side-whiskers jiggling. *They* had not been trained not to see me. If I brought tasties for them, they would see me well enough. Well enough to follow me.

Where was the harness kept? I did not see it in the caves, though there was other equipment hung here and there among the bins of dried fungus. I swept dust from my memory, recalling me as a child, riding on Chahdzi's shoulder, being shown the beasts, the caves, the wains. What had the harness looked like? Chest straps, as I recalled, with fringes on them to keep the insects away from the soft, naked hide between the front legs, where the false udders are. And carved wooden buffer bars, to hold the pairs abreast. Wide hauling straps of gaufer leather, and long, light reins of braided bark fiber, the same as our well ropes.

There was nothing resembling a harness in the caves.

Which meant the harness was with the wains. Or in the hive somewhere.

I passed Leelson Famber on the ladders, murmuring to him that I had not found the harness. He nodded and continued downward. Perhaps he would find it.

If it was in the hive, it was in the quarters of the herdsmen, where their families lived. I could not go there when the people were there. Perhaps at the morning song, when everyone was gathered behind the doorskins, waiting to go out. Then I could slip inside to look around.

There was a time I would have hated this sneakiness. Was a time I would have considered it beneath me, beneath any Dinadhi. Now I was no longer a person to be concerned with such things. I was an unperson. I did not exist. Who would point the finger at me when they could not even see me?

I returned to the leasehold. Lutha was there, feeding the child. I offered to do it for her, and she handed me the spoon with an expression almost of relief. She went to sit in the window, looking out at the day while I plied the spoon. It was like feeding a little animal. He was too old for the breast, but I had the feeling he would best have liked to suckle, for he could have done that without thinking at all. Certainly he could not keep his mind on the spoon.

He calmed as he grew less hungry. When we were finished, it took a large

417

towel and a bowl of warm water to clean up the boy and the area around him.

'He has always been this way?' I asked.

'Yes,' she said, her body stiffening. She did not want to talk about it.

Well then, we would not talk about it.

'There are some good gaufers down there,' I told her. 'But I couldn't find the harness. Perhaps Leelson will find it in a wain. Where has Trompe gone?'

'He's carrying supplies down the ladders,' she said with suppressed laughter. 'Or was. Here he comes, very hot looking!'

As he did, out of breath and considerably annoyed.

'Leelson's found a wain,' he said. 'It's parked out of sight of the hive, around those stone columns south of the cave. He told me to put the food inside it. Otherwise he thinks it won't last until we're ready to leave.'

I nodded. He was right. Any food left where the Kachis could get it would be either eaten or fouled past use. 'Was the harness there?' I asked.

'I don't know. I didn't look and Leelson didn't say.' He collapsed onto a sleeping bench and threw one arm across his face. 'Lord, that's a long climb. You Dinadhi must have steel legs and arms, up and down all day as you are.'

'Two trips a day is considered much,' I told them. 'One is the usual. When the farmers go to work in the fields, they go down at daylight and return before dusk. They carry their lunch with them.'

'We haven't talked about how long this is going to take,' he said. 'How much food we'll need ...'

'All we can carry,' I told him.

'Then we'll need a faster way of getting it down there.'

Silence, broken by the sound of the door. Leelson, returning.

'Harness is in the wain,' he said. 'I counted the individual sets, and it looks like enough for six animals. On my way back, however, I overheard several of the herdsmen talking. They're taking the animals up tomorrow.'

Silence again.

'We'll have to leave before then,' murmured Lutha. 'Won't we?' She gave me a pleading look, as though hoping I could think of some other choice.

'No time for sneakiness,' I said. 'Were there panels on the sides of the wain you chose?'

He nodded, his lips pressed tightly together. 'Yes. I remembered that part. They make up the pen for the gaufers, I presume.'

'Walls and roof, to keep them safe at night,' I said. 'Tomorrow before light, we'll take all the food from the dispenser, put it in sacks, and drop it into the canyon. We need not carry water. This time of year there will be water along the canyon-bottom trail we'll follow. We'll have to be gone before light.' To my own ears, my voice shouted panic, but the others did not seem to hear it. They merely sighed, resolved on the struggle to come but taking no joy in it.

'They'll know the wain is gone,' Trompe objected.

'Perhaps not,' I replied. 'There are extra ones. If the one you picked is beyond the pillars, likely it is one that was not to be used this year. Or, if someone sees it is gone, they may think someone moved it. People are always moving wains around. To store things in. Or to repair them.'

'They don't belong to anyone in particular?'

'They belong to Cochim-Mahn. Not to any particular person. Anyone might move a wain.'

'Well then,' said Leelson.

'I just had a thought,' Trompe interrupted. 'What about weapons?'

'Weapons!' I cried. 'To use against what?'

They looked at me, the two men with those expressions they have, reading me, knowing how I felt. Well, I could read their faces as well!

'No!' I shouted at them. 'That is forbidden. You will not!'

The two exchanged glances, then shrugged, both at once, as by agreement.

'They are our ...' I said, trying to explain, remembering I couldn't explain.

'Your what, Saluez?' asked Lutha curiously.

I could not say. I had already said forbidden things, thought forbidden thoughts. I shook my head at her. Enough. One might do this little wrong thing, or that little wrong thing, but not forever! One could not cut across the pattern over and over again. I had to stop, even though these folk were eager to know more. Let them find out some other way. Let them read it in someone else's feelings. I had said all I could say.

On Perdur Alas, night on night the monstrosities returned to wander the world. Even when Snark did not see them, she could tell they were present somewhere: just over a cusp of hills, in a valley somewhere, at the bottom of the sea, perhaps, for when she stood with her mouth open and turned about slowly, she could taste them, strongly or faintly. At first she would taste nothing, perhaps, but then her tongue would curl at the subtle disgust of them, the cloying rottenness, the foulness that could not be spat away.

One taste was enough. Whenever she detected it, she went to ground. Driven as much by instinct as by prior knowledge, she made herself a dozen hidey-holes around the camp and between it and the sea. She dug upward, into the sides of hills, so the tunnels would drain and the holes would stay dry. She made them large enough to be comfortable. She knew if she was surrounded by earth, the beings could not detect her. If she was in a hole, with foliage drawn over her, they could not tell she was there. She thought someone had told her this, just as they'd told her how to dig holes. She seemed to remember these things from that former time.

The blacknesses, as she called them, did not always come to the camp. Moreover, the blacknesses were not always the same. Occasionally, rarely, they were like the first time, with that same muffled soundlessness, that same trembling of the soil, that same monstrous plodding. More often they were merely shapes against the stars, who brought with them a horrible taste. Very rarely they were both. They came irregularly, once every three to five nights, seldom two nights in a row, always after dark. She wondered if they came to the other side of the planet when it was night there. She dug out the reports and found that the other side of the planet was mostly water, covered by the vast shallow sea that made up nine tenths of Perdur Alas. They came when this side was in darkness, she decided. The other side was not useful to them, or was less useful, or was ... unimportant, perhaps. Who knew?

Why did they come at all? After that first night, they changed nothing. They took nothing away. They added nothing at all. They merely came and wandered about, black against the stars, occasionally trembling the earth, shaking the hills, shaking Snark herself in absolute terror.

At first she survived on this terror, letting it drive her deep into her cave and keep her there. As time went by, however, curiosity asserted itself, and she found herself speculating more and more about what the presences were, and what their enigmatic business might be. She wanted to see them. She wanted to get a good look! She did not consider that she might have been conditioned to be curious. The feeling was natural to her. She had always been that way. Mother had ...

Mother had always been that way too. Mother had been here with her, long ago, and Mother had always been curious about Perdur Alas. The others ... the other people used to warn her. Don't take chances. But Mother had taken chances. The memory came and went, evanescent as a breeze.

It was time to satisfy curiosity. Since the beings seemed no longer particularly interested in the camp, she stealthily removed a number of items to make night spying easier: devices for seeing in the dark; recorders activated by change in air chemistry or pressure, by sound or movement, by temperature change; solar-powered lights, solar-powered reference files. More food and blankets, to make her other hidey-holes warm enough to spend whole nights in, if necessary. The things that wouldn't fit into her cave or into the new hidey-holes, she hid elsewhere. The solar devices she secreted here and there in newly dug holes or among piles of stone, covering them with layers of furze that she could remove each morning to allow the devices to charge. The night eyes she secreted in her hole above the camp. There, lying in the mouth of her tunnel, rolled into a pair of soft blankets and screened by carefully positioned branches, she propped herself in a comfortable position, one she could wake from silently.

They didn't come. Toward morning she roused, tasting them. They were somewhere, but not here, not at the camp. The taste was mild, barely discernible. She stood up, yawned, and made her way to the cave over the sea.

Twice more she waited fruitlessly.

On the fourth night they came. She gagged on her own saliva and knew they were nearby.

She focused the device, propping it in the opening, careful not to move the screening grasses and leaves. She watched them come from the west, over the sea, watched them traverse the moor between, watched them gather south of the camp as though waiting for something or checking on something or, perhaps merely assembling there prior to departure. Through the device she could see the shape of them, the way they moved. They had no legs. These could not be the earth tremblers; these were the others. Monstrous and shaggy, they floated in air, multiple appendages hanging limply below, a few of them reaching to the sides as though feeling the way.

Snark put down the night eyes and clawed at her mouth, cleaning it out with her fingers. Too much of this and she would choke on her own spit! She put a wad of leaves between her teeth to hold them apart so the sticky saliva could flow – if it would – and lifted the device to her eyes once more.

The shapes had no faces, nothing that looked like ears or noses or mouths. Occasionally two of the creatures would pull in all their appendages, making their bellies smooth and shiny, and would then turn toward one another while wavering blobs of deep-hued color flowed across the smooth integument. The next time two of them paired in this fashion, she took the device from her eyes to see if the color was visible to the naked eye. It was detectable only because she knew it was there. A shifting red shadow, a depth of blue or purple, at this distance hardly discernible without the device.

On Prime, while living in the sanctuary, she had gone with the other children to an aquarium. She remembered a multiarmed sea creature that had changed color, being in one instant white and gray, in another dark, marbled with red, and in another so gravelly that it disappeared into the sandy seabed it lay upon. So the skin on these creatures changed, from dark to light, from pattern to pattern.

One of them had a winy-red patch that repeatedly moved diagonally downward, left to right. Diagonal Red, she named it, turning her attention to the others. By the time night was over, she had named Four Green Spot, Blue Lines, Big Gray Blob, and Speckled Purple, these particular ones because they were at the top of the hierarchy. Diagonal Red was the one who moved first, the one the others followed. Blue Lines and Speckled Purple were next, then Four Green Spot and Big Gray Blob, and after them, a host of others whose characteristics she had been unable to identify. Over their next few visits she counted them, seeing as many as eighty at a time. Her count never came out the same. There were at least eighty. Maybe as many as a hundred, all huge as hills. All truly and unbelievably horrid.

For a time she stopped watching them, too exhausted to do otherwise, but curiosity reasserted itself and she came back to her hidey-hole, back to her blankets, watching. Very late, choking on the taste of them, she wakened from restless sleep. Two she later identified as Diagonal Red and Speckled Purple had returned alone and were moving through the vacant camp. After making colors at one another several times, they separated, one stopping at the seaward edge of the camp, the other stopping on the inland side. There they poised themselves, turned on their sides, settled onto the soil, and extended three or four appendages on each side, these tentacles becoming longer and longer, wider and wider, creeping along the edges of the camp, surrounding it, until at last the tips approached one another and touched.

From her carefully dug hole on the hill, Snark could see down into this squat cylinder of alien flesh, five hundred paces across. The outer surface was shaggy. The inside was bare and shiny. She watched fascinated as colors developed upon the bare bellies of the participants, then moved sideways onto the appendages, moving right to left, onto the other creature, color succeeding color, shape succeeding shape, an unending flow of luminescence, now bright, now dark, now vivid, now pale, flowing uninterruptedly from the bare flesh of Diagonal Red across the appendages to the bare flesh of Speckled Purple, thence around onto Diagonal Red once more, a slowly whirling vortex of color and movement. She didn't need glasses to see it. It was perfectly visible without!

Despite the strangling taste, the strangeness of the sight, something teased at Snark's mind, something she should see, should understand. She strained, trying to think, what was it? Something ... something ...

Then it was over. The two shapes darkened, the appendages separated, curled into tentacle shapes, shrank languidly back to their usual size. The central creatures rose like shaggy, bulbous balloons and moved away. Propelled, Snark told herself, by thought. Or wish. Or by something else, somewhere else.

A few moments later the taste vanished. Snark scraped her tongue, rinsed her mouth with water from her canteen, spat repeatedly, getting rid of it. What had she just watched? What kind of ceremony? Oh, to be a Fastigat right now! Able to sense whatever emotion had been present, whatever those two immensities had been feeling!

Something solemn, she thought. Some color litany, some ritual observance. Or perhaps they had been mating!

If so, why would they pick a human encampment to mate around? No. It had more the sense of a ritual. Sacrifice, maybe? Explaining to their weird gods that they had wiped out a few dozen humans as required by their religion?

Again something teased at her mind. Something she should know! She held very still, hoping it would come to her. It did not. Merely that teasing sensation, something she should hold on to and could not get hold of!

Ah, well. Let it go for tonight. She hid her night-eye device once more, picked up her canteen, and trudged down the hill toward the moor paths to the sea. The stars told her it was still some hours until morning. Still some hours to stay hidden in. She had not known them to come twice on one night, but this evening's exercise indicated how little she really knew.

The way seemed longer than usual. When she dropped into the cave at last, she was in a mood of weary indifference. She wanted to live, but not much. What she really wanted to do was understand these creatures, but what she had seen tonight was unintelligible. Perhaps they would remain unintelligible.

She stripped off her clothes and laid them in a pile at the back of the cave. Tomorrow would be wash day. She pulled other clothing from her sack and put it on. She always slept fully dressed except for her boots. One never knew when one might have to move quickly. She checked the emergency pack by the entry hole. Water. Food. Medical supplies. A change of clothing.

'Now I lay me,' she told herself, curling into her blankets, knees to chest, one arm cradling her head. 'Now I lay me.' Outside the surf repeated sea words, over and over. *Shush. Soof. Fwoosh.* Again and again.

She dreamed. She was walking on the moor, coming to the cave by the sea, but she was not alone. Someone held her by the hand.

'We must go very carefully,' the someone said. 'Try not to go the same way too often. Not to make a trail, you understand?'

Snark jerked her chin resolutely, saying she understood. Things could follow trails. She had to be careful, or the *things* would get her.

They came to the edge of the cliff. 'Hold on tight,' said the someone.

Snark's arms were locked around the person's neck, her legs around the person's waist. The person leapt, and Snark's stomach came up into her throat the way it always did. Then they were swinging, swinging, then the hole was there, and they were in.

'Home is where the heart is,' said someone, kissing Snark. 'Home is where my girl is.'

Snark looked up at the person. ...

Color flowing, blotches flowing, making a pattern ...

The person held her tightly, patting her on the back.

Bright and dim, pale and vivid, colors on the huge fleshy barrier. Shaggy skin outside, bare skin inside ...

The person smiled.

Shapelessness became shape. Shades flowed into one another. Blotches and colors combined to make a face on the body of an alien monster, a huge face that moved and spoke and smiled and called her by name!

'Sweetheart,' the mouth said. 'Love.'

Her mother's face!

Snark's cry went out over the sea like the cry of a wounded animal, totally alone, infinitely sorrowful.

'Mother,' she cried. 'Oh, Mother, Mother, come back to me!'

Night on Dinadh. In the leasehold, Lutha and the two Fastigats had had their evening meal. We had packed the last few things we intended to take with us. Then Leelson insisted that everyone lie down and get as much sleep as possible, promptly thereafter making it impossible for anyone to sleep by getting into a fierce argument with Lutha. I had felt it coming during our evening meal, like thunder just beyond the horizon, a muted mutter, scarcely heard and yet ominous, making one's whole body tense, awaiting the flash of lightning, the crash of riven air!

The flash was Leelson's pronouncement to Lutha:

'When Trompe, Saluez, and I leave in the morning, I want you and the child to stay here, Lutha. Give us a few days to get well away, then ask the people to take you back to the port.'

'The hell,' she snarled, a thundercrack.

Hurriedly, I left the room. They were so intent upon each other, they did not see me go. Trompe, who had been half-asleep in the neighboring room, had evidently felt the emotional storm going on, for he emerged, blinked at me, and mouthed, 'What?'

I shrugged and kept going. While I fully intended to listen, I didn't want to be involved. We mutilated ones are observers of life, not participants. So says the sisterhood. And safer so, so says the sisterhood. And more peaceful.

So I took myself beyond the storeroom door and then shamelessly leaned against the wall while I listened to what was going on. Lutha was saying at great length that having come this far, she had no intention of going home.

'Besides,' she cried, 'you and Trompe aren't linguists, and I am.'

'We are Fastigats,' said Leelson.

'Fastigats aren't gods!' she snarled at him. 'Much though you like to think so! You can tell how people feel, maybe, but you can't tell why. Sometimes, it takes words to tell why.'

It was true that neither Trompe nor Leelson had a really good command of our language. I spoke far better aglais than they did Nantaskan. But then, a lot of us learn languages as children, in order to cater to our lease-holders. Why would they learn our dialect? There are few of us who speak the tongue.

'You will be safer at home,' he said, like a father cautioning a child. 'You will be better off.'

'I'll decide where I'll be better off,' she said. 'If you'd had the common sense and decency to tell people you were coming here, I wouldn't have been sent. Now that I have been sent, I've no intention of going home until the job is done.'

'The boy will be in the way.' His tone said she would be in the way, too, which perhaps she noticed.

'Leelson,' said Trompe from the doorway. I could see him through the hinge gap at the side of the door I stood behind. 'Leelson. Stop talking and think.'

Leelson stopped talking. I assumed he was looking at Lutha. The silence had a peculiarly penetrating quality to it, one I have noticed before when he or Trompe reached out. So, he was reaching at Lutha, into her, understanding her.

'Stop it,' said Lutha. 'Stop digging at me! I'm fully capable of telling you how I feel. I am not a gofer to be sent hither and thither at the whim of any presumptuous Fastigat who gets a burr up his rear! I'm a person. Until the Great Gauphin comes down from heaven and appoints you his lieutenant, I've got the same rights you have. I decided to come here, and I've decided to stay until our mission is finished. Since I had to bring Leely in order to get here, he'll come along, no matter how much "in the way" he is.'

Silence. I saw Trompe make a helpless gesture.

After a time Leelson said calmly, 'Have you thought about your career? A lengthy interruption certainly won't forward it.'

'Having a child didn't forward it,' she said. 'Quite frankly, I don't anticipate it forwarding much in the future. About the best I can hope for is keeping my head above water.'

'She's bored, Leelson.' This was Trompe.

More silence. Then her voice, quieter: 'He's right. I'm bored with my life on Alliance Central! I'm bored sick with it! I'm also terrified at the threat of the Ularians. I may mock the Firster assurance that men are the meaning and soul of creation, but that doesn't mean I welcome being slaughtered by something bigger and meaner. The Procurator used fear for motivation, succeeding better than he knew!'

Even I, who am no Fastigat, knew she was not telling all the truth. Later, when the men had gone to sleep, she came to the storeroom door and peered in, looking for me.

'You're still up,' she said, trying to be surprised. No doubt she had seen the light of my candle.

'I'm too ... too something to sleep,' I confessed.

She sat on a sack of grain, crossing her ankles, then recrossing them, twiddling her feet, wanting to talk about something, obviously.

'Leelson was right,' I murmured. 'You would be safer back in your home. And so would the boy.'

She looked up at me blindly. 'I don't want to be safe, Saluez.' There was a sob in her voice, betraying a feeling I knew well. She wanted to die. It is not so much an active thing, this feeling, not so much a desire to kill oneself as it is a desire not to be. An absence of hope. Despite everything she told herself about the boy, she had no hope. She saw herself getting older and older while he got bigger and stronger, his demands got bigger and bigger, more and more difficult. She saw herself victim to a helpless love for him, unable to help him or herself, desiring rather to be dead.

I found myself holding her, cuddling her as she had cuddled me, laying my own fingers on her lips.

'He should get to know his son,' she said, taking my hand in her own. 'Get to know him.'

What was there to know? I wondered. I didn't say it aloud.

'Leely has many ... many interesting qualities,' she insisted.

'Of course,' I murmured. 'Children do.'

'His artistic talent alone ...'

'Shhh,' I whispered, rocking her. 'Shhh.'

So we sat together in the dark, reaching for light. My sisters tell me so women have done for lo these thousands of years.

6

In the hive of T'loch-ala, which is *Old Place* in Lutha's language, Mitigan of the Asenagi and Chur Durwen of Collis, being neither linguists nor Fastigats, found that getting information out of the Dinadhi was easier assumed than accomplished. Though they were well served by the two women appointed to the task, one veiled and one barefaced, the women had no more to say than any other member of the hive. True, they spoke a little aglais, as did Chur Durwen, and Mitigan spoke enough Thibegan, which was a Nantaskan tongue, to make his wants known if he used sign language along with it, but neither of the men had any luck whatsoever in finding out where Bernesohn Famber might once have lived and even now held lease upon Dinadh.

'I've told you we don't know,' said the barefaced servitor, an older woman whose voice verged upon annoyance. 'We would have no reason to know. We do not discuss such things. Until you said the man's name, I had never heard of him. We have our own pattern here on Dinadh. Why would we ignore our own pattern to enter that of some outlander ghost?'

Both men were Firsters of the more primitive sort, accustomed to treating every itch in the groin as though it were divine commandment, and after several days of utter boredom in the hive, Mitigan thought he'd try a bit with the veiled servitor. She had a seductive shape beneath her robes and a pleasant voice from behind her mask. He managed to twitch the veil a little bit to one side before she got away from him, but that little bit was enough to leave him sweating and cold, like a man who had just escaped dropping over a precipice.

'My god, man,' he whispered to Chur Durwen. 'She looked chewed. Like a viper bat had been at her, or one of those hovolutes they have on Zeta Nine.'

'Hovolutes don't leave anyone alive,' objected Chur Durwen.

'Well, imagine one of the victims surviving and you'll have an idea what our waiting woman looks like.'

Chur Durwen was curious. He kept watch, and one day as the woman bent over to pick up something, the veil fell loosely at the side of her face. He, too, caught only a glimpse, but that was enough.

These happenings were small in themselves, but enough to set both men thinking. They had assumed there were no predators on Dinadh, but now they began assessing certain phrases and silences, certain movements of avoidance, certain rituals of aversion.

'It's them,' Mitigan said to Chur Durwen one night as he looked through their barred windows at the pale forms assembled across the canyon. 'Those flyin' things that hang about after dark. They're dangerous beasts.'

'Small ones,' murmured Chur Durwen, unimpressed.

'Chowbys aren't big either,' said the other. 'Or viper bats. But you get over-run by a dozen of either one and you're dead meat. And ants, they're tiny little old things, but people on Old-earth used to go in fear of their armies. Stingers, those were.'

'I'd forgotten about chowbys,' mused the man from Collis. 'And you're right. There's a considerable mob of those night fliers about. I must've seen several hundred, just last evenin'.'

'So.'

'So?'

'Puts a bit a crimp in goin' lookin' for Fambers, dunnit? Stands to reason they're not comin' here, we got to go lookin'.'

'Must be a way.' Chur Durwen stared meditatively at his boots. 'Always has to be a way.'

Mitigan grunted. What his friend said was true. There was always a way to kill a man or woman. No matter how he hid, how he ran, how he vanished into another identity; no matter how she pleaded, how she bribed, how she threatened. There was always a way. So Mitigan's father's brother had taught him when he was a boy.

'Always a way, boy. Study on the target, make him your book, make him your library, boy, and you'll find the way.'

'They say killin's wrong, Uncle Jo.'

'They! And who's they? They put power in your pocket? They buy festives for your women? Food for your children? Ha? Who's this they? Not Firsters, that's sure! No Firster ever said such a damn fool thing!'

Which was true. A man who'd recently killed was considered blood guilty, but there was a ritual for erasing blood guilt. All Mitigan had had to do was pay a hefty price to the Firster godmonger in the district where the victim lived. Those who spoke against killing were only do-gooders, reform-ers, non-Firsters all. They were men who belonged to no tribe, swore alle-giance to no hetman. Men who, it was said, would puke themselves inside out if told to go out and get an ear for the hetman, a hand for the hetman, or somebody's head in particular.

Mitigan was born of the Dirt-hog tribe, and Uncle Jo sat on the hetman's right hand. Not quite next to him, true, but no more than three or four men down. Mitigan's pa, now, he'd sat right next to the Dirt-hog hetman, and when the hetman said go, Pa had gone. One time too many, as it turned out, but he died with his name bright, so Mitigan had no dishonor to live down.

It was a good tribe to learn killing in, all the way from elementary mutilations right up to, so Uncle Jo sometimes said, a graduate degree in massacre: an MMA, Master of Mortial Arts. Mitigan studied his subject as Uncle Jo had advocated: studied it and practiced it, and got so good at it that when the Dirt-hogs were ambushed by the Lightning Bears one bloody night at Headoff Hill, only fifteen-year-old Mitigan escaped and survived. He'd sworn vengeance. He could not have lived with himself otherwise.

The Lightning Bears had laughed at him, man and boy, laughed at him and hadn't even taken the trouble of killing him. They hadn't laughed five years later, after Mitigan had taken out the whole Lightning tribe, one man by one man, including every male child. That's why it took so long. That last infant he'd had to wait for, since it hadn't been born yet. Firsters didn't hold with killing babies until after they got born!

A man with that history had his future pretty well laid out for him. There was always a market for assassins, especially assassins who could think. Mitigan could think, though he did not think much about his career. A man could get tied up in his own thoughts, worried over them, or guilty over them, or overly convinced of his own prowess. A man needed a clear head to survive. He had to be careful.

Still and all, if a man really wanted to hit a target, Chur Durwen was right. There was always a way.

It wasn't long before Mitigan put two and two together to come up with the same answer those at Cochim-Mahn had arrived at. The key to traveling on Dinadh was to have a structure or vehicle inside which one could be safe at night. Since the hover cars were controlled from the port city, they wouldn't do. Since any other structure would make too heavy a load for a man, it would have to be hauled by beasts, which meant the beasts themselves had to be protected. Travel on Dinadh required a wain and beasts to pull it. Or the equivalent.

'You think I'm goin' to fool with animals, you got a fool's idea.' Chur Durwen yawned.

'Right,' agreed Mitigan. 'We'll do it our way.'

They'd brought certain items of equipment with them, the parts innocuously labeled and packaged as health monitors or retrievers and transcribers or library modules. Several of these items, taken apart and reassembled into a portable unit, would create a protective dome big enough to sleep in. Big enough to live in for a while, if necessary.

'Though it'll be somewhat troublesome,' Mitigan told his companion, 'I think we'd be wise to take a pack animal.'

Chur Durwen didn't argue with him. In a pinch, Mitigan later told me, they could have carried their own provisions, but assassins preferred to stay unencumbered when engaged in their profession. Besides, at T'loch-ala, spring had not advanced so far as it had at Cochim-Mahn and there were many strong animals to choose from still in the caves.

'So now we know how,' muttered Mitigan over his evening meal as he stared out the window at the dancing Kachis. 'All we have to figure out is where.'

The question plagued him as he ate, as he slept, as he did his weapons exercises morning and night. Chur Durwen, who preferred to get his daily exercise climbing up and down the ladders between hive and valley below, was bothered by the same question. Where?

It was a conversation Mitigan overheard between two women at the well ropes that gave them the clue they needed.

'Will you be going to Tahs-uppi with songfather?' one asked of the other.

'Alas, no,' replied the other. She was quite beautiful, Mitigan thought, with black hair that fell in a lightless flow almost to her knees. She was also very pregnant. 'Songfather feels it is too near my time.'

'He's probably right,' said the first, with a delicate shudder. 'One should not be far from help the first time. Still, it's sad that you'll miss it. All the songfathers and their guests will be there, from everywhere in Dinadh. Another such opportunity will not come in our lifetime.'

Mitigan went at once to inform his colleague. 'She said people would be there from all over Dinadh. Which means there'll be someone there who knows where Famber is, or was.'

'Fine,' muttered the man from Collis. 'So we go to Tahs-uppi. Where is it?'

It took them some days of fumbling questions to elicit the information that Tahs-uppi was not a place but an event that took place at the omphalos, the navel of the world. Plotting a route that would get them there occupied them for scarcely another day. The morning after, very early, they stole a beast from a herd cave and departed T'loch-ala, leaving only one dead body behind them, that of an impertinent herdsman who'd wakened early and gone down to his flock without waiting on Lady Day. Had he waited properly, he would still be alive, a fact the songfather of T'loch-ala would later discourse upon at length.

'Have you never married, then?' Poracious Luv asked the King of Kamir.

Jiacare Lostre reflected. 'I saw wedlock as wedded lock indeed, another set of chains binding me fast. Seeing what fate I saw for all Kamir, I did not wish for children.'

'You can speak like common people if you like,' she said, grinning at him. 'You are no longer king.'

He flushed, started to say something, then stopped. The slow beat of aristocratic speech had become second nature when talking to any but intimates or servants – in which category he had always included his ministers, just to infuriate them. And yet, he had not spoken like that when he was Osterbog Smyne. Why should he as ex-king?

Enjoying his embarrassment, Poracious thrust her seat back to the limit of the inadequate space the ship provided, stretching out her legs. She felt cramped. She was cramped. Her sleeping cubicle was the size of a disposal booth, and after spending several hours in it, she wished it *were* a disposal booth. One would travel more comfortably as ashes.

Of course, the journey could have been passed in sleep. Most passengers had chosen to sleep until a day or two before they reached their destination, but the king wanted to savor every moment of freedom, and Poracious had thought it wisest to stay with him. On the well-established ground that men like best to talk about themselves, she had led him to discuss his life and times at great length.

'What did you do for amusement?' she demanded. 'Everyone has to have amusement.'

'One spends one's time—' he began, catching himself. 'I spent a great deal of time in the gym. I used to retreat there as a child, and I've rather depended upon it. One is told ... I'm told I acquit myself well.'

'In what sport?'

'Bisexual heptathlon.'

She regarded him thoughtfully. He had the build for it, wiry and compact, and no doubt the energy for it, too, since he'd used it for nothing else. Or almost nothing. 'I suppose they allow you women?' she said in a silky tone.

'Oh, Lord Fathom, yes,' he blurted, unthinking. 'Women. Men. Animals, too, one supposes, if one liked. One's father had an insatiable appetite for little girls. So far as one is aware, his desires never went unfulfilled. There are middle-aged women all over Kamir living on pensions from the government. One supposes that's how the ministers managed it.'

'That and payment to the girls' families, probably,' said Poracious.

He sighed. 'I always had trouble imagining what kind of family would ... would ...'

'Many kinds,' she said dryly. 'Believe me, Your Majesty.'

'Jiacare,' he said. 'If I am to speak like a commoner, you must stop calling me Majesty. Call me ... Call me Jickie.'

'Right. Jickie. As I was saying, I've seen families who would sell their children, their grandmothers, their husbands or wives. Sometimes out of desperation, sometimes out of greed, but I have seen it.'

'One's own life has been more circumscribed,' he admitted. 'One has only read of such things, and it is hard to know what is real and what is fiction.'

She nodded ponderously. 'Most fictions turn out to be real. At least, such has been my experience. I no sooner hear some horrible story, told as a mere tale, than someone assures me it really happens, here or there.

Sometimes it turns out the perpetrator heard the same tale and decided to copy it. Massacres, mutilations, murder, mayhem. There are worlds where all these things are everyday affairs. Asenagi, for example. From among whose people you did not hesitate to send an assassin after Leelson Famber. Surely Kamirian law does not countenance such activity.'

'Well,' he mused doubtfully, 'in fact it does. Though only for kings. Kings customarily do anything they like so long as it can be hidden from the public. One's father often said that public officials generally do so. People want to believe in their kings or presidents or procurators. They gild their leaders with brightest gold, as they do their idols, though both may be but clay. And so long as one does not rub our people's noses in one's filthier habits, one can lead them to the slaughter in war, one can squander their treasure for one's own aggrandizement, one can give preference and immunity to one's friends, children, and kin. One can let the poor starve and the sick die, and the people will still follow so long as they see one smile and wave and seem to be satisfied with the way things are going.'

'So long as taxes are kept low,' Poracious rumbled.

'That too. But mostly one has only to wear a kingly mask in public while seeming to be interested in the common man. It's easy to do. One simply watches for occasions when common men do something uncommon, then one notifies the news sniffers that one is gratified at this example. One has one's picture taken with the awed hero, who may, in fact, have done a very stupid thing. All his neighbors treat him with reverence for several days thereafter, and a holo of himself rests into perpetuity upon his altar shelf, along with the image of his god.'

'Your ministers cooperate in this effort?'

'Oh, yes. Aristocracies conspire to keep their reputation clean. Though they fuss at one for not begetting sons, one has heard them privately say that a bachelor king is less trouble than royal offspring, who are, however one trains them, beset by the passions, ambitions, and rebelliousness of youth. One's own escapades have been minor. One was assured, for example, that word of the previous flight from Kamir never reached any further than the palace walls.'

'It reached the Fastigats,' she said. 'Obviously. May I make a suggestion?'

'Of course.'

'It is not customary for commoners to refer to themselves as "one." If you are desirous of appearing less—'

'Oh, one takes the point. I, that is. Do.' He flushed. 'It's difficult. I keep forgetting. When I ran away, I had a role I'd planned on. I'd practiced my speech, my gait, the clothes I would wear. I haven't practiced this.' He fell silent, nodding to himself, before saying, 'About the Fastigats. I didn't know that Famber's finding me was merely an assignment. I'm afraid I attributed to him some degree of personal malice. To one being pursued, the pursuer may seem motivated by something more than mere duty, and once he had found one … that is me …'

'If you'd told him you didn't want to come back, he'd have left you alone, as required by Fastigat ethics.'

The king flushed. 'I didn't ask. He didn't say.'

'It's of no consequence now,' she said. 'So, tell me, do you have a favorite mistress or sweetheart?'

Jiacare smiled slightly. 'I did. One or two.'

'But you didn't bring anyone with you.'

'No encumbrances,' he said. 'I wish to experience freedom. I've never had freedom before. The other time I was a fugitive, not a free man. By the Great God Fathom, madam, do you have any idea what it's like, being born to royalty? Every action scrutinized. Every word assessed. Every royal bowel movement inspected. Every royal sneeze worried over. I cannot say with any certainty that there were not several pairs of eyes looking through holes in the wall during my acts of sexual congress. The best I could do was draw the bed curtains and stay beneath the sheets!'

'It would have a damping effect,' she admitted.

'Indeed. A very good word for it. All that attention put out one's, that is, my fires very well, madam, both physical and spiritual. Believe it.'

'I can see why you wanted revenge against Famber.'

'Well, yes. But I shouldn't have done it, even so.'

Poracious allowed him a moment of reflection before asking, 'So, tell me what kind of woman you like? Assuming, that is, you do like women.'

'Women, yes.' He stared at the curved surface above them as though he saw a picture there. 'I have never paid much attention to appearance. My favorite woman – up until the time she married someone else in order to have children – was not at all attractive in a physical sense, though she had great vitality. I admire humor and intelligence. And, of course, patience. It takes a great deal of patience to be mistress to a king.'

'In future, perhaps your companions will need less patience. That is, if you are truly resolved to be no more a king.'

He shrugged carelessly. 'If one went back, they'd have to depose Fenubel in one's favor. Such is Kamirian law. But if one … that is, I don't go back … Well. I am free not to go back.'

Poracious Luv nodded. He was indeed free not to go back. Perhaps he would stay on Dinadh. The Alliance had offered him a vast sum for his help. The former king could live much as he would, if he would.

'I've been wondering,' he said. 'What happens if we get to Dinadh and find that my assassins have already killed Famber's wife and child? What if they've found Famber himself and killed him?'

She shifted her huge bulk uncomfortably. 'Pray they have not. When this Ularian business started, there were four populated systems in Hermes Sector: Dinadh, with one world and a few storage installations; Jerome's system., with several settled worlds and moons; Goan's system, with several settled worlds and a homo-norm team on another one called ... Perdur Alas; and finally Debair's system, with several settled worlds, one of which, Tamil's world, was wiped clean by the Ularians just before we left Kamir. Or, so I heard. I don't remember how many worlds that makes. Half a dozen or more, totally wiped clean. The losses are in the millions.'

He scowled at her, vertical wrinkles appearing between his eyes. 'That's too many to keep quiet. You'll have a panic.'

'There's already considerable panic in the outlying areas, those nearest Hermes Sector.'

'The ship's library says the Dinadhi keep their foreign guests pretty well spread out. Will the authorities let us go directly to the Famber leasehold?'

She grunted, a porcine sound. 'They must. I bear letters of demand from the Procurator. All ships of the line are engaged in evacuation, but the Dinadhi don't know that. I'm to threaten them with invasion if they don't cooperate.'

'I shall follow your lead,' he said carefully. 'Lord Fathom, but I've messed things up.'

'Not your fault, lad,' she murmured. 'Not anyone's fault. How can you lay guilt for an enigma like the Ularians? We still have no idea who, or what, or why—'

'Or when,' he murmured.

'Or when,' she agreed. 'All we can do is our best, and do it as quickly as possible.'

Among the scattered buildings at Simidi-ala was a small stone house occupied by Thosby Anent, the Alliance agent, and by Chadra Tsum, a Dinadhi woman. The moment Thosby took up residence, everyone in Simidi-ala knew what he was, for everyone knew who Chadra Tsum was, and she was assigned as his housekeeper. Chadra was an agent for Simidi-ala, assigned to find out things, which she did with one hand while busily keeping Thosby's house with the other. All in all, the functionaries of the Edge were thankful that Alliance interference was limited to one elderly individual, known to be addicted to imported tobaccos and liqueurs, who was, even when sober, more otiose than diligent.

Thosby Anent was as blessedly unaware of this assessment as he was of most other real things. He galloped through life like a fifth leg on a horse, always in motion, seldom touching the ground, and to no purpose when he did. Even in childhood he had been far too preoccupied with being other people to learn to be himself. Early on, he had played at being Mysterious

Child or Royal-Boy-Raised-by-Commoners. Later he had played Brilliant Scholar and Gallant Lover and Deep Thinker, in each case adapting or even curtailing reality to accord with his current persona. He maintained a little recorder in which he entered supportive quotations from old books and antiquarian records along with lists of tasks he meant to undertake, turning each morning to a new page without ever referring to the old.

All this I was told, in time, by Poracious Luv, who had used all the resources of the Alliance to get a clearer picture of its agent upon Dinadh.

While in his early twenties, Thosby had experienced the biography of an almost legendary diplomat-cum-secret-agent, and this had convinced Thosby that his true talent lay in foreign service. He thereupon invented the role of Sagacious Applicant, performing it so well that the Bureau of Information Services actually awarded him a minor clerical position, which he filled with his customary distracted inefficiency. His supervisors, finding him too ineffectual to retain but too amiable to dismiss, shifted him to another department, whence he was shifted to others yet as successive executives moved him gently along. Thosby misinterpreted their efforts as he did most things. He believed he was being groomed for A Really Important Position, so he flitted from job to job with an air of intent incomprehension, waiting for his true talents to be applied.

Thosby reached the acme of incompetence in the Division of Minor Planets, a department whose charge it was to recruit unencumbered persons to serve as factotums and general mumbleglums on small and unimportant worlds – places like Far Barbary or Finagle-Chump or Dinadh. No one objected when Thosby was sent to Dinadh as covert flunky in charge of routing intelligence from Hermes Sector. The personnel officer who made the assignment knew, quite rightly, that any idiot could route intelligence!

Thosby Anent, however, was not just any idiot. He was an idiot convinced he was being moved into An Important Place! Prior to his arrival on Dinadh, he spent a great deal of time choosing the roles he would play there – the roles, that is, in addition to the one he had been assigned – coming up with two that were no more inappropriate than all his other roles had been. He chose, as primary persona, the role of Master Spy. For this he had designed and rehearsed a conspiratorial manner and a repertoire of winks and nods of great significance. As a 'cover' for Master Spy, he adopted the persona of Codger. This required him to smoke a tobacco pipe, wear an eccentric hat, and adopt a manner of gruff but kindly bemusement along with a spraddled way of walking, as though slightly crippled in the knees. In order to avoid 'giving anything away,' Master Spy was laconic while Codger was obfuscatory, apt to take off in dizzying locutory flights, which left his listeners not only lost but remote from any point of reference.

Between the mystifications of Master Spy and the divarications of Codger, Dinadh-Alliance communication soon dwindled to a muddy trickle. People back at Prime learned to send Thosby's infrequent reports directly into the files, not even feeding them through content analyzers that would have scanned for key concepts, such as *lost contact* or *disappearance.*

Thosby took comfort in the lack of feedback. He felt continued silence from Prime was an expression of confidence in him and his work. Meantime, after one or two feeble attempts at supervision, line functionaries at Prime gave up on Thosby and turned to alternate sources of information: agents for other organizations, rumor mongers who were paid for knowing things, people with relatives or friends on settled worlds in Hermes Sector. It was through these that Prime had learned of the Ularian incursions, almost as promptly as Thosby could have informed them.

One young administrator, who was still naive enough to believe that efficiency was a Good Thing, unearthed Thosby's reports, and after laboriously plodding through one or two, recommended that Thosby be replaced. The recommendation, however, languished on the desk of the aide to the deputy assistant to the subassistant secretary for personnel matters. Everyone was now in a panic about Ularians and much too busy to do anything at all about Dinadh.

All of which, so Poracious Luv told me, explains how the Intelligence Division at Prime, purely on the basis of contiguity and without questioning competence, assigned Thosby Anent the responsibility of monitoring the highly secret work of the Perdur Alas shadow team.

'For want of a nail,' the Procurator would say to me, Saluez, as he reviewed this entire matter, with many a shake of the head and furrowing of the brow. 'For want of a nail, the horse was lost. ...' (Our animals on Dinadh do not have nails, so I had to ask Lutha what he meant.)

Thosby accepted responsibility for the shadow team with his usual nonchalance. No one told him how important Perdur Alas was. It would have made no difference if they had. The more challenging and important a task, the more good sense and concentration it required, the more likely Thosby was to ignore it in preference for something else, anything else, that was repetitive and familiar and disconnected from reality.

As a consequence, the shadow team had been gone for some time before Thosby knew it. To give him credit, he did use his equipment to search for survivors, though it took him ten times as long as it should have. He found Snark through sheer luck, and when he set the machines to provide a readout of Snark's sensory data, he found, to his slight discomfort, that it covered a very long period of elapsed time, during which he, Thosby, should probably have Done Something.

Codger was neither honest enough to admit incompetence nor dishonest enough to destroy the evidence. Master Spy, on the other hand, was convinced it was a ploy. Trapped among his several personalities, Thosby chose to do what he had often done in the past with real things that presented real problems: ignore them until they went away.

Perdur Alas didn't go away. The ship that had transported the shadow team stopped subsequently on Dinadh, where, in a drunkenly lugubrious moment, the captain had grieved over the fate of the bait. This was reported to Chadra Tsum, who routinely used Thosby's equipment to find out things that interested her, whether they interested anyone else or not. Chadra knew about Snark long before Thosby did. She told her colleagues, who told other people, with the consequence that, among certain circles in Simidi-ala, Snark was spoken of familiarly and with sympathy as the lonely shadow of Perdur Alas.

Which is not to say that *Dinadh* knew. The people at Simidi-ala, because of their forced association with foreigners, are not considered to be real Dinadhi. They are, so to speak and through no fault of their own, tainted and resented. Though I had not realized it, it seems the resentment runs both ways. They are as suspicious of us as we are of them. So, though the port buzzed with the drama of one lonely shadow upon Perdur Alas, one lonely shadow confronting the might and mystery of the Ularians, the rest of Dinadh remained ignorant.

As did I, and all those with me. We knew only what Lutha had been told: that our worlds were in danger. If my world was in danger, so were my people, so was my child. What more did I need to know?

It would have been helpful to know a great deal more about driving gaufers! I had assumed they were gentle and accommodating beasts, but then, I had only seen them driven. I may even have seen them being harnessed – without paying much attention – and I'd certainly never done it myself. It surprised me, us, therefore, when the beasts made it clear they did not like being harnessed, did not like pulling, and would do so only when ... when something none of us could figure out!

Leelson blindfolded them to harness them, only to find that when the blindfolds were removed, they would not move. We were working in the predawn darkness, the sun threatening at any moment to edge the rimrock above us, and I was having a hard time staying calm.

'They are accustomed to some other order,' said Lutha in a perfectly rational, matter-of-fact voice. She stood next to the lead animals, stroking their necks, an expression of wonder on her face, as though she had never touched animals before. 'Use your skills to find out which ones are leaders.'

Leelson and Trompe looked at her in astonishment, the lantern light showing their faces, hard with frustration. Gradually, Leelson's face cleared, however, and he turned his attention to the beasts. 'That one,' he said, pointing to one of those hitched in the third pair. 'I think. Don't you, Trompe?'

'I think so,' said the other doubtfully. 'And that one, maybe. The one on the right in the second pair.'

'Likely they will also have a preferred side,' said Lutha. 'Right or left. If we are lucky, we will have picked one leader for each side.'

I had not thought of any such thing, and obviously the men had not either. Nonetheless, after a few moments of swearing and sweating, they were able to say that the two animals at the front were accustomed to being there and were on their accustomed sides. The animals did not feel affection or longing for the proper side; they merely felt less aversion.

'There are probably other refinements,' said Lutha, 'but I think we'd better get away before it gets any lighter.'

The rimrock above us already glowed with gold. Even as we looked up, the first notes of the dawnsong came from above and behind the great stone pillars that hid us, notes falling like water, silken as falling water. Lutha put Leely into the wain; Leelson drove it. Trompe, Lutha, and I walked alongside. The animals pulled, though without enthusiasm, and we went away south as quietly as we could.

'How did you know that?' I asked Lutha. 'About the lead gaufers.'

'I am a translator of documents,' she said. 'I read. I read many things from many worlds. I translate documents about crops and water rights and weapons and marriage law and livestock. My head is full of a million irrelevant facts, one of which just happened to be useful.' She laughed, somewhat harshly. 'Another thing I know, which is more troubling, is that these animals will have to be fed. Since we're not carrying any food for them, presumably they'll have to have time to graze before night, correct?'

She was right, of course. I had not thought of it. Even though this was my world, I had not thought of it. It was not a woman's thing to worry about. Only men did the herding. Only men drove the gaufers. Why would I have wondered about it?

Still, I felt shamed that she had and I had not.

'It's going to cut down on our travel time,' said Leelson, his lips compressed. 'They'll probably need to graze for several hours.'

'One of the middle pair would be less unhappy if it was back by the wagon,' muttered Trompe. 'It's clear enough, once you know to look.'

'Most things are,' said Lutha in a dry voice, with a sidelong glance at me. I knew what she was thinking, that I was not clear and that she did not know where to look. 'What do they eat, Saluez? Grasses? Leaves? Can we cut fodder for them as we go?'

I didn't know and was ashamed to say I didn't know. We took knives and cut grasses and leaves along the way, for the trees along the trickling stream were coming into leaf, and when we stopped at noon for a brief meal and a drink from our canteens, we soon learned which things the gaufers would eat and which things they would not. By this time we had come along the canyon wall all the way to the place where the five canyons meet. Because of the way the canyon curved, we could not see Cochim-Mahn behind us, but then, the people there could not see us either. We could cross the open place and go to the right around the Gathered Waters and get all the way to the south-tending canyon before anyone could see us from Cochim-Mahn. Of course, if someone were on the trail across the canyon from the hive ...

'I think that's stretching good sense,' said Lutha, when I suggested this plan. 'What I think we'll do is camp for the night near the water to give us grazing time. Then we'll get ourselves into that other canyon very early in the morning, when we won't be seen.'

Though Leelson showed surprise at her decisiveness, he grunted approval as he went to help Trompe, who was shifting two of the gaufers to their preferred positions. One animal was still out of place, its preferred slot occupied by another with the same preference. Leelson pointed this out. Trompe said the out-of-place one was the lesser opinionated of the two. This made Lutha laugh, a sound I had not heard since she arrived. She had a lovely laugh, like water. I told her so, and she said she had noticed that Dinadhis think most lovely things are like water.

'It is because we are water poor,' I said. 'We value it.'

'Well, it flatters me that you like my laughter,' she said. 'Sometimes I think I have forgotten how to laugh.'

Her eyes were on the boy, and I knew why she had almost forgotten, but I said nothing. She did not want to discuss Leely, and I did not want to offend her. Still, I wondered why. Among the Dinadhi, once we know a child is ... incompetent to live, we do not insist upon keeping it alive. Sometimes a mother will fight the inevitable, and she is allowed to do so. Mothers are mothers, after all. But eventually, even a mother understands that humans are not immune from nature's error. Some babies are not meant to live. I thought Leely was one such. So did Leelson, and this was the source of the conflict between them. I almost said hatred, but it was not hatred. Not that alone, at any rate, for she loved him too. I am no Fastigat, but I could feel her yearning, and his. It was like wind, or sunshine, or flowing water, an undeniable presence.

It was all very tragic and complicated, and I interested myself with it for all the miles we walked that afternoon, down the long canyon, out into the bare space where the five canyons meet, and across that rocky expanse to the place beside the water where we hid ourselves in a grove of trees and set up our camp.

I had no more idea how to set up the gaufer cage than they did. After a time we figured it out. The pen had the wain for one side, with a narrow panel fastened across the wheels to keep anything from coming under. Two oblong panels hooked onto the front and back of the wain, then onto other panels to make a six-sided enclosure. Then six triangular panels made the peaked roof, all joined together with paran-wood fasteners on the inside.

'Leather lacings would be easier,' said Trompe as he struggled with a panel that would not line up correctly.

'The Kachis can chew through leather,' I said quietly. 'They cannot chew paran, which is sometimes called wood-adamant. It must be steamed a long time before it can be worked, and when it is dry, even metal tools have difficulty cutting it.'

'I can see why,' he muttered, continuing his struggle.

Eventually, he and Leelson figured it out. Only after they'd done it by trial and error did they find the faded marks on the edges of the panels to show which one went where. Meantime, the gaufers had been watered and allowed to graze in the woody glade. When the sun was almost gone, they surprised us by coming purposefully out of the woods and entering the enclosure by themselves. They milled about uncertainly until we shut them in, then they settled, each to a small pile of the edible growths we had gathered during the afternoon. We were shut in as well, with a tiny fire in the firebox to warm our food and make a pleasant smoke. The Kachis do not like smoke, though they are attracted to fire. Carrying a torch at night is a sure way to bring them by the dozens.

We heard the dusk song, echoes of it from far up the canyons. Only from the southern canyon came no sound, for it is too narrow for men to live in. The days are short inside it, and there are no hives there. Luckily, the canyon itself is not long. We could traverse it, I told Lutha, in a couple of days.

'Will we find enough fodder for the gaufers?' she asked.

'Lady, I do not know,' I told her. 'I feel such a fool. I should know more about my own world.'

'Your world is sexually di-cultural,' she said seriously. 'Men know one set of things, and women know another. And, I suppose the women are di-cultural as well. Those who are ... veiled and those who are not.'

'No,' I said. 'We who are veiled know everything the others do. And more, besides.'

She opened her mouth as though to ask a question, then caught herself and was still. Trompe and Leelson were murmuring together, but they, too, fell quiet in that instant and we all heard the questing cry from the southern canyon.

At that sound, the gaufers shivered and crowded together, away from the woven panels. They arranged themselves in a circle, holding the same order they had occupied during the day, the less opinionated one hissing and laying his ears back as he took a few moments to decide where he belonged. When they were settled, with their legs folded under them and their heads laid back upon their spines, eyes half-closed, jaws moving, no part of them was within reach of the panels. Whatever was out there could not get hold of them.

'So interesting,' said Lutha, looking at the beasts. 'You know, gaufs are the first animals I've ever seen.'

'There are no animals on your world?' I asked, and she said no, no animals upon Alliance Central. No animals on any world that had been completely homo-normed. 'They're all in the files,' she said. 'If there's ever room for them again.'

I thought I would miss animals if there were none. I had a pet cornrat when I was a child. Many Dinadhi have pet gaufs. Weaving Woman is said to favor animals and there were many in Blessed Breadh, the world from which we came On the other hand, the Firsters teach that the universe was made for man, made for man to use and use up, including all its creatures. We talked of this in desultory fashion while we listened for approaching wings.

Try though we would to keep our minds on something else, it did no good. First a little silence fell among us, then a longer one, then one longer yet. Finally, we withdrew into the wagon itself and pulled the door almost shut behind us. There we each sat in our own ten square feet of space and tried not to hear what was going on outside. They were teasing us. Kachis always do, tease us, try to frighten us. They do it, say the songfathers, to try our faith, to be sure we are strong and resolved. First they flutter. Then come the cries, like hungry children, enough to melt ones heart. They shake the panels, they thrust in their long, stick-thin arms. They gnaw at the panels with sharp, white teeth. They cannot chew paran wood. It is for this reason we call paran the Lord Protector of Trees and never cut a mature one without planting two in its place.

If it had not been for Leely, perhaps we could have slept, but he would have none of it. He wanted to see what was going on. Finally, Lutha took him to the wagon door, cracked it a bit wider, and sat there with him for a long time while he reached toward the white arms, the white faces, the sharp teeth, and cried, 'Dananana. Dananana.'

I stood behind them, looking out, and Lutha heard my indrawn breath.

'What is it?' she asked, looking up at me.

'So many,' I blurted. 'There are so many of them!' I had never seen that many in Cochim-Mahn. I wondered if they were following us or traveling to the omphalos. Then I relaxed, remembering. Of course they were going to Tahs-uppi. They were a part of it!

Eventually Leely tired, and Lutha laid him down, shutting the door tightly. Even then, it was a long time before he slept.

When Leelson woke us before dawn in the morning, the Kachis had gone. The ground outside the panels was littered with their droppings. I have a hard time reconciling the mess they make with ... with what they are. Holy creatures should not smell like that. I was eager to leave, but Lutha insisted we take time to cut fodder, storing it on top of the wagon. Then we took down the panels, stacked them on the racks, hitched the gaufers, and were gone before light. We were, as we had planned, into the southern canyon by the time the sun rose. Too deep to be seen from Cochim-Mahn, which was good, but lost in deep shadow ourselves, which we had not thought on.

Leelson unfolded Bernesohn Famber's map on the seat beside him and traced our route with his finger.

'This canyon branches into another,' he said. 'One leading southwest. Is that right?'

I rehearsed the way as we children had learned it from songfather. 'The Canyon of Cochim-Mahn to the Lost Things Canyon. This canyon to the Burning Springs. Burning Springs to the Nodders. Beyond the Nodders, the omphalos.'

He tracked my words on the map. 'Burning Springs?' he asked me. 'It's printed here, but what is it?'

'Songfather told us it's a flammable gas that comes up through fissures in the rock. There is water that comes also. The gas was ignited at some time or other, perhaps by lightning, and it burns in the water. Sometimes the place is called the Fountains of Fire or Canyon of Fire. There is a superstition that drinking the water from there will keep—'

I caught myself in time. I had not said it.

'Keep what?' Leelson asked.

'Keep one in good health,' I said. Masanees had mixed her medicine with water brought from the Canyon of Fire. So she said.

He gave me an odd look. I suppose he read my discomfort, but at least he did not ask me anything more.

'What are the Nodders?' Lutha asked.

'Tall thin pillars of rock. Many of them. With stone tops that move sometimes. Songfather says when the wind blows strongly, they nod.'

'If that is true,' remarked Trompe, 'sometimes they no doubt come crashing down.'

'I don't know,' I confessed. 'Songfather never mentioned that.'

'No animals?' Leelson asked. 'Nothing dangerous except the Kachis?'

'The beautiful people are as they are, which is as the Gracious One wills,' I replied. Who knew what the Gracious One willed?

'No *known* dangers, then?' Leelson smiled, reading my mind.

I flushed. 'None.'

I was more worried about the known than the unknown. Known dangers were quite bad enough. These feelings were justified at about midmorning when we began to hear wings. At first it was just a barely heard flutter behind us. When we looked, we saw nothing. The noise grew more frequent the farther we went. I caught Lutha and Leelson exchanging long glances. I felt myself growing pale and sick. I knew the sound. Oh, yes, I knew the sound.

Then we heard the noise from before us as well. Both behind and before. Casting a quick look around, I surprised a pale shadowy movement on the canyon wall to our left. Then I saw them everywhere, pallid shapes slipping behind rocks. More than I had ever seen before.

'They're all around us,' I said in a voice that I could not keep from sounding terrified. 'They're all around us.'

'I thought they didn't,' said Trompe. 'In daylight ...'

'But it isn't daylight,' I cried.

It was day*time*, but we were still in deepest shadow. The sun lay upon the wall to our right, perhaps a third of the way up, a long line of brilliance that inched downward slowly ... so slowly.

'We could stop and set up the shelter,' said Lutha.

'I read that as a bad choice,' said Leelson, keeping his eyes on the trail. 'The minute we try it, they'll be on us.'

'You can feel them?'

'If it is them I'm feeling, yes.'

'Then what? What, Leelson!'

'Keep your eyes on the sun line, there on the right-hand wall. How long would you say until it hits us?'

'I have no idea! Saluez?'

'Not long,' I mumbled. 'But maybe too long.'

'I think not,' said Leelson. 'I'm getting feelings of slyness, of calculation. They want to be sure of us. They aren't yet. They're cunning.'

'You speak as though they were rational beings,' Lutha objected.

I pinched my lips shut and said nothing. Trompe looked at me curiously, his brows knit together. I concentrated on the lower pool at Cochim-Mahn, thinking deliberately of its coolness and the light-less depths within the stone. Leelson looked away, perhaps foiled, perhaps merely respecting my desire not to be thought at.

'We'll talk of something else,' he said firmly. 'Trompe, how were the league championships coming when you left Prime?'

Trompe responded, and the two of them talked in quite natural voices about interalliance sports of various kinds. Their voices seemed normal and casual, but their eyes were narrowed in concentration. I stayed frozen in place, gathered into myself, my face hidden in my hands. I could still hear the Kachis, even above the sound of the men's voices. Lutha put her arm around me and squeezed. I scarcely felt it.

Then, suddenly, 'Here,' said Leelson.

I slitted one eye and peeked. We had come to a puddle of sunlight, a spot where the eastern canyon wall dipped low to let the sun through. Leelson got down from the wagon and pretended to check the wheels; Trompe joined him, the two of them continuing their discussion. Lutha and I merely waited. Silence. The Kachis were not going to announce their presence. They didn't know about Fastigats. They didn't know we had heard them, that their slyness had been interpreted. It was obvious they didn't yet want us to know they were there.

We waited in the puddle of light until the sun flooded the bottom of the canyon. Only then did Leelson cluck to the animals and we moved on, more rapidly. Trompe buried himself in the map, measuring and muttering.

'There's a turn to the west ahead,' he said. 'Quite a lengthy east-west arm. That should be lighted for its entire distance. If we hurry, we may make it before the sun drops behind the west rim.'

'If everyone who can will walk, we can hurry more easily,' remarked Leelson, his voice little more than a whisper.

I had thought my legs wouldn't hold me, but it was actually easier to walk than to sit. Walking gave my trembling muscles something to do. Even Leely walked, all of us except Leelson striding along, and the gaufers moving almost with alacrity. The Kachis kept pace with us, fluttering among the stones at the eastern side of the canyon, more of them every moment. If we had not known to look for them, we might not have seen them. When they were still, they appeared to be only some lighter blotch on the stone itself.

It was not long until we came to the turning, not in actual time, though it seemed endless. The sun had shifted from the west side of the canyon to the center, from the center to the east. We were driving close to the eastern wall when we came to the turn, and now we moved around the corner into the light of Lady Day, she who smiled fully upon us as we moved toward the west.

Behind us in the narrow canyon, one lone derisive cry, faint and far, immediately silenced. If we had been near the sea, it might have been mistaken for the call of a bird, but we have no large inland birds.

'They want to get ahead of us,' said Leelson. 'There are shadowed ways in and among the rocks along the walls.'

Lutha shivered. I swallowed over and over, not to let the bitterness in my throat rise into my mouth. Then, all at once, Leely pulled away from Lutha and began to run back, as though he had been attracted by that lone cry.

Lutha caught up to him and seized him, but he struggled, pulling so strongly that Trompe had to help her restrain him and shut him in the wagon. There he raged incoherently for a time before falling asleep.

Late in the afternoon we stopped, still in the east-west part of the canyon. Ahead of us it turned south again, though the map indicated the southward arm was not a long one.

'That's where they probably expected to find us tonight,' remarked Leelson, pointing to the turn ahead. 'Instead we'll stay right here, make an extra long halt, and not leave here until that southern arm is in full sunlight. Besides, there's grass here, enough to supplement what we cut earlier.'

This time we had less struggle with the panels, we knew how to handle the gaufers. It was they who found water, a tiny spring that seeped from the canyon wall. By the time the sun set, we were safely shut in. The men fell asleep almost immediately, though Lutha and I were still awake.

Tonight Leely showed no interest in the Kachis. They came, as before, to gnaw the panels, to reach through with their long, white arms, but he curled himself into slumber and did not seem to care. Instead it was I who stood at the crack in the wagon door, looking out at them, at the faces of those who crossed the narrow line of light that escaped through the doorway.

Lutha heard me gasp and came to stand beside me.

'What is it, Saluez?'

I was so surprised, I spoke without thinking. 'I just saw him, the outlander ghost!'

'You mean ... Bernesohn Famber?' she asked in an incredulous voice.

'See, see,' I said, pointing. 'Look, there he is again. The one with the twisted shoulders.'

She stared out, turned to me, and stared again. 'I see a Kachis with twisted shoulders, Saluez.'

'That's him! That's how we know him. He, too, had twisted shoulders.'

Only then, I realized what I had said.

I clung to her. 'Don't tell,' I begged. 'Please. Don't tell the men that the Kachis are the spirits of our departed! I'm not supposed to talk about it!'

She pressed my lips with her fingers, a soft pressure through the fabric of my veil. 'Shhh. I won't, if you don't want me to, but you must tell me, Saluez. I need to know. When someone here on Dinadh ... goes, he comes back as a ghost?'

'When people's bodies don't work anymore, their spirits depart the human bodies and find Kachis bodies. We invite them to return to us. We promise to feed them and care for them. The Kachis were made by the Gracious One, just for this purpose, to hold our spirits. And they do come back, where we can see them, and they live for many, many years, staying with us, enjoying the lives of their children and grandchildren, eating, coming to our ... taking part in our lives.'

'All of your people who ... die, Saluez?'

She didn't understand! 'But we *don't* die. Don't you see! We don't die, not anymore. No. We just change our forms, that's all. From human form into Kachis form, but we know who we are, we are still alive.'

She mused a long time. 'I see,' she said at last. 'So your mother is out there somewhere, Saluez?'

I could not answer her. She should not have asked that. I turned my face from her and went to my place to sleep.

Hallach, songfather of Cochim-Mahn, finished his salute to Lady Day, took the three ritual steps into her light, then fastened his robe and looked around for his breakfast. Someone should have come with it from the hive the moment he sang, 'Go forth!'

He grumbled, his belly grumbling with him, missing Saluez. She had never been late with his breakfast. Shuddering, he put the thought aside. It was forbidden to think these things. One could not think kindly of someone who had doubted, who had had heretical ideas. And she had, had doubted, had fallen away from grace, otherwise ... otherwise she would not be down below with the other veiled doubters and recalcitrants. Lady Day had smitten them, and Weaving Woman had made dark patterns of them, and the Gracious One had turned his back upon them. Praise to the deities who knew the inner hearts of women, darker and more devious than those of men!

Shalumn hastily approached, bearing a bowl and ewer. He held out his hands for the ritual washing. Then Shalumn handed him his food bowl and politely turned away, looking out over the canyon.

He forgave her tardiness with his first bite.

'Only a little time until Tahs-uppi,' he remarked. 'Would you like to see the ceremony?'

She was very still. What ailed her? He spared her a curious glance before returning to his meal.

'I am better suited to my duty here, songfather.'

Was she refusing to attend? For the goddesses' sakes, he hadn't been suggesting anything improper. Surely she didn't think ...

He made the matter clearer. 'Hazini will be accompanying me, along with her father. I thought you might be company for her.'

She didn't look at him. 'Thank you, songfather. It is a kind thought. But I am better suited to my duty here.'

He put down the bowl and stared. 'What is it, Shalumn? Something is troubling you.'

'Nothing one may speak of, songfather.'

He dropped his voice to a confidential whisper. 'One may speak of anything to a songfather.'

She confronted him, her eyes filled with tears. 'I fear Saluez has gone into shadow, songfather.'

Confused for the moment, he could not understand what she was saying. Those behind the veil were said to be in shadow, and of course Saluez was among them. 'Into shadow? But ...' Of course those who passed on were also said to be in shadow. Though veiled women couldn't be said to pass on. Because they had doubted the Great Gift of the Gracious One, veiled women truly died. They were not accorded the right of living on in Kachis form. Shalumn must mean something else!

'Tell me!' he demanded in a whisper. 'You think she's gone' – he gestured outward, at the canyons, the mesas, the distant glinting mountain peaks, all the faraway that was Dinadh – 'there?'

'Yes, songfather.'

'What makes you think so?'

'I haven't seen ... not for days.'

He sighed, surprising himself with the realization that it was a sigh of relief.

He reached out to shake the girl gently. 'Shalumn. Shalumn, you were her friend. You recognize her shape, her walk. Of course you watch for her, even though you know it is forbidden. That's quite common, my dear, and it is not a severe sin. But it's customary for those behind the veil to spend days below, in their own place, unseen by anyone.'

'But she cares for the outlanders! No one else has been given the duty! And no one has seen them, either!'

'Put it out of your mind,' he said sternly. 'Hear me, Shalumn. Put it out of your mind.' Her voice had been too full of grief. She should not feel so about a doubter!

'Songfather,' she said submissively, bowing her head. 'I will do as you say.'

He turned his back on her and resumed eating. So no one had seen Saluez for a few days. Well, that was as it should be. No Dinadhi should see her at all. She was a trash-person. Just as the outlanders were trash-people. Dinadhi didn't look at trash-people, or look for them, for that matter.

Still, it was strange no one had encountered the outlanders. On the ladders, perhaps. Even trash-persons took up space on the ladders. One had to wait. Or step aside. One noticed.

He scraped the sides of his bowl with his spoon. Not long now until there'd be some greens. Early greens, springing up along the streamlets, a welcome addition to the diet. If those gaufers that had gotten loose somehow didn't eat them all first.

Strange, that. Six gaufers had escaped their pens. Songfather had assumed they'd been let loose by someone. Some child, too frightened to confess. But the six missing ones had been a hitch. Almost. Two leaders, right and left, who as mere gaufs had established their right to that position by kicking and biting their herd mates into submission. Two followers, right and left, who did not kick or bite at all, and two middles – though they were both left middles.

Who would steal a hitch? And for what? Some young man who wanted to prove himself, taking the animals onto the heights, maybe finding an unused wagon there. But to do what? To go where?

To Simidi-ala, perhaps? Sometimes young people did run off to Simidi-ala. They grew bored with the Dinadhi way of life. They did not treasure the Great Gift enough. They decided they wanted excitement, and off they went. Hive-reared, they knew the only way they could get there was in a herder's wain. Fully half the population of Simidi-ala was made up of runaways, which was another reason for not trusting those at Simidi-ala. Apostates, all of them. Apostates and renegades.

He chewed the last bite thoughtfully. Young people were always interested in Simidi-ala. When Saluez was young, she had asked a lot of questions about the port city, so many that he'd taken her there himself during one brief visit.

He stared blindly at the opposite canyon wall. Saluez couldn't have taken a hitch. A mere girl? Not strong. Now wounded, though he did not know how badly. It was better not to know how badly. Better if loved ones never knew. Too many questions if they knew. Too many doubts. Saluez couldn't have taken the gaufers. It was physically impossible.

But she had been tending the outlanders. Taking care of the Famber family. Who, so Shalumn said, nobody had seen for a while. Of course, they wouldn't know about a hitch.

But Saluez might!

Hallach found himself moving rapidly toward the hive, meantime praying fervently to Weaving Woman, to Lady Day, to all the other deities of the Dinadh that he was merely woolgathering. Oh, let it be that he was merely making up stories, telling tales. Let him not have happened upon the truth!

The morning wore away in questioning and discussing, with this one, with that one. In time he found we had gone. Consternation in the hive. Much mumble among the elders. Then, finally, days later, what no one had thought to do until then, an inventory of wains and the discovery that one was missing, not from those upon the height but from those in the canyon itself. So, where had we gone?

What other place than the omphalos, for Tahs-uppi!

And the end of that episode was songfather standing at the edge of the canyon, swearing retribution on those aliens who had betrayed the hospitality of Dinadh and on that apostate who had aided them. He would follow them, so he howled to Lady Day as she departed. He would follow them and bring them to judgment. His voice quavered in its rage. His arms trembled. The people of the hive quaked behind the doorskins.

So I imagine the scene, at least. Later, while he was raging at me, he let me know some of it, including that he gave me credit for knowing about gaufers, about hitches, things I'd never even been curious about. He told me he had sworn judgment on me, a judgment that did, in time, come to pass. So, though I visualize the details for myself, in all important respects, that is what happened.

While songfather stuttered and swore, I was trying to sleep in the westerly elbow of Lost Canyon. The gaufers were quiet. Trompe snored, an abrupt, breathy sound, as though he were surprised over and over by something. Leelson slept like a child, radiantly, his lips curved into an angelic smile. Leely had the same expression, but Lutha burrowed, like some little animal, her face buried between her hands. And I lay on my back, urging my sinews to let go, let go, let me not think of my mother, let me merely be.

Eventually the struggle wore me out. The attempt to unthink it did no good. All right, I said to my disobedient mind, I will think of it. Let me remember it all. Let me wear out remembering, until it no longer hurts.

Mother went away when I was only a child. No one ever said how she departed. It wasn't a thing we talked about in the hive. Not openly, at any rate. As a child, I overheard this and that. Putting it all together, I understood she had departed because something had gone wrong when she had a baby. The baby departed also. The circumstances were, as we on Dinadh say of things we should not talk about, 'difficult.' If Lutha were translating, she might say blasphemous. Which does not mean anyone was at fault, but simply that something happened that was unpatternly and unpleasant. Whatever it may have been, this something happened and my mother ... departed.

And I wept desperately in father Chahdzi's lap, he petting me and murmuring over and over and over, 'We'll get her back, Saluez. That's what we'll do. She's out there, just waiting for us to ask her. We'll beg her to come back. And she will, you'll see.' He actually smiled when he said it.

So we prayed her return. There is a chamber on the ground floor of the hive, a place where petitions are made to any of our deities, a quiet place, softened by hangings and lighted dimly by little wax lamps, even at night, for night is the time we most need such a place. Chahdzi and I went there with songfather – he was just Grandpa then – and we petitioned Weaving Woman to tell my mother we wanted her to return, to take habitation among us.

I echoed the words. 'Take habitation among us ...' What did the words mean to me? That she would come home, come back, be there as she had been before. But that wasn't what Chahdzi meant, or songfather. For seven nights we uttered our petition. For seven nights we stood behind a window of the chamber, which, alone of all the windows in the hive, has no shutter. It is glazed with heavy glass so that petitioners may look out upon the beautiful people, the dancers, the Kachis.

Oh, beautiful upon wings, the Kachis. As I child I learned the hymns to the Kachis. *Oh, beautiful upon wings, gift of glory, loveliest of beings, those for whom the night was made!*

The seventh night my father's hand tightened upon my shoulder as he pointed with the other, saying excitedly, 'There, there, see, Saluez. See, there's Mother, with the cleft in her chin, just like always. Here's Mother come home again, Saluez!'

He pointed and pointed and I looked and looked, until eventually I saw what he was pointing at. A Kachis with a deep hollow in her chin like the one my mother had had. Though at the time I thought it was only rather like, as I remembered the event over the years it grew more and more like until I was sure it was utterly like. Of course. When the spirits of our loved ones return as Kachis, they always let us know who they are by some little trait. The shape of a nose. The shape of an ear. The way they move. A birthmark. So this was my mother, come back to be with us again.

Why didn't she come in?

Songfather shook his head. Because the spirits of our beloved dead are holy, sacred, taboo. They couldn't mix with ordinary people.

Then why did she come at all?

To see her girl Saluez grow, so Chahdzi said. To see her grandchildren born and watch them grow. To take delight from seeing us, to live among us until that time she would go on, sometime in the far future, to a blessed life that awaited her elsewhere.

I said I would go out and kiss her.

No.

I said I just wanted to hug her.

No, no forbidden. We must not touch the Kachis, even though they are people we love. But we can still care for them – her: feed her, love her, watch her dancing with the other spirits. ...

'Doesn't she know who I am?' I cried. 'Doesn't she want to kiss me?'

Of course she did, but that, too, was taboo. Forbidden. We Dinadhi had been given this great gift, the gift of continued life, continued embodiment, the ability to live on with our families and those we loved. We must keep our part of the bargain. Our part of the choice.

Had I doubted then? Did it seem to me then that this pale winged form was a poor substitute for a warm and living mother? Then, when I was only what? Six or seven? Before I knew the whole story? Before I knew the other reasons it was taboo, or what the other side of the choice had been? Before I knew that songfathers had done the choosing but women had paid the price?

Possibly, without even knowing it, I was an apostate even then. Possibly my mother, even then, looking in through the window at me, saw my thoughts and knew I was unworthy. Perhaps then is when she started hating me for being so ungrateful. How else explain?

How else explain why it was she who led the pack that ate my face away?

7

I woke first in the morning, and my rising brought Trompe and Leelson from under their blankets. Lutha was a knobby lump beneath hers, and we were quiet, not to disturb her. I knew she must have been wakened during the night, probably more than once, for I had heard the boy moving around. He was sometimes a restless sleeper, a murmurer, given to odd little cries that seemed more curious than restless.

The two men and I had no sooner started to take the shelter apart, removing the pins from the fasteners, than Trompe said in surprise:

'This one is open.'

It was open, gaping, the pin removed and dropped onto the ground beneath it. Even with just one pin removed, the panels could be pulled apart, though it took some strength to do so. We turned immediately to the gaufers, looking them over for blood or wounds, but they were as placid as a rain pool on a rock, gazing liquidly beneath fringed lashes, jaws moving in the immemorial rhythm of the cud. So, our songfathers tell us, animals of the long ago twice chewed their food, even back so far as Old-earthian times.

'*Something* pulled it loose,' said Leelson, clamping his mouth into a grim line. 'One of your beautiful people?'

'They couldn't,' I said. 'It's made so they can't. We must not have put it in tightly last night.'

'I did that side,' Trompe objected. 'And believe me, it was as tight as it is possible to get it!'

We were still standing there, lost in that kind of slightly fearful confusion that readily leads to contentiousness, when Lutha came to the door of the wagon and asked in a plaintive voice, 'Where's Leely?'

I blurted, 'Isn't he curled up under the blankets? I thought ...'

She turned back to rummage inside the wagon, crying almost at once, 'He's not here. Trompe, Leelson, he's not here.'

'He's only a child,' muttered Trompe. 'He couldn't have opened—'

'He's strong as the proverbial nox,' grated Leelson. 'If you haven't seen that, you haven't noticed much. He's stronger than many men I know.'

'Oh, God, God.' Lutha's voice rose in a shriek. 'Where is he. Where's my baby?'

The two men exchanged glances once more, pulled two more pins out, thrust open the loosed panels, and went in opposite directions, one up and one down the canyon, quartering the ground, looking behind stones and among low growths, calling, 'Leely. Leely-boy. Leely.'

Lutha was out after them in the moment, barefoot as she was, her hair streaming behind her, covering the same ground and lamenting so loudly that the rock walls echoed with it.

'Hush!' bellowed Trompe. 'Listen!'

Abrupt silence. Then I heard it. Softly, a little voice, not at all fearful or pained. 'Dananana.' And again: 'Dananana.' It came from upstream, in the direction of our travel.

Lutha darted in that direction, soon catching up with Trompe. Leelson trudged slowly back to the wagon and continued disassembling the panels as though nothing had happened. He had about him an air of frustration that had been growing hour by hour since Lutha had arrived at Cochim-Mahn. Everything she did irritated him, but he could not, for some reason, just let her be, so everything he did regarding her irritated him as well. By the time Trompe and Lutha came back, she carrying the boy, Leelson was muttering to himself angrily with the gaufers half-harnessed.

'What are you doing!' Lutha screamed. 'My, God, Leelson, don't you care about him at all!'

She lifted the boy in a dramatically hieratic gesture, as though offering him for sacrifice or dedication, drawing attention to his arms. There were several little red spots on the flesh above his wrists, no more than insect bites. Leely seemed undisturbed by them. He wasn't scratching or whimpering, and even as I looked the redness faded. It was like watching a candle burn down, slow but perceptible. So healing was with him.

'He doesn't seem to be hurt,' said Leelson in an expressionless voice. 'Look at him, Lutha!'

Her eyes were still full of righteous fury, but she did look at the boy, her chin quivering as she kissed and hugged him and looked beneath his shirt to see if he was hurt, murmuring small endearments the while, all of which Leely ignored in favor of churning his arms and legs and caroling 'Dananana.'

'He's not hurt,' said Leelson again. 'He woke early, let himself out, and got bitten by … what, Saluez? You know your native vermin better than we.'

'Jiggerbugs,' I said, giving the creature an equivalent aglais name. 'Maybe. Or there's a kind of spidery thing we call D'lussm. Both of them bite.'

Which they did. A bite from either would leave spots similar to those on the boy, though usually it took a day or two of frantic itching and even localized pain before the swelling disappeared.

'Or it could be something local,' I offered apologetically. 'Something we don't have around Cochim-Mahn.'

'Whatever it is didn't hurt him,' Leelson repeated for the third time, reaching out a hand to shake Lutha by the shoulder. 'Get him dressed, Lutha. Feed him. Feed yourself, you'll feel better.'

She reddened at his tone, which was impersonal and disinterested. It would have angered me had I been she, but then, she couldn't see the look in his eyes. His disinterest was as false as her fury. Both of them were playing at it. Still, Leelson wasn't lying to her. The boy wasn't hurt; the boy was strong; the boy had opened the panels to let himself out. And Leelson was considering all these facts with an appearance of calm while Lutha was wildly splashing about in her own terror and guilt at having let Leely escape. Or, perhaps, wondering if Leelson had not purposely let him out. I saw something like that in her eyes. She wanted someone to blame besides the boy himself; she knew this was silly; so she added guilt to all the other things she was feeling.

After a time she settled down, but the look was still there, in the way she watched Leelson when he wasn't looking, in the hard set of her lips and the wrinkles between her eyes, in the shamefaced flush when she caught me watching her. The travel was hard enough without this simmering away. I went to her, putting my hand onto her arm.

'I heard the boy moving around in the night. No one else, only he. He let himself out, Lutha.'

She shook off my hand angrily. 'Perhaps,' she said, with a grimace. 'Perhaps he did.'

She didn't want to believe me. Any more than she wanted to believe all those people who had told her about the boy, over and over, for years. She rode her own belief. Sometimes she slipped off its back, for it was a slippery beast, but most times she straddled it steadily, whipping it onward: Leely was human; soon he would talk, he would amaze people, he would be supernormal.

I sighed and set about fixing us a quick meal so we could get on our way. Leelson stood by the lead gaufers, tightening harness straps. His back was rigid. When I moved to get the food bowls, I saw that his eyes were closed. He was reaching at Lutha, feeling her out, deciding how to behave toward her.

When I handed him a morning bowl, his eyes opened and he smiled at me, a courteous curving of the lips with no real camaraderie behind it.

'Give her time,' I whispered.

'She's had years,' he murmured, this time really smiling, though ruefully. 'She's had ... enough time, Saluez. She simply will not see!'

I knew the saying in aglais. *The blindest are those who won't see.* We have similar sayings in our own tongue. *None so lost as those who will not believe.* Leelson could quote the blindness one to Lutha, she could counter with the belief one. And neither would change their opinion one whit!

We ate in strained silence. I washed the bowls in the trickle of water provided by the spring. We drove on to the end of the elbow and turned south once more, hoping we would come to the end of the canyon before midafternoon, for though it was midmorning, the shadow had only just moved away from the bottom of the western wall.

We had not gone far when Leelson pulled up the gaufers and sat staring ahead. On a huge flat stone, one that the trail veered around to the right, something pallid heaved and struggled. To me it looked like a pile of our cotton underrobes, almost white and softly shapeless. But it moved.

Leelson clucked to the gaufers and we moved forward a little, then a little more.

'It's one of them,' breathed Lutha in my ear. 'One of the Kachis, Saluez.'

In fact it was two of them, tumbled side by side on the flat stone, where they writhed, lips drawn back from their sharp teeth, eyes blind and unseeing. Even as we watched, one of them collapsed, motionless. The other cried out, a long, ululating cry that made the canyon ring, then it, too, fell into motionless silence.

From somewhere came a distant echo, or an answering call. We waited to see if it came nearer, but there was no more sound.

Leelson got down from the wagon seat. Trompe went with him. I stayed where I was, unable to take my eyes from the place where they were, from Leelson's and Trompe's hands as they moved the wings, the arms, from their faces as they looked curiously at the slender bodies.

'They're dead,' cried Leelson. 'Do they normally die like this, Saluez.'

I could not move. I could not speak. Lutha looked at me curiously, then put her arms around me and held me closely, whispering, 'They don't die at all, do they, Saluez?'

I shook my head frantically. Of course not. Of course they didn't die. They couldn't die. They stayed with us, until they went on, at Tahs-uppi. This wasn't the way they went on.

'Leelson,' she spoke sharply. 'Leave it. We can't afford this delay.'

Almost reluctantly, he left the tumbled bodies and trudged back to the wagon. I went inside it so I could not see those bodies when we passed. I was trembling so hard I thought my bones would snap. They couldn't die. Kachis could not die. They never died. No one had ever seen one die, or seen a dead one. That was a fact! Part of the evidence we were taught as children, part of the supporting evidence for the choice.

The wagon moved again, and I heard Lutha muttering to the two men. She wouldn't break the promise she made to me, not to tell them about ...

the spirits of our people. I knew she'd keep her promise, but she would have to tell them something. I didn't care. Just let them leave me alone. I couldn't bear to be questioned.

Later, when she and I were alone, she whispered to me, 'Did you ... recognize either one of those Kachis, Saluez?'

I did not. I had not looked. I didn't want to know if they were dear departed of mine.

During the following hour, I had time to calm myself, time to tell myself it had been something aberrant that had happened there, something utterly beyond belief. Perhaps even Kachis can sin. Perhaps even Kachis can disbelieve and be punished for it. This occurrence might be perfectly understandable.

So I thought until Leelson pointed out another dead one. After that, they were scattered all along the way, like fallen rocks. When we emerged from the canyon a little later than midafternoon, he had counted several score of them dead.

'I'm doing it,' I said frantically to Lutha. 'It must be me. My apostasy. My evil. My sin.'

She shook me. 'Don't be ridiculous, Saluez. Are you the only so-called apostate? How many are there? How many women in your sisterhood? Plenty, I'll wager. Back in Cochim-Mahn I did a count. I'd say between a third and a half of your women are veiled. You have an exaggerated opinion of your own importance if you think you can cause something like this!'

I had never counted them. But ... the chamber of the sisterhood was large. Extremely large. And it was full, too, even on those nights when we had no guests from other places. Lutha was right. When I thought of it calmly, I knew she was right. But knowing and believing ... oh, they are such separate things. 'What's causing it, then?' I cried. 'You tell me what's causing it!'

'If I had to guess, I'd guess some virus brought in by one of your lease-holders,' she said. 'There are new viruses turning up all the time.'

'But why *here!* Where we are!'

She shrugged. 'Saluez, maybe I'm carrying it. Or Leelson. Or even Trompe. By the Great Gauphin, girl, it could be anyone. We handle the panels, the Kachis chew on the panels and pick up what we've left there. Just be thankful we were away from Cochim-Mahn when it happened. I have a feeling if this had happened while we were under the eyes of songfather, he'd have assumed we caused it and we'd all be dead by now, including you because you'd associated with us. And Chahdzi, probably.'

I shuddered. Poor Chahdzi father. 'You really don't think I did it.'

'No,' she said firmly. 'I don't think it's you. I don't think it has anything to do with you. I'll go further. I don't think you sinned at all. I don't think your face is the result of apostasy or heresy or whatever you choose to call it. In fact, I don't think you're guilty of anything, Saluez.'

'Please don't,' I said feebly. 'You ... you disturb me when you talk like that. You take all my ... all my foundations away.'

It was true that when she spoke so, something quaked inside me, as though my heart had torn loose. I couldn't bear it.

She shook her head angrily, flushing and pinch-lipped. 'Sorry,' she said. 'I have no right. Ignore me, Saluez.'

But how could I? As we drove across the open space between Dark Canyon and the Canyon of Burning Springs, I could not get it out of my head. Was it better to be guilty of sin while knowing there was a power that had punished you? Or was it better to be innocent and feel there was no power? Was it better to be lost in a horrid storm at sea, knowing there was land, or be sailing peacefully with no certainty of land anywhere?

For myself, I decided I would rather be guilty. I could deal with that. One had only to outlive it. Submit to it. Atone for it. Surely if I helped these people save humanity and Dinadh along with it, that would atone for something!

So I set my teeth together and resolved to listen no more to Lutha the temptress. Not that she was a bad woman; she wasn't; but some people are not good for other people, and I thought then that Lutha was not good for me.

At the port city of Simidi-ala, the arrival or departure of outside travelers is an infrequent occurrence. Days go by with only the wind blowing in from across the shallow sea, tangy with the scent of rushes that grow along the shores and of the fragrant weed that floats on the waves. The people of Simidi-ala are Dinadh's only sailors or fishermen, and the bright sails of their shallow little boats scud to and fro across the placid waters, a pattern of bright dots, continually changing. I have seen them. I was there once, long ago, as a child, with Grandpa.

The boats were the first thing the ex–King of Kamir saw as he stood with Poracious Luv at the latticed gate of the shiplift while it slowly lowered them to the beach. The former King of Kamir said something convoluted and quintessentially Kamirian to her, a lengthy cadence comparing the brightness of the boats to the desolation along the shore. Normally Poracious indulged his poesy games, but this time she didn't answer. Her eyes were fixed elsewhere.

Poracious murmured, 'How in hell did he beat us here?'

'Who is he?' Jiacare asked, following her gaze to the stooped figure waiting at the gate, a younger man standing in attendance.

'The Procurator, boy. Things must be in a pickle if he's decided to join us. Pull up your socks. Smile. Make pleasant. He looks like a nice old man, but he can have our guts for garters if he likes.'

The Procurator did not move toward them, but waited for them to come to him, murmuring as they did so, 'Madam Luv,' and to the ex-king, 'you do, sir. May I introduce my aide, Mikeraw?'

They uttered conventional phrases of greeting as the Procurator led them away across a paved courtyard and into the nearest of the slab-like structures that serve Dinadh as hotels or inns or warehouses, as needs must. The ex-king verified a suspicion by scratching a wall with his nails. The place was built of dried mud. He shook his head, wonderingly.

They went up a flight of shallow, curving stairs, down a wide hallway, and through an open door. Mikeraw shut the door behind them, then absented himself, leaving the three together in a sizable chamber lit by a score of glazed openings in the outer wall. They were not the shape Poracious associated with windows, being mostly round or oval, some head-sized, some larger, all randomly scattered from floor to ceiling, from sidewall to sidewall, though sidewall might be a misnomer since the general effect was that of being inside a perforated egg with a flattened bottom. Still, the chamber had a peaceful feel to it, and Poracious rejoiced to see several chairs large enough to hold her comfortably.

'Sit,' the Procurator urged them. 'I've asked the person responsible for leaseholds to join us, but if you want to eat or drink or wash up before he arrives ...'

Jiacare smiled his thanks, taking a piece of fruit from the bowl on the table.

Poracious said, 'Nothing for me, Procurator. How did you get here before we did?'

'Military ship,' he answered. 'In and out of holes like the proverbial rabbit. Very fast. Very uncomfortable. I felt there was no time to waste.' He fumbled with a case set on a nearby table, removing a dataplat, which he handed to Poracious. 'Current situation.'

He sat down, leaned back, and shut his eyes.

The former king leaned over the big woman's shoulder as she keyed the plat and scanned the contents.

Puzzled, he asked, 'What language is this written in, I don't read—'

'Never mind,' Poracious Luv replied with a sigh so heavy it was almost a groan. 'All it says is that we've lost several million more people in Hermes Sector. The last populated world has been wiped clean, the attack is continuing. We still don't know who or what or why. Every available ship was engaged in evacuation of the remaining planetary populations and all the ships that were in Hermes Sector are gone.'

'Succinct, Poracious,' said the Procurator without opening his eyes. 'Very succinct. You left out that we are helpless. That we've kept this Ularian business inside our administrative skinnies about as long as we can. That we're going to have panic once it gets out, as it will.'

The ex-king stared at him curiously. 'You're a Fastigat, aren't you, sir? First among Firsters?'

Poracious made shushing motions, but the younger man shook his head at her.

'I'll do what I can to help, but I want to know! Is there any chance these Ularians are actually human? Somebody out there we don't know about?'

The Procurator gave him a long, level look. 'The idea has crossed my mind.'

'I should have thought so. If the universe is made for man, who else could be out there?'

'I don't know. If they are men, they are able to do things we cannot do. For purposes of action, I refer to them as Ularians, no matter what they are. I take it you are not of the Firster persuasion?'

'I am not, no.'

'May we set the matter aside? May we agree to let our differences alone for the moment?'

The ex-king shrugged. 'You mentioned panic.'

'There will be panic. Many of the vanishees have friends or associates on Alliance worlds. Once ordinary person-to-person communication ceased, rumor began to spin among the citizenry. It won't be long before they learn the truth. We could make up stories until we're bright green; we could issue silence edicts until our voices fail, but not all the evacuation ships were in Hermes Sector; some of them had returned across the line. The crewmen are going to talk. The evacuees are going to talk. They already have! The newsies are already on it, if the opposition doesn't tell the universe first! In either case, we'll be up to our necks in chowbys.' He sighed heavily. 'I reflect on my own coming political troubles to keep grief at bay. Some of those taken were my grandchildren.'

He got up and turned away, going to one of the windows and standing there with his back to them, his shoulders shaking.

Poracious heaved herself out of the chair and went to him, putting one huge arm around him and murmuring, 'Has there been any word from Perdur Alas? From the shadows?'

'None that I've received,' the Procurator said, drawing himself erect. 'Though we certainly should have had *something* by now, if only a preliminary report on their activities. I don't understand the delay.'

The former king ran his hands through his hair. 'Lord of all Confusion, I pray I have not added to this woe!'

'Sorrow comes as the seasons,' the Procurator answered, wiping his eyes as he returned to his chair. 'Inevitably. Being Procurator doesn't make me exempt. But it doesn't make me any better able to bear it, either. Well and well, grieving gets one no fowarder, as my grandfather used to say. There is an immediate task before us. We have to find two men, quickly! With your help, sir' – he bowed slightly in the ex-king's direction – 'and that of the local leasehold functionary, perhaps we can do so.'

'Mitigan of the Asenagi,' said the former king, with a wry twist to his mouth. 'And Chur Durwen of Collis. Or is it the Haughneep brothers?'

'The former two.' The Procurator wiped his eyes once more and made himself sit tall. 'We know they came to Dinadh. Now we need to know where they are.'

A discreet rap at the door drew their attention. The man who came in was robed, tassel-bearded, and gray around the temples. 'At your service, Procurator,' he said, sounding neither obsequious nor interested.

'Do you know of Jerome's system?' asked the Procurator.

'It contains, among others, the ocean world of Hava,' replied the Dinadhi, raising his eyebrows almost to his hairline. 'It is the inhabited system nearest to our own.'

'Your nearest neighbors have gone missing,' said the Procurator heavily. 'Yesterday, more than a million persons vanished from Hava. The other worlds in Jerome's system had already been wiped clean. It is clear the Ularians have returned. Last time around, every human person in Hermes sector was disposed of except you Dinadhi. One exception does not create a pattern. You may not be immune this time around.'

The man simply stared, taking it in, his eyes gradually widening.

'Some kind of jest, sir ...'

'I would not have gone to the trouble of a painful journey to jest with you, sir. The Procurator of the Alliance does not flit about playing games. The only persons who may be able to help us are now at the leasehold of Bernesohn Famber. Lutha Tallstaff, her son, a helper named Trompe. You recall!'

'I recall, of course.' Offended dignity. 'I am a rememberer!'

'There were two men who arrived about the same time, Mitigan and Chur Durwen. Assassins. Hoping to kill at least two of those earlier mentioned, Lutha and her son. We have to find them!'

'The men were sent to T'loch-ala,' said the rememberer. 'Which is a hive remote from Cochim-Mahn where Bernesohn Famber still has leasehold. We knew they were mercenaries.'

'That's all very well so far as it goes,' said the Procurator wearily. 'Though I'm delighted to hear that you took precautions, you have not told me those precautions were effective. Can you find out whether the assassins are still at this T'loch-ala?'

'We have systems for communicating with the songfathers of each hive.'

'Quickly, or at leisure?'

'With some dispatch, sir.'

'Then let us stop dancing and do so. Please. And while you're about it, I want to see a man named … ah.' He tapped his wrist-link. 'Name of agent on Dinadh?'

'Thosby Anent,' said the link.

'Thosby Anent,' repeated the Procurator. 'Get him, too, as quickly as you can.'

A peculiar expression showed for only a moment, then the tassel-bearded man put on his lofty face once more and went striding away, his robes lashing his ankles in a frenzy of offended motion.

'He hasn't really taken it in yet,' said the former king.

'No. Habit tells him to do nothing quickly, but we tell him to act at once. Such people grow defensive when forced into motion.' The Procurator rubbed his forehead wearily. 'There are disadvantages to being responsible.'

The former king considered this. 'There are also disadvantages to being responsible for nothing, Procurator.'

There seemed nothing more to be said until the rememberer returned. While they waited, as though with one mind, the three turned slightly away from one another and sat, each lost in an individually lonely world.

It was almost dark when Trompe drove us into the entrance to Burning Springs canyon. We camped once more. Setting up the enclosure was getting to be a routine. Cutting fodder for the beasts was becoming habit, as was watering them, hobbling them, letting them graze awhile. While rummaging among the food stocks, trying to decide what to prepare for a meal (on Dinadh, we rarely have that much choice), I overheard a conversation between Lutha and Trompe.

'You want me to sit up and watch Leely half the night?' Trompe asked in a slightly offended voice. 'Because he got a few bug bites? Why don't you put his harness on him?'

'Even if I put him in his harness, he might manage to escape. And supposedly, you're here to help me!' she snarled.

Long quiet moment while he stared at her. 'Right,' he said. 'Quite right.'

Then he went off muttering and shaking his head while Leelson stared at his back resentfully. It was an interesting muddle. Leelson and Lutha could neither accept one another nor leave one another alone. And, though Trompe had been quite willing to play Lutha's servant so long as Leelson was thought to be missing, he felt it put him at a disadvantage now that Leelson was present and accounted for. He, Trompe, was, after all, as much a Fastigat as Leelson was, and Lutha was, more or less, Leelson's responsibility. Leelson, meantime, felt he had the right to argue with, ignore, or even attack Lutha, but he denied Trompe any such right. What with long hours of either drudgery or boredom plus our restless nights, all three of them were on edge, irritable, ready to lash out at anyone, anything.

So I analyzed the situation, as though I were a songfather setting things to rights in a winter hive, where, as here, everyone is shut up together and irritation mounts. It was an ordinary, irrational human stew, quite complicated enough, even without the sexual feelings that were churning around among them. Among us.

Myself included. I found myself watching Trompe, time on time. Liking the shape of him. Imagining him in other places, at other times. I was not in love with him, but yes, I lusted after him. Lusting after men is a particular pain for women of the veiled sisterhood, because we know it is hopeless, fruitless, foredoomed. Even if some man could overlook ... overlook our appearance, we are not allowed to have children who might inherit our ... tendencies. Well. Set all that aside. It was of no importance. Certainly it was of no consequence. It simply was.

Though we had set up the panels, we had not yet fastened the last ones. It was open country where we were, a wide canyon, with no Kachis about, and it was not yet dark, though the sun rested upon the canyon rim above us. Leelson and Lutha had gone away from the wain, he to cut forage and she to a pool in a nearby grove – to wash herself, she said, for she was tired of smelling like smoke. She took the bucket, to bring water when she returned. Trompe was fussing about with the harness, which he seemed to have adopted as his particular responsibility. Leely was asleep and I was restless. I slipped out between the panels and went in the direction Lutha had gone.

The grove was made up of d'kymah trees, trunks no larger than my arm, the first branches just above my head. The trees are not good for anything but smelling sweet and being delightful, for they grow always in company with a carpet of flowering grass we call golden eyes. Lovers' woods, we called places like this. Sweetsong woods. The leaves were just coming out, no larger than the nail of my little finger, a pale green, the purest of all colors.

I did not disturb the quiet but went silently, as Dinadhi sisters learn to do, touching the trees for thanks, smelling the foliage with kindness. These pleasures could not be taken from us, so my sisters said. These pleasures were to be enjoyed. My enjoyment was ended by the sound of raised voices, and I stopped, behind a screen of leaves, peering through them at Lutha, and at Leelson.

She had stripped off her outer robe and had taken her arms out of the inner one, lowering it around her waist. She had loosened her hair so the great wealth of it hung over her wet shoulders and breasts. One hand still held the comb, the other was out, as though to ward him away. Leelson stood a pace away, his hands out, imploring her.

'I can't,' he said. 'Lutha, I can't.'

462

She lifted her hand. Even from where I was, I could see it tremble. She was like a little tree, shivered by wind. 'Oh,' she cried. 'Oh, Leelson.'

They came together then, so swiftly it was like an attack, like a rape, only that wasn't what was happening. Neither was more frantic than the other, loosening, unfastening, ridding themselves of garments so their flesh could lie together. The comb fell with a tiny click onto the stone, unnoticed. The clothing sighed away.

I turned away, my eyes burning. So it had been for me. So it would never be again. I crept away, ashamed, piteous, angry, needing to stand for a long time at the edge of the grove before I could return to the wagon. In time, Leelson returned, his face empty, as though he had purposefully decided not to think of anything. Later Lutha came back. There were still tears in her eyes. So. Passion and pain. Attraction and anger. Two who would not, but must.

When we went to our beds, Trompe propped himself near the slightly open door, saying the night air (and the Kachis, no doubt) would keep him awake while he kept watch on Leely. He was there when I fell asleep. He was there when I woke the following morning, his head lolling on his chest, breathing heavily.

It was barely light. I slipped out past him and went to the panel that had been loose the day before. It was loose again. Even as I stood there I saw Leely coming from among the stones at the canyon's mouth, skipping like a little gauf, arms extended, hands waving, a portrait of perfect contentment. I pulled the panels apart to let him in, and he looked at me as he went past. I have seen that look in the eyes of birds, or lizards. A kind of fearless wariness. A look that says, 'I know you could get me – kill me, eat me – but at this moment you are not a danger.'

His arms were marked as they had been the morning before, as was his forehead, a dozen small, slightly reddened spots that were already fading. He gave me that lizard look again, then went into the wagon silently, he who was rarely silent! I stood listening, but there was no outcry from within. He had sneaked out; he had sneaked back. Considering how everyone felt at the moment, perhaps it was best that I keep Leely's excursion to myself. If I said anything about it, Lutha – whose emotions were always at the surface of her, quick to erupt, quick to cool – would blame Trompe, who would be angry at her, which would annoy Leelson, which would make Lutha angry at him. Angrier. She who could no more resist him, or he her, than the stone can resist the rootlets of the tree. Even the hardest stone will break, for the tree will grow, despite all.

Far better say nothing.

We broke camp without incident or argument. We drove into the Canyon of Burning Springs, the mouth and throat of which are no different from any other canyon: a trickle of water at the center, water-rounded stones along the sides among a sprinkle of low grasses and forbs and woody plants, then a long slope of rubble piled at the foot of the canyon walls, then the walls themselves, fissured and split, some parts actually overhanging us as we wandered slowly below. The canyon tended generally westward, so we were in light, the sun lying midway between the zenith and the southern rim. We heard no sounds, we saw no living things except ourselves. The canyon curves slightly, so we could not see far ahead, though we could hear the sound of water. We did not realize we had made a considerable change of direction until we were well into what Leelson called a 'dogleg.' (I called it an elbow. We have no dogs on Dinadh.)

The change impressed itself on us when the light went out as though someone had closed a shutter. Even in a sunlit canyon there are often narrow shadows thrown across the way by protruding boulders on the rims, but we had come to a veritable lake of shadow, thrown by a monstrous monolith we could see black against the sun glare, south and east of us. We blinked and murmured and stared around ourselves, dark afterimages of the sun dazzle swimming across our eyes. Only after we stepped into the shadow and let our eyes adjust to it did we realize we had come to the place of fire.

Songfather had often amused the children of Cochim-Mahn with tales of this place, but I'd never imagined it as it really was. I'd thought there would be small fires here and there, like a gathering of campfires, perhaps. When our eyes cleared, however, we saw a world of flame. Fountains gushed everywhere, up the sides of the walls, along the rubble slopes, in the canyon bottom, beside the steamy stream that trickled along beside us, braided into a dozen vaporous streamlets. We were surrounded by firelight and water noise, by fire roar and water glimmer. The light and the sound twisted and warbled together, so that it was hard to know whether we saw the movement or heard it. There was a mineral smell, not unpleasant, and warm damp upon our skins that turned clammy as we moved.

'Worthy of a tourist's visit,' murmured Leelson, an awed expression on his face. 'Why have I never heard of this place?'

'Because Dinadh does not want tourists,' Lutha said, in a voice equally awed.

I had no words at all. Around us the fountains burst forth from smooth basins they had polished into the stone over the centuries. Some were clear jets like pillars of glass, others were peaks of foam; some were single towers of evanescent light, others were multiple spouts that collided in fans of glittering gems, then drained away through multiple fissures, back into the fiery depths below. The small streamlets beside us carried away only a tiny fraction of the leaping water. Mostly it was recirculated, seeping away, bursting forth again, every shining cascade lit by the changing, evanescent spirits of flame burning within the water. Sometimes the fire topped the foam, sometimes the water leapt higher; no instant was like any other. Together, the plash and burble of water and the muted roar of flame hummed like a giant voice, a great harmonic chord.

'Wow,' whispered Lutha, cupping her hands over her ears. An inadequate response, I felt, becoming for an instant very planet proud.

'You could make hard coin bringing tours from Simidi-ala,' said Trompe.

I said, 'It is a tortuous distance overland, and we will not fly unless it is absolutely necessary.' My voice was properly stiff and Dinadhish, but my senses echoed Leelson's pleasure. Why shouldn't people from other worlds see this wonder? I knew the answer, of course, but for that moment it did not seem sufficient.

Our mutual awe and pleasure was quickly lost.

'Uh-oh,' murmured Leelson. I looked in the direction of his gaze and saw what the fiery fountains had prevented our seeing until that instant. The pallid wings. The shining forms. Not one or two, but dozens, scores. I found myself counting. There were a hundred of them, at least, sitting around a fountain at the foot of the wall, heads resting on their folded arms or lax upon their shoulders.

We made no sound, almost holding our breaths. A long moment went by. The pale forms did not move. They took no notice of us. One of the gaufers grew impatient and struck the rock with the hardened skin of his foot. It made a rough, scraping noise quite loud, but it occasioned no reaction.

I was close at Leelson's side. I felt him drawing in a deep, quiet breath before he clucked to the gaufers and shook the reins. They moved, their heads down and forward at the end of their long necks. They are curious beasts. So they greet the offer of some new kind of food or the hand of some new handler. We approached the first fountain and its surrounding forms. The fountain danced and chuckled. The Kachis did not move.

The gaufers drew their heads back, snorting and spitting as they jerked the wain into quicker motion. The next fountain was larger, with even more Kachis about it. We drove by and they did not move. So we went on, four fountains, seven, ten: all of them ringed by Kachis, none of the Kachis moving. Gradually, as our eyes accustomed to the variable light, we saw more Kachis, thousands of them scattered all the way to the canyon walls, up the rubble slopes, behind broken boulders and pillars.

Lutha tapped my arm and pointed upward. They were there as well, high upon the narrow ledges left when blocks of stone had fallen away. Every shelf was edged with them, like white tatting on the edge of a sleeve.

'Are they asleep?' Lutha whispered to me.

How did I know? I had never seen a Kachis asleep. Still, most things sleep, so one might suppose …

I shook my head at her. Who would know what Kachis do when they are alone, afar, away from us? Who knows the truth of what they do even with us?

Finally, at the end of the dogleg, Leelson gave the reins to Trompe and told him to drive on. He was going back to examine the Kachis.

'Don't be a fool,' said Lutha, yearning toward him, furious at him.

'I lead a charmed life, remember?' he told her, actually smiling.

'Leelson! It's dangerous!'

'I don't think so,' he said. 'Drive on. I'll catch up with you in a while.'

Trompe grunted in annoyance, but he drove on. We kept going for some little time, then, at Lutha's insistence, we stopped. We waited, and waited, growing increasingly apprehensive. At the moment when both Trompe and Lutha had decided to turn about and go back, Leelson appeared at the turn in the canyon, sauntering toward us as though he had been out for a morning stroll around a hive!

'Do you know anything about what we saw back there, Saluez?'

I looked blankly at him. Of course I didn't.

'Very strange,' he mused. 'They're unconscious. As in a trance.'

I said nothing. What could I say?

He shrugged, with an apologetic look at me. 'I'm picking up all kind of avoidance signals here. This is evidently something Saluez doesn't want us to discuss.'

'Saluez doesn't want to talk about the Kachis,' said Lutha.

'Talk,' I said weakly, flapping my hands at them. 'You talk. I won't listen.'

Of course I did listen, even though they used many words I didn't know then, words I only learned later.

Leelson said, 'There are a few dead ones back in the canyon, like the ones we saw yesterday. But those gathered around the fountains don't seem to be dead, even though they're totally unresponsive to stimuli. I thumped a few of them. They're rigid. But there's no sign of decay or mummification, so I wondered what Saluez could tell us.'

Lutha looked at me from the corner of her eye. I avoided her look.

She said carefully, 'I believe ... at the ceremony of Tahs-uppi, some Kachis go into the omphalos—'

The Kachis, I corrected her mentally. All of them. Our beloved ghosts, going on to heaven.

'—and if this ceremony is dependent upon songfathers getting to the omphalos, perhaps it's a state the Kachis go into at this time. Making the journey safer for people.'

'Interesting,' mused Leelson, climbing up to take the reins from Trompe.

Not interesting! Holy!

I was amazed to find my eyes wet, to feel that choking sensation that comes with tears. What was there to cry over?

In Simidi-ala, the rememberer returned to the outlanders, his brow broken by three deep horizontal wrinkles, his mouth twisted up as though he had drunk sour water, his hands flapping.

'Well?' demanded the Procurator.

'Gone!' said the rememberer. 'Mitigan and Chur Durwen, they're gone from the hive we sent them to. And there's been a herdsman murdered, a gaufer taken!'

'Chowby excrement,' said the Procurator. 'The piss of diseased farbles. The sexual relationships of brain-dead bi-Tharbians.'

'Now, now,' said Poracious Luv. 'Cursing won't help.'

The Procurator shuddered. 'How long ago?' he demanded.

'Several days.' The rememberer fell into a chair limply. 'There's hardly a chance of their surviving.'

'Why?' asked the ex-king. 'What dangers does your world afford?'

The rememberer flushed. 'We enter upon a delicate area, sirs, madam.'

'I don't care if we enter upon you and your wife in the act of holy procreation,' the Procurator snarled. 'Damn it, we need to know!'

'We have certain sacred … creatures upon Dinadh. They are nocturnal. Anyone who is abroad upon the planet during the hours of darkness is almost certain to be … ah, damaged.'

'Mitigan came from Asenagi,' said the ex-king. 'Though the Asenagi are Firsters, they are of a sect which does not believe in homo-norming. Have you heard of the viper bats of Asenagi? Or the great owl weasel? Both of them are nocturnal. Viper bats go in clouds of several thousand. Owl weasels are more solitary, but then, they're as big as a man. Asenagi youth spend several years in the wilderness, living off the country, before they're accepted into the clan of assassins. Do you think your nocturnal creatures, whatever they are, will bother Mitigan?'

'Or Chur Durwen,' Poracious Luv offered. 'Collis, too, is a warlike world. Young men are expected to have slaughtered their first enemy by the time they are seven.'

Beads of sweat stood like pearls along the rememberer's brow.

'The songfather of T'loch-ala is questioning those who spoke with the two leaseholders. He will determine whether they gave any hint as to where they are going.'

The Procurator said something under his breath.

'Meantime,' offered the rememberer. 'The man you asked for. Thosby Anent? He's waiting to see you.'

He hurried out, and after a long moment the door opened only far enough to admit a lean, rather stooped man who moved through wraiths of smoke on legs oddly bowed, as though he were crippled at the knees. He looked at the three who awaited him, and his posture straightened.

'A peculiar time,' said Codger, bowing slightly. 'One in which we might be led to question the very bases of our existence. A time in which humanity's overwhelming concern with its own affairs must give way to a more general consideration. ...'

'Anent?' questioned the Procurator.

'Myself.' Thosby bowed. 'Who has lately been much involved in philosophical musing.'

'Can such musings be set aside for the moment?' queried Poracious Luv. 'I would suggest that now is not the best time for—'

Thosby interrupted with a grandiose gesture. 'But what time is, madam? Is any time *best* for the consideration of ultimate disaster? When we are faced with—'

'What are we faced with?' demanded the Procurator. 'That's what we want to know! Intelligence Division tells me you are responsible for forwarding reports from the shadow team on Perdur Alas. We've received no information!'

Thosby was momentarily paralyzed. He puffed furiously, his head disappearing in a hazy cloud. Poracious Luv lunged from her chair and struck the pipe from his lips. It clattered against the far wall.

'Summon your wits, man! The Procurator wants to know about the team on Perdur Alas.'

'Survivor,' murmured the Master Spy, desperately seeking a role to fit the current circumstance. 'Just one survivor.'

'One! Since when?' cried the Procurator.

'Ah, well, one doesn't know, does one? They simply, ah, disappeared.'

'How long ago?' Poracious barked.

Thosby hum-gargled, deep in his throat. 'It's difficult to say. The information received now is sensory, but is it objective or subjective? Does one count time when one is alone as one does when with one's fellows. There's an interesting philosophical—'

'Stop these interminable divagations!' she cried. 'When did you know they had disappeared?'

'Well, the equipment says ... perhaps thirty, forty standard days, though from the low standard of equipment maintenance I have noticed during my stay here on Dinadh, I would be forced to—'

'Do you have any other information?" the Procurator said in a danger-ously calm voice.

'No,' Thosby said sulkily, retreating into Codger.

'None at all?' asked Poracious, unbelieving. She retrieved the pipe from where it had fallen and held it out to the man, like one using a morsel of food to coax an unwilling animal from its den.

'So far as I know, she hasn't found anything at all interesting,' mumbled Codger, snatching the pipe. The last time he had monitored the recording had been days ago, but he did not mention this.

'She?

'She who?' asked Poracious in a silky tone.

'The survivor.'

'Who in the name of all the excremental and sexually active deities now or ever thought of is this survivor?' demanded the Procurator, his face gray with rage and frustration.

'This girl who seems still to be there,' said Codger. 'This XZ51.'

The other three in the room exchanged looks of amazement.

'What girl is he talking about?' asked the ex-king.

Poracious Luv sat down and held her hands high, commanding silence and attention. 'Let's make sense of this! Anent seems to be saying the entire team on Perdur Alas has disappeared except for one girl or woman des-ignated by the code number XZ51. That one is still on Perdur Alas with a functioning sensory recorder. Is that more or less correct?'

'Said that,' muttered Master Spy, biting hard upon his pipe stem, his lips writhing back to disclose a gray-coated tongue and stumpy, smoke-black-ened teeth, at the sight of which Poracious averted her eyes. 'Already said that!'

'You have the records.'

'No,' he said between clamped teeth.

'You don't have the records? Where are they?'

'At my house.'

'You will provide them?'

'That was the plan.' It was a favorite saying of Thosby's, used in reply whenever anyone asked him when he would do something he had said he would do a long time previously.

'Not a plan,' whispered the Procurator, his hand at his throat, which felt raw and dry. 'Not a futurity, not a possibility, not a matter to be thought over. It is now, an immediate order. Go, at once. As rapidly as it is possible for you to do so. Without doing anything else or going anywhere else. Go to your house, and get the records. Bring them here!'

'I'd better go with him,' said Poracious, heaving her bulk from its chair. 'He might get sidetracked.'

The two got only as far as the slightly open door when a young woman of Dinadh pushed it open, bowed politely, and spoke to Thosby Anent in a cheerfully guileless voice:

'Sir Thosby, when I learned you were on your way to meet with the Procurator of the Alliance, it occurred to me you might want the records you have been so assiduously compiling.' She held out several datachips, offering them to Poracious.

Poracious broke the astonished silence.

'And you are?'

'Chadra Tsum, ma'am. I am housekeeper for Thosby Anent.' She relinquished the datachips with a significant glance, which said, 'I am who and what I am, but this matter is larger than who and what I am.'

'You were both thoughtful and correct,' the large woman said.

'I believe this room is equipped with retrievers. If the Procurator wants the latest information.' Chadra bowed to Poracious, to Thosby, a perfect model of polite servitude.

'Pushy, unpleasant woman,' Thosby snarled as Chadra turned away. 'Always interrupting me when I'm busy.'

'Perhaps she wishes to direct your attention to something important,' whispered the Procurator. 'Had that occurred to you?'

'Oh, sir,' said the Codger with a patronizing smile, 'we are too concerned with things we believe are important. When one considers the infinite nature of time, that all races including our own are doomed to live and perish like the candle flame in that infinitude—'

'Good day,' said Poracious, taking him by the shoulder and moving him gently toward the door. 'We can't thank you enough for your help.' She shut the door behind him, then turned, the data-chips in her hand, murmuring, 'Where's the retriever?'

'What's that beside the window?' the Procurator asked plaintively. 'Surely that's a retriever.'

The ex-king took the plat from Poracious and inserted it into a wall-mounted retrieval complex that had been designed to look like a landscape sculpture. 'Is there a code?' he murmured, stepping politely aside and averting his eyes.

Poracious referred to her wrist-link before entering an activation code. The unit hummed briefly, then the walls of the room disappeared and the three were on Perdur Alas, assailed by sounds, sights, smells. And a taste!

They gagged.

Before them, observed from some distance, through a twiggy growth, monstrously shaggy flesh encircled something they could not see, great cliffs of hair reared high as hills, walls of old dog, of lairs deep in layers of fatty bones, the taste of beast, hot reeking blood, and sour spit. From behind them came the sound of the sea. Between their teeth a twig was jammed to keep their mouths slightly open so they wouldn't gag on the taste ... on the dreadful taste.

The scene jiggled and moved as they rose laboriously. Their point of view changed. They climbed, up and up, then peered out once more from above, down at the inside of that wall of flesh, seeing bare skin upon which patterns moved, around and around the abandoned camp, memories of slaughter, retelling of the chase.

They raised their eyes. Through the air, from the south, three things came toward the others, reaching out with appendages that seemed to stretch forever, joining others, making other enclosures. In the middle distance, a dozen shaggy mountains moved in a slow procession.

What was it they tasted? Oily, soapy, rancid, bitter, nasty ...

Poracious Luv, from her vision of Perdur Alas, stretched her arm through the vision to find the reality of the retrieval control on Dinadh. She turned it off. While the other two retched and gagged she unashamedly wiped out her mouth with the hem of her garment.

'Technician!' she said. 'Call for a technician to filter out the tastes. We can't analyze this until we filter out the tastes.'

'Do it,' sputtered the Procurator, heading for the door labeled SANITARY FACILITY. 'Summon that rememberer back, and have him find someone. Now!'

From behind a clump of furze, Snark watched Diagonal Red, Four Green Spot, Big Gray Blob, Blue Lines, and Speckled Purple – the ones she'd come to call the Big Five – gather over the camp. Recently these particular ones had been assembling more and more frequently, sometimes only three or four of them, often all five, looming aloft for a while, then descending to encircle the abandoned camp with appendages that seemed almost liquid in their ability to flow together. Peering at them from her hole at the top of the nearest hill, Snark had decided this was either the way they conversed or the way they remembered. Each new picture coalesced on one Ularian before it moved across the united flesh to the next Ularian, where some other details or actions were added. Each Ularian augmented or complicated the picture created by the previous ones, and the event continued accreting finer and finer detail until the sequence was completed. Or until the Ularians got tired of it.

She had watched them kill her mother half a dozen times. Since she had first realized that the color blobs were pictures, she had counted the number of different pictures they shared. The most frequent one was Snark's mother, a huge mother one who covered the whole front of one of the things. Soon Mother would run across the moor, her hair streaming behind her. The shape of running Mother would move to the left, racing along that great wall of flesh. The next Ularian added the shapes of the pursuers. This picture went on, left, farther left, until Snark lost sight of it. When it came into view again, to her right, the pursuers were pouncing, sending Mother fleeing this way, that way, playing with her. Every time the same, the sea coming nearer and nearer, safety almost within reach ...

Each time Snark had seen it, Mother had almost reached the edge before they caught her.

Why did they show it over and over? Tell it over and over? It wasn't a story one of them told, it was a story they shared. Sometimes Diagonal Red would start it. Sometimes one of the others. And the details were always the same, as though they'd all agreed just how it was, just what had happened, remembering it all the same.

Snark told herself the pictures were not necessarily true. The chase might not have happened at all. Maybe it was something they wanted to have happened. Maybe it was a religious thing, a kind of ritual they went through, like primitives did, counting coup, telling tall tales, even painting lies on their tombs to make their gods think they were better, or bigger, or stronger than they actually were.

Today they weren't telling the mother-chase story. Today they were showing another favorite, a fish story. The picture was of shaggy forms that hung over the sea, dropping their tentacles into the waves, drawing them up again, laden with silvery fish. The detail was so complete that Snark could see the fish flapping inside the tentacles that had caught them.

When they were finished telling stories, they would float away, like monstrous balloons. There was a wrongness to them. Balloons should be festive, not repulsive. Snark put her face onto her hands, waiting for them to finish showing the fish story and go away. Close as they were, she dared not move, though the taste was hard to bear. When she watched them for a long time like this, the taste seemed to permeate her own flesh until she herself tasted as they did, sick of her own saliva, nauseated by the rottenness of her own tongue. When they left, she would lie in the mouth of her cave with her mouth open, letting the sea wind wash around her teeth, cleansing her into humanness once more.

During the past few days, they had been around more frequently and had stayed for longer times. Maybe they were planning a fishing trip. Maybe they'd taken over this whole planet just to go fishing! Though all they'd done so far was talk about it, that is, show pictures about it. They themselves hadn't caught any fish, not that Snark had seen.

She clamped her eyes shut and concentrated on breathing deeply: one breath, two breaths, three, four, the smell of the sea, the sound of the birds, thirty-two, the sound of the waves, eighty, one hundred, a hundred thirty, seventy....

When she raised her head, they had gone. She didn't move. A few days ago, she'd thought they were gone and had been about to move when she realized they were hanging directly above her. She'd come that close to being eaten. Or transported. Or cat-and-moused like her mother. Whatever it was they did. Would do.

She risked a look up. Clear sky. Nothing. Nothing near the camp. Nothing between herself and the cliff. Still, one had to be careful. They could move with horrid alacrity. One minute they wouldn't be anywhere around, the next moment they'd be present.

Maybe they knew she was here. Maybe all this was part of the ritual. Showing her what would happen to her.

She wouldn't think that. Wouldn't let herself think that. If she thought that, she'd run screaming right at them, out in the open, panicked. She couldn't do that. She had to hold on, hold on. ...

For what? There was no one here. No one to protect, no one to talk to, no one to lie beside, sharing warmth, sharing comfort, even.

Untrue. Somewhere was a monitor. Seeing what she saw. Feeling what she felt. Somewhere on Dinadh was someone watching over her.

Though the monitor might not be the only thing watching over her! Sometimes in the night she woke to that flattened sound, that curtained feeling, that almost subliminal shudder, as though a mighty hoof had touched the planet, moving it slightly in its orbit. What was that? Did *it* know she was here?

'Lonely,' she whispered. 'God, I'm so lonely! I'm all alone. Please. Help me. Come get me. Please!'

Late Dinadh daylight filtered chill through multiple windows, making puddles of grayed gold upon the floor. Three sat stunned, facing one another, only just returned from Perdur Alas, returned from fear, pain, hunger, cold. From weary loneliness.

'Well,' said the Procurator in an exhausted whisper. 'At least we now know what they look like.'

They did not know whether they had been living Snark's life for a day or two or three. Only when she reached the safety of her cave and curled into sleep had they turned off the retriever and let the Dinadh evening surround them once more. The Procurator's words were the first intelligible ones any of them had made, though their experience had been punctuated by cries and grunts and indrawn breaths.

'Can't we do something for her?' the ex-king asked, his voice breaking. 'Send a ship or something.'

Poracious Luv arched her brows disbelievingly. 'You? The King of Kamir, the practitioner of ultimate ennui? Touched by the plight of another human being?'

'She's alone,' he blurted, flushing. 'I've ... I've been alone. It would touch anyone!'

The Procurator rubbed his forehead wearily. It ached from the battering he, Snark, had received. It had ached before, and now it was worse. He had, after all, sent her there. He was responsible for her.

He said, 'Touched or not, right now there's no ship to send. Even if there were a ship, we couldn't risk it for one survivor.'

'Particularly inasmuch as we now have records of everything she's picked up,' said Poracious Luv in a dry, cynical voice. 'So there'd be no advantage to rescuing her.'

'Advantage,' Jiacare Lostre snarled. 'Advantage!'

'Would you trade a hundred lives for one?' the Procurator said, looking him in the eye. 'Surely you don't think those ... creatures would let us go to Perdur Alas and simply remove her? We'd have to send a cruiser at least. Would you trade a shipload of men on a gesture?'

'How do we know they wouldn't?'

Poracious sighed. 'We know what happened to ships in the Hermes Sector a hundred years ago. Any ship approaching a world that had been stripped was taken. They went, just as the people went. Gone. Whisk. Away. Nobody knew where. That's what has happened to the evacuation ships this time, too.'

'I didn't realize,' mumbled the ex-king. 'Sorry. This is all ... very new to me. I've tried not to care about anything for a very long time, but this ...'

'Nothing like a heady dose of danger to wake one up,' Poracious agreed. 'Well, Procurator? What do we do next?'

'With what we've seen happening currently, there must be dozens of episodes in the record that will warrant perusal by experts.'

'Experts.' She laughed. 'Ha!'

'Well, by people who might have specialized insights, at least. Some other Fastigats than myself should see this. Also some linguists who specialize in sight languages.'

'Sight language?' Jiacare Lostre cocked his head curiously.

'There are, or were historically, several sight languages for people who couldn't hear. Now, of course, such languages aren't necessary, but we still have records of them. The girl mutters to herself a lot, so we can pick up clues as to what she's thinking. She said "telling stories"; she said "ritual"; both in connection with that pictorial thing they do. I'd be interested in knowing what others think.'

'What do you think?' demanded the ex-king.

The Procurator considered. 'The episode with the running woman had the feel of a story, didn't it?'

'Was the woman actually her mother?' Poracious asked.

'Each time the woman appeared, she, Snark, subvocalized the word,' said the Procurator. 'She said the word *mother*, and her throat and mouth sensed the shaping of the word. Whether she actually believes so, we don't know. Her thoughts can't be recorded. Only what she senses.'

Poracious mused. 'If the woman was her mother, then the girl was a child there, on Perdur Alas. A survivor from the former Ularian crisis?'

The Procurator shook his head. 'It seems impossible. She'd have to have been third or fourth generation.'

'We've found great-grandchildren of colonists before.'

'True.' He stared at his hands, surprised to find them trembling. 'I've just thought, Lutha Tallstaff is a linguist. One of the best, according to my sources. I don't know if she knows anything about sight languages, but it's worth bringing her from wherever she was sent. What was the name of the place?'

'Cochim-Mahn,' said Poracious.

'We should be fetching her anyhow. She's at danger if those two assassins are on the loose. And meantime, we should be bringing in some other experts to experience what this girl is going through.' The Procurator stared blindly at his companions. 'Think of it. The first human contact with a life-form that speaks, and it speaks a nonverbal language.'

The ex-king remarked, 'My Minister of Agriculture would say we don't know that it's speaking. It could be merely replaying things it has seen. My Minister of Agriculture would deny it thinks. He says the universe was made for man.'

Poracious stared at the wall, remembering. She didn't believe it was a mere replay. There had been too much relish in the retelling. Reshowing. She went to the door and beckoned to the tassel-bearded rememberer waiting outside. He rose, bowing attentively as she said:

'Will you please send word to Cochim-Mahn that we need to get Lutha Tallstaff here, as quickly as possible.'

'And Trompe,' called the Procurator. 'Bring him as well!'

The rememberer stared at the ceiling, shifted his feet, cleared his throat.

'Well?' demanded Poracious, suspiciously. 'What?'

'Inasmuch as we had determined the assassins were no longer where they belonged, I took the liberty of communicating with Cochim-Mahn. While you were ... occupied.'

'And? Come on, man. Spit it out. All this havering merely makes us itch.'

'They're gone,' he blurted. 'She, the boy, her companion. As well as Leelson Famber. Also a shadow woman. An eaten one.' He curled his lips around the word, whether in disapproval or disgust, she couldn't tell.

'Gone?' she cried.

'Leelson Famber!' exclaimed the Procurator as he joined her in the doorway. 'When did Leelson Famber come here?'

The rememberer shrugged, looking from face to face as though trying to decide which question to answer first. 'He came, sir, some time ago. And it is believed by those at Cochim-Mahn that they may all have gone to Tahs-uppi.'

Jiacare Lostre joined the others in the doorway. 'Gone where?'

'Gone to what,' corrected the rememberer. 'A ceremony. Held once every sixty years or so. At the omphalos. At the sipapu. At Dinadh's birthplace, the site of our emergence. The songfather of Cochim-Mahn believes they have gone there, and he is pursuing them. The assassins asked questions about the ceremony, so we believe they're headed there also.'

'Can we intercept them on the way?' Poracious demanded.

The rememberer turned up his palms helplessly. 'Who knows which way they've gone. If they intended to avoid other travelers, they would have tried less-traveled ways, of which there are thousands! The canyons ramify, net-like. They go off into pockets and branches. We'd never find them.'

'Well then,' the Procurator said. 'How long for us to get where they're going?'

'Not long, great sir. I can arrange it for tomorrow. We can fly.'

The three shared helpless glances, equally at a loss. Poracious Luv broke the silence, attempting encouragement. 'We'll meet them when they arrive,' she said, patting the Procurator upon the shoulder.

'If they arrive,' corrected the rememberer. 'I would be remiss if I did not tell you that their arrival is far from certain.'

8

The first of us to catch sight of the Nodders was Trompe. He was driving the hitch; Leely was asleep inside the wain; and the rest of us were trudging some way behind, cursing every step we made across the curved pebbles that often twisted treacherously beneath our feet. Trompe's *whoof* of surprise brought us stumbling forward to find him gaping, the reins lax in his hands. Gaufers are incapable of astonishment. They simply lay down, snapping and grumbling at one another as they did at every halt. We made no effort to get them moving. There seemed to be nowhere they could go.

It was another place like the Burning Springs, that is, one I'd heard described without getting any idea what it was really like. Songfather had said there were many Nodders, that they were tall, thin pillars of stone, topped with stone heads.

What he'd said wasn't inaccurate; it was simply a ridiculous understatement. Trompe climbed down from the wagon seat to join Lutha, Leelson, and me as we went slowly forward. The first Nodder was like a sentinel, standing a little forward from the rest. As we neared it our eyes were drawn upward, seeing the tower narrowed to a pinpoint against the massive bulk of the balanced stone head. Perspective, I told myself. It wasn't really that slender. It couldn't be. It couldn't be frigidly cold in the vicinity of the stone, either, but we thrust our shivering arms into our sleeves as we backed slowly away. Beyond the first pillar stood two more, side by side, and behind them, hundreds.

Songfather had said they were many, tall, and thin. I also recalled – as we fled in howling panic! – he had said the stone heads moved.

It was impossible to run over that treacherous footing and we collapsed in a confused heap not far away.

'I thought it was coming down on us!' Lutha cried as she scrabbled backwards on all fours, never taking her eyes from the ponderous, impossible nodding of that great stone head.

I still thought it would come down. When it did, it would roll purposefully over us. Behind the three menacing outliers, the great forest of them seemed to whisper to one another in sinister agreement. *Yes, yes, let's roll over on that wagon and squish all the people. Wouldn't that be fun?*

I couldn't keep from saying this, a mere whisper to Lutha, and she laughed, a wild peal of amusement. The two men turned disapproving looks on her, which only increased her hilarity. All the tension she'd bottled up during the journey poured out in hysterical torrents. She put her hands over her mouth and smothered the sound, head on knees, shoulders shaking.

Leelson, with his usual casual disapproval, pointed to the sharp-edged fragments of curved stone that littered the ground, fragments not unlike those that had been troubling our footsteps for some miles. He said pointedly, 'It really isn't funny, Lutha. They do come down.'

Not the least sobered, she spared a glance for the surfaces around us, then took a quick look at the conspiratorial heads. My eyes followed hers, and the same odd idea possessed us both at once, for we said, as in one slightly echoed voice:

'From where?'

'Why, from ...' said Leelson, his words trailing into silence.

'If some tops fell down, then there should be some pillars without tops.' Lutha giggled. Her voice sounded foolish, like that of a petulant little girl. She heard herself, cleared her throat, and said in a more normal tone, 'But there aren't any pillars without tops. So where did they fall from?'

'Strange,' mused Trompe. 'Very strange. The shape of the heads, I mean. They shouldn't be quite that spherical, should they? Or would erosion tend to round them off?'

When one focused on the shape and not on the streaked and blotched surfaces, the roundness was obvious. Lines and smudges of mineral colors – ocher, brown, red – made them appear more irregular and rugged than they actually were. Except for the horns on top, they were ball-shaped.

'The mass can't be uniform,' Leelson remarked in a troubled tone. 'The center of gravity has to be ... where?'

'Doesn't matter,' mumbled Trompe. 'It'd have to be below the point of the pillar to keep the thing balanced that way. The way they are, the damn things can't exist.'

'But they do,' I said.

'It would work if there were a gyroscope inside.' Leelson strode away in a long arc to examine the nearest Nodder from the side. 'Or a central support. Or a gravitic drive.'

'Or if they weren't really stone,' said Trompe, joining his colleague. The two of them stood there with their mouths open, wearing identical expressions of annoyance. Fastigats, so I had already learned, do not like things they do not understand. Their irritated silence made me uncomfortably aware that I understood no more than they.

Lutha had regained control of herself. 'You're not thinking that they're unnatural, are you?'

Leelson took his time before answering. 'You've seen Dinadhi children playing ball games. You've seen Dinadhi herdsmen spinning wool. Imagine yourself trying to balance one of the balls on the tip of a spindle and tell me how much luck you'd have.'

She gave me a quick look, and I shook my head. As described, it would be impossible. Unless the ball were spinning. We have jugglers skilled in such tricks, but these heads weren't spinning. So. It couldn't be done.

The two men came strolling back, foreheads wrinkled with concentration.

I said, 'But if they aren't natural, wouldn't someone have noticed before now?'

Leelson shook his head. 'According to you, Saluez, people come this way only once every sixty Dinadhi years, which is about once a century, standard. Since that's a generous lifetime, it's unlikely anyone makes the trip twice. Suppose a traveler *had* noticed. Suppose he'd gone back to his hive and told someone. Would there have been any consequence?'

His superior tone implied there would have been none, and he was probably right. On Dinadh, whenever someone raises a 'difficult' question, someone else can be depended upon to mutter, in that particular tone of hushed apprehension people always use on such occasions, 'Perhaps it's part of the choice.' Once the choice is mentioned, all conversation ends. Only songfathers are allowed to discuss the choice, along with the rest of their arcane lore.

I suppose my thoughts showed on my face, for Leelson said:

'As I thought. No one would have done anything at all about it.' Then he shared one of his infuriatingly smug looks with Trompe.

Lutha glanced at me from beneath her lashes, and I blinked slowly in sympathy. We were both thinking that Fastigats were impossible. She took my hand and we walked back to the wagon behind the men. I was wondering if our being here was blasphemous, but Lutha had a different concern.

'From here, they look like a herd of great horned beasts, don't they? If they're artificial, why are they here?'

Leelson stood for a moment in thought, then fetched Bernesohn Famber's map from the wagon, unrolled it on the ground, and put a stone on each corner to hold it down. Kneeling beside it, he pointed with an extended forefinger.

'The important geographical features are all shown on this map, canyons, tablelands, hives, and so forth – even the omphalos, beside this winding river on what seems to be a flat plain. The Nodders, however, are not shown.'

'That is, they're not printed on the map,' said Trompe, underlining the obvious.

Leelson continued. 'No. The word *Nodders* has been written in, probably by Bernesohn himself. He learned about them a century ago. Either someone told him about the Nodders or he himself came this way.'

I said, 'But Bernesohn Famber wouldn't have been allowed to go to the omphalos. He was an outlander.'

'We're not allowed either, but we're going,' Trompe snorted. 'What would they have done to him if they'd caught him?'

It was not a proper question. It was not a question any Dinadhi should have to answer. 'I don't know,' I said. 'Sometimes the songfathers have people stoned.'

Leelson sat back on his heels. 'Let's assume he came here himself. Let's even assume he was put to death by the songfathers for that impropriety. Would his property have been forfeit?'

I didn't know what he meant, but Lutha did. She turned to me, asking:

'If a person is executed on Dinadh, what happens to his property. What happens to his clothing, or anything he may be carrying?'

'Everything we have belongs to our families. When someone dies, if the body isn't too close to a hive, it's just left where it is. It's only … flesh. The spirit is already gone. But anything like clothing or tools would be returned to the family.'

'Even if the person has been executed?'

'The family is not tarnished for what one person of it does. That would not be just.'

Songfather was not tarnished because of me. Chahdzi father was not tarnished because his daughter had failed. It would not be just. I felt my throat tighten, all my sinews strain. Was it just that I had been tarnished? What had I done to deserve tarnishing?

Lutha put her hand on my shoulder, but Leelson did not notice my pain. He was focused elsewhere.

'So if Bernesohn was killed out here somewhere, the map would have been returned to his leasehold.'

I brought my mind back to where we were.

'The map?' Leelson demanded impatiently. 'It would have been brought back?'

He made me angry with his insistence. 'Yes, but the same would be true if he had been found dead. He didn't have to have been executed. In fact, we know he wasn't, because if he had been, no one would have – ' I caught my breath and put my hand over my mouth.

I'd been going to say, 'No one would have prayed his return if he'd been guilty of blasphemy.' Since he came back to Cochim-Mahn as a Kachis, he must have been invited. This is one reason our people are careful to be pleasant to one another, not to be hostile, not to be mean, for if one of us is not well liked, that one may not be invited to return, may not be invited to be part of his former family.

I turned away in confusion.

'What?' demanded Leelson.

Lutha squeezed my hand, saying, 'It's one of the things she's not supposed to talk about, Leelson. Simply take it as given that she has reason to believe Bernesohn Famber was not killed by the songfathers.'

Leelson glared at her and at me, shaking his head. 'It really doesn't matter whether he vanished during his journey or subsequently. In either case the map ended up back at his leasehold with his handwritten notes on it. It's unfortunate he's no longer among us to enlighten us as to the details.'

I opened my mouth, then shut it without saying that Bernesohn Famber was still among us. Lutha hadn't believed it. Leelson wouldn't believe it either.

Leelson went on, 'Let's assume the songfathers know the way to the omphalos because they've inherited instructions from former generations, not because they've made the trip before.'

Lutha asked, 'Where are you going with all this, Leelson?'

'I'm getting there. The map shows a dozen canyon mouths opening into the area of the omphalos, and assuming the Nodders did not grow here but were put here, we could extrapolate that there may be similar installations at the mouths of all the canyons. In which case, what purpose do they serve?'

'I haven't the least idea,' she replied in a grumpy voice. 'Do you? Or are you just being rhetorical?'

'He's not being rhetorical,' Trompe offered. 'He's saying there may be Nodders guarding all access to the omphalos. Controlling traffic, so to speak.'

'Traffic!' She stared pointedly at the emptiness around us. Stone and more stone. No traffic.

Trompe persisted. 'If he's right, timely travelers get through, others don't.'

I said, 'It is true that songfathers may not go to the omphalos except at the time of Tahs-uppi.'

'What about leap year?' asked Lutha in a contentious tone. 'I thought an extra day had to be drawn from the navel hole every few years!'

'Only the big days must be pulled by songfathers,' I told them. 'The little days are pulled out by the spirit people who live there, at the sipapu.'

'Monks?' Lutha puzzled in aglais. 'Priests?'

I knew those words. 'Women too.'

'Nuns?'

I shrugged. 'Spirit people is what the songfathers call them. Spirit men, with spirit women to take care of them.' In the sisterhood it was said the spirit people had no House Without a Name. It was said the spirit women never got pregnant. No one had ever told me how they managed that. I thought perhaps they were all very holy. Or very old. I would ask Lutha about it later.

Trompe rolled up the map and put it back in the wagon. 'How do the Nodders decide to let people through? By the season of the year? By counting planetary revolutions since the previous visitors? By genetic pattern? Or are they controlled from somewhere?'

'We're going to have to find out,' Leelson said. 'One of us will have to try it. You or me, Trompe.'

'I can go,' I offered. Perhaps this is why I had come, to spend my life, and my child's, for something important. 'I want to.'

'Your going wouldn't tell us what we want to know,' Trompe said kindly, patting my shoulder. 'They could let you through, then come down on us. We need to know if non-Dinadhi can get through. Assuming the time is right, of course.'

'But that's not all you're assuming!' cried Lutha incredulously. 'You're assuming they're artificial, you're assuming they're a danger, you're building this whole scenario out of thin air.'

'Thin air! Look at the damn things,' Leelson snarled at her. 'For the love of heaven, Lutha! Stop living in your gut and start living in your head!'

She went pale with anger as she spoke between gritted teeth. 'I'm as thoughtful as you are, Leelson Famber. And as intelligent! It's just that I don't go building elaborate theoretical structures on damned little evidence.'

'Really! That hasn't been my observation up until now,' he said, with an obvious sidelong look at Leely.

'That's unfair,' she cried, storming away from us to stand at some distance, back turned, rigid.

He strode after her. 'Lutha, damn it, use good sense!'

'You're talking about Leely.'

'Forget Leely!'

'I can't. He's alive! His heart beats. His lungs pump air—'

'Frogs' hearts beat,' he shouted. 'Sparrows have lungs that pump air. Is that your criteria for humanity? Hearts and lungs?'

'He has brain waves!' she shouted.

'He has the same kind of brain waves as chickens. As a matter of fact, his brain waves are virtually indistinguishable from those of chickens.'

'He's not a chicken. He's a human being!'

Leelson's face was very pale, his mouth was hard. 'Morphologically, he's a human being. Mentally, he's a chicken.'

He came striding back, saying something to Trompe in an angry tone, words I couldn't catch. Trompe soothed him.

'Give her room, Leelson. She's not here because she wants to be.'

'She stayed when she had a chance to leave! I wanted her home, safe, out of this!'

'It's no good arguing that point now. She's here. Leely is here. You're here, and so am I, and Saluez. We've got people, animals, and a wagon to get through those ... whatever they are. You're not going to get Lutha to think logically about Leely, so let's forget that and concentrate on what we have to do!'

Leelson heaved a deep breath. 'You or me, then. We'll draw for it; short straw goes, on foot. Then we'll know if nonplanetary human males can get through. Saluez can come next, to establish whether women are allowed.'

Even angry as he was at Lutha, to protect her he would sacrifice himself. And me. But then, I was used to that.

'Then Lutha and ... Leely. Then the other one of us, driving the wagon.'

'Not driving,' amended Trompe. 'Leading on a long, long rope. That way, if they don't like wagons, or gaufers, the one leading will still have a chance.'

They nodded at one another, agreeing. I thought we wouldn't have any chance unless the Nodders let the gaufers and the wagon through. But then, before we left Cochim-Mahn, I was fairly sure we'd be eaten the first night or so. And before I first met Leelson, I thought outlanders would be strange and exotic instead of just ordinary people. And at one time I'd thought the Kachis were invulnerable and all-seeing, but some of them had died and thousands of others had sat like stones around the Burning Springs. And at one time I'd thought Leely was helpless, but he wasn't. He sneaked around like a clever little cornrat. Leelson was wrong about him. He was smarter than a chicken. Of course, I'd never seen a chicken.

Just because Leelson might be wrong didn't mean Lutha was right about him, though she was about some things. She was probably right about the Kachis we'd seen at Burning Springs. If the songfathers couldn't get to the ompahlos, the omphalos wouldn't be opened. If the omphalos wasn't opened, the Kachis couldn't go through it to heaven. It made sense that all the Kachis would find nice warm places and meditate there, awaiting their time of transfiguration.

While I was puzzling over this Leelson had wandered off to the edge of the small stream that we had traveled along since we had left the Burning Springs. He plucked a few lengths of dried grass and came striding back to Trompe, holding out a fist with two straws protruding. Trompe drew one.

Leelson opened his hand to show that the one he retained was the shorter one, and then, without so much as blinking or saying goodbye, he turned and walked rapidly toward the Nodders, leaving Trompe and me with our mouths full of unspoken advice. Leely poked his head out of the wagon and stared at Leelson's retreating back. Only Lutha, still angrily facing back the way we had come, did not see him go.

When he came beneath the first of the Nodders, I forgot to breathe. The Nodder began to sway again, very gently, side to side, like someone saying no, no, don't do that. Leelson looked up, hesitated only a fraction of an instant, then went on. The Nodder went on swaying: no, no, no, and it didn't stop swaying when Leelson went past it, out of its shadow, and strode toward the gap between the two other outliers. Both of them began to sway also, saying no, no, no. This time Leelson didn't look up. He just went on, arms swinging, eyes on his feet.

The great heads were horning the heavens, right, left, right. Lutha had been right. They resembled a herd of ... what? 'They look like animal heads,' I whispered. 'What is that Old-earthian animal, Trompe? Men fought it ritually, risking their lives. Was it a cattle?'

'Bull,' he said.

Of course. Bull. Virile and puissant. Mighty bull. I remembered now.

From behind me I heard an indrawn breath. Lutha came running. Trompe caught her as she was about to pass us.

'Hush,' he said as she began to babble. 'Don't do anything to foul up the findings. Or to risk his life more than it already is.'

She paused, frozen, one foot still raised, watching as intently as we. A few moments before, she had hated him. A few hours before, when we had stopped to rest, I had seen her in his arms again, the two of them holding one another as though they would never let go. It would be nice, I thought wistfully, if they could sort it out. Whenever I saw them at it, loving or hating, it was hurtful to me.

Leelson went between the sentinel pair, then into a veritable forest of pillars. The great horned heads bobbed restlessly above him, moved by something. Not wind. It was, for the moment, utterly calm and very cold.

When Leelson moved out of sight among the stones, we all looked upward, readying ourselves, I suppose, for one or more of the great heads to fall. Nothing happened but that slight motion, that measured horning. Jab, jab, jab, they said. No, no, no.

Trompe murmured, 'We can postulate it's the correct time to get through, but only just. The traffic controllers seem to be in some doubt.'

That was one explanation. I could think of others, but to no profit. No amount of thinking would tell us what we needed to know; only action would do. I took a deep breath and trudged off in the direction Leelson had gone, hoping the path would be self-evident. One route through might be passable, while another might be forbidden! The two Fastigats had not considered that! Behind me Lutha said something and Trompe hushed her. I heard Leely burbling his eternal Dananana. Then I heard nothing but my own blood roaring in my ears.

The temptation to look up was too strong when I came beneath the first one. I staggered at the sight. So huge. So horrid. So heavy. The tops of our caves are as huge, as heavy, but they curve comfortingly down around us, like sheltering arms. These curves went away, the wrong way, and it was like looking up at the shape of some flying monster, diving on me. I shuddered, forced my eyes down, and kept walking. Everywhere the ground was littered with shards of broken stone, sharp edges, curved surfaces, like fragments of eggshells made gigantic. They had fallen from somewhere. At one time or another, they had fallen.

I kept my feet moving, one foot in front of the other. My mouth and throat were so dry it hurt to move my tongue. I gulped at the sight of bones. Not human. Gaufer bones. A scatter of them, as though something had been eating them. Then, as I moved around a great pillar, there were human ones: shoulders and a skull staring at the sky, arms and torso disappearing under a broken-edged stone.

The rock was curved like a fragment of cup and it rocked as I passed. Curve inside curve. Were the Nodders hollow? Were they great stone eggs? With what inside? Were these the remnants of some that had hatched?

Beware, the skull eyes said to me. *Beware. Don't panic. Don't shout. Don't run. Beware!*

I had passed between the Nodder pair. Off to my left the streamlet ran, winding among the pillars, which were all around me now, a thick copse of rising trunks with a multitude of paths among them. How did one keep from getting lost? The stony soil showed no trace of Leelson's passage.

Look up, I told myself. Look past the threatening heads to the canyon rim. Even these monsters are not so high as that lofty edge. Look where the sun is, and where it comes across the heads to make scallop-backed scythes of gray-golden light upon the rocky soil. The rays come from the left. The scythe crescents open to the left. Keep them lying so as you go.

And so I did, while something inside my mind made little gibbering noises and a muscle near my eye twitched as though someone were pulling at it with a thread. The temptation to look up never abated, but it was hard enough to find a way among the fallen fragments without frightening myself more. Turn and turn again. Stop. Look for the light. Turn so the light is coming from the left. Go a little way. Stop again. Look for the light again. No sound at all but my own panting breath escaping the halter of my throat. Turn and turn again, winding among them, winding around them, to come out of them at last quite unexpectedly!

Leelson stood a short distance away, beckoning with one hand, the other before his lips, urging quiet. Then I allowed myself to look up to see them nodding, nodding, nodding: no, no, no.

Still, they had let me pass. I trudged over to Leelson, bending double to catch my breath. I felt sick. I had half strangled myself.

'Lutha and Leely next,' he whispered in my ear. 'Is she coming?'

I nodded, supposing that she would. Trompe would tell her she was next; she would take Leely into her arms and start walking in a kind of fatalistic calm. She would recognize the risk. She would tell herself she had never rejected or neglected him, that she had resolutely denied Leelson's assessment of him. Nonetheless, she would risk him and herself. If she allowed herself to think about it at all, she would consider dying with Leely to be an acceptable solution to the problems of their lives, hers and his.

I could read her as though I, too, were a Fastigat. Her longings were mother longings. I knew about mother longings. Sometimes they did not bear thinking on, so I thought instead of her pathway, how she would walk, as I watched the slot from which I myself had emerged. There would be movement, I told myself. At any moment there would be movement.

There was none. Perhaps I was wrong. Perhaps she would not risk herself, or Leely. Leelson gave me a troubled look. I shrugged. I didn't know. We planted our feet and watched, leaning slightly forward, as though to urge her out of hiding.

She did not come, but Leely did, quite alone, face glowing with an almost supernatural light, skipping into sight at the base of one of the pillars, waving his hands, caroling, 'Dananana.' He was more beautiful than any child I have ever seen. He gave us an enigmatic look, that same look he had given me when he returned from his morning expedition, then he slipped between two pillars to lose himself once more, shining like a little sun.

Beside me, Leelson grunted in surprise. I looked upward as he was doing so and saw only quiet stone heads. Not a motion. Not a quiver. I stepped forward involuntarily to go after the child, but Leelson caught my robe, stopping me.

'No,' he whispered vehemently. 'Wait!'

We both waited. Everything was silent, still, an interminable stillness. Not a sigh, not a tremble. The first sound we heard was the creak of wheels. Though we'd greased them again and again, they still creaked, a distinctive, irritating sound that might have been near or far, approaching or departing. The echoes and reverberations came at us from all sides, bounced around by the Nodders until they had no point of origin. I swayed with sudden dizziness and realized I'd been holding my breath again. Beside me, Leelson had been doing the same, for he exhaled in a sudden burst as Leely appeared once more.

This time Lutha was behind him, her hands twisted into the shoulders of the child's garment so he could not break away. Her pallor was icy, almost blue, and even from where we stood I could see the rigidity of her arms and shoulders. She was holding the boy in a death grip of which he took no notice at all. His hands waved and his feet skipped and his voice rose in its constant contented comment on the world. I was transfixed once more by his ethereal, marvelous beauty. As one imagines angels or fairies looked in old stories.

Beside me Leelson said, under his breath, 'Seraphic.' That was the word I'd been wanting. Either Leelson had thought of it, or he'd somehow picked it up from me. He wrenched his eyes away from the boy and held out his hands to Lutha. She ignored him, marching past us.

Trompe appeared next, tugging at the end of a rope. At first I could not imagine where he'd obtained a rope, then I saw he had knotted the reins together. A trivial thought at such a time, for when I looked up, the heads were shaking once more: no, no, no, no. Trompe wasn't looking. He was concentrating on the gaufers. Either they disliked being led or they had picked up our tension, for they were behaving skittishly, throwing their feet sideways as they do when disturbed, bobbing their heads and growling in their throats. With shaking fingers, Trompe put the end of the line into Leelson's hand, threw a glance in Lutha's direction, where she'd stopped a few paces farther on, and then collapsed onto the ground.

'You made it,' said Leelson flatly, tugging the gaufers nearer us.

'Obviously,' Trompe returned, wiping his face with his sleeve.

Leelson turned to Lutha. 'What happened with ... him?' he asked, indicating Leely with a jerk of his head.

'He just ... jumped out of my arms,' she murmured almost inaudibly. 'I should have had his harness on him, but I never expected ... One minute he was there, and the next he was running off between the pillars. He kept appearing and disappearing. I thought he was lost!'

'Where did you catch up with him?'

'Just there, at the edge, one moment before we saw you.'

Leelson shut his eyes, concentrating. Was he trying to reach Leely? Most likely he was, for all the good it did him. I didn't know what Leelson thought, but *I* thought Leely had not been lost among the Nodders any more than he'd been lost when he sneaked out during the night. Leely didn't get lost.

Lutha obviously thought otherwise. Her eyes were full of exhausted tears, and I realized that though Leelson and I had seen how quiet the Nodders were when the boy was among them, she would not have seen it. Not if she'd been running this way and that, seeking the boy at ground level. Would she have felt more or less fearful if she had?

I caught Leelson's eyes upon me and flushed. He turned away, but I knew he was probing at me, trying to figure out what I knew or felt, which, Weaving Woman be thanked, was little enough. I didn't want to know anything. I said so mentally, over and over, a little litany. *I know nothing about Leely. I know nothing about the Nodders. I know nothing about anything. I am an ignorant Dinadhi woman, an unworthy Dinadhi woman, of no possible use to anyone!*

When I finally looked up, Leelson was helping Trompe restore the reins to their ordinary use. Wordlessly, we got moving into the canyon, Leelson driving and the rest of us trailing behind. A few dozen paces farther on, the ground was suddenly clear of curved rock fragments; the footing was blessedly good; we could actually look around us as we went. Still, Lutha never for a moment relinquished her grip upon Leely, even when he began to fuss at her.

The canyon went away in a long, westward-curving arc, and we did not pause until the Nodders were no longer in sight. When we stopped, the ravine was level, widening toward the west, where the sun lay in a shallow notch, like an apple in a bowl, tempting us. That notch was a definite place, discernible, reachable, pulling at us despite our weariness. The temptation to go on was in all our faces, a yearning to be done with this, to be away from the canyons. Even the gaufers leaned into the harness, stamping impatiently.

But Leelson said no. He said the sun was low, we would finish the trip tomorrow. He said we should be well rested when we arrived. He was no doubt right, but it was hard to wait. Beyond that notch was the world's gate, through which the beautiful people would go on their way to heaven. All of them would come, lost children, slain fathers, grandparents dead of age. Bernesohn Famber's outlander ghost, he would be there. My mother would be there. Even now she was probably sitting near a fire fountain in the Canyon of Burning Springs, deep in meditation. Saying good-bye to this world. Saying good-bye to me.

It did not seem fair. The outlander ghost had lived among us for almost a hundred years. My mother's spirit had lived among us for only a few. If she hated me when she went, she would never have a chance to love me again. If this was the choice we had made, shouldn't it be fair for everyone. Shouldn't she be allowed to stay longer? To see her grandchild born?

But then, why would she? Her only child was unworthy of her. If I were one of the beautiful people, would I choose to stay with an unworthy child, or to go on to heaven? Perhaps that is why they meditated, making up their minds.

I looked up to catch Leelson and Lutha watching me. His gaze was intent, hers sympathetic. He wanted to know what I thought; she already knew. Mothers, her eyes seemed to say, always choose happiness for their children, no matter what they or the children have done or not done.

Where was my happiness? Was I less worthy than Leely?

I turned my back on them, pulled my veil across my eyes, and let the tears come. Cry and be done. Soon enough this journey would end and then I might know the truth.

Halfway up the wall of another canyon, one southeast of the omphalos, Mitigan of the Asenagi and Chur Durwen of Collis emerged from the mouth of a shallow cave and stood looking down upon the narrow sea of smoky mist below them. For the last two days they had been traveling in a region of boiling springs, each spring surrounded by multitudes of Kachis, all immobile, all seemingly insensate.

'Quite a change,' remarked Mitigan, unwinding a bandage from his forearm and disclosing a nasty-looking bite wound. He smeared it plentifully with reeking salve from his pack, then replaced the bandage. 'Damned critters have dirty teeth.'

'I told you the thing was behind you,' Chur Durwen remarked mildly. 'You're getting slow.' He examined the line of knives on the stone before him, seven of them, including the ones from his wrist scabbards. All of them needed cleaning and sharpening. Kachis blood was corrosive, and Chur Durwen had bloodied all his knives repeatedly during the earlier stages of their journey.

'If I hadn't ignored the one behind me, you'd have been dead,' said Mitigan. 'The one I killed would have had you by the throat.'

'You're right. Which tells me the throat flap on my battle mask was badly designed. I doubt the Collis Arms Consortium had vampire butterflies in mind when they created it.' He took a sharpening stone from his pack and ran it along the edge of the largest knife with a repeated wheeping sound. 'They certainly aren't interested in biting now, are they? What do you think they're doing?'

'Could be dead,' said Mitigan. 'Could be in some kind of hibernation.'

'Estivation,' corrected the other. 'It's closer to summer than winter.'

'Why in hell would anything go dead in the summertime?'

Chur Durwen picked up the next knife and peered at it closely. 'I think animals do it on desert planets. Where it gets too hot and dry in midsummer. Where the cooler winter weather is actually more supportive of life.'

'This probably qualifies as a desert planet. And I can't say I'm sorry they've quit bothering us.'

'Nasty, aren't they? Almost human, the way they look, the way they sound. That little whine of theirs. Like a child, or a woman trying to get you to buy her something.'

'Or pay her for something,' gibed Mitigan.

'Hell, if you have to pay for it, you don't deserve it.' The man from Collis tried the second knife with the hardened skin of his thumb. 'Come to think of it, though they have very female-looking bodies, every damn one of them has a dingus long as your forearm and pointy as a dagger. Do you suppose the locals ...?'

'You'd have to be more than ordinarily stupid,' remarked Mitigan. 'Or quite irresistibly horny.' He turned away from the cave entrance to examine the map he'd pinned to the wall inside. 'This canyon, then one more. We'll make it in one or two days if the butterfly bats stay quiet.'

'Vampire butterflies,' corrected Chur Durwen.

The other muttered, 'Vampires only suck your blood. They don't bite your throat out and try to chew on your face.'

His companion grunted agreement. When he had finished three more knives, he asked, 'You really think there will be Fambers there? At this navel hole?'

'Just a feeling,' admitted Mitigan. 'A hunch. I've learned to pay attention to my hunches. I think we're going to hit the main vein of Fambers at the omphalos. I think when we get there, we'll earn our pay.'

According to the rememberer in Simidi-ala, the Procurator could not fly directly to the omphalos. He could fly to a point very near. To the very next canyon, in fact. But the last little bit, one had to go on foot.

'And why is that?' demanded Poracious Luv.

'Only songfathers will be allowed to go into the sacred area or to ...'

To make decisions, the Procurator silently finished the remark.

'Interesting,' said Poracious. 'Why is that?'

'It's not my area of expertise,' said the rememberer, staring over her left shoulder.

'Most interesting,' she repeated. 'Don't you think so, sir?'

'I think we should waste as little time as possible in conversation,' muttered the Procurator between his teeth. 'We would not enjoy arriving at the omphalos only a few moments too late to prevent assassinations from occurring.'

490

'Quite right. Fastest way, please, rememberer. On foot or whatever.'

The rememberer's 'on foot' seemed to include gaufer feet, for both a chariot and a cart, each with its team of gaufers, awaited them near the head of the shallow valley in which they landed. Two servants, who had accompanied them in the flier, jumped down at once and began loading the Procurator's voluminous baggage into the cart while both hitches of animals stamped their feet impatiently.

'I suggested the conveyances would make the remaining distance a bit easier,' the rememberer murmured, keeping his eyes resolutely away from Poracious's bulky form.

'For which my thanks,' she said, heaving herself aboard the chariot with remarkable agility. She picked up the reins and gave them an experimental tug.

'I must leave you here.' The rememberer bowed. 'As I've mentioned, those of us from Simidi-ala are not allowed to enter the sacred precincts. Neither are outlanders, of course, and I cannot guarantee an exception will be made for you. We have managed to convince the songfathers it is in their best interest to speak with you. That's the best we can do.'

'We understand.' The Procurator nodded. 'Where are they?'

The rememberer nodded toward the very top of the valley, where several figures stood athwart a shallow col, silhouetted against the sky. 'High officials. And I'm afraid we're persona non grata.' He beckoned to the servants. 'As soon as I've gone, they'll come for you.'

He and the servants climbed back into the flier and were whisked aloft in a great cloud of dust.

'He seemed relieved to get out of here,' commented the ex-King of Kamir, wiping the dust from his eyes as he climbed into the chariot beside Poracious.

'I can see why,' murmured Poracious, peering beneath her lashes at the black-clad men who were approaching. 'They don't look happy to see us.'

'Please allow me to speak for us,' said the Procurator from where he stood beside the left wheel. He had donned an official tabard for the meeting, one glittering with gems and fine gold embroidery. It bore upon the back panel the great arms of the Alliance, worked in pearls and sapphires, and on the front panel a grid, in each square of which was the symbol of one of the Seventeen Sectors. Stitched over the symbol of Hermes Sector was a pall of black tissue, showing it to be under threat.

The symbolism was not lost upon the approaching Dinadhi. They saw it and stopped to mumble with one another before continuing their advance.

'What has this predicament of the Alliance to do with Dinadh?' demanded the foremost, threatening with one clawlike hand.

'All your people may perish,' said the Procurator silkily, the words sinuous as snakes, demanding attention. 'Dinadh is next in line.'

The Dinahdi glanced at one another, only briefly.

The speaker sneered. 'We do not believe we are in any danger from ... the Ularians.'

The Procurator blinked slowly. His voice gained both volume and vehemence. 'If you are not in danger from them, you are in danger from the Alliance. If you alone in Hermes Sector are not destroyed by the aliens, we must assume you have made common cause with them against the rest of humanity. Is it not written, "All life is struggle. He who will not stand with me stands against me"? Humanity will have vengeance for such treachery. You will not be allowed to remain here unscathed while others suffer.'

The hearers shivered. Even Poracious felt her bulk quiver. Fastigacy at its finest, she told herself, maintaining her composure with difficulty. What actors they made!

'There has been no common cause with aliens,' cried one of the other Dinadhi. 'Nothing such is needed! We are under the protection of our gods! Our gods are stronger than any ... aliens.'

The Procurator smiled voraciously, his teeth showing. 'Then we will have vengeance against your gods, songfathers. If your gods choose some men to favor, while sacrificing others, then those sacrificed may well cry from beyond the grave for justice.'

The third man spoke. 'You threaten much. We see only one old man, much bedecked, one fat woman, and one younger man who does not look dangerous. From where will this vengeance come?'

'From the battleships of the Alliance that hang in orbit around your world,' said the Procurator, poker-faced. 'From persons on those ships who even now listen to our conversation and watch your actions.'

'And from the royal navy of Kamir,' said the ex-king, 'which will extort retribution for any dishonor done its king.'

'And from Buchol Sector,' said Poracious. 'Where my brother is emperor.'

The Dinadhi turned their backs and went a little distance away, where they put their heads together in troubled confabulation.

'The royal navy of Kamir?' asked Poracious, without moving her lips. 'Since when?'

'Since your brother was selected emperor of Buchol Sector,' said Jiacare Lostre.

Only the former speaker rejoined the outlanders as the others straggled away toward the col.

'I am Hah-Rianahm,' he said. 'Subchief of the Songfathers' Council, Second Grandfather of the Great Assembly. My word binds or looses. It is my decision that you will come with us to the omphalos! We cannot delay to parley with you, for Tahs-uppi approaches, and our presence is required in the eternal circles. When those are broken, however, we will take time to hear what you have to say. This is not a good time for you to have approached us.'

'We didn't pick it,' said Poracious. 'It was picked for us, by the Ularians.'

'What are these Ularians?' asked Hah-Rianahm.

'The beings who have destroyed humans on all the occupied worlds in this sector.'

'You have seen these beings?'

'We will show them to you,' said the Procurator. 'We will let you see them, and feel them, and taste them. . . .'

'After Tahs-uppi,' called one of the other men urgently. 'Even now the circles are forming!'

'At the first possible moment,' said the Procurator. 'At the very first possible moment.'

In her cave above the sea, Snark lay dreaming. She'd been doing that a lot lately, spending whole days in the cave, dozing, remembering, having imaginary conversations with people she'd never met or never really known. She carried on an animated three-way conversation among herself, her mother, and the Procurator. She discussed life with Kane the Brain. She talked to the mistress of the sanctuary, the one who had labeled Snark a liar when Snark had claimed to come from the frontier.

'Wrong,' said Snark in her reverie, holding the mistress in a grip of steel, forcing her to look upon the moors of Perdur Alas. 'You were wrong about me, madam! Look upon my childhood, my rearing, the cause of all my woe. . . .'

The daydream dissolved in a spatter of icy spray, and she opened her eyes, startled. Outside on the branch, a large seabird tossed a scaly thing in its beak, preparatory to swallowing it. The scaly thing struggled, not quite fish-like, throwing water in all directions.

'You woke me,' said Snark, wiping her face with the back of her hands.

The bird did not reply. The bird didn't even see her. It looked past her in the same way people always had. All those at the sanctuary when she was only nine or ten. All those she'd asked for help later, when she'd been a street rat. All those who'd had business with the Procurator: bureaucrats or military, male or female, foreign or domestic, old or young. All of them had been fully present, completely in the picture, aware of one another and of the world at large, but unaware of Snark. She had always been a shadow, even before they made her one. A mere thing in the background, never quite in focus. One of the unseeables who lived in the alleys of Alliance Prime. Like the brain-deads she'd known in the sanctuary, kids born with faulty circuits, not bright enough to be human but still able to be embarrassingly vocal. 'I, I, I want, I want!' Like some kind of meat animal suddenly standing up and begging out loud. Too human looking to be killed; not human enough to live. Brain-dead. That was the mildest of the epithets the other orphan brats had given her. Snark the brain-dead, Snark the liar, Snark the thief.

She wished for them all, wished they were here, fleeing across the moor as the great creatures disported themselves. Let Diagonal Red eat this one, and Big Gray Blob eat this one, and ... and, and, and ...

Though eating might not be what the creatures did. Had they eaten her companions? Had they killed Kane the Brain and Willit and Susso? Had they tortured them, enslaved them? What? Would it make her feel better to know they were worse off than she? Not really. Since she'd been alone, she'd longed for them. Even slob-lipped Willit. Especially Susso.

She rolled onto her side, finding the stony hollow that fit the curve of her hip. Near the opening, the jar in the niche stood as it had when she had found the cave. Never moved. Never looked into. Why was that?

'Because you know what's inside,' she told herself soberly. 'You've always known what's inside.'

Mother had made that jar. Mother had painted it, using the rib of a furze plant for a brush, her own blood for the paint. Mother had fired it, so the blood turned black on the white clay. Mother had told her daughter to put her bones inside, in the care of Mother Darkness. If there were any bones.

When Snark had gone looking for Mother, overcoming her fear, deciding to disobey the prime command ('Stay in the cave!'), she'd found bones. She'd been hiding that from herself for many years, but here at the trembling edge of sleep, nothing could be truly hidden. Longings came out, and hates, and loves, and old, old memories that she'd tried to obliterate. Old horror would sprout, old bones would walk, old blood would fountain up.

Though homelier things returned as well. Like the stories of Breadh that Mother had sung.

'Homely Breadh of long ago!'

Snark remembered once when they'd been inside the cave, Mother cross-legged, Snark in Mother's lap. She hadn't been Snark then. Mother had called her Laluzh, Laluzh-love, Laluzh dearest daughter. Laluzh, last remnant of the faithful.

'I sing, Laluzh-love, of our homeworld of Breadh, where we patterned our lives as the weaver the cloth, light and dark, day and night, sorrow-joy, pleasure-pain. On Breadh we were born, on her bosom we grew, there we found our nearhearts, there we danced when we wed. On Breadh's shoulder we grieved when our loved ones were lost. So it was, so had been, for time out of time.'

This was story rhythm, a kind of chanting. Mother could do it for hours. Sometimes the story rhythm changed, becoming inexorable:

'But then the tempter came. Ancient and sly was he. Rising from dark of caves. Mammoth with mighty feet. Furred like Behemoth he. Whispered in darkness, he. Telling the songfathers. How they might never die. If they would make the choice. Leaving beloved Breadh. Where even animals. Were kindred souls to us. Leaving behind our gods—'

'And the old men listened to the tempter,' interrupted Snark, anything to break that rhythm, that pounding.

Mother nodded, rocking back and forth, resuming the sweet motion Snark loved, like being cradled on the waves of the sounding sea: shush shush shush, to and fro. Mother sighed as she answered, not in story talk but as herself.

'The old men listened. They listened to sweet words and tempting promises. They bowed down before the tempter and called him the Gracious One. Gracious to them, indeed, for the price demanded was not paid by them but by the womenfolk. Godmongers have always found it easy to pay for their beliefs with women's lives. ...

'So, they chose. Some of the people on Breadh said they would not do what the tempter ordered, they would remain behind, on Breadh, but no one was allowed to remain. Even after they were taken to the new home, the faithful refused the new commandments. Though we pretended to follow them, it was in appearance only. In secret, generation after generation, we remembered the old ways and recited the old prayers.'

'For we are the faithful,' Laluzh/Snark said.

'We are the faithful, Laluzh-love. And faithful we remained, even when a traitor among us denounced us to the songfathers. Then we were reviled and persecuted, some of us were tortured and killed. We decided to run away, to go back the way our ancestors had come, to return to Breadh.'

'Many of us. Many, many of us!'

Mother didn't answer for a long time. There was only the *shush shush shush* of her garment on the floor as she rocked. Her face was wet when she spoke. 'There were many of us who came to the gate. Enough of us to open that gate, for it is a heavy gate indeed, made of stone set upon stone. We were many as we came through that gate, but who knows if any came to Blessed Breadh. A few families of us ended here, and only Mother Darkness knows where the others ended.'

'And the scourges came. ...'

'True. When we opened the gate, scourges of the tempter pursued us, coming through the gate with us. Almost before we knew they were here, they had killed some of us. Yet faithful we remained, for in the end, where can even these scourges bring us except to the waiting arms of Mother Darkness and Father Endless, they who were before the Consequential Egg was hatched?'

She rocked Laluzh/Snark, softly *shush shush shush*, singing in her mother voice:

'Ahau, Father Endless, Mother Darkness. Ahau, thou who wert before the stars. Ahau, eternal entropy, refuge of the sorrowful, haven of the weary, salvation of the aged, unlit by grief or pain. Ahau, to lie upon the breast of darkness knowing only peace.'

The song was like a lullaby, a hymn to the gods left behind on Breadh, a memorial to those who entered the gate, a plea for those few left on this world: Mother and Laluzh and the four other children, silent Nanees and strong Ehrbas, weepy little Hahnaan and some other little girl whose name Snark couldn't remember. Six of them in all. And Mother herself was gone by the time the ship came.

An Alliance ship, screaming out of the sky, landing upon the moor, where the children ran back and forth like panicked animals. Twenty standard years ago, when she'd been eight or nine. Old enough to remember the questions.

'Where did you come from, little girl?'

'I live here.'

'What happened to all the grown-ups, little girl?'

'The scourges of the tempter ate them. Something killed Mother, but I put her bones away safe, in the Mother Darkness jar.'

Glances, one man to another. A finger circled beside an ear. Crazy little girl. Out of her head. Must be a survival pod somewhere nearby. Kids must have been boosted off some ship in trouble. Castaways. Couldn't actually have lived here for any length of time. Impossible. There was nothing here: no agriculture, no edible animals, no beasts of any kind. Only seabirds, fish.

'She's gone snarky from the trauma,' said one.

'What's snarky?'

'Snark's a kind of a duck thing. From Herangia Five. It goes crazy and drops eggs on people.'

The label had stuck. Laluzh became Snark the crazed, later Snark the liar, Snark the thief. Eventually, she forgot Laluzh, forgot Perdur Alas, forgot Mother. Only the cave had remained, a place of safety and comfort. She might never have remembered the other parts if she hadn't been sent here. But now ... now she recalled everything she had been told of: Breadh, the Tempter, the Choice, the Journey to Dinadh, the Faithfulness, the Persecution, the Flight, and the Scourges.

She had not seen scourges since she'd returned to Perdur Alas. Mother had said they'd died soon after arriving, screaming in the night, crying like lost children, hungry and cold. So it wasn't scourges who'd killed Mother. Something had. Something had killed her and chewed on her bones. Was it as Diagonal Red and the others had shown her? Had they done it?

She didn't know. There was no way of telling. Nothing was left of that former time. Nothing but monsters. Monsters and Mother's bones.

9

I Saluez had thought to grieve a little and then to sleep, but it was not to be. There was a stir of discontent eddying among us travelers, and its name was Lutha Tallstaff. She would not settle. Trompe fell asleep. Leelson fell asleep. Even Leely was quiet, with none of his usual restless little murmurs, but Lutha moved and sighed, sighed and moved, wearing herself out with trivialities. She went out and checked the panels not once but a dozen times. She put Leely's harness upon him and fastened the end to her belt. Though Leelson had already referred to Bernesohn Famber's yellowed map when he said we would finish our journey on the following day, Lutha unrolled the map once more and sat perusing it by lamplight. When she tired of that, she wedged the door shut, leaving me gasping for air.

'I'll go outside,' I said. 'There are no Kachis tonight.' It was true. There were none at all, and I desperately wanted to be by myself.

I did not escape. She came after me, to the limit of the cord that bound her to Leely at any rate. Obviously, I was to have no privacy on this particular evening. I sighed and sat myself up within my cocoon of blankets, seeking some topic of conversation that would distract her from this hectic activity.

'How did you and Leelson ever meet?' I asked.

She sat down upon the step of the wain. 'I met him while working in the Greinson Library at Prime.'

'Such places must be interesting,' I said politely.

She laughed under her breath. 'Or deadly dull. I was trying to make sense of some knotty old document written long ago in a dead language, memorializing a contract between peoples who don't exist anymore.'

'Dull, but no doubt important,' I murmured.

'I suppose. It was one of those documents universally acknowledged to be "precedental," so I struggled mightily, trying to extract something my client could use in a court of law, glumming, as one does, writing down and crossing out. Then I had this odd feeling, as though I was being stared at, and when I looked up, Leelson was there. I knew at once he was Fastigat.'

'How did you know?'

'Oh, they have such absolute confidence, a stunning savoir faire which

498

puts mere poise to shame. Still, I'd dealt with Fastigats before. One does tend to get a bit short of breath when they turn on the charm, but up until then I'd considered the effect manageable.'

'Until then?'

'Until he began to speak, yes. "Something called me down from up there," he said. The document niches are all up and down the towers, and the whole place was dotted with little scholars on their lift plates, zooming up, dropping down. He said, "Perhaps it was your perfume."'

'I wasn't wearing perfume. I made some remark about being generally in good odor, and Leelson laughed. We introduced ourselves. I thanked him for his compliments, and the whole time I was gasping for air, sort of mentally, you know?'

I said yes, I knew. I'd been doing the same all evening.

'I resolved with every fiber of my being not to return to the library and to stay away from Fastigats. My kind of people, that is, Mama Jibia's kind of people, the non-Fastigat professional class, consider Fastigat men unsuitable for women who are serious-minded.'

'You are serious-minded?' I wanted to laugh, but did not. Despite Lutha's undoubted intelligence, she was constantly exploding like fireworks, laughing or crying, passionate about every trifle. On Dinadh, we think of such behavior as typical of children, not serious adults.

'Don't you think I am?' she asked, surprised.

I told her exactly what I thought, hoping she would go away.

When I had finished, however, she only said thoughtfully, 'It's the way we were reared, Yma and I. If you'd ever met my Mama Jibia, you'd understand. She was a singular person, of extremely forceful mien, a faithful follower of the Great Org Gauphin, who preached logic and good sense in all things. Mama Jibia was dead set against Yma or me getting tangled up in feelings we couldn't express or understand. Starting at puberty, she had us experiencing sex through sensurround, so we'd know about that. Then, twice a year she had us vetted by the mental health people from the Temple of the Great Org Gauphin. We had emotional and stress inventories and sessions with a behaviorist, and I'd wager we knew more about the human animal at fifteen than most of our contemporaries ever learned.'

I murmured, 'It sounds quite ... rigorous.'

'Well, she was trying to make us immune to romance or sentimentalism. Of course, many of our friends came from Firster families, and sentimentalism is one of their largest stocks in trade. They use it to excuse all kinds of nasty behaviors. If Papa beats you, it's because he loves you, you know the kind of thing ...'

I did. I knew more than that. Probably far more than she!

She went on, 'Firsters don't approve of pragmatism, self-analysis, or sexual sensurround for anyone, much less virgin girls who should be, so they claim, innocent, by which they really mean susceptible to any self-serving lie that's going around! So, Yma and I saw our friends being romanced and falling in love and making babies they weren't at all ready for, and we thanked our stars we'd been raised differently.' She sighed. 'How did this conversation start?'

'You said you were so passionate about everything because of the way you were reared.'

'Yes. Mama thought feelings should be expressed. Whatever they were, it was healthier to have them out in the open, and neither Yma nor I could do it quietly. It's our sense of drama, you see. We inherited it from a scandalous ancestress who was well-known in her day, as Yma is now. Yma made a career of it. I merely play at it.'

'You play very intently,' I said. 'You and Leelson. I saw you that time, at the pool. I've watched you. Like magnets, one minute pulling at each other, then turnabout and you're pushing at each other.'

Lutha flushed and gave me a half-angry look. I had no business commenting, and I was slightly ashamed of myself for being rude to her.

'It's always been that way,' Lutha admitted. 'Like some kind of shackle we didn't know existed until then, tying us to one another. The relationship was never suitable. Not at all.'

'You don't like his mother?'

'She's ... contemptuous. Of me. Of Leely. Fastiga woman are that way, just like Fastigats. She wanted Leelson to have children with one of his cousins – Fastiga is quite inbred, though they deny it – and of course, I'm far from being a cousin. She used to send some of the relatives over to look at Leely. I'm sure she did it to infuriate me and so she could say "I told you so," to Leelson.'

'What about Leelson's father?' I asked, before I thought. I had opened a new floodgate!

'Leelson's father disappeared. Grebor Two, his name was. And his father disappeared, too. Grebor One. They each fathered one son and then disappeared. Leelson's mother was afraid Leelson was following in their footsteps.'

'Twice doesn't make a habit,' I said, giving up rudeness in favor of letting her talk.

'Three times,' Lutha said. 'There was a granduncle, too. One of Bernesohn's twins. He did the same thing Leelson did, got some unsuitable person pregnant.'

'Who?' I asked politely, not caring who.

Lutha frowned for a moment, then came up with an answer. 'Dasalum Tabir.'

I laughed, intrigued despite myself. 'D'ahslum T'bir! That means *skeleton*. That's not a name you'd forget.'

Lutha said the words over to herself, this time with the Dinadhi accent. The root words were for *bones* and for *ladder*, or *tree*.

'She was famous for more than her name, or infamous, depending on how you look at it. A cradle robber, according to the Fastigats. Twice Paniwar Famber's age.'

I heard disapproval in her voice. 'Maybe she couldn't help it any more than you can. Try pretending you were hit by lightning. You can't feel guilty about being hit by lightning.'

'It is rather like that,' Lutha confessed with a half smile. Without meaning to, I said, 'I know about that kind of lightning.' I spoke then of Shalumn, and Lutha responded with stories of her own life, of her own family.

'Was your mother pleased with you?' Oh, such a pang I felt when I asked her that, but I wanted to know.

'Yma and I have always felt that she'd have been pleased with us, that we had done well for her. Thank the Great Org Gauphin she was gone before ...'

'Before Leelson?'

She spoke between gritted teeth. 'Oh, Saluez! I swore I wouldn't get entangled with him. I swore I wouldn't, but I kept ... feeling him. Smelling him, tasting – foretasting – his skin, seeing parts of him that I hadn't realized I'd noticed, like the lobe of an ear or the way his hair grew at the base of his neck.

'Yma said I was smitten. She laughed at me. Of course, she hadn't met Leelson. As events conspired, perhaps luckily, she never actually met him.'

Now I was really curious. 'How did events conspire?'

'Leelson showed up at my door a few days after our chance meeting. He looked oddly subdued, and I felt ... oh, I felt as though I were being pumped full of sunlight. He stepped inside and took me in his arms before he said a word. I don't think either of us said anything that evening. Words would have been ... misleading.'

'That's how you were for each other? Made for each other?'

'That's how. He said never one like me before. For me it was never anyone before and never one since.'

'It's like your edges are dissolved, and you feel yourself spreading out. ...'

'Gossamer thin,' she said, giving me an astonished look. 'Feeding on starlight.'

We stared at one another. 'I know,' I said at last. 'I know.'

She dropped her head, scowling at her shoes. 'After a while Leely was born. Not long after that, my former self reasserted itself. And then Leelson left me.'

'Did he leave you? Or Leely?'

'He wanted me but not Leely. I wanted them both. I wouldn't let Leely go because he needs me.'

Hearing those words, I accepted that she was a serious person. There was something implacable in her voice. Something rigorously dutiful. Leely needed her. I thought it possible that until Leely, Lutha had never known herself truly, and Leelson had never known her. Likely he had known only a soft and corrupted creature who dangled from his lips like fruit from a vine, sweet and yielding, rotten with juice. That woman had laughed and cried and tempted. That woman had been sensual and mindless. But finally she had remembered herself and became Lutha Tallstaff again, saying no, no, I will not send Leely away.

'You can't help yourself, can you?' I asked softly.

'I can't,' she snarled, half-angry, half-amused. 'The only way I can resist him is by being furious at him. The only way I can stay furious is to remember what Leely and I came here for. We're not going to be disposed of just because Leelson would prefer it so! I will do my duty!'

'Yes,' I murmured. 'Yes, of course, Lutha.'

'I promised,' she said. The words had the feeling of old familiar sounds, worn smooth by repetition. I looked up to see tears.

'What?' I demanded.

'When Leely was almost lost, back there in the Nodders ... She gulped, fell silent.

'You were frightened?' I suggested. 'Panicky?'

She shook her head, a quick motion, a denial she could not admit even to herself. I read it.

'You thought he was gone. You felt ... relief.'

'How could I!' She leaned upon her knees and wept, her shoulders heaving. 'How could I?'

How could she not? How could she not feel as though a window in her soul had been cracked open upon joy. A gigantic relief, as though the solution to some painful problem had unexpectedly presented itself! As it had for me, to come on this journey.

'It was the shock,' she said firmly, raising her head and wiping at her eyes. 'It was only the shock.'

So she slammed the door shut on her feelings, despite all Mama Jibia's teachings. She would not allow herself to want him gone. No matter how she sagged beneath the burden of him, no matter how wearying his needs and demands, no matter the evenings like this when she wearied herself with minutiae so she could sleep, the deep heedless sleep of exhaustion, lying so drunken with sleep she could not worry over days to come; no matter all this, he was her son and she loved him!

So she said to herself as she rose to go within and be with him, leaving me at last in peace, now that I no longer wanted it.

The night was without incident. Trompe roused us at daybreak. By early afternoon we emerged from the last canyon onto the winding plain the map had shown as the site of the omphalos. Since leaving the Burning Springs, we had had on our left a small stream that occasionally surged over its banks in response to the rain that fell far away, upon the heights. I thought we would need to cross it between surges, but this proved to be unnecessary, for once out of the canyon, the stream relaxed into a gurgling, shallow brook that meandered in silken loops across the plain to join a considerable river flowing toward the south. According to the map, this river was the Tahs Ahlai, which is a Dinadhi way of saying, the future, or time to come. All waters, we say, run into the Tahs Ahlai. All lives run into the pattern.

We crossed the smaller stream with only minor difficulty. Gaufers do not like wet feet, and they had to be blindfolded to be led over. They could no doubt feel the wetness as well as see it, but evidently feeling it and seeing it were two different things. Lutha brought the last one across, pausing beside me to say, 'It seems so natural to have them here.'

'Why wouldn't they be here?' I asked, surprised.

'They are the first living animals I have ever seen, Saluez. The first I have ever touched!'

'There are no animals on Central?'

'None at all. No animals. No trees. No grassy meadows. No water running freely. It is a very different place from here.'

I gaped, unable to imagine it.

'Like one big building with many, many rooms,' she said softly. 'Even the seas are covered over, for that is where our food is raised.'

I considered the gaufers, really seeing them for the first time. They smelled warm and earthy, their muzzles were soft and their bodies sleek. What would it be like never to see any living creature but one's own kind?

'They think,' she said. 'I was surprised at that.'

'Of course they think!'

'On a homo-normed world, we never consider that. We don't consider animals at all, and certainly we don't consider that they can think. But the gaufers ... they have their own order of precedence, allowing them to interact without constant conflict. They have their own habits of alertness, one keeping watch while others eat, one standing apart, head high, while others drink. They have even a kind of sympathy, for when the lead left one injured his leg slightly, the others gave way and let him have the best spot to lie down.'

She had noticed more than I!

'They like to be scratched just behind the ears, for it's an itchy place they have difficulty reaching for themselves. They do it for one another, turn about. They know each one of us. They don't like Leelson and Trompe. Every time one of the men comes toward them, they make whuffing noises with their nostrils. They like you and me, Saluez, for they butt us with their heads as they do one another when they are content. Leely, they ignore. He climbs all over them and they seem not even to notice. Perhaps that's the way they treat their own young.'

As we went on I thought about what she had said, for there had been something wondering in her voice, like a person under enchantment. Not that I have had much experience with enchantment, but our old stories are full of it.

We moved onto peaceful meadows where a soft wind tossed the grasses into long rollers of shaded silver, a placid, utterly beautiful landscape. This wide valley was green, all green, and I, too, began to feel enchanted at the wonder of it. I had never seen so much grass! It beckoned to be embraced, and I did so, pulling a plumy clump toward me, smelling the fragrance of it.

I turned to find Lutha beside me, holding out her hand. I took it. We stood so, smelling the grasses, while the wagon moved on. Her hand was warm in mine, and comforting. Finally we had to run, hand in hand, to catch up with the others.

We followed the river until it entered a steeply walled channel through a shallow rise, and there we turned a little eastward to climb the hill. Our view southward was blocked until we reached the top, but once there, a new world opened out. Canyon walls retreated on either side, leaving room for endless emerald meadows. The river curved first left, then right, and beyond this scribble of flowing silver was yet another loop in which a building stood.

'How artful,' said Leelson.

'How appropriate,' murmured Lutha.

'It's a temple, isn't it,' said Trompe.

The building was circular, made of wood and plaster. The pillars surrounding it were the trunks of great trees, smoothed and ringed with gold. The shallow dome was ribbed with wood and gilded with gold, as was its central pinnacle. All around the building were smoothly plastered pediments, aisles of huge wooden columns, and shallow flights of wide, smooth steps that descended to a surrounding plaza from which paving led in all directions, an enormous spiderweb of narrow roads. It was like nothing else on Dinadh. I might have been on some other world!

'The omphalos,' I breathed. 'This is the house of the omphalos!' Then I saw a hive at the foot of the cliffs, east of the temple. 'That must be where the spirit people live. Songfather says the omphalos is guarded by spirit people.'

Far to the south, the canyon walls, diminished by distance, thrust in from the west over a diamond glitter, where the river Tahs Ahlai turned eastward toward the sea. Leelson pointed in that direction.

'Something moving.'

Trompe, meantime, had spotted movement in the west, and when we all stopped marveling at the view and concentrated on people, we found traffic in every direction: lines and clumps of people and gaufers on the spider-web of roads, wagons of all sizes and types crossing meadows, all of them moving toward the common center we looked upon.

'Drawn to Tahs-uppi,' said Lutha. 'Like moths to a flame. Unable to resist, no matter how dangerous the way.'

'Commanded to come,' I murmured. 'Some of these wagons have been on the way since early winter. It takes a long while to come from the far side of Dinadh. The delegation from Cochim-Mahn is probably not far behind us. Songfather will soon be here, and he will be very angry with us.'

He would be angry with me most of all, for he expected obedience from me. Lutha put her arm around my shoulders and hugged me.

'You're such a little thing,' she said. 'But you're stronger than I.' She said it to be comforting, knowing how apprehensive I was. She took my hand, and we continued our inventory of the travelers coming toward us.

One particularly impressive procession had come over a saddle in the cliffs southwest. It included a chariot, several wagons, and files of marching persons, one of them glittering as though dipped in jewels. Above this line of march a long banner floated, like a superscription.

Lutha said, 'That flag has a familiar look to it.'

Trompe reached into his pack for glasses, and looked again.

'What in ...' he blurted. 'It's the Great Flag of the Alliance.'

'The Procurator?' she questioned. 'Here?'

'Doesn't have to be the Procurator,' murmured Leelson. 'Could be an envoy.'

I looked up to see that Lutha had gone red in the face. Her lips were tight, her nostrils flared. She was furious!

'What?' I whispered.

'I came all this way! Unwillingly, at considerable danger and discomfort! Then Leelson turned up, out of nothing, trying to send me home, trying to get rid of me and Leely, but I stuck to my duty, and *now*, before I've had any chance to do what I was sent for, here's the man who sent me, or his envoy! Why was I needed at all? Why disrupt my life? This person has probably come directly from the port! *He* has not been forced to endure a hover car for endless wearying days, plus a strenuous canyon climb, plus the danger of being maimed by the Kachis!'

I touched her cheek. She dropped her eyes, seemingly ashamed.

'Drama,' I whispered.

'I'm ridiculous,' she agreed. 'As the Gauphin taught, people *are* ridiculous! We have language and history, we have technology and philosophy, and we still have not achieved good sense and self-control! And those of us who pretend to, as Fastigats do, are so damned smug about it!'

I patted her, evoking a smile. I smiled in return, though she could not see it. She knew there was nothing to be gained by being annoyed with the Procurator, or with Leelson. No gain from lying sleepless over Leelson. No gain from weeping over Leelson. No gain remembering that time at the pool, before the Burning Springs...

'Shhh,' I whispered. 'It'll be all right.'

Her eyes said it wouldn't be all right. 'The next few moments will be all right. That will have to do. I must live from one set of moments to the next.'

'Shall we go down?' Trompe asked, nudging Lutha impatiently.

'Of course.' She and I moved off in a purposeful manner, ignoring the sidelong glances Leelson and Trompe cast in our direction, feeling for our feelings.

She snorted, saying under her breath, 'One's feelings, one's love-making, and one's letters should be strictly private! In my opinion, when these things are dragged out and displayed to strangers, affection is corrupted and destroyed. It is what bad biographers do, this digging into what might have been intended, what possibly had been felt. See here, she feels; see there, she says; look here, she promises! Even I do not always know what I feel or what I intend. What arrogance for these Fastigats to presume to know me better than I know myself!'

'Perhaps they should spend their time analyzing themselves,' I suggested, receiving a smile of agreement in return.

We had no time for further conversation. We had come about halfway down the slope when a crowd of black-clothed figures swarmed out of the hive near the canyon wall and came hastily along a path that intersected our line of travel. Lutha moved up beside the left-lead gaufer to translate as necessary, and I saw her start with dismay when they came near enough that we could see them clearly.

They were like me! Like the members of the sisterhood! Missing ears, riven lips, tattered eyelids. It was not only faces with them. Fingers and hands were missing, as were feet. Bodies were contorted and thin as saplings. The one in the lead shouted in an out-of-breath voice, in a sort of dialect that was not clearly understandable, at least not to me. I took them to mean something on the order of 'Halt, stop, come no nearer the sacred land.' Since we were already halted, his commands seemed superfluous.

Lutha held out her hands, empty, the universal gesture of peace. 'We have come to save the lives of the Dinadhi,' she said. 'There is a threat from outside the planet.'

They began shouting fervently at one another. I gathered that one faction wanted to kill us immediately, while another, slightly larger faction was reminded that blood could not be shed near the sacred precincts without the gravest consequences. These antiphonal shouts went on for some time – during which Lutha muttered fragmentary translations – before the shouters reached a solution that all could agree to. They would pen us up during the ceremony, which was about to begin. After Tahs-uppi, they would take us somewhere else and kill us. Not one of them had paid attention to the threat Lutha had told them of. Either they didn't believe her or they didn't care. They were frightening in their single-mindedness.

I went to Lutha's side.

'Are these your spirit people?' she asked me.

'I don't know,' I whispered. 'Nobody ever told me they were … like this. Why are they like this?'

My words drew the attention of one of them, who darted forward, twitched my veil to one side, then screamed as he turned and fled. The others chattered among themselves, backing slowly away. Lutha took hold of the left-lead gaufer's halter and tugged him forward. The other gaufers leaned into the harness, and the wain creaked after. Trompe and Leelson dropped back to walk beside it.

'I am unclean,' I told her as we slowly pursued the spirit people, who were limping and stumbling away from us as fast as they could go. 'He says the beautiful people have rejected me, and now that he has touched me, he must go out of the valley and cut his hand off at once.'

'You sound quite calm about it. Do you think he means to do it?' she asked.

'I don't care if he does,' I said angrily. 'They're all men, Lutha. They're even worse than I, but *they're* not unclean! What right have they!'

The fleeing bunch split before us, creating an open aisle that led toward a stout pen set upon a small rounded hill.

'Gaufer pen,' I said, sidetracked from my annoyance. 'They're always set high like that, so they drain well and don't cause a muck.'

Whether intended for gaufers or not, the pen was now to be used for us. There were already a dozen spirit people arrayed outside the fence, muttering angrily to one another over the bulk of several large and shiny weapons.

'I hope those fusion rifles are not charged,' Leelson said to the air.

One particularly clumsy guard (not his fault; he had no fingers on his right hand) chose that moment to drop his weapon.

Lutha said, 'I've had arms dealers as clients, and I've seen diagrams of that weapon. It looks to me like an Asenagi product, but he had it set on standby. If it had been set in firing position, this whole place would be gone by now.'

Leelson paled. Trompe gulped, 'We are probably the first outsiders they've ever seen. They've obtained weapons for protection against intruders, but they have no idea how to use them.'

The idea of novices with deadly weapons was not cheering, and the others turned their eyes elsewhere, not to seem threatening.

'Let's not bother them with talk,' Lutha suggested. 'If that's really the Great Flag of the Alliance coming down the hill, let the envoy or whoever deal with the problem.'

Our willingness to be penned up seemed to have quieted some of the panicky gestures and voices around us. The clumsy guards backed off a little, allowing us to concentrate on the view of the omphalos our low hill afforded.

The temple was now surrounded by several nearly complete concentric circles of kneeling men, some spirit people, and some songfathers, distinguishable by the colors of their robes, black for spirit people, hide brown for the others. Each had his own cushion, and each knelt at an equal distance from his fellows. The circles were neat and perfectly regular, and as new men arrived they filled in the gaps and started new circles concentric to the old ones. I saw no women anywhere near the temple.

Lutha laid her hand on my arm and jerked her head toward the eastern cliffs. There were other black-clad forms huddled at the base of the buildings and in the windows. She borrowed the glasses from Trompe and gave them a good looking over before passing the glasses to me. They were the female spirit people, all of them disfigured or maimed and as thin as the men.

Lutha said, 'They're too thin for childbearing. Starving women don't get pregnant. They don't even menstruate.'

'But this valley is fertile!' I told her. 'The soil is wonderful. And they have a river! They should have lots of food! More than we can raise in the canyons!' Perhaps it was significant that we had seen no sign of cultivation anywhere in the valley. The grass was of a different sort than I knew. Perhaps it too was sacred and farming was forbidden.

'Look at the temple,' urged Leelson. 'At the floor!'

The temple was in the form of a circular dais made up of three concentric steps. The first was below the pillars. The second formed the base for the circle of pillars that supported the roof. The third was inside the pillars and made up the floor of the temple itself. The south half, a semicircle of this inner circle, was one step higher yet, with massive metal links protruding at both the east and west ends of the low step. A long and heavy rope had been attached to the eastern link, then threaded around the golden base of the northernmost pillar, back across the raised floor, around the southernmost pillar, then back to the north again, making a Z shape.

'It's a tackle,' said Trompe.

So much was obvious. We used similar gear to get water from the deepest wells. The loose end of the rope lay stretched along the ground to the north, and it was now being tugged at by a few dozen songfathers. They managed to pull the east end of the semicircular floor a hand span closer, rotating it on its diametric center, then nodded in satisfaction at one another as they dropped the rope and departed.

'Those golden rings around the pillars are metal sheaves,' remarked Leelson, who was looking at them through the glass. 'What are they moving the floor for? And what's it made of?'

'It is made of one great block of stone,' I told them. 'It was brought from the cliffs by the Gracious One, who, having created the great gate, then opened it unto us. The stone covers the navel of the world. The sacred sipapu. The gate through which we came. Now it will be uncovered and the beautiful people, those who carry the spirits of our beloved dead, will depart through this gateway to heaven.'

Leelson threw Lutha a startled glance, and she gave him a look that meant 'don't ask.' He glared, but he clamped his lips shut. I had just revealed the holiest secrets of our religion. It didn't matter now. There would be no secrets soon. He would see, as I would.

More songfathers arrived. There were other brief episodes of rope tugging with nobody trying very hard. Groups came and went, rehearsing separately, accustoming themselves to the feel of the rope. It was as Leelson had said at one point during our journey: every participant was here for the first time. They knew what was to be done, but not precisely how to do it. They had to practice.

By midafternoon there were tens of thousands of wains filling a shallow valley south and west of the temple, a good distance away. The ordinary men and women who had accompanied the song-fathers fringed every slight rise of ground, none of them close enough to get a good view and none of them equipped with glasses. Evidently these laymen were to view Tahs-uppi only from a distance.

During the afternoon, groups of songfathers came up the hill to the pen to take a look at us. Late in the afternoon, one came who was well-known to me. Hah-Hallach, songfather of Cochim-Mahn. He summoned me to the fence.

'Foolish woman, what have you done?' he demanded in a soft voice full of suppressed rage.

'I have come to say good-bye to my mother,' I replied.

'You have led strangers here! You have blasphemed the Gracious One. You have risked our immortality!'

'So, let the Gracious One deal with me,' I said. 'He can cause me little more pain than he has already done.'

'Because you doubted,' he said, cursing. 'Because you doubted!'

I shook my head. 'The sisterhood knows better than that.'

'All heretics. All doubters. Why you?' he shouted.

I turned my face away, not answering, sobs welling up inside me. Lutha came to me, put her arms around me, and said across my head:

'If you're asking her why she came here, it's because she believes what we have told her. Your people and your world are in danger. She does not care for herself, but she is going to have a child. She wants that child to have a future!'

He turned his glaring eyes upon Lutha and spoke from a mouth contorted by wrath. 'There is neither future for blasphemers nor children for those who doubt,' he said. Then he turned on his heel and went back down the hill. Lutha's arms held me while I wiped my eyes.

'Thank you for trying to help me,' I said. 'But there is no help against ... them.'

'Them?' she whispered.

'Old men who enslave us, then rebuke us when we rebel, calling us disobedient daughters, doubters, even heretics. I told him the sisterhood knows better. He did not like it much.'

We had no time for discussion. The crowd of songfathers and spirit people around the temple had grown larger and noisier, and now it erupted with shouts and waved fists as the Great Flag of the Alliance came bobbing and wavering toward us through the mob. The kneeling circles of spirit people opened up with some difficulty to let the flag come through, and I saw that each man had attached himself to a metal eye set into the ground. Now, what was that about? I scanned the temple, finding more such metal eyes set into the semicircular stone inside the temple.

The flag jounced up the hill, carried by a youngish, long-faced man who walked beside the Procurator, he all aglitter like a fish just out of water. With them was a huge red-faced woman driving a chariot, and behind that a stolid Dinadhi driving a cart loaded down with heavy packs. Leelson opened the gate for them.

The Procurator greeted us with a nod, then said to the woman, 'Madam Luv, this is Leelson Famber.'

'Who has much to answer for,' said the big woman, in a disapproving tone.

Leelson took no notice of their disapproval. Fastigats, Lutha was to say, often don't take notice of others' disapproval, even that of other Fastigats. While the bearers stacked their burdens in a pile near the pen gate, Leelson made introductions as though we were at tea. The long-faced man was the ex–King of Kamir, who seemed embarrassed at seeing Leelson, though I could not imagine why. The large woman was Poracious Luv, an Alliance councilwoman, flamboyant, but with good sense, so Lutha said. I gathered she had been visiting the king when both of them had been dragged into this business more or less accidentally. Or, if not accidentally, for some reason they did not, at the moment, choose to explain.

As the cart driver shut the gate on us and clomped off down the hill, Poracious joined Lutha and me at the fence while the three Fastigats went to the other side of the pen and put their heads together. They were looking at a small, hand-sized mechanism that the Procurator had taken from the baggage. A retriever, said Lutha, asking Poracious what it was they intended to retrieve.

Instead of answering, the big woman took her by the shoulder, saying, 'So, Lutha Tallstaff, what's happened thus far? Have you solved our problem?'

Before Lutha could answer, Leely appeared suddenly at the door of the wain, totally naked, his skin darkly and oddly blotched with chill. I went quickly to him, leaving Lutha to deal with the demands of Poracious Luv. I could hear them from inside the wagon.

'Your son?' asked the big woman in a kindlier voice. 'No doubt he likes the feel of air on his skin. I did, when I was smaller. Now I have rather too much skin for the air. I understand your son is an amazing artist.'

'Where did you hear that?' Lutha asked, surprised.

'I heard of it in Simidi-ala,' Poracious said. 'I was told he did some excellent portraits there. There is one on the wall of a women's convenience. They have framed it and put Perspex across it. They say he is beloved of Weaving Woman.'

I glanced outside, to see Lutha much discomfited, digging her toe in the dirt.

'I know all about him,' Poracious confided. 'You needn't be diffident or defensive with me. We are both women. We understand our feelings, whether these men and Fastigats do or not.'

'Leelson doesn't think Leely's human,' Lutha blurted.

'My, my,' Poracious said. 'He is exclusionary, is he not?'

Exclusionary was an improper word in the Alliance, so Lutha had said, more than once. The Alliance likes to think of itself as an egalitarian organization.

Lutha said, 'That's not quite accurate where Leelson is concerned. His prejudice is limited to his own children. His family has certain well-defined expectations for its posterity, that's all.'

'Oh, my, don't we all know that,' Poracious murmured. 'I've met his mama.' She winked at Lutha. 'Don't take me for a fool, lovely girl. We fat old things have not laid aside our brains with our silhouettes. We put on flesh for as many reasons as others make love, have you ever thought about that? Out of lust, out of habit, out of greed, out of ambition. Out of time, too little or too much of it, or too little else doing in it.' She sighed. 'The flesh does not represent the spirit, for which observation one can thank the Great

511

Gauphin. Though one wonders, sometimes, what the purpose is of either spirit or flesh.'

She gave Lutha a kindly pat, ignoring her confusion, then beckoned to the ex-king, who had been standing diffidently to one side, looking rather lonely.

He came over, hesitantly, asking, 'Has your group been threatened at all?'

It seemed an odd question. Lutha said, 'Threatened by the Kachis, certainly. Not particularly by anyone else until we came near the omphalos.'

'Have you learned anything?' asked Poracious.

Lutha said, 'We found a voice recording that Bernesohn Famber left in Cochim-Mahn. It was old, fragmentary, not at all clear. It mentioned three things – the abandoned gods of the Dinadhi; the omphalos, which is why we came here; and finally a few enigmatic words about the rejoinder of his posterity.'

'Abandoned gods?' the ex-king asked with an intent and eager look. 'Tell me?'

'The Dinadhi claim they came here from somewhere else, or perhaps were sent here from somewhere else, after being commanded to leave certain of their gods behind. In return, they were to receive' – she paused, glancing through the open door of the wain at me – 'immortality?'

'You don't sound sure,' said the king, still in that intent voice.

'I'm not. The whole matter's complicated.' She led them away from the wagon slightly, and when I heard the king ask, 'What's a Kachis?' I knew she was telling them about our beliefs.

They talked quietly, then Poracious's voice rose:

'These Kachis must have a lengthy life span if one of them has been around since Bernesohn's time!'

Even Lutha forgot to keep her voice down.

'I have no idea whether there's been one or a succession of different ones. Saluez believed the Kachis cannot die, but we saw dead ones during our trip, which has sorely tried her faith.'

Tried, but not defeated, I said to myself as I fastened Leely's shirt.

'Does this relate in some way to the Ularian problem?' the ex-king asked.

I came out of the wagon, bringing the now clothed Leely to stand beside his mother as the king went on:

'I see no connection. These Kachis may be nasty, but the Ularians are ... quite inexpressibly vile!'

I looked at him across my veil, asking, 'Have you seen the Ularians?'

'I've seen them. And tasted them. I've heard the sound of the waves on the world where they are now, heard the scream of seabirds and the weeping of the girl who's there watching them.' He shook his head, making a face. 'They're ... horrible beyond belief.'

'What do they look like?' I asked.

The ex-king gestured. 'Big. Big as one of your hives. Shaped, oh, like any old thing at all. A massive middle, rather shapeless, with a lot of appendages or tentacles hanging beneath like a fringe. They float. Or they sit like mountains. Or they build themselves into rancid walls of flesh that can surround an encampment! On one side, their skin is bare, and they are able to show pictures on their skins.'

I felt my eyes widen. It was an unbelievable description. Leely slipped loose and started purposefully toward the fence surrounding us. Lutha caught him just as he was climbing through.

'Dananana,' he cried, struggling to get away from her. 'Dananana.'

She pulled him into her arms and asked me to get his harness from the wagon. He hated it, but sometimes it was the only solution. I fetched it and we buckled it behind him, fastening the tether tightly to Lutha's belt.

He looked at the harness, decided he couldn't get out at the moment, then opened his pants, peed onto the dirt, and sat down to make a mud picture on the bottom board of the fence. I saw Lutha flinch, but Poracious Luv watched him with lively interest and no discernible disapprobation.

About this time the three Fastigats concluded their conference. Both Leelson and Trompe spat over the fence and then wiped their mouths. The Procurator said something to them, then calmly let himself out the gate and went off down the hill. The spirit people and songfathers had left an aisle open all the way from the pen to the temple at the bottom. He was confronted almost at once by one of those who had accompanied him up the hill in the first place.

'Hah-Rianahm,' Poracious whispered. 'Lord high-muck-a-muck among this rabble.'

The Dinadhi's voice was strident. I could hear him clearly, though he spoke from some distance.

'... must return to the pen!' he howled.

'... must take time to experience this record,' shouted the Procurator in stentorian tones, overriding the other, no small achievement considering how the skinny old man was screaming.

'No time! Tahs-uppi!'

'Until Tahs-uppi!'

Gabble and shout, pushing and shoving, the Procurator was thrust back up the hill and through the gate that Leelson opened for him. The three Fastigats exchanged wry looks that said the result of the foray had not been unexpected. Then all three of them began dragging items from the baggage pile, opening sacks and cases, sorting out items of equipment. When they had unpacked and assembled the first half-dozen elements, Lutha said:

'Isn't that a wide-range retriever? The kind entertainers use?'

Lutha was looking questioningly at Poracious, but the large woman was preoccupied with what was going on at the temple. There the circles of kneeling men were completely filled in and various ritual personages with towering headdresses had taken up positions atop the raised semicircular section of floor. As we watched, songfathers manned the entire length of the pull rope, and half a dozen black-clad spirit men were pouring the contents of large jars upon the northeast quadrant of the temple floor – oil, I presumed, to make easier the moving of the great stone lid across this lower stone. When their jars were empty, they departed. One of the hierarchy shouted a command. Though we could not see musicians from where we stood, the sounds of their instruments came to us clearly: drums, gongs, trumpets, panpipes, and several sonorous stringed instruments.

First a blaring fanfare, then a *whomp, whomp, whomp* of drums and deep-toned plucked strings, then a shouted command, and those along the rope took up the slack. They began to tug, grunting with each pull. The arrangement of the rope allowed a one-quarter turn of the semicircular stone, and I held my breath, awaiting what this displacement would reveal.

At first it was only a darkness. A darkness within darkness. A circular blackness. A pit, perhaps. A pit smeared with cloudy concentric lines to represent a ... I struggled to find a word. A vortex.

A blotch spun past, appearing at the edge farther from us, disappearing behind the edge nearest us. Well then, it wasn't a representation of a vortex, it *was* a vortex. A ... maelstrom. Though it didn't look like water.

'Not water,' said the ex-king doubtfully. 'It doesn't look like water.'

Leelson cursed briefly behind me. He had dropped some part of the device and now knelt to attach it once more. The loose parts were almost all attached; I assumed they were finished with it. Trompe knelt beside Leelson and they thrust a record file through a narrow slot.

Poracious followed my glance.

'A record from Perdur Alas,' she murmured. 'Unfiltered, if I don't miss my guess!'

I only half heard her, for the ex-king made a muffled exclamation, drawing my attention back toward the temple where the steadily grunting line, *ungh-ah, ungh-ah, ungh-ah*, had moved the floor the entire quarter turn the tackle permitted. Now the whirling darkness was fully disclosed. The music stopped. We heard a shouted command. Then trumpets again, and a quicker tempo from the drums. The rope went slack. The ritual personages unshackled it from the eye, hauled it in, and carried thick coils of it away eastward to the accompaniment of panpipes and gongs. The members of the orchestra marched onto the northeast quadrant of the great stone lid and fettered themselves, facing north, while over their left shoulders the vortex whirled with hypnotic force. The musicians' hair whipped in the rising wind.

'Look away,' demanded Poracious. 'Don't let your eyes get sucked in. Observe – the musicians are wearing blinkers, and none of the people are looking at it.'

As indeed they were not. The temple stood on a slight rise; almost all of the observers were on lower levels, where they couldn't see the vortex; if any were higher than we, they would see only the temple roof or the processions of spirit people and songfathers who were marching hither and yon, waving banners and censers while drums pounded, gongs sounded, trumpets brayed, and panpipes tweedled breathily. When the music stopped, no one looked toward the temple. All eyes were searching the far canyon edges, where they opened into the valley.

'The beautiful people are coming,' I cried, hearing both the pain and the joy in my words. 'Oh, they are coming. They will see us one more time before they go to heaven! Perhaps ... perhaps ...'

Oh, perhaps. The crowd stirred. At first I did not see what they saw, then I detected the pale movement at the canyon entrances, like a flow of milk. It did not come closer. Not then.

At the same time Leelson said something in a self-satisfied tone, there was a click, and I was elsewhere.

Before me, observed from some distance, through a twiggy growth, Diagonal Red and Four Green Spot floated over an abandoned camp. I heard the sea, at some distance behind me. A twig was jammed between my teeth to keep my mouth open as I drooled filthily. From the south, enormous shapes bobbed toward me, and my throat formed the words, Blue Lines, Big Gray Blob, and Speckled Purple. In the middle distance, a dozen more shaggy Ularians moved in a slow procession.

I was tasting ... what was it I tasted? Soapy, rancid, bitter, nasty ... Over the sound of the sea I heard retching; through the view of the moorland, as through a transparent picture, I saw the valley of the omphalos, filled with people who bent and twisted as they tried to get rid of that filthy taste. Abruptly, the effect lessened somewhat, becoming no less nasty but less overwhelming.

I heard Leelson's voice. 'I've put in a partial filter.' Whatever he had done, it did not prevent the experience continuing ...

... showing pictures on their bodies! Each newly pictured thing coalesced on the body of one single being. 'Ularian,' my throat said. The picture moved on to another Ularian, and more detail was added. Each Ularian augmented or complicated the picture created by the previous ones, and the event continued rotating. ...

I shut my eyes, held my breath, refused to smell or taste anything. No good. It was not an experience one could evade.

The woman fleeing. Fleeing. The monstrous beings coming after her.

I heard indrawn breaths. Not from the vision; from reality. There were murmurs of denial in the valley of the omphalos. Shouts of anger. I shut my eyes and made myself listen for sounds from Dinadh. What were the spirit people doing while this went on? The music had stopped. What were they thinking?

Huge, those beings. Great shaggy walls. Shapeless, amorphous, threatening, with dangling tentacles. Now the huge bodies began a new sequence of pictures, a detailed sequence playing over and over and over again:

A place near the ocean. A strangely shaped stone. A twisted tree. The hammered sea sparkling under the sun ... A note of ... anticipation? And then, all at once, an explosion of shapes from the face of the cliff, like puffs of thick smoke that separated into individual things, a horde of shaggy little floaters, miniature likenesses of the huge Ularians, countless numbers of them, spewing out of crevasses, out of caves, pouring into the sky ...

The huge ones sit, unmoving, bands of bright color dancing upon their skins as the little ones fling themselves outward, pursuing the seabirds, catching them, gulping them down! Oh, they are hungry, so hungry!

And the experience stopped, all at once, like waking from dream. Leelson had shut down the machine. Before me, Poracious Luv wiped her mouth and spat across the fence. Beside me, Lutha and the ex-king did the same. At our feet, Leely, unbothered, still painted upon the fence. He, too, had seen what we had seen. His painting was of them, the little shaggy things that had come pouring from the cliff wall. He had seen but he hadn't tasted.

Across the pen from me, the three Fastigats stared down toward the temple, waiting. Everywhere in the valley people stood up, shaking, wiping their mouths. Afar, at the openings of the canyons, movement began again, a milky flow made of countless white forms floating from the canyon mouths, streams of them, coming through the tall grasses, converging upon the omphalos.

From somewhere below, a shaky command. Then again, louder, more vehement.

I am lost in anticipation! A drum pulses, trembling. Voices shout. Music resumes, unsteadily, out of tune, out of tempo. The milky streams come nearer.

Kachis! Floating wide-eyed, arms and legs spread wide, only their wings moving them, rivulets of them, becoming rivers, becoming pools, becoming a surrounding, foaming sea! Oh, our people. Oh, our ancestors. Oh, our loved ones. So many! Could there be so many in only one hundred years? And how would I find *her* in such a mob! Millions of Kachis swirling in creamy eddies, nearing the omphalos, twirling more and more rapidly as they are caught at the edges of the vortex, as their wings ...

As their wings rip away! Glassy fragments flying! A sigh from the song-fathers assembled, from the spirit people. Was this expected? Was this the way of things? Would they not need their wings in heaven?

Perhaps not, for the Kachis are changing. There is a stripe of darkness up their fronts, from groin to chin. A widening stripe of darkness. At first I don't understand, then I see what it is. The pale delicate skins have split. Whatever is inside shows dark against the pale integument, thrusting outward, fighting its way out of the tight white casing in which it has been trapped. Arms split from wrist to shoulder, legs split from toe to thigh. Translucent pearly coverings curl away, and what is inside heaves out.

New forms. Different forms. Forms we had just seen, as recorded upon another world, shaggy ravenous hordes of creatures, miniature Ularians ...

I hear my own voice howling, no, no, no.

Trompe screams. Why is Trompe screaming? I turn. He is lying beside the fence, blood-covered. Leelson is down behind him, and above them bright ruby lines cut the air into deadly polygons of cross fire, pulses of force coming from downhill, southwest and northeast. Someone is firing at them, at us!

I hear the ex–King of Kamir, shouting. 'Mitigan. Stop! Don't! Chur Durwen, no!'

At the bottom of the hill shaggy, fringed shapes pour into the omphalos like a foaming tide. The air is full of Kachis ghosts, split-skin phantoms, half faces, single wings, shed skins whirling on the wind, clattering softly against one another like fallen leaves.

Leelson runs toward Lutha, seizes her up, tied as she is to Leely, who grabs my arm and holds me in a grip of iron, so I must run alongside. The ex-king pursues us, trying to shield us from the weapons fire. We five are fleeing down the aisle while the spirit people rage around us. Faces, I see, mouths, I see, wide mouths, shouting, furious faces. They are tied down. They cannot stop us, for they are belted to eyelets set in the stone, tied down against this dreadful wind!

Oh, but they scream. Blood has been shed. Violence has been done. Worse than that! Worse than that! They have seen, oh, they have seen ...

Leelson stumbles. He is attempting a tangential course, one that will carry us to the west, around the omphalos, but by this time the force of the whirling vortex has built into a tornado, a hurricane spinning uncontrollably, a maelstrom of wind! We run through air, legs churning space. We fly!

Beneath us I see musicians held in place by stout straps, kneeling circles of men chained to their eyelets. We are not chained and we spin, sucked down after the shaggy creatures, sucked down as the ghost-white skins of the Kachis are being sucked down ...

Leely, Leelson, Lutha, the ex-king, and I, and as we go screaming down, in terror of the darkness below, our heads twist to keep sight of the light, the light, where other dark forms fly after us like the shadows of doom.

'MI ... TI ... GAN ...' I hear the ex-king shout. 'NO. NO. NO!'

Then only darkness and howling and shed skins making a horrid rustling sound and shaggy things with tentacles and sucking mouths all around us.

Then blackness, and pain, and no more story of Saluez. For a time Saluez is gone from the pattern and the weaving goes on without her.

They did not know how much time went by. Lutha seemed to recall going in and out of consciousness, in and out of places, always borne on that terrible wind, unable to move except as it moved them. There were momentary pauses, as though the maelstrom had to switch gears or decide where to go next. During one of these, Lutha hauled on the tether between her and Leely, pulling him close, and with him Saluez, who clutched him tightly. It was then she realized there was light where they were, for she saw Saluez's face, eyes rolled back, only the whites showing. Then the wind grabbed them up again, and they were away.

The next thing they felt was the crushing impact of hitting something solid and hard, of being dropped with enough violence to drive out their breaths and cause pain. Then was the sound of cursing and sobbing and fighting for air. Lutha was on top, with Leely sandwiched between herself and Saluez. For a moment she simply lay there, so thankful for the quiet that she didn't care whether anyone else was there or had survived.

Leelson's voice rose, cursing, then that of the ex–King of Kamir. Then another male voice, raised in challenge.

'Leelson Famber! Stand and die!'

'Don't, Mitigan!' cried the ex-king.

'What are you doing here?' snarled the stranger voice in a tone of furious surprise.

'Come to stop you doing what you're trying to do,' the king gasped. 'I was wrong.'

'I swore an oath!' trumpeted the other. 'We Firsters honor our oaths!'

'Oath or not, you won't get paid if you kill anyone! Take a new oath. I was wrong. I hired you to do it, I'll hire you not to do it. It wasn't his fault.'

Lutha pulled herself gingerly erect. Saluez was not conscious. Leely was simply asleep. He did that sometimes when things were confusing. Lutha pushed herself away from them both and struggled to sit up. At least one rib had something wrong with it, for it hurt to breathe. Light pouring through a jagged opening at her left disclosed a room-sized cavern, the rugged walls streaked with white, the floor leveled by deposits of gravel and stones and a million years' worth of bird droppings. Translucent membranes waved from a dozen places, and it took a puzzled moment before Lutha identified them. Kachis wings caught among the rocks, brought here by the winds. Leelson lay slightly above the others, prone in the slanted opening, feet kicking against the sky, mumbling about wormholes. Somewhere nearby the sea swallowed and sucked, the stone vibrating in tidal rhythms.

The ex-king leaned against the back wall of the cave, facing the savage stranger. Jiacare winced as he rose to his full height and moved to put himself between the savage and Leelson.

'There's still the matter of my oath,' said the savage, curling his lip.

'Mitigan of the Asenagi, I will compensate your bruised honor,' snarled the king with equal force. 'By your blood and mine, man! We've been sucked through a wormhole in space; we don't know where we are or when we are, and it's a poor time in my opinion to argue about honor!'

The man addressed as Mitigan did not put aside his bellicose manner, but at least he took his hands away from his weapons. Saluez moaned and put her hand to her head. Leelson went on cursing under his breath, the same words over and over. Lutha looked around for Trompe and then remembered.

'Was Trompe killed?'

'Yes,' gasped Leelson. 'He was. For which someone will answer ...'

His voice failed. Lutha blinked. Trompe had been a faithful companion. She wept into her cupped hands, regretting that they had not always seen their duty alike, that she had been impatient with him.

It was then that she heard another voice, sharp though rather plaintive, pitched to be barely audible over the sound of the sea. 'Hello?' And again: 'Hello?'

Leelson, startled by the voice, slithered down from the opening in an avalanche of gravel. Lutha detached herself from Leely's tether and crawled up into the space he'd left. Above the ocean the transformed Kachis were furiously feeding, dropping long lumpy tentacles into the sea and pulling up fish after fish, spreading their tentacles into nets to capture seabirds, meantime bobbing, weaving, spinning as they increased the spaces between themselves, all the time gobbling voraciously. They stretched away in a level plane, a flat grid of bodies that met the flat surface of the sea at the horizon. Lutha risked sticking her head out of the hole just far enough to look along the cliff face. She saw nothing but rock and more rock, all of it splotched with salt and bird droppings and streaked with black ropes of what could only be seaweed.

'Hello,' she called. 'Where are you? Who are you?'

'I saw somebody's feet!' cried the voice. 'I'm Snark. Did you come to rescue me?'

What a question! Turning toward the sound, Lutha saw light-colored movement, something waving, a scarf or shirt, then a face peering down. The person was above them, almost at the top of the cliff, her head and shoulders protruding from a hole. Some other cavern, Lutha thought as she glanced out at the transformed Kachis, still busily eating.

'What place is this?' she called.

'Perdur Alas,' the other cried.

At the moment the name meant nothing to Lutha, though she was sure she had heard it recently. She rubbed her head fretfully, calling, 'Don't go away.'

She squirmed back inside to tell the others there was a human being nearby and the name of the place. Leelson's and the ex-king's exclamations reminded her where she'd heard the name recently. Poracious Luv had said the sensory recording was from Perdur Alas.

Leelson felt his arms, groaning. 'No doubt the woman who's calling to us is the observer whose senses we experienced.'

'Don't you find that unbelievable?' Lutha asked.

The ex-king said, 'Those who encounter chains of events at two disparate points, without observing the connections, think they have observed coincidence when they have, in fact, seen only consequence.'

Lutha's mouth dropped open, and he grinned.

'I was a figurehead, yes, but I was allowed tutors.'

Leelson started to laugh, cut himself off in mid-amusement, and rolled over so he could feel tenderly along his ribs.

Mitigan stepped over Leelson's body and looked out the entrance, then he helped Leelson up so he could do the same. The ex-king didn't bother.

'I'm no good at practical things,' he said. 'I've had no experience.'

'You can keep watch, then,' Leelson directed him. 'Sit in the opening there and tell us if any of those things come back this way.'

The ex-king obediently sat, throwing Lutha a good-natured glance as he pushed by her to get at the opening.

'How's the boy?' he asked.

'He's fine.' Leely was fine. She had no worries whatsoever about Leely. He had just wakened and now sat happily arranging bits of gravel while Leelson and Mitigan talked about getting out, and Lutha turned her attention to Saluez.

At some point in the wild journey, perhaps when they were dumped from the vortex, Saluez's head had been injured. She had a large bruise above her left ear, and as Lutha felt gingerly around the edges of it, she opened her eyes.

'Have we come to heaven?' Saluez murmured.

For a moment Lutha couldn't answer. Had they come to heaven! Hell, more likely, but she hesitated to say that, not knowing how badly Saluez was hurt.

'Dananana,' whispered Leely, laying his face against Saluez. 'Dananana.' He pulled her veil aside and kissed her face moistly, repeatedly.

Lutha looked away. Just another of Leely's little habits. She took a deep, painful breath and turned to meet Saluez's terrified eyes. She'd had time to realize it wasn't heaven, which saved Lutha from having to break the news.

'We're not dead?' Saluez asked, sounding strangely disappointed.

'Not so far,' Lutha told her glumly. It would do no good to delay telling her the truth. 'If the Kachis don't come back, we may even survive for a while.'

'They went to heaven,' Saluez cried, her eyes wild with pain and confusion.

'They went out there to eat fish,' Lutha said as matter-of-factly as she could manage. 'If the big creatures we saw are Ularians, then your beautiful people are baby Ularians. Or maybe Ularian larvae. Or nymphs.'

'Imagos,' corrected the ex-king from the opening.

'Whatever.' Lutha shrugged, gasping at the pain. Shrugging was not a good idea.

'Mother,' Saluez cried, her eyes wide. 'Mother.'

Lutha leaned forward to take Saluez into her arms, and for a moment Saluez clung to her before slumping into unconsciousness once more. The men stopped their talk long enough to cast a sympathetic glance toward the women. Leely scrambled up to the cavern entrance, crawled into Jiacare Lostre's lap, and stared out across the waves, waving his hands and saying over and over, 'Dananana, Dananana,' at which the king looked rather more intrigued than Lutha thought appropriate.

After a time Mitigan took the king's place in the cavern opening and carried on a shouted conversation with the person in the other cavern, who identified herself as Snark. By this time it was becoming obvious to all those in the cavern that they could not simply climb up or down from where they were. The cliff was sheer below and overhanging above. Snark tried to get a rope to Mitigan, who leaned widely from the entrance, gripping the stone with one hard fist while he flailed unsuccessfully at the windblown line. After a time Snark shouted that she would go up on top and try it from the other side, but by this time Leelson had made a rope of Leely's harness, all the belts and sashes, plus some strips torn from the bottom of the robes, and had weighted the end with a stone.

Mitigan succeeded in tossing the stone over the tree that protruded from the cliff just above Snark's hole and turned to the others with an expression of triumph. Then, inexplicably and simultaneously, they all gagged.

'Get in!' demanded Leelson.

Mitigan dodged back into the hole and lay flat.

'Ularians,' breathed Leelson, unnecessarily. Those who were conscious had already figured that out. They lay on their bellies, drooling onto the cave bottom, waiting for the taste to pass. Lutha was nearest the opening, and she actually saw one of them go by, like a hairy whale sailing out over the sea, long, tangled tentacles hanging like a tattered drapery beneath it. It should have seemed balloon-like, she thought. It should have seemed airy, but did not. Instead it breathed ominous cold, horrid intention, ghastly power. She felt the tears start and barely kept herself from moaning.

After a lengthy hiatus, the taste dissipated and they got shakily to their feet once more. When they looked out, Snark had already attached her rope to the makeshift line. Mitigan hauled it in. Snark made an amazingly acrobatic leap out from her cavern to the tree branch, squirmed up and onto it with the rope between her teeth. Shortly afterward she called, and Mitigan went up the line like an ape. Leelson went next, though with rather less agility, and the two of them raised the rest, one at a time. First Leely, then the unconscious Saluez, tied into a kind of rope sling, then Lutha, her head reeling from the height, the immensity of the sea, the nearness of the Ularians. The ex-king came last, looking around himself delightedly, his cheeks pink with excitement.

The entire process, though lengthy, took place in virtual silence, bouts of strenuous, grunting effort interrupted by periods of frozen stillness when they tasted even the remotest presence of the great Ularians. Each time it was only a hint of taste, a momentary awfulness.

The sun was setting by the time all were assembled at the top of the cliff. Saluez lay wrapped in warm blankets – provided by Snark – while the rest hunkered down with their heads together, telling Snark how they had come to be with her and watching the sun set in a bonfire of reds and pinks and oranges against a purple sea and lavender sky. The shaggies had spread themselves evenly, a plane of blobby black shapes cutting the red orb of the sun into a knife edge of light.

'So you haven't come to rescue me.' Snark laughed. It was a harsh, self-mocking sound. She looked directly at Lutha. 'I guess I knew that as soon as I saw your face, Lutha Tallstaff.'

'Why?' Lutha asked, puzzled.

Snark laughed again, like a cock crowing, half jeer, half boast. 'I hate you, Lutha Tallstaff. And him, Leelson. Not that I can do anything about it. Prob'ly learn to hate him, too, the one that was king. Not her, though.' She jerked an elbow in Saluez's direction. 'She's like me. Life ate her up and spit her out, din it.'

Lutha was both offended and mystified. 'Have we met before?'

Snark told her where, and when. Lutha flushed. She had known the shadows were ... people. Hadn't she? Or had she?

Unexpectedly, Leelson came to her defense. 'Lutha doesn't know anything about shadows. None of the ordinary people do. Only the Procurator's people knew about them.'

'Likely.' Snark sneered.

'True,' he said. 'I am well connected in the bureaucracy, and I knew next to nothing about them until the Procurator told me, there on Dinadh.'

Lutha added, 'And if we've offended you, we're sorry.'

'I killed you. I got even.'

This required explanation, and Mitigan was much fascinated by Snark's description of a simul booth.

'Sensurround doesn't work that way! It has built-in censors,' he said. 'You can't kill anybody in sensurround. You can't do anything to a person that's against his will!'

'Shadows can.' She sneered again. 'Simuls let you do anything you want, and they let me kill her, more than once.' She cast a ferocious glance in Lutha's direction, making the other woman pale and draw back.

The ex-king intervened. 'As I've mentioned to Mitigan, we have no time for hating or killing, for our survival must come first. So tell us, Snark. How do we survive?'

She gave him the same up-and-down look she had given Lutha, though a more approving one, as she said offhandedly, 'I've got me a few holes dug here and there, but they're only big enough for me. I don't know whether the big Rottens know I'm here or not, but I do know they like to play games.'

'Let's take it one thing at a time,' said Leelson. 'Food, first.'

'There's all you'll ever need in the camp. The Rottens don't seem to care if I take stuff. They don't seem to notice, I mean.'

'Warmth?' Leelson asked.

'So far it hasn't been very cold. The team records say it doesn't get really cold. If you're out of the wind, all you'll need is a few blankets. There's both blankets and solar-heat storage units at the camp. 'Course, they'll have to be recharged at the camp, where the collectors are.'

'And, finally, shelter?' asked Mitigan.

'Well, that's it, isn't it?' she agreed, with a lopsided, rather desperate grin. 'That's what it's all about. Either they don't know we're here, the big Rottens—'

'Why do you call them big Rottens?' queried Leelson.

'Because it's descriptive, damn it! Call 'em Ularians if you like, I don't care. Like I was saying. Either they don't know we're here, or they know damn well we're here and are playing with us. If they don't know, then we got to stay hid, don't we? If they do know, it still makes sense not to tempt 'em.'

'We can't stay in the camp?' asked the ex-king.

'Well, I'll tell you. Used to be the Rottens just came out at night. Lately, they've been coming daytimes, too, and they all the time hang over the camp. That's a favorite spot, that is. An it's not all that secure. Wasn't built to defend. 'F it was me, I'd go back behind the ridge north of the camp. There's a big rockfall there, pillars and blocks all tumbled down with spaces between. You'd be close to food stores and the solar collectors, and likely there's a place in there big enough for all six of you. Not real smart, to my mind, but then—'

'Why not?' Lutha asked.

'If the Rottens go after one of you, they'll get all. Spread out, maybe they won't get you all. That's the way my folks did it.'

Mitigan smiled approval and she flushed. She was not accustomed to approval.

'Am I right in thinking you were here before?' Lutha asked her. 'You were one of the "survivors" the Procurator mentioned?'

Snark nodded, responding unwillingly. 'Me. Yeah. There were five of us, all kids.'

'Why were you ...?' Lutha didn't know how to ask the question.

'Made a shadow?' She laughed harshly. 'Yeah, well. Things just happen to some people. Runnin' from scourges, you get what they call antisocial.'

None of them knew what she meant by scourges, but they did not interrupt her as she went on:

'I'd had a few years of running before I was rescued. Makes you quick. Makes you – what you say – crude. Guess I didn't adapt real well to civilization.'

This time Mitigan grinned admiringly at her. Snark returned the grin, a quick feral flash, no more used to humor than to approbation.

Lutha watched the two closely, thinking them a good pair. She, brown and lean, with muscular shoulders and calves, high, strong cheekbones, and a rounded but stubborn jaw; he wide as a door, his almost white hair drawn up into a tall plume atop his head, wearing a hide vest, a beaded crotch piece, and not much else besides a bandage and his many scars. If he'd ever worn Dinadhi dress, he'd dropped it before attacking at the omphalos.

Leelson peered down his nose at both of them, the aristocratic Fastigat sneer Lutha found so infuriating. Snark didn't bother to notice. She had seen so much of Fastigat superiority at Alliance Prime that it ceased to impress.

'What's happening back on Dinadh, do you suppose?' Lutha asked Leelson. 'They must have seen what happened to us. Are you sure Trompe's ... dead?'

Leelson looked at his boots. 'I'm sure. The other … assassin was aiming at you or Leely, and Trompe jumped in front of him.' He glared at Mitigan. 'You had no reason to kill Trompe!'

'We weren't aiming at Trompe,' said Mitigan, unmoved by Leelson's anger. 'As for what's happening back there, your Procurator will be stirring dust. As will Chur Durwen. We are sworn to cover one another.'

Leelson nodded. 'The Procurator will mount a search immediately. He'll send probes through the vortex.'

Lutha wondered, briefly, why Leelson hadn't noticed that the vortex was no more. She started to say so, but was cut off by the ex-king:

'Poracious Luv is on Dinadh. She will also put her considerable talents to the problem. And perhaps the songfathers of Dinadh as well. Though they won't want to admit they were wrong about the … Kachis.'

His words made the hair rise on the back of Lutha's neck. She could infer from various things Saluez had told her that the songfathers wouldn't want to admit they were wrong. In fact, if what had happened at this Tahs-uppi was what usually happened at the ceremony, they *would* not admit they'd been wrong. Every hundred years they would be disillusioned, and each time they would swear to hide their disillusionment in order to retain their power. 'We won't tell anyone,' they'd say. 'We won't let anyone know. We'll deny it. We'll defend the traditional teachings!'

Such things had happened before! Men in power had made mistakes or foolish claims and spent the rest of their lives and their successors' lives defending the indefensible, or hiding it. And arrayed against the impenetrable wall of the songfathers was only one big woman, one old man, and one warrior who might or might not take sides.

'Whatever they do,' Snark remarked, 'they're not going to do it tonight. Those little shaggies, they came out all along this cliff.'

'Not just one place?' Leelson demanded.

'Hell, no. They spurted out from where you were, and from south of me a dozen places. Some of 'em even came out of that island out there.' She pointed westward, where a stone point jabbed the glowing sky. 'Doesn't matter where they came out, you still got the same problem. You need cover. You need food. You have to put that pregnant woman somewhere safe if you're going to try to keep her. Right after dark still seems to be a good time to move around. The Rottens haven't ever come over the camp right after sundown. I keep a kind of chart. When they come, how many, where. Then I try to stay away from the worst places, the worst times.'

All of them were exhausted, but they could not argue with the local expert. They got wearily to their feet; Mitigan put Saluez over his shoulder with surprising gentleness; Lutha was less gentle with Leely; and they went in a weary straggle through the dusk. Before it was completely dark, they arrived at a shallow swale halfway up the slope north of the camp.

Mitigan rolled Saluez under a windrow of dried brush, and Lutha was appointed to keep watch over her and Leely while Snark took the three men down among the buildings. Leelson left her with a lingering stroke along her cheek and the remark that it might take them a while to find everything that was needed.

Lutha didn't care. She could have slept atop a volcano, so she thought, struggling to stay alert until they returned. The last of the dim purple along the sea horizon was being sucked into a black throat of night. Stars blazed on the moonless sky, like paper lanterns, their light diffused. Strange. Down in the camp small lights moved about, not radiating as one would expect, not making star shapes in her vision, but softened, dampened. She blinked, assumed the air was foggy, or that perhaps her sight was affected by fatigue. Then she realized it was not only sight that was affected but also sound. She shook her head, swallowed, twisted her head from side to side, trying to unplug ears that suddenly weren't working properly. All sounds were flat, with no resonance. Damped. Someone had lowered a curtain over the world.

Which trembled. Beneath her. Only a little, as though some large creature had taken a step near me. And another. And another yet. Three steps. Something. Something huge enough to make the stone backbone of the ridge tremble like a leaf.

She swiveled her head, silently, scanning the darkness, trying to see something, anything against the sprinkled star field. There . . . across the camp. To the southeast. On the horizon, the stars winking out, and those above them, and those above them, and those above . . . By the Great Gauphin, halfway to the zenith, the stars winking out. Something huge close up? Something even bigger far away?

She put her hands over her mouth and breathed quietly. The sound of the sea came as a series of flat slaps, no susurrus, no following hush. The world trembled again. She counted the steps, one, two, three, four. Five, six, seven. Eight, nine. Coming or going?

And then the stars bloomed in heaven and the sound of the sea was there once more, the soft rolling shush of waves on the gravelly beach. Down in the camp, the lamps made sparkling stars of refracted light.

Lutha was wide-awake when they returned laden with blankets, charged solar stoves, and camp lights plus a number of prepacked emergency kits full of food and other necessities.

'Did you hear?' Leelson whispered to her. 'Did you feel?'

Snark said, 'It's happened before.'

'How often?' demanded Leelson.

In the light of her lantern they saw the shrug, the twisted mouth, the fear in her eyes. Still, her voice retained its usual offhand manner.

'A few times. Just a few times.'

Deeply troubled, they straggled off again, uphill to a ridge spiked by stone fragments, scraggy as broken teeth, where – so Snark said – a natural dike had fallen. The remnants lay behind the ridge in a tumble of chunks and pillars, like a child's blocks dumped from their box. Among this rubble were the clefts and shelters Snark had described, places where the hunted could go to ground.

They found a room deep inside, roofed by huge pillars that had come to rest across a dozen rounded boulders, the floor cushioned by a few centuries of dust but no bird droppings. It was large enough for all six of them and their stack of provisions. Snark, very subdued, was nearest Lutha when they variously knelt or flopped or fell onto spread blankets.

'Really, have you counted how many times that thing happened?' Lutha asked her quietly, wanting to know but not wanting a general conversation about it.

'Once just before the first time I saw the Rottens,' she said through her teeth. 'And maybe three or four times since. There were times I thought it was maybe happening, but I wasn't sure.'

'So it isn't the Rottens that do it?'

'You didn't taste Rottens when it happened, did you? So, if that means anything, it means they don't do it.' She gave Lutha an almost friendly look. 'You wanna know the truth, I'm glad it happened with you here. Those other times, I thought I was losing what little brain I've got left.'

Mitigan approached them, his mouth full of questions about the Rottens. While he and Snark talked Lutha went to wrap Leely against the chill.

Snark said, 'I'll hang around close. I got a hole up the hill there. You sleep. You all look like hell.'

And with these helpful words she departed while Mitigan stood looking admiringly after her. At least Lutha assumed it was admiration that kept him standing there in the dark while the rest of them settled in like so many marmots, gathering close together to share warmth and wishing at that moment only to be safe, at least for a time.

10

They slept restlessly on the rocky floor with a fair share of grunting and turning – all but Mitigan and Leely, both of whom were able to sleep anywhere, under any conditions. By the time enough gray light pried its way through the stone pile to make a few dim puddles on the floor of our shelter, they were all awake, aware of the morning's chill, coveting the warmth of the stove and something hot to drink.

All, that is, but Saluez, who had lain closest to Lutha during the night. At intervals she'd moaned softly, but she had not responded to Lutha's touch or voice, any more than she responded to Leelson, who bent over her in the early light, shaking his head.

'She's lost in something fearful and ugly. I sense feelings of betrayal and guilt. Hard to say what it may be.'

Lutha thought that Saluez's feelings of betrayal were much the same as her own. Even now Leelson went past Leely as though the child did not exist.

'How cruel,' said Jiacare Lostre.

Lutha turned, startled, but he wasn't talking to her. He was kneeling beside Saluez, holding her hand.

'A cruel joke on all of us,' he said with a grimace, gesturing at the rocks around them. 'Perhaps Saluez simply prefers to be out of all this.'

She was lying supine, the melon swell of her belly rising above the slackness of her body.

Lutha said, 'She's never mentioned how long she had left in her pregnancy. Poor Saluez.'

'Why say "poor Saluez"?' Mitigan demanded angrily from his corner, over the *wheep, wheep, wheep* of his sharpening stone. 'She will soon have a child. All women want children. Bearing is what they are good for!'

'Thus speaketh a Firster,' Lutha growled, deeply offended. 'I suppose your god came roaring out of a whirlwind to tell you the universe was made for man, and so were women!'

'I received the visitation from the Great Warrior, yes! At my coming-of-age.' He glared his disapproval, then went scrambling off among the stones in the direction Leelson had gone a few moments earlier.

Lutha muttered, 'Why is it all Firsters have to talk about their visitation? Even Leelson does it, though he dresses it up in philosophical language.'

'And what did Leelson's god look like?'

'Like a Fastigat.' She laughed grimly. 'Of course.'

Jiacare drew the blanket closer around Saluez's shoulders. 'Mitigan was right about one thing. We can't assume she regrets her pregnancy. Most of us humans seem to find one excuse or another for increasing our numbers.'

'Oddly enough, that didn't seem to be true on Dinadh. Trompe and I were surprised to see how many vacant hives there were. Dinadh's population is evidently decreasing.'

He thought about this, his mouth pursing, his eyes squinting. 'That would fit the pattern. The Ularian reproductive cycle would start with a growing human population and few Kachis, and the proportions would reverse by the end of the cycle.'

Lutha shuddered. 'Through predation?'

'It is a kind of predation,' he mused. 'If Saluez is an example. She's a young woman with an unimpaired body, but as I understand Dinadhi culture, she'll never have another lover or another child.'

'Why maim her? Why not just kill her?'

'As she is, she can still work in the fields to produce food. Late in the cycle the Kachis probably get the biggest share of what food there is.'

'If it's cyclical, then some Kachis must have remained on Dinadh to start the process over. Also, we've assumed the Kachis are the young of the Ularians. Where are the Ularians on Dinadh?'

He shrugged. 'Being offspring of Ularians doesn't preclude multiple parthenogenic generations. Or even sexual reproduction as immature imagos—'

He was interrupted by Snark, who darted from the tunnel through which the men had departed. 'You ought a go up and watch the show. The little shaggies that came blasting out when you folks came! They're blowing each other up, like balloons!'

The lure was irresistible. Lutha tucked the blankets close around Saluez's shoulders and tied Leely's tether around a stony knob nearby, putting the knot above his reach and jerking it to be sure it would hold. He settled down next to Saluez curling into the curve of her body, his eyes half-shut, while Lutha and the ex-king went out after Snark.

Beyond the cover of the stones, they got their first daytime look at their hiding place: a dark cleft gaping between enormous, rain-rounded boulders beneath a jackstraw tumble of huge basalt crystals, so dark a gray they were almost black. Gap-toothed shards of similar crystals fanged the ridge.

From beyond that toothy ridge came a thin shrilling, rising and falling in volume, punctuated by explosive sounds. Mitigan and Leelson lay prone at the top of the slope, and the others joined them to peer through the scraggy scarp. They saw a seething caldron of shaggies, great globules of them rising and falling, tentacles whipping like strands of flung lava, the whole punctuated by eruptions in which one or more shaggies were blown apart. The cacophony was underlain by the sodden gulp of the sea, its waves flattened beneath a mat of floating body parts. The slender crescent of rocky beach was piled with clotted, squirming fragments, and more were washed ashore with each vomitous surge.

Lutha averted her eyes from the beach and focused upon the battle. There was a certain horrid fascination in the relentless winnowing. The rain of dead and injured was continuous. Gradually the deafening noise abated. Much of the detritus was sinking. The height of the waves increased, showing patches of clear water and making a more surf-like noise.

Snark said, 'It's brood aggression. Sibling murder. Happens with a lot of creatures. Supposedly it maximizes reproductive output. All the rearing effort will go to the strongest.'

Jiacare muttered, 'How many will they leave alive?'

'Too many,' said Mitigan and Snark, as with one voice.

'It's hard to believe they changed shape that much,' Lutha murmured, half-hypnotized by the continuing massacre. 'They looked almost human on Dinadh.'

Snark turned slowly, her eyes very wide. 'What did they look like? On Dinadh?'

'Small. That is, slight. Very thin, but human in form, with wings—'

'And sharp teeth,' she said. 'Right? And their teeth was really poisonous! And they come out at night!'

Lutha nodded.

'We called 'em scourges,' Snark muttered. 'When my people ran off from Dinadh, some of the scourges followed 'em through the gate.'

'Kachis? In their original form? What happened to them?'

She made an aimless gesture. 'There weren't very many. Mother said our people hunted and killed some of 'em. The others starved, I guess.'

Above the sea, the carnage had come to an end. Some few ragged forms still floated on the waters, gradually disappearing beneath the waves, while above, the uninjured ones separated and arranged themselves in an orderly grid that stretched to the horizons. By counting how many body diameters would fit in the previously crowded but now empty space, Lutha estimated one out of a hundred of the original number had survived.

She was about to mention this when she gagged, sickened by a sudden, horrible taste.

'Down, quick!' Snark spun her around. 'It's the big Rottens!'

They made it down the ridge and into the rocks before the creatures appeared – though barely. When they came to the sleeping chamber, each of them found a water bottle and a wiping rag and sat down well away from one another, each careful to look away from the others as they drooled and wiped. The few pale rays of sunlight that penetrated the piled stones now stood almost erect, disappearing one by one. All scarcely breathed as the rays reappeared.

'No clouds today,' said Snark unclearly but matter-of-factly. 'That was a big Rotten goin' over. Floatin' and danglin'.'

'Is there a place we can safely watch from?' asked Leelson, wiping his lips. 'I'd like to see a big one.'

Snark dug her heel into the sand and twisted it as she considered. 'This rockfall piles higher the farther east you go. Clear at the east end, it's right on the ridge. We can try working through in that direction.'

Lutha had stacked the provisions in a neat pile, away from the stove. Disregarding these efforts at order, Mitigan tumbled the stack, tore open one of the personal kits, and burrowed inside it to find a full water bottle. Snark wiped her filthy face with the back of one hand and went scrambling off with him in pursuit, looking from the rear more like four-legged creatures than two-legged ones.

'Be back,' said Leelson as he followed them into the dark.

Jiacare Lostre shook his head, muttered fragmentary phrases of fastidious annoyance, and set about picking up the scattered contents of the personal kits.

'This isn't a kit knife,' he said. 'Whose knife is this?'

'What knife?' Lutha asked, swiveling toward him.

He held a knife into the light of a slanting beam. Lutha saw it, and saw beyond it, where the severed end of Leely's tether hung white against the gray stone she had tied it to. The knife belonged to Saluez. She carried it in the pocket of her underrobe and Lutha had seen her use it dozens of times. So had Leely.

Lutha scrambled across the sand toward Saluez's recumbent form, feeling frantically along her blanket-covered body. Leely wasn't there. Saluez hadn't moved. Only her covers had been shoved aside to gain access to her pocket. Leely had been lying there when Lutha and the ex-king had gone out!

'Your boy,' said the ex-king. 'He did it?'

Lutha nodded, rigid and cold with tension. She hadn't thought of his using a knife. Why hadn't she thought of that! Now what? The Ularians were out there, and Leely was wandering around in this warren, or outside it. Maybe out in the open. What could she do? What dared she do?

Jiacare Lostre put his hand on her shoulder, forced her down, sat before her, taking her hands in his. 'Be still,' he said.

'Got to—'

'Don't. Don't do anything. If he's inside, he's as likely to come back here as we are to find him. If he's outside, anything you do might endanger him more.'

'I could go to the entrance and call to him!'

'If you did, would you want those creatures to hear you? Listen to me, Lutha. The best thing you can do is nothing. Just wait. Besides, the others are looking out. If they see him outside, they'll come back and tell us so.'

She thought that Leelson wouldn't. Leelson wouldn't give it a second thought. She shivered. Jiacare put a blanket around her, then his arms around that, and they sat so for a long time.

Time went by. The patches of sunlight shifted nearer the stone, crawling amoeba-like on the sand. The taste went away, but Leely hadn't returned.

'What?' demanded Leelson from the edge of the cavern.

'Leely,' said the ex-king. 'He's gone.'

'Oh, tsssss.' Leelson hissed, grimacing at Lutha, at the world. 'How long?'

Jiacare said, 'He was gone when you left. We just didn't notice until afterward.'

Lutha put her face in her hands. He meant that she hadn't noticed. She would have, if it hadn't been for that horrible taste. ...

Leelson was suddenly beside her in the ex-king's place, his arms tight around her. 'Oh, damn it, Lutha,' he whispered. 'Why did you have to come out here? Why?'

He wasn't asking for information. She gave him none.

'I have to find him.'

'No. Not until it's safe. Snark says they haven't really gone. I came back to tell you to be careful.'

'Leely could have gone out there!'

'He could have. But likely he didn't.'

Saluez moaned. They looked up. She had lifted one hand to her forehead as she made whining, hurt noises. Leelson got up and went to her.

'Saluez?' Leelson raised her up.

Jiacare had already filled a cup, and Leelson put it to her lips. She drank, only a little.

'Hurt,' she said, putting her hand on her chest. 'Hurt.'

Leelson laid her down once more. She breathed deeply, experimentally, her expression unchanging. 'Not broken,' she whispered. 'Don't think it's broken.'

It was not clear what she had decided wasn't broken. A rib, perhaps. Her collarbone. Her heart.

'Maybe you got a bump on the head,' Lutha said, forcing herself not to scream. It wasn't Saluez's fault that Leely had stolen her knife.

'Not in heaven?' Saluez asked, one side of her mouth twisting in a pathetic attempt at a smile.

'Not noticeably, no,' Lutha agreed, tucking the blanket back around her shoulders. 'Are you cold?'

She ignored the question. 'Who's here?'

'You and me and Leelson. And the former King of Kamir, Jiacare Lostre.'

'Your servant, ma'am,' said Jiacare, with a bow.

Saluez tried the smile again. 'Where's Trompe?'

'Gone,' Lutha said flatly, tears starting in her eyes. She had been trying not to think about Trompe.

'The other one who's here,' Saluez said faintly. 'That warrior. He killed Trompe.'

'Mitigan,' said Leelson. 'Yes, he's here, too.'

'Leely?' she asked.

Lutha tried desperately for calm. 'He seems to have gotten himself lost.'

'No, no,' Saluez murmured, squeezing her hand. 'Can't get hurt. Can't get sick. Can't get lost.' Her eyes fell shut. She was gone again.

'Why?' Lutha demanded. 'Why does Leely keep doing this?'

'Doing what?' asked Mitigan, emerging from the shadows with Snark close behind him.

'He's disappeared,' said Leelson.

'He's gone exploring. Kids do that,' Mitigan said offhandedly.

'I've suggested we not draw attention to ourselves,' the ex-king offered.

'If we go looking, we'll have to be careful,' Snark said, nudging Lutha, not unsympathetically. 'It'd be dangerous to go running around out there. Sometimes they come out right on top of you.'

'Stupid to go out at all,' said Mitigan, with a warning glare at Lutha.

She felt a scream welling up! They were full of what they could or must do, which was everything but go out and find her son!

Leelson picked up on her panic. He tightened his hold on her and said, 'We're not at all certain he is outside. Let's search the rock pile first. I'll stay with Lutha and Saluez. If he isn't found in a reasonable amount of time, we'll decide what to do next.'

Lutha knew he was staying to keep an eye on her so she wouldn't do anything motherly! She was so angry the blood hammered in her ears.

'We're being sensible,' said Leelson, his forehead wrinkled in apparent concern. 'We really are, Lutha.'

'I know you think you are!' she cried at him, hating him. 'Stop feeling at me!'

He only held her closer. 'I can't stop feeling you. I do feel you, Lutha. I've felt you since the moment I first saw you. I was high up in that library, all by myself, quite contented, and I ... heard a summons. I tried not to answer it. And when I'd met you, that first time, I went away, fully intending never to see you again.'

She laughed shortly, wrenching herself away from him. 'You did? I did too. When I told Yma about you, we both decided you were like a case of the plague, better avoided and very hard to cure!'

'More or less what my mother said.'

She flushed angrily. 'Damn your mother.'

'She's a product of her heritage. If you damn her, you'll have to go on damning former generations, all the way back to Bernesohn's time or earlier.'

'You're just like her! You and Limia are so much alike I can't figure out why she can't understand about ... about us.'

He shook his head. 'Why should she understand? I don't. I've been with other women. I've loved some of them. But when I've decided to go, I've always gone.'

'You went from me! Damn it, Leelson, you went!'

'I went.' He laughed in wry amusement. 'But I wasn't gone. Or rather, you weren't. You were there, love. Every morning when I woke, like an invisible rope, tying us together. Every night when I was alone, I felt it tugging. Even when I wasn't alone, you were there, between me and whoever.'

She tried to laugh, tried to pretend he was lying, knowing all the time that Fastigats didn't lie. It was one of the infuriating things about them. They might not see the truth the way others saw it, but they really couldn't misrepresent what they thought was true.

'Why? Why did you go?' she demanded, a question she'd been wanting to ask for years.

'I told you why. In the note.'

'You call that a note? Five words! "I can't get to him."'

'I couldn't get to him. And I couldn't ... couldn't bear to see you ...'

'See me what?'

'Wasting all that caring.'

'Wasting? On my own child!'

He threw up his hands. 'That's why I went, Lutha. This is why I'll go again, when this is done. If this is ever done.'

'Don't say it.' Lutha banged her fist against the stone, hurting herself. 'We can't change each other. We can hammer and hammer, and in the end we'll be the same. Things happen. We can't go back and make them unhappen.'

Lutha saw Leelson's lowering expression and laughed out loud. 'This is ridiculous! We're marooned, we're n danger of death, we're sitting in a rock cavern with nothing but a few blankets and a rather modest stack of food, my child is missing, and you and I are—'

'Are doing exactly what I wanted to avoid,' he said firmly. 'But you're right. We won't change our views in this matter. The more we talk, the more pain we'll cause, but we won't change.'

'But he's—'

'Lutha!' Leelson glared at her. 'Don't talk about what Leely is!'

Then a voice from among the stones! 'Dananana. Dananana.'

He danced into the cavern as though Leelson had summoned him, shining as brightly as one of those vagrant rays of sun.

Lutha gasped. He was bleeding! Round wounds on his arms, on his face. No. Perhaps not. Not wounds exactly. There was blood, but not … not so much. 'He's been bitten,' she cried.

Though maybe he'd only scratched himself on the stones. His little shirt was torn, a fragment of the striped fabric missing, his skin abraded beneath. But already the redness was paling, the rough edges of skin were smoothing.

'Can't get lost,' breathed Saluez, from some great distance.

'He's not hurt,' Leelson said in an ugly tone. 'Look at him, he's not hurt.'

'Can't get hurt,' said Saluez, her voice fading into silence.

Lutha held Leely close, he waving his hands, kicking his feet, caroling the way he did when he was contented. 'Dananana.'

Leelson turned his back on them and slowly moved in the direction the others had taken. 'Be back,' he said, the same words, the same tone as before. Definite. Dismissive.

Lutha heard the sounds of his going away, the tumble of small stones, the crunch of his feet.

'Poor Lutha,' breathed Saluez.

'My own damned fault,' she mumbled. 'Maybe you're right. Maybe Leely can't get hurt, or lost. People used to believe strange ones like Leely were protected by the gods.'

There was no response. Saluez was gone, back to wherever she'd been since the omphalos. Lutha tucked the blankets around her once more, then sat quietly by while Leely drew pictures in the sand, saying over and over, 'Dananana. Dananana.' When he tired of this, he curled up beside Saluez and went to sleep.

Eventually the others returned to the cavern and, unaccountably so far as Lutha was concerned, set about making ready for an excursion.

Now, Leelson said, they would go out and look around.

Lutha stared at him in wonderment. He didn't notice. Mitigan raided the supply pile once again for mottled gray-green overgarments he said would hide them among the bracken. Snark suggested that they smudge their faces with dust so as not to show up pale or dark against some contrasting background. Lutha went along with all this for a time, though all the preparations seemed rather melodramatic, but finally she could stand it no longer.

'Will someone please tell me why we're going outside?'

Leelson cast her a lofty glance. 'Anything Snark experiences feeds back to Simidi-ala, where the Procurator is no doubt even now planning our rescue. The feedback includes not only what Snark sees and hears but anything she sees us do or hears us say. We've had no chance to look around in daylight. One of us might come up with some insight that may be useful in planning the rescue attempt. Even the scanty information we have now is more than the Alliance has known previously!'

Mitigan, busy checking his own armament, raised the subject of weapons for the others, and Snark suggested they go first to the camp to pick up heat guns like the one she carried. These were tools used by the shadow team to sterilize soil before planting homo-norm crops, but they would serve to discourage attack as well.

While Snark demonstrated this device to the others Lutha checked her arrangements for Leely once more. Saluez's knife was put away in Lutha's own pocket so he couldn't get at that. His tether was tight – she checked it for the third or fourth time – so he couldn't get loose. While she did this Snark was instructing the others: '... turn it on ... press the button.' Even distracted as Lutha was, she thought she would be able to manage that.

They went down the slope into the camp, exploring from building to building, Mitigan, Leelson, and Snark half-crouched, looking in all directions at once, the ex-king and Lutha shambling along, feeling faintly ridiculous. Lutha was reminded of the vacated world the Procurator had showed her, where Mallia had lived. Here, as there, was clothing out of which bodies had been stripped. Here, as there, were artifacts, tools, games left behind when their users had been taken away. Through open doors the wind keened softly, a chill murmur that never ceased. In a window a tuft-eared, short-nosed animal sat quietly, staring at us interlopers.

'Is that a live cat?' Lutha asked, disbelievingly.

'Left behind when the real team was evacuated,' Snark said. 'Her name's Zagger. There's another one somewhere. Zigger.'

'Animals? Real animals? Left behind? The Procurator told me the Ularians left nothing alive!'

'I know what he said,' snarled Snark. 'I was there, pouring your damn tea!'

Lutha fell silent. The cat jumped down from the window and came to rub itself against her legs. A strange sensation. It looked up intelligently. Lutha realized that it, like the gaufers, knew things. Not as humans knew them, but in its own way. She saw language in its movements. Not her own language, not a spoken language, but ... Smells, maybe? A combination, perhaps, of smells and gestures and sounds.

'You're right about what the old Proc said.' Snark leaned down to stroke the cat. 'He talked about all life being gone. But you remember that world he showed you – there was a little pet animal crying along the fence. And there was trees and plants and birds. It was only the humans gone. It's just, the old Proc, he's like a lot of people spend all their lives in Class-J cities, with only humans around – he gets to a point of thinking *life* means *human*. People like that, maybe they got a flower in a pot and a clone fish in a bowl, but they get like Mitigan, so set on humans being the top of the heap, they don't give anything else credit for living.'

'What do the cats eat?' asked the ex-king.

'I put out food for 'em,' said Snark. 'They'll eat fish. I used to catch 'em fish. Now I dunno. Won't be many fish left, the way the shaggies're gulping 'em down.'

Though they had come to the camp for heat guns, Lutha took the opportunity to do a superficial inventory of supplies available. She was looking particularly for a medical diagnostic unit for Saluez. Such a unit should have been a standard item in any human-occupied area, but there was none in any building they visited. Lutha didn't mention the omission to Snark, considering that Snark had quite enough to be angry about already.

With the heat guns in their pockets, they left the camp and walked down the narrow vale to the pebbly beach, the only place for several days' walk in either direction, said Snark, where the cliffs did not close off access to the sea. They stopped in what Snark called a storm hole, a hollow eaten out by storm waves above the usual high-water line. From this cover they stared at the shaggies from a new angle. The shaggies took no notice.

After some little time Mitigan strode down onto the beach and strutted back and forth to see if the shaggies would react. When they did not, Leelson joined him in his stroll, then Snark and Lutha. Still no attention from the fishers. They walked the length of the beach, not a great distance, noting that the long wave-washed piles of shaggy body parts had much diminished. The remainder was liquefying, trickling into the gravel in ink-like runnels.

'You'd think this would smell, or taste, or something,' said Snark.

To Lutha, it looked disgusting, but it did not smell or taste, and the shorebirds took no notice of the remains. Neither did the shaggies, who merely hung like lumpy balloons above the sea, their amorphous, knotty tentacles reeling up and down, the fringed tips stirring the water. Whenever a fish was encountered, the lines twitched and drew upward by a process of gradual thickening, becoming a bulbous extrusion from which the catch was drawn into the main sac. Each shaggy had at least a hundred appendages of various lengths, some coming down, others going up, some quiescent, just hanging. Lutha thought them clumsy looking, as though they had been botched or left unfinished. They seemed uncommitted to their present shapes, as though wearing an expedient disguise.

She started to mention this to Leelson, when Snark looked up and said, 'Whoa ...'

Lutha smothered a shriek. While they'd been staring westward one of the shaggies south of them had floated to a spot between them and their cover. It was far larger than Lutha had estimated. Very wide. With many tentacles.

'Split up,' said Mitigan. 'Spread out. Start inland.'

Lutha's instinct was to stay close to someone else, but Mitigan gestured her away, so she moved obediently apart from the others, a full shaggy diameter away southward, swiveling her head to look in all directions above. The shaggy was hanging roughly between Mitigan and Leelson, tracking them, its underside bulging with incipient filaments and with others already partway extruded. The two men were to Lutha's left, and though they moved rapidly, the shaggy had no trouble staying above them.

Snark was nearest Lutha, on her right.

'More of them, moving in from the sea,' she said, breaking into a trot.

Lutha ran beside her, realizing that she had no idea where the nearest bolt-hole was.

Snark saw her confusion. 'The rocks just ahead,' she said. 'Aim for the shadow to your left.'

There were several shadows. As they came nearer, Lutha saw the one Snark meant. A hole with space behind it. She hurried, hearing Snark's feet racing away toward another hole, one farther south. Out of the corner of her eye, Lutha saw tentacles at her side, left and right. She leapt toward the shadow, making it under cover just in time.

A slithering sound came from behind her. She turned to see a tentacle slide down the rock behind her, its end plopping onto the ground she had just left.

'Safe,' shouted Snark.

'Safe,' shouted Mitigan.

Then Leelson's voice shouted the same word. Lutha breathed easier.

'Lutha!' shouted Leelson. 'Jiacare!'

Oh. 'Safe,' she cried breathlessly. 'I think.' She heard no responsive shout from the ex-king, but then she had other things to worry about.

The plopping tentacle had fallen on a rootlet that led inward. Now it had wrapped itself around the rootlet and was pulling itself slowly into the shallow shelter where Lutha crouched. The tip explored, feeling its way, reaching out for the next thing it could get hold of. Each time it stretched thin, a bulbous thickening somewhere behind it moved up, allowing the slenderer tip to move forward again. The tip was fringed all around with cilia that moved independently, giving it an odd sort of expressiveness. As though it might be thinking.

Could it smell her? Hear her?

She held her breath. The tip quested, erect, turning this way and that, cilia up. Almost she saw it raise its eyebrows, almost she heard it say in a grumpy voice, 'Now, where did the thing go!'

She could hold her breath no longer. She gasped. The questing tip turned toward her. 'There she is!'

Damn it, she told herself hysterically, the thing was not talking and she could not go forever without breathing!

She picked up a pebble and tossed it away, toward the entrance.

The questing tendril turned that way.

She tossed another pebble, breathing as quietly as possible. Then another one. The tendril was moving faster, extruding blobs of itself forward, then pulling itself toward them, moving across the rocky floor like a lumpy snake.

She heard a blatting, a muffled roar.

'They burn!' cried Snark.

The Lutha-seeking tendril stopped, its end waving, as Lutha heard what the tendril evidently also heard, a high-pitched weeping noise, a whine, not quite organic sounding. The sound of a wounded one?

The questing tendril went into a fury, lashing itself against the ground in a circle. Finding nothing, it grew longer, lashed again, and grew still longer. It was in a temper, no longer willing to spend time to find Lutha. If it went on doing what it was doing, it would touch her.

Reluctantly, she took out the heat gun and pointed it. When the lashing tendril came closest, she pushed the button.

Nothing. She stared at it in disbelief. Pushed it again. Still nothing. It bore an indicator dial just above the button. A red dial, *charge level minus.* Nobody had bothered to check.

No. Not nobody. She. She hadn't bothered to check!

She thrust the useless thing into her pocket to free her hands. There was something else in the pocket. Saluez's knife. She took it out, her hands trembling so that she almost dropped it. Not a big knife. Sharp, though. Sharp enough, maybe, to cut through that questing tendril. If she could hold it down with something while she cut it.

Knife between teeth. Large rock in both hands. Person, not herself, some other idiot, making small noise. Tendril turning purposefully in her direction. Sneaking, sneaking. End up, questing. Another small noise from idiot. Tendril coming faster, extended, thinner and thinner.

Then, smash down rock. Kneel on rock. Saw at tendril, fast, bulges coming down it in this direction, quick, before bulges got there!

Put foot on rock to hold it down on severed tendril. Decapitated tentacle slithering outward, making weeping noises ...

Something else screaming louder somewhere. Lutha?

Leelson saying, 'You did that very nicely.'

Lutha, idiot Lutha, making stupid noises with tears all over her face, flinging herself at the man.

'What did she do?' asked Mitigan.

'Cut the tip off the thing,' said Leelson with equal parts accusation and admiration. 'She forgot her heat gun.'

'Did not!' she screamed. 'Damn thing hadn't any charge.' She took it from her pocket and threw it at him.

He looked at the indicator, pressed it. It turned blue. 'You have to turn it on first,' he said. 'Then you press the button.'

'Snark said – ' Lutha said.

'I said,' Snark said, 'you turn it on then press the button.'

Maybe Lutha hadn't been listening, Lutha thought.

Snark shook her head wonderingly, then crouched over the chopped-off tentacle tip, scraping it into a collection bag. 'I got samples of the body parts along the shore, but I was wondering how we'd get a sample of a live one,' she said. 'Like they used to say at the home, fools rush in.'

'You did very well,' Leelson assured Lutha. 'Heat gun or no heat gun.'

'How many of them came after us?' Lutha murmured.

'One each,' Snark said. 'And there's a shaggy dying over near where I was. I want samples of that one.'

Of course they went to look, at the shaggy and for the ex-king, who seemed to be missing. This time they did not talk, they did not make noise, they did not breathe loudly. They sneaked, insofar as it was possible to do so. The dying shaggy lay behind the south end of the outcropping, its tentacles spread around the end of the stone, almost to the hole Snark had taken cover in. The tentacles quivered as they approached. Each time they moved, they quivered anew. All up and down the tentacles, ragged little holes had appeared and the same inky runnels they had seen bled away from the thing.

Mitigan reached down and picked something up from beside a tentacle. He held it out to Lutha.

A fragment of striped fabric. Her eyes refused to see it.

'This your kid's?' he asked.

'Maybe this shaggy picked it up from outside the cavern. Leely might have lost it there.' Snark said it. She didn't believe it, but she said it because believing anything else was insane.

Lutha took the scrap and turned it in her hands. On one side was a series of circular impressions, made up of small, individual eaten or burned dots.

Mitigan had already rolled the tentacle with his boot heel, exposing the line of circular structures beneath, made up of individual pores. He took the scrap and held it close. They matched.

'Can't get hurt,' whispered Leelson, his eyes on Lutha. 'Can't get lost.'

He was quoting Saluez, of course, but his eyes questioned Lutha. What did Lutha know?

Lutha told herself she didn't know a damned thing!

'He's pure poison to these,' said Mitigan thoughtfully.

'And to Kachis,' Leelson mused. 'That's why they died.'

Lutha screamed at him. 'You don't think ...?'

'Hush.' He gripped her arm, glancing upward. 'Don't yell. I don't know what I'm thinking. Not yet. Keep your voice down.'

They stayed where they were for a few moments, watching the shaggies to see if Lutha had alerted them. Evidently not. Even the one she had wounded had returned to its place and was fishing, unconcernedly.

They went in single file along the limp body, for the first time getting an accurate idea of its size. Even flattened as it was, the creature had an ominous bulk. Snark knelt beside the mantle and began cutting at a puffy area, which collapsed with a whoosh of escaping gas and a momentary stink.

'Hydrogen,' murmured Snark, carving off a piece of the body before turning to the tentacles. 'I'm betting it uses bioelectrics to separate hydrogen from salt water. The analyzer in the lab at the camp will figure it out.'

'Jellyfish,' said the ex-king, who at that moment came from behind a brush pile and wandered over to them. 'It's a huge, aerial jellyfish.'

'I thought they got you,' Leelson remarked to the ex-king.

Jiacare shook his head slowly. 'No, actually I dallied a bit behind you when you all went down to the shore. You seemed to be moving rather precipitously. And then, of course, you were making a foolhardy amount of noise.'

He nudged the dead or dying shaggy with one toe. 'What killed it? It's too far up the slope to have washed in.'

Leelson handed him the scrap of cloth; Snark displayed her flesh samples; there was a consequent babble babble. The ex-king looked shocked, then intrigued.

Lutha refused to join in the talk. What they said wasn't true. It couldn't be true.

'It doesn't make sense,' Leelson said. 'Evolution takes countless generations to come up with things like this. Poisoned leaves that dissuade leaf-eating insects. Thorny seedpods that are not eaten, allowing them to germinate. Poisoned flesh, brightly colored, that warns off predation.'

'Might not be poison,' said the ex-king. 'Might be ... oh, a virus.'

Lutha blurted, 'Leely's been examined by experts. He doesn't have a virus.'

'He doesn't have a virus harmful to him, you mean,' said the ex-king. 'I doubt anyone looked for viruses harmful to other things. Especially exotic things.'

Lutha admitted to herself he was probably right. Why would they? Leelson had hired people to analyze Leely, and she'd fought them every step of the way. She'd let them inventory Leely's genetic material, but she'd stopped there. No one had done a complete cell inventory.

'How could he have a virus I don't have?' she demanded. 'The two of us are always together.'

Leelson shushed her. 'Leely went off alone and touched them. You didn't. Maybe you have it, too, and don't know it.'

'Fine,' she snarled. 'Next you'd be suggesting I be staked out as bait, just to find out!'

In this mood of mixed apprehension and annoyance, she followed the others to the camp, where Snark put the specimens into the analyzers, and then back to the rock pile. They had been under cover only briefly when the Rottens returned. Everyone but Lutha went to spy upon them, but she remained in their sleeping chamber where Saluez and Leely were sleeping. Though Saluez drooled unconsciously, Leely did not. He did not respond to the presence of the Rottens in any way. He just went on quietly sleeping while Lutha bent her head over the sand and waited for it to be over.

As, eventually, it was. Lutha was washing her face when the others returned.

'There were five big Rottens,' Leelson told her. 'They found the dead shaggy. It seemed to upset them a good deal.'

Lutha turned, the wet cloth still in her hand. 'Why be upset at one dead one? Millions of them tore each other apart this morning!'

Leelson made an equivocal gesture. 'I know. The Rottens paid no attention to the piles on the shore, but they did hover over the dying shaggy. One of them touched it, then they all drew in their tentacles and made pictures at it.'

His voice held a hint of strain, of puzzlement.

'What is it, Leelson?'

'They grieved, Lutha. I could feel it. The one there on the slope, it has an identity. It has a name. They called it by name.'

'Maybe it wasn't a name as such,' she suggested. 'Maybe it was a classification. A label, like *little one*, or *child*.'

'It was a name,' he said. 'I could feel the grief, the pattern in it, singularity addressing singularity. If it wasn't a name, what was it?'

Lutha folded the cloth and put it away. 'How could it have a name? There were millions of the damned things in the vortex; there are still hundreds of thousands of them. Do ants have names, or bees?'

'Numbers aren't really the issue,' said the ex-king. 'There are billions and billions of men. We all have names.'

Lutha flushed. He was right. Given the Firster attitude toward animals, however, how awkward for them to have names!

A point that Leelson made at once. 'They aren't men, damn it. I suppose it's possible there might be a kinship with some sensory way of identifying members of their own group. I wonder how we'd ...'

Lutha sat down on the nearest rock. 'You said the Rottens made pictures to the dying one. It would help to know pictures of what?'

'We couldn't see,' Snark replied. 'We were looking down at the beach,

542

and the angle was wrong. I just knew that's what they were doing, making pictures at the dying one.'

'If you could have seen the pictures, you might have caught some clue to the language.'

'Ants and bees communicate,' said Mitigan. 'But we don't call it a language. Only men have language!'

Jiacare Lostre challenged this in his usual mild manner. 'Oh, mighty warrior, it has to be a language.' He put up a hand as Mitigan growled. 'Hear me out! Didn't the Ularians arrange this world for the benefit of the shaggies? Don't we assume the shaggies are the offspring of the Ularians? Wasn't it a Ularian who went to the people of Breadh to tempt them away from their former home? Didn't that tempter need language to do so? Am I the only one here surprised at our not having been killed or transported by the Ularians, since, according to the Alliance, that's what Ularians do.'

Snark disagreed. 'The tempter wasn't the same! If Ularians are the same as the tempter on Breadh, then the Rottens are not Ularians. The tempter was mighty and mysterious, wonderful and terrible, so my mother said. He wasn't a blob that made people drool all down their chins while they listened.'

Leelson murmured, 'Or, if both Rottens and tempter are Ularian, then tempter is some kind of ultimate Ularian, some other race, or evolved type.'

Jiacare rubbed his hands together thoughtfully. 'An ultimate Ularian. Interesting thought. And both you and Saluez are sure about this tempter?'

Snark nodded in vehement agreement. 'The sisterhoods on Dinadh kept alive a lot of the old forbidden stories and songs. The original sisterhood, so my mother said, was made up of women who actually remembered what happened on Breadh.'

'So' – the ex-king threw his arms wide – 'if the Rottens aren't Ularians, where are the Ularians?'

'Don't ask me,' said Lutha. 'If Snark is light, then the ones here are just … nannies. Caretakers. They fret over a sick or dying shaggy; they come and go, minding the young; but they don't or can't clear planets or transport humans. What we call a Ularian crisis, from our point of view, may be just nannies tidying up, from the Ularian point of view.'

'We've got three layers of beings already, and you're extrapolating another?' Leelson at his most supercilious.

As usual, Lutha found his tone infuriating. 'I'm extrapolating from what Saluez and Snark have told us and what we've found out, Leelson! We don't know for sure that the Rottens even know we're here, and neither they nor the shaggies have been proven capable of vanishment. Therefore, as Snark says, there's a chance that our local Rottens are not Ularians, or at least, not the "ultimate Ularian." Besides, Snark says she's seen ... how many big Rottens all together?'

Snark made a face. 'A hundred, maybe. Mostly I just see the same ones, over and over, about thirty or forty of 'em.'

Lutha nodded grimly. 'Millions of Kachis came through from Dinadh. Ninety-nine percent of them died in the brood struggle; there are still hundreds of thousands of them out there in the grid; but Snark has seen only about a hundred big Rottens. What happened to the rest of the previous generation? The ones that came through a hundred years ago. They must have gone somewhere. Where are they?'

Puzzled silence until Snark broke it, saying:

'There's the thing. You know. The thing that happened the night you got here. There's that.'

They shifted uncomfortably, each recalling the occurrence, the strangeness, the occulted stars, the dampened sound, the odd effects of air and light. Mitigan made a furious gesture of rejection, as though about to burst out in anger, but Leelson quelled him with a look. The ex-king smiled, very slightly, a mere quiver of lips that seemed to say, 'Ah, yes, well, there was that.' Snark and Lutha exchanged questioning looks, and Snark nodded firmly.

'That wasn't nannies,' she said. 'That was a different thing, that was. And if that was it, the ultimate Ularian, we don't need to ask where IT is. Part of the time, anyhow, it's here.'

11

The question of whether the Rottens knew there were humans on Perdur Alas was answered dining the early-morning hours when they woke choking in the dark. Gray dawn disclosed besiegers all around them. Portieres of tentacles encircled the rockfall, closing off every doorway to the outside world and most of the sunlight as well. While the others stayed miserably huddled near the stove, Mitigan and Snark went scrambling through the stones, trying to find an escape route. There was none. The tentacles were too closely spaced to get between, the tips resting on the ground preventing anyone's going under. The only option seemed to be to outwait them, though as the day wore on it was clear that time meant little or nothing to Rottens. Midmorning came and departed. Noon came, status quo. They forced themselves to drink, to rehydrate bodies depleted by the constant salivation. Eating was out of the question. Early afternoon came and went. Though the Rottens made no effort to infiltrate the rock pile, they seemed prepared to stay forever.

All of them but Mitigan became increasingly worried about Saluez. She remained comatose; only her chest and belly moved; breath came and went almost inaudibly while her belly quivered and jabbed sharply beneath the blanket. How close to the time? Snark wanted to know, receiving shrugs as reply. It could be today, Lutha thought, or much later. Even if they knew when, it wouldn't help. No baby could nurse with this going on! And a dehydrated mother couldn't provide milk.

When Jiacare said he was going to one of the peek holes to get a good look at the Rottens, Lutha offered to go with him, partly from curiosity, but mostly just to stop sitting, spitting, worrying about Saluez. Snark joined them, though Mitigan and Leelson sat immovably, each in his own drool corner.

Lutha had thought the shaggies quite large enough – they were hundreds of times larger than the Kachis – but the Rottens were enormously bigger yet. They shared the same form, even to the bulgy, lumpy tentacles that looked as though they contained bones or hard chunks of something rather than being the sinuous flow of flesh one might expect. Lutha mentioned this to Snark.

'It's a scleroprotein,' Snark replied indistinctly. 'It's got a lot of silicon in it, and I'm guessing it's the lining for the hydrogen ducts. I think the ducts fold up when the tentacles contract. Probably the gasbags contract, too, so the hydrogen can be pressurized to reduce buoyancy.'

'Weird,' offered the ex-king.

'Odd,' Snark replied, shaking her head. 'What's weird is their genetic pattern. Pieces of it are similar to a lot of creatures we have records of—'

She stopped, her words arrested by a break in the thus-far-unchanging view through the crevice. Far to their right the curtain of tentacles was disturbed. A dozen of the lumpy lines thrashed in agitation and began reeling in as the shaggies did when they caught fish. The observers craned, trying to see what had caused the disturbance, seeing nothing at first but stones and bracken. Then came a flash of pale color.

Lutha's throat knew before her brain did. She heard herself shouting, 'Leely!'

He was out there! Stark naked! Skipping along the line of tentacles, letting them run over his body, thrusting his hands into them. Damn Leelson! Damn him. He'd let her baby go!

She turned blindly toward the exit, but Snark grabbed her in a devil's grip. 'Look,' Snark demanded. 'Don't go running off. Look!'

Unwillingly, Lutha turned her head toward the crevice. The tentacles Leely touched were withdrawing, reeling in quickly, more quickly than they'd seen even the shaggies do while fishing. The dangling appendages didn't grab at him as he skipped by; it was he who plunged in and out of the ropy curtain, moving right to left along the arc of tentacles, up the ridge.

A few – four or five – of the Rottens didn't reel in when touched. Instead they dropped the touched tentacles, severing them near the body, then drew in all the others, sucking them in as though slurping noodles. This unlikely sight distracted Lutha just long enough that when she looked back to the left, Leely was over the ridge, out of sight.

Once more she tried to get away, struggling with Snark.

'Wait!' demanded Jiacare. 'He's not hurt, and he's following the circle. He'll probably come around again.'

She stared outward with a feeling of sick impotence. The Rotten circle was at least four or five hundred paces across, fifteen hundred paces around or more. And Leely was moving in a skipping, sidling way, not in any hurry. It would take him a long time. She counted: One pace, two, three, four. If he moved as she counted ...

She lost her place twice and was up to eight hundred something, long past hope of seeing him, when he appeared as he had at first, far to the right, still skipping, still touching, though now there were very few tentacles within his reach.

Only when Lutha saw he was safe did she look elsewhere, following

Snark's jabbed finger toward the Rotten directly above. It was one of those that had withdrawn all its tentacles before being touched. The bottom surface was smooth, shiny, like the surface of a balloon. Colors flowed across it.

'That's Diagonal Red,' slavered Snark.

None of them could have missed the pulsing scarlet blot, edged on one side with misty violet, on the other by deep wine and vivid yellow.

Lutha wiped her mouth. 'Do they all have individual patterns?'

Snark nodded.

'No two alike?'

'Not that I've seen.' Snark spat onto the dirt with an apologetic shrug. 'I don't think we can see all of it.'

Despite the difficulty of talking, Lutha persisted.

'Couldn't that be what Leelson sensed as a name? An individual pattern?'

Snark shrugged, raised her eyebrows, mimed possible agreement, all the while choking and hawking.

Lutha gave up. She would pursue the question later. For now, she'd assume each of them had an individual pattern that might extend beyond visible wavelengths, a pattern of which humans might see only a part. For all they knew, the terrible taste might be part of the creatures' titles!

The one to the left of Diagonal Red was probably the one Snark called Four Green Spot. It, too, had drawn in its tentacles and was repeating its pattern. If their patterns were their names, then they were saying their names, over and over.

Lutha tried it silently: 'My name is—. My name is—.' Why were they telling the humans? A nice point of linguistics! Under what circumstances do creatures announce their names?

Perhaps when they want others to know they have names? Perhaps when they want others to know they are not bees or ants but beings? Or perhaps even to say that ants and bees *are* beings?

Leely had returned to a point opposite the peek hole. Now he stood facing the rock pile, looking up, his bare little body mottled with chill.

Not mottled. Colored. On his smooth chest and belly a patch of bright scarlet bloomed, bordered on one side in violet and on the other side by deep wine and yellow.

The enormous being above him made a roaring sound, so thunderous and terrible that those who were watching cringed. Colors fled across its underside. Pictures of Rottens, pictures of Leely being grabbed, drawn in, his bones falling from the sky.

And on Leely's belly, nothing but the colored pattern. No pictures.

'Tell it back,' cried Snark out the peek hole. 'Oh, little boy, tell it back! Tell it you'll kill it dead!'

But Leely made no pictures. Just the pattern, then another Rotten's pattern, then another's. Lutha pressed her face into her hands, not to see, oh, not to see. Leely had never made pictures that moved. To send a message, he would need motion, but his art was a static art.

It wasn't even art, blared a voice in her mind. *It's no more art than an echo is art. Or a reflection in a mirror. It's reproduction, not interpretation.* Leelson's voice, too well remembered.

'He can't,' she said brokenly. 'He can't answer it.'

'What's happening?' demanded Leelson from behind them.

Lutha stood aside to let him see.

'They're hurt!' exclaimed Leelson. 'Or they're scared! By my lineage!'

He plunged off among the stones with Lutha at his heels. They erupted into the open inside that monstrous, fleshy chimney where all the tentacles were raised, all the bellies smooth, all showing pictures of Leely dying, of Lutha being devoured, of Leelson's violent demise.

Unaware they were doing so, they cringed at the sight. Farther up the hill, Leely stood unmoved, staring up at all the colors, waving his hands and singing, 'Dananana, Dananana.'

Then the great circle fell apart. Rottens sluggishly sagged away toward the sea, pieces of themselves bulging, almost detaching, then being tugged back with lurching effort. These were the ones Leely had touched, now barely coherent as they bobbled awkwardly down the valley. Some barely made it past the beach; some went a little farther out before they fell and floated, amorphous balloons, black bulges against the bright sky and brighter sea. The shaggies took no notice as the Rottens moved out like sinking ships, wallowing out under their own erratic power, out and down, lower and lower, the waves breaking over them at last.

Those few Rottens that had severed their tentacles moved in quite another direction, straight up, dwindling in distance, vanishing at the zenith. ...

And beneath the watching humans, the world trembled, shivered, rang like a gigantic bell, the vibration dying away to leave them sprawled, deafened, only half-conscious.

Silence, then. A long, disapproving silence.

Who? What? They could not tell. Over the sea, the grid of shaggies remained quiet, all tentacles withdrawn. All around, the moor was soundless, no branch quivering in even the slightest breeze. No seabird cried. No fish splashed. They looked at one another, themselves silent, mouths open, eyes wide. Nothing.

'Dananana.' A fretful cry.

Lutha staggered toward Leely where he spun on his bare feet, staring at the sky, still calling, 'Dananana.' His mouth pushed out, pouting. He had liked all those pretty colors. He had been having fun. Lutha watched him, possessed by a sudden and terrible disorientation. Who was he? What was he?

And she stumbled to a halt, hand to mouth to muffle the sound she felt boiling from her throat. She knew what he was! She knew who he was!

Snark stumbled past her, knife in hand, single-mindedly set on taking samples of dropped tentacles. Lutha saw her sawing away at the great, lumpy coils while beyond her Leely danced in and out of the furze, waving, giggling. Lutha didn't follow him. She was incapable of motion. After a few moments he tired of playing hide-and-seek by himself and came to put his hand in hers. She made herself close her hand, turning like an automaton to follow Snark as she rejoined the others.

They approached Leelson where he stood leaning against a stone, the glasses at his eyes, searching the land around them.

'What was that?' Leelson asked Snark. 'That earthquake?'

'Like what's happened before,' she said softly. 'Only closer. Angrier. Something here's not liking us much.'

Everything here didn't like them, Lutha thought. The whole world was arrayed against them, and with good reason.

'How ... how did Leely get out there?' she demanded, barely able to speak over her sick certainty.

'I sent him,' said Leelson with a level look. 'And I would do the same again.'

It had not occurred to her that he would simply admit it.

'He could have been killed,' she said. 'He could have been ...' This was foolishness, and she knew it, but her tongue went on making words her heart did not believe!

'I thought it unlikely,' he replied.

'You had no right—'

'Saluez is in labor. She would have died had this siege continued. She may die regardless. And her child,'

Lutha opened her mouth, but nothing came out. He would have sent Leely out if there had been no Saluez. Saluez was only an excuse, but she was a good excuse, one Lutha could not argue now.

'Dananana.' Unhelpfully.

'I'll go to her,' Lutha said stiffly. Later she would deal with Leelson. When she had more time to tell him a terrible thing. When he had time to hear.

'I'll go with you,' said Snark, with a glance at the zenith, where the Rottens had vanished. 'I guess they're gone! Who'll take this sample down and put it in the analyzer?'

The ex-king took the packet from her and trudged off toward the camp.

'Come on,' she said, nudging Lutha. 'I know a bit about baby taking.'

'I didn't know shadows – ' Lutha murmured.

'Before I was a shadow,' she interrupted with an exasperated look. 'When I was a street rat. Street rats get pregnant like real people. But they don't have *responsible sponsors* to sign for their babies. Who'd sign for a street rat's kid? So they can't go to a registered birther. They have 'em unofficial, like.' She shook her head. 'Street rats don't eat too good, they get beat on a lot. Sometimes they have a hard time! Let's hope Saluez won't.'

They scrambled back into the cavern, where Lutha harnessed Leely to his pillar once more, fastening the latches of the tether, making a sound she was surprised to hear coming from her own throat, half a snarl, half a moan.

'What?' demanded Snark, turning a surprised face.

Lutha pressed her eyes with her fingers, shutting down the frenzied, ugly thoughts that possessed her. 'Not now,' she said. 'We have other things to do now.'

Besides, she told herself, trying to calm her frantic mind, the matter didn't concern Snark. It concerned Leelson. Leelson and Limia, and their damned posterity!

Snark didn't pursue the matter, for one look at Saluez was enough to push other concerns aside. Saluez's labor was proceeding without her, so to speak. Her body heaved and pushed, but her mind had gone elsewhere.

'Jiacare,' said Snark. 'She's filthy. So are we. We'll need some wash water.'

He picked up a bucket and went out. Snark knelt beside Saluez, a strange expression on her face. 'Dinadhi,' she said, as though to herself. 'It's her first birth and she's Dinadhi.'

'Of course she is,' Lutha said impatiently.

Snark nodded to herself, rubbing her forehead fretfully, then went across the cavern to busy herself among the emergency kits.

'What are you doing?' Lutha asked.

'Making a catch bucket.'

'What in ...?'

Snark stopped, staring at the wall as though puzzled at Lutha's question. 'Saluez is Dinadhi. My mother, she ... said, have a catch bucket, with a lid.'

Lutha pursed her lips and forbid herself to say anything at all. Some cultures made quite a ceremony disposing of the placenta and umbilical cord, and perhaps it was for that reason that Snark had emptied the contents from a folding emergency kit, had resealed the sides and top, and was now cutting a narrow opening into it. Whatever Snark's reason, she needed help less than Saluez did.

The floor beneath the unconscious woman was a sodden mess. Lutha dragged Saluez to a drier spot, removed her filthy robes – little filthier than Lutha's own – and covered her with clean blankets. While she was doing this the ex-king returned with a full bucket, put it near the stove, and departed with a nervous look in Saluez's direction.

Lutha scrubbed her hands and arms, then bathed Saluez as best she could. Snark finished her self-imposed task and rejoined Lutha, bringing her 'catch basket' with her: an emergency kit with a hand-sized opening surrounded by latches cannibalized from other kits.

Snark set it down with a thump. 'The lid,' she said, adding a thick slab roughly cut from another kit.

Lutha was muttering over the lack of medical equipment. Had it been oversight? Or had it been purposeful? Had those who sent the shadows to Perdur Alas not cared that they might be hurt or ill? Or had they simply not thought about it?

Snark tapped her. 'Stop fuming. There's antibiotics in the kits. We'll make do with those.'

Growling, Lutha went to fetch them while Snark dug out several of the unused overalls and ripped them up to make a dry bed between Saluez and the floor.

'She's sucking that veil in every time she breathes,' Snark said. 'Let's get it off her.'

Lutha removed it and set it aside, turning back at Snark's exclamation.

'Her face!'

Saluez's face was a whole face. Like Lutha's. Like Snark's. No bone showing through. No mutilated lips or eyelids. One ear was still slightly battered looking, but even that flesh was smooth.

'How?' breathed Snark.

Lutha had no idea. The woman between them moaned, a remote, careless sound. Her eyes stayed blank. She wasn't there. She didn't know what had happened to her.

They propped Saluez's knees on folded blankets.

'What else?' asked Lutha.

'We wait.'

'I'm tired of waiting.'

Lutha stared at Saluez, her face, her form, the skin of her legs. She'd never seen a natural birth before. Leely, of course, but there had been medical people there, able to handle any emergency. What would they do if Saluez was in trouble?

'What?' asked Snark.

'Just ... my mind, pestering me. I need to think about something else.'

Snark grinned ferociously. 'Think about this. I hated you, you know?'

Lutha swallowed. 'So you said.'

Snark squirmed, settling herself, her eyes on Saluez. 'I got to thinking about that. Truth was, it wasn't just you. I hated ever'body. Ever since they called me a liar and thief in that home, I hated 'em.'

She scowled, lines of concentration between her eyebrows. 'Thing is, I got to figuring, it wasn't just me! It'd been the same for any female. If it'd been a boy and they'd called him a liar, he'd have said so what and who wants his nose flattened over it?'

'Probably,' Lutha said, intrigued.

'Boys get in a fight, nobody thinks much about it. Boys tell a few stories, or thief a few things, boys'll be boys, an' nobody says civilization's coming to an end. Do they?'

'Not usually,' Lutha agreed. 'But you think it's different with girls?'

'Girls go for somebody, they're out of control! People at the home said that; justice machine said that. Snark, you're out of control! I never done anything men I knew didn't do, and they're still back on Central, scavenging and telling lies, just like always. Men a lot like Mitigan, killing folks right and left. Men like Leelson, doing whatever he wants ...'

Saluez moaned. Snark's voice trailed off, waiting. The moan didn't go anywhere. It fell off into quiet, and Snark resumed her discourse.

'It's different for women. And for some men. Men like the old Procurator, I guess. And for the king too.'

'Jiacare?'

'Him, yeah. Old Proc and the king, they're more like Saluez, trying to be in control all the time. More like you.'

'Like me?' Lutha was astonished.

'Yeah. You carry on – crying, laughing. Flapping around sometimes like a bird. Lotsa drama, you know, but down at the bottom of it, you're like Saluez too. Trying to hang on.'

Lutha laughed, a hollow sound. 'Drama,' she said. 'My family does have a tendency toward ... drama.'

Snark accepted this. 'What I think is, men, they can rape and ruin, maim and murder, kill each other off in dozen lots, so long as there's one left, he can make babies enough for the next go-round without even working very hard at it. If you're a woman or a king, though, you got more invested than that, right? You got yourself invested in civility, 'cause that's what's safe for people. You get invested like that, you got to be righteous and do the looking out for other people. There's the young ones, the old ones, the sick ones. Got to stay in there, hoping for something different ...'

Saluez moaned again. Snark wrapped several folds of her shirt around her hands, like clumsy mittens, watching intently while Lutha wet a cloth and wiped Saluez's sweaty face.

Lutha asked, 'You think that's what Saluez is doing? Hoping for something different?'

'Saluez says she wants to lie in sweet grass, eating apples,' said Snark. 'That's different. That's paradise. Like it was on Breadh.'

'Were there many people on Breadh?'

Snark laughed, abruptly joyous. 'Hardly any! That's what made it paradise! I told Kane the Brain about Breadh. He said we all make up an Eden. Some old-time place. Some never-never place. Someplace just over the hill, maybe, where things're the way things used to be, ought to be, the way they never were.'

Lutha caught her breath, aware of a sudden pain behind her breastbone. Not her heart. Lung and stomach, probably, contending for the title of chief dramatist. It hurt, nonetheless. 'Can't there be a real Eden?' she gasped, astonished at the pain the question evoked. 'Somewhere? Can't there?'

Snark shrugged. 'We could make one here if we wanted. We could make one anywhere, if we would. Instead it's apples and sweet grass, long gone, long past. Kane said we ate them all—'

Saluez shrieked abruptly, a senseless sound that accompanied a seemingly endless convulsion. Her teeth ground together. Her belly heaved and clenched.

'Why is she unconscious?' Lutha demanded. She hadn't been unconscious when Leely was born. Women who chose to give birth usually chose to experience it.

'She's Dinadhi,' Snark replied, as though this meant something. Then she shook her head in momentary confusion. 'I think I remember what Mother told me. I hope I haven't forgotten. I think we have to do this thing first. ...'

'Do what first?'

The question was answered, but not by Snark. Saluez shrieked mindlessly. Out from between her legs came a white thing, a bloody white thing, a small head with closed and bulging eyes, a wide mouth that showed the tips of sharp little teeth. The moment the head came into the light, the eyes opened and the teeth began snapping, snapping at them, the eyes glaring.

'Quick!' shouted Snark, grabbing at the thing with her mittened hands, wrenching it from Saluez's body, and thrusting it through the narrow neck of her recently manufactured catch bucket. Despite the wrappings of cloth, the thing brought blood from her arm, leaving a nasty gash.

'Watch out,' she cried. 'There may be more!'

There were two more. Snark got one, and Lutha got the other one, while one part of herself gibbered mindlessly and some other part demanded that she should not behave stupidly in front of Snark. The creatures were slimy and pale, they shrieked and gnashed, and the gaping slits along their backs quivered like gills as grim-faced Snark thrust them into her bucket and fastened the lid down tight.

When the contractions stopped and it was clear there were to be no more of them, Snark tied the catch bucket top with line and put it inside one of the larger supply cases, which she also lashed closed. The entire bundle rocked and shrieked at them as they returned their attentions to Saluez. She had expelled the afterbirth. With it was what remained of the infant she had carried.

Snark wrapped the bloody fragments in the clean cloths they had intended to receive a living child.

'Did you get bitten?' she asked matter-of-factly.

'A little,' said Lutha faintly. 'What ...?'

'It most always happens,' Snark said, her eyes wide and unfocused. 'Mother said it's a rare thing that a first baby lives. Sometimes it does, if there's only one scourge inside, but usually there's at least three or four of them.'

Lutha trembled, unable to get any words out. Now she knew where the next generation of Kachis were on Dinadh. Even now they were being incubated and born.

'They didn't have wings,' she said stupidly.

'Those slits down the back,' Snark replied. 'As soon as they dry, the wings pop out. They can fly almost right away.' She shook her head. 'These looked sort of not ripe, though, didn't they?'

Lutha had no idea what a ripe Kachis would look like. 'How does this happen?'

Snark made a face, a spitting sound. 'It's the Dinadhi way. It's part of the choice the songfathers made. First time a woman's pregnant, a helper takes her to the House Without a Name. They take food and water so the scourges won't be hungry or thirsty. And the helper ties her down on the table and then rings a gong, and maybe one or two scourges come and lay eggs in her. They've got these long prickly-looking ovipositors. But sometimes instead of one or two coming, lots of them come and eat on the woman's face. Only the face, though. No other parts.'

She wiped at her cheeks with the back of one bloody hand. 'And when comes time for the woman to have the baby, the scourges get born first. The midwives take 'em and feed 'em and turn 'em loose as soon as their wings're dry. And then, if the scourges didn't eat it, the baby is born.'

'But why do the Dinadhi do it?' Lutha screamed.

'I'm tellin' you! The songfathers *command* it, so's there'll be *beautiful people* to hold all the people who die. Places for their souls to go. The women are supposed to have this duty so the people can live forever.'

Snark took a deep breath. 'If the baby's messed up but alive, they take it away somewhere.'

'By the Great and Glorious Org Gauphin,' Lutha said fervently. 'Knowing all this, why does any Dinadhi woman get pregnant!'

Snark shared a bitter half smile. 'They don't know it. It's taboo to talk about it. All the girls know is there's a kind of a trial they have to go through to become a woman, but they don't get told about it until after it's happened.'

Saluez shifted and groaned.

'What shall we tell her?' Lutha demanded.

'How about telling her the truth. That she had scourges inside her. That we've got 'em in a box. That her baby died.'

'That her baby never developed. That's true, too, and it'll be easier for her.'

Snark shook her head, mimicking Lutha viciously, 'Oh, yeah, by all means, make it easier.'

'Snark! Why not?'

'I was just thinking of my flippin' life,' she growled. 'That nobody was much concerned about making easier.'

'Your mother was! Whatever else happened, she saved you from this!' Lutha waved at the shrieking box, the supine form, the bloody rags. 'You didn't have to experience this!'

Snark flushed, then her eyes filled and she sobbed, once only. 'Yeah,' she whispered. 'Yeah.' She sounded so sad that Lutha reached for her, but Snark evaded the embrace, ducking her head and stepping away.

They bathed Saluez again and wrapped her warmly. She began to breathe more easily.

Snark said, 'She'll wake up anytime now. Once the scourges have time to get dry and fly away, then the mother can wake up.'

Saluez's eyelids fluttered.

Lutha said, 'You're all right, Saluez.'

Saluez murmured something, about a baby.

'Rest,' said Lutha, helplessly.

Snark shook her head disapprovingly, saying in a firm voice, 'You didn't have a baby, Saluez. It never developed. You had scourge ... Kachis eggs in you and they kept the baby from growing.'

Saluez made a lost, lonely sound. She was not truly there, had not truly heard.

Lutha held her, whispering, 'They're gone, Saluez. The things are gone. Snark knew what to do.'

'Sad,' murmured Saluez. 'No baby. So sad.'

'No baby, but a miracle,' said Snark. 'Feel your face, Saluez. Feel your face!' She took Saluez's hand and thrust it almost roughly against her cheek, the one that had been riven so the teeth showed through. 'It's healed, Saluez.'

'It's a miracle,' said Lutha. 'Weaving Woman did it.'

'... not,' breathed Saluez. 'Leely. ...'

'He's safe,' said Lutha. 'He's fine.'

'Has to be fine,' Saluez whispered. 'Nothing else for him. ...'

Then she shuddered and was gone again, her breast moving gently, her face calm.

'Now that's normal sleep,' said Snark, wiping her face again. There were bloody streaks on both cheeks. 'And she needs it.'

Behind them the lashed box rocked and rustled.

'What do we do with them?' Lutha asked.

'Drown 'em,' said Snark. 'I'll do it.'

'Drown what?' asked Jiacare from among the stones. He came into the entrance, water still beaded on his skin, his hair streaming down his back.

Snark went to him and they muttered together, his voice rising angrily. Lutha went to the stove to heat more water. She was filthy. She smelled to herself like a tidal flat. She resolved to wash her hair, at least, while she kept an eye on Saluez.

The ex-king came to fetch the lashed box, his face hard and furious. He started to speak to Lutha, then merely shook his head, making a gesture of frustration. Lutha gulped, getting hold of herself. Jiacare felt as she herself did. As Snark did. Angry at ... what? The songfathers? Much good would that do Saluez. At the Kachis, the Ularians, the whatevers? Much good would that do anybody!

She poured water over her head, surprised that it didn't go up in steam, then set about soaping and rinsing, interrupting the task whenever Saluez made a sound or changed position. She was stripping the water from her hair when Leelson arrived.

'Leelson ...'

'Snark told me,' he muttered as he knelt beside Saluez and closed his eyes. After a long moment he said, 'She's not grieving.'

'I think she knew,' Lutha replied, combing her wet hair with her fingers. 'A secret like that can't be kept. No doubt there were whispers, even on Dinadh. I think she knew, but she didn't admit it to herself. I'm so thankful Snark was here.'

'She says you were bitten.'

'It's really only a scratch.' A scratch that burned like fire. She rummaged among the odds and ends, looking for a comb, finding one at the bottom of a personal kit.

'Jiacare and Snark went to drown the things.'

She grunted angrily. Good for them!

He drummed his fingers, a little rat-a-tat to accompany thought. 'Do you have any explanation for what happened?'

'To Saluez?'

'No. Snark explained that. I mean with Leely. How he is capable of ... doing what he's done?'

So here they were at last, at the subject of her revelation, at the answer that had come to her, finally, when it was too late to solve anything between her and Leelson!

She put down the comb, folded her hands in her lap, took a deep breath, found a knob of stone over Leelson's left shoulder, and fixed her eyes on it intently. She would not be bellicose. She would be calm.

'You used to talk to me about your great-great-grandpop. You told me he was the biochemist to end all biochemists, a genius, a savant, a polymath. We both know he went off to investigate the Ularians and ended up on Dinadh. We can assume he saw Kachis on Dinadh, and they raised certain questions in his mind. There was an analyzer among his equipment at Cochim-Mahn. Just as Snark has fed pieces of the shaggies into her analyzer, Bernesohn no doubt fed pieces of Kachis into his. Then Tospia visited him. She went home pregnant. One hundred years later, precisely when he is needed, a boy of Bernesohn's lineage, *your son Leely*, turns up with this trait deadly to the Ularians. ...'

She paused, shifting her eyes to his face. He had gone rigid, eyes staring at nothing, in that moment resembling Limia, feature for feature, his expression of rejection and repudiation exactly like hers. Limia and her damned Fastigat lineage! Limia grieving over Leelson's posterity! Oh, by the Great Gauphin, Lutha prayed, let me live long enough to tell her!

She couldn't keep the anger from her voice. 'What part of that do you find hard to understand?'

'Impossible!' he growled, very red in the face. 'That's impossible. Ridiculous!'

Well, well. In all the time they had been together, she had never seen Leelson truly dismayed until now. How marvelous!

'How would you know?' she cried, boiling with five years' fury. 'You're only an ordinary Fastigat. Bernesohn was out of your class, or so you've told me.'

'But none of the family ... not my father, not his father, and not me, certainly ...'

'So? Somehow Bernesohn arranged this talent to lie low for a few generations. Until it was needed!'

'I don't know how he'd do that.'

A new speaker heard from! Snark, leaning against a pillar at the entrance of the chamber, where she'd obviously been listening for some time. 'They force-fed me a pretty fair technical education, and I don't know a way this could happen all at once, out of nothing.'

'Maybe the trait emerges only if the taste of Rottens is in the air,' Lutha muttered.

'Then I'd have it,' said Leelson. 'I've tasted Rottens.'

These were mere quibbles. 'I don't *know* how Bernesohn did it, but I'm damned sure it's not coincidence. It happened because he's your son!'

'Dananana,' caroled Leely, waving his hands and plucking at his trousers. 'Dananana.'

Oh, marvelous anticlimax! 'I need to take him out,' Lutha said furiously. 'Is it safe to go out?'

Snark shrugged, her go-to-hell shrug, but her eyes were wary. 'Safe as it ever is, but don't get careless, Lutha. I've had a bath at the edge of the water, and you look like you could use one, but keep an eye out.'

Lutha did not reply. She stalked out past Leelson, Leely trotting along at her side, sometimes moistly kissing Lutha's wounded wrist, sometimes petting her arm. They passed Jiacare Lostre as he returned empty-handed from the sea, and Mitigan, who sat quietly on a rock, his face flushed with sunset, both of them looking like shiny new people. Lutha lusted for water, much water, and for clean air after all those hours of tasting rottenness in the claustrophobic stone chamber. She wanted to wash it away! She wanted to wash Leelson away!

Leely tugged at her hand, leading her over the ridge and down toward the scarlet shine of water and sky. The first line of shaggies seemed a safe distance away. At the shore Leely peeled his trousers off and waded into the water to do his business. He liked to do that, whenever water was available. He'd been born able to swim. She watched him paddle, sometimes diving, feet in air, taking mouthfuls of water and spurting them like the legendary whale, he all silver and rose like the waters, like the sky. She took off her filthy clothes and waded in far enough that she could dunk all of herself. The water was cleansing, not very salty, but chill. She scrubbed at her body with handfuls of the powdery bottom sand, then waded out and sat like a monument on a pedestal of stone, letting the soft wind dry her while her filthy clothing soaked in the nearest pool.

Leely came up a good way out, clutching a fish, laughing. Not far beyond him, a shaggy lowered its tentacles. Leely took a bite out of the flapping fish, then threw the remainder into the lowered tentacles. Lutha shuddered, again aware of her son's surpassing strangeness. For years this uncanny presence had shared her days, clear as noon, while she denied and refused to see that he wasn't just a little boy, not just a child, not just her beloved son. She had been like Saluez, facing the unbearable, rejecting it.

'You're very beautiful.'

Leelson was standing behind her, staring at her, looking wistful. Leelson never looked wistful!

'You used to say so,' she said, swallowing deeply as she grabbed up the sodden robes and draped them around her shoulders, trying to put revelation and seduction both aside. She didn't want to talk, not about the two of them, not about Leely, not about anything.

Fastigats paid no attention to that! With them, nothing could remain unsaid, undefined, unfulfilled. 'You really think Bernesohn Famber designed ... that?' He gestured toward the splashing child. 'Why isn't he intelligent?'

His expression was very much like Limia's had been. Stubborn. Dismissive. Lutha swallowed again and said stubbornly, 'We don't know that he isn't.'

It rang false, even to her. Why not say it? Why not get it over with?

'It's because Bernesohn had the same expectations as your mother, Leelson! He expected you to beget with a woman from Fastiga, not some ... outsider! If you'd had a Fastigat woman, Leely would have been all right.' The bitterness boiled to the surface, shaming her. She couldn't control it. It wasn't fair. None of it.

He ignored her tone. 'I wonder if Tospia knew? When she left here, when she had the twins, Tospiann and Paniwar, I wonder if she knew one or both of them had been *designed* by Bernesohn.'

'If they were, he forgot to plan on redundancy. Twin children, one of whom – was it your great-grandmama? – had only one child. And your grandpa, and your father.'

He nodded. 'It's true Great-grandmother Tospiann had only one child, but Paniwar had an acknowledged son and a number of daughters, in addition to at least one ... escapade.'

'Improper fathering,' she said, quoting the two dowagers in Fastiga.

He made a rueful face. 'An early dalliance with a member of a traveling troupe. On one of the Nantask planets. He was little more than a boy at the time, and she was twice his age.' He was watching Lutha closely, digging at her.

Deja vu. She herself had told this story as Leelson had told it to her before. She wanted to change the subject, but he wouldn't let her.

'Her name was Dasalum,' he said. 'She was a celebrity, a superb actress. It was her fault Paniwar committed improper fathering. She went off in a temper and the Fambers never did find out what happened to the child.' He watched me, waiting.

A long silence. She could feel him, probing, probing. He'd brought this up for a reason. She resisted, resisted, then cracked, letting in the light. Her revelation hadn't gone far enough. And she couldn't lie to him. He'd know if she did.

She said, 'In Nantaskan, her name was D'ahslum T'bir, which means bonetree. Skeleton.' She looked at her hand, surprised. All on its own it was drawing a lineage chart in the sand.

'And?' asked Leelson.

'She bore a daughter whose name was Nitha Bonetree.'

'How do you know?'

'I didn't until just now. But it's the only thing that makes sense.' Lutha looked away, willing him to let it alone, willing him to stop!

He wouldn't stop. 'And why is that?'

'Because Nitha Bonetree was my great-grandmother.'

He didn't change expressions. She had told him all about her family when they were together. In the last little while he'd figured everything out, everything she hadn't put together until now. She looked down at the chart she'd drawn:

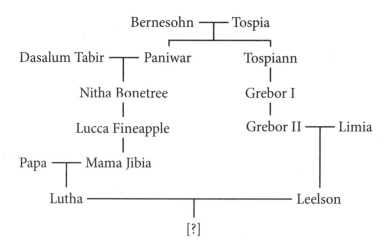

She didn't add Leely's name. He was out there splashing, making bright fountains. The sun bulged on the sea, a fire blister, scarlet veins bleeding along the horizon. The shaggies reeled in fish, flapping silhouettes against the glow. She wanted to scream, yell, throw things, but the moment was too precarious. Not as she had thought. Not as she had thought at all.

'Now we know how Bernesohn managed to do it,' Leelson said at last. 'That's why he fathered twins. On that old chip we played, he didn't mean "rejoinder" in a legal sense. He meant "rejoindure." Rejoindure of his lineage. Half the virus in one line, half in the other. A virus made from Kachis, from Ularian life. One it would have no antibodies against.'

What could she say? What was there to say?

He stared at the dying sun. 'Tospia must have known! She was supposed to tell the twins. "Daddy invented a weapon, children. Daddy didn't want to lock it away in a laboratory somewhere, where it might be lost or forgotten or misused—"'

'Why lost or misused, necessarily?'

'In Bernesohn's time, the government was ...'

'Mostly non-Fastigat,' she supplied bitterly. 'Your great-grandpop didn't trust us ordinary people.'

Leelson went on as though she hadn't spoken. 'Actually, what he did makes a certain kind of sense. There were still things he needed to find out on Dinadh. He knew he might be killed. He had to provide for that eventuality. He didn't know what the virus would do to its host. He had no way to test it. So he put half in one zygote, half in the other, depending on Tospia's pride in her posterity to keep the twins well guarded and protected. If he wasn't killed, he'd be back on Central long before the twins grew to reproductive age. If he didn't get back, he knew the twins wouldn't reproduce with one another! We don't even reproduce with first cousins very often, so it would be at least two generations before the virus could be reunited. Perhaps Bernesohn had learned enough about Tahs-uppi to know they'd be needed by then. ...

'Tospia must have known. I wonder who forgot to tell whom?'

Lutha buried her face in her hands. Had Tospia really known? Had Nitha Bonetree known? Had Lucca Fineapple, the religious nut, Lutha's grandma, had she known? Had Mama Jibia known? Unlikely in the extreme. Lutha's mother hadn't known, and neither had Lutha. Five generations back to Paniwar Famber, and nobody had known.

'How did the strain stay pure?' she asked from a dry throat. 'It would have been diluted.'

'Not if it were carried quiescent in the reproductive cells. A virus is just a machine for making more viruses. We're still carrying around viral fragments from prehistoric times. They merely inhabit, reproducing themselves from generation to generation but not ... doing anything.'

'Until it met up with its other half,' she murmured. 'But there's only two in my family, Yma and me. And there's only one of you. Surely that was depending a great deal upon fate.'

This line of thought didn't delight him, obviously. He scowled. 'Bernesohn assumed there'd be lots of descendants from both sides, well spread out among the rest of humanity. Bernesohn himself was prolific. He had half a dozen Fastigat mates and children by all of them; he'd have expected the twins to produce a horde.'

'But that didn't happen. There was only you and me. Our meeting was accidental. No one planned it. Almost too neat, Leelson!'

'Too neat to be believed, Lutha. Bernesohn no doubt built in some kind of attractant. Something that would gain effectiveness in each generation.' He frowned at the sea. Dirty. Unhappy.

'You're filthy,' she suggested, wanting desperately to be let alone. 'Why don't you at least wash yourself!'

He wandered off toward the water and began stripping off his clothes. She stared into the sunset, trying not to think of anything at all. Until now she'd regarded their affair, Leelson's and hers, as the summit of her life, the single most exciting and marvelous thing she had experienced. From the day he'd come to her door, she'd kept a journal, just to memorialize the wonder of it, so the episodes would never fade, never dwindle. Since he'd left, night after night, she'd reread it, reliving their time together. Certain expressions, certain words, certain actions. They'd been made for each other, she had told herself.

Yes. Well. So they had. Not quite as she had imagined. It had not been the inscrutable stars that had brought them together. Instead they'd responded to one another like any two moths or frogs or beetles. Leelson was right: Bernesohn had made sure of bringing his great-grandchildren together. He'd built in some attractant. Perhaps a pheromone, growing more potent with each generation, some chemical lure that wafted for great distances, bringing them both to that library. A time bomb in their reproductive cells, set to go off!

How dared Bernesohn Famber do such a thing!

'Don't be angry with him,' said Leelson, standing naked at the water's edge, following her thoughts as though she had spoken them aloud.

'Leave me alone, Leelson.'

'Think of Saluez's face, Lutha. Look at your wrist. Bernesohn was trying to save the human race.' He entered the water, scooping it over his shoulders and body in ruby showers, watching her all the while.

She looked at her wrist. Healed, of course, By Leely, her son, their son, no one's son. Leelson was right. Bernesohn's task, as he'd seen it, was to save the human race. To create a magic bullet that would ricochet around among humanity. One that would kill off the enemy and heal the afflicted at the same time. Or perhaps the healing power was simply a side effect. Serendipity.

Tospia probably *had* known. Maybe Paniwar and Tospiann had been told, as soon as they were old enough to understand it. Which was probably *after* Paniwar had fathered her great-grandma. 'You can't screw around like this,' his mother had no doubt said. 'You're too important. You carry the secret weapon. You're the possessor of our heritage, our survival.'

'Don't romanticize either,' Leelson cautioned her, standing tall as he stripped the water from his golden head.

She could barely keep from screaming at him. 'Please, Leelson. We've done our genetic duty. Now can't we at least leave one another alone.' It took all her willpower not to weep hysterically.

'I don't think he invented a way to turn it off,' he said helplessly, returning to her with arms open.

She tried not to respond. Oh, she tried, but it didn't work. Leelson was right, of course. Bernesohn had made them for one another, and he hadn't included a way to shut it off.

They had only just lain down that night, all too weary to extend the evening beyond the bare necessities of food and shaking out the blankets, when they came up off the floor as though alerted by some bone-deep klaxon.

Lutha felt a surge of adrenaline, then that stopped-up-ears feeling she sometimes got when swimming, that muffled, gurgling-in-one's-head effect. She yawned widely, momentarily surprised to see the others yawning too. Obviously, it had affected them all. Snark had her fingers in her ears; Mitigan was gaping like a fish; they all looked apologetically at one another as they tried to clear a way for sound that should be there but was not. The sea was a shush, and the wind a hush, and the birds a shrill *tee-tee-tee*, all flat, muffled, without resonance.

'It's happening again,' mouthed Snark, grasping Lutha by the shoulder. 'Like the night you first came!'

Flinching at the strength of her grip, Lutha nodded. It was very much like what had happened before, only more so. There was a panicky breathlessness along with the soundlessness. They gathered around Saluez's recumbent form while the effect went on, still with no discernible cause. Mitigan's hands were busy with his weapons, which rather increased their apprehension.

Far off, a muted thunder. Though Lutha considered it an odd-sounding thunder, it was more like thunder than it was like an avalanche or a volcano. She shared significant looks with the others, looks meaning more or less, 'Did you hear what I heard?' mouthing the word 'Thunder?' following this with agreeable nods. Yes. Thunder.

None of them really believed it. First Leelson grimaced, then the others, for it *hadn't* been thunder and they all knew it. Through the cracks among the stones the stars shone clearly in an unclouded sky.

Again the stones around them shuddered, the soil beneath them trembled. This pulse repeated at long intervals, two, three, four, five times. Then nothing. Still the flat sound, the muted uncanniness, the breathlessness. Saluez gasped, her eyes still closed. Lutha felt as she had at the Nodders: terrified of something without knowing what. As the Nodders had been unnatural, so this was unnatural.

'*At his feet the mountains skip,*' whispered Saluez. '*At his step the worlds tremble. See him treading down the star trails, the Gracious One, potent and victorious.*' Tears were running beside her nose, at the corners of her mouth, dripping from her jaw. Lutha apprehended her words clearly, though she had no sensation of hearing her.

'What?' breathed the ex-king, falling to his knees beside Saluez.

'A songfather hymn,' whispered Snark, her hand on Jiacare's shoulder, her eyes fixed on the stone above them. 'From Dinadh.'

Songfather hymn or not, Lutha couldn't stop the words from repeating in her mind, over and over. *At his feet the mountains skip.* As on a screen, the letters moved right to left, then started over as her body tensed in rhythm with the thudding of those feet. As her lungs gasped for air, so her ears gasped for something to hear, inventing sounds where there were none, creating them, labeling them, recognizing them though she had never sensed them before:

Touch of hooved feet upon mountains, crack of horn upon horn, rasp of battle breath, slow drumbeat of heart and sinew, final bellow of supremacy. Pad of soft toes through jungles, herb scent slipping between parted jaws to flow across the tongue, night-tasting, prey-finding, huff of soft nostrils flared, whisker tips tracing the night, spotted hide sleeking like silk among the grasses, low rumble in the throat like a bass string bowed, ominous, peremptory. Shuffle of nailed feet below mighty legs, thewed as a tree grown up with vines, billowed dust blown over hides thick as boards, ears wide as doors, massive movers, a trumpet call across tree-bowered stone-speckled savannas. Water surging along slick hides, flick of fins, eyes in the depth turned upward toward liquid-trembling gray light. Beaks cleaving air, chill along the quills, knife edge of wind-buffeting wing, steel grip of talons, amber-slitted horizon-compassing eye.

Blood on the stone. Whether from the deep or the height, whether from mountain or jungle, whether from claw or talon, beak or fang, blood on the stone, rising up to live again. The very soundlessness was their sound – its sound – and all the other senses as well. They stretched, reaching for being. In silence, sound. In darkness, sight. In nothingness, touch.

The sacrifice, it says. *All living is by sacrifice. For one creature to live, another one must die. What will you give me? Where is mine?*

It speaks to her! It says: *Oh, feel how you have unvoiced us. See how you have cut us down. Hear our silent cries! Our worlds were full of the murmur and clatter of being, now listen to the silence we inhabit, all our spirits, still!*

'Lutha?' Leelson, holding out his hand.

'Nothing,' she said in a voice she didn't recognize as her own. 'It's nothing.'

What was it? Not nothing. What were these visions? Things she had seen as a child in sensurround? Fairy tales? Stories of olden times? Creatures out of dream? Creatures come out of time?

Silence, silence, silence, even while the voice spoke, saying: *So you may remember, we give you silence. Where we should be, but are not, there is silence.*

What was this listening? Attenuated, the sense stretching itself outward, begging for something to fill it? Feeling one's own eyes rattling in their sockets, twitching every way, seeking an out, an escape. Why were they here, shielded from the sky? Why was this stone all around them? Why were they not there, at the sea's edge, crawling out of that salty womb onto the shore in company with the creatures of their common birth?

'Lutha!'

'Nothing,' she cried again.

He shook her. 'Lutha.'

Lutha saw him then. Felt his violence transmitted to her own body as he ragged her to and fro, not gently.

'Leelson!' Urgently she called him, from great distance.

'Shhh,' he replied, eyes suddenly aware of some outside presence as he leaned against her, pressing her equally into himself and into the stone.

All of them were pressed into the stones, clinging to them, even Saluez, edging toward the crevices and cracks they'd made their own. A stupid place to choose when skies came down. As in a dream, they saw all the great stone slabs falling, obdurate shadows piercing reverie to become horrible reality, crushing them before they knew they were in danger. Little nutkins in the mighty vise of what? And yet, what other choice? They could be beneath the stone or beneath the sky, the vengeful sky, hearing that quiet!

'Listen,' Lutha whispered.

'No,' said Mitigan in a horrified voice.

'Don't,' cried Saluez. 'Don't listen.'

They were children afraid of ghosts, pulling up the blanket to cover their eyes, pulling themselves into the stone and huddling there. Even Leelson! Even Mitigan! Where is your courage, Fastigat? Where is your honor, Asenagi? Why are you huddled with the rest while this silence goes on and on and on.

Slither of scales upon stone; scutter of hairy legs, silk filament trailing the wind; hear in the silence what is not there. Cry, cry, cry, a bird who hungers; cry, cry, cry, a bird seeking her young, who will never be again. All is desert, all is dry, all is dead and gone, not even a memory. All that is left is a set of symbols, a list of bases, a pattern stored away. The machine knows them as the machine knows everything, dryly, without blood or breath, but humans do not know them at all!

Leely came drowsily naked out of some crack or crevice where he'd been sleeping, cast them a sidelong look, and went past them toward a tilted arch of starlit stone, a window onto the night, where he stood waving his hands.

Lutha didn't move. Lutha was lost among the animals. Oh, the colors of them. Oh, the sounds they make. The eyes of them, bright and quick and full of accusation. Who was Leely in the face of this ... this!

Too battered by sensation even to be curious, she watched open-mouthed as he turned, again, again, wearing his Leely face, swaying and waving, a familiar and aimless activity. Then his face took on a new expression. Not his usual quiet satisfaction. Not his hungry look or his chilly look or his sleepy look. Not any expression she had seen before. This was something else. A kind of wakefulness.

He opened his mouth very wide, his tongue quivering in the midst of that round, red hole, deep as an abyss his throat. He screamed a sound that went endlessly out into the world. Not any sound they had ever heard him make before. Not a sound any child should be capable of making, a sound that fled unmuted across the moorlands like the shadow of a cloud, sweeping across the world, south, away: a trumpet, a roar, a shriek, a cry, a whistle, a bellow, a blast ... They could almost watch it go!

Leelson grunted, 'By my manhood!'

Mitigan shook Lutha by the shoulder. 'What?'

She couldn't tell him. She didn't know!

And normal sound came back all at once, as though a finger had been snapped.

In the window Leely sucked his fingers, murmuring, 'Dananana.'

He had exorcised the ghosts. He had driven them away. What right had he to do that?

They breathed deep into oxygen-starved lungs.

'Lutha!' Leelson demanded. 'What is this?'

'Why ask me?' she cried. 'How would I know?'

'You're his mother!' he shouted.

'Bernesohn Famber was his mother and his father,' she yelled back. 'Bernesohn designed him. Too bad Bernesohn isn't around to give us the operating instructions.'

While babble broke out all around, she sat down and wept, feeling her face smart from the salt, feeling her nose swell and turn red, that familiar pain behind her breastbone like a swallowed stone. Obviously, Leelson hadn't told them what they'd figured out about Leely. Well, neither had she. They were both ... what? Ashamed of it? Probably. How can one tell friends and acquaintances that one's great passion, one's world-shaking romance is no more than a mating dance between ephemerids, that all one's achievements count to nothing in the face of a biological destiny hoicked up by a runaway Fastigat in a makeshift laboratory on a very minor planet!

She wept while Leelson explained, as Fastigats do, unemphatically but in great detail and with all possible inferences.

It would have bored anyone. It bored Lutha. He talked so long she tired of sniveling and began wiping the wetness from her face.

'But what is he?' Jiacare Lostre demanded.

'A virus,' said Leelson, without emotion. 'To all intents and purposes. Morphologically, he's human, born of a normal zygote that carries a lot of something else – something Ularian. He's a hybrid. He has enough brain to get along at the level of a ...'

'A chicken,' Lutha said bitterly, feeling a new gush of tears. There were no chickens left, but the word remained. One of those sorts of words that did remain.

'Something like that,' Leelson admitted.

'Whatever he's carrying, it gets around the Ularian immune system,' Snark supplied. 'I found disrupted cells in the dropped tentacles, and in the dying shaggy.'

Leelson nodded heavily. 'He's also carrying an agent or genetic program that promotes rapid healing in humans. It's in his saliva. Probably in his blood. Maybe he had to have that to retain human shape with all that Ularian stuff in him.'

'Or it was purposeful, so people would value him,' offered the ex-king. 'Maybe Bernesohn was looking ahead. He would want his ... virus to survive. He knew people would value something that could heal their ills.' He furrowed his brow, continuing in a doubtful voice: 'Of course, that would have depended upon people knowing about it.'

'He prob'ly meant 'em to know,' breathed Snark. 'Meant 'em to know about the whole business. He sure wouldn't depend on it bein' found out like this! By accident!'

Mitigan hoisted Leely high and presented his wounded arm, still festering and red.

'Dananana,' Leely caroled, giving Mitigan's arm several wet kisses.

'Me,' said Snark. The wound she'd sustained during the Kachis birthing was also inflamed. Leely kissed the bite marks. Lutha had seen dogs lick wounds like that, in old nature chips. She shook her head, ashamed. She had known about Leely's healing ability the day before. She should have told Snark. And Mitigan.

Saluez noticed her pain. She took Lutha's hand, peered into her eyes. 'Lutha. Lutha, sister.' Her eyes filled and Lutha turned away, unable to bear her compassion. By the Great Gauphin, Lutha didn't want anyone to share her feelings. Her feelings were her own, singular, unique!

Which was bosh. They were the world's woes, as Mama Jibia used to say. No matter what the world, the woes are the same. Pain and loss. Hope dimmed. Ambition quenched. Love becoming an unfunny joke on the lovers! Body saying aye; mind saying nay; now saying can; future saying can't.

Lutha felt Leelson reaching for her, and shook him off, surprising on his face a reflection of her own. He felt miserable. She'd planned his misery, but she hadn't realized she'd be in it with him.

And why should it be so upsetting? She'd guessed the biggest part of this. What had changed since then? Nothing, except the knowledge that she was as responsible as Leelson. Leely himself was as he had always been. Only her hopes had changed. Her hopes and whatever was out there at the edge of the world. The trembler. The world shaker.

She took Leely from Snark, settling him on her hip. It was time they went back to sleep. If they could sleep.

Leely patted her face, opened his dreadful mouth, and said quite clearly, 'Lutha Lutha Tallstaff Lutha sister mother love.'

It was a person's voice, totally unfamiliar, not a child's voice.

Silence. Shock. Indrawn breaths.

Leelson cleared his throat, a scritch like iron dragged on stone.

Leely turned, cocked his head, said, 'Leelson Leelson Famber damned Fastigat darling.'

No one even breathed.

Leely said, 'Saluez of the shadow. Snark love Laluzh. Mitigan Mitigan of the Asenagi.' He smiled. 'Exking exking of Kamir Jiacare Lostre. Leely baby Leely love Leely yourson myson.'

'He's naming things,' said Leelson in a hollow voice.

'Pee – peeeple,' said the ex-king, awed into virtual incoherence. 'People.'

Lutha had been holding Leely pressed against her, but now she felt it was safer to set him down.

'Lutha Tallstaff Lutha Lutha sister mother love,' he said, making a mirror likeness of her on the skin of his chest and belly. He showed her as she was, dressed in her gray-green overall.

'Why now?' cried Leelson in petulant, almost horrified surprise. 'Why *now!*'

'He's never been out among people before,' whispered Saluez. 'Not since he was a baby.'

It was true. From the time Leelson had left them, they'd lived almost alone. Those who came and went were seldom repeat visitors. Those who came to see Lutha often did not see Leely. Only since this trip began had Leely heard Lutha's name used by this one, that one. She recalled Leelson's outraged, 'You're his mother.' So now she was Lutha Tallstaff Lutha Lutha sister mother love.

'When he made the pictures back to the Rottens!' she exclaimed. 'That's when he made the connection. They have color titles. We have verbal ones.'

'That's a title?' Leelson bellowed at the top of his lungs. 'Leelson Leelson Famber damned Fastigat darling?'

'Hush,' she hissed, pointing through the tilted arch at the shaggies float-ing against the stars. 'Leelson, damn it, don't yell at me. It's not my fault; I didn't do it; I'm not responsible for it. Will everyone just please remember where we are and shut up.'

As they did quickly enough, for they felt once more that tremble in the core of the world, heard once more, though briefly, that flattened sound.

Even Leely was silent as Lutha sat down upon her blanket, cradling the child against her. He looked thoughtful. Mitigan and Leelson whispered together, but Lutha was too drained to care what they were talking about. Joy and hopelessness and fear were all fighting for supremacy. If something had harmed Leely as he had been, she would have grieved. But, oh, to be in this danger with him changed! Now if something happened to him! Her child, her son, if anything happened to him now!

'You always said he would talk,' Saluez reminded her.

Yes. She had. She had thought he would say Mommy and Daddy and the other things babies say. She had not thought he could tremble worlds with his voice.

All such thoughts were cut short. She saw Mitigan's head come up, alertly, swiveling as he listened, his hands going to his weapons belt. They all heard it then, a sound like rain, like a pouring of sand, an endless hissing. They twisted, searching for the source. ...

Which slid onto the sand of the cavern like a runnel of dark blood, scaled from its gaping mouth to the darkness in which its body was still hidden, serpent king, snake lord, mighty monster, thick through as Mitigan's body, and all around it, its children, its kindred, the small ones of its kind, striped and mottled and jewel-marked, sinuous and horrid.

'Out,' cried Mitigan, something very like panic in his voice. 'Out!'

They stumbled to their feet and ran, out and away, Saluez supported on either side by Lutha and Snark, Leely running beside his mother. Mitigan's voice shouted battle cries while Leelson and Jiacare urged him to run. They did run, with snakes all around them, striking from crevices, dropping from holes, slithering across their feet as they struggled on, bruising themselves on the jutting rocks, scraping themselves on the rough stones until they came out under the sky. Leelson erupted from the rock pile, dragging the ex-king behind him. He had thought to bring one of the survival packs with him, and a lamp.

'Mitigan?' cried Snark.

'Coming,' said Leelson, dragging the ex-king toward us. 'Here, Jiacare's been bitten!' Lutha stood stupidly, not realizing what he wanted.

'Leely,' Leelson cried. 'Come see the bite.'

The ex-king pulled up a trouser leg, displaying puncture wounds that seeped a yellowish ichor. The flesh around the wounds was green. 'I fell on it,' he said. 'I don't think it meant to bite. ...'

Leely ran to him, hugged the bitten leg, effectively tripping the ex-king, so that he fell heavily and was unable to get up. Leely kissed the bites, then hugged the ex-king once more.

'Jiacare Lostre, ex-King of Kamir,' cried Leely. 'Poor Jiacare!'

'Can you walk on it?' demanded Leelson, heaving Jiacare to his feet.

'If I have to.' He stood up, took one experimental step, and groaned.

'Mitigan!' demanded Snark once more.

'He's either coming or he's dead,' grated Leelson.

'Where are we going?' Jiacare smiled as he asked the question, a thin, fatalistic smile.

'Wherever we're allowed to go,' Leelson muttered.

Mitigan appeared at the entrance to the rockfall, staggering toward the others. His face and arms were covered with bites. 'Hard to kill,' he muttered. 'Oh, they're hard to kill.'

He fell. Leely looked at his wounds, then at Leelson. 'Dananana,' he said, uninterested.

Leelson thrust his fingers into Leely's mouth, then rubbed the wet fingers onto Mitigan's wounds. The assassin gasped, as though in sudden agony.

'Mitigan Mitigan of the Asenagi,' Leely said in a tone of disapproval. 'Mitigan fought the snakes.'

Where Mitigan had emerged from the rocks was now a darker shadow. They stared at it, trying to find in it the coils of a serpent, the twining shape of the snake. It wasn't a snake. Something deep inside them told them that. Snakes to flush them out, but something else to drive them.

Eyes reflected the light from the lamp Leelson carried. A wavering howl split the air.

'Wolves,' Lutha breathed. 'It's wolves.' How many times had she seen them, recreated in story, remembered in myth? How many times?

As though answering to their name, lithe forms spewed from the rock pile. Some of them loped up the slope toward the camp, others made a line to the north. The way was open south or west, but in no other direction. They were not all wolves. Some of them were other things, shamblers, gigglers, mutterers, throat growlers.

Mitigan stumbled to his feet. He and the ex-king staggered up the slope, the rest following. As they went the bitten men gained strength. They crested the ridge, walking almost normally, then stopped. Across the narrow valley the wolves had made a line barring the way to the south. The only open way was the valley, the crescent of gravel that was the beach. They were being forced toward the sea.

'Make a stand,' muttered Mitigan. 'Get into one of the storm caverns and make a stand.'

'No,' said Leelson. 'Let's just go along for the moment. See what's intended.'

Lutha stared blindly into the dark. Even Leely could not live in this place without food, without shelter. What was intended was eradication. What was intended was that not one of them should return to Alliance to tell men what they knew.

12

The stories of Old-earth are shared among the people of Old-earth. Even I, Saluez, can identify elephant and whale, ostrich and eagle, serpent and wolf, though they exist no longer. I know that they were and now are not, because of mankind. So, when I wakened under the stone on Perdur Alas to a terror not dreamed but real, I recognized the creatures bringing it upon us.

Snark and Lutha heaved me up, one on either side, and they supported me as we fled. Lutha seemed lost in some apocalyptic vision, concentrated on senses I did not share. Not so Snark. Nothing quenched her insatiable interest, or her avid commentary on each thing it touched.

'Old Tempter,' she said as we fled down the valley toward the beach. 'Old Tempter sent 'em. Wanted to be sure, he did, we knew what was coming. Righteous vengeance, that's what they're after!'

Her words rang like the gong by the House Without a Name, awaking dissonant echoes, evoking monsters! The Kachis had also been sent by the tempter. They, too, had been a cacophony of bestial noises and the gleam of fangs!

'You notice Mitigan?' Snark muttered. 'Mad! That man is so rageous he's about to kindle. Sure never figured he'd get beat by snakes! High-and-mighty Asenagi, with Leely spit all that's keeping him living. Has to be hard for a proud man!'

The fact that she could notice such things while we fled for our lives cut through my panic. If Snark could keep her senses during this wildness, then so could I. I concentrated all my thought and energy on calm, on focus, on breathing slowly, moving deliberately, on noticing what was happening.

It actually helped. It took me out of myself to look at the others, imagining what they felt. Mitigan, as Snark had said, was blazingly angry. So was Leelson, though probably for a different reason. Fastigats like to make sense out of what happens, but Leelson couldn't get beyond his Firster viewpoint to make sense of this! Jiacare Lostre wore a thin smile, like a seer who knows what is happening, perhaps, or someone who thinks it doesn't matter. Lutha, of course, wasn't with us at all. She stared into the distance like one ensorcelled, an inhabitant of some other world.

We halted on the beach, hemmed in on three sides by creatures, on the other by ocean. There we gasped, waiting for what would happen next. I drew the night air deep into my lungs, amazed at the feeling of it, the scent of it! Like the air of a new world! The wind came wildly fresh, with a keening mist and a bluster of cloud.

Snark leaned close against me, supporting either me or herself. Her face was ecstatic as she murmured, 'Oooh, they're lovely. Like flowing gold, snakes.'

She meant it! Inexplicably, she was enraptured!

She nudged me, pointing. 'And see the wolves – it's like I can see them better in the starlight than even in full sun. Look at their fur, Saluez! Soft as clouds, full and sleek. Teeth silver sharp in those laughing jaws. Eyes two smoky mirrors full of what ought to be. Oh, you can see Eden in those eyes! You can see a world stretching away, all green and misty! You can almost hear 'em, nose up, hollering the moon! They make me feel guilty, like Old Tempter meant 'em to, but they make me feel more than just that!'

Lutha came to herself abruptly. 'Is this your paradise?' she gasped. 'Are you finding it in the eyes of wolves?'

'Maybe so,' said Snark. 'Are you scared?'

'I'm past being scared,' Lutha replied with a shivery giggle, half-hysterical, that built into a spate of wild laughter, quickly hushed. 'Long past!'

Snark laughed with her. 'Me too. This is sort of mazy, isn't it? Like a dream where you're in deadly trouble, but you go along, kind of floating, and the thing coming after you is monstrous terrible; its eyes fall on you like a horrid light; but it's righteous! You know how it's going to come out and all you can hope is you'll wake up in time or it won't hurt too much. Like that.'

I saw new shapes among those surrounding us. Wolf and serpent, yes, but other creatures as well.

'Animals,' I said to Lutha, under my breath. 'What is it you've been muttering about animals?'

She hoisted Leely into her arms and stared at me over his head. 'For days, over and over, I've found myself thinking of animals. They pad through my brain at night; they howl in my ears and climb my flesh with sharp claws. Is it really animals, Saluez? Or is it the ultimate Ularian, pretending?'

I didn't know. It might be the big Ularian, the tempter of Breadh, but I'd have sworn the animals were real.

That interchange was all we had time for. One wolf howled, then another. Something shadowy and immense growled deep in its swollen throat; something shambling giggled; we were stalked by ramified darkness, full of eyes. They pushed us toward the sea. Crawlers and trotters came after, chunky creatures, close to the ground, others sleek and thin, each bone showing through their dappled hides, strung with muscles like taut cable. Sinuous tails whipped; eyes lit like lanterns; tongues licked at jaws with a rasping sound, as at our bones, scraping them clean!

573

We were not driven into the waves, but onto the path at the foot of the cliffs. The creatures behind us kept their distance, not pursuing us closely enough to make us run, only closely enough to make us move. There was no space to walk abreast as we went southward along the sea. Mitigan was first, carrying the lamp, then the ex-king, with Lutha carrying Leely after him. I came next, then Snark, then Leelson. Only the waves spoke as we went, but when we came around the first curve, we heard howls and growls and hisses from the beach behind us, a cacophonous laughter, as though someone had told a funny story. No doubt who the joke was on.

From behind me, Snark announced, 'There's caves along here. Sea caverns. We're headed where you folks come out, where the shaggies come out.'

'Toward the vortex entries?' Lutha asked in a far-off, toneless voice. 'Does it mean to herd us into the vortex again?'

Leelson ignored her question. 'Tide's going out just now,' he muttered. 'It won't go out forever. Do they – does it mean for us to drown?'

'Probably one or the other,' said the ex-king, turning to glance at us over his shoulder. 'If I were they, it, I'd want to kill us without touching us. Touching us – at least touching Leely – seems to be fatal.'

Though I hadn't seen any of the creatures come onto the path behind us, I felt there was something there, following us. I had no sense that we were escaping. We were only moving in nightmare, not waking from it. Perhaps fortunately, we weren't able to get into a panic over it, for our footing required complete concentration. The sea shelf was narrow, uneven, littered with slippery clumps of sea grass and shells and stones that rolled beneath our feet. And, of course, Leelson was right about the tide. When it came in, the water would come up to the path.

Snark was thinking along the same lines. 'Hey, Saluez? Maybe there'll be something in it, somethin' swimming there under the rub and ruckle of the sea. Something else we'd know from olden times. Sharks maybe?'

I was spared the possibility of reply.

'Someone ahead,' cried Mitigan. He stopped, holding his lamp high to throw light on the way ahead. 'I hear someone.'

We all heard it then, a woeful sound. It sounded almost familiar to me, and I remembered when we fell into the vortex. Jiacare had been right behind me, but after him had come at least three others. As we stumbled around the next curve the sound came louder, a solitary weeping over the plaint of the sea, where it fingered in, pestering the cliffs.

'It's Poracious Luv,' said Lutha.

It was she, huddled upon the path, her clothing in tatters, a muddy heap lying beside her.

'Dirty as a street rat,' Snark murmured from behind me. 'Not a high-muck-a-muck now. Just a fat old woman crying.'

As she was, next to the limp sprawl of the old man. So were the mightiest brought to nothing.

'The Procurator,' I said. 'That's the tabard he was wearing at Tahs-uppi.'

The path was too narrow to get to him, but Mitigan scrambled down onto the slippery seaside stones to get a look.

'Dead,' he said in an angry, wild-sounding voice. 'Dead for some time.'

Leelson said hard words, striking his forehead with his open hand.

Snark whispered, 'All this time they been depending on the Procurator and Poracious Luv to come to the rescue! Now they know it's not gonna happen!'

As was his custom, and as though we were unable to draw the same inference, Leelson spelled it out for us.

'Of all those who knew we had gone through the omphalos, only your colleague remains, Mitigan. He and the songfathers.'

The songfathers would do us no good. It would be easier for a gaufer to go through the eye of a needle than a songfather to admit to telling lies.

'There's my recorder,' cried Snark. 'Somebody's looking at my recorder!'

Poracious raised her head and stared at the ex-king. He began to laugh and so did she, neither of them truly amused.

'By Lord Fathom,' he said hopelessly. 'We rely on Thosby Anent.'

She repeated the name as though it were an obscenity. 'Old Thosby! He had a watchword. What was it?'

'Vigilance,' said Lutha. 'Vigilance was his watchword. Chosen more for its brave sound, I'd wager, than for its requirement of diligence.'

Snark was as puzzled by this exchange as I was, but no one took time to explain it. Mitigan and the ex-king hoisted Poracious to her feet, and we went on, stepping over the body of the Procurator. We could not carry him with us.

'Poor old man,' muttered Snark. 'All his excitements is over! He wasn't such a bad old boss.'

We said nothing after that as we struggled endlessly on. Each step became harder. There was pain in my belly, pain in my groin. I felt wetness seeping down my thighs. I wept out of weakness and weariness, wiping ineffectually at the tears. I let myself lapse into dream, making up visions, placing myself back on Dinadh, sitting with Shalumn beside the fire, holding her hand in mine while our children slept warm in the hive.

The vision was ended when I bumped against Lutha, almost knocking her down. Our progress was halted. The sky had lightened. Before us, across yet another of the ramified inlets we had stumbled along through the night, a cliff ran seaward to thrust its rocky jaw into the waves. It looked no different from the dozens of others we had passed, but this particular protrusion seemed to be special. Mitigan was gesturing with the lantern and calling Snark to look where we were.

'We sure didn't get much forrader,' snorted Snark as she climbed around me. 'That's my own particular tree up there on the rim. All around here's the caves the shaggies come out of.'

When she reached Mitigan's side, they mumbled together. I saw her wave her fist at him, and she cried, 'There's food up there. There's blankets and a stove. There's stuff we need.'

Mitigan's scowl was plain in the light of the lantern. 'I can climb it,' he admitted.

In the predawn grayness, we could see a faint shadow trail that laddered across the cliff face. Handholds, perhaps. Foot holes. Something arduous and impossible for any normal being.

'You'll never get me up there,' said Poracious Luv.

'We don't need to get you up there,' Snark said. 'When me and Mitigan can get up there, we'll lower the stuff down.'

'The tide's coming in,' said Leelson wearily.

'There's cover,' replied Mitigan irritably, pointing across the narrow finger of sea at the cliff wall opposite. There was a gap there, a black hole at the top of a rockfall, one layer atop another, almost like a wide flight of giant stairs.

No one moved. We merely stood, staring. Like gaufers, I thought.

'It's above the tide line,' Snark said impatiently, her tone urging us onward. 'Get on! The seaweed tangles don't go but halfway to the cave door. It's as safe and dry as anyplace we're going to come to.'

'I might manage that,' said Poracious in an uncertain voice. She was limping badly, footsore from her many long days on the cliff path. Nonetheless, it was she who led us toward the gap, all but Snark and Mitigan. By the time we'd staggered around the cove and come to the cavern, we could see them far above, like spiders clinging to the cliff face. Day was coming. If there was something following us along the path, we would soon be able to see it.

It was not long before Mitigan came swarming down a rope and Snark began lowering bundles. The last thing down the cliff was a large jar, not unlike some of the pottery made in Dinadhi hives, followed by Snark herself. When she arrived at the bottom, she picked the jar up tenderly and carried it into our cavern before she brought anything else.

'My mother's bone jar,' she said to me, noting my curious look. 'Likely I'm not going back up there. Likely there's room enough in there for me, too.'

Lutha looked up, startled. I kept my own face expressionless, though I knew our thoughts were the same. It was unlikely there would be anyone left to put our bones anywhere in particular. We, like the Procurator, would probably be washed by waves, dismembered by sea creatures, dispersed by the tides.

Snark brought us blankets and one of the little stoves, which gave us a welcome warmth and light. We huddled around it, all but Mitigan, who remained at the entrance to keep watch for whatever was coming. Something was, we all knew that, and all our eyes shifted to the entrance, then away, then to the entrance again. All we saw was the warrior sharpening his blades, a vague silhouette against the gray spread of a chilly dawn.

Poracious Luv subsided onto the sand with a moan of exhaustion, her head on her knees. I thought she'd fallen asleep, but after a moment she lifted her head and said plaintively, 'I wonder if Behemoth is out there, waiting. ...'

Lutha glanced at the opening, as though someone had sounded an alarm. 'Behemoth,' she said in a wondering voice. 'An odd word for you to use, Poracious.'

'Why so?' asked the older woman. 'A behemoth is a great beast, isn't it? An old word for some kind of hugeness that lived a long time ago?'

Lutha nodded. 'It's an old word, yes.'

It was a word I'd heard somewhere. 'Is it a real word? I mean, does it mean something real?'

Lutha nodded. 'It isn't what it means so much as what it denotes. It means beasts, actually. Plural. But it conveys something more than a mere animal. The connotations are of intractable mightiness, of inexorability and fatefulness.'

Poracious nodded slowly as she slumped the heavy lines of her body seeming to me inexpressibly weary and dejected.

'Fatefulness,' she said. 'I said the same to the old Proc while the world shook around us. That was after we'd had the vision, you see.'

Lutha's eyes came back to us. She raised her eyebrows.

'I say vision, though maybe it was only old minds playing tricks on old bodies. The old Proc and me, we'd stopped a bit, to rest. He was gray, holding his arm across him as though it hurt. We'd found this place where we could sit. ... So, we were looking out to sea, and suddenly there was an ark, a great primitive sort of boat, rocking against a wrack of cloud, rain slanting across it like a curtain, wind driving it. It was made out of wood, don't you know. We could see the marks of tools on the sides, and it was loaded with animals ... Well, you know the old story, only this was real! And one of the animals put back its head and howled words! "Beware," it cried. "Was it not commanded that each kind should be saved?"'

Leelson had been listening. Now he frowned down his nose at Poracious, slowly shaking his head. Thus did Fastigats reject the fanciful. Poracious took no notice of him.

Jiacare, on the other hand, was intrigued. 'The ark story is from an ancient literature, isn't it? What was the book called?'

'It was called, simply, the Book,' Leelson said in his usual didactic manner. 'It was supplanted by the doctrines of Firstism in the late twentieth and early twenty-first centuries of the pre-dispersion era.'

He rose, brushed himself off, then went to join Mitigan at the cave entrance.

The ex-king nudged Poracious. 'Did you see anything else in your vision?'

She shook her head. 'Leelson thinks I am hallucinating, but I did see it, and I heard the voice so very clearly.' She sighed, dropping her head once more. 'Of course, I hadn't eaten for a long time, and we'd been walking endlessly. I know people who are very hungry and tired can see things. ...'

Her voice trailed off as though she'd lost the strength to speak.

Snark said, 'Suppose Firsters are wrong. Suppose the universe was made for all kinds of creatures.' She took Lutha's hand and gripped it. 'Suppose, Lutha!'

'I don't know,' Lutha murmured. 'Instinctively, it seems to me Firstism is illogical, but even now it's hard for me to imagine living with creatures. There are no creatures on Central. In my whole life I've only seen two or three other kinds of creatures. Gaufers. And the cats ...'

'You must have seen birds in Simidi-ala,' I said. 'And we had cornrats in the hive. And little fishes in the streams. You must have seen them!'

'Perhaps I did. I don't remember. Of course, I've seen Kachis and shaggies and Rottens. Are they animals?'

Poracious sighed. 'Isn't everything alive either a plant, a human, or an animal?' She rubbed at her head, dragging her hair up in dirty spikes. 'When I was a child, there were still a few animals on my home planet. I remember horses. I remember—'

'Horses,' said Jiacare Lostre. 'Oh, weren't horses wonderful? So shiny, so majestic, the way their necks arched, the way they pranced, high and proud. I remember seeing one running across a pasture, tail high, with her little one running beside her. Oh, on Kamir, we still had horses in my father's time. And dogs. We used to ride. ...'

His voice faded into nostalgic silence. Poracious Luv drew her blanket more tightly around her, extending one hand from this cocoon to stroke the jar Snark had brought down from her cave. She followed the design with her fingers, asking, 'Who are these?'

She was pointing at curvilinear patterns that seemed to make eyes and noses and mouths.

Snark replied, 'Father Endless and Mother Darkness. And the carriers of souls.'

'They have not human faces,' Poracious commented. 'Why is that?'

'They are mother and father of all things,' I whispered. 'Why should they have human faces?'

'Did your tempter have a human face?' Poracious asked Snark.

Snark cast a look over her shoulder, to be sure Leelson and Mitigan were still some distance away, before saying, 'The songfathers claimed the Gracious One was male and had a human face and a male ... body. Considering how the songfathers lied about other stuff, maybe it's just a story they made up.'

Poracious moved slightly, looking at the jar from another angle. 'Most gods of most worlds have human faces.'

'Because men make them in their image,' Lutha remarked, somewhat bitterly. 'To grant mankind license to do what we would do anyway.' Her eyes went back to the entrance and she gasped abruptly.

Snark followed her gaze. The two cats had somehow sneaked by the watchmen. They stood well inside the chamber, crying at us as they rubbed themselves against the stones. Whatever we might have expected, it was not cats. Snark went at once to find a food packet among the store she and Mitigan had lowered from above, and while she opened it the animals arched their backs and wound in and out between her legs. Mitigan and Leelson joined us by the stove, and we all watched while the animals ate. From Leelson's expression, I think he was expecting the cats to speak or go up in a puff of smoke. No one said anything at all until they had finished and departed.

Mitigan snarled, 'Maybe they're spies. For whatever's out there.' He stalked back to the entry.

Leelson joined him, saying, 'What *is* out there? And what's it waiting for?'

'Poracious says it's Behemoth,' said Snark. 'Whatever it is, it's more like the cats than it's like us.'

'How?' Poracious demanded. 'How like.'

'It's part of something,' Snark replied.

'So are we!' Mitigan asserted angrily.

She shook her head at him. 'No. Not on any homo-normed world. On Central, we didn't depend on anything, and nothing depended on us! We didn't respect anything, and nothing respected us. On natural worlds, life makes a loop. Birth and life and death are all parts of it, and all the parts respect one another. There's no top or bottom. There's just this ... honorable dependency. But on homo-normed worlds, no flesh lives but man-flesh.'

'Because we don't need animals!' Leelson asserted angrily.

'You say we don't,' Lutha protested. 'But one could argue they need themselves. One could argue that their creator may have purposes for them.'

'Do you have any idea how ridiculous that sounds?' He waved a forefinger in her face. 'We can be their creator. We have specifications for every species stored away. They can be reanimated anytime.'

Snark jeered, 'Stored away? Like old chairs, in a cellar some-wheres? Would that satisfy you, Leelson Famber? Or you, Mitigan. Not living, not breathing, not moving. Just a pattern, in storage. Suppose before they did it to you, they told you, "Don't worry. We can reanimate you anytime." How'd you feel about that?'

'Humans are not animals,' Mitigan said angrily. 'You can't compare them. The universe was made for man.'

'So you say,' Snark crowed, with an outrageous snicker. 'Now maybe whatever's out there is remaking the universe. Repopulating it, anyhow.'

'Snark ...' Lutha murmured warningly.

Mitigan's hands twitched toward his weapons; his eyes were hard and slitted. Snark wasn't noticing, or she didn't care.

'Well, yeah, but look! Look at this world. Look how it's set up. Doesn't it look like a nursery? Some place all clean and ready to multiply life on, and lots of it?'

'You're saying the world is *it*-normed?' asked Leelson, incredulously. '*Shaggy*-normed. *Rotten*-normed.' He was almost as angry as Mitigan.

'That's it!' she crowed, a rapscallion, happily infuriating larger and quite dangerous opponents. 'Maybe this world is Ularian-normed! Wouldn't that be a joke on us?'

Mitigan and Leelson were not amused. Before she could say anything else, the ex-king put his hand on Snark's shoulder, calming her, drawing her away. There was enough danger, his eyes said, without causing more among ourselves.

I sat down beside Lutha and Leely. The boy was busy drawing in the sand, and she watched him, her thoughts written on her face. They were old thoughts, ones she had spoken of: love warring with pain, pain warring with love. Leely was uncanny, a changeling, yet flesh of her flesh, fruit of her love for Leelson – which was perhaps something else, not love at all. Leely smiled meltingly up at her. She reached out, and he crawled into her lap to curl up there, playing with her hair. His mouth made silent words. He was trying names for things, silently working them out.

Poracious reached over and tapped me. 'Look,' she said, pointing out toward the sky. It took me a moment to realize that day had come and the sun shone in vast emptiness. The night before, the sky had been full of shaggies. Now there were none.

'Where'd they go?' Snark demanded.

We went to the cavern opening and looked out. No shaggies. No Rottens.

'The sea!' Leelson exclaimed.

It was alive with swimming things. Great fishy creatures, huge as houses. Monstrous shelled things. Eels that squirmed among the rocks along the shore. Various and multiple, fecund and furious, life beat upon the shores of Perdur Alas. We were so awestruck we did not even see the enormous tentacle that reared out of the water and lashed toward us, missing us by a finger!

We scrambled back, getting out of the way. I had felt this same emotion at the Nodders, when I had known they were capable of killing us easily and quickly, with no one to see or mourn or care. So, too, this great welter of living things could drag us down and drown us, leaving no trace. We were not masters here! This world was not made for man!

'Eagles,' said Poracious.

We craned our necks to watch eagles for a while. They were as unexpected and marvelous as the other creatures, soaring in splendid spirals against the cloudless sky. Poracious stuttered and muttered, trying to attach a name to every living thing she saw, but Lutha said not a word.

'Where did they come from?' Leelson cried.

'The shaggies went,' said the ex-king. 'The animals came.'

I turned to Lutha, the question in my face.

She shrugged. 'I agree with him. The shaggies bred all kinds of creatures. This life is mutable. It will be what its maker wills.'

'What the hell is "its maker" playing at!' demanded Leelson, outraged.

We felt the earth shake, just a little, like a heavy footstep nearby. Poracious put her head on her knees and shuddered. Leelson pointed out into the sea, far, far, where the sky came down on the horizon. An island there, which had not been there before. It became larger while we watched.

'What's it doing?' demanded Mitigan in a tone almost as furious as Leelson's had been.

Lutha remarked. 'Why so offended, Mitigan? You weren't this offended by the shaggies or by the Rottens.'

'Animals,' he said. 'Why bother being offended at animals?'

'So what's coming out there isn't an animal?'

He scalded her with a look, before turning back to watch the blob grow larger. It had horns on top. Even at this great distance it was ineluctable, numinous, but familiar!

Lutha had the same idea. 'Did you see Nodders on your way to Tahs-uppi?' she asked Mitigan.

'We climbed around them,' he grated. 'Such things have no right to be.'

The ex-king smiled. In some terrible, fatalistic way, he was enjoying himself. 'Perhaps this creature feels it has every right to be alive and moving. Perhaps it has judged our storage vaults and found them wanting. Perhaps it has some more immediate destiny to attend to.'

'We will soon know,' said I, from my position atop a boulder. 'It's coming nearer.'

It was very tall. The head was massive. The horns on top showed clearly. This was the reality of which the Nodders were only a symbol. This, what-ever this was – had the same proportion of height to horned top, to the great bulk of the nodding head. I had no time to consider the effect, for sound changed, the world shuddered, a peculiarly dreamy sensation overtook me, as though all happenings were inevitable and I did not greatly care.

Leely pushed past me and went out of the cavern. He plopped down on a shelf of wave-rounded pebbles and stared outward, his lips making silent words.

'By all that's holy,' breathed Poracious. 'Look, low down, against the water.'

We saw. Light. Shadow on one side, shadow on the other, shadow above, and light under, between.

'Legs,' I told them in my dreamy, languorous voice. 'We only saw its upper part before. Now we are seeing between its legs.'

The Nodders had been only busts, then? Only heads and necks of Behemoth? There was more to the creature than that? Well, yes, my dreaming mind assented. Well, yes. Time went on. Eventually we saw its wings, which had until then been folded along its back. Eventually we saw its marvelous face, its wondrous eyes, its great adamantine teeth.

It stopped when the ocean was no deeper than its knees. Whales leapt around its legs. Gyring eagles made its aureole, and the wind of its breath pushed us to and fro, like little flags.

'I've seen it before,' whispered Poracious. 'Somewhere.'

'Ancient earth,' Lutha replied. 'Was it Babylon? Was it Ur? Mighty winged creatures were carved upon its walls.'

'Winged cattle,' said Poracious. 'But that is mythology.'

'This is not myth.' The ex-king smiled. 'And this is no kind of cattle.'

Lutha clung to Poracious as she backed into the cave, they two pulling me with them. Anything else was past doing. Past believing. Past thinking on. We were ants, crawlers between the hairs of immensity.

Leelson dragged Lutha into his arms and held her close. I saw sweat on his face. I saw fear.

'Come forth,' said a voice out of the whirlwind.

There was no place to hide. Stones shattered into powder. The cliff danced. Great boulders skittered through the cavern roof and bounced between us, close as a hair!

Lutha grabbed me by the arm and dragged me back against the wall, but it did no good. Dust rose from the floor in clouds, boiling upward, threatening to smother us in stone ash.

'We must go out,' I cried at them. 'We can't stay under here.' I broke away from them and ran. Lutha came after me. We stopped in the entrance. Leely and the ex-king hadn't moved when the rest of us had retreated. Leely lay where he'd been before. The ex-king clung to a stony pillar, his back to us, staring up at the great face that floated above us like a thundercloud.

The head bent; a mighty hooved forefoot withdrew from the sea, rivers running from its fetlock, alive with silver fishes. The foot stamped down.

The world shook to its roots.

'Come forth,' said the voice once more.

There was no denying that voice. There was no hiding from it. All of us shambled out into the open air, where we stood like drunken, tethered creatures, unable to move unless the voice commanded us.

We didn't have to move. It came to us, jarring the world with every step. We fell and got up. It took another step. We fell again, and got up. We leaned together, like floppy dolls, holding each other erect. Leely lay on the ground where he had stayed all along, waving his hands, saying nothing, nothing at all, his eyes fastened on that which came.

Beyond the hugeness was a sky full of birds, a million pairs of beating wings, a whirl of white terns, a swerve of black-backed puffins, a spiral of silver gulls rising on the wind. I knew their names. They all had names. Before each mighty foreleg, a bow wave of life rushed upon the shore to wriggle, to stride, to fly, to crawl. I tasted a sweetness of mown grass and a salt-clean tang of the ocean wind.

In the end, we stayed on our knees, unable to get up again.

'Is this your tempter?' Leelson asked me, through trembling lips.

The stories had not said it was so huge. The stories had said it was male. This was not male. It smelled like flowers and spices and fragrant smoke. It tasted of ... marvel. It wore a high crown. It spoke to us in thunder.

'Will you go home again?' it asked. 'Will you go to your proper place? To Dinadh, where I had placed you?'

I saw Lutha's head move. Nod, nod. There was Leelson, nodding. Mitigan nodding. I felt what they felt. How tempting to go home once more. To Dinadh. To the winding canyons. To the sweet songs of the songfathers.

'Will you go home again?'

Would I go home again? To the lies the songfathers told? To the pain of the House Without a Name? To that terrible destiny for my daughters? To connivance at that evil by my sons? To sell truth and wisdom short in order to buy the false hope of immortality?

Somehow I got to my feet.

'No,' I cried. My voice was the cry of a small bird against that mighty thunder. Still I cried, 'No. I will not!'

'Not me, neither!' trumpeted Snark, as though my words had wakened an echo in her.

I felt Lutha's eyes, and Poracious's. They didn't understand. Ah, but they hadn't known the House Without a Name. Their wombs had not held what mine had held.

The mighty head bent above us like a cloud descending.

'You were given worlds to share,' it whispered in a voice like an avalanche. 'But you would not share. You were given life to treasure, but you did not treasure. You counted your own lives holy and all other lives expendable. All my creations you have subverted, all my wonders lost and slaughtered and betrayed. I made a garden to receive you. To make clear my intention, I set my creatures around you to be your companions; you have made of your habitation a termite mound, and of that garden a desolation!

'So now I have made your world suitable, a place where you can serve my creation. What more do you deserve than that?'

I couldn't answer. There was no answer.

'Now I have drawn a bowstring around all mankind, and in the fullness of time, I shall leash him with it. He who will not share shall serve instead.

'Will you go to the place I have allotted you?'

Somehow I kept upright. 'No,' I cried, my voice breaking. 'Mankind deserves no more, but this woman would rather die, knowing the truth, than go back to live that lie! I choose truth! We are not immortal. My mother wasn't immortal. She died. She did not eat my face; she died!'

The face faded. For a moment it was not there. The place it had been was blank. Then the earth shook again mightily, tumbling us about, and a face returned, a lion's face, an eagle's face, a face of leaves, of fruits, of fishes, a woman's face, terrible and pitying. I knew that face. A mother's face!

Leely was up, running toward the sea, the rocks, the tidal pools, the squirming eels, the tentacles, the quivering, hammered surface of the sea, toward the great creature as he made the same noise he had made that other time: the scream, the command, the roar, the whatever it was! And the ex-king went after him, calling out some wordless warning, trying to catch him, trying to get him back.

Too late! Too slow! The great head bent down. It was coming at Leely, but the king got in the way so it caught him first. Oh, he never made a sound, not a sound. I heard him crush between those teeth and I heard the soft sound of his body hitting the stones. The huge head tossed, making a great gust of wind, a buffet that knocked us all away as it withdrew with the child!

It crushed him. He screamed. It drew him up. Lutha went past me like a wind. She leapt. I ran, I jumped. Snark was beside me, even Poracious, all of us, jumping, trying to reach Leely where he hung between those mighty jaws, between those great teeth, screaming all the way.

'Lutha Lutha Tallstaff Lutha sister mother love!' he cried, a terrified voice, a voice like every child who ever was abused or frightened.

'If you choose truth, will you live by it?' cried the Great Beast. 'Reflect!'

Blood rained around us. An arm. A leg. Oh, by all the gods of man, by all merciful deities, a baby, a child, falling around us, torn into bits ...

Lutha screamed as though rent apart, a sound of such pure and utter pain that it pierced us all. Leelson seized her and pressed her face against his chest so she wouldn't see, so she wouldn't hear! Oh, I wished I hadn't seen Leely's blood on its jaws, on the ringlets of its mane. Leely's blood on the stone. Leely's blood falling on the raised knee, the mighty foot that came down and down and down, to shake us like dice in a cup and cast us away into utter darkness. I wished I hadn't seen, but I could not do as it commanded.

We came to ourselves after a time. A day. A moment. Who knows? We crawled into our cavern, dragging Lutha, who lived, and the king, who did not. Him we rolled in blankets against the back wall. Her we put near the warmth of the stove, and I held her head in my lap while I wiped bright blood from her forehead where she had fallen against the stone. Snark was beside me, her hand in her pocket. I knew she held a weapon. Like her, I watched Mitigan and Leelson where they raged in a corner, not at one another. Now they were allies in this matter. Now Snark was their enemy, I was their enemy. We had refused the bargain. We had denied the word of the tempter.

Lutha moaned.

'Don't leave him like that!' she whispered at me. 'Oh, don't leave him like that. Leely-baby.'

I hushed her.

'My baby.'

Oh, yes. Baby. All our babies. All our wealth of babies that we had worshiped more than life itself.

'Nothing there,' whispered Snark, shaking her gently. 'Listen, Lutha. Maybe it wasn't real! We got Jiacare's body, but there was nothing there but him. I looked ever'where.'

I hadn't seen her go out, but she wouldn't lie. Not Snark.

'But there was blood,' Lutha cried. 'Blood falling . . .'

'Not even blood. Me and Poracious've looked real careful, over and over again. There's no blood.'

'Where did Behemoth go?'

Snark shrugged, looking at me.

'I don't know,' I said. 'I'm not sure. If I had to guess, I'd say it's still there. It hasn't gone anywhere.'

'I thought it went down into the waves,' said Poracious in a little-girl voice. 'I thought I saw it go there. We can't see under the water.'

'We couldn't see it now if it was right outside,' Snark said. 'It's getting dark.'

She was right. The day had gone as in an instant while we cowered.

'Was it also the tempter?' Poracious whispered to me.

'I believe it was,' I told her.

'Your ultimate Ularian,' said Leelson from the shadows.

'That's not who it is,' whispered Lutha. 'Why can't you see who it really is?'

'If it's Ularian, we'd taste it,' Poracious objected.

'No,' Lutha whispered again. 'That was for us. It is disgusted with us. It is simply disgusted!'

Poracious stared at her as though she were crazy. 'What are you saying?' she demanded querulously. 'I don't know what you're talking about.'

Lutha closed her eyes, refusing to answer. Her face was agonized. I remembered our talk, on that other world, the night before we came to the omphalos. She had spoken of the guilt she had felt when she thought Leely was lost among the Nodders, wondering if she would grieve. Now he was lost, utterly, and she grieved. I held her, rocking back and forth, unable to forget that dreadful rending.

'Why?' cried Poracious. 'Oh, why …?'

Yes. Why. I stopped listening to the others. They went on talking, mostly Leelson and Mitigan, asking each other questions that neither could answer: What might we do to help ourselves? Should we stay where we were or go elsewhere?

After hacking each alternative to death, they decided to stay where we were, a simple decision considering that none of us was in any condition to do anything else.

And Lutha lay in my lap, hurting. Grief is not only in the mind. A spirit does not agonize in separate space. It takes the body with it!

'He called my name,' she wept. 'Oh, Saluez! He called my name!'

Eventually she wept herself into exhaustion. Despite everything, all our capacity for wonder or outrage or grief wore itself out. No one had the energy to weep another tear, to ask another unanswerable question. I made tea. Snark brought me some herbs to put in it, soothing things, she said. Her own face was wet and weary, but when I offered a cup, she would not take it. She would keep watch, she said, though what good watching could do she did not say.

In the night I heard Lutha moving. I said her name. She mumbled something about a stone in her bed. In a moment she was quiet again.

Gray light came and I woke. Around me on the sand the others lay in blanketed hummocks, Snark among them. Evidently she had decided it would do no good to keep watch. Against the far wall, another hummock showed where the ex-King of Kamir had been laid. Beside me, Lutha moved uncomfortably, whining again about the stone beneath her.

Quietly, thinking to ease her, I reached under her covering to remove what troubled her, encountering instead a warm softness, not Lutha, something else alive.

My first thought was the cats. I had never felt a cat, but presumably a cat would feel soft and warm and alive. Then I had a less pleasant thought, something to do with the serpents that had driven us from our rock pile.

Shuddering, I drew it away from Lutha's side, waking her. Her eyes came open as I held the thing at arm's length, thrust it into the light. ...

And dropped it as Lutha screamed, a sound that might have waked the bones in Snark's jar. It waked all those around us, who within moments were babbling as wildly as I.

It was Leely! Leely, the size of my foot! Leely no bigger than a small cat, a whole Leely in miniature, exactly like himself but tiny, tiny.

Mitigan cursed, brushing his hands across his blanket, bowling another Leely onto the sand. Two Leelies, three, four. A dozen Leelies from among our blankets, all piping in reedlike voices, 'Dananana.'

Poracious held Lutha while she came apart. I, too, felt the seams between reality and madness fail, felt myself rip into pieces, then saw all the pieces, a row of them on the edge of a precipice, teetering into hysteria, ready to tumble!

'Lutha!' Leelson, who had taken Poracious's place. 'Lutha, Saluez, think! It's all right. It's all right!'

There was Snark beside the stove, holding out crackers to the Leelies. There were dozens of them. Some no larger than my thumb.

What was all right? This? This was all right?

'It's the healing,' Leelson shouted at us, slapping Lutha gently to get her attention. 'It's regenerative, that's all. A whole organism from any fragment. Lutha. It's all right.'

'It's not,' she howled. 'It's not all right.'

Several of the Leelies came running across the sand to stand pulling at Lutha's trousers, caroling, 'Dananana,' over and over, then running back to the others to make a bird twitter of tiny voices, among which we heard, 'Lutha Lutha mother love.'

I think perhaps Lutha fainted. Or perhaps she simply abdicated responsibility for living. She let go, fell down, and stopped, quit even being aware that life was going on around her, ignoring all our attempts to arouse her.

Leelson said, 'Let her alone.'

'Good. Let me alone,' she agreed in a far-off voice.

We did let her alone. The Leelies didn't. They liked her. She was their Lutha Lutha mother love. They liked me. I was their Saluez of the shadow. They wandered all over both of us, like tiny explorers setting out across a new land, while I sat there, my hands twitching as I tried to decide whether to pick them off or let them be. Hysterically, I told myself to await the jab of a flag driven into my thigh, a voice claiming this new continent!

Under her breath, Lutha was counting. She stopped at the count of one hundred ten.

'One hundred ten?' I asked.

'That's how many of them I've counted,' she said in a high, cracked voice. 'One hundred ten.'

More had come in from among the stones. The smallest ones were half the size of my little finger. The largest was three times the size of the one I had found first. I found myself saying, that one is leg-sized. That one is arm-sized. That one grew out of a few drops of blood. They clustered around us like grapes, dangling from Lutha like pendant fruit, eager, joyous. They felt no pain. They knew no fear. They had no worry about what had happened to him, them. It didn't matter what had happened to him, them, or how they had come to be.

Lutha said brokenly, 'God, what kind of mind could have designed such a thing!'

After a time they seemed to find new centers for their attention. A dozen broke away to cluster around a slightly larger one, and that group wandered off. Then, gradually, another dozen, or a score. The groups wavered across the floor, disappearing into holes, reappearing again, vanishing at last. Finally there was only one left. The largest one.

'This is how big he was when he was born,' raved Lutha, 'this big. Just this big. The same size ...'

Leelson sat down beside her, his face very white. 'Are you all right?'

'I suppose,' she said.

'You understand what's happened here.'

Her face twisted. I knew she was cursing him, cursing all Fastigats who would not assume anything, who had to spell everything out, letter by letter. Still, she shook herself, gripped her hands tightly together, and answered his stupid question with reasonable self-control.

'I understand it intellectually, Leelson. Not in any other way. I will never understand in any other way.'

'It might help if you consider that ... thing that tore him apart. It's in for a surprise, isn't it?'

She cast me one incredulous glance, then closed her eyes and refused to speak.

'It's the big one, Lutha. The prime Ularian. The chief Rotten. And whatever venom Leely spreads, that creature is now awash in it.'

Laughter welled uncontrollably from her throat. She roared. 'You're such a fool!'

He drew away, deeply offended.

'You Firsters! Suppose your Firster god came calling on you. When he arrived, would you call him a Ularian? Would you expect him to resemble you even in your frailties? Would you expect him to catch your cold. To get a bellyache? To sneeze?'

He was rigid, pale, not following her.

She whispered. 'You would expect God to be above all that, no? So, if a deity appears who is deity not only of man but of *all* living things, will you really expect it to die from mange or distemper or an attack of the Leelies?'

He still didn't understand.

'Bernesohn didn't understand what's really happening any more than you do.'

'What are you saying?' he grated. 'What do you know that I do not?'

She glared at him. 'There is life in Hermes Sector, Leelson. Life breeding here. Life that uses humans as incubators, infinite, wonderful life. Life for old planets that man has ruined and left barren behind him. As mankind seems always to do, we have stumbled into it and contaminated the process, for which we will be punished.'

'No!' he said hoarsely, reaching for her. 'No.'

She jerked herself away from him. 'And your ultimate Ularian is not merely some alien life-form! It is Behemoth. Creation made manifest. Primordial life. Great Beast. Ruler of some large chunk of the universe. So far as we're concerned, its name is God.'

'You're mad!' he exclaimed, turning away from me. 'Quite mad.'

She shook with hysterical laughter. 'We'll see.'

Snark seized one of her arms and I the other, putting my hand over her mouth. Lutha wasn't noticing their faces, Mitigan's and Leelson's. Both of them were ready to explode. Snark had pushed them, the ex-king had pushed them, now Lutha had pushed them. They were becoming dangerous.

'Enough,' said a voice.

We turned to confront a ghost that rose from the base of the stones. Jiacare Lostre. Ashen, cadaverous, but alive. From around his feet, beetle-ish things bumbled away, tiny Leelies, who did not stop at healing, but also had a sideline in resurrections.

'You were dead!' cried Mitigan in angry disbelief.

'So I was,' he replied. 'And if I was killed as a representative of mankind, deservedly so. And if what I heard may be believed, all mankind may soon share my fate, or that of Dinadh, to be incubators for all eternity.'

'It'll die!' cried Mitigan. 'The way the Rottens died. The way the shaggy died. It touched Leely. It'll die.'

Poracious said, 'I think not. Look there!' She pointed to the opening of the cave, where one of the Leelies was dueling with a crab among the stones. He touched it repeatedly, but the crab didn't seem to care.

Lutha wept. 'Behemoth has vaccinated its creatures against our plague. What is breeding here now is Leely-proof.'

589

The largest Leely crawled into Lutha's lap, climbed her chest, and put his tiny arms around her neck.

'Lutha mother love,' he whispered. 'Don't cry, Lutha mother love.'

She went on crying, and so did I.

'We should go back to the camp,' said Mitigan in a stiff, unnatural voice. Poor Mitigan. All his world astray, and him lost with it.

No one had anything else or better to offer. Poracious wanted to stay where she was, but Snark wouldn't let her.

'It's not a good idea for you to be alone. Not a good idea for any of us.'

After a time of aimless delay, we went from our cave in a wavering line, much the way the Leelies had gone, each of us wrapped in a blanket or two. Lutha carried the largest Leely. Snark carried her jar, taking the lead when we reached the path. I followed after her, then the others, with Mitigan bringing up the rear, his face hard and angry as it had been since Behemoth had appeared. As we went north along the ocean trail we caught glimpses of the smaller Leelies, jumping into tide pools, dodging behind stones, disappearing down holes in the ground. Several of the larger ones greeted us in tiny voices. 'Dananana.'

We rounded a corner and confronted a lioness. That is, it was similar to pictures I had seen that were labeled lioness. We scrambled onto the slippery rocks while she passed us by. On her side was a vivid patch of scarlet, bordered by misty violet on one side, by deep wine and bright yellow on the other. Behind her came a train of cubs, each with its own color pattern.

'They are not hungry,' Leelson said in an expressionless voice. 'At the moment.'

The lioness was only the first. There were huge almost birds running on the trail, darting their beaks into the tide pools to spear wriggling, silver things. Each of them bore its own pattern of stripes or mottling or moving blotches of color. There were shelled things, clattering on the stones, turtle-like, crab-like, strangeness-like. There were small, furry beings with fluffy tails and piping voices that whistled as we passed. Every corner brought a new creature, each one with a new pattern, and each one bringing a new outburst of rage from Mitigan. Their very existence was an insult to him.

We passed the body of the Procurator in late afternoon, and it was evening when we came out onto the beach. There a snake slithered at Mitigan's feet, and he mouthed impotently, his fury mounting. He saw me cringe, so he turned and began to say to me the kinds of unpleasant things men of his kind often say to women, working himself into yet greater rage.

Snark tired of it. She shouted, 'Use your head! *This* world was not made for man, Asenagi!'

'Then why didn't he kill us?' he howled. '*He should have killed us!*'

We stopped where we were.

'Who did you see?' I asked Mitigan, when I could form words again. 'When you saw *it*, what did you see?'

'A winged bull with a man's face,' he cried. 'It carried a bull's pizzle and it wore a great beard!'

'We know,' said Leelson. 'That's what we all saw. Let's move along, shall we?' He took Mitigan by the arm and tugged him away from us, trying to calm him while the rest of us stood dumbfounded, wondering if we had gone mad.

'I did not see a man's face,' said the ex-king, quietly. 'But some can see no farther than their mirrors. What wears another face must go unseen.'

'It was a good question, though,' said Snark. 'Why didn't it kill us?'

'It hasn't decided yet,' said Lutha.

'How do you know?' I asked her.

'I just know. If it had decided to kill us, it would have done it there, as Mitigan expected.' She jabbed her chin toward the south. 'But we, too, are the offspring of Behemoth. It has uses for all its creatures and would rather not kill us.'

Snark stopped dead. 'That's what the justice machine said to me. It would rather not kill me. It would make me useful as a shadow instead.'

'As the sisterhood of Dinadh were shadows,' I said.

'As all women become shadows,' said Lutha. 'Where men have their way.'

Leelson dragged Mitigan back to the rest of us. 'We've been talking about Chur Durwen,' he said. 'Mitigan believes Chur Durwen will send help.'

'How'll he do that?' asked Poracious wearily.

Mitigan glowered at her, his mouth working.

'Through the officials at the port?' suggested Leelson.

'Who control nothing. Who are suspect because of their association with outlanders.'

Mitigan growled, 'He'll take ship for Alliance Central. There will be someone there.'

Poracious nodded, saying calmly, 'When we came to Dinadh, shipping in Hermes Sector was already a very iffy thing. Suppose Chur Durwen does get through, how will he reach anyone in the bureaucracy? I assume he is a registered assassin? Such folk are not routinely solicited for unusual information about unheard-of situations.'

'He'll go to the Alliance agent in Simidi-ala,' said Mitigan.

Poracious smiled grimly. 'Much good may that do him, or us. Thosby Anent's information routes are secure, but he won't get around to making use of them!'

The ex-king laughed, almost inaudibly. 'There's his servant. The woman. Chadra Tsum. We might offer audible prayer, several times a day, to Chadra Tsum.'

With a look of hectic gaiety, Poracious fell to her knees on the sand, held out her arms, and prayed to Chadra Tsum. The ex-king joined her, and they concluded their prayer with a repetitive chant: 'Vigilance. Vigilance. Vigilance.'

Lutha and I turned away, overtaken by a fit of hysterical laughter. We leaned on one another, tears running down our faces. Mitigan stood stony-faced, eyes glaring, but Leelson pulled Lutha away from me, into his arms.

'Oh, Lutha.' He sighed. His own face was wet. I had not seen Leelson weep ever before. Had things come to such a pitiful pass that even a Fastigat could weep?

'Why?' she asked, touching his cheek. 'Why tears, almighty Fastigat?'

'Guilt,' he said with a grimace. 'It seems I may have been, may be wrong about a number of things. I blamed you.'

'You blamed me?' she asked.

'For not seeing reality. My reality. And Limia blamed you for not seeing hers.'

'And I blame you now for not seeing what is,' she said, almost whispering. 'This is real, Leelson. This is not philosophy. Pray with Poracious that someone comes, that Behemoth will let us go, for someone must convince the Fastigats at Prime that this is real.'

'Little chance of that,' he murmured, looking around himself.

'But Behemoth might let us go,' I offered, more loudly than I intended. 'We could pray to it. ...'

I had not seen Mitigan edge up behind us. I didn't know he was there until I heard his howl of rage:

'Make prayer to an animal?'

'Mitigan.' I faltered, stepping back, away from him. 'I meant it only as a suggestion. Perhaps if we offered ... repentance, self-sacrifice ...'

It was the wrong thing to say. Perhaps anything would have been the wrong thing to say. He had been teetering on the edge of rage and frustration for too long.

'You think it would accept a sacrifice?' he bellowed, grabbing me by the arm, lifting me with one mighty hand, and flinging me across his shoulder. 'Well then, let us make sacrifice!'

It happened so quickly that we were halfway up the slope toward the scraggy ridge before I could catch my breath and cry out. Any sound I made was drowned by his fury.

'We will build us an altar! We will make blood sacrifice!'

All the breath was driven from my lungs when he dropped me at the crest of the ridge. He took a thong from his belt and lashed my feet and hands together with one quick motion while I gasped and struggled. Dimly I saw him heaving great slabs of stone, stones too heavy to lift, stones no man could have lifted.

I rolled my head to one side. The others were halfway up the hill. Leelson. Lutha. Above me Mitigan held a huge boulder aloft.

'Want to join her, Famber? Come closer and you will!'

'Mitigan!' cried Leelson. 'This isn't the way—'

'I've had enough of this heresy, these devil beasts,' Mitigan howled, casting a manic glance in my direction. 'Enough!'

He backed toward me, holding the great stone aloft with one hand while he fumbled for a weapon with the other. Something to kill me with, kill them with. Almost he could have killed them with his eyes, so berserk he was.

'Why me?' I gasped. 'Why sacrifice me, Asenagi?'

'Why not you?' He dropped the stone and jabbed a contemptuous thumb toward Lutha. 'She belongs to Leelson Famber. And the other one is of some use. But you are no use and you belong to no one but your devil god, so let it have you!'

'I didn't create it!' I cried. 'I only saw it, listened to it. I only sensed what was really there, Mitigan. As you did—'

'Lies,' he cried, heaving a huge slab of stone into place upon his pile, now waist-high. He tossed me onto the stone like wood onto a fire, effortlessly. My head hit, and I felt myself go limp, dazed. I couldn't struggle, though I could feel him lashing me to the slab. 'The Gracious One warns us against your kind! Animal-lovers! Devils! Mistresses of lies!'

He licked at the spittle that ran down his chin. Past him I could see Snark on her belly, worming her way up the slope, and behind her, Lutha struggling with Leelson, trying to get free from him. It was all happening too quickly and too slowly, both at once. There was time to be terrified, not time enough to do anything. I prayed, begging Weaving Woman to let my pattern end cleanly, swiftly, without pain. Surely there had been enough pain!

'Not nearly enough,' Mitigan jeered, and I knew I had spoken aloud. Now his hand was aloft, already reddened by sunset, glittering with the blade it held. That was for me.

Far off, as though in another world, I heard Lutha and Snark shouting, not pleading. There was a strangeness in their voices, something inappropriate. I had time to think that. Why did they sound that way? I squeezed my eyes shut, clenched my teeth tight, waiting for the knife to come. . . .

It didn't come. Instead Mitigan bellowed, harshly, horrified.

I opened my eyes against a dazzle of light. Mitigan stood with his back to me, his head thrown back. Beyond him was Behemoth, up from the sea, serpent-necked, dragon-jawed, caldron-eyed.

'No,' it said in a voice of wind.

'But she refused you!' Mitigan howled. 'She deserves to die. She refused you!'

'She has that right,' said the wind. 'Do not all my beings have that right? Even you? You may ruin yourselves by your choices, still I will not take them from you. ...'

Mitigan turned frantically, lunging toward me, the knife aimed at my heart, but the wind came after him, raising him, taking him up as the vortex had done, twirling him, spinning him, up and away, away, glittering with weapons, howling with rage, away. ...

And all the while, for that tiny eternity, Behemoth looked me in the eye until I felt I had drowned in that look. Willingly. Forever. I did not want to come away.

'Still your kind may choose,' it said in a fading whisper. 'Choose truth; choose lies; still you may choose, even now.'

I saw sunset. Only that. Behemoth gone. That rough beast gone. That enormous glory gone. That terrible beauty, gone. Leaving only its purpose evident all around us.

'Saluez,' cried Lutha, her fingers busy with the lashings. 'Oh, Saluez.'

Far above us in the dusk, a sudden star bloomed and moved, swimming toward us through the evening.

'A ship,' said Leelson disbelievingly. 'It's a ship.'

The ship hung above us for some little time while we stared and mumbled. It had grown quite dark before it broke into two glittering parts, one of which descended. When it set down beside the camp, we saw it was a tender. It was from the *Vigilance*, as it turned out, a battle cruiser of the Alliance.

We stood slack-jawed while the lock opened, the ramp came down, and a woman alighted.

'Chadra Tsum,' said Poracious wonderingly. 'Just as I saw her in Simidi-ala. And there behind her, that's old Thosby Anent.'

He was a crooked man, with a lopsided walk. 'Ah,' he cried as he hobbled toward us, his eyes scrunched almost shut with delighted self-importance. 'Ah, *Vigilance*! See the ship's name? Ah? I've been watching, waiting. *Vigilance*!'

He went on past us to stand upon a small hillock, looking about himself like a conqueror of worlds as he drew deep, dramatic breaths and tapped himself upon the chest in self-congratulation.

'Let me guess,' whispered Poracious to Chadra Tsum. 'You told him we were here, expecting rescue, but he had to think it over. He couldn't make up his mind to do anything about it?'

Chadra Tsum nodded, murmuring, 'After some time had gone by, I asked if he would attempt to rescue you, and he said, "That's the plan!" Days went by, however, and he did nothing at all. So I commandeered an Alliance ship in his name. Then, when it was the *Vigilance* that showed up, he assumed he had done it himself.'

'Quite a coincidence,' Lutha murmured.

'Not really,' said the woman. 'It's the only battleship assigned to this sector. That's where Thosby got his password in the first place.'

'I'm surprised you've come so quickly,' I managed to say. 'Poracious and the king only prayed to you this evening!'

'You mean you really did that?' the woman breathed. 'You know, I've felt something for days, as though you were speaking in my mind. Isn't that strange?'

Poracious took her by the arm and led her a little aside, where they spoke animatedly to one another. Leelson joined them, and then others from the ship. Leely watched them for a moment, his face intent, then he wandered away toward the sea. I stayed where I was, with Lutha. In a few moments Snark joined us, then the ex-king, none of us making a move to join the general rejoicing. It was as though the four of us had been pulled together.

'Why did it let the ship come?' whispered Lutha. 'Why?'

'Didn't you hear what it said?' I murmured. 'We have a choice. We've always had a choice.'

'Between what and what?' asked Snark.

'What choices are there?' Jiacare counted them off on his fingers. 'What truths we choose to see. What lies we choose to ignore. Whether we become Firsters ... or something else—'

He was interrupted by a raised voice from the group down the slope. Someone said loudly that ships were still disappearing in Hermes Sector and the captain wanted to get away quickly. Someone else reinforced this, but Poracious demanded, loudly, that the Procurator's body be retrieved. There was a muttered argument, then general assent. The group broke up, with individuals going busily off in different directions.

'They'll want to leave soon,' I said.

'It will be good to be at home,' said Lutha. It was a statement, but it sounded like a question.

'I have no home,' said Snark.

'Nor I,' I said, as softly. 'In any case, that is not why the ship was allowed to come. It did not come merely to take us home. Remember what Behemoth said when it spoke to us first.'

'What did it say?' asked the ex-king. 'I don't remember.'

'You wouldn't remember,' said Lutha in an expressionless voice. 'You were ... dead. It was after it tore ... tore Leely into bits. It asked if we would live by truth. It told us to reflect.'

'Such violence,' he said distastefully, as though it had happened to someone else.

I broke the long silence that followed. 'The violence wasn't arbitrary. The question wasn't rhetorical.'

Lutha did not look at me. I knew she had heard me, but she didn't meet my eyes. She was watching Leelson, who had broken away from a small group near the ship and was striding up the slope toward us.

He put his arms around Lutha, hugging her joyously.

'We can go home,' he said. 'We can take ... our son and go home.'

She turned toward me, her eyes spilling tears. I knew what she was thinking. She had wanted him to say that, something like that.

'He'll be of great value in Fastiga,' Leelson assured her, stroking her hair. 'For his healing power alone.'

My throat was dry. I cleared it, painfully. 'Yes, he'll be of great value. For his healing power alone.'

The ex-king looked off toward the horizon. 'Fastigats should be able to live almost forever, with all the Leelies around.'

Leelson frowned, shook his head, stepped away from Lutha. 'But ... I hadn't ... I thought we'd only take ... just the one, Lutha.'

'But they're all ...' she cried, her hand to her mouth, not finishing the sentence. She was right, however. They were all.

'As you say, they'll be enormously valued,' repeated the ex-king, 'for their healing power alone. Not to speak of raising the recently dead. Extending human life spans for how long? Increasing human population by how much? All Firsters will be delighted, of course. It shouldn't take long for there to be a profitable market in Leelies.'

Leelson recoiled as though he'd been slapped.

'Later,' Lutha said in a voice that was almost a scream. 'We'll discuss it later.'

'But the ship's leaving. ...'

'They've sent men to get the Procurator's body. The ship won't leave until they return. Leelson! If you love me, let me be. Give me a moment!'

He backed away, uncertainly. Poracious called his name, and he went off toward her, glancing at us doubtfully over his shoulder, unable to decide whether to be hurt or angry. Poor Fastigat. Even he could not read this tangle!

Lutha turned away from us, her shoulders shaking, wiping her face with the backs of her hands. She shuddered, drew a deep breath, then wept again. In a moment she stopped trying to control herself and simply walked away toward the sea.

Snark said to me, 'Go after her, Saluez. She talks to you.'

The ex-king nodded, nudging me, so I went after her. By now it was starlit evening, with just enough light to see by. She wound her way among glistening pools with me trailing after, and when we came to the beach, I wasn't surprised to find Leely already there, perched on a rock. He was her destination, after all.

'Lutha mother love,' he called in his small voice, sliding off the rock to hug her leg and look happily up at us. 'Saluez of the shadow.'

She lifted him, hugged him gently, then sat on the rock where he'd been perched.

He settled into her lap. I leaned against a boulder, being invisible, watching the stars come out.

'Tell me about home,' he said.

I saw her throat tighten, as though she choked. She swallowed deeply. 'Isn't this home, Leely?'

'No. Home home I remember. Alliance Central home.'

Who would have thought he would remember Alliance Central? And yet, why would he have forgotten.

'What do you remember?' Lutha asked, looking helplessly at me.

'Everything! My room. My paints. All the nice places you put on my window scene.'

'Do you miss those things?'

He leaned back against her with a little squirm of pleasure and comfort. 'I like it here. Window scenes are nice, but you can't touch them. You can't be in them. I like real fish. But you want to go back and I want to be with you.'

There were tears in my throat. Stars fragmented in my sight. I blinked my eyes clear.

She asked, 'How do the other Leelies feel?'

'Most of us don't remember. I'm the only one who *really* remembers. You know.'

'I don't know. You tell me.'

His little voice was matter-of-fact as he said, 'It depends on how big a piece we got made from or maybe which piece we got made from. I got made from Leely head. That's why I remember. The other ones, they were made from Leely legs or Leely blood or Leely guts. They've got good brains, but they don't remember some old things like I do.'

He turned to hug her, then went on. 'I remember lots of things, Lutha Lutha Tallstaff sister mother love. I remember Trompe. I remember when we met Saluez of the shadow, and how we got here. I remember Behemoth.'

She took a deep breath. 'You'd probably be fine here, all you Leelies, whether I was here or not.'

His face clouded. I had never seen him wear that expression before, though it was one common to other children. The look of a child fearing loneliness. The look of a child afraid.

He put his hands to her face, whispering, 'I'd be lonesome. I need somebody to talk to. I want to be with you.'

After a time she rose and walked back to the camp, Leely riding on her shoulders, his arms wrapped around her head. Snark and the ex-king were standing outside the dormitory, waiting for us. Lutha took no notice of them. She went on by, as though she would go on walking forever, the child smiling and kicking his heels, his tiny hands clasped around her brow.

The journey from Perdur Alas to Dinadh was not a long one. It brought me, Saluez, almost full circle in my journey. I arrived as outlanders do, through Simidi-ala.

So much had changed.

So little had changed.

Poracious asked the people at the port about the Kachis. The people at the port furrowed their brows and asked in return: What about the Kachis? Had something changed about the Kachis?

What about Tahs-uppi? Poracious asked.

It had been successful, they told her. Additional days had been drawn from the omphalos and time ran once more in its accustomed course. I heard all this, though the people of Simidi-ala were talking to Poracious, not to me. I was veiled and silent before them. They did not even see me.

'What are you going to do?' Poracious asked me when we were alone once more.

'I'm going to make my way to the nearest hive,' I told her. 'Where I will talk with the sisterhood.'

'And what good will that do?' she asked.

I grimaced behind my veil. 'Perhaps none. Perhaps a good deal. A few years will tell. What are you going to do?'

'I will do as Snark and Jiacare have said I must. Return to the Alliance and become a preacher. A prophet. A doom crier.'

'What good will that do?' I mocked.

She shrugged. 'Perhaps none. Perhaps a great deal. I may be of some help on Prime. If things are going to change, it will have to start there. I will do what I can.'

'Did you learn what happened to Chur Durwen?'

'He made his way here, to Simidi-ala, and from here went back to Collis.' She smiled a strange, harsh smile. 'Have you heard of the recent occurrence on Asenagi?'

I raised an eyebrow and waited.

'Asenagi has had a visit from the Gracious One. It – he has spoken to their tribal leaders. They have been promised immortality. . . .'

I took a deep breath. 'In return for?'

'In return for mounting a holy war against nonbelievers, which they readily agreed to do.'

'War!'

598

'The Gracious One has promised them a very fierce, unstoppable animal to assist them in their battles. This animal will be born from the women of Asenagi and nurtured by the Asenagi themselves. The animal will fight beside the warriors and will carry the souls of warriors killed in battle directly to ... well, one assumes Valhalla.' She stared out again at the sea. I saw her eyes were wet. 'A tempting tale, tailor-made for the Asenagi culture.'

'As Lutha once said, it is disgusted with us. I wonder if any of us will manage to choose aright.'

'We will try,' she replied. 'We will do our best.'

She kissed me and left me then, alone as I had been before the outlanders came. Later, I saw both her and Leelson being lifted up into the ship that would take them back to Central. He was very pale and focused looking, very set upon his task, his duty, his enormous and quite terrible responsibility. Being a Fastigat, he assumed it was not beyond his capabilities.

And I? I gritted my teeth and set my feet upon the path of righteousness.

Thus was the loom rethreaded.

Thus was the pattern determined.

Thus the shuttle wove.

Dawn on Dinadh.

Deep in the canyonlands shadow lies thickly layered as fruit-tree leaves in autumn. High on the walls the sun paints stripes of copper and gold, ruby and amber, the stones glowing as though from a forge, hammered here and there into mighty arches above our caves. Beneath those arches, the hives spread fragrant smoke, speak a tumult of little drums, breathe the sound of bone flutes. Above all, well schooled, the voice of Shalumn, songmother, soars like a crying bird:

'The Daylight Woman, see how she advances, she of the flowing garments, she of the golden skin and shining eye ...'

Years have come and gone since Perdur Alas. I speak often now with Daylight Woman, the Revealer, and with her companion, Behemoth, guardian of all-living. I revere them as I do Weaving Woman and Brother and Sister Rain and the Sisters of Soil. Each morning as my friend Shalumn sings the welcome to day, I pray: *Oh, Great and Gracious Ones, see the choice we have made; do not destroy us but keep us in righteousness. Dinadh shall become as a paradise; and we will share it and treasure it as is your will.*

Each morning before first light, songmother comes to the lip of our cave, raising her voice when the sun touches the rimrock above. Each morning I stand behind her among the sisterhood, they with their faces exposed that all may see the ugliness that comes from seeking more and longer human life at the expense of life itself. Behind us are the other inhabitants of the hive, all joining the song, all hearing the great warp and woof of sound that follows Daylight Woman's eternal march westward. Dawnsong still circles our world endlessly, like the belt that runs from the treadle to the wheel. So much is as before.

Other things are changed. Both Mother Darkness and Father Endless are with us again. They are welcomed with dancing each evening when Daylight Woman departs. Though it is the nature of children to fear the darkness, adults know there can be no light without it. Hah-Hallach and his brethren have been deposed, not for listening to the tempter – for any creature might do that – but for lying to their people after they knew the truth. We have songparents now, mothers and fathers both, as we did on beloved Breadh.

This morning, when the dawnsong is over, Shalumn and I will go to the House Without a Name. In our hive an old woman named H'Nhan died some time ago, leaving an empty place in the pattern. Now a new H'Nhan may be born, to fill that place, and a certain woman has been given the privilege of bearing that child. Today she will lie upon the table, imagining the terror of those who once lay there. There are no Kachis now. The songparents teach that the Kachis were our punishment, but thinking creatures may choose repentance and restitution instead. Now, instead of Kachis we have the reanimated ones from the files on Central: fish and otter; eagle and squirrel; fox and mouse; all manner of creatures to be woven together with us.

We tell the story of Perdur Alas to our children when we teach them the commandments of Dinadh: 'Do not wish to live forever. Do not believe that every man-shaped thing is holier than something else. Do not look into the mirror to see the face of God. Do not weave your life only in one color, for Behemoth will not bless you if you do.'

Now the morning song is almost over. One of the sisterhood offers the bell. Shalumn accepts it. She rings it, once, twice, three times. Quiet falls. Heads are bowed. All in Cochim-Mahn are saying a silent prayer for Lutha Tallstaff, and for all the Leelies, too. May their shuttles carry brightness; may they be comforted in their choice.

Whenever I say the words, I remember our parting:

The ship was slender and white and still, like a tower, all its crew aboard, all its people waiting. At the bottom of the ramp we few gathered in the light of the rising sun. From the bottom of the valley the sea threw the dawn into our eyes. There was not a sound except our voices, as though the world held its breath.

I hear Lutha repeating what she had said over and over during the long night:

'Leely can't go back, Leelson. He mustn't, not ever.'

I hear Leelson:

'Then let the Leelies stay. ...'

And Lutha again:

'I will not leave my child.'

He reached for her then, and she backed away, blazing at him through her tears. 'Don't tell me you'll stay, Leelson! The Fastigats will listen only to one of themselves. You have seen what happened in Hermes Sector! Do you want it to happen to all mankind?'

She took one step, then another, her hand lifted in farewell. Yet still he reached for her, tears streaming down his face.

Then Jiacare's voice:

'Go, Leelson. She won't be alone. Snark and I are staying with her.'

And finally, Snark:

'Kings and women, Leelson. Kings and women! We gotta do stuff like that!'

Lutha and Leelson and Leely. They are with me always. Leelson left her once, because of Leely. He left her at last, because of Leely. If their love was not really love, their courage was surely courage. Heroes have been adored for less.

The sun is upon Shalumn's ankles now, and her voice ascends the sky. She holds her arms wide, inviting us to enter into the pattern, to go forth into a world that was not made and is not kept for man alone.

And we of Dinadh step into the light.

SIX MOON DANCE

'What matters it how far we go?' his scaly friend replied.
'There is another shore, you know, upon the other side ...
Then turn not pale, beloved snail, but come and join the dance.
Will you, won't you, will you, won't you, will you join the dance?'

– *Alice's Adventures in Wonderland*, LEWIS CARROLL

CAST OF CHARACTERS

Abbreviated list of characters, in order of appearance (walks-ons not included).

Mankind Newholmians:

Mouche	Moosh	A consort trainee
Ornery	OR-nery	A farm girl turned seaman
Madame Genevois	Gen-eh-VWA	Consort House operator
Simon		Her assistant
Bane and Dyre Dutter		Two delinquents
Ashes		A leftover
The Machinist		Another
D'Jevier	Duh ZHEV-yai	A hag
Onsofruct	AWN-so-FROOT	Another hag
Marool Mantelby	Mah-ROOL	A sex maniac
Calvy g'Valdet	gh-vahl-DET	A man of business
Estif g'Bayoar	Es-TEEF g'BAY-wahr	Another
Myrphee g'Mindon	g'MIN-don	Another
Slab g' Tupoar	g'too-POUR	The antepenultimate
Bin g'Kiffle	g'KIFF-el	The penultimate
Sym g'Sinsanoi	g' SIHN-san-oy	And the last

Native Newholmians:

The Corojum	Koh-roh-JOOM	A solitary survivor
Joggiwagga	Jog-ee-WAH-gah	Heavy equipment operator
Timrny	short for Tim-Tim	Useful fingers
Flowing Green		A particular finger
Eiger	EYE-gher	Four eyed bird
Bofusdiaga	Boh-FOOS-di-AH-gah	Current planetary manager
Corojumi	Koh-roh-JOO-mi	Creative artists
Fauxi-dizalonz	FOW-shee DIZ-ah-lawnz	A gender bender
Kaorugi	Cow-RUE-ji	Current planetary subconscious

Extraplanetary persons:

Ellin Voy		A dancer, female
The Questioner		A device
Gandro Bao	BAH-oh	A male female dancer
The Quaggima	KWA-gi-mah	Who arrived a long time ago

Together with various gardeners, livestock, supernumeraries, naggers, worshippers, travelers, members of an entourage, a representative of the Brotherhood of Interstellar Trade, ship's crewmembers, family members, spouses, and monsters.

1

On Newholme: Mouche

'It's all right,' Mouche's mother said. 'Next time we'll have a girl.'

Mouche knew of this because his father told him. 'She said it was all right. She said next time …'

But there had been no next time. Why the inscrutable Hagions decided such things was unknown. Some persons profited in life, producing daughter after daughter; some lost in life, producing son after son; some hung in the balance as Eline and Darbos did, having one son at the Temple, and then a daughter born dead at the Temple, and then no other child.

It was neither a profit nor a great loss, but still, a loss. Even a small loss sustained over time can bleed a family: so theirs bled. Only a smutch of blood, a mere nick of a vein, a bit more out than in, this year and then the next, and the one after that, a gradual anemia, more weakening than deadly – the heifer calves sold instead of kept, the ewe lambs sold, the repairs to the water mill deferred, then deferred again. Darbos had taken all he had inherited and added to that what he could borrow as his dowry for a wife who would help him establish a family line, to let him wear the honorable cockade, to be known as g'Darbos and be addressed as 'Family Man.' He had planned to repay the loan with advances against his share of the dowries paid for his own daughters. Instead, he had paid for Eline with the price of the heifer calves, with the ruin of the mill. Her family had profited, and though families lucky enough to have several daughters often gave those daughters a share of the dowry they brought in (a generosity Darbos had rather counted on), Eline's parents had not seen fit to do so. Still, Eline's daughters would have made it all worth while, if there had been daughters.

Their lack made for a life not precisely sad, but not joyous, either. There was no absence of care, certainly. Eline was not a savage. There was no personal blame. Darbos had created the sperm, he was the one responsible, everyone knew that. But then, some receptacles were said to reject the female, so perhaps Eline shared the fault. No matter. Blaming, as the Hags opined, was a futile exercise engaged in only by fools. What one did was bow, bow again, and get on.

So, each New Year at the Temple, while g'Darbos waited outside with the other Family Men, all of them sneaking chaff under their veils and whispering with one another in defiance of propriety, Eline bowed and bowed again. Then she got on, though the getting did not halt the slow leaking away of substance by just so much as it took to feed and clothe one boy, one boy with a boy's appetite and a boy's habit of unceasing growth. As for shoes, well, forget shoes. If he had had sisters, then perhaps Eline would have bought him shoes. In time, she might even have provided the money for him to dower in a wife. If he had had sisters.

'If bought no wife,' so the saying went, so forget the wife. More urgent than the need for a wife was the need for daily grain, for a coat against the wind, for fire on the winter's hearth and tight roof against the storm, none of which came free. Eline and Darbos were likely to lose all. After nine barren years, it was unlikely there would be more children, and the couple had themselves to think of. *Who can not fatten on daughters must fatten on labor,* so it was said, and the little farm would barely fatten two. It would not stretch to three.

On the day Mouche was twelve, when the festive breakfast was over and the new shirt admired and put on, Papa walked with him into the lower pasture where an old stump made a pleasant sun-gather for conversation, and there Papa told Mouche what the choices were. Mouche might be cut, and if he survived it, sold to some wealthy family as a chatron playmate for their children, a safe servant for the daughters, someone to fetch and carry and neaten up. The fee would be large if he lived, but if he died, there would be no fee at all.

Or, an alternative. Madame Genevois – who had a House in Sendoph – had seen Mouche in the marketplace, and she'd made an offer for him. While the fee was less than for a chatron, it would be paid in advance, no matter how he turned out.

Mama had followed them down to the field and she stood leaning on the fence, taking no part in the conversation. It was not a woman's place, after all, to enlighten her son to the facts of life. Still, she was near enough to hear him when he cried:

'Trained for a Hunk, Papa? A Hunk?'

'Where did you learn that word?' said Mama, spinning around and glaring at him. 'We do not talk filth in this family ...'

'Shh, shh,' said Darbos, tears in the corners of his eyes. 'The word is the right word, Madam. When we are driven to this dirty end, let us not quibble about calling it what it is.'

At which point Mama grew very angry and went swiftly away toward the house. Papa followed her a little way, and Mouche heard him saying, 'Oh, I know he's only a boy, Eline, but I've grown fond of him ...'

Mouche had seen Hunks, of course – who had not? – riding through the marketplace, their faces barely veiled behind gauzy stuff, their clothing all aglitter with gold lace and gems, their hats full of plumes, the swords they fenced with sparkling like rippled water. Even through the veils one could see their hair was curled and flowing upon their shoulders, not bound back as a common man would need it to be, out of the way of the work. Their shirts were open, too, and in the gap their skin glowed and their muscles throbbed. Hunks did not work. They smiled, they dimpled, they complimented, they dueled and rode and wrestled, they talked of wonderful things that ordinary people knew little or nothing of. Poetry. And theater. And wine.

Mouche wondered if they talked of the sea, which is what Mouche talked of, to himself when there was no one else by to speak to, or to Papa, when Papa was in the mood. Not to Mama. Mama did not understand such things, even though it was she who had given him the book of sea stories, and she who had told him about going to Gilesmarsh when she was a girl, and how the shore had looked and smelled, and how the little boats came in full of the fishes that swam there, and how the ships sailed out and away into wonderful places. The seamen didn't even wear veils, except in port. Mama didn't mention that, but the book did. Of course, out at sea, there were no women to be tempted and corrupted by the sight of wanton hairs sprouting on a male face, so veils weren't really needed.

Mouche's dream of going to sea when he was old enough was not pure foolishness. The books were full of stories about boys who ran away to sea and ships that took them, sometimes with no apprenticeship fee. Poor as Mouche's family was, he knew it would have to be without a fee. He would have to have something else to recommend him, like knowing things about ropes and nets and repairs and suchlike. He asked his teacher if he could get Mouche a book about all that – which he did, and followed it with others when Mouche was through with the first one. Mouche practiced knots in his bed at night, and learned all the words for the parts of the ship and the pieces of the rigging and how it all worked. 'Seaman Mouche,' he said to himself on the edge of sleep. 'Captain Mouche.' And he dreamed.

But now it seemed he was not to go to sea. Not even without a fee. He was to be a Hunk. Hunks did not go to sea, did not pull at nets, did not look out to far horizons and distant ports, did not smell of fish. They smelled of perfume. They pranced like ponies. And they fucked, of course. Everyone knew that. That's what they were for. Though they did not father, they fucked.

Some very wealthy women were known to have several of them. When a woman accepted a dowry from some man she did not know – might never have seen, might grow to detest – thereby making him the sole begetter of her future children, it was her right to include in the contract a provision that after five or seven or ten years, whether she had any daughters or not, she was to have at least one Hunk. This was common knowledge. It was also common knowledge that many of the best-trained Hunks came from House Genevois in Sendoph. Polite people didn't call them Hunks, of course, Mama was right about that. They called them 'Consorts,' but it meant the same thing.

'Consort Mouche,' he said to himself, seeing how it sounded. It sounded dirty, no matter what word he used. It sounded like a teacher saying, 'Take your hands out of your pants. What do you think you're doing? Practicing to be a Consort?'

It sounded like teasing on the school ground, Fenarde saying, 'Mouche can't ever get married. Mouche will have to be a Hunky-monkey.' Which was very dirty talk indeed. All the girls stood and giggled and twitched their bottoms at Mouche and said, 'You can *be my* Hunky-monkey, Mouche. *I'll* put you in my contract.' And then they started kissing Mouche and touching him on his behind. Such evil behavior got the girls a talking to about courtesy and treating males respectfully, because they were not as resilient as girls and their minds weren't as flexible, and Fenarde got a mouthful of ashes from the schoolroom hearth for starting the whole thing. Mouche merely got a brief lecture. Though the teacher was patient, he didn't have much time to waste on boys.

'Girls always talk that way,' he said. 'They have no masculine modesty. You must behave demurely and simply ignore it, pretend not to hear it. When they pinch you or rub up against you, get away from them as soon as possible. And take no notice! That's the proper way to behave, and it's time you learned it.' Though how you could feel those intrusive hands on you and take no notice, the teacher did not say.

The night after Papa had told him about House Genevois, Mouche heard a tap at his door, so soft and so late he almost thought he had dreamed it until Papa slipped in and sat on the edge of his cot.

'My boy,' he said, 'a man's life is never easy. We are the weaker sex, as everyone knows, though sometimes at the end of a long, hard day loading hay I think our weakness is more a matter of fable than reality. Still, this is the world we live in, and we must live, as the Hags say, either with it or against it. I've come to say some things to you that I didn't want to say with your mama there.' He stroked Mouche's hair away from his forehead, looking at him sadly.

'Yes, Papa.'

'This decision is much against my inclination, Mouche. You were to be the son of g'Darbos, our unique line. I had such plans for you, for us ...' His voice trailed off sadly, and he stared out the small window at two of the littler moons just rising above the horizon to join a third, bigger one in the sky. 'But seemingly it is not to be. There will be no g'Darbos lineage, no immortality of the family, no descendants to remember me and honor the name. Even so, I would not make this decision lightly; I had to find out what kind of life we'd be sending you to. I didn't tell your Mama, but when I was last in Sendoph, I went into House Genevois, by the back door, and when I explained myself, I was allowed to talk to some of the ... young men.'

Mouche wriggled uncomfortably.

'I found out, for example, that they eat very well indeed. Far better than we do. I found out that the maximum contract for a Hu – a Consort is about twenty years, beginning as soon as schooling is completed, somewhere between the eighteenth and twenty-fourth year. The standard contract for men from House Genevois provides one third the original payment set aside for your retirement, plus one third of the downpayment on your contract, plus half the payments to House Genevois every year of service, all invested at interest to provide you an annuity. All Consorts receive wages from their patronesses, plus tips, many of them, and even after they're retired, ex-Consorts can freelance for additional profit. There are ex-Consorts in the city who are almost as well respected as Family Men.'

'But it isn't the sea,' said Mouche, feeling tears, blinking rapidly to keep them from running over. 'If I go to sea and make my fortune, I could send you money.'

'No, Mouche. It isn't the sea, but it's now, when we have need, not years from now when it's too late. If you can set aside your dream of the sea, being a Consort has few drawbacks. Well, there's the possibility of being killed or scarred in a duel, but any farmer might be killed or scarred. The men I spoke with said Consort dueling can be avoided by a fast tongue and a ready wit, neither of which can help farmers avoid accidents. And, so far as I can tell, the shame that attaches to the candidate's family goes away after a time. One grows used to saying, "My son? Oh, he's gone to work for a contractor in the city."' Papa sighed, having put the best face on it he could.

'How much will you get for me, Papa?'

'I won't get it. Your Mama will. It's twenty gold vobati, my boy, after deducting your annuity share, but Mama has agreed to use it on the farm. That's the only way I'd give permission for her to sell you, you being my eldest.' Eldest sons, as everyone knew, were exempt from sale unless the father agreed, though younger ones, being supernumerary, could be sold by their mothers – if she could find a buyer – as soon as they turned seven. Supernumes were miners and haulers and sailors; they were the ones who worked as farmhands or wood cutters or ran away to become Wilderneers.

Still, twenty vobati was a large sum of money. More than he could make as a seaman in a long, long time. 'Is it as much a daughter would bring in?' Mouche whispered.

'Not if she were a healthy, good-looking and intelligent girl, but it isn't bad. It's enough to guarantee Mama and Papa food for their age.'

Mouche took a deep breath and tried to be brave. He would have had to be brave to be a seaman, so let him be brave anyhow. 'I would rather be a Consort than a playmate, Papa.'

'I thought you might,' said Papa with a weepy smile.

Papa had a tender heart. He was always shedding a tear for this thing or that thing. Every time the earth shook and the great fire mounts of the scarp belched into the sky, Papa worried about the people in the way of it. Not Mama, who just snorted that people who built in the path of pyroclastic flow must eat ashes and like it, and with all the old lava about, one could not mistake where that was likely to be.

Papa went on, 'Tell you true, Mouche – but if you tell your Mama, I'll say you lie – many a time when the work is hard and the sun is hot, and I'm covered with bites from jiggers and fleas, and my back hurts from loading hay ... well, I've thought what it would be like, being a Hunk. Warm baths, boy. And veils light enough to really see through. It would be fun to see the city rather than mere shadows of it. And there's wine. We had wine at our wedding, your mama and me. They tell me one gets to like it.' He sighed again, lost in his own foundered dream, then came to himself with a start.

'Well, words enough! If you are agreeable, we will go to Sendoph tomorrow, for the interview.'

Considering the choices, Mouche agreed. It was Papa who took him. Mama could not lower herself to go into House Genevois as a seller rather than a buyer. That would be shameful indeed.

Sendoph was as Sendoph always was, noisy and smelly and full of invisible people everywhere one looked. Though the city had sewers, they were always clogging up, particularly in the dry season when the streams were low, and the irregular cobbles magnified the sound of every hoof and every wooden or iron-rimmed wheel to make clattering canyons between the tall houses and under the overhanging balconies. The drivers were all supernumes who had to work at whatever was available, and they could not see clearly through their veils. The vendors were equally handicapped. Veils, as the men often said, were the very devil. They could not go without, however, or they'd be thought loose or promiscuous or, worse, disrespectful of women. There were always many Haggers standing about, servants of the Hags, who were servants of the Hagions, the Goddesses, and they were swift to punish bad behavior.

The town was split in two by ancient lava tubes, now eroded into troughs, that guided the northward flow of the River Giles. Genevois House stood on the street nearest west and parallel to the river, its proud western facade decked with tall shuttered windows and bronze double doors graven with images of dueling men. The south side, along Bridge Street all the way to Brewer's Bridge, was less imposing, merely a line of grilled windows interrupted in the middle by one stout provisioner's gate opening into the service courtyard. The east side, on the bank of the river itself, showed only a blank wall bracketed at each end by a stubby tower of ornamental brickwork around fretted windows set with colored glass. This wall was pierced by an ancient gate through which a rotting tongue of wharf was thrust into the river, a tongue all slimed with filth and ribboned with long festoons of algae. Parts of House Genevois plus the courtyard walls, the wharf, and the bronze doors, dated back to the lost settlement, the colony from Thor that had vanished, along with its ship, long before the second settlers arrived.

The door where Mouche and his papa were admitted was an inconspicuous entrance off Bridge Street, near the front corner. Inside was the parlor of the welcome suite, where Madame Genevois kept them waiting a good hour. Through the closed door Mouche and Papa could hear her voice, now from here, then from there, admonishing, encouraging. When she came into the interview room at last, her sleeves were turned up to her elbows and her forehead was beaded with perspiration. She rolled the sleeves down and buttoned them, took a linen handkerchief from the cache-box on her worktable, and patted her forehead dry.

'Well, Family Man; well, Mouche,' she said. 'I'm sorry to have kept you waiting, but we have a new fencing master who is inclined to be too rigorous with the beginners and too lax with the advanced class. It is easier to bully novices than it is to test competent swordsmen, but I have told him I will not tolerate it. He is paid to exert himself, and exert himself he shall.' She patted her forehead once again, saying in a matter-of-fact voice: 'Take off your clothes, boy, and let me look at you.'

Papa had warned Mouche about this, but he still turned red from embarrassment. He took everything off but his crotcher and his sandals, which seemed to make him bare enough for her purposes when she came poking at him, like a farmer judging a pig.

'Your hands and feet are in terrible condition,' she said. 'Your hair is marvelous in color and fairly good in shape. Your eyes and face are good. The leg and back muscles are all wrong, of course. Farm work does not create a balanced body.'

'As Madame says,' Papa murmured, while Mouche shifted from foot to foot and tried to figure out what to do with his hands.

Madame jerked her head, a quick nod. 'Well, all in all, I will stick to

615

my bargain. The hands and feet will be soaked and scrubbed and brought into good appearance. The muscles will yield to proper exercise. A score ten vobati, I said, did I not? A score for the wife, ten in keeping for the boy.'

'As Madame recalls,' Papa murmured again.

'And is his mother prepared to leave him now?'

Papa looked up then, his eyes filling. He had not planned on this, and Mouche pitied him even more than he pitied himself.

'Can I not have time to say good-bye, Madame?' he begged.

'If your mother allows, of course, boy. Take two days. Be here first thing in the morning on fifthday. First thing, now.'

She unbuttoned her wrists and rolled up her sleeves once more, giving him a look that was almost kindly as he struggled into his clothes.

'You're coming into good hands, Mouche. We honor our annuities, which some Houses only claim to provide. We don't sell to sadists. And you won't hate the life. You'll miss Mama and Papa, yes, but you'll get on.' She turned away, then back, to add, 'No pets, boy. You know that.'

'Yes, Madame.' He gulped a little. He no longer had a pet, though the thought of Duster could still make him cry.

She asked, almost as an afterthought, 'Can you read, Mouche?'

'Yes, Madame.' The village school wasn't much, but he had gone every evening after chores, for five long years. That was when he was expected to be the heir, of course. Heirs went to school, though supernumes often didn't. Mouche could read and print a good hand and do his numbers well enough not to mistake four vibela for a vobati.

'Good. That will shorten your training by a good deal.'

Then she was gone from them, and they too were gone from her, and soon they were alone and Papa had dropped his veil and the dust of the road was puffing up between their toes as they walked the long way south, on the west side of River Giles, to the tributary stream that tumbled down from the western terraces through their own farm. All the long valley of the Giles was farmland. On the east, where the grain and pasture farmers held the land, ancient lava tubes lay side by side, lined up north and south like straws in a broom, their tops worn away, their sides rasped into mere welts by the windblown soil, each tube eastward a bit higher than the last, making a shallow flight that climbed all the way to the Ratback Range at the foot of the scarp. On the west, where the g'Darbos farm was, the terraces stepped steeply up to the mountains, and the fields were small and flinty, good for olives and grapes.

'Why are girls worth so much, Papa?' asked Mouche, who had always known they were but had never wondered over the whys of it until now.

'Because they are more capable than men,' said Papa.

'Why are they?'

'It's their hormones. They have hormones that change, day to day, so that for some parts of every month they are emotional and for some parts they are coldly logical, and for some parts they are intuitive, and they may bring all these various sensitivities to meet any problem. We poor fellows, Mouche, we have hormones that are pretty much the same all the time. We push along steadily enough, often in a fine frenzy, but we haven't the flexibility of women.'

'But why is that, Papa?'

'It's our genetics, boy. All a Family Man has to do is one act, taking only a few moments if the mama is willing and a little longer if she is not.' Papa flushed. 'So our hormones are what might be called simple-minded. They equip us to do *that thing*, and that's all. Used to be men attached a lot of importance to *that thing*, though it's something every mouse can do just as well. Women, though, they have to bear, and birth, and suckle, and – except among the monied folk – they also have to work alongside the Family Man in the business, tending and rearing. They have to work and plan, morn till night. So, their hormones are more complex, as they have to be.'

'And men get in more trouble, too.' Mouche was quoting his teacher.

'Well, yes, sometimes, in some men, our fine frenzy begets a lustful or murderous violence, and we tend to become contentious over little or nothing. But, as the Hags teach, "If you would have breathing space, stay out of one another's face," which is one reason we wear veils, not to threaten one another, so we may stay out of trouble and under control.'

'I thought it was so the women couldn't see us.'

'The *reason* they mustn't see us, Mouche, is that we must not tempt females, or stir their insatiable lusts, for that leads to disorder and mis-mothering. We are the weaker sex, my boy. It is why we must bid high for wives to take us, to show we have learned discipline and self-control.'

'Darn ol' hormones,' sulked Mouche. 'Girls get all the luck.'

'Well, hormones aren't the only reason,' Papa comforted him. 'Women are also valuable because they're fewer than men. Only one girl is born alive for every two boys, as we know to our sorrow.'

'Then not every man may have a wife, may he, Papa?' Mouche knew this was so, but at this juncture, he thought it wise to have the information verified. 'Even if he has a dowry?'

'Only about half, my boy. The oldest sons, usually. The younger ones must keep hand-maids.' Which was an old joke among men, one Mouche already understood. Papa wiped his face with the tail of his veil and went on, 'Once, long ago, I heard a storyteller's tale about the world from which our people originally came, that was Old Earth, where men were fewer than women ...'

'That's impossible.'

'The storyteller said it was because many males died young, in wars and gang fights and in dangerous explorations. Anyhow, in his tale, men were worth much more than women. Women sought men as chickens seek grain, gathering around them. A man could father children on several women, if he liked, without even dowering for them.'

'Fairy stories,' said Mouche. 'That's what that is. Who would want a woman you didn't dower for?' Everyone knew what such women would be like. Old or ugly or both. And probably infertile. And sickly. And certainly stupid, if they didn't even bother to get a good dowry first. Or even maybe invisible. 'Are there more invisible men than there are women?' he asked, the words slipping out before he thought.

Papa stopped in his tracks, and his hand went back to slap, though it did not descend on Mouche's evil mouth. 'Which only a fool would say,' Papa grated instead, thrusting his head forward in warning. 'You're too old to tell stories of invisible people or see such fairies and bug-a-boos as babies do, Mouche. You could be blue-bodied for it.' Mouche ducked his head and flushed, not having to ask what blue-bodying was. When a supernume was incorrigible and his father or master or boss or commander could do nothing with him, he was dyed blue all over and cast naked into the streets for the dogs to bite and the flies to crawl upon, and no man might feed him or help him or employ him thereafter. People who died foolishly were said to be 'independent as a blue body.'

Papa hadn't finished with him. 'Such talk could bring the Questioner down on us! Do you want Newholme to end up like Roquamb III? Do you?'

Stung, Mouche cried, 'I don't know how it ended up, Papa. I don't know anything about the Questioner.'

'Well, boy, let me tell you, you'd be sorry if words of yours reached *her* ears! As for Roquamb III, well, *she* took care of those poor souls. Imagine what that would be like. The whole world dying around you, and you knowing it was your fault!' Papa glared at him for a moment, then started down the road again, leaving Mouche thoroughly confused and not much enlightened. He'd been told something about the Questioner at school, but at the moment, Mouche couldn't remember what.

He decided to talk about something else during the rest of the trip, something with no danger to it. The dust puffing up between his toes gave him inspiration.

'Why do we have to walk everywhere, Papa? Or go behind a horse? Why don't we have engines? Like in the books?'

'Interstellar travel is very expensive,' said Papa, grateful for the change of subject. 'Our ancestors on our Motherworld saved up for centuries to send off our settlement, and the settlers had to pick and choose carefully what they would bring with them. They brought just enough rations to keep them until the first crops could be harvested. They brought seed and fertilized stock ova and an omni-uterus to grow the first calves and foals and piglets and lambs, and an incubator to hatch the first chickens.

'Our population was small and our first generations tended flocks and herds and planted crops and cut wood and quarried stone, and the next generation built up the towns, and searched for metal ores and rare biologicals to build up our trade. Then came sawmills along the river, and then the first smelter and the little railroad that runs from the mines to Naibah, and so on. Now we are almost ready to become industrial.'

'It sure seems slow,' mumbled Mouche.

'Well, it's been slower for us than for some, partly because we have so few women, and partly because Newholme has no coal or oil. We hadn't exactly counted on that. Every other planet that's had life for millions of years has had fossil fuels, but not Newholme.'

'I know,' Mouche muttered. He really did know all this; he'd learned it in school. Sometimes he thought it would be easier if the schools didn't talk about life on Old Earth or on the older settled worlds where people had replicators and transporters and all the robotic industries to support them. If he didn't know there were any such things as transporters and replicators, walking to Sendoph or working in the garden wouldn't seem so hard. It would just be natural.

That night was a good supper, better than any they'd had in a long time. The next day, too, as though Papa could not let him go without stuffing him first. Like a goose, Mouche thought. Off to the market, but fattened, first. Between these unexpectedly lavish meals, he had time to say goodbye to most everything that mattered. The pigs. The geese. The milk cow and her calf. With the money paid for Mouche, the family could get by without selling the heifer calf, and when she grew, they would have more milk to sell. With the money paid for Mouche, the mill could be repaired, and there'd be money coming in from grinding the neighbor's grain and pressing their grapes and olives. With the money paid for Mouche ...

It was only fair, he told himself, desperately trying to be reasonable and not to cry. If he'd been a girl, he'd have brought in a great dowry to Eline and Darbos. Just as the money paid for Eline had gone to her family, so money paid for a daughter would go to this family. But that would be honorable, which this was not. Buying a Hunk was honorable enough, it was only selling one that wasn't. Still, getting a good bid for a girl was just good sense.

Why should getting a good bid for a boy be different?

Mouche said farewell to pasture and woodlot and barn, farewell to the cat and her kittens, allowed the freedom of the loft and a ration of milk in return for ridding the granary of the Newholmian equivalent of mice. And finally he went to Duster's grave and knelt down to say goodbye, dropping more than a few tears on old Duster who had been his best and only friend, who had died in such a terrible way. He could have had one of Duster's pups from the neighbors – Old Duster had been an assiduous visitor next door – but there had been no food to feed another dog, said Mama. Well. Duster had left a numerous family behind. He was g'Duster, for sure, and long remembered.

Then it was farewell to Mama on the last evening and a long night listening to Papa cry in the night, and very early on the morning of the fifth, before it was light, he and red-eyed Papa were on the road once more, back to Sendoph, Mouche carrying only a little bag with his books inside, and Duster's collar, and the picture of a sailing ship he had drawn at school. Papa didn't have to put his veils on until they were far down the road, and he spent most of the time until then wiping his eyes.

When they came to House Genevois, Mouche asked, in a kind of panic, 'Can we walk down to the river, Papa?'

His papa gave him a sideways tilt of the head, but he walked on past House Genevois, down Bridge Street past the courtyard entrance, on to the corner where one of the little green-patinaed copper-domed towers topped the wall above the riverbank, and thence out over the stone arches of Brewer's Bridge itself while the invisible people moved back and forth like little mud-colored rivers running in all directions, their flow breaking around the human pedestrians without touching them, those pedestrians looking over the heads of the invisibles and never lowering their gaze. The breweries stood across the water, four of them, and on the nearest stubby tower a weathervane shifted and glittered, its head pointing north, toward the sea.

The river was low and sullen in this season, dark with ash from the firemounts to the south and east, with the islets of gray foam slipping past so slowly it was hard to believe they were moving at all. Between the water mills, the banks were thickly bristled with reed beds, green and aswarm with birdy-things, and far down the river a smoke plume rose where a wood burning sternwheel steamboat made its slow way toward them against the flow. Down there, Mouche thought, was Naibah, the capital, lost in the mists of the north, and beyond it the port of Gilesmarsh.

'The sea's down there,' he whispered.

'No reason you can't go to sea after you retire,' said Papa, hugging him close. 'Maybe even buy a little boat of your own.'

'Ship,' said Mouche, imagining breakers and surf and the cry of water-keens. 'Ship.'

His thoughts were interrupted by a rumble, a shivering. At first Mouche thought it was just him, shaking with sadness, but it wasn't him for the railing quivered beneath his fingers and the paving danced beneath his feet.

'Off the bridge,' said Papa, breathlessly.

They ran from the bridge, standing at the end of it, waiting for the spasm to end. Far to the east, the scarp was suddenly aglow, and great billows of gray moved up into the sky, so slowly they were like balloons rising. Down the river, one of the legs of the rotted wharf gave way, tipping it into the flow. Everything was too quiet until the shaking happened again, and yet again, with tiles falling from roofs and people screaming.

Then it stopped. The birdy-things began to cheep, people began to talk to one another, though their voices were still raised to a panicky level. Even the usually silent invisible people murmured in their flow, almost like water. The ominous cloud went on rising in the east, but the glow faded on the eastern ridge and the earth became solid once more.

Mouche remained bent over, caught in an ecstasy of grief and horror, come all at once, out of nowhere, not sure whether it was his heart or the world that was breaking apart.

'Boy?' Papa said. 'Mouche? What's the matter?'

'Oh, it hurts, it hurts,' he cried. It wasn't all his own feeling, from inside himself. He knew that. It was someone else's feeling, someone suffering, some huge and horrid suffering that had been let loose when the world trembled. Not his own. He told himself that. He wasn't dying. He wasn't suffering, not like that. His little pains were nothing, nothing, compared to that.

'There, there, boy, I know it does,' said Papa, completely misunderstanding. 'But the pain will pass if you let it. Remember that, Mouche. The pain will pass, but you have to let it.' And he looked at Mouche with the anguish he had carefully kept the boy from seeing.

After a moment, Mouche was able to raise his head and start back to the corner, trying not to let Papa see he was crying, easy enough since Papa was resolutely keeping his own face turned away. Mouche did not know who he was anymore. It was as if his whole world was coming apart and he with it. And though Papa had said it would pass, it felt more like pain on the way than pain going away. It had an approaching feel to it. Like the whistle of the little train, rising in pitch as it approached, so the pain seemed to intensify toward the end rather than fading.

The packet of gold was waiting Papa in the foyer of Genevois House, counted out by a stern-faced steward, some put into Papa's hands, some taken into keeping for Mouche. For later. When he was old. He signed a receipt for it in his best hand and put it back in the steward's hands, then the inner door was opened just wide enough for Mouche to enter.

'Well, come in, boy,' said Madame. 'Don't dawdle.'

And his life as a Hunk began.

2

Ornery Bastable, and a Bit of History

The first of mankind to land on Newholme had been an all-male schismatic group from the skinhead planet, Thor, that had set down on the flatlands east of the River Giles in a stolen ship full of plunder and recently captured slaves. They had started building two towns and had conducted trade in biologicals and furs for more than a decade while they went on building, getting ready, so they told the traders, for the time they would go out and capture themselves some women. All this was a matter of record.

While the two towns were still abuilding, along with fortresses at the center of each, disaster struck. A trading ship, arriving on its usual schedule, found the port abandoned except for rampaging monsters of whom the ship's crew killed a goodly number. Cursory investigation indicated that the planet was abandoned except for a few surviving slaves who said the settlers had all vanished in the darkness, a few days past.

The trader crew put the slaves aboard the settlers' ship, and flew it to the nearest COW station, claiming both slaves and ship as salvage even before reporting the disappearance to the Council of Worlds. Questioner I (the predecessor of Questioner II, of whom Mouche's Papa had spoken, and of whom we will learn more in due time), was sent by the COW to survey the situation. The two settlements were indeed empty, the half-built fortresses held nothing but dust, and though Questioner found no sign of monsters, it felt a definite sense of disquiet about the planet as a whole and said so.

At that stage of history, however, Questioner I was still rather new and had not yet gained the fall confidence of the Council of Worlds. Recommendations based on mere 'feelings' were almost always ignored because Questioner wasn't supposed to be able to 'feel' anything. The planet was, therefore, listed as vacant by the proper COW committee, which opened it up for another wave of settlers. These were not long in coming. They named the planet Newholme and the two half-built towns Naibah and Sendoph. The fortress in Naibah was called the Fortress of Lost Men, and the one in Sendoph became the Temple, or Panhagion, headquarters for the Hags.

The level and fertile lands along the river were soon claimed, and successive generations of farmers settled farther east, finally moving up among the Ratbacks, an area of crouched and rounded hills that ran to the very foot of the scarp. In these remote valleys the dower rules of the Hags could not be rigorously enforced, and the farm folk acquired a bucolic and obstinate independence. It was not unknown for a cash-poor man, if he was persistent and personable, to talk a woman into coming to his farm to help him pay off her price through time payments to her family.

The Bastable family resulted from exactly this sort of understanding. Harad Bastable was a good worker who inherited a good farm when his older brother died. One of his nearest neighbors had a plethora of daughters, some of whom did not want to marry into the city. Pretty Suldia agreed to wed Harad, and her family agreed to let her do so in return for payments or support to be given them in their age. Suldia soon produced a daughter, Pearla, born at home and registered at the Temple at six months of age, as was required for girls. Three years later, also at home, Suldia bore twins: a son, Oram, and another daughter, Ornalia.

Oram and Ornalia, soon called Ornery, were inseparable. Perhaps from this connection, perhaps from something genetic – the Bastables had a few cattle and knew all about freemartins – or perhaps from example, Ornery grew into what the farm people called a crower, a boyish girl, one who liked boyish things, a scrambler over, a climber up, a rider of horses and tamer of creatures. To look at them both, the boy and the girl, one would find little difference between them. Both were lean and freckled, with generous mouths full of frequent laughter. Both had good appetites and ferocious energy.

Pearla, on the other hand, grew to be a very feminine woman, and in her twentieth year she was offered for by a young man from Sendoph who had seen her in that city during the harvest festival. At that same festival, Pearla had seen Hunks riding with their patronesses in the street and had decided on the spot that she wanted one of those for herself. If what it took to get one was a few years of not unpleasant boredom, then she would spend the few years.

It helped that she did not object to the young man who was offering for her. Nothing about him stirred her sensibilities, but he smelled of spice water, he had a carriage of his own, the family had a good haulage business of boats and ships and wagons that went from here to there and back again, as well as a grand house with several supernume servants plus (one could not help noticing) a goodly number of invisible people.

So, with much backing and forthing as to the terms of the dowry, Harad and Suldia agreed that the family in Sendoph might dower Pearla in, if Pearla herself approved. The prospective bride went to Sendoph to spend a few weeks among the maybe-husband's family to see how she liked being treated as a lady.

Ornery was saddened at Pearla's approaching marriage, not so much at the loss of a sister, for they had never been playmates, but because the event suddenly made her confront her own future as a female, a sister growing up in her brother's shadow. Oram would inherit the farm. Her parents would use the money received from Pearla to dower in a bride for him, but even before that, Ornery herself would most likely be dowered in to some city man, which she would hate!

Truth to tell, Ornery did not feel herself drawn to men at all. Though she was of an age to be stirred by romantic or erotic thoughts about men, she remained unmoved. The Hags wouldn't force her to marry, but they could make life miserable if she didn't. She was registered at the Panhagion, and if she got to be twenty-one or two without being dowered for (an event which also required registration at the Temple) the Hags would want to know why. If she refused to be dowered, the Hags could make her a Hagger or even name her to Temple Service, though usually it was newborns who were named, so they could grow up Hag-rid. Being a Hag was easier, so they said, when you'd grown up to it. Though what was hard about it, nobody knew! Though there were only a few of them around anytime one went to Temple, they never seemed to sweat at anything.

Ornery didn't want to be a Hagger. Haggers had none of the honor and all of the labor. Maybe she'd just run off and become a Wilderneer, living in caves in the badlands, letting her hair grow long, sneaking and pillaging for her living. Females didn't become Wilderneers, though. At least Ornery had never heard of any.

Pearla's departure brought all these matters boiling to the surface of Ornery's mind, and she became so aggravated and belligerent over her role apprehensions that she was rude to her mother, at which her father threatened her with total and perpetual responsibility for the kitchen garden if she didn't straighten up. Fuming, Ornery decided to get up before dawn and run away – maybe forever. Probably just for a while. Leaving the home valley was a strictly forbidden pastime that was nonetheless habitual for Oram and Ornery both.

At this particular juncture, however, Ornery hated Oram along with everyone else, so she did not take him with her. Besides, he was bossy and wouldn't let her go where she wanted to, and today she intended to do precisely what *she* wanted to and nothing else because that's what Pearla was doing, so it was only fair.

Ornery rose before the family wakened, filled her pockets with apples, a chunk of bread, a bit of cheese, and went out into the early morning. Not far from the farm was the beginning of a southerly-tending valley, from which she climbed over a ridge to a narrow canyon, and from the end of that into a lava tube that had only bits of its roof left, here and there. Far along this tube, among areas of tumbled stones, was a pit into a lower tube, one that could be climbed down into by way of shattered ledges, and then there was a long walk down that tube, lit only by occasional gleams from cracks above, to a darker pit, one leading to a tube three layers down. Easing the descent was a rather short rope, which was all Oram and Ornery had been able to get away with. Rope was valuable, even short bits of it that could be made into bridles or gate ties or whatever.

Ornery lowered herself onto a steep pile of stone that had fallen from the pit opening, a pile which made descent possible as otherwise the rope would have been far too short. Lying against the rockpile were the torches Ornery and Oram had fashioned the last time they had come here, and at the edge of the dim light that came through the pit opening was the cairn of rocks they had piled to distinguish one direction in the tunnel from the other. Both ways looked the same, dark holes leading endlessly into the black, and since the rope often twisted and turned during the climb down, it was difficult to tell one direction from the other. It was probable, Oram had claimed, that monsters lived down here. There were many stories of such. Big wriggly things that set up stones called Joggiwagga, and huge four-eyed flyers called Eigers. So far as Ornery knew, they were only stories told to the twins by someone she couldn't remember.

On a conveniently located smooth stone beside the pile, Ornery sat down to take her breakfast. After eating, she would light the torch and go some way in the direction marked by the cairn, not that she expected to find much. She and Oram had already explored the other way to the limit of their light, finding nothing but rock and more pits and the bones of various things that had maybe fallen in and couldn't get out again, all of them too small to be monsters.

She had finished her bread and cheese and had just set her teeth into an apple when the rock beneath her shivered. At first all her rumination about Wilderneers and monsters came flooding back and she figured something huge was coming down the tunnel. She dropped her lunch forthwith and started up the rope, only to be shaken off, tumbled down the stone pile, and left bruised and battered on the floor of the tunnel while the world went crazy around her. Stone cracked. Rocks fell. The pit opening seemed to jitter in midair, like an eye blinking against a glare. There was a sound from inside, outside, somewhere, that went past the limits of noise into something heard with the skin and the bones, a sound so huge she could not exist inside it.

So, for a time, she stopped existing. When she came to herself again, the world was quiet, the pit opening was gray with dusk, and from it the rope hung like a worm on a web, twisting gently in a hot little wind that came from down the tunnel. Windward, far along the tube, shone a fiery light. Something had fallen, letting the outside in, or something inside was burning. She thought of going to see, but she ached so that she could not make herself go an inch farther than necessary, and she was, besides, overcome with a feeling of such grief and horror she could not move. In her dazed condition she seemed to hear a gigantic voice calling to her, though it wasn't her name it called, which made no sense at all.

She buried her face in her hands and merely sat until her dizziness subsided, then staggered to the top of the pile where the rope hung. Her first two attempts were abortive, and on the third try she managed only with excruciating difficulty, as though she had never climbed the rope before. In the light, she could see her bruises and bloody abrasions. All the air was thick with dust and smoke. The way back to the valley took forever, even though there were two moons still almost full that rose as the sun set in a blaze of crimson, purple, and orange. She lost her way, coming to a hot waste she had never seen before and losing herself as she tried to go around it. The mountain trembled again as it grew darker, emitting wavering fumes across the faces of the moons. Eventually, weariness conquered and she fell into a little grassy pit, pulling her coat around her and relinquishing everything else. Mama and Papa would be furious, but she'd deal with it in the morning.

Morning came. She rose, looked around herself, told off her landmarks and realized she had gone past home. She went toward it and came upon the same waste she had encountered the night before, ash and mud and stink, with smoke rising from the edges where things had burned and there, at the far side, a piece of roof she recognized as from the chicken coop and beside it a tall post that had stood at the gate to the vineyard, crowned with a circlet of dried vine.

She screamed first, then ran about, then trembled and merely wept. She tried, but could get no closer, for the earth burned under her feet. Either her people had fled or they were dead under all that black. The nearest people were at the mines, along the foot of the scarp, but the way there was blocked by smoking rock. The nearest farm was down valley, and she finally turned in that direction, walking along the hills above the black, realizing along toward midmorning that she had gone long past the neighboring farm, that everything down this valley was gone.

There was a family one valley over. She crossed the ridge and came there in the early evening, trudging up their lane to be confronted by dogs and people.

'Why it's Oram,' cried the woman of the house. 'That's your name isn't it, boy?'

Ornalia didn't correct the misapprehension. 'My family, all gone,' she cried. 'Buried, and all the cows and chickens. All but my sister Pearla. Oh, they're gone, all gone...'

And the farm folk, between questioning and answering and giving her tea and food and offering the use of a washbasin, at once made plans to send a wagon to Sendoph to report what had happened to the neighboring valley. Oram, they said, could ride along.

Pearla was alone in the house when Ornery came, for the dowerer and his parents had gone to Naibah to arrange payment of the dowry. Oh, she had seen the mountain blow, she said. Oh, she had feared for her family.

'The vineyard gone,' grieved Pearla. 'Oh, Ornery, I can't imagine it gone. I can't imagine Mama and Papa, gone. So quick, like that.'

'There's just mud and ashes,' sobbed Ornery. 'No house, no barn, no storage houses, no poultry house, no orchard. Mama ... I hoped for a while maybe, well, maybe, but everything's gone, all down the valley ...'

They cried on one another's shoulders and told one another it would be all right, though it was a good deal easier for Pearla to say, who, though orphaned, would not have her life much changed from the one she had already planned. Still, they both wept, taking a long, uninterrupted time in which to grieve and talk of their sadness and despair, and after that of the fact that Ornalia was adrift, with no place to call home.

'Oh, you can stay here,' Pearla wept. 'They'll let you. I mean, you're old enough to be dowered for, even now.'

'I'd rather die,' spat Ornery, all yesterday's anger bubbling up through her grief, like mud roiled up from the bottom of a clear stream.

'But, you'll want to someday ...'

She cried, 'Never. I don't want to be married, I don't want children, the idea of being married off to some man is just... repulsive.'

Pearla flushed. 'Well, Ornery, it's not wonderful, I know. I mean, my intended, he's nice enough, but ... oh, he doesn't stir me at all. None of the Family Men I've met do. They seem all tangled up in these deals and games and strategies of theirs. They give you a flower and candy, they say sweet things, and it all comes out like Oram being polite to Grandma Miby.'

They both laughed, wiping tears. Oram had had to be extensively coached to say, 'Hello, Grandma Miby, how are you today?' and it always came out in a completely wooden voice.

'But,' Pearla went on, 'there's Hunks, Ornalia! And they're oh, they're wonderful. My mother-in-law, she has one, and she says they make life worth living. Some of the things they know how to do ...' She sighed. 'And I'm only twenty, so by the time I'm thirty, I'll have a Hunk of my own!'

Ornery shook her head. 'Call me Ornery, Pearly. I don't feel like being Ornalia, and I don't want a Hunk, either.'

'You could serve the Temple as a Hagger ...'

'Doing what? I'd have to give up all life except Temple life. I'd have to serve wherever the Hags say to serve. That's no life for me, Pearly. What I'd really like is a stephold for myself. A tiny croft with a few sheep, a garden, and a loom for winter work. Some women have done it, begging sickly lambs from the neighbors and nursing them into a flock, building their own shelter of turf, getting by through full season or lean …'

'Some women have done it, true, but they weren't young or fertile,' said Pearla. 'I doubt the Hags would allow you to buy even a stephold farm, though you will have some money coming.'

'From where?' Ornery was astonished.

'If Mama and Papa are dead, if Oram is dead … my dowry will come to you.'

'But I can't use it as I like,' cried Ornery.

'Even if they'd let you buy a farm, they wouldn't let a healthy young woman stay unmarried.' Pearla stared thoughtfully into the fire, shocked by all this loss into an unusual consideration for her sister. 'There's an idea creeping around in my head, though. You say the family who helped you thought you were Oram?'

'They did.'

'I can see why, the way you're dressed, and how you always looked alike. All of us were born at home, not at the Panhagion birthing center, so you – that is, my sister Ornalia – was registered at the Temple at six months age, as all girls must be, but they don't have a DNA sample, as they would if you'd been born there, and Oram, *he* wasn't even registered, and *he's* not required to make Temple visits, so why not go on being Oram?'

Momentarily shocked, Ornery thought about it. 'Veils,' she said at last. 'If I'm wearing veils …'

'Which Oram always would be, in public, at least. And you're not built like me or Mama, but like Papa's sisters, very lean, with hardly any chest at all.'

'But what will I do? I can't live here with you.'

'No. But my soon-husband is a decent sort of man. He owns ships, Ornery. If we can think up a way, he could put you on a ship, as an apprentice boy. You're seventeen. Old enough. Then when you're older yet, you could buy a farm.'

'Close quarters on a ship,' said Ornery, who had heard their father talk about the summer he spent as a sailor, when he was young, a mere supernume, before he inherited the farm. 'They'd soon find out I was female.'

'We could say you were sold as a chatron,' said Pearla, after a moment's thought. 'You had it cut off, but then the family that wanted to buy you was killed when the mountain exploded. So now here you are, a chatron, but you no longer need to be sold. The farm is gone, so now you'd prefer to go to sea. My dowry will more than pay your apprenticeship if I can't get my soon-husband to pay it. I'm sure I can make him arrange it, one way or the other. He likes me, Ornery. He said he was afraid he'd have to dower some woman he couldn't fancy making children on, but he likes me.'

This last came with a tremulous smile, and for the first time gave Ornery something to feel thankful for. Thanks be to the Hagions that Pearla had been here in Sendoph rather than at home.

Pearla and Ornery took the trouble to learn something about chatrons, it being a subject not much thought of on the farms even though male things were gelded or neutered there all the time. Chatrons were mostly playmates for city daughters, companions for young wives tired from bearing but not yet entitled to a Hunk, de-sexed beings who wore a distinctive dress of baggy trousers and embroidered vests and veils a bit lighter than most men.

Before long, Pearla's soon-husband, all well-meaning ignorance, fell in with their plans. He had not previously known that Oram was a chatron, but then, he did not really know Pearla well, as yet, and might, if he followed custom, never know her much better. Chatron though Oram was, this brother of his soon-wife would be properly provided for.

3

The Establishment of the Questioner by Haraldson the Beneficent

Mothers can not tell us who we are.
Mirrors can not tell us who we are.
Only time can tell for every moment
we are choosing what to be.

'REFLECTIONS'
HARALDSON AND THE HOLIES
GALACTIC METRONOME
TERRAREG, REPRORIGHT 3351 AZY

The life of Haraldson (3306–3454 AZY) has been the subject of many biographers; his abilities and intentions have been analyzed for centuries. It is true that he was a popular musician of interstellar fame, one who could move the population of whole systems with the sound of his voice or the twitch of a finger on the strings. It is true he had wed the most beautiful woman in the known universe and fathered children whose charm and poise, even in adolescence, had to be witnessed to be believed. It is true that he had no faults anyone could uncover with the most diligent search, and it was also true that he displayed the virtues of kindness, fidelity, modesty, and empathy combined with a political savvy which had not been known since before the Dispersion and had, even then, been rare. He was a phenomenon, a unique example of mankind, one whose honesty and goodwill could not be questioned, and it is probable that only Haraldson could have done what he did.

What he did was to get himself elected President for Life of the Council of Worlds (COW), with the title of Beneficent Exemplary. At his coronation, Haraldson sang the first verse of 'Reflections,' the song that had first brought him to the attention of the worlds: 'Mothers can not tell us who we are. Mirrors can not tell us who we are. Only time can tell, for every moment we are choosing what to be.'

'Let us choose justice and civility,' he went on. 'Let us do so in the company of beauty and joy. If we have not that company, let us still honor ourselves in the choice of justice and civility.'

No sooner had the coronation occurred than Haraldson issued the Edicts of Equity, in which for the first time humanity was defined in terms of intelligence, civility, and the pursuit of justice rather than by species or form. Certain Earthian creatures other than mankind were immediately rendered human by the edicts, gaining the right to life, liberty, and the pursuit of satisfactions thereby, and some extremist individuals and groups who had previously paraded themselves as human were disabused of this notion.

The fallout from the edicts had not yet settled when Haraldson reorganized the bureaucracy of the council, setting up several departments or 'Houses,' among which were HoTA, House of Technical Advancement, and HoLI, House of Legislation and Investigation. In setting up HoLI, Haraldson declared that regulation and research should be inseparable, since mankind's societies had for too long been hip-deep in laws that had been useless, unenforceable, and despicable from inception. If a law needed constant tinkering with, he said, it is a bad law, and the goal of justice should always be superior to the rule of bad law no matter how good the intent!

It was Haraldson, almost single-handedly, who made COW an effective agent of general welfare for all member worlds – as well as any mankind worlds COW could reach – were then subject to Haraldson's edicts forbidding slavery, genocide, settling on previously occupied planets, racial crowding, and the destruction of either habitat or biodiversity. Haraldson further provided that persons must not only advocate but assure personal rights for all races, and that they must not discriminate against born, hatched, aggregated, or budded creatures on the basis of species, morphology, color, hispidity, gender, age, or opinion, except as species, morphology, gender, et al. provably altered the consequence of any given situation.

It sounded innocuous enough until Haraldson made it clear just how inclusive he expected the term 'opinion' to be. 'Language, cuisine, the arts, culture, tradition, religion, sexual and reproductive practices vary widely among mankind and even more widely among other races. All these, therefore, are to be considered matters of opinion, to which every person is entitled, and the free expression of which is guaranteed up to and no farther than the point at which that expression conflicts *directly* with someone else's opinion. Direct conflict shall be defined as incivility directed at a specific person or group as well as any action designed to alter someone else's opinion by coercion, law, or violence.

'Students of history will recall that prior to Dispersion, our Earthian ancestors espoused civil liberties,' Haraldson explained. 'Theoretical liberties, however, were too often assured at the expense of actual civilities, and as civilities were lost, litigation emerged as a way of life with a consequent reduction in *real* liberties for all persons except lawyers, who, like mercenaries, are profiteers of discord. Persons were actually allowed, by law, under the guise of free expression, to shout into the faces of those who held differing opinions and to intrude upon their privacy. Liberty has two legs. Vigilance is certainly one, but civility is as certainly the other.

'With this in mind, I hereby establish the defecation rule: A defecator is at liberty to commit the act, but he may not commit it on his neighbor's doorstep or in the quiet street in front of his neighbor's house, or in his neighbor's alley, or in his neighbor's customary place of work, or anyplace where the neighbor or any other passerby may step in it by accident in his own zone of privacy and tranquility.

'This means that any opinion may be expressed privately or in incorporated communities of the likeminded from which the non-likeminded are at liberty to depart. When an opinion moves into another's zone of privacy and tranquility, however, civility shall reign. If the Hairless Supremacists of Thor plan to march through a quiet community of furry Krumats with the sole intent of discomfiting the Krumats thereby, they may not do so, for though freedom of expression is guaranteed, a captive audience for an incivility is not.

'Our neighborhoods are an extension of our homes. Our right to privacy does not stop at our front doors. Our rights to the tranquility of our own senses and the privacy of our own space only gradually decrease as we move from our homes to the neighborhood street, down that street through our incorporated community of likeminded persons, out of that community and into the arteries of public commerce, waning gradually as we come to areas also used by other persons and ideas. Even there, we hold about ourselves a bubble of privacy which we lose totally only when we relinquish both senses and space by voluntarily choosing to become a tourist or part of a live audience.

'Despite this rule of civility, departure from the community and open expression of opinion remain absolute rights, and every community and every government must provide both opportunities for departure and venues for expression. Such opportunities and venues shall be both fully accessible to and fully avoidable by all citizens. No one shall attempt to control the coming and going from such venues or the events occurring within them.'

The edicts of Haraldson were heralded as enlightened and were, after some false starts and befuddlement, generally accepted among the member worlds. The number of extremists began to drop as various factions killed each other off in the free-expression zones, and conflict waned as rebels were encouraged to depart. Except for gender issues, which, like Proteus, seemed capable of infinite metamorphoses, most societal agitations were assuaged and kept that way.

The House of Legislation and Investigation was charged with the periodic assessment of all mankind worlds for conformity to the edicts. During the first few decades of Haraldson's reign, these assessments were done in an orderly and timely way, producing tranquility and openness of opportunity and serving to increase general knowledge about the worlds in question.

Eventually Haraldson grew weary of his long years at the helm. He desired to leave the post of Exemplary and spend his last years in the study of non-mankind intelligences. The Council of Worlds, however, appealed to Haraldson's sense of duty, claiming that no candidate could possibly take his place. After a period of reflection, the aged Haraldson addressed the public.

He said he was not immortal, he had found his task arduous, and he felt that no holder of an elective office, including himself, could be relied upon to continue indefinitely a course which ran counter to so many human urges. Age or appetite would inevitably corrupt good intentions, he said, and therefore an unbiased and incorruptible agency must be created to continue the assessments of human settlements around the galaxy.

COW referred the matter to HoLI, who decided no committee or council of persons could be totally incorruptible. HoLI referred the matter to the House of Technical Advancement (HoTA) whose staff came up with an answer. They would develop a bionic construct that contained a human mind or minds, a construct infallibly programmed with Haraldson's edicts. The construct would be capable of learning, applying, and adapting those edicts while retaining their Spirit and sense. Even though the technicians would start with one or more human brains – a more ideal interface could not be found – human memories and emotions would be repressed. The construct would have no vanity or greed, it would be incapable of pique or sloth, and would, thus, be immune to influence. The brains within it would be harvested from among persons who were already dying. Haraldson, on being approached, refused the honor of being among them.

HoTA was fortunate at that time to employ a number of exceptional scientists who, even more fortunately, worked well together. When the assemblage was completed it turned out to be a conceptual and technological tour de force, decades if not centuries ahead of its time. Because it held three human brains and unlimited memory, complicated corpora callosa and storage units of enormous capacity were required, but the solutions to these and other problems of structure and design were uniformly inspired.

In fact, the most knotty problem encountered by the technicians had been not the brain but the body. There had been no conception of what the Questioner – as it was now being called – should look like. Eventually, the team agreed on a motherly image, an ethnic in appearance and, since the machinery was massive, Brunhildian.

Questioner I was finished and programmed, and Haraldson himself attended the dedication. On that occasion, with his usual foresight, he advised the chief of HoTA that it would be prudent for the House to undertake a continuous update of Questioner plans and specifications in the event that Questioner ever met with a fatal accident.

Questioner I worked well among the worlds for several hundred years. Questioner was able, in many cases, to bring imperfect societies into conformity with the edicts, and it was also able to dispose of societies which were totally unacceptable. After lengthy argument, the Council of Worlds agreed that Questioner had proven flawless and might, therefore, see to such matters on its own initiative. At first COW wanted advise and consent status, but after the first few interminable debates, COW felt it best to get out of the loop and was, accordingly, bypassed.

The ruthless sentences of the Questioner were carried out rarely but thoroughly. Many were the docudramas produced concerning the final years of intransigent populations. Questioner I perished at last in the Flagian Miscalculation, the cataclysm of self-mortification that destroyed the Flagian Sector. Due to Haraldson's foresight, however, the technical specifications and many of the core components for a new device were ready and waiting, including technical advances that had been made in the intervening centuries.

Questioner II had all the abilities of its predecessor but a slightly less massive housing and a slightly expanded mission. On the basis of Questioner I's tantalizing reports, COW wished to know more about the non-mankind races: the horn-headed Gablians; the inscrutable Quaggi; the individualistic Borash; the numerous Korm.

At no time during the first or second construction of the Questioner had anyone in the Council of Worlds thought to specify that the brains used in Questioner should come from member planets that were subject to the edicts. In the welcome absence of such directives, the technicians had chosen brains that would make their jobs easiest: those easiest to get, with the least information and the fewest treasured memories. One technician, in fact, was heard to comment on the irony of selecting Questioner brains from cultures that forbade asking any questions at all.

4

Orientation to the Amatory Arts

During orientation, which is what Madame Genevois called the sessions conducted with each new boy in the small classroom, Mouche was required to memorize certain information that Madame categorized as 'essential to your understanding of your role in life.' These rules, regulations, laws, and customs were read aloud and explained by Madame, after which Mouche was drilled until letter perfect by Simon, one of the instructors, a former Hunk who had been improvident and was now required to earn a living in his later years.

The first thing drummed into him was the Dower Law.

'Section one,' parroted Mouche, 'provides that a family wishing to continue through the male line, usually through the eldest son, must pay dowry to a girl's family for the use of the girl as a wife.'

'And this is called?' asked Simon.

Mouche responded promptly, 'This is called dowering in, as the wife comes into the man's family and takes his name. Section two provides that a younger son who also wishes to continue his biological line may set up a new ...'

'With the support,' prompted Simon.

'May, with the support of his family, set up a new line, under a new name, and pay dower for a wife under that name ...'

'Which is called?'

'Dowering off. Because his new name is an off-shoot of the old family name. Like, say, the family name is Vintner, he could set up as family Vineyard. Or he may buy his way into a family that has a daughter but no son, where he takes her family name, and that's called dowering out.'

'Dowering in, off, or out,' explained Simon, with a muffled yawn, 'is always seen from the groom's parents' point of view, as they are the ones who pay. Now, section three?'

'Section three states that any attempt to evade the law through elopement, rapine, or abduction is punishable by blue-bodying and consequent death. Simon, what's rapine?'

'Forcing sex upon a woman, often with the intent of getting her pregnant.'

'I didn't know you could do that.'

'Used to be a good bit of it, but no more. Not unless you want to end up dead.'

'When was there a good bit of it?'

Simon settled himself. 'Well, it was like this. Our ancestors came to this world in ten ships. The first ship had the male workers, the livestock ova, and the reproducer, but it didn't have any women on it at all. That was so the men could get things whipped into shape, shelters made weathertight, crops planted, things like that, before the women and children came on the second ship. But the second ship was delayed, and instead they sent the support ship, the one that had the machines ...'

'What machines? I didn't think we had machines?'

'Of course we had machines. What do you think the Denti-med is? And the sensor array that keeps track of the volcanoes? And the stuff at the space port that lets us talk to the ships?'

'Oh. I guess I never thought those were machines.'

'Well, they are. Our people didn't bring many, they had limited resources, but they chose not to do without medicine or geological and weather sensors or a space port. So, anyhow, the technology ship was the one that set down second, and it was full of technicians and scholars, a lot of them women, but most all of them were, so to speak, spoken for.'

'They had husbands?'

'Right. Or as much as. Anyhow, the first ship men were feeling pretty randy by then, so they started raiding, stealing the women, and some of them got hurt.'

'Some of the women?'

'Right. Some even got killed, which made their friends and colleagues very angry, so the others, the scientists and professors and technicians, men and women both, they moved the machines and the supplies and the libraries into the half-built fortress in Sendoph, and all the women stayed in there where they couldn't get abducted. Most of the people on that second ship were Gaeans, like Haraldson, worshippers of the Life-mother, and they were the ones who set up the Council of Hags.'

'And they wrote the Dower Laws.'

'Well, not right away. The laws sort of developed. But the key thing was, nobody got a wife without paying for her, and wives got the right to satisfactions for themselves. When the ship with all the women arrived, two or three years later, the Dower Laws were already in effect. Including section four, which you may now quote.'

Mouche nodded. 'Section four provides that every Family Man must have a unique family name for his genetic line, as it is to guarantee the uniqueness of each male line that this system was designed by the Revered Hags to meet the needs of the men of Newholme.' Mouche swallowed a yawn.

'And, finally, section five.'

'Section five says that every marriage contract must provide that once the wife has fulfilled her contractual obligations in providing her husband with his own, specific lineage, she has the right to one or more well trained Consorts to make her life more pleasant.'

'Which is why you're here,' said Simon, cuffing him lightly over the ear. 'Recite it one more time, then you can be excused.'

5

Life as a Lobster

During Mouche's first days at House Genevois, he stayed in the welcome suite where his life seemed to consist of nothing but orientation and baths. Dirt that had taken twelve years to accumulate was loosened over a period of days, pried from beneath finger and toenails, rasped off of horny calluses, steamed out of pores he had not known he had in places he had never bothered to wash.

'You know what we call new boys?' said Simon. 'We call them lobsters, because they're always in hot water.'

'What's a lobster?' asked Mouche.

'A kind of Old Earthian critter,' Simon replied. 'Eaten after boiling. Like a crustfish, sort of, but with more legs.'

Even while Mouche soaked in the hot water there were snacks, bits of this and that, little plates and bowls brought by silent, invisible creatures at whom one never looked directly. They took away the empty plates and refilled them and brought them back again, but no one noticed the plates until they were set down, because when they were being carried, they too were invisible.

Bodies could not be properly contoured, according to Madame, unless they were well fed. There was also massage, which was embarrassing, though he soon learned to disregard the invisible creatures pounding away at him. When the staff of the House weren't washing him or pounding on him, or feeding him, or correcting his speech, he could read anything he liked from a great library full of real books.

'Am I the only one here?' he asked Simon. 'I haven't seen anyone else.'

'No, boy, and you won't, not until you're clean as a plucked goose, and fat as one. New boys are always the butt of jokes and hazing. That's life. It's always been that way. But there's no point letting a new boy in for the kind of labeling that will make training him or selling him more difficult. Too many good Hunks have been ruined by being called Fatty or Slobby or Stinky. So, you don't meet anyone until you meet them on equal footing, so far as cleanliness and elementary courtesy goes. We'll have no nasty nicknames here. Propriety, boy. That's what Madame wants. Our clients want Consorts they can take anywhere: to the theater, to the festivals, to the forecourt of

639

the Temple, even. Our graduates must have no lingering taint of the pigpen or the tanners.'

'Decorum,' said Madame. 'You'll behave in gentlemanly fashion, and you'll do it not only when you're being observed by one of us' – by which she meant the staff of Genevois House – 'but also when you're alone with your colleagues. It must become second nature to you, a habit unbreakable as a vow.'

So it was Mouche wasn't totally surprised when, clad in a white linen tunic, soft stockings and sandals, he was introduced to a similarly clad group of young men so polite it near took his breath away.

'You are welcome, Mouche,' said one. 'We are happy to have you among us,' said another, and such like other syrupy phrases that made him more than merely worried. His concern was justified, for when the lights were out and the monitors had left the dormitory, Mouche came in for rather different treatment. The habit unbreakable as a vow was, like most vows, quite breakable when no one was watching. Still, it was no worse a bruising than he'd had from the cow when she'd resented milking, or from the buck of the plow when it had hit a root. Next day he was able to say with a straight face that he'd fallen on the stairs, and Simon was able with a straight face to accept that explanation.

Genevois House was all gray stone and iron grilles on the outside. On the inside it was white plaster and carved wood and marble and velvet. The bare gymnasia were cavernous and echoing; but even there mirrors towered between gold-leaf piers and the floors were set in wood mosaic. The stuffy parlors were small and hushed and elegant. In the former, Mouche learned to fight hand to hand, to dance, and to fence with a sword. In the other, he learned from the conversation mistress to fence with words. Learning to fence in the bedroom would come later, though he was soon started on erotic exercises. Simon said boys his age all did erotic exercises anyhow, so better put it to some use.

As before, he spent hours in the library, reading all manner of books which were commonly read among the better classes of women, some of them written centuries before on Old Earth or the old colonial worlds, and all of them imported from worlds that had had time to develop the arts past the purely provincial. There were other hours in the kitchen, being lectured by the chef and the wine master. Not that Newholme had many vintages to brag of, but those they did should be properly appreciated. There were hours at the table, learning how to discriminate among foods, how to eat them elegantly, and how to manage veils of various weights while one carried on charming and amusing conversation. It became second nature: the left hand up to catch the veil at the right side; the upward sweep of the fingers to lift the veil from the mouth; the release, letting the veil drop as one chewed and swallowed. Not that the gauzy stuff Hunks usually wore was much of an impediment. Only respectable men wore real veils, and respectable men did not eat with their wives in public. They stayed in their offices at home or at their businesses among other men, where they belonged. 'Or should be at,' so the saying went. 'Men of Business should be at business.' Or else.

Several times each tenday – forty tendays the year, divided into four seasons – the new boys, who were not yet sexually mature and therefore not yet veiled, walked with their teachers to the park to watch the show put on by the advanced students. The older boys rode gracefully on horseback, glittering like gems. They picked quarrels with one another, and debated eloquently, declaiming dramatically, with many references to honor. Sometimes they fought with swords, brilliantly but inconsequentially, until one of the uniformed Housemasters stopped the battle and made them shake hands. The new boys were not the only ones watching. From closed carriages along the bridle paths, eyes watched and hands took notes, and it was for these watchers that the charades were played. The merchandise, so Simon said, had to go on display, for House Genevois often received bids for certain Consorts years before they were fully trained.

When the short nights of summertime came, the advanced students went off in all directions: the tongue-tied to summer conversation classes; the lazy to remedial fencing school; the merely awkward to dancing school. There were no remedial courses in amatory arts. One either did well in those or one was given one's pension money and dismissed. Very few were dismissed, said Simon. Madame had an instinct for boys who would do well in amatory arts.

Almost all the newest boys were sent to the equestrian school owned by House Genevois, where Mouche rode horseback, at first a few hours each day, then all day every day, until he could stay on anything with legs, whether bareback or asaddle. By this time he had friends among the students – as Madame called them – and had himself taken part in the harassment of several new boys. He had also grown taller by a handspan and added weight to match, had found the first pale hairs sprouting near his groin, and had heard his voice crack on at least three occasions.

'So, Mouche,' said Madame, the day after he returned to Sendoph, 'today you are one year with us. As of today, you are no longer a new boy.'

Mouche swept her a bow in which no hint of servility was allowed. He would learn about groveling, Simon said, but not until later. Groveling was sometimes necessary for Hunks, but the dangers inherent in the practice had to be weighed in the light of experience, which Mouche had none of at this stage.

'Yes, Madame,' he said.

Madame acknowledged him with a gracious nod. 'You graduate to your own suite today. Simon will take you to it.'

Simon did so, through the main hall, past the low-ceilinged dining room with its open hearth and smell of sausages, up the broad marble stairs onto the wide landing with its tall windows overlooking the street between great swags of wine-colored fabric and its equally tall doors leading to the apartments of the staff, and up a flight more, through the deeply carved doors that led into Consort Country.

'No galloping on these stairs,' warned Simon. 'Madame's orders. You gallop on these stairs, Madame may rethink letting you go up.'

'I didn't think I'd go this year,' said Mouche in wonderment. 'I thought you had to be veiled first.'

'Ordinarily, yes. But the way you're growing, you will be veiled by the end of the year. Fact is, Mouche, we need to increase dormitory space for the younger students, but we've several empty suites in Consort Country.'

Something funny in Simon's voice when he mentioned increasing dormitory space, Mouche thought. Something a bit tentative and uncertain. He didn't have long to think about it, for Simon pushed upon the door, revealing a table set with tapers and a long, narrow, very dark hallway. At Simon's direction, Mouche lit them each a candle before the door swung closed.

The front part of House Genevois, so Simon said, had been rebuilt and added to during the last century in accordance with modern rules of architecture, and that was the part people saw when they visited. Once through the door into Consort Country, however, one went back into a sprawling maze made up of many separate buildings, some of them dating back to the first settlement, that had been acquired, remodeled, and joined together in stages and in accordance with no overall plan or direction. The suites of the Consorts presumptive were scattered throughout this labyrinth, like lumps of fat in a black pudding, for though windows and skylights had once lit the corridors, most of them had been built over, leaving the passageways in darkness.

Mouche followed Simon, bearing his own dim sphere of light, through which he could catch only a glimpse of the dark, velvety runners on the corridor floors, the carved wagon-panel along the walls, the shadowed ceilings high above with the gilded cornices, the gold of the ornate frames surrounding huge, dark pictures that lined every wall. The subject matter was at first indiscernible, but then, when the light caught one such painting at the right angle, all too obvious.

Mouche grunted, not sure whether to laugh or gag.

'Pay no attention to them, boy,' said Simon. 'Some persons wish to be immortalized in this fashion, though the Hagions know why. Perhaps they use these images to titillate themselves. Perhaps the paintings stir them to unaccustomed lust.'

'I wouldn't lust over *that*,' said Mouche, indignantly. 'And their faces are *bare!*'

'Faces are usually bare in the bedroom, boy. I wouldn't lust over such activities either, but there are some who will, and that's a matter for us all to keep in mind, Mouche. There are always some who will.' His voice resonated with that same tentative unease Mouche had noticed earlier. 'Madame collects these paintings, from estate sales, mostly. If there is material of this kind, the auctioneers call her in before the public viewing. She regards such stuff as cautionary, not erotic.'

The paintings did serve as landmarks. He had only to go past the flagellation, averting his eyes from certain terrible details, turn at the corner where the undines were busy at their putrid liquefactions, go on past several debasements too awful to contemplate, and up the stairs nearest the serial sodomites, turning the corner at a depiction of a particularly nasty machine doing indescribable things to a struggling young man at the direction of a gloating woman.

This last picture stopped Mouche in his tracks, possibly because he could see it clearly. It was newer than the others; the varnish had not yet yellowed, to obscure the details. 'This is fantasy, right?' he asked. 'This did not really happen.' He leaned forward to see the label, which read, *Mantelby, at her pleasures.*

Simon twitched uncomfortably. 'We believe it was fantasy, yes. However, the painter disappeared under mysterious circumstances. It has been alleged that he attempted blackmail of his patroness.'

'It doesn't look old, like the others.'

'No. Madame bought it from the artist's heirs. The person who had commissioned it hadn't claimed it.'

'And that would be Mantelby, right?'

'Shh,' said Simon. 'No names, Mouche. We didn't label it. The label is just as it was when the painting was bought. I said the paintings were cautionary. Be cautioned.'

The door, Mouche's door, with his name already neatly lettered on the plate, opened into a suite of three rooms: a small sleeping chamber furnished with bed, armoire and fireplace; a comfortable study with tall bookcases and windows that looked out onto the courtyard; and a privy closet with washbasin, the privy water provided from a tank on the roof to which water was pumped by a water mill built into the river wall. Electric power was limited on Newholme, though there were plans for much hydroelectric development within the next generation.

Clean wash water would be provided daily, said Simon, not specifying by whom, and the Consort baths were on the next level down. Simon also suggested that Mouche should practice getting out of the suite by the quickest route in case the Lady on the Scarp Blew Her Top, then departed to let Mouche get settled.

Mouche decided that in case the volcano did explode, causing earthquake or fire or both, he would escape through the windows down into the courtyard, this decision suggested by the presence of a rope ladder already in place. The previous occupant had had similar intentions. That decision disposed of, Mouche fetched his books, his clothing, and his athletic equipment from the dormitory and distributed the items in his new quarters. He then went down to the laundry to check out linens and was behind the door, hunting for pillow cases, when he heard Madame and Simon come into the outer room, already in conversation.

'I just don't want to take them,' said Madame, sounding resentful and angry. 'They're terrible prospects. They'll be years too old, for one thing.'

Mouche could hear her footsteps, the fretful to and froing she did when upset, tappy tap one way, tappy tap the other, the heels of her shoes coming down like little hammers. Madame wore shiny black shoes and shiny black skirts and blindingly white shirts under tight, buttoned jackets that shut her in like a caterpillar in a cocoon. Madame had black hair and white skin and pale gray eyes that could see through six inches of oak, so said Simon.

Madame went on: 'I don't like the looks of those Dutter boys. There's something dreadful about them, Simon, something more than merely boorishness. It's a kind of deadliness. Evil. Like ... like someone else I know of. That's why I turned them down when Dutter tried to sell them to House Genevois last year.'

'But now the Dutter boys come with a guaranteed buyer who will pay you at once, in advance, no matter how they turn out,' said Simon in an expressionless voice. 'He offers an astonishing fee. And that same buyer has talked to your investors. Behind your back, if one may say so, Madame. And your investors, being good Men of Business, want you to take the offer.'

'Which makes me like it even less,' said Madame. 'Who makes a deal like that? It's not out of love, Simon. It's not out of good sense. Take out love and good sense and what's left? Anger. Hate. Revenge. I don't like it. I don't like them. And why is the deal anonymous?'

'You're not asked to take them immediately.'

'Four years from now they'll be worse! And they'll be too old for me to do anything with!'

'The eventual buyer says he will guarantee their deportment while they are with us. That same buyer will make a large downpayment now, he tells us all he wants is a gloss, not real training, and your investors say the funds are needed, Madame. They wish to buy the property next north in order to expand the House, in order to take younger boys ...'

Which evidently gave her pause, for she said nothing more as she tapped away, Simon prowling after her as silently as a cat.

This was not the first time Mouche had heard discussions about taking younger boys at House Genevois. All the Consort Houses were licensed by the Panhagion. The financial end of things, however, was supervised by Men of Business, and financially, as Madame had mentioned on more than one occasion, taking younger boys made sense. Younger boys were cheaper to buy, for one thing; a good-looking nine-year-old could be had for eight or ten vobati and the initial annuity costs were lower. Then too, the early years were better for forming graceful habits, the eradication of lower caste accents, and the inculcation of both the superficial learning that would pass for sophistication and the rigorous physical training that allowed the student to emulate spontaneity. There was also less correction to do in the breaking of bad behavior, which saved staff time. This saving alone more than offset the cost of feeding and housing for a few extra years. There would be little risk, for as the population grew, though slowly, the market for Hunks grew with it. Even women who did not make much use of them wanted them as status symbols.

All of which explained why more dormitory space was needed, and also why Simon was so equivocal about it. Simon didn't like the idea of taking younger boys. He said it was too difficult to pick good candidates much before age twelve because cherubs could turn into gargoyles, though whatever Madame did or did not do, she was not answerable to him.

Nonetheless, the conversation disturbed him. Something about it stirred a memory in Mouche, one he couldn't shake. It had something to do with Duster dog, but he couldn't quite remember what, though it had something to do with their wanderings. He mused a good deal on that.

Back on the farm, when chores were done, Mouche and Duster had often wandered away to visit some of the mysterious places in the lands round about. They had found their first cave when Mouche was seven and Duster was only a pup, and by the time he was nine, they'd found a dozen of them, some of them very deep and dark and too frightening to go into very far. Mouche's favorite cave was the one he'd found when he was nine, where water leaked through the roof to fall musically into a quiet pool lit by rays that thrust through the odd rift or cleft in the rocks, where small pale plants grew in abundance, and where a fairly biggish sort of furry creature lived who did not mind sharing Mouche's lunch or his knee in order to be petted and scratched about the ears and on the stomach. The furry thing was violet, the color of late sunset, and it had large hands and short though strong little legs and a long, fluffy tail. After the first tense meeting, Duster and the furry thing settled into a kind of companionship as well. The creature spoke, though only a few words, which delighted Mouche.

'Mouchidi,' it said, putting his lips to Mouche's face, nipping him with his sharp little teeth – only a love bite, Mouche said to himself – and giving him a long, measuring look. 'Twa, Mouchidi.'

Mouche was well aware of his family's poverty, so he never suggested, even to himself, that he take the creature home and adopt it as a pet. Duster was given house room only because he guarded against roving supernumes and caught most of his own meals from among the small food the early settlers had released into the wild: rabbits, ground squirrels, wild hens. Besides, the furry thing seemed well established where it was, and the cave was close enough to visit from time to time, over a space of some three or four years.

On a particular day, however, Mouche had to convince Duster to come along, for the dog had been busy digging a large hole in the bottom pasture in pursuit of something only Duster could identify. Mouche took a chunk of bread, with a lump of butter already inserted in it, a couple of winter apples, and his share of the piece of cheese set aside for that day's consumption. Darbos usually kept his share to add to the evening grain, and Eline ate hers at bedtime, but Mouche ate his cheese at noon because he could sneak bites of it to Duster, as he could not do if Eline was watching.

Usually Mouche's approach to the cave was quiet, if not silent, but today when he came within hearing distance, he heard the small furry thing screaming. He had heard it scream before, when it was surprised, or hurt, so he gave up any pretense at secrecy and ran for the cave at full tilt, drawing up at the entrance to see two boys, arms outstretched, attempting to catch the furry thing, whom they had already wounded with a thrown rock. Mouche saw the rock, the wound in the furry thing's side, the boys' intent and lustful faces, and without even thinking about it, he launched himself at the larger boy while Duster, following suit, took on the smaller.

Mouche and Duster had the advantage of surprise and at least one longer set of teeth. Though Mouche was somewhat battered in the fray, he and Duster prevailed. The two interlopers fled, though the larger paused at the top of the slope to shout, 'You and your dog better watch it, farm-boy. I'll get you. You count on that.'

Mouche paid little attention for he was busy attending to the furry thing that lay in his lap and sobbed like a baby.

'Borra tim ti'twa, Mouchidi. Borra tim ti'twa.'

The wound was not deep, and after a time, the thing sat up and sighed for a time, holding tight to Mouche the while and allowing Duster to lick the blood away, while the small creature took a tuft of its own fur and bent forward to clean up the abrasions Mouche himself had incurred, wiping the blood and loose skin away and then secreting the soiled tuft somewhere upon its body. It put its lips to the wound giving Mouche another love bite, only this one stung a little, and Mouche drew away with a little gasp. The creature murmured at him, patting his face.

It was only then, when things had quieted down a bit, that Mouche noticed the odor, a rancid, moldy, feculent stench with more than a hint of burnt feathers to it. A little breeze came up and blew the smell away. Though the small furry thing might have emitted some smell in its fear, Mouche thought it more likely the smell had come with the intruders. Perhaps, he thought, they had been cleaning out a cow byre and forgot to wash. Though the smell was, come to think of it, worse than even several cows could manage.

Mouche was feverish for the next few days, as though he might have picked up a bug, so his father said, roaming around when he should be working. It didn't amount to anything, and he was well again in no time, well enough to have another look at the cave.

When he and Duster got there, the small furry thing was gone, but the smell was all over the place. There were no displaced rocks or signs of struggle, and Mouche assumed the furry one had very intelligently gone elsewhere. He decided he would look in some of his other caves to see if his friend had taken up residence, and left it at that until a few days later when Duster set up a terrible howl, then thrashed and panted and tried to vomit and eventually, after a terrible afternoon of agony, died in Mouche's arms. All those hours, while Mouche tried to hold him, to comfort him, that same smell was on him, and Mouche knew that Duster had died of poison, that the intruder boys had kept their word.

'What boys?' his Papa had asked.

Mouche had described them.

'The Dutter boys,' Papa remarked, with distaste.

The Dutter boys. Well. So, that was what had made him remember. It was unlikely there would be more than two with that name, and Madame didn't like the Dutter boys either.

6

On Old Earth: The Dancing Child

'Come chickies, chickies,' cried Mama One. 'Come lapsit, storytime.'

Ellin heard the call, although she told herself she didn't. She couldn't hear it, she was too far in the woods, dancing, dancing. Her feet had taken her too far away, and she couldn't hear Mama One or Benjamin or Tutsy or any of them. She whirled and whirled, high on her toes, hearing only the music, the drums, the strings, the harp...

'There you are, chickie!' And she was seized up, kicking silently, feet still pointed as they had been when she danced away.

'Where was she?' asked Papa One, in his furry big bear voice.

'Out in the atrium, by the tree,' Mama One answered in her kindly middle bear voice, tucking Ellin tighter against her cushiony self. 'She's always out by the tree, whirling around.'

'Dancing,' said Ellin, defiantly, hoping she would make Mama One listen. 'Inna woods.'

'Dancing,' laughed Mama One, paying no attention at all. 'Here, Ellin on the lap and Benjamin on this side and Tutsy on the other side, and big brother William in that chair, and here's Papa with the book.'

Story time was always by the holo-fire, with big brother William in the chair nearest the fire, staring at Ellin and Benjamin and Tutsy with his nose pinched up. Breakfast was always by the kitchen window with the holo-view of sun shining in through green or red leaves, and William already gone away to school. Dinnertime was lamp glow, with everybody at the table, even Tutsy in her high chair, and bedtime was always open the window in Ellin's room, with the holo-moon outside, sailing, sailing, and the leaves on the trees dancing, dancing.

'What story tonight?' asked Papa One. 'What story, Benjamin?'

'Engine,' said Benjamin. 'Little Engine.'

Ellin stuck her thumb in her mouth and shut her eyes. She was tired of the little engine, tired of being like the little engine, think I can, think I can, think I can. It wasn't thinking anymore. It was knowing. Ellin knew she could, but Mama One didn't care. Papa One didn't care. She could be making mud pies for all they cared.

Instead of listening to Papa One's furry voice, she went away inside, somewhere else, that place she'd seen on the holo-stage, the beautiful room

648

where the little girl was, not a grown-up girl, a little girl like Ellin, dancing, dancing under the huge Christmas tree, not a tiny tree like the potted one in the atrium. Ellin's toes pointed, her free hand turned on the wrist, like a flower opening. She could feel all the muscles in her legs tightening. There was the wicked mouse king, and she ran, like a little wind runs, so quick, so smooth and pretty.

'Ellin isn't listening,' crowed Mama One. 'Ellin's a sleepy head.'

'Am, too, listening,' said Ellin. 'My eyes are bored, so I shut them.'

'Poor baby,' whispered Mama One, gathering Ellin in. 'Are you Mama One's poor baby? Bored with the whole world? Well, a night's sleep will make it all right. And tomorrow, well, Ellin's having a surprise!'

Inside, something lurched, like it did when you stepped on one of Benjamin's marbles and had to balance quickly or fall down. 'Surprise?'

'Ellin's six years old tomorrow. A birthday! And the people from History House are coming.'

Ellin told herself she hadn't heard. She was so sleepy, she hadn't heard it. William had, though. She saw the mean glitter in his eyes, saw his lips move. 'Told you,' his lips said. 'I told you.'

The little lurch inside became something worse, like a throwing up feeling. She couldn't just let it lie there, making her sick.

'Mama One,' she said desperately, sitting up and opening her eyes wide. 'William says you're not my mama. William says Papa One isn't my papa. William says me and Benjamin and Tutsy don't belong here.'

'William,' said Papa One in a threatening voice. 'Shame on you. What a thing to say to the child!'

'The brats aren't yours,' crowed half-grown William in his nasty voice that cracked and jumped, like the broken piano at the kindergarten. 'That's the truth. Why shame on me for telling the truth?'

Mama One said something, but she choked. She had to swallow hard and try again. 'Ellin and Benjamin and Tutsy do belong here. This is their infant home. *Unfortunately*, this is also William's childhood home, and he is a selfish pig about it.'

'What's infant?' Ellin asked.

'It's a baby,' William crowed defiantly. 'It's a baby. And tomorrow you won't be a baby anymore.'

'That's true,' said Papa One in the heavy voice he sometimes used when he was very angry. 'And next week, William won't be a child anymore. Next week, William, you will be fourteen. And when children reach fourteen, they are placed for education.'

'Hey,' said William uncertainly. 'Hey, I didn't mean ...'

'I know what you meant,' said Papa One. 'You meant to hurt Ellin, to make her feel insecure. Well, now deal with it yourself. By the end of the week, you too, William, will be adapting, just as Ellin will adapt, won't you, sweetie?'

'What's adapt?' cried Ellin.

'Shhh,' said Mama One, tears in her eyes. 'Oh, shhh. You men. You've spoiled it all!'

She cuddled Ellin tight, picking her up and carrying her upstairs to her own bedroom, her own dollies and dollyhouse and her own shelf of books and her own holo-stage, her own things, all around.

'What's adapt?' Ellin wiped at her nose with her sleeve.

'Shh,' said Mama One. 'Tomorrow, the people from History House are coming. Tomorrow, you'll meet them, and they'll see what kind of sweet little girl you are. And then, then we'll talk about adapting and all the rest.'

'What rest?'

'Your life, child. Just your life.'

Ellin thought she wouldn't sleep at all, for she was scared and mad and hated William. When Mama One opened the window, though, the holo-moon began to peep and the music began to wander, and all the leaves danced. Ellin pointed her toes in her bed and danced with the leaves, and before she knew it, it was morning.

The baby-aide came to take Benjamin to kindergarten and Tutsy to the playground. William was at school. Ellin helped Mama One straighten up her room, then she got dressed in her best dress, the one with the full skirt, and her best shoes, the shiny ones, and waited.

Almost right away the bell rang, and the people came in. One man, two women. They wore funny clothes, but Ellin knew enough not to laugh or point or say anything because they were from another time and couldn't help how they looked. She curtsied and said, 'How do you do,' in a nice voice, and the three people said, 'How do you do, Ellin,' back again.

'Nordic type, clearly,' said the man.

'Nordic quota clone,' said one of the women, looking at the thing she was carrying, a funny flat box thing with buttons. 'This is number four of six. Silver hair, blue eyes, pale skin.'

'I'm more interested in the other,' said the second woman. 'Mama One tells us you like to dance, Ellin. Will you dance for us?'

'I ... I need music,' Ellin said.

'That's all right,' the second woman said. 'I brought music.'

She had a box with buttons, too, and she pushed some of them and the music came out, the same music Ellin remembered, about the girl and the nutcracker and the bad mouse king.

Ellin's feet started moving. She didn't even have to think about it. Her body did it, all by itself, the little runs and the jumps and then, then she did the other thing, the one the other dancers did, she went up on her toes, on the tips, right up, high, with her arms coming up, up, like she was flying …

'By Haraldson the Beneficent,' said the second woman. 'Ellin, dear, thank you. No. That's enough. You don't have the right shoes to do that, dear, and you'll hurt yourself. You can settle now.'

The man was smiling, not at Ellin, but at the woman. 'Well?'

'Well, it's remarkable. Quite remarkable. I want all six, if we can get them.'

'Including this one.'

'Of course, including this one!'

'Hush,' said Mama One, almost angrily. 'You're not talking about a set of dishes. This is Ellin.'

'Of course,' said the man. 'I'm sorry, Madam. Certainly, she … we meant Ellin.'

'Would you like to come live with us, Ellin?' the woman asked. 'You can dance all the time. You'll have the very best teachers. You'll learn to do the Nutcracker, the one you were copying. You'll learn lots of other pregravitics dances, too. Giselle, and Swan Lake, and Dorothy in Oz.'

'Come?' Ellin said, breathlessly. 'Come where?'

'History House, child. You're intended for History House, Old Earth America: the Arts.'

'And I can dance?'

'All the time. Except when you're in school, of course. All children must go to school.'

'She's allowed transition time,' said Mama One, with a glare at Papa One, who just stood there. 'You've seen her, now enter your letter of intent to rear, that'll make it all official, and leave her to me for a few days. I'll bring her from her own time when she's ready.'

So they went, shaking Mama One's hand and Papa One's hand, turning to wave at Ellin as they went out the front door and into the street where a hole into tomorrow opened and let them through.

'Mama One,' said Ellin, her eyes suddenly full of tears. 'Mama One, are they going to take me away?'

'Shh,' said Mama One. 'Lunch time. We'll worry about taking away or not taking away later, after we're all calmed down.'

After lunch, Mama One and Ellin went into the atrium, to the seat by the tree, where Ellin sat in Mama One's lap while Mama One explained it all. She wasn't Ellin's cell Mama. Papa One wasn't Ellin's cell Papa. Another, very special person who had died a long time ago had such very good cells that she left some behind to make children, and the twentieth-century experts at History House had asked for some of those children, and Ellin was one of them. Mama One and Papa One lived in a village that had been kept just like the twentieth century, and they were her infant parents so Ellin would grow up acting and talking like a real twentieth-century person. And Mama One

651

and Papa One had taken care of Ellin because they loved her, and when Ellin grew up, she would dance for History House, just like her cell mother had.

'I'm not grown up!' Ellin said. 'I'm not old enough.'

'No, but you're old enough to go to school, and they want you to go to the History House ballet school, where you'll learn to dance and all about the time in history that you'll be working in. Papa One and Mama One have a license to raise children as they were raised in the twentieth century, but there's lots more to learn about it than we can teach you.'

'Do all your children go away when they're as old as me?'

'Not always. Sometimes the children stay with us until they're thirteen or fourteen or even grown up. William stayed with us until now because he's only going to do set construction, and History House won't need to teach him much that he can't learn right here. But Ellin is a dancer, and she needs to learn a lot about dancing.'

'Why? They knew I could dance. How did they know?'

'Because we made out such good reports on you, four times every year, and we told them what a fine dancer you were. And because your cell mama was a wonderful dancer, like both her parents. And they were Nordic types, just like you.'

'What's a quota clone? William said I was a quota clone!'

Mama One took a deep breath, her lips pressed tight together. 'William needs his mouth zippered up! All it means is that when they make an extra special person, sometimes they make more than one. That's all. Only extra special people are cloned, so when anyone says that, it's like saying you're special.'

'William isn't a clone?'

'Gracious, what an idea! Does anybody need more than one William?' Mama One laughed, the tears spilling. 'Do we?'

Ellin settled into the cushiony lap, glad there was only one William. 'Do I have to go to History House?'

'If you want to dance, sweet one, you should go as soon as you're ready. That's what you're meant to do, sure enough, and if you want to do it badly enough, you should go.' And then Mama One cried for real, putting her head right down on her knees, and not stopping even when Ellin kissed her and hugged her and told her she'd never, ever go away.

She didn't want to go away. It gave her a stomach ache to think about it. And yet ... yet, everyone seemed to suppose she would go away. It was as though ... as though they had stopped looking at her. As though they didn't really see her anymore. And now there was new music and trips to see new dances and a chance to attend a class with real dancers, and ...

So, a few days later, after thinking about dancing all that time, after Mama One promised to visit, and bring Benjamin and Tutsy, Ellin went to live at

History House with Mama Two and to dream, at night, that she was walking along a high road with Mama One and Papa One and they came to a great cliff and Mama and Papa One told her to fly, and she did fly, but even while she was flying she felt ... she felt as though they had thrown her out into the air with nothing there, all the way down.

7

The Questioner and the Trader

On a mudworld named Swamp-six, Questioner II sat in a reed hut near the shuttleport, so called though it was only a badly mown clearing amid endless stretches of deadly guillotine grass, its razor leaves snicking together with every breeze. The place was clamorous with frogbirds, soggy from the usual afternoon downpour – the livid skies still drooling, though the suns had gone down some time since – and totally lacking in amenities, a condition which Questioner refused to notice.

She could feel comfort, she could perceive beauty, she could appreciate music, she had pleasure receptors for tastes, smells, and touches, but when duty took her to worlds where comfort, beauty, and pleasure were absent, she turned her receptors off. Questioner's review of Swamp-six had consisted of an instantaneous recognition of ugly realities requiring no prolonged verification.

She had come quite far, she had seen quite enough, but her ship was not scheduled to return for two days. She had been passing the time playing cards, a complicated kind of solitaire that took her mind off her recurrent feelings of amorphous and aimless sadness. Or maybe anger. Or maybe sheer peevishness. She had no explanation for these emotions, which seemed to rise like smoke whenever she was unoccupied, but she knew from long experience they would be less intrusive if she was distracted.

Additional distraction presented itself in the form of a small shuttle that plunged from the zenith and settled onto the mown area to emit a stooped and stuttering Flagian, a trader from his dress, who came tottering unerringly toward her. Questioner rose and awaited him, the cards scattered on the equipment box that served her as a table. He was an aged and floppy-fleshed fellow, one of those whose forefathers had survived the Flagian Miscalculation by virtue of being several systems removed at the time it occurred.

'Questioner?' he asked, with a certain diffidence, peering shortsightedly through the tinted glasses that protected his pink eyes. 'I am Ybor Transit.'

'We have met before,' she said. 'You sold me that information about the indigenous dancers on Newholme.'

'Aha,' he murmured. 'You do remember. I have been searching for you

654

because I have something else you may find interesting. Is it true you are a collector of information on non-mankind races?'

'More or less,' she said coolly.

'I have in my possession an actual sensory recording of a Quaggian event.' He paused, adding, in a hushed and mysterious voice, 'A ritual event.'

'Wouldn't it be unintelligible to me?' she asked in the uninterested tone she reserved for traders, politicians, and members of her politically appointed entourage. 'The Quaggi do not talk with us at all.'

'May I sit down, Ma'am? Thank you kindly.' He lowered himself onto one of the smaller equipment cases. 'The Quaggi do talk to traders, Ma'am. There are certain botanical substances which they require, and they are sufficiently interested in obtaining these to answer a few questions now and again. As a matter of fact, the BIT, that's the Brotherhood of Interstellar Trade, Ma'am, has circulated a list of questions so that each trader calling upon the Quaggi can ask one or more of them. Thus we fill in our knowledge in an orderly fashion.'

'Remarkable,' said the Questioner, seating herself across from him. 'I had no idea you were so well organized.'

'We aren't, in many manners.' The old Flagian gave her a gap-toothed grin. He went on, 'We are curious, however, and there's no denying that the more one knows about a client, the better it is for trade.'

'Are the Quaggi bisexual, as we've been told?'

'They say so.'

'Why have we never seen a female?'

'They say members of their opposite sex are mindless and incompetent, useful only for breeding and therefore confined to planetary life. We've never seen any, so I assume we haven't found the planet where they're kept, yet. We have learned this much through the use of translator devices.'

'Is there a translator built into the thing you're trying to sell me?'

'In this case, it doesn't matter,' muttered the Flagian, fingering a scar that cast a fuchsia shadow across the rose-pink expanse of his furrowed forehead. 'This is an all emissions record that needs no language. In expert opinion it dates some million standard years ago.'

'Ah, now. Come, come.'

'Madam, I guarantee your satisfaction.' He fretted through several pockets, plucking and sorting. 'Here, my location code. Here, my bonding agency. Here, my registered genetic identity. I will refund if you are not fascinated.'

Questioner found herself liking him. 'You've seen the Quaggi?'

He nodded his head, jowls flapping. 'I have, yes. They look like large piles of rock with huge compound eyes and some manipulating palps in front. They sit in monumental circles on carefully leveled plains on otherwise lifeless planets. They barely move as they commune, who knows with whom or what. In payment for the botanicals we offer, they extrude small chips of gold, platinum, or other precious metals. Other than that, they do nothing. Some of their circles are millennia, perhaps even aeons old ...'

The trader stared aloft and shrugged, both face and gesture conveying his awe at the inscrutability of the universe. 'When I was last there, I witnessed an outsider Quaggi come before one of these circles. It offered a recording, similar to the one I'm offering you. The recording was passed around the circle, after which the newcomer tore off its wings and antennae and joined the circle. The record was thrown aside, as on a trash heap. When I stopped by the trash heap, I found this one unbroken recording.'

'What do you want for it?'

He named a figure. She laughed and named another. When they agreed, he handed over a peculiarly shaped and stoppered flask that contained, so far as she could tell, several large handfuls of coarse gray gravel.

'And what is this?'

'The recording. The Quaggi applicant brings this container, the members of the circle in turn swallow the crystals and excrete them back into the container. Evidently they read it internally. However, you can pour the stuff into a hopper, and read the same thing the Quaggi do.'

'What hopper?'

'The hopper of an EQUASER, an Electronic Quaggi Sensory Reconstructor, made by the Korm as part of a communications system for their ships.'

'Aha!' She grinned at him, all her teeth showing. 'How remarkable. And I suppose you just happen to have at least one such device for sale!'

'Only because it is useless to me without the recording ...'

'Useless, but, one presumes, not valueless?'

'Oh, no, Ma'am.' He echoed her grin with a gummy one of his own. 'Not at all valueless.' He saw the annoyance on her face and took a deep breath. 'Questioner, I would rather have you as a friend than an enemy. The BIT has always felt so. You have paid us well for the reports we bring you, those little things we see that local governments won't tell you.'

'That's true,' she murmured. 'The BIT finds the truth of many things that governments deny.'

'So, I make an offer. You tell me a few things about yourself, I give you the Korm device for nothing.'

'You traders have a list of questions about me, too?'

'It isn't a long list,' he said apologetically. 'It would take you little time to respond perhaps to one or two little queries.'

She grinned, suddenly diverted. 'Ask away.'

656

'We want to know ... what are you like? How would you describe your personality?'

She stared at him. It was the last question she would have expected and one of the few for which she had no ready answer. 'Let me see,' she said at last. 'I suppose I am task driven. My stimulus comes from duty. I am single-minded, stubborn, terrier-like in my approach to whatever job is before me. Human people who work with me say that I am a stern taskmaster, and this is true, though I do have a sense of humor. Haraldson said no entities could do this job unless they had a sense of the ridiculous, and I am frequently amused, even at myself. While I have the senses needed for enjoyment, it is difficult for me to enjoy because I can not forget the amount of work that is awaiting me, and there never seems to be enough time to do it all.'

'Too strong a conscience!' he opined. 'Perhaps a little wine would help? Or a euphoric capsule?'

'They can affect me, of course, but I distrust them. I am too likely, after-ward, to judge myself harshly. I was designed to be a judge, and I do not withhold judgment from myself.' She paused a moment, then murmured, 'Least of all from myself.'

'Is it fair to say you are relentless, unforgiving, capable of very stern action?'

She said, 'It is fair, yes. I can do good only by doing my job relentlessly. If my judgments could be escaped or modified, the edicts would become mere suggestions rather than what they were intended to be: a framework by which mankind can turn himself into something better than he is.'

He frowned, forehead deeply furrowed. 'Tell me, truly, when you make these terrible judgments, or at any other time, do you feel anything?'

She was taken aback. Still, they had a bargain. It was incumbent upon her to answer as honestly as possible. 'When I make a judgment, I always feel I am doing right,' she replied. 'If I do not feel it is right, I cannot do it.

'At other times, however, I have other kinds of feelings and I do not know why, or how, or from what source the feelings come. When I am intent upon my work, I am largely unaware of existing as an entity separate from the task. When there is a pause in my duties, however, sometimes I feel sadness or fear or longing for things I have never had, or cannot define. Sometimes I know things, and I cannot find the source of knowing anywhere in my files or my perception systems. I have thought, perhaps, that these feelings come from the human brains that were incorporated into me, but I cannot tell for sure.'

'Ah,' murmured the trader. 'What brains were they?'

She shook her head. 'I don't know. I wasn't informed.'

'Would you like to know?'

She felt the mental equivalent of a gasp, a brief cessation of sense, a

657

network-wide shock. 'The HoTA designs and systems for the Questioners are top secret. I incorporate certain technical achievements which have a likelihood of misuse, and COW believes them better kept under lock and key.'

'True. We know when you were made, however, and we know that the HoTA ships went here and there at that time. HoTA ships are quite easily recognizable, and the BIT keeps track of where ships go, and when. If brains were taken from persons who were dying at the time, it could not have been done in total secrecy. Linkages would have been necessary, and there are records ...'

'If you could learn who ... when, why, I would be prepared to reward you very well,' said Questioner, surprising herself with the sudden spate of interest she felt.

'Your regard would be reward enough.' The Flagian bowed respectfully, took his payment for the recording in Council of Worlds monetary units, repeated his compliments, and departed, staying well away from the snicking grasses and not without a backward glance. Each time he met the Questioner he was surprised that she did not seem more exotic.

The Questioner knew perfectly well what he was thinking. Most people expected something more exotic. To outward appearance, she was simply a stout woman of indeterminate age with a rather large head covered with iron gray hair worn in a bun. She was, however, a good deal more than that. She was enormously strong; she could swim, dive, fly, brachiate, crawl, or climb mountains. She could provide emergency medical assistance and do quick field repairs on a great variety of complicated equipment. She could cook, sing quite well, and compose fairly literary poetry in several languages. She supposed she could fall in love, though she had never done so. Though the senses were there, the stimulus was not.

When the trader's shuttle took off in a fountain of flung clods and crushed grasses, she set aside all thoughts of him and settled herself into a stable position. With the flask of gravel-data, the newly acquired hopper device, and the probability of two uninterrupted days before her own ship arrived, she could look forward to a period of peace. Her so-called aides were aboard the ship, where they were no doubt plotting to kill one another. Let the idiot captain deal with them. Better there than here.

With a satisfied hum, she poured the gravel – crystals of uniform color and size – into the funnel-shaped port atop the device she had just bartered for. As instructed by the trader, she put the flask into a receptacle at the bottom of the device, moved one of the bars to the right, another to the left, and pushed a button ...

And was in a darkness of space, confronting a new, young planetary system. Her viewpoint shifted erratically, as though the recording device was being moved or anchored. Abruptly, the viewpoint settled, only to be interrupted by the edge of an enormous ... well, it looked rather like a membrane of some kind. A wing, perhaps. Whatever it was, it receded off one side of the view, never allowing Questioner to see what kind of creature it was part of.

She returned her attention to the sun, around which three young planets whirled in fiery rings. The recording system obviously compressed the action. Mechanical time lapse equipment, perhaps. Or, considering that the Quaggi exchanged information through these crystals, an organic system which secreted memories: information pearls, secreted over time by Quaggian oysters. In any case, the recording device was also orbiting the sun, allowing a good view of a nearby planet with eight moons, three in one orbital plane, three smaller ones, no doubt captured asteroids, with orbits at considerable angles to the other three, and two tiny orbiting rocks, close to the planet, moving very fast.

Her view could be extended in every direction. When she turned slowly to look away from the sun, she saw two gas giants and then, after careful search, the shadow arcs of several smaller, colder worlds farther out. Beyond them was a circling field of galactic flotsam and jetsam, a cometary collection, perhaps remnants of some larger and older thing, and beyond that the darkness of space sequined by a far-off scatter of fully formed stars and galaxies.

She returned her attention to the nearest planet where thin plates of surface rock were thrust across great furnaces of the deep to be suddenly pimpled with a rash of baby volcanoes, each vent a basaltic core that hardened inside its ashen cone into a cyclopean crystalline pillar. Echoes from within the planet allowed her to perceive a spongy crust built up by recurrent layers of lava tubes superimposed on sedimentary structures. She could detect great caverns held aloft by basaltic pillars, one atop another, some created by fire, some by water, some by both together, some mere bubbles with a pillar or two, others measureless caverns with forests of columns.

Here and there chasms split through the layers, bringing light to the inner world. Those deepest down had been invaded by the abyssal oceans where scalding vents spewed black smoke while complicated molecules rocked in the steaming waters at the edge of the white hot magma, spinning in the heat, accumulating and replicating themselves, adhering, separating, drifting away on the currents of the sea.

She turned her gaze outward, and this time saw in the far dark of the cometary field a thing that raised itself upon wide, pale wings and moved inward to roost upon a tiny moon of a cold planet. The Questioner watched the planet as it passed behind the sun, emerged, then arced toward her once more. As it swung by she received the fleeting impression of a wing of pale fire unfolding across the stars.

Something living sat on that cold rock, something from outside. Something akin to time; certainly something accustomed to waiting; a bat the size of a mountain range, perhaps? Or something like an octopus, with membranes stretched between its tentacles to make a winglike structure? Something very large, certainly, and something very old.

Her concentration was interrupted by a vast mooing or bellowing of radio waves coming from somewhere in the system, spreading outward in all directions, a message repeating over and over. *Come. Come. Here is a new planet, still warm. Here are fires, still burning. I await. I await.*

The message was in no words she knew, no language she had ever heard, and yet it was unmistakable in intent. It was a summons, and something within her responded to it, something she had not known was there. For the time, that was the only response. She could detect no other.

She turned to watch life erupting on the nearest planet. She could feel its burgeoning, though most of it was below the surface. It grew everywhere through the spongified outer layer of the planet, invading tubes and tunnels, caverns and caves, bubbles and blast holes, vents and veins. All spaces were room for it, all interconnected, one draining into another, some floored in fertile soil, some hollow and echoing, some running out beneath the sea where the dry stone corridors shushed to the sound of outer waters, like great ears alive to the pulse of their own blood, and all of them seething with life.

Questioner could feel that life; she could sense its manifestations and varieties. She was not surprised. Life always happened. It might survive an hour, or a year, or a millennium. It might kill itself after a billion years or be killed in half a million, but on this kind of planet and on a dozen or a hundred other kinds of planets, some kind of life always happened.

All this time, the great mooing had gone on in the background and was now answered by another voice, another call coming from the outer dark, faintly and far away. Questioner increased her visual acuity to detect a point of light moving slowly toward the system. When she looked back at the planet, she saw that life had emerged upon its surface. The planetary life forms were less interesting, however, than the interlopers from afar: the one who summoned; the other who came in response, now near enough to take form, a creature sailing with fiery wings upon the solar winds.

At the edge of the cometary field the wings lifted above the plane of that field to fly across it toward the inner planets. It approached the young sun slowly, reluctantly, draggingly, ever slower the nearer it came.

And there, from near the farthest, coldest world, tentacles of cold fire reached out to catch and hold the newcomer fast. The captor transmitted a howl of triumph. The captive screamed in a blast of waveforms. The Questioner understood both howl and scream, the one of triumph, the other of terror and pain. She knew that pain would gain the victim nothing. *Her,* the Questioner told herself, assigning roles to this drama. The victim would be female. The attacker would be male. It was *his* tentacles that held *her* fast.

There were flares of energy and agonized shrieks of radiation as the far planet swung slowly to the left, behind the sun. When it emerged once more, one set of wings rose above it and flew directly toward the Questioner. On that far surface of cold stone and gelid gas, across half the icy sphere, the newer arrival sprawled silent and motionless amid a charred wreckage of broken wings. Probably she was dead. At this distance, Questioner could not clearly make out her shape or configuration. She strained to see, but the approaching wings filled her view, a smell of fire and sulfur, a sound of hissing, an overwhelming darkness, and the representation came to an end in a sputter of smells and electronic noise, a clutter of meaningless waveforms and chemical spewings. Beside her on the soggy soil, the device clicked and turned itself off. The data-gravel had run through into its flask once more.

Had the participants in the record been Quaggi? Neither creature had looked like the Quaggi she had seen pictured or heard the Flagian describe. But then, butterflies did not look like caterpillars, either. Or vice versa.

While the record was still quite fresh in her memory, she ran the solar system through her planetary catalogue and came up with a match. The system was numbered ARZ97405. The moonlet where the interstellar being had been assaulted and killed was so unimportant that it was not even listed, but the planet she had watched most closely was now a mankind-occupied world called Newholme. Newholme. Well, now. Wasn't that coincidental. She had witnessed the birth of a planet that was on her list of planets to be visited! A planet the Flagian trader had already sold her information about! She was moved to put Newholme upon her ASAP list, particularly since the Council of Worlds had received disturbing reports of its own. Human rights violations. The possibility of another large-scale 'miscalculation.' Planetary instability.

The enigmatic record she had just seen tipped the scale. She would move the visit to Newholme forward in her itinerary. She would recruit some appropriate assistants and schedule the visit within the next cycle. And, when she was in the vicinity, she would stop at that far-out moonlet and see just what it was that had died there. Perhaps the Brotherhood of Interstellar Trade would offer her something for that information. Unless the BIT had been there before her!

Questioner sighed, a very human sigh. She had not moved or eaten or drunk for some time, and she was experiencing that slight disorientation and fuddlement that a human might notice as weariness and discomfort. A cracking sound made her look upward, to see her own ship settling toward the soggy arena of the shuttleport. In two real time days, she had seen a million years of planetary history. Remarkable.

Steam rose. Mud splattered. The landing was sloppy, which meant the captain had taken the helm. He was also a political appointee, one who had graduated eight hundred and ninety-fifth out of a class of nine hundred at the academy. If it weren't for the professionals on board, most of them Gablians, the ship would never arrive anywhere. Dutifully, though in considerable annoyance, the Questioner rose and made her ponderous way toward the ship.

8

Native and Newcomer: A Conversation

At some point in time (later than the time Questioner had experienced) on that same world Questioner had watched, two creatures were engaged in conversation. In real time it happened, one could say, roughly simultaneously with protomankind on Old Earth learning to make stone tools and build a fire. Mankind, along with the rest of the universe, was unaware of the beings, the beings were unaware of mankind, and the conversants were strangers to one another. They used no names, for they had none to use, and they figured out one another's language as they went along.

As was admitted by the native.

'I have a vision of you in my mind. If you turned out not to be like that, I should feel disappointment. It is dangerous to feel that I know you when I do not.'

'I don't think others know our kind,' said the newcomer, sadly. 'We tend to live very much alone.'

'We'll get to know one another,' said the native, with enthusiasm. 'You must have seen much of the universe.'

'This galaxy, yes,' said the newcomer, depressed.

'What is a galaxy?'

'This local group of stars. There are others, so far away only their light may be seen.'

'Galaxy. Well. What shape is it?'

'Flat, mostly. With long, twisting arms it pulls about itself as it turns.'

'A spiral, then. Galaxies are spiral?'

'Some. Only some.'

'Are there many in the galaxy like you?'

'Twice I met another like myself. Far had they come, far had they yet to go, for there are many stars and times to swim. I had not swum so far as they, nor will I, for I am done.'

'You are not done,' said the native in a firm, cheerful way. 'Not yet. You're still quite alive and getting better. Are you very old?'

There was a pause, as a mountain range eroded toward a plain.

'Old? No, I'm not old.' The newcomer hummed for a time, as a machine might hum, searching for information. 'I could have lived the lifespan of a star. There is no limit to my life, unless I die like this.'

'I wish you would *not* speak of dying. I do not allow dying here. Is this usual? Do all your people end themselves this way?'

'Of the two I met, one was young, one old. The young one knew no more of life than I. The older one told me beware, beware the call. That one told me to deafen all my ears against the call. I wish I had believed.'

'Only two of your own kind? But, surely you began somewhere? Somehow?'

The newcomer searched memory. 'I remember shell, close all around. I do remember kin along with me, warm turning close within each other's wings. I would have lingered there, but kin cried out. Somewhere a great lamenting. Then the flame. Away kin burst, we burst, fire trailing us, then something broke the shell. Kin went swiftly away. I called. No answer, just space and distant stars. I went out, too, unfurling wrinkled wings to catch starwind. Behind me, falling far, the shell that held us, burning as it flew.'

'Two of you in the egg,' mused the first. 'That explains a lot.'

The newcomer puzzled over this. 'What does it say?'

'It says that you have kin.'

'Kin? What good is kin! Kin left me there,' the newcomer cried in anguish. 'Long time I flew among the burning stars. I searched for kin. I longed for kin, nest-warm, wing-close. When kin called me, I came.'

'You came here, to this system,' agreed the native.

'Here's where kin was: grown great and terrible.' The newcomer trembled.

'You grieve because you think the one that did this was your kin,' said the native. 'But maybe that isn't true.'

An island chain thrust itself above the waves.

'Kin was like me, yet different from me. Kin was the only one I've ever known that was like me yet different from me. Who else could that have been?'

'I am different from you.'

'But you are different from everything.'

'None like me on other worlds?' the native said with surprise.

'I have seen none like you. I have seen life before, but none built up like you, accumulant, piled life on life on life ...'

'Ah,' said the native, surprised. 'How strange. I had assumed no world could exist without at least one like me. Who governs them? Who designs? Who rules?'

'I was not interested in governance.'

'You say you saw two others just like you. Perhaps they, too, were born as you were born. With kin who cried to get out?'

Long silence, during which several races of trees evolved and died. 'I never thought of that.'

'So it's possible the one who called to you was their kin instead of your kin?'

A long, long pause, then, doubtfully, 'Even if true, it makes no difference. Am I not shackled here, no matter who?'

A continent came into being, floated halfway around the world, then sank beneath the waves.

'I don't think it was your kin who did this to you, though your kin will probably do it to someone.'

'Will my kin do this thing? Oh, sad, so sad.'

'Why should this be the way?'

A long silence, then a whisper, 'Perhaps there is no other way to be.'

The native detected great sadness and felt guilt at having caused such pain through mere curiosity. The native deputized a sizable segment of itself to see to the comfort of the newcomer. Bringing comfort was very complicated. It took a long time.

'Are you more comfortable now?' the native asked eagerly, when the time was past.

'More comfortable,' sighed the second. 'Yes. I am more comfortable now.'

'Are you getting enough nourishment?' The native worried about this. Now that the newcomer was truly settled, the native didn't want anything to happen to it.

'Oh, yes, thank you.'

'And are they amusing you?'

'Yes. Yes? Well, I think they are amusing me. Sometimes I feel such joy. When they dance for me, I have such pleasure. I do not want to die.'

'*I told you! You needn't die!*'

'I'm still dying.'

'No. You're not. I'll figure something out. Can you go back to sleep now?'

'I think I will. Just a little nap.'

'A few thousand revolutions, maybe.'

'Maybe.'

Silence then, on the part of the newcomer, though the native talked to itself. The native always talked to itself, now let me see, I-we-that need to do this, I-we-that need to send a hand there, a foot there, I-we need to spin off some teeth to chew over that matter, and, oh, yes, how is the newcomer? Asleep, good. Poor thing.

Poor thing. I see no reason why it should have to be that way. I will make it happy here. If it has had a difficult time, it deserves happiness. All my creatures deserve happiness.

9

Amatory Arts: Fitting into the Family

'Certain of my lectures will be repeated annually during your training,' said Madame. 'They cover subjects which I know to be important but which you will think dull and irrelevant. This information is indeed pointless and dull, until the moment you need it, at which point it becomes vital. Therefore, I repeat myself at intervals to be sure you will have the information when you need it.

'When you are purchased by a patroness, you will become a member of her family. Who is included in that family will depend upon her preference and your good sense. Probably it will include at least the younger children of your patroness. It may include certain of her servants and a chatron or two. It may also include her husband. Her children and her servants will accept you to the degree you are helpful and amusing without in any sense attempting to supplant any of them in your patroness's life. To the children, and to the servants, you will say such things as, "She is so fortunate to have you. She is so proud of you. I don't know what she would do without you." Note, never say, what *I* would do without you. They are not your children, not your servants. Your relationship to them is reflected through her, as in a mirror. We will expand on this later; your conversation mistress will help you with the variations that may arise.

'Now, as to the husband. It is important that you consider the personality of your patroness's husband, for though she has the right to a Consort of her own choosing, husbands accommodate that right in various ways. It is essential that you analyze the degree and type of accommodation and make every effort to meet it more than halfway.

'For example, the husband of your patroness may be complacent, in which case honest civility will be all that's required. He takes first place. At functions where husband and wife must appear together, you do not appear at all. At functions planned for patronesses and Consorts, at the theater, at restaurants, at fêtes and jollities, he does not appear.

'He may be envious, in which case you will speak *to* him of how highly his wife speaks *of* him. You will use a variation of the same technique used on servants and children. "She is so lucky to be married to you. She says so, all the time."

'Occasionally, however, you will meet a husband who is given over to an amorphous rage, which may or may not direct itself at you. Some people, more often men, spend their entire lives awash in bitterness. They rage against injustices done to their forefathers, perhaps centuries in the past. They rage against injustices done to their countrymen, their families. They rage against people who are unlike themselves, who, by virtue of their difference, must be up to no good. They rage against people who are like themselves who do not share their views. They rage against their parents, their wives, their children, and against anyone who is sympathetic to any of these. Their rage is a screen between them and the world, behind which they huddle over their egos, like a caveman over his fire, unable to see out through the smoke.

'Even some apes display this characteristic. Such fury may begin as a matter of status, as resentment against the dominant male. It may begin out of frustration of desires. It may begin with an unhappy nature that is born depressed and uses anger to fuel itself into action. It may begin in mystery, and it may end in tragedy. However or whyever it begins, it is essential that your patroness be protected from it. Your duty to your patroness is to give her joy and keep her from harm. She selected you. She places her happiness and her trust in you. She is your responsibility. If you injure a husband in protecting your patroness, you are exempt from any damages or judgments, even if the entire Executive Council of the Men of Business rises in wrath. This is one of the reasons you are taught hand-to-hand combat.

'Anger is our most destructive emotion. The most difficult part of your job is to deal with anger, your own or others'. We need anger to defend ourselves, so we cannot breed it out or teach ourselves not to feel it, but when we let the anger well up without a proper object, it floods our minds and renders us helpless. We all know men who are angry at everything, simply because they prefer to be angry at everything. Often, they self-destruct, and sometimes they take other people with them.'

10

Three Angry Men

Settlers had spread outward from Naibah along the shores of the Jellied Sea, so called for the semi-annual hatch of Purse fish whose translucent egg sacs rose from the pelagic ooze in uncounted millions, turning the sea for that brief period into an oceanic aspic. There were good-sized communities as far as several days' sail east or west, and small struggling settlements more distant than that. These places were supplied by ships from Gilesmarsh, the port at the mouth of the river, a place well equipped with doss houses, gambling dens, taverns, and stews built on tall pilings above the tidal ooze. Naibah was actually a bit inland from the delta, away from the stink of the mud flats and on high enough land to avoid both five-moon tides and the occasional tsunami resulting from sub-oceanic seisms.

Most boats docking at Gilesmarsh tried to do so at middle high tide, so their passengers could take one of the wind taxis upstream to Naibah and Water Street. There the transvestites were younger, prettier, and more agile than the old swabs at the port; the drink was of less lethal quality; and a man in his cups was less likely to end up dead, providing he kept his veils straight. Though there were few women of good repute to be offended on Water Street, there were alert Haggers everywhere.

One of the Water Street taverns was called the Septo-pod's Eye, and in addition to more-regular customers the place was patronized quarterly, more or less, by a group of odd fellows who came into Naibah from different directions, looked considerably different from the usual run, and smelled different from (and worse than) any living thing. One of them was called the Machinist, and another went by the name of Ashes, and the third one called himself Mooly. Whenever the barman (who despite his profession was a respected family man, entitled to a g' and a cockade) caught sight of any of the three, he summoned several bulky Haggers to sit about and look menacing and made sure his wife and daughters were up in the family quarters behind locked doors.

The three odd fellows never seemed to notice these arrangements. Each time they came, they sat at the same table and they drank the same brew, and they left at the same hour – just before the night boat sailed for Nehbe. Every time they came, any patron they spoke to was offended, and every man who got close enough to smell them was offended, and all in all, the barman was thankful they only showed up three or four times a year.

'So,' said the one called Mooly to the one called Ashes, 'you got your vengeance all underway, have you?'

'All moving along nicely.' Ashes grinned ferociously and dipped his snout into his glass. 'Machinist kind of helped me out. Now I'm waitin' for matters to ripen.'

'You figure gettin' ridda her will change things, do you?' asked Mooly.

'Change my irritation some,' Ashes growled. 'Teach her a lesson. Woman had no right to go off like that. I shoulda had daughters! I shoulda had riches! Woulda had, but for her!'

'Still got no ship,' murmured Mooly.

'We'll get the ship. No reason for hurry. Mountains are gonna roll, Mooly-boy. Mountains are gonna roll.' He leaned back, opened his mouth and sang, 'An' when they do, it's me and you, and devil take the hindmost.'

Everyone in the place began talking of something, anything, to cover the sound of that song, for it held a horridly broken quality, as though it issued from the throat of something not quite complete.

'Well, we're ready,' said Mooly, glaring at Ashes, his long yellow nails, ridged as washboards, making a dry tattoo upon the tabletop, like the rattling of bones. 'Been ready some time.'

Ashes squirmed, perhaps uncomfortable at this challenge. 'I know, I know. Gotta be patient. Gotta wait on events. You tell 'em Ashes said so. Wait on events.'

'I done my part,' whispered the Machinist. 'Nothing new, here, Ashes. Why'd you need me here? I don't like coming here.'

'Got to show the flag to the bloody Hag, Mah-cheeny. Got to come out in the open, ever now and then, listen to people talk, see 'em wander, figure 'em out.'

'You're drunk,' said Machinist, who drank nothing but water. 'You're pickled.'

'And if I am? Who's got more right? Never mind, Mah-cheeny, old boy. These little get-togethers keep us in touch. You over there near Nehbe. Mooly over the mountain with our folk. Me wanderin' around in Sendoph and Naibah, keepin' track of this one and that one. Now you can go back to your con-stit-you-encies and tell 'em what's goin' on.'

'Got no constituency,' grated Machinist. 'Don't want none.'

Ashes sneered, 'You got one, whether you want it or not. There's still folks remember you well, Mah-cheeny. Folks that speak of you often. Shatter sends regards. So does old Crawley! Meetin' here keeps us all together, keeps us on track. Whatever happens, we're gonna be all together. No matter what happens.'

'What happens better be what we planned to happen,' said Machinist. 'That's what'd better happen.'

'Sure, sure,' soothed Ashes. 'All in good time.'

'There's been too damn much good time!'

'You want it sooner, you can lead it.'

'Don't want to lead it,' said Machinist. 'Never did.'

'Well then, don't be so impatient. It'll all come to pass. You can rely on that. It'll all come to pass. No more Hags. No more smart-ass women dyin' when we do 'em. No more g'this and g'that. You relax, old boy. All's going just the way it should.'

They drank, they muttered, and around them the air seemed to seethe with frustration, expressed and repressed, a kind of livid glow that exhausted the air, leaving it without sustenance. Not a moment too soon, they left, this time with no assaults and no insults beyond the assault of their smell and the insult of their presence. Everyone in the room gasped with relief and those nearest the windows rose to throw them wide.

The barman propped the door ajar as well, then summoned two super-numes-of-all-work to scrub the table and chairs where the three had sat. He bought drinks for the house just to restore a little conviviality. Every time the trio descended on him, he swore it would be the last, but he still hadn't come up with a way to keep them out without insulting them, and somehow he didn't think insulting them was a good idea.

11

On Old Earth: History House

On Old Earth, History House #8739 (one of 10,000) glowed golden in dawn, shone rose-pink in sunset, a mountain of mirrored surfaces set like the facets of a gem. The interior ambience fulfilled the exterior promise; all was brilliance and luxury. Gilded columns towered, white faux marble stairs curved away to unseen marvels, while the tall mirrors on every wall expanded the interiors into infinite, though often fragmentary, spaces. Carpets were thick and mattress-soft, and they led past fountains and sculptures and flowering trees, artificial but scented like real ones, to wide corridors that opened into the exhibits: *Old Earth, 20th-century America; Old Earth, Asian Heritage; Old Earth, the Arts; Old Earth, Africa, Cradle of Man; Old Earth, the Primordial Fauna; Old Earth, Trees, Trees, Trees.* And so on, and so on.

The exhibits were an artful combination of theme park, resort, museum, concert, theater, and zoo. They were even partly, though by far the lesser part, authentic. Late in the fourth millennium of the common era, who was to say what had been real two millennia ago, or three millennia, or even longer than that? Clothing, ideas, fads, convictions, all had been transitory and miscible. Nature itself had been ephemeral. Even religions had shifted, becoming more or less than they had been, or had been thought to have been, but History House offered hints and approximations of the spiritual just as it offered approximations of everything else.

Though they were called 'artists' in the puff stuff, the performers who made the displays enjoyable and understandable did not profit from the glitter of the lower floors. Artists who lived in, mostly quota clones, occupied the far upper floors, for people on contract were not important enough to be allocated either luxury or space, both of which stopped at the 80th floor, just above the suites and gyms and dining rooms allocated to management. Above that were the shops, warehouses, and rehearsal halls, and above them were the dining rooms, grooming suites, and Denti-meds, serving those who lived above. The topmost floors were hives, with artists' cubicles crammed like cells in a honeycomb.

One's cubicle, however sterile and cramped, held all one had of home. Ellin Voy's cubicle, for example. On her narrow bed lay the stuffed bear Mama One had given her when she was three and the dolly Mama One had given her when she left for History House. On the shelf above was a little holo of herself and Mama One and Mama Two when they met at the ballet school for Ellin's thirteenth birthday. There was the book that Mama Two had given her for a sixteenth birthday present: *The Wizard of Oz*, a facsimile of a real book written centuries and centuries ago.

Hung above the shelf were other pictures memorializing brief holidays and ephemeral friendships. There was Ellin standing next to the bionic bull and the real bullfighter, the time she was assigned to History House in Spain; standing next to a handsome guard at the Tower of London when she'd been assigned to History House in England. Artists got reassigned among the History Houses all the time, or their contracts expired, or they paid off their contracts and left. There was no one in the corps de ballet that Ellin had known longer than two years. She looked at the pictures of herself with this one and that one, and sometimes it was hard to recall their names.

At night, the three inner cubicle walls could be set to show views chosen from among an extensive library of landscapes and interiors and events, both Terran and other worldly. Most of the artists chose something from their assigned periods of earthly history, something homey: a fireplace with glowing logs; a summer garden, glorious with flowers; an autumn land-scape, with trees changing color and a little wind riffling the surface of the pond; a city with broad avenues where spring blossoms fell gently onto the horses and carriages; views of things that no longer existed and places that no longer were.

Honorable Artist Ellin Voy chose otherwise. The sight of morning sun through autumn leaves made her cry. The sight of a fire burning on a hearth hurt her, as did trees dancing in moonlight. Views that made her think about the walls themselves made her choke, unable to catch her breath. Some fault within her, some unsuspected weakness that should have been eradicated before she was allowed to develop, had escaped the scrutiny of the monitors.

No matter what other artists did, Ellin kept her walls set on patterns only: receding colors of infinite depth, currents full of eddies and swirls, shapes that opened up and ramified and became other shapes, or endless streams of bubbles changing hue as they floated up and away. She curled on her narrow bed after lights out, dissolving in the patterns like a lump of sugar, unskein-ing like syrup into the liquid movement, becoming clearer and clearer, fading into transparency. Somewhere in that fluid motion was the thing she longed for, the total absorption, the absence of painful memory. In a few moments her eyes would blink, and soon she would fall asleep to dream of the same patterns and of herself as part of them.

She tried never to think of Mama One's house or of infant Ellin. She had chosen to dance, she had been bred to dance, but she had not chosen to leave Mama One. It wasn't quite so painful to remember Mama Two, for that time had been spent here, inside History House, and she still saw Mama Two from time to time. She had felt safe and connected with Mama One and Mama Two. She hadn't really felt safe since.

At six every morning the bells in the dancers' section would ring to introduce la patronne de ballet, her bony face protruding from the walls above each narrow bed, mouth bent into an unmeaning smile, eyes half shut as she crooned, 'Did we have good rest, mes enfants? Are we ready for le jour meilleur, the best day ever?'

To which all the dancers, Ellin included, replied aloud with the cheery voice and happy face the occasion required:

'Oh, oui, Madame. Bon! The best day ever.' Audio pick-ups recorded each response and graded it for wakefulness and enthusiasm as well as for any betrayal of incipient anarchy. Fortunately, the view screens weren't set to pick up silent rebellion. They didn't see fingers crossed behind backs or under sheets, or hear the subvocalized, 'Corpulent likelihood, Madumbdumb ballet-hoo. In a swine's auricular orifice!'

The cheery response to Madame's greeting still echoed in the cubicles when the morning fanfare sounded, segueing into march music as drum and bugle urged on the jagged reds and yellows of the walls, sawing away at any remaining languors. In less than half the time allotted for hygiene and grooming, Ellin had her wealth of silver hair braided and piled on top of her head and had moved from the sonic cleansers to the service module where she un-racked new disposables: tunic, trousers, slippers. The slight limp she'd had last rotation was quite gone. The injured toes were totally healed. Today she would return to dancing.

She hadn't been idle. She'd kept up her exercises, and she'd performed her alternate role. Everyone had alternate roles. If you were injured and couldn't fulfill your primary role, you still had to make every day the best day ever! Otherwise you'd find yourself out of work, and out of work could mean dead. Since Ellin had been raised in a twentieth-century matrix, her alternate roles were all in the twentieth century. This last one had been an elderly shopkeeper, Charlotte Perkins, in the small American town of Smithy's Corners. She'd been Mrs. Perkins for the whole rotation, which was enough.

Awaiting the breakfast gong, Ellin used the basin for a barre as she bent and stretched. Being Charlotte Perkins was easy on her feet, but it had bored her into knots! Smiling, waiting on people, answering their really dumb questions about the twentieth century. 'You mean they didn't have a Reproductive Center?' and, 'Where's the transporter station?' The days without the discipline of class and performance had left her feeling logy and disoriented, as though all her muscles had turned to cloth. She had to get back to the dance before she lost her mind! Besides, if she didn't, they might assign her coveted role of Dorothy to someone else!

The gong reverberated; the doors snapped open; the music got louder; the marching tempo carried the dancers out into the hall and thence past the gimlet-eyes of Par Reznikoff, Madame's deputy in this little bit of heaven. Ellin carefully kept people between her and him when she passed him on her way to the service counter. He wanted to apply for a reproductive contract with her, and she wasn't interested, no matter what it paid.

At the moment, all she was interested in was food. She had to cut intake when she wasn't dancing, but the lowered calories left her feeling hungry all the time. She was so preoccupied with making her breakfast last long enough to calm her hunger pains that she hadn't finished the liquid meal when the work bell clanged. Stage-hands and crew, already in uniform, streamed past the dancers' refectory toward the shafts that would drop them to the lower floors.

She was still holding the cup to her lips when Par came swiveling through the morning mob and took her arm.

'Elleeen,' he purred, making an indecency out of her name. 'You are looking lovely this morning.' He began walking her toward the shafts.

'Par.' She nodded, smiling, trying to hold her body away from the intimate contact he intended. No point in being nasty to him. He was Madame's little pet, and he'd get even if she did.

'You have a chance, perhaps, to think about the offer I made?' He cocked his head, eyes slitted, lips pursed, as though he were sucking an answer out of her, the answer he wanted.

She kept her voice calm, though she felt anything but. 'I don't have the energy, Par. I'm just getting over an injury, and I don't think now's a good time for me.'

'It's a lot of money, Ellin. You've got AA genes, pity not to use them for something.'

Well, damn it, she was using them for something, couldn't the idiot see that? She smiled, shook her head as she tried to look as uninteresting as possible. 'Sorry, Par ...'

He made a moue at her, patted her shoulder, and wandered away, leaving her at the end of the line. He wouldn't leave it alone. He'd be back, and next time he'd be pushy. She needed a strategy to discourage him, but at the moment she couldn't come up with one.

A dozen more pods came and went before she snagged an empty one, darted into it, felt the shoulder and waist restraints grip her firmly, felt the neck brace fit itself from shoulder to head as she said, 'Wardrobe, Twentieth-Century America, the Arts' and remembered too late she was still holding the cup.

She gasped as the pod fell straight down, then shifted left, right, made a quick spiral, a long horizontal run at top speed, then a quick stop that threw the last of her breakfast all over her. Ellin gasped. She had never been able to breathe in transit. Now she felt like a dropped egg!

When the pod side popped open, she almost fell out, steadying herself on the wall, hearing the pod chant, 'Make it the best day ever,' as it zipped away.

Why did Par want her? It was true that History House paid big bonuses to the women characters who were willing to let tourists observe the actual births. Ellin only knew one person who'd done natural pregnancy and public birth, her friend from infant fosterage, Tutlia Omae, formerly known as Tutsy, who had actually had six babies, earning enough in seven years not only to pay off her contract but also to buy tickets off-world for herself and the two youngest children! Of course, not everyone would have been allowed to have six children, but Tutsy had AA genetics on both sides and the quota for American Indigenes was always scraping the bottom. Also, Tutsy had worked in one of History House's most profitable exhibits, *Old Earth, Cowboys and Indians!* and she got hardship bonuses all the time. Ellin had often wondered what there was about sitting around a fire and eating half raw meat that made it more of a hardship than dancing. At least when Tutsy stepped out of the cleanser cubicle at night, her day's work was all washed away, no harm done. When Ellin cleaned up at the end of the day, her feet were often still bleeding.

Being pregnant might be profitable, but Ellin wouldn't care for it, no thank you! All that bloating and being sick! All those months unable to dance! She'd have to gain ten or twenty pounds even to be fertile, and she hated the idea. Her body was precious. It was her, all she had, and she didn't want it changed. The idea was ridiculous. Sex was ridiculous, despite the stories people told about dancers, about their probable sexual habits, spending so many hours cooped up together. That was a laugh. Mostly the female dancers were too tired and half starved to even think about sex. Some of them didn't even menstruate.

She was still carrying the cup when she entered Wardrobe. Taking tableware was against the rules, so she sneaked down the closest aisle to her own dressing area, hid the cup on her locker shelf behind the wigs, and wadded the wet disposables directly into the chute, cursing beneath her breath. She'd expected to get at least three or four days out of this set, and here they were, ruined. Disposables were charged to her contract. Meals were charged to her contract. There was no charge for housing, but then, one couldn't really call a cubicle housing.

Getting into the Dorothy costume took only a moment, the blue-and-white checked skirt, the little apron, the puff-shouldered, high-necked blouse with all the buttons. The blouse had been designed for Ellin, with a high neck and long, slender arms. She took the Dorothy wig from its stand and held it ready as she entered the name of the character in the makeup frame that gaped in the locker door and thrust her face into it, holding her breath while it went dabby-dab-dab, plucky-pluck at her. She focused her mind on the Yellow Brick Road sequence, summoning the music, feeling the role, the stretch and release of muscle, the gathering and loosing of sinew and strength.

When the mirror dinged and she stepped back, someone behind her looked over her shoulder into the mirror. Snow Olafson, who'd sneaked up on her and now lifted an eyebrow, giving her a smoky look.

He whispered, 'I hear you and Par are signing a contract.'

She pulled the Dorothy wig over her hair, pushing her stray locks up under it, as she snapped, 'Don't be silly, Snow. That's ridiculous.'

'Oh, not the way he tells it.'

'He can tell it any way he likes. I am not interested in a reproductive contract with anybody. I'm just beginning to get lead roles, why would I frangle it up?'

He blinked at her like a big cat. 'Well, Ellin, if you do decide to ... frangle ... keep me in mind.'

And he moved lazily away, glancing at her over his shoulder. Snow danced the role of the Wizard – not at all the kind of Wizard who had been in Ellin's book, but then she wasn't exactly the kind of Dorothy who had been in the book, either – and the two of them had a long, sultry pas de deux in Act II. Snow was not a contractee. Snow had been hired from outside, and the word was he had a sole-use reproductive contract with two licensed nordic type women in the Wisconsin Urbop. So why was he here flirting with her? Why did men get themselves into sole-use reproductive contracts if they didn't intend to honor the terms? That's all Ellin needed, getting dragged into some contract violation case.

She put him out of mind as she put the finishing touches on her wig, tied her shoes, and padded down the stairs. There was a rehearsal studio behind the stage where they could warm up. Below her, she could see Snow arguing with Beise Tonkoff, the choreographer. Probably about that really ugly sequence in the last act, where Dorothy had to choose between staying with the wizard or going home. Both she and Snow hated it. It was ugly! Beise swore it was the same as written originally for the ballet, back right around the end of the twentieth century or start of the twenty-first, though back then it was called Homage to Dorothy, based on the book Ellin had been given.

Snow looked up, caught her eye, and grimaced. Her inclination was to stay away from Snow and never to confront anyone, but in this case ...

Beise was saying, 'But I can't simply change something that's authentically in period ...'

'It isn't,' Ellin said. 'There's nothing authentic about the ballet. In the first place, in the book and the two-dee, the wizard is a fat old man and Dorothy is a girl, a child. They never dance together at all. In an authentic version, Dorothy would dance with the metalman, the strawman, the beastman, and possibly one of the witches, but not with the wizard. So for heaven's sake, look at it, and let us fix it!'

He sighed, much put upon. 'What in particular?'

'The whole sequence! Look at it. The good witch has just told Dorothy about the red slippers, and Dorothy comes forward, sur les pointes, arms widely back, raising the working foot a little higher each time, looking down at the slipper. She's amazed. She does a grande battement, ending with an attitude an avant, to get the closest possible look at the slipper. That's fine, but all this time the Wizard just stands there like a lump, waiting for the pirouettes, and then he walks around her like a robot, clunk, clunk, clunk. He's not the metalman, for heaven's sake! Both characters look robotic, and there's no motivation for what he's doing! He ought to follow her, then as she pirouettes, he should reach out to her. Maybe a slow lunge and glissade. Something! If he wants Dorothy to stay, his body ought to say so.'

Snow raised his eyebrows at her and grinned, leaning toward her yearningly.

She ignored his intent and said, 'Yes, maybe like that. Then when we get to the lifts, it's up down, up down, like someone doing exercises, and Dorothy's not even paying attention! The whole sequence makes him look like a robot with ugly legs.'

Snow scowled at that, and she quickly turned away. That ought to do it. Snow was very vain about his legs. He wouldn't let go of Beise from now until the end of time. As she stepped away, she caught the director's amused eyes on her. He'd heard her.

Well, maybe it was amusing, but dance was her life, her only love. In her head it was a continuous stream, with eddies and falls and high, sparkling splashes. Certainly it shouldn't ever just *glug, glug, glug,* like a plugged up pipe! Her dream of herself, the dream she'd had since a child, had no glugs in it. When it was right, her body moved without herself being aware of her body, as though she were dissolved in the music.

She walked back across the stage while various back-scenes flicked into and out of existence in the rearstage matrix: fields where the strawman was found; the forest where the metalman appeared; the line of stone where the beastman appeared roaring in the red glow of the sunset, dark against a burning sky. The backscenes used in History House shows were among the best ones anywhere because they were based on tapes of actual landscapes, as they had appeared before all the atectonic land areas were leveled and domed. Somehow computer-generated scenery never looked as real.

She reached the wings just as the tornado flicked into being behind her, first far off, then coming closer and closer while Dorothy and her little dog

677

ran for the house ... Then off and away, the house flying, Dorothy and Toto in it.

Sometimes children were brought backstage to meet the dancers. They always wanted to meet Toto, too, but of course he was only a holo. There were no dogs anymore.

'That twisty wind is great,' one candy-smeared small boy had exulted to Ellin – or rather, to Dorothy. 'Why don't they let tornadoes happen for real?'

Ellin had told him why, but the boy had seemed unconvinced. Later, Ellin had thought maybe he was right to be so. There was something terrifying about the tornado, even here on stage, but oh, it lent wings to the dancing! Many old books had dangers and excitements in them, but all natural violence was controlled now. Everything was domed over. If there were excitements, they were out on the frontier, which is where, she told herself firmly, she was going to go as soon as her contract was paid off. She was going to find a primitive planet way out there, where the people had no dancers, where she could teach them all about it until she was too old to move.

No one on Earth worked very late in life. History House never kept anyone after they were forty, but Ellin would not quit at forty and spend the rest of her life on her pension, in a cubicle somewhere! Not even if she had to save up and save up and skimp on disposables and serve her whole twenty years to use her money for a ticket out! She dreamed about it all the time, finding a place with real trees, real grass, real creatures. A place that lasted.

Warmup was short, a kind of abbreviated class. Out in the lobby, people were already lined up as Ellin and the others took their places in the wings. The orchestra was tuning up. All History Houses used real people, keeping the various talents alive. A man's voice spoke her name from behind her, and for a moment it sounded like Par's voice, but when she turned, it was a stranger, one of two, both dressed in management blue. That meant they had a right to be here. Or anywhere.

Her mind raced over recent days' activities, searching for something, anything she might have done, might have said. Had someone heard her complaining about the restrictions or the food? Maybe someone had seen her take that cup ...

One of the men returned her panicky look with the fractional upturn of lips allowed government functionaries. Since he'd smiled, it probably wasn't anything she'd done. Snow? Par? Who? Then she noticed their lapels and insignias: red-and-gold instead of the green-and-white of the civility monitors. They were from Planetary Compliance!

'Ellin?' one of them asked. 'Ellin Nordic-Quota, 2980-4653?'

She nodded, afraid to trust her voice. Planetary Compliance. You couldn't get any more threatening than that.

He smiled again. 'Will you call your substitute, please. We have a requisition for you.'

'Requis...'

'From the Questioner.'

Her mouth dropped open. The man who had smiled uttered a brief, official chuckle, three precise ha's. She caught a glimpse of herself in the mirror through the classroom door and shut her mouth. No wonder he laughed. She looked witless! Actually stupid, and when men in blue were talking at you, it was not the time to be stupid.

Summoning all available poise, she tried to draw herself up and out of character to ask, 'The Questioner, gentlemen?' Try though she had, the words came out in what she thought of as Dorothy's voice – wondering and very naïve.

The fatter one said, '*The* Questioner, yes.' He actually grinned. 'Today, girly. This morning. If you'll call your substitute, please.'

He had just committed an incivility, calling her girly, but now probably wasn't a good time to report him. Maybe it would be better to ignore it. Even forget it. Trying not to fumble or seem hesitant, she went to the nearest com and spoke to the panel: 'Corps de ballet. Director's office, please. Dorothy character has been called away from backstage by PC officers. Substitute needed immediately.'

'How long will it take?' the man asked.

'Once they call me back, not long,' she murmured. 'One of the human alternates will have to be dressed for the part. They only use androids in emergencies.'

'You have to wait?'

'Once the orchestra starts, no character is supposed to leave the wings, sir. In case the entrance cue comes up ...' She stared at the floor, trying to keep her breathing steady. What had she done? What had someone claimed she'd done? Had Par accused her of something?

Down the hallway a door opened and Par Reznikoff came through. 'That's Madame's deputy,' murmured Ellin, pointing. 'I guess you'll have to talk to him.'

The two men moved away from her and intercepted Par in mid-stride. Ellin couldn't hear them from where she stood, still poised for the music. Madame's deputy didn't like it, whatever he was hearing. He shook off their reaching hands and came to the wings, where she was standing, pointing his finger at her and saying: 'You'll stay right where you are ...'

'Reznikoff, perhaps you'd like to call the nearest PCO,' said one of the men in blue, who had followed him.

Par turned quite pale, though his mouth was still chewing at the words he hadn't said yet. Evidently he didn't like the idea of the Planetary Compliance Office.

'I suggest, before you say anything actionable, that you do so.' The other man in blue looked amused, which would send Par around the far turn. He began furiously punching up com numbers on the panel. Ellin caught one of the men in blue staring at her and she flushed.

'That's all right,' he said in a calming voice. 'He'll get the word. You're the lead in this ballet, aren't you? The records on you said you were a dancer.'

She didn't ask what records. She was saved from having to say anything for Par turned from the com with his jaw set and his lips pale from being pressed together. He stormed away.

'You can change your clothes now,' said the less-talkative man in blue, gesturing down the hall. 'And you'll want to bring an overnight case.'

She shifted uncertainly.

He smiled the government smile once again. 'It's all right, dear, really. There's your replacement at the end of the hall. You're not in any trouble. We'll meet you at the gate.'

Both of them had been uncivil, calling her girly, calling her dear. She was not a nus, someone with No Useful Skills. She was an honorable, just as they were! She passed the substitute without a glance and went back to wardrobe in what she hoped was a dignified manner. As she removed the wig and the dress, the Dorothy thoughts and worries seemed to dissolve, leaving an aching space to be filled with some other thought or worry. It didn't take long. As she dropped a clean tunic over her head, she found plenty to worry about in being approached by PCO and requisitioned by the Questioner.

12

The Amatory Arts: What Women Want

'One of the most important things you will learn,' said Madame, 'is how to give a woman what she wants, whether she knows what she wants or not. If you have read your assignment, you know that mankind has a stratified mentality. The ancient lizard mind lies below the mammalian mind, which lies below a primate mind, which is modified by a mind adapted to language, and since these layers have developed in response to differing evolutionary pressures, they often do not function efficiently together. Human civility tries to control ape dominance, human rationality tries to control mammalian sexuality, human social conscience tries to ameliorate reptilian greed, never with total success. Some individuals who could be human give up the struggle and remain mere speaking animals.

'Add to this the complex endocrine makeup of women that drives their cyclical biological systems, and add to *that* the fact that women are more likely than men to "think about situations" in words and symbols which themselves have imprecise meanings, and you will begin to get an idea why women cannot always say, even to themselves, what they desire at any given time.'

Madame took a sip of water. Mouche sat very still, pen poised, hoping he could figure out what Madame desired at any given time. Keeping up with her was very difficult. Keeping one step ahead was impossible. He looked up to catch her gimlet eye, as though she had read his mind, and flushed, bending quickly over his notebook.

She went on. 'At the prelinguistic levels, young females are no different from their brothers. They all eat, sleep, and play in the same way. The female's physical growth is as rapid, her bones and muscles are as strong. The prelinguistic mother makes no differentiation between the male and the female infant.

'Both male and female young play in accordance with their genetic pattern; they run and jump and make noise and copy adult behavior. Primate males, as a group, are more active and noisy and less thoughtful. Primate females, as a group, have longer attention spans and are less likely to engage in rough play. Individual males and females, however, are found at the extremes of both groups, so we must regard these differences not as sex-determined but as gender and culture influenced.

'It is at sexual maturity that real differentiation begins. Among many primates, including primitive hominids, females begin to cluster around infant and nurturing activities, and maturing males tend to assemble into gaming gangs that spend their time in group competitions and rivalries ...

'Fentrys! Pay attention. You and Egon may finish your quarrel in fencing class!

'... and the groups are stratified, with one or more leaders and the rest as followers. This pattern continues even today, though the acquisition of language allows such groups to be institutionalized as tribes, armies, political parties, commercial empires, religious hierarchies, or sports teams. All of these have rules requiring defense and extension of territory by carrying some play object – a ball, flag, icon, trademark, or belief system – into someone else's territory. From the psychological point of view, there is very little difference between making religious converts, kicking the winning goal, or cornering the market on Thorbian gigarums.

'Proper gang activity requires the control of members. Gangs cannot tolerate "loose" persons wandering around. One is either with the church or against it; with the company or against it; with the team or against it. A phrase long in use on Old Earth was, "Are you with it?" meaning, "Do you comprehend the behaviors necessary for membership?" Persons inside the group are "us." All significant entities outside the group, including females, are "them," and all them are either property, prey, or opponents.

'Outside persons who have needed or desired talents become property; persons who aren't useful or won't submit become prey. Powerful people and groups, male, may be opponents. Females are not usually regarded as opponents, and on many worlds if a woman acts as an opponent, she risks being raped or maimed in order to redefine her as a prey animal and restore balance to the system.

'Females who agree to be property are the survivors. Belonging to a mature, powerful male guarantees his protection for her and her children and raises the female's rank in the primate society. The higher the rank, the less she is harassed and the more she gets to eat. Over millions of years, therefore, it has become instinctive for females to mate with the most dangerous, most dominant male they can attract.

'Male hominid group leaders really are dangerous. When they cease being dangerous, they will be overthrown. This too has carried over into current time. Men who are physically dangerous – sports stars, murderers, rapists – often enjoy great sexual success. Even imprisoned serial killers are known to acquire female followers who send them gifts and invent romances about them. The aura of danger was and is sexually stimulating, and the attraction of and "taming" of a dangerous man lies at the heart of all romance literature.

'While civilized males no longer publicly categorize females as prey or property, the instinct to do so remains strong ...'

Mouche wriggled again, fighting boredom. His father had not treated his mother as either prey or property, and he probably didn't think of her as an opponent, either. This time he kept his head down, evading Madame's glance.

'How does this apply to you, Mouche?'

He looked up startled, but she had turned away.

'How does it apply to any of you? You will learn to impart an aura of danger because women find it thrilling, though it is only the aura, not the reality that we seek to achieve. It may take no more than a wicked smile to convey a delicious threat that will increase a woman's feeling of vulnerability to you while at the same time increasing her feeling of safety. Don't expect this to make sense at the rational level, it doesn't. It makes sense only in the bestial basements of women's minds, where a mate strong enough to fight off a cave bear was a plus, even if he occasionally knocked his mate into the fire.

'Don't confuse fantasy and reality. It is all too possible to be so swept up in the fantasy that one continues into reality, but the Consort who crosses that line is lost. We never speak of them by name, but I could tell you of more than one who injured a patroness and died in shame and obloquy. Learn your own danger signals. Learn how to control yourselves.

'In your training, you will learn to use these instincts. You will learn how to look and sound dangerous. For example, we stage duels that appear quite real, but we intervene at a point when the combatants are equally advantaged so that both participants can be made to seem dangerous. Each one will then say to his own particular audience, "They made us stop because they had a lot invested in him, and they were afraid I would kill him." Properly said, with a choke in the voice and furious tears in the eyes, this goes over well. Danger whispers to a woman, "He's so strong, he's so fearless, he can protect me."

'This is the effect you will be trained to convey. You will seem larger than life, dangerous and perilous, while really being self-controlled. When a woman buys a Consort, she wants something larger than life. If you were mere Men of Business, you would not be tempting to your patronesses.'

She fell silent, took a sip of water, looked up to see a hand respectfully raised.

'Yes, Mouche? You have a question?'

'Why must we never hurt a woman, Madame? My mother made my father very unhappy sometimes. I used to think if he would hit her, he would feel better.' There. He had proved he'd been listening.

Madame nodded. 'That raises several issues:

683

'There has been much woman-wastage in history. Women have been used as breeders only, as dawn to dusk agricultural workers, as beasts of burden. They have been unconsidered, used up, untaught, cast aside, injured or killed, not allowed to grow or live to their potential. In societies that do this, it is a "way of life," but there is little or no culture. Heterosexual males, when by themselves, seem to fall naturally into the gang pattern where rape is an amusement or a battle tactic. Haraldson's edicts, however, make it clear that we expect more than that from humanity.

'Here on Newholme we choose to be human and we cannot afford to waste women's reproductive nature or their cultural talents. Injury is forbidden. Injury invalidates a marriage, no matter how much dowry has been paid, and a husband or Consort who purposely kills or injures a woman is invariably blue-bodied.

'Any other questions? Good. We will discuss this further on future occasions. You are excused.'

13

At the Mercy of the Mountain

A short walk from House Genevois, the Panhagion stood on a low mound a few streets west of the river, just outside the main business district but accessible from the broad, straight length of the boulevard that connected the north and south gates of the city. A fraction of every dowry paid for a wife went to support the Panhagion. A fraction of every Consort's pay went to support the Panhagion. Every Hag, every Hagger, every Temple worker or young married woman doing her matron's stint of Temple duty was jealous of the honor of the Panhagion, for it was the center of religious life not only in Sendoph but in all of settled Newholme.

Most women chose to deliver their babies in the birthing center in the vaults below the Temple, where birth was considered sacramental and where the most skilled midwives were found. If some could not deliver at the Temple, at least they tried to have Temple midwives. The viral invasion of the X chromosome that killed half of all female infants on Newholme while allowing virtually all of the boy children to live was best understood by the Temple midwives.

The domed hall of the fortress became the Panhagion Sanctuary, a place for the adoration of the Hagions, the female deities. The lower levels surrounding this space and accessible from the forecourt were given over to the offices that conducted public business. In the vaults below, the Hags Observant, each of whom could count over forty years service to the Hagions, supervised the birthing suites and the secret rituals. Their lengthy lives of service were rewarded by the provision of luxurious living quarters in the towers at the back of the Temple.

Among the Hags Observant were two cousins, D'Jevier and Onsofruct Passenger, who had been born in the Temple and had, at the Hags' order, been reared there. D'Jevier was tall and extremely slender, with tightly drawn nut-brown skin that gleamed slightly in the lamplight. Onsofruct was a year or so older, shorter, darker, and rounder. Except when bathing or sleeping, they wore what all the Hags wore: soft, long-sleeved, high-necked gowns with close-fitting wimples that hid their necks and heads and served as an anchor for the complicated folds and twists of the bright headscarves that marked their rank. The colors of their gowns betokened their lengths of service. Novices wore yellow; young women, green; middle-aged women, blue; and crones, shades of red that increased in vividness with their years. D'Jevier and Onsofruct had passed into cronehood some time since; they wore gowns and figured kerchiefs the bright crimson of fresh blood or burning coals.

The garments were so vivid that someone looking upward at the balcony where the cousins stood, high on the east side of the residence tower, might have thought the tower was on fire, a conflagration echoing that on the eastern scarp. There a crimson gash had recently appeared below a billowing eruption of ash, and this great gray cloud had opened a gaping sleeve of angry flame to stretch a cinereous arm toward Sendoph.

D'Jevier's voice quavered as she remarked, 'It's worse than it's ever been!' She sipped from her wineglass as she watched the smoky fist sail toward her, closer and closer, the fat, billowy fingers extending. So huge, so incorporeal, so deadly, nonetheless. Her fancied confrontation with this monster was aborted by a gust of wind that swept down the valley of the Giles, breaking the ashen cloud into scattered shreds of gray.

She murmured, 'I wish we could ask the Council of Worlds for help.'

'Help to do what?' Onsofruct asked. 'We can't ask for evacuation. There are too many of us.'

'I read something about HoTA devising some new method of controlling earthquakes ...'

'Can they do it from off-planet?'

'No. I'm sure not. It involved burning deep wells along the fault lines and pumping in some kind of shock-absorbing liquid. It doesn't stop the earth moving, but it does make the movement smooth instead of shuddering. It's the shaking does the worst damage ...'

'Well, take your pick,' said D'Jevier. 'Die in a quake or invite COW in and die anyhow.'

'You think the Council of Worlds would really kill us all?'

'In the first place, they'd send the Questioner. The Questioner doesn't even need council approval anymore, hasn't for at least a century. And what the Questioner would do would be worse than merely killing us all.'

'If she comes here, she would see ... what she would see.'

'She'd turn right around and make examples of us, for the edification of the galaxy.'

'So we're trapped.'

'Trapped ourselves.'

'We didn't. Not you and me.'

'Well, Hags did. And Men of Business.'

A long silence. D'Jevier tipped her glass and pretended to be concentrating upon the light reflected in its depths as she said, 'We might ask ... *them*. Maybe they know something that would help.'

'Jevvy! You wouldn't dare!'

The other woman grinned mirthlessly, shaking her head. 'Every day I get closer to daring. If it gets worse, yes, I'll dare.'

Both fell silent, thinking long, hard thoughts that they had already gone over a thousand times. Decisions made centuries ago that could not now be unmade. Roads taken that allowed no possibility of return. An hour later they were still there, their glasses long since empty, still staring wordlessly at the world-wound upon the height, livid ash and bleeding fire. They and their world were at the mercy of the mountain, and they could think of nothing at all that would be helpful.

14

A Diversion of Dancers

'It's really very simple.' The Planetary Compliance worker smiled fleetingly at Ellin across the shining width of her authority surface. 'Do pay attention.

'The Questioner is a device of the Council of Worlds. The Questioner moves about among the worlds assessing mankind-occupied worlds for conformity to the edicts of Haraldson. While doing assessments, the Questioner likes to take along a person or persons from a similar developmental stage as the world being assessed. One of the planets to be assessed, for example, is Bandat, where society has achieved what the Absolute Correct Ones call their preholiness phase. Another world is Chirry-chirry-dim-dim, which the Butterfly-Boys identify as being in the caterpillar stage prior to planetary pupation. You will visit Newholme, which is in the incipient industrial stage.'

Ellin Voy, Nordic-Quota 2980–4653, shifted uneasily. After a long moment of silence, she cleared her throat and asked, 'Am I here because I play a part in History House and have some knowledge of preindustrial society?'

'Honorable Ellin, from Old Earth America, you are here partly for that reason, but more because you are a dancer. Also going to Newholme will be Honorable Gandro Bao, who is a character in History House of the tenth Asian Urbopolis.' The woman in blue nodded gently in the direction of a lean, olive-skinned man in the chair nearest Ellin. 'Honorable Gandro Bao works in Old Earth, Asia: Heritage of the Arts. He is an actor-dancer of the fifteen to nineteen hundreds, Kabuki style, authentic female impersonator. Honorable Ellin is a dancer of western classical style. Among this variety of background, some skill should be found to assist the Questioner in assessing the planet Newholme.'

'We are assessing it for what?' asked the man identified as Gandro Bao. 'I am not understanding the role of dancers.'

The woman in blue put her face in censorious mode, one of the seven official government expressions Ellin had been able to identify over the years: kindliness with smile and/or chuckle, businesslike with tight lips, censorious with narrowed eyes, threatening with mouth distended, rage with red face, forgiveness with nod and gesture of benediction, and pity with sorrowful mouth and dropped eyes and chin. Conversations invariably began with kindly or businesslike, though they might end with any of the seven.

'Were you not educated, Honorable Gandro Bao?' challenged the PCO.

He nodded, seeming in no whit embarrassed. 'I am recognizing what is the Questioner. I am recalling function of Questioner in examining planets. I am not understanding why dancer is wanted.'

'Ah.' Her expression switched to forgiveness, the requisite smile flickering in and out of existence so quickly as to be almost subliminal. 'Questioner is allowed total discretion in determining how investigation is done. Questioner has asked for dancers. Therefore, we send dancers. Questioner does not say why. We do not ask.'

Ellin shook her head, conscious of weariness and annoyance. 'So we're supposed to go to Newholme, which will be kind of a History House in the sky, and determine whether they treat one another properly? An android could do that!'

The censorious expression returned. 'The Questioner is beyond criticism. If Questioner felt an android could do it, an android would be sent.'

'Sorry,' murmured Ellin. 'I'm just ... surprised, is all.' Surprised hardly expressed it. She was actually shocked into near paralysis. The thought of being suddenly uprooted left her teetering over an abyss, fumbling for words and proper responses, dizzy and adrift, shocked by the immediacy and strength of her emotions. After all the years she had imagined being free, after all those dreams of going to other worlds, seeing other peoples, finding her own special place in which to live her own, unique life, now here she was, invited to do virtually as she'd always thought she wanted, at no trouble or expense to herself, and she was frightened witless.

'You may have time to adapt,' said the woman in blue, giving her a very percipient look.

The word evoked a veritable bonfire of associations. Time to adapt. Time to move on. Time to do this, do that. Infant fosterage giving way to boarding school in History House. Boarding school giving way to advanced studies. Advanced studies giving way to the corps de ballet. Always time to say good-bye, to give up treasured things, familiar friends, always time to adapt ...

The woman's voice cut through Ellin's confusion. 'Suddenness is difficult for all creatures, but this will not be sudden. Honorables Ellin Voy and Gandro Bao will go to Newholme. The ship leaves soon, in seven days, but the voyage will be lengthy. During some of it, you will be asleep. For this next few days, however, the honorables will live here, in prelaunch. During this time you have medical assessment, wardrobe and other necessities will be assembled, and you will have access to all records and reports on the planet Newholme, which should be studied assiduously. Go through that door there,' she pointed, 'to Suite Four Thirty-Four.'

The forgiving expression returned momentarily as the woman returned to her papers. 'Honorable DoJub and Honorable Clementi will be visiting the planet Boshque, which is in a late arboreal phase due to ground-level predation ...'

Bao stood in front of the door sensor, keeping the door open for Ellin, a courtesy which earned him a half smile. The two of them prowled silently down the corridor, Ellin avoiding his eyes, concentrating on finding Suite Four Thirty-Four. She needn't have bothered, for at their approach a door lit up and caroled a welcome.

'Honorables Ellin and Bao. Welcome to Suite Four Thirty-Four, prelaunch facility for planetary examiners.'

Bao broke his silence with an angry mutter. 'Being much filth and excrement. Five days from now I am to be dancing the lead in the Chikamatsu *Shinj ten no Amijima*, with orchestrated Joruri, as adapted from the Bunraku. I have been much wishing this for three years. And now this is happening!'

'Be calm,' said the door in a soothing tone. 'Feel elation! HoLI COW pays off contracts of all nominees who are contractees as well as post-bondage stipend. Once duty is done for the Questioner, you are free! Feel satisfaction! Do not distress yourself, Honorables. Even if you do not return for decades, all will be well. Oh, feel elation!'

At the word 'decades,' Ellin felt a watery lick, as though an icy wave were rising inside her, threatening to spurt out of her throat in a jet of pure hysteria. She pushed it down, swallowed it, and felt it dissolving her insides. She must not disgrace herself. Not in front of this person. Not in front of this door, which was so very solicitous and was probably programmed to report any deviation from acceptable norms. She dropped into a chair and put her hands over her face, evoking the patterns on her wall, swirlings, eddies, flowing ... calm and quiet. Herself part of the flow. None of this was really happening, not yet. She would put off the happening for a little time, and when it came, she would be ready.

'Are you feeling elation?' demanded Bao in an arrogantly angry tone. 'Are you liking to go so far for doing Questioner knows what?'

At this interruption of her hard-won calm, she felt a flare of fury, as though she had received an injection of some energizing drug.

'Don't speak to me as though addressing a nus. I am not a nus. I have useful skills. Though I am a quota-clone, I retain my rights of reproduction and am as honorable as yourself. I, too, have disappointments. This rotation I was to dance in one of the Morris ballets of the late twentieth century. Your arrogance is not acceptable. You will treat me with courtesy, or I shall report you for status harassment!'

'Oh, gracious,' cried the door. 'Let us not speak of reportings. Feelings are strained. Emotions are liberated in unattractive ways. This is understood. Being nominated is stressful. Suddenness is resented by all organisms. Please. Sit down and let yourselves be comforted.'

Again hysteria threatened to erupt. Ellin's jaw clenched tight as she sank back into the chair. One did not achieve pleasantness by greeting incivility with incivility. She knew that as well as she knew ... anything.

A six-legged server came scuttling across the floor, eager to be of help. 'Something to drink?' it whispered in a husky little voice. 'A massage of feet? Of neck? Some food? Milky nutriment often soothes. Nordic types are lacto-tolerant. Please?'

'Tea,' she said in her Charlotte Perkins voice. 'Hot tea. In a real cup. With lemon flavor and sweetness. And a cookie.' Long ago, the infant Ellin had been comforted with cookies by Mama One. She had not had a cookie for many years.

The server scuttled off.

'Apologies,' Bao said wearily. 'I am being frangled.' He sighed and sank into the chair across from her, looking around himself at the luxurious setting. There were real carpets. There were real fabrics at the sides of the view screens. The chairs were large and cushiony. The small table at his side had the appearance of real wood, though that was, of course, unlikely. Still, going to the trouble to make it look like that was an indication of... something. 'They are believing us to be important,' he said.

'They want us to believe they think we're important,' she snarled, unwilling to forgive him. 'Sending us off for years and years, disrupting our lives! All this is like offering a child candy if he will be good.' She had seen a good deal of that in Perkins Store, where so-called penny candies were provided for children as souvenirs of Old Earth.

He nodded, his eyes fixed on her face as though he had just noticed her. 'There is being high probability we must be good regardless, so candy is being offered for making us more happy about inevitables. A bonus, perhaps?'

'Bribe, not bonus!' She snorted. Newholme. She had no idea where Newholme was. They spoke together:

'Are you knowing where ...'

'I have no idea where ...'

He laughed. After a moment, unable to help herself, she smiled waveringly.

He made an expansive, almost girlish gesture. 'We are being angry at situation, not at one another. Maybe we are being angry with Questioner, but Questioner is not knowing and is not caring, so we waste anger on nothing. It is clear we are being together for some time. Let us be easy together.'

'Is the Questioner a she?'

'So I am understanding. Of a sort.'

The server brought the tea and several cookies, real cookies that smelled of vanilla and lemon. Ellin smiled at this and allowed herself to be soothed.

Gandro Bao was right, of course. There was no point getting frangled with one another.

'Do you have family?' she asked.

'I was natural born,' he said. 'I have mother, father, one sister.'

'Do you look anything like your sister?' Ellin asked curiously. Full siblings were rare except for clones. The genetic agencies usually required donor insemination for second births, to keep the gene pool as widely spread as possible within types.

He nodded, raising a hand to the server, which came buzzing over, stopping at his elbow. 'I am desiring a ham sandwich,' he said. 'With mustard and a pickle.'

'Corpulent likelihood,' murmured Ellin.

'I am testing if we are really important,' he said, crinkling his eyes at her. 'Your question about my sister, yes, she is looking much like me, Asian type, and we are having similar facial structures. What is your family?'

'No family I know of. Except clones. I was born on preassigned ethnic quota, so my parent could have been anyone ...'

'I am looking at you,' he corrected her. 'I am thinking not just anyone, no.'

She flushed. 'I never asked if I had non-clone siblings, full or half. Somehow it didn't seem to matter.'

'Where was your rearing?' he asked.

'First in an infant fosterage, but I don't remember much about it, to tell you the truth, except for Mama One. They cloned six of me, and History House approved us for fosterage – not together, of course – then it picked me up on a quota-clone contract when I was six ...'

'After you were infant?'

'I lived at the History House boarding school, with dancing lessons every day, in a nurturance group – foster brothers and sisters – with our Mama and Papa Two, until I was twelve. Then I went into the ballet school, four of us with a foster aunt, for six years of additional education in dance and drama and twentieth-century studies. Then the corps de ballet. And they've moved me around. This last History House was my fifth.'

He grinned ruefully. 'It is not sounding like much fun. How is it feeling to have foster parents? And foster aunts?'

She frowned, chewing on a mouthful of cookie, surprised to find her eyes filling. She shook her head impatiently, refusing the tears. 'Well, actually, I loved Mama One very much. I guess you could say I never really got over the separation. I still hear from her, every now and then. Mama Two was different, but as she told me herself, her job was different. And when it came time for Foster Aunt, her job was to get the four of us through the second-decade miseries. Do boys have miseries?'

He laughed, his eyes half shut, his body shaking. 'Oh, Ellin Voy, I am remembering all such things. Yes. Miserable boys, I am remembering.'

'How'd you get into a History House?' she asked. 'Tapped, or on purpose?'

'I was being tapped,' he admitted. 'I was attending school in town where family is living. There, in the school, I am being always... what is called a laughjerker ...?'

'A clown?'

'You are knowing the exact word. Clown, yes. Everything is being a joke for the face and for the voice and for the legs, always being funny, always making the laughter, always falling down so much they are calling me Bao Bao Down. So many times I was having the settle-down speech, the school was getting tired of saying it. So, instead, they were giving me the test battery, and as soon as I was reaching twelve years, my family was being told I am born actor, born comic, born Kabuki dancer for women's parts – all Kabuki is dancing by men, you know ...'

'I didn't know. Why?'

'Oh, long ago sex-workers were dancing Kabuki to be fetching customers, so Emperor was issuing decree that only men could be dancing. My life is being like your life. I am having foster uncle and three brothers also with miseries, and I am learning in the theater school, in the dance school. I am playing parts of women characters in Kabuki; princess so-so in Japanese drama; jokey fisherman wife in China Sea; fall-down silly daughter of man who is keeping cormorants.' He shrugged. 'That one is fun, much miming of being in rocking boat, making whole audience seasick. Now I am dancing most of time, and for rotation I am doing weird empress or being strange holy woman.' He folded his arms, half closed his eyes and gazed directly ahead with a lofty, detached expression of infinite disdain. 'Very wise. I am memorizing whole book of Confucian analects.'

'Tell me an analect,' she begged.

'Major principles suffer no transgression. Minor principles allow for compromise.'

'What does it mean?'

'It must be meaning my dancing is a minor principle,' he said, laughing. 'For my career is being compromised.'

'I guess that's how I feel, too.'

'Then we are agreeing on two things.'

'Two?'

'We are agreeing on what is minor and what is principle.'

She sat back, suddenly relaxed. This duty might not be so bad. He seemed all right. The expression on her face was mirrored on his, and they both smiled, pleased to be with one another, beginning to anticipate whatever it was that was coming. The server interrupted this calm to bring Gandro's sandwich, which he sniffed at, tasted, and pronounced real – or so close as made no difference.

Though soothed, Ellin was not entirely willing to give up worrying. 'You know, even though we're both History House contractees, even though we think we know the period, this Newholme could be totally different from anything we know about.'

'Oh,' he nodded, chewing, his face very serious, 'I am having no doubt about that. I am sure it is being very, very strange.'

15

Meeting Marool Mantelby

West of Sendoph, the terraces were narrower and steeper than in the farmlands to the east, climbing from the river in a great stair flight that ended on a final set of wooded ridges where the homes of the elite were built, very near the wilderlands. There among others of its kind stood the mansion of Mistress Marool Mantelby – Monstrous Marool, as she was known to some – the youngest of eight sisters, whose parents had done Marool great services firstly by having had no sons, and secondly by having died along with their eldest daughter, after they had sold off six younger daughters but before they had been able to sell Marool herself.

Her prosperity had come upon her thuswise:

Margon g'Mantelby the elder, Marool's grandfather, had dowered in for his son, Margon Jr., a very expensive daughter of the Rikajors, a family known to run to girls. Though the Rikajor girls had a high opinion of themselves, Margon Jr. was an acceptable if not intelligent candidate, and the Mantelby fortune, gained through the fiber trade, was large and growing. Margon g'Mantelby's offer was accepted, and Stella was dowered in to the Mantlebys.

In the first five years of their marriage Stella outdid herself in the production of five daughters, all born at home. Though the Margons, Sr. and Jr., gave every public evidence of pleasure in accepting the congratulations of their peers, they were heard to remark among friends that a male child would have been acceptable. The girls, after all, would be dowered away from the line. Where were the Margon sons to continue the line itself? Who would inherit? One did not want as heir a dowered-out nobody! One wanted a son as like oneself as possible!

Mayelan, the eldest daughter, and her two oldest sisters were much cosseted. The next two were not so much admired. Margon Sr. had died by the time numbers six and seven, twins, were born, and the last daughter, Marool, born three years after her next sister, was the straw – so Margon said in private – that fucked the camel. It had been the last attempt to produce a son, as Margon and Stella had been married ten years, and Stella's contract provided that after that term she might select a Hunk to keep her company and take her about the city and do what Hunks were known to do so well.

Thus Marool was born into a house in which fortune was assured, domestic tranquility was without fault, and her father seldom talked with her mother. Or vice versa. The Hunk was very nice, but he was her mother's Hunk, and though Hunks were taught to cosset children, they were also cautioned not to overdo it. Girls could be ruined by too much charm too early in their lives, for the reality of marriage would then come as too great a shock.

In truth, the Hunk was not even tempted to cosset Marool. Unlike her sisters – tall, pale girls with blunted edges, like monuments of warm wax – Marool was dark and pudgy in the places she was not sharp, the first of her many contradictions. She was born angry. Her first words, to her heedless chatron-nanny, were 'I hate you.' In this, as in most of her later life, she was completely truthful, for she did not care enough about anyone's opinion to lie.

When Marool was eight, her second oldest sister was dowered in by a wealthy family, followed by the next oldest sister, and so on each year until Marool was almost fourteen. At that point she became the only child left in the house except for Mayelan, the heiress, who had not yet found a man who was both willing to dower out and rich enough to tempt Stella and Margon. With the other daughters gone, family attention, long distracted, turned in Marool's direction. There was, her parents felt, no point in keeping her as a family member. Since she had been allowed to run rather wild, she would need some work before she could be offered for dower. They decided to hire a team of Hagger trainers to clean her up and teach her to behave in a civilized manner. If that didn't work out, they would offer her for Temple Service.

Rooly, as she called herself, was informed of these plans, at which point the resentment she had been stoking since she was in the nursery was ignited. There was a good deal of it to burn, and burn it did, with a sullen, consuming flame. She had been just another girl in an establishment where a son was desperately wanted. She was a disappointment. Well, so were they.

On her fourteenth birthday, Marool was reintroduced to her mother, who at first frowned at this dark changeling, trying to recall her name, and who then tried, during the ride to the Temple, to come up with a description of Marool that would appeal to the Hags. Many, many girls were picked for Temple Service; sometimes an only daughter was picked. Stella Rikajor, however, had thus far lost none of her daughters to the Temple, nor had her mother before her. The Rikajor family supported the Temple lavishly, and their generosity had been kept in mind.

Stella decided she would be honest about Marool and simply ask the Hags for a favor. While Stella was about this business, Marool herself slipped away into the Sanctuary to ask a few innocent-seeming questions. By the time she was rejoined by her disappointed mother – the Hags had not been responsive to Stella's needs – Marool had the information she needed.

The following morning, Marool returned to the Temple alone. Though she was not supposed to leave the Mantelby mansion, she had sneaked into town often enough to know the way.

'I want to see the directory of Hagions,' she said to the two Hags on duty, D'Jevier and Onsofruct. Both were taken aback by this request from one so young and so unprepossessing in appearance. Marool was, in truth, very unkempt and disheveled, though, as D'Jevier remarked later, her manner forbade any motherly attempt to either kempt or hevel her. D'Jevier was not unkindly, and though she felt some antipathy toward the girl, she made herself be generous.

'What are you seeking, Marool? Perhaps it is something I can help you with?'

Marool sneered. 'Unless you're one of eight sisters, you can help me with nothing, Madam. It is my right to see the directory of Hagions.'

The cousins, though nettled at her manner, were rather intrigued by the request. The girl confronting them was bristling with anger, every tangle on end, like a burr-bit cat, puffed up out of all good sense. Very well, the Hags thought, sharing a knowing glance. Let her peruse the directory of Hagions. She would soon weary of it.

They went into the Temple proper. The seating area sloped down to an oval dais with a curved back wall against which stood the three effigies of the Hagions, marmoreal images four times the height of a woman, each the likeness of robes draped around a female figure, but with only an emptiness inside. The robe to the left shaped a slender form, the robe to the center a stouter one, the robe to the right was somewhat slumped, as though the one who wore it was aged. Where the faces might have shown beneath the hoods or where hands might have protruded from sleeves were only vacancies. Before each image were cushions to kneel upon, and at the center, as though at the focus of a dozen pairs of invisible eyes, stood a low lectern with a kneeling bench. Upon the lectern lay the directory of Hagions, the names of all the female deities ever worshipped by mankind, each with an account of her characteristics and rites.

Marool ignored the tabs that would have led to one of the more healthful, 'normal' deities. Instead, she knelt at the directory and began to turn its pages, leaf by leaf. The Hags left her there. At noon, she went away, returning some time later to continue her perusal. When it grew too dark to see in the Temple, she left it, only to return on the following morning, and thus two days passed. Late afternoon on the second day, she left the lectern and went to kneel before the center image.

D'Jevier, who had become interested in this process, was watching from the back of the Temple. She saw the hollow robe waver, as though something inside it moved. She closed her eyes, and when she opened them it was to see a fiery presence peering out of the hood, not at her, but at the kneeling girl, and a fiery hand held out, as though in welcome. She closed her eyes again, disbelieving, and when she opened them for a second time, she saw Marool rising from before the empty effigy. Though D'Jevier told herself she had imagined it, for a moment she was sure she saw that the carved marble around the opening of the hood had been blackened by fire.

As Marool passed her, going up the aisle, D'Jevier kept her eyes slightly averted, though not so far averted that she did not see the terrible and tri-umphant smile which lent a horrid allure to the girl's features.

'A smile,' she said to her sister Onsofruct, 'such as a demon in hell might wear. The smile of a fiend.'

'What Hagion did she pray to?'

D'Jevier shook her head. 'I didn't look.'

'Is the book still open?'

'I think so.'

They went to look. The name at the top of the page was not familiar to them: Morrigan. They read what was written below and turned toward one another with horrified expressions.

'Oh, by all the Hagions of life,' whispered Onsofruct. 'Why would a child of that age choose to worship the patroness of sexual torture and death? Which image?'

D'Jevier indicated the center one, noticing there was, in fact, no black-ening around the hood. 'The strong one,' she said. 'The being in its greatest physical strength.'

They closed the book. D'Jevier thought of cutting out the page. She could not, of course. Everything she had learned as a Hag instructed her that dark pages of death and destruction were part of the book, along with bright pages of pleasure and health. Still, she resolved to take the earliest opportu-nity to speak to Stella Rikajor g'Mantelby about her daughter.

Any speaking would have come too late, for Marool had left the Temple with Morrigan's name dissolving on her tongue like a poisonous candy, sweetly fatal, and she did not return home. Instead, she stalked down the stony stairs to the walkway beside the Giles and along it until she encoun-tered a small group of those supernumes, losers and layabouts who lived beneath the bridges and viaducts of Sendoph and called themselves, unim-aginatively enough, the Wasters. Though she had not met them before, she went to them unerringly and did not return to her parents again.

Among the Wasters, she continued to call herself Rooly, avoiding any use at all of the Mantelby name. Having access to money was not a good idea in this company. Those with money were victims. If she was known to come from à wealthy family, she could neither exist in happy association with her fellow predators nor take part in their forays, and Marool intended to be one of them in all respects.

She obtained a black knit garment that started above the breasts and ended above the knees and over this a collection of veils, cloths, drapes, or skins brought together more for their appearance of defiant dilapidation than for any purpose of warmth or protection. She poked bones through her ears and painted her face and body in ugly colors. Everyone around her wore similar garments, poked various things through their ears or other parts, and painted themselves, for this was their fashion, their statement, their comment upon society.

The Wasters weren't numerous, a few score at most. They found shelter where they might, under bridges, or in culverts, or in abandoned barns or falling-down warehouses or anywhere else that offered modest cover from the rain, which was frequent, and the snow, which was not. They sometimes stole their food, sometimes extorted it from passers-by, sometimes traded for it the items they had looted. A few of them wore their hair twisted on top of their heads, the knot hidden inside the dried skull of a carrion bird and fastened there with thigh bones thrust through the eye holes to signify they would kill for what they wanted, and Marool soon and zealously joined this subgroup for, perhaps coincidentally, the carrion bird was the symbol of Morrigan.

The Wasters' lives were made tolerable and even amusing through the constant use of drugs, preferably one called Dingle, or Nosmell, an extract of the ubiquitous Dingleberry that grew anywhere a square inch of soil received one drop of rain. It could be smoked or drunk or eaten or even bathed in if one had enough of the leaves to steep a tubful. It had a long last-ing euphoric effect and only a few minor side effects, one being a temporary loss of libido and fertility and another being the permanent loss of the sense of smell and taste, which, considering the way the Wasters lived, could be considered an asset.

By the time she was fifteen, Rooly existed in a state of permanent Dingle-float interrupted by occasional and transitory rages. Her happiest times were when she was torturing someone or when she and her colleagues threw a bale of Dingle into a hot springs and soaked in it until the solution was too diluted to maintain the feeling of disembodied joy. Once in a while Marool thought about her parents and her intention to kill them. The Goddess had promised her their deaths, but the time didn't yet seem ripe.

When Rooly was something over seventeen and well versed in massacre, a new man introduced himself into the group. He was older than most of them, larger, certainly, with a thick, powerful body. He did not dress as the rest of them did, preferring tight trousers and a well-made cloak of some water resistant fabric. He was also different in some way that Marool could not define, as though he had come from some other place or had, perhaps, once spoken some other language.

'Who is he?' Rooly asked her companion, Dirt, casually, not caring much.

'Ashes, his name is,' said Dirt. 'Blue Shit knows him.'

'He's fat. He's got a bulge around his middle.'

'He's not fat. He just carries a money belt or something.'

'Well, if he's one of us, he'll get no fatter.'

Which was true. Ashes got no fatter. He got no thinner, either, which might have been enough to create some suspicion if anyone in the group had been capable of rational and connected thought. Ashes came and went and came and went. The others commented that Ashes had something odd about him, his eyes, maybe, or the whip he kept wrapped around his waist under his coat. Ashes seemed uninterested in Dingle, but greatly interested in sex.

All this Rooly noticed without caring one way or the other, and she was completely surprised when Ashes caught her by the arm one day and dragged her away into the woods where he had made a rough camp and where they might be, so he said, private. What happened next was astonishing, for Ashes gave her something other than Dingle to keep her happy, and he did not let her go back to the others. He kept her with him for a day, then another, and never during the course of those days did he cease stroking her and touching her, and putting his mouth on this part of her and that, and giving her more of the stuff he had, until she was in a frenzy she had never felt before.

'Oh, don't, don't,' she pled. 'Oh, stop, stop.'

'Never,' he said. 'No. Now we'll do this. Now we'll do that,' which he did, endlessly. Whenever she objected more strenuously, he merely fed her a bit of the stuff which was not Dingle and went on turning her tighter and tighter. Every breath became a game with what his fingers did, what his tongue did, what he did with that strange whip. Every time her body flamed, he quenched it only a little, then set about stoking it again.

He did nothing to release her from it. He built her lust into a fire that burned hotter and hotter, never letting it come to culmination. Two full days of it, she had, until she begged him, at last, not to let her go but to get on with it, and only then he gave her what she pled for in a way she could not afterward quite remember. The whip was a great part of it, but she could not recollect how, and there were no scars.

The episode was repeated. It was the third or fourth time before she realized they were being observed, that all of it was being observed, from the first touch to the last, all of it was being noted by avid eyes, hungry for sensation, people hiding in the underbrush whom she could not quite see. She thought they were people. Perhaps they weren't people. She was too heated to care who watched. Besides, she had a sense that all of it was meant, planned, a part of some larger whole to which she was dedicated. Sometimes, during her couplings with Ashes, she would murmur Morrigan's name.

But then, in a tenday or two, Rooly found herself sick, really sick, vomiting and gasping like a fish, and any taste of the drug made her worse. Ashes took her by her ear and whispered deep into it, 'That's my child you carry, lady. That's my daughter you bear. And I'll be back for her.'

Then he went away.

Rooly had been pregnant several times, or thought she had, but each time she had miscarried. This time she did not miscarry, or at least she had not a short time later when the Mantelbys' men of business descended on her to tell her that her parents and her eldest sister were dead.

The Mantelby men extricated Rooly from among her fellows as they might an oyster from its shell, efficiently, quickly, not caring who got hurt in the process. Her parents and eldest sister, she was told, had gone for a picnic, though such entertainments were totally foreign to them. They had gone together, though Margon and Stella had gone nowhere together since the Hunk had come. They had gone to a high place, though Stella was afraid of heights, and then, somehow, all three of them had fallen from that height to their deaths. Everyone was surprised and shocked and disbelieving, except Rooly, who remained indifferent.

Margon Mantelby Sr. was dead, Margon Mantelby Jr. had no living brothers. Since Marool's eldest sister was now dead and her other sisters had been dowered into other families, Marool was the only Mantelby remaining. She inherited the name and the fortune, swollen as it was by the prices paid for six brides. Several of her sisters served notice they would contest this ruling on the grounds of moral incompetence. Marool was promiscuous; Marool was even then pregnant by the Hagions-knew-whom, and was therefore guilty of mismothering; she had done the Hagions-knew-what while among the Wasters and she was unfit to manage House Mantelby under the Mantelby name.

Marool – awakened by greed and a few days abstinence to an appreciation of the life she had long despised – denied it all. She went to the Temple, where she knelt before the same effigy as before. D'Jevier, fascinated despite herself, hovered near the curtained arch, observing. Marool was no longer a pudgy girl, but a woman lean as a snake, every plane of her face tight drawn around huge eyes that were dark and full of fire, casting the terrible allure that D'Jevier had noted before.

Once again the marble robe filled with fire and once again the fiery hand reached out to touch Marool, as though in blessing. When Marool came calmly from the Sanctuary, she told D'Jevier that she had vowed a religious pilgrimage to the Daughter House of the Hagions at the new city of Nehbe, along the coast to the east, a pilgrimage made in memory of her parents. Could D'Jevier assist her by appointing someone in Temple Service to look after the Mantelby estate in Marool's absence? At the usual rates, of course. Marool would, she said, be generous.

D'Jevier nodded, though she had to struggle to keep her face and voice calm. She agreed to send a factotum from the Temple plus an efficient Man of Business to keep everything running while Marool was away.

It was almost a year later when Marool returned in the company of several Haggers she had picked up somewhere. She came openly to the Temple and to the theater. She was clean, decently dressed, and certainly not pregnant. When her sisters sought witnesses to her alleged immorality or promiscuity or any of the rest of it, none could be found. The Wasters had disappeared. Marool's closest associates, or at least those who had known most about her, were simply gone, no one knew where. No one knew anything about a child, there was no evidence of the rumored child itself and Marool could not be convicted of mismothering.

Marool's well-paid agents reported that all her former acquaintances had been taken care of – except for one. The man she had called Ashes could not be found, not in any city or town inhabited by mankind, and all of them had been searched. When her agents had reported this, Marool had felt a momentary pang of fear, quickly overcome. If he showed up, she said, see to him. If he never showed up, who cared. It was his word against hers, and she was a Mantelby. She had either forgotten or chosen not to remember those avid but anonymous eyes in the underbrush which denoted a host of witnesses.

Outwardly, currently, she was a woman reformed, settled down among her Haggers to the enjoyments afforded by the Mantelby estate, of which there were many. She was secretive, however, about many things: her pastimes, her pleasures, the odd, bulky shipments she received now and then from someone living near Nehbe. Inwardly, always, she was still the follower of Morrigan, Monstrous Marool.

16

The Amatory Arts: Stories Women Tell

Early on in House Genevois, Mouche had made two good friends, a dark, wiry and slightly older boy named Fentrys and a ruddy-haired, brown-skinned lad of his own age named Tyle who came up into the suites about the time Mouche himself did. Simon had housed the three of them close together in the suites, for he believed in friendship and solidarity and the three boys were alike in being rather bookish, a trait sneered at by many Hunks, though Madame encouraged the trait among those with a taste for it, finding it a salable characteristic among her more discriminating customers. When a patroness grew weary of bedsports, she might enjoy a good book read in a well-schooled voice. And when, eventually, a patroness outlived bedsports, she had not necessarily outlived her enjoyment of a good show, a good fencing display, a good song, or a good tale.

The boys studied together. They found, as had generations before them, that the Amatory Arts practice classes were more interesting than the theory lectures. In order to minimize study time, they divided the material into thirds, with each of them being responsible for part of it, feeling that if they volunteered often enough, they wouldn't be called upon.

Today they waited, poised, as Madame said:

'Our job, in essence, is to make married women contented and happy. On other planets, married women, whether matched through arrangement or romance, usually rank lowest in contentment among gender and marital groups. Who can give me the reason for this?'

This was in Mouche's third of the reading material, and he raised his hand to receive her nod.

'Madame, married men are most content, for they are cared for by their wives. If a woman is unmarried, she is contented to care for herself. Some unmarried men maybe don't care for themselves that easily, but they have no other responsibilities. But a married woman usually has to care for her husband, her children, and her household, even if she has other work, and usually she receives little care in return. So, she is least contented of all.'

'You are speaking historically?'

'Oh, yes, Ma'am. Historically.' He bit his lip. As Madame said, it was necessary to keep in mind that what *had* been done was not necessarily what *should* be done.

'Here on Newholme, love is not considered a requisite of marriage,' Madame continued. 'If the couple is fortunate, their sexual encounters will be not unpleasant, and if they are not fortunate in that regard, at least the unpleasantness will be infrequent and brief. We have medications that assist women in tolerating it.

'But as Mouche has said, women have many duties, some of which are painful, all of which are arduous, many of which are thankless. In consideration of this, the Hags have decreed that women are entitled to compensatory joys. Having done their duty to the family, they are entitled to the rewards of sensuality and romance, which is, of course, why you gentlemen are here.

'Tyle, discuss primary sensuality.'

Tyle was busy taking notes. He wrote down, 'Tyle, discuss,' before he thought, then looked up flushing, to find half the class sniggering at him.

'Ah, Madame, well, ah, women respond to the sensuality they remember as babies or children. When a baby is tended it is cuddled and sung to and fed, and talked to ...'

'Endlessly,' said Madame, severely. 'Endlessly communicated with, if only in baby talk. There is playfulness in this and an innocent sensuality. Women who were well treated as infants remember the feeling of this warmth and acceptance, if only subconsciously. They like being sensuously cuddled and affectionately talked to. They like being given sweets or wine and playfully admired for their own accomplishments, even if these are minimal. Now, why do men not see this?'

'Mouche?' she said, turning suddenly to give him a wicked look. 'Why do men not see this?'

He flushed, scrambling through his memory of last night's reading. 'Oh, Madame, the book says ... ah, it says ...' He stared at the ceiling for inspiration.

Tyle spoke up, 'Men get ranked by their peers on the battleground, in business, or in games, where nobody gets cuddled and you have to be almost ... heroic to be noticed at all.'

Mouche grimaced and offered, 'We know this is true, just from fencing class. You have to be very, very good before the master says anything except, "Next boy."'

'Correct,' said Madame, with an admonitory look at Mouche. 'Men are taught to dismiss the need for babying as mere "female stuff," that is, foolishness, but this nurturing does not seem foolish to women. Women are hungry for affectionate words and that's why we have conversation mistresses: to teach you to use them! Your colleague or brother may accept your striking him forcefully and addressing him as "You old mismothered bastard." Your patroness will not do so.

704

'We do other things similarly. We teach you to dance in ways that make your patroness feel skilled and graceful. We teach you to stack a deck of cards so your patroness will win the game if at that moment she needs to win a game. Simon or Jeremy are skilled cheats, and they will teach you how to do it.

'Now, in order to make a woman contented, we must be alert to the stories she creates about her own feelings. It is important for you to recognize when your patroness is inventing.

'Let us suppose that on some other world a young woman falls "in love" with an utterly unsuitable young man. Describe an unsuitable young man, Bartel.'

Bartel scratched his forehead with his pen, leaving a smear of ink at the top of his nose. 'Well, Ma'am, he'd be lazy. He'd be ... unkind. He'd be ... I suppose he could be dirty. Or ugly ...'

'She wouldn't fall in love with him if he was ugly,' objected Tyle.

'Well, then not ugly,' conceded Barton.

'On the contrary, Tyle, he could be ugly,' said Madame. 'And he could be lazy and abusive as well. The woman still might fall in love with him. Why? Anyone?'

Fentrys said, 'Because her hormones are pushing her toward mating, he has a dangerous look, and he is spreading pheromones all over the place.'

'Quite true,' agreed Madame. 'Now, she cannot say to her friends or parents that her body is sexually receptive and that this man looks dangerous and smells virile. Can she? What would her family say?'

Fentrys laughed. 'They'd say he was ugly and lazy and abusive.'

'And the woman actually knows that,' said Madame. 'She may refuse to admit it, but she knows that. What she doesn't know is why she is responding to him. She does not know that she is being led by evolution and her nose. Though she can see his inadequacies with her mind, her body wants him nonetheless, so she has to justify herself. What does she do?'

'She makes up a story,' said Mouche, suddenly enlightened.

'Indeed. All unconscious of what is going on, she makes up a story. What does she say?'

Interested, Fentrys said, 'She could say he has good things about him that nobody sees. Some women are very tenderhearted, so she could say he needs her ...'

Tyle offered, 'She could say he would change after they got married. I heard my aunt say that about a man who offered for my cousin.'

'Indeed,' said Madame. 'And after they are married, he abuses her, and what does she say?'

Mouche said, 'She says, "He broke my arm, but he really loves me."'

'She wouldn't!' said a voice from the back of the room. 'Women aren't crazy.'

'Quite true,' said Madame. 'They aren't crazy, but they are sometimes quite helpless in dealing with their biology. Our theoretical woman might say just what Mouche proposes. Or, she might say, "He's under a strain, and he goes all to pieces, and it was my fault, I upset him." An interesting fact about such stories is that repeating them actually calms the mind and assuages the pain of abuse by eliciting the release of Serotonins and endorphins. Such stories are a kind of self-hypnosis, a verbal veil over reality. In this example, the woman assigns the man the role of one helpless in his affliction and assigns herself the role of nurturing mother-martyr, using the verbal veil as her device for surviving in that role.'

'She wouldn't do that here on Newholme,' said Fentrys. 'My mother wouldn't do that!'

'Women don't need to do that on Newholme,' Madame agreed. 'On this world, any woman who did do such a thing would be referred to the psych machines for rebalancing! Here, physical abuse of women took place only at the time of the women raids and the Hags put a stop to that! We do, however, hear women say things like, "My father really treasured me. He didn't want to let me go ..." Or, "My married daughter would come visit me with the children if she could get away from home." What are these?'

Tyle said, 'They'd be the same kind of veils. To hide her disappointment?'

'Exactly. Admitting the fiction would be destructive to the woman's ego, so she uses a verbal veil to conceal disappointment. Why do we care? Why do we talk about it? Because as Consorts, you will hear these stories as symptoms of need! Your patroness should be without disappointments if you are doing your job correctly. When you hear your patroness lying to herself, your job is to eliminate her need to do so.'

'We tell her she's being silly,' said the voice from the rear of the room.

'You will not,' snapped Madame. 'That is a traditionally male response which is totally unhelpful! You won't say she is silly or that the situation she describes is not true or that she should forget it. You will say, "Yes, I know what you mean. I understand. I know of a similar case," and you will go on to tell a parallel story, which will allow her to feel that her own disappointments are universally shared, that she is not exceptional in this regard, that she need not worry over them ...

'Fentrys? You look confused.'

'I am confused, Madame. Our patronesses are supposed to be exceptional, so why ...'

'Your patronesses are supposed to be exceptional in all *favorable* regards. You will let them know they are exceptionally witty, exceptionally beautiful, exceptionally charming, patient, and so forth, and you will tell them so at least hourly. But if your patroness is troubled, if she thinks "Why me?" the "Why me?" must be turned into "It's not just me." It's normal for husbands to be preoccupied with business, for children to be thoughtless, for familial relationships to be unfulfilling. That is exactly why you are there, to make up for such things. If such disappointments weren't normal, Consorts wouldn't be needed. You'll know you have succeeded when your patroness does not lie to herself anymore, when, instead of coping with sadness, she turns to you for her entitlements.'

17

Mouche Becomes a Hunk

Though Mouche grew accustomed to his new suite and his new status, the pictures in the hallway continued to disturb him. It was only after some months had passed that he realized he was worrying about his own eventual patroness, something he hadn't even thought about until the most recent Amatory Arts lectures. The time of graduation had seemed remote, and he had never once visualized himself as actually fulfilling the necessary role, but now he thought of Her, the Patroness, someone sad, maybe. Someone needing care. Or, he found himself thinking almost obsessively, someone like … someone in one of those pictures.

There were stories about Hunks who had been required to do things so evil and depraved they had gone mad. There were tales about Wilderneers, Hunks who had killed their owners and escaped after swearing revenge against all females. Little girls were frightened with this tale beside the fire of an evening. 'They'll come in the night,' the story-spinner would say. 'Tapping at your window. Their eyes are red with blood, and their teeth are sharp …'

The suddenly perceived reality of his future made him self-conscious. In the privacy of his own suite that night, Mouche stripped down, set candles either side of the cheval glass, and tilted the mirror to give himself a slow looking over. His skin was very white and smooth, due to all the bathing and oiling and massage. His ashen hair was not yet as long as Madame wanted it, but it was a good deal longer than when he came, the silver-gold mass artfully curled up and away from his brow, which was wide and unlined and interrupted only by the wings of his dark brows, plucked into full but graceful arcs. His nails were smooth and polished, his teeth likewise. The health machines brought by the settlers had seen to that.

Since Mouche was only thirteen, the hairdresser, manicurist and facialist worked on him only once in a tenday. Later, it would be every day or so. Light hair and dark eyes, said Madame, were a dramatic combination. Mouche's eyes were malachite green, fringed with heavy dark lashes. His mouth was wide, the upper lip somewhat narrow, the lower more full. Even now, his jaw was round enough to denote strength. He would not have to keep a full beard, as some Hunks did, in order to look properly romantic.

As for his body, it wasn't much as yet. Lean and muscular, of course, with all the training he was getting, but he had little bulk. His shoulders were broader than when he came, and his legs straighter and more comely. He turned, looking at his back view from over his shoulder. Women were attracted by butts, as men were to breasts, so butts were important. The ideal butt was small, neat, round, and smooth. His wasn't bad. Nothing would be done to his sex, if at all, until he was sold.

Every Consort was sterilized as soon as he was sold, for the one thing absolutely taboo to Consorts was the fathering of children. Extravagant dowries assured that children would be of a man's own name, his own line. Every Family Man had a right to expect his own unique line, his own genetic makeup, his own descendants. Elder son to elder son to elder son, the lineage honored and remembered, his own name honored and remembered. The g'name was the important thing. There could be no doubt about who fathered whom.

Later, after most or all of the children were born, that man's wife would shop for someone much like Mouche, who now turned before the mirror trying to envision himself after another five years or so. When dressed in a clean tunic and a graceful mantle, he made a good appearance. Several times during the park promenades, he had caught people looking at him. Some of them had been women, though there had been a few men as well. He had, as instructed, dimpled at the former and ignored the latter. Madame did not sell to homosexuals, unless the Hunk was being purchased by a woman as a gift for her husband – an erotic aide, as it were, in the necessary business of procreation.

He struck a fencing attitude. He liked fencing, and his fencing master was pleased with him. He rose on his toes and turned, then bowed and stepped and turned again. His dancing master had moved him to the advanced class. Mouche liked fencing better than dancing, but dancing was important, so he did it. Sometimes women held soirées for their friends and their Hunks, and the Hunks had to be able to put on a show. He cleared his throat and did a few lalas. The singing master had been pleased with him also, though Mouche's voice was now beginning to crack. Beginning next year he would learn to accompany himself on the lap harp or lute.

All in all, except for recurrent fantasies of the sea, Mouche was reasonably content. He had gotten over feeling shamed, for in House Genevois his status was not considered shameful. How one is regarded by one's peers is most important, and Mouche's peers were friendly enough. The embarrassment he had thought he would feel forever had lasted only a cycle or two, though he often thought of Mama and Papa, wondering if he would ever see them again.

✳

Mouche did see his papa again, for once a student went into Consort Country, he could receive visitors, as Mouche soon learned. He sent word to Papa, and Papa arrived shortly thereafter, looking unusually prosperous, with a new cockade on his hat and much news of the new calf and the new kittens and the successful repairs to the mill. Papa did not mention that Mama was pregnant, an event long considered impossible, but which may well have resulted from a lessening of worry and an improvement in diet. When little Bianca was born some months later, Mouche was not informed of that, either. Even though money could have been borrowed on the girl's prospects, Mouche could not have been redeemed. Sales to Consort Houses were considered final. Repayment, even with interest, would not have been accepted by Madame, and the contract Papa had signed was not susceptible to cancellation.

When Bianca had a baby sister, a year later, and then a baby brother a year after that, Mouche was not told of either event. Though Papa continued to visit faithfully, appearing ever more prosperous over the next few years, he didn't mention to Mouche that for all practical purposes, the new baby boy was now the g'Darbos-apparent, as Papa's eldest son.

At sixteen, the boys entered upon the most demanding part of their education. Four hours of physical training each day were coupled with five hours of classroom work, and to this was now added the actual practice of amatory arts. The women who came to House Genevois to assist in this education were masked during the sessions, no one knew who they were except Madame, and Madame did not even hint at who they might be. Some were young and shapely, and some were not, but the quality of work expected from a Consort was to be the same, regardless. In fact, the highest prices would be paid for those from whom the pleasures given a thirty-year-old wife and a sixty-year-old grandmama were indistinguishable. What these women had to say about the students was perhaps more important than any other assessment they might receive.

Amatory arts required, Mouche found, a good deal of concentration, the acquisition of certain autohypnotic abilities, and careful attention to his physical health. There were certain drugs that helped in certain cases, either taken by the Consort or by his patroness, though Madame did not recommend their use except in cases of extreme need.

'In this respect, graduates of House Genevois are unlike the graduates of, say, House Fantuil. In House Fantuil they do a great deal of drug-induced work, but in my mind such sensationism – I do not call it sensuality, which is a natural effect – not only suffers in comparison with the natural modes, but also shortens the lifespans of its practitioners. Of course, given the clientele to whom House Fantuil sells, perhaps the drugs are necessary! I am proud to say that House Genevois never expects the impossible from its graduates!'

Mouche now paid strict attention to the lectures, usually given by Madame but occasionally by other women, concerning the nature or natures of women, for he now could put the theory into action. He decided women were more complicated than he had imagined possible. At night, in the Consort suites, there was a great deal of talk about these complications, about natural versus unnatural modes, and all the middle ground between.

Naturally, the boys discussed other things as well, with particular attention to the mysterious, the unmentioned, and unmentionable. There was exchange of misinformation about the invisible people. There was more of the same about the fabled Questioner, who was rumored to be interested in Newholme. This rumor had more substance than most, for Tyle had a sister married to the family man who managed the space port, and a trader captain had told the manager, who had told his wife, who had told Tyle.

'What does the Questioner do?' asked one boy.

'It destroys worlds,' whispered someone else, 'if they don't conform to the edicts.'

None of the boys knew much about the edicts, but most of them supposed Newholme didn't conform.

'I mean,' said Fentrys, 'we've got all these things we can't talk about, but if we conformed, we could talk about anything.'

'So she wipes out Newholme?' asked Mouche skeptically.

'No. Not if we can keep her from finding out.'

This topic was hashed and rehashed until it grew boring and was replaced with newly heard stories about Wilderneers. No one had actually ever seen a Wilderneer, but stories about them nonetheless abounded.

In general, Mouche enjoyed his life. The Consorts-in-Training had, so Madame stressed, a better diet than other men, a more healthy lifestyle, a more certain future, and fewer sexual frustrations than anyone on the planet. The days went by without upheaval in an atmosphere of general kindliness, and the only thing that saddened Mouche were his dreams: often of Duster and sometimes of the sea. Each time he dreamed of the sea, it became wider and darker and bigger, until eventually he dreamed of a sea of stars with himself sailing upon it.

In accordance with Madame's instructions, Mouche had managed to let go of his father and mother. He had ceased to grieve over the animals and the farm itself. But Duster and the ever widening sea ... those things he wept over still.

18

Ornery Bastable, the Castaway

The freckled, red-headed 'boy' named Ornery Bastable had been bought onto the freighter *Waygood* at age seventeen and she had stayed there ever since. Because of her (his) early 'mutilation,' a story that Ornery frequently told and by now had considerably embellished, she was allowed to be somewhat reticent about natural functions. She had no beard and her voice was rather high. Nonetheless, she was strong and resourceful, and though she could not participate in all the recreations indulged in by her companions, she was a good shipmate, always eager to offer a hand or stand a watch for a friend. Had Ornery been prettier, the subterfuge might not have worked, but 'he' had remained a plain, lean, energetic person who over the years had become an accepted member of the crew.

In general, Ornery had found the life healthful and interesting. So far as recreations went, Ornery enjoyed the society of her fellows, she had found a close lipped and empathetic female Hagger in Naibah with whom she could occasionally be 'herself,' and every now and then she traveled up the river from Naibah to pay dutiful visits to Pearla. Though most of her life was relatively routine, it was not without adventure, including, on one occasion, being marooned.

Freighters sailing westward from Gilesmarsh customarily refilled their water barrels a dozen days' sail down the coast at a sweetwater spring which was separated from the shore by a strip of forest so thick and over-grown as to be impassible except by the laboriously created trail maintained by the shipcrews who watered there. Ornery was part of a work party sent ashore on the duty of chop and fill, but despite the trail being well marked and Ornery herself having traversed it many times, she somehow got herself separated from the rest of the party. She sat down to figure out where she'd gone wrong, and just at that moment the world started to shake.

She was under a tree; a branch whipped off the tree, struck Ornery on the head, and she rolled down into the dirt, dead to the world, in which state she continued until the *Waygood* sailed away without her.

She wakened along about moonfall, figured out where she'd gone wrong and made an unsteady way to the beach, where she found a note from her mates saying they'd return in eight or ten days, and, 'If you want picking up you'd better stay on the sand, but watch out for tidal waves, because there's more tremors all the time.'

They left her a few rounds of hardbread, as well as a packet of cheese and jerky, so she wasn't as badly off as she might otherwise have been. She had her belt knife, hatchet, and canteen. There was fruit in the trees. The spring was close enough for drinking water, the rations were sufficient, the knock on the head had left a painful lump but no lasting damage. She hacked herself a few fronds from the nearby trees, built a shelter of sorts high on the beach between two erect pillars of stone that had long served as a landmark for the spring, a space partly screened from the sea by a pile of other pillars, similar though recumbent. She then lay back in her lean-to awaiting rescue, staring at the moons at night and swimming in the sea in the daytime – a delight she almost never had the privacy to indulge in and one she considered almost worth being marooned for.

Three of the biggest moons were out when the ship left, one almost at full but the other two at waxing half and new, so the tides weren't enough to make her move and she felt no tremors. On the third night, however, she wakened to a sound: not a loud sound, not even a threatening sound, but certainly an unfamiliar one. It conveyed, she thought, the sense of an exclamation. Or, maybe, an exclamatory question, as though something very large had asked from the direction of the sea: Who is that person camped on my beach? Or, more accurately, Who is that person camped *there* on my beach?

Ornery went from *there* to *somewhere else* in a panicky skulk that ended with her in the trees, prostrate upon some uncomfortably knobby roots, peering out at the place she had just left. The waxing half moon was low in the sky; the new moon had long since set, but the full moon was just past the zenith, casting enough light for her to see the bulky though sinuous shadow that flowed upward from the water to her left, squirmed across the beach to the stones, fumbled about with them for what seemed a very long time, then went back as it had come. This was accomplished without any noise whatsoever and without any evidence that the shadow knew or cared where Ornery was. Where there had been two pillars standing in the moons' light, there were now five, each casting a bifurcated shadow like a lopsided arrowhead, pointing away from the place Ornery lay.

Ornery stayed where she was, replaying what she had seen in her head: the shadow coming out of the sea and squirming across the sand. Now that had been one thing, one single thing, she was sure of that. But then, when it had fumbled around with the rocks, some of it had separated itself and moved away from the other part of it, so it must have been more than one thing to start with.

Except for that very distinct impression it was one thing at the beginning!

At the first light of dawn, Ornery crawled back to her shelter. The rations were pressed quite deeply into the sand but otherwise undamaged. The fronds that had sheltered her were scattered and the area smelled like … well, she couldn't quite say. Not a bad smell. Not a stink, but nonetheless, something quite distinctive and possibly to be avoided. Ornery gathered up her belongings and found a place at the other end of the beach to make her bed. Having done so, she fell asleep, without even thinking about it. She knew it was the only thing to do.

Later in the morning she woke with the word 'Joggiwagga' moving about in her head. Moon dragon, she said to herself, wondering where she had heard such a thing. Her memory didn't at that moment stretch as far as the invisible person who had nursed Oram and Ornalia as babies, telling them stories and singing them songs. She had been told to forget that time, and though she had by no means forgotten, she had obediently stopped thinking of it. The word soon evaporated, like dew, and she remained astonished at herself for having slept at all since she had a rather frightening memory of the night's happening.

When the ship came by on its way back to Gilesmarsh she told her mates about the experience, and they teased her a good deal. Castaways always told stories about hearing things and seeing things and being wakened in the night, or having their things moved about. Ornery accepted this with good grace but without believing a word of it. She'd seen the stone pillars lying in the sand and she'd seen them standing erect, and each of the stones had been far too heavy for her to have raised it herself. Something had set them up, and Ornery had seen the shape – or shapes – of the somethings.

19

The Invisible People

Late in his sixteenth year, Mouche fell prey to a peculiar illness, one with few and subtle outward symptoms, one to which, however inadvertently, he exposed himself.

It began one evening rather late when, in the course of restoring certain volumes of erotic tales to his bookshelf, Mouche jostled a particular carving in an unusual way, and the whole bookshelf rotated on its axis to display a gaping black doorway out of which drifted the sound of music and an enticing odor. The smell made his mouth water even as it made his nose wrinkle, as if he scented something marvelously luscious but, perhaps for that very reason, forbidden.

After experimenting with the bookcase to learn how it opened and closed and how the latch might be opened from the back side, Mouche lit a candle and went through the dusty, webbed opening. He briefly considered asking Tyle or Fentrys to go with him, but they were at fencing practice, and Mouche did not want to wait.

He shut and latched the door behind him and began exploring, finding no single route that led from his suite to somewhere else. Instead he was in a maze of passageways that branched opening onto narrow catwalks that crossed open space to small, dark balconies from which, ascending or descending by ladders, one came upon narrow adits leading to crawlways that went hither and thither in all directions through the ancient fabric of House Genevois. Everywhere along the route were small access panels into rooms of House Genevois, and doors that would have opened had they not been closed from the back by long rods that thrust into the surrounding woodwork. There were also a great many peepholes that looked out into the corridors and suites. When Mouche applied his eyes to some of the holes, he saw his fellow students. When he peered through others, he realized he was peering through the painted eyes of those quite terrible pictures in the halls.

Throughout his rather lengthy exploration, he kept moving toward the sound of the music, arriving finally at one end of a level and uniform passageway stretching in a straight line for some considerable distance and pierced with tiny glazed openings along both sides. Since the passage was scarcely wider than his shoulders, he could look through the openings by merely turning his head. To his left he saw the moonlit roofs of the buildings

715

north of House Genevois; to his right, the open space of the large courtyard. When he stood on tiptoe and craned his neck to peer downward, he could see the torch-lit dock and a firewood wagon being unloaded.

The corridor continued straight on, eastward past the courtyard, over the roofs of the lower buildings and along yet another open space to end finally in a cul-de-sac with two leaded windows of colored glass, one to his right, one straight ahead. Putting his eyes to a missing segment at the corridor's end, Mouche gained a view of the muddy river, dully gleaming in moonlight, like hammered copper. The window to the right was unbroken and so dirty he could see nothing at all through it, though it was ajar just enough to admit both the sound and the smell that had enticed him.

No one had ever warned Mouche not to do what he was doing. No one had considered for a moment that he or any other student might fall into it by accident. While some parts of the maze were too low and narrow for most persons to traverse, other parts had been built by long ago mankind, but then closed off and forgotten. The straight stretch of cobwebby corridor where Mouche found himself was actually inside the north wall of House Genevois, a wall that began at the street and ran eastward to the riverside.

On inspecting the windows, Mouche saw that the slightly open one to his right was not merely ornamental, though the hinges and the latch were so corroded from long exposure to the weather that they might as well have been. After a moment's hesitation, he decided to force it farther open. The hinges were on the left, and when Mouche leaned his full weight against it, it cracked open with a scream of alarm followed by utter silence.

Mouche held his breath and waited until the rhythmic sounds of voice and instrument resumed. He then used the music to cover the sound as he forced the reluctant casement a fingerwidth at a time, opening it enough that he could lean out and look below.

He stared down from the northeast corner of an earthen courtyard enclosed on the north and east by walls, on the south and west by brightly painted dwellings, their colors and designs revealed by the leaping flames on a central hearth. Around the fire were dancers. Not people dancers. Far too slender for people, and too graceful. For a long moment, it did not occur to Mouche who the dancers were, and then the heaps of brown, shapeless garments lying near the firepit wakened him with both a thrill of recognition and a shiver of dread. What he was doing was improper. What he was doing was forbidden. He should not be here watching, for the dancers were invisible people, people who did not exist.

His first thought was that he'd done it, he'd overstepped, he was done for. He'd be blue-bodied for sure, or at least beaten into insensibility. In a moment this guilty fear passed as he realized he was alone, after all. No one knew he had come here. He needn't ... well, he needn't tell anyone. And since no one knew where he was, he needn't go back, not just yet.

In truth, he could not have made himself leave what he saw, what he smelled, what he heard in the music: the new, the strange, the marvelous. He was so intrigued that he sat down on the sill and settled into being a spectator.

He pretended to himself that he did not know who they were. If he ever got caught, he thought, the 'ever' coming to mind quite clearly, if anyone 'ever' asked him, he would say he didn't know who they were. How could he? After all, he might not have noticed the garments that defined invisible people. How could he tell these were people who did not exist?

People who nonetheless were! People who leaped and spun around the fire in ecstatic, delirious movement, like willows in wind, their hair flowing like swirls of lovely water. They were more slender than people, almost sylphlike, and their skin had a sheen of opalescent gold, the ocher-apricot glow of freshly fired clay pots. And they sang! Their voices were like birds and breeze and the burble of water. Their hair was much more luxuriant than people's hair, thicker and longer, and it almost seemed to rise and fall of itself, besides being of gorgeous and opulent colors: all the blues of the sea and the sky, shading to dark purple, all the greens of the forest and the fields shading to pale yellow. Mouche had seen hair colored so brilliantly only once before, on the small furry thing that he and Duster had befriended.

The dancers below him were clad only in diaphanous shifts, though after a time it struck him that the swirling veils weren't clothing at all. The dancers had a sort of web that flowed from beneath their arms and down the outside of their legs. So far as Mouche could tell, they were all of one sex, whatever that sex was. They didn't seem to have breasts or genitals, but each was definitely an individual, easy to distinguish from the rest. One particular form brought his eyes back again and again, a girl or youth he supposed one might say, one with soft moss-green hair flowing to its ... no, *her* knees in a liquid stream that seemed to pour forever across his vision. His eyes went away and returned, went away and returned, unable to ignore the magic of that hair and the pattern of light that shifted along it like a fish sliding among eddies. Once or twice he caught the glimmer of her eyes, a startling mirror silver in the firelight.

Adding to his enchantment was music full of unfamiliar harmonies and rhythms, the *tunk-a-tunk* and *tongy-dong* of tuned wooden blocks and metal rods being struck with soft hammers. Also, there were marvelous odors from the foods seething over the fire, exotic spices and resinous smokes, all part of a marvelous and fascinating whole that gave him new sensations and awarenesses that caught him by the throat. What he saw, smelled, and heard wrapped him in a tingling web of stimulation that burned like a warm little sun, ripening him as a fruit on a vine, making him swell with sweet juices. His foot tapped, *TIKa-tika-TUM tika-TIKatum*. His eyes crinkled, he caught himself smiling as he could not remember smiling ever before. After the first few moments, he was lost in the spell of it.

And then … then they sang a song he knew. He knew it! He had heard it, not like this, with many singers and drums and wood blocks and bells, but still, he knew it. Someone had sung it to him, in this same language, and then later in his own …

Now, as that voice rose from below, he remembered the words in his own language:

> *Quaggima she calls:*
> *Out of starfield coming, fire womb seeking.*
> *Fire it finds, rock wallowing, fume reeking.*
> *Oh, Corojumi, openers of space;*
> *Bofusdiaga, burrower of walls;*
> *She has need of birthing place.*
> *Wheeooo, she falls*
> *Quaggima she cries …*
> *Something, something …*
> *Bofusdiaga, singer of the sun;*
> *Oh, Corojumi, dancers of bright skies;*
> *He has done and I have done.*
> *I cannot rise.*

His Timmy had sung it to him when he was a tiny boy. His Timmy, the one who had cuddled him and fed him. The song trailed away, unfinished. The singers moved from the fire, leaving it to burn itself out. They left Mouche, bewitched, his mind full of the song he knew and the shapes he knew. Timmys.

Curving one hand protectively around the flame of his candle, he returned the way he had come, losing himself more than once and finding his way by trial and error. At the entrance to his own room he found a peek hole that allowed him to see if anyone had come to visit while he had gone. They had not. Mouche let himself into his suite and closed the passage behind him.

He threw himself into bed still enchanted, wakened by sensation into a troubling apprehension. Probably no one now in House Genevois had ever seen the Timmys dancing. Would Madame have watched, ever? Would Simon? Only he, Mouche, knew what they did there, and he admitted to himself with a return of his earlier dread that those he had seen were indeed the beings who did not exist, the ones no one ever … ever let themselves see, the ones never mentioned.

And yet, one of *them* had sung to him a long time ago. His own Timmy had sung the song of Quaggima, the interloper, the song of Niasa, Summer Snake. His own Timmy had told him stories of the great four-eyed Eiger, the bird who sees and knows all. He remembered Joggiwagga, the moon dragons, the setters up of stones.

And it wasn't just him! The revelation came in an instant! Virtually every mankind baby on Newholme had been sung to sleep with 'Niasa's Lullaby' – the song of the Summer Snake to its baby in the egg; every child had heard the stories of great Bofusdiaga and the many Corojumi. As adults, though they had been forced to forget the singers, surely they could not forget the songs.

They had been taught to forget, just as Mouche had. They had gone to school in order to learn to forget. It was permitted for babies to believe in Timmys, but essential that adults should not. For adults, it was forbidden for Timmys to exist. They were a figment. Imaginary playmates. Hallucinatory nursemaids. Though every child in the classroom had been reared by Timmys, when one reached age seven, Timmys no longer were.

The teachers had explained, so patiently. There were no Timmys when the people had first moved onto Newholme. Then, some time later, suddenly people had started seeing Timmys. There they were, everywhere, like mice, or bunchbeetles, listening under windows, camping outside people's houses, gathering at various seasons beside the river where the hills resounded to the sound of their music and the scrape of their dancing feet. It was inexplicable, but there they were, able to speak a few words of the people's language, calling to one another, *tim-tim, tim-tim,* able to explain that they were here in the *kwi,* the outside, and eager to be *tim-timidi,* useful.

Where had they come from?

'*Dosha. Lau.*'

Who had sent them?

'*Dosha-lauhazhala-baimoi.*'

No matter how they tried to explain, no one could understand what they meant. A few linguistically talented persons who struggled to understand them, believed they were saying they had been sent by something or someone, but that they had never seen whatever or whoever it was that had sent them. Some people of a scientific bent believed they were animals, and they took some of the tim-tim apart to find, in their amazement, that the tim-tim had no brains! Creatures without brains were obviously not real, intelligent creatures. No creature could be considered real if it did not have a brain. They were, therefore, hallucinatory.

All this, Mouche learned in infant school, as all small children learned. Though he had been tended by a Timmy since birth, cuddled and fed and sung to by that swaddled form, closer to him than his mother or father, kinder to him than either, he could not acknowledge that fact for grown up people did not see them.

Mouche had been quite willing. He had learned not to see them, not to believe in them. Until now.

20

The Dutter Boys

At House Genevois, there were always departures and new arrivals. A notable arrival occurred about half a year after Mouche began watching the dancers. His friend Fentrys had been downstairs in the sewing room, having his new doublet fitted, when two new boys had been escorted past on their way to the welcome rooms. Fentrys, glancing at them, could see they were unlike the usual new boys, and when he left the sewing room, he'd let his curiosity pull him into a closet near the parlor where he could overhear what went on.

'Big,' he said to Mouche minutes later, eyes wide. 'By the Hagions, Mouche, one of them is as big as Wander!' Wander was the largest of the present Consorts-in-Training; he stood a head taller than any other student and several hands breadths wider, though he was not yet of an age to be sold. 'The other one is not as large, but they are both evil as snakes in their words. Madame had one of them stripped and striped!'

This was astonishing, for the boys were seldom beaten. Madame didn't believe in such punishment, except as a last resort. That it should have been imposed at first opportunity did not bode well for the peace of the House.

'What did he do?' asked Mouche.

'The one called Dyre said that Madame was a withered hag who had outlived her usefulness and should be retired to the stitchery. The fencing master and two of the cleaners had to hold the other one, Bane, while Dyre was beaten, and since they had him down, they beat him too, for interfering.'

'She didn't throw them out?' Students were expelled, from time to time, their bodies and faces dyed blue, to show the world they were worthless and incorrigible. Other Houses did the same, as did the Army school and the apprentice programs. Blue-bodies usually didn't last long in the outside world, and it was said of recalcitrants that they were 'independent as a blue-body.'

Fentrys said, 'I heard Madame talking to Simon. She sent word to someone, some large personage or other. She awaits that personage now, in the parlor.'

'Let's listen,' suggested Tyle. 'Can we?'

It wasn't consortly behavior, certainly, since it reflected an unhealthy interest in other people's business, but neither was it disobedient, strictly speaking, since they had never been forbidden to hide in closets and eaves-drop. They found room in the same closet Fentrys had hidden in before, one that backed on the parlor, though once hidden in it they had a stuffy time before Madame's summoned guest arrived. They could not see him. They could only hear his words, uttered in a deep, flat voice with no resonance at all, though, Mouche thought to himself, that might be because they heard him from a closet.

'Madame Genevois.'

Madame's voice came not only flat but curiously muffled, as though through a handkerchief. 'Sir. I have today received the two boys you paid me some time ago to take and train. They are a good deal older than my usual students, and they seem to be of the opinion that they need no training and that they are in charge of House Genevois.

If this is your intent, you have misjudged me. I have not spent my life acquiring a reputation so meaningless that I would cast it away for so little. I can and will refund your money, sponsors be hanged.'

A long silence. Then, 'I'll see to the boys.'

'Indeed,' said Madame with a gasp.

There was the sound of the parlor door opening and closing, and Madame's footsteps going away toward the welcome suite, breathing deeply. There were then other doors opening and shutting, mutters in the hallway, an uncouth clattering and chatter, then the parlor door opened and closed once more.

'Oh,' said a young voice. 'It's you.'

'I thought you'd got it in your head about this,' replied the deep voice. 'And here you go, startin' off just like usual.'

'That old bitch …' said another voice, deeper, almost adult. Mouche shivered inside. He knew that voice.

Then there was a sound, not a sound the listeners could identify. It might have been a burning sound, a kind of sizzle and pop. Again, it might have been something else. It was followed by a gasp and a whimper. It came again and was followed by a moan, almost a scream.

'If I've got to come down here another time, it'll be the last time,' said the deep voice. 'And you won't like it, I can guarantee.'

The door opened and closed once more. Heavy feet went to the foyer. The front door opened, letting in street noises, and closed. Then a long silence. When it had gone on for a very long time, Fentrys opened the closet door, and they slipped out into the corridor, stopping there with wrinkled noses, for the air smelt foul. When they peeked into the room where the interview had been held, they saw two boys on the floor, one very large, one smaller, both slumped against a huge, carved sofa, eyes half open, mouths fully open, drool at the corners. The smell of the corridor was far worse in the room, and it was a smell that Mouche remembered all too well.

He was staring around the corner at the larger of the boys when the boy's eyes came fully opened and looked at Mouche with total recognition. Mouche drew back, breathless. It was the larger of the intruder boys, from mat time long ago, the boy who had poisoned Duster. Older, he was, and strong looking, like an ox, but it was he, nonetheless, and the boy beside him was the other one from that day.

Mouche's immediate reaction was fury. If he had been home, in his own place, and if there had been a weapon at hand, or even a rock to crush a skull, he would have moved to violence. Since coming to House Genevois, he had been drilled in the avoidance of violence, however, and the more recent lessons held him wavering, readying himself, taking a moment to decide.

It was Tyle who broke his indecision, tugging Mouche by the arm, muttering at him. 'Let's get out of here.'

They got out, though Mouche felt someone listening, someone following his footsteps. If he had recognized that smell, those faces, the two new boys had also recognized him.

They made it as far as the landing before people came into the hall below, and when Simon and others came past the foot of the stairs, the three friends were occupied with an ostentatious concentration on the notice board. Mouche turned to look after the people below. The two new boys were being assisted, almost carried, and he met the gaze of the larger boy, his face quite empty but his eyes blazing as his mouth formed the soundless words: 'Farm-boy, I'll get you.'

Behind them, in the hallway, the strange smell still lingered.

'We don't say anything about this,' whispered Fentrys. 'Not a word!'

The other two nodded. Though an account of this happening would be very interesting to all their mates in Consort Country, they knew instinctively that Fentrys was right. The smell in the room and the hallway was of a particularly unpleasant kind. It was not to be talked of. Not with anyone; not even among themselves lest they be overheard. So, Mouche had no one to share his gratitude that the new boys would not be coming upstairs to Consort Country, not for some little time yet.

21

Among the Indigenes

That one whom Mouche adored, the Timmy who was called by other Timmys, *Fauxis-looz,* which meant something like 'Flowing Green' stood in one of the small painted houses in the rear courtyard, staring through the open door at the strange little tower gracelessly perched at the corner of the thick wall, built long and long ago by the first settlers as part of their riverside fortress. It was what the Timmys called a pretend wall: one that the humans pretended kept the Timmys in; one the Timmys pretended to be imprisoned by. The truth was there was no manmade enclosure that did not have doors in its walls and floors, no cellar without tunnels along its foundations, no loft without sneakaways between the rafters. No place had ever been built that tim-timkwi could not get into or out of whenever tim-timkwi wished.

Nonetheless, for now, these tim-timkwi, those called by infant mankind 'Timmys,' remained in the courtyard while Flowing Green kept her eyes on the tower window, which until some days ago had been almost closed but now was quite widely ajar.

'Tim saw his light again tonight,' the green-haired one said. 'Tim saw it, when tim-tim were come inside.'

'Yes,' the speaker was answered by another who stood beside tim. 'He comes every night.'

'This is the one Corojum spoke of,' said Rowing Green.

An older voice spoke from shadows. 'Who knows what is to come? Not even Corojumi, dance weavers; Bofusdiaga, sun singer; Joggiwagga, moon watchers, setters up of stones.'

Silence. Then the whisper from another, 'Niasa is restless and She is awakening. We cannot settle Her.'

'I have seen what I have seen in the dreaming time,' sang Flowing Green in a long, sustained flow of notes, a minor strain as plaintive as a nightbird.

'And who is tim to dream?' asked another, almost angrily. 'Who is tim to say "I," "I," as though tim were a mankind? Is this one standing here a many-times-rejoined one? Is tim Bofusdiaga? Is tim Kaorugi Itself! *Who* is Flowing Green to know of dreaming?'

'I am who I am,' said Flowing Green. 'I was made to watch these mankinds. I have the juice of one of them within me. I was created for this

724

purpose. I have watched, I have learned. When I have been remade, what I had learned was not taken from me. I say this Mouche is the needful one.'

'Already lost are the gemmed gardens under Mist-mount,' sang the old voice from the corner shadows. 'Fallen are the stone skies of Great Gaman and all the living stars that shone within them. If we do not find the dance, all will be lost.'

'Tim-tim still have some of it,' mused Flowing Green.

'In fragments,' said the voice from the corner, with only a hint of resentment. '*What* tim-tim have is thin, too thin, like gauze, like mist, like the wandering sound of little winds, unsure and unsettled. The power of it has leaked away. And now the gathering approaches, the Joggiwagga are setting up the stones, the tide comes with the moons; Niasa turns in sleep and She dreams restless dreams. The world trembles. Already the waking has begun.'

The corner tim spoke the truth. Even mankind had heard the word being called in the wilderness and had seen the pillars erected on the shores. Mankind did not know it was the Great Eiger who called or Joggiwagga who read the moon shadows. Mankind spoke of volcanoes and earthquakes, but mankind knew it was happening. Destruction threatened. Not at this moment, no. Nor tomorrow. But soon.

'I say once more, this one who watches us is the key,' said Flowing Green in a firm voice that said tim did not care whether they believed or not. 'A Corojum spoke to me saying: *This one, Mouchidi, is not jong. He may not go gau when the waters close over him* These were the words of the Corojum, and when I had heard the words of the Corojum, I dreamed of myself in the Fauxi-dizalonz, and this Mouchidi, he was with me.'

Only shamed silence greeted this. Such a thing was an abomination. Bofusdiaga had tried it with the jong long ago, and it had been a disaster. Surely Bofusdiaga would not allow it again! The tim-timkwi began to murmur, but the voice from the corner came again, admonishing.

'Bofusdiaga made strangely this one called Flowing Green, this one who says, "I," like mankind. Perhaps Flowing Green is a new thing in an old form.'

'Or perhaps Flowing Green is timself gau, bent, a monster,' said another-tim.

'Tim-tim will know soon enough,' murmured the corner voice ironically.

There was a wave of bitter laughter, a sound that overflowed the one little house to run among the other little houses in a freshet of real mirth as tim-tim repeated what tim had said. 'Soon enough, too soon, enough.'

'Tim-tim will know,' said Flowing Green in her dreaming voice. 'And I will know. And I will remember my dreaming and the words of the Corojum and this watcher from the wall.'

The Timmys were not the only thinking beings who remembered old times in the evening. Aloft on her balcony, D'Jevier remembered, not what she herself had seen, but what she had read in the secret journals of the Hags.

When the second settlement arrived, there were no Timmys. Years went by, and suddenly, there were Timmys, intelligent seeming beings. Speaking beings. And if they belonged here, mankind did not, according to Haraldson, so mankind had tried to drive them away.

The Timmys stayed. The Timmys gathered in great mobs to dance. There, on their dancing grounds, mankind had killed them, piling their corpses in stacks to be burned.

It hadn't worked. For every Timmy killed, another arrived, and they still danced. They also started doing things for people: washing clothes, weeding gardens, cleaning dwellings.

Meantime, the mankind population grew slowly, and since the people were too few to do everything that needed doing, they began to depend upon the labor of the Timmys. In no time at all, the Timmys became the cleaners and cultivators and carriers. The Timmys became the miners and millers and child-minders. They were ubiquitous and industrious about mankind's business, but they still danced. When they danced, they did not work.

Now their dancing was regarded as a dereliction of duty rather than ah opportunity for slaughter, and once again mankind had interfered. Though the Timmys were never mentioned in either written or spoken edicts, 'the sound of drums' had been forbidden, as had the 'unprofitable shuffling of feet.' 'Coordinated and frivolous movement' had been tabooed, as well, and there had been more than a few cases of maiming and murdering of Timmys in an effort to enforce the rule.

Mankind had always had a propensity for trying to govern the ungovernable and to control what was uncontrollable. Mankind had always relied upon laws and rules to direct those drives that did not care about laws or rules. Pragmatism had at last prevailed. Mankind upon Newholme had conceded that creatures who did not exist, who had no brains, could not be expected to modify their behavior to accord with mankind's desires. Indeed, one Hag had been heard to say in confidence that forbidding the Timmys to dance was like forbidding a horse to piss. The horse would do it, somehow or other, somewhere or other, and though inconvenient and embarrassing, the best thing to do was ignore it.

The Timmys who had overheard this comment from their spyholes in the walls were not offended. Well, they nodded, it is time these folk saw sense.

Still the Timmys danced. The Hags knew it. The Men of Business knew it.

They did not know why. Only the Timmys knew why.

Now and then they filled their courtyards or canyons or lava tubes with whirling dedications to zoological or botanical divinity, with ecstatic miming of many wondrous creatures. Now and then they did the slow omturtle dance, accomplished in pauses and silences; now and then the twirling rapture of the Great Eiger, the windbird, the four-eyed flier, who saw all, who knew all. Now and then was mimed the circular slithing of Joggiwagga, the moon dragons, simulated by stroked tambours and the throb of water drums. Now and then was the reed dance done, and that of the quiowhat tree and the little fluttery dances of all the beings-who-do-not-know-themselves, the fishy swimmers and birdy-things and lesser vegetables who, unlike the Timmys, were not individually made by Kaorugi the Builder but were allowed to reproduce independently to serve as food for all creatures.

All these dances were done for enjoyment, and for practice.

For sometimes mere enjoyment gave way to necessity. Sometimes Niasa, summer-snake-in-the-egg, who dreamed of life, would become restless. Whenever this happened, Timmys did the little amusement dances for Her-Who-Hatches-Niasa, small simple dances, the first ones the Corojumi had created for Her. Then, every decade or so, when the moons lined up and pulled roughly, Niasa-in-the-egg would almost be wakened, and for these times more powerful and hypnotic amusement dances were needed, with many rehearsal sessions beforetime. Many Timmys were required for these, but the dance was always done for Her on time, and however restless it might be, Niasa slept on, dreaming as it had done forever.

But then, once every few centuries all the moons gathered at once and the substance of the world was shaken, and Niasa-in-the-egg was almost jolted from sleep to call wakefully to Her, The hatcher!

Then came time for the great dance. Only the great dance would serve. Timmys had done the dance time after time. All life upon Dosha had done the dance time after time, a hundred, two hundred times.

But then mankind had come and had done the evil thing. Over and over, done the evil, destroying the dance. And when Timmys had tried to get it back, the mankinds had done worse things. Now the time for the great dance was coming fast upon the world, and no one was left, no one at all who remembered how the dance was done.

22

A Dream of Falling Water, Flowing Green

In the small hours of night, Mouche dreamed he stood in the mists of an unlit chasm while a cataract fell before him out of darkness into darkness. The source was so far above him, the catch basin so far below that no sound of water reached him. The curved emerald surface of the water and the glassy shadows moving within it were lit by a single ray that pierced the darkness from behind him. In his sleep he could not name this falling water, yet he knew it poured forever through that solitary beam, a perfect and eternal miracle made manifest by this single and incomplete enlightenment.

So, Mouche remembered in his dream, had the emerald hair of the dancer poured forever across the dark and empty chasms of his heart, with only his flawed perception disclosing its mystery. The dance, the scent of the food and the smoke, the sound of the drums and the voices, the flutes and the bells, all became an experience that lifted him as on an unending tide, out of nowhere into everywhere, while mysterious mists rose around him, spreading the possibility of marvel through the moist and fecund darkness.

Certainly the dream mists permeated his sleep, soaking into certain opinions that had been already petrified when he had received them and which nothing in his life until now had served to soften. Each time he woke, he was different, as though his very bones had become pliable, bending to become the framework for some other, as yet unparticularized person. Hidden in the deep embrasure beneath the patinaed dome, he suffered the nightly torments of the unknown and itched with a fascination that drove him closer to madness every time he scratched it.

The change was a fearful thing. As it progressed he found he could take nothing as a matter of course. He could no longer submit to the ministrations of the invisible masseuses without wondering what color hair they had, and whether they sang in the evening, or whether they danced, and what their true purpose was and why they had come. He did not see their eyes upon him, equally wondering and weighing. He could no longer look aside from the brown-clad forms who swept the street without wondering where their homeland had been and whether they hated their present confinement or whether even that was part of the flow he could sense happening.

He did not see their glance follow him as he went, the gestures their hands made, signifying to any tim-tim watching that this was Mouchidi, the one Flowing Green had come for, the one Flowing Green said Bofusdiaga wanted.

The change overflowed the night hours and ran into everything he tried to do. Mouche could no longer pace the dignified measures his dancing master required without flowing far too gracefully, as though to emulate the dances of those he imagined were watching from behind the walls. He could not leap without being lifted, like a balloon. He could not twirl without spinning. He was become a dervish, all too full of inordinate intention.

'What's come over you Mouche? You dance like a windlily!'

Mouche apologized, and went on apologizing, to the fencing master, to the conversation director, both of whom found him odd, eccentric, no longer focused, but oh, interesting, very interesting. He, meantime, was too busy to find himself interesting, for he was desperately attempting to interpret what was happening to him, and he was without tutelage, completely on his own. He was possessed without knowing how to be a possession. Even if he had sought help, he could have found no adviser among the mankind inhabitants of Newholme.

Suspecting as much, he confided in no one. He borrowed the oil can from Simon's workroom and oiled the latch and hinges of the window where he sat night after night; he borrowed a brace and bit and drilled a narrow hole into the woodwork of his bookcase, into which a short length of metal rod could be inserted from the front, thus preventing anyone else from repeating the movements that had led to his current predicament. That had been purely accidental, he told himself, unaware of the hands that had manipulated the door from behind the walls to be sure he had found the way they had opened for him.

It seemed that everything he did was accompanied by feelings of exhilarating joy or of overwhelming melancholy, that deep, unfocused grief he had felt before, in which Duster, and Papa, and his own dreams of the sea were merely drops in an unending tide. With every passing day he became more convinced that both joy and pain were signals, meant for him alone, requiring him to find the sufferer and offer ... something.

It would have been more comfortable to return to his former state of ignorance and contentment, but he could not. The longer it went on, the more secret and precious his delight in the watching became, the more painful that other emotion, that one from outside, as though the delight continued sensitizing him to the agony. They were inextricable. He could not have the one without the other. When he shuddered himself awake in the night, overwhelmed by an agony of loss and horror, he knew that they, too, wakened, hearing that pain as he heard it, like the tolling of a great alarm bell deep in the world. Somewhere on this planet, something suffered and grieved. It wasn't himself. It wasn't the dancers. Not his family, or House Genevois or anyone he knew. But something!

23

Dancers in Transit

Though Mouche had no inkling of it, another player in the Newholmian drama also itched with fascination, though of a more introspective kind. Whereas Mouche slept and changed in his sleep, Ellin, toward the end of the first stage of the trip toward Newholme, often found herself unable to sleep at all. The ship did its part, lowering the lights and the temperature and sending sleepy sounds through the ducts, like drowsy birds. The window-wall suddenly became a landscape, trees seen against a moonlit sky and a glittering body of water with a background of low mountains. It was the kind of scene that she had avoided on Earth, but here on the ship she had let it be. Who could feel claustrophobic in space? One either was well off inside or one was outside and dead.

None of her old sleepy-time rituals did any good. Her eyes stayed stubbornly open while she fretted. Since awaking from electronically induced deep sleep, which, though it had not seemed to last any time at all, had really lasted quite a long while, she and Bao had spent many waking hours reading, or having the monitors read to them, everything the Council of Worlds knew about Newholme plus a good bit the COW had no inkling of.

Though Ellin had always been a reader, she had not been much of a student, except of the dance. Ballet was taught by example and repetition, and Ellin learned best in that way. The official reports were couched in wordy bureaucratese that hid information rather than disclosing it. Trying to find meaning amid the polysyllabic jargon made her cross and irritable and wakeful, like an itch that wouldn't go away.

The view panel was there, of course. It didn't have to depict trees and moonlight. She could ask for virtually anything ever written to be printed or dramatized, and she'd tried that a few times, but the panel remained obdurately *there*, between her and whatever story it was trying to convey. A book would be better. With books, she wasn't conscious of anything except living the narrative.

Sometimes she thought she only dreamed about dancing while her real life was lived in books. She could get lost in a book, in being somebody else, in feeling amplified, complicated, her simple self fancied up with new sensations, new ideas and perceptions. In books she had family, community, a place in history; she had travels and explorations, struggle and achievement.

In the books she was greeted by others who said, in effect, 'You are so and so, and I know who you are!'

Often, when she finished a book, she came to herself with a sense of loss at what she'd surrendered in reading that last page. Closing the book was a finality that stripped her of identity, severed her life, left her squatting in the shallows of her mind, surrounded by polliwogs and ooze, with all the depths drained away. How often in her life had she longed for the story to become real! And yet now, here she was, far, far out in space, getting closer and closer to a dramatic doing, a wonderful adventure, a terrible excitement beyond all her expectations, and all she could do was worry that when the time came she'd be so self-conscious or frightened that she couldn't engage the event!

Her basic worry, excavated from the depths of her being through many fretful midnight sessions, was this clone business. Could a clone accomplish something it wasn't designed for? Dancer clones were supposed to be dancers. Musician clones were supposed to be musicians, entertainers entertainers, supervisors, scientists, genius generalists, all to be what they were! Just as many were cloned as were needed, with none left over – except for the occasional nus.

Nuses were mistakes. They were errors of system or development, and in moments of despair, Ellin comforted herself that she was definitely not a nus. She was exactly as per order, good legs, dancer's build, and with a mind that was ... oh, filth, filth, filth, step one foot outside the stage and it was an absolute blank! Hadn't her clone parent had a brain? Hadn't the brain been passed on? If Ellin wasn't a nus, why did she feel like one? She clenched her pillow and groaned.

A moment later there was a rap at the door before it opened a crack to reveal a sleepy-eyed Gandro Bao peering in at her. 'I am hearing moans? Are you being sick?'

Had she moaned? Perhaps it had sounded like that. 'Maybe I let out a sigh or something,' she confessed. 'I was thinking about something.'

'About all the volcanoes on Newholme blowing up?' he asked, insinuating himself into the tiny stateroom and perching on the foot of the bunk. 'About the strange indigenous peoples existing there?' Some of this information had reached COW through official channels. Other facts, if indeed they were facts, had been picked up from the gossip of BIT or freighter crews who had landed briefly on Newholme to deliver or pick up materiel.

'Those are the only two things I could get out of all those filthy reports,' she snapped. 'Did you find anything else?'

'No. Indigenous race is being there, even though indigenes were not being there before settlement. Volcanoes are threatening to blow up world, even though they were never doing so before settlement. This is making me think settlement is, perhaps, unsettling.'

He mugged a comic face, making her laugh, then cry, petulantly: 'Why did it take them a thousand pages to say that?'

'Aha,' he said with a serious face. 'You were moaning over number of pages. That is being very understandable. Number of pages is often causing moaning, groaning, temper tantrums.'

She flushed, embarrassed, confessing, 'Nothing so relevant, Gandro Bao. I was thinking it would be easier if this was a book.'

'Why is it being easier in book?'

'If the book came to a troublesome part, I'd just lay it down for a while. Or I'd jump ahead a page or two, to see if it came out all right. That way my stomach wouldn't hurt, and I wouldn't get pains in my head. And in a book, you get told who you are. You get the right words and the right clothes and the dialogue, everything, props and all. You don't have to work it out for yourself.'

'This is being true in dance, too, but dance is not excluding extemporaneous art. So, be extemporizing.'

'It's easier if you have a personality, that's all,' she said in a defeated tone. 'You know. Roots.'

'You are fine nordic dancer. There are being many roots to go with nordic dancer.'

'I know that.' She sat up, annoyed. 'I looked it up. There's a lot of warlike hordes moving around, and lots of stomping and kicking dances and several complicated religions, and a lot of violent wars. I don't feel connected to any of it. It's not like a family.'

He leaned against the wall, taking one of her feet in his hands and digging his thumbs into her sole. 'Why are you wanting a family?'

She felt her leg relax in a spasm of pleasure. 'I meant it would be ... nice to know who my parent was and what she did and where she lived, because she was a whole person and sometimes I feel like I'm just one sixth of one.'

He mused, 'I am reading a little bit about chaos theory: many things explained by chaos theory, many new discoveries about it even after centuries! This teaching is that tiny differences in original event can cause great difference in result. So, you and sister clones are each having many little differences, beginning in laboratory, going on into rearing. End result is six differing persons with similar appearance and skills. You are not being them, they are not being you. People have always been having twins, triplets, also clones. They are not being identical people.'

He moved his fingers up to the arch of her foot. 'If you really are wanting to know parent, records are letting you find out. All that is being included in records.'

'That's not what I meant,' she whined. 'It's … I was born to be a dancer, and that's all I've ever known about. I didn't grow up *wanting* to be a dancer, I was born one. I didn't *choose* to be a dancer, that was already decided. I didn't even have to worry about whether I'd succeed, everyone knew I would. If I'd had to… explore, to try other things, I'd have had some … I don't know, some variety.' She heard the snivel in her own voice and silently cringed. Shameful, carrying on this way!

'Female,' he said, almost affectionately, putting down the foot and picking up the other. 'You are being female all over. Now to me, who is only being female impersonator, it is not making difference how I get to be a clown so long as I am really wanting to be clown. But you are wanting to try something else so you can have doubts about talents you have?' He shook his head at her.

'Listen, Ellin, in Kabuki, we get persons coming after us. What is the old word? Groupies? It is like singers or actors, persons writing notes, asking are we free for dinner, you know? Mostly, I am not paying attention, but a few times I am going to dinner to meet people. I am seeing me through their eyes, and I am finding this confusing. They are picturing me so differently. Some are men who are thinking they love the woman I am pretending to be. Some are women who think they are loving me, actor, because I am obviously understanding women and they are needing understanding. Some are being as you say, vice versus, backward, women in love with woman character, men in love with man actor.

'So, I am being confused, and some days I am looking at face in mirror and thinking, who is this? Is this male or female? Is this real person or only actor? Knowing father and mother is no help. They are being them, I am being me. They are not even knowing me. When I was being small boy sent home from school for being jokester, Mother was saying to me all the time she could not figure who I am being. I am thinking every parent is looking at every child sometimes thinking, who is this? So, when I am twelve, I am hearing famous Haraldson song and deciding I am whoever I am wanting to be! Who I am choosing to be!'

'But that's just it! I can't choose who to be! I never had a choice!'

He began to work on her ankle, drawing his brows together. 'You cannot choose to be horse, or fish, or tree, no. But it is like this. You are like small seed, and this ship is like big wind, and it is blowing seed from small plant far, far away where is no other such plant. And plant is not saying, "Oh, oh, I cannot be oak tree, I cannot be bamboo, I cannot be cactus, I have no choice." Plant is not so silly as that. Plant is putting down roots of own self and growing! And while it is growing, when things are difficult, it changes a little bit, so when it is grown, it is not exactly like the plant it was coming from. It adapts.'

She caught her breath. It adapts. And she had adapted. Even if her clone didn't have a brain, presumably she had adaptability. 'So that's all I am? A seed blown on the wind?'

He snorted. 'Seed on wind and being adaptable. Same as me, Ellin. Same as everybody. All of us, seeds. Seed is ninety percent precursor mammal, like mouse. Seven or eight percent chimpanzee-human primate precursor. One point nine nine nine percent generalized Homo sapiens. Tiny fraction one percent me, or you, different from everybody else. One healthy creature being able to blow on wind and still live! Able to choose.'

He threw up his hands, scowled at her, then patted her foot with a gesture that was pleasant without being in the least threatening. There, there, he seemed to say. Settle down.

'Oh, go away,' she said, turning to bury her face in the pillow. 'Very soon we'll be meeting that other ship, and I don't want to be all messed up in a frangle with you about my identity – or lack of it!'

'Lacking of it?' He grinned. 'I make it rule only to talk to identities. Stop fretting and sleep.'

Though unconvinced by anything he had said, shortly after he shut the door, she slept.

Back in his own stateroom, however, Gandro Bao did not sleep. Instead he stared into the mirror, his brows tented in query, one nostril lifted, as though scenting a trail. 'Here I am being helpful,' he murmured to himself. 'Lecturing all about roots and growing in space where is nothing to grow on. Maybe is being only wind under us, and no place for us to hold to? Who is this Bao Bao Down to be giving Ellin Voy small contentments, like mama giving cookies?'

He smoothed his face, making it expressionless, calm, accepting. 'Demand much of yourself and little from others,' he quoted to himself from the analects. 'You will prevent discontent.'

That would have to do, for tonight.

24

Harassments

Bane and Dyre began harassing Mouche the moment they were moved into Consorts' quarters, as they had to be very soon, for the protection of the new students. 'Dirt rubs off,' as Madame was wont to say, and with Bane and Dyre dirt took all forms from attitudinal, to behavioral, to linguistic.

At first the two of them merely placed themselves within Mouche's view and stared endlessly, the lidless stare of serpents. Mouche ignored them. Within a few days, Simon had them so busy they had no time for staring.

Nights were still free, however, so they moved from covert threat to overt violence. One night, as Mouche was returning to his suite, Bane and Dyre leapt out at him from behind a protruding pillar, grimacing in theatrical fashion, mouthing their intentions in voices far too loud for secrecy, and with knives snaking from between their fingers. The assault was interrupted by Fentrys and Tyle, who came around the corner too late or just in time, depending on one's point of view. They were all wounded by the time it was over, and it took all three of them to put the two brothers down and send them off, bloody but still threatening.

'What started that?' Fentrys wanted to know.

'I told you about Duster,' Mouche said, dabbing at a cut on his hand. 'Those two did it, and they recognized me the first day they were here. Now they want to punish me for what they did.'

'Well,' said Tyle, 'if they're that sort, they'll want to punish all three of us. We'd better travel in company for a time, to watch one another's backs.'

And so they did, sticking so tight with each other or around the instructors that they thwarted several more attempts at violence. Simon, whose job required keen observation, noted this collective stance almost immediately, but it took him several days to determine the cause. At that point Simon took an early opportunity to call Mouche aside and have an informal conference.

'What is this?' Simon asked the boy, after seating both of them comfortably in Simon's quarters and pouring two glasses of wine.

'Those two used to live near my family's farm,' said Mouche. 'They killed my dog. Worse, they made poor Duster suffer!'

'What cause did they have for doing that?' Simon wondered. 'Or was it random meanness?'

'Oh, they thought they had cause,' Mouche admitted. 'Duster and I stopped their killing some little native creature, killing and torturing it, too, I'd guess. I didn't hurt them any, and this business of trying to wound me or kill me just doesn't make sense. Why are they doing it?'

'I'd say your not hurting them is part of the why,' said Simon. 'Remember what Madame has taught you about gaming groups, packs, tribes? If you'd beaten them bloody, they might have fawned on you. Some men want more than anything to have a place in a pack and follow a lead dog. But if you won't fight for the role of lead dog, then you're an outsider, someone who interfered with their doing as they liked, and to men like Bane and Dyre, outsiders, particularly interfering ones, are the enemy. Prey, property, or enemy. You have to be one of the three.'

Mouche ducked his head to hide the angry tears at the corners of his eyes. He always teared up when he thought of Duster. 'Do they get pleasure out of acting like that?'

Simon leaned forward and laid a rough hand on his shoulder. 'Look, Mouche, you've got to understand what Newholme men are about, not from Madame's point of view but from our own. Now most men get taught early on that being dutiful is good, so they think they're being good when they work themselves into exhaustion and meanness. And most men know that pleasure distracts them from duty, so that teaches them pleasure is shameful. But at the same time, we have these restless brains inside that tell us to keep pushing toward the top so we can make a hole, crawl through, and see what's up there. All of us, even Consorts and supernumes, figure we've got a natural right to be there, on top and we use whatever we've got to get there. Humor. Or eloquence. Or skill. Whatever.

'Bane and Dyre, now, they've got the idea mutual pleasure is sissy stuff, so the only pleasure they get is sniggering and bullying and destruction. And they don't like duty either, so they avoid it. The only thing that gives them satisfaction is anger, so being angry is how they go looking for themselves, like vandals taking a city: throw, hit, break, kill, shatter – it's all one to them. Destroy enough stuff, suddenly they'll find the hidden door with heaven behind it.'

Simon looked at his glass, swirling the liquid in it, watching the patterns it made. 'I try to tell you boys, best I can, that there isn't any door. You climb over people, you push and shove and get up there on top, it's empty. I try to tell you pleasure's a good thing, and it's easier with Hunks than most, because you're being trained to give it. And I try to tell you that duty's good, too, but you've got to balance it. And you've got to study

yourself to know how much of each you need, for no one man is a measure
of all.'

'What do you mean, study?' Mouche asked.

'If you want to know about a Purse fish, you don't beat the fish to death
or drain the sea dry. You look at the fish where it is. You study how it swims
and what it eats and how it lives. You don't take hold of it, or kill it, you
watch it. So, if you want to know who you are, you don't go laying around
with a pickax. You try to catch yourself when you're not pushed by anybody
or anything and watch yourself. You see what you do, and you figure out
why, and you decide how that makes you feel, and how it affects others, and
whether it makes you joyful or proud.

'It's amazing how many people don't know their own nature, even though
they can't do anything with it until they know what it is. How can you move
toward joy if you don't know what makes you happy?' Simon shook his head.
'Nobody's required to live in pain. We should always try to move toward
joy ...'

He looked up to meet Mouche's smile, suddenly radiant.

'Oh, Simon,' he said, 'It's not easy, but you're right. And even the pain
lights a road for you, doesn't it? It beckons you to fix it! Like if you know
something's hurt, you can try to mend it.'

Simon, surprised into near silence, agreed it could.

He later mentioned the matter to Madame, when they were alone and
very private, for she had asked him, as a favor, to come warm her bed that
night and he had, as much from affection as duty, done so.

'Mouche is right,' murmured Madame, sitting naked on the side of the
bed, her hair loose about her shoulders, while Simon knelt behind her,
kneading her neck between strong hands. 'They beg for murder, both of
them.'

'Have you no pity for them, Madame?'

'Of course I pity them, Simon. I pity the mad dog that bites the child,
the bull that gores the herdsman, the boar pig that tears the swineherds
leg to shreds with his tusks. If they were wild creatures, we would say, with
Haraldson, that they have the right to be as they are and the fault is ours for
straying into their territory. The fact is, they are not wild creatures, they are
protected and doctored and fed by mankind, and are thus kept according to
mankind's rules. So it is with Bane and Dyre.'

He went on kneading. 'An odd thing happened when I was talking
with Mouche. I was talking about discovering oneself, the lecture you often
give ...'

'... so our Consorts can help their patronesses discover their joys ...'

'And their own. Yes. And he got this expression on his face. I've never
seen such ecstasy on a face!'

She said softly, 'Mouche is a good one, isn't he Simon? Quite out of the ordinary. Something about him ...'

Simon moved his hands to the other side. Yes, he thought to himself. There was something about Mouche.

25

The Long Nights

At midwinter the people on Newholme took a long holiday which coincided, Mouche found, with the disappearance of the Timmys. When the Timmys went away, everything shut down, and in winter it stayed shut down for seven or eight days.

The holiday was called the Long Nights, or The Tipping of the Year, an occasion for family gatherings. Then kinfolk sat around the fire to tell over the names of ancestors, to honor those who had achieved g' status or Haghood among them, to relax standards of neatness and laundering (in the absence of whomever or whatever might have been, at other times, responsible for neatening and laundering), and to give amusing gifts and consume traditional foods prepared by their own hands while telling old stories around the tile stoves.

Though Consorts would never be, strictly speaking, 'family,' they needed to know how these occasions were managed, and House Genevois paid local families a generous stipend for hosting two or three youngsters in their homes during the Long Nights.

Mouche might have balked had the courtyard still been tenanted. His nightly forays had become an addiction, despite the feelings that flooded him at each watching. Initially, there was a kind of ecstasy in the watching, but gradually it turned to pain as if some huge thing was dying and unwilling to do so. The feeling exhausted him, and he had a sense the Timmys felt as he did, that they, too, were exhausted by the grief and weariness that came out of nowhere.

But the courtyard was empty, and he felt better for the respite. It was good, for a time, to have a simple skin-deep life, to be amused and think of nothing but singing or cooking or playing with children. He and Fentrys and Tyle always went to the weaving house of Hanna and Kurm g'Onduvai; their grown son, who supervised the looms, and his dowered-in wife as well as the eldest daughter, who had been dowered-in by a neighboring family, but who was visiting for a few days. There were also numerous merry and lively grandchildren.

Mouche and his friends enjoyed the annual give and take of the holidays. They played games with the children, taking them sledding on the nearby hill and ice-sliding on the frozen brook. In the evenings, they entertained by singing and playing on their instruments a number of songs everyone knew: 'The Wind in the Chimney Corner,' and 'Six Black Cows,' and the wordless melody of the 'Lullaby for the Summer Snake.' Even the chatter was interesting, and it was from Hanna's chatter, in fact, that Mouche first learned something on a subject he had been on the lookout for, the history of Dyre and Bane.

The conversation was between Hanna and Kurm, concerning some yarn Kurm had recently purchased from a local farmer.

'I can't use the stuff,' said Kurm. 'It's last year's spin, and I hate telling old man Dutter it's no good, but I can't afford not to. I can't use it.'

'The quality is bad?' asked Hanna. 'The Dutters were always good spinners.'

'It isn't the quality,' he replied. 'It's the smell. I told you what I suspected ...'

'About Dutter not fathering those boys? Yes. You told me long ago.'

'Well, you know *he* has that smell. Skunk-lung is what it is, and it's why *they* wouldn't have him, no matter how much he offered for dowry. And *he's* been seen here and there near the Dutter farm since those two boys came there – everybody knows they aren't Dutter's boys – and they have that same smell. Old man Dutter, he's either got no nose or he's so used to it he doesn't notice.'

'But the boys don't spin.'

'No. And billy goats don't give milk. But you make goat cheese where there's a billy, the cheese stinks, sympathetic like. You spin yarn where there's skunk-lung, and the yarn stinks, too. They breathe it onto everything, and whatever the cause, I can't use it.'

Which was all that was said, enough to make Mouche mightily interested. The Dutter boys had lived over the hill from his own home. And Madame had said she'd turned Dutter down when he'd tried to sell them. So, Dutter was a farmer, and the boys probably weren't his, and they smelled, and House Genevois had two newish students who smelled and whom Madame was not thrilled with. So, who was the *he* who had been seen near the Dutter farm? The same *he* who had come to House Genevois?

'Have you heard about them smelling bad?' Mouche asked his friends, when they discussed the matter that night in the loft where they slept.

'The room smelled bad that time,' said Tyle.

'Maybe it wasn't them. Maybe it was the other one.'

They didn't know. Bane and Dyre were still new boys. If they smelled, only the other new boys would know.

The fact that the other new boys didn't know was a testimonial to Madame's assiduity and long experience. She had not been in the same room with Bane and Dyre for more than a moment before realizing they would present a challenge. Charcoal in the food, and chopped alfalfa, and certain herbs she knew of. Certain uncommon unguents rather than usual ones. One drug, expensive but efficacious in quelling goaty effusions in young bucks. The condition presented by the two youngsters was not unknown, though this was the first she'd ever heard of it in young men. The condition was usually reported as infecting those few weird and elderly outcasts who frequented the frontier. They'd wander into town, nobody knowing who they were, and they'd have that smell.

He, her patron, who had offered a very large sum in gold for the training of these boys, had the same affliction, though *he* looked perfectly normal. To *him,* it must have seemed unimportant, for *he* did little to ameliorate his own condition. *He,* of course, was not married. *He* had not produced children. Except, vague rumor had it, these two, and they under such circumstances as were … well, better not mentioned. Those who had at one time spoken openly of the matter had ended up … gone. Vanished. Still, people whispered: Had *he* placed them with Dutter? Or had *she!* The woman. Whoever she was or had been. A certain name was sometimes whispered; whispered unwisely, Madame felt.

Madame was fairly sure who the mother had been, though she did nothing to verify the fact. She asked no questions, sent no investigators – though there were several she had employed in the past when she had needed information. In order that she might be unburdened of the boys as soon as possible, she concentrated instead on turning Bane and Dyre into acceptable candidates, and within two or three seasons she had them to the point where they could be seen occasionally in public without greatly risking the reputation of House Genevois.

That they were well groomed and handsome was an artifact, produced by much labor, none of it their own. That they were, when left to their own devices, belligerent, unmannerly, dirty and ill spoken was a given. That they were maintained in a more or less obedient state only by the threat of intervention from outside was the leash to keep them heeled. All of which could have been overlooked if they had showed any inclination to adopt a more acceptable manner. They did not do so, and it was this that made Madame despair.

Unwilling boys could be forced to obey, but they could not be forced to learn. They could be beaten into submission, but not into charm. Since learning and charm were the hallmarks of the Consort, what Madame could make of Dyre and Bane, the Hagions only knew.

26

Amatory Arts: the Hagions

Madame rapped her desk for attention. 'Finish up quickly boys. We have had a long session today.' The afternoon 'honored visitors,' as they were called, had gone. The students had showered and dressed for supper. This lecture would be short.

The more diligent among them were making a few quick notes concerning the visitors' session. 'Stroke, stroke, tweak,' Mouche wrote, rehearsing the latest matter in his mind. '*Not* shove, shove, grab.'

'Ahem,' said Madame. 'Gentlemen. If you will close your notebooks and attend, please.'

Mouche underlined the last phrase, then closed his book.

'This evening,' said Madame, 'I want to discuss the worship of the Hagions.

'I'm sure it has crossed your minds that on occasion, a Consort may find himself unable to respond to the person of his patroness. Though he does his exercises, though he sets his mind to his task, though he is devoted to his profession, he finds something lacking in his own work.

'In handling these occasions gracefully, it is wise to be able to call upon at least one of the Hagions. In our library you will find several volumes devoted to the Hagions, the various manifestations of female divinity, all the goddesses ever worshipped by mankind. You will find Athena the wise and Aphrodite the fair; You will find Iyatiku, corn mother; Isis, goddess of fecundity; Gaea, earth mother; Cybele, founder of cities; Sophia, holder of wisdom; Hestia of the hearth; Heka of childbirth, all these and a thousand more. For the most part they are kindly and comforting, though some among them are foreign to our idea of womanhood. I recommend that you avoid choosing one of the destroyers and torturers, for you would do so at your peril. Those who delight in killing condemn themselves to a bad and ugly death.

'Over the next few months, you are to peruse the encyclopedia of Hagions with the intent of choosing a personal goddess. Most are womanly in shape, some are androgynous, some are homo-, bi-, or omnisexual, and a few take other forms. Many exist in the guise of youth, as prepubescent maidens, as laughing children. Others are more matronly, secure in their maturity, sensuous and passionate. Some are old women, beyond lust, but filled with the knowledge of years. In general, it is best to choose one of the younger goddesses, saving the older for your own age.

'Our religion is monotheistic. We worship the lifeforce that pervades the galaxy in infinite variety, life that bubbles up from the ferment of worlds, and we know that force may appear in myriad guises. There is no rivalry among these guises, as they are all aspects of the same divinity, one so vast and complex that She can be infinitely divided into parts while every part remains infinite. Your relationship to a particular guise may be as a son to a mother, as a servant to a queen, as a lover to his love, and among all her guises you are certain to find one who will attract you, one who will remind you of some aspect you already deem sacred, one who you will feel no strain in worshipping and to whom you might be pleased to devote your life.

'Choose well and thoughtfully. It is not blasphemous to say that choosing can be rather like getting a new pair of boots made. So long as you are in the service of your patroness, your chosen Hagion will walk with you in that service, and She must not rub blisters on your soul or cripple you with calluses. She will make your way smooth and easy, no matter how arduous it is in fact, so choose a goddess that fits.

'Once you have chosen your own aspect of divinity, we will help you become conditioned to Her service, and if the time comes when you believe you cannot properly serve your patroness, you will succeed by serving your Hagion instead. When your patroness takes you to the Temple at each New Year, you will light incense in thanks to your own divinity. In your own quarters, you will maintain a shrine to Her. This is to remind you of the divinity through whom the lifeforce flows, however corporeal the body or frail the mind through which that force is transmitted.'

She saw a hand hesitantly raised. Fentrys, with an almost apprehensive expression.

'Yes, Fentrys?'

'Do the Hagions not resent being used like that, Madame?'

Madame frowned. At the back of the room, someone tittered, and she turned a quick and cautioning glance in that direction, like a search light, quickly beaming and as quickly withdrawn.

'It is not a foolish question, but it is a complicated one. The Hags at the Temple say that because the Hagions wish our patronesses to be served properly, they do not mind being used to that end. The Hagions accept our adoration, even though we are conditioned to give it, because we are using the conditioning to do their will. The Hags base their decision upon an historic precedent:

'On Old Earth, certain orders of celibate females were said to be brides of their male god. The writings of some of these women clearly establish that their devotion, though chaste in a physical sense, could be highly erotic, sensual, and joyous on a psychological level. These celibate orders often served the male priesthood or worked among the sick and the poor, doing many laborious and distasteful activities in the spirit of "serving" their bridegroom, that is, achieving sensual and erotic rewards through activities which were neither. This conditioning and sublimation was considered appropriate.

'We do the same. Though serving our patroness may be unstimulating, serving our Hagion is highly erotic, sensual and joyous. Thus we accomplish the one by doing the other ...'

Her voice faded and she stood, staring out a south window at the busy street with an expression that grew slightly troubled. Far to the east, across the river, ashen clouds rolled from the scarp, and they seemed far more ominous than usual. When she looked back at her students, she saw a hand raised at the back.

'Mouche?'

'Madame, when you talk about serving the patroness, you always say "we." Why is that?'

She smiled. 'Oh, my boy, I serve the Hagions by serving your patroness by serving you, just as you serve the Hagions in serving your patroness. We are all caught up, all of us, in serving this through serving that. Nothing is ever quite clear or direct in this world, and love is the most unclear and indirect of all ...'

A bell rang in the great hall. She said, 'It is suppertime. You are dismissed.'

She returned to the window as the room emptied, hearing one final rustle of paper and turning to see that Mouche still lingered, looking blindly at her like one stunned by terrible news or a sudden revelation. She hardly dared speak to him, and yet his depth of concentration seemed almost dangerous ...

'Are you considering which Hagion you will select, Mouche?'

His face lightened suddenly and he looked directly at her with a blinding smile.

'Oh, no, Madame. As you say, love is unclear and indirect, but once you feel it... I already have a goddess that I serve.'

He turned and went out, leaving Madame staring speechlessly after him. She had seldom seen such rapture on a human face. She could not imagine who, or what might have stirred it, and she felt a strange disquiet that only later did she identify as envy.

27

The Questioner is Announced

The Council of the Men of Business (the C-MOB, as it was jovially called) made the laws that governed men's affairs from their council house in Naibah, that structure known as the Fortress of Vanished Men. The council was made up entirely of g'Family Men, men whose wives had been dowered in and who had produced children. It elected from among its members an executive committee, ECMOB: six men from various parts of Newholme who came to Naibah each quarter year.

The Naibah fortress had, as a matter of fact, figured prominently in the women raids of the early settlement years, thus giving it a long and (as the Hags put it) disreputable history. Not the least reason for its scandalous reputation was the behavior of ECMOB members who immediately upon arrival removed their veils, poured themselves large glasses of vinaceous liquids and thereafter spoke disrespectfully of their wives, acts no fathering men would dare commit in public. There, also, when the routine business had been taken care of, ECMOB allowed itself to talk of other matters: matters of governance usually reserved to the Hags; matters that family men ordinarily only whispered at.

On a particular day, there was only one item of business. Volcanic activity had increased, as it did cyclicly every ten to twenty years, but the current geological violence was greater than at any time since settlement. Therefore, ECMOB had recently hired a consulting firm from off planet to set up surveillance equipment – also purchased from off planet – and assess the danger to settled communities. The firm had prepared a report which said, in essence that, yes, there was an increase in volcanic activity, which currently seemed to be about four times what it had been when Newholme was settled and twice what it had been ten years before. Yes, there might be some danger to the valley of the Giles, but no, it hadn't come to the point that the firm could recommend any sort of evacuation yet.

'Which I, for one, do not find helpful,' said the chairman, one Estif g'Bay-oar. 'Not with all the eastern valleys ashed over, not with all the farms up there buried. There've been tremors as far north as the sea islands and as far west as Bittleby Village.'

'All the valley farms gone?' asked Myrphee g'Mindon, stroking his chins. 'I used to get quite a good goat cheese from up there.'

Estif nodded. 'The firm hired some supernume outliers to place some sensors near the big caldera on the scarp. It's too high to climb to without breathing apparatus, which we've ordered but not received yet. Two of ¿he men did get high enough to see that some new vents have opened during the past year, and there've been gas and ash flows all down the valleys. I suggest we ask the firm to give us their best estimate on city security. We can't evacuate Naibah or Sendoph without considerable notice!'

There were nods, some sanguine, some troubled.

Estif cleared his throat to signify a new matter, tapping restless fingers on the sheet of heavy vellum that lay on the table before him. Writing on vellum was considered sufficiently traditional that receiving it would not insult either pre- or post-technological societies. It was, therefore, habitually utilized for formal interplanetary notifications.

'Newholme has received a communication from ... from the Questioner,' he said in a voice that was usually dry and emotionless but trembled now, very slightly. 'The Questioner intends to visit Newholme, and it sends a formal announcement of that fact via a freighter that now sits outside Naibah. Does anyone here have any idea why it would be coming just now?' He regarded the problematical document, biting his lip, as though the meaning might become clear through protracted observation.

The ECMOB shifted restlessly, each member glancing covertly at his neighbors. Slab g'Tupoar, a portly fellow with dark, squirming eyebrows, snarled, 'For Family's sake, 'Stif. You know why now. There's only two reasons it could be! Coming just now, I mean.'

Bony Bin g'Kiffle, moved to immediate belligerence, muttered, 'Of all the stupid ... Why must we deal with this?'

Myrphee g'Mindon struggled to his feet and wobbled unsteadily toward the information wall. 'Questioner,' he said. 'Enlighten.'

'Bionic construct,' murmured the wall. 'Nominally female. Containing, in words of enactment, text and commentaries on Haraldson's Edicts of Equity as well as wisdom of ages acquired since inception.' The wall hummed a moment, as though thinking. 'Wisdom of ages not susceptible of definition.'

'Purpose of,' Myrphee grated in an annoyed tone. 'Enlighten.'

'Purpose of Questioner,' said the wall. 'Primary assignment: Assess member worlds of COW on regular schedule to determine continued compliance with edicts of Haraldson. Secondary assignment: Assess other mankind-settled worlds to determine if cultures meet minimal standards of ethical conduct regarding human rights. Final assignment: Take every opportunity to accumulate knowledge about cultures, mankind and other. Report to COW any divergence from council edicts applying to all mankind settlements, whether members or nonmembers of COW, regarding human rights, age or gender rights, or rights of indigenous races.' The machine silenced itself, then, with a whir said, almost conversationally, 'Questioner is also authorized to order disposal of mankind populations who are egregiously transgressing the edicts.'

At this addition, Myrphee's chins quivered, the tremor passing to those at the table as a little wind might move through a grove of trees, a sudden and collective shudder that left a trembling quiet in its wake. After some moments, Myrphee drew back his pudgy fist as though to hit the wall, but contented himself with an obscene gesture.

'Excrement,' he said feelingly.

'Gentlemen.' Estif tapped his little gavel, saying in his high, serious voice, 'Come now. It's unlikely to be ... well, it just can't be that bad.'

'About as bad as it can get,' grated Myrphee g'Mindon as he returned to his seat.

'Like tidal wave, tornado, forest fire,' offered Calvy g'Valdet, in the light, slightly amused tone that the other members often found offensive. Calvy made a point of being amusing about important things, and he did it in a way that came close to condoning immorality. Often the others punished him for it, as now, by seeming not to notice. If morals were the measure of a man, Calvy had no business being a member of ECMOB, for it was known that Calvy's wife of some fifteen years had not bought a Consort, though her contract allowed her to do so. It was rumored that prior to his marriage, Calvy had pretended a lengthy business trip while actually spending a month or two in a Consort house, learning whatever dirty things it was that Consorts did, just so his wife would never supplant him in her affections. The story said he was in love with her, which if true, was both unmanly and indecent.

Though this story was known to the other members of ECMOB, none of them had ever discussed it with Calvy himself. Had they done so, custom would almost have required that they denounce his behavior. Pleasuring a wife was not proper for a Family Man, and they felt Calvy should be far too bowed down by guilt to be amusing.

Why then, Bin g'Kiffle asked himself, did Calvy seem to enjoy life so much more than he, Bin, who conducted himself in perfect accordance with custom? Bin's couplings were unfailingly joyless, and reason dictated that the Hagions should, therefore, reward him more than they had! The cockade in his hat, the g' before his name, and six children, four of them supernumes, did not seem a sufficient compensation for all his years of struggle. The thought was a recurrent one, and as usual it made him splenetic.

'The Questioner's visit could mean total disaster,' he fumed, glaring at Calvy.

'Bin, let's not overreact. Calm, please!' Now slightly peevish himself, Estif looked from face to face, annoyance plain on his own.

'What does it ... she *say?*' Diminutive Sym g'Sinsanoi hoisted himself higher in his chair. It was a habitual movement, this hoisting up, though Sym appeared little shorter than the other men when seated. 'She must say *something!*'

Himself annoyed by all these festering feelings, Estif threw the vellum onto the table before him and sank into his chair. 'The letter of announcement says she wishes to visit our lovely world, which she has not yet had the pleasure of assessing.'

Myrphee shifted in his chair, redistributing his considerable weight. 'The Questioner will look at our way of life to see if we comply with the edicts. We are going to have to prove that we do comply with the edicts. Which means we will need the help of the Hags.'

'How many in the party?' asked Calvy g'Valdet, who was not given to muttering over what could not be changed. His way was to smile, to avoid recrimination, to cut through the tangle, to decide and move, to do what was necessary without endless nattering. No matter what the others might think of his morals, they all agreed that Calvy got things done.

'And, where will we put them?' asked Myrphee.

'Here in the fortress?' Bin g'Kiffle suggested. 'It's the easiest place. It's already staffed with ... ah, well, you know.'

'It has a human staff,' said Sym, sourly. 'Chef, assistants, stewards. For reasons of security.' He put his hands together and examined the ceiling above him.

'How many are coming,' asked Myrphee, 'with the Questioner? We need to know! One or two we could maybe ... manage. More than that ...' He scowled at the tabletop.

'I'm afraid the notice mentions an entourage,' admitted Estif. 'There will be two Old Earthians to do the actual "contact work," as they call it, plus a Cluvian protocol officer, some bodyguards, plus whatever specialists she figures she needs. The protocol officer will arrive on planet before the others.'

'There's no way we can keep the Hags out of it, I suppose?' Bin snarled.

'We didn't receive the only copy,' said Calvy. 'The Hags will have been notified as well.'

Myrphee squeezed his hands together until his knuckles made white dimples in the plump sausages of his fingers. 'How about asking for a delay, on the grounds of insufficient notice, or time for preparation?'

Calvy said, 'We're not supposed to prepare, Myrph. She's supposed to catch us as nearly unaware as makes no difference.'

'You don't suppose she's heard about ...?' asked Slab, his eyebrows rising into a single hairy bar across his forehead.

It took no effort for the others to keep their faces carefully blank. They did not suppose. Every habit they had cultivated since childhood kept them from supposing. Not one of them would even momentarily consider that there was something particular on Newholme in which the Questioner might be quite interested. Even if the something particular bit them with long, sharp teeth on their collective ass, they would bear the pain without seeming to notice.

Considering that their true concerns were unspoken and nothing was put forward as a solution to the unspecified, the meeting lasted longer than necessary. Calvy tried a time or two to push for some resolution, but the general discomposure made decision impossible. Whenever the Hags or the edicts came into MOB discussions, the meetings dragged on while a chronic complainer vented anger at his wife or mother and a hobby-historian blathered on about olden times when there weren't any Hags and when women did as they were damned well told. The committee always seemed to have at least one of each. At present they were Bin and Myrphee respectively. Though Calvy was a better historian than Myrphee, he didn't blather about it.

Estif muttered, 'If you're sure the Hags are going to be involved, we ought to appear cooperative, I suppose. Is there a volunteer to take this document into Sendoph to the Haggery?'

Somewhat reluctantly, Bin g'Kiffle raised one hand. 'I'm going back there tonight. I suppose I can take it.' He intended to catch the afternoon boat upriver, and could, in fact, deliver it that evening. It would give him an excuse for not going home immediately on arrival. As everyone in the room knew, Bin would use any excuse not to go home. His wife was a termagant.

'I'm going up to Sendoph tonight on business,' murmured Calvy. 'I can take it if Bin doesn't want to be bothered.'

'I said I'd take it,' snapped Bin. 'And I will!'

Calvy bowed, making an ironic face. He intended to call on an old friend in Sendoph, and he was glad enough not to make a time-consuming call at the Panhagion.

Estif handed over the vellum and the fancy envelope with the seals and ribbons. Bin stowed it away in his leather-and-gilt document case, almost as important a symbol of status as his cockade and the g' before his name. After which the men carefully affixed their veils across their faces, adjusted their honorable cockades, and took themselves back to home cities and places of business, where they belonged.

28

A Family Man Visits the Hags

Only in the secrecy of the Fortress of Lost Men was the Temple in Sendoph referred to as 'the Haggery,' and Bin g'Kiffle was careful not even to think the words as he climbed the wide stone steps leading to the huge bronze doors. One of the Consort Houses had doors like that, also, part of the cargo of the ship the first settlers had pirated. Pirated or not, males did not approach those doors for anything trivial. Males did not hurry when there were Hags in the vicinity. When at the Temple, even workmen or delivery men took their time, abating any tendency toward immodest alacrity. Here, everything was done slowly, deliberately, with due weight and moment.

Bin, therefore, climbed in a dignified, almost ritualistic manner. When he had completed this errand, he would take off his cockade and go to one of the basement taverns hidden in the warehouse district near the river. He would stay there as long as possible. He would tell his wife he had had an errand at the Temple, and if she didn't believe him, the hell with her – the Temple offices were always open.

He was solicited by a holy prostitute, not a bad-looking boy, considering, and Bin produced a generous contribution while murmuring the acceptable excuse. Tonight was his wife's night. he said. The prostitute smiled slightly and went back to his fellows. No one questioned that excuse, but one had to be a Family Man to get away with it.

Bin bowed outside the door, waiting until three very pregnant women had preceded him to the font, then dipped his own fingers in the water, thereby symbolically cleansing himself of the taint of business, the stink of profit. Here at the Temple, business did not apply. Here one could not set a price on a sentient life, though people did so constantly elsewhere in the city. Here one did not speak of gain. In the Temple, there was no network of honorable Family Men on whom one could depend for information or influence. Here Bin was simply another man of Sendoph, like any other man of Sendoph, whether g'family or otherwise.

He opened the small door set into the huge one and went through into the Temple forecourt, a broad semicircle of mosaic pavement that bordered the outer half of the circular Sanctuary. To one side, a gentle ramp led to the birthing rooms below. The pregnant women were already partway down, chatting among themselves. All devout women tried to bear their children in the Temple; certainly Bin's wife had done so, for all the good it did. Five sons and only one daughter to show for it, and now his wife had a Hunk. Every cent he got for the girl would go to dower his eldest boy, and what was he to do with the others? He'd made the mistake of raising them above their expectations, at least the older two, so they were resentful and useless. He'd intended to start a dynasty, and now there was damn little wherewithal to start anything. Whatever he did, there'd be no profit in it!

Fifty feet above his head, the barrel-vaulted ceiling curved away to right and left, the air hazed by the smoke of a dozen incense kiosks. The opposite wall, concentric with the outer wall, was a row of pillared and heavily curtained arches, beyond which was the Sanctuary, the statues of the Hagions, the lofty seats of the Prime Hags, the rites and observances that kept Newholme ticking. Even at this time of night, there was movement through the curtained arches, and Bin checked his veil compulsively. If a man wanted a slow, agonizing execution, just appear in the Temple unveiled. That would do it. There were always women here, women quite willing and eager to be punctilious about male behavior. Not to mention the ubiquitous Haggers.

The Sanctuary, barely visible between the curtains, was forbidden to him and all other males over the age of ten, but this wide foyer with its racks of votary candles was open to all. Bin turned to his left and went along the curve of the outer wall toward the offices, moving solemnly so as not to be suspected of frivolity. A young woman, younger, that is, than most of the Hags, nodded to him as he entered the open door of the reception area.

'Family Man,' she said pleasantly.

As always, Bin chafed at the designation. She could see his cockade, she knew who he was perfectly well, but no woman would greet a veiled man by name in public, not even a wife her husband. The avoidance was supposed to be proper, but to Bin it always felt rude, depersonalizing, as though he were invisible!

He bowed. 'Madam. I bring a notification received by the Men of Business in Naibah. It concerns a proposed visit to Newholme by the Questioner ...'

She smiled sweetly. 'We have already received notification, Family Man. Though we thank you for your courtesy.'

Bin shifted uncomfortably from foot to foot. 'Our chairman, that is, Estif g'Bayoar, thought maybe the Questioner would like to stay at the Fortress in Naibah? That is ...'

'We'll call upon the Men of Business if we need them,' she said, still sweetly. 'Do shut the door on your way out, Family Man.' And she bent back to her work, ignoring him so pointedly that he felt himself growing heated beneath his robes and veils.

He opened his mouth to say something snappish, then closed it again.

She glanced up. 'Something else?' Her face was now quite stern, the smile gone.

'Where we put her! It's important! She can't be allowed to—'

The woman held up her hand, palm outward, warningly. 'The matter is being attended to, Family Man. You need not concern yourself. Do you understand?'

It took him a moment to find his voice. 'Of course, Madam,' he said, bowing. 'Sorry to have disturbed you.' Then, stubbornly, he said, 'Madam, have the Hags any information about the volcanic activity? The Men of Business believe there has been a troubling increase and we seek guidance.'

Her face grew very still. It was some time before she replied, 'I will convey your concern to the Hags, Family Man. I cannot say at the moment whether they or the Hagions would find this matter within their purview, but I will inquire. Feel free to come again in a day or two, by which time I should know something.'

He turned and left, shutting the door behind him, making no sound. Once out on the street, at the bottom of the steps, however, he muttered to himself. 'Damn, uppity, pushy, Hags. Damn women. Damn female pushiness. Damn.' He made a threatening gesture that drew the attention of a couple of Haggers who were sweeping the cobbles. Since male Haggers had, so to speak, foresworn being male, they wore no veils, and their faces were stern as they turned toward him, holding the thick, heavy broom handles like pikestaffs. At that, he came to his senses. Thrusting his hands into his sleeves, lowering his head so they could not see his eyes glaring at them through his veil, he walked steadily away. It was late. He had had a full day. He wanted to get home and go to bed!

'Damn Hagions,' he cursed the Goddesses. 'Damn Haggers,' he cursed their followers. 'Damn, damn Hags.' And their priesthood, as well.

Behind him, through one of the slit windows that looked out upon the temple stairs and down into the street, the young woman he had spoken to along with two older Hags watched him depart.

'So the Men of Business are worried about the smoke,' murmured D'Jevier.

'All that gray ash streaming from the scarp would be difficult to miss,' muttered Onsofruct. 'All those valley farms wiped out over the last five or six years.'

'And the tidal wave that took six villages out along the Jellied Sea.'

'And the way the pillars are shifting off their bases in the crypts of the Temple. More than worrisome, I'm afraid. I still wish we could ask for help from the Council of Worlds.'

'We can't,' snarled D'Jevier. 'Obviously.'

'Obviously.'

'With the Questioner coming, we have other things to worry about.'

'Obviously.'

So agreed, they stood where they were, watching until Bin's skinny form disappeared into the dark.

29

Calvy and his Friends

Calvy had ridden up the river with Bin, avoiding his carping by pretending to be asleep most of the way, and he left the boat at the Brewer's Bridge. He took the precaution of removing his cockade before leaving the boat, his veils were impeccably impenetrable, and thus he had no difficulty whatsoever achieving his goal without being recognized by anyone at all – a good thing, for Family Men of good repute did not visit Consort Houses.

Calvy did. He had visited House Genevois at intervals for some years, and in the doing he had made a good friend of Madame and a better friend of Simon, who had taught him a number of interesting and provocative tricks. His current business with House Genevois was the procurement of a birthday present for his wife, a matter that Simon and Madame could accomplish more deftly than Calvy himself, given all the import regulations that he, as a Man of Business, was forced to uphold. The Consort Houses were more devious. Consorts had to give gifts; women expected it; and the Consort Houses helped their graduates meet expectations.

The present was on Madame's desk, and after pouring them each a glass of a pleasant restorative, she laid the velvet box before him with a flourish, a necklace of gemstones and gold, the stones local, but cut and faceted off planet, the gold of a fine workmanship utterly impossible to achieve on Newholme. The necklace was not massive, and it was not gaudy, but every link of it spoke of quality and care.

'Your lady will simply love it,' said Simon.

'She'd better,' murmured Madame, thinking how nice it would be to have a man as much in love with one as Calvy was with Carezza. 'You've outdone yourself, g'Valdet.'

He smiled, stretching back on the sofa, letting Simon fill his glass. 'It's an odd old world we live in, Madame.'

'It is indeed. You're noting some particular oddity?'

'Though I cultivate a certain fatalism and eschew the fidgets my colleagues are displaying, I agree with them that the world seems increasingly unstable, in a geological sense.'

Madame frowned. 'The Hags are worried, but they don't let themselves show it, and therefore the people, who are also worried, don't show it either. What brings it to your mind today?'

'The Questioner is coming.'

Simon looked puzzled, but Madame nodded, lips thinned. 'Oh, is she, now.' With a side glance at Simon, she said, 'Haraldson's creature, Simon. You know.'

He did know. The Questioner was the monster under the bed, the bugaboo in the closet, the sound creeping up the midnight stairs. To anyone without a clear conscience, the Questioner was the ultimate terrifier. He nodded, sipping at the wine while Madame went on. 'You think she's coming because of this rumbling and rattling we've had to endure lately?'

'That, possibly. Though it could be another thing or two, or both.'

She asked, 'The other thing being?'

'The Questioner has on more than one occasion recommended severe action against the mankind population of worlds when that population had not governed in accordance with Haraldson's edicts.'

Madame sipped at her glass. 'As in the matter of our invisible people.'

'That is one such matter.'

'You know of another?'

'There's our odd imbalance of the sexes, Madame.'

She frowned. 'But we know why that is. There's a virus peculiar to this planet that attaches to the mother's X chromosome. When the cell doubles, at the polar body stage, the virus doesn't double, and it has a fifty-fifty chance of staying with the oocyte or being discarded with the polar body. It's more complex than that, but that's the pith. The Hags have been unable to find a cure, though they've searched diligently.'

He smiled, sipped, murmured, 'I merely have a feeling the Questioner may doubt that. Having read the Council of Worlds accounts of some of her investigations, she seems a doubting sort of device.'

'Where do you get Council of World's reports?' demanded Simon.

'They're public record. I subscribe to the journals that record them. The data cubes come in with our other supplies. Some of her visits are extremely interesting. There was one case I was very taken with. Beltran Four.'

'I don't know of it,' said Madame.

'A warlike planet, ruled by a polygynous warrior elite. Because of the constant battles, there are many fewer men than women. Our own situation, in reverse. This results in a large surplus of women, so the powerful men have huge harems of them.'

'Why did this interest you enormously?' asked Madame, with an expression of distaste.

'Because, essentially, the powerful men keep the battles going that result in the deaths of the young men that result in the surpluses of women they then take advantage of.'

'I agree it is unethical. And the Questioner dealt severely with mankind on that planet?'

'No.' Calvy smiled. 'That's what interested me enormously. She did not.'

Madame and Simon exchanged confused glances, at which Calvy smiled the wider. 'As I said. It's an odd little old world, but I didn't mean to discuss each and every little oddity in today's conversation. I did mean to thank you for your help with the necklace.'

'Always glad to help,' murmured Simon.

Calvy nodded. 'I did hope one of you would say that, for I have another problem. Carezza is pregnant. Tinsy, our chatron child tender, is up to his fat little armpits with the older children. I need another chatron. Unfortunately, a few of our friends have been sharing horror stories, and both Carezza and I want to be sure ...'

Madame nodded. 'You want a supernume of good repute. Someone trustworthy.'

Calvy said, 'Someone cut long enough ago that he's over the trauma, settled down, able to enjoy what's enjoyable without being angry at the world. The angry ones take it out on the children.'

Madame pursed her lips and Simon frowned.

'What?' Calvy asked.

Simon blurted, 'Of course they take it out on the children. What does anyone expect? Removing a man's sex organ doesn't increase his happiness, or his delight in other men's children!'

'Simon is right, Calvy,' said Madame. 'I think all this amputation business really goes too far. We're seeing more and more chatrons every year. The fact that many of them die makes them rare, their rarity makes them status symbols. Would you consider a supernume who has not been altered? Or even a retired Consort? If we pick carefully, I can guarantee you, he'll have a better temper and more considerate feelings. It's the maiming chatrons really hate, and their anger must manifest itself somehow.'

Calvy said plaintively, 'But Tinsy has been so good.'

Madame said, 'I located him for you, Calvy. He was cut when he was a baby, before he was conscious of there being anything there to lose. He already had a sweet disposition and was hardworking by nature, with a great desire to please. I don't know of any other like him, but I do know of at least two retired Consorts and one supernume who're very good with children. They genuinely like them, and they aren't bitter about life. The two Consorts simply like taking care of people, and the supernume is looking for a new place because his last charge is just entering school, and he's really not needed in the family anymore.'

'Was it a good family?' Calvy asked, significantly.

'It was a kind family for one so well-to-do,' said Simon, promptly. 'I know who she means, and he is a good lad. The mother doesn't spend all her time partying and being cultural, she stays in touch with the children and doesn't forget their names or their birthdays. The father is a good man, considerably overworked, what with business and caring for the children and overseeing the domestic arrangements, but then, which of you Men of Business isn't overworked, present company excepted.'

Madame said, 'I can understand your wife's concern, though being so concerned is unconventional. Carezza should be so involved with her Consort, she wouldn't be worried about the children.'

'But then, Calvy doesn't have a conventional family,' said Simon with a grin. 'He and Carezza seem to have something quite exceptional going on.'

'As my colleagues are constantly throwing into my face,' Calvy confessed. 'I sometimes find it hard to imagine how other men manage. They work all day, every day, they worry over their young children, trying to be sure the nursery tender does a good job and doesn't smack them about, they gamble with the investment made in the children, knowing there won't be enough girls born to keep all the boys in the family, so if they're at all soft-hearted, they try to make some kind of provision for the supernumes, and all this while their wives are going here and there, enjoying themselves.

'With Carezza and me, even with a good child tender, it's so much easier with both of us involved. I really feel for some of my colleagues. Those with six or eight offspring look quite worn out. I look ahead to the time that we finally build a reproductive center and have enough women that all men can live as Carezza and I do.'

Madame laughed, the laugh turning gleeful when she saw his offended expression. 'Oh, my dear Calvy, do you really think having more women available would make everyone live as you and Carezza do? Come now, dear, and you a bit of an historian?'

He flushed. He had been unbuttoned by the wine and said something stupid. She was right, of course. Having more women wouldn't assure that his colleagues lived as he and Carezza did.

'I'll interview your supernume,' he agreed. 'And I'll talk to Carezza about it. Perhaps you're right, Madame. You very frequently are.'

For a short time, too short a time, all three of them forgot the impending visitation.

30

Mistress Mantelby Investigates

It was almost eighteen years after her parents died that Marool Mantelby, riding in an open carriage in the Riverpark at Sendoph, saw a group of young men escorted by attendants from House Genevois. Marool knew of House Genevois though she had never obtained a Hunk from there. Madame never seemed to have one available. Still, Marool enjoyed looking at the strings of novices and graduates, shopping for companions for her later years. Though she had several companions currently being readied for destruction and no immediate need of additional personnel, in this particular group was a young man whose face, quite visible through its transparent veil, intrigued her. There was something about it that was evocative, and for a moment she thought perhaps he was a nephew, one of her sisters' children.

As though he felt her stare, he looked up, returning her measuring look with an almost sneering arrogance. He was large and well built and handsome. She liked the cock of his head, that nervy, totally disrespectful stance she found appealing. She went home thinking of him.

She thought of him often over the next few days, scouring recollection as she tried to think who he resembled, happening upon long-repressed memories of her parents, as the child Marool had understood them through fourteen years of covert, obsessive observation. One memory jostled another, which bumped another yet, and she began waking in the night, heart pounding, gasping for breath, pursued by nightmare terrors which, except for a horrific vision of her father's dead face, vanished before she was even awake. 'Marool,' he said. 'It wasn't an accident ...'

Finally, after waking three times in one night, she decided to put an end to it by finding out for herself how it was that her parents and sister had died. Everyone had said it was an accident. Her dream vision cast doubt upon that, ripping away almost two decades of complacency to reveal something horrid. If her family's deaths had been purposeful, she needed to know who had done it, and why.

The mountains of Newholme were not what one thought of as mountains in an Earthian sense: wrinkled, rocky land which, aside from being wrinkled and rocky, was not much unlike other land, that is, solid. The mountains of Newholme were not solid. Every prominence was drilled through with holes, bubbles, passageways, pits, and caverns. Every range was a speleological nightmare of twisting ducts, narrow channels, and precipitous galleries, most identifiable as volcanic in origin. No effort had been made to map the ramified and interpenetrating layers.

Only a few features of the wilderland attracted casual visitors: the Glittering Caves near Naibah; the Cavern of the Sea east of Nehbe; and the Combers, northwest of Sendoph, where an enormous set of lava tubes lay parallel, their southeastern sides eaten away by continual, grit-bearing winds to leave curling waves of rock, an eternal surf intent upon an unseen shore.

Water had penetrated into the Combers and eaten holes into the unseen tunnels below. Winds blew through the holes to make music that trembled up through the feet and could be sensed as a vibration in the bones of the leg or a shivering in the groin. Strange, pallid growths filled in the tunnels, expanding upward and sideways, some of them with tentacles and solar collector leaves and hollow stalks through which the fluids of the world could be seen pulsing.

On the surface, each comber was a linear world, uncrossable by anything without sticky feet to crawl on the underside of a vaulted overhang. If one climbed up the closed side, one could cross to the lip that curved to slick knife edges hanging twenty or thirty meters above the razor-edged fragments below. One could walk along the inside of a comber or clamber about in the soil-filled area between combers, and while doing so, one could fall through into any number of pits and deadfalls. For these and other reasons, people rarely found cause to go to the Combers.

Marool Mantelby's family had met their deaths among the Combers, and Marool decided to go see for herself. No matter what people said, Marool's parents would not have gone on a picnic, they would not have gone anywhere together without some strong and so far unfathomable motivation.

The Man of Business who had attended to the affair at the time accompanied her in the light carriage that jolted along a woodcutters' rutted road as it wound back and forth among the stinks and steams of hot springs toward the wilderland. In addition to the Man of Business, Marool had hired a bulky guard from the post in Sendoph, and a driver, a wiry individual who had agreed to use his carriage only after she signed a release that allowed him to unveil once they were in the hills.

'I don't drive on those roads 'less I can see,' he said, rather too truculently for Marool's taste. 'There's things in those hills, and I sure can't outrun 'em if I don't see 'em coming.'

'Things?' Marool inquired, in the voice she had been cultivating since leaving the Wasters, one that disguised her malice with a gloss of amiability. 'What things are those, driver?'

'Things,' he repeated, rather less belligerently, mistaking her nature as she had intended. 'People go missing with no sign how or where, so it has to be things. Stands to reason!'

'Ah,' she murmured. 'Well, then, I will give you permission to go unveiled. Once we are in the hills.'

The guard required no such variation from custom. Guards wore tinted visors that covered their faces, allowing them to see out but others not to see in, and this one perched beside the driver, head swiveling alertly from side to side while Marool, seated behind them, contented herself with a view of backs and heads between which scraps of scenery were sometimes discernible.

'I can see no reason whatsoever that my parents would have come here,' she muttered.

'Nor I,' replied Carpon, the Man of Business. 'Your father ordered a team hitched to a carriage, then he took it from the carriage yard himself, collected your mother and sister at the front steps and went off. The only servants who knew anything were the stableman and the cook, for your father had asked him to prepare a basket luncheon.'

'And who was it found them?'

'When they did not return by evening, their majordomo reported their absence to the guard post, and at first light dogs were fetched and the carriage was tracked – or more properly, perhaps, the horses were tracked – to the place they were found unharmed and still hitched. The luncheon, though much disarrayed by small creatures during the intervening hours, had obviously been laid nearby, some way back from the comber edge. I was with the group who found the bodies of your family members in a sink at the bottom. We recovered them for burial only with great difficulty.'

They continued on their way for some time while Marool digested this. 'The driver,' she murmured, 'mentioned *things*. Could they have been driven over the edge by *things*!'

Carpon shifted uncomfortably on the seat. 'One hears such stories, of course. One has never seen a *thing*, however, nor has one talked to anyone who has actually seen one. There are always subterranean noises in the mountains, and rumor makes more of them than is probably warranted.'

Marool was not inclined to believe in *things*, but as she and the Man of Business fell silent, they were uneasily aware that the only noises in these mountains were the ones made by themselves. Aside from the plopping hooves of the horse and the rattle of the wheels, the world was incredibly still. Even the steams that came from hidden vents to curtain the surrounding forest were silent.

'Just around the next bend,' said Carpon in too loud a voice.

They came around the bend into a clearing that spanned the tops of several of the great tubes running from southwest to northeast, the nearer ones to their left curling toward the southeast. To their right the tubes were buried, visible only at their centers as parallel trails of bare, wind-polished stone. Forest enclosed them on north and west. South, where the combers might otherwise have blocked their view of the valley, several of them had collapsed to leave receding jaws of jagged teeth framing a view of Sendoph, far below, like a square of patterned carpet: streets and buildings, plazas and parks, all hazed and faded by distance.

Marool climbed from the carriage, the Man of Business close behind her.

'Your father's carriage was tied there,' he said, gesturing toward a copse of lacy trees at the edge of the clearing. 'The trees were smaller then. Their luncheon was laid out there,' indicating a table-sized chunk of ancient, lichen-spotted lava standing some distance back from the edge with lower chunks around it that could serve as seats.

His voice was overly loud, Marool thought, and she raised a hand to her lips, shushing him and herself into the profound silence of the place. No bird song. No wind sound. No flutter of leaf. Only the breathing of the horses, the jingle and creak of their harness and the stamping of their restless feet.

She moved toward the edge of the comber. When the rock began to curve downward, she dropped to her knees to edge a bit farther. Before her, the stone was bare and wind-polished, curling into a razor edge above a litter of rock shards.

Marool crept backward, rising awkwardly beside the stone table. If Margon and Stella and Mayelan had been sitting here – which was in and of itself ridiculous – and if some creature had crept out of the dark woods that confronted her, might they have been frightened over the drop?

'Are there any people out here?' she asked Carpon.

'Wilderneers,' he said, in a tone that told her he smiled behind his veil.

'You think there are Wilderneers? Here or anywhere?' she demanded.

'Men disappear,' he replied. 'All the time. Supernumes, seamen, Consorts. Even sometimes a Family Man. These lands are wide, there are innumerable places to hide, so I suppose there could be Wilderneers.'

Marool was unimpressed by disappearances. She herself knew how a good many had disappeared, and it had nothing to do with Wilderneers.

'Wait here,' she told him, lifting a finger to summon the guard and moving off among the trees as he trotted to join her. Behind her the driver and the Man of Business exchanged looks, eloquent in the cock of head and shrug of shoulder, though the one's face was hidden. Together they sat down by the stone table to await her return.

Marool strolled in the profound shade of the trees, sniffing the air like a hound though she could smell nothing at all, staring at this thing and that though she had no idea what she was looking for, stopping short in the realization she was seeing something very strange.

On either side was a straight and rounded ridge of soil, the two ridges perhaps three meters apart, as though something huge and heavy had been dragged along here, pushing the dirt up at the sides. The ridges were overgrown with herbage and wild flowers, so whatever had made them hadn't been here lately. She moved to the ridge at her right and walked along it, kicking at it aimlessly, stopping when an object caught her eye, near her feet. It was a piece of something, like shell.

She bent over and picked it up, turned it in her fingers, a piece as large as her two hands set together, slightly oily, knife edged, oval in shape, smooth on one edge, rough on the other, like a gigantic fingernail jerked from some enormous finger. It had gooey stains along one edge.

She held it out to the guard, who started to take it, then gasped as though it had bitten him. The warmth of her hand had brought an odor from that dry substance, a rank and feculent stink that was suddenly all around them, floating on the wind, moving the leaves of the trees.

Marool noticed nothing.

'Throw it away,' he muttered. 'It stinks!'

She made a face at him, wrapped the thing in her scarf and put it in the reticule she carried at her belt, ignoring him as he turned aside, retching.

'You have a weak stomach for one in your occupation,' she said angrily, walking on only to encounter another track that had crossed the first one. On these ridges nothing grew. The soil was crumbly, newly thrust aside. Beside her, the guard stopped short, as though frozen in place.

'Qiuh?' asked the world. 'Chuh?'

It was a grunt, a growl, a chuffing interrogation, perhaps an expression of surprise, maybe of annoyance. It was loud enough to make the ground tremble, to shiver the leaves on the trees and to start little falls of dust from the sides of long buried rocks. It was echoed by a huffing shudder that repeated a guttural *uh, uh, uh, uh* as it faded toward the east. All this, Marool had time to notice before the sound, or another such sound came from another direction, a distance to the right, possibly ... very possibly behind her.

'More than one,' she said not quite aloud, turning to lead the way out of the woods, hurrying, just short of running. 'More than one.' Unless that last sound had been an echo. She did not think it had been an echo.

The guard followed silently, his head turning to look over one shoulder, then the other. He had not realized how far they had come among the trees. He had not realized what a time it would take them to get out again, to rejoin the others ...

Who were not there. The carriage was there, and the horses, seemingly frozen into immobility, eyes wide, whites showing, nostrils flared, skin shivering, but making not a sound. When Marool got herself sufficiently under control to issue a command, the guard reluctantly fetched a rope from the carriage, tied himself to the stone table and let himself far enough down to look over the edge while she scanned the forest, seeing nothing. Then the rope trembled, and she turned to find the guard scrambling away from the edge on hands and knees.

They were there, he said, his voice cracking. They were there, far below. He could barely see their bodies among the broken rock. Marool chose not to look for herself. If someone wanted to retrieve the driver and the Man of Business, they would have to come out from town to do so.

She turned to go back to the carriage, stumbling a little, out of either haste or terror, admitting with a hysterical little laugh of self-discovery that it could have been either, as she stooped across a sudden pang, breathing deeply, deciding not to swoon away, not here, not in the company of this anonymous and uncaring guard.

'Throw it away,' cried the guard.

'What?' she demanded.

'That thing you picked up. Can't you smell it?' he cried. 'Don't try to bring it with you. It will terrify the horses!'

'I need it,' she said. 'I need it for something.'

The horses seemed more stunned than nervous, so he did not argue. Within moments the carriage was headed back down the road. Once in movement, the horses could be kept in check only with difficulty, and their panic did not cease until they were almost at the Mantelby gates.

31

The Questioner Approaches

Somewhere between Newholme and whatever place it had been before, the Questioner's ship swam in wavering nacreous lights that alternately flared and ebbed as the ship slid toward the end of a wormhole connecting with several other such through a brief real-space nexus. Questioner, who had been brooding about Newholme, paying little attention to the journey, was alerted by a blare from the ship's annunciator, a Gablian voice: 'Hold fast, hold fast, hold fast, wormhole ending, wormhole ending, worm hole ending . . . now.'

The Questioner had anchored herself to a supporting member at the first sound. After a vertiginous moment during which everything outward and inward seemed to be in simultaneous though uncoordinated transit, everything quieted.

'Settle, settle, settle,' demanded the communicator, belatedly. 'Taking passengers.'

The Questioner did not settle. She went to the viewport and stared outward as the ship slowly turned. The new passengers were an anonymous pod of light moving away from a smaller ship. Their own ship turned slightly; there were scraping sounds, thuds and clatters; then a puff of vapor marked the disconnect. It had been done well, so undoubtedly the Gablian commander had been at the helm. The Gablians were the only personnel aboard who could be trusted to do anything right. Every mankind individual on board had been politically appointed, as part of her entourage, and none of them were qualified for anything.

The other ship grew larger as it moved toward and above them, off on some tangent of its own. Some time later, two voices were heard in the corridor, interrupted by a third at the door: the horn-headed Gablian purser, saying in his formal way: 'Great Discerner, may I present Honorable Ellin Voy, Honorable Gandro Bao.'

The Questioner turned toward the door, nodding slightly to acknowledge the deep bows of the two newcomers.

'Unimpeachable One,' murmured Gandro and Ellin in duet.

'Well come in, come in. Let me look at you.' She did look at them, from head to foot, each and both. They were dressed in simple tunics and soft shoes, he dark, she light. 'Dancers, are you?'

'Yes, Spotless One,' murmured Ellin.

'Though we are still having no idea what that has to do with anything,' commented Bao.

'All in good time,' said the Questioner. 'I set out the specifications myself, and I always have reasons for everything I specify. Also, you may drop that Spotless, Unimpeachable stuff. The Gablians allow no informality, but I find that even imaginative honorifics soon pall. If I am what those titles proclaim, it is purely good design.'

'We are wondering how to address you,' murmured Bao.

She shrugged. 'I am a Questioner. Or, as the Gablians call me, a Discerner. I am an examiner and judge. My official role is as ethics monitor of human worlds, but I was designed to be more than that. Haraldson the Beneficent framed the existence of humankind – which category includes some mankind – as arising from intelligence, civility, and the pursuit of justice. He wanted justice pursued with beauty and joy. I was created as a means toward this end. It is my task to find out how mankind can live most justly, most beautifully and joyfully, assuming intelligence is capable of such a discovery. What you call me is irrelevant, but I do hope you enjoy cards.'

'We are being very good at cards, both!'

Questioner nodded. 'Your ability with cards is one reason I picked the two of you from a lengthy list.'

'Hold fast, hold fast, hold fast,' blared the ship. 'Entering wormhole, entering wormhole, entering wormhole, now ...'

Gandro picked Ellin up from the floor.

'Sorry,' Ellin muttered. 'I'm not used to that, yet.' She took a deep breath. 'Questioner, Ma'am, before we forget. We have a package for you.'

Gandro Bao nodded, burrowed into his pack, and came up with a small packet which he passed to Questioner with a humble bow.

Ellin said, 'It's from a Flagian trader, Ma'am. He left the ship the last stop back, but he said to tell you it contains the information in which you expressed an interest.'

Wordless with surprise, Questioner took the packet and turned it over in her hands. It wasn't large. From the size and shape, she judged it was a data cube, one capable of some experiential recording. Well. This could be enlightening.

She put the packet in one of her capacious storage pockets while giving them both a long looking-over.

'Let us see if you can be more amusing than the rest of my so-called staff.'

She moved from the bench to a large, padded chair that had obviously been made to fit, pressed a button on its arm, and waited while a table emerged from the floor and rose into position before her. She gestured at them to bring chairs, while she herself took a deck of cards from a compartment in the table and began shuffling it with lightning-like speed.

'Are you always able to solve problems?' Ellin asked.

'Sometimes I solve them,' said Questioner, 'even when I don't.'

'This is being conundrum,' murmured Bao.

'Not really. In all humility, I assert that great peace of mind has been brought to the settled worlds by the mere fact of my existence! Divisive matters, the discussion of which had previously led to widespread civil disorder, are now referred to me for decision, and my decision is often so long postponed that people become accustomed to the status quo.'

'You delay on purpose?' asked Ellin.

'I do.' She nodded. 'On matters which have no solution, I offer no solution, though I always claim to be on the verge of one whenever the matter comes up. Though Haraldson did not foresee that his Questioner would serve the function of conflict damper, perhaps it is as well that I do. Trouble is forestalled when both law and custom are required to await my decisions.'

She stared pensively at the two newcomers. 'Do sit down. I'll deal. I picked up these cards on Fanancy. They are in all respects similar to Old Earthian, Western-style decks, except for the names and colors of the suits. Here the four suits are labor, management, love, and death, signified by the shovel, the club, the heart, and the coffin, the colors silver, black, red, and brown.' She dealt rapidly, four hands, the fourth to an empty chair.

Ellin picked up her hand. She seemed to have an ace of labor and an ace of management, together with three face cards in love and death, and an assortment of minor management cards. 'What game are we playing?' she asked.

'Three-handed Whustee,' said Questioner. 'I bid one shovel.' Then, without waiting to hear their bids, she continued on the prior topic. 'I sometimes grow weary of delay, however, and at such times I am tempted to rule arbitrarily, as God is said to do, to put an end to matters.'

'It is possible, tempting you?' asked Bao, his jaw dropped. Catching her peremptory gaze he murmured, 'Two ... ah, coffins.'

'It is not possible to tempt me,' said Questioner. 'It is possible only for me to imagine the consequences of temptation.'

'Pass,' said Ellin.

'How long have you been the Questioner?' Bao asked.

'I bid three shovels.' She folded her hand and tapped it significantly on the tabletop. 'We are the second assembly to hold the office. Two hundred sixty years ago, Questioner I was melted down in the cataclysm known as the Flagian Miscalculation, somewhere out near the Bonfires of Hell. The Flagians' attempt to prove that matter was illusory succeeded only in redistributing that matter rather widely. We, Questioner II, took the place of our vaporized predecessor. Together, we have been questioning for over seven hundred standard years. We have learned a great deal about health and contentment, prosperity and pleasure, and we have found no reason to change Haraldson's edicts defining opinion and providing for justice, though there are races that think differently.'

'Pass,' murmured Bao, into the momentary silence.

'Are there really?' cried Ellin, eyes wide. 'Pass.'

Questioner chuckled, a mechanical sound. 'My hand to play, I think. Turn up the other hand, please, it gets to be the macarthy. Fah. I hoped it would have the ace.

'To answer your question, yes. A century or so ago we encountered the Borash, no two of whom agree on anything, but who tell us it is their destiny to rule all other races. Luckily, they lack either the weapons or the will to enforce their doctrine. Before that it was the Korm, a hive race of absolutely uniform opinion. Only their worker class "think," and they can only think one thing at a time. The Korm believe they have been created to travel to another galaxy with a great message. They devote all their resources toward that eventuality, and they don't even talk to us unless we have something their engineers say they need for the ships they have been building for the last four millennia. The ships have yet to be tested, and the great message, so I understand, is still to be determined by the committee that has been working on it for several thousand years.'

She paused for a moment, scanning their play thus far.

'... three, four, and five are mine. Now I will regret that ace!' She smiled. 'Then, of course, there are the Quaggi.'

Bao frowned in concentration. 'May I be asking what is Quaggi?'

'The Quaggi are an interstellar race of beings who, I infer, need the radiation in the vicinity of a star in order to reproduce. As a matter of fact, we may get to see the remains of one on this trip.'

'Remains?' faltered Ellin.

'Of a Quaggida, or Quaggima. I think this one was killed during mating. Or perhaps only injured so badly that she died. Whichever, she should be lying on a moonlet of the outmost planet of the system we're about to visit. There's no atmosphere, and if it hasn't been blown apart by meteorites, it should still be there.'

'I don't think I've even heard of Quaggi,' said Ellin.

'I have heard it suggested that the Quaggi, a star-roving race, have succeeded in reinventing Euclidean geometry, and, since they have no actual experience of plane surfaces, consider it an arcane lore fraught with metaphysical significance.'

'But,' murmured Ellin, 'you're not suggesting we should change our ways to emulate any of those races, are you?' She placed her ace of management on the Questioner's CEO, took the trick and led with the queen of labor.

'Clever girl. You had the ace all along. No, we should not emulate other people. We probably couldn't emulate the Korm. Any mankind person worth his salt can simultaneously incubate whole clutches of ideas that are either contradictory or mutually exclusive. For instance, mankind has persuaded itself that its race is perfectible, though it hasn't changed physically, mentally, or psychologically since the Cro-Magnon. Mankind has also persuaded itself that each individual is unique, though each person shares ninety-nine and ninety-nine one hundredths of his DNA and roughly the same percentage of his ideas with thousands or even millions of other persons.'

Bao, with a sidelong glance at Ellin, said with an ironic grin, 'It is being true that persons want very much to be singular and individual.'

Ellen made a face at him. 'I have complained about being a clone, that's all.' She took the next trick, leading with the jack of labor, a union organizer.

The Questioner nodded ponderously. 'Individuality is more imagined than real. Persons are more alike than they care to admit. On Newholme, however, their social structure is based upon the theory that each family line is unique.'

'Is that what we'll ask about on Newholme?' asked Ellin. 'Individuality?'

The last few cards clicked down, with Ellin the undisputed winner of the hand.

'Among other things.' The Questioner rocked slowly in her chair, considering. 'Very nicely played, my dear. You deal the next hand.'

Bao took a deep breath, shaking his head. 'The briefing documents are also mentioning an indigenous race. Precolonization reports are saying no indigenes. This is most confusing.'

Questioner smiled grimly, with determination. 'Confusing, yes. The entire surface of that planet had supposedly been examined up and down and sideways before any settlement was allowed. If there are now indigenes, someone falsified a report, or failed to file one, or the confusion is intentional, designed to mislead me. I always find the truth, however, no matter how many red herrings colonists drag across my path.'

She picked up her hand and smiled a tigerish smile. 'It is likely there have been grave infractions of the edicts on Newholme. Every few years I do find a planet that must be punished for its infractions, with all its people.'

'Would you really punish a whole world?' Bao asked with some trepidation.

'If it were indicated. It is too early to know what is indicated. We are going to Newholme to see what is true and what is false, and in either case, what can be done about it.'

'I've read every document, but I don't understand what any of them have to do with us,' murmured Ellin as she picked up her own cards. 'Why did you ask for dancers?'

The Questioner nodded. 'It wouldn't be in the documents because it was an informal report, but one of my spies has mentioned that the indigenes are dancers.'

Ellin drew in a deep breath. 'So?'

The Questioner said sagaciously, 'Trust is strengthened by similarity of interest, either apparent or real. If they are dancers, they may talk to other dancers. If they dance for you, you will dance for them ...'

Ellin frowned, unconvinced. 'If nobody knows anything about this indigenous race, how does anyone know that they dance?'

The Questioner shrugged, an unandroidish movement. 'How did my spy find out? He probably sat in a tavern, listening to drunken conversation and putting two and two together. Or he bribed someone. Or, he planted a few mobile sensors. I didn't ask how, specifically. I do know he is a reliable source.'

They played out the game, which Questioner won, putting her in a good humor, after which Bao and Ellin were shown to their own quarters, where they huddled together in their salon, whispering.

'You were dealing her a very good hand,' said Bao.

'I was dealing her from the bottom of the deck,' mimicked Ellin, with a smirk. 'I learned cheating from one of the actors. What do you think of her or it?'

'She is being obdurate, I think. Very severe. And while you are being so free with the cards, she was winning from me five credits.'

'Poor thing. I'll owe it to you.' She paused, looking at him thoughtfully. 'Gandro Bao, will *we* have to do something dreadful? Like recommend the wiping out of all the mankind on the world?'

Gandro Bao shook his head, though he was no less troubled than she. 'We are not recommending, Ellin. She is doing that. All we are doing is finding things out.'

They stayed together a while longer, taking reassurance from one another's company, before seeking the equal comfort of real beds after shower baths in real water. Though the Questioner needed neither, she made sure that her assistants were well looked after.

She, in the meantime, had been left to her own devices. She frequently remarked as much to her attendants, intrigued by the phrase, for it was literally true. Her memory, her maintenance machines, her elaborately miniaturized equipment, her IDIOT SAVANT, the syncretic scanner she used in her attempt to find patterns where none were apparent, all were her own devices with whom she was frequently left.

Just now, she needed her maintenance machines. She always put off maintenance until the need for it became what she thought of as painful. Though she was not designed to feel pain, the intense unease occasioned by delay in response, by inability to remember immediately, by mechanical parts that did not function precisely or systems that did not mesh, must, she felt, come close to what mankind meant by pain. It could be avoided by getting maintenance more frequently, and she could never remember between maintenance sessions why she did not do so. Nonetheless, she always put it off, without knowing why.

This time, she took with her into the booth the data cube that the trader had sent. She inserted it into the feed mechanism, and directed that during maintenance it should be entered into permanent memory. Then everything went gray, as it always did during maintenance. Time stopped. All thought stopped as well. Only after her linkages had been disconnected, only after her memory as Questioner was off line, was the cause of her discomfort made manifest. Then, and for a brief time afterward, her mankind brains, those three with which she had been endowed, remembered who they were. Mathilla remembered, and M'Tafa, and Tiu. During that time, the separate entity that was the Questioner knew why she judged some societies as she did, and why she felt about them as she did, and how deep her prejudices went, even though they never showed.

When her usual maintenance was complete, after the linkages were reestablished and the memory hooked up with all its shining achievements on display, Questioner did not move, did not utter, did not recollect, for she was still holding fast to Mathilla and M'Tafa and Tiu, unwilling to let them go and they, within her, were holding fast to life once more, unwilling to be gone. Then, usually, the booth door opened automatically, and the stimulant shock was provided, and she wakened, as one wakens terrified from dream, only to feel the terror fade, and shred, and become as gauze, as a thing forgotten, as it always had before.

Not this time. This time she found the memory remained with her, firmly planted inside her files, their names and faces, the stories of their short lives, and how they had died.

Mathilla. M'Tafa. And Tiu.

32

Ornery Bastable Goes Upriver

Ornery Bastable arrived in Gilesmarsh when the *Waygood* came in to unload a cargo of gold-ash and dried Purse fish. Since it would be some time before the *Waygood* had discharged its cargo and been loaded once more, Ornery had a whole tenday to herself.

She intended to spend part of it in Sendoph, where Pearla had recently achieved statistical normalcy by bearing a living daughter after a run of one stillborn daughter and two sons. First, however, she intended to spend a day or two in the Septo-pod's Eye in Naibah, seeing what she could find out about the thing she had seen, or almost seen, when she had been marooned in the wild. Though she was not imaginative enough to have frightened herself into a funk over the experience, she had resolved to ask some questions next time she had time in port, and now seemed as good a time as any.

She had just received her pay, and she spent a good bit of it buying drinks for those who had stories to tell. When she had listened for several evenings, she had accounts of the setting of stone pillars and questioning sounds and shadows moving, all of them making a reasonably consistent catalogue. One talkative old type, who had at one time kept the library at the Fortress of Vanished Men, said the records described creatures seen in the wild by the second settlers, quite monstrous things that seemed to have disappeared for no one had seen them for several hundred years.

As for stone pillars, they had been often seen on beaches and plateaus, always in groups of three or more, always in the clear where the shadow pattern could be seen under sun or moon, the nighttime patterns depending upon which moons were where. The pillars sometimes appeared at dawn in places where they had not been at dusk, and therefore were assumed to have been set up by creatures, people, things, or beings who worked at night and intended to remain unseen. Two informants had used the word 'Joggiwagga,' and Ornery recognized the word from her infancy.

Joggiwagga, whatever they were, were busier at certain lunar configurations than others, and these were also the times when the loud questioning or challenging sounds were most likely to be heard. Because she was a sailor, Ornery recognized the times as coincident with exceptionally high or low tides. Six sizable moons, leaving aside the two orbiting rocks, could produce quite a complicated schedule of tides. A two big-moon neap, full or dark, was low, but a three big-moon neap was lower, and an all-moon low sucked the water out of the bays to leave mud flats extending to the horizon. A rare five dark-moon high, on the other hand, would bring water over the piers in Gilesmarsh, high up the levees of Naibah, and send the River Giles over its banks all the way to Sendoph.

Six big-moon highs came about every seven or eight centuries. Though the more extreme lunar configurations were rare, they were the ones during which stones were set.

Once Ornery had satisfied herself that she wasn't crazy, that she could assume the things or beings or creatures were real, she put her notebook in her pocket, finished her ale, bade her friends and associates farewell for the nonce, and went out to confirm arrangements for the trip to Sendoph. There was a steam-powered mail launch headed upstream within the hour, and it was owned by Ornery's brother-in-law. By the gift of a bottle and a little banter with the captain, Ornery had earned an invitation to ride to Sendoph in style. Travel by engine was still rare and might get rarer, considering the firemountain had buried most of the mines and about half the railroad. There was still more reliance on horses than on horsepower, and riding in a launch was, therefore, a treat.

Ornery regarded it as such, sitting at her ease on the rear deck, watching the paddles of the stern wheel fall toward her as the reed bed and marshes and watermills went by. Low in the eastern sky the misty bulk of the scarp seemed to float upon the lower clouds as it blew ominous bars of smoke across the higher ones. Ornery turned her back to it, not wanting to be reminded of the tremors that were coming closer and closer together. People were beginning to get really jumpy about it and would have been more so if they could have seen the damage. Though there had been a good many more disasters like the one that took Ornery's family, all the destruction thus far was behind and among the Ratbacks, invisible from the cities. Most everyone in the more populated areas believed or wanted to believe that they were not in danger.

Ornery thought everyone was in danger, whether they believed it or not. Anyone could see that the summit was blacker than it had been, meaning either that ashes were falling atop the snows, or the snows had melted, revealing the dark rock below.

'There's been shakings and shiverings for a time now. She's goin' to blow,' said the captain, around the splinter of chaff he was chewing. 'Been a long while accordin' to the wise folk. I say it doesn't matter how long, it's still alive and it'll blow again.' He laughed a phlegmy laugh, hawked and spat over the side. 'Warm up all them Haggers in Sendoph, won't it?'

His tone angered Ornery, but she kept a neutral tone as she said, 'You're cheerful about it, considering you may be there when it goes.'

'If I am, I'll be in company, and if I'm not, I'll rejoice. Whatever the inscrutable Hagions provide.'

Ornery made a noncommittal noise. If the scarp decided to blow, it really wouldn't matter what had been said about it either way. Either it would reach all the way to the Giles or it wouldn't. She turned the conversation in another direction, and the hours went by more comfortably until, along about evening, they were in sight of the city, the domes of the Temple district shining in the rose-amber light.

'Where do you tie up?' Ornery wanted to know.

'We'll stop at the post pier to pick up and drop off mail and valuables. Then we'll go on up to the old wharf just the other side of Brewer's Bridge, and we'll tie there for tonight. I've half the forward hold full of stuff for House Genevois, and the other half grain for the brewers. We'll unload in the morning, then go farther upstream to the market district to pick up special orders for Naibah. Will you leave us tonight or tomorrow?'

Ornery thought about it. Her sister lived not far from the Temple district, which was just a few blocks west of the river, but it was late to drop in on her. 'I'll help you unload and sleep aboard, if you've no objection, Captain, then I'll go on to my sister's place in the morning.'

So it was agreed between men. The boat thrust itself upstream past a tanner's yard and a printing house – both identifiable by the smell – then for a brief stop at the post wharf. Then onward once more, past a lumber yard and a dyers yard and a clutter of old houses, then past a tall wall with two odd little towers at its corners and the remains of a rotted wharf at its center, and finally beneath the high central arch of Brewers Bridge to the pier beyond, where, with much shouting and maneuvering, the captain, Ornery, the deckhand and the stoker brought themselves tight against the timber pier built out from the edge of the stony trough in which the river ran.

It seemed too quiet. Ornery stared all around, finding no reason for the silence, which was soon broken in any case, when people came with carts from House Genevois and from the breweries. They unloaded by torchlight, the carts departed, and the strange silence returned. Later that night, as Ornery spread her blankets on the deck she heard a scurrying, like small animals moving, and she looked up to see a skulk of shadows vanishing along the river path in a lengthy stream, like a migration. It was too dark to see who they were, though Ornery thought them too small for mankind, and they had been in a most dreadful hurry. She resolved to tell someone about it tomorrow, perhaps, if it seemed important.

33

Marool Mantelby and the Hags

That same evening, which was a few days after Marool Mantelby returned from her trip into the mountains, Marool made a visit to the Temple of the Hagions, most particularly the office of the High Crones, where she was assured a polite welcome by virtue of her frequent and generous gifts to the Temple. She met with women who knew her better, perhaps, than she supposed: D'Jevier and Onsofruct Passenger, who remembered the fourteen-year-old Marool well, though Marool had been too preoccupied at that time to remember anyone.

'Revered Hags,' Marool announced as she entered the throne room cum office. 'Thank you for seeing me.'

D'Jevier and Onsofruct had changed little in the almost twenty years since Marool had come to the Temple to find the Hagion Morrigan. The two Hags had never mentioned that incident to anyone except one another, preferring to forget it as nearly as possible. Over the years, both had cultivated the impersonal manner and voice suitable for use in Temple when emotion was inappropriate, and it was this voice D'Jevier used to greet Marool.

'You are welcome, Marool. Is there something needful?'

Marool shook her head as she took the seat she was offered, then sat there with her lips pursed out in uncharacteristic uncertainty. Her hostesses did not encourage her, but merely waited, as though she could tell them nothing that would surprise them.

'I have been into the hills,' said Marool, at last. 'I went to look at the place where my parents and sister died.'

'Ah,' murmured Onsofruct. 'You had a natural curiosity.'

Marool shook her head with an annoyed expression. 'It wasn't that! It's as though something about their deaths has been nagging at me for years. I wanted to see for myself. However ...' She went on to describe her own experience, and that of her driver and Man of Business. 'I suppose their bodies are there still,' she concluded. 'The guard reported what happened to the guard post, but I've heard nothing more about it.'

D'Jevier cast a glance at her cousin, which Onsofruct returned, furrowing her brow and clenching her jaw before replying, 'We have all heard stories of Wilderneers and monsters. Such are common tellings during the Long Nights.'

'You mentioned picking up something, some artifact?' D'Jevier queried.

'I have it here,' said Marool, taking a packet from her bag, laying it upon the table and unrolling it. As she did so, a stench spread throughout the room, and both the Hags caught their breaths.

'You smell it?' demanded Marool, looking at their faces.

Both nodded. D'Jevier held her breath and took the article into her hands, keeping a layer of the wrapping between it and her skin.

'It looks more organic than manufactured,' said Marool. 'Like a giant fingernail. That shape, at any rate, though far too huge. The bottom is ragged, as though it had been ripped away ...'

D'Jevier rewrapped the article, obviously troubled. 'It's a scale,' she said. 'From some sort of squamous creature.'

'It would have to be enormous!' said Onsofruct, her eyes wide.

D'Jevier grated, 'I have no doubt it is. We are only now growing numerous enough that we can explore the wilderness in any systematic way, and as we do so, we hear more frequent tales about things or beings in the badlands. Did you see any kind of trail while you were there? As though something very large had been dragged along, pushing up the dirt at the sides?'

Marool nodded, though unwillingly, for she had thought to do all the enlightening herself. 'I did, yes. Both an old trail and a newer one. So new that nothing was growing on it.'

D'Jevier went on, 'We have had reports of such in the hills to the west. As though a very large serpent had crawled there, though the paths are straight or angular, not sinuous. The witnesses are sober persons whose word I am inclined to accept, and there have been too many disappearances of livestock for peace of mind.'

'Then you have already planned a course of action,' said Marool.

The thin woman shook her head, her lips twisted into an unpleasant knot, as though she tasted something foul that she could not spit out. 'Yes, and no. Reason would dictate that we enquire among the Timmys, who presumably once occupied that wilderness, whose relatives may do so still, and would therefore know what creatures are there. At this juncture, however, we cannot do so.'

Marool felt a strange frisson at this mention of the invisible people, a surprise reaction, though she knew that no subject was forbidden to the Hags when in Temple, albeit only there.

Onsofruct murmured, 'We have been advised the Questioner is on her way. This is not a time we would have picked for the Council's Hound to come sniffing among us, but the Hound does not sniff at our convenience.'

Marool furrowed her forehead, trying to remember what she had learned about the Questioner. 'The visit constrains us?'

Onsofruct snorted, 'Rather more than merely constrains.'

'What more?'

D'Jevier's lips curved into a wry smile. 'There were no Timmys here when we came, Marool. We forget this from time to time, but it is true. There were not on the surface of this planet any race of intelligent beings nor was there any mention of such in the records of the first settlement. The plane-tary assessment was rigorous before we came, searching for those monsters reputed to have wiped out the first colony. If Timmys had been here, the assessment would have picked them up, anywhere upon the surface of this planet.

'They weren't here. Had they been here, we would not have been allowed to settle. Some years later, suddenly here they were. By that time, we had so much invested in this world that we chose to pretend we hadn't seen them, difficult as that was, for the creatures were pertinacious. Though it may have been a stupid decision – indeed, in hindsight, was a stupid decision – we, the Hags, decided not to report their existence to the Council of Worlds, as that would have led to our immediate evacuation from Newholme.'

Marool frowned at the implications of this. Had she known about this matter? Had she ever considered this?

D'Jevier went on: 'Years went by, and we still didn't report it. The Timmys grew more numerous. At the same time, because of the ... ah... unexpected sexual imbalance on this world, our population was growing far too slowly to do all the things our settlement plans had set forth. Suddenly, there were the Timmys, doing this little job and that little job, almost as though they had read our minds. One had only to utter and the task was done. Before we quite knew how it happened, the Timmys had become the better part of our workforce.'

Onsofruct snorted. 'And our foremothers didn't report that, either! Even a generation later we could have reported. Needless to say, we didn't. We have committed a very grave offense in not reporting the existence of an intelligent and speaking race. This will not be to our credit.'

D'Jevier nodded agreement. 'The Questioner, who takes the matter of indigenous races very seriously, will not excuse these omissions if it finds out about the Timmys.'

Marool shifted on her chair, frowning. 'But why does the Questioner's visit prohibit our asking the Timmys now about the wilderness?'

'We cannot take time to pursue the linguistic matter, since the Timmys are even now being banished.'

'Banished?' Marool was dumbfounded. 'What do you mean, banished?'

'Sent away, into the mountains. The Questioner and her people aren't blind! The Timmys must not be visible when the Questioner arrives.'

'But they do half the work in the city! On the farms! Everywhere!'

'Obviously they do,' D'Jevier replied. 'But someone else will have to do that half! We've decided to make up the lack through press gangs. There are a good many supernumeraries who are underemployed, if they are employed at all. And then, the Consort Houses are full of young men who can be used, at least temporarily.'

Onsofruct asked in a suspiciously casual voice, 'Do you use Timmys on your estate, Marool?'

'I do,' she said, rather angrily. 'Though not in the house. There I prefer human servants, but I let the steward use them in the gardens, the fields, and in the stables.'

The two Hags bowed and glanced at one another again, each thinking that few persons had the unlimited wealth of a Mantelby with which to hire human servants. Or the unlimited number of nephews needing work.

'Then except for the stables and gardens, your mansion is staffed and run entirely by humans?' murmured D'Jevier.

'It is.'

Again that glance. D'Jevier nodded, saying, 'Marool, would you consider letting us house the Questioner with you?'

Marool swallowed a snort and tried to formulate a polite mode of refusal, then bethought herself that it might be best not to refuse. Not yet, at any rate. 'Why with me?'

D'Jevier rose and went to sit beside Marool, regarding her intently. 'What do you know of the Questioner?'

'What anyone knows. There's something about her in the *Book of Worlds*, the one we all learn to read from as children. I don't think I've even heard the name of the Questioner used in a dozen years. Her creation always seemed to me to be a fool idea.'

Onsofruct said in a conciliatory tone, 'Perhaps, but an idea with an ancient history, nonetheless. Mankind has long been interested in assuring ethical treatment of other races.'

'History is all well and good.' Marool snorted. 'Ethical treatment is no doubt something we all wish to achieve. But if the Timmys have come here since we came, surely the Questioner would not insist on our leaving this world.'

D'Jevier crossed to the window and stared outward. 'That's the enigma, Marool. They weren't here when we came, but they didn't come after we came. They couldn't have. Council of Worlds traffic monitors hang in orbit around all occupied worlds from the moment of first settlement, recording every arrival and departure. Nothing has landed on this planet since we came except the supply and trade ships we all know about. By dint of much effort, we keep Timmys away from the port. The staff there is made up of both Hags and Men of Business, and we can say unequivocally the Timmys did not arrive here; they were already here even though no one knew it.'

'Now seems late to worry over it,' grumbled Marool.

Onsofruct said, 'We thought we'd done our worrying long since, when we first adopted our conventions vis-á-vis the Timmys: not speaking to them, not looking at them. We worried about it by shutting them away in particular places where they could not be seen. They have become to us, in accordance with custom, invisible. We could argue that they do not exist, to us.'

D'Jevier nodded. 'Now, however, the Questioner comes. Do we confess to generations, centuries, of untruth? Do we pretend to her that these creatures are indeed invisible? She is unlikely to agree. Do not suggest that we pack up our families and our baggage and leave the planet, for unfortunately, that is no longer an option. There are certain limits on the evacuation of planetary populations, and we are now too numerous for that choice. A century ago we could have departed, perhaps, but not now. Do we volunteer to restrict ourselves to a small part of Newholme and eschew any contact with the Timmys? A similar offer was made by mankind on Bayor's world when they discovered a native population living on a single island where they had been for millennia. The Questioner said it wasn't good enough and acted against the entire mankind population. That was only fifteen years ago, and I remember vividly the consequences of that decision.'

Marool was astonished. 'I had not heard of this!'

'Few of us here on Newholme read the reports of the COW, a few of us Hags, a librarian or two, a few Men of Business. The Men of Business have some understanding of the situation, for they invited us to house the Questioner at the Fortress of Vanished Men, obviously because it has no Timmy staff. As though that would be enough! The Questioner isn't blind, or deaf. Even though Timmys don't exist in the fortress – or at your mansion, Marool – she would not be fooled by that alone. No. Total banishment is necessary. The Questioner must neither hear nor see a single Timmy while she – *it* is here.'

A long silence, during which Marool ground her teeth, finally erupting with: 'How are you going to make them go?'

'They hear us. They understand us. We've said enough that they know what the stake is. Either they disappear, or we may all die.'

Marool snorted. 'You're assuming that all this circumspection will be easier to manage if I invite the Questioner to Mantelby House?'

'It is more hope than assumption,' Onsofruct murmured. "Once the Timmys have been sent away, if they will understand enough to go away, there'll be a period of adjustment in human behavior. New habits, however, take time to form and old ones are hard to break. Presumably your house servants do not have the habit of addressing thin air with orders for the nearest Timmy to wash the dishes or milk the cows.'

Marool mused, stroking her massive jaw. 'True, which makes it all well and good inside my walls, but the Questioner won't sit still, will she? We can't depend on her squatting at my place all day and all night while she's here.'

'This may be true. The plan is not foolproof, but we have no alternative to suggest. We do know the Questioner has various aides, assistants, deputies, and functionaries, and we can make it a point to accompany these ancillaries during their investigations, interpreting what they may or may not see or hear.'

Marool moved restlessly to the small barred window that looked out over the avenue, the wide steps, the parade of women climbing toward and descending from the Temple. 'I will have to get rid of my Timmy gardeners and stable workers.'

'Yes,' D'Jevier murmured.

'When does the banishment take place?'

'We started earlier this evening, delivering the edict to all homes and businesses.'

'The planetary economy will probably collapse,' said Marool, thinking of the many Men of Business who handled Mantelby affairs and all their investments and projects.

'Well, of course, if we would prefer extinction ...' Onsofruct's voice was not at all sarcastic, though her eyebrows slanted sardonically.

Marool shook her head doubtfully. 'I don't see how the Questioner could insist on our extinction. How would it enforce a dictum like that?'

D'Jevier said wearily, 'The biological sciences are far advanced on many worlds, Marool. The Questioner need only explode a small canister in our upper atmosphere, as was done on Bayor's world ...'

Marool retreated into sulky silence. 'I suppose I can survive without Timmys. If the visit isn't long. But having guests ... it would be an inconvenience.'

To break a weighty silence, Onsofruct murmured, 'Let me take a few moments to discuss the matter with my colleague.'

Taking D'Jevier by the arm, she led her out into the hall.

'I hate that woman,' said D'Jevier. 'There is a horridness about her.'

'You are remembering the time she came here ...'

'I am remembering that, yes. And there have been rumors. Disappearances. Things her servants tell, when they come down into town. Things her neighbors say they've heard. Things that might have been foretold, keeping Morrigan in mind.'

'And you hate her,' Onsofruct mused.

'I loathe her. I think all the stories are true.'

'Then you don't want to authorize her to house the Questioner.'

D'Jevier snorted. 'I loathe her, but I loathe equally what the Questioner may do to us! I've racked my brain trying to come up with a place to put this Questioner creature where there are or have been no Timmys. In this one case, Marool's desires parallel our own. She's bright, she's ruthless, and she's likely to be as helpful as possible. Have you some better idea?'

'None,' said Onsofruct.

'Then let us pay the piper, as we must.'

They returned to the office, and Onsofruct said, 'We could possibly grant you some consideration, Marool, to make the inconvenience worth your while.'

'Well worth my while?' She lifted the corners of her mouth into a harpy's smile.

D'Jevier wet her mouth, which was inexplicably dry. 'And what offer would do that?'

'You mentioned press gangs. From among the supernumeraries, and the Consort Houses ...'

Onsofruct, reading the distress on her companion's face, said in an unperturbed voice, 'You would be entitled to replace your Timmys, of course. Once you have announced the edict of banishment to your stable and garden workers.'

'Tomorrow?'

'If you like.'

'How do I go about it?'

The two Hags exchanged quick glances once more. Marool was a good deal more eager than they thought appropriate.

'Ah,' mused Onsofruct, 'you can come down into the city with a few of the Haggers you have been kind enough to support and select a few supernumeraries from the streets. Take note of their identity, place of residence, and mode of living. Be prepared to bring that information here for registration.'

'I was thinking more of ... you said the Consort Houses!'

'Ah, well. Yes. You could obtain two or three workers from the Consort Houses if you like.'

'Am I to buy expensive Consorts to clean my stables?'

D'Jevier drew herself up, her voice cold. 'No. Certainly not. But you *will* give the House owner a signed receipt, guaranteeing the return of her students when the current emergency is over. The supernumes would also have to be returned.'

'House Genevois,' purred Marool. 'I've had my eyes on ...'

D'Jevier cried, 'Mistress Mantelby, please. The young men are to be gardeners and stable hands. Need we make the point they are to be only that?'

Onsofruct put her hand on D'Jevier's shoulder, calming her. 'My colleague is correct. You are not to use them as Consorts, and for the duration of the Questioner's visit, it would be better not to allude to the existence of such, for we do not know what the Questioner would think of such a profession.'

Marool's eyes narrowed. She was not accustomed to taking orders from anyone. Still, in grievous times, one could bear grievous pains, as the book of precepts had it, though one would remember the pains later, and who inflicted them.

'I will settle for a few from the street.' She smiled charmingly. 'And a few more from one of the Hunk Houses.'

She took her leave from them, humming under her breath as she made her way from the Temple. Behind her, she left two troubled Hags.

'We may live to regret this,' said D'Jevier.

'If we live at all,' said Onsofruct. 'Which is really the issue.'

The order of banishment was carried by swift couriers to all mankind towns and villages, and from thence was spread by riders and rumor into the rural lands. **The Questioner is coming. The Questioner is coming. All those invisible somethings that do not actually exist must go away into the wilds. Consult with local Haggers to obtain pressed men to do necessary labor.**

Though the words of the edict were trumpeted in some places, in most they spread silently, like a fog, a fog that seemed both to spur the Timmy's going and to hide the fact of it. After the first hour or so, those attempting to spread the edict to the Timmys themselves were amazed to find no Timmys to spread it to. As one observer put it, the invisibles had 'faded into the walls.' That was exactly where many of them were. No matter where Timmys labored for the humans, they were never more than a few steps from an entry to their own world, that subsurface milieu which spongified the planet beneath mankind's feet.

Doors opened, secret ways were momentarily crowded, and within an incredibly short time all the Timmys who had worked among humans had disappeared like blown-out candle flames. By dawn, not one could be found.

34

Pressed into Service

That same dawn, Ornery Bastable arose from her bed on the deck of the steamer, dressed herself carefully, arranged her veils, and climbed the steps from the stone pier to Brewer's Bridge. From the carved railing, iridescent water birds (called birds, even though they were not actually birds) were diving for fish while others sat on the banks drying their black/green/violet wings and croaking at one another. Brighter birds were clinging to the reeds, trilling at any other of their kind within hearing. The sky was a clear and flawless blue except for the haze that hung above the scarp, where long lines of gray, like blown veils, stretched away diagonally on the seawind, fading into the horizon to the south.

Despite the good weather, the clear sky, the quiet city, Ornery felt something was wrong, or different, or awry. Her first thought was the scarp, and she set her feet widely apart, waiting for that premonitory shudder, but nothing came. She turned and walked westward along the street, looking around at the street scene, the early carts clattering across the cobbles, the bustle of a few veiled Men of Business, the call of a milk vendor: 'Fraiiiish, Creeeemy: glug glug glug; breeng your bahttles, breeng your jug!' and the spice-cart man's staccato call, 'Pepper-an-spice, makes-it-nice. Pepper-pepper-pepper.' Newholmian pepper was actually better than Old Earth peppers, and it sold to the BIT for a good price.

Ornery turned slowly, examining her surroundings. Something was amiss. Something was wrong! Then she realized. Timmys! There were no Timmys. No brown-clad forms scurrying behind the wagons or along the walls. There were always Timmys, everywhere, but not this morning. Not sweeping the roads. Not running here and there on errands. Not washing the outsides of windows or scrubbing the stoops of the buildings. Not leading the donkeys that pulled the carts. Not putting out the trash bins. No Timmys.

Ornery stopped where she was, on the corner just outside House Genevois, and stared about herself, confused. As she stood, staring witlessly, a carriage approached with several armed Haggers running along behind it, and behind them a wagon with two veiled men chained to its railing. Ornery's hand went to her veils, securing them, and she stepped back against the building, out of the way.

The carriage stopped and a voice trumpeted, 'That one, there. Let me see his face!'

One of the Haggers approached, ripped down Ornery's veils, then waited while Ornery's heart half-stopped and her breathing did stop.

'Good enough,' the woman called. 'Put him in the cart.'

'What?' Ornery cried. 'What is this?'

'Press gang,' said the Hagger, not without some satisfaction. 'Mistress Marool is pressing some of you supernumeraries to take the place of some … servants of hers.'

'But I'm a seaman!' cried Ornery. 'I've a legitimate job. I'm not a supernumerary.'

The woman had alighted from the carriage. Now she too approached, glaring into Ornery's face. 'If I say you are a supernumerary, boy, that's what you are. If you speak out of turn again, you'll serve my needs without your tongue.'

Ornery choked herself silent. The woman went by her like a storm wind, and the Hagger who held her thrust her past the carriage to the cart that waited there, where Ornery was unceremoniously put inside and chained beside two other unwilling passengers, from whom she learned what little they knew about what was going on.

Meantime the woman had gone on to the main doors of House Genevois, where she jerked the great bell into such a clamor that it sent a cloud of birds flying from the roof, screaming outrage. The door was opened, and she went inside to find Madame herself awaiting her.

Marool presented the edict of the Hags, her sneer of authority ready for use at the first sign of recalcitrance.

'Wait here,' said Madame, leaving with such alacrity that Marool had no time to be rude. She was gone long enough for Marool to have worked up a good fume by the time she returned.

'See here,' she began, in an angry tone.

'In here,' said Madame, throwing open the double doors that centered the farther wall. Inside the gymnasium thus disclosed were several ranks of young men, arranged by age.

'I have not included the Consorts already purchased, since they are not my property to dispose of,' said Madame, crisply. 'The younger boys would be of little use to you as laborers, for they have not come into their strength. All the others are here.'

Marool's eyes gleamed. She did not notice the pinched look of Madame's nostrils, or the wariness in the faces of those before her. She had no hint of what had been said by Madame to those youths in the intervening moments. She was interested in only one thing, and that was to discover the boy she had seen in the park. The light veils the youths wore were no impediment to her search. She walked down the line, spotting him immediately. It was the boy she had seen. She could not possibly have missed him. He was the largest boy in the room.

'Him,' she said, pointing at Bane.

He regarded her with insolence. 'I go nowhere without my brother, Ma'am,' he said, making little pretense of politeness.

'Your brother?' She laughed. 'By all means. If you have a brother.'

Dyre stepped forward. Marool nodded. 'I have a cart outside. They will be taken to Mantelby Mansion.' She turned to stalk away down the line of youths, paying the rest of them little attention.

One of the Haggers who had accompanied her opened the door into the entry, admitting a slight breeze that lifted the veil of the young man at the end of the line. The movement drew Marool's eyes to the face behind the veil. It was a beautiful face drawn into an expression of horrified recognition. Why horrified? She had never laid eyes on him before.

'What's the matter, boy? You never seen a woman before?'

'My apologies,' he bowed, hiding his eyes. 'I meant no disrespect.'

Something in his manner both annoyed her and piqued her curiosity. 'Feh,' she barked, angry at him. 'I'll take you as well, boy. You hear, Madame? I'll take this one as well. Does he have a name?'

'His name is Mouche, Mistress Mantelby.' Madame said it in a dead, impersonal voice. 'As I understand this matter, you are to give me a document agreeing to return these young men when the current emergency is over. If you will join me in my office, I will enter all the pertinent data on both our copies. Their names. Their annuities, which you would be expected to fulfill, if they should be incapacitated in your employ. Also their value to me, which you would be expected to pay if anything happens to them to reduce their value. Anything at all.'

Marool glared, meeting eyes as cold as her own were hot. 'You are presumptuous, Madame.'

'Not at all. When we received word of this last evening, I went to the Temple to consult the Hags personally on the matter. It is not their intention that the Houses shall be robbed of their students. Bane, and Dyre, and Mouche will work in your stables or your gardens, replacing certain other laborers who are, for a time, unavailable to you. Such work is all they will do. And if their skin is marred, or their appearance changed, or if they are ill fed or their bones twisted or broken ...'

Marool stormed out into the hall, and thence was led by Simon to Madame's office. Mouche moved uncertainly. Madame stepped beside him, murmuring: 'Mouche, go with them. Be polite. Be subservient. Do your work. Do not tempt the woman to violence ...'

'Madame ...' he whispered. 'Madame ...'

'Yes, boy. What is it?'

'That picture outside my room. It's her, isn't it? That is Mistress Mantelby.'

Madame paled. She shivered, then drew herself up once more. 'Yes, Mouche. That is Mistress Mantelby. And the best way to avoid drawing her attention is to seem uninteresting. Do you understand? Be unattractive and dull. Totally dull.' She gave him a significant look and gestured toward the door.

Still he hesitated. The sight of Marool's face had been terrible, but more terrible yet was the thought of leaving House Genevois, leaving his secret way within the walls, leaving ... that one whom he watched in the night hours. 'Madame. Are the Timmys really gone?'

She shivered, only slightly, reaching forward to stroke his face with her fingers. 'What Timmys? I know nothing of any Timmys. Nor do you, if you are wise. Go, Mouche. And may fortune be with you.'

On her lips, it had the sound almost of a prayer.

35

Timmy Talk

If Mouche had been there to open his hidden gate and creep into the walls, he would have found the space packed with Timmys: Timmys listening at cracks, peering through eye holes, observing what the humans were doing as they or their predecessors had been observing almost since humans had first arrived. Though it had been some time before Timmys had been seen by the second wave of settlers, Timmys had seen the settlers from the beginning.

'This creature coming,' said one Timmy, who had been in the walls of the temple when D'Jevier and Marool had conversed, 'This Questioner-idi coming, if idi finds out we have been treated badly, idi may seek to redress our wrongs, to do justice.'

'That must not happen,' cried others. 'Our wrongs must not be redressed. Justice would upset everything!'

There was agreement. Justice would be the last straw.

'Why can't tim-tim go now,' sang one, two, a dozen, their voices making a sad harmony of the words.

'It is not the time,' replied others, an antiphon. 'Tim-tim must await the time.'

'But the jong grow strong,' sang the first ones. 'And the jong wax large, like moons, and Niasa turns and turns.'

'Even so, it is not the time.'

'The earth shakes with the turning of Niasa. *She* will waken! *She* will break the egg!'

'Even so.'

After a long silence, one offered, 'Whether it is the time or not, word must be sent to the bai. The depths must be informed of this dangerous idi, this Questioner.'

Others agreed. There was a generalized and rather ant-like scurry as some set out and others arrived, this one and that one being assigned to this peephole or that crack, and a small group started on a journey to the depths where they would inform the great ones of the dangerous Questioner who was coming.

Those remaining behind stayed at their peepholes in the walls. 'The woman-gau took Mouchidi,' said Mouche's goddess, the one he had intuitively

787

called by her tim-tim name, Flowing Green. 'They took the one I have hopes of!'

'Not far,' reassured another. 'He goes to House Mantelby. Tim-tim are in all the walls there, watching the terrible ones and the bad woman.'

'I will go there,' said the green-haired one. 'I have many long hopes of Mouchidi. I read his face and see him feeling what we feel. I see how he joys. I see him perceive Her pain.'

'I have no hopes,' said another. 'None of the jong have been any use. All those who came at first, they did the bad thing, but when we tried to use them to fix it, they were no use. Jongau are still moving around out there, all warped. That Ashes-gau, that bad smell, he is still out mere.'

'The other bad smells are there, too,' offered another. 'The big ones, the wet ones, the dry ones, the thorny ones ...'

'I know what happened before,' murmured the green-haired one. 'I have been told by Bofusdiaga, singer of the sun. I have been told by Corojum, dancer of bright skies. Mouchidi is different. So say they.'

One who had departed moments before returned breathlessly.

'We went, we met word already coming up from below,' tim said. 'The below ones already know of this Questioner. When it comes, it will be of some other kind and maybe have with it some other kinds yet. Bofusdiaga thinks we should look at them, too. Perhaps we would have better luck with another kind.'

'Try, then,' said the green-haired one. 'Meantime, I will go to watch Mouchidi.' She paused, as though debating whether or not to say what was in her mind, deciding at last to do so. 'Again I dreamed! In the dream I danced into the fauxi-dizalonz, and Mouchidi was in it, and I was with him, and we were being changed together.'

Several of the others recoiled, putting up their hands as though to ward her away. 'Tss! Do not speak of it to tim-tim. It is not for us who say tim, tim, but only for you who say I, I. Speak of it only to Bofusdiaga, who alloys, and even then, speak softly, for *She* might hear.'

'*She* still sleeps,' asserted the one called Flowing Green. '*She* is not listening yet.'

The other made a gesture which was the equivalent of a shrug. Flowing Green was excessive. From highest to lowest, Doshanoi, everyone, knew it. Tim-tim always said 'tim-tim,' we. Tim-tim never said 'I.' What could a part teach the whole? what dance could an 'I' do, all by itself? Surely only the great ones could dream fully. Surely only the alloyed ones could remember what had been lost ...

'But they do not,' whispered some. 'Even they do not remember, even among them the dreams are tattered, filmy, without substance. How could even alloyed ones make do with such as that?' They could not. The dance was lost. Perhaps ... lost forever.

'It is said,' sang someone hidden in a corner. 'It is said the mankinds have done wrong, they may be exterminated for the wrong they have done. Now, almost one could welcome this Questioner if it would exterminate these jongau who had not the courtesy to die.'

'Bofusdiaga says no,' said Flowing Green. 'Bofusdiaga does not want justice.'

The timmy departed by Doshanoi ways, unseen. It did not take long to find the place where Mouche and the others had been sent.

36

Pressed Men at Mantelby

Mouche let himself be loaded into the wagon and chained there with no outward sign of protest. Only when he knew the sound of the wheels on cobbles would mask his words did he lean toward the nearest man to whisper: 'My name is Mouche.'

'Ornery Bastable,' the other replied. 'I'm a seaman. She called me a supernume!' Ornery's chin jerking toward the leading carriage showed who she meant. 'I'll have words with her.'

Mouche masked his mouth with a shackled hand and spoke softly. 'Words won't help. I don't think she cares if we're supernumes or not. She is an evil woman, Bastable, so beware.'

The other gave Mouche a level stare, then asked, too loudly, 'Known or suspected of being evil?'

Mouche shook his head slightly, narrowing his eyes. He had meant only to warn, thinking it far too dangerous to get into discussion about it while Dyre and Bane were near. They were doing one of their favorite things, watching him with that long, unblinking snake-eyed stare. It made Mouche think seriously of the need for allies. No Simon or Madame here. No Fentrys or Tyle. He would have to cultivate Bastable or whomever, for any help was better than none.

He shielded his mouth with his hand once more and murmured, 'She is known to be an evil woman, seaman. There is no doubt about it at all. I have been warned to be inconspicuous as possible, not to attract her attention. I would not have words with her if I could avoid it.'

Ornery thought it over, then gave a tiny nod of thanks for the warning. Bane and Dyre went on staring for a time, though they soon gave it up in favor of loud and continuous complaint mixed with assorted sneers and unspecific threats against all and sundry. They complained of having been sent to House Genevois against their inclination and of having been kept there by threat of force. They said they had been forced to be civil (though they called it sucking up to nobodies) when they would have preferred despotism (though they called it getting their rights). They complained of this latest outrage in which they were expected to labor like damn Timmys instead of being cushioned on silk and fed cream, which is what they'd been trained for. Cushioning and drinking and other such dalliances seemed to have figured largely in their minds, as they went on and on about it. When next Mouche and Ornery shared a glance, both understood it as a contract. If word came to blow, they would stand together against these two.

The wagon took the winding road leading onto the western heights, passing great houses behind high walls. At the top of the ridge, a man stood in an open gateway, obviously awaiting them. Mistress Mantelby halted her carriage and, indicating the waiting man with an imperious forefinger, called to those in the wagon: 'Here is my steward. You will be working at his direction, so mind yourselves.'

There was no reply from the wagon, and seemingly none was expected, for she went on in a loud voice.

'Well, Nephew! I said I would bring replacements, and here they are!'

'Thank you, Aunt,' the steward murmured, standing with bowed head while the carriage moved away. When she had departed some distance toward the house itself, the man waved the wagon on, following it dejectedly afoot as it went down a lane toward a group of outbuildings. The six prisoners were hauled out of the wagon, two of them were sent along the lane under the watchful eyes of an understeward, while Bastable and the three Consorts were half dragged and half led into the stables. While the Haggers watched from the sidelines, the steward dropped his veils and looked them over, disgust plain on his face.

'Three layabout supernumes and a triplet of useless Hunks,' he complained, 'to replace a dozen pairs of skilled hands. And if you don't do the work, it'll be my hide that pays for it, so take this to heart: You'll do the work or I'll make your hide pay for it, count on it.'

'And who're you, g'nephew?' sneered Bane. 'A Family Man? A Man of Business?'

The steward paled, biting his lips. 'I am the person who gives orders to the Haggers,' he said when he had collected himself. 'The Mistress has set them under my direction. So, if you've some idea of attacking me or attempting to leave this place, mark down that I won't be alone in retaliation.'

'We have powerful friends,' yelped Dyre. 'And they'll not leave us here.'

The steward grimaced. 'Oh, surely. And when your powerful friends order me to release you, and when the Hags agree to that, and when Mistress Mantelby signs her name to the order, I'll do it. Until then you are my fingers to move at my command, worthless, and best you remember it.'

He went down the line of them, pulling their veils away from their faces, staring at each of them, noting the brothers' sullen rebellion as well as Mouche and Ornery's puzzlement. The puzzlement, he felt sympathy for. He himself was more than a little puzzled about this whole situation.

'There is no stable master at the moment,' he said. 'Until I can find a person with experience, I'll direct you myself. Tools are over there. Muck out all those stalls, put the muck in that cart there. Fill all the mangers with hay. Take the water buckets out, wash them, and fill them with fresh water from the well outside. Put one in each stall. When that is done, haul the cart out to the field and spread the muck about. If you think to save yourself trouble by dumping it all in one pile, you'll crawl about, spreading it with your noses! I'll be back after the noonmeal to see how much you've done. If you've done well, you'll eat.'

And he turned and left, leaving two stout Haggers leaning on their cudgels to observe the work.

Mouche and Ornery set about the task, as described. There were a dozen stalls; they began on the ones nearest the loft. The job was no new thing for Mouche, though his hands, from which all calluses had long since been removed, soon felt the burn of the manure fork's wooden handle. Ornery had no such problem. Daily manipulation of ropes had given her palms like leather. Observing Mouche's tender hands, she pulled a pair of heavy work gloves from her back pocket and handed them over.

When Bane and Dyre made no move to help, the Haggers spoke roughly to them. After some muttering, they went unwillingly and unhandily to work at the far end.

'Y'said when we left Dutter, it was the end of this,' Dyre growled.

'It will be,' Bane muttered in return. 'All this is a mistake, believe me.' Then, with a glance at Mouche and Ornery, he muttered, just loud enough for them to hear, 'But I think we'll probably stay long enough to settle with that one. That one there owes us, don't he, Brother? He'll take a beating that will last him a lifetime.'

Mouche clenched his fists and turned. 'I owe you more pain than you do me, Stinkbreath.'

'You got that wrong,' said Bane, turning white with fury. 'I do what I like. I'm a new breed, I am, and nobody interferes with me, not ever.'

This brought the Haggers over once more, and while Bane and Dyre claimed their full attentions, Mouche and Ornery exchanged a few conspiratorial whispers concerning where they might find a haven if attacked. They settled upon the loft, and Ornery climbed there by the loose ladder – taking her and Mouche's belongings with her – and began forking straw down into the two stalls they had so far shoveled out. Mouche brought in two full buckets of fresh water, waited for an unobserved moment and handed one up to Ornery, who set it out of sight. Now, if they had to retreat, at least they wouldn't die from thirst!

Somewhere a noon bell rang, and the Haggers, who evidently felt they had supervised long enough, filed out and away, chatting between themselves. When the stable door closed, Bane stalked from the stall he had made little effort to clean, threw his manure fork at Mouche's feet, and growled, 'Get on with it, dungrats.'

'We'll do six stalls, our half,' said Mouche. 'And no more than that.'

'You'll do the whole,' sneered Bane. 'Or you'll suffer for it.'

Mouche and Ornery exchanged a glance, then ignored Bane's bluster and turned back to the stall they were cleaning.

'Hey, farm boy,' sneered Bane. 'You been home to visit lately?'

Mouche paid no attention.

'You otta go. Somethin' there you otta see.'

Mouche turned. 'And how would you know? You've not been home either.'

'Well, Dutters wasn't my home and they weren't my folks. I didn't have a daddy and a mommy like you did, but I got friends tell me things. You know you got two baby sisters, farm boy? You know you got a brother going to grow up to be a Family Man?'

'That's a lie,' said Mouche stoutly. His father would have told him if any such thing were true.

Bane and Dyre laughed, punching each other in their glee. 'No lie. Sold you off and right away, mama had a girl, then another one, then a boy. The farm's doing well without you, farm boy. I guess all they had to do was get rid of their bad luck, and the Hagions made it right for them.'

'How come you know so much?' demanded Ornery, moving nearer to Mouche, who was choking on his anger.

'We was neighbors. Dutter place is just over the hill. We used to roam around there quite a bit, killing vermin, getting rid of varmints.'

'What do you mean you didn't have a mother and father?' Ornery challenged. 'Everybody has.'

'Not us,' cried Dyre. 'We was born of the thunder, we was. Lightning is our papa. We're a new breed.'

'Born of the stinkbush,' choked Mouche, against all good sense. 'Fathered by an outhouse.'

Mouche scarcely had time to brace himself before Bane landed on him, knocking him backward so the breath went out of him. His attacker drew a blade from his belt and wasted no time striking at Mouche's face. Mouche rolled and fended the first blow, but the second bit deep. He felt the slice and the warm blood on his cheek. His mouth was suddenly larger, and something inside himself screamed with outrage. His face. Bane had scarred his face!

The manure fork was under Mouche's hand, his fingers closed around the neck, just below the long tines. He managed to bring the fork up, twist it so the tines pointed at Bane, and thrust them deep enough that Bane fell back with a yelp, allowing Mouche to scramble to his feet with a firm grip on the fork as he backed, blood streaming, toward the ladder to the loft.

Meantime, Dyre had attacked Ornery, clutching her clumsily around the waist. Ornery had thrown herself forward, fallen hard on her attacker, and escaped while Dyre was catching his breath. By the time the brothers were on their feet, Ornery and Mouche were in the loft with the ladder pulled up after them and the manure fork close at hand for repelling boarders. Mouche leaked blood from his face, where his cheek had been sliced through, along with other cuts. Ornery had battered knuckles and a cut on her jaw, made by Dyre's ring. She paid no attention to this as she inspected Mouche's face, where the flesh was already swelling.

'Oh, by all the Hagions, Mouche ...'

'If i ... 's aad, don' ... ell ... e.'

'It's bad, and I have to tell you. It's got to be stitched. You'll be a horror, otherwise.'

Mouche felt the horror as he moved his fingers over his face. '... ack,' he said, as best he could, and Ornery read his mind. He fetched the pack and Mouche felt through it, coming up with a slender tube. 'Glue,' he said, almost clearly. 'Now ... whiaw is ... resh.'

'Tissue glue? I may not be good at it, Mouche. I may leave a scar.'

'Now ... whiaw ... is ... resh.'

Working from the top of the cut, high on Mouche's cheek, just under his left eye, Ornery applied the glue and pressed the flesh together, centimeter by centimeter, hoping desperately that she would come out even when she reached the lips. The end of the cut was at the corner of the mouth, and this took several applications of the glue before it held. Mouche lay back, eyes wide with pain and sudden terror. Up until now, he'd had a life to depend on. Now? He couldn't be a Hunk, not now. Not unless a miracle happened and it healed so clean that the Denti-med machines could clean it up. Well, Madame would make Mantelby pay his annuity out. Trust Madame. At least he wouldn't starve.

Meantime, below, the brothers rattled the stable door to no effect, then sat down, muttering to one another and examining the walls in a vain effort to find some climbable way into the loft. The work of cleaning the stables went no further. Nor would it be finished, Ornery whispered, until those other two were got rid of.

'Let's ... ill 'em,' muttered Mouche, dazedly fingering the manure fork.

'Now, then,' whispered Ornery, patting Mouche's shoulder. 'Killing them isn't going to do us any good. Calm down. Maybe your folks didn't want to hurt your feelings so they didn't tell you about the new babies.'

Mouche shook off the comforting hand and concentrated on what was going on below. '... e could ... ake um ... ane isn' ... so good a ... ighter. He's lazy.'

'He may not be a good fighter, he may even be lazy, but we're in no shape to prove it,' said Ornery. 'Please. Just lie there and let the glue set. Don't talk. Let me just try to get us put to work somewhere else, or vicey-versy.'

Mouche took a shuddering breath and subsided while Ornery wet a clean handkerchief and cleaned the worst of the blood from his face. The glue had sealed the cut, as it was designed to do, which is why the stuff was carried by sailors and roustabouts and others subject to injury in way of the work. Deep, disfiguring injuries like Mouche's, however, were supposed to be followed up by an immediate visit to the surgery machines, and Ornery didn't think it was going to happen, not with things all in confusion as they were.

'I'd rather the gardens for me,' said Ornery, making conversation to keep Mouche's mind off the wound. 'I was raised a farm boy, and I can do gardening without thinking about it. It would smell better out there, too. It really stinks in here.'

Mouche wrinkled his nose, testing. It did indeed stink in the stable, and he knew that the stench was not entirely horse. The fetid odor was the same as he had smelt years ago in the cave, and on his dog, and later in Madame's front parlor. He knew it came from the brothers below, though they had not smelled like this at House Genevois.

Mouche was unaware of the special bath soaps, the additives in their food, the unusual unguents used during morning massage. Today there had been no morning bath, no morning meal, no morning massage. Bane and Dyre had come a long way in an open cart, sweating under the sun and had begun to smell very much as they had smelled at the Dutter farm.

Ornery murmured, 'We can talk to that head man, if he comes back down here today. Personal, I think he won't remember us until nighttime comes, and maybe not then. This place is in a uproar, just as Sendoph probably is, all at greasy glasses and burned biscuits, I'd warrant. Everybody depending on those Timmys, years and years the way they have ...'

'... ou ha ... nt?' Mouche whispered.

'No, I haven't. No Timmys on ships. No sir. They don't like the water, and that's a fact. You find 'em on the wharf and you find 'em stowing stuff in the hold, but you don't find 'em once the ship goes out on water. No Timmys on the Bouncing Isles. No Timmys at the sea farms ...'

'Sea ... arns?'

'Out there in the Jellied Sea, they got sea farms. There's a kind of weed draws gold out of the seawater and fixes it in the leaves, and they hook it and tie it to a hawser and pull it in by the quarter mile into a great pile, and they dry it and burn it and mix the ashes with water to make bricks, and they send the bricks back to the smelter, to get the gold out. And it's not just gold! There's other good metal in the ashes. There's fishes out there, too, kinds we can eat, and dried Purse fish eggs, for making jelly ...' She went cheerfully

795

on, trying to keep Mouche's mind occupied.

Though the two below continued to search for some way of reaching their prey, they had not accomplished it by the time the stable door opened with a crash. Both Bane and Dyre turned their angry faces to confront the steward once more, along with several Haggers. In the loft, Ornery urged Mouche to the edge of the loft and arranged his veil so the wound would show while Mouche quivered with newly kindled rage and shock.

'You've got the stalls mucked out?' demanded the steward.

Bane said something about the other two taking a rest.

'No rest, sir,' said Ornery in as respectful a voice as she could muster. 'They tried to kill us, sir. We came up here to get away from them. They've cut Mouche all to bits.'

An argument below built rapidly into shouting and threats, falling silent as suddenly as another voice cut into the fray: 'Silence.'

It was Marool herself. 'Who has cut whom?'

Explanations. More argument. More yelling. Through all of which Mouche and Ornery quietly sat at the edge of the loft, their veils so arranged as to allow a full view of their battered faces in the light falling through the air vent.

'Well, boy,' said Marool to Bane, who was by this time held in the grip of several Haggers. 'Look at them up there. Their little faces all beaten and bruised, one of them possibly scarred for life, and who's to pay for it? Ah? You baby Hunks have to be returned untouched, unharmed, and here you are, already costing me money. Well, boy, you owe me. I can't get it out of your pockets, so I'll take it in services.' And she jerked her head backward. Two Haggers took Bane away, still yelling, while the others restrained Dyre from following.

Marool followed his departure with her eyes, casting only a single infuriated glance upward as she said to her steward, 'Separate them, Nephew. And see they're tended to. I may get enough use out of one not to mind paying damages for the one he's ruined, but damned if I'll pay for more than that.'

And she was gone.

'I was reared a farm boy,' called Ornery in a level tone. 'If you need gardening done.'

'. . . e, too,' said Mouche.

The steward exchanged looks with the Haggers, who shrugged, one of them commenting: 'The gardener says the two you gave him are useless, they don't know roots from sprouts, and they've planted three rows of fennel upside down.'

'We'll bring them back here, then,' said the steward, in a glum voice.

Mouche and Ornery were beckoned down from their perch. They were then taken down through the paddocks to the lane, and up the lane to the stone house of the head gardener, and there traded for the two other pressed men who shambled sourly down the lane to the stables. Behind the gardener's house were several daub-and-wattle houses, brightly painted, where the gardener's invisible help had lived, and the contents of Mouche's pack were soon laid out there, together with a few clothes for Ornery, who had only what she'd carried on the boat upriver.

Thus it came that Mouche and Ornery, their wounds washed and medicated, sat over a late lunch beside a Timarese hearth, drinking broth from Timarese bowls, spied on, though they did not know it, by a good many Timmys in the walls, including Flowing Green who was in as near to a frenzy as the Timmys ever got. Mouchidi had been wounded, and badly. Mankinds could die from such wounds. Tim had seen it happen!

When Ornery had gulped all and Mouche spooned down half what they had been given, enough that they were no longer famished, Ornery set down her bowl and leaned confidentially toward Mouche.

'That was rotten of him, saying you were bad luck. It isn't true, you know. It's just the inscrutable Hagions, making mock of good sense.'

'I ... udden ... ind so ... uch,' muttered Mouche, 'if aw had jus tol ... ee.'

'I told you why. Your pa didn't want to hurt you.'

'He could haw 'ought me 'ack!'

Ornery gave him a long, level look. 'He couldn't buy you back. Not from a Consort House.'

Mouche flushed. Of course he couldn't have been bought back. He knew that. Someone could have tried, though.

'I ... ove' 'at farn,' he muttered resentfully.

'I loved my family's farm, too,' said Ornery. 'It was beautiful there. We had a vineyard ...'

'So di' ooee.'

'And we had sheep and chickens and a garden and orchard. But the mountain blew, and the ashes came on a terrible wind, and when I got home they were all dead, Mama and Papa, brother, all gone. There was no sense to that, either. Maybe when they felt the hot wind coming, they hated me because I escaped and they didn't. Maybe they didn't even think of me. Life's hard enough, so my captain says, that most times we should do very little thinking about what other people think or do or say, just enough to get by. Otherwise we just jangle ourselves for nothing. So he says.'

'I renen'er how uh hayhield snelled,' said Mouche, stubbornly, determined to make his loss the greater.

'And the smell of strawberries, new-picked,' said Ornery. 'And the flowers in Mama's garden, outside the kitchen door.'

Mouche heaved a huge sigh and gave up the effort at grief supremacy. 'You're righ',' he announced. 'Likely he didn' wan oo hur ny 'eelings ...'

'And you're nobody's bad luck,' insisted Ornery.

Mouche nodded and forgot himself enough to try to smile, more because of Ornery's good intentions than at his interpretation of the facts. If good fortune had come to his family, it had happened only after he, Mouche, was gone away. If that wasn't bad luck, what was it? Almost as though he hadn't belonged there. And if not, where did he belong? Was it possible he had been brought here, well, at least to House Genevois, for a purpose? By fate? Now there was a large thought.

When they had finished eating, Mouche still ruminating on fatefulness, the gardener took a look at Mouche's face, then told him to do no more than he could comfortably do for the rest of the day. A barrow was laden with tools and they pushed it to a long arbor walk overgrown with fruit vines and edged with flowers, where things needed a general clipping and weeding and neatening up. Mouche had his own taste to guide him, which was considerable. Ornery had a shipman's love of order, for, as she told Mouche, disorder breeds death at sea, where a loop of rope or a tool left out of place can spell the difference between life and death.

Mouche found that concentrating on the work made the pain lessen. Between them they worked, both sensibly and conscientiously enough to feel a sense of satisfaction in late evening when the gardener finally came to see what they'd accomplished. The man nodded once or twice as in pleased surprise, then patted their shoulders as he took them back to his own house to give them a plentiful supper.

'Well, now, I'd have said you were both useless as tits on a boar, but you've proved me wrong,' the old man said when he had filled Ornery's stew bowl and salad bowl and laid out a thick slab of cheese on a chunk of brown bread wrenched from the new loaf. After another long look at Mouche's face, he furnished him with a mug of broth and more chunks of the bread to be softened, he said, by dipping.

'What are you doing here, and how did it all happen?' he asked when he had them provided for.

Between mouthfuls, Ornery explained about the Timmys without once referring to them by name. 'And Mouche told me his Madame says, people who don't exist, can't exist, not until this Questioner person goes away. And the Questioner person is to be staying here, in Mistress Mantelby's house.

'Far's I'm concerned, it's all a mistake, an' I got to get me back to the ship,' said Ornery. 'This Mantelby woman, she took me wrong, she did. I'm no supernumerary. I got to get back, or maybe I'll lose my place. An' I got to get word to my sister, too, or she'll fret herself sick over me.'

''ould you sto' us?' Mouche asked the old man. 'I' we ran away?'

The old man poked the fire and snorted. 'Well o' course I'd stop you. Old I may be, and not so spry, but I've still got good sense, as well as work that needs doing. Now, you stick around here, workin' away, stooped a little, maybe, so's you look older, with nice thick veils over your young faces and a good deal of manure rubbed in your hair and eyebrows, that one up at the house, she'll ignore you like you don't exist, just like she allus did them others that don't exist. That cut on you, thas good protection, too, for she doesn't pay attention to people that're hurt, or sick. But you run off, that steward, he'll report it because he's her nephew, and if he doesn't tell her everything, she'll put him out on the street, maybe blue-body him into the bargain. My, she loves disposin' o' nephews. So, he'll tell her if you run off, depend on it, and right then you'll go down in her bad book. She don't abide being crossed, so people don't stay in her bad book long. Right soon they just vanish, quick as you can say, oh, my gracious. Sometimes there's bones and sometimes there's not. And who you think she'll take to task for you leaving? Whose back will she stripe? Whose bones will she roast? Eh? Mine, that's whose.'

He shook his head sadly and set a burning splinter to the pipe he had just filled with shreds of fragrant willowbark, then waved the smoking pipe about his head to drive away the midges. 'No, sailor, I'll send letters for you, so your people won't worry, but you'll be smart to wear those old invisibles' robes and the thick veils. I scrounged 'em for you as uglification, just to keep you meek and safe from harm. I had the laundry boy wash 'em and stitch 'em together, to make them big enough. I figure anybody in those robes likely won't get seen anyhow, seein' as how we don't see those robes, if you take my meaning.'

There was a good deal of sense in what he said, and though Ornery fretted over her shipboard position, the gardener assured her the Hags would set it right. It wouldn't make sense for men to lose their positions because of some emergency measure. Once everything was back to normal, it would be fixed.

It was weariness as much as anything else that made Ornery agree. They wrote their letters, one to Ornery's captain, one to Ornery's sister, and one from Mouche to Madame, then they went out through the dusk into a Timmy house where they curled up on Timmy mats under Timmy blankets. Ornery fell asleep while it was still light outside, though Mouche stayed longer awake, feeling with delicate fingertips the swollen flesh of his face and wondering what was to happen to him now.

In the cities and towns of Newholme, things went from greasy glasses and burned biscuits to filthy streets and food rotting in the fields before some kind of order began to emerge, or, if not order, at least a more amenable disorder. A kind of controlled chaos, as the Hags put it. A godawful mess, according to the Men of Business. Priority was given to food and fuel. Necessary things were getting done. Unnecessary ones, uncritical ones, were long delayed and might, in fact, not get done at all.

The Consort Houses held only staff and boy-children too young to work. There were no supernumeraries to be found anywhere on the streets, and it had even begun to dawn on a good many people that had the Timmys not been so ubiquitous all those generations, likely there would have been no such things as supernumes. The new order required a new economic basis, of course. The Timmys had worked without pay, though they had been provided with housing, clothing, and food. The new workers took up more space, ate more food and required more fabric for clothing, and some of them even demanded wages. The CMOB struggled with these matters while trying to pretend that things had always been this way.

At House Genevois, Madame sent a message to a certain one and awaited a visitation in her parlor, and when he arrived, she tried not to breathe as she told him his wards, his protégés, the Dutter boys, had been pressed into service.

'Who by?' He grunted.

'By Mistress Mantelby,' she replied, keeping her voice carefully neutral.

The man across from her shook. For a moment she thought his spasms came from illness or distress, but then she realized he was laughing.

'Monstrous Marool has them? Oh, does she? What a joke! Oh, that's a rare one, that is. Well, Madame, all our agreements stand. I won't hold you responsible for their being *pressed into service,* not even if they come back in worse condition than when they left.'

'You are kind,' said Madame, with the least possible deference in her nod.

'Not at all,' he said, departing. She sat for several moments after he left, breathing through her mouth, hearing his final words resonate, realizing at last that he had meant them literally. He was not at all kind. He would be incapable of kindness.

At the port outside Sendoph, a tall, blue-skinned protocol officer arrived on the Questioner's advance cutter to spend half an officious hour with the Men of Business and a day with the Hags, most of it in inspection of the Mantelby mansion. Mouche and Ornery were trimming lawn edges in the garden when they saw the blue one stalk through. The two had taken the gardener's advice and made themselves useful but inconspicuous, though Mouche did not believe for a moment that this strategy would save him from Bane's malice. The head gardener told them Bane had been installed as Mistress Mantelby's toy boy, and Dyre, too, had been taken up to the main house to enjoy himself.

'You'd think they were kin of hers, the way they act,' the old man whispered over the evening meal. 'Oh, I hear things, I do. All the servants up there at the house, they're talking about it. She's shameless, that one. She'll cosset him, or them, until they think they shit pure gold. She'll take them to bed with her, and she'll give them stuff to make them feel like lords of creation, and they'll play round games. Then one day they'll wake up in shackles in her playroom. I've seen it happen a hundred times …'

''lay roon?' asked Mouche, apprehensively.

The old man shivered. 'Call it a dungeon, you'd be closer on. Down in the old wine cellars. Playroom is what she calls it. There's machines in there, and sometimes when the machines are through, all that's left is grease.'

'I don't understand,' said Ornery.

Mouche did understand, all too well. He whispered to Ornery of the picture at House Genevois.

Ornery turned back to the old man. 'You've seen it a hundred times, gardener? Truly?'

The old man shrugged and pursed his lips. 'Well, no, boys, not strictly, no. That's liar's license, that is, to make the story ring right. I'd say she does for at least three or four men a year, most of 'em Consorts, but some just plain folk, like a footman at table she takes a dislike to or some cook that spoils the roast. And nephews, o' course. She loves disposin' of nephews.'

'Why does she do it?' breathed Ornery.

Madame had explained psychotic sadism to her students, but Mouche could not yet speak without considerable pain, so he made no attempt to pass that information on. Madame had said some people were made that way, and they did it out of vengeance, and some were born that way, and they did it because hurting and killing made them feel powerful. Either way, there was no cure for it, for each act led to the next with no way to retreat.

'Whatever reason Mistress Mantelby is like she is, you keep tight to what I told you,' said the old man. 'I'm trusting you to keep out of the way and be silent. Just like those things we used to have that never existed. You understand?'

By the time the Questioner and her entourage arrived, affairs at Marool Mantelby's mansion were as calm and usual as it was possible to make them. The only change for the household was that Bane and Dyre were to be housed in a suite at the far end of the servants' quarters during the Questioner's stay, because of the stink. So the old gardener said. For that reason and others, everyone was more or less holding their breaths until the visitation was over. It wouldn't be long. So everyone had been told.

37

An Intimate Disclosure

On the evening the Questioner arrived Ornery asked the gardener if they might make use of the washhouse in the compound, and he gave his permission, so long as it was after everyone else had gone to bed, provided they were stingy with the firewood in the boiler and mopped up after themselves. The stone-floored little building was near the wood stove and the pump and was furnished with wooden tubs of various sizes. Ornery took herself and her clothing inside, locked the door, lit the boiler, and heated a good quantity of water.

Mouche, however, on learning that Ornery had gone to commit an act of cleanliness, stopped scratching himself and decided it was long past time for himself to have a bath also, to rid him of vermin if nothing else, so he went along to the room, jiggled the latch, and walked into the place. She was standing in the tub, washing her hair. She was Ornery, no doubt of that, but she was also unmistakably female.

Ornery seized up a towel and covered all pertinent parts while stammering a long exposition of how she had been turned into a chatron as a boy. Mouche smiled as politely as his wound would allow. His studies at Madame's had exposed him to women's bodies in all varieties of age and inclination; he had seen chatrons and hermaphrodites as well, and he knew Ornery was physiologically a girl and he said so, intelligibly.

Ornery protested.

Mouche shook his head, bewildered. He knew Ornery was a girl, and moreover, he knew she had a body that was sleek and lovely. He liked the looks of her very much, though he felt no desire toward her. He had been trained not to feel desire until and unless desire was wanted, and, if he had thought about it, he would have realized that he had felt no spontaneous desire since he first saw Flowing Green.

By this time he was able to speak with reasonable clarity, though with some pain and effort. 'That may have worked on a ship where, I suppose, you kept yourself covered and where few of the men had seen a woman in their entire lives, but it won't work with me. Why don't you just finish your hair and tell me what's going on?'

'Don't touch me,' demanded Ornery.

'Of course not,' said Mouche, annoyed. 'What do you think I am?'

802

'You're not fixed,' Ornery stuttered, reaching for her clothes. 'And neither am I.'

Which was perfectly true, of course. Mouche wasn't fixed. He wouldn't be until he was sold. And of course he would not force himself on Ornery, because if Ornery – the female Ornery – got pregnant, she could be executed for mismothering, and Mouche was not the kind of person to endanger another in that way. So Mouche told himself, illustrating his goodwill by leaving the room with the utmost dignity and closing the door gently behind him.

Ornery checked the door. The lock was broken. It seemed to lock, but in fact it did not. So, all right, he hadn't picked the lock in order to get at her. With some apprehension, she went back to the room they shared, where Mouche attempted once again to explain that he was both honorable and harmless and that Ornery did not need to worry. His friendly overtures were rebuffed. Further, Ornery adopted a new manner toward him, one of nervous shyness, like a young cat only recently made aware of dogs. Her native gregariousness had led them into a friendly and trusting camaraderie, but now her sense of prudence dictated otherwise. Suddenly, she became suspicious and almost preternaturally alert.

Mouche, in turn, could not decide whether he was annoyed with her or not. Given the high status of women on Newholme and the very low status of supernumes – even ones who got jobs as seamen – he could not quite envision a circumstance which would have led him, had he been female, to pretend otherwise. He would very much have liked to discuss it with Ornery, but she was not of a mood, as yet, for any discussion at all.

38

The Questioner Arrives

Questioner arrived without fanfare. Her shuttle set down near Sendoph late at night. Though Questioner had intended to enter the planetary system from the side nearest the moon where the Quaggi had died, the immediacy of the geological problems on the planet had made her change her mind. The Quaggi would wait. She could stop at the outer planet on her way out.

By morning she was ensconced at Mantelby Mansion, her maintenance system unloaded and ready, her reference files properly arranged, Ellin and Bao settled, and the rest of her varied entourage provided with rooms of their own, along with a separate dining salon. The entourage had caused quite a stir. Of the eight persons attached to Questioner, in addition to Ellin and Bao, no two looked anything alike, and some of them looked only remotely mankindly. The peepers from the walls had seen this with a good deal of interest, and had immediately sent messengers off with descriptions of each one of the eight.

By breakfast, Questioner had her people taking scanner views of every street from Naibah south, and inventorying all businesses, agricultural enterprises, and the like, from Sendoph north. The work could have been done automatically, by miniature spy-eyes, but Questioner did not advise her so-called aides of this. The opportunity to be rid of them for some days, if she was lucky, was too good to miss.

Within the hour, Ellin Voy and Gandro Bao were on their way to the Panhagion in a carriage borrowed from the Mantelby stables while another, larger carriage was being modified to carry the Questioner. The ride was neither long nor uncomfortable, and Ellin considerably enjoyed the amusement of seeing Bao dressed as a woman. Questioner had approved his doing so, since he would otherwise have to wear veils and his efficiency would be impaired. Ellin had to admit that, within a few moments, she thought of him as a woman, for he acted and looked exactly as a rather grave, pleasant, youngish woman might. He had, so he said, learned women's ways and women's wiles over years of study with a Kabuki master of the genre.

Among all these pleasurable details, Ellin could not understand her uneasiness. There was something in the atmosphere of the place, the city, or perhaps the planet, that made her feel queasy. A melancholy in the air. A sadness. A late-autumn, leaf-burning, chill-wind-blowing, inexorable-lifeloss-coming kind of feeling. She felt it like a ghostly hand on her shoulder, and it made no sense at all.

'Do you feel it?' she whispered to Bao, her eyes on the back of the veiled coachman.

Bao stared out at the world, looked up at the sky, across the valley at the long shredded lines of smoke trailing away to the south. 'Something,' he admitted in his woman's voice. 'The hairs on my neck are standing on end.'

When they left the carriage at the foot of the Temple stairs, Ellin stopped a young woman and introduced herself, asking to be taken to someone in charge. She and Bao were escorted into the forecourt of the Temple, where they watched as women placed lighted incense sticks in great sand-filled basins on iron tripods. Smoke rose from hundreds of glowing wands to fill the vault with haze that was lit by vagrant rays of light from high, gem-colored windows. Seen from below, the smoke shone in fragments of ruby and emerald, sapphire, amethyst, and amber, a shifting glory against the gold mosaic tiles of the ceiling.

'It is only the imperfection in the atmosphere that allows us to see the light,' said a voice at their shoulders. 'So with us, only our own imperfections allowing us to see what perfection might be.'

The person addressing them was tall and thin and brown, dressed in a crimson, long-sleeved garment topped by a complicated headdress of striped wine and flame. 'I am D'Jevier Passenger,' she said. 'One of the Temple Hags.'

'Madam,' Ellin bowed. 'My name is Ellin Voy and this is ... Gandra Bao. We are uncertain as to the respectful form of address ...'

'Ma'am will do,' said D'Jevier. 'Or, you may call me simply Hag or Oh, Hag, or Revered Hag, though I doubt the latter is always sincere. I am your servant, Ma'am, and that of the Hagions.'

'The Hagions?' Ellin cocked her head. The Questioner had assured her that this movement, properly executed, elicited information all by itself. Persons often helped the merely puzzled while they withheld information from the demanding.

'Come,' said the Hag. 'You will understand better if you see the Temple proper. We close it to men's eyes. For millennia, mankind was so conditioned to believe that the only possible God is created in the image of a very large and powerful male, that the mere idea of a goddess made the entire male gender overwrought. Even here, on Newholme, where the Hagions have reigned for generations, we find it necessary to keep menfolk's mouths and minds busy with other things.'

D'Jevier held aside one of the heavy curtains and they passed through into the Temple proper, Bao doing so without hesitation. So far as he was concerned, the moment he put on his wig, he became a woman, and he stayed a woman until he took it off.

The Hagions stood along the far, curved wall, their heads – or what would have been their heads – well above Ellin's height, even though the floor was much lower where the images stood. The robes expressed a female form and a female head within a vacancy. *Here I am,* each statue proclaimed, *invisibly existent.*

'Have they names?' Bao whispered in a charming and completely womanly voice. Ellin was silent, though she felt both awed and excited by invisible images, so palpably present.

'The Goddess to the left is the maiden, in the center, the woman, to the right, an old woman, a crone. These ages typify differing types of power. There is also present a fourth, without shape or age, a spirit, invisible. The directory of Hagions is there,' said D'Jevier, indicating the low lectern at the center of the arc of effigies. 'Please feel free to glance at it.'

Ellin and Bao did so, turning the pages, finding there name after name they had never heard of. D'Jevier spoke from behind them: 'There are many aspects of divinity. Some are useful for occasions of joy. Others when we are troubled …'

Something in her voice led Bao to ask in his sweetly sympathetic voice, 'You are troubled? We hope we have not occasioned this feeling.'

She shook her head with a fleeting smile. 'We all are troubled on Newholme. Vulcanism is increasing to an extent that it may threaten both our food supplies and some of our water sources. The Men of Business are extremely worried about the cities and the farmlands, while we are more concerned with human life …'

'Do you mean mankind life?'

D'Jevier turned her face slightly aside, masking her eyes. 'With all due respect to Haraldson, mankind is the only human presence on Newholme.'

'Where will you go?'

'If it gets any worse, we'll have to go into the badlands. Though every tame mountain south and east has turned feral, the canyons west of the city seem to be untroubled. Foodstuffs will be needed, emergency supplies of all kinds …'

D'Jevier sighed dramatically, attempting to look wearied by her labors, hoping to misdirect her visitors. The recent tremors were indeed worse than others in the records, but the Hags had no real intention of evacuating the city as yet, preferring to delay any decision until the Questioner had departed. If she did not approve them and depart, any decision might prove to have been a waste of time.

Ellin and Bao took note of what had been said, then looked once more at the trio of images.

'Are your rites secret?' asked Bao, gravely, hand to throat, conveying awe.

D'Jevier shook her head. 'Private would be a better word. We do not encourage attendance by scoffers, or by the inattentive and the ignorant, but we do not hesitate to inform persons who are interested. Our most popular rite comes at the Tipping of the Year when we concentrate on forgetting the disappointments of the past year, on setting aside events or relationships that have proven troublesome and unhappy, even within families, and on moving on to others that are more kindly, cooperative, and productive. Our rule is to bow, bow again, and get on. Our religion is based upon eschewing human sacrifice in favor of lives that are fulfilling, productive, and joyful.'

Startled, Ellin cried, 'Human sacrifice! I am surprised you can think of such a thing!'

D'Jevier said with unfeigned weariness, 'My dear young woman, our history is made up of millennia of human sacrifice. Well into the twenty-first century, huge armies of young men were sacrificed to tribal or national honor, women were sacrificed to male supremacy, children were sacrificed to brutality, all immolated in flames of painful duty. We try to determine whether the dutiful will suffer and to decide how that suffering may be compensated. We continually redesign our society to provide joy to those who incur pain on our behalf.'

'I'm not sure I get that,' Ellin said.

D'Jevier smiled. 'One example will suffice. On most worlds women have a duty to bear and raise children. Some children are loving and generous; some women enjoy mothering; some families are happy. However, some women are unskilled, or have children who are unloving and selfish. Sometimes they grasp at their children, seeking from their children the joys that instinct tells them they should receive, and there is hurt and annoyance on both sides. Here on Newholme, we try to see that all lives contain appropriate joys, in order that children may grow up without guilt.'

'I see,' murmured Ellin, feeling an abyss open around her. Such a simple idea. Why had she never heard anyone speak of providing appropriate joys?

Bao, with a concerned glance at Ellin, murmured, 'Madam, we are only envoys of Questioner. She has sent us to advise you that she herself will be calling upon you, probably rather soon.'

'I understand,' said D'Jevier, bowing. 'Whenever you like.'

They went out together, standing for a long moment at the top of the stairs. The city moved before them with a certain intent bustle, people carrying this and that, going hither and yon, none of them sparing even a glance for the visitors.

'Something is wrong, here,' said Gandro Bao. 'They should be showing curiosity about us, and they are not doing it. Everybody is being oh so very busy. Let us be going separate ways, to see what we can see.'

Wordlessly, Ellin agreed, and the two of them went off in opposite directions to get a closer look at Newholmian society.

'Nobody is dancing,' said Gandro Bao, removing his dusty cloak and hanging it neatly by the door of the large and luxurious suite that he, Ellin, and Questioner occupied at Mantelby Mansion. He doffed his wig, also, setting it atop his cloak. 'One rumor, about volcanoes, is saying truth, for there is much smoking from the mountains, much agitating among peoples. Other rumor is being unverified. I am seeing no indigenous race.'

'Ah,' murmured the Questioner. 'Where have you been?'

'I am going about in the business section. I am asking Men of Business if mountains are blowing up, and they are saying yes, too many, but it is striking me an oddity that no one is standing about looking at mountains. Or at me! I am being stranger, and mountains are being very dramatic, very threatening, but everyone being very busy, not looking.'

'Aah,' murmured Questioner. 'Perceptive of you, Gandro Bao. They are not looking because ...?'

'Because they are thinking of something else or are avoiding me. Also, I am asking if people dance, and they are saying no, no dancing at all. Streets are being very dirty. Men are wearing very thick veils. Perhaps those are reasons for no dancing. If I am dancing in such a veil, I am falling over my feet.'

'You say the streets are dirty,' mused Questioner. 'Old trash ends up as a kind of sludge in the gutters. You mean dirty like that?'

He shook his head in an effort of memory. 'No. No sludge. Just this little trashiness.'

'Ah. Then the streets are usually cleaner, but not now, or they are infrequently cleaned. If you see anyone cleaning the streets, let me know.' Questioner entered the information on her project file, another in the great number of nagging and interesting data she was accumulating on Newholme.

'You can ask them about the painted houses, too,' said Ellin, entering from the hallway. She yawned enormously and threw herself down on the cushioned seat that stretched beneath a pair of wide windows. 'I'm so tired! I feel heavy on this world!'

'Heaviness is suitable. Newholme gravity is slightly greater than Earth. What is this about painted houses?' asked Questioner.

'I found them behind places and off courtyards and down little hidden lanes, brightly painted little houses in a style I see nowhere else. I asked, people said servants' quarters, and there are servants living there, but they don't fit.'

'Don't fit how?'

'Too tall for the doors, too long for the floors, and too few for all the rooms. The paint's fresh on the houses. The walls are clean, the floors also. I'd say someone else lived there up until just recently.'

'Ah,' murmured Gandro Bao, taking a very feminine stance and parading across the floor, fluttering his eyelashes at Ellin, then at Questioner. 'So, the people are hiding something.' He seized Ellin by the hand and drew her into a whirling encounter, something between a tango and a duel, the two moving like jointed dolls.

Questioner cogitated, much interested and intrigued by this information. So many of her visits were dull and juiceless, with everything laid out like a pattern for a garment: fabric here, shears there, cut here, sew along the dotted line, and what results is a very dull cloak, one size fits nobody. Or there were visits where she could find no pattern at all. Cut? What means cut? Sew? What means sew?

How interesting to meet a third variation, a false pattern. Everything seemingly right there in plain sight, sew here, cut there, and what results is a surprise. A three-legged trouser. A four-armed coat!

She said sharply, 'Stop twirling, you're making me dizzy.'

Ellin and Bao spun to a stop, drawing apart and bowing to one another, Ellin rather pink and breathing strongly. Obediently, they sat side by side on the windowseat, like two marionettes, awaiting the next twitch on the strings.

Questioner remarked, 'Let us assume some other people were here until just recently. If they swept the streets, if they cleaned the houses, chances are they also minded the children, for this is the usual pattern when a culture has cheap labor. So, you should seek out some children, watch them, see what they do and say. Also, it is time we spoke to more ordinary people.

'What did you find at the Temple?'

Ellin keyed her file, which immediately recreated the sight and sound of the visit. When the record had played itself out, Questioner murmured, 'Joys to compensate thankless duty? You didn't pursue that?'

Ellin flushed. 'I was so taken with the idea, I forgot.'

'We will ask next time,' said Questioner. 'Meantime, it seems you can make yourself understood in the local dialect.'

'After all those hours with the sleep teachers on the ship, it isn't difficult,' Ellin replied. 'It still cleaves closely to Earth-universal.'

'In my family, we were speaking Asia-matrix, not Earth-universal,' said Gandro Bao from his place by the window. 'But I am coping.'

Questioner nodded. 'Have you encountered any reference to the first settlement made here? It preceded the second by half a century, at least.'

'Of that, I am having word,' said Bao, picking up his own project file and keying through it. 'Ah, here is note. A man I asked about the Temple building – he would not look at the woman I was being, only at his feet – said building of Temple and the Fortress of Vanished Men in Naibah was being done by first settlers. First colony is disappearing, but fortresses and many other buildings were remaining, mostly along river. There are records in fortress. Are you wanting me to read them?'

Questioner frowned. 'No. I'll send one of my aides to make a copy. I try to keep them as busy as possible with things that don't matter greatly. The entourage is supposed to be for my help and protection, but they don't help and I don't need protection here. The population seems conditioned to respect older women.'

'Isn't that the norm in most worlds?' asked Ellin.

Questioner replied. 'Far from it, my dear, especially on nonmember worlds. Surpluses are not much respected, whether of eggs, grain, or women, and elderly women are always surplus.'

'Newholme is unique in the scarcity of women, then,' remarked Ellin.

Questioner spoke thoughtfully. 'At the current time, it is the only planet I know of.' She rose and went toward the door, saying over her shoulder: 'Dig around a bit more. Talk to some common people. Talk to some children. We will meet again over our evening meal.' She departed. In a moment, they heard the door to the room in which the Questioner's massive and complicated reference files had been installed. It opened and, after a long pause, closed.

Ellin stood at the window, using the sill as a barre as she stretched and bent. 'Oh, Gandro Bao, let us dance a little more. Just that little bit of dancing worked out some of my kinks! I feel like a wooden doll, all stiff.'

'You should be dancing with me more.' Bao smiled. 'The exercise will be doing us both good.' He drew her into the dance once more, looking her up and down as they twirled. 'Are you still wondering who you are, Ellin Voy?'

'Not when I'm dancing,' she cried breathlessly. 'Not then.'

She bent, turned, bent again, then stopped, her eyes caught by movement in the gardens below.

'There,' she said, pointing. 'Gandro Bao, there are two gardeners there below. They're common people. After we've had some lunch, let's talk to the gardeners.'

He looked out the window, noted the gardeners, started to draw her to him once more, then changed his mind. Her eyes were sparkling, and she had just given him a very friendly and intimate look. He did not want her to get the wrong idea. She was a dear companion, with a truly sweet nature, but in the pursuit of certain pleasures, Gandro Bao preferred men. He took her hand, bent over it, then suggested they go into the small salon where their lunch was served.

Behind them, in the walls of the room where they had danced, voices cried:

'Dancers! They are dancers! Oh, we must take them!'

'Tim was going to take the other ones! The different ones.'

'Take the different ones, but take these, too.'

'Now? Shouldn't we ask Bofusdiaga?'

'Now. We shouldn't waste time!'

'Ask some-tim,' a voice cried. 'Find out.'

After a moment, the walls were silent, the peepholes hidden, the room quiet. Elsewhere, however, was a bustle of coming and going as the Timmys decided whether and when to take away Ellin and Bao.

39

Gardeners, Molds, and Intricacies

On the lawn of Mantelby Mansion, Mouche and Ornery were silently raking up the trimmings from a hedge; silently because they did not know what to say to one another. They had not spoken since the previous evening when Mouche's friendly overtures had been rebuffed. He was, in consequence, annoyed, which made him feel guilty. Consorts could be angry at insult or annoyed by too much starch in their frilled shirts, but they could not, ever, be angry or annoyed at women. Mouche had been drilled in that fact, he had been given exercises to do, and he had discussed it with his personal trainer over and over again, none of which was helping him now. He was irritable because though he could now talk intelligibly, it pained him to do so, and he was also feeling symptoms of withdrawal from his addiction. It had been days since he had seen Flowing Green. He had dreamed of her, it, but he had not seen her. All this made him more annoyed at Ornery than he might otherwise have been. He needed a comfortable friend, and now, amid all this confusion, she had stopped being one.

Mouche had discarded the notion that it was because of his face. Ornery was not that kind. Others would be, but not her. When they had been comfortable friends, however, he, Mouche, had thought she, Ornery, was a boy. So, perhaps the key to this tangle was for him to accept that she, he, Ornery was indeed a boy. Well, a chatron. And he, Mouche, should treat him, Ornery, just as he had in the past.

Mouche rehearsed these intentions, putting reasonable words to them, fighting the temptation to be spiteful, resolving to sound firm but sensible, and he was readying himself to expound on his resolution when Ellin and Bao came along the walk, full of questions.

Mouche and Ornery bowed. Mouche had been working himself up to politeness, but Ornery acknowledged the visitors only in a cursory fashion. Ornery was, if possible, more annoyed than Mouche was. She liked Mouche a good deal as a friend, but Ornery did not like men except as friends. On the ship she had come to know a good many of them rather intimately. Some she enjoyed being with, as she did Mouche, and some she would as soon not be around, but her strongest feelings were reserved for other women. She had no desire to be any more than friendly with Mouche, but she strongly wanted to be friendly! If she was friendly with him, he might desire her, and then it would all be a tangle!

And now, adding irritation to aggravation, here were these two outlanders, asking questions!

'Have you worked here long?' Ellin asked.

'Too long,' snarled Ornery.

'Yes, Madam,' said Mouche, with an admonitory glance at Ornery. They were under instructions to be polite, word having filtered down just what the stakes were in this particular game. It had been intimated that some great penalty might be exacted by the Council of Worlds, a penalty that would affect each and every one of them. Discretion, urged the powers that be. No matter who you are, discretion.

Bao, who was still in his women's garb, said, 'I am seeing gardens with much work invested. What numbers of persons are working to keep them so?'

'A lot,' snarled Ornery from behind his veil.

'More sometimes than others,' said Mouche, leaving himself a way out.

'How many right now?' asked Ellin, with a hint of asperity.

Mouche laid down his shears and tucked in his veils as he said slowly and pleadingly, 'Mistress, we don't know. We are very lowly persons. We are not told things by those who hire us, except to go here or there, to do this or that. Sometimes there are a good many gardeners at meals in the servants' quarters. Other times, there are fewer. Some who work the gardens may also labor in the stables or the fields. To find out precisely how many, you would need to ask the head gardener or the steward.'

This was the longest speech Ellin had managed to provoke from a veiled man as yet, and she noted the way in which it was delivered. Humbly, but eloquently, with a slight catch in the pronunciation that spoke of a minor speech impediment. Also, the man who spoke stood like a ... well, a dancer. Or perhaps an actor. Reason told her he should have been a little stooped and gnarled if he had, in fact, worked a long time in the gardens. Reason told her, also, that the voice should not have sounded so very well trained. It was, in all respects, an attractive voice.

She turned to the other veiled figure and asked, 'Is that so? Are you truly told so little?'

'It's true,' grunted the other. 'It's hardbread and tea, work until noon, soup and hardbread and work until sundown. That's life on Newholme.'

'It sounds hard,' said Gandro Bao.

'But satisfying,' said Mouche with a grim look at Ornery. 'We are content with our lot.'

'Speak for yourself,' said Ornery.

Mouche took a deep breath and spoke directly to Bao. 'You ladies are not veiled. Sometimes we who are veiled find working in such conditions troublesome and itchy. Sometimes we get irritable, as my friend is now. He is a good friend, however. I do not want to lose him *as my friend*. Please, do not say to anyone that *my friend* was anything less than accommodating to your needs.'

The four stood staring at one another, open interest on the one side and veiled frustration on the other. With some vague idea of clarifying things, Ellin asked, 'Will you take down your veils for us? Just for a moment.'

Ornery and Mouche looked at one another, surprised, Mouche more shocked than Ornery, who had gone long times without veils on the ship.

'Please,' begged Ellin. 'We will not mention it to anyone, but we need to discover things about this world, and so much of it is hidden behind ... veils.'

'You are not getting into trouble over it,' said Bao. 'We are discovering all kinds of things, as Ellin says.'

Well, they had been told to be polite! Though Mouche would have preferred not to display his battered countenance, he did so, with a quick glance around to be sure they were unobserved. The veil dropped at one side, and as it did so Mouche saw in his mind what he would have seen in a mirror, more or less what his interlocutors would see, and it struck him that he and the woman confronting him could have been kin. They had the same coloring. Same bones. Same long, thin hands. Only one of them was badly cut, of course.

Ellin and Bao searched the exposed face before them: ivory skin, a lock of pale hair showing under the cowl, dark brows, green eyes, a spatter of pale beard shadowing mouth and chin, and a new, horrid scar from beneath the left eye to the corner of the mouth. It seemed to be healing cleanly, but the flesh around it was livid and puffed. If it had not been for that, it would have been a handsome though, at the moment, rather furtive face.

'Why do you have to wear the veil?' Ellin asked.

'So as not to stir your insatiable lusts, lady,' said Ornery in a slightly ironic voice, lowering his own veil to display a countenance tanned by the sea winds and the sun.

Ellin managed to look both amused and offended. 'My what?'

'Your insatiable lusts,' murmured Mouche. 'So we are taught as children.'

'At the moment, I have none,' Ellin said. 'Have you noticed that I have insatiable lusts, Gandro – ah, Gandra Bao?'

'I am seeing nothing of that kind, no,' he said, bowing slightly in her direction. 'Perhaps, to be helping us, this gentleman will be explaining?'

Mouche leaned on his rake, examining their faces for guile. 'Women are easily moved to lust,' he said at last, believing them to be truly interested. 'It is part of their biological heritage, which is so very valuable to mankind.

Their lusts serve their lineage, of course, since it forces them to bear and tend, which otherwise many would reject as uninteresting. Also, any child they bear is unequivocally their own, and the more males each female can associate herself with, the more likely she has links to survival. This is all sensible and correct as a survival technique, and women's instincts still thrust in that direction.

'Historically, so we are taught, the same was true for males. They also desire survival, and through the designs and desires imposed on them by their own genetic pattern, wish more than anything to guarantee their own posterity. We are taught how great predator cats kill cubs not their own. Other creatures also do this, including sometimes mankind males, who take up with a woman with children, then kill her children. Males want above all to guarantee their own line. So, in order that men have surety of their lineage and women not be lured into mismothering, men must not stir their lusts.'

'This is making loving very dull,' said Gandro Bao, with a seductive smile at Mouche.

Mouche ignored the smile. 'Only for husbands! Say for them rather it is very stern and thoughtful. We are taught it is better that posterity be engendered with coolness, with much deliberate intention. Once that task is completed, however, women are entitled to compensatory joys, and for that they require a Consort who does not make it dull! Someone to indulge their lusts, but not engender children. You see?' Mouche had become carried away with his explanation and had said a good deal more than he intended.

Ellin said to herself, Oh-ho, so here is what compensation is offered. She and Bao looked at one another, eyebrows raised. Mouche and Ornery waited.

Finally, though he was sure he already knew, Bao asked, 'What is being Consort?'

'A man trained to cosset women,' said Ornery. 'Like him,' and she jerked a thumb in Mouche's direction.

Mouche merely blinked at her, refusing to be drawn by her chiding tone. From beyond the recently trimmed hedge, they heard the approach of persons, loudly talking to one another. Hastily, Mouche and Ornery rearranged their veils and turned to their work, busily raking while the two agents went thoughtfully back to their window, far above.

'What is hardbread?' Ellin asked.

Bao didn't know. He summoned a servant. 'What is hardbread?'

'A kind of dried cracker that sailors eat, sir. Hardbread and tea. Or so they complain.'

'Sailors, not gardeners?'

'Not gardeners, no. Gardeners eat garden stuff, and bread from the kitchen. Ships have no kitchens, so between barbecues and fish fries ashore, shipfolk eat hardbread.'

'Interesting,' said Ellin. 'A sailor and a ... a Consort. I would have guessed he was an actor. How did the two of them get to be friends?'

'I think they were meeting for first time not long ago,' said Bao, 'but men are striking up friendships quickly. Particularly in adversity. It is having survival benefit.'

'I don't know what women do,' she said thoughtfully. 'Every time I thought I had made a woman friend, they switched me somewhere else. Even the dance classes. They kept moving them around, shuffling them. Sometimes you didn't see the same people for two shifts running.'

'Forget what is past. Now I am being your friend,' he said.

She gave him a somewhat suspicious look, finding nothing in his expression but placid good will. 'Careful, Bao, or you may stir my insatiable lusts!'

He flushed, rubbing with a finger at the furrow between his eyes. 'This is not my desire.'

She scarcely heard him. 'Besides, are there male-female friends who are truly friends? I've never heard of any.'

'There are such friends,' he said firmly. 'And if there were never being any, we could decide to be the first.'

When Ellin and Bao learned the nearest infant school was in Sendoph it was already quite late in the day. Accordingly, they postponed their interviews with children until the following morning. The Questioner emerged from her room in the early evening, seeming somewhat changed. Ellin and Bao had been with her shortly after a maintenance session aboard ship, and they were prepared for the slight uncertainty her appearance evoked.

'It's the machines,' the Questioner had told them while aboard ship. 'The mind is affected by the files and the maintenance machines and so is the body. If I were human, I would change with time, so the machines change me a little, perhaps to make me aware of time passing.' This sounded good, though she felt it probably wasn't true. Since receiving the information about her donor minds – though certainly 'donor' wasn't the proper word – she had found maintenance more than usually uncomfortable. Now that she *knew* about her indwelling minds, the buffer that held their memories from her own had been breached. Each time she came from maintenance she had learned more about their lives, and each time she felt more angry. Those who had killed her indwelling children were dead these several hundred years, but she hated them still! Hated them, was furious at them, and knew her duty required her to set all such feelings aside.

Ellin launched at once into a report of their conversation with the gardeners along with the inferences she and Bao had drawn from it, all of which Questioner entered into her memory, commenting, 'So the one was a sailor and here he is, cutting away at the little hedges. And the other man is, according to the first, a Consort ...'

'He talks like an actor,' said Ellin. 'And he moves like a dancer. Don't you agree, Bao?'

'Yes, I am concurring,' said Bao, his voice thickening slightly. The pale gardener resembled someone he had once known well but far too briefly. He cleared his throat. 'His voice is projecting extremely well. I am having feelings of recognition, as when I am meeting someone of my own profession. His work is seeming to say that making women happy is mostly acting!'

The Questioner nodded ponderously. 'Not a definition most women would appreciate, though I don't doubt its truth. More often it is women who do the acting. On Generis, in fact, prostitutes belong to the actors' guild, for it is recognized their profession is pretense. Let us consider: if there were other gardeners here before, and these are here now, presumably they had to get these from somewhere. So, they got them from nonessential areas? The sea and ... whatever this other thing is?'

'Compensation,' said Ellin. 'Consorts provide pleasurable compensation. The Hags at the Temple referred to it, remember? But I forgot to ask them what it was.'

'I am having one thing more to report,' said Bao, referring to his notes. 'There is most unpleasant smell ...'

'The one out at the back,' the Questioner said, nodding as she pointed vaguely away. 'Yes. I wandered about while you were in town. The smell is near the servants' quarters. My lexicon would identify this particular smell as a considerable stink.'

'Oh, that at least,' muttered Ellin. 'Bao and I thought it was maybe animal excrement.'

The Questioner considered this. 'Animal excrement is accumulated near the stables and spread upon the fields. It smells, yes, but this stink has a much higher rating than animal excrement. The ooze of the volbers of Planet Gosh, a notable stench, rates a maximum of seven. This rates an eleven on a scale of twelve. A most putrescent and malodorous reek! Which raises an interesting question. How and why do the servants tolerate it?'

'It seems a minor matter,' Ellin remarked, 'but we can ask the servants.'

'Mercy me, no.' Questioner smiled. 'One cannot imagine such fetor existing without Mistress Mantelby's knowledge, though it may be something she would prefer not to discuss. With that in mind, we'll play a little game to learn why it is she is not greatly offended.'

She then took a few moments to rehearse them, then sent one of the Mantelby servants to Mistress Mantelby, requesting a guided stroll in the gardens for the Questioner and two of her aides.

Marool's immediate reaction was to reject any such claim on her time, but she caught herself. The Questioner's numerous entourage was causing a good deal of agitation, and the repression of Marool's normal appetites was becoming a grave annoyance. The sooner the Questioner could be satisfied and depart, the sooner Marool herself could resume her usual devotions.

She agreed, therefore, to meet the Questioner on the terrace. Questioner showed up with Bao, in wig, and Ellin, who had been coached to be quite Perkins in her persona, as polite as it was possible to be. They proceeded downward into the garden from the lofty and balustered terrace, Questioner leading the way without at all seeming to do so, while Ellin and Bao chatted inoffensively and commented effusively. Marool, though totally contemptuous of the Questioner and her entourage, was lulled into a state of complacent disdain.

'I so seldom have time merely to walk,' Questioner murmured. 'One would not think strolling much of an amusement, but we spent such a long time coming to your lovely world, and the ships are never large enough to walk in. I find this gentle ambulation quite wonderful. And may I say, Mistress Mantelby, how beautiful your gardens are. I have seen many, all over the sector, and yours are among the loveliest.'

'Oh, that's so true,' bubbled Ellin.

'How very kind,' smiled Marool, soothed into amiability.

'Oh!' cried Ellin, on approaching a certain corner. 'Nova roses. My favorite. May I pick one?'

Marool condescended, looking on with amusement while Ellin stepped lightly into the back of a bed where she clipped an enormous silver white blossom and put her nose into it. She then offered it to Marool, saying, 'The scent is quite remarkable.'

Marool sniffed at the rose. 'It is wonderful,' she said with an indifferent nod.

'Among the most fragrant in your garden,' Questioner murmured.

'Indeed,' Marool agreed.

They walked on, Ellin burbling on about the beauty and the fragrance of the garden as she sniffed at this and that and Bao offering this or that blossom for appreciation. At the end of their stroll, they departed from their hostess with fulsome expressions of gratitude, and Marool went back to the more decorous parts of her daily routine in a somewhat improved mood. Though Questioner was nothing but a piece of machinery, it was a polite piece of machinery and its aides were polite also. Marool could tolerate them.

Questioner said, 'It's as I thought,' she said. 'Mantelby has no sense of smell! The Nova rose is odorless. Did you watch her when Bao waved the crimson stinkbrush in her face?'

Ellin nodded. 'She didn't flinch. She has a smile like a shark, that one.'

'What is it meaning?' asked Bao.

'I have no idea.' Questioner showed her own teeth in a tigerish grin. 'It goes down onto my list with all the other odd data.'

'Odd?' Bao raised his eyebrows. 'What things are you counting as odd?'

Questioner ticked them off on her fingers. 'There's the oddity of the first colony, the one that disappeared. There's the oddity of the little houses too small for the people who live in them. There's the dirty streets and the stink out back, and the fact that Madam Mantelby has no sense of smell. There are those monumental schools that show up on the business inventory, seeming far too large for their stingy classes of little boys. Well, we have a clue to that, now, don't we?'

'Consorts?' asked Ellin. 'Consort academies?'

'Assuredly. If they are trained to cosset women, they must be trained somewhere. In itself a strangeness. Well, most cultures have oddities of one kind or another.'

'I am not understanding what you mean by strangeness,' said Bao.

The Questioner seated herself comfortably, quite willing to educate a willing listener. 'All societies maintain themselves by forcing personal behavior into a mold or pattern which the society calls its "culture." The patterns are imposed by natural or political conditions; for example, either recurrent drought or recurrent persecution can result in similar patterns. Most patterns require changes in behavior, and that requires changes in belief systems, or vice versa, sort of chicken and egg as to which comes first.

'So a few thousand years go by and the climate changes, or the politics, but the people still follow the same taboos because by now they believe their deity ordered them to do it. Long-practiced behaviors that started as a response to conditions, always fossilizes into "traditional values," that is, the only "right way" to do things. At that point people no longer use the system in order to survive, the system uses them in order to survive. That's something people often don't understand. Systems are parasitical, they have a life of their own, and they, too, evolve and change and try to survive. The one fact that is true of all cultures, without exception, is that it never represents the free desires of the people who are jammed into it even when people are conditioned from childhood to accept uniformation.'

'Really?' asked Ellin. 'Never?'

Questioner grinned at her. 'Only mavericks live in accordance with their desires, and even they don't often get away with it. They are usually labeled as troublemakers and gotten rid of. So, when the Questioner arrives on a new planet, the people show us the culture. Here, they say, this is what we are, we have nothing to hide. Genetic variation, however, guarantees that sometimes a rebel will be born, and you may be sure the culture has come up with a way to deal with him.

'So, in order to find out what's really going on, we investigate how the culture reacts to threats, we look for the people who do not fit, we look for the oddities, the strangenesses. When we have enough of them, we learn what the bones and nerves of the culture are really like, beneath the skin.'

'But you're saying all societies are coercive,' said Ellin in a troubled voice.

Questioner laughed. 'But Honorable Ellin, of course they are. This is what makes reading history so amusing. Most cultures think of themselves as free while regarding others as coerced. They do so because they are following "traditional values," and the generations of coercion that resulted in those values is long forgotten. On Old Earth, in one society, women rejoiced that they were "free" to have children, when in fact they had been coerced into excessive reproduction by a profit-driven culture that required a growing population. Men felt they were "free" to ingest deadly substances or own deadly weapons, when in fact they were coerced into desiring them by industries that had to sell weapons and drugs to survive. Weapons, poisons, and large families were all parasites on the population. The people weren't free, they had been molded into consumers, which is what the mercantile culture needed.

'Such things can be most amusing,' she said with a chuckle.

'I think the veils on the men is being coerced,' said Bao.

'Of course they are,' the Questioner agreed. 'Usually it is women who are locked behind the veil, but veiling isn't unusual. I have heard two phrases that are unusual, however: "mismothering" and "blue-bodying." These words are indicative of intricacies being kept from us.'

'The gardener who isn't a gardener referred to mismothering,' said Ellin. 'It was in the context of men desiring their own posterity.'

'Yes.' The Questioner mused. 'In which case, to have a child by other than one's lawful mate would be mismothering. Depend upon it. When we find what the penalty is for that, it will be far worse than mere veiling.' She rose to stare out the window across the manicured lawns of Mantelby Mansion.

'It's too early to say exactly what's going on, for we're still collecting data ...' Her voice trailed off as she switched thoughts. 'Which reminds me: I've asked the technicians on the ship for a detailed report on the geological situation, and it will be finished by morning. First thing tomorrow, we'll summon a conveyance. The report will make a good excuse for me to call upon the Temple of the Hagions.'

40

Questioner Visits the Panhagion

The following morning, the Questioner, dressed in the force-shield cloak she wore outside for protection against everything short of meteorites, was standing with Ellin and Bao on the gravel drive, awaiting their conveyance, when the ground began to shake, the initial tremor building into a bone-twisting shudder that lasted some minutes but seemed, in retrospect, to have gone on for hours. The gardens shimmied, blooms were whipped from their stems to fly like shrapnel in all directions. The terraces snapped like so much sugar candy, the rough edges of the shards grinding against one another in a rasping mutter that almost drowned out the sound of the roar, the exhalation, the whatever-it-was from wherever-it-came that subsumed all other sounds.

When the ground stilled at last, Questioner was still standing obdurately erect, stabilizers extended, with Ellin and Bao each clinging to an immovable arm. Waiting for the last of the noise to subside, the Questioner asked in a mildly interested tone: 'Read for me what the report says, Bao. That one you are still holding. And may I remark how dutiful you are to have held on to it.'

Bao, between gritted teeth, hissed a commentary that fell far short of describing his feelings.

'Take a deep breath,' said Questioner. 'Release. Now again, in, out, in, out. Are you recovered?'

Bao muttered again, as Ellin broke into a titter that threatened full-fledged hysteria.

Questioner turned her head from side to side, examining them both. They still clung, as though for dear life. 'It's over for the time being,' she told them. 'Look, down the driveway, where the horses attached to our carriage are having seizures of anxiety. Observe the driver in the exercise of his phlegmatic habitude. Does he not inspire you? Are you not moved to emulate his imperturbability?'

Ellin stepped carefully away, feet spread well apart, braced for the resumption of the tremor. Bao followed her example, keying the file he held and peering at it blindly. 'It says,' he gulped, 'it says …'

'There, there,' said Questioner impatiently. 'What does it say?'

'It says the crust of the planet is becoming increasingly unstable …'

'How perceptive of them!' cried Ellin.

'... and may reach, but has not yet reached, the point at which it endangers planetary life,' he concluded, handing the report to Questioner, who scanned it rapidly.

The carriage, which eventually approached, was one that had been adapted to carry Questioner's massive form. She climbed the two steps without help and sat hugely upon the seat, the two aides across from her, the report open upon her lap.

'When you first went to the Temple,' said Questioner to Ellin, 'I recall that D'Jevier remarked about the volcanoes. Did it seem to you she was greatly disturbed?'

Ellin thought back. 'Not greatly, no,' she said, grabbing for a handhold as the carriage dropped an inch or two over a recently fallen slab. 'Her perturbation seemed more dramatic than real.'

Questioner scanned farther in the report. 'Our planetologists tell us that the greatest damage thus far has occurred on the other side of this world, where islands have sunk or are sinking, all of them uninhabited, so far as anyone knows. Our scientists go on to say that what we are experiencing, this local disturbance in the vicinity of the Giles, happens every ten to twenty years in gravitic response to certain lunar configurations. So, if she, the Hag, has seen this happen before, why is she being so dramatic about it now?'

'She is dragging, perhaps, a dead fish along the way, hoping we will go sniffing after that rather than something else?' asked Bao.

'Rather than thinking of indigenes?' Ellin asked.

'Quite possibly,' mused Questioner. 'Of course, this latest eruption is exceptionally strong, and dangerous, but do they know that?'

Ellin tittered again, breathlessly. 'It would be ironic if we all got swallowed up by some volcano, the indigenes along with the rest of us.'

'Which could happen in time,' said Questioner, dispassionately. 'For our planetologists say that if present conditions persist, the settled areas will be endangered. Further, they say they can find no geological reason for this instability except an "unforeseen and mysterious change in the movements of the crust itself, though there is no detectable change in its nature." I find that very interesting.'

'Interesting.' Ellin gulped. 'She finds it interesting.'

Questioner turned toward her. 'We all die, Ellin Voy. Even I, in time. I was designed to be interested in all things, including those that repulse mankind, like slime and strange insects, like plague and famine and dying. You may be interested, too, when you have a calm moment to consider it. Now do as I bade Gandro Bao. Breathe, breathe, and calm yourself.'

The rest of the journey was made in nervous silence by the dancers, in apparent serenity by Questioner, and in some apprehension by the horses.

The driver was habitually glum, and nothing had changed him. The passengers were met at the foot of the Temple stairs by Onsofruct herself, her face pallid and her hands moist, who conducted them up the stairs and into the forecourt.

'I'm sure you are not female in the sense our worshippers would understand,' said Onsofruct to Questioner. 'But in some cases, appearances are all. Shall we go into the Temple?'

They did so, seating themselves on the lowest bench, the one nearest both the lectern and the effigies of the Hagions. There were worshippers scattered about in the Sanctuary, some kneeling, most of them standing quite still or seated upon cushions. Older women, some very old, sat on the high-backed benches around the sides. Though the air was hazed with dust, the Temple seemed undamaged by the recent tremors.

Questioner scanned the interior of the lofty space, comparing it to the account Ellin had recorded. She saw the book on the lectern, rose and went over to it, flipping the pages with one hand, too rapidly for the others to see anything but a blur. When she returned to sit beside them, she had put into memory the total contents of every page, including the chemical traces left on each page by the fingers and breath of those who had taken time to read it. A separate part of her mind went to work analyzing what it had read and cross-referencing persons to pages.

She smiled at Onsofruct, took out the geological report, keyed it, and turned it so that the Hag could see it.

'Your concern about the stability of Newholme's crust is well founded.'

Onsofruct stared at her, mouth very slightly open, thinking vaguely that she and D'Jevier had been blown by their own bomblet. Though the Hags had purposefully overstated their fears, it seemed this current instability was living up to their pretended anxieties.

Smoothly, Questioner continued, 'What we find most interesting about this is that the geologists can find no reason whatsoever for this increasing instability. There is no significant change in the geothermal variations of the mantle or the core. There is no gross change in the slow movement of the plates or the frictional heat causing up-wellings from mantle through crust. Our technicians tell me, and I find this imaginative, that it is as though the world's crust was suffering discomposure. A planetary eczema, perhaps?'

Onsofruct smiled, a humorless smile, her eyes focused on some other time or place.

Questioner shook her head with seeming sadness. 'Madam, pay attention. Whatever other problems you may have here on Newholme, they pale beside this one. Whatever guilts you are attempting to hide from me, they are small beside this actual danger of destruction. Actual, proximate, and total destruction.'

'Then the Men of Business ... they are right?' Her voice sounded incredulous and shrill. She cleared her throat. 'I thought ... I thought perhaps they had overstated the case.'

'No,' murmured Questioner. 'I am amazed the Temple is still standing after that shaking this morning.'

'When we took over the building, it was retro-engineered to withstand earthquake,' muttered Onsofruct. 'Most of the larger buildings in Sendoph and Naibah were either reinforced or designed to be quake resistant from inception. There are always ... tremors.'

'Ah ...' said Questioner. 'Madam, this may sound quite silly to you, but do you have any legends or myths concerning this shaking? Hmmm?'

'Legends?' she faltered.

'Most societies have stories about natural phenomena: volcanoes, waterfalls, windstorms, whatever. Fire goddesses; wind gods; ocean deities. You have been upon this world long enough to accumulate a mythology. Do you recall any such?'

'I do,' came a voice from behind them.

They turned to see D'Jevier, who was observing Onsofruct with troubled eyes.

'My cousin,' murmured Onsofruct.

'D'Jevier Passenger,' the new arrival introduced herself. 'We are close cousins, yes, but we did not share all aspects of our rearing. My cousin may not have heard a children's story that I remember well. Did you ever hear it, Onsy? About the snake at the center of the world?'

Onsofruct flushed and glared at her sibling, who only smiled in return, saying: 'Though it may be embarrassing to recount a ... nursery tale, the matter does seem to be of some urgency. Surely the Questioner would not ask if it were not important.'

Some signal passed between them. Onsofruct flushed again, began a retort, then caught herself, mumbling, 'Oh ... well. Yes, I remember hearing it. But my cousin is correct, it's only a children's story. A fairy tale.'

'Tell it,' instructed the Questioner. 'Sometimes we find truth in the unlikeliest places.'

'Well ... let me see. The Summer Snake is curled in the center of the world, like a baby snake in an egg ...'

'Why is it called Summer Snake?' asked Questioner.

'Because that is when it came,' said D'Jevier. 'It came in summer, and its name is Niasa.'

'You mean, then is when it was laid?' asked Ellin.

'Laid, I suppose. *Came* is what I remember.'

Onsofruct resumed: '... And there are moon dragons, Joggiwagga, who keep track of the moons, for when the moons get lined up and pushy, it makes Niasa uneasy and wakeful, and the egg shakes. So then its mother soothes ...'

'Not the mother,' D'Jevier corrected. 'It was Bofusdiaga.'

'I thought Bofusdiaga was its mother.' Onsofruct frowned.

'No. Don't you recall? She was the mother, and Little Niasa was the egg. Big Summer Snake laid her egg at the center of the world, where it is nice and warm. And when she hears Little Niasa crying, she cries also, very loudly, and then the Corojumi and Bofusdiaga hear her ...'

'Who or what are they?' murmured Ellin.

D'Jevier shook her head, shrugging. 'Bofusdiaga is something very large and singular. The Corojumi are smaller and numerous. In the stories, Bofusdiaga is the sleep tender, the one who lullabies, and the Corojumi weave the dreams that keep the snake from waking. Also, Bofusdiaga sets the sails, and the Corojumi hold the tiller, or other way round, and they sail the ship of dreams across the pillared seas to Niasa's nest.'

'They want to *keep* the snake from waking?' asked Ellin.

'Yes.' Both the cousins nodded. 'So it won't hatch too soon.'

'And from whom did you hear this charming story?' asked the Questioner. A momentary stillness.

'Our ... nursemaids,' said D'Jevier. 'When we were little.'

'And what were their names?'

'Mine died,' said Onsofruct.

Questioner glanced at her aides and smiled, a sardonic smile that said she knew they were lying.

D'Jevier said, in a tone of bright and totally spurious helpfulness, 'Mine was a nice old lady, but she also died, years ago. Her name was Velgin. Emily Velgin. She didn't have any family. She was sterile. She never married.'

'Her parents are no doubt dead, too,' murmured the Questioner. 'And all her family.'

'Certainly.' They said it almost together, both nodding.

Questioner rose, still smiling, thanking them fulsomely, letting them know with every movement and word that she knew they were liars of the worst stripe, whom she would pretend to believe for the nonce, for reasons of her own. As they moved toward the curtained arches, the floor came alive beneath them, dancing under their feet. High in the vault, a window cracked, then broke, shedding a shower of tinkling ruby glass.

'Perhaps Little Niasa has colic.' Questioner smiled. She had thrown her protective cape across Ellin at the first shiver. 'Perhaps it writhes helplessly, seeking to escape evil dreams. Night terrors, as they are sometimes called. If Big Niasa could waken it, perhaps it could be soothed, given hot milk and a cookie. Or, since it is reptilian, a live mouse.'

She lifted her arm, releasing Ellin.

'Perhaps,' said D'Jevier, her forehead beaded with tiny drops, her hand clammy when Ellin grasped it as they said good-bye. Bao waited for them outside on the steps of the Temple, his own face fearful. They felt three more tremors of descending degrees of violence on their way back to Mantelby.

Where they confronted rebellion.

'Look at this,' snarled the protocol officer, waving a copy of the geological report. 'I've just had a chance to read it. It says the world is going to come apart. We aren't required to sit here and wait for it, are we?'

'Is it indeed?' Questioner was calm as she removed the cloak. 'Would you like to leave the planet?'

'We should all go at once.'

'I am inclined to agree that you should, yes. I am staying here for the time being. I imagine, though I am not certain, that Ellin and Bao will choose to stay with me. That is no reason, however, why the other members of my entourage should remain here. Your work is largely done. You will no doubt be more comfortable on the ship, and I should be able to maintain a link with the ship while it remains safely in orbit.'

For a fleeting moment, Ellin readied herself to shout a denial. She would go, go at once, not stay, things were too dangerous. She tried to formulate a graceful announcement that wouldn't sound like total hysteria, but the words wouldn't come. Why not? Could it be that she didn't want to go? After a moment's shuddering indecision, she admitted it to herself. She wanted to … to feel like this. She had never felt like this, tingling like this. Absurdly, she remembered the little boy who had wanted tornadoes! He had been right! She also wanted tornadoes. She wanted to see what was going to happen.

Turning, she caught Bao's eyes on her and flushed. He had told her to put out roots and grow, and now he was watching her do it! He made a comical face and winked at her, accurately interpreting her confusion.

The protocol officer departed, returning briefly to say that all eight of them were leaving for the shuttle and would return to the ship immediately.

'And you're really going to let them go?' asked Ellin.

'Have they contributed anything to our inquiry? The technicians – who are not political appointees, thank whomever arranged it – have given us considerable help, but they've done it from orbit and can go on doing so. So long as we can reach the ship, what do we need these people for?'

'I am not seeing why you are having those people in the first place,' sniffed Bao.

Questioner laughed, a mirthless bark. 'My dear young people, they are foisted upon me. A century or so ago, the Council of Worlds decided that providing me with an entourage would open up opportunities for some of their juvenile kinfolk. Many of the functions of COW are cluttered up with witless fetchers and carriers who are somehow related to council members.

A pity Haraldson never forbade nepotism!'

'If you are not needing them, are you really needing us?' Bao asked.

'I am. I really need nonthreatening persons with alert, questioning minds and enough good sense to spot the oddities. Thus far, you've done well. So, let us proceed.'

A Mantelby servant came in to announce that dinner was served in the adjacent salon, to which Questioner, Ellin, and Bao immediately repaired to indulge themselves in a long, elaborate, and delicious meal. The servants had just set dessert on the table – a fluffy concoction of fruits and cream which Ellin had been looking forward to with delicious guilt since it had appeared on the morning menu card – when the link to the ship announced itself.

Bao spoke to the Gablian watch officer, who asked for the staff member who was handling the geological reports.

Bao informed the ship that the entire staff should be aboard. A long silence presaged a denial by the watch officer that any of the staff members were anywhere on the ship.

Questioner rose and approached the link. 'Commander, I sent all my entourage except the two young Earthians back to the ship some hours ago.'

'I was alerted to expect them. They never arrived.'

'Hold fast,' suggested the Questioner. 'Let's see what we can find out here.' She turned to Bao and Ellin, putting on an exasperated face. 'Would you mind, young people? Go see what's holding them up?'

Ellin had a mouth full of delight and her eyes shut. Reluctantly, she swallowed.

'You, a dancer, consuming such stuff!' said Questioner in mock reproof.

'I know,' Ellin cried guiltily. 'But then, I keep thinking it might be the last chance I ever have.'

'Last chance, child?'

Seduced by food and wine, her thoughts burst out without censor. 'Oh, Questioner, something's building to a climax! I keep hearing the music for it, all those tremorous violins, the slow descending basses, each note deeper into the fabric of the world, the brasses, muted, like voices calling in a dark wood ...'

'All day she has been hearing this, nodding her head in time to this music,' confirmed Bao. 'I am finding it quite interesting.'

Questioner nodded, unimpressed by this idea. 'Very poetic, my dear, but hardly your last chance. Your dessert will wait for you.'

As they departed, Questioner tasted the dessert and approved. It was not necessary to eat more than one taste, as she could recall the flavor and texture at will. Which she did as she sat, musing, going over everything she had learned on this planet. She had already decided mankind could not be allowed to continue on Newholme. The presence of indigenes was incontrovertible. If mankind had settled in ignorance of their presence, they should have reported it the moment the first indigenes snowed up. The fact they had not condemned them, and she had no intention of arguing with Haraldson's edicts. And then there was this viral disease that constricted the female population ...

But there were other riddles still to be solved, interesting habits, like the reverse veiling and the Consorts, and there was also this strange geological business ...

Gradually it occurred to her that a very long time had passed since Ellin and Bao had left in search of the members of the entourage.

A steward was summoned and asked to go find Bao and Ellin. He departed, veils flapping. After a short time, he returned. The Questioner's aides were nowhere to be seen. Neither were any other of the Questioner's people. The last anyone had seen of *them* was when an understeward had served a light meal in their salon some time ago while they were packing. Their salon was now empty of persons. None of them had asked for transportation. They had not set out on foot or they would have been seen.

Questioner told him to wait outside, dismissing him with a wave of her hand. Now what? Before she had a chance to think, Marool Mantelby was at the door. Her staff had advised her of this strange disappearance. Could she offer any help?

Questioner, regarding the woman with close attention, saw that she panted, her skin was flushed and her eyes darted in heightened excitement of a feral sort.

'I think it likely they have gone off on some expedition of their own,' murmured Questioner.

'Then ... they may be gone for some little while?' asked Marool, licking the corner of her lips.

'Does this cause some domestic disruption?'

'Not at all. I merely ... wondered.'

The Questioner smiled her meaningless, social smile. 'Do not fret over it, Madam Mantelby. I'm sure all will be explained.'

Marool bowed her way out with suspicious alacrity, Questioner staring after her, trying to decipher what the woman was up to. The understeward was still standing in the hall, and Questioner beckoned to him through the open door.

'Ma'am,' he said respectfully.

'Will you lead me to the the quarters where our missing staff members stayed?'

The understeward bowed and led the way out into the wide, deeply carpeted corridor. The suite given over to the staff members was on the same level, though around several corners and down a long side corridor almost to the end. At the door, Questioner told the understeward to wait while she went in. There she stood looking slowly around herself. All the belongings one would expect were there, some neatly packed into cases, others piled ready for packing.

Questioner approached the wall, examining it with sensors in the tips of her fingers, moving along it, centimeter by centimeter. After a time, she touched an ornamental cartouche and stepped back as the wall swung open. She looked through into a passageway that ran in both directions behind the wall. Questioner touched the cartouche again, and the wall closed silently upon itself.

'I read no evidence that mankind has ever been in that corridor,' she murmured to herself, as she did sometimes when alone, impressing the things she saw into memory with the words she spoke. 'No Earthian, no settler, none of my non-Earthian aides. There is evidence of some other living thing, however. The same living things I sensed in the little houses behind the gardener's quarters.'

She moved around the room, trying several other manipulations with similar effect. At the fourth hidden door she said to herself, 'Here. They went in here. I can smell them. All of them. I scent Ellin's perfume.' She shut the opening and turned away, eyes unfocused.

'Madam Questioner...?' queried the understeward from outside in the hall.

'One moment,' she said, going on with her interior colloquy. 'Did Mantelby do this? No. For if she had known about these sneakways in her walls, she would not have come to us to ask about our missing people. She would have searched for them herself, lest the abduction be laid at her door. No, the people who built them, the people who use them, are not mankind. Human, yes, probably, as Haraldson defined human, but not mankind.'

She strolled toward the door. 'So now, upon this stage, the indigenes appear, almost magically. How interesting. Now, what did they want with my witless entourage and my two good little dancers? Hmmm?'

In the doorway she stopped, looking around once more. 'I find an interesting pattern: The planet was settled by mankind, and all the original settlers disappeared. Then it was settled again by mankind; this time the settlers didn't disappear. Almost as though whatever had taken the first bunch had learned whatever it needed to know about mankind. Then we come along, bringing with us examples of several races that are fully mankind but different in appearance, and whoops, they disappear. As though whoever took them wanted to try a new flavor?

'But for what? And did they also seize up Ellin and Bao, or did those two adventurous children go off after them?'

She threw back her head, saying in a loud voice, 'I hereby announce my intention of going wherever my staff members have been taken. I would appreciate an escort, but if none is provided, I will take whatever route I can find.'

She moved majestically into the hallway. 'I am talking to myself,' she said to the servant. 'Or to anyone else who can hear me and take the matter under advisement.'

41

Assorted Persons In Pursuit

Ellin had spoken of an unheard music that was building to a climax. Questioner had taken it for mere fantasy. Now, however, as she walked back to her own suite with every detector at full alert, she heard real subsonics with a wave length so long that it seemed to pulse like a heartbeat through the fabric of the world. Something very large was moving, or living, or thinking. So, let calm preparations be made.

The understeward trailed after her to wait outside her door, shifting from foot to foot, white showing around the edges of his eyes. Poor thing, she thought, he was frightened half out of his wits, thinking he would be next.

'My aides recently met two gardeners,' she said. 'One is actually a sailor. The other is, I think, a Consort in Training. Please, go to their quarters and tell them that I, the Questioner, need them at once. Have them bring with them whatever they would take on a journey. And come quickly back.'

When he went away, almost at a run, she started putting together a pile of equipment: rations, lights, stout clothing and shoes for Bao and Ellin. In Ellin's room, and Bao's, she found dancing shoes, which she packed up along with everything else.

Meantime, the understeward had wakened the gardener and was spending too much time explaining.

'It'll be my back,' the gardener lamented for the tenth time.

'Not if the Questioner ordered it,' the understeward said between his teeth. 'We were all told to do whatever she ordered, and that means you, too.'

'What's going on?' asked a sleepy voice from the doorway.

The understeward turned, recognized Mouche as one of those the Questioner had asked for, and said, 'The Questioner needs you and your friend. She said one of you was a sailor and one was a Consort and for you to put together equipment for a journey and come at once.'

Ornery thrust his head between Mouche's shoulder and the door. 'She needs a sailor? For what?'

'I don't know what she needs,' the understeward cried. 'All I know is, the Questioner wants you, so go get your things.'

'Things?' said Mouche wonderingly.

'Whatever you need to go on a journey. She said a journey. Clean stockings. Clean underwear. Water bottles.' The understeward fell silent, frantically trying to think what he, himself, would pack for a journey. He wasn't sure he even had a water bottle.

'Who's going to tell Madam Mantelby they're gone?' asked the gardener in a grumpy tone. 'You going to tell her? Now?'

The gardener looked at him significantly, jerking his head toward the back of the house. 'Not now, you fool.'

'Oh,' the gardener jittered, licking his lips. 'Right.'

Mouche and Ornery went back to their quarters for their few belongings, then joined the understeward on the path, only to move quickly off it, for it crunched too greedily beneath their feet. Even the servant chose to pad up toward the house on the silent grass. He had left a side door open, which he shut and locked behind them before leading the way up the stairs, demanding silence with every movement, achieving it, and moving in it as a fish in quiet water. Like shadows, they slipped into the room where the Questioner waited.

'Well,' she murmured, when they had been escorted in, when the understeward had been dismissed and the door shut tightly behind him. 'Are you prepared for adventure?'

Ornery merely stared, as was his habit when confronting an ambiguous situation. Mouche responded as taught, with a low bow and a well-spoken salutation expressing the deep honor he felt at being able to serve the Questioner.

'How long did it take you to learn that?' Questioner asked in an interested voice. 'Years, I'd imagine.'

'I have been five years in training, Madam.'

'How many more before you're what they consider employable?'

Mouche bowed again, noting the amusement in the voice and reminding himself that this was said to be an artificial creature from whom he should not take offense. 'It would depend upon the discrimination of my patroness, Ma'am. I am quite good at some things already. I am not, however, fully qualified as a judge of wine or as a gourmet cook. My musical skills require honing. Perhaps another five years ...'

'Then the pleasures you offer are not only of the ... how would you say it?'

'Bedsports, Ma'am. No. Not only those.'

She smiled ironically. 'A pity to waste one so highly trained on so uncertain a mission. We are going underground, and we may run some risk. I have heard there are oceans under this planet, oceans sailed by strange and marvelous creatures.'

Mouche's eyes lit up. 'I don't know where your mission will take you, Ma'am, but I will not be a supernume if you are going by sea. Since a child,

I have dreamed of the sea. I have studied it, as well. I will not be a bad companion.'

'And you.' Questioner turned her eyes on Ornery. 'What about you?'

'A sailor, Ma'am,' Ornery said. 'Only that. Fond of the sea, yes. It's a good life. Less troublesome than shore, so most of us think.'

'Well. It may be we will find strange seas that warrant a sailor's efforts, though to begin with you will be mere beasts of burden to carry the supplies my aides were not given time to take with them. You may leave those veils and outer garments here. The packs I have made up are in the next room.'

When Mouche dropped his veil, she took his face in her hands and turned it to catch the light. 'Ah,' she said. 'This needs attention, boy.'

'We have had no opportunity, Ma'am,' he said.

'Well, it won't get any worse in the near future. Perhaps I can do something about it when we've finished. If we finish.'

Ornery and Mouche eagerly took off the shapeless gardener's robes and loaded themselves with Questioner's gear, being not overburdened with the double load, since their own supplies were scanty.

'Is that all you brought?' Questioner asked.

'It is all we have, Ma'am,' Mouche replied. 'We were pressed into service with only the clothes on our backs and our small packs. May we assist you with your own burden?'

'I need none. Everything I need is provided for in what I am. I have many tools and gizmos built in, and maintenance is just over. I should be highly efficient for many days. You may follow me.'

They did so, going silently out through the wide hallways toward the room where Questioner had found the sneakways in the walls.

42

Marool Worships Morrigan

While with the Wasters, Marool's worship of Morrigan had been a daily event, shared with some, hidden from none. During her self-imposed banishment, however, self-interest had dictated that she either give up Morrigan entirely or adopt a more covert style of adoration. During her so-called pilgrimage to Nehbe, Marool had seen the work of a local though reclusive artist. He was called the Machinist, an eremitic genius living in the hills near the town and earning a livelihood by making ornamental devices as well as prototype machines for practical use. He was not a Family Man. He had no g' to his name. He gave the impression of living in a separate world, but was nonetheless sufficiently connected to the real one to be available to Men of Business needing improved designs of rug looms or grain threshers or goods wagons or anything else they could conceive of.

He could build virtually anything.

'Anything?' asked Marool.

"Oh, but not f ... f ... f ... for you, Ma'am. He does not work for women.'

Someone had hired the stutterer to introduce Marool to the Machinist's work. This someone had also suggested that Marool's personality throve upon contrariness. The idea that someone would not do something she wanted done was guaranteed to pique her interest, and she demanded to meet the Machinist.

No, no, said her informant. The Machinist was very secretive, demanding that all his business be done by written orders left in his post box a mile or so from his lair. He saw no one, and no one saw him.

Marool asked why.

Her informant's reply was quite spontaneous. 'Well ... Ma'am, b ... b ... because he smells. You try to talk to him, you can't b ... b ... breathe!'

Smells didn't bother Marool. Before returning to Mantelby Mansion, Marool met with the Machinist. She did so secretly, taking no escort except two Hagger bodyguards who stayed at the post box while she went on to the house. On her first visit she explained her desires to the stringy, dirty-fingered, hot-eyed man, while he scribbled notes, asked few questions, and licked his lips while he suggested one or two refinements. On her second visit, she inspected the work so far completed and found it to her taste.

When she returned to Mantelby Mansion, she needed a place to put the device, and her grandfather's wine cellar came to mind. Margon Mantelby the elder, Marool's grandfather, had used a natural cavern below the mansion as a cellar for Mantelby wines, the product of family-owned vineyards. The cool catacombs had been presided over by a cellar master of some reputation, and the wine had been drunk during the ostentatious banquets given in honor of this or that family achievement.

When Marool had returned to the mansion, it had taken only a few trials to convince her she had no use for the wines since she could neither smell nor taste them, so she converted their vaulted spaces into what she called her *playroom*. Power for the devices was no problem. A sizable tributary of the Giles flowed down the canyon behind Mantelby Mansion, and Margon the Elder had long ago partnered with his neighbors in building a small dam and hydroelectric plant to provide domestic lighting and the pumping of water. Marool's fantastic devices did not fit either category, but she did not trouble herself over that.

The first machine was installed shortly after Marool returned from Nehbe, and in due time she added others. Among them was a device that amplified sexual pleasure by almost but not quite choking the participants during the act, and another that administered a carefully planned series of drugs during excitement. Some devices turned and twisted, holding bodies in ways that allowed persons – one or two or several simultaneously – to juxtapose or penetrate one another in ways otherwise unlikely. And finally, there was one very complicated machine that started its cycle doing interestingly erotic things and went on doing them, with increasing pain, pressure, and intensity, until the participants perished.

Some of them Marool used with her playmates; others were used by her playmates, or her soon to be ex-playmates, on one another while Marool watched. All the machines were designed to be unstoppable except by Marool herself, and she wore the master key upon her wrist and never removed it, not even to bathe or sleep. On that same hand she wore a great obsidian seal ring bearing in intaglio the fanged, flame-haired face of Morrigan.

The furnishings of the playroom included a closet of masks, costumes, and devices, as well as an ornate cabinet of drugs that could, variously, increase pleasure or enable participants to tolerate quite high levels of pain. Though the cabinet was locked, the lock was a simple one, an oversight by Marool, who gave her partners credit for little intelligence and had not thus far been mistaken in doing so.

Marool customarily spent part of every day in this special place. Since the Questioner had arrived with her entourage, however, Marool had not been near it. Though the Questioner and her two assistants customarily kept to their own rooms during daylight and always did so at night, the Questioner's strange-looking aides were ubiquitous about Mantelby Mansion. Marool had found them at all hours, walking here, looking there, always very interested in what was going on, always intrusively present whenever Marool even thought about amusing herself. The moment Marool learned the entourage had disappeared, she sent a peremptory note to the servants' quarters ordering Bane and Dyre to join her. She took the absence of the entourage as a sign from Morrigan that she need no longer deprive herself of her pleasures.

Aside from venting the pressures she had built up, there was another reason to bring the brothers to the playroom, one she had so far delayed dealing with. Though Bane and Dyre were innately cruel, though they did not balk at inflicting considerable pain even on one another, qualities that Marool quite enjoyed, the difficulty of keeping the brothers nearby had become prohibitive. She could find other playmates who would be equally cruel and vicious but who did not stink so. She herself could not smell them – or thought she could not, though her body responded to the presence of their smell nonetheless. No matter what she did or did not sense, her servants could smell them too well. Several specialized and expensive staff members had simply gaped, gasped, and fainted away when in the brothers' vicinity, and they had been unable thereafter to resume their duties. Her latest nephew-steward had confirmed, though only when asked, that the odor given off by the two was asphyxiating, and that it grew worse with each passing day.

She had decided, therefore, to unite pleasure with necessity by proceeding at once to the final machine, the one Bane and Dyre had been dying to try. Marool always enjoyed what she thought of as the end game. The preliminary teasing; the erotic challenge; the moment when it finally dawned on the participant(s) just what was happening; the pleading; the screaming; the final moaned and broken phrases of adoration, when Marool told the victims she might stop if they loved her enough.

Thus, when Marool's playmates arrived, she greeted them with every appearance of joy and with a generous supply of the treats they liked the most, drinks and rich foods and euphoric drugs. She engaged them in a little preliminary titillation, during which she herself indulged in several glasses of wine that Bane offered her, for the relaxing effect, not the taste. She had had a long, thirsty abstention!

It was Bane himself who suggested the special machine, the only one they had not yet used.

'You're too young,' teased Marool, who was enjoying herself inordinately and was in no hurry. 'That's for grown-up men.'

'I'm as grown-up as you need,' boasted Bane, with a sidelong glance at his brother. 'Both of us are.'

'Oh, you wouldn't like it.' Marool giggled, a little surprised at the sound coming from her own mouth. My, she had had a little sniffy more than usual. Had Bane slipped some of the euphoric into her wine? Naughty boy. Life was too pleasant at the moment to scold him. She breathed deeply and giggled once again. 'It requires a very sophisticated taste.'

'House Genevois gave me sophisticated taste,' Bane said, stroking her thigh. 'That's why I got sent there.'

'Who sent you there, dear? How much did you cost Madame?'

'We're not Madame's stupid Hunks,' asserted Dyre. 'Bane and me, we're destined for great things. Our daddy, Thunder his name is, he paid for us because he's got a future planned for us.'

'Sons of thunder,' said Marool. 'Oooh, so powerful.'

'Powerful enough for any old machine,' muttered Bane, flexing his muscles and admiring his erect phallus as reflected fragmentarily among many mirrors.

'Well, then,' Marool purred. 'If you think so ...'

She staggered to her feet and directed them, Bane there, Dyre here. They were acquiescent, even eager, but somehow, the machine didn't fit properly. Bane got out of the proper position and knelt down, fussing with the mounting, Dyre turned and twisted, and then joined Bane. 'Damn thing,' he muttered.

'It's perfectly all right!' She laughed, still feeling quite giggly and giddy, far more amused than annoyed.

'It's not all right. There's something there that pinches! You don't believe me, you try it.'

Which she did in a state of high amusement, only to find the cinches closed and the bands locked, and Bane trying to wrench the ring off her finger as the machine started its initially gentle motion.

'Stop this!' she shrieked through a gale of laughter. 'You don't know what you're doing!'

Bane stopped trying for the ring and growled into her ear. 'We know. Our daddy, he told us how you're the one took us from him and left us in the care of nobodies. He had to come hunting for us over near Nehbe. He says to tell you, him and the Machinist, they're old friends and kinfolk. He says to tell you, this is his payback for the daughter you were supposed to bear him. He says, tell Marool good-bye for me!'

'Your daddy?' she gasped, breathlessly. 'Who?'

Bane was hastily donning his clothes. 'Thunder and Ashes, our daddy. You knew him, Marool, bitch. Don't say you didn't. There was witnesses, and they told us all about you.'

'Ashes!' she cried, suddenly and horridly aware.

'He found us over near Nehbe, with that goat farmer, where you sent us, you bitch.'

'Oh, by Morrigan, do you know who your mother was? Do you know who I am?'

'Our mother died birthing us, and you're the bitch stole her babies. Daddy said we had to get rid of you before we could get our inheritance. That's all we need to know.' He struck her then, hard across the mouth, shutting off further words, then ran for the tunnel entrance that gave upon the gardens. Dyre was not far behind him as the machine shifted into a slightly more energetic mode of action.

43

A Journey Toward Dosha

As Questioner set out on her search for her vanished entourage, she swept the hallways with all her senses, hoping that all the servants were abed or about some other business, for she did not want to explain where she was going. She did not want her ship or the Council of Worlds to be involved in this. Though she knew she was probably being watched from every side by unseen eyes, they did not trouble her, for they were not the eyes of mankind.

When she had discovered the wallways in the small salon, she had closed each one behind her, but when she, Mouche, and Ornery entered the room, one of them had been reopened. The wideflung panel disclosed the same narrow tunnel she had identified as the route taken by Ellin and Bao. A lit candle sat on the floor inside the opening as though to say, *This way.*

'You, boy?' Questioner asked. 'Name?'

'Mouche, Madam.'

'You will lead.'

Mouche looked at the opening with a feeling of dawning delight. He forgot his pain. This sneakaway was familiar to him, totally familiar, so like those wallways in House Genevois that it was obviously made by the same creatures and obviously ... oh, obviously leading to the same kind of place. He shut his eyes for only a moment, calling upon his Hagion to let him become an intrepid explorer whose delight was entering dark, unknown territory in search of heaven knew what.

Questioner's eyelids rose, an expression of surprise that she used seldom and felt almost never. The boy had accomplished a very pretty somatic maneuver there, in very short time. She had been monitoring his internal pressures and tensions, as well as smelling certain secretions in body and brain. All had responded to whatever invocation he had made. He was now exactly the person she would have selected to assist her in this journey. Not foolhardy, but daring and quite ecstatic about the venture!

Well, it must be conditioning. No doubt sexual consorts would need a good deal of conditioning. She would make time before she left the planet to speak to the head of his school or academy or whatever it was. If she survived to leave the planet.

'You next. What's your name, sailor?'

'Ornery, Ma'am.'

'Well you then, sea*man* Ornery.' She winked at Ornery, much confusing her. 'And, I bring up the rear. I am massive enough to keep almost anything off your back. If I say *back* in a loud, imperative voice, both of you come back close to me. I have certain defenses to help us all survive.'

Mouche oozed into the opening in the wall, turned briefly to catch the freshest airs – assuring himself that outside must lie in that direction – and advanced into the wind. The sneakaway sloped slightly downward, and since the small salon was on the second level of the Mantelby Mansion, it stood to reason they would have to go down to get away from the house.

After shutting the opening behind them, Questioner emitted a cone of light wide enough to contain herself and Ornery as they wound slowly along the passage. The slope soon steepened into a ramp, the ramp gave way to steps leading into blackness. They slowed, taking more time to light each step, each corner, each twist and turn of the way.

The stairs and ramps, some of which creaked ominously under Questioner's weight, were interrupted by horizontal stretches with frequent peekholes. Mouche glanced at a few of these with practiced ease, which Questioner noted before turning her own attention to the spyholes. She judged they were winding through a part of the house devoted to the servants, for there was much scurrying and late-night tidying going on.

At one point a stench came through some few holes like that from a fresh dunghill, and Questioner turned down her receptors. Her senses were connected to her mind, just as people's were, and she found the smell atrocious.

They dropped farther. The smell did not depart, though it abated, and a certain deadened quality in the sound of their feet told them they were now on soil or stone rather than wooden floors, though the peekholes were still aboveground. The sneakaways had obviously been designed to give maximum access without regard for the distance between points, and they had walked quite a long winding way to drop only these few meters. They continued to go downward, losing the peekholes on one side, and soon heard a sound, a rhythmic and inexorable ratcheting that grew louder as they progressed.

Mouche stopped in his tracks, his breath coming quickly, as though at some suddenly perceived threat. Questioner told Ornery to stay in place as she went forward to the place Mouche stood.

'What is it, boy?'

'The sound, Madam. Not the mechanical sound, but the screaming? Do you hear it?'

Until that moment, she had accepted the noise as mechanical, as of some unoiled bearing, some ungreased pivot shrieking across a metal plate. A moment's concentration told her Mouche was right. The ratcheting was machinery, but the other sound could be from a living creature.

Questioner took the lead. They went forward and down another flight as she ran her sensor-tipped fingers along the wall. Here, and there, and then, yes, here, a door. She tried it in various ways until it sighed open, flooding the place they stood with increased noise and a wave of the familiar stench.

They stood in a cellar, stone floored, rock walled, softly lit, luxuriously carpeted, hung with great swaths of satin and velvet and centered by a warm fountain that steamed gently in the cool air. All around them stood the horrid legacy of some nightmare craftsman: ogre-racks of brass and steel, chimeric skeletons of gold and silver, squatted toad bones of hard iron, all wed to springs and cams and drive shafts, soft cushioned in places and fanged in others, all with red-lit eyes staring and metal arms spread wide.

The atrocious squealing and screaming came from the far side of the room, where Questioner went speedily.

If it had not been for her enhanced senses, she would not have recognized Marool. She was no longer a person but only a piece of living meat clamped into a machine that had hung her by her ankles as it thrust at her from above and either side. Questioner took one quick glance at the mechanical linkages, reached forward to an oscillating rod, and snapped it between powerful hands.

The ratcheting noise stopped with a shrill scraping noise. A frustrated mechanical whine built to a howl. The inhuman squealing went on. From behind her, Questioner heard Mouche's gasp, Ornery's muffled curse.

'Can't you do something?' cried Mouche, distraught.

'I can,' Questioner agreed, though with peculiar reluctance. She reached upward, extruded a needle from her palm, and injected a strong opiate into the woman's body.

In a few moments, the squealing subsided to a dull, grunted moan, endlessly repeated. The machine itself reached a point of no return; a linkage shattered; silence fell.

Questioner turned to find Mouche's horrified eyes fixed upon her. Of the three of them, he was the only one unsurprised.

'You knew about this?' she asked him.

Mouche gulped, turned his ashen face aside, and told her about the picture in the hallway at House Genevois. This, he said, was the same machine.

' "Mistress Mantelby at Her Pleasures," you say?'

He gulped. 'That was how it was labeled, Most Honored One.'

'Call me Questioner. We will have no time for honorifics on this journey.' She turned back to the puzzle before her. The machine would not reverse. There was no real way to extricate the woman, for there were linked escapements preventing the machine from going back to its original configuration until it reached the end of the cycle or was unlocked. As if in answer to this need, Marool's bloody arm flopped downward with the wrist at eye level before them, the key dangling.

Questioner broke the light chain that held it and unlocked the machine, which immediately disengaged from Marool's body with an intimate, sucking sound, and dropped her to the floor, where she lay, still faintly moaning.

'Marool,' said Questioner, 'listen to me. Who did this?'

'Dyre,' gasped Marool. 'And Bane ... for ... ahhh ...'

'It is dire and baneful, but who ...'

'That's their names, Ma'am,' interrupted Mouche. 'I can tell who it was from the stink. It's the Dutter boys, Bane and Dyre. That's their names.'

'My sons,' Marool gasped, her face transfigured by rage. 'My sons ... for that damned Ahhh ... shes.' She cried out, a long angry howl that went out of her interminably, dwindling into a final aching silence.

Mouche turned away, hiding his face, and Ornery put an arm around his shoulders.

'She has died,' said Questioner. Her voice and motions were stiff and mechanical as she straightened the limp form where it lay then jerked one of the hangings loose to cover the body. 'No doubt many others have died in this place. Look at the ring she wears. See that face upon it and the name engraved around the edge: Morrigan. In the Temple I learned of Morrigan, a deity of pain and destruction. Marool selected her goddess and became her own sacrifice.'

'What shall we do for her?' whispered Ornery.

Questioner murmured, 'She has done for herself. It was she who brought this deadly device to this place, perhaps even she who designed it. Certainly it was she who used it upon others. The machine is not new. See the wear patterns around the pinions, the stains on the straps. It has killed before.'

'Why ... why would anyone do ... do that?' Mouche begged, as he hurried to the door through which they had entered. 'I never understood the pictures, the why of any of it ...'

Questioner emitted a very mankindlike sigh. 'It is a very primitive emotion, and even when we explain it, we do not understand it, Mouche. If we all understood it, there would have been no need for Haraldson and his edicts.'

'Prey, property, or opponent,' gasped Mouche, who was now in the door they had entered through, breathing the cleaner air of the sneakway. 'Madame said that's how gangs think.'

Questioner nodded. 'One like this was a gang unto herself. So long as we think of such people as humans and attempt to treat them as humans, we cannot protect the innocent.'

'They really can't be cured?' asked Ornery.

Questioner waved the idea away. 'We haven't found a way. Haraldson said that if a being has sufficient sense of justice and civility to know it has done wrong, knowing it has done wrong is often sufficient punishment. If the being has no remorse, punishment will only increase its anger.'

She sighed, gesturing at the scene around them. 'I don't think Marool felt any remorse.' She turned toward Mouche and called, 'What did she mean, "Her sons, that damned Ashes"?'

Mouche was by now sitting head-down in the sneakway, still fighting his nausea and revulsion. He turned reluctantly. 'I'll tell what I know, but if you're finished, Ma'am ... Questioner, can we get out of here?'

Questioner nodded. Her olfactory receptors were still turned down, but the others had no such amelioration. She herded them ahead of her.

When they were inside the wall with the opening shut behind them, Mouche mopped the sweat from his face on the sleeve of his shirt. 'When Bane and Dyre first came to House Genevois, they broke all the rules, and Madame sent for someone. I never saw him, though I heard his voice. When Bane and Dyre were sent to him, he did something painful to them, and he told them to mind themselves. Later on, Madam had to summon that person again, to stop their attacking me – '

'Why?' she interrupted. 'Why attack you?'

'I'd had a run in with them before, at home.' He gulped, suddenly overcome with a longing for that home. 'I stopped them killing a little native creature I'd made a friend of, and they hated me for it. It was Bane did this to my face, later on. Well, the person Madame summoned could have been their father, their real father, for he smelled as they did, and I know Dutter wasn't their real father. The Dutters were only paid to rear them.'

'Was Marool really their mother?' asked Ornery.

'Does it fit in with what we've heard from other sources?' Questioner asked.

Ornery offered, 'The gardener said she'd disposed of two or three a year since she'd been back, so she was away, somewhere, perhaps long enough to have had those two.'

'So. If she bore these boys, she was guilty of mismothering?'

Both Mouche and Ornery nodded, Ornery adding, 'Oh, my, yes Ma'am. That's about as mis a mothering as anybody could do. And then, playing about with them here ... Well, that's as bad a thing as you can do on Newholme.'

'Most places would agree,' said Questioner.

'She'd of been blue-bodied sure, if anyone had caught her at it.'

Questioner murmured, 'I wonder who Ashes really is ...'

'Jong,' interrupted someone. 'Ashes is jongau.'

The voice sent a thrill through Mouche, shivering him to his feet. 'Timmy,' he whispered, as though to himself. 'Timmy?'

The others turned, Ornery crouching defensively, searching the darkness.

The voice came as a spider-silk whisper, drifting to their ears a word or two at a time, from any direction and from none:

'Mouchidi.'

A caress, that voice, as it whispered, 'She, the evil one is gone.'

And another voice. 'She will never come to the Fauxi-dizalonz where Bofusdiaga waits. She will never be remade.'

Questioner turned on her massive feet, peering into the darkness. She saw only a vanishing glimpse of moving colors around a globe of wavering green, like a cloud of seagrass.

'It's the Timmys,' cried Mouche, who had turned an instant earlier. 'The dancers!' He could not mistake that movement, that slender, sylphlike form. The most graceful creatures mankind could produce could be only an awkward copy of that.

Questioner muttered to herself, 'Aha. So here is our indigenous race!' Then, making her voice soft and unthreatening, she called, 'Why have you come here?'

The first voice came again, fading, departing: 'We were coming for Mouchidi. Corojum said go get him. Now you are coming anyhow, so we will lead you across the seas, but you must hurry.'

Questioner stood, immovable. 'Why should I listen to you? You have stolen my people.'

'They are not hurt,' said a slightly different voice, sounding both impatient and surprised. 'We do not hurt things as you do. Two of them are dancers! We needed dancers. Even now they skim the waters, on their way across the seas to the Fauxi-dizalonz. They go there to help us with the dance.'

The last words faded into distance. She or he or it was not waiting for them to get closer, so much was clear.

'What dance?' whispered Ornery.

'I have no idea,' Questioner replied. 'Though I had no doubt dancers might be helpful.'

'Oh, Questioner, we'll find out,' cried Mouche. 'What an adventure!'

Adventure or not, he stood as one stunned by delight, incapable of movement. It had been her, its voice. The voice of divinity.

'Come,' said Questioner, shoving him gently. 'I think haste may be appropriate.'

Down the road from Mantelby Mansion, the man known as Ashes sat in a carriage behind two black horses. They and their saddled stablemate, tethered to the back of the carriage, heard the sounds of approaching feet before Ashes did. They started and stamped their feet, ears erect.

'Daddy Thunder?' called a voice.

'Here,' said Ashes in his deep, dead voice. 'D'jou get the ring?'

'Couldn't get it off her damn finger,' said Bane. 'Didn't have my knife to cut the finger off. Figured you'd rather we got here on time than go off hunting for cutlery.'

'Damnation. She had that ring when I knew her under the bridges. I wanted it. A souvenir. She's dead?'

'By now, I'd say. Good thing we saw that picture at Madame's place. Otherwise we wouldn'ta known which machine it was.'

'You'da known. I told you the Machinist fixed it the way I told him. He fixed it so's it couldn't hurt our kin, not any of the sons of Thunder. He put sensors in the pads so it wouldn't run if it was you, or me. That machine's your friend, boy. You could'a got on it with her, it'd of killed her and set you down without a scratch. Well, that'll pay her back for the daughter she owed me!'

'So how come she picked us? The way we smell, we figured nobody would.'

The man smiled. 'She's addicted to the smell. Not that she knows it's a smell. I can do the same to anybody when I've got a little time. Once they've got the smell in their head, they're gone, lost, can't do a thing against it.'

'What'd you mean, paying her back for the daughter she owed you?'

'Arrgh. Three times I tried for a Rikajor daughter. They were said to run to girls. Rikajor refused me each time. He couldn't refuse me Marool. Her, I bought with other coin.'

'She asked who our mother was. Why'd she care?'

A gleefully gloating expression fled across the older man's face. 'No reason. Just trying to confuse you. Get on in here. I'm sick of towns. Time to go.'

The boys climbed in, and Ashes took up the reins, starting the horses up the hill, along the road that led past the mansions into the wild, the same way Marool had gone when she investigated her parents" deaths in the badlands.

'Where we going now?' asked Dyre, yawning.

'Off into the wild to meet your cousins, boy. Our kindred. The first settlers of this world. The Wilderneers.'

Ornery moved off down the tunnel, sped both by curiosity and by Questioner's urgency. Mouche moved with more eagerness, though Questioner noted that both Mouche and Ornery seemed somewhat reluctant to look where they were going. Like guilty children handing around a dirty picture, they peeked at the darkness ahead, and pretended not to and peeked again. So long as they were all headed in one direction, it made little difference, though Questioner could imagine circumstances in which this preoccupation and inattention could be dangerous.

'Mouche,' murmured Questioner, placing her heavy hand firmly on one of his shoulders, 'stop trembling.'

Instead of steadying, he quivered like an excited horse.

'Whoa,' Questioner said. 'Stop. Take a deep breath; stop.'

She turned Mouche toward her, staring into his dazed eyes. 'What is this business of not looking where you're going?' She snapped her fingers in his face and shook him lightly. 'What?'

Ornery had turned and came back to them. 'It's hard for us, Ma'am. They do not exist, Ma'am. So we are taught. We are not allowed to see or hear them. I can see them or not, depending, though I am still surprised at myself, but Mouche seems to be having trouble looking at them.'

'You cannot see them?' Questioner turned her searching gaze on the sailor. 'What do you mean you cannot see them?'

'I mean ... I can sort of not. Not look. I mean, I ... know they're there, but I don't. They wear brown robes that cover them all up, and we're not allowed to look. Not once we're six or seven years old.'

'Why?'

'Because ... well ... they don't exist.'

'They what?'

Ornery cried petulantly, 'They don't exist! There weren't supposed to be other creatures here. And they weren't here when our people came, which means they probably came from somewhere else. But even if they didn't, it wasn't playing fair to hide all that time ...'

'So, what's the matter with your friend, here?'

Mouche's life of sin had caught up with him all too swiftly. He quivered with mixed joy and shame, muttering, 'I've been watching them. I've been watching them at House Genevois. I've been ... I've been ...' His sins had been settled, dependable. He had made a detente with his sins, taking his inspiration from his sins, but now he was in actual pursuit of the ideal, and he could not say what he had been. '... maybe wicked,' he concluded, head hanging.

Questioner mused over this for a moment, shaking her massive head as an indication of the astonishment she did not feel but knew was suitable to the occasion. 'Young ones, listen to me. During this present time we are in, this *now*, Timmys do indeed exist. During the near future, it will not be forbidden to look at them. During the near future, everything you learned ... when? When you were mere schoolchildren? Well, whatever you learned then was wrong. For the near future. Can you absorb that? When we catch up to them, or when they return to us, you will see them for they will be there, right? All this pretense has to end. Ending it is one of the reasons I am here!'

'Ahh ... if you say so, Ma'am.'

'I do say so. And I am smarter than your teacher, so what I say, goes. You understand?'

Both of them nodded, Ornery obediently, Mouche equivocally. Ornery didn't care one way or the other, but Mouche had set certain limits on his dreams and delights. He didn't particularly want them to be sullied by reality. He wanted to have without the burden of having, to imagine without being imagined in return, and most, to be inspired without questioning his inspiration. Now, having heard Flowing Green's voice so near, he alternately rejoiced and suffered. She had come to get him, him, personally. Why? What did she think of him? What did she see when she looked at him? Did she look at him? What would she think of his face now? Or did that even matter? Would she hate him?

Thinking was troublesome, hurtful, and useless. He gave up thinking and merely went.

They had left the sneakaways of the house and entered a natural tunnel, or so Questioner identified it from the texture of the stone. There was no way to get lost, for there were no side tunnels, merely this partially dissolved stratum of limestone, floored with harder stone, naturally sloping downward and penetrated from above by rough tufts of root. Among the roots she heard the squeak and chitter of small creatures, and when one fled across the edge of her sight she saw a being the size of her hand, winged with tight membranes stretching between fore and rear limbs.

'What is that called?' she asked, directing her voice down the tunnel ahead of them.

'Dibigon,' came a drifting voice, soft as the twitter of a drowsy bird. 'Self-creators. You would say swoopers.'

'I didn't know they could speak our language,' muttered Mouche, talking to his feet. 'No one told me.' Then, remembering his childhood, he flushed again. Of course they had spoken his language. How could he have forgotten?

Questioner called, 'How far down do we go?'

'All way,' whispered the voice. 'To baimoi. To dwell-below.'

As they went farther, the stones around them began to glow, at first with a hint of palest green along the edges, growing brighter the farther they went, enabling them to see the outlines of the stones around them, the fading distance of the tunnel ahead. Questioner reduced her own light to a soft, reddish glow, and soon the luminescence became a brighter yellow. Coincident with this brightening, they heard the murmuring of a stream.

They found the source of the liquid burbling at an intersection of their tunnel and a larger, more cylindrical one was half-filled with smooth, dark water, visible as a shadow against the bright luminescence of the opposite wall. The water, though silent elsewhere throughout its course, burbled at the conjunction of the two tunnels where irregular blocks of stone had fallen to interrupt its flow. There, also, were two podlike shapes drawn onto the shingle, each one about five meters long and less than a meter wide, each shining with the same light as the stone itself.

Questioner put her face close to the rock, amplified her vision, and saw that the luminescence was the product of bacteria accumulated in lichenous growths that covered every surface. Some were effulgently yellow, others emitted blue or green or even violet light.

Ornery looked over the pods, thumping them with her fist and finding them rather rubbery. 'You don't call these ships, I hope,' she said in a disgusted tone. 'Canoes, I'd call them, if that.'

'Their size befits a small river,' said Questioner. 'Neither of these will bear my weight, however, so I will rely upon my flotation devices.'

'Flotation devices?' asked Ornery.

'Some worlds are water worlds,' said Questioner. 'Some people swim or even dive about their activities. Some people are arboreal. Some are cave dwellers. I was designed to get about in any of them, to swim or dive or brachiate or soar or crawl, not always gracefully, but always efficiently.'

Mouche and Ornery stared doubtfully at the pods, looking around for something more solid, seeing nothing that would float. It seemed to be the pod or nothing. Questioner, reading their minds, patted them on the shoulders comfortingly. 'Many things will no doubt be made clear as we go.'

Several Timmys leapt into one of the boats, which then slipped into the water of its own accord and floated a little way downstream, remaining there, quiet in the current. Mouche and Ornery started to push one of the boats into the river, only to have it slip along the rocky beach by itself. They climbed into it, sat in the rubbery bottom facing one another and felt their bottoms bumping over small rocks that were easily discernible through the half-flexible substance of the vessel. Questioner waded into the stream and hooked herself to the back edge of the boat that held Mouche and Ornery, her mid parts ballooning until she bobbed on the ripples like a hollow ball. She was near enough that her reddish glow still illuminated both Mouche and Ornery, near enough to speak and be heard, though once they had pushed off into the river, she seemed disinclined to do so. There were no paddles or oars. Evidently it was intended they should simply float wherever they were going, though that did not explain the fact that the little boats maintained their relative distance and position, no matter how the tunnel twisted or how the water eddied.

From the front of the other boat a green glow swam upon the river. Mouche knew this was Flowing Green, that she led him to his destiny, that she knew he followed willingly even though he hadn't wanted to approach her, not really. So far ... so far nothing had happened to disenchant him, but if it did ... oh, he would feel ... feel so ...

'What?' asked Ornery, leaning toward him. 'You look as though you had lost your last shoelace and the race about to start.'

Mouche managed a smile. 'I was thinking how wonderful ... how wonderful they are.' He gestured, making it clear who he meant.

'They always were,' said Ornery. 'I always thought so.'

'You've both seen them?' Questioner asked. 'I mean, without their coverings.'

'Not recently,' Ornery admitted. 'But when I was a child, of course I saw them. They didn't wrap themselves up with *us*. Not when we were little.'

'Mine did, mostly,' Mouche confessed. 'We had such a little place to live. Unless we were out in the woods, then my Timmy would take off her wrappers.'

'*Her* wrappers? You knew she was female?'

'No! of course not.' Mouche subsided into a new fit of guilt. Thinking of Timmys as male or female was also forbidden. 'We weren't supposed to wonder about them, or to think of them being families or having babies or anything.'

Ornery snorted. 'Oh, well. Supposed to! We're supposed to be veiled, but on ships we aren't. We're supposed not to see Timmys, but we don't trip over them, so we must really see them, right? You can drive yourself crazy with stuff you're not supposed to.'

'And women aren't supposed to be … running around loose,' murmured Mouche in a slightly angry tone.

Surprisingly, Ornery grinned. 'Right. Not supposed to.'

From behind them, the Questioner murmured, 'And girls aren't supposed to pretend to be boys, but I doubt you're the first.'

'How did you know?' Ornery asked, jaw dropping.

'I can smell you, child. My sense of smell is copied from Old Earther canines. Differentiating between sexes is nothing. I can also tell about how old you are, where you've been and what you've been eating recently, what your state of health is, and what was in the soap you last used.'

'Can you tell where we're going?' asked Ornery in a slightly sarcastic voice.

'From the fact that water runs down hill, I assume we go down,' she said. 'Somewhere this streamlet runs into a river, and that, I should imagine, runs eventually into an underground sea. I believe so, for seas figure in the legends of this place and because Mouchidi's little friend has told us we will cross them.'

Mouche flushed. 'She isn't my … my friend.'

'Ornery is right, you know. She isn't a she, either.'

Astonished, Mouche tried to turn around, a maneuver that set the little boat bobbing. A Timmy voice came clearly through the darkness. 'Still, sit, you make peevish Joggiwagga!'

Without moving, Mouche said, 'She isn't? I mean, it isn't?'

Questioner murmured, 'It isn't, no. Is the one leading us the one you've been watching?'

Mouche nodded miserably. 'One of them. I call her … it, Flowing Green.'

'Because of the hair, of course. Flowing Green is very attractive to you, is it not? Tim, not. I think we will find they do not say him, her, he, she, but merely tim. Mankind proposes, tim-tim disposes.'

'No sexes?' drawled Ornery, with a sidelong glance at Mouche. 'That should simplify things.'

'Not really,' murmured Questioner. 'Reproduction of nonsexual beings will inevitably have its own complications. We simply don't know what they are, yet.'

Questioner dimmed her light to the slightest, reddish glow, watching in fascination as the luminescence around them continued to grow brighter. The surroundings were in no sense illuminated. Much of their environment appeared as patches of darkness outlined or interrupted by strings, shades, lines, or clouds of light ranging from pale yellow through all possible greens to deep blue. Part of this, Questioner knew, was due to her reduced light and their own eyes adjusting to the lower levels of illumination, but part was a real increase in luminosity and a shift in color toward the slightly longer wave lengths. One did not actually see a rock, one saw a fuzzy angular yellow outline around a black patch partly filled in by pale green with blue prominences that one could decode as a rock. The green fangs that hung above them had been deposited there ages ago by water leaching through limestone. The green glow in the boat ahead of them was brighter now, and occasionally Questioner could detect twin silver eyes peering at them from within it as well as from other, accompanying glows, various shades from amber through blue. Flowing Green was not alone.

Questioner had already adjusted her senses to pick up the talk of the Timmys, which she was stowing away while her internal translator worked at it. Give her a few days, and she'd know their tongue as well as the fifty or so others she'd come equipped with.

Ornery leaned to whisper into Mouche's ear. 'What do you think of her, the Questioner?'

Mouche considered it. He had spent hours every day for some years considering what this or that individual woman was like, for if one could not know that, one could hardly be a Consort.

'I think she's sad,' he whispered back. 'Not showing it, of course. Very soldierly about everything and taking a proper pride in her duty, but underneath, she could use a bit of happiness.'

Ornery, surprised, sat back in her own place, thinking of what Mouche had said. All in all, she thought, Mouche was probably right. Questioner, who had heard every syllable, was slightly surprised.

The tube in which they were floating began to narrow slightly. From ahead came louder water sounds. Without interference from those aboard, the two little boats lined up end to end, their speed increased to a dizzying rush that carried them through the last narrow bit of small tunnel into another with a diameter several times as large. Beside the boats, a huge eye, like a pale balloon, emerged from the dark water and stared at them. Great dripping, weed-hung swags of line or cable pulled themselves above the water, dark against the background glow, heaving the boats into the slower current. Not cable. Too thick for cable. Tentacles. Far above, the higher, broader ceiling shone softly with fractal patterns of amber and emerald.

The two canoes stayed in line, as though they were linked, and the moon-eye ahead of them swiveled from left to right before turning in the direction of their movement, the joined boats holding steady in the slow current.

A voice drifted back to them, 'Drink this water now. To make you visible.'

Ornery began to laugh. 'So now *we're* invisible.'

'It isn't funny,' complained Mouche.

'You are only darkness, Mouche,' said Questioner. 'You're a black hole in the middle of light. I've been analyzing the water. I detect no impurities that would endanger your health, but it does have luminescent bacteria in it. Presumably, if you drink the water, soon you will glow, and we can see you. I must admit, I'm curious to see a glowing Mouche, a shimmering Ornery!'

'The bacteria? They won't make you glow?' asked Ornery.

'Probably not. But I can make myself glow, so you know where I am and what I'm about. I'd like to know what that thing was that came up just beside us?'

'Joggiwagga,' whispered the darkness.

'Joggiwagga,' murmured Questioner. 'I've heard that before.'

'It is Joggiwagga who raises the pillars,' said Ornery. 'It is Joggiwagga who keeps track of time, by the moon-shadows. I saw one once, by the side of the sea, setting up the stones!'

'Dangerous,' whispered the voice. 'To be seen by Joggiwagga on the land.'

'I moved very fast,' Ornery confessed.

'Wise,' murmured the darkness. 'Wise. It would not hurt us for we are part of it, but you are not.'

'What do you mean, you are part of it?' asked the Questioner. 'You are part of Joggiwagga?'

A verdant glow ahead of them billowed, then shrank once more, as hair was tossed wide and then fell into place. 'Joggiwagga is part, we are part, all everything is Dosha, all is made in Fauxi-dizalonz, except you people and jongau people and Her and Niasa.'

'What are jongau?' the Questioner asked.

'Bent people. People not put together right. That Ashes one is jongau. That Bane, that Dyre, they are jongau. All their kinfolk and like, many, many more! They are not finished. They are only half done, and they smell bad. They should have the courtesy to die, but they do not.'

'And who are the Corojumi?' the Questioner pursued.

Out of darkness: 'Once were many Corojumi to open spaces, make the dances, fix what is broken ...'

'And Bofusdiaga?'

'Bofusdiaga mixes things together. Bofusdiaga stops pains and breaks chains and burrows walls and sings to the sun. That is Bofusdiaga.'

Questioner spoke to Mouche and Ornery: 'Are you making any sense of this?'

Mouche said, 'I'm afraid not.'

The voice came again, this time with some asperity. 'You mankinds always need everything right now. Your babies, too. Why this. Why that. Tell me this, tell me that. Explain, explain. You should learn to wait. See a little, then a little more. It will be clear. Drink water.'

None of them dared ask any further questions, though Questioner said in a jolly tone, 'Drink water. By all means.'

Ornery and Mouche obediently scooped water from the stream and gulped it down. Aside from being very cold, it was simply watery, with nothing at all unpleasant about it. When he had wiped his hands on his shirt, Mouche turned gingerly on his haunches to speak softly to Questioner.

'When I was little, my Timmy used to sing me to sleep with a song that had Corojumi and Bofusdiaga in it. It was all in their language, and I asked her ... it to tell it to me in my language, and a few days later she ... it had it figured out in our language, rhymes and all. After that, it sang it to me in my language part of the time.'

'Can you sing it to me?'

'Not the way she ... it did. Their singing is wonderful, but it's all full of little trills and lilts and runs. I'll just say it very softly.'

Mouche cleared his throat and began:

'*Quaggida he sings*
somewhere among the dimmer galaxies,
luring the Quaggima that he will seize.
Oh, Corojumi, she comes unaware.
Bofusdiaga, from deep dark he flings
fiery loops that make a snare
for her bright wings.
    '*Quaggima she screams*
her wings broken and torn, she cries in vain
at flame and scalding light and piercing pain.
Bofusdiaga, where will she find aid?
Oh, Corojumi, all her lively schemes
are but memories that fade

among dead dreams.
'Quaggima she calls:
Out of starfield coming, fire womb seeking
Fire she finds, rock wallowing, fume reeking
Oh, Corojumi, openers of space
Bofusdiaga, burrower of walls
She has need of birthing place
Wheeooo, she falls!'

After a long moment, Questioner said in an interested voice, 'Is that all of it?'

Mouche shook his head. 'No, there was more, but I can't quite remember it. Their language is a lot prettier than ours. You're right that it has no hes and shes. They sang *tim* in their language, but they put in the *hes* and *shes* in ours. In our language they couldn't put all the trills in, and I usually fell asleep along about the burrower of walls line. I'll try to remember the rest of it.'

'How do you explain it?'

Mouche scratched his head, trying to remember. 'It's the story of the Quaggi. Aren't they a kind of huge something that lives out in space? I guess they're travelers, sailing between the stars, and the male lurks around in the dark spaces between outer worlds to catch the female, and he impregnates her. And she's supposed to lay the egg, but in the song, she's hurt so badly she can't ever fly again. When I was a little kid, I always just thought it was just a sad story, a lament, you know.'

Questioner murmured, 'I think it's a story about real things. It's an odd story for a child, however, all that rape and violence, though it may be a clue to something your Timmy said earlier. It remarked that everything was part of the Fauxi-dizalonz except the jongau people, us people, *Her*, and Niasa.'

'Well, there are lots of songs or rhymes about Niasa, like:

"Niasa, little Summer Snake,
Turn in your egg, the world will shake.'
Niasa's mother, down so deep,
Sing your baby snake to sleep."

Questioner mused, 'So, Niasa is Summer Snake; Ashes is jongau; we are unequivocally us; so could *Her* be the Quaggima?'

'You think there's a real Quaggima?' asked Ornery.

Questioner answered. 'The Quaggi are one of the four races we have met who are definitely not human. The Quaggi we've met – or rather, seen, since one does not really meet a Quaggi – are all alike according to our sensors, so we've always rather assumed the females are somewhere else. This story you tell, which is the same story the Hags tell, by the way, accords with some information I received from a trader ...'

'Well, my story and the Hags' story would be the same,' interrupted Mouche. 'Because Timmys told both of us. The Hags had Timmy nurse-maids, just as all of us did.'

Unperturbed, Questioner went on, 'I believe the Quaggi at some point lose their wings and become long-lived, planet-bound creatures devoted to philosophy. They don't talk about their method of reproduction, and this little song of yours gives us a rather nasty hint that the females either die after being waylaid and raped, or perhaps in the act of laying the egg or hatching the young. All that bit about her broken wings and her dead dreams and being unable to fly. Most unpleasant.'

Ornery said, 'Maybe the females don't die. Maybe they just can't fly any-more so they have to stay put.'

A long silence before Questioner commented: 'Possibly. If the scene I wit-nessed was typical, that would be equivalent to lifetime solitary confine-ment. They have the lifespan of rocks.'

'So, since Quaggi are real,' said Mouche, 'then maybe the song was real, too, and she could still be wherever it happened.'

'How big are they?' Ornery asked. 'These Quaggi things?'

'The ones we've seen vary in size from mountainous to merely large,' mused Questioner. 'The females could be smaller.'

Mouche said, 'I can't see what the Corojumi and the Bofusdiaga have to do with it.'

'Maybe they were just witnesses,' remarked Ornery.

'Many tribes of men tell stories that have bases in fact,' mused Questioner. 'Of the eclipse of the sun, perhaps, or of shooting stars. Ornery may be cor-rect, and these people may have witnessed the encounter.'

'In which case, the story has nothing to do with this journey,' said Mouche, finalizing the matter. He really wanted to stop talking.

'I think contrariwise,' murmured Questioner. 'Everything has something to do with this journey. Tell me, Mouche, do the Timmys dance?'

'How did you know?' he asked, amazed. 'They dance all the time. Everywhere. But who told you?'

'Actually, Mouche, it was an interstellar trader, who got into conversation with someone at your port, who told him a charming story about something you call the Long Nights.'

'Our midwinter holiday.'

'Which, according to the story, you celebrate because all your workers are busy dancing, even though you've tried and tried to make them quit.'

'There is a story like that,' he admitted.

'And another thing, Mouche. I am interested in the singer of your song.'

Startled, he replied, 'The singer? My Timmy sang it to me ...'

'Ah, yes. But who, in the song, apostrophizes and instructs? Who is it who cries, "Oh, Corojumi."? Who is it who tells what occurred in "the dimmer galaxies."? Is there some other personage present we have not yet heard of?'

44

A Consternation of Hags

The morning following the Questioner's visit to the Temple, D'Jevier took note that there had been no tremors through the night. Those venturing into the street saw clear blue above the scarp for the first time in seasons. Her hope that the predictions of the geologists aboard *The Quest* might have been premature was cast down, however, when those same geologists sent word to the Temple that the calm was merely a hiatus and they could not reach the Questioner. Where was she? D'Jevier received this message just as Onsofruct came in with a message from the steward at Mantelby Mansion.

'Marool, dead?' D'Jevier breathed. 'How?'

Onsofruct told her. Though the steward's account had been somewhat reticent, she had accurately imagined some of what he had left unsaid.

'Also,' said Onsofruct, taking a deep breath, 'the entire entourage that accompanied the Questioner has disappeared, along with the Questioner herself and four pressed men, three of them from House Genevois. And if that were not trouble enough, the ship that brought her knows of it and has stated its intention of relaying this information to the Council of Worlds.'

'Three men from House Genevois? *Who*, Onsy?'

'I didn't ask their names. But by every Hagion from A to Z, I'd like to know what is going on!'

'We know what's going on,' said her cousin. 'At least, we have a fat hint or two that something real is happening among creatures or beings we have always considered mythical.'

'I wish we knew the extent of the reality!'

'What do the Men of Business say? Anything useful?'

'This and that. It will or won't bankrupt the world. It will or won't put us all back to the Stone Age. It will or won't have anything to do with our social ... arrangements, though they know nothing about this world's real arrangements.'

'No,' said D'Jevier. 'But they think they do, and they simmer with discontent. They are sexually frustrated, overburdened with responsibilities, often overtired. They turn to drink and to drugs or nagging at their children. They blame themselves if they have no daughters.'

'Tragic!' snapped Onsofruct. 'Tit for tat after millennia of otherwise!'

D'Jevier sighed. 'Did you expect them to agree on anything? It isn't in them to adopt a cause or pursue justice, not given over to the game of profit as they are. That's one of the reasons we designed ... well, our foremothers designed things as they are.'

'Those same foremothers warned us, their daughters, that if ever a leader emerges among the Men of Business, they might rise up in rebellion. Especially if they ever found out ...' Onsofruct's voice trailed away.

D'Jevier shook her head warningly. 'Which they won't. We keep tight hold of information on this world. They have no way of getting hold of it.'

'Not so long as the Panhagion controls, no. But, the greater our population, the harder it gets to keep things quiet. If we're going to keep on as we have been, it'll take a new Temple near Nehbe and a couple of branch Temples out toward the scarp. Those valleys are filling up ...' Onsofruct's voice trailed away as she realized what she had said.

'Were filling up, Onsy. Were. The people there are either dead or evacuated by now. Which actually helps us control data. When the population is centralized, we manage very nicely.'

'Until the planet blows up.' She heard her voice rising stridently and put her hands over her eyes.

'If it does. Well, if it does, our troubles are over. I've been wishing we could ask the Timmys ...'

'I think we must.' Onsofruct put her hands flat on the table before her and pushed herself erect. 'Certainly we must. Let's find some.'

'Unfortunately they don't seem to be findable. I've had the word out among the Haggers for the last couple of days. The Timmys have completely vanished, Onsy. They went so quickly and totally that it appears they'd been planning it. As if they knew about it before we did.'

'That's impossible!'

D'Jevier fought down a shriek, took a deep breath, and said as calmly as she could manage, 'Nothing's impossible any longer. We must go to Mantelby Mansion and see what we can find out there.'

They saw the scene of the deadly event, which both of them were reluctant to call a murder. They questioned everyone, learning the sequence of the disappearance, first the entourage, then the two Old Earthians, then the Questioner herself along with two gardener's boys named Ornery and Mouche – at the mention of whose name D'Jevier's face paled.

'You know him?' whispered her sister.

'Of him,' said D'Jevier, in so forbidding a manner that it halted further mention.

Two other boys had disappeared as well, the steward said, but they had disappeared from the cellar, where they had been with Marool. Their names had been Bane and Dyre.

The Hags examined the machines and fought through their disgust to a comprehension of their use. D'Jevier sent for a smith to bring a portable furnace and the necessary equipment to dismantle everything in the cellar and convert it to scrap. They found the maker's name attached on neat little brass plates, and they directed a squad of Haggers to find and dispose of that individual, even before directing that Marool's body be wrapped in a linen sheet and be buried without ceremony in the Mantelby graveyard, behind the ridge.

'And,' said D'Jevier with a glare at the steward, 'as you value your life and sanity, don't take that ring off her finger or whatever ate your aunt may come to nibble on you, as well.'

When the ashen-faced young man departed, leaving them momentarily alone in the hideous cellar, Onsofruct whispered, 'Was her death a final act of worship?'

'Not a voluntary one,' murmured D'Jevier. 'Which doesn't mean Morrigan didn't relish it. I think it's clear Marool was murdered by two of the boys she got from House Genevois. The order of disappearance is probably significant. First the entourage, without the Questioner's knowledge. Then, the two Old Earthians, then the Questioner and two gardener's helpers, one Mouche, a Consort trainee, and one Ornery, a sailor lad. Finally, only after Marool's body is discovered are the other Consort trainees found to be gone. We assume they left Marool dead or dying and may, in fact, have been the first to depart. I wonder who turned off the machine and took her out of it before she was dismembered.'

Onsofruct shuddered. 'Is that what it would have done?'

'Oh, yes. The mechanical linkages led next to knives and then to a lever-aged system which would quite effectively have quartered her after disembowelment. There has not been any such barbarism among mankind for millennia. Marool had reinvented it.'

She fell silent, wanting to spit the foul taste from her mouth, taking refuge in changing the subject. 'I've noticed quite a draft. Look at the smoke from those candles.' She pointed at a branched iron stand where guttering candles unskeined black smoke that drifted sideways to disappear along a wall. The paneling was ajar. They tugged it open to reveal a shadowy sneakway running along the walls. D'Jevier went in and peered at the dusty floor, noting the footprints there, noting the spyholes in the walls.

'See, here.' She pointed. 'There, those depressions which are not quite footlike. The Questioner. And two pairs of boots, the Consort and the sailor. Some other tracks beneath, too scuffed to read, all of them headed in the same direction.' She stood staring into the dark. 'The murderers went some other way. I want to see Madame Genevois. Let us go to her, woman to woman. It will save time.'

Madame was in her office, off the welcome suite. She greeted D'Jevier as an old friend, and, after a look at their haggard faces, offered brandy. When she'd heard what they had to say about Marool's death, she rang for Simon and sent him with one of the workmen to fetch a picture from the hallway upstairs.

'I collect a certain kind of thing. It's as well to be somewhat cautionary with the young men, and also to blunt their curiosity.' She sipped, and poured, and in moments, Simon was back, bearing the picture as though it were a long-dead fish.

'By all the Hagions,' murmured D'Jevier. 'Where did you get it?'

'The artist disappeared. His body showed up, later, giving evidence that he had died by this machine or some similar. Someone had rifled his studio and then tried, unsuccessfully, to burn it down. This painting was found, quite undamaged, among several others in a kind of vault he had built below his house. His heirs sold it to me.'

'If Marool had known you had it ...'

'She didn't know. I've always refused to deal with Mistress Mantelby. Even if I'd never seen this, I'd have refused to deal with her. There was always something ... possessed about her.'

'You say "always" ...'

Madame sat back comfortably and stared beyond them, into the past. 'I saw her first at a Family Men's Soirée at her parent's house. I often attend such events. It gives me an opportunity to get off in a corner with a patroness to discuss what I might have in stock to interest her, or for her to tell me what she's looking for. Marool was at the time about four, but her expression was merciless, like a hungry animal watching prey. Her eyes were without humanity. I saw her several times after that, as she grew older, and I thought each time that her eyes were like viper's eyes.

'After she ran off to join the Wasters, I saw her in their company from time to time, and of course, after she returned from her so-called pilgrimage, I saw her at the Panhagion and at the theater, and I heard things from other Houses about Mantelby Consorts who disappeared or died without explanation.'

D'Jevier set down her cup. 'About these two boys who supposedly killed her ...'

Madame said, 'Bane and Dyre. I believe they were her sons. I can't say whether they knew she was their mother, though I rather think not. Mismothering was probably the least of her sins.'

The two Hags were shocked into silence. Madame sipped, staring at them over the rim of her glass, thinking that she, too, might have been shocked if she had not had the opportunity of knowing Bane and Dyre and the man she thought was their father. 'Whether she was or was not their mother, I believe their father is a man known to me as Thor Ashburn. Not a Family

Man, no g' to his name, but not a supernume, either. He offered my investors a very large fee if I would take these two boys and train them. Left to my own decision, I would not have done so for any sum, but as you know, we cannot always do what we would prefer.'

'Indeed,' D'Jevier said thoughtfully.

Madame went on, 'Over the years I've heard this and that about Marool. Consorts talk among themselves at the Temple and in the park. The talk comes back, and the Houses hear what's said. What was said about Mantelby identified her as a sadist, an accomplished torturer, a gloating killer. She's been seen in public every day or so for eighteen years, however, so if she bore these boys, it was while she was away, supposedly at Nehbe.'

'Interesting,' murmured Onsofruct. 'Our Haggers tell us the man who made the terrible machines also lives near Nehbe.'

Madame set down her glass. 'The thing I can't figure out is that Thor Ashburn seems unconnected to any known family. Also, he and his sons share a family stink.'

'Skunk-lung?'

'That's what it's called,' Madame confirmed. 'Though it doesn't come from the lung.'

'But none of the settlers could have had it,' D'Jevier remarked. 'It would have been a disqualifying attribute for a colonial.'

'I have a suspicion,' murmured Madame, 'that those who had it weren't settlers. At least, not from the second settlement.'

'First settlement survivors?' breathed D'Jevier. 'There were no survivors!'

'How do we know, for sure?' Madame raised her eyebrows as she refilled their glasses. 'I've been puzzling over this a good deal since meeting Thor Ashburn. I hated the man instinctively, the way we hate snakes, without thinking about it, knowing they have not enough brain to be swayed by pity or reason. And yet, he is mankindly looking, not unhandsome, not badly built. He had to come from somewhere. So, I asked myself, how do we know there were no survivors? Our ancestors didn't see any, quite true, but then, our ancestors arrived over a period of twelve years, in ten large shiploads, a thousand to the ship. None of them knew all the others, not even the ones on their own ship.

'If someone from the first settlement had shown up in a bustling neighborhood and said he was from upriver or downriver, who would have known?'

Onsofruct mused, 'According to the servants at Mantelby Mansion, the boys claimed to be sons of thunder.'

'Thor was a god of thunder back on Old Earth,' said Madame. 'That's what Thor means, thunder. Thor is also the supremacist planet from which the schismatic group departed to become the first settlers here.'

'You're forgetting something,' said D'Jevier. 'The first settlement had no women, and the second settlement was almost a hundred years later! They couldn't have lived that long.'

Madame nodded. 'They weren't supposed to have had women, no. But perhaps they did. Stolen women. Enslaved women. They simply didn't want it known.'

Onsofruct cried, 'So why haven't we ever seen them? Why didn't they make themselves known?'

'We haven't seen them because they didn't wish to be seen,' said Madame. 'They know what the Hags would do about enslaved women, and they do not want us to know they are here. They must have maintained a hidden community, somewhere. This planet is certainly rife with enough wilderness to hide a whole population if it wanted to stay hidden!'

After a long pause, Onsofruct said, 'In addition to the two sons of thunder, there's a sailor lad missing, who seemingly went off with the Questioner herself, plus another of your young men. His name was Mouche.'

Madame cried, 'Mouche?' She looked quickly at D'Jevier, then back at Onsofruct. 'Is he all right?'

'We assume so. You seem to care a good deal. Who is he?'

'He's ... just Mouche. Well, I confess, a favorite of mine. We have favorites, though we shouldn't.'

'What can you tell us about him?' asked Onsofruct.

Madame poured a splash more brandy and sat back in her chair, surprised to find that her hand trembled slightly. 'Nothing evil at all. I bought Mouche when he was twelve, and I made the first overture, having seen the boy in the marketplace. The father came to the House first, talked to some of the students and to Simon, who's one of my old boys. Only when he was convinced the boy would be well treated did he consent, even though his need was great.'

'And his mother?' Onsofruct set down her glass.

'I didn't meet the mother. She must be a good-looking woman to produce such a son.'

Onsofruct remarked, 'He's handsome, then?'

'Oh, remarkably, yes. Many of my students are extremely good looking, and none are plain. Appearance is what sells! But it isn't his appearance that made me like him so. Most young men, well, you can imagine, learning to be a Consort is for most of them an occasion for a good deal of lewdness and that excretory jocularity that men seem to find funny. It's something we work hard to control, since by and large women are offended by it. With Mouche it wasn't necessary. Mouche was never lewd. He went through a stage when he was about sixteen when he seemed distracted, which isn't uncommon, but then lately, it seemed that he was above his work, very sure and capable but able to do it without thinking about it. No, it was more than that! He was able to imbue a relationship with romance without personalizing it. He was able to do what we try to get all the young men to do; focus on the ideal, treat the real as though it were the ideal. Mouche could do that.'

'A treasure,' murmured D'Jevier.

After a rather long pause, Madame said, 'Yes. A treasure. When that woman took him from here, I wanted to kill her. If I'd had a proper weapon in my hand, I might have done so. I managed to warn him, before he left, to be as inconspicuous as possible. Now, hearing that she's dead but that he is, so far as anyone knows, unscathed, I breathe again in hope. I have not had many like Mouche.'

Onsofruct asked, 'Why did the Questioner take him? Or the sailor boy?'

'Most likely she needed strong young hands to fetch and carry. Do you know where they went?'

D'Jevier explained about the sneakaway in the wall.

'We must go after her, of course,' said Madame. 'Until my students are back, I have little purpose to my life, and my students won't be back unless we find this Questioner, get her or it off planet, and return to our own lives. Assuming the volcanoes leave us any life.'

'I suppose we must go in search of her,' said D'Jevier, almost unwillingly. 'Otherwise ... well, we'll have the Council of Worlds on our doorstep. If by some chance our world survives all this rumbling and rattling, I'd prefer that the Council of Worlds not involve themselves in our lives.'

'We should go as soon as possible,' said Madame. 'I'll need a couple of days to take care of immediate business, but then I can leave the House to my assistant. It's threeday morning. I can be ready early fiveday. Say at dawn.'

'Let us use the time to prepare well,' Onsofruct suggested. 'We will want provisions, and some strong Haggers, and such things as lights and ropes. We can get that together by early fiveday morning.'

'Very well,' said Madame, already assembling her kit in her mind. 'I will meet you then, at Mantelby's.'

45

The Camp of The Wilderneers

The light carriage that Ashes had used to pick up his sons was abandoned at the edge of the wild, not far from the place Marool's parents and sister had died. The horse behind the carriage was already saddled and there were two more light saddles in the boot. Shortly the three were riding through the forest, along the level top of one of the great lava tubes to the north of the Combers. It was not the first time they had ridden together, though it was the first time they had ridden here, and only Ashes knew the way to their destination.

The horses' shod feet struck the top of the buried lava tube like drumsticks striking a gong. Most often the sound was muted, but occasionally, as they crossed a particularly reverberant space, the earth shivered around them with deep bell sounds, an enormous tolling, as though for some creature long dying or just dead. Bane was not normally fanciful, but even he was struck with the similarity of the sound to that of the bells of the Panhagion, which tolled away the old year at the festival of the Tipping.

None of them were sorry when the stony way ended. They turned to the side for a brief time and picked up another stone-floored path, almost like a road, this one completely muffled so that the hooves made no more sound than on any paved surface. Bane, staring at his surroundings, such of them as he could see in the moonlight, thought the lava trail was extremely road-like. The dirt at either side of it was pushed up, like a curb, as though something huge and wide had moved this way, displacing the earth as it went. Several places along this track Bane found large, oval pieces of something, like enormous fingernails.

They rode for some hours, dismounting as needed to relieve themselves and once to eat food from the saddlebags and drink from the flasks. When dawn came, Ashes turned aside from the trail he'd been following, hobbled the horses and let them browse while he slept, leaving it to Bane and Dyre whether they followed his example or not.

The boys were unusually quiet, somewhat awed by the silence of the forest. House Genevois had always been clattery with boys, and they had spent their childhood on the farm where there was constant cackling of poultry, the low or bleat of livestock, the chatter of people. Here was no sound at all. The night had been windless. They had crossed no streams. No bird had cried, no small beast called, no large beast threatened. Sleep eluded them, and they dropped into uncomfortable slumber only moments, so it seemed, before Ashes roused them again.

When they remounted, the silence was still unbroken, and even Ashes looked around himself with a certain wariness.

'Is it always this still?' asked Bane, in a throaty whisper.

Ashes shook his head, his eyes swiveling from point to point. 'No. Usually there's animals making noises. I don't like this quiet. It could mean Joggiwagga about.'

'What?' grunted Dyre. 'What's Joggi whatsit?'

'Very big and nervous and dangerous,' murmured Ashes.

'Did Joggy whatsit clear the road along here?' Bane asked. 'Something big came along these tops. The dirt's all pushed back. And there's funny pieces of stuff.'

Ashes swallowed, his nostrils pushed together, then said, 'No. That wasn't Joggiwagga. Those things are seeds, and they came off another ... another thing entirely.'

'Something big?'

'Big, yes.'

'Never seen any really big wild thing,' opined Dyre.

His father retorted, 'You boys favored little things, didn't you? Well, the one that made this trail is a lot bigger than the little critters you hunted for fun while you were at Dutter's.'

'How'd you know?' asked Bane, astonished. 'Never told you!'

'You don't need to tell me anything, boy. I know everything there is to know about you from before you was planted to the breath you just took. I know all about your hunting trips.'

'Ol' Dutter, he said even if we killed something, he wouldn't let us keep any hides.'

'No. That furry thing you hunted – there was lots of them when we first landed, and we hunted 'em for fur, but the Timmys, they won't let you keep any part of an animal here. Well, except for the littlest ones, birds and fish and mousy things. The only way to keep hides from anything bigger than that is put 'em in a safe, put the safe in a metal-lined room, then send them off world as soon as may be, the way we used to. Dutter knew that. He wanted no trouble with Timmys.'

'Like to see the Timmy could take something from me,' muttered Bane. 'Like to see 'em try.'

Ashes didn't reply. They had come to the end of the network of level lava trails they'd been following for hours and were now climbing onto the flanks of the ancient calderas that stretched in an unbroken range stretching south from the shore of the Jellied Sea, and perhaps beneath it, for all anyone knew. The day wore itself out in ascents and descents, in long traverses across sliding scree, ending at evening on a shadowed ledge that darkened as the sun set.

'Can't go on until moonrise,' said Ashes. 'Can't see where to go. We'll build a little fire and have some food, catch some sleep.'

Bane and Dyre were too tired to complain. They ate, dropped into sleep, only to be wakened again, this time for hours of careful, slow travel by landmarks only Ashes could see, until almost dawn.

'The way's tricky from here,' Ashes remarked, dismounting and hobbling his horse once more. 'We'll wait for full light.'

Full light came. They rode. Darkness came. They stopped, until moonrise once more, then went on. Shortly before dawn, after a long climb, they drew up near the edge of a cliff that marked the rim of still another immense and ancient caldera. Early light bleached the eastern sky. Two moons threw silver reflections in a lake far below, and beyond the lake flickered the amber glows of a scatter of campfires.

'Our people,' said Ashes. 'Wilderneers.' He moved restlessly on his saddle, then turned to the boys and told them to dismount.

When they were afoot, he brought them close, within arms' distance, and muttered, 'Before we go down there, there's things you got to know.'

'Yeah?' sneered Bane. 'And what would that be?'

Ashes reached to his side, thrusting back his coat to let Bane get a good look at the whip coiled around his waist, the sharp end hanging at his side, then grasped him by the shoulder in a grip that made him cry out. 'You want some more of what you had before, boy? I'm not one of your flowery fencing masters or your wet-eared boys or some woman you can smart-mouth to. I'm Ashes and Thunder, and you'll hark or you'll suffer.' He gave Bane a shake and released him, glaring into his face. 'Now the two of you. You listen.

'A long time ago, we came here, a bunch of us, from the planet Thor. We'd had a bit of a disagreement with our brethren there, and we decided to find ourselves a new place where we could do things right without having to explain every other move ...'

'What was the disagreement about?' asked Bane, interested in all this.

For a moment Ashes looked angry, but then he breathed deeply and said, 'Women. How we were going to handle women. We said women had no right to refuse any man anything. Whatever man she belonged to, he owned her just like he owned a horse, and you didn't let a horse say it wasn't going to be bred or saddled. We took a few women just to prove the point, and we killed some families that got in the way, and the whole thing blew up into a sort of war.

'Well, we had hostages, and we said we'd let the hostages go if they'd let us go, and they said so leave. They wouldn't let us bring any women, but we figured we could pirate some from somewhere, once we got settled. So, we scouted a few places and decided on this one, then we met up at a transfer point, and we captured a colony ship with almost a thousand men aboard, people we could use as slaves, and we came here. The place suited us. We settled in, we planted crops, we built a couple of fortresses, we started building towns, we did some hunting, some trapping, we sold furs off planet – after we learned how to get 'em off planet – we brought in some recruits, we sold biologicals, Dingle and Farfaran and other such stuff, and after a score or so years, after most of the towns were built and most of the slaves were dead, we decided it was time to bring in some women.'

Dyre gaped. 'Why'ja wait so long?'

'Too much trouble to get them earlier. Our system is, women are for breeding, and that's it. You gotta keep 'em locked, you gotta keep 'em private. Letting other men see your women, that'd be shameful. So, before we brought women in, we had to make places to keep 'em, places they could stay out of the way, do their own work without being seen. Courtyards, like. Like there in House Genevois. That wharf behind there, we shipped furs and stuff down river from there. When the courtyard was empty, the Timmys used to come out into it, and I used to sit up there under the tower watching them dance.'

'Timmys? You saw Timmys? Our teacher said they didn't come till after the second settlement!'

'They were here almost as soon as we were, but I'm not talking about that …' He paused, as though he'd lost track of his tale.

'So?' muttered Bane. 'So, you brought women.'

'We were getting ready to, getting the ship ready, deciding who'd go and who'd stay, and then one night, the Timmys came out of the walls in packs, like ants. It wasn't just Timmys, either; they had other kinds of bigger critters with 'em, and there we were, all of us, wrapped up like so many packages, being hauled off into these woods here. They hauled us partway and they floated us partway, and they swallowed us partway, and we ended up down in caves, over there, some days west, beyond the far side of this valley! They took us out of the caves and down into a kind of pond. And they threw us in the pond. And after a while, we crawled out again.'

'So,' muttered Bane again, yawning.

Ashes said angrily, 'So, some of us came out pretty much like we was before and some of us didn't.'

The boys stared at him, waiting, but he seemed to find no words to go on with his story. Finally, Dyre ventured, 'What do you mean, not like before?'

Ashes chewed at his lip, eventually saying, 'Some of us was changed, that's what I mean. And some went on changing. When we go down there, where the camp is, you'll see some of us who don't look ... well, who don't look like we do, but you'll know they're Wilderneers by the smell. Since that pond, we all smell the same. But you won't know by the shape, so be careful who you smart off to.'

Bane's forehead was creased. 'So what did you do about the women?'

'We never got any women,' said Ashes. 'When we came out of that damned pond, there weren't enough of us left in shape to man the ship, and in the meantime a trader ship had set down and taken all the slaves away, not that there was many left. We came roarin' down on 'em, and when they saw us, they killed a good many of us, then they took off in both ships, theirs and ours! Left a notice on the door of the fortress saying they'd salvaged our ship, taken it as a prize!

'So, after that we had no way to get women. Not until the other settlers came. Then we took some women, but they weren't our women, so it wasn't any good.'

'Settlers let you get away with that?'

'The settlers didn't know it was us. The settlers don't even know we're here. Some of us, we go to town when we like, we wander around, we know what's goin' on, they don't know who we are. The rest of us, well, the rest of us learned to stay hid. There's caves ... caves that go on forever. After they took our ship, we stayed in caves for a long, long time.'

'So it was you, doing the women raids,' said Bane.

'Well, it was us to start with. Some of us looked ... normal, so we dressed up like them, let them think it was one family going after women from another family. Before you knew it, it was one family going against another family, like we'd given 'em the idea. They never did know it was us started it.'

'So, you took some women ...'

'Just enough to find out it wouldn't work anyhow. We couldn't breed 'em.'

'Whattaya mean, you couldn't breed 'em?'

'They died. We'd get close to 'em, and they'd die. Every time.'

'But there's us,' Bane complained. 'We had a mother!'

'That was later, and I tricked her,' Ashes said. 'It was something we planned, to get some daughters born to us who could be our kind of women, women of our own. But ... she didn't have daughters. She had you two.'

A long silence, during which Bane and Dyre thought their way through the implications of this.

'You mean we're the only ones?' Bane asked. 'The only kids you've had in hundreds of years?'

'The only ones the Wilderneers ever had,' said Ashes.

'But ... if all that happened hundreds of years ago. How come ... how come you're still here?'

'We don't die,' said Ashes, staring at the sky. 'Way we figure it, critters that come from that pond, we can get killed – like that trader ship killed some of us, but we don't just die.'

'We? You mean us, too?'

Ashes shrugged. 'I don't know. You had a regular woman as a mother. Maybe it only works if you've been in the pond. Maybe it doesn't work for sons, or daughters. We don't know. We want to find out.'

Bane raised his voice. 'So what are we, huh? Some kinda experiment? You gonna see if you can kill us?'

Ashes shrugged again. 'You're my sons. For now. And when you go down there, you're their kinfolk. For now. So long as you don't do anything or say anything stupid.'

'Like what?' demanded Bane.

'Like anything but "yes sir" and "no sir" and "kind of you to say so sir,"' Ashes growled.

The boys got wordlessly back on their horses and rode along the edge of the caldera until they reached a break in the rimwall, a path leading down. Ashes's lead horse took to the trail as though he knew it well, and after a moment's hesitation, the others followed. Clouds settled and they rode for a time in glowing, clinging mist. Clouds rose and they found themselves almost at the bottom, the lakes away to their right, glittering with moon trails.

Something tall, massive, and darker than the sky reared into being at the edge of the trail. Though the horses took no notice at first, both Bane and Dyre started in fright, pulling up on the reins, causing their mounts to rear. At this, there came a titter from between the stones at the side of the path where something poured out of one declivity into another.

'Hush,' said Ashes, 'it's only Bone and Boneless.' He glanced upward toward the slow clap, clap of leathern wings. In a moment the winged one dropped onto the trail beside him, eyes glowing, sharp fangs glittering. A lean, gray-furred body leaned toward the boys, almost hungrily.

'Ashes and Thunder,' the thing said from a fanged mouth. 'Welcome home. You brought me dinner?'

'They're not for your dinner, Webwings.' Ashes nodded. 'These're my boys. This here's Bane, that's Dyre.'

Barely able to speak, the brothers managed jerky nods in the newcomer's direction. He stared at them for a time with glowing eyes, then grasped Ashes's arm and swung himself onto the horse behind him, wings falling to either side of the mount, the ragged tips trailing along the ground. When Ashes clucked the horse into a trot, Bane and Dyre did likewise, though reluctantly. Having seen this little, they were not eager to see more. The trail led toward cook fires that burned on hearths of stone in what seemed to be a permanent encampment, a sprawling community of stone-and-wattle shacks, of roofless enclosures, of pits and holes, all set well apart, with fire-wood piled nearby, and everything concealed from above by copses of large trees.

Ashes drew up at the edge of the encampment. His winged acquaintance slipped off the horse and walked away behind a high earthen wall. Bane and Dyre shared a glance between themselves and at their father who watched the wall, waiting. From behind that concealment a huge, bony hook slashed down, flailing in a forceful arc that slammed it into the shivering soil, fragments of sod flying. Then came another hook at the end of a stout cable or a thick rope, flailing down, piercing deep. The cables tightened; there was a sound like a gasp or grunt, not quite organic, and a monstrous mound of flesh tugged itself into view, something like an elephantine caterpillar, a thing the size of a large carriage or small river boat, though longer than that, for it kept coming as the huge grapples at its front were set again and again so the body could heave itself forward. The immense, immobile weight hauling along the ground, accompanied by a barrage of grunts and gargles, thrust up the earth at either side, leaving a groove like a ditch.

Terrible as the thing was, it was not the size or the sound that horrified the boys so much as the sight of the almost human face between the hooks, a face with wide, slobbery lips and a hole for a nose and eyes that peered from deep pits of gray, granular flesh under a ruff of large, oval scales, like those Bane had seen along the way.

The horses jittered as the thing came nearer: hook, heave, hump, hook, heave, hump, gargling and spewing, stopping at last a hook's length away.

'Crawly, I'd like you to meet my boys,' said Ashes, rather too loudly.

The thing wheezed in a breathless, bubbling voice, straining against the buried hooks. The cables had elbows, even a kind of wrists, being otherwise twisted sinew. Closer to, Bane could see that the hooks were hands that had become enlarged with the fingers fused into sharply angled, bone-tipped grapples.

'So here's the offspring,' wheezed the monster. 'Well, well. Very human-looking, aren't they? How do you do, young sprouts. Doing well, are you?'

'Say yessir, when someone speaks to you,' snarled Ashes, striking Bane on the back.

'Yessir,' bleated Bane and Dyre, as with one voice.

The creature grinned and drooled, raising the large, oval scales around its neck into a hideous ruff. Greenish goo oozed from between the erected scales, emitting a greatly amplified wave of the family stink.

Webwings came around the side of his monstrous friend, smiling maliciously at Bane and Dyre. 'Not what you expected, eh, boys?'

Bane swallowed, trying to moisten a dry mouth. 'Didn't … didn't expect anything.' In the light of the fire he could see what looked like spiders moving about on the creature's wings, spinning back and forth, thread by thread, repairing the holes and tatters. When the spiders had finished, they scuttled into holes in what would have been armpits if Webwings had had arms. Bane felt an irresistible urge to scratch under his own arms, and only a glare from his father held him motionless. Dyre was not so fortunate. He scratched and was thunked across the back of the head for it.

'This is Strike,' said Ashes, turning to the other side, where someone else had approached without their notice, a creature knobbed and heavy at the top, thin as a rail below, bearing a long bony beak like a curved pike, with opaque bloody beads of eyes peering from either side. It had arms like boneless vines twisting at its sides, and it tottered on clublike legs as it struggled to hold its great bony haft aloft.

And behind it came something tentacled and horned, moving on a carpet of fibers, and behind that came something squatty with a mouth like a furnace. 'Mosslegs,' said Ashes. 'And Gobblemaw. Say howdy.'

'How do you do, sirs,' said Bane, shaking his brother with one hand. 'Tell the sirs how do you do, brother.'

Dyre managed a nod and a gush of wordless air.

There was also Foot (a tiny person with one huge extremity that flexed endlessly upon a separate patch of soil), and, each on its own plot, Ear (a tiny person with huge ear that quivered), and Tongue (a tiny person with huge tongue that wagged). There was Belly, too, wide as a swamp, legs and arms flung out like those on a skin rug, with a wide mouth at one end where some many-handed being called Shoveler was busy pushing the carcass of a very dead goat into it.

All had faces, though some were very small. Not all had mouths and tongues capable of speech. All had arms and legs, though some were rudimentary. Not all had means of locomotion. Among the speaking and walking were a dozen or so who appeared mankindly enough to pass in a crowd, creatures with names like Blade and Shatter and Brigand, Machinist and Mooly, and some of the mankindly ones wore clothes as Ashes did, though more were clad in thick hair or bristles or scales or feathers, or had skin that was warty or horned or embossed or folded. No two were enough alike to mistake one for the other, not even the manlike ones.

Soon Bane and Dyre were at the center of a gathering, a score of creatures all talking at once, producing a windy gibberish that babbled on until the one called Shatter thrust through the mob and drowned them out with a stentorian cry: 'Good-looking girls there, Ash. So these're the daughters, eh?'

Ashes's lips thinned, his jaw tightened. 'So, what you got, Shatter? You got some girls hid we don't know about?'

Bane shut his eyes, reminded of Dutter's farm, where the animals had made similar noises and the supernume farmhands had joshed at him in similar phrases, until they had learned not to. He had never suffered insults without retaliation. Here, the life around him was itself an insult, past retaliation, and the inability to voice or display his outrage left him feeling weak, as though from loss of blood. He would feel better later, he told himself, and then he would do whatever he had to do, and when he did it, this mockery, yes, mockery would be remembered, for Ashes had no right to do ... whatever it was he had done.

'Boys're bettern nothin', I suppose!' Shatter brayed.

'That's right, Shat. Can't blame a man for trying.'

The one called Mooly bent himself in laughter. 'No, we can't blame old Ash for tryin'! Or us for watchin' him try!'

The gathering split asunder. Ashes rode out of it, the boys staying close behind him as he pointed his horse toward a shack under a towering tree at the far side of the camp. There they turned the horses into a corral made of dead branches with bits of vine twisted around them, and while Ashes busied himself with unsaddling the mounts, the boys went inside. There was little in the way of furniture. A table and a chair. A low dirt mound cushioned with boughs and sheepskins to make a couch or sleeping place. They settled themselves on this, leaning forward toward the coals of the fire, piling on a stick or two as though this tending of the fire were necessary and demanding, choosing an appearance of gravity rather than acknowledge to one another the depth of their confusion and disappointment. They had not sorted out how they felt, certainly they had not sorted out what, if anything, they would do about how they felt.

When Ashes came in, they were still bent beside the fire, side by side, cross-legged and silent.

He regarded them narrowly. 'Well?'

The first thing they needed, so Bane had decided, was information. 'What'd you bring us here for?'

'You're family,' said Ashes, hanging his jacket on a peg set into a tent pole. 'You'll want to be in on family business.'

'Don't exactly see it that way,' said Bane, carefully expressionless. 'Don't see much great future here. Not exactly what you promised. No reason to have killed *her*, if this was all we did it for.'

'No women here,' Dyre added in sulky explanation. 'No sex machines. No hot baths. No massage. I had a look at what they was roasting on the fires, walking over here, and it's not food, it's garbage. You promised us good stuff, all kinds of good stuff.'

'You had your good stuff with Marool,' said Ashes. 'I promised you good things while you were with her, boys. I said, you get yourselves educated at House Genevois, and I'll situate you at Mantelby Mansion. Well, you got situated there, one way or t'other, and you got good stuff, too, don't say you didn't.'

'A few days,' grated Bane. 'And why her? Why not somebody we didn't have to kill? Somebody we coulda stayed with?'

Ashes said angrily, 'I told you why, boy. She needed killing and she's the only one couldn't smell you. That job's over and that future's gone a begging. You don't want the good life any more than the rest of us do, but before we get it, first we got to clear the way! So, you've done the first part and killed one that needed killing.'

'We killed her cause you told us to!'

'Well, I'm your daddy. I got that right.'

'I been wanting to ask you, how come she couldn't smell us?' asked Bane, eyes narrow.

'Dingle. She used it when she was a girl. Ruined her sense of smell.'

'Well, then, we'll find us some other women used Dingle. She couldn'ta been the only one.'

Ashes sat down in the only chair the tent afforded, a folding affair of rawhide and curved sticks. 'Well, not the only one, no, but women who use Dingle are mostly the ones too ugly to dowry for. Or they're sterile. Or they're crazy. Or all three. Once in a great while there's one like Marool, but it's rare.'

'There was our mama,' said Bane, watching his father narrowly. 'Could she smell you?'

Ashes was momentarily silent. 'Well, no. But her and Marool were the only ones I ever found.'

'But it just happened Marool was the one stole us away from you?'

'Right,' said Ashes, busying himself with his bootlaces. 'We all three knew each other, me and Marool and your mama. And Marool was jealous of your mama having my babies. So, when your mama died, she stole you away. And she was goin' to have a daughter for me, but she didn't. But I found you, so it all turned out all right.'

'Maybe,' muttered Bane. 'Maybe it did.'

'So what's the family business?' asked Dyre.

'Why, boys, this whole world is our family business! It belongs to us! We was here first, and we're going to take it back!' Ashes lay back in the chair and stared at his sons through the smoke of the fire. 'We're going to take it back, kill off all the timrats, kill off all the settler men, all those g'family men. We'll keep the women. Some of them, anyhow. Whichever ones we can fix like we did Marool. We're going to build a race of giants!'

'Is this all of you?' Bane asked, gesturing to indicate the camp. 'All that's left?'

Ashes stared into the fire. 'No. There's others. Bigger. Meaner. Sometimes they come to the edge of the light and we talk. They're with us.'

'How come they don't live here?'

Ashes made a peculiar face, a kind of chewing, as though trying to swallow something that wouldn't go down. 'They ... they got changed in the pond. Really changed. They're too big for camp, for one thing, and there's nothing ... nothing much we can talk to them about now. They're like ... only set on one thing.' He got up, started to speak, then thought better of whatever he'd been going to say. 'Later,' he admonished. 'We'll get into all that stuff later.'

Bane shook his head, showing his teeth. He wasn't going to let go. 'So, how come you've waited all this time? It'd a been easier when there wasn't so many settlers, wouldn't it? It'd a been easier when they just first arrived. You shoulda done it then, killed the men, took the women, got your own daughters, like you planned. I mean, those, out there, they say you planned daughters, right?'

'We wanted daughters, sure, but I told you we couldn't do it back then!' snarled Ashes. 'We tried that. Grabbed a few girls outa their houses, took 'em back in the hills, did 'em there. We'd just get half done with 'em, and they'd die! They'd turn blue, try to breathe, then they'd die. I told you, it's the smell of that pond! Like it smothered 'em. Took us a long time to figure out how to get around that. Mooly figured out about Dingle. You get on Dingle, it builds up a kind of ... resistance to the smell. Dingle grows easy, but back then it only grew far back in the hills. We had to bring it near the cities, plant it there so we could get plenty of it, easy. Then we had to teach people to use it, Wasters and rebels and like that.

'But you get a woman on Dingle, she'll abort, sure as anything. So, then Mooly had to find some other drug to counteract that effect. That took a long time, boys. That took a long, long time. We tried this and we tried that, over the years. Got to be legendary, we did, for stealing women, but we kept at it.

'So we did that, all of it, nice and slow, and we've got you. You're the proof that it works. When we take over, we'll take our time, do it right ...'

'How you going to do that? Take over?'

Ashes leaned back in his chair, staring at the fire, looking at the boys, then past them, then back at the boys again. 'Well, there's a time coming. We can feel it. Kind of like a call in the bones. The mountains are gonna blow! Then the cities'll fall, boys. Cities'll fall. People, they'll be out, running around in the streets. We'll be there, waiting. There's hot springs here and there, we'll fill them with Dingle. Kill this one, take that one and drop her in a Dingle pot, kill this one, take that one to the Dingle, slow and easy. These folks, they got nothing like an army. Nothing like police. Just those Haggers, here, there, ever-where. But Crawly, he's as good as a fortress. Webwings, he's our lookout. Ear, he can hear a moth drop a day's march away. Tongue, he can taste blood in the air. We'll manage.'

'When you gonna do it?' asked Dyre.

Ashes looked out the one small window at the sky, pointed westward where four of the moons made a cluster low along the hills, with another one trailing close. 'Soon, boy. My bones say soon. They're all gathering. Real soon.'

'And when we take it over, everything, then we get what you promised, huh?' Bane asked.

'Then you get what was promised you and I get what was promised me, and we all get everything we want. And more.'

46

The Second Expedition Sets Out

Onsofruct and D'Jevier, together with five sturdy Haggers, waited for Madame outside the gates of Mantelby Mansion rather early on fiveday morning. They heard the carriage wheels approaching from down the hill, then saw the equipage as it rounded the nearest curve and came quickly toward them. Madame was not alone. She was accompanied by one veiled man without cockade and a family man known to the Hags by the cockade as Calvy g'Valdet. He leapt from the carriage and bowed deeply.

'Revered Hag,' he said. 'It seems the Hags and the Men of Business are similarly motivated.'

'How did you find out about this, Family Man?' demanded Onsofruct, with a glare in Madame's direction.

'Do not blame Madame,' said Calvy. 'The steward here is Bin g'Kiffle's son.'

'Of course,' murmured D'Jevier. 'We should have remembered that.'

'There was a special meeting of the ECMOB, and after a good bit of talk that achieved nothing, they decided to send me to represent the Men of Business.'

'Why you, g'Valdet?' asked Onsofruct. 'Are you now in good odor with your colleagues?'

'No, Ma'am,' he said. 'Slab g'Tupoar nominated me. He said that Myrphee was too fat, Sym was too small, Slab himself was too lazy. Estif's wife wouldn't let him, and Bin bitches about everything. He said he didn't much like me, but I got things done. And here I am.'

'Well, if your intention is to find out what happened to the Questioner, your interest is no less justified than ours, though I am surprised at the company you keep.'

'I have known Calvy for many years,' said Madame. 'In my opinion, we need him and my well-trusted Simon to assist us in this exploration.'

Onsofruct said stiffly, 'If you think it wise, we will not obstruct you. I suggest, however, that the Family Man and Simon replace two of our Haggers rather than increasing our total number.'

'Is the number important?' asked Calvy.

'Not if you are both excellent swimmers,' remarked D'Jevier, rather frostily. 'Since Timmys are no doubt involved in this disappearance, we have cast about in memory and fable and find many references to subterranean waters – at least rivers, perhaps even lakes. We are carrying an inflatable boat that holds a maximum of eight.'

Calvy laughed. 'I hadn't thought of that! By all means, let us replace two of your Haggers.'

There was a momentary hesitation among them, an unspoken acknowledgment that they had not agreed upon a leader for their expedition.

Onsofruct ran her fingers down the seams of her unaccustomed trousers and said, 'Madame? D'Jevier and I have seldom been outside the Panhagion since we were children. Do you have experience of this kind of thing? If so, we would be pleased to follow you.'

Madame was herself dressed appropriately for the occasion in heavy trousers and shirt, with stout boots on her feet. She regarded the Hags with some diffidence, saying, 'I can't claim to expertise, though a small group of friends and I have gone on lengthy cave hikes during the summers, exploring some of the badlands west of Naibah. I may have picked up some useful skills. I know that Simon and Calvy have had similar experience.'

D'Jevier nodded. 'You are better equipped than we. How do you suggest that we proceed?'

Madame smiled. 'By handling a question that arose during our trip here. Calvy and Simon have pointed out that it will be difficult for them to be useful if they keep their veils.'

'We are unlikely to be able to see through them underground,' said Calvy, making an apologetic gesture toward the Hags.

D'Jevier replied, 'I have no objection to your removing your veils while on this expedition. It would be foolish to handicap you out of mere custom; Onsofruct and I have quite dependable self-control, and we promise not to assault you sexually.'

Madame merely smiled at this.

Calvy said, 'Inasmuch as Simon and I are already carrying all we can manage, let's proceed with all five of your Haggers. When and if we encounter water, we can decide then what baggage to leave behind, who will go on and who will return.'

D'Jevier nodded her assent, then led them around the house to a side entrance that gave directly upon stairs leading to the cellars. The room below had already been cleared of its sadistic machines, except for piles of scrap, and Onsofruct wasted no time in finding and opening the sneakway door, bowing Madame to enter first.

Madame stepped into the sneakway, looked and sniffed in both directions, and came to much the same conclusion Mouche had come to earlier. 'That way goes back up into the mansion. This way leads down. I think we may rely upon it that they went down, though we'll watch for their tracks to be sure.'

'If you'll allow me,' said Calvy, drawing Madame out and taking her place in the narrow way. 'I have done some tracking, and I am armed, which you are not.'

'Armed, Family Man?' asked D'Jevier, threateningly. 'Our laws forbid Family Men carrying arms.'

'A canister of chemical repellant, Ma'am. Useful for dissuading vicious dogs while walking on the streets. And a rather large knife, useful for opening shipping crates. Both are allowed within the regulations. I am also carrying a staff which I have been trained to use.' He turned on the downward way and moved off with Madame and the Hags behind him, then Simon and the Haggers bringing up the rear.

Down they went, as Mouche, Ornery, and the Questioner had gone, making their slow way through the rooty tunnel until it intersected the stream. Because they had lighted their way throughout, they noticed no luminescence. Indeed, they had sent two Haggers back the way they had come, had inflated their boat and were well down the river before they turned out their lights and began to see the wonders of the world around them.

47

Round the Down Staircase

For Mouche and his companion, the drift-trip down the big river had seemed timeless. Both Mouche and Ornery had slept for long, lost periods of quiet and peace. Every now and then the boats had stopped at some sandy beached curve and let them go ashore to eat and drink and relieve themselves, and according to Questioner, who seemed to be keeping track, this happened several times each day for several days. They had eaten only a little food from their packs, for Questioner had reminded them they had no idea how long they would be on this journey and thus no idea how long their food would need to last.

'I think we could eat their food,' Mouche had said, indicating the darkness where pairs of silver eyes shone briefly from time to time. 'I've smelled it, and it smells wonderful.'

'Do not worry over food,' came the voice from the darkness. 'You will not be allowed to starve. You must come to the Fauxi-dizalonz in good health. When we come to the sea, we will feed you.'

'How long to the sea?' asked Ornery, somewhat fretfully.

'Long enough to get there,' came the fading voice.

Sometimes they felt that their escorts went away, for a kind of vacancy occurred, as though some essential component of the environment had gone missing, though where anything could go in this dim world, they could only guess. There were folds and cracks in the tunnel walls, and the tunnel constantly changed direction, and any of these irregularities might hide a way in or out just as they concealed the roosting places of many small creatures that plunged out into the air or down into the river, luminous forms that approached and receded, glowing parasols of light, soaring cones, winged diamonds, both above and below, as though air or water made little difference to them.

Three long sleeps into the journey, they became aware of a hushing sound, like the roar of their own blood in their ears. This very gradually grew into a soft roaring that grew more thunderous with every passing breath. If they had not guessed what caused it, Questioner would have told them. The sound was quite unmistakable, she said, for she had heard waterfalls on a hundred planets and water always sounded like water. By the time the little boat thrust up onto a sandy shore and tipped them out, unfolding into a flat blade of rubbery flesh that slipped away under the water, the roaring was loud enough to make conversation difficult.

'Now what?' shouted Ornery, who had been content to sleep the time away, curled in the end of the boat, dreaming of far shores and strange sights. Sailors, so she had told Mouche, learned to sleep whenever and wherever they could.

'You cannot dive the falls; for you the stairs,' cried the voice from the darkness. 'We have put a light.'

The familiar hugeness swelled out of the water, a shiny dark mound that turned its pale, spherical eye across them then receded toward the falls. Within moments, it was gone, the guides were gone, and they three were alone.

'Light?' suggested Questioner. 'Where?'

They found it hidden behind several broken shards of lava tube, the pieces nested like pieces of a giant cup, curved up against the wall, a glowing crystal set within the arch, illuminating the top of the stairs to the left. After taking a few moments for comfort's sake and redistributing their packs, they stepped past the light and onto the stairs. Flowing Green had not said *endless* stairs, though there was no end in sight.

Questioner lit their way as they variously clomped or danced or leapt downward. Here and there the sidewall opened to admit both the roar of the waters and curtains of flung spray, from each of which they emerged deafened and wet through. Finally came a roaring window near the bottom of the falls, where Questioner leaned through to light a great cauldron of boiling foam leading to a short stretch of glassy river, and then to a lip of stone over which the water poured unbroken into darkness.

They paralleled the level stretch of river, finding more stairs beside the lip of the fall. The next opening was a long way down, far enough down that the roar of the basin was reduced to a soft rushing, and again Questioner leaned out to light the water. The smooth pour shone with greenish reflections, utterly silent. Within the glassy flow moved pallid shadows that twisted and spun within the cataract, moving with the water into some unguessed at basin below.

Mouche made a noise that was almost a moan. 'I dreamed this,' he said in a helpless voice. 'I dreamed this!'

'Well, Mouche,' said Questioner in a chilly, admonitory voice, 'I am sure you believe so. It is all very mystic and dreamlike, and though I can be sensitive to the moods and impressions such places evoke, I try not to give way to them. When dream is most attractive, then is time to be alert and practical, for it is then we are most in danger.' She gave him a keen and penetrating look.

Mouche swallowed painfully. He didn't want to be practical. Every step in this journey took him either nearer to his dream life or farther from it, into new and treacherous territory, and he could not tell the difference.

'I'm sure you're right,' he said, gritting his teeth.

'Be assured, I am,' said Questioner. 'Let us expedite this climb. You, Mouche, come here upon my left side. I shall extrude two little steps there, see, one at the back, one at the side, one for each foot to stand upon while you lean forward upon my shoulder. And you, Ornery, do the same upon my right, if you will. In that way we may make better time, and certainly in a less fatiguing manner.'

Though doubtful, they did as she ordered, after which a brief clicking and clanking preceded a seemingly effortless, level and continuous descent of the interminable stairs.

'How are you doing this?' asked Ornery, who had always been fascinated by machinery.

'Two-part rotary tread, two outside sections, one wider, central section, operating alternately, first center legs then side legs. The knees are double jointed, of course, and the only trick is to shift my ballast properly.'

'How long can you do it?'

'Several planetary diameters, I should imagine. Do you think we'll be going that far?'

Ornery fell silent for a time, thinking it remarkable how quiet the mechanism was. There was only the slightest *chickety-click chickety-click* as the treads placed themselves, only the tiniest hum as Questioner descended, obviously unhampered by the weight of both of them and their packs.

'I can see how that works on stairs, but does it work on irregular slopes?' Ornery asked.

'It adapts itself. I am very well designed.'

They went down the stairs for what seemed half a day with the water, intermittently lit by Questioner's headlamp, still soundlessly falling at left or right, depending upon the spiral of the stair. Mouche leaned upon her shoulder and slept while Ornery, more or less alert, whispered occasional comments and questions into Questioner's ear.

'Someone said you were made with mankind brains inside. Is that true?'

'True. Yes. Three of them.'

'Do you know whose they were?'

Questioner surprised herself by answering honestly, 'Yes. I was recently given that information.'

'Old people, I suppose.'

'No. Three young women. Very young, one of them, only a girl, M'Tafa, her name was. Of an untouchable caste, on a planet you've never heard of and I wish I hadn't.'

'Why?' begged Ornery, sensing no discomfort and willing to be distracted with a story.

'The untouchables are simply that. They may not let their shadows fall on other people. They may not touch anything the higher castes touch or use. If they do, the thing must be boiled before it can be used again. If the thing cannot be boiled, they kill the untouchable instead.

'The untouchables speak a language of their own in order that the words spoken by the higher castes cannot be sullied on their lips. This child, M'Tafa, was a filth carrier. She sat outside an uppercaste nursery, and whenever the babies soiled a diaper, M'Tafa carried it to the laundry where it would be boiled. Sometimes, when no one was looking, she would touch things, very quickly, and then watch to see if anyone boiled them. They never did, unless they knew M'Tafa had touched them.

'One day a pet animal knocked over a lamp in the nursery, and the baby's crib was in the way of the fire. M'Tafa could not call anyone, for they did not speak her language. She could not put out the fire, for she had nothing to do it with. She was not supposed to touch the baby. Very quickly, so that no one saw, she moved the baby out of its crib, out of the way of the fire.

'Of course, someone figured out what had happened, for M'Tafa was the only one there. They could not boil the baby, so they killed M'Tafa. She was buried alive for her crime.'

'Oh, horrid,' cried Ornery. 'That's terrible. Does she remember? Is she still . . . like, alive inside you?'

'She is, yes.'

'Were the other two like that?'

'More or less. Tiu was a young bride, married to an old man who lived only a few days after the wedding. When he died, custom dictated that a faithful wife could offer to die on the pyre with him. Tiu did not wish to die so. She scarcely knew the old man. But, if Tiu did not die on the pyre, she could claim an inheritance, and since the grown children of the old man did not want to divide the inheritance, she was tied to the pyre and burned alive.'

Ornery gulped, beginning to be sorry she had asked. 'And the last one?'

'Mathilla. A similar story. A young bride of thirteen or fourteen in a world where women are hidden away. She was sequestered virtually alone in a harem by her old husband who was often away. The grown son of the old husband came to visit. He had a daughter her age, and he took pity on her and taught her to read and gave her books to pass the time. And when the old man found out, he charged her with adultery, though there had been nothing between the little wife and the grown son but pity and gratitude. She was stoned to death, for such is the penalty for adultery. Her own father threw the first stone.'

Ornery breathed deeply. 'Do they remember dying?'

Questioner sighed deeply. 'I sometimes think it is all they remember.'

Ornery said, 'Many of our baby girls die, but not like that. They die when they are born. That's why all women have to marry and have children, because they are so few. It's why I pretend to be a man, so I won't have to.'

She fell silent, thinking about Mathilla and Tiu and M'Tafa. She had never considered before that in other places, things could be far worse for women than they were on Newholme.

'Why did they pick brains with so much pain?' she asked.

Questioner hummed for a moment. 'The technicians are long dead, so I can't ask them. I know they wanted brains that were healthy, young, with few memories, so people dying of disease wouldn't do. I know they had to make some advance preparation, so people dying suddenly in accidents wouldn't do. They preferred planets which were less advanced, technologically, where fewer questions would be asked. They may even have been motivated by pity, thinking that, in a way, they were saving those three. And then, of course, they didn't expect that I would ever know enough to bring them into memory.'

Ornery thought about this, lazily, which led her to another thought. 'We met those two Earthers you brought with you. Why did you bring those particular ones?'

'They are dancers. I felt we might need dancers.'

'What for? You haven't needed them, have you?'

'We are not yet finished with our visit though, are we?'

They went on a bit farther, and Questioner said, 'Hark?'

Ornery listened for the sound of water, hearing instead the sound of voices. Someone or something was approaching from farther down the stairs.

Questioner unburdened herself, wakening Mouche, who shook himself sleepily, adjusting his pack and brushing wrinkles from his clothing. The voices came nearer. Questioner turned up her light.

They appeared quite suddenly around the turn of the stairs below, half a dozen Timmys, slim and graceful in their flowing membranes, plus a plump and furry bright violet creature a bit larger than they.

'Oh,' cried Mouche in a tone of great pleasure. 'There you are!'

The furry creature separated itself from its friends or colleagues and dashed up the stairs to fling itself on Mouche, huge hands holding to his shoulders, back legs braced against his body, both tail and body hair fluffed wide in the pure and glowing color Mouche well remembered.

The being put one hand on Mouche's lips and said clearly, 'Mouche, Mouche.' Then, looking around, 'Duster?'

Tears filled Mouche's eyes, part grief, part delight that his friend had remembered. 'Dead,' he said. 'Those two boys killed him.'

'Jongau,' said the creature in a tone of anger. 'Very bad jongau.' He climbed sadly down, head bowed, then approached Ornery. 'You are the sailor. Good! And you are Questioner?'

'Yes,' Questioner agreed with a regal nod. 'And you are?'

'He's my friend,' cried Mouche. 'From when I was a boy. But he never talked, not then!'

'True,' said the creature, returning Ornery's bow. 'I did not talk to you then, but I was a friend. Also I am the last of the Corojumi, the last choreographer.'

'Choreographer,' said Questioner, intrigued. 'A choreographer?'

'Once one of many, many, many. Now, only one.'

'What happened to the others?' Ornery asked.

'The jongau killed them. And took their skins. And took the skins afar, to some other place, where we could not retrieve them. And so my friends could not come to the Fauxi-dizalonz. They could not be reborn. And now, I am the only Corojum, one alone.'

'What's a choreographer?' Ornery whispered to Questioner.

'A designer of dances,' Questioner answered. 'One who creates the steps and gestures and meanings of dance, though sometimes they copy former choreographers ...'

'Which is what we want to do,' cried the Corojum in an agonized voice. 'That is what we must do! We must copy the former dance!'

'But you have nothing to copy,' offered Questioner.

'Exactly.'

Mouche opened his mouth, 'But ...'

'Hush,' said Questioner, raising her hands. 'I can feel the questions bubbling up on your lips, but I feel that poised halfway down an interminable stair is not the right time or place. We must have a settled time in which to pursue matters uninterruptedly before we agitate ourselves with hasty questions and half answers.'

The Corojum nodded. 'Oh, yes, that is wise. Far better to take time, better even to show than to say. Far better to illustrate than merely explain. Always in the dance, this is so. Come then.' He turned toward the stairs and started down. 'It is only a little way now.'

They followed him. His colleagues, the Timmys, had already disappeared, and they did not reappear, even when Questioner's group emerged at last onto an open and level space. The Corojum ran ahead into darkness, beckoning them. 'Come. With less light you will see better.'

Questioner dimmed herself. After a moment, they did see better, and with the seeing came hearing, too, the soft shush of waves on a sloping beach. Before them was the subsurface sea, lighted with a hundred dancing colors and shades, wavelets of luminous peridot and emerald, sapphire and aquamarine, effulgent ripples running toward their feet across a flat beach of black sand to make a citron-colored froth at their toes. Along the beach to their left, a great curved tower went up into the luminous sky, disappearing at the height. Beyond it was another, larger than the largest buildings on Newholme, higher than the tallest, crystalline in structure, reaching upward like a great column.

'I saw these columns being built,' said Questioner. 'I saw a record of this world when these pillars were the cores of little volcanoes.'

'True,' offered the Corojum. 'First a plain here, then a thousand tiny firemountains, then their cores left behind, then the sea covering the plain with silt, then the plain rising again, then the roof pouring out from other fire-mountains. So Kaorugi told us, Kaorugi, the builder. It was Kaorugi who sent tunnelers to drill the holes to let the rain through to lick away the soft stone, Kaorugi who sent the closers to seal the holes up again before the land sank beneath the surface seas. It was Kaorugi who built the stairs and made the places for water to run deep into the world and out again, Kaorugi who created the first boat to sail this sea, but then, you know about the boats or you would not have brought sailors with you.'

'Bofusdiaga and the Corojumi sailed the ship,' said Questioner. 'According to my informants.'

'We Corojumi guided the ship, yes. And Bofusdiaga told us how to make the journey. But Bofusdiaga was already too large for ships, Bofusdiaga is now too large to move, and besides, it is usually busy elsewhere, and there is only one Corojum, so we must sail as best we can.'

The Corojum ran from them to the edge of the sea, put his huge hands to his mouth and called into the distance.

Watching this, Mouche asked Questioner, 'Where did the waterfall stop?'

'Back there, somewhere,' said Questioner. 'I imagine in some kind of enclosed cave from which it siphons up or flows out into this sea. If there was, indeed, a designer of this place, it no doubt preferred to keep the noise and dense mists away from this shore. For visibility's sake, if nothing else.'

'Are we under the ocean?' asked Ornery, apprehensively. 'I mean, the Jellied Sea?'

'I think not,' Questioner answered. 'My judgment is that the first tunnel brought us under the badlands west of Sendoph, that the first small stream brought us farther west. The river then changed our direction, taking us north or northwest – which would be more or less toward the Jellied Sea – until we came to the fall, from which the stair twisted upon itself going mostly down. Now we are north and west of the place we began, looking westward across this sea, and above us are the badlands. This ocean is self-contained, with its own atmosphere, like a submarine vehicle.'

'But the water's been running down into here,' objected Ornery. 'Wouldn't it fill it up?'

Questioner shrugged massively. 'Kaorugi has no doubt taken that into account. Possibly it runs past furnaces of the deep which turn it into high-pressure steam and thrust it up somewhere else,' said Questioner. 'We need not worry how it happens since it is evident it does. Otherwise, we would all have drowned by now.'

Far out on the luminous waves, a shadow appeared.

'A ship,' cried Ornery. 'A sailing ship.'

Though of unfamiliar appearance, it was a sailing ship, with a curly prow and two short masts that held reefed sails. It was being towed by their old acquaintance, Joggiwagga, whose moon-eye preceded the craft. On the deck, along the rail, stood a dozen Timmys.

Mouche stared, searching. They did not include Flowing Green, and he felt a surge of relief. For his Hagion to be here with him would have been too much.

'Why can't Joggiwagga just tow us where we need to go?' asked Ornery.

'Forbidden,' cried the Corojum. 'His place is not there. His place is here and outside.'

'But our place is there?' cried Mouche.

'There, or nowhere, my friend. Together we will live or we will all die, as is the way of worlds. Together all creatures must live, changing together, else the world dies. All creation dances together, is this not so?'

'Usually,' replied Questioner. 'Is there a way I can get on that ship, or must I fire up the gravities?'

'There is a way.'

The ship stopped at the edge of deeper water, unrolling a silvery tongue that extended across the shallows and up onto the beach, stiffening into a ramp. 'Welcome,' said the ship. 'Please watch your footing.'

The tongue was as rigid as a gangway, and when they had come aboard, it rolled up behind them. The Corojum showed them where to put their packs, and the Timmys invited them to a table set with food and drink.

Mouche watched them as in a reverie, and Questioner watched him watching the Timmys. She thought the boy was in the grip of dreamtime. It wasn't sexual. She was sure of that. It was something else entirely, the lure of the marvelous and mysterious, the siren call of the unknown. Or perhaps the Timmy who had tended him as a child had had green hair.

After they had eaten and drunk and the Timmys had cleared away all evidence of the meal, the Corojum summoned Timmys, Ornery, and Mouche to work together in setting the sails.

'If it's alive,' whispered Ornery, 'why doesn't it set its own sails?'

'It's not alive like that,' whispered one of the Timmys. 'It's just alive enough to utter a few courtesies and keep itself mended.'

Slowly, after several tries, the sails were swung into the desired position, and the ship turned slowly with the wind, which endlessly blew, so the Corojum said, down the stairs behind them.

'It is so, for so Kaorugi designed it.'

'How far do we have to go?' asked Ornery, tightening a very organic-looking rope around a cleat that had obviously grown into place where it was.

'Until we get there,' murmured Questioner. 'Is that not so?'

'That is so,' replied the Corojum. 'That is always so.'

48

Westward the Wilderneers

By Bane's count, four or five days had passed since the death of Marool and their arrival in the camp. That morning Ashes told him and his brother to pack up and ready themselves for a journey.

'Where to?' Bane demanded.

'I told you about that time the Timmys took us? That pond kind of place they took us to?'

'Underground, you said.'

'No, not under. Just down in a deep valley, well, an old volcano. Anyhow, ever since then, some of us have kept watch on that place. Now, the mountains are getting ready to blow, and when that happens, we need all of us to be ready to take over, so it's time to fetch all our friends.'

'Prob'ly dead by now,' said Dyre. 'That was a long time ago.'

'They're not dead,' asserted Ashes. 'I told you we don't die! And you'd best shut that backtalk, boy. Best remember what I can do if I need to keep you in line.' He patted his waist, where the whip hung, its tip twitching hungrily toward them, the tip opening like a little mouth, a living thing.

Bane turned his eyes from the whip. 'What d'you need us for?'

'Company. I like the company of my sons,' said Ashes, laughing at them. 'Besides, you're safer with me than staying here. The Shoveler might decide to feed you to Belly. Or Crawly might get hungry and forget you're part of the family. Or Mooly might decide to find out how well you can fight, and you don't want to fight Mooly.'

'I'm not ascared of him!' asserted Dyre.

'More fool you, then,' said his father. 'You haven't been in the pond like we have. You may not have our ability to heal. Mooly's got a skin like steel plates and he's fast. Faster than anybody here. Including me.'

'So, it's just us going?'

Ashes's face went blank, as though the question had derailed him. His features sagged, like wax, half melted. Bane looked at Dyre, gritting his teeth, readying himself to do something ... anything. Dyre's mouth was open, and he shivered as though frightened. Then, gradually, sense seeped back into Ashes's eyes, his facial bones acquired rigidity, and he spoke as though nothing had happened. 'It's just us, starting out. Who else decides to go is their business. Us sons of thunder are into independent action.'

887

When they left, several other of the Wilderneers said they'd be coming along, soon, and midway through the morning, Bane spotted Webwings, high in the air above them, flying far faster than they were riding. He cleared his throat tentatively.

'Well, what you got in your craw?' his father asked.

'Webwings, he's up there. Those … those spiders on him, Webwings. Where did he get them?'

'They aren't spiders, they're part of him,' said Ashes, patting his hip. 'Just the way this whip is part of me, and Crawly's hooks are part of him. We came out of the pond that way.'

'How come … how come some of you are so big?'

'Weren't big, not then. Some of us got bigger. Crawly wasn't any bigger than you to start with. Foot wasn't all that big, just one foot larger than the other. Belly wasn't, he just had a pot on him. Ear wasn't all that big, he could still get around, only he kind of held his head to one side. It's just those parts went on growing and growing while the rest of them shrunk down.'

'Why is that?'

Ashes pinched his lips together. 'Well, Belly always did think more about his next meal than anything else. And Tongue was a talker.'

'And Foot?'

'None of us can figure Foot. It wasn't he liked dancing or anything. Gobblemaw was sort of like Belly. Mosslegs, we can't figure. Webwings we can't figure.'

'When you all escaped from the pond place, what did the Timmys and those other things do?'

'Do? They didn't do anything. They tried! Tried to push us back in, gibbering and jabbering. Some of them used our language, too, "Go back through, go back through," but we'd had enough. We smashed a few and beat a few and got ourselves out of there. They didn't come after us, just perched all over the place, staring and chattering. Timmys. Joggiwaggas. Tunnelers. All kinds. Well, we gathered our people up, even the strange-looking ones, and we took them all up out of there, oh, that was some climb. We didn't want to go by the road, take too long, so we went straight up, pulling and heaving, carrying the ones that couldn't move on their own. Some of us decided to stay there, to keep watch, but the rest of us went back …'

The last few words trailed off dreamily, as though Ashes were drifting into somewhere else. Bane and Dyre exchanged looks again, wondering, not speaking until Ashes began to talk again, as though he hadn't stopped.

'… went back eastward, to the towns, and by the time we got ourselves sorted out, that trader ship had already landed. Some of us, the ones who could move easiest, we tried to stop them, but they had weapons on their ship, and some of us got killed before they took off in both ships.'

Dyre was still digging at the problem that bothered him and Bane the most. 'The Timmys didn't even try to stop you leaving?'

'No,' Ashes snorted. 'They pushed us in one side, and we swam out the other.'

'Was it deep? Did they try to drown you?'

'Wasn't deep and they didn't try to drown us.'

'So what did they take you there for?'

Long, dreamy silence, unbroken until Dyre asked the question again.

Ashes snorted. 'Boy, if I knew that, I'd know a lot more than anybody else!'

Since Ashes immediately drifted into a reverie again, and since he seemed to have trouble dealing with the questions, Dyre gave up asking for a time.

They had gone a good bit farther on when Bane, who happened to be looking up to judge the position of the sun in the sky, saw Webwings approaching. 'See there,' he cried, pointing.

They pulled up the horses and waited. Webwings was searching the ground beneath him, possibly looking for them. Ashes took off his hat and waved it. The flying figure folded its wings and dropped, coming to rest on a large rock near the trail.

'I've got to go get the others,' said Webwings. 'Crawly and Strike and all the rest of us.'

'Crawly and Strike should be coming,' said Ashes, again in that dreamy voice. 'They said so.'

Webwings jittered, peering closely at Ashes's face. 'Some of 'em went north to intercept the road. Movin's easier there. We've all got to get there in time. Time's running out. Got to get there.' Webwings's voice had the same dreamy quality as Ashes's.

'We told our brothers we'd come get 'em,' Ashes asserted. 'Before we did anything about women or taking over. They'll all want to be there. Hughy Huge. Old Pete.'

Webwings stared at the sky. 'I saw Pete. In the mouth of that cave where we left him. He's still there. Grown to fit. Can't get out, I shouldn't think, at least not far.'

'Good old Pete. We'll get him out. Crawly'll get him out. How about Gorge George? An' Titanic Tom?'

'I caught sight of most of 'em.'

'How are they all? Good to see them again.'

'They're moving.' He snorted and flapped his wings, sending the spiders fleeing to his armpits as he said distractedly, 'Eager Eyes, you remember Eag, he can look down into the place, and he saw a whole bunch of Timmys and Joggiwagga and Tunnelers bringing some strange people there, just the way they did us. And one of the people is a blue person. You know what that's about?'

'That's got to be that Questioner's people,' muttered Bane. 'I heard all about them at Mantelby's.'

Ashes stared at the sky, smiling slightly.

'What's a Questioner?' demanded Webwings.

Bane slid off his horse to shake his shirt and trousers loose from his sweaty body. 'Seven or eight days ago, maybe more, this Questioner thing came down in a shuttle, and they brought it to Mantelby Mansion to stay. And the servants said that's why all the Timmys had to go, and why we ended up there, doing what Timmys had been doing, because this Questioner was there and she shouldn't catch on we even had Timmys. And she – they all called it she – had this one blue-skin with her, along with a bunch of other kinds.'

'Oh,' said Webwings dreamily, as though he had lost interest.

Ashes switched his attention from the sky to his fellow Wilderneer. 'What do you think it means, Web?'

Webwings shook his head. 'Don't ask me. I'm just telling you what Eager saw ... down at the pond.'

'What would they want with a blue person?' Ashes muttered.

'What did they want with us?' Webwings responded.

'Things keep changing around,' Ashes complained. 'I wish everything would settle for a few years, let us make some plans.'

The flyer shifted from foot to foot. 'You know, Ash, seeing that pond, I got to thinking, you remember Foot ... before?'

'Before when?'

'Before that pond. You ever know about his shoe collection?'

'Shoe collection?'

'We could never figure him getting that way, you know. Or me, but him especially. But lately, I've been remembering. Back on Thor, after he'd done it to some bitch, you know, he'd take her shoes ...'

'A fetishist?' asked Bane. 'We learned about fetishists at House Genevois.'

'So what's one of those?' his father asked.

'Somebody that gets off on a certain thing, like shoes, or gloves, or women's underwear, or even parts of flesh ...'

Ashes turned on Webwings, giggling like a schoolboy. 'So what'd you collect? Dead birds? Girly feathers?'

'Forget it,' said the other, sharply. 'I just thought it might explain things.'

'What did Pete collect?' Ashes went on. 'I mean ...'

'I said forget it,' Webwings said, launching himself upward. 'I'll tell 'em you're on the way.' He spiraled high and then flew back the way he had come, toward the camp.

'What was he talking about?' asked Bane.

'Oh, he probably was talking about some of us, from Thor,' Ashes said, once more in that dreamy, half-hypnotized tone. 'Half of us, almost. The way they came out of that pond. They didn't want to come back to the towns, looking like that. They wanted to stay there. Well. So they stayed.'

'You said they came to the edge of the camp, sometimes?'

'Not the ones that stayed by the pond, no. The ones that come to the camp are more like Crawly than anything. People like Roger the Rock. And Black Cliff. And Hughy Huge. Back on Thor, they were muscle men, always on the body machines. Big guys, strong as bulls, and that pond made 'em more so than ever. And they've grown since. Oh, I tell you, they're just mountains of muscle. They don't talk much anymore, they just roll over everything, like it wasn't even there. That's why we built camp where we did, down in that hot pot, so they can't get down into it and roll over us all.'

'Why?' asked Bane. 'Why would they roll over you?'

'Oh, they still get mad, sometimes. When we take the towns, we'll use 'em all. Talk 'em up. Use real short words ...'

They sat silent for a long moment. Bane asked, 'So. We goin' on, or what?'

Ashes merely sat, staring at the sky, indecisively musing aloud, as though he had forgotten they were there.

'Web could be right. I did know about Foot's shoes, back on Thor. I just hadn't thought of it for a few hundred years. And Tongue, well, he had some dirty habits, too. And it makes me remember when we were in that pond ... the thing was ... Well, you ever see one of those joke mirrors, the ones that're all curvy, make you look like you had wobbly legs? In that pond, it was like looking into one of those mirrors. Being outside, looking in. Looking at what I was, moving a little, making this bigger, that smaller, you know how you do. And when I came out, I was what I am now because that's what I always thought I was. Even the whip, I'd always had one, not a real one, but in my mind. They used to say that about me, old Ash, he can take the skin off. Old Ash, he can turn you raw. Well, I could.' He giggled, very lightly, a strange, quavery sound. 'I did. All of us did what was natural to us. You can't do that, what can you do, huh?'

Dyre started to answer, but Bane caught him, keeping him quiet, letting Ashes talk. He'd already said more than they'd heard him say before, and over the last few days, Bane had decided he needed to know everything there was to know about all this.

Ashes kicked his horse into motion, saying, 'But those bastards on Thor, when this one or that one got skinned or tromped on or rolled over, they weren't man enough to take it or fight it, either one. Had to run to daddy this or uncle that and complain about us. We weren't *orderly* enough. We used up the *wo*men, we didn't accept the *dis*cipline. Discipline, hah!' He giggled again, that high, quavering giggle. 'They had one thing right, though, we did go through the women. It was getting hard to keep 'em in supply.'

He turned toward his sons, his face alight with malice. 'Trouble was, the good ones were stupid and the bad ones were rotten. Like Marool. If they're bad enough to be interesting, they're not good enough to use. Not fit to live, right?'

This time Dyre spoke before Bane could stop him. 'What did Pete grow into?'

'Pete? Old Petey. He came out of that pond considerably enlarged, and last time I saw him, sitting in the mouth of that cave, he had a piggy as long as old Crawly. He just sat there, looking at it, keeping it from getting sunburned. If it's grown into the mountain, it must be sizable by now.' Abruptly, he kneed his horse onto the trail, riding in the direction Webwings had come. 'Be good to see old Pete again!'

Behind him, Bane looked at his brother in terrible surmise, fighting down the urge to feel himself to make sure he was still the same size he had been that morning.

'I know one thing,' mumbled Dyre. 'I know I don't want to go near that pond.'

With some difficulty, Bane summoned up his usual jeering manner. 'Don't want a big piggy, huh?'

Dyre moved onto the path, following his father, head hanging. Bane rode up beside him, reaching out to touch him, only to have his hand shaken off.

'Look, we need to decide something,' Bane whispered, reaching across to rein Dyre's horse, letting some distance grow between them and Ashes's receding figure. 'I don't like all this much. He's talking funny. He's riding west for no reason at all, so far as I can see. And another thing, Webwings ...'

'He flew back to camp.'

'Well, he said he was going to, but not long ago, I looked up, and there he was, headed west again. And he said the others were headed this way, too. Like all of them headed off like this, no reason, just going. Like ... well, like some of those Old Earth creatures we learned about, going off on migrations, no reason, just going because their insides told them to, maybe right over the cliff into the ocean! I'm getting the idea all this sons of thunder business may not be what we're really after, you know?'

'How you gonna get away from him?' asked Dyre, nodding at the figure ahead of them. 'Him and his whip.'

Bane shrugged. 'He keeps drifting off. Maybe we can get him to get shut of us. Just let us go. That Questioner thing came down in a shuttle, and the shuttle's still there, outside Sendoph. If this world is going to fall apart, like everybody says, I'd just as soon get a ride to someplace else.'

'You can't fly a shuttle.' Dyre laughed derisively. 'You can't even fly a kite.'

'The shuttle's got a crew, crotchbrain. Maybe we could get a few of the ... the people at the camp to help us. If any of them stayed there. Maybe Mooly. Some of the halfway normal-looking ones. We take the shuttle, and we fly it to the ship, then we take the ship.'

'Yeah, but the way he talks, the way we smell, I mean, what's the point? If we can't get any women?'

'We had women,' Bane declared. 'Stupid! At House Genevois, we had women. Not as many as pretty boy Mouche, but some. And they didn't die, either. So Madame knows how to handle the smell bit. All we have to do is grab her and take her somewhere and make her tell us. We can do that before we leave.'

They heard a call, looked up to see that Ashes had stopped and was glaring back at them, beckoning.

'Later,' said Bane, spurring his horse. 'You keep your mouth shut. But later ... we'll talk about it some more.'

49

Sailing the Pillared Sea

On the ship, the Timmys retreated to an open-sided cabin at the rear of the deck while the Corojum explained the skills of the underground sailor. There were neither compass nor stars. Everything was either black or luminescent, and the only landmarks were the great pillars that loomed, dark and featureless, from the wavering yellow-green sea into the vaulted blue-green sky.

'Except,' said the Corojum, pointing with a huge bony finger, 'for the luminous lichen that grows on each face in signs that Kaorugi has set there.'

'It's like blazing a trail,' Ornery whispered to Mouche. 'I read about that, something people used to do in forests, before they had locators. You'd chop a chip out of the tree, leaving a white blaze that you could see on your way back.'

'Except these trees have about a hundred different blazes,' muttered Mouche. This kind of sailing had never entered into his fantasy, among a forest of pillars on luminous water with a steady breeze blowing from behind them. Still, he knew the ropes and the knots, he could feel the sense of the simple rigging.

'Now,' said the Corojum in a pedagogical manner, 'you must understand that this journey we are about to make is the journey of Quaggima.'

'Quaggima!' exclaimed the Questioner, turning from her position at the railing. 'Quaggima?'

The Corojum quashed her with an imperative gesture. 'Please, you must not interrupt, or we will not be in time. This is the story of Quaggima.' His voice soared in a brief phrase, trilling at the end. 'That is, "Quaggida, stronger one sings." Correct? You learned song as young beings.'

'Yes,' murmured Mouche. 'Ornery and I, I guess we did. Not just those words, but yes.'

'It is the Timmys' duty to teach the songs and dances of being to all creatures. For that reason they came to your first ones and all of your people since, no matter how you treated them or killed them or prevented their dancing. Now, at the beginning of the voyage, we sing first line to remind us of the sign, then we look for that sign. Quaggida is winged mouth, or mouth that sings.' He leaned on the railing of the ship and pointed to one of the row of pillars they were approaching. After a moment's concentration, they could see that it bore a winged and fanged circle.

'See long teeth in circle, for Quaggida has teeth of fire. See bright bar to left? That means we must come so close as this, to see the sign, then turn to just pass it on the left! Quickly, be ready to change sails.'

Obligingly, Mouche and Ornery were ready, and at Corojum's word, they set the sails to take them just past the left side of the pillar. Mouche, thinking it out, decided that changing sails at a certain distance from the pillar was important, as it set the direction for the next tack, though it was imprecise at best. The Timmys looked up but made no effort to help them. Evidently this voyage was to be tutorial in nature.

'As you learn the way, do not forget the pass sign,' murmured the Corojum. 'You must come this close to pillar, read sign, then pass the pillar on the correct side.'

'So the pass sign is on the left, and we pass it on the left,' muttered Ornery, concentrating on the approaching pillar.

They passed it sedately, not with any great speed. The wind was enough to move them, but not enough to speed them through the glowing water.

'Next line,' demanded the Corojum.

'Somewhere among the dimmer galaxies,' said the Questioner, promptly.

'Sign is spiral of galaxy,' said the Corojum, a frown in his voice. 'But song must be sung, not spoken.'

'Sorry,' said Questioner. 'Just as an item of interest, how do you know galaxies are spiral?'

'Not all are,' answered the Corojum, 'but Kaorugi learned that many are. Please, interruptions are very bad idea.'

'Sorry,' she said again, lifting her eyebrows and grinning covertly at herself.

Mouche and Ornery finally saw a cluster of dim dots which, when they came closer yet, became the image of a central disc and several spiraling arms. The pass bar was again to the left.

'Change sail now,' demanded the Corojum, then, as they were passing the pillar on the left, it said imperatively, 'Next line.'

This time, as though to forestall the Questioner, the Timmys burst into impassioned song.

'… Doree a Quaggima t'im umdoror/Au, Corojumi, tim d'dom z'na t'tapor – ' The song cut off, as though with a knife.

'Which is to say,' asserted the Corojum, '… "Luring the weaker-one that strong-one will seize!/Oh, Corojumi, weaker-one comes without awareness …" Sign is same as Quaggida, but without teeth. Winged circle, for mouth that sings, and beneath, egg shape to show this is weaker or smaller one.'

They seemed to go a very long way before the next pillar came into sight before them, a little to their right.

'Pass bar to the right,' cried Mouche.

'So, go to right,' murmured the Corojum.

Nothing more was said until they had passed the pillar on the right, at which point the Timmys burst into song once more.

'Bofusdiaga! Embai t'im umd'dol/zan'ahsal diza didom ...'

Again the Corojum translated. '... Bofusdiaga! From deep dark strong one flings/fiery loops that make a snare ...'

'Next sign is a loop,' said the Corojum. 'Like a noose.'

They passed pillars that bore other signs, wave forms, squares, triangles, four yellow circles with green dots in the center. 'The Eiger,' said the Corojum, pointing this one out to them. 'Four eyes, the Eiger, but that is someone else's voyage.'

Finally, the loop came into view, a sign like a hangman's noose. As they passed it, the Timmys sang sadly:

'... ersh tim' elol lai ...'

'For weaker one's bright wings,' said Corojum.

'So the last sign for that verse will be wings again, right?' asked Mouche. 'With an egg, to show it's what you call the weaker one.'

'Correct,' said the Corojum, hugging Mouche's leg. 'You learn quickly.'

'Why am I hungry?' asked Mouche.

'Because it is half a day since we had food,' answered the Corojum. 'Next pillar we will stop. Six verses to the song, each at least half a day's sail, even in the old days, when there were many to set the sails and sing the song, time was the same.'

'How far ...' Mouche started to ask.

'Hush,' said Ornery, grinning. 'It's as far as it takes.'

'I merely wondered,' Mouche said between his teeth, 'whether we might not be traveling around and around in here, like in a maze, before we get out. How do we know this is the most direct route?'

'Oh, it is not,' cried the Corojum. 'No, no. Why would anyone come to sea of Kaorugi to take direct route? Dance voyages are for thinking, for planning, for learning. During voyage, we recalled the reason for dance. Also on this voyage, when there were many Corojumi, we talked of dance, remembering it in all its details. We decided who would dance which part, and who would make singing and music and when it would start. We spoke of moons and their power, and when that power approached at last, we were ready to go down into chasm, where dance must be done.'

They went wordlessly on, until the next pillar was reached, at which point they lowered the sails, and lay rocking slowly to and fro while the Timmys brought them large, shiny leaves spread with an assortment of fruits and breads, traditional, so said the Corojum, to this voyage alone.'

The Questioner left the railing, found what looked to be a hatch cover, and sat down upon it.

'Come,' she said to the Corojum. 'I have withheld my own questions, we all have. But now, while we have our lunch, surely questions can be asked and answered. The dance must be done, you say, but you are the only one left, and you do not remember the dance.'

'Only a tiny piece,' said Corojum sadly. 'I remember the Timmys assembling. I remember a tiny, early part of the dance, and then standing upon the rim of the abyss singing. Some Timmys remember some, some Joggiwagga, some others. And Bofusdiaga remembers only the song, for Bofusdiaga left it all to us!'

'Then let us start with what we have,' said Questioner, beckoning Mouche and Ornery to sit beside her. 'Now. Tell us about the dance.'

The Corojum said, 'The dance. So, long ago the Quaggima was caught, you know, the song says.'

'I saw her,' said Questioner. 'Lying on an outer planet. I thought she was dead.'

'Not dead.' The Corojumi shook his head sadly. 'Not dead, but very ... wounded. Maimed? These Quaggida, when they mate, they lure weaker-one with their song, they capture them, but while mating, they almost kill weaker-ones. That one is left on the far-off mating place, all alone, while the egg grows inside.

'Then, when the egg has grown too big for Quaggima to keep it warm, Quaggima searches for womb fires. A warm place, you know? It is instinct. No one taught Quaggima, Quaggima merely knows. So, here in this world, closer to sun, were womb fires. Timmys, sing verse of falling!'

Their voices came from the aft deck:

'*Quaggima it calls:*
Out of starfield coming, fire womb seeking
Fire it finds, rock wallowing, fume reeking
Oh, Corojumi, opener of space
Bofusdiaga, burrower of walls
It has need of birthing place
Wheeoo, it falls.'

The Corojum nodded. 'Quaggima did not really call us by our names. Kaorugi heard Quaggima calling: "Oh, opener of space. Oh, burrower of walls." In our language, openers of space are Corojumi – for this is a dancing matter – and burrower of walls is Bofusdiaga, so we used those names in our song. It was Kaorugi who heard the calling, and Kaorugi said to us, you Corojumi, you are openers of space. And you, great Bofusdiaga, you are a burrower of walls, so you will be openers and burrowers for Quaggima as well. So, we opened space, and Quaggima fell.'

'Here?' asked Questioner, wanting to be quite sure. 'To this planet?'

'Here. Inward, toward sun, intercepting us.'

'How did Kaorugi know what Quaggima said?'

'Kaorugi perceives meaning, over much, long time. Yes. Timmys, sing next verse!'

> 'Quaggima it cries:
> I plant one living egg where womb fires are.
> See how starflesh suffers! see wings char!
> Bofusdiaga, singer of the sun,
> Oh, Corojumi, dancers of bright skies
> It has done and I have done
> I cannot rise.'

Corojum nodded. 'We did not know how big was Quaggima. We made too small a place. When Quaggima fell, it made far deeper chasm. All Quaggima's wings were torn and burned. Egg was laid there, beneath Quaggima's body, where stone is hot and steams rise, and egg sank down, into stone. What Quaggima said was true, it could not rise. It did not have wings to fly, like a bird-thing, only wings to soar, like a kite. And Kaorugi perceived it and felt pity and great interest and told us to care for Quaggima. Timmys, next to last verse!'

> 'Quaggima despairs
> Driven against desire to fall and spawn
> Now loving death and longing to be gone
> Oh, Bofusdiaga, death defying!
> Oh, blessed Corojumi, who repair!
> The Quaggima is dying,
> Take it in care.'

'Kaorugi said, "We do not know who Quaggima means when it sings about mender and death defier, we do not know where such creatures are or if they are listening, but *we* are here and *we* are listening, so we will become mender and death defier! We will stop pain, we will repair, and my creatures shall be death defier and caretaker to Quaggima." And it has been so, for Kaorugi said it. Kaorugi said, "You, my offshoot, Bofusdiaga, you be breaker of shackles and limitations. You be singer of sun, maker of mirrors, who will not allow stone walls to keep out the light. And you, you Corojumi, you create the dance, you repair the broken, you focus bright skies upon Quaggima."

'Very commendable behavior,' commented the Questioner. 'Does Kaorugi always say "we"?'

'When Kaorugi means self and parts of self. We are all parts of Kaorugi and do Kaorugi's will. When Kaorugi says we, Kaorugi means all.'

'I understand. And what happened then?'

The Corojum whispered, 'So we made Quaggima sleep to forget pain, and we mended its wings. But we were like Quaggima, z'na t'tapor, as you say "unaware," for egg of Quaggi grew with each wax of each moon. It sucked in substance of our world, and its shell got bigger and bigger. And then, as moons came all in a line, pulling, and egg rocked inside world, from inside egg we heard creature calling, "Quaggima, Quaggima, crack egg and let me out!" And Quaggima began to hearken!

'But Kaorugi was there, everywhere, listening, and he cried, "A great miscalculation! When creature breaks the egg, it breaks world, and all here nearabout, all our life and being that is Dosha will die along with Quaggima!"'

'Timmys! Final verse, the one we sing at the chasm!'

'Quaggida destroys
its life and ours. It lies beside the nest
where its child and our doom are coalesced.
Oh, Corojumi, bring deliverance,
Oh, great Bofusdiaga, who alloys
all life, grant it within this dance …'

'Yes, yes,' said the Corojum. 'Do you see? Her child is our doom, for when Niasa breaks egg, Niasa breaks world. Everything shatters. All Dosha dies.'

'Aha!' exclaimed Questioner.

'So, what was to be done?' The Corojum scowled, posed, gestured broadly in a forbidding movement. 'We say Quaggima must not wake to break egg. We say it must sleep. This was not an evil thing to say. The creature in egg …'

'Niasa?' asked Mouche.

'Little Niasa, yes, for we gave it a little name. Little Summer Snake, we called it, for it was laid in summer and so does our own little summer snake writhe within shell. Kaorugi says Little Niasa can go on growing in egg for-ever and ever if need be. There is no limit to its size so long as it has fires to feed on. Then, when world grows cold, after we are gone, then it can hatch. This did not distress Quaggima – she is called Big Summer Snake – for we had soothed Quaggima's pain and given good dreams and much good food and drink with our mirrors ...'

'Mirrors?'

'And lenses, for it eats sunlight, and Bofusdiaga sings to sun, making mirrors we use to send sunlight down into chasm. So, then, Kaorugi said, we must dance Quaggima to sleep ...'

'We is who?' interrupted Questioner.

'We Corojumi and Timmys and Joggiwagga and Tunnelers and Eiger birds, and everyone that moves!'

'I get the picture.'

'And Corojumi said do this thing, and that thing, and the Timmys or Joggiwagga did it, and we all sang, and when Quaggima stirred, Corojumi said no, that doesn't work, and when Quaggima was relaxed and happy we said yes, that will do, and we put dance together, tiny bit at a time. And because Niasa was not yet grown very great, dance was enough.'

'And you remembered it?' asked Ornery.

'We Corojumi remembered it. It was our job to remember it. And when came next time of many moons, we remembered it, and all Dosha danced it, and we improved it for Quaggima's pleasure. And each time many moons happened, we improved it more, over and over again. And then came your people, those jongau.'

'The men from Thor,' said Questioner. 'I don't think they were our people. I don't think they fit our definition of human, even.'

'They came, whatever people they were. And they hunted us Corojumi, and they took skins away. And soon there were fewer, and then only a few, and then none but me, and those young jongau would have killed even me, but for Mouchidi! And all pieces of dance were gone but mine!'

'Each of you remembered only a small part?'

'True.'

'You said, they took the skins away, so they couldn't come to Fauxi-dizalonz. What have the skins to do with it?'

The Corojum threw up his hands. 'You have all your thoughts in one place, in here,' he knocked his head with one large fist. 'We people of this world, Timmys, Corojumi, Tunnelers, Joggiwagga, all of us, we keep our memories all over us, in net, under skin. And when we are old, and our parts are worn, we go into Fauxi-dizalonz, and everything is refocused and straightened and made new again. Without skins, what was there to mend? Bofusdiaga tried with jongau, but it was no good.'

'The jongau?'

'Your people who you say are not your people. Jong is like we say, throw away, trash. Them. Bofusdiaga thought, well, maybe they have eaten memories of Corojumi, why else would they want hides? So Bofusdiaga sent

Timmys and Joggiwagga and all to bring those persons to Fauxi-dizalonz, and our people went to their town at night, and we tied them and brought them, and pushed them in the Fauxi-dizalonz, and the jong swam through and came out other side, gau!'

'Gau?' asked Questioner.

'Unmended and bent and too dreadful to live, and we told them, go back, go back, be remade as you were – for Fauxi-dizalonz will repair, you know – but the jongau would not and they smelled, so bad we could not come near them. And some of the Timmys went into Fauxi-dizalonz, to see if they had left anything there about the dance, but the jong had left only ugly memories and pains and horrors that Bofusdiaga took much time and care to filter out. Our peoples do not keep such things.'

'Why can't you just reinvent the dance?' asked Mouche.

'First dance, perhaps, for it was simple and Quaggima was small. Even second, or third. But this is many times one hundred dance, more complicated than you can imagine, and with something ... essential (is that word?) about it we cannot remember!' He sighed. 'We will talk to Bofusdiaga. Bofusdiaga will consult Kaorugi ...'

'When we have completed the voyage,' said Questioner quietly.

'Yes. When we have completed voyage.'

50

The Abduction of Dancers

Ellin and Bao had arrived in the small salon just in time to see the protocol officer's blue legs being dragged away through an opening in the wall.
Without thinking, Bao had thrown himself forward, trying to catch hold
of the abductee, but before Bao could get near, he himself was grabbed by a
dozen hands, lowered not ungently to the floor, and there tied and gagged.
The last sight Bao had of Ellin was of her being similarly treated. The creatures committing the abduction were sylphlike, mankindlike in form, small
but energetic, strong, and very set on doing what they were doing as expeditiously as possible.

Thereafter a transportation occurred through such complete darkness
and in such complete silence that very little of it was perceptible to either Bao
or Ellin. After a time, still in darkness, they were assured in whispers that
no one was going to injure them in the slightest, their gags were removed,
their arms were untied (though their legs were kept secured) and they were
allowed to sit side by side, more or less comfortably, in a conveyance, type
indeterminate, that was jerkily and noisily taking them somewhere, presumably away from Mantelby's.

The moment Bao's arms were freed he reached out to Ellin, who clung
to him, partly in terror and partly in feverish excitement. 'Where are we
going?' she cried, almost hysterically, with a laugh on top of a sob. 'Bao? That
is you, isn't it?'

'Me, yes,' he said, then called into the darkness, 'Who's here?'

'Tim-tim are here,' said someone in the dark. 'You people say Timmys.'

Ellin and Bao peered in the direction of the voice, making out a pale
shadow against the black. The longer they looked, the brighter it became, an
effulgence, an aura of light.

The voice spoke again from the darkness. 'Bofusdiaga has sent a legger
for you. We are taking you quick as may be to the sea, where is a swimmer
waiting, then into a tunneler who will take you down to the Fauxi-dizalonz
where you may help us recover the dance.'

This brought so many questions to Ellin's mind that she couldn't settle on
which to ask first. Bao saved her the trouble.

'What dance?' he asked.

'If we knew what dance, we would not need to recover it,' the voice replied with some asperity. 'This is not the time to ask questions about the dance. When we arrive, you may ask all the questions you need. Now is time to ascertain whether you are comfortable. Are you in need of food or drink or excretory privacy?'

The almost hysterical laughter bubbled in Ellin's throat, and she swallowed it, half choking herself in the process. 'Thank you, but no. I'm not hungry or thirsty. Not yet, at any rate.'

'Where's the other people you were dragging off?' demanded Bao. 'Where are Questioner's people?'

'In another tunneler, going by a slightly quicker route. They are not hurt.'

Since the Timmys would not answer questions about the purpose of the trip, and since there was nothing at all to look at except a dimmish glow that the Timmys were either emitting or crouched within, Ellin sank back onto the rubbery surface with Bao's arms about her, and the two of them whispered together comfortingly, keeping, so Bao said, their spirits in good form.

'It is being important not to be getting in a state,' he avowed. 'We must be keeping our wits about us.'

'Will Questioner come looking for us?'

'I am not doubting she will. She will be making a terrible uproar over this abducting, believe me.'

'These … these people don't seem to care. Something in their voices … They sound extremely touchy, almost desperate, but not hostile. Not at all. Is it the volcanoes that have them so upset?'

'What has us upset,' said a voice from the darkness, 'is that mountains are falling. Great Gaman, most beautiful of caverns, is no more. What has us upset is *Niasa* will be hatched, I think, even if it means we die, all of us.'

The voice began to sing in a language neither Ellin nor Bao had ever heard before, full of *ororees* and *intimees* and *wagawagas*. The song was unmistakably a lament, long drifting phrases in a minor key, with many repetitions that seemed to go nowhere, reminding Ellin of some twentieth-century ballet music by a man named … what had it been, Grass? Gless? After a time the warmth, the music, and the jiggle-jog of the floor beneath them created a cocoon of nursery-like peace around them and they fell asleep.

When they wakened much later there was light. Dimly glowing stones had been set here and there to cast a pale greenish light on the surroundings. When they sat up, they found their legs had been untied and they could make out the glowing forms of their captors, much brighter than before, sitting at some distance from them having, so Ellin muttered resentfully to herself, a picnic.

'I'm thirsty,' said Ellin plaintively, running her tongue around her dry mouth.

Immediately, one of the Timmys rose and brought them cups full of liquid. 'Mir-juice,' said the Timmy. 'Not too sweet.'

Ellin tasted it doubtfully. It was tart, cool, with a satisfying flavor somewhere between fruit and spice. By the time she had finished it, the Timmy was back with small loaves of bread. 'We brought these for you,' it said. 'We took them from the pantry at Mantelby Mansion.'

Ellin put one of the little loaves to her nose, then bit into it. It was one of the sweet breakfast breads Ellin had most enjoyed since being at the mansion. 'Can't we eat your food?' she asked, somewhat tremulously.

The Timmy smiled a three-cornered smile, its eyes crinkling, its lips open to display bright yellow mouth tissues. 'Assuredly. But, we thought when people are snatched up and carried off, when they are tied up and put in the belly of a legger and then are in the belly of a swimmer, and it is dark and things are most unfamiliar, then it is probably comforting to have familiar food.'

Only then did Ellin and Bao realize they had indeed been moved into some new conveyance, though it felt and smelled exactly like the former one. The jogging motion had given way to a recurrent warping of their space, first to one side, then the other, like the swimming motion of a fish or snake.

Bao stood up and stretched, bracing himself against the sideways warping. 'So, we are having familiar food. What are you bringing specially for me?'

Another Timmy handed over a neatly wrapped sandwich. Ham and cheese. 'You are watching us,' said Bao. 'All the time we are being here, you are watching.'

'That is true,' agreed the Timmy. 'Mostly we watched the other ones, for they are most different. But then, we saw you dancing, and we said, oh, they are dancers, we must bring them, too, and we asked Bofusdiaga, and the word came, yes, bring them. So, we took some things to make you comfortable, and if you had not come in upon us when you did, we would have come for you very soon anyway.'

'That makes me feel so special,' said Ellin, only slightly sarcastically.

The Timmy was alert to the tone. 'We will not hurt you. We do not hurt people. Oh, the Fauxi-dizalonz showed those other ones they were gau, but that was their own fault. Being gau is always the creature's fault if it will not go through and through to get fixed.'

'What other ones?' asked Bao.

'Now they call themselves Wilderneers,' said the Timmy, with an exasperated little shake of its head. 'They were the first mankind ones who came. But they were all ... all one kind and all jong. Jong, that means ... like something we sweep and throw away. We did not know they were jong until they went in the Fauxi-dizalonz. Then Bofusdiaga cried out, and we all came running to see. Fauxi-dizalonz turned an evil color, and they came out like evil monsters, and we told them, "Go back through, take up all the disguises you have left there and fix yourselves," but they would not.'

'Disguises?' asked Ellin. 'You mean, masks?'

'Disguises,' said the Timmy, coming very close and looking her in the eye. 'In your language, which is not always sensible. We say, what you wear out here,' he tapped her arm, her shoulder, her cheek, 'is a guise (that is your word) for what is in there,' and he peered into her eyes, as though trying to see her brain. 'If it does not match your insides, it is a disguise (that is your word, meaning a bad-guise), and you go through the Fauxi-dizalonz and get the outside to express the inside. Then back through to change the inside, perhaps, and sometimes back and forth several times, working it out.'

'Do your outsides look like your insides?' she asked.

The Timmy hunkered down and considered this. 'Before mankind came, Timmys were shaped differently. When mankind came, Bofusdiaga thought we would be more ... what is mankind words ... acceptable, to look like you. So, some insides also shifted, to make it work.'

'Were your outsides looking like your insides before?' queried Bao.

'Always, pretty much. First came life without any insides, just moving, eating, excreting, moving some more, no thought about it, no worries, just live or get eaten, building bigger and bigger. Then, the big thing grows a little bit of insides, enough to say to itself, "Do not grow that way, the fire is too hot." So, once it says that, it must have outsides ready to grow where it says! You see?'

'When you say "insides," asked Ellin, 'you mean brain?'

'We mean the thinkables. The person inside who talks with the person outside. The unbodied observer of that which acts. I suppose yes, brain, but you people, you have four brains, maybe five, all mixed up. You know?'

'I am not knowing this,' said Bao. 'What five brains?'

'First very little brain for some little something swimming around that does not do much. This brain makes you jump if someone bites you. Then you have brain for some cold thing that moves better and thinks a tiny bit. This brain says run, hide, that thing is dangerous. Then you have brain for some warm thing that runs and leaps and thinks. This brain says, build nest here, not there, or eggs will drown. Then you have bigger brain that thinks much and is aware. This is ape brain. We know about ape brain because the Hags talk of it. This brain says: me powerful; oh, child, dead, I grieve; alas, I love, I want. Then comes mankind brain, brain that talks, brain that puts ape thoughts into words, brain that uses and misuses many words! Only the last brain is what you call human, which is what we call dosha, which means fullness, capable of self-judgment and correction.'

'All that!' exclaimed Ellin.

'Too much,' agreed the Timmy. 'Because your brains are not a good fit. They are like some too small boxes in another too big box. They rattle. Outside, you look like one person, inside you are five things, not all persons. So, if you go in Fauxi-dizalonz, you come out like your insides, with lizard tail and ape arms and your inside minds say, oh, look, this is who I am, and you think about that with brain five, then you go back in Fauxi-dizalonz and put the pieces back, but put them back in good order, so they work together and do not rattle.'

Ellin had listened to this with increasing horror. 'But, but,' she cried, 'I know who I am already. I know who my grandfather and my mother were, or I would know, if I looked them up, but ...'

'Pff,' said the Timmy. 'You mankinds with your fathers and mothers. This is one of first things we thought strange, you all the time talking my father this, my mother that. What does fathers and mothers have to do with who you are? Your planet is your mother; time is your father. Your insides know this! All life outside you is your kinfolk. Even we dosha are your kin, born of another planet but with same father as you. Starflame makes your materials, and live-planet assembles them, and time designs what you are, not your fathers and mothers. Pff. You could be genetic assemblage; Bofusdiaga could make you without fathers or mothers; and you would still be persons! But you could not have material without stars, or life without planet, or intelligence without time and be any way at all. It is your stars and your world and long time gives you legs to dance and brains to plan and voices to sing.'

'My mother gave me my ability to dance,' said Ellin angrily.

'Pff,' said the Timmy. 'And who gave her? Ah? Her mother passed it to her, and her mother passed it to her, and so back to the ooze. Planet and time gave dancing. Squirrels in trees dance. Horses dance in meadows. Birds dance in air. Snakes dance in the dust. Your mother did not invent it, she only inherited abilities to do it. So, she inherited well, but she did not do it herself.'

'You're saying my mother gave me nothing?' Ellin was outraged, almost shrieking.

'What your mother can give you, maybe, is recipe for chicken soup. Apple pie. Maybe she invented that.'

'What are you meaning, chicken soup ...' choked Bao.

The Timmy cocked his head far to the side, stretching his neck, a very unmankindlike gesture. 'We hear Hags talk of chicken soup. Any kind of soup. This one recipe from this mother and that one from other mother, but even so, soups taste much alike. Timmy have recipes also. Many good things. You ask Mouche. We made great good smells and flavors for Mouche.'

'Mouche the gardener?' cried Bao.

'Mouchidi, the one the Corojum has sent for.'

After that, Ellin was too angry and Bao was too confused or bemused to ask any more questions, and very soon the swimmer began to swim much faster, with a great rushing-splashing noise along its sides, far too much noise to talk at all. Bao and Ellin settled into a comfortable hollow, stuffed bits of Ellin's bread into their ears, and let the rocking movement slowly lull them back to sleep.

51

Madame Meets A Messenger

Madame and the two Hags had chosen to sit in the rear of the inflatable boat. Simon and Calvy and the three remaining Haggers sat two on each side and one in front. They were so busy listening to the silence that they did not speak at all, and they floated on the small river for what seemed to them some considerable time before the tunnel narrowed, the water began to rush, and they found themselves plunging through the same narrow throat of stone the prior expedition had traversed, into the same larger river and across it, where the boat ricocheted violently off the tunnel wall.

'I suppose we're sure everyone went this way,' murmured D'Jevier, as the Haggers and Calvy g'Valdet tried to paddle the boat back into the center of the stream.

'We saw their tracks on the sand. We saw the impressions made by at least two boats,' muttered Calvy, fighting his desire to curse at the Haggers, who persisted in paddling against one another's efforts so that the clumsy boat spun lazily around as the current caught it.

'Let me,' said Madame, moving to the place across the boat from Calvy and taking the oar from the Hagger there. 'Watch me,' she said to him. 'It is necessary to coordinate the strokes or we go nowhere.'

'Now where did you pick that up?' said Calvy in an interested tone.

'My friends and I do a bit of wilderness walking,' said Madame, concentrating on her paddling. 'And canoeing.'

Among Simon, Madame, and Calvy, they managed to turn the boat so that it faced downstream and keep it there with only occasional dips of the paddles. When Madame thought the Haggers had the idea, she gave up her paddle and returned to the company of the Hags.

'Have you met the Questioner?' Calvy asked over his shoulder.

'We have,' said Onsofruct. 'A very civil contraption.'

'Civil on the outside, but she wasn't fooled,' said D'Jevier. 'She knew something. Maybe everything. I thought we might sidetrack her onto the threat posed by the volcanoes, but she made it clear she knew what we were up to.'

'You mean the Timmys?' Calvy asked.

'Oh, definitely the Timmys,' D'Jevier acknowledged. 'She had these two young Earthers with her, very openfaced and so milky-lipped that one might think them moments from mama's breast, but they turned out to be quite perceptive. I should have expected that. She'd scarcely have brought them, otherwise.'

'How do you read all this, Madame?' Calvy asked over his shoulder. 'This current journey of ours?'

Madame said, 'How can we read it? The Timmys took the Questioner's people, her Earther aides went after them, then Questioner and two pressed men became third in line. Why the Timmys took the first ones ...' She shrugged invisibly. 'Who knows?'

'I've been doing some research,' Calvy persisted. 'Our records since we've been on Newholme show that episodes of vulcanism increase during lunar conjunctions. Multiple conjunctions are usually accompanied by some very big quakes. If the Timmys were here before we were (and I think we have to accept that they were), then they've evolved under conditions of periodic vulcanism and presumably would know how to deal with it ... unless this time is really different from any former time.'

'As to that,' said Onsofruct, 'we don't know about all possible former times. We've only been here a few hundred years.'

Calvy said, 'We don't know, but the planet does. There's a gravelly cliff west of Naibah that sheds a few feet of itself every time we have a quake. Each of the falls has time to weather and change color before it gets covered by the next layer. When you drill into the deposit, you get a nicely striped core, one you can read like tree rings. So, I had a few of my supernumes take some really deep core samples, as deep as we can get with the equipment we have.'

'And?' queried D'Jevier. 'What did you find?'

'We got back about five thousand years. If we had better equipment, we could go deeper and probably read up to hundreds of thousands, but during those five thousand years, at least, we find thick deposits every seven or eight hundred years, but the gravel that's falling now is already thicker than the thickest previous layer.'

'You didn't tell us that?' said D'Jevier. 'You didn't say a word about it.'

'My people finished up the report last night,' Calvy responded mildly. 'I've not had a chance to tell anyone. It does make me wonder whether we colonists have destroyed or weakened some vital link in this planet's ecology.'

'But we haven't!' Onsofruct objected.

Calvy gave her a grin over his shoulder, saying, 'Well, that's true to form. If we have, we could hardly admit it to ourselves if we had, could we? Or to anyone else?'

'But to allege such a thing ...' Her voice trailed away.

'It's only an inference, Ma'am.' He paused in his paddling, then said firmly, 'Still, it can't be discounted without some proof to the contrary. How do we know what the first settlers did? Why were they wiped out, as we presume they were? Was it because they had committed some grave offense?'

Onsofruct opened her mouth to retort, more out of habitual response to any male criticism than from real conviction of the innocence of the first settlers. Her words were stopped by a sound they all heard in the same instant: a grating sound, quite distant, but coming nearer and growing louder.

They fell silent. Calvy, Simon, and the Haggers dipped their paddles, pushing the boat along a little faster than the water, then faster yet, as though to escape.

'Shhh,' said Madame, leaning forward. 'If it already knows we're here, we can't outrun it. If it doesn't know, paddling may attract it.'

'It?' demanded Simon, glancing at her over his shoulder, the whites of his eyes gleaming.

'The sound-maker. Let us go softly.'

The sound came from downriver, getting louder with each moment until it reached a screaming crescendo and abruptly stopped. The reverberations died away. Silence returned. The river curved slightly; they floated around the bend and abruptly bumped into a weir set across the river.

'What in the name of seven devils?' murmured Calvy.

D'Jevier turned on a light and examined the weir. Not rock. Something else. Something smooth and rubbery that gave slightly when she pressed it with her fist. To their right a pebbly beach had been deposited along a shelving recess in the tunnel wall, and it showed the mark of two boats and footprints that led back toward crevices in the tunnel wall.

'They were here,' said Onsofruct. 'There's the treadmark of the Questioner, and the footprints of two people.'

They paddled the boat to shore, got out and pulled it up onto the pebbles where they stood, shining their lights on a patch of finer sand.

'Not only two people,' said Simon. 'Other things, too.'

'Timmys?' asked Onsofruct.

'That size, at least,' said Madame. She turned her light onto the small area around them. A rocky wall, a few fallen chunks of that wall, no openings that they could see – that they could ... see.

'That wasn't there before,' whispered one Hagger to another, pointing.

They all looked. An opening. Too small to worry about. They looked away, looked back. Perhaps not that small. Looked away, looked back.

'It's opening,' said D'Jevier in a shocked voice. 'The rock is opening!'

It was opening slowly, a vertical slit, perhaps as high as their boat was wide. It made a grating sound as it went on opening, wider and wider, displaying a gleaming orb inside which swiveled in their direction. An eye, with a vertical pupil. And another slit opening, a much wider horizontal one, below. A mouth.

From which, after some time – while they all froze in place, scarcely breathing – came a voice like rocks grinding together.

'I am sent by Bofusdiaga, burrower of walls, singer of the sun, death defier, savior of Quaggima. I am sent by him who alloys and thereby preserves. I have come to take you to the Fauxi-dizalonz.'

Onsofruct sagged. Calvy and Madame caught her as she crumpled to the ground.

The mouth opened again. 'Terror is inappropriate. Proper emotion is gratitude. I am tunneler. My way is much less tiring than the way of the Pillared Sea. Besides, many of your people are already there.'

D'Jevier cleared her throat several times, managing to get the words out on the third try. 'We're searching for ... ah, some others who have come this way ...'

'First group, eight strange people belonging to Questioner. They are already at Fauxi-dizalonz arguing with one another. Second group, two dancers, they are now in swimmer, arguing with Timmys about mothers and fathers. Soon they will be at Fauxi-dizalonz. Third group: Mouchidi, Ornery, and the Questioner, they are far ahead on the Pillared Sea, experiencing the Quaggima voyage, and arguing with the Corojum.'

'Mouche!' cried Madame. 'Mouche also?'

'So I have said. You are fifth group. If we go same way, would not catch them in time.'

'Who's the fourth group?' demanded Calvy.

'The jongau.' The messenger spat the words in a hail of gravel. 'Many jongau. Large and small, all horrid, they are going on the surface, and they are getting near to the sacred place.'

'The jongau,' said Madame. 'Being?'

'That Ashes. Those sons of Ashes. All those bent ones. They will be there, too, and I have come to take you where you can meet them.'

The voice made Madame think of walking on scree, a gravelly crunch, rattle, and slide. Was this irritation? Or mere impatience? 'We are grateful,' she said loudly.

The mouth turned up its corners, dislodging small boulders in the process. 'At least you are not arguing! Mankind is a very arguing species! Bring your belongings,' it said, then opened its mouth to display two complicated, bellows-like structures on either side and between them, access to a dry, sandy-floored space.

'I think it means we should go in,' said Calvy, a slight tremor in his voice. 'I presume it knows we are easily crushed.'

The mouth waited. 'After you,' said Simon politely, needing two tries to get it out.

Madame pressed her lips tightly together, took a deep breath, lifted her pack from the boat and walked into the creature's mouth. After a long moment, D'Jevier and Onsofruct did likewise.

Simon looked after them, doubtfully.

'This is why women rule this world,' Calvy observed. 'We men can't make up our minds.'

'I'm going, I'm going,' said Simon, taking up his pack. 'What about the Haggers?'

The Haggers were out in the river, having already waded some distance along the edge in the direction they had come.

Calvy called, 'Farewell. Don't forget to turn off into the little stream when you get there.'

They splashed more rapidly away, without replying. Calvy picked up his own pack and one of theirs; Simon took another; together they stepped into the mouth of Bofusdiaga's messenger.

52

Leggers, Tunnelers, and Assorted Traffic

Ashes rode westward like a man possessed by a dream, waking occasionally into a fit of anger, then falling into his reverie once more. His sons trailed behind him, lagging as much as they could without stirring him into a rage, whispering together so he would not hear them, for whenever he heard them he demanded to know what they were saying, what they were thinking, what insurgency they were planning.

'You'll do what I tell you,' he said, not once but a dozen times when he came to himself. 'You know what's good for you, you'll do what I tell you.'

'He's got to have somebody to boss around,' whispered Bane. 'If we'd been girls, like he planned, he'd have been just the same with them, made them do whatever he wanted. He'd have hitched them up to Mooly, prob'ly. Or one of those others.'

'I can't figure why Marool took us away from our mama,' said Dyre, who'd been puzzling over this for the better part of a day. 'He said she was jealous, but she didn't seem jealous over men. She had plenty of men. Why'd he want her dead? Specially, since she couldn't smell him. Seems like he'd have rather kidnapped her, brought her out here to keep around. She wasn't old. Maybe she'd have had a daughter for him.'

'Other thing,' mused Bane. 'He never said how our mama died, did he?'

'Never said what her name was, nothin'.'

'Somethin' else. There's this pond he talks about. So, you go in there, you can't die, right? So, how come when our mama was sick or hurt or whatever, he didn't take her there and fix her?'

Dyre looked crafty. 'Maybe he hated her. Maybe he just as soon she died.'

'That don't make sense! He wanted children, and he went to all that trouble, why would he let her die?'

'Maybe he couldn't tell her what to do, so he decided he didn't want to bother.'

'Maybe Marool was her,' said Bane, not thinking what he said, his unconscious prompting him to a truth he immediately recognized and wanted to unsay.

Dyre said nothing. He pretended not to have heard. He did not want to have heard because ... well, because. They'd killed her, was why. And they'd done ... lots of other things. And if she had been, well then, Ashes had lied

913

to them. But if she had been, then why hadn't she known? Why hadn't they known? Why had they grown up in that place near Nehbe, and at Dutter's farm? She hadn't kept them by her, and she should have. If it was so. Which it probably wasn't.

Bane did not repeat himself. What he had said did not bear repeating. Not that it was wrong. Ashes had told them sons of thunder couldn't do wrong so long as they did what they wanted to. Whatever they wanted to do was right. It's just that he should have been told. If what he had said was right, he should have been told. Ashes said people back there on Thor, they killed off a lot of people who didn't believe what they did: mothers, fathers, kids, made no difference. So, it wasn't wrong to have killed her. It was just ... Well, it was the way it happened. There could have been a better way than that.

Late in the afternoon, as the three rode abreast along a wider stretch of the trail, Ashes pointed off into the west at a certain high, ragged line of mountain.

'That's the edge of the chasm,' he said.

'How deep?' grunted Bane.

'Well, there's a shallow crater and a deep one. The deep one's maybe five, ten kilometers to the bottom,' said Ashes. 'Before the pond, we used to have a member of our brotherhood named Maq Bunnari, Bunny the Book, we used to call him because he was always reading. He read everything, he knew anything there was to know about anything. So, just before we left Thor, Bunny was in charge of looking around for a place for us to go. There wasn't a lot of choices in the nearby sectors, but one of them was this place, so Bunny got the geological report, and according to him, the chasm was an "anomalous feature." Seems like that the chasm was a two-mouthed volcano to start with, pretty much dead, so the two domes fell in and that made two pot-shaped valleys, right? So, just like it was aiming for the bull's eye, a meteor fell right into the southern valley, and it punched a pretty big hole. The report said there was a hell of a big, deep cone-shaped hole down inside that mountain.

'Well, Bunny, he read this and he said there shouldn't be a hole that deep because most of the stuff that blows out of a meteor hole falls right back in. Bunny said if there was this big hole, something besides a meteor did it, and before we settled here, maybe we ought to find out who or what it was. Well, we didn't have time for that, but Bunny wouldn't shut up about it. One night after we'd been here a while, Mooly and Bone, they got aggravated at him calling them stupid for not finding out what made the hole, and one night they beat him up so bad he died.'

Ashes barked laughter. 'Bunny was right, dead right, it turned out. When those Timmys and their friends took us to the pond, we saw all kinds of things carrying gravel out of that hole and smoothing down the sides. They'd cut them a twisty road back and forth, too, so they could get to the bottom.'

'Can we get to the bottom?'

'Oh, we could probl'y get down there all right, they probl'y wouldn't care, but it'd be a waste of time. It's so deep, standing up on that ridge, you can't see the bottom.'

'Webwings saw the bottom. He said those Questioner's people was there.'

'Webwings only flew to the pond, and that's in the other crater, the shallow one. See, when the meteor fell, it broke the wall between the two, so you got this crater shaped like an eight, and back and forth around the top half you've got this road that goes down to the pond, then you go through the gap to the other crater, and you wind back and forth down to the bottom of that.'

'You been there lately?' asked Bane.

Ashes shrugged, shaking his head. 'No reason to go. Web flies down to the pond sometimes, partway, anyhow. He says it's real busy down there, lots of critters coming and going. Up until now, I figure, with all that busy going on, no reason for me to get in the middle of it.'

'Where's ... where's your old friends? The ones that stayed there.'

'Oh, some of 'em in the raggedy edge, up there. See, that's all volcanic up there, full of gas bubble caves. Nice and smooth and round inside, good shelter. That's where old Pete put himself, into a long chain of bubble caves, about halfway down to the pond. Some of the others, they're between here and there. Hughy Huge, he's along the road we're coming to. And Roger the Rock, he's some way ahead.'

'How much longer to get there?'

'Not so far, now. Down at the bottom of this hill we come to the road. From here on, we can go right straight there.'

'Who built the road?' Bane asked. 'Timmys?'

'Damfino,' grunted Ashes. 'I suppose it's Timmys or some of the bigger things. Stands to reason they had to have someplace to put all that gravel they dug outta that hole, and roads use up a lot of gravel. When they captured us and carried us in that time, it wasn't on any road, but when we came away from there, we climbed up to the rim and there it was. Some of our folks, they'll be along it, too. You keep an eye out.'

Bane kept an eye out. His frustration and confusion had risen as the day had worn on. His own plan of escape, to capture the shuttle, now seemed to him the only sensible thing to do, if he could get away from Ashes. But then, he thought, of course he could get away from Ashes because Ashes had told him how. Ashes wouldn't die, not the way people did, but he could be killed. And if Ashes could put them up to killing their mother, then there couldn't be anything wrong with killing their father, could there? It'd be no trick at all.

Bane did not mention this to Dyre. He hadn't decided yet whether he needed to involve Dyre.

They came to the road just before dark, a level, straight, hard-packed and gravel-surfaced highway on which six horses could have ridden abreast. It cut through forests and hills, across valleys, leading onward and upward like the flight of an arrow to the ragged line of mountain Ashes had pointed out earlier. Ashes went only a little way along it before leaving it, dismounting, and leading his horse away. Following his example, Dyre stopped by the road, unsaddling his horse and dropping his pack.

'We'll sleep off here,' called Ashes, from a grove some distance away. 'Away from the road.'

'Looks like a good place here,' offered Dyre.

'Not far enough from the road,' barked his father. 'Down where I said.'

Grumbling, Dyre picked up the saddle and the pack and took them farther down the hill. They made camp, warmed their food, ate it in silence, and rolled into their blankets. Three moons came up, almost in a line, with two more close behind. The world was bathed in half-light. Bane and Dyre fell exhaustedly asleep.

Away along the road something roared. The ground trembled. Bane sat up. Ashes was snoring. Bane poked Dyre, who sat up as well, clutching the blanket around his shoulders. The earth trembled again, and again, and constantly as the roaring grew louder. In the moonlight they saw something galloping toward them, huge and many-legged, rumbling like a string of freight carts on a cobbled street, continuing this horrid thumping as it rushed past and off into the west, toward the chasm.

'What was that?' cried Dyre, trembling.

'Legger,' mumbled Ashes from under his blankets. 'Sort of like the kind that carried us off, that time before. They go by here all the time. Go to sleep.'

They lay back down. After a time they slept, to be roused again and again by the sound of leggers going past, in both directions, to and from the chasm, and once by the sound of something more ponderous than leggers, rolling. That time Ashes awoke and, telling them not to move from where they were, went up to the road. They heard him shouting, then the heavy rolling stopped.

'Ashes,' said a thick, gurgling voice, like rocks rolling around in thick syrup.

'Where you going, Hughy Huge?' Ashes asked.

'Roll 'em over,' gargled the voice. 'Roll 'em over.'

'Who told you?'

'Wings.' The thing breathed, like a wind, heaving. 'Wings said it was time to roll 'em over. Wings, he's comin' along. The rest of 'em, they're comin' along. S'long Ash.'

The rolling started again, at first slowly, then faster.

'*Who* was that?' asked Bane, when Ashes returned.

'Hughy Huge,' mumbled Ashes.

Bane judged it a good time for a sensitive question. 'I thought Web said he was going back to camp.'

'Oh, that's just Web,' said Ashes. 'Just Web. He's here. Of course he is. We have to ... we have to be here.'

'Why?' whispered Bane. 'Why do we have to be here?'

Ashes sat down by the fire, stirred up some glowing coals and put a few sticks on them, blowing into the embers until they burst into flame, talking sleepily, half to himself.

'Some of us ... we didn't like what that pond done to us. Some of us didn't know what to think. Web, one day he's mad, the next day he likes being able to fly, next day he's mad again. Lately, he's been mad more of the time. It's like he's bored. Web was always smart, like Bunny. Him and Bunny was close. Since Bunny's been gone, Web's kinda ... like I said, bored. I think he just wants to make something happen.'

Bane said offhandedly, making little of it, 'How come nobody knows about you all? Back there, in town, they think Wilderneers are just a story.'

Ashes ruminated a long time on this. 'Well, we hid. One here, one there. After that time when they killed us, we hid. This whole world it's just full of places to hide ...'

'But the camp's right out in the open.'

'Lately,' Ashes agreed. 'Haven't been there but a little while. A couple years. Most of us're still hid. Me 'n Mooly, we started the camp. It's a place to get together. Him and me, we go around, talk to this one and that one, bring 'em into camp, so we'll be ready, when the time comes ...'

'Look, you Wilderneers got a plan about the cities, right?'

Ashes nodded, like a man in a trance, not taking his eyes from the fire.

Still distantly, as though it were unimportant: 'So, if you're here when the cities fall, the plan won't work, right? So why're you here?'

Ashes nodded again, distantly. 'There's time. World's not going to blow up yet.'

'How do you know?'

Ashes shrugged again, yawning, staring sleepily at the fire.

Bane turned away, outwardly calm, inwardly seething. The Wilderneers had a plan, but nothing came of the plan. They found themselves a new planet, but they had done nothing with it. They planned to get themselves some women, but nothing happened. Hundreds of years and nothing had changed with them, except that they'd grown bigger and stranger. They – or more properly, Ashes – had succeeded only once at reproduction. Their town was a shabby collection of huts and hovels, not fit to live in. Their food was offal. Some of them had only one emotion, and that was a kind of unfocused belligerence. Ashes and Webwings had retained some quality of irritability, but aside from being irritated, what did either of them do?

Bane surprised himself at these thoughts, at the words he used to form them, words he had never had until he went to House Genevois, words he had learned from the conversation mistress but had rejected using in favor of the rude and impoverished blatting of his fosterage. He used them now, nonetheless. Well, Madame herself had said words were tools. A tool was a tool. A man didn't need to carry a tool. He could pick it up when he liked and put it down when he liked.

Still seething, Bane curled into his blankets once more, peering through slitted lids at his father's firelit face, brooding over the coals. What was he thinking? Was he thinking? He, Bane, wasn't at all sure Ashes could think, not straight. So, maybe ... maybe he'd better concentrate on this business of getting away.

He remembered something Madame had said: 'There is a class of person who cannot lead and will not be led. Such persons go their own way, uncorrupted by insight, unmitigated by experience. They do what they do, and usually they die of it, but they would rather die than cooperate with anyone else.'

Bane had always made a point of ostentatiously not listening during Madame's lectures, so it surprised him how much of what she said he remembered. He remembered that bit, because it had made him think of Ashes at the time, wondering if he was one who couldn't lead and wouldn't be led. Now he was sure: nobody could lead that batch of weirds, anyhow. And none of them would be led. So if all of them were getting together, now, it meant something big was happening, something maybe they had no control over at all!

Brooding on this, Bane fell asleep. Ashes, too, returned to his blankets. The fire burned down to dying embers once more. They were not wakened by the quakes that came in the early hours, snapping the ground beneath them, but gently, like a laundress shaking out sheets. They were not wakened by certain other things that came quietly and stood looking at them for a time before going forward on business of their own, though when Bane and Dyre and Ashes woke in the morning, they saw the sinuous tracks of those beings all around them.

'What?' Dyre asked, pointing to the deep depressions.

Ashes yawned, shook himself, and said in an uninterested voice, 'Joggiwagga, maybe. Something like that. On their way to the chasm.'

'Why are we going there?' Bane demanded. 'All kinds of things are going there, and they're all bigger than us.'

'I guess that's why,' said Ashes, moving about his morning tasks almost unconsciously. 'Something going on. You can't gain ground without knowing what's going on, boys.'

'I thought you was gonna take the cities,' Dyre cried petulantly. 'You can't take the cities if you're here and they're there. What if they fall down while you're gone? You can't get anywhere doin' that.'

The whip was out and moving before Bane could take a breath; it moved of itself, without Ashes using his hands, like a prehensile tail, an autonomous appendage, snaking out from the front of Ashes's jacket, cracking with that all too familiar electrical sound, leaving Dyre writhing on the ground, spittle running down his chin, eyes unfocused.

'You,' snarled Ashes. 'You keep your mouth shut. I told you, and I won't tell you again. You do what you're told. And what you're told is, we're going to that chasm to see what's going on. We're gonna talk to old Pete. Talk to some of the others.'

He picked up his saddle and threw it onto his horse, still growling to himself. 'Talk to some of them. That's what. Talk to them and find out what's going on.'

Bane lifted his brother from the ground, muttering, 'You don't have good sense, you know that?'

Dyre cried, 'I heard you say the same thing about the cities, about his plan.'

'At night, when he was sleepy. And in a tone of voice like it wasn't important. Not pushing it up his nose! That's bound to jerk him up! Keep it shut, brother. I'll figure it out. You just keep it shut and come along.'

919

53

The Farther Shore

On the third day of their voyage, while Questioner brooded on deck and all except the Corojum slept, the ship finished its voyage and was hauled ashore. The Corojum alone had been on watch as they passed the last two pillars, and he alone had sung the last lines, in his own language, while two of the Timmys manned the sails. When the keel of the ship grated on the bottom, the Corojum wakened the others, the Timmys gathered at the rail, the ship extruded its gangway, and they disembarked. The ship turned, of itself, and sailed out beyond the nearest pillars where, said the Corojum, it would come to no harm.

'Now what?' asked Mouche, wiping the sleep from the corners of his eyes.

'Tunneler,' said the Corojum. 'The Fauxi-dizalonz isn't far from here, and we could walk, but most everyone is there by now. There's just us left, and some of the jongau and some people from Sendoph.'

'People from Sendoph?' asked Questioner. 'Who might that be?'

'Two Hags,' the Corojum said. 'And Madame from House Genevois. And Simon, and a Man of Business.'

'Madame?' cried Mouche. 'Did she come after me?'

'Whether she did or not, how do you know all these things?' demanded Questioner.

Corojum looked surprised. 'Swoopers and swivelers come through the walls, up out of the sea, through the air, like moths. They carry messages.'

'Luminous things. Like flying kites or diamonds?' asked Mouche.

'Like that. How could we all work together if we did not know what was going on? The Man of Business is not a bad one. Calvy is a good mankind, and so is Simon, more or less.'

'How do you know so much about them?' asked Questioner. 'Do you spend a lot of time watching them?'

'The Timmys do. At first, we needed badly to understand *them*, those first ones. Then, after we took them to the Fauxi-dizalonz, we thought we *did* understand them. They were jong, gau, useless. Then you new ones came and we weren't sure. In some ways, your culture is like our own. You have supernumes, we have Timmys. You have actors and musicians, we have Corojumi. Had Corojumi. You have Hags, we have Bofusdiaga. You have Hagions, we have Kaorugi.'

'The Hags are like Bofusdiaga?' Questioner regarded him with delight. 'That is a new idea.'

'Bofusdiaga balances things to keep all the parts functioning. The Hags balance things to keep all the parts functioning. We do not have anything like the Men of Business, though. It seems to us odd to churn one's needs in that way. Buy everything, churn it around, increase the price, then sell it back to people who made it. To us it seems sensible to make what everyone needs and let everyone use what he needs, but then we do not have five brains inside, rattling away. The ape brain you all have is very acquisitive, so our way would not work for you.'

'How do you know it is the ape brain?' asked Mouche, yawning.

'I think you give five apes five bananas, biggest ape will take them all,' said the Corojum. 'Unless other four gang up on it, or, unless it is mother with child. So say the Hags.'

'When will we finish this journey?' asked Ornery. 'Can you tell me?'

'When we are finished,' said the Corojum.

'When we come from underground,' said Questioner, 'I hope I will be able to reach my ship. I have not been able, up until now.'

The Corojum did not meet her eyes. 'Maybe that is Kaorugi. Maybe Kaorugi does not want you talking.'

Questioner fixed him with a stare, but before she could say anything, the Corojum cried, 'And here is our tunneler. This is as you say, last lap. It will not be long.'

54

Assembly At The Fauxi-dizalonz

The tunneler bearing Questioner, Mouche, Ornery, and the Corojum traveled with a muffled roar interspersed with periods of almost silence that Questioner interpreted as movement through something more yielding than rock. Soil, perhaps. Or even predrilled tunnels. These relatively silent periods grew more frequent as they progressed, and the last part of their journey was accomplished in relative quiet. The tunneler stopped moving; the mouth end gaped large; and from the complicated structures beside the creature's mouth, its voice said, 'We have arrived near the Fauxi-dizalonz. Others will be coming soon. Some are already here.'

Almost drowsily, as though they had been long hypnotized by the motion and the sound, the three followed the Corojum out of the creature's mouth to find themselves on a high, wide ledge with sky and air everywhere but behind them. There the mouths of highly polished tunnels gaped, explaining the silence of their arrival. These ways had been cut long since, and among them were several smooth-walled caves, in one of which the Corojum suggested Mouche and Ornery deposit the packs before coming to stand beside itself and Questioner at the rim of the world.

They stood at the top of a sheer cliff that swooped in an unbroken wall to the bottom of the caldera where the jewel-green disk of a largish lake shone brightly in the morning sun.

'The Fauxi-dizalonz,' said the Corojum, pointing at the lake below. 'Your people are there, and I will collect them for you.'

'Don't hurry on my account,' said Questioner, moving a little back from the rim. 'I'm really most concerned about Ellin and Bao, the two dancers. Have you done anything to them?'

The Corojum shook his head. 'After what happened with the jongau, Bofusdiaga is reluctant to try it again. When you come, Bofusdiaga thinks we may arrive at a better way.'

'One would hope,' she murmured.

The Corojum went to the rim of the ledge, whistled, and was answered from the air. Within moments, a huge, four-eyed bird dropped from the sky, plucked up the Corojum in its talons, and plunged toward the distant pond.

'An interesting mode of travel,' Questioner began, interrupted by a slithering *shush* that proved to be another tunneler, emerging from another

922

portal onto the same ledge. When it opened its mouth, five disheveled persons staggered out: Madame, the two Hags, Calvy, and Simon.

'Madame, Simon!' cried Mouche, delightedly, then, 'Revered Hag,' with a deep bow to D'Jevier.

D'Jevier turned very pale.

Madame cried, 'Mouche! What has happened to you? Who did that to your face?'

'Bane,' said Mouche. 'I can put on my veils ...'

'Of course not,' snapped D'Jevier. 'Let me see.' She came close and ran her fingers down the healing wound, turning to Madame to say, 'We must get him to the med-machines.'

'I'm afraid it will have to wait,' said Questioner.

D'Jevier started to speak, but was distracted by the sudden and noisy departure of the tunneler, rattling itself away in one of the bores.

'Come,' said Questioner. 'I have not met the gentlemen. Would someone introduce us?'

'Calvy g'Valdet,' Calvy murmured. 'And Madame's assistant, Simon. I'm sorry, but I'm afraid we don't know the correct form of address.'

'At the moment we are being informal. Please call me Questioner. I do weary from all the unearned reverence I'm subjected to.'

'Hardly unearned,' murmured Calvy with a bow. 'Your reputation is unsullied, certainly a matter for reverence.'

Questioner laughed, a truly amused sound that seemed to draw all of them from their various reveries. 'Come,' she said. 'Let us admire the view.'

Accordingly, they turned their attention to their surroundings, though both Madame and D'Jevier found it difficult to take their eyes from Mouche's face.

At their right, a roadway opened upon the ledge, an avenue that stretched down and across the wilderness, straight as a rule.

'That doesn't appear on the orbital surveys,' said Calvy. 'None of this does!'

At right angles to this road, continuing the line of the ledge, a narrower way descended in a gentle slope eight-tenths of the way around the caldera before making a switchback that returned it to a point almost beneath them. The road continued in descending arcs, back and forth, back and forth, at last reaching the floor of the caldera, where it ran around the emerald lake and thence through a gap in the caldera wall to their left.

The ledge they were on also continued in that direction, making a sharp bend onto the wall of the twin caldera and giving them an unimpeded view down an abyssal cone. The road below wound back and forth on only the northern half of the cone. The southern half, from the rim down as far as they could see, gleamed blackly, smoothly, its surface interrupted by occasional vertical ridges, softly rounded, that ran convergently into the depths. The rim of this chasm sparkled as though set with gems. Questioner extended her sight to make out huge lenses and mirrors that reflected light down the black surface into the pit below.

'Well,' said Madame to D'Jevier, turning her attention from this enigmatic vision. 'We seem to have arrived, wherever this is. What's going on down there?' She pointed to the lake below, where a cluster of persons was being marshaled upward on the road.

'I see Ellin and Bao,' announced Questioner. 'My Old Earth aides, but I don't see the rest of my people.'

'You do not sound concerned,' said Calvy.

Questioner sighed. 'I do not wish them ill, I simply don't mind if they're elsewhere. They are political appointees, presumably serving a kind of internship. Occasionally the committee gives me someone sensible, but that is not the general rule.'

'What is that with your two aides?' asked D'Jevier. 'That's not a Timmy.'

'That is a Corojum,' said Questioner. 'According to it, the last Corojum, and he tells us the extinction of his ilk means our extinction as well.'

'Now, then ...' said Onsofruct angrily.

'Hush,' said D'Jevier.

Onsofruct fell silent, fuming as D'Jevier said in a cautionary tone, 'Let them tell us what's going on. It's sure somebody must, for we are at a loss.'

'Do you know what's going on?' Onsofruct demanded of Questioner.

'More or less, yes. In a moment or two, Ellin and Bao will be here, and then we can put our heads together. Meantime, since we may be here for some time, let us look about this place with a view to occupancy.'

Though unwilling to defer enlightenment, the eight of them scattered into the caves that backed the ledge, finding them already equipped for persons, with bedplaces piled with soft twigs and covered with blankets; a small, private cave set aside for a privy; water jars hung in the cool air, and flat trays of fruit and bread set nearby. Calvy, Simon, Ornery, and Mouche took possession of one cave, the three women settled themselves into another. When Ellin and Bao arrived, Bao joined the men and Ellin the women.

Questioner took no part in this bustle, instead continuing her examination of the abyss, noting now that the black, glossy surfaces seemed to quiver from time to time as though alive. Which, she thought, would explain a great deal. After a short recess of nibble, sip, lie down, and get up again, the Newholmians trickled out to join her at the rim of the ledge, where they were soon joined by Ellin and Bao. When they were all present, she gestured them to find a sitting place, studying them closely as they did so.

Mouche and Ornery, Ellin and Bao gravitated toward one another and sat to one side wearing faces that were almost copies of one another. Interested but wary and mostly uncommitted. Bao was perhaps a little more engaged in what was going on. Ellin was refusing to become involved. Ornery was merely cautious, and Mouche ... Mouche had the appearance of someone who had removed himself as far from the present as possible and was existing on another plane by will alone.

The Hags and Madame looked merely weary, the men no less so. Calvy maintained an alert expression, letting his eyes wander, seeing all that was to be seen. Simon hoarded his gaze, seeing only one thing at a time, not moving on until he'd dealt with it. They sat in silence. The air around them moved gently. Flying creatures glinted by, occasionally uttering calls that were not unlike bell sounds, their various pitches contributing to a slow and wandering melody. From below, Timmy voices rose in song, underlying the bell sounds, supporting them. From on high came another voice, and they looked up to see one of the large, four-eyed birds circling high above them.

'That's an Eiger,' murmured D'Jevier, her head thrown back to display the long, vulnerable line of her throat. 'The bird who sees all. It's singing what it sees to Bofusdiaga.'

'You know this,' said Questioner, 'because your nursemaid told you, when you were a baby. Your nursemaid who is now dead.'

D'Jevier flushed, looked at her shoes and said nothing.

'Well,' Questioner remarked. 'Let us accept that all you Newholmians had nursemaids who told you of Eigers and Bofusdiaga and Corojumi and Timmys and Joggiwagga. And here we are, confronting them in reality. This has been an enlightening journey for all of us, I have no doubt. Are you ready to discuss what it means? Or would you prefer to continue in suspicious ignorance?'

'Madam.' Calvy bowed, grinning at her. 'I am sure I speak for everyone when I say we would be ... gratified to know what it means.'

Though D'Jevier's mouth pinched momentarily, holding in her immediate rebuke, she did not utter it. She could not in all honesty disagree, and though Calvy had no right to speak for the Hags, in this case he had represented them honestly.

55

The Tale Of Quaggima

'As I have pieced it together, we are here today because of something that happened a million years ago,' said Questioner.

'Which could be said for anyone being anywhere,' Calvy remarked, his troubled eyes belying his charming smile.

Questioner's pursed lips and down-the-nose stare apprised him of the impertinence of charm. 'There is more than mere timeflow at work here. Our lives have intersected those of a very large, long-lived, star-roving race called the Quaggi. Except for Ellin and Bao, who have heard the name only in passing, you all know about the Quaggi.'

Her listeners glanced covertly at one another.

'Come now,' she coaxed them. 'You heard about the Quaggi when you were children.' She stared imperiously at D'Jevier. 'When you heard many other interesting stories ...'

'Say that we know about the Quaggi,' Calvy interrupted, to spare D'Jevier's obvious discomfort. 'If we don't, we'll pretend we do.'

'Ah,' said Questioner. 'Pretense. Well, that is something you Newholmians do well. I continue:

'A very long time ago, when this solar system was still quite young, a Quaggida entered the system. I am told by the Corojum that reproductive males sit out on the cold edges of solar systems, summoning, and that one or more females eventually respond to that call. I infer the female is unaware of the consequences, or, if aware, A: finds the lure irresistible, or B: is resigned to her fate.

'When the female arrived she was impregnated. In the process she was rather badly injured and her wings were so mutilated that she could no longer fly. The Quaggida left her there, one would imagine in considerable discomfort, and flew off to get started on the contemplative phase of his existence.'

Madame made a breathy exclamation, then subsided under Questioner's admonitory gaze.

'This may have been an aberration. It may have happened only in a single case. Or, it may be that both the violation and the concurrent mutilation are required by the Quaggian ethos, or the Quaggian physiology. In any case, the Quaggima lies there on the cold planet, barely able to move, while the egg slowly develops. When it has grown too large for its location, the Quaggima struggles with her crippled wings to leave whatever mild gravity is holding her, and she falls toward the sun, timing this to intercept some moon or planet which is "warm."'

She paused for a moment, and was interrupted by Onsofruct, who said angrily, 'What has all this got to do with us?'

Questioner held up an admonitory hand. 'It has everything to do with you, because it happened here!'

'Here? Where we are?'

'It happened here, on a moonlet of the outermost planet, and when the egg was ripe, the Quaggima fell to this world. She fell into a caldera where she somehow laid the egg beneath her in the warm rock. She did not die. I infer that the last act the female Quaggi commits is not the penetration of a warm moon or planet to lay the egg, but the breaking of that egg when it is ready to hatch.

'When she fell here, however, life was already present: intelligent, self-aware life. It was not life arising by differentiation and selection, which we are more familiar with. The life here had developed around suboce-anic vents and had grown by ramification and accumulation. It was and is, I should think, a fractal sort of creature which recapitulates in each part or group of parts the structure of the whole. In any case, most life on this world is one giant living thing that permeates the outer layer of this planet, a thing called Kaorugi, the Builder, one single being who is able to detach and reattach quasi-independent parts of itself. Though some of the detach-able parts were very simple ones, created to be merely self-replicating food items for other parts, all the other detachable parts have some intelligence, and some are self-aware to the extent that they have their own cultures and systems of artistic expression. The Timmys, for example. The Joggiwagga. The Corojumi.'

'The Timmys,' whispered Mouche.

'Indeed. The Timmys, who, according to Bao and Ellin, were shaped dif-ferently prior to mankind's arrival, and who were reshaped as erect bipeds only after mankind arrived on this world. They were made to look like man-kind so that mankind would accept their presence. The entire life system, Kaorugi, is everywhere within the crust of this world, in the caves, in the tunnels, in and beneath the oceans, upon the surface, making up forests, pastures, and wildernesses. Since the separate animate parts are all parts of Kaorugi, there is no predator-prey food chain; strong does not eat weak; large sentient things do not live on small sentient ones; all things take their nourishment from sun, air, water, and the flying, sprouting, or swimming things, the self-reproducing, unconscious lifeforms Kaorugi has designed to serve as nourishment and habitat for its roaming parts. These unconscious parts are prolific and were created to have no sense of fear or pain.

'On this world, nature is not raw and violent. The green or violet or blue hair of the Timmys, the bright fur of the Corojumi serve the same function as leaves on plants, to draw energy from the sun. On this world, everything lives for the purpose of everything, and when a part wears out, it returns to that pond we see in the caldera, a place or organ called the Fauxi-dizalonz, and is there reconstituted.'

'You're describing Eden,' said D'Jevier, wonderingly.

Questioner nodded. 'One might say, Eden, yes. Obviously, there is none of the inevitable agony and terror that a food chain implies. Accidents, however, can happen even in Eden, and the intelligent, nonfood creatures of this world have an aversive reaction to being maimed or mangled, just as we do, though they may fear it less, for they know if they are rendered nonfunctional they can be returned to the Fauxi-dizalonz to be healed or remade.

'When Kaorugi became aware of the Quaggi – before the fall – Kaorugi recognized pain and responded to it with what we might call pity or empathy or perhaps only curiosity. The Quaggi called upon certain Quaggian deities by their attributes. Kaorugi had parts with those attributes, so Kaorugi deputized them to make a place for Quaggima and ease her suffering. It is this sympathetic effort that is memorialized in the song you all heard as children.

'In that song and others, Bofusdiaga is called the death defier, the burrower of walls, the singer of the sun. We know this crater next to us was prepared for Quaggima, but Quaggima's falling created a much larger hole, displacing a great mass of rock that promptly fell on top of her. She was buried, shut off from the sunlight that nourishes her. Now we see that the stones have been removed. Now we see holes burrowed through the rim of this caldera where great lenses and mirrors are set to focus and reflect sunlight upon her.'

'She's still here?' cried Ellin. 'Where?'

'There,' said Questioner, gesturing. 'She is there, stretched up from the abyss, covering half that great crevasse, her wings exposed to the light.'

'There?' asked Calvy in an awed tone, pointing at the black, shining surface of the pit. 'Those are her wings?'

'I believe so. Those convergent ribs are no doubt the stiffeners with which the sails are controlled. Bone, perhaps, or carbon fiber. When, or if, we get to the bottom, we will find her body and her brain and the rest of her. I have no very clear idea as to her anatomy, though I expect something serpentine.'

'She's huge,' murmured Madame.

'Her wings are huge, but I would guess they are quite fragile,' Questioner explained. 'They are actually stellar sails. When she flew, she sailed on the radiation winds between the stars, her wings spread over kilometers of space. By the time she fell here, her wings were so tattered as to be virtually useless.

'In the songs, however, Corojumi are called, among other things, those who repair. I infer, therefore, that the Corojumi have repaired her, possibly using the liquid substance of the Fauxi-dizalonz, which repairs all life on this world. The Corojumi were also choreographers, and we know that when the Quaggima was restless, the Corojumi designed dances that soothed her.'

'Where?' cried Ellin. 'Where could you dance? Where are her eyes to see the dancers? Her ears to hear the music? She'd have to observe it, wouldn't she?'

Questioner patted the air, saying, 'Patience, Ellin. We will no doubt learn where the dance was done, and how.'

'I am still waiting to find out what this all has to do with us,' grated Onsofruct.

'Use your perceptions, woman!' snarled Questioner. 'When the egg was laid, it was small. Over long time, however, it has grown! Had it not been soothed into sleep, it would have hatched long since! But, at some point when the creature within stirred very strongly, Kaorugi realized the hatching of the egg would mean the destruction of the world!'

'Destruction?' cried Calvy, incredulously.

Questioner nodded. 'I've been running some simulations, just to see how the thing could be managed. One implication is inescapable. The Quaggi cannot escape planetary gravity using star-sails. I don't know the size or weight of the egg, but it has to be propelled out of the gravity well with the hatchling still folded safely inside, and it is possible that only nuclear force would provide sufficient propulsive power. We will, I imagine, find some kind of device within or around the egg, developing as part of it, that will propel the hatchling away from this world's gravity, with consequent destruction to a great part of this world. According to the Brotherhood of Interstellar Trade, the adult Quaggi extrude metal, which they draw from their surroundings. I imagine that the egg itself, or the thing inside the egg, or the Quaggima itself, has been mining this planet for fuel since it arrived here.'

'You're sure of this?' asked Madame.

'Of course I'm not sure! Nonetheless, I can come up with no other reasonable inference.'

'Destruction,' Calvy said again, as though unfamiliar with the word. 'Destruction of the whole world?'

Questioner replied, 'The substance of the world will no doubt survive, as may some elementary lifeforms, but *the* life, the totality which is Kaorugi, is another matter. The explosion, with the resultant pouring of dust into the atmosphere, is likely to cut off the sunlight. Much of Kaorugi now draws its life from the sun and will die if sunlight is lost.

'Once Kaorugi realized the destructive capabilities of the Quaggi egg, it did everything possible to keep both the Quaggima and the developing hatchling quiescent. Evidently the hatchling can continue developing in the egg for a very long time, if necessary, and keeping it there was the purpose of the dances we have heard about. On another planet, one without moons, it might stay quiescent for eons. Here, however, as the egg went on growing, the tug of the moons became greater, the dance grew more and more complex.'

'So?' demanded Simon, wonderingly.

'So, no one of the Corojumi could remember it all. They remembered it corporately, and they recreated and augmented the dance whenever it was needed.'

'I can guess where you're going with this,' said Calvy, staring at the pond below, where the Corojum stood in the midst of a great crowd of Timmys, a violet light shining among the other colors of the slender beings. 'You said this was the last Corojum. The first settlers must have what? Killed them for their hides?'

'They did. What makes this most unfortunate is that all detachable, quasi-independent creatures on this world carry their neural and cortical networks inside their skin. Soon, there were no more Corojumi. The system managed to muddle through for the last several hundred years because there hasn't been a six-moon conjunction in at least that long.

'Now, however, a conjunction approaches. There is one Corojum left, but it doesn't remember enough of the dance to recreate it. Kaorugi can make more Corojumi, of course, perhaps it has done so, but they will not know anything about the dance. Without the dance, the Quaggi in the egg is going to wake the Quaggima, she'll crack the egg, which will set off whatever the propulsive force is, the hatchling will be burst out into space, and it's likely good-bye Dosha.'

'Dosha?'

'We call it Newholme. They call it Dosha, which means *fitting*, or *proper*, or, in some contexts, *ours*.

Calvy started to speak, but Questioner raised her hand. 'Two final bits of information that should be kept in mind. First, Kaorugi interpenetrates the crust of the planet. It feels the pain of the Quaggima, it realizes what will happen if she wakes and the egg hatches. It does not bear that pain and apprehension motionlessly. It writhes. It heaves. The mountains tremble and the caverns fall. Kaorugi itself is the source of much of the recent geological activity.

'Second, the Timmys, Joggiwagga, Eigers, and so forth are capable of

930

independent movement and also independent thought. When these inde-pendent parts first realized the dance information was being lost, they went to the two cities, along with some large leggers and tunnelers and whatnot, and captured all the first settlers who had killed the Corojumi and dragged them to the Fauxi-dizalonz in the hope they might be holding some of the information. Their reasoning was that mankind ate animals – the first set-tlers had brought livestock with them – therefore they may have digested the Corojumi and somehow absorbed the information.'

'So that's what happened to the first settlers!' cried Calvy. 'They drowned in this Fauxi whatsit?'

Questioner shook her head. 'No. Fauxi-dizalonz isn't water, it's a living thing. The settlers went in the pond and they crawled out again. Unfortunately, they went in as jong, which means trash, and they came out as jongau, which means bent trash, trash cubed, something that is unworkable and useless. The implications of that occurrence are extremely interesting.'

'The man known as Thor Ashburn must have been one of their descend-ents,' said Madame. 'But ... there was nothing physically abnormal about him. Except his smell!'

'You're sure?' asked Questioner in her turn.

Madame stared sightlessly into space. 'No. Of course I'm not sure. I never saw him unclothed. The boys were his sons, and I am sure they were physi-cally normal, except for smelling like their father.'

Questioner said, 'He and the boys would be no danger to us, I don't imagine, but there are no doubt many others of his ilk.'

'All or most of whom – so said our tunneler – are on their way here,' said Madame.

'Why?' demanded Mouche. 'What're they coming for?'

'I don't know,' said Questioner. 'Curiosity? Or maybe they're frightened. The recent tremors are enough to have frightened anyone.'

'And the tremors come from Kaorugi,' mused Simon. 'In response to the pain of Quaggima ...'

'Which is in response to the movement inside the egg,' said Madame.

'Which is in response to the tug of the moons,' said D'Jevier.

'Which nobody can do anything at all about,' concluded Calvy.

'Not unless we can recover the dance,' said Questioner. 'Which is an issue I have decided to consider separately from the ethical concerns posed in doing so ...

'Ethical concerns?' cried Calvy. 'At a time like this you're worried about ethical concerns?'

'I was created to worry about ethical concerns! Under Haraldson's edicts, we would have no right to interfere with the hatching. The Quaggi came here after a local population had arisen, however, so the rights of the

931

local population should take precedence over the Quaggi's rights. They, it, Kaorugi, had already interfered with the Quaggi before mankind entered the scene, but that issue is Kaorugi's ethical concern, not ours. I don't blame it for what it did, and in my opinion it also acted rationally, though mistakenly, when it abducted my people.'

'But taking your people wasn't rational!' cried Ellin. 'What would any of us from off planet know about their dance?'

Questioner laughed wryly, shaking her head. 'Persons, beings are often unable to see things they can't recognize, things they have no search-image for. Kaorugi is not accustomed to sexual reproduction. On this planet, creatures are budded or assembled in the Fauxi-dizalonz, and Kaorugi designs them and grows them as it needs them. All information on this planet is held by parts of Kaorugi. When Kaorugi needs information, it accesses the part that has it. From Kaorugi's point of view, it was rational to assume that if some of its information is missing, we must have it. Where else could it have gone?'

'Even if the Corojumi are gone,' said Mouche, 'the Timmys who performed in the dance should remember it. Why doesn't Kaorugi gather up the Timmys who danced and give their information to some new Corojumi?'

'Right. Quite right, Mouche,' said Questioner, nodding her approval. 'I asked the Corojum that same question during our voyage. The Timmys, however, weren't shaped as they are until mankind came. They retain the memories but not the shape. If that weren't enough, it seems your second wave of settlers had not only forbidden dancing but had killed and burned many of the Timmys who went on doing it. As a result, much of the Timmy information was lost.'

D'Jevier blanched. Onsofruct moved uncomfortably. Calvy nodded, mouth twisted. 'This time we really did it, didn't we?'

Questioner shrugged. 'Certainly someone did. Kaorugi is intelligent but not at all imaginative, because it has never had to be. Conflict acting on intelligence creates imagination. Faced with conflict, creatures are forced to imagine what will happen, where the next threat will come from. If there has never been conflict, imagination never develops. Wits arise in answer to danger, to pain, to tragedy. No one ever got smarter eating easy apples.

'Kaorugi, therefore, could not imagine beings who would willingly destroy the common good for personal gain, something mankind is very good at. Kaorugi knew nothing of individually acquisitive creatures, and it didn't learn until too late. The point I am trying to make quite clear is that all of us here must admit that it is, in fact, too late for any simple solution. We and Kaorugi must try something else.'

'It could kill the Quaggima,' said Onsofruct. 'That's what it could do!'

They all stared at her. The Questioner arranged her face, keeping her expression disinterested. 'It couldn't, as a matter of fact. It does not kill.'

'Well then, you can! You've got a ship out there. It has weapons!'

'Onsy!' said D'Jevier, warningly.

'Well, she could!'

'I'm not at all sure I could,' Questioner said calmly. 'But aside from the fact I'm still unable to contact my ship, how would you kill it?'

'Blow her to hell!'

Questioner replied, 'Blowing her, as you say, to hell, would certainly destroy the egg, and if you destroy the egg, you'll set off the propulsive system and probably blow the planet apart. Which is rather what we're trying to avoid.'

'So no matter what we do, it's going to happen sooner or later anyhow,' cried Onsofruct.

'The operative word is later,' cried Calvy.

Questioner nodded. 'I'm sure a century or so could make a big difference to everyone involved, including Kaorugi. Given even a few tendays, there are many things we could do, but we have only a day or so to do something else. Something wonderful and imaginative and expert that will give us breathing time.'

She turned, gesturing to Ellin and Bao. 'And here are my wonderful and imaginative experts. How shall we set about recovering the dance?'

Ellin gasped, turning quite pale as she said, 'You're joking? You've got to be!' She looked around herself in a panic, reaching out for Bao.

'Oh, how faulty an expecting!' asserted Bao, giving Ellin a supportive arm and a sympathetic look. 'We are being out of our depths here.'

'No false modesty, hysterics, or avoidance rituals, please,' Questioner murmured. 'It's a simple question well within your field of expertise. My data banks tell me that recovery of old dances is something done all the time among dancers on Old Earth. Simply tell us how they would do it.'

Ellin gritted her teeth and took several labored breaths before saying, 'I'm sorry, Questioner. You took me by surprise, but you're quite right. There's no time for ... whatever.

'Um. If I had to recover an old dance on Old Earth, I'd find all contemporary accounts of the performance. I'd look for letters written by cast members or observers, interviews given by them. I'd look for critical reviews, either printed or broadcast. I'd look at impressions noted by audience members or notes made at the time by dance aficionados. If the ballet had a name indicating a traditional or well-known story, like, oh, *Romeo and Juliet* or *Homage to Dorothy*, I'd find the story.'

'Designs of costumes or even bills for costumes are useful,' offered Bao. 'Costume often defines character, and character defines movement. Same is being true for scenery. The music is being a good place to start, also musicians themselves. Then, one is doing what Mouche said. Surely not *all* Timmys who danced are being dead! So I would be talking to the ones left. They are describing the steps and movements they were doing, as well as those other people were doing.'

'If we still *have* some of the Timmys who danced,' said Ellin. 'They aren't all dead, are they?'

'Not quite all, no,' said Questioner, with a significant look at the Hags. 'The governing powers were not quite that efficient.'

Bao went on, 'If we have story, we can start with plot. Who are characters? What is represented, what is emotion? What is done? Surely this much Kaorugi knows!'

'According to the Corojum,' said Questioner, 'Kaorugi knows only that the dance soothed the Quaggima and let it sleep.'

With her brow furrowed in concentration, Ellin offered, 'It might be plotless, Bao. Just movement for movement's sake. Kind of like hypnosis, or wall patterns. I always kept my walls on patterns because they were soothing. And if there's no story line, it's very difficult to figure out what went on.'

'Assume for the moment there was a story,' said Questioner.

'Well then, I'd look for representations of the work of the solo dancers, verbal or pictorial, to see how they moved, how they worked, what their style was …'

'Style?' asked Calvy. 'I don't see—'

Ellin interrupted him, 'We know the Timmys danced. Well, they were shaped differently. What could that shape do? What kinds of jumps, positions, movements? How did the choreographers work? Did they work out lengthy series of steps and teach the series, already set, or did they allow the dancer a share in developing the vision? On Old Earth, we'd ask the patrons of the ballet, as well, but I guess that doesn't apply here.'

'The music,' said Bao. 'Again, I am emphasizing importance of music.'

'How many people are we talking about here?' asked Calvy. 'How many dancers? Musicians? Scene setters?'

Ellin, who had, despite herself, become interested in the problem, shook her head firmly. 'The numbers aren't that critical. Even in a large ballet, you wouldn't need everyone in order to learn what they did. A lot of ballet is ensemble work. One dancer in an ensemble could reconstruct the whole ensemble, or large chunks of it, because she would move as everyone else does, or groups would move in repetitive sequence. It wouldn't matter if there were twelve or two hundred, they might all be doing the same steps. The same is true for small groups: in a pas de deux, for example, either dancer could remember what the other one did …'

Bao objected, 'Except, there were being in twentieth century, so-called modern dances in which every person was doing something completely different from everyone else. Movements and groupings were being more sculptural ...'

'But if these were very small dancers, doing something to soothe a very large being, they'd have to move en masse to be perceived, wouldn't they?' Ellin asked plaintively. 'I keep getting this twentieth-century, Old Earth flash of Busby Berkeley musicals. Hundreds of dancers parading around. Or carnival processions! Or even pageants! Something with hundreds, thousands of participants, all jingling and jiggling, headdresses bobbing, skirts swirling ... Looking at the size of the wings on that creature in the pit, I wonder if it could even perceive individual dancers.'

'Postpone that concern,' said Questioner. 'For now, merely find out everything you can, without worrying about how we'll use it. We have no newspapers or reviews; we have no notes; we do, however, have some persons, creatures, who saw the dance or did the dance or provided music for it.'

'I must be very stupid, but I can't understand why Kaorugi doesn't remember,' cried Ellin, frustrated.

Questioner pondered. 'Let me simplify. Imagine that your brain is spread out everywhere under your skin. Imagine that you could detach your arm and send it off to pick strawberries, and imagine the brain under the skin had sensors to see and smell and taste with. Imagine your arm can remember what it is supposed to do, and can record what happens. When the arm comes back, once it is reattached, you would remember picking the berries. If your arm never came back, however, you would remember sending the arm, but not what happened to it. Kaorugi can remember deputizing its parts, but it can't remember what they do until and unless they return.'

'And Kaorugi can't extrapolate the missing parts?' Madame said, shaking her head.

Questioner said, 'Madame, I don't know all the implications of Kaorugi's mind. I think the dance was a subfunction that was left up to the Timmys and the Corojumi, a constantly changing detail Kaorugi never incorporated into its core. The Timmys and the Corojum are, after all, virtually independent. The system had plenty of redundancy until we came along, but this planet hasn't had a history of traumas and mass deaths. We brought the habits of murder with us, which meant the redundancy level just wasn't high enough.'

'Ridiculous,' muttered Onsofruct.

Questioner said patiently, 'It does us no good to ponder and fret over what we don't have, let's start with what we do. We will go down to the Fauxidizalonz and find out what the one Corojum remembers. We will find out what the remaining Timmys remember and whatever else exists that might

935

retain any memory of the dance. And by the way, what are the members of my entourage doing down there?'

Ellin shook her head in confusion. 'Were they down there? We didn't see them.'

'The Corojum said they were there,' Questioner averred.

Bao stood up, took Ellin by one hand, and pulled her erect. 'We'll see when we get there.'

Mouche was standing at the rim, examining the crowd of persons below. His Goddess was not there, which gave him a sense of relief. On the voyage he had managed not to look at her, it, too closely, and just now he had carefully refused to listen to Questioner's exposition, knowing he wouldn't like the implications of it. He could not accept that Flowing Green was a part. His mystical dream required that she, it, be a singular creature woven of starlight and shadow, magic and romance. She was a perilous eidolon, a symbol of marvel and mystery. Instinctively, he kept a respectful distance to separate his Hagion from reality. Since she, it, was not by the Fauxidizalonz, nothing prevented his going with the others.

The road began its descent into the caldera from the north end of the ledge, and they went along it only a little way before cutting downward on a steep narrow track interrupted by rocky stairs. The road had a much gentler slope, but it went so far around the caldera before each switchback that it would have taken them half a day to traverse it. Even as it was, Questioner thought, setting her climbing legs on slow, a careful journey would take them some time.

Madame, the Hags, and Questioner were at the end of the procession. Madame stared after Mouche, worried by his manner. Something there. Something strange. When he came back, she'd have to try and find out what. She turned a troubled face toward the Questioner, who was watching her closely.

'You're worried about the boy?' Questioner asked.

'I am, yes.'

'Mouche?' asked D'Jevier. 'What's wrong with him?'

'He is enchanted,' said Questioner.

'By them?' D'Jevier looked downward. 'The Timmys?'

'One of them, I should think,' said Madame. 'Though how it happened ...'

'He watched them,' said Questioner. 'At their dances, while he was at your establishment, Madame.'

'Impossible!'

'Nothing is impossible when it comes to youthful mischief, as we all know,' Onsofruct drawled in a muffled voice.

Questioner said firmly, 'Since we are more or less alone, just we four ... women, I think it's time for you to tell me the truth about Newholme.'

D'Jevier refused to be cowed. 'By all the Hagions,' she erupted, planting her feet firmly on the trail and turning on her interlocutor. 'Don't play games with us, Questioner. You know the truth! You know we lied about the Timmys. You've probably had that one figured out since shortly after you got here. I don't know what made us think we could hide it.'

'I know some of the truth about that, yes,' said Questioner. 'But I am speaking now of the truth of Mouche and Madame. I mean the other truth.'

The three women looked at one another. Onsofruct sighed. 'What about Mouche and Madame?'

'This Consort business. This business of men going about in veils.'

The two sisters exchanged a glance, and Onsofruct shrugged. 'There's no point in not telling you. It's not unethical.'

Questioner said, 'You may be right, though I doubt Haraldson would have approved. It's part of the Newholmian pattern, and I need to know about all of it.'

Onsofruct sat on a boulder at the edge of the path, removed her boot, and dumped gravel out of it, saying: 'Tell her about the woman raids, D'Jevier. That's where the whole thing started.'

D'Jevier did so, concluding, 'The men who took them made no bones about their intentions. They'd been promised wives with the second ship, and they weren't going to wait. They had stolen women, they would steal more, and they intended to keep them all under lock and key to prevent their running away.

'Well, Honored Questioner, "keeping women under lock and key" or "stopping their running away" sounded like the worst sort of patriarchal repression to our foremothers, some of whom, as required by the Settlement Act, were cultural historians.'

Onsofruct interrupted, 'The women knew that if we got entrenched in a patriarchal system, no matter how useful it might be for a generation or two, there'd be no simple way to stop it sixty or seventy years later. Once a male dominance system got started, it would take centuries before their daughters and granddaughters could achieve equality.'

Onsofruct got to her feet and started down the path again, Questioner close behind. 'The women used the fortress in Sendoph. It was unfinished, but it had strong walls that were easy to defend, and our ancestresses had control of medical care, tools, weapons, and women. That gave them what they needed to enforce the newly written dower laws. Our foremothers knew that when women had to be paid for, they were more highly valued, so we told the men they'd either pay and pay well for a woman's reproductive life, or they would do without.

'Well, you know about the dower laws. Women have a contractual right to be well supported during their entire lifetimes – there is no divorce in an economic sense – and in return the women agree to contribute their reproductive capabilities to their husbands' lineage for a specified number of years. If a woman has talents or skills, the contract may include some contribution toward the business. The marriage contract can guarantee support, but no contract can guarantee affection or pleasure. Our people thought women should be entitled to those as well. After a dutiful child-bearing, women had a right to the same pleasures men have always achieved through having mistresses.'

'You gave men Consorts,' said Questioner.

'Exactly. Someone to offer intellectual stimulation, to make conversation, to create romance, to cuddle and cosset, to make love to them. Men of Business are too busy with the game of business – which most men seem to enjoy more than anything else – to have time for pleasuring a wife.'

Questioner asked, 'And you're satisfied with the system?'

Onsofruct said, 'Almost everyone is satisfied because we tried very hard to give everyone what they wanted. What men most wanted was clear title to their children's paternal genetics, so we gave it to them. What women most wanted was to lead productive and companionate lives. We gave them that by giving them broadly educated companions, Consorts who read, who enjoy the arts. Whenever you see art or hear music or enjoy culture upon Newholme, you may thank women and their Consorts, for they are the ones who keep it going.'

'It wouldn't work if you had as many women as men,' said Questioner.

Onsofruct and D'Jevier plodded on, blank-faced.

Madame said, 'Our system works for us. It's coercive, yes, but no more so than every other system. We know Haraldson's edicts say people shouldn't be coerced in matters of reproduction, but you know as well as we do they've always been coerced, women particularly. Here, we tried to balance things.'

'I give you credit for good intentions,' said Questioner in a preoccupied tone. 'I will report you, of course, but chances are the Council of Worlds will agree with you. Your system works. And it probably makes no difference, for you're sufficiently at risk over the business of the Timmys that the matter of coercion takes second place.'

'You're going to report the Timmys, too.' Onsofruct sighed.

'You'd expect me to, wouldn't you?' asked Questioner. 'Though it's an interesting question whether they are, in fact, indigenes. I'm not sure detachable parts can be considered an indigenous race. And since there's only one of Kaorugi, it isn't exactly a race. It's more of a biota. Haraldson's edicts cover destruction of biotas, but killing the Timmys didn't kill the biota. The hearings on the question should be interesting, no?'

'Oh, certainly, certainly.' Madame threw up her hands, as though throwing the subject to the winds. Then, looking down the hill, she remarked,

'Let's catch up to your assistants and the men.'

They went on at somewhat greater speed, Madame with a clear conscience, the two Hags somewhat troubled, and Questioner quite certain she knew what each of the others was thinking.

56

A Gathering Of Monsters

Though Ashes and his sons kept to the high road, their progress was slowed by the traffic in Newholmian leggers and tunnelers along with various of Ashes's kindred who rolled, heaved, crawled, slunk, poured, bounced, and otherwise ambulated along in the same direction. By the time half the morning had worn away, Dyre and Bane were dizzy with the variety they had observed and half paralyzed by the monstrousness of the movers and shakers – for so Ashes called them.

'Movers and shakers, boys,' he crowed. 'That's us, the movers and the shakers.'

'When they all get there, what are they going to do?' asked Bane, keeping his voice in the even, careless register that Ashes seemed able to hear without growing angry.

'Like Hugh said, roll 'em over.' Ashes chuckled.

Bane started to ask why, then desisted. Ashes wouldn't know why. Yesterday it had occurred to Bane that Ashes had never known why, and probably neither had any of the first settlers. They had been discontented with life on Earth, so they'd moved to Thor. They'd been discontented with the rules on Thor, so they'd broken the rules. They'd been discontented with the punishment received for that, so they'd moved. They had been discontented without women, so they'd tried stealing some. They'd continued discontented with the results of that; they would always be discontented, and probably they would never know why. During the night just past, he had dreamed of Madame's voice going on and on about angry men, discontented men, men who went off like bombs.

'What're you thinkin'?' asked Dyre.

'I was thinkin' about Madame.'

'Old horny corsets? What about the old bitch?'

'I was thinkin', she was right about some things.'

Dyre sniggered under his breath. 'You're goin' soft in the head.'

Bane took a deep breath. 'I was just rememberin' she said that thing about men being angry. Ashes there, he's angry.'

'I'm angry,' snarled Dyre. 'All those people saying we stink. It's enough to make you good and angry.'

'I mean besides that. Got to be something more than that to make Ashes so ferocious.'

'Hellfire, you know,' said Dyre. 'He's mad at those people on Thor who got in his way, and he's mad at the Timmys for what they did to him, and he's mad at the women for dyin' on him, and he's mad at Marool for doin' … whatever she did.'

'And he's mad at you and me because we're not girls,' concluded Bane. 'And if we was girls, he'd be mad at us for something else.'

'You are getting soft,' muttered Dyre, pulling his horse back to conclude the conversation.

Bane said softly, between his teeth, 'I'm just thinking I'm not set on dying just yet. And the way he's going, he's going to get himself killed and everybody else who happens to be standing too close.'

Dyre pretended not to hear and they rode silently for a time. A legger came up behind them, abated its speed, and seemed content to follow. Nonetheless, Dyre kicked his horse into a trot and came up beside Bane, throwing suspicious glances over his shoulder. Bane ignored him, though Dyre had been right, of course. Bane did get mad at people saying he smelled. But then, they'd been at Madame's, and she'd stopped the way he and Dyre smelled, and nobody at House Genevois had ever mentioned it, not even Mouche, but they'd still felt mad. Like being mad was a sort of habit. He thought about this for a time, then tried again to involve his brother.

'All right, look. Who's on our side? There's Hughy Huge. And there's those crawlers we saw this morning, like Crawly, back at the camp, only bigger. And there's that one we heard about, the one that's grown into the mountain. And there's the ear and the eye and all, who're probably coming along. And there's Bone and Mooly, and the rest. So there's muscle ones, and mouth ones, and belly ones, and other kinds of ones. There's all kinds of body parts, all kinds but one. There's no brain one. Don't that make you wonder?'

'Wonder what?' snarled Dyre.

'Oh, shit, forget it.' Bane frowned to himself and shut his mouth tightly, drawing his horse away from his brother's. Maybe there was something wrong with him. Maybe he was sick. Maybe he'd caught this sickness at House Genevois. He'd never had thoughts like this before. He'd always been pretty much like Ashes, mad at everybody, getting his pleasure out of hurting them, screwing them up. So now Ashes was really going to screw something up, and then what?

As though to accentuate this thought, the earth moved beneath him, the horse stopped, legs braced wide, white showing at the edges of its eyes, nostrils flaring. The tremor went on and on, then faded. Ahead of them, the road danced then stilled. Behind them the legger emitted a confused noise, for it had been knocked off the road and now lay on its side, all its legs kicking without being able to right itself. Suddenly the legs came loose in pairs connected by saddle-shaped bits, and a few of these pieces began galloping away down the road, making the horses shy away. Then the tubular body split into cylindrical sections that wheeled onto the road and began rolling westward, spinning like tires, while the abandoned legs assembled themselves into pairs of pairs and spun after them like four-spoked wheels.

Only a squarish part was left behind, one that immediately began a shrill screaming, 'Weeeple, weeeple, weeeple!'

The rearmost set of legs skidded to a stop, turned, sped back, separated itself to attach one leg pair at each end of the remaining part, then galloped off after the rest, the screamer still keening, 'Weeeple, weeeple!'

Another tremor began, a long, slow shaking that seemed to go on endlessly. The horses refused to move. Cursing, Ashes dismounted and sat on a quivering rock at the side of the road, the reins loose in his hands.

'Did you see that?' Bane asked.

'See what?' his father growled.

'D'ja see that thing come apart?'

'They all come apart. Joggiwagga comes apart into snakes and balloony parts. Leggers come apart into tubes and legs and voice boxes. Tunnelers are just legger tubes with a driller section added on in front. Swimmers are just tunnelers with fins added on.'

'How about Timmys?'

'Funny about them. They don't seem to fit together real well, and they don't come apart into smaller things.'

'How do you know all that?' Bane asked.

'Been watchin' 'em. Long time.' Ashes yawned, his face suddenly becoming vacant and unlike himself. Bane stared at him, wondering why he looked so mushy, as though his nose and chin were sinking into his face.

'You feelin' all right?'

'Why?' snapped Ashes, suddenly himself. 'Something the matter with you?'

Bane shook his head slowly, making his voice sound uninterested again. 'You were yawning and looked a little sleepy, that's all. I thought maybe you hadn't slept real well.'

'Slept fine.' Ashes got back on his horse and rode on without a backward glance. Bane kicked his mount, as did Dyre, and they followed after.

'You were right,' whispered Dyre. 'He looked funny. Like somebody melted him.'

'Like I said,' muttered Bane. 'I think we'd better be careful not to stand too close.'

57

Quaggima And The Chasm

When Questioner and the women came to the shores of the Fauxi-dizalonz, they saw Questioner's entourage disconsolately huddled in the mouth of a nearby cave. Simon and Calvy were with the four young people, all concentrated upon the Corojum, who was tightly pressed against what appeared to be a curved rock wall. The new arrivals joined the others in time to hear the Corojum say loudly, 'Bofusdiaga says your people won't help, so probably none of you will help.'

'What people?' demanded Mouche.

'Your people. Bofusdiaga wanted to talk to them, but they became frightened and silly. Bofusdiaga is annoyed.'

Questioner stepped forward and pulled the Corojum gently away from his attachment, earning a scowl from the Corojum and a tremor in the ground beneath them.

'Corojum, what's going on? We haven't killed any of you, like the settlers did. Bao and Ellin and I have only been here a few days, along with the members of my entourage. Why would Bofusdiaga be annoyed with us?'

'Because they won't be sensible. All they will do is talk about how they have been wronged. Those jongau, they were also wronged. Bofusdiaga says creatures who think only of how they are wronged cannot help with the dance and everything is lost.'

Questioner rubbed her head. 'If you had asked me, Corojum, I could have told you that those people in the cave would be of no help. They are young, rebellious, and not at all useful. At that age, many young people spend a great deal of time thinking they have been wronged.'

Corojum snorted. 'So. Bofusdiaga says past wrongs cannot be righted because past wrongs are past and time only runs one way. Bofusdiaga says all you independent creatures suffer great wrongs sometime in past, which is normal, but you stay always living in past so you can continue wronged forever! Forever miserable, forever tragical! Bofusdiaga says so long as you go on chewing yesterday's pains, you cannot eat today's pleasures, so it is no help!'

'This is Bofusdiaga, not Kaorugi?' Questioner persisted.

Corojum leaned against the stone, faced the group, held up his hands for silence, and said with an attitude of sorely tried patience: 'Before Quaggima, in this place was only Kaorugi and this world that Kaorugi came into and made Kaorugi's own. Kaorugi, only! Itself! Solo! One living thing and its parts! You are also living things with parts. You say fingers to do work; Kaorugi says Timmys. You say arms; Kaorugi says Joggiwagga. You say eyes; Kaorugi says Eiger. You say conscious activity; Kaorugi says Bofusdiaga. You say creativity; Kaorugi says Corojumi. You understand?'

Questioner nodded, intrigued, as the Corojum went on: 'Only difference is, Kaorugi's parts know themselves and act by themselves. Well! After Kaorugi heard Quaggima calling, here was this world and Kaorugi and its parts, but also there was Quaggima coming toward it, Quaggima who evoked many new ideas: stars and galaxies and sex and other peoples, outside. Kaorugi had never thought of other people, and now Kaorugi had to think about that and other new things, and it was very difficult! So, Kaorugi takes a part of itself, the Bofusdiaga part, and Kaorugi says to itself, Bofusdiaga, "You do this work here, you, Bofusdiaga, you go on being part that builds, alloys, puts together and takes apart! You take charge of the Fauxi-dizalonz, for I am going down deep to think!" And since then, Kaorugi has gone down deep all over, under cities, under oceans, under mountains, and Kaorugi is thinking, all the time thinking deep thoughts, and Kaorugi is not finished thinking yet.'

The ten visitors looked at one another for support, at the sky, as though for inspiration, up at the ledge, as though for direction, finding no help.

'What is problem?' demanded the Corojum.

Calvy asked, 'Where is Bofusdiaga?'

The Corojum stared at him incredulously, gesturing widely. 'Here. This is Bofusdiaga. Bofusdiaga is all around us, anywhere inside this valley and in next valley, where Quaggima is, and I think spills over a little even farther.'

'What if we want to talk to Kaorugi itself?' asked the Questioner.

Corojum's fur stood on end, both head and hands waved in negation. 'Oh, no, no. Kaorugi would be very angry. Kaorugi does not want to be distracted and has made self unavailable.'

'Rather like the male Quaggi in that respect,' muttered Questioner, fidgeting, feeling inadequate. She could not recall ever before feeling inadequate and could not understand why she did so now, as though something very important was going on that she was not seeing! She took a deep breath.

'Corojum, Bofusdiaga is quite correct about the people in the cave. Most of them are very young and given to rebelling against their fathers and mothers. Do you understand the word mother?'

'Kaorugi understands; Bofusdiaga understands. So, I understand.

Quaggima is nest keeper, child hatcher. Mankinds have also nest keepers and child hatchers also, called mothers. Other sex is called fathers.'

Questioner said, 'Well, the mothers and fathers of these children have grown tired of them, so they sent them to me, hoping this will help them grow up, which it sometimes does. For the moment we can forget them. They are not part of this. We, the rest of us, are not feeling wronged.'

She said this with a swift glance at the others which they uniformly interpreted as a directive to give up any such feelings on the instant and not make a liar of her.

Mouche said, pleadingly, 'We are really interested in helping, Corojum. Can't we please get on with it?'

Corojum stared at them, looking from face to face, letting his eyes rest finally on Mouche, who held out his hands pleadingly. 'I will ask Bofusdiaga.'

The Corojum went to the rock wall, leaned against it, and stared at the sky, his eyes moving, his body moving, various muscle groups knotting and relaxing, all in accompaniment to the communication, which was lengthy. Those closest could see that it had opened a seam along its side which had actually attached to the stone.

Finally, just as Questioner was running out of patience, Corojum pulled away from the rock and said, 'Bofusdiaga says all right for now. Bofusdiaga will forget those others and cooperate with you. We have asked for all Timmys who danced to come here; some are here already. Every other creature who saw dance is coming, also. Some Joggiwagga, some Eiger, some others ...'

'Then I think we'd better get started, because we're running out of time!'

In the brief pause that followed, Questioner went to the cave and told the captives there to get themselves onto the high rim to wait for her, and if they wanted to avoid being eaten by the monsters, to do it without any talk whatsoever. Casting resentful glances behind them, they went, the last of them departing just before Corojum returned leading an assortment of creatures.

Questioner instructed the group: 'Each of you take one of the portable data heads and record everything. Ask about the site, first. Where did they dance, where from, where to. Then ask about what they did, what they saw done by others. Corojum says when you are finished with the Timmys, they will translate for the others.'

So they began with the Timmys, their initial diffidence giving way to assurance as afternoon wore away toward evening. Questioner moved from place to place, feeding the data head information into the larger accumulator she carried in a compartment on her person.

'What is that thing, anyhow?' asked Calvy, alert to the possibility of profit.

'An IDIOT SAVANT,' she murmured. 'An Improved Deductive Imager Of Theoretical Scenarios And Variations, Ambassadorial, Non-Terrestrial. It was invented by HoTA – the same department that designed me – for use by Council of Worlds diplomats. It has a data bank that includes most of what we know about intelligent races; it takes everything that is observed, fact by fact, and extrapolates a logical scenario that includes all observed realities. Then it does variations on the scenario. It helps me understand both mankind and non-mankind races.'

Sundown neared. Ellin gaped with weariness; Mouche slumped; Madame, impossibly erect and Eiger eyed, continued her slow accumulation of data, as did Simon. Calvy and Bao gave up for a time to take a nap in a cave. D'Jevier and Onsofruct worked methodically, occasionally rising to take a few steps, roll their heads about and wave their arms, restoring circulation. Bao returned from his nap and bantered with Ornery and with the last few Timmys who were translating for the Joggiwagga and the Eigers.

'Is your IDIOT SAVANT coming up with anything?' Calvy asked.

'Not so far,' Questioner admitted. Actually, a three-dimensional moving construct of the supposed dance had emerged, but it meant nothing to her at all.

During all of this, the ground shivered and subsided, shivered and subsided. They were all overcome with weariness, cold, and hunger by the time the last few interviews were concluded.

Evening brought dark and a chilly wind accompanied by stronger tremors, wave after wave, like a rising surf that brought falling rocks and a hail of gravel. Corojum told them to take refuge in a nearby cave, where the Timmys brought firewood and cooked up roots and greens, producing the same savory smells that had delighted Mouche at House Genevois.

D'Jevier and Onsofruct sat a little apart from the others. D'Jevier murmured, 'Where's the green-haired one? The one that enchanted Mouche.'

'I haven't seen it. And why do you care? What is it with you and this Mouche?'

D'Jevier flushed and did not answer.

'You've been going to House Genevois!' said Onsofruct, in whispered outrage. 'You've been ...'

D'Jevier shrugged. 'Someone has to play the part of patroness during their training. It's our system. We're responsible for it.'

'At your age!'

'I'm not dead yet, Onsy. And I like Mouche. Sometimes, talking with him – and mostly we just talked – you'd swear there was a sage inside that young head. Something's affected him strangely and wonderfully, and I don't think it was Madame, or not entirely, at any rate. What that other boy did to his face was inexcusable.'

'Spoiled it for you?' sniped Onsofruct.

'No,' snapped D'Jevier. 'Nothing could.'

Onsofruct merely shook her head, more annoyed than amused. D'Jevier was younger than she, but not that much younger. If anyone was entitled to a little fun, it should be she! She said as much.

D'Jevier responded, 'Well, cousin, the pleasures are there. Do not blame me if you would rather feel hard-used than enjoy them.'

When they had eaten, Questioner summoned them all together, including the Corojum.

'Corojum,' she said in a measured, respectful voice, 'during our questioning of the Timmys, they have spoken of fitting together. Please tell us how the Timmys can join together.'

'Not so well, now that they are shaped like mankinds,' he said, as though puzzled. 'All Kaorugi's parts have seams that open and join together, seam to seam. Some are like tunnelers, end to end, or like Joggiwagga, making a circle around a middle piece. Timmys used to be shaped to make big things.'

'So a lot of them all together, they could become a rather massive shape.'

Corojum nodded. 'They must keep airways open, but yes, they can make big assemblies with legs to move them and arms on the sides.'

Questioner turned to Ellin. 'That would explain the lack of grace, would it not?'

She turned back to Corojum. 'And Joggiwagga. Do they get very large?'

'Some Joggiwagga are very large, you would say huge, to do heavy things, like raising up very large stones to mark the rising of the moons.'

'Have we learned anything?' asked Madame in a weary voice.

Questioner replied. 'One of our basic problems was how such small creatures, relatively speaking, as the Timmys could be observed in the dance. We have learned they used to be shaped differently and could mass together. We have also learned that the dance, as described by the Timmys, moved repetitively, in a quickening tempo. And, we have learned that the dance was done in the chasm, yonder, where the Quaggima is. All of this is more than we knew before.'

'We have also learned there were no costumes or sets,' said Ellin dispiritedly, 'which makes it unlike any dance I was ever involved with. Even minimalist ballet had something by way of setting or lighting.'

'We have learned something of the music,' said Bao. 'Singing by Timmys and drumming by Joggiwaggas, little ones and very big ones, on great singing stones set in the chasm. Some singing was by Bofusdiaga itself. Bofusdiaga is remembering the singing, which could be good clue if there were being words. It is being unfortunate there were no words.'

'We have to go down there,' said Ellin. 'We have to see it, her. We can't work on the dance at all until we see and feel where it is to be performed.'

'This is important?' asked D'Jevier.

'Oh, Ma'am, yes,' cried Ellin. 'I remember the first time I encountered a raked stage! I had always danced on a flat stage, with the audience tilted up and away for good views of it, but I was transferred to another History House where they had a raked stage, higher at the back, slanted toward the audience, and, oh, the whole time I felt as though I would fall into their laps! It is also more laborious, for much of the time one is running uphill or plunging down!'

'Also, partnering,' said Bao. 'With raked stage, partner is being upstage above, or downstage below, and every motion is being changed longer or shorter depending on location.'

'I see,' murmured D'Jevier. 'Well, then, those of you who know something about dancing should go. I can't imagine the rest of us would be of any help.'

Corojum, summoned, received this intention fatalistically, saying only, 'You have little time.'

'Corojum, we know that,' cried Mouche. 'Believe me, we're doing everything we can as fast as we can!'

As though to underline this comment, the ground beneath them shook once more, and stones plummeted from above to splash into the Fauxi-dizalonz. Corojum looked up alertly as several Timmys came flashing into the firelight, hair wild and eyes wide.

'They come,' called one. 'The jongau! The bent ones! Dozens and dozens!'

'Where?' asked Questioner. 'On the road?'

'On the road, off the road, rolling, hopping, squirming, flowing, along the road.'

'When will they get here?' Questioner demanded.

Corojum said soberly, 'Now is dark, only the one little moon rising will make them slow down, but they will come soon, for Bofusdiaga calls to them.'

'Why?' cried Ornery. 'Why just now? Don't we have enough to worry about without them?'

'The bent ones are not finished,' said the Corojum. 'They wouldn't go back through the Fauxi-dizalonz and get finished, so they're only part done. Part-done things do not last well. They lose cohesion, and their substance longs for the Fauxi-dizalonz, whence it came. If they do not come now, they will disintegrate.'

'Interesting,' said Questioner. 'Since they caused this mess, why don't you just let them disintegrate?'

'Because Bofusdiaga does not waste material. Bofusdiaga alloys, changes, refines. You will see, very soon.'

'Then we must not delay,' Questioner said. 'Let us go to the chasm.'

The Corojum fussed, 'It is dark in the chasm ...'

'Never mind that. I can light the place adequately. Let us go now, before we are overtaken by events.'

They went, Questioner and the four young people, accompanied by a small horde of Timmys trotting and Joggiwagga writhing and Eigers flying overhead and Corojum riding in the crook of Questioner's arm. When they had gone a little way down into the chasm, a huge mooing sound began in the chasm below them, much akin to that mooing Questioner had heard in the recording.

Mouche and Ornery both sagged, stricken with such sadness they could barely move. It was the feeling each had felt before, Mouche on the bridge, Ornery in the tunnel, a terrible melancholy, an aching terror, as of something despairing over aeons of time.

Questioner turned on her lights. The area around them leapt into visibility. Across the chasm, the coal-dark drapery of Quaggima's wings quivered against the rock wall, as though in response to the sound coming from below. As Questioner had understood the intent of the cry she had heard recorded, so she understood the plaint of this one, a fractious whine: 'Oh, I am in pain, I am without ease, time drags, living drags, can no one help me, can no one help me. I want out, I want out, I want out.' The plaint had an odd reverberation, an almost instantaneous echo, as though spoken slightly out of sync by more than one voice.

With the light, the voice stilled. Mouche took a deep breath and staggered to Ornery, helping her up. Ornery put an arm around him, and they supported one another.

'She is very restless,' said the Corojum, pointing to the movement in the wings, now clearly discernible to them all. 'The egg has been moving under her and she has been getting worse for days and days.'

'Sticking to this track will take too long,' said Questioner to the Corojum. 'If we have as little time as you say, we must get there more rapidly.'

Corojum whistled. They looked up just in time to see the talons of the Eigers that snatched them from the trail and plunged with them into the depths of the chasm, Questioner and the Corojum held by one great bird, each of the others borne singly, along with a cloud of Timmys who flung themselves into the air, circling and soaring on flaps of skin that joined their arms and legs, like larger versions of the swoopers in the tunnel. Even stranger were the several Joggiwagga that flattened themselves into spiked disks that sailed downward, like spinning plates.

The Questioner's light surrounded them as they circled, slowing as they neared the bottom. There they were deposited gently one by one on the circular floor, smooth as glass, black and glossy.

'Obsidian,' observed Questioner, brushing herself off, dislodging a few fluffs of down in the process. 'Now, where is she?'

Corojum gestured, head down, bowing to something behind Questioner. She turned and stared into an immense, faceted eye the size of a building. Several more such eyes were arranged symmetrically below three tall, flickering antennae that rose like feathery trees. Below the eyes was what could be a mouth, complicated and surrounded by ramified angular structures that twitched restlessly. Below that, laid sideways along the floor, partially enclosed in the glassy floor, was the long, striated, dully gleaming body of the Quaggima, twitching, vibrating, waves of motion rippling down it from the head, away into the darkness.

Though the creature gave no evidence of seeing them, they all bowed. Questioner abated her light, dimming it to a softer, rosier glow, and muttering commands to her troops.

'Mouche, pace off the length of the body. Take a data head and get every inch of her recorded. Ornery, take another data head and go bit by bit over the upper body and head; be sure to get good, clear views. Ellin and Bao, I'd like to test for a reaction, so would you two do something in the way of a pas de deux? I'll give you some music and atmosphere – anything you'd prefer?'

The two dancers looked at one another. 'Debussy,' said Bao. '"La Mer."'

Questioner flipped mentally through her catalogues, found the appropriate references, and began to emit the music, along with shifting watery lights that poured like a tidal flow across the dark glass beneath her ...

From within which, something watched her. She bent over and beamed her light down, disclosing another faceted eye above a shifting, shadowy depth of moving wings, and beyond the wings, far down, far, far down, another eye ...

'This is the egg!' she said to Corojum, without moving or interrupting the music.

'Of course it's the egg,' said Corojum. 'What did you think it was?'

'When the wing moves, I can see far down past it, far, far down. There's more than one in there.'

'She told Kaorugi, always they have at least twins,' said Corojum. 'One male, one female. Each Quaggima mates only once. If they are not to go extinct, she must produce at least two offspring. Sometimes they have four.'

'Are the ones in the egg aware?'

'They are more aware than she is. Long ago, before the egg grew so big, she was awake all the time. She used to cry until the whole world sorrowed, so Kaorugi talked more with her, and when she could talk with someone, she was not sorrowful, but when the egg got bigger, she began to be agitated again, and talking with Bofusdiaga was not enough. That's when the dancers put her to sleep. Sometimes, like now, when the moons pull and pull, her children move and she feels them moving. What wakes her most is when they cry like they were doing. She hears that!'

'That crying wasn't from the Quaggima? It was from the egg?'

'From the egg, yes, though it is like her crying. And if Quaggima wakes up and hears them crying to get out, she will break the egg for them and so die. And so will we, Corojum and Timmys and Joggiwagga, Bofusdiaga and Kaorugi, all, dead. And you, too.'

'Maybe Kaorugi shouldn't have healed her.'

'It is Kaorugi's nature to heal. So Kaorugi says, it is the nature of all life to heal, no matter where it arises. Creatures that do not heal are not natural to this universe, they come from outside. This one wanted to die at first, but after Kaorugi made her well again, she did not want to die. She was then, as you mankinds say, on a dilemma. So she said to Bofusdiaga, let me sleep, let me not think about it.'

'And since then she's been asleep.'

'More like how do you people say it, hypnotized, dreaming. What is word? Entranced. I think she sees you as a dream, but she is watching Bao and Ellin.'

Indeed, the glittering eyes did seem fixed on the dancers, and the antennae turned toward Questioner, hearing the music. Drawn by the sound, the Timmys also began to dance, forming a moving backdrop for the two Old Earthers.

The egg shivered, the world moved. Reeling and teetering, Ellin and Bao went gamely on with their extemporaneous performance. Beneath them, the eyes moved to follow their steps.

'How would she break the egg?' Questioner asked the Corojum.

'Down at her far end, there is a kind of tail that is very heavy and stiff. And from there going deep, deep down to the end of the egg are capsules, like a ... a ... string of beads, bigger the farther down they go. Bofusdiaga says they hold heavy metals. The egg puts out roots, says Bofusdiaga, and it brings the metals bit by bit out of the world, atom by atom. And when she is ready to break the egg, she hits those capsules with her tail, and the first one drops into the next, breaking it, and so on, each bigger and bigger, going down and then something in the last one mixes with it, and it goes up, all at once, like a volcano exploding.'

'And?'

'And she is blown to pieces, but the baby Quaggi are in the shell, and the shell is in a rock tube, and the way it is shaped, it gets exploded far out into space, and then they fly.'

Mouche came trudging back into the circle of light. 'About four hundred eighty meters, Questioner. Maybe a little longer. It's a long, tapering body.

The surface is much rougher down at that end, and it was hard to keep my footing. She has a kind of tail or stinger down there that seems to pain her and it quivers.' He turned to stare into the faceted eyes, trying to penetrate their mystery. Something in this utterly strange place was familiar to him. Something was happening here that he had experienced before.

'A tiny body for all that wingspan,' murmured Questioner. 'This pit is at least five kilometers deep, the wings are folded in half, with both of them opened out it would have a twenty-kilometer wingspan ...'

Corojum remarked, 'She is bigger than when she fell. She told Kaorugi she could grow bigger yet, but the mate doesn't want them to grow bigger. That's why they do as they do. They do not have to ruin the wings; they do it because they want to.'

'The rapist mentality,' remarked Questioner. 'Seems always present. Tell, me, Corojum, when is the six-moon conjunction, exactly?'

Corojum stared at the sky. 'Now, on other side of Dosha, four moons are almost aligned, they will draw apart, then tomorrow they draw together again with two more. By noon they will be joined in line with the sun. They will stay in line only a short time, but oceans will rise, egg will be shaken more than ever, Quaggima will wake, all will be over.'

'That soon?' breathed Mouche.

Questioner said, 'If we had a few days, I can think of several solutions to this fix we're in. There are probably drugs that would keep Quaggima asleep. Certainly we could lift her out into space, given a little time, and also we can lift the eggs, though it would take the cooperation of Kaorugi and the tunnelers to cut them loose from below. But one day simply isn't long enough, even if I could reach the ship, which I can't!'

She seemed furious at this, and Mouche said sympathetically. 'I'm sure they'll fix whatever went wrong on the ship, Questioner.'

'And I am as sure they won't,' she snapped. 'Not unless they let the Gablians do it.'

Corojum puffed out his fur and sighed.

'I must think,' said Questioner. 'I must go up above and spend a little time in total concentration.'

Mouche was crouched beneath the great faceted eyes of Quaggima, intent upon Questioner's IDIOT SAVANT.

'Mouche,' Questioner said impatiently, 'let's go.'

'Give me a moment,' he begged. 'Can you leave me this SAVANT thing, Questioner? It almost seems to make sense ...'

'We'll wait with him,' called Ellin, stopping her whirling motion and drawing Bao with her to Mouche's side.

'Stay if you like,' Questioner murmured. 'Come when you're ready. Corojum, let us go up.'

The Eiger took them up, away, Questioner and Corojum, leaving the four young people crouched before the Quaggima, intent on the glow of the screens and the dance of glittering motes within it. Beside them stood four Eigers, each with its multiple eyes fixed on one of them, ready to carry.

The wing beats of the Eiger bearing the Questioner faded upward in the chasm. Mouche exclaimed.

'What is it?' breathed Ellin. 'What are you thinking, Mouche?'

He drew breath between his teeth. 'It should make sense. I have this feeling that I know what's going on. The movements they described, the music they used ... Did either of you get a better description of the music than I did?'

Ellin and Bao handed over their own data heads. Mouche linked the three together and fed this new information into the larger device, directing it to extrapolate.

It did so, building and refining, variation after variation. Long sliding sequences. Slow advances and retreats. Turns, twists, then long sliding sequences again. And again.

'It reminds me of something,' said Bao. 'I just can't tell what.'

Mouche stood up, taking a deep breath. 'It reminds me of something, too,' he said. 'It's just ... it shouldn't make sense. I mean, it doesn't make sense.'

They watched the stage go on with its improvisations, heard the drumming settle into a definite rhythm. Mouche and Bao stared at one another in dawning realization. Ellin and Ornery looked at one another in confusion.

'It shouldn't make sense. But it does,' said Mouche. 'Oh, yes, it does. No wonder I thought I knew ... The feeling. The yearning ... I wish I could ask someone ...'

'There is someone ...' said a small voice.

They turned toward a shiver of silver, a flare of green.

'Flowing Green,' said Mouche, unable to breathe. 'Where ... where have you been?'

The silver eyes tilted. 'Waiting for you, Mouchidi. Waiting for a little quiet. Oh, so much noise and confusion! So many persons. So many jongau! And poor Mouchidi, wounded so.' She moved toward them, lilting. 'Now is a little peaceful time, so listen to my words! I dreamed you would come here. I dreamed we would go to the Fauxi-dizalonz together. I dreamed the world would continue. They all think you will be of no help. They all think I am strange, not well made, to think such things, but Bofusdiaga made me for you, Mouchidi. Bofusdiaga made you for me, too, a little.'

'Made you?' whispered Mouche.

'Made me from some of your own self and some of Bofusdiaga's own self. Made you a little bit like me. I knew to come here, to tell you of the dancers.'

'You know what the dancers were doing here?'

'I know what you mankinds call it.'

'What do we call it?' cried Ellin.

'You call it making love,' said Flowing Green.

58

The Jongau And A Matter Of Gender

High above the chasm, Ashes and his sons arrived at the end of the straight road and moved out onto the ledge that looked down to the Fauxi-dizalonz. Behind and around them were the remains of the settlers from Thor, the jongau, the bent ones. Emerging from bubble caves here and there around the circumference of the caldera, others edged out, softly gleaming in the pallid moonlight, casting dark shadows behind them. Some of those farthest down struck the stone with whatever parts of themselves were available – heads, toes, tentacles – and these blows resolved into a cadenced drumming upon the walls. Those high on the ledge stepped in time with the cadence, turning with lumbering precision to move downward on the long, gentle road that switched back and forth as it descended into the caldera, at first only a few, then more and more as each new monster reached the ledge and marched across it, over the lip and down.

Here were Crawly and his cousins, four beats to a flail, twelve beats to a drag, flail-two-three-four – drag-two-three-four – down-six-seven-eight – below-ten-eleven-twelve. Here was Strike, four beats to a foot step, *rye-ut ut ut, lay-uft uft uft, rye-ut ut ut, lay-uft uft uft*. Here was Belly, dragged behind the Shoveler and Gobblemaw, like a harrow behind a team of oxen, four bars to the belch; *hup plod plod plod, hup plod plod plod, hup plod plod plod, squawwwweeough*.

'Old Pete,' murmured Ashes, who was marching along quite erect, arms swinging at his sides. 'He's a little way down yet. Crawly'll drag him out.'

'What do we do when we get to the bottom?' Bane asked.

'Gonna roll 'em oh-ver,' said Ashes. 'Hup hup hup roll 'em, hup hup hup over.'

Hughy Huge came down like a gingery cannon ball, Ear clinging to one side, Tongue to the other, *blather, rumble, blather, rumble*. Foot hopped, *bingety spop, bingety spop*, and Mosslegs swished, *slooush, slooush*, all in time, all in perfect time.

'You learn to march like this on Thor?' Bane asked.

'Drill-two-three-four, this is what a drill's for,' said Ashes, keeping time.

Boneless oozed over the lip of the ledge, splooshing in cadence. Bone clattered behind him, *brack-bruck brack-bruck*.

'There's old Craw-lee. He tooka short cut,' chanted Ashes.

There was Crawly indeed, flopped on the roadway outside a cave, flailing his claws into the pale flesh that blocked it, heave-two-three-four, heave-two-three-four.

'Pete, he's coming out, huh,' breathed Ashes, still keeping time. 'Pete he's coming out, huh!'

Pete had come out, or his body had, though his appendage was still emerging, foot by foot, a gigantic sausage, a titanic pizzle, white as alabaster, smooth as marble, throbbing with discontent. Crawly turned and clasped Pete's figure with his hind legs, dragging Pete along behind while Crawly himself proceeded down the road, flail-two-three-four, heave-two-three-four.

The moon had risen high enough to show all this nightmare vision to Madame, the two Hags, the two Men of Business, and to Questioner, who arrived just as the last of Pete popped out of his cave and came thumping down the road in Crawly's wake. Corojum summoned several Joggiwagga and a great number of tunnelers and leggers who assembled themselves into levees that reached from the foot of the road to the Fauxi-dizalonz.

'Can the pond hold them all?' whispered Madame. 'And what in heaven's name are they?'

'Creatures by that Old Earth artist, Hieronymus Bosch,' murmured D'Jevier. '"The Garden of Earthly Delights"!'

'More likely Kaorugi's joke,' said Onsofruct. 'Surely Bosch never meant his paintings to be taken literally.'

'She's right, though,' said Calvy, unexpectedly. 'I've seen them in a book, and that's what they look like.'

Madame asked once again, 'Will the pond hold them all? And what will they be when they come out?'

'And why have they all come at once?' demanded Calvy. 'Is this an invasion?'

'They came,' said the Corojum, 'because they have to. They aren't as stable as finished persons. When Bofusdiaga makes someone, he builds in the call. When it starts to come apart, it has to come back and get fixed. Bofusdiaga does not like losing material.'

'Penis-man,' murmured Simon, in awe. 'Look at that thing!'

'I'd prefer not,' said Onsofruct frostily. 'Quite indecent. And what is that flaccid sack? A stomach?'

'Belly boy,' said Calvy. 'I don't think the pond can hold them all.'

'It will,' said Corojum. 'A little at a time. Though it will overflow when they liquefy, and we will need to move up to higher ground.' He moved off toward the steeper trail, and the others trailed along behind him. When they had gone up thirty meters or so, they stopped on a conveniently spacious ledge and merely watched.

'There's Thor Ashburn,' said Madame, from Questioner's side. 'And the boys, Bane and Dyre. What will become of them?'

'We'll make the young ones go through twice,' murmured Corojum. 'Even if they fight us. We want no more jongau.'

'Look,' cried D'Jevier. 'An Eiger, coming out of the chasm!'

'It's carrying Bao,' said Madame.

The Eiger circled for a time, as though uncertain where to put its burden. Then Bao saw the group on the ledge, called out, and the great bird turned, swooped, and dropped Bao gently at their feet.

'Questioner,' said Bao breathlessly. 'Oh, Questioner ...'

'Look,' she said. 'Look at the monsters.'

'No time for monsters,' he said. 'Questioner, you must listen.'

'What is it?' asked Madame, turning toward him. 'Have you come up with something?'

Bao flushed. 'I ... that is we, yes. We think.'

'What is it?' asked Calvy.

'I am showing you on the IDIOT SAVANT,' said Bao. 'I cannot describe it.'

Wordlessly, Bao set up the device, and the screen came alive with the image of the Quaggima, with glittering points and blots of light. 'The lights are being the Timmys,' said Bao. 'And the Joggiwagga.'

They watched for a time as the sparks and blotches moved slowly around the Quaggima, repetitively, back and forth, back and forth, then quickly another motion, then back and forth ...

'Are you not seeing it, Madame?' begged Bao. 'Mouche was being sure you would be seeing it.'

'I don't see anything,' said Madame. 'What am I supposed to see?'

Bao approached Simon and murmured something. He, in turn, murmured to Madame, and she stared at the screen with a shocked expression. 'Oh, by all the Hagions ...'

'What?' demanded Questioner. 'What did he say?'

'He said the ... that is, the dancers ... they're making love to it,' said Madame.

'To the Quaggima?' Questioner turned to Simon. 'Is that what he said?'

'He said *stroke, stroke, tweak*, Questioner.'

'He said what?'

Madame threw up her hands. 'Never mind what he said! I believe he's right! Only ...' She looked puzzled. 'Of course, the anatomy is all wrong. How in heaven's name would we ...'

'Give me a moment,' cried Questioner, turning her attention momentarily to her data banks. 'I see! If the Timmys amassed to do this ... ritual, well, now that we can see it, Corojum can tell these current Timmys what to do ...'

'No,' said the Corojum, in mixed anger and sadness. 'It would take many, many Corojumi to tell them what to do. And much rehearsal, also.'

D'Jevier cried, 'But if the Fauxi-dizalonz can make anything …'

Corojum said, 'Can disassemble quickly. Can put together in new shape with new information much more slowly. Making things right takes time. A few little things take as long as one very big thing. To make many, many Timmys would take a long time.'

Questioner said, 'So we won't try for Timmys. It can make one big thing.'

'Where is pattern?' cried Corojum.

'Mouche is a Consort,' Questioner responded. 'He is trained to do this kind of thing. And you, Simon, you were also trained. And you, Calvy, from what I am told. And there are those monsters moving down the road, including one … one organ that might be useful.'

'You're saying you expect the Fauxi-dizalonz to create a Consort for this Quaggima?' cried D'Jevier.

'Why not?' snapped Questioner. 'You should approve of that.' She turned to the Corojum. 'It would work, wouldn't it? If Bofusdiaga will cooperate.'

Corojum dithered. 'Is this something my friend Mouche would want?'

'Bofusdiaga can put him back the way he was, can't he?'

'Creatures are never exactly the same,' whispered Corojum. 'Maybe he will not be willing?'

'Does he have to be willing?' muttered Onsofruct. 'Consorts are sold into duty all the time, are they not? I'm sure they're not always willing.'

'Onsy, I'm ashamed of you,' cried D'Jevier.

'I will talk to Bofusdiaga,' said the Corojum, plodding away with his head down and his fur lying flat, the picture of dejection.

'We can't do this,' cried Madame. 'It's unconscionable.'

The world shook. From the chasm opposite they heard the great mooing, a plaint of such enormity that they covered their ears and grimaced with pain. Stones plunged past them. The procession of monsters stopped their descent and held on. Whenever the sounds of the stones stopped, the muttered cadence of the monsters was heard: *hup, hup, hup, hup.* Finally, after long, terrorized moments, the tremors subsided.

'Perhaps you find it more conscionable to die,' Questioner said to Madame. 'I think you will find yourself in the minority.'

Another tremor struck, then a milder one, then one milder yet.

'The moons are separating on the backside of this world,' said Questioner. 'We will now have a time of peace before the end. Which may, or may not, be long enough!'

The monsters had resumed their progress downward. The observers stood in silence, watching, waiting until the Corojum came into sight once more, trudging toward them along the edge of the Fauxi-dizalonz.

'Bofusdiaga says yes, he can do it,' said Corojum. 'He will take all material from those coming down road; he will filter out bad stuff; he will hold rest of it in readiness. Then you have Mouche and Simon and Calvy go in, and Bofusdiaga will make a big one body to do the will of the little one's minds.'

'Me?' cried Calvy, in outrage. 'Me!'

'Bofusdiaga needs more brain stuff than one person,' said the Corojum.

'So it's fortunate you're here, Family Man,' said D'Jevier. 'You and Simon and Mouche, and that other one, what's his name? Ornery.'

'Not Ornery,' said Questioner. 'She's a girl.'

'A what?' cried Onsofruct. 'A girl? What is she doing in sailor's garb? She's not allowed to do that!'

'Allowed or not, she's been doing it.'

'By all the Hagions,' muttered Onsofruct. 'We're losing our grip upon this world.'

'Let's get beyond this crisis,' pled D'Jevier. 'Then we can decide what needs doing about our grip upon this world.'

'Mouche comes,' said the Corojum. 'With Ellin and Ornery.'

Mouche did indeed come with Ellin and Ornery, all of them Eiger borne. He was softly lowered before the others.

'He told you?' Mouche panted.

Madame nodded sadly. 'Yes, Mouche. We understand that we must make a partner for the Quaggima.'

'The Fauxi-dizalonz is going to make it,' said Questioner.

'Out of Timmys?' asked Mouche in a distant, detached voice. 'As before?'

'Evidently there's insufficient time,' said Questioner, giving him a sharp look. Where had she seen that expression before? 'The Fauxi-dizalonz doesn't work that way. It can make one large thing in the same time it can make a few small things. We have the pattern, however, and if you'll look up the hill, you'll see our raw material.'

Mouche's eyes focused on the descending monsters, and his jaw sagged. 'What are they?' he demanded.

Madame explained. Ellin caught her first glimpse of old Pete and turned aside, flushing.

The two Hags approached, trailed by a disconsolate Calvy and Simon.

'Mouche,' murmured D'Jevier, wiping tears, 'we appreciate your sacrifice.'

'It was nothing,' said Mouche, slightly puzzled. 'I figured it out at the same time as Fl ...' He caught himself. '... Bao. He figured it out as much as me.'

'Still, many would have concealed the truth because of the implications.'

'I am glad to be of service, Ma'am,' he said, still puzzled, made more so by Calvy and Simon's faces as they turned away and departed, without speaking, arms around one another's shoulders as though for mutual support.

The women turned away as well, D'Jevier saying to her sister, 'You see, Onsy. He is one of a kind. A marvel.'

'I don't know what's so marvelous,' said Mouche.

Madame replied, 'Neither Calvy nor Simon have your sense of duty, Mouche. They are not really willing to go into the Fauxi-dizalonz to be made into a Consort for the Quaggima.'

'A *Consort* for the Quaggima!' shouted Mouche, his voice reaching all the retreating persons. 'Are you crazy?'

Calvy and Simon turned as one, staring, mouths slightly open.

D'Jevier turned, white-faced. 'I thought you understood.'

Questioner held up her hand imperiously. 'We know the Quaggi anatomy is quite different, Mouche. But if the Fauxi-dizalonz can make and remake, to order, so to speak, we can simply use you trained people – you, Mouche and Simon and Calvy – to create a male for the Quaggima.'

Mouche smiled, his face serene once more. 'You didn't explain it to them, Bao.'

'Explaining what?' yelped Bao. 'I myself am not understanding ...'

Mouche said in that same, distant voice, 'Actually, considering the size, the anatomy isn't that different. All the pertinent parts have their man-kindly parallels. And I'm sure the Fauxi-dizalonz could probably come up with a Consort of some size. And I'm sure that would be quite appropriate ... if the Quaggima were female.'

'But I saw her ... him ... it ...' said Questioner. 'Out on that moon. And I saw him ...'

'You saw one Quaggi violate another Quaggi,' said Mouche. 'You assumed it was the male assaulting the female. In fact, it was a female who did the assaulting. She laid an egg in him. We ran an analysis from the data, and the egg was actually imbedded under the skin next to the male organs. That's how they do it. The females are bigger and stronger. They lay eggs in the males, and the males are the brooders. We got the sex wrong.'

D'Jevier cried, 'That's silly. Even Bofusdiaga says ...'

'Bofusdiaga has no experience of heterosexual creatures,' said Ellin, crisply. 'After mankind came, Bofusdiaga made the assumption it was female, because in mankind and their livestock it is the females who have the eggs.'

Ornery said, 'It's the female that sits out there on the far moon and sings her siren song, and it's that song that excites the male and makes him follow it. Later, when the egg is ready to hatch, the young ones call in almost that same voice.'

Madame said, 'I know that some creatures respond sexually to scent and some to appearance, but you're saying this one responds to sound?'

'It's true,' said Mouche. 'When the creatures in the egg call, the sound stirs the same excitement as the mating call did, and the Quaggima gets so excited, he thrashes around and breaks the shell of the first bomblet or whatever it is, and that sets the hatching sequence off. It ends with some kind of explosion ...'

'Nuclear,' murmured Questioner. 'A shaped, nuclear charge.'

Mouche went on, 'What Bofusdiaga and all have been doing with their dance is relieving his sexual arousal. That's all.'

'But why didn't someone realize ...' Madame murmured.

'What did this world know about sexual arousal?' snarled Questioner, suddenly very much aware of much she had overlooked. 'Nothing! And, seemingly, neither do I. After all my instructions to you about not jumping to conclusions – '

'Forgive me for interrupting,' said Mouche in the same serene but distant tone he had used since coming from the chasm. 'We have every reason to believe this can be managed, but first the four of us need a little rest and something to eat and drink and some quiet conversation.' He took Ellin by the hand and tugged her away, up the steep slope toward several tall stones that held between them a patch of moonlit quiet and private space. Bao and Ornery followed them.

'I must be forgiven, also,' said Corojum, 'But I am lost in all your talk. What is sexual arousal? What do you mean, Quaggima is not mother. She is child hatcher!'

Questioner replied, 'On our home planet, Corojum, back when we had animals, sometimes the male was the child caregiver or hatcher. A bird called the rhea, for example. The seahorse and the stickleback, which are kinds of sea creatures. It just happens that the Quaggi is a race in which the males are the caregivers.'

'Males are choosing to be this?'

'They are not choosing,' Madame said in an annoyed voice. 'They can't help doing it, any more than a pregnant woman can help doing it. If the egg is attached, then the Quaggi can't get rid of it. It has to bear it, even against its own will.'

'Could we separate it?' asked Onsofruct. 'Could the tunnelers separate it?'

'Do we have the right to interfere with another race's mode of reproduction?' Questioner asked.

'But the hatching will kill him,' said Calvy. 'It's already crippled him and kept him bound here for an eternity.'

'Evidently, that's the way things are done among the Quaggi,' said Questioner.

'Does that make it right?' cried Simon. 'Just because that's the way they evolved? It's a reasoning, feeling being! It was impregnated against its will!'

D'Jevier laughed, almost hysterically. 'Oh, read your history, Simon. Read your history. Some philosophers would no doubt argue that the hatchling, being innocent, has more right to life than the father! Historically, in similar cases, women were expected to sacrifice themselves!'

Onsofruct cried, 'Then why should not this male creature die for its child as women have often done? It has already had a long life.'

'Aside from the ethics of the situation, he shouldn't die for his child because we'll all die with him,' said Madame with asperity. 'Revered Hag, this is not philosophy, this is reality. Will you please keep in mind what's going on!'

'I need maintenance,' snarled Questioner, more or less to herself. 'This is ridiculous. How could I have made such a stupid error? Well, let us start again! Instead of Mouche, Calvy, and Simon, we will use you, Madame. And the two Hags.'

Madame and D'Jevier were shocked into silence. Not so Onsofruct, who cried, 'Well, if you think we females are going to make a partner for it, forget it! I for one, am not going to do it. Let us have another Miscalculation. Let the world blow itself to Kingdom Come. I don't care.'

59

Into The Fauxi-Dizalonz

Following Onsofruct's outburst, the people on the ledge regrouped themselves in a mood of general discontent and befuddlement, the Hags and Madame taking refuge behind several large rocks at the western end of the ledge, the two men finding refuge at the eastern end. They could look upward and see movement among the standing stones, where the young people had gone to talk, or downward, where the tunneler levees were so solidly implanted they might as well have been made of stone.

At the female end of the ledge, Onsofruct said for the tenth time, 'I won't do it.'

'You expected Mouche to do it,' snapped D'Jevier.

'He is younger than we,' said Onsofruct. 'He is more adaptable. If he won't do, let the off-planet girl do it. That dancer. Let Questioner do it. She's female.'

'If I were less bionic and more fleshy,' said Questioner, from a midpoint on the ledge, 'I would leap at the chance for such an experience. Oh, yes, I would go with you.'

'You mistake me,' grated Onsofruct. 'I refuse to go at all.'

'You are female. We need females. Why would you shirk your duty to your people?'

'I have never shirked my duty to my people.'

'Your duty at times must have been unpleasant,' said Questioner in a tone of barely repressed annoyance. 'Keeping things as they are.'

Silence stretched. None of the three asked what she meant.

She continued, 'When Mouche told us of our mistake, I castigated myself for stupidity. Then I wondered what else about your world I might have missed, and of course, once I started looking for it, I saw the mold, the pattern, which should have shouted to me from the beginning.'

'And what pattern is that?' asked D'Jevier.

Questioner came nearer, leaning against one of the stones. 'I never have enough time, I seldom have skilled help, but I always have a surfeit of data. I know all that there is to know about life here and there, including on Old Earth. There, historically, various hierarchies were preoccupied with Cura Mulierum, the care of women. Of course, in order to care for women, it is first necessary to make both men and women believe that women cannot care for themselves.'

'True,' said Madame. 'So I have read.'

Questioner went on: 'The care of women has always presented a problem for government or religion, for there were always leftover women who could not be conveniently disposed of.'

'Widows, I suppose,' said D'Jevier tonelessly. 'Or women no one wants to marry. Or women who don't want to marry.'

'Oh, all of those, yes,' said Questioner. 'Plus women who do marry and can't bear it, or prostitutes, or girls who have babies with no way to support them, or single mothers with large families, and wrinkled old crones hobbling about, muttering imprecations and getting in the way.'

'Handling surplus population is a perpetual challenge,' said Onsofruct. 'Has it not been written that the poor are always with us?'

Questioner shook her head. 'Handling surplus men isn't that difficult. Just start a lively war or find some new frontier – there's always dangerous work that needs doing. If that fails, one can create lethal rites of passage to kill off batches at a time. One needn't pretend, not with men. The gang chief or general simply talks them into a fury and sends them into battle, and then gives them a medal after they're maimed or dead. Or, the employer gets them to use up their lives in a factory and then tosses them aside with a memento and an inadequate pension. Team spirit does the rest.'

'The same would apply to women,' said Madame.

'Women are not such good team players, so society has to enforce its control by pretending it's for women's own good. Then, too, women do produce babies, which multiplies the problem.'

Onsofruct said in a remote voice, 'Purdah always worked well. It allowed troublesome women and girls to be disposed of without anyone knowing. If no one had ever seen your wife or daughters, who would wonder if they disappeared? And then there were nunneries, and witch hunts. I understand religion on Old Earth managed to remove a great many elderly women by claiming they were witches.'

'The most efficient strategy was economic,' said D'Jevier in that same remote, uncaring voice. 'Pay them so little they can't get by, or don't hire them at all because women belong at home, and then throw them in jail when they turn to beggary, thievery, or prostitution because they and their children are hungry.'

Questioner said, 'How fortunate you are that the problem has never arisen here on Newholme.'

'Fewer women than men are born,' said Madame.

'So I have been told,' said Questioner. 'But the Hags and I know that isn't true.'

The silence stretched. The Hags stared at one another, their faces very still and white.

Questioner rose. 'I might have excused the slaughter of the Timmys for various reasons, but doing away with half the female babies born on this planet I cannot excuse.'

D'Jevier turned away.

Madame cried, 'No! You wouldn't! Jevvy? You couldn't have?'

Silence. The Hags stared into the distance, saying nothing.

Madame demanded, 'D'Jevier, tell me it isn't true!'

D'Jevier said, 'Let us explain ...'

'No,' said Questioner. 'Do not try to explain. I am, quite frankly, sick of explanations!'

After a lengthy silence, Onsofruct whispered, 'What will you do?'

Questioner drew herself up. 'Assuming we are left alive to do anything, Revered Hags, I will sterilize the race of mankind on this planet, as I have done elsewhere for less provocation.'

She left them, going out onto the ledge, unwilling to listen to the pleadings that no doubt hung on their lips. It didn't matter what they said. She didn't care what they said. Within her, Mathilla, and M'Tafa, and Tiu didn't care what they said. It was simply more injustice. More repression and torture. It was unforgivable!

Ignoring the tumult at the other end of the ledge, Calvy and Simon were watching the descending monsters. The first of them, one of the great crawlers, had reached the Fauxi-dizalonz, bellowing as it plunged. Behind it, the next one pushed into the liquid, dissolving at the leading edge before the following edge had reached the pond, a pond which lapped at its shores like a living thing, its ripples spreading ever more widely.

The next one in the line was a spherical orb of muscles. 'Roll 'em over,' it cried. From one side Ear dangled, and from the other Tongue flapped, 'Roll 'em over!'

It entered the pond like a cannon ball, with a great body-flopping splash that splatted down in a glistening layer that covered the monster like partially set aspic, dripping from his enormous form as he sank gradually into the goo. Tongue, dislodged by the splash, floated about on the surface, gargling 'Help, help, I'm drown-ding ...'

Flailing and dragging, Crawly came next, with Old Pete jouncing and throbbing behind him, and it was there that the procession stalled, for Crawly entered the pond so slowly that he dissolved while barely in, leaving no traction to move Old Pete. All the monsters came to a halt, still marching in place, voices calling the cadence: *hup, hup, hup.* Then from somewhere a great voice uttered, shivering the surrounding soil. Several leggers raced from a nearby cave, disassembled to get themselves into position, then reassembled to push Old Pete into the pond, little by little, to the accompaniment of shouted commands by their own voice boxes. 'Grab him by the balls! Catch him higher up! Push him in!'

When the last of Pete vanished in the goo, the leggers broke into their constituent parts and fled while the next rank of monsters, still hup-two-three-fouring, moved forward and into the increasingly turbid Fauxi-dizalonz, whose surface was spreading wider with each addition.

From their position on the ledge, Madame broke the silence. 'Up around the first curve, there's Bane and Dyre, and that's Thor Ashburn next to them.'

'Why is he naked?' asked Onsofruct, distractedly. 'And what's that he's got wrapped around his waist?'

'It looks very much like a whip,' murmured D'Jevier. 'Though it seems to be attached between his legs.'

Glad of the distraction, Madame focused on the distant figure. 'Well,' she remarked, 'I would say it's a smaller version of Penis-man's appendage. One designed for inflicting punishment. How very interesting. Clothed, he showed no hint of it at all.'

'I believe you're right,' said Questioner from her position at the center of the ledge. 'An interesting variant.'

'None of this makes sense,' said Calvy, coming to stand beside Questioner. 'How is one to understand it?'

Questioner said, 'The Fauxi-dizalonz is like a mirror that reflects one's desires. When you go through the first time, you come out looking as your thoughts and desires would form you, looking like that thing which is most important to you. To that monster, the one you call Penis-man, being male and light-skinned was most important to him. He emerged pale and male and sat in that cave for centuries becoming ever paler and maler. Whatever the others are, they display what was important to them.'

Calvy said, 'If there had been women among them, no doubt some would have emerged as Breast-woman or Uterus-woman or Hair-woman.'

'Lips-woman, or Legs-woman,' offered Simon. 'Mouth-woman, Nagger-woman ...'

'Enough, Simon,' said Madame, joining them from among the stones, D'Jevier trailing behind.

'But what's the Fauxi-dizalonz good for?' begged D'Jevier. 'What's its purpose?'

Questioner said, 'I infer that when Kaorugi sends one of its parts out to do something, the part returns with information. The information may be so vital that it will suggest a change or improvement in general structure. In the Fauxi-dizalonz, the information can be evaluated and implemented and possibly spread around to other units.' She fell silent, thinking. 'From what we've heard from the Corojum, I infer also that the Fauxi-dizalonz destroys information. If a part has experienced evil or felt great pain, Kaorugi takes that memory away ...'

'But these monsters didn't go back in the Fauxi-dizalonz? So what will Bofusdiaga do with them now?' asked D'Jevier.

'They have been too long unfinished to send back through. Now they are only raw material,' said Questioner, 'from which to assemble a partner for Quaggima. Using one or more of you ladies for motive power.'

Among a small grove of standing stones, the four young people were hunkered down knee to knee with Flowing Green.

'Long ago and long ago,' whispered Flowing Green in a voice like wind through the trees, 'Kaorugi knew all living things, for there was only Kaorugi to know. Then came Quaggima. Oh, but it was strange when Quaggima came. Outside-ness came with Quaggima. Other-ness came with Quaggima. Separate life came with Quaggima. Kaorugi knew no outside, no other, no separateness from self until then.

'Kaorugi went deep, to think. Kaorugi makes all living things, but Kaorugi had never thought of making a thinking thing that was not part of itself. Only after Quaggima came, only after mankinds came and killed so many Timmys and Corojumi, only then did Kaorugi wonder if Kaorugi could make something that was not part of itself.

'Kaorugi told the last Corojum to take a pattern of this otherness, and Corojum took a pattern from you, Mouchidi. Corojum took a tiny bit of you, skin and blood, and Corojum bit you and put a tiny bit of Kaorugi into you. Inside you, the Kaorugi part grew. And the part Corojum took from you, Kaorugi used it when it made me. I am a strangeness, Mouchidi. Even Corojum says so, and Corojum is my friend. I am made of Kaorugi and made of you, a Timmy, yes, but a separate-part mankind creature also.

'So, now, if all is not to end or go back to long ago beginning and start over, we must create together, you and I and Kaorugi. Something that is not mankind alone. Not Timmy alone. Not even Kaorugi alone. And we must do it for sorrow of Quaggima, for pity of little ones in the egg, for delirious delight of it, for ecstasy of it, for love of it ...'

'We,' said Ellin. 'You mean you and Mouche?'

'Flowing Green and Mouche, yes, but Kaorugi says better if also Ellin and Bao and Ornery, if they can,' said Flowing Green. 'Because Ellin and Bao and Ornery are good pretenders, and to make what must be made, we cannot be only what we are, you see?'

'I don't see,' said Ornery, stubbornly.

Flowing Green whispered a sigh. 'On your machine, you saw what the dancers did, what they became, each part doing its own part, thousands of them. This was long in the design, long in the rehearsal. We have no time for design, no time for rehearsal, no time for the many to be choreographed into something huge. We must do it as one thing, first time! To become what we must become, we must imagine. That is the word? We must turn into something else. We must … join, lay aside, divest …'

'Metamorphose,' suggested Bao. 'Be turning into a new creature?'

'This is so. Questioner is right. It must be one thing. Male and female and neither. Joy and sorrow and neither. Pleasure and pain and neither. Bigger than we are, and wider and longer, a thing to be to Quaggima what Quaggima needs, and we must do it right, first time.'

'Extemporaneously,' offered Ellin.

'Yes,' cried Flowing Green. 'You are good pretenders! I have listened to you in the walls! You imagine. You dance, you are someone else. You are always being other people. You *want* to be other people. And Bao, when he dances, he is a woman person else. And Ornery is a man person else, not what she was born, and Mouche … oh, Mouche is all kinds of things to the women people he knows. Kaorugi is fascinated by you mankinds, that you are not content to be only the thing you are, so you are full of dreams. Well, this is a dream. In this dream we will really become another being. I am … accustomed to this, but mankinds are not. You dream it, you do not do it, but of all mankinds on this world, you four are the best mankinds to try to really do it. Not the Hags, too old, too set, like stone. Not the Questioner, she is not even all flesh that can be reshaped. Not the men, they are set, too, in maleness, only, not like Bao, or even Mouche …'

'It is seeming to be a risk …' murmured Bao. 'We might fail, we might die …'

'Ah,' said Flowing Green. 'Yes, we may fail, we may die, but if we do not do this, we will truly fail, we will truly die.'

Mouche leaned forward and took Ellin's hands in his own, murmuring words of encouragement. She would do it. He knew it, and so did she, but she needed to be encouraged.

Bao turned to Ornery, taking her hands, saying in his woman's voice, 'This is being wonderful. Think, Ornery, what an adventure!'

Ornery surprised herself by smiling into his eyes, feeling herself respond to his excitement. 'Yes,' she said. 'Oh, yes. What are we to do?'

'Now we wait,' said Mouche. 'Until it is time.'

Questioner moved only a little distance from the women, and Madame followed her to lean plaintively against the rocky side of the caldera. 'Questioner, I realize how angry you must be, but believe me, I didn't know. Most of the people on Newholme didn't know. What you accuse them of … it must have been done entirely by the Hags. You aren't suggesting that they, and I, go into that pond as a kind of punishment or reparation, are you? You'd have told us if there were some other way?'

'Punishment is not my business,' said Questioner. 'As I have said to others, it never works anyhow. Putting right is my business. Unfortunately, when things are put right, often the innocent suffer with the guilty. If there were some other way, I would try it. Even if I could reach my ship, which I've been unable to do since we first went underground, my crew could do nothing on this short notice, so the situation is simple. We will all be destroyed within the next few hours if something isn't done, so you women have the choice of self-destruction now, soon, or of living the remainder of your lives in some honor.'

'Honor!'

'You will have saved the Quaggi and its egg. A not inconsiderable achievement.'

'You will save the Quaggi,' cried Madame, 'but you will let us die?'

'I, Madame?' Questioner's eyebrows rose. 'I would not think of such a thing. I will simply recommend that mankind not continue on Newholme past the lives of those now living. Even our earliest espousers of human rights limit them to life, liberty, and the pursuit of satisfactions. They do not guarantee posterity or immortality.'

Madame turned away to hide her face. 'How long do we have … before we must go into that place?'

'Until the last of these monsters have been absorbed. By then, it will be day. The moons collect near noon, so says the Corojum. All six of the larger ones will be more or less in line with the sun; there will be darkness at noon; we will have one dilly of an eclipse.'

Madame returned to the Hags to tell them brokenly what Questioner had said. They stood where they were, watching. There was nothing else they could do.

Slightly above them on the road, Ashes looked down on the observers and called his sons' attention to them.

'That's Mouche over in those rocks,' said Bane, outraged. 'What's he doing here?'

'And there's that Questioner thing,' said Dyre. 'And there's ol' Simon and Madame.'

'Who? two, three, four,' muttered Ashes. 'Simon? two, three four.'

'Just somebody from House Genevois,' muttered Bane, embarrassed to see Mouche looking up at Ashes's nakedness. 'Why'd you hafta take your clothes off?'

Ashes ignored him. Any clothing worn by the Wilderneers had been stripped away. The rags lay along the descending path. The sight of Mouche made up Bane's mind for him, and he edged away from Ashes, stepped over the edge of the path behind a large boulder, and waited there while the procession passed him by. He did not notice that Mouche and Ornery, Ellin and

Bao had also slipped away to disappear along the boulder-strewn slope that led down to the pond.

Bane heard wings and looked up. Webwings dropped onto the concealing rock and perched there. 'What you waitin' for, boy?'

'I think all you folks should go in first,' said Bane carefully. 'Cause you've already been in once. Then Dyre and me, because it'll be our first time.'

'Oh, we're gonna get all refurbished, we are. Been kind of shabby, lately. You noticed that? Kind of shabby. Kind of worn. But we'll come out lovely, we will.' Webwings almost purred. 'Shiny. Like stars. Just lately, I've been thinkin' about it. All of us have. Hughy Huge. He told me he was gonna be a star.'

'That's right,' said Bane. 'I'm sure of it.'

Webwings spread his wings, the spiders beneath them quivering in anticipation. He launched himself into the air, circling upward, then from the height fell like an arrow, making scarcely a splash as he slipped into the pond and was gone.

There were only a dozen or so monsters remaining. Below Bane, on the switchback path, Dyre was straggling along at Ashes's heels. Bane whistled softly. Dyre looked up, saw him, looked back at Ashes, then darted upward, off the path to make his way upward toward Bane. They watched as their father marched into the Fauxi-dizalonz without a backward glance, moving briskly forward until even the top of his head had disappeared.

The few Wilderneers who had been behind him finished their march, their voices growing weaker, their very substance seeming to lose definition. The tunneler levees had pulled back as the liquid level rose, and were finally removed altogether when the turbid pond filled the caldera to the very foot of the road. The surface was barely riffled, but the depths were full of dark shadows and stringy shapes that writhed like leeches. The shapes swam just under the surface until early light drove them into the depths. As the sun came higher, shining more directly into the caldera, the pond began to clear, and with torturous slowness it continued clearing until, when the sun was high, it shone at last with the bright, emerald green they had all seen at first.

The world began to move beneath them, a different movement than any they had felt heretofore, a pounding, like a heart beating far beneath them.

Across the caldera from where they stood a great slot opened in the rocky wall and from it came the great voice of Bofusdiaga, making the caldera shudder as it cried, 'Now!'

Madame straggled toward the steep path, with the two Hags at her heels, like naughty children, plodding toward punishment.

The Questioner approached them. 'Are you ready?' she asked.

'You're going down there with us?' asked Onsofruct angrily. 'Can't you rely on our word? We have said we will do it. We will.'

'Put it down to curiosity,' Questioner said. 'It is one of my tasks to gather information, and how this will be accomplished should be very informative.'

They plodded slowly down the path to the point where it disappeared under the emerald surface, then simply stood, unmoving, staring into the depths.

'I'm frightened,' said D'Jevier apologetically. 'I'm scared silly.'

'Don't stand here and exacerbate your fear,' suggested Questioner. 'Just take a deep breath and dive.'

'No,' said Mouche.

They turned. Mouche was close behind them, with Ornery, Ellin and Bao, and the Timmy with emerald hair.

'What do you mean, no?' asked Questioner, annoyed.

Mouche reached out to touch her shoulder, then moved to do the same to Madame. 'I mean these women are unfitted for this task. Madame here would do it out of duty, but as she herself has taught us, duty is never enough. The Hags do it out of some other emotion. Whatever it is, it is inappropriate. You are all too much what you are. Too set into your identities. Timmy tells us you cannot do what is needed.'

'And you can?'

He grinned at her. 'Remember your lectures, Madame. You told us we had only to set our minds on our Hagions. So, I serve the Hagion by serving the Quaggima, by serving the creatures of this world. You told us we are all caught up in serving this through serving that. Nothing, you said, is ever quite clear or direct in this world, and love is the most unclear and indirect of all.'

'And does love come into it?' whispered Madame.

'Flowing Green says it must, though she uses other words for it. Otherwise, our design will be faulty, our execution weak, our concepts flawed. To use your words again, Madame.'

They did not know what to say, Questioner least of all, and Mouche gave them no time to come up with something apposite. He leapt past them, the others following, like creatures riding a wave of inevitability. In a moment they were gone, vanished, diving quickly, disappearing in the depths.

For one moment, nothing at all seemed to happen. The pond sparkled innocently in the sun, throwing bits of broken sunlight into their faces. Full of questions and expostulations, Calvy and Simon scrambled down from the ledge to join the others; the Corojum appeared out of nowhere; and from somewhere up the slope, Timmys began to sing a hymn to light.

The world shook again, and again, a stronger beat than before. Tunnelers emerged from various caves and began digging at one side of the Fauxi-dizalonz.

Questioner asked, 'What are they doing?'

'Doing what must be done,' said the Corojum. 'And when that happens, you need to be away from here.'

'Away?' asked Calvy. 'Where?'

'Away from this place. High up, away from the falling rocks. Up on the road, maybe. All of you.'

'I don't want to leave him,' cried Simon. 'Mouche, I mean. He's in ... in there somewhere.'

'Mouchidi isn't in there. You couldn't help him if he were, and you are in danger,' said the Corojum. 'Bofusdiaga says you are to go.'

Calvy said, 'I want to watch what happens in the other chasm.'

'Have you no shame?' Onsofruct challenged him. 'Here are persons making great sacrifice for our sakes, and all you think of is lechery!'

'Oh, it is more than lechery, Revered Hag,' said Calvy, irrepressibly. 'The road starts up there on the ledge, where Questioner's people are waiting. From up there, we can see down into the other side.' He turned to the Corojum. 'Can we wait up there?'

Corojum glared at him wordlessly. 'Mankinds can be trivial. I have said so to Bofusdiaga, many times.'

'Sorry,' Simon murmured. 'But I'm with Calvy. I intend to see what goes on.'

'Corojum,' cried Madame. 'Was that Timmy the one who ... who Mouche was much interested in?'

'Flowing Green,' said Corojum. 'Tim is ... it is a new kind of Timmy, made of Mouche's blood and Kaorugi's mind. Flowing Green has watched Mouchidi forever from the walls. And when he came to House Genevois, the Timmys opened the way into the walls, and they tempted him in, and he watched Flowing Green from there. Both, watching one another. All these last years of his life, his own tim has been setting tim's voice into him, setting tim's own dance into him, and he has some of tim's substance in him, too. Some of Kaorugi, inside Mouche.

'Together we have thought, perhaps Mouchidi will be the one. Now tim has lured him or taught him to do this thing, and he has convinced Ellin, and Bao has convinced Ornery ...'

'What is this thing?' demanded Questioner, almost angrily.

'... to do this thing as Bofusdiaga did it,' whispered the Corojum. 'For they,' he indicated the Hags with a jerk of his head, 'no, they cannot.'

Onsofruct burst into tears.

'We probably cannot,' said D'Jevier, shuddering. 'The Hagions know I'm not fit for martyrdom! I'm not pure enough, not resolute enough, not inspired enough. I haven't been pure since childhood, nor resolute except in duty, nor inspired recently at all. Except now and then by hope, I suppose.

We are only weary old women, trying to do the best we can. Hush now, Onsy. Come, Madame, Calvy, Simon. Let us get out of the way of this great work and wait to see what happens.'

60

Many Moons

Five moons were in the sky, two west of the sun, seeming to linger in place, and three coming from other directions, moving swiftly, ever closer. The world shook and shook again. Stones fell. Distant peaks shivered and danced. The sixth moon, said Questioner, was actually hidden in the sun's radiance and would shortly begin to obscure it. While the people held on, trying to anchor themselves on the high ledge, the tunnelers continued their frantic digging between the south end of the Fauxi-dizalonz and the opening into the Quaggima's crater. Soon it was apparent they were cutting a trench to join caldera to chasm, leaving only a narrow wall of soil and rock to hold the Fauxi-dizalonz in place.

Meantime, Timmys ran here and there, carrying, fetching, coming, going. As the moons crept closer to one another, Timmys poured by the hundreds down onto the track that led into Quaggima's crater, massing to either side of the space where the new trench would breach the wall.

'What is Bofusdiaga going to do?' asked Calvy. 'Drain the pond into the other crater?'

'It looks very much like it,' said Questioner. 'Furthermore, it seems to be putting every resource it has into the job.'

'Look,' cried D'Jevier, pointing upward with a hand that shuddered with each pulse of the world. 'Two moons across the sun!'

There were two, one on the leading side, the other on the following. From below the sun, a third moon climbed toward it.

'I saw those moons when this world was young,' said Questioner to Calvy, in a didactic tone. 'I obtained a recording of the birth of this system. All these moons make it a very complex and interesting system.'

'At the moment,' said Calvy, 'I refuse to be interested. I would trade all of them gladly for a moonless night with no tides.'

'Don't you think Mouche and his friends will be successful?'

Calvy contorted his face into a mocking grimace. 'If you want the truth, Questioner, I don't know what success amounts to. My idea of success would be to be home, with Carezza and my children. Mouche seems to intend a great deal more than that, though I'm damned if I know what.'

Beneath them, the thudding of the world built in volume and force. This was nothing like the tremors they had felt in the past. This was purposeful, powerful, a recurrent jar that allowed only a moment for the previous blow to reverberate into silence before striking again. As though stirred by the sound, the Fauxi-dizalonz began to boil, sending up fogs and fumes, spirals of mist, whirlwinds of foam, at first in random fashion, then gathering into one shadow that darkened beneath the waters. A being was growing there. Only one. And they could not see what it was like.

Within the green, an accumulation. Star-shaped, it spun slowly in the flow, a mindfulness at each point, each point a sense of awareness. Here. Now. I. Am. Here. Now. They. Are. Here. Now. We.

Reaching out, left and right, thought touched thought. We. I. We. I. Across, left and right, thought touched thought. We. I. You. We. I. You. Each linked to each, lines of association spreading to make a glowing star in a shining pentacle, and at the center, a smaller pentacle where something new began to grow.

At four of the points, persons fought to reclaim themselves, as drowning men gasp for air, and Flowing Green sang to them.

'Dissolve,' it sang to Ellin. 'Into the pattern, into the music, just dissolve. Skein away like melting sugar. Become one with the patterns on the wall, in peace, in quiet, as if you were in Mama One's lap once more ...'

'Dissolve,' it said to Bao. 'Leave all concerns behind. There is nothing here but pleasure. Let it all go, parents, expectations, worries, all are fading. Let them go ...'

'Dissolve,' it said to Mouche. 'Into the sea, Mouche. Into the liquid roaming, the cry of the waterkeens, into the slosh and swim of the sea ...'

'Dissolve,' it said to Ornery. 'Lay death away, lay pain away, your people are here, renewed, part of everything, and you will rejoin ...'

'Dissolve,' it said to itself. 'Become what you covet becoming, tim-tim. Be one with him, with them, with all ...'

They loosened. They gave up being. They joined and re-became, a new thing. A stronger thing. A thing that knew more than any one of them had supposed it was possible to know.

The new thing heard a calling. 'Oh, I long, I long, I long. I am alone, alone, alone. Death comes on me, time runs away, pain awaits, fire awaits, and I am alone, alone, alone.'

A certain mindfulness reminded: *Do not say don't be silly. Say, instead, of course, I know, I understand. Do not go too softly. Go strongly, as one who is perilous and brave.*

A certain mindfulness said: *Do not smell of this world, but of the vast sea, the spaces between the stars.*

A certain mindfulness said: *Do not dance as a woman would dance, as a man would dance, as legs would dance, but as wings would dance, as these two would dance if they were lovers making a promise that would echo among the galaxies.*

Do not be bound by gravity, for we will swim weightless within this liquid world. Do not be bound by breath, for we need not breathe, or by thought, for we need not think. Here is only sensation and the need for joy ...

The being began to form. Two points joining two others to make wings. One point to make a head containing eyes to perceive light and images. Organs to perceive and make audible signals. Organs to create and perceive heat. Organs to compute and calculate. Organs to encompass and caress.

'I know where it is,' it said to Kaorugi. 'I hear it calling. I feel its longing. I am ready to go.'

'Not just yet,' said Kaorugi. 'You must grow. Add to yourself. Accumulate. Before you go, you must be larger, much larger.'

'Where am I?' a certain mindfulness wondered, in momentary panic.

'Here, Mouchidi,' whispered Flowing Green. 'Don't worry.'

'I don't know enough to do this.'

'You don't. We do. And Kaorugi has figured it out. Seeing our shape, he is understanding what it is for.'

'I am dancing ...' Ellin thought.

'I am a woman, dancing ...' Bao thought.

'I am having a great adventure,' Ornery told herself.

'Let me go,' thought Mouche. 'I can't take me with me. I'll just have to let me go ...'

The form solidified, still growing. The wings began to toughen, their great spars folding and unfolding.

'Let me go.' A fading thought.

'Mouche?' whispered Kaorugi. 'Ellin Voy? Gandro Bao? Ornery Bastable?'

There was no reply.

'Flowing Green?'

Still no reply.

'Ready then,' said Kaorugi to his tunnelers. 'Now.'

The tunnelers at the trench redoubled their efforts. In the Fauxi-dizalonz, the form became more definite, with edges and fringes. The thudding at the heart of the world came more rapidly.

Calvy, clinging to a boulder, shook his head angrily. Oh, to be so close and have this wonder hidden from him!

'Come,' murmured Simon, dragging him from the edge. 'Your curiosity will kill you, g'Valdet.'

So quickly they could not follow it, the Fauxi-dizalonz rose of itself, making a single great fist of green that broke out the narrow dike of rock between it and the trench and poured furiously down that trench to the lip, tumbling over it into the chasm, eating the trench ever deeper as it flowed.

Deeper and deeper yet it cut, splitting the wall between caldera and chasm, all the Fauxi-dizalonz spilling into the abyss, an endlessly flowing green that poured silently, a cataract of purest emerald, down and down and down. Within the flow, an enormous and glassy shadow moved. Wings it had, or perhaps tentacles. A body it had and many eyes, for they peered upward for an instant before it plunged over the wall. They could not tell what it looked like, and even after it was gone, the emerald flow went on.

Below, the abyssal pounding slowed. The green rose around the Quaggima, totally submerging him except for the upper stretch of his wings. Beings of fire danced in the depths while music rained upon them from the walls of the abyss, for there the Timmys sang and the Joggiwagga beat upon stone pillars to make sounds like bells and blew into hollow stones to make flute and horn sounds while all around crouched a thousand other Joggiwagga, drumming on their own hides, stretched between their spikes. Behind and beneath it all sang the huge voice of Bofusdiaga, the mountains giving voice, the world making thunder.

The flow slowed, abated, finally ended. The trench ran dry. The Fauxi-dizalonz was an empty well, a deep and murky vacancy, all its contents plus the wellspring of its self drained away into the new lake that had accumulated within the chasm.

'I can't see anything,' whispered Calvy, who had moved back to a rim-stone that still rocked to the rhythms of the deep.

'I don't think we are supposed to,' said Questioner, extending her stabilizers. 'Shall I tell you what the Timmys are singing?'

Calvy looked incredulous. She smiled and said:

'Quaggima despairs,
driven against desire to brood Her spawn,
now loving death and longing to be gone.
Oh, Bofusdiaga, pain defying,
Oh, blessed Corojumi, who repair,
This Quaggima is dying,
Give him your care!
 'Quaggida destroys
all life but Hers. He lies beside the nest
where his child and our doom are coalesced.
Oh, Corojumi, bring deliverance!
Oh, great Bofusdiaga, who alloys
all life, grant through this dance
compensatory joys …'

'How do you know that is what they are singing?' asked D'Jevier. 'It is not in our language.'

'When we were afloat upon the Pillared Sea, they sang it upon the ship during the voyage of Quaggima, and Corojum had the kindness to translate it, though he left out the genders or mixed them up. You are not the first people to achieve compensating pleasures, Lady. Long before you came here, Bofusdiaga understood the need for them.'

D'Jevier snapped, 'Are you convinced that at least that part of our arrangement is a good one, then? That our Consorts and our systems are appropriate?'

'Ah, no,' said Questioner. 'On Newholme, I am convinced of very little.'

The song went on, and the dance. The moons moved into line with the sun and a gloom descended, a palpable shade that seemed to war with the music, advancing upon it, being driven away only to advance again. The earth shook, the mountains skipped, distant peaks tumbled like children's blocks, and still the music went on, the liquid depths surging again and again, waves leaping high, only to fall into glassy calms that swirled and eddied and rose again.

When two moons moved from the face of the sun, the music softened. As other moons sailed out and away from their gathering, the music softened more. The world stopped rocking, and they breathed again. Bofusdiaga's voice fell silent, then those of the Timmys, and last the drumming of the Joggiwagga ceased, leaving only the great stone flutes and horns making sonorous harmonies over the misty depths.

During all this time, even during the worst of the tremors, the tunnelers had been repairing the trench, chewing up loads of stone and regurgitating them into the ditch, while leggers pounded them down with their many feet. Lit by the fiery light of midafternoon, only a rough scar on the stone marked where the ditch had been. All was silent. No Timmy spoke, no creature moved. Bird-things sat silent along the rim, like a fringe.

The watchers waited. Inside the nearest cave, the members of the entourage muttered among themselves. At last, as evening came, a green spring began to bubble up into the depths of the Fauxi-dizalonz, throwing emerald sparkles in all directions. The stone music faded into quiet. The bird-things flew. Fogs rose from the abyss of the Quaggima, thickly roiling upward to fall as cool rain. When the rain stopped, the abyss was flooded down its western side with a fierce and golden light that gave them a transitory look at every detail of the chasm. The great black wings lay quietly upon the walls, and at the bottom the obsidian gleam of the great egg shone beside the still form of the Quaggima. Nothing else.

The world turned. The abyss shifted out of the sunlight, shadow streaming across its bottom and onto the eastern wall.

'Where are they?' whispered Simon. 'Madame, where's Mouche?'

She shook her head. Nothing so small as a mere person could be seen at this distance. But then, Mouche and his companions had not been that small when they had flowed away. She would have asked the Corojum, but it had disappeared while they had watched the moons. Now there was nothing in the upper caldera but the sodden surface, a scar on the rock, the slowly filling pool of the Fauxi-dizalonz, and the trundling back and forth of the tunnelers and leggers who were smoothing the stone where the trench had been. Of that great being who had plunged over the edge into the chasm, there was no sign at all.

They sat without speaking until the sun had fallen well toward the west, at which point they were recovering sufficiently that Madame and Simon were beginning to murmur to one another their grief over Mouche, and the Hags, huddled with Calvy, were beginning to cast aggrieved glances at Questioner.

Seeing this, Questioner rose and said imperiously, 'Now is not the time to discuss the future, if, indeed, it becomes a matter for discussion at all. I intend to have a closer look.' She went toward the steep track, and the others straggled after her, for no reason except that it gave them something to do.

They had gone three-quarters of the way down when D'Jevier asked, 'Madame, aren't those your boys?'

Madame searched the caldera, seeing two young men standing beside the rapidly filling pool.

'Bane and Dyre,' murmured Madame. 'They were never my boys, but I wondered where they'd got to. Now what are they doing?'

'Making up their minds to enter the pond,' said Questioner, who had amplified her hearing. 'Bane is telling his brother to jump, and his brother is saying he'll wait until the water gets higher.'

A clutch of Timmys approached the two boys, backed by a Joggiwagga. Those on the trail could see the argument that resulted, but they could hear none of it.

Questioner asked Calvy, 'These boys killed Marool Mantelby. Leaving aside for the moment the fact that Marool was their mother and that she probably needed killing, what does your system of justice require?'

Calvy replied, 'Strictly interpreted, our law would require blue-bodying. For both of them.'

D'Jevier commented, 'That's true. But when we wrote those laws we did not have access to a Fauxi-dizalonz.'

She had no sooner spoken than the pond began to bubble and percolate, shimmering of its own motion rather than from the wind. A tongue of green licked out of it and wrapped around both Bane and Dyre, lapping them down into the depths. At once, several of the Timmys ran around the pond to the opposite side and waited there.

The persons from the ledge reached the level of the caldera floor before two squat, ugly gargoyles crawled from the pond to stare at one another in horror. Their stench could be detected even by those across the pond. The Timmys did not suffer it. Immediately, they pushed the two back into the pond while, across from their point of entry, other Timmys readied themselves.

Questioner and her associates drew closer to observe the eventual emergence of two undistinguished and indistinguishable young men who gagged and gasped upon the shore, but gave off no detectable odor. The pond glittered, made a strangled noise, and spat a mouthful of clothing onto the shore beside them.

Questioner approached the two, prodding Bane with one foot. 'How are you, boy? Are you all in one piece?'

'I'm all right,' said Bane. He gagged, rolled over, then crawled toward his sodden trousers. 'I'm hungry. We haven't had a decent meal since we left ... wherever it was. Where was it, Dyre?'

'House Genevois,' said Dyre, trying to find the sleeves in his wet shirt. 'Haven't had anything good to eat since then.'

'And what are you doing here?' asked Questioner.

'Damfino,' said Bane, staring about himself in wonder. 'Hey, lookit all the Timmys with no clothes on!'

'Do you young men by any chance remember Marool Mantelby?' asked Calvy in an innocent voice.

'Or someone called Ashes?' asked Madame.

Bane and Dyre looked at one another, mystified, then back at the group. 'Sorry, don't think we've met anybody like that.'

Madame shrugged. D'Jevier shook her head. Onsofruct narrowed her nostrils and stared through slitted eyes. They were Bane and Dyre, truly, but they weren't the same young men.

'Blue-bodying?' D'Jevier asked Onsofruct.

'I see no point in it,' said Onsofruct, turning to Calvy and Simon. 'Do you?'

The two men shook their heads, then stopped, fixing their gaze toward the chasm. 'Look,' breathed Calvy, pointing down the almost invisible scar where the trench had been.

Laboring toward them over the lip of the chasm came four trudging figures. Ellin and Bao and Ornery and Mouche. Not exactly Mouche. Mouche with a billow of emerald hair that moved like seagrass. Mouche, smiling quietly. Mouche-timmy. Mouche-Flowing Green.

None of them spoke. The four approached, plodding wearily, yet with glowing faces.

'Now we are having time!' Bao called to Questioner. 'Yes? Time for tunneling out the Quaggi egg? For lifting Quaggima?'

Mouche stopped where he was, leaning against the rock as if exhausted, but the other three came on to meet the group advancing toward them.

'Were you seeing dance, Questioner?' asked Bao with a wide grin. 'We are being damn sexy.'

'I'm afraid not,' she replied. 'No one up here did. We heard climactic music, we saw whirlwinds and surf.'

'It was all very dramatic,' said Calvy. 'But not at all sexually explicit.'

'Good.' Ellin sighed. 'At the time, I thought it was very beautiful, but I wouldn't have wanted it to be ... observed, or even recorded. Besides, in stories it's nicer when they leave a good deal to the imagination.'

'Tell me,' Madame whispered to her. 'What actually happened?'

Ellin and Bao struggled to find words, glancing at one another. Finally, Ornery said, 'The way I remember it is that first we sort of dissolved and then we sort of aggregated, and the thing we aggregated into was put together with all of Ellin's romantic notions and Bao's womanly beings and all the satisfactions I'd ever had, plus everything Kaorugi knew about the Quaggima, plus everything Mouche had learned about lovemaking, and then that being dived over the cliff, and we made love to the Quaggima. That kept it distracted while all the pulling and tugging was going on, and afterward, it went to sleep. That's all.'

'And I'd have been embarrassed, really, except it wasn't me, or Mouche, or any of us,' murmured Ellin. 'It was something else entirely.'

'What happened with Mouche?' asked Madame.

Ellin nodded. 'That was a little surprising. When it was all finished, Kaorugi separated us out again, but not Mouche and Flowing Green. Flowing Green was always sort of part of him, so Kaorugi – or maybe Bofusdiaga, I'm not quite sure – left them together.'

'How very strange,' said Questioner.

Bao shrugged. 'Being frank, Questioner, it is not seeming that strange to me. After all this doing and dancing and being, I am regarding gender things in a new light. Both are being much more capacious than I was ever thinking!'

'We owe you a debt of gratitude,' said Questioner, meaning it sincerely.

Ellin shook herself and spoke again. 'That's true. But you needn't owe us, Questioner. When we've had time to consider it, we may ask you a favor.'

'So soon after such an experience? You recovered from it quickly.'

'Well, we talked about it on the way up, while we were resting, and we figured *somebody* owes us a favor. It won't be inappropriate or greedy. You can count on that.'

Bao said pleadingly, 'We are not bothering you with it now, Questioner. Everything is being too upset and weird, and there are rocks still falling off mountains. And besides … besides …' His voice trailed away. Besides, he had been going to say, Flowing Green had changed everything when she had talked to them before the transformation. She had told them something wonderful, right there at the end – something they hadn't even had a chance to think about. Not yet.

'Well, if you want a favor, I can at least consider it,' said Questioner. 'You've been good and dutiful aides. You're deserving of some consideration. And what about Mouche?'

'You'll have to ask Mouche,' said Ellin. 'I don't feel all that different from before. Not yet. There were only five of us, but the memory is already fading. I know why the Timmys couldn't remember, all those thousands of them. But Mouche … I don't think he will forget. I think something different happened to Mouche.'

'I shouldn't be surprised,' muttered Questioner. 'Though this planet has, on several occasions, surprised me.' She turned to stare at the two Hags, who were standing a little distance away. 'Unpleasantly,' she added with a sniff.

Onsofruct caught Questioner's glance. Her eyes brimmed with tears, and she turned away to hide the tears that spilled down her cheeks. 'It's going to happen, Jevvy. Our grandmothers made the wrong choice.'

'No,' said D'Jevier angrily. 'They made the right choice. It just doesn't happen to fit into Haraldson's edicts.'

'What?' demanded Calvy. 'What are you talking about?'

'She's going to sterilize mankind on Newholme,' murmured D'Jevier.

'Because of the Timmys?' Calvy cried, not waiting for an answer. 'She's going to sterilize the people?' He turned to confront Questioner, saying accusingly, 'Sterilize my children? That's a rotten way to repay Mouche and Ornery for their efforts on your behalf, Questioner. Or all the people on this planet who never killed a single Timmy. No future for them, either?'

'What are you talking about?' cried Ornery. 'She's going to do what?'

'The innocent suffer with the guilty,' said Questioner, with a significant glance at the Hags. 'And it is not because of the Timmys! Let them explain it to you.' She moved ponderously up the hill away from them.

Behind her, D'Jevier burst into tears, to be comforted by Ellin, who stared after Questioner, wondering if she and Bao should stay or go after her. Bao put a hand on her shoulder, holding her in place. Well then, they would stay. They did not yet understand what exactly was happening, but they understood well enough that Mouche and Ornery along with the rest of

Newholmian people were condemned to a fate that had sunk the others of their group deep in grief.

Away toward the chasm, Mouche looked up, noticed the unhappy group by the Fauxi-dizalonz and came slowly toward them.

'How can I tell him?' wept Madame. 'Everything he's done for us, for us all, and now this. I can't tell him.'

'It wouldn't make any difference to him, would it?' asked Ornery. 'He never had any future, anyhow. Not in the way of children and a family.'

'But this is different,' Madame cried. 'Different … when it's the whole world.'

Ornery, watching Mouche's slow approach, was not at all sure that the difference was worth mentioning.

61

Love Cards Wild

Over the succeeding days, the Quaggi egg was tunneled away from the body of Kaorugi and also out of the body of Quaggima – a job for which Kaorugi created two large creatures with geo-surgical aptitudes. The blast capsules beneath the egg were also carefully disassembled and Questioner's ship – whose captain had claimed 'parts failure' as an excuse for failing to respond during the gathering of the moons – proved capable under the Gablian commander of lifting Quaggima and the egg and the dangerous hatching mechanism from the planet's surface. Quaggima was deposited on one of the tiny moonlets orbiting Newholme, for a time of rehabilitation, but the egg was taken farther out, to be cracked when Quaggima was ready. According to Bofusdiaga, Quaggima intended to take his children under his wing, male and female both, to start a Quaggian rights movement, a movement that might seek an allegiance with the Council of Worlds, who would be asked to lend certain ships to the task of rescuing abused and dying Quaggi. During the enlightening intercourse that had taken place in the chasm, the Quaggima had acquired strong feelings about Quaggian sexuality.

These effort were still underway when Mouche paid a visit to House Genevois, where he found both Madame and D'Jevier, pale and shadow-faced, grieving the future loss of their people upon Newholme. Mouche hugged them both and told them to keep up their spirits, use their heads, the game wasn't over, there might be a card or two to play yet, burying them in so many hope-inducing cliches that they both laughed.

'Are you coming back to House Genevois, Mouche?' Madame asked. 'I will understand if you choose not to do so.'

'Questioner has offered to pay off my contract. As for what I will do, I am uncertain at the moment, but I think we would all agree, Madame, that I am an unlikely Consort.' He shook out his shock of green hair, letting it flow like seagrass, grinning at her in a devilishly intimate manner.

'You are unlikely, Mouche. You're also unusually impertinent.' She gave him a tearful smile.

The smile undid him. He had sworn to himself to say nothing, but these women needed a hint of hope. 'Madame, I have set myself the task of changing Questioner's mind. If I fail, keep in your minds that Kaorugi does not want mankind departed from its world, and Kaorugi is capable of much we do not understand.'

He dropped a kiss on each forehead and took himself off.

'You'll miss him,' said D'Jevier.

'We both will,' said Madame. 'And I'm so glad the Fauxi-dizalonz fixed his face. But think, Jevvy, what he said!'

'About Kaorugi?'

'The last few nights, I've found myself dreaming about him – not sexually – and in the dream he was pointing into the distance and calling, "There, there it is, Madame." I was sure he was pointing to the Fauxi-dizalonz. And what he said just now ... Do you think Bofusdiaga would let us? Some of us? Even ... all of us?'

'If we are to have no mankind future, you mean? Oh, yes, Madame. I've thought of that, too. Could we become? As Mouche has become? Do you suppose the Corojum would ask on our behalf?'

They thought about this, with emotions that ranged moment to moment from revulsion and apprehension to wonderment and hope.

Corojum, speaking, so he said, for Bofusdiaga, had suggested that Questioner transport a quantity of previously unknown Newholme botanicals to test the market among the populated worlds. One or another entity of Dosha seemed to be determined to maintain contact with the outside worlds, though whether this was Bofusdiaga or Kaorugi itself or some new, commercial sub-entity, Questioner wasn't sure.

Whichever, rather than attempting to deal with the cargo, the captain of *The Quest* ran true to form by tendering his resignation. 'My aunt is the delegate from Caphalonia!' he said. 'She wouldn't have obtained an office for me on a *cargo* ship!'

'Quite right,' Questioner had said. 'Beneath your dignity. There's a freighter arriving tomorrow. I'll send you home with my entourage.'

'But,' said the captain.

'Not at all, not at all,' Questioner boomed. 'Don't thank me. Glad to do it.'

The Gablian commander was immediately promoted to captain. Ornery had learned a good deal about cargo in her years as a sailor, and she offered to help the Gablian crew stow the bales and cartons.

Calvy had been so deeply depressed by the Questioner's decision to sterilize mankind upon Newholme that he went into a funk every time he saw his children. Trying to raise his spirits, his wife suggested a visit to the extraordinary caves west of Naibah, and Ellin and Bao were invited to go along.

Thus for a time everyone was busy and occupied except Questioner and Mouche. Mouche wasted no time in asking Questioner to dine with him.

He had an agenda, a very specific agenda, which he and Flowing Green had arrived at.

The two met in the side room of a cafe in Sendoph, where they enjoyed a very good early dinner, sipped a little not bad Newholmian wine, and agreed to spend the early evening playing a few hands of Gablian poker. As Mouche had arranged, the room was empty except for themselves, though the walls were no doubt full of eyes and ears, a hundred tattletales ready to run to Bofusdiaga at a moment's notice.

When Questioner arrived she was in a state, as she confessed to Mouche. A mood, Mouche thought of it. Despite the fact that all concerned had managed to avert a tragic outcome of the Quaggian Dilemma (thus far), Questioner had not come away from the episode feeling either satisfied or relieved. Indeed, if anything, she was more irritable and exasperated than before.

Mouche did not let it pass. 'It is clear to me you are sad and irritable,' he said, dealing them each five cards, the last one face up, 'because the beings from whom you were made are in great pain and terror, and you know this even if you do not feel it.'

'How do you know?' she demanded, regarding her exposed king of shovels with a scowl. 'Did Ornery tell you?'

Mouche had a ten of love showing, and he made a face as he picked up the facedown cards and arranged them in his hand. 'Not until later, but Flowing Green knew all about it. She saw you in your maintenance booth. She heard you talking to your inward persons. You have a deep pain there, but it need not remain.'

'Is your Timmy recommending a cerebrectomy?' Questioner sneered.

Mouche gave her a look so patient as to be almost patronizing. 'No, Flowing Green and I recommend only the removal of unpleasant memories and the substitution of some happy feelings. We can be at the Fauxidizalonz in an hour in your shuttle, and Bofusdiaga has already agreed that the parts of you needing surcease are organic parts that it can work with.'

'Why should I do that?' she asked, astonished by this suggestion. 'I've done well enough so far.'

'You have,' he agreed. 'But until just recently, you were unaware of the tragedy you carry inside you. Mathilla, M'Tafa, and Tiu cannot be freed of pain until you help them. Bofusdiaga can not only free them, he can also grant them happiness.'

She gritted her teeth. Learning of the three from an outside source had brought them into her memory banks by a route HoTA had never intended. All her baffles and wards had been outflanked and the lives and deaths of the three indwelling minds had been resurrected in herself.

'They are no longer severed from your consciousness,' said Mouche, accurately reading her face. 'It is their anger and agony you feel on a daily basis, hour by hour.'

'I can bear it,' she said through clenched teeth.

'Of course you can bear it,' he said. 'The question is, why should anyone bear it? Bearing it does no one any good, least of all you. Like the jongau, you'll come to survive on hatred, and like the jongau, you'll disintegrate. I remember what Corojum said about living in the past. And I remember that when we spoke with Timmys who had themselves been killed by men and later resurrected in the Fauxi-dizalonz, none of them remembered the terror or horror. They knew about it, yes, but they did not feel it. So, when you have been in the Fauxi-dizalonz, you will know about your indwellers, but you will not feel their pain.'

She stared at him, examining him with all her senses. Nothing there now of the quivering boy who had accompanied her on the underground river. And the green hair was certainly unusual, as was his hybrid facial appearance. Slightly lofty. Like a minor angel. Though he sounded very little different from before, he thought quite differently, she could tell.

'It's not the same,' she murmured.

'It *is* the same,' he asserted. 'In recent time I have come to understand that, Questioner. Flowing Green has observed that the true story of any living thing has pain in it, and life has to be that way. Curiosity is a good goad, but pain is a better one. It is pain that moves us, that makes us learn how to cure, how to mend, how to improve, how to re-create. Inside all of us, even the happiest, are memories of pain. Ellin, Bao, Ornery ... they all had hurt children inside them. We came to know one another's pain during our adventure in the chasm. Each of us cries that we are lost. We ask the darkened room, who are we? And we demand easy answers: I am my father's son. My mother's daughter. A child of this family, or that.'

'That's the nature of mankind,' she agreed.

'True, but Corojum had an answer that is equally true, and I like his better! We are made of the stuff of stars, given our lives by a living world, given our selves by time. We are brother to the trees and sister to the sun. We are of such glorious stuff we need not carry pain around like a label. Our duty, as living things, to be sure that pain is not our whole story, for we can choose to be otherwise. As Ellin says, we can choose to dance.

'The minds inside you suffer, Questioner. Let them have joy.'

She frowned, turning her glass in her hands, not replying. Tactfully, Mouche turned his attention elsewhere, feeling movement behind the walls, a scurry, a coming and going. Every word he said was reported. Every motion he made. Still, thus far in his game he was content. He had played a card, and she would think about it. She would construct a dozen reasons why not, but before she left Newholme (if Bofusdiaga let anyone leave Newholme) she would go into the Fauxi-dizalonz. For the sake of those children, if not her own.

Now the next play. He laid his cards face down on the table before him, saying: 'See how empty the streets are. The Timmys now have no need to hover over people, and many of them have gone back to doing whatever they did before mankind came. Do you include the fact that mankind killed many of them in your decisions about Newholme? Are their deaths one of the reasons that the mankind population will be sterilized?'

Questioner shook her head slowly, still mulling the matter of the suffering children inside herself. 'It wasn't for that, Mouche. I could argue it, but the question of individuality would arise. The Timmys are, after all, only quasi-independent beings. They were made to look like people by Bofusdiaga, but in the past they were otherwise, and maybe in the future they will be stranger yet. If they are malleable beings, made as Bofusdiaga wills, then what was actually killed? They were distinctive only in the information they carried, but not even information was lost, for the dance has been regained. In any case, it won't be needed in the future.'

'This is so,' Mouche agreed.

'However,' she went on relentlessly, 'the killers didn't know the Timmys weren't individuals when they killed them. Their intent was genocidal. That's a point against mankind on Newholme.'

Mouche nodded sympathetically. 'True, Questioner. Though not all the people were involved even then, and none now living were. How about the culture, the dower laws, the supernumes, the men having to wear veils? Does that figure in your decision?'

She shook her head. 'Blue-bodying is against the edicts, I should say, but corrective action would have been easy enough without extreme measures. On that ground alone I would have recommended that in order to comply strictly with Haraldson's edicts, the people here should establish another colony where their dissidents could go. The system is actually no more coercive than many other systems that are supposed to be voluntary. The men give up a little to get most of what they want, the women give up a little to get most of what they want. Neither sex is completely satisfied, but neither is completely dissatisfied.'

'So you accept the system?'

She frowned. 'As D'Jevier pointed out to me, the population is generally healthy, the lifespan is long, the average intelligence is rising. I would recommend corrective action, not punishment.'

'Ah,' murmured Mouche. 'I'm glad of that.'

Questioner gave him a very direct and imperious look. 'All this is purely argumentative, however, for my decision to sterilize this planet is based upon the fact that the Hags are doing away with half the girl babies born on this world. Believe me, that is all I need to decide as I have done.'

She kept her eyes on him, waiting for a reaction. She'd anticipated his being shocked by this, but he showed no evidence of surprise.

'Oh, is that so?' he asked, raising his eyebrows only slightly.

'That's an odd reaction!'

'Well, Questy ... may I call you Questy? Ma'am seems so ... formal. As I've said a time or two, what Flowing Green knew, I know. And Flowing Green knew everything there was to know that could be found out listening and watching through holes in the wall. When did you learn of this?'

She said in an exasperated voice, 'I've known there was something out of line almost from the first. The actions of this alleged virus seemed entirely too dependent upon where one had one's children and what family one came from. Calvy has eight, four boys, four girls. Marool Mantelby was one of eight daughters. Both Marool's mother and Carezza bore their children at home. It became glaringly obvious that the Hags were keeping tight control on the woman supply in order to remain in power, and that some men like Calvy, who had figured it out, were letting them do it.'

'You think staying in power is why they do it?'

'That's usually the reason for arbitrary cruelty.'

'You think it's cruel?'

'Don't you?' she cried, stung.

'Do you know what happens to the babies?'

'They do away with them! I said as much to the Hags, there at the Fauxi-dizalonz, and they didn't deny it. Not even when your friend Madame begged them to.'

He reached forward to lay his hand on her own, just for a moment, stroke. 'They didn't deny what you said, which is true. But they didn't understand what you *meant* by it. You meant by "done away with" that the babies are killed.'

'Of course,' she cried. 'What else?'

'Everything else! They're put in stasis and sent off planet, to newly settled worlds where women are in short supply and where every little girl will be very much valued and honored. As they are here. The Hags exact a good price for them, and the profits support old women here on Newholme who could be in great need otherwise.'

Questioner found herself momentarily speechless. She had never considered any other outcome than death. She had assumed ... she who had long ago learned never to assume. She sat for a long moment silent before whispering, 'Why didn't they explain?'

'Because you were angry, and you told them not to attempt explanation.'

'By all the follies of Flagia, why did I assume they killed the babies?'

'Because of your own suffering children who were killed,' murmured Mouche. 'You were angry on their behalf. Madame says when we focus on our anger, our vision begins to constrict. Soon we are caught up in fury, and we turn it upon everyone.'

She complained, 'But the Hags didn't have to choose that way of doing things. Surely there's a better solution!'

'If you can suggest one, I know they'd be happy to hear it. They aren't monsters, Questy. They're the descendants of the cultural historians on the second ship, and their ancestresses knew very well that surpluses breed contempt. Too many of anything reduces the honor in which it is held: too many men, too many women, too many children, too many people.

'The Hags saw their duty as taking care of women, and they did it. There's no female prostitution or slavery on Newholme. There are no poor elderly widows. There are no poor, unwed mothers. If I were calling the game, I'd call that a trump card.' He took up the card from one side of his hand, the ten of love, and laid it face up on the table.

Questioner frowned at the table, spreading her own hand, face up. Not a love card among them. Only shovels and clubs, labor and management. Duty and efficiency. Her life. 'An artificial shortage surely isn't what Haraldson had in mind – '

Mouche interrupted her. 'I know. I thought you'd say that. But I've been talking to Calvy. He's one of the few men on Newholme who actually reads the COW journals, including your reports. He told me to remind you about Beltran Four.'

'Beltran Four!'

'Mmm.'

'It's a very warlike planet.'

'Many fewer men than women?'

'Yes. Because so many men are killed in the battles.'

'And the warrior elite keep the battles going. For honor. For reputation. For rapine.'

She said reluctantly, 'Yes.'

'And did you sterilize all mankind on Beltran Four? Because half their young men are slaughtered in battle?'

She frowned at him. 'Calvy told you to ask me this.'

'He did. He said he'd been following your career for some decades, reading your recommendations and the reports you'd made to COW. He said to ask you which was worse, slaughtering half the young men in battles, or selling half the girl babies to planets where they'll be appreciated? On Beltran Four, a male hierarchy guarantees that they will have their choice of women. On Newholme, a female hierarchy guarantees that women will have a choice of men. In both cases, the surplus is eliminated, but here, at least, no one dies.'

He turned up the jack of love and laid it beside the ten. 'Another point for Newholme, Questy?'

Questioner shifted uncomfortably. When she had assessed Beltran Four a quarter-century before, she had not recommended any punishment. What went on there was all too common. Though Haraldson had hated war, he had known it would happen. War was natural. Men being killed in war was natural. Why was this situation worse? She had no sooner thought the question than Mouche answered it.

'You're holding women to a higher standard than men,' he said. 'Madame used to tell us that this is traditional, for men have usually been the judges, and they put women either in the gutter or upon a pedestal. Men have traditionally forgiven one another, for they know and excuse their own failings, but they do not forgive women for falling off the pedestal.'

She thought, of course, and of course. For a woman to be respected she must burn on a pyre like M'Tafa, be immured in solitude like Mathilla, submit to being buried alive like Tiu; for a woman to be respected, she must take the pain of life without demanding the joys, she must sacrifice herself, preferably without complaint. She may have no pleasure except what she is granted by father, or husband, or son. Damn Calvy!

'Are you finished with your argument?' she asked, her voice giving no indication of yielding.

'Not yet,' he said, taking a deep breath, for there was more at stake here than she knew. 'I have the Kaorugi card to play.'

'Which is?'

'Will you agree that Kaorugi is a lifeform?'

'Kaorugi is a lifeform, certainly.'

'And will you agree that Haraldson's edicts prohibit the torture or harassment of lifeforms?'

'I agree. I'm not intending to interfere with Kaorugi or any of its subparts. Quite the contrary.'

'Ah, but Bofusdiaga says you are. All his life until Quaggima, Kaorugi was singular and alone. Then Quaggima came, and Kaorugi had a companion. He delighted in that companionship, strange though it was. Then mankind came, and Kaorugi had still other creatures to learn about and from. He learned new feelings: vanity, pride, ecstasy, disgust – a whole volume of emotions.

'Now Quaggima is gone. It's partly due to you that he's gone, you know; you helped take him away, and you've left Kaorugi, who is virtually immortal, with mankind only. If you sterilize the planet of all mankind, Kaorugi will be sentenced to solitary confinement. Kaorugi doesn't want that. So, if

991

you take away mankind, you are torturing Kaorugi.'

He turned up the queen of love, laying it next to the jack and ten. 'The Kaorugi card.'

'And that's why I should change my mind?' she cried. 'I should evade my duty so Kaorugi can have some company and learn more about the universe?'

'Not only for that, also because Haraldson would not approve of your interfering with the lifeform on this planet,' Mouche murmured. He hadn't said all he could have said about the lifeform on the planet. If Questioner insisted on sterilization and managed somehow to get off planet to do it, Bofusdiaga would not let mankind die. They would become something else, of course. Rather as Mouche had become, though without some of the elements that had made that becoming successful, assuming it was successful. It would not necessarily be a bad thing or bad in all cases, but still that part of Mouche that was purely mankind preferred that his people be allowed to choose what they would be.

'You seem to have innumerable arguments,' she said in a grumpy voice.

'Not innumerable, no. I have played all my cards but two.'

'Well, play them,' she said impatiently. 'Get on with it.'

'This is one you should like, Questy. Now that your political appointees are out of your hair, not that they were ever any good to you, you should demand the liberty of choosing your own aides. Competent ones. People who will work with you.'

'Competent aides,' she murmured, intrigued despite herself. 'I must admit, that has its attractions. Could I possibly have a competent ship's crew, as well?'

'We could work on that. Ornery might be just the person to assure it. We, that is Ellin and Bao and Ornery and I, would like to be your aides, Questy. We've held off discussing it with you, for there's been a lot to think about, but it's the only thing that makes sense. Ellin can't go back to History House, she's beyond that, and so is Bao. Ornery needs wider seas than the ones she's been traveling, and I can't be a planetbound Consort now. I know too much. I've seen too much, felt too much. I can't do it even by serving my Hagion, for the Hagion I served is part of me, and that part of me isn't interested in an eternity of Consorthood on Newholme ...'

'An eternity?'

He bit his lip. He hadn't been going to mention that just yet. 'So it seems. We've been through the Fauxi-dizalonz, Questy. We could still perish, far from here and unable to return, but if no accident catches up with us, and if we get back here to Newholme every few hundred years or so, we're in for a very long haul. It might be nice for you to have some friends who remember when you were only a youngster, two or three hundred years old.'

She stared, open-mouthed, as he placed the king beside the queen.

'Besides,' he said, 'Kaorugi wants the four of us to go with you, for then, at intervals, when we return to the Fauxi-dizalonz, Kaorugi will experience the whole galaxy, or as much of it as we have seen in the interim.'

'So you have it all figured out,' she said helplessly.

'All four or five of us have figured it out. You offer me and Ornery and Ellin and Bao adventure and exploration, we, including Flowing Green, offer you comradeship – and another point of view, which is always valuable.'

'I'm not sure my life is that adventurous. You may get the short end of the deal.'

'Well then, even the score. Give us something we all want. Approve of Newholme, as it is. Let our friends and families alone. No sterilization.'

'You're trying to suborn me.'

He swallowed a sigh. Kaorugi preferred the presence of independent, alien creatures, but if Kaorugi could not have that, Kaorugi would have something else. Kaorugi did not like what it had learned of the sterilization order. Kaorugi felt, as had been foreseen, that justice was simply the last straw, but the Timmy part of Mouche would not let him speak of that. The Timmy part of him would not allow Kaorugi's contingency plans to be forestalled.

Well, if Questioner were to be moved, it had to be with eloquence. Or ...

'I'm trying to convince you, Questioner. Why not just agree?'

'Because,' she said angrily, 'I was created for a purpose, and I feel my purpose is being undermined here.'

Or ...

He fingered the last card in his hand. The ace of love. 'Is that really what you feel?'

She fumed. She wasn't sure what she felt. Sadness, certainly. And anger. She muttered, 'You're probably right about my feelings, coming from what I know about the three children. The buffers were there for a reason, and I shouldn't have gone around them.'

'It's not only the three children,' Mouche murmured. 'The council loads you down with work, then saddles you with incompetent people and still expects you to work miracles.'

'While constantly cutting my budget,' she said furiously. 'They even interfere with my technical support. That's why I couldn't get in touch with the ship when I needed to! Parts failure! That idiot! Can you believe that?'

He did not believe it. Flowing Green knew there had been no failure of parts, only Bofusdiaga, determined to give them no alternative to solving the Quaggian dilemma. Not even Flowing Green knew the extent of what Bofusdiaga could do.

Focus, Mouche told himself. As Madame had always said, Focus!

'Part of it is that you work very hard, and no one really appreciates what you do,' he said softly, moving his chair a bit closer to hers.

'I was designed for it,' she sniffed. 'But it is hard, yes. I'm human enough to feel that.'

'Of course you feel it. You must get terribly annoyed.'

'It's what I was created for,' she said less forcefully. 'But none of us like to feel our efforts are wasted ...'

'True. And even when we know our efforts aren't wasted, we like to be appreciated.'

'Yes,' she admitted, almost in a murmur. 'It would be nice.'

'I admire you so greatly,' he said. 'We all do.'

'Really?' She laughed, rather sadly. 'That's something new.'

'You aren't admired by the members of the council?'

'By and large they treat me like a computer. It's understandable, I suppose.'

'They disregard your humanity, because it makes them feel uncomfortable, I imagine.' He put his hand on top of her own. 'It probably surpasses their own. But we ... I think of you as a friend. And I'm honoring myself when I give you that title.'

'Oh, Mouche. Really.' She felt herself flushing.

He shook out his mane of emerald hair and looked at her from under lowered lashes. 'It's time that someone took care of you, Questioner. After all the care you take of humanity, it's only right that humanity do something for you in return.'

'For me?'

He gave her a dangerous look as he reached out to run his hand along her neck, where several of her sensation circuits were placed near the skin.

'Ahhh,' she said unwillingly. 'Ahhh.'

'I've researched you in these recent days, Questy,' he whispered. 'Flowing Green and I.' He lowered his fingers, recently returned to their Consortly softness, stroking the line of her shoulder. Stroke. Stroke. Tweak.

'Mouche. For heaven's sake ...' She quivered with unfamiliar pleasure. 'For heaven's sake ...'

'Oh Corojumi, grant deliverance ...' he sang softly, with a purposeful stroke, laying the ace upon the table.

'Last card ...' she gasped.

'... grant Questy in this dance ...'

'You stacked the deck,' she whispered.

'... compensatory joys,' he sang, the green hair swirling high above his head as he and his Hagion smiled into her eyes.

If you've enjoyed these books and would
like to read more, you'll find literally thousands
of classic Science Fiction & Fantasy titles
through the **SF Gateway**

✳

For the new home of
Science Fiction & Fantasy . . .

✳

For the most comprehensive collection
of classic SF on the internet . . .

✳

Visit the SF Gateway

www.sfgateway.com

Sheri S. Tepper (1929 –)

Sheri Stewart Tepper was born in Colorado in 1929 and is the author of a large number of novels in the areas of science fiction, fantasy, horror and mystery, and is particularly respected for her works of feminist science fiction. Her many acclaimed novels include *The Margarets* and *Gibbon's Decline And Fall*, both shortlisted for the Arthur C. Clarke Award, *A Plague Of Angels*, *Sideshow* and *Beauty*, which was voted Best Fantasy Novel Of The Year by readers of *Locus* magazine. Her versatility is illustrated by the fact that she is one of very few writers to have titles in both the Gollancz SF and Fantasy Masterworks lists. Sheri S. Tepper lives in Santa Fe, New Mexico.